THE NOVELS OF
THOMAS LOVE PEACOCK

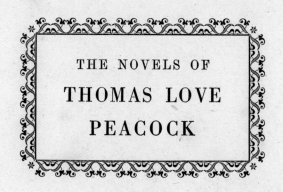

THE NOVELS OF
THOMAS LOVE
PEACOCK

Edited with Introductions and Notes by
DAVID GARNETT

LONDON
RUPERT HART-DAVIS
1948

Printed in Great Britain by Butler & Tanner Ltd., Frome and London

CONTENTS

Biographical Introduction . . . vii

Bibliographical and Textual Note . xix

Peacock's 1837 Preface . . . xxi

HEADLONG HALL 1

MELINCOURT 91

NIGHTMARE ABBEY . . . 345

MAID MARIAN 435

THE MISFORTUNES OF ELPHIN . 541

CROTCHET CASTLE . . . 639

GRYLL GRANGE 763

BIOGRAPHICAL INTRODUCTION

THE reader who wishes to study Peacock's life will find the latest information in Mr H. F. Brett-Smith's introduction to the Halliford Edition of Peacock's works. It is however a rare book. In any case he should also read Mr Priestley's sympathetic and sensitive biography in the English Men of Letters series (Macmillan, 1927); he who wishes to trace all the influences which went to make up Peacock's novels and poems should read *Un Épicurien Anglais : Thomas Love Peacock*, by M. Jean-Jacques Mayoux (Nizet et Bastard, 1933), to whom I wish to express my acknowledgments for the assistance which his book has been to me.

Here I shall give a brief sketch of Peacock's life; in the separate introductions to each of the novels I shall try to explain those of his opinions without a knowledge of which points in the novels might be misunderstood.

Thomas Love Peacock was born at Weymouth on the 18th of October, 1785. His father was a glass-merchant of whom little is known; his mother was the daughter of Thomas Love, formerly master of a man-of-war, who had lost a leg at Rodney's crowning victory of the 12th of April, 1782, off Dominica. Peacock had an uncle in the Navy and a cousin who became an Admiral. Another of the Loves was an eccentric and corpulent bookseller in Weymouth. Samuel Peacock died when his son was three years old, and widow and child went to live with her parents on the Thames at Chertsey.

Thomas Love was a cheery old man who liked good living, good wine and hot punch and was fond of singing catches, tastes which his grandson shared later on.

Peacock was a remarkably beautiful child and it is said that Queen Charlotte stopped her carriage to give him a kiss. He grew up into a strikingly handsome man. At Chertsey he developed a life-long love of the country, particularly of the valley of the

Thames, and of taking long walks. He had a great love for the beauty of natural scenery, and his novels contain many passages to show it.

His mother was a well-educated woman, with a particular liking for Gibbon. She taught her son much herself. He went to school, as a day-boy, at Englefield Green, from the age of six to nearly thirteen. After that he was entirely self-taught.

He and his mother moved to London when he left school, and after a brief period of working in an office, he does not seem to have sought employment again. For several years Peacock is said to have frequented the Reading Room of the British Museum, becoming in time one of the best classical scholars of his day and acquiring a wide knowledge of Greek, Latin, French and Italian literature. In old age he also learnt Spanish.

Soon after he went to London he gained the eleventh prize offered by the *Juvenile Library*, for an essay. Leigh Hunt won the fourth prize in the same competition. In 1804 and 1806 Peacock published his first volumes of poetry, *The Monks of St. Mark* and *Palmyra*. In 1807, he fell in love with a girl called Fanny Falkner, whom he used to meet in the ruins of Newark Abbey, eight miles from Chertsey, and they became engaged. Her parents disapproved of the connection and broke the engagement off by indirect means. Fanny was hurriedly married to someone else and died the following year. Thirty-five years later Peacock wrote these verses, which I insert as a specimen of his poetry at its best. They were particularly admired by Tennyson.

NEWARK ABBEY

AUGUST, 1842

WITH A REMINISCENCE OF AUGUST, 1807

> I gaze, where August's sunbeam falls
> Along these gray and lonely walls,
> Till in its light absorbed appears
> The lapse of five-and-thirty years.

If change there be, I trace it not
In all this consecrated spot :
No new imprint of Ruin's march
On roofless wall and frameless arch :
The hills, the woods, the fields, the stream,
Are basking in the self-same beam :
The fall, that turns the unseen mill,
As then it murmured, murmurs still :
It seems, as if in one were cast
The present and the imaged past,
Spanning, as with a bridge sublime,
That awful lapse of human time,
That gulph, unfathomably spread
Between the living and the dead.

For all too well my spirit feels
The only change this scene reveals :
The sunbeams play, the breezes stir,
Unseen, unfelt, unheard by her,
Who, on that long-past August day,
First saw with me these ruins gray.

Whatever span the Fates allow,
Ere I shall be as she is now,
Still in my bosom's inmost cell
Shall that deep-treasured memory dwell :
That, more than language can express,
Pure miracle of loveliness,
Whose voice so sweet, whose eyes so bright,
Were my soul's music, and its light,
In those blest days, when life was new,
And hope was false, but love was true.

Peacock's granddaughter Edith Nicolls states that he always wore
a locket containing Fanny Falkner's hair and that in the last weeks
before his death he had frequently recurring dreams of her. Peacock
was a man free from false or affected feelings ; he was naturally and
sincerely rather sentimental than passionate, a man of loyal friendships and deep undying attachments.

Peacock made close friends at this period with Edward and
Thomas Hookham, sons of the Bond Street bookseller and librarian,
They published all his books from 1810 to 1837. He was still corre-
sponding with Thomas after his seventieth year.

A*

In the autumn of 1808, Peacock became private secretary to Sir Home Popham, commanding the fleet in the Downs. He found life on board " a floating Inferno " in which it was impossible to write poetry or to pursue any rational occupation. He gave up the job the following spring and set off to visit the sources of the river Thames on a walking tour which provided material for a long poem *The Genius of the Thames*, which like his other long poems is laboured and has little merit.

The following winter Peacock visited North Wales and fell in love, but far less deeply, with Jane Gryffydh, the daughter of a Welsh clergyman. She was a well-educated girl and was able to talk to him intelligently of books. Peacock's letters to Hookham show that at this period he was reading Æschylus, Sophocles and Sallust and Cicero ; Rousseau, Boileau, a work on the origin of religion by Dulau and Dupuis ; Tasso and four other Italian poets ; Spenser and nine other English ones, Hume's essays, Dr Johnson's *Rambler*, Horne Tooke's *Diversions of Purley*, a history of Persia, and Zimmermann *On Solitude*. He went for immensely long walks with his dog Luath (named after Cuthullin's dog in Ossian's *Fingal*) and gloried in the mountain scenery, going out with Dr Gryffydh one night to view the Black Cataract at midnight. Peacock was twenty-six years old, had no prospects and no money, and he parted from Jane Gryffydh without making any declaration.

She had fallen in love with him, but he was able to assure his friend Hookham soon afterwards that " Richard is himself again." Peacock paid a second visit to North Wales the following spring but he is not known to have seen Jane Gryffydh. Eight years were to elapse before they met again, and during this period Peacock had many passing flirtations and at least one serious love affair—that with Marianne de St Croix. The description which Miss Ilex gives of her lover in *Gryll Grange* is a portrait of Peacock, and the dog is also identifiable as his dog Luath.

" He delighted in the society of accomplished young women, and in that alone. It was the single link between him and the world. He would disappear for weeks at a time, wandering in forests, climbing mountains, and descending into the dingles of mountain-streams, with no other companion than a Newfoundland dog ; a large black

dog, with a white breast, four white paws, and a white tip to his tail :
a beautiful affectionate dog : I often patted him on the head, and
fed him with my hand. He knew me as well as Bajardo knew
Angelica. . . . Well, my young gentleman, as I have said, was a
sort of universal lover, and made a sort of half-declaration to half
the young women he knew : sincerely for the moment to all."

Shelley never saw Jane Gryffydh, and his reference to the " milk-
white Snowdonian antelope " does not tally with what we know of
her appearance, any more than its mate, the cameleopard, does with
Peacock.

In the autumn of 1812 Peacock first met Shelley in London, no
doubt through Hookham, who was Shelley's bookseller. Shelley
was just twenty. The two men had in common an enthusiasm for
literature, particularly for Greek literature. Equally important,
they were poets. But whereas Shelley was a great poet, Peacock
was a minor one. Fortunately, however, Shelley admired Peacock's
poems.

Peacock did not share many of Shelley's enthusiasms, and the
reason why his friends and hangers-on called Peacock a " cold
man " was that he thought they were ridiculous.

Peacock did not however think Harriet was silly ; he liked her
and remained her friend, speaking up for her during her life and
long after her death.

Harriet, though she was deeply in love with Shelley, was beginning
to tire of his vagaries and to long for a more conventional existence,
which her hateful sister urged her to demand. When Peacock went
to stay with the Shelleys at Bracknell it was natural that Harriet
should feel he was on her side. For at Bracknell Shelley was surrounded by sentimentalists, who shared his views on religion and
politics but, as Peacock says of them :

" Every one of them adopting some of the articles of the faith of
their general church, had each nevertheless, some predominant
crotchet of his or her own which left a number of open questions for
earnest and not always temperate discussion. I was sometimes
irreverent enough to laugh at the fervour with which opinions,
utterly unconducive to any practical result, were battled for as
matters of the highest importance to the well-being of mankind :

Harriet Shelley was always ready to laugh with me, and we therefore lost caste with some of the more hot-headed of the party."

Peacock's visit to Bracknell was short, but it made an indelible impression and his friendship with Shelley provided him with characters, one of whom, J. F. Newton, the Zodiacal mythologist who believed in a return to the golden age, reappears in more than one of his novels.

Yet Peacock was far from being a mere scoffer. He shared many of Shelley's political views, in particular his love of individual liberty, and his hatred of a Government founded on corruption and pocket-boroughs, which, after the defeat of Buonaparte, was engaged in imposing police-states in Europe and curtailing the liberty of the subject at home. Like Shelley he could not forgive the apostasy of the Lake poets from their earlier principles, and Southey is roughly handled in most of his novels. He applauded Cobbett's radical individualism, and his hatred of slavery led him to abstain from the use of sugar and rum, the products of slave labour.

Peacock was however incapable of abstract enthusiasm—of enthusiastic belief for its own sake. He clung to realities and to the good things he knew. When Shelley fell passionately in love with Mary Godwin, aged sixteen, and, after vainly attempting to persuade Harriet to join in a *ménage à trois* as the sister of his soul, eloped with Mary, Peacock maintained his friendship both with Shelley and with Harriet. The Bracknell reformers, on the other hand, were scandalised.

Peacock's defence of Harriet and his temperate statement of the facts, many years later, led to his being the target of violent and quite unjustified attacks by my grandfather, Richard Garnett, who however, in later years, expressed his regret for his " unjust and uncharitable " words. The reason for the attacks was that Richard Garnett shared the concern of his friends, Sir Percy and Lady Shelley, to prove that Shelley had not " forsaken Harriet for Mary merely because he liked Mary better "—which " could not be justified by any code of morality "—but that " after an insanable breach with Harriet he had transferred his affections elsewhere, which would have had the approbation of Milton."

Dr Leslie Hotson's discovery of Shelley's letters to Harriet, which

were filed by the Westbrook family to deprive Shelley of the custody
of his children, has shown that these hopes, so important to lovers
of Shelley in 1862, were vain, and vindicated Peacock's reputation
for loyal friendship and disinterested truthfulness. Shelley had
in fact been blind to the enormous moral importance of being
off with the old love before he was on with the new. He loved
Mary passionately and Harriet tenderly and would have liked to
live with both of them together. Although Peacock liked Harriet
and did not like Mary, and was disliked by her, he saw that Mary
was intellectually better suited to Shelley. After Harriet's suicide,
Shelley consulted Peacock and an Etonian friend, Sir Lumley Skeffington, as to whether he should marry Mary. They advised him to
marry her at once and Shelley did so. Shelley was maturing rapidly
and his friendship with Peacock grew steadily closer until he and
Mary left England forever. He appointed Peacock, who had already
acted as his agent in some business matters, as the executor of his
will, and left him a legacy of £2000, which he accepted, when it
became payable, in 1844.

In the summer after Shelley's departure Peacock suffered a
financial loss, and at the beginning of 1819 he heard of a vacancy
in the office of the East India Company. After an examination he
was appointed one of the four assistants in the Examiner's Department, the other three being the Utilitarian philosopher James Mill,
Edward Strachey and J. J. Harcourt. Peacock's test papers were
returned to him marked by the examiners : " Nothing superfluous
and nothing wanting," which is not only, as Mr Priestley pointed out,
an excellent description of his prose style, but also of the construction of the best of his novels. Ten months after his appointment
and a breach with Marianne de St Croix, Peacock proposed marriage
to Jane Gryffydh by letter and was accepted. He had not seen her
for eight years. The marriage was marred by the ill-health of his
wife and the death in 1826 of their second daughter, whose loss was
very deeply felt by both parents. Mrs Peacock remained a nervous
invalid from that time, incapable of any family responsibilities.
Altogether they had three daughters and one son, and adopted a
cottage child who resembled the little girl who had died.

In 1823 Peacock bought a cottage for his mother at Lower Halliford on the Thames between Shepperton and Walton, and moved his family to one adjoining it. He himself stayed in London from Monday till Friday evening and visited Halliford at week-ends.

His mother died in 1833 ; her death was a great loss ; he had been devoted to her, and had read and discussed his books with her, in manuscript, before their publication. After her death he did not write another novel for twenty-five years. The interval between *Crotchet Castle* and *Gryll Grange* has been ascribed to the loss of her encouragement and appreciation.

Peacock proved an extremely capable administrator and rose to succeed James Mill as Examiner at a salary of £2000 a year. When he joined the Company, mails were carried round the Cape on sailing ships and only reached London twice a year. Peacock investigated alternative routes, recommended and secured the adoption of steam vessels to carry the mails, personally supervised their construction and tests before they were sent round the Cape. Thanks to Peacock, there were mails from India once a month. He was also responsible for armed steamboats being sent up the Indian rivers for combined operations with land forces. These facts should be borne in mind by those who think of him as a hater of innovations.

When he first went to the India House, he found there the leisure more characteristic of Government Departments than of great commercial ventures and he described it as follows :

> From ten to eleven, ate a breakfast for seven :
> From eleven to noon, to begin 'twas too soon ;
> From twelve to one, asked, " What's to be done ? "
> From one to two, found nothing to do ;
> From two to three began to foresee
> That from three to four would be a damned bore.

There was time for Peacock to make many friends, and to write verses and novels. It is said that for a considerable period he used to dine once a week with Jeremy Bentham. Peacock, in spite of his hatred of political economy, was a practical Utilitarian in his views. He saw a good deal of his colleague James Mill, though he did not like him. Edward Strachey was a close friend. In later life his closest friend was John Cam Hobhouse, Byron's intimate friend. Although an extremely good talker, Peacock was rather a recluse than a diner-out—he liked his friends but not society. He was musical and passionately fond of the Opera, of which he wrote a number of reviews.

In 1844 Peacock's eldest daughter, Mary Ellen, married a naval officer, Edward Nicolls, and was left a widow before the birth of a child Edith, who grew up to be Peacock's favourite companion. Five years later Mrs Nicolls married a young solicitor's clerk with literary aspirations, called George Meredith. The Merediths were very poor, and after Peacock's wife died in 1851 they went to live with him. Mary Ellen Meredith was six-and-a-half years older than Meredith (not nine, as he stated), and although a son was born the marriage was a failure, not owing to the difference in age but partly because she was as brilliant and intellectual and every bit as well educated as her fiery young husband. In 1856, the year before the Mutiny, Peacock retired from India House, and went to live permanently at Lower Halliford. He seems to have found his son-in-law tiresome and the baby noisy and took a cottage for the Merediths on the other side of the village green. There he would play cricket with his grandchildren, there he would preside over the May-day festivals that he loved, when the little girls went garlanding and one or other of his granddaughters was crowned Queen of the May.

But though Peacock may not have liked Meredith, he influenced him greatly. In Mr Priestley's words, it was owing to Peacock that " Meredith became the creator of a new kind of fiction, in which romantic narrative is fused with intellectual comedy." M. Mayoux has enumerated a number of examples, some important, some trifling, of Meredith's indebtedness to Peacock. Unfortunately the debt did not extend to prose style and for many readers Meredith's great powers in the creation of character and the management of a plot— so infinitely greater than Peacock's—can only be dimly seen through the Amazonian forest of tangled literary verbiage, of intertwined metaphors and similes. The Meredith marriage broke up in 1858 when Mary Ellen left her husband to go abroad with Henry Wallis, the painter. This relationship did not last and she returned to England and died in 1861, unforgiven by her husband, who deprived her of her son. Meredith's side of the story would appear to be recorded in *Modern Love*, published the year after her death and four years after their final separation.

Peacock spent much of his time in his library, to which his grand-child Edith alone was allowed access. On one occasion she took in Thackeray, who had unexpectedly called to see her grandfather, and though Peacock was affable to his visitor, he gave her a terrific scolding afterwards. *Gryll Grange*, written when he was seventy-three, shows us Peacock in his old age, full of vigorous intellectual life and power, but mellower.

Peacock's death was brought on by an outbreak of fire, of which he had developed a morbid terror. He refused to leave the library, shouting, " By the immortal gods, I will not move," but when the fire had been put out, he took to his bed and remained bedridden, dying in January 1866, aged eighty-one.

Peacock has been a favourite author whose work I have read and re-read many times in the last thirty-five years. But my apprecia-tion of his novels has grown very greatly since I began to edit him. I believe that he is a writer whose thought one should understand as well as his wit. He is full of allusions and obscurities which it is better to understand than to take in one's stride. I know of few other writers (T. S. Eliot is one of them) whose work is so full of phrases taken from the great literature of the world and so fortified with quotations.

Like Eliot, Peacock may misquote a line to suit his own purposes. On one occasion, for example, he deliberately changed Wordsworth's meaning to its exact opposite. M. Mayoux, indeed, accuses him of " la rage de la citation inexacte," but I am convinced that, unlike Eliot, the great majority of Peacock's misquotations were accidental. He had a wonderful verbal memory but often it betrayed him. Just as many writers think and write in the threadbare commonplaces of current journalism, so Peacock thought and wrote allusively in passages taken from the works of other writers whom he admired. He used them, for the most part, as parliamentary orators of the old school used them—to gain the goodwill and respect of their audience. But he also used them, I believe, to give a certain remoteness and perspective to his characters. Their very culture detaches them from the everyday world and sets them upon a stage, framed by a proscenium of the Classics and illuminated by footlights of the Moderns—from Chaucer and Rabelais downwards.

Against this view must be set the fact that he wrote at a time when there was a very much larger class whose education consisted of a thorough knowledge of ancient and modern literature and wisdom, so that to give an authority for an opinion was to advance an argument in its favour.

To-day education is so much more a knowledge of the theories and practice of the last two or three decades that references to ancient authority would be considered irrelevant. The use of continual quotation was therefore less unreal when Peacock wrote than it would be to-day.

It may be difficult for the contemporary reader to realise how numerous these allusions are. I am conscious that I may have missed a number of them. Many that I have not missed I have failed to identify.

A problem arises from Peacock's frequent inclusion of songs and verses in the text of his novels, for it is not always possible to tell whether Peacock is himself the author of a verse or not. In some cases I have been able to show that Peacock inserted a passage from his earlier work within quotation marks and with the attribution of " Old Song." One such is not included in Mr Brett-Smith's index of Peacock's verses in the Halliford Edition, on which I might otherwise rely. It seems probable to me that several passages which I have failed to identify are really by Peacock himself. But in spite of such shortcomings, I hope that by attempting to provide an edition with explanatory notes, I shall enable nine hundred and ninety-nine persons out of a thousand to understand Peacock's novels better than they would otherwise have done, to laugh louder and more often and to love him more.

As long ago as 1927, Mr Priestley pointed out that in *Gryll Grange* Peacock satirises the modern world ; that the mole-hills he turned into mountains have actually become mountains. That is even more striking today : the mountains have grown larger and we are living in their shadow. Peacock's novels are full of cranks and system-mongers. Today they have become the statesmen who plan

our destinies and direct our actions.   Enjoying the abundant fruits
of their activities, there is a peculiar relish for us in hearing how the
systems were first gaily propounded at breakfasts where rounds of
beef were demolished and at suppers where political economy and
planning never lacked the accompaniment of bottles of Burgundy
and bumpers of Madeira.

Shelley summed up Peacock's novels in his *Letter to Maria Gisborne*
so perfectly that there is nothing that need be added :

> his fine wit
> Makes such a wound, the knife is lost in it ;
> A strain too learnèd for a shallow age,
> Too wise for selfish bigots ; let his page,
> Which charms the chosen spirits of the time,
> Fold itself up for the serener clime
> Of years to come, and find its recompense
> In that just expectation.

It would be gratifying if this edition were to enable Shelley's hope
to come true.

DAVID GARNETT

BIBLIOGRAPHICAL AND
TEXTUAL NOTE

PEACOCK'S novels were first published in the following years: *Headlong Hall*, 1816; *Melincourt* (three volumes), 1817; *Nightmare Abbey*, 1818; *Maid Marian*, 1822; *The Misfortunes of Elphin*, 1829; *Crotchet Castle*, 1831; and *Gryll Grange*, 1860. *Headlong Hall* was published anonymously. All the others were published as: " By the Author of ' Headlong Hall.' "

In 1837 four of them (*Headlong Hall, Nightmare Abbey, Maid Marian* and *Crotchet Castle*) appeared together as Volume LVII of Bentley's Standard Novels, with texts containing minor revisions by the author. The first collected edition of Peacock's works appeared in 1874 (dated 1875) edited by Sir Henry Cole and published by Bentley in three volumes. This edition has no textual significance, but it does contain the valuable Biographical Notice of Peacock by his grand-daughter Edith Nicolls.

In 1891 Messrs J. M. Dent published an edition of the works in ten volumes, edited by my grandfather, Richard Garnett. This text proves, on examination, to be corrupt and unreliable. In the volume called *Calidore and Miscellanea* were first collected some of the best of Peacock's stray fragments and essays, together with *Recollections of Thomas Love Peacock* by Sir Edward Strachey, Bart.

In 1895–97 Messrs Macmillan published an edition of the novels with introductions by George Saintsbury, and in 1924 appeared the first of the ten volumes of the Halliford Edition of the Works, edited by H. F. Brett-Smith and C. E. Jones and published by Messrs Constable. The last volume appeared in 1934. This was the first modern edition to establish a definitive text.

The text of the present volume is therefore that of the Halliford Edition, reproducing in each case the last edition which Peacock revised himself; that is to say the Bentley volume for the four novels therein contained, and the first editions of the other three. Obvious misprints (including even a few which had crept into the Halliford Edition itself) have been silently corrected. The names of the speakers in the formal dialogues, which Peacock printed above each speech, have been brought down and run into the first line of the speech to save space.

In Peacock's own footnotes the names of books and periodicals have been italicised, to harmonise with my own notes. Otherwise the texts are as Peacock left them, with all their manifold inconsistencies of spelling, italics, capital letters, and so forth. All Greek accents save rough breathings have been omitted from the first three novels, in deference to the opinion and example of the author, who applied to them, in one of his notebooks, the lines of Martial:

> Turpe est difficiles habere nugas :
> Et stultus labor est ineptiarum.
>
> (It is silly to concentrate on trifles and only
> a fool expends his efforts upon nonsense.)

There is only one Greek word in *Maid Marian,* and by the time Peacock came to write *The Misfortunes of Elphin* his opinions had mellowed.

My thanks are due to Messrs Constable, Mr Michael Sadleir, Mr Brett-Smith and Mr Jones for their friendly co-operation ; to Messrs Dent, who have been so good as to allow me to make such use as I wished of my grandfather's introductions and notes ; to a classical scholar of Oxford University, who wishes to remain anonymous, for supplying me with translations and references for the Latin and Greek quotations ; and to Professor Roberto Weiss of London University, for similar help with the Italian quotations.

Lastly, I have received great help with the notes giving references for quotations, and the letter G. which distinguishes my notes from Peacock's own (marked with the letter P.) must here be interpreted as the symbol for the collective wisdom of many friends, without whose help this edition would be far more imperfect than it is.

D. G.

PREFACE

TO VOLUME LVII OF BENTLEY'S 'STANDARD NOVELS'

containing *Headlong Hall, Nightmare Abbey, Maid Marian* and *Crotchet Castle*

ALL these little publications appeared originally without prefaces. I left them to speak for themselves ; and I thought I might very fitly preserve my own impersonality, having never intruded on the personality of others, nor taken any liberties but with public conduct and public opinions. But an old friend assures me, that to publish a book without a preface is like entering a drawing-room without making a bow. In deference to this opinion, though I am not quite clear of its soundness, I make my prefatory bow at this eleventh hour.

"Headlong Hall" was written in 1815 ; "Nightmare Abbey" in 1817[1]; "Maid Marian," with the exception of the last three chapters, in 1818 ; "Crotchet Castle" in 1830. I am desirous to note the intervals, because, at each of those periods, things were true, in great matters and in small, which are true no longer. "Headlong Hall" begins with the Holyhead mail, and "Crotchet Castle" ends with a rotten borough. The Holyhead mail no longer keeps the same hours, nor stops at the Capel Cerig Inn, which the progress of improvement has thrown out of the road ; and the rotten boroughs of 1830 have ceased to exist, though there are some very pretty pocket properties, which are their worthy successors. But the classes of tastes, feelings, and opinions, which were successively brought into play in these little tales, remain substantially the same. Perfectibilians, deteriorationists, statu-quo-ites, phrenologists, trans-cendentalists, political economists, theorists in all sciences, pro-jectors in all arts, morbid visionaries, romantic enthusiasts, lovers of music, lovers of the picturesque, and lovers of good dinners,

[1] Actually 1818. G.

march, and will march for ever, *pari passu* with the march of mechanics, which some facetiously call the march of intellect. The fastidious in old wine are a race that does not decay. Literary violators of the confidences of private life still gain a disreputable livelihood and an unenviable notoriety. Match-makers from interest, and the disappointed in love and in friendship, are varieties of which specimens are extant. The great principle of the Right of Might is as flourishing now as in the days of Maid Marian : the array of false pretensions, moral, political, and literary, is as imposing as ever : the rulers of the world still feel things in their effects, and never foresee them in their causes ; and political mountebanks continue, and will continue, to puff nostrums and practise legerdemain under the eyes of the multitude ; following, like the " learned friend " of Crotchet Castle, a course as tortuous as that of a river, but in a reverse process ; beginning by being dark and deep, and ending by being transparent.

THE AUTHOR OF " HEADLONG HALL."

March 4, 1837

HEADLONG HALL

HEADLONG HALL

All philosophers, who find
Some favourite system to their mind
In every point to make it fit,
Will force all nature to submit.[1]

---

[1] Swift. *Cadenus and Vanessa.* G.

Headlong Hall was first published in 1816

CONTENTS OF
HEADLONG HALL

CHAPTER		PAGE
	Introduction by David Garnett . .	7
I	THE MAIL	9
II	THE SQUIRE.—THE BREAKFAST .	13
III	THE ARRIVALS	18
IV	THE GROUNDS	22
V	THE DINNER	27
VI	THE EVENING	38
VII	THE WALK	44
VIII	THE TOWER	51
IX	THE SEXTON	56
X	THE SKULL	60
XI	THE ANNIVERSARY . . .	63
XII	THE LECTURE	67
XIII	THE BALL	70
XIV	THE PROPOSALS	81
XV	THE CONCLUSION . . .	88

INTRODUCTION TO
HEADLONG HALL

HEADLONG HALL was written in 1815 at a time when Peacock was constantly seeing Shelley, and the book is largely concerned with the ideas which Shelley and his friends habitually discussed. Shelley loved argument, which he thought was the best way of arriving at the truth. Although he was emotionally unstable and passionate, these qualities did not appear in conversations with his friends. He was always charmingly good-tempered in an argument and always open to conviction, and when he disagreed he did so calmly and gently. Nor did he lack a sense of humour; for holding absurd opinions does not prevent a keen sense of the ridiculous. Shelley was also free from vanity and could discuss whether the story he had told Peacock was a delusion or a fact, without showing any irritation or resentment.

The belief that mankind has deteriorated from a golden age and that human evils have sprung from the adoption of a carnivorous diet was adopted wholesale by Shelley when he was writing *Queen Mab*, from his friend J. F. Newton, the author of *Return to Nature, or a Defence of Vegetable Regimen*. Newton himself does not appear personally in *Headlong Hall*. Shelley was a vegetarian in his own home, but when he was travelling he " lived on what he could get " like Mr Escot in the inn on the Holyhead road. On the boating expedition up the Thames, Shelley became so unwell from living on a spurious lemonade made of powder, and on tea and bread and butter, that he thought he would have to give up the trip. Peacock prescribed three mutton chops well peppered, which Shelley ate and was immediately cured.

Like all Peacock's novels except the romances, *Headlong Hall* is formed on the simple plan of assembling visitors at a country house

7

where they carry on discussions, eat and drink abundantly, dance and sing, fall in love and are married off in the last chapter.

In *Headlong Hall* there are three philosophers with whose foibles the author shows more sympathy than with the other visitors; they may be regarded as serving as mouthpieces for Shelley, Peacock and Hogg, Mr Escot's views being based on Shelley's when he wrote the notes to *Queen Mab*, Mr Foster's partly on Shelley's, partly on Peacock's utilitarianism, Mr Jenkison's on Hogg's cautious conservatism.

The other visitors are based on the authors of books and reviews which Shelley and Peacock had read, but whom Peacock had not met, or personify follies of the age. There are the landscape gardeners who had been quarrelling in print over theories of the picturesque, there is Mr Cranium who personifies the craze for phrenology, there is an omniscient and conceited gentleman, Mr Panscope, whose interest in metaphysics alone links him with Coleridge, there are the Edinburgh reviewers and poets, and a female novelist whose work Peacock had read, all puffing each other in order to get puffed in return. Several of the characters in *Headlong Hall* are taken out of Peacock's plays *The Three Doctors* and *The Dilettanti*, which were not published till 1910 from manuscripts given by Peacock's granddaughter, Edith Nicolls, to the British Museum. They were published against her wishes and there are many imperfections in the text of that edition. Mr Brett-Smith reprinted the plays accurately in the Halliford Edition of Peacock's works.

The Three Doctors was written before 1815. The setting is that of a Welsh Country House and the play begins with Squire Hippy and his butler Shenkin making confusion worse confounded. Other characters are Marmaduke Milestone, who exhibits his plan for Lord Littlebrain's park, and Mr O'Fir, who is pulled out of the water like Mr Cranium, but is otherwise a "picturesque tourist" like Sir Patrick O'Prism.

The Dilettanti includes a violinist, Mr Chromatic, and a painter, Mr Shadow. Peacock drew on both plays in writing *Headlong Hall* and *Melincourt*, but they contain few ideas and no philosophers.

D. G.

HEADLONG HALL.

HEADLONG HALL

CHAPTER I

THE MAIL

THE ambiguous light of a December morning, peeping through the windows of the Holyhead mail, dispelled the soft visions of the four insides, who had slept, or seemed to sleep, through the first seventy miles of the road, with as much comfort as may be supposed consistent with the jolting of the vehicle, and an occasional admonition to *remember the coachman*, thundered through the open door, accompanied by the gentle breath of Boreas, into the ears of the drowsy traveller.

A lively remark, that *the day was none of the finest*, having elicited a repartee of *quite the contrary*, the various knotty points of meteorology, which usually form the exordium of an English conversation, were successively discussed and exhausted; and, the ice being thus broken, the colloquy rambled to other topics, in the course of which it appeared, to the surprise of every one, that all four, though perfect strangers to each other, were actually bound to the same point, namely, Headlong Hall, the seat of the ancient and honourable family of the Headlongs, of the vale of Llanberris, in Caernarvonshire. This name may appear at first sight not to be truly Cambrian, like those of the Rices, and Prices, and Morgans, and Owens, and Williamses, and Evanses, and Parrys, and Joneses; but, nevertheless, the Headlongs claim to be not less genuine derivatives from the antique branch of Cadwallader than any of the last-named multiramified families. They claim, indeed, by one account, superior antiquity to all of them, and even to Cadwallader himself; a tradition having been handed down in Headlong Hall for some few thousand years, that the founder of the family was preserved in the deluge on the summit of Snowdon, and took the name of Rhaiader, which signifies a *waterfall*, in consequence of his having accompanied the water in its descent or diminution, till he found himself comfortably seated on the rocks of Llanberris. But, in later days, when commercial bagsmen began to scour the country, the ambiguity of the sound induced his descendants to drop the suspicious denomination of *Riders*, and translate the word into English ; when, not being well pleased with the sound of the *thing*, they substituted that of the *quality*, and accordingly adopted the name *Headlong*, the appropriate epithet of waterfall.

> I cannot tell how the truth may be :
> I say the tale as 'twas said to me.[1]

The present representative of this ancient and dignified house, Harry Headlong, Esquire, was, like all other Welsh squires, fond of shooting, hunting, racing, drinking, and other such innocent amusements, μειζονος δ᾽ αλλον τινος, as Menander expresses it.[2] But, unlike other Welsh squires, he had actually suffered certain phenomena, called books, to find their way into his house ; and, by dint of lounging over them after dinner, on those occasions when he was compelled to take his bottle alone, he became seized with a violent passion to be thought a philosopher and a man of taste ; and accordingly set off on an expedition to Oxford, to inquire for other varieties of the same genera, namely, men of taste and philosophers ; but, being assured by a learned professor that there were no such things in the University, he proceeded to London, where, after beating up in several booksellers' shops, theatres, exhibition-rooms, and other resorts of literature and taste, he formed as extensive an acquaintance with philosophers and dilettanti as his utmost ambition could desire ; and it now became his chief wish to have them all together in Headlong Hall, arguing, over his old Port and Burgundy, the various knotty points which had puzzled his pericranium. He had, therefore, sent them invitations in due form to pass their Christmas at Headlong Hall ; which invitations the extensive fame of his kitchen fire had induced the greater part of them to accept ; and four of the chosen guests had, from different parts of the metropolis, ensconced themselves in the four corners of the Holyhead mail.

---

[1] Scott : *Lay of the Last Minstrel*, Canto 2, St. 22. G.
[2] *Fragm.* 301 K. G.

These four persons were, Mr. Foster,[1] the perfectibilian ; Mr. Escot,[2] the deteriorationist ; Mr. Jenkison,[3] the statu-quo-ite ; and the Reverend Doctor Gaster,[4] who, though of course neither a philosopher nor a man of taste, had so won on the Squire's fancy, by a learned dissertation on the art of stuffing a turkey, that he concluded no Christmas party would be complete without him.

The conversation among these illuminati soon became animated ; and Mr. Foster, who, we must observe, was a thin gentleman, about thirty years of age, with an aquiline nose, black eyes, white teeth, and black hair—took occasion to panegyrize the vehicle in which they were then travelling, and observed what remarkable improvements had been made in the means of facilitating intercourse between distant parts of the kingdom : he held forth with great energy on the subject of roads and railways, canals and tunnels, manufactures and machinery : " In short," said he, " every thing we look on attests the progress of mankind in all the arts of life, and demonstrates their gradual advancement towards a state of unlimited perfection."

Mr. Escot, who was somewhat younger than Mr. Foster, but rather more pale and saturnine in his aspect, here took up the thread of the discourse, observing, that the proposition just advanced seemed to him perfectly contrary to the true state of the case : " for," said he, " these improvements, as you call them, appear to me only so many links in the great chain of corruption, which will soon fetter the whole human race in irreparable slavery and incurable wretched-

[1] Foster, quasi Φωστηρ,—from φαος and τηρεω, lucem servo, conservo, observo, custodio—one who watches over and guards the light ; a sense in which the word is often used amongst us, when we speak of fostering a flame. [P]

[2] Escot, quasi ες σκοτον, in tenebras, scilicet, intuens ; one who is always looking into the dark side of the question. [P.]

[3] Jenkison : This name may be derived from αιεν εξ ισων, semper ex æqualibus—scilicet, mensuris, omnia metiens : one who from equal measures divides and distributes all things : one who from equal measures can always produce arguments on both sides of a question, with so much nicety and exactness, as to keep the said question eternally pending, and the balance of the controversy perpetually in statu quo. By an aphæresis of the α, an elision of the second ε, and an easy and natural mutation of ξ into κ, the derivation of this name proceeds according to the strictest principles of etymology : αιεν εξ ισων—Ιεν εξ ισων—Ιεν εκ ισων—Ιεν 'κ ισων—Ιενκισων—Ienkison—Jenkison. [P.]

[4] Gaster : scilicet Γαστηρ—Venter,—et præterea nihil. [P.]

ness : your improvements proceed in a simple ratio, while the factitious wants and unnatural appetites they engender proceed in a compound one ; and thus one generation acquires fifty wants, and fifty means of supplying them are invented, which each in its turn engenders two new ones ; so that the next generation has a hundred, the next two hundred, the next four hundred, till every human being becomes such a helpless compound of perverted inclinations, that he is altogether at the mercy of external circumstances, loses all independence and singleness of character, and degenerates so rapidly from the primitive dignity of his sylvan origin, that it is scarcely possible to indulge in any other expectation, than that the whole species must at length be exterminated by its own infinite imbecility and vileness."

" Your opinions," said Mr. Jenkison, a round-faced little gentleman of about forty-five, " seem to differ *toto cœlo*. I have often debated the matter in my own mind, *pro* and *con*, and have at length arrived at this conclusion,—that there is not in the human race a tendency either to moral perfectibility or deterioration ; but that the quantities of each are so exactly balanced by their reciprocal results, that the species, with respect to the sum of good and evil, knowledge and ignorance, happiness and misery, remains exactly and perpetually *in statu quo*." [1]

" Surely," said Mr. Foster, " you cannot maintain such a proposition in the face of evidence so luminous. Look at the progress of all the arts and sciences,—see chemistry, botany, astronomy——."

" Surely," said Mr. Escot, " experience deposes against you. Look at the rapid growth of corruption, luxury, selfishness——."

" Really, gentlemen," said the Reverend Doctor Gaster, after clearing the husk in his throat with two or three hems, " this is a very sceptical, and, I must say, atheistical conversation, and I should have thought, out of respect to my cloth——."

Here the coach stopped, and the coachman, opening the door,

---

[1] Foster, Escot and Jenkison, though not in any way portraits, are the mouthpieces of ideas discussed by Shelley, Peacock, Hogg, and Shelley's friend, J. F. Newton. Foster voices Shelley's faith in perfectibility, while Escot's ideas are derived from Rousseau's *Discours sur l'inégalité* and *Emile* and from Rousseau's disciple, Lord Monboddo. Jenkison voices the mundane attitude of Hogg. G.

vociferated—" Breakfast, gentlemen ; " a sound which so gladdened
the ears of the divine, that the alacrity with which he sprang from
the vehicle superinduced a distortion of his ankle, and he was
obliged to limp into the inn between Mr. Escot and Mr. Jenkison ;
the former observing, that he ought to look for nothing but evil, and,
therefore, should not be surprised at this little accident ; the latter
remarking, that the comfort of a good breakfast, and the pain of a
sprained ankle, pretty exactly balanced each other.

CHAPTER II

THE SQUIRE.—THE BREAKFAST

SQUIRE HEADLONG, in the mean while, was quadripartite in his
locality ; that is to say, he was superintending the operations in four
scenes of action—namely, the cellar, the library, the picture-gallery,
and the dining-room,—preparing for the reception of his philosophical
and dilettanti visitors. His myrmidon on this occasion was a little
red-nosed butler, whom nature seemed to have cast in the genuine
mould of an antique Silenus, and who waddled about the house after
his master, wiping his forehead and panting for breath, while the
latter bounced from room to room like a cracker, and was indefatigable in his requisitions for the proximity of his vinous Achates, whose
advice and co-operation he deemed no less necessary in the library
than in the cellar. Multitudes of packages had arrived, by land and
water, from London, and Liverpool, and Chester, and Manchester,
and Birmingham, and various parts of the mountains : books, wine,
cheese, globes, mathematical instruments, turkeys, telescopes, hams,
tongues, microscopes, quadrants, sextants, fiddles, flutes, tea, sugar,
electrical machines, figs, spices, air-pumps, soda-water, chemical
apparatus, eggs, French-horns, drawing books, palettes, oils and
colours, bottled ale and porter, scenery for a private theatre, pickles
and fish-sauce, patent lamps and chandeliers, barrels of oysters, sofas,
chairs, tables, carpets, beds, looking-glasses, pictures, fruits and con-
fections, nuts, oranges, lemons, packages of salt salmon, and jars

of Portugal grapes. These, arriving with infinite rapidity, and in inexhaustible succession, had been deposited at random, as the convenience of the moment dictated,—sofas in the cellar, chandeliers in the kitchen, hampers of ale in the drawing-room, and fiddles and fish-sauce in the library.[1] The servants, unpacking all these in furious haste, and flying with them from place to place, according to the tumultuous directions of Squire Headlong and the little fat butler who fumed at his heels, chafed, and crossed, and clashed, and tumbled over one another up stairs and down. All was bustle, uproar, and confusion ; yet nothing seemed to advance : while the rage and impetuosity of the Squire continued fermenting to the highest degree of exasperation, which he signified, from time to time, by converting some newly unpacked article, such as a book, a bottle, a ham, or a fiddle, into a missile against the head of some unfortunate servant who did not seem to move in a ratio of velocity corresponding to the intensity of his master's desires.

In this state of eager preparation we shall leave the happy inhabitants of Headlong Hall, and return to the three philosophers and the unfortunate divine, whom we left limping with a sprained ankle into the breakfast-room of the inn ; where his two supporters deposited him safely in a large arm-chair, with his wounded leg comfortably stretched out on another. The morning being extremely cold, he contrived to be seated as near the fire as was consistent with his other object of having a perfect command of the table and its apparatus ; which consisted not only of the ordinary comforts of tea and toast, but of a delicious supply of new-laid eggs, and a magnificent round of beef ; against which Mr. Escot immediately pointed all the artillery of his eloquence, declaring the use of animal food, conjointly with that of fire, to be one of the principal causes of the present degeneracy of mankind.[2] " The natural and original man," said he, " lived in the woods : the roots and fruits of the earth supplied his simple nutriment : he had few desires, and no diseases. But, when he began to sacrifice victims on the altar of superstition,

[1] Strikingly reminiscent of Hogg's account of Shelley's rooms at Oxford (Hogg's *Life*, Ch. III). The confusion in which Shelley habitually lived probably suggested this passage to Peacock. G.

[2] See Shelley : *Queen Mab*, Note to Canto VIII, ll. 211–12, which contains all of Mr. Escot's argument here. G.

to pursue the goat and the deer, and, by the pernicious invention of fire, to pervert their flesh into food, luxury, disease, and premature death, were let loose upon the world. Such is clearly the correct interpretation of the fable of Prometheus, which is a symbolical portraiture of that disastrous epoch, when man first applied fire to culinary purposes, and thereby surrendered his liver to the vulture of disease. From that period the stature of mankind has been in a state of gradual diminution, and I have not the least doubt that it will continue to grow *small by degrees, and lamentably less*,[1] till the whole race will vanish imperceptibly from the face of the earth."

" I cannot agree," said Mr. Foster, " in the consequences being so very disastrous. I admit, that in some respects the use of animal food retards, though it cannot materially inhibit, the perfectibility of the species. But the use of fire was indispensably necessary, as Æschylus and Virgil expressly assert, to give being to the various arts of life, which, in their rapid and interminable progress, will finally conduct every individual of the race to the philosophic pinnacle of pure and perfect felicity."

" In the controversy concerning animal and vegetable food," said Mr. Jenkison, " there is much to be said on both sides ; and, the question being in equipoise, I content myself with a mixed diet, and make a point of eating whatever is placed before me, provided it be good in its kind."

In this opinion his two brother philosophers practically coincided, though they both ran down the theory as highly detrimental to the best interests of man.

" I am really astonished," said the Reverend Doctor Gaster, gracefully picking off the supernal fragments of an egg he had just cracked, and clearing away a space at the top for the reception of a small piece of butter—" I am really astonished, gentlemen, at the very heterodox opinions I have heard you deliver : since nothing can be more obvious than that all animals were created solely and exclusively for the use of man."

" Even the tiger that devours him ? " said Mr. Escot.

" Certainly," said Doctor Gaster.

[1] An echo of Prior : *Henry and Emma*, l. 323. " Fine by degrees and beautifully less." G.

"How do you prove it?" said Mr. Escot.

"It requires no proof," said Doctor Gaster: "it is a point of doctrine. It is written, therefore it is so."

"Nothing can be more logical," said Mr. Jenkison. "It has been said," continued he, "that the ox was expressly made to be eaten by man: it may be said, by a parity of reasoning, that man was expressly made to be eaten by the tiger: but as wild oxen exist where there are no men, and men where there are no tigers, it would seem that in these instances they do not properly answer the ends of their creation."

"It is a mystery," said Doctor Gaster.

"Not to launch into the question of final causes," said Mr. Escot, helping himself at the same time to a slice of beef, "concerning which I will candidly acknowledge I am as profoundly ignorant as the most dogmatical theologian possibly can be, I just wish to observe, that the pure and peaceful manners which Homer ascribes to the Loto-phagi, and which at this day characterise many nations (the Hindoos, for example, who subsist exclusively on the fruits of the earth), depose very strongly in favour of a vegetable regimen."

"It may be said, on the contrary," said Mr. Foster, "that animal food acts on the mind as manure does on flowers, forcing them into a degree of expansion they would not otherwise have attained. If we can imagine a philosophical auricula falling into a train of theoretical meditation on its original and natural nutriment, till it should work itself up into a profound abomination of bullock's blood, sugar-baker's scum, and other *unnatural* ingredients of that rich com-position of soil which had brought it to perfection,[1] and insist on being planted in common earth, it would have all the advantage of natural theory on its side that the most strenuous advocate of the vegetable system could desire; but it would soon discover the practical error of its retrograde experiment by its lamentable inferiority in strength and beauty to all the auriculas around it. I am afraid, in some instances at least, this analogy holds true with respect to mind. No one will make a comparison, in point of mental power, between the Hindoos and the ancient Greeks."

"The anatomy of the human stomach," said Mr. Escot, "and the

[1] See *Emmerton on the Auricula*. [P.]

formation of the teeth, clearly place man in the class of frugivorous animals."

" Many anatomists," said Mr. Foster, " are of a different opinion, and agree in discerning the characteristics of the carnivorous classes."

" I am no anatomist," said Mr. Jenkison, " and cannot decide where doctors disagree ; in the mean time, I conclude that man is omnivorous, and on that conclusion I act."

" Your conclusion is truly orthodox," said the Reverend Doctor Gaster : " indeed, the loaves and fishes are typical of a mixed diet ; and the practice of the Church in all ages shows——"

" That it never loses sight of the loaves and fishes," said Mr. Escot.

" It never loses sight of any point of sound doctrine," said the reverend doctor.

The coachman now informed them their time was elapsed ; nor could all the pathetic remonstrances of the reverend divine, who declared he had not half breakfasted, succeed in gaining one minute from the inexorable Jehu.

" You will allow," said Mr. Foster, as soon as they were again in motion, " that the wild man of the woods could not transport himself over two hundred miles of forest, with as much facility as one of these vehicles transports you and me through the heart of this cultivated country."

" I am certain," said Mr. Escot, " that a wild man can travel an immense distance without fatigue ; but what is the advantage of locomotion ? The wild man is happy in one spot, and there he remains : the civilised man is wretched in every place he happens to be in, and then congratulates himself on being accommodated with a machine, that will whirl him to another, where he will be just as miserable as ever."

We shall now leave the mail-coach to find its way to Capel Cerig, the nearest point of the Holyhead road to the dwelling of Squire Headlong.

CHAPTER III

THE ARRIVALS

In the midst of that scene of confusion thrice confounded, in which we left the inhabitants of Headlong Hall, arrived the lovely Caprioletta Headlong, the Squire's sister (whom he had sent for, from the residence of her maiden aunt at Caernarvon, to do the honours of his house), beaming like light on chaos, to arrange disorder and harmonise discord. The tempestuous spirit of her brother became instantaneously as smooth as the surface of the lake of Llanberris ; and the little fat butler " plessed Cot, and St. Tafit, and the peautiful tamsel," for being permitted to move about the house in his natural pace. In less than twenty-four hours after her arrival, every thing was disposed in its proper station, and the Squire began to be all impatience for the appearance of his promised guests.

The first visitor with whom he had the felicity of shaking hands was Marmaduke Milestone, Esquire, who arrived with a portfolio under his arm. Mr. Milestone [1] was a picturesque landscape gardener of the first celebrity,[2] who was not without hopes of persuading Squire

---

[1] Mr. Knight, in a note to the Landscape, having taken the liberty of laughing at a notable device of a celebrated *improver*, for giving greatness of character to a place, and showing an undivided extent of property, by placing the family arms on the neighbouring *milestones*, the improver retorted on him with a charge of misquotation, misrepresentation, and malice prepense. Mr. Knight, in the preface to the second edition of his poem, quotes the improver's words :—" The market-house, or other public edifice, or even a *mere stone with distances*, may bear the arms of the family : " and adds :—" By a *mere stone with distances*, the author of the Landscape certainly thought he meant a *milestone ;* but, if he did not, any other interpretation which he may think more advantageous to himself shall readily be adopted, as it will equally answer the purpose of the quotation." The improver, however, did not condescend to explain what he really meant by a *mere stone with distances*, though he strenuously maintained that he did *not* mean a *milestone*. His idea, therefore, stands on record, invested with all the sublimity that obscurity can confer. [P.]

[2] The landscape gardener and improver, Humphry Repton, who succeeded to the position of " Capability " Brown. (See *Mansfield Park*, ch. 6.) Repton, Payne Knight and Sir Uvedale Price had been attacking each other's views violently. Shelley described them as " ill-trained beagles . . . snarling at each other when they could not catch the hare."

Headlong to put his romantic pleasure-grounds under a process of improvement, promising himself a signal triumph for his incomparable art in the difficult, and, therefore, glorious achievement of polishing and trimming the rocks of Llanberris.

Next arrived a post-chaise from the inn at Capel Cerig, containing the Reverend Doctor Gaster. It appeared, that, when the mail-coach deposited its valuable cargo, early on the second morning, at the inn at Capel Cerig, there was only one post-chaise to be had; it was therefore determined that the reverend doctor and the luggage should proceed in the chaise, and that the three philosophers should walk. When the reverend gentleman first seated himself in the chaise, the windows were down all round; but he allowed it to drive off under the idea that he could easily pull them up. This task, however, he had considerable difficulty in accomplishing, and when he had succeeded, it availed him little; for the frames and glasses had long since discontinued their ancient familiarity. He had, however, no alternative but to proceed, and to comfort himself, as he went, with some choice quotations from the book of Job. The road led along the edges of tremendous chasms, with torrents dashing in the bottom; so that, if his teeth had not chattered with cold, they would have done so with fear. The Squire shook him heartily by the hand, and congratulated him on his safe arrival at Headlong Hall. The Doctor returned the squeeze, and assured him that the congratulation was by no means misapplied.

Next came the three philosophers, highly delighted with their walk, and full of rapturous exclamations on the sublime beauties of the scenery.

The Doctor shrugged up his shoulders, and confessed he preferred the scenery of Putney and Kew, where a man could go comfortably to sleep in his chaise, without being in momentary terror of being hurled headlong down a precipice.

Mr. Milestone observed, that there were great capabilities in the scenery, but it wanted shaving and polishing. If he could but have it under his care for a single twelvemonth, he assured them no one would be able to know it again.

Mr. Jenkison thought the scenery was just what it ought to be, and required no alteration.

Mr. Foster thought it could be improved, but doubted if that effect would be produced by the system of Mr. Milestone.

Mr. Escot did not think that any human being could improve it, but had no doubt of its having changed very considerably for the worse, since the days when the now barren rocks were covered with the immense forest of Snowdon, which must have contained a very fine race of wild men, not less than ten feet high.

The next arrival was that of Mr. Cranium, and his lovely daughter Miss Cephalis [1] Cranium, who flew to the arms of her dear friend Caprioletta, with all that warmth of friendship which young ladies usually assume towards each other in the presence of young gentlemen. [2]

Miss Cephalis blushed like a carnation at the sight of Mr. Escot, and Mr. Escot glowed like a corn-poppy at the sight of Miss Cephalis. It was at least obvious to all observers, that he could imagine the possibility of one change for the better, even in this terrestrial theatre of universal deterioration.

Mr. Cranium's eyes wandered from Mr. Escot to his daughter, and from his daughter to Mr. Escot ; and his complexion, in the course of the scrutiny, underwent several variations, from the dark red of the piony to the deep blue of the convolvulus.

Mr. Escot had formerly been the received lover of Miss Cephalis, till he incurred the indignation of her father by laughing at a very profound craniological dissertation [3] which the old gentleman delivered ; nor had Mr. Escot yet discovered the means of mollifying his wrath.

Mr. Cranium carried in his own hands a bag, the contents of which were too precious to be entrusted to any one but himself; and

---

[1] Saintsbury has pointed out that the name Cephalis occurs in *Les Mariages Samnites*, one of Marmontel's *Contes Moraux*, which he believed greatly influenced Peacock. G.

[2] " Il est constant qu'elles se baisent de meilleur cœur, et se caressent avec plus de grâce devant les hommes, fieres d'aiguiser impunément leur convoitise par l'image des faveurs qu'elles savent leur faire envier."— ROUSSEAU, *Emile*, liv. 5. [P.]

[3] " Scientific " phrenology was first formulated by Drs. Gall and Spurzheim. Both visited England, lectured, and obtained a large following in the early years of the century. Controversy on the subject was vigorous, and by 1832 there were 29 phrenological societies in Great Britain. G.

earnestly entreated to be shown to the chamber appropriated for his reception, that he might deposit his treasure in safety. The little butler was accordingly summoned to conduct him to his *cubiculum*.

Next arrived a post-chaise, carrying four insides, whose extreme thinness enabled them to travel thus economically without experiencing the slightest inconvenience. These four personages were, two very profound critics, Mr. Gall and Mr. Treacle, who followed the trade of reviewers, but occasionally indulged themselves in the composition of bad poetry; and two very multitudinous versifiers, Mr. Nightshade and Mr. Mac Laurel, who followed the trade of poetry, but occasionally indulged themselves in the composition of bad criticism. Mr. Nightshade and Mr. Mac Laurel were the two senior lieutenants of a very formidable corps of critics, of whom Timothy Treacle, Esquire, was captain, and Geoffrey Gall, Esquire, generalissimo.[1]

The last arrivals were Mr. Cornelius Chromatic, the most profound and scientific of all amateurs of the fiddle, with his two blooming daughters, Miss Tenorina and Miss Graziosa; Sir Patrick O'Prism, a dilettante painter of high renown,[2] and his maiden aunt, Miss Philomela Poppyseed, an indefatigable compounder of novels, written for the express purpose of supporting every species of superstition and prejudice;[3] and Mr. Panscope, the chemical, botanical, geological, astronomical, mathematical, metaphysical, meteorological, anatomical, physiological, galvanistical, musical, pictorial, bibliographical, critical philosopher, who had run through the whole circle of the sciences, and understood them all equally well.[4]

Mr. Milestone was impatient to take a walk round the grounds, that he might examine how far the system of clumping and levelling could be carried advantageously into effect. The ladies retired to enjoy each other's society in the first happy moments of meeting:

[1] Richard Garnett erroneously identified Gall with Gifford. M. Mayoux points out that Geoffrey Gall is Jeffrey of the *Edinburgh Review*. This fits in with the identification of Mac Laurel as John Wilson (Christopher North). Mr. Priestley identifies Mac Laurel with Campbell. Nightshade appears to be Southey. G.

[2] Based upon Sir Uvedale Price, Bt., author of *An Essay on the Picturesque*, in which he argues against formal in favour of natural beauty. G.

[3] Based on Mrs. Amelia Opie, the novelist and widow of the painter. G.

[4] Based on an insufficient knowledge of Coleridge. G.

the Reverend Doctor Gaster sat by the library fire, in profound meditation over a volume of the "*Almanach des Gourmands*" : Mr. Panscope sat in the opposite corner with a volume of Rees's Cyclopædia : Mr. Cranium was busy up stairs : Mr. Chromatic retreated to the music-room, where he fiddled through a book of solos before the ringing of the first dinner-bell. The remainder of the party supported Mr. Milestone's proposition ; and, accordingly, Squire Headlong and Mr. Milestone leading the van, they commenced their perambulation.

CHAPTER IV

THE GROUNDS [1]

"I PERCEIVE," said Mr. Milestone, after they had walked a few paces, "these grounds have never been touched by the finger of taste."

"The place is quite a wilderness," said Squire Headlong : "for during the latter part of my father's life, while I was *finishing* my *education*, he troubled himself about nothing but the cellar, and suffered every thing else to go to rack and ruin. A mere wilderness, as you see, even now in December ; but in summer a complete nursery of briers, a forest of thistles, a plantation of nettles, without any live stock but goats, that have eaten up all the bark of the trees. Here you see is the pedestal of a statue, with only half a leg and four toes remaining : there were many here once. When I was a boy, I used to sit every day on the shoulders of Hercules : what became of *him* I have never been able to ascertain. Neptune has been lying these seven years in the dust-hole ; Atlas had his head knocked off

[1] "From Towyn I shall proceed to Aberystwith, and from thence to the Devil's bridge at Hafod."—Peacock to Hookham, 9 April 1811.
It appears probable that the description of Headlong Hall and of its owner was inspired by Hafod House and grounds, which belonged to Colonel Johnes. Mr. Geoffrey Grigson has recently suggested (*Cornhill Magazine*, No. 970, 1947) that Colonel Johnes and Hafod House inspired Coleridge, who passed that way in 1794, with material for Kubla Khan and Xanadu. Hafod House was burnt down in 1807 and Peacock saw the ruins. G.

to fit him for propping a shed ; and only the day before yesterday we fished Bacchus out of the horse-pond." [1]

" My dear sir," said Mr. Milestone, " accord me your permission to wave the wand of enchantment over your grounds. The rocks shall be blown up, the trees shall be cut down, the wilderness and all its goats shall vanish like mist. Pagodas and Chinese bridges, gravel walks and shrubberies, bowling-greens, canals, and clumps of larch, shall rise upon its ruins. One age, sir, has brought to light the treasures of ancient learning ; a second has penetrated into the depths of metaphysics ; a third has brought to perfection the science of astronomy ; but it was reserved for the exclusive genius of the present times, to invent the noble art of picturesque gardening, which has given, as it were, a new tint to the complexion of nature, and a new outline to the physiognomy of the universe ! "

" Give me leave," said Sir Patrick O'Prism, " to take an exception to that same. Your system of levelling, and trimming, and clipping, and docking, and clumping, and polishing, and cropping, and shaving, destroys all the beautiful intricacies of natural luxuriance, and all the graduated harmonies of light and shade, melting into one another, as you see them on that rock over yonder. I never saw one of your improved places, as you call them, and which are nothing but big bowling-greens, like sheets of green paper, with a parcel of round clumps scattered over them, like so many spots of ink, flicked at random out of a pen,[2] and a solitary animal here and there look- ing as if it were lost, that I did not think it was for all the world like Hounslow Heath, thinly sprinkled over with bushes and highwaymen."

" Sir," said Mr. Milestone, " you will have the goodness to make a distinction between the picturesque and the beautiful."

" Will I ? " said Sir Patrick, " och ! but I won't. For what is beautiful ? That which pleases the eye. And what pleases the eye ? Tints variously broken and blended. Now, tints variously broken and blended constitute the picturesque."

---

[1] This passage, from the word " Neptune " to the word " horse-pond,' is taken almost verbatim from Peacock's farce *The Three Doctors*, except that " twenty years " has been reduced to " seven years." G.

[2] See *Price on the Picturesque*. [P.]

" Allow me," said Mr. Gall.   " I distinguish the picturesque and
the beautiful, and I add to them, in the laying out of grounds, a third
and distinct character, which I call *unexpectedness*."

" Pray, sir," said Mr. Milestone, " by what name do you distinguish this character, when a person walks round the grounds for
the second time ? " [1]

Mr. Gall bit his lips, and inwardly vowed to revenge himself on
Milestone, by cutting up his next publication.

A long controversy now ensued concerning the picturesque and the
beautiful, highly edifying to Squire Headlong.

The three philosophers stopped, as they wound round a projecting
point of rock, to contemplate a little boat which was gliding over the
tranquil surface of the lake below.

" The blessings of civilisation," said Mr. Foster, " extend themselves to the meanest individuals of the community. That boatman,
singing as he sails along, is, I have no doubt, a very happy, and,
comparatively to the men of his class some centuries back, a very
enlightened and intelligent man."

" As a partisan of the system of the moral perfectibility of the
human race," said Mr. Escot,—who was always for considering things
on a large scale, and whose thoughts immediately wandered from the
lake to the ocean, from the little boat to a ship of the line,—"you will
probably be able to point out to me the degree of improvement that
you suppose to have taken place in the character of a sailor, from the
days when Jason sailed through the Cyanean Symplegades,[2] or Noah
moored his ark on the summit of Ararat."

" If you talk to me," said Mr. Foster, " of mythological personages,
of course I cannot meet you on fair grounds."

" We will begin, if you please, then," said Mr. Escot, " no further
back than the battle of Salamis ; and I will ask you if you think the
mariners of England are, in any one respect, morally or intellectually,
superior to those who then preserved the liberties of Greece, under
the direction of Themistocles ? "

" I will venture to assert," said Mr. Foster, " that, considered
merely as sailors, which is the only fair mode of judging them, they

---

[1] See *Knight on Taste*, and the *Edinburgh Review*, No. XIV.   [P.]
[2] Two rocks at the entrance to the Bosphorus.   G.

are as far superior to the Athenians, as the structure of our ships is superior to that of theirs. Would not one English seventy-four, think you, have been sufficient to have sunk, burned, and put to flight, all the Persian and Grecian vessels in that memorable bay? Contemplate the progress of naval architecture, and the slow, but immense, succession of concatenated intelligence, by which it has gradually attained its present stage of perfectibility. In this, as in all other branches of art and science, every generation possesses all the knowledge of the preceding, and adds to it its own discoveries in a progression to which there seems no limit. The skill requisite to direct these immense machines is proportionate to their magnitude and complicated mechanism; and, therefore, the English sailor, considered merely as a sailor, is vastly superior to the ancient Greek."

"You make a distinction, of course," said Mr. Escot, "between scientific and moral perfectibility?"

"I conceive," said Mr. Foster, "that men are virtuous in proportion as they are enlightened; and that, as every generation increases in knowledge, it also increases in virtue."

"I wish it were so," said Mr. Escot; "but to me the very reverse appears to be the fact. The progress of knowledge is not general: it is confined to a chosen few of every age. How far these are better than their neighbours, we may examine by and bye. The mass of mankind is composed of beasts of burden, mere clods, and tools of their superiors. By enlarging and complicating your machines, you degrade, not exalt, the human animals you employ to direct them. When the boatswain of a seventy-four pipes all hands to the main tack, and flourishes his rope's end over the shoulders of the poor fellows who are tugging at the ropes, do you perceive so dignified, so gratifying a picture, as Ulysses exhorting his dear friends, his *EPIHPEΣ 'ETAIPOI*,[1] to ply their oars with energy? You will say, Ulysses was a fabulous character. But the economy of his vessel is drawn from nature. Every man on board has a character and a will of his own. He talks to them, argues with them, convinces them; and they obey him, because they love him, and know the reason of his orders. Now, as I have said before, all singleness of character is lost. We divide men into herds like cattle: an individual man, if you strip

[1] Trusty comrades (Homer: *passim*). G.

him of all that is extraneous to himself, is the most wretched and contemptible creature on the face of the earth. The sciences advance. True. A few years of study puts a modern mathematician in possession of more than Newton knew, and leaves him at leisure to add new discoveries of his own. Agreed. But does this make him a Newton ? Does it put him in possession of that range of intellect, that grasp of mind, from which the discoveries of Newton sprang ? It is mental power that I look for : if you can demonstrate the increase of that, I will give up the field. Energy—independence — individuality — disinterested virtue — active benevolence — self-oblivion—universal philanthropy—these are the qualities I desire to find, and of which I contend that every succeeding age produces fewer examples. I repeat it ; there is scarcely such a thing to be found as a single individual man : a few classes compose the whole frame of society, and when you know one of a class you know the whole of it. Give me the wild man of the woods ; the original, unthinking, unscientific, unlogical savage : in him there is at least some good ; but, in a civilised, sophisticated, cold-blooded, mechanical, calculating slave of Mammon and the world, there is none—absolutely none. Sir, if I fall into a river, an unsophisticated man will jump in and bring me out ; but a philosopher will look on with the utmost calmness, and consider me in the light of a projectile, and, making a calculation of the degree of force with which I have impinged the surface, the resistance of the fluid, the velocity of the current, and the depth of the water in that particular place, he will ascertain with the greatest nicety in what part of the mud at the bottom I may probably be found, at any given distance of time from the moment of my first immersion."

Mr. Foster was preparing to reply, when the first dinner-bell rang, and he immediately commenced a precipitate return towards the house ; followed by his two companions, who both admitted that he was now leading the way to at least a temporary period of physical amelioration : " but, alas ! " added Mr. Escot, after a moment's reflection, " Epulæ NOCUERE repostæ ! " [1]

---

[1] Protracted banquets have been copious sources of evil. [P.] [Virgil : *Georg.* III. 527. G.]

CHAPTER V

THE DINNER

THE sun was now terminating his diurnal course, and the lights were glittering on the festal board. When the ladies had retired, and the Burgundy had taken two or three tours of the table, the following conversation took place :—

SQUIRE HEADLONG. Push about the bottle : Mr. Escot, it stands with you. No heeltaps. As to skylight, liberty-hall.[1]

MR. MAC LAUREL. Really, Squire Headlong, this is the vara nactar itsel. Ye hae saretainly descovered the tarrestrial paradise, but it flows wi' a better leecor than milk an' honey.

THE REVEREND DOCTOR GASTER. Hem ! Mr. Mac Laurel ! there is a degree of profaneness in that observation, which I should not have looked for in so staunch a supporter of church and state. Milk and honey was the pure food of the antediluvian patriarchs, who knew not the use of the grape, happily for them.—(*Tossing off a bumper of Burgundy.*)

MR. ESCOT. Happily, indeed ! The first inhabitants of the world knew not the use either of wine or animal food ; it is, therefore, by no means incredible that they lived to the age of several centuries, free from war, and commerce, and arbitrary government, and every other species of desolating wickedness. But man was then a very different animal to what he now is : he had not the faculty of speech ; he was not encumbered with clothes ; he lived in the open air ; his first step out of which, as Hamlet truly observes, is *into his grave*.[2] His first dwellings, of course, were the hollows of trees and rocks. In process of time he began to build : thence grew villages ; thence grew cities. Luxury, oppression, poverty, misery, and disease kept pace with the progress of his pretended improvements, till, from a free, strong, healthy, peaceful animal, he has become a weak, distempered, cruel, carnivorous slave.

[1] i.e. " you are at liberty to sit up drinking until daylight." G.
[2] See Lord Monboddo's *Ancient Metaphysics*. [P.]

THE REVEREND DOCTOR GASTER. Your doctrine is orthodox, in so far as you assert that the original man was not encumbered with clothes, and that he lived in the open air ; but, as to the faculty of speech, that, it is certain, he had, for the authority of Moses——

MR. ESCOT. Of course, sir, I do not presume to dissent from the very exalted authority of that most enlightened astronomer and profound cosmogonist, who had, moreover, the advantage of being inspired ; but when I indulge myself with a ramble in the fields of speculation, and attempt to deduce what is probable and rational from the sources of analysis, experience, and comparison, I confess I am too often apt to lose sight of the doctrines of that great fountain of theological and geological philosophy.

SQUIRE HEADLONG. Push about the bottle.

MR. FOSTER. Do you suppose the mere animal life of a wild man, living on acorns, and sleeping on the ground, comparable in felicity to that of a Newton, ranging through unlimited space, and penetrating into the arcana of universal motion—to that of a Locke, unravelling the labyrinth of mind—to that of a Lavoisier, detecting the minutest combinations of matter, and reducing all nature to its elements—to that of a Shakespeare, piercing and developing the springs of passion—or of a Milton, identifying himself, as it were, with the beings of an invisible world ?

MR. ESCOT. You suppose extreme cases : but, on the score of happiness, what comparison can you make between the tranquil being of the wild man of the woods and the wretched and turbulent existence of Milton, the victim of persecution, poverty, blindness, and neglect ? The records of literature demonstrate that Happiness and Intelligence are seldom sisters. Even if it were otherwise, it would prove nothing. The many are always sacrificed to the few. Where one man advances, hundreds retrograde ; and the balance is always in favour of universal deterioration.

MR. FOSTER. Virtue is independent of external circumstances. The exalted understanding looks into the truth of things, and, in its own peaceful contemplations, rises superior to the world. No philosopher would resign his mental acquisitions for the purchase of any terrestrial good.

MR. ESCOT. In other words, no man whatever would resign his identity, which is nothing more than the consciousness of his perceptions, as the price of any acquisition. But every man, without exception, would willingly effect a very material change in his relative situation to other individuals. Unluckily for the rest of your argument, the understanding of literary people is for the most part *exalted*, as you express it, not so much by the love of truth and virtue, as by arrogance and self-sufficiency; and there is, perhaps, less disinterestedness, less liberality, less general benevolence, and more envy, hatred, and uncharitableness among them, than among any other description of men.

(The eye of Mr. Escot, as he pronounced these words, rested very innocently and unintentionally on Mr. Gall.)

MR. GALL. You allude, sir, I presume, to my review.

MR. ESCOT. Pardon me, sir. You will be convinced it is impossible I can allude to your review, when I assure you that I have never read a single page of it.

MR. GALL, MR. TREACLE, MR. NIGHTSHADE, AND MR. MAC LAUREL. Never read our review ! ! ! !

MR. ESCOT. Never. I look on periodical criticism in general to be a species of shop, where panegyric and defamation are sold, wholesale, retail, and for exportation. I am not inclined to be a purchaser of these commodities, or to encourage a trade which I consider pregnant with mischief.

MR. MAC LAUREL. I can readily conceive, sir, ye wou'd na wullinly encoorage ony dealer in panegeeric : but, frae the manner in which ye speak o' the first creetics an' scholars o' the age, I shou'd think ye wou'd hae a leetle mair predilaction for deefamation.

MR. ESCOT. I have no predilection, sir, for defamation. I make a point of speaking the truth on all occasions ; and it seldom happens that the truth can be spoken without some stricken deer pronouncing it a libel.

MR. NIGHTSHADE. You are perhaps, sir, an enemy to literature in general ?

MR. ESCOT. If I were, sir, I should be a better friend to periodical critics.

SQUIRE HEADLONG. Buz !

MR. TREACLE. May I simply take the liberty to inquire into the basis of your objection ?

MR. ESCOT. I conceive that periodical criticism disseminates superficial knowledge, and its perpetual adjunct, vanity ; that it checks in the youthful mind the habit of thinking for itself ; that it delivers partial opinions, and thereby misleads the judgment ; that it is never conducted with a view to the general interests of literature, but to serve the interested ends of individuals, and the miserable purposes of party.

MR. MAC LAUREL. Ye ken, sir, a mon mun leeve.

MR. ESCOT. While he can live honourably, naturally, justly, certainly : no longer.

MR. MAC LAUREL. Every mon, sir, leeves according to his ain notions of honour an' justice : there is a wee defference amang the learned wi' respact to the defineetion o' the terms.

MR. ESCOT. I believe it is generally admitted, that one of the ingredients of justice is disinterestedness.

MR. MAC LAUREL. It is na admitted, sir, amang the pheelosophers of Edinbroo', that there is ony sic thing as desenterestedness in the warld, or that a mon can care for onything sae much as his ain sel : for ye mun observe, sir, every mon has his ain parteecular feelings of what is gude, an' beautifu', an' consentaneous to his ain indiveedual nature, an' desires to see everything aboot him in that parteecular state which is maist conformable to his ain notions o' the moral an' poleetical fetness o' things. Twa men, sir, shall purchase a piece o' grund atween 'em, and ae mon shall cover his half wi' a park——

MR. MILESTONE. Beautifully laid out in lawns and clumps, with a belt of trees at the circumference, and an artificial lake in the centre.

MR. MAC LAUREL. Exactly, sir : an' shall keep it a' for his ain sel : an' the other mon shall divide his half into leetle farms of two or three acres——

MR. ESCOT. Like those of the Roman republic, and build a cottage on each of them, and cover his land with a simple, innocent, and smiling population, who shall owe, not only their happiness, but their existence, to his benevolence.

MR. MAC LAUREL. Exactly, sir : an' ye will ca' the first mon selfish, an' the second desenterested ; but the pheelosophical truth is semply this, that the ane is pleased wi' looking at trees, an' the other wi' seeing people happy an' comfortable. It is aunly a matter of indiveedual feeling. A paisant saves a mon's life for the same reason that a hero or a footpad cuts his thrapple : an' a pheelosopher delevers a mon frae a preson, for the same reason that a tailor or a prime menester puts him into it : because it is conformable to his ain parteecular feelings o' the moral an' poleetical fetness o' things.

SQUIRE HEADLONG. Wake the Reverend Doctor. Doctor, the bottle stands with you.

THE REVEREND DOCTOR GASTER. It is an error of which I am seldom guilty.

MR. MAC LAUREL. Noo, ye ken, sir, every mon is the centre of his ain system, an' endaivours as much as possible to adapt everything aroond him to his ain parteecular views.

MR. ESCOT. Thus, sir, I presume, it suits the particular views of a poet, at one time to take the part of the people against their oppressors, and at another, to take the part of the oppressors, against the people.

MR. MAC LAUREL. Ye mun alloo, sir, that poetry is a sort of ware or commodity, that is brought into the public market wi' a' other descreptions of merchandise, an' that a mon is pairfectly justified in getting the best price he can for his article. Noo, there are three reasons for taking the part o' the people : the first is, when general leeberty an' public happiness are conformable to your ain parteecular feelings o' the moral an' poleetical fetness o' things : the second is, when they happen to be, as it were, in a state of exceetabeelity, an' ye think ye can get a gude price for your commodity, by flingin' in a leetle seasoning o' pheelanthropy an' republican speerit : the third is, when ye think ye can bully the menestry into gieing ye a place or a pansion to hau'd your din, an' in that case, ye point an attack against them within the pale o' the law ; an' if they tak nae heed o' ye, ye open a stronger fire ; an' the less heed they tak, the mair ye bawl ; an' the mair factious ye grow, always within the pale o' the law, till they send a plenipotentiary to treat wi' ye for yoursel, an' then the mair popular ye happen to be, the better price ye fetch.

SQUIRE HEADLONG. Off with your heeltaps.

MR. CRANIUM. I perfectly agree with Mr. Mac Laurel in his definition of self-love and disinterestedness : every man's actions are determined by his peculiar views, and those views are determined by the organisation of his skull. A man in whom the organ of benevolence is not developed, cannot be benevolent : he, in whom it is so, cannot be otherwise. The organ of self-love is prodigiously developed in the greater number of subjects that have fallen under my observation.

MR. ESCOT. Much less, I presume, among savage than civilised men, who, *constant only to the love of self, and consistent only in their aim to deceive, are always actuated by the hope of personal advantage, or by the dread of personal punishment.*[1]

MR. CRANIUM. Very probably.

MR. ESCOT. You have, of course, found very copious specimens of the organs of hypocrisy, destruction, and avarice.

MR. CRANIUM. Secretiveness, destructiveness, and covetiveness. You may add, if you please, that of constructiveness.

[1] Drummond's *Academical Questions.* [P.]

MR. ESCOT. Meaning, I presume, the organ of building; which I contend to be not a natural organ of the *featherless biped*.[1]

MR. CRANIUM. Pardon me : it is here.—(*As he said these words, he produced a skull from his pocket, and placed it on the table, to the great surprise of the company.*)—This was the skull of Sir Christopher Wren.[2] You observe this protuberance—(*The skull was handed round the table.*)

MR. ESCOT. I contend that the original unsophisticated man was by no means constructive. He lived in the open air, under a tree.

THE REVEREND DOCTOR GASTER. The tree of life. Unquestionably. Till he had tasted the forbidden fruit.

MR. JENKISON. At which period, probably, the organ of constructiveness was added to his anatomy, as a punishment for his transgression.

MR. ESCOT. There could not have been a more severe one, since the propensity which has led him to building cities has proved the greatest curse of his existence.

SQUIRE HEADLONG—(*taking the skull.*) *Memento mori.* Come, a bumper of Burgundy.

MR. NIGHTSHADE. A very classical application, Squire Headlong. The Romans were in the practice of adhibiting skulls at their banquets, and sometimes little skeletons of silver, as a silent admonition to the guests to enjoy life while it lasted.

THE REVEREND DOCTOR GASTER. Sound doctrine, Mr. Nightshade.

MR. ESCOT. I question its soundness. The use of vinous spirit has a tremendous influence in the deterioration of the human race.

MR. FOSTER. I fear, indeed, it operates as a considerable check to the progress of the species towards moral and intellectual perfection.

[1] Plato's definition of Man. G.
[2] Mr. Cranium must have rifled the grave in the choir of St. Paul's where the visitor is informed that a monument to Wren is superfluous : "Si monumentum requiris, circumspice." G.

Yet many great men have been of opinion that it exalts the imagination, fires the genius, accelerates the flow of ideas, and imparts to dispositions naturally cold and deliberative that enthusiastic sublimation which is the source of greatness and energy.

MR. NIGHTSHADE. *Laudibus arguitur vini vinosus Homerus.*[1]

MR. JENKISON. I conceive the use of wine to be always pernicious in excess, but often useful in moderation : it certainly kills some, but it saves the lives of others : I find that an occasional glass, taken with judgment and caution, has a very salutary effect in maintaining that equilibrium of the system, which it is always my aim to preserve ; and this calm and temperate use of wine was, no doubt, what Homer meant to inculcate, when he said :

Παρ δε δεπας οινοιο, πιειν ότε θυμος ανωγοι.[2]

SQUIRE HEADLONG. Good. Pass the bottle.

(Un morne silence.)

Sir Christopher does not seem to have raised our spirits. Chromatic, favour us with a specimen of your vocal powers. Something in point.

Mr. Chromatic, without further preface, immediately struck up the following

SONG.

In his last binn SIR PETER [3] lies,
　Who knew not what it was to frown :
Death took him mellow, by surprise,
　And in his cellar stopped him down.
Through all our land we could not boast
　A knight more gay, more prompt than he,
To rise and fill a bumper toast,
　And pass it round with THREE TIMES THREE.

---

[1] Homer is proved to have been a lover of wine by the praises he bestows upon it. [P.] [Horace : *Ep.* I, xix. 6. G.]

[2] A cup of wine at hand, to drink as inclination prompts. [P.] [*Od.* VIII. 70. G.]

[3] In Peacock's farce *The Three Doctors* Squire Hippy has inherited the property from Sir Peter Paxarett, of whom he complains : " That old sot Sir Peter thought of nothing but liquor and pipes ! " Later he sings :

" Couldn't that old sot, Sir Peter,
　Keep his house a little neater ? " G.

None better knew the feast to sway,
　　Or keep Mirth's boat in better trim ;
For Nature had but little clay
　　Like that of which she moulded him.
The meanest guest that graced his board
　　Was there the freest of the free,
His bumper toast when PETER poured,
　　And passed it round with THREE TIMES THREE.

He kept at true good humour's mark
　　The social flow of pleasure's tide :
He never made a brow look dark,
　　Nor caused a tear, but when he died.
No sorrow round his tomb should dwell :
　　More pleased his gay old ghost would be,
For funeral song, and passing bell,
　　To hear no sound but THREE TIMES THREE.

(*Hammering of knuckles and glasses, and shouts of Bravo !*)

MR. PANSCOPE. (*suddenly emerging from a deep reverie.*) I have
heard, with the most profound attention, every thing which the
gentleman on the other side of the table has thought proper to
advance on the subject of human deterioration ; and I must take the
liberty to remark, that it augurs a very considerable degree of
presumption in any individual, to set himself up against the *authority*
of so many great men, as may be marshalled in metaphysical phalanx
under the opposite banners of the controversy ; such as Aristotle,
Plato, the scholiast on Aristophanes, St. Chrysostom, St. Jerome,
St. Athanasius, Orpheus, Pindar, Simonides, Gronovius, Hemster-
husius, Longinus, Sir Isaac Newton, Thomas Paine, Doctor Paley,
the King of Prussia, the King of Poland, Cicero, Monsieur Gautier,
Hippocrates, Machiavelli, Milton, Colley Cibber, Bojardo, Gregory
Nazianzenus, Locke, D'Alembert, Boccaccio, Daniel Defoe, Erasmus,
Doctor Smollett, Zimmermann, Solomon, Confucius, Zoroaster, and
Thomas-a-Kempis.

MR. ESCOT. I presume, sir, you are one of those who value an
authority more than a reason.

MR. PANSCOPE. The *authority*, sir, of all these great men, whose
works, as well as the whole of the Encyclopædia Britannica, the entire
series of the Monthly Review, the complete set of the Variorum

Classics, and the Memoirs of the Academy of Inscriptions, I have read through from beginning to end, deposes, with irrefragable refutation, against your ratiocinative speculations, wherein you seem desirous, by the futile process of analytical dialectics, to subvert the pyramidal structure of synthetically deduced opinions, which have withstood the secular revolutions of physiological disquisition, and which I maintain to be transcendentally self-evident, categorically certain, and syllogistically demonstrable.

SQUIRE HEADLONG. Bravo! Pass the bottle. The very best speech that ever was made.

MR. ESCOT. It has only the slight disadvantage of being unintelligible.

MR. PANSCOPE. I am not obliged, sir, as Dr. Johnson observed on a similar occasion, to furnish you with an understanding.[1]

MR. ESCOT. I fear, sir, you would have some difficulty in furnishing me with such an article from your own stock.

MR. PANSCOPE. 'Sdeath, sir, do you question my understanding?

MR. ESCOT. I only question, sir, where I expect a reply; which, from things that have no existence, I am not visionary enough to anticipate.

MR. PANSCOPE. I beg leave to observe, sir, that my language was perfectly perspicuous, and etymologically correct; and, I conceive, I have demonstrated what I shall now take the liberty to say in plain terms, that all your opinions are extremely absurd.

MR. ESCOT. I should be sorry, sir, to advance any opinion that you would not think absurd.

MR. PANSCOPE. Death and fury, sir——

MR. ESCOT. Say no more, sir. That apology is quite sufficient.

MR. PANSCOPE. Apology, sir?

[1] This observation, which is older than Dr. Johnson, is quoted by Coleridge, among whose projects was one for an encyclopædia. " Intelligenda," he says, " non intellectum adfero." G.

MR. ESCOT.   Even so, sir.   You have lost your temper, which I consider equivalent to a confession that you have the worst of the argument.

MR. PANSCOPE.   Lightning and devils ! sir——

SQUIRE HEADLONG.   No civil war !—Temperance, in the name of Bacchus !—A glee ! a glee !   *Music has charms to bend the knotted oak.*[1]   Sir Patrick, you'll join ?

SIR PATRICK O'PRISM.   Troth, with all my heart : for, by my soul, I'm bothered completely.

SQUIRE HEADLONG.   Agreed, then : you, and I, and Chromatic. Bumpers !—bumpers !   Come, strike up.

Squire Headlong, Mr. Chromatic, and Sir Patrick O'Prism, each holding a bumper, immediately vociferated the following

GLEE.

A heeltap ! a heeltap ! I never could bear it !
So fill me a bumper, a bumper of claret !
Let the bottle pass freely, don't shirk it nor spare it,
For a heeltap ! a heeltap ! I never could bear it !

No skylight ! no twilight ! while Bacchus rules o'er us :
No thinking ! no shrinking ! all drinking in chorus :
Let us moisten our clay, since 'tis thirsty and porous:
No thinking ! no shrinking ! all drinking in chorus !

GRAND CHORUS.

By Squire Headlong, Mr. Chromatic, Sir Patrick O'Prism, Mr. Panscope, Mr. Jenkison, Mr. Gall, Mr. Treacle, Mr. Nightshade, Mr. Mac Laurel, Mr. Cranium, Mr. Milestone, and the Reverend Doctor Gaster.

A heeltap ! a heeltap ! I never could bear it !
So fill me a bumper, a bumper of claret !
Let the bottle pass freely, don't shirk it nor spare it,
For a heeltap ! a heeltap ! I never could bear it !

---

[1] Congreve : *The Mourning Bride*, Act I, Sc. 1 :

" Musick has Charms to sooth a savage Breast,
    To soften Rocks, or bend a knotted Oak."   G.

"ΟΜΑΔΟΣ ΚΑΙ ΔΟΥΠΟΣ ΟΡΩΡΕΙ!"[1]

The little butler now waddled in with a summons from the ladies to tea and coffee. The squire was unwilling to leave his Burgundy. Mr. Escot strenuously urged the necessity of immediate adjournment, observing, that the longer they continued drinking the worse they should be. Mr. Foster seconded the motion, declaring the transition from the bottle to female society to be an indisputable amelioration of the state of the sensitive man. Mr. Jenkison allowed the squire and his two brother philosophers to settle the point between them, concluding that he was just as well in one place as another. The question of adjournment was then put, and carried by a large majority.

CHAPTER VI

THE EVENING

MR. PANSCOPE, highly irritated by the cool contempt with which Mr. Escot had treated him, sate sipping his coffee and meditating revenge. He was not long in discovering the passion of his antagonist for the beautiful Cephalis, for whom he had himself a species of predilection ; and it was also obvious to him, that there was some lurking anger in the mind of her father, unfavourable to the hopes of his rival. The stimulus of revenge, superadded to that of preconceived inclination, determined him, after due deliberation, to *cut out* Mr. Escot in the young lady's favour. The practicability of this design he did not trouble himself to investigate ; for the havoc he had made in the hearts of some silly girls, who were extremely vulnerable to flattery, and who, not understanding a word he said, considered him a *prodigious clever man*, had impressed him with an unhesitating idea of his own irresistibility. He had not only the requisites already specified for fascinating female vanity, he could likewise fiddle with tolerable dexterity, though by no means so *quick* as Mr. Chromatic (for our readers are of course aware that rapidity of execution, not delicacy of expression, constitutes the

[1] " There arose a din and a clatter." Homer : *Il.* IX. 573. G.

scientific perfection of modern music), and could warble a fashionable love-ditty with considerable affectation of feeling : besides this, he was always extremely well dressed, and was heir-apparent to an estate of ten thousand a-year. The influence which the latter consideration might have on the minds of the majority of his female acquaintance, whose morals had been formed by the novels of such writers as Miss Philomela Poppyseed, did not once enter into his calculation of his own personal attractions. Relying, therefore, on past success, he determined *to appeal to his fortune*, and already, in imagination, considered himself sole lord and master of the affections of the beautiful Cephalis.

Mr. Escot and Mr. Foster were the only two of the party who had entered the library (to which the ladies had retired, and which was interior to the music-room) in a state of perfect sobriety. Mr. Escot had placed himself next to the beautiful Cephalis : Mr. Cranium had laid aside much of the terror of his frown ; the short craniological conversation, which had passed between him and Mr. Escot, had softened his heart in his favour ; and the copious libations of Burgundy in which he had indulged had smoothed his brow into unusual serenity.

Mr. Foster placed himself near the lovely Caprioletta, whose artless and innocent conversation had already made an impression on his susceptible spirit.

The Reverend Doctor Gaster seated himself in the corner of a sofa near Miss Philomela Poppyseed. Miss Philomela detailed to him the plan of a very moral and aristocratical novel she was preparing for the press, and continued holding forth, with her eyes half shut, till a long-drawn nasal tone from the reverend divine compelled her suddenly to open them in all the indignation of surprise. The cessation of the hum of her voice awakened the reverend gentleman, who, lifting up first one eyelid, then the other, articulated, or rather murmured, " Admirably planned, indeed ! "

" I have not quite finished, sir," said Miss Philomela, bridling. " Will you have the goodness to inform me where I left off ? "

The doctor hummed a while, and at length answered : " I think you had just laid it down as a position, that a thousand a-year is an indispensable ingredient in the passion of love, and that no man, who is not so far gifted by *nature*, can reasonably presume to feel that passion himself, or be correctly the object of it with a well-educated female."

" That, sir," said Miss Philomela, highly incensed, " is the fundamental principle which I lay down in the first chapter, and which the whole four volumes, of which I detailed to you the outline, are intended to set in a strong practical light."

" Bless me ! " said the doctor, " what a nap I must have had ! "

Miss Philomela flung away to the side of her dear friends Gall and Treacle, under whose fostering patronage she had been puffed into an extensive reputation, much to the advantage of the young ladies of the age, whom she taught to consider themselves as a sort of commodity, to be put up at public auction, and knocked down to the highest bidder.   Mr. Nightshade and Mr. Mac Laurel joined the trio ; and it was secretly resolved, that Miss Philomela should furnish them with a portion of her manuscripts, and that Messieurs Gall and Co. should devote the following morning to cutting and drying a critique on a work calculated to prove so extensively beneficial, that Mr. Gall protested he really *envied* the writer.

While this amiable and enlightened quintetto were busily employed in flattering one another, Mr. Cranium retired to complete the preparations he had begun in the morning for a lecture, with which he intended, on some future evening, to favour the company : Sir Patrick O'Prism walked out into the grounds to study the effect of moonlight on the snow-clad mountains : Mr. Foster and Mr. Escot continued to make love, and Mr. Panscope to digest his plan of attack on the heart of Miss Cephalis : Mr. Jenkison sate by the fire, reading *Much Ado about Nothing* : the Reverend Doctor Gaster was still enjoying the benefit of Miss Philomela's opiate, and serenading the company from his solitary corner : Mr. Chromatic was reading music, and occasionally humming a note : and Mr. Milestone had produced his portfolio for the edification and amusement of Miss Tenorina, Miss Graziosa, and Squire Headlong, to whom he was pointing out the various beauties of his plan for Lord Littlebrain's park.

MR. MILESTONE.   This, you perceive, is the natural state of one part of the grounds. Here is a wood, never yet touched by the finger of taste; thick, intricate, and gloomy. Here is a little stream, dashing from stone to stone, and overshadowed with these untrimmed boughs.

MISS TENORINA. The sweet romantic spot! How beautifully the birds must sing there on a summer evening!

MISS GRAZIOSA. Dear sister! how can you endure the horrid thicket?

MR. MILESTONE. You are right, Miss Graziosa: your taste is correct—perfectly *en règle*. Now, here is the same place corrected —trimmed—polished—decorated—adorned. Here sweeps a plantation, in that beautiful regular curve: there winds a gravel walk: here are parts of the old wood, left in these majestic circular clumps, disposed at equal distances with wonderful symmetry: there are some single shrubs scattered in elegant profusion: here a Portugal laurel, there a juniper; here a lauristinus, there a spruce fir; here a larch, there a lilac; here a rhododendron, there an arbutus. The stream, you see, is become a canal: the banks are perfectly smooth and green, sloping to the water's edge: and there is Lord Littlebrain, rowing in an elegant boat.

SQUIRE HEADLONG. Magical, faith!

MR. MILESTONE. Here is another part of the grounds in its natural state. Here is a large rock, with the mountain-ash rooted in its fissures, overgrown, as you see, with ivy and moss; and from this part of it bursts a little fountain, that runs bubbling down its rugged sides.

MISS TENORINA. O how beautiful! How I should love the melody of that miniature cascade!

MR. MILESTONE. Beautiful, Miss Tenorina! Hideous. Base, common, and popular.[1] Such a thing as you may see anywhere, in wild and mountainous districts. Now, observe the metamorphosis. Here is the same rock, cut into the shape of a giant. In one hand he holds a horn, through which that little fountain is thrown to a

[1] *Henry V*, Act IV, Sc. 1. G.

prodigious elevation. In the other is a ponderous stone, so exactly balanced as to be apparently ready to fall on the head of any person who may happen to be beneath : [1] and there is Lord Littlebrain walking under it.

SQUIRE HEADLONG. Miraculous, by Mahomet !

MR. MILESTONE. This is the summit of a hill, covered, as you perceive, with wood, and with those mossy stones scattered at random under the trees.

MISS TENORINA. What a delightful spot to read in, on a summer's day ! The air must be so pure, and the wind must sound so divinely in the tops of those old pines !

MR. MILESTONE. Bad taste, Miss Tenorina. Bad taste, I assure you. Here is the spot improved. The trees are cut down : the stones are cleared away : this is an octagonal pavilion, exactly on the centre of the summit : and there you see Lord Littlebrain, on the top of the pavilion, enjoying the prospect with a telescope.

SQUIRE HEADLONG. Glorious, egad !

MR. MILESTONE. Here is a rugged mountainous road, leading through impervious shades : the ass and the four goats characterise a wild uncultured scene. Here, as you perceive, it is totally changed into a beautiful gravel-road, gracefully curving through a belt of limes : and there is Lord Littlebrain driving four-in-hand.

SQUIRE HEADLONG. Egregious, by Jupiter !

MR. MILESTONE. Here is Littlebrain Castle, a Gothic, moss-grown structure, half-bosomed in trees. Near the casement of that turret is an owl peeping from the ivy.

SQUIRE HEADLONG. And devilish wise he looks.

MR. MILESTONE. Here is the new house, without a tree near it, standing in the midst of an undulating lawn : a white, polished, angular building, reflected to a nicety in this waveless lake : and there you see Lord Littlebrain looking out of the window.

[1] See *Knight on Taste*. [P.]

SQUIRE HEADLONG. And devilish wise he looks too. You shall cut me a giant before you go.

MR. MILESTONE. Good. I'll order down my little corps of pioneers.

During this conversation, a hot dispute had arisen between Messieurs Gall and Nightshade; the latter pertinaciously insisting on having his new poem reviewed by Treacle, who he knew would extol it most loftily, and not by Gall, whose sarcastic commendation he held in superlative horror. The remonstrances of Squire Headlong silenced the disputants, but did not mollify the inflexible Gall, nor appease the irritated Nightshade, who secretly resolved that, on his return to London, he would beat his drum in Grub Street, form a mastigophoric[1] corps of his own, and hoist the standard of determined opposition against this critical Napoleon.

Sir Patrick O'Prism now entered, and, after some rapturous exclamations on the effect of the mountain-moonlight, entreated that one of the young ladies would favour him with a song. Miss Tenorina and Miss Graziosa now enchanted the company with some very scientific compositions, which, as usual, excited admiration and astonishment in every one, without a single particle of genuine pleasure. The beautiful Cephalis being then summoned to take her station at the harp, sang with feeling and simplicity the following air :—

LOVE AND OPPORTUNITY.

Oh ! who art thou, so swiftly flying ?
  My name is Love, the child replied :
Swifter I pass than south-winds sighing,
  Or streams, through summer vales that glide.
And who art thou, his flight pursuing ?
  'Tis cold Neglect whom now you see :
The little god you there are viewing,
  Will die, if once he's touched by me.

Oh ! who art thou so fast proceeding,
  Ne'er glancing back thine eyes of flame ?
Marked but by few, through earth I'm speeding,
  And Opportunity's my name.

---

[1] From the Greek ushers armed with whips. The term is also applied to the ciliate protozoa. G.

> What form is that, which scowls beside thee ?
> Repentance is the form you see :
> Learn then, the fate may yet betide thee :
> She seizes them who seize not me.[1]

The little butler now appeared with a summons to supper, shortly after which the party dispersed for the night.

CHAPTER VII

THE WALK

IT was an old custom in Headlong Hall to have breakfast ready at eight, and continue it till two ; that the various guests might rise at their own hour, breakfast when they came down, and employ the morning as they thought proper ; the squire only expecting that they should punctually assemble at dinner. During the whole of this period, the little butler stood sentinel at a side-table near the fire, copiously furnished with all the apparatus of tea, coffee, chocolate, milk, cream, eggs, rolls, toast, muffins, bread, butter, potted beef, cold fowl and partridge, ham, tongue, and anchovy. The Reverend Doctor Gaster found himself rather *queasy* in the morning, therefore preferred breakfasting in bed, on a mug of buttered ale and an anchovy toast. The three philosophers made their appearance at eight, and enjoyed *les prémices des dépouilles*. Mr. Foster proposed that, as it was a fine frosty morning, and they were all good pedestrians, they should take a walk to Tremadoc, to see the improvements carrying on in that vicinity. This being readily acceded to, they began their walk.

After their departure, appeared Squire Headlong and Mr. Milestone, who agreed, over their muffin and partridge, to walk together to a ruined tower, within the precincts of the squire's grounds, which Mr. Milestone thought he could improve.

The other guests dropped in by one's and two's, and made their respective arrangements for the morning. Mr. Panscope took a little ramble with Mr. Cranium, in the course of which, the former professed a great enthusiasm for the science of craniology, and a great

[1] This stanza is imitated from Machiavelli's *Capitolo dell' Occasione*. [P.]

deal of love for the beautiful Cephalis, adding a few words about his expectations : the old gentleman was unable to withstand this triple battery, and it was accordingly determined—after the manner of the heroic age, in which it was deemed superfluous to consult the opinions and feelings of the lady, as to the manner in which she should be disposed of—that the lovely Miss Cranium should be made the happy bride of the accomplished Mr. Panscope. We shall leave them for the present to settle preliminaries, while we accompany the three philosophers in their walk to Tremadoc.

The vale contracted as they advanced, and, when they had passed the termination of the lake, their road wound along a narrow and romantic pass, through the middle of which an impetuous torrent dashed over vast fragments of stone. The pass was bordered on both sides by perpendicular rocks, broken into the wildest forms of fantastic magnificence.

" These are, indeed," said Mr. Escot, " *confracti mundi rudera* : [1] yet they must be feeble images of the valleys of the Andes, where the philosophic eye may contemplate, in their utmost extent, the effects of that tremendous convulsion which destroyed the perpendicularity of the poles, and inundated this globe with that torrent of physical evil, from which the greater torrent of moral evil has issued, that will continue to roll on, with an expansive power and an accelerated impetus, till the whole human race shall be swept away in its vortex."

" The precession of the equinoxes," said Mr. Foster, " will gradually ameliorate the physical state of our planet, till the ecliptic shall again coincide with the equator, and the equal diffusion of light and heat over the whole surface of the earth typify the equal and happy existence of man, who will then have attained the final step of pure and perfect intelligence." [2]

[1] Fragments of a demolished world. [P.]

[2] Shelley wrote to Hookham on 19 February 1813, asking for literature on the precession of the equinoxes, and in a note to *Queen Mab* stated : " It is exceedingly probable . . . that this obliquity will gradually diminish, until the equator coincides with the ecliptic. . . . There is no great extravagance in presuming that the progress of the perpendicularity of the poles may be as rapid as the progress of intellect ; or that there should be a perfect identity between the moral and physical improvement of the human species." G.

"It is by no means clear," said Mr. Jenkison, "that the axis of the earth was ever perpendicular to the plane of its orbit, or that it ever will be so. Explosion and convulsion are necessary to the maintenance of either hypothesis : for La Place has demonstrated, that the precession of the equinoxes is only a secular equation of a very long period, which, of course, proves nothing either on one side or the other."

They now emerged, by a winding ascent, from the vale of Llanberris, and after some little time arrived at Bedd Gelert. Proceeding through the sublimely romantic pass of Aberglaslynn, their road led along the edge of Traeth Mawr, a vast arm of the sea, which they then beheld in all the magnificence of the flowing tide. Another five miles brought them to the embankment, which has since been completed, and which, by connecting the two counties of Meirionnydd and Caernarvon, excludes the sea from an extensive tract.[1] The embankment, which was carried on at the same time from both the opposite coasts, was then very nearly meeting in the centre. They walked to the extremity of that part of it which was thrown out from the Caernarvonshire shore. The tide was now ebbing : it had filled the vast basin within, forming a lake about five miles in length and more than one in breadth. As they looked upwards with their backs to the open sea, they beheld a scene which no other in this country can parallel, and which the admirers of the magnificence of nature will ever remember with regret, whatever consolation may be derived from the probable utility of the works which have excluded the waters from their ancient receptacle. Vast rocks and precipices, intersected with little torrents, formed the barrier on the left : on the right, the triple summit of Moëlwyn reared its majestic boundary : in the depth was that sea of mountains, the wild and stormy outline of the Snowdonian chain, with the giant Wyddfa towering in the midst. The mountain-frame remains unchanged, unchangeable ; but the liquid mirror it enclosed is gone.

The tide ebbed with rapidity : the waters within, retained by the embankment, poured through its two points an impetuous cataract, curling and boiling in innumerable eddies, and making a tumultuous

[1] This embankment, for which Shelley raised money, was constructed by Peacock's acquaintance Madocks. G.

melody admirably in unison with the surrounding scene.[1] The three philosophers looked on in silence; and at length unwillingly turned away, and proceeded to the little town of Tremadoc, which is built on land recovered in a similar manner from the sea.[2] After inspecting the manufactories, and refreshing themselves at the inn on a cold saddle of mutton and a bottle of sherry, they retraced their steps towards Headlong Hall, commenting as they went on the various objects they had seen.

MR. ESCOT. I regret that time did not allow us to see the caves on the sea-shore. There is one of which the depth is said to be unknown. There is a tradition in the country, that an adventurous fiddler once resolved to explore it; that he entered, and never returned; but that the subterranean sound of a fiddle was heard at a farm-house seven miles inland. It is, therefore, concluded that he lost his way in the labyrinth of caverns, supposed to exist under the rocky soil of this part of the country.

MR. JENKISON. A supposition that must always remain in force, unless a second fiddler, equally adventurous and more successful, should return with an accurate report of the true state of the fact.

MR. FOSTER. What think you of the little colony we have just been inspecting; a city, as it were, in its cradle?

MR. ESCOT. With all the weakness of infancy, and all the vices of maturer age. I confess, the sight of those manufactories, which have suddenly sprung up, like fungous excrescences, in the bosom of these wild and desolate scenes, impressed me with as much horror and amazement as the sudden appearance of the stocking manufactory struck into the mind of Rousseau, when, in a lonely valley of the Alps, he had just congratulated himself on finding a spot where man had never been.

---

[1] The impression here recorded may have influenced Peacock in the choice of subject of *The Misfortunes of Elphin*. G.

[2] Peacock had stayed at Maentwrog, 8 miles from Tremadoc, in 1810 and Shelley stayed nearby at Tanyrallt in 1812. G.

MR. FOSTER. The manufacturing system is not yet purified from some evils which necessarily attend it, but which I conceive are greatly overbalanced by their concomitant advantages. Contemplate the vast sum of human industry to which this system so essentially contributes : seas covered with vessels, ports resounding with life, profound researches, scientific inventions, complicated mechanism, canals carried over deep valleys and through the bosoms of hills : employment and existence thus given to innumerable families, and the multiplied comforts and conveniences of life diffused over the whole community.

MR. ESCOT. You present to me a complicated picture of artificial life, and require me to admire it. Seas covered with vessels : every one of which contains two or three tyrants, and from fifty to a thousand slaves, ignorant, gross, perverted, and active only in mischief. Ports resounding with life : in other words, with noise and drunkenness, the mingled din of avarice, intemperance, and prostitution. Profound researches, scientific inventions : to what end ? To contract the sum of human wants ? to teach the art of living on a little ? to disseminate independence, liberty, and health ? No ; to multiply factitious desires, to stimulate depraved appetites, to invent unnatural wants, to heap up incense on the shrine of luxury, and accumulate expedients of selfish and ruinous profusion. Complicated machinery : behold its blessings. Twenty years ago, at the door of every cottage sate the good woman with her spinning-wheel : the children, if not more profitably employed than in gathering heath and sticks, at least laid in a stock of health and strength to sustain the labours of maturer years. Where is the spinning-wheel now, and every simple and insulated occupation of the industrious cottager ? Wherever this boasted machinery is established, the children of the poor are death-doomed from their cradles. Look for one moment at midnight into a cotton-mill, amidst the smell of oil, the smoke of lamps, the rattling of wheels, the dizzy and complicated motions of diabolical mechanism : contemplate the little human machines that keep play with the revolutions of the iron work, robbed at that hour of their natural rest, as of air and exercise by day : observe their pale and ghastly features, more ghastly in that baleful

and malignant light, and tell me if you do not fancy yourself on the
threshold of Virgil's hell, where

> Continuò auditæ voces, vagitus et ingens,
> *Infantumque animæ flentes,* in limine primo,
> Quos *dulcis vitæ exsortes,* et ab ubere raptos,
> *Abstulit atra dies,* et FUNERE MERSIT ACERBO ! [1]

As Mr. Escot said this, a little rosy-cheeked girl, with a basket of
heath on her head, came tripping down the side of one of the rocks on
the left. The force of contrast struck even on the phlegmatic spirit
of Mr. Jenkison, and he almost inclined for a moment to the doctrine
of deterioration. Mr. Escot continued :

" Nor is the lot of the parents more enviable. Sedentary victims
of unhealthy toil, they have neither the corporeal energy of the
savage, nor the mental acquisitions of the civilised man. Mind,
indeed, they have none, and scarcely animal life. They are mere
automata, component parts of the enormous machines which
administer to the pampered appetites of the few, who consider
themselves the most valuable portion of a state, because they consume in indolence the fruits of the earth, and contribute nothing to
the benefit of the community."

MR. JENKISON. That these are evils cannot be denied ; but they
have their counterbalancing advantages. That a man should pass
the day in a furnace and the night in a cellar, is bad for the individual,
but good for others who enjoy the benefit of his labour.

MR. ESCOT. By what right do they so ?

MR. JENKISON. By the right of all property and all possession :
le droit du plus fort.

MR. ESCOT. Do you justify that principle ?

MR. JENKISON. I neither justify nor condemn it. It is practically
recognised in all societies ; and, though it is certainly the source of

---

[1] " Straightway heard they voices and a mighty wailing and the sobbing
voices of little children on the threshold—children whom the black of
doom had snatched from the breast before they had had their share of
life and drowned in bitter death." Virgil: *Æn.* VI. 426–30. G.

enormous evil, I conceive it is also the source of abundant good, or it
would not have so many supporters.

MR. ESCOT. That is by no means a consequence. Do we not
every day see men supporting the most enormous evils, which they
know to be so with respect to others, and which in reality are so with
respect to themselves, though an erroneous view of their own miserable self-interest induces them to think otherwise ?

MR. JENKISON. Good and evil exist only as they are perceived.
I cannot therefore understand, how that which a man perceives to be
good can be in reality an evil to him : indeed, the word *reality* only
signifies *strong belief*.

MR. ESCOT. The views of such a man I contend are false. If he
could be made to see the truth——

MR. JENKISON. He sees his own truth. Truth is that which a man
troweth. Where there is no man there is no truth. Thus the truth
of one is not the truth of another.[1]

MR. ESCOT. I am aware of the etymology ; [2] but I contend that
there is an universal and immutable truth, deducible from the nature
of things.

MR. JENKISON. By whom deducible ? Philosophers have investigated the nature of things for centuries, yet no two of them will agree
in *trowing* the same conclusion.

MR. FOSTER. The progress of philosophical investigation, and the
rapidly increasing accuracy of human knowledge, approximate by
degrees the diversities of opinion ; so that, in process of time, moral
science will be susceptible of mathematical demonstration ; and,
clear and indisputable principles being universally recognised, the
coincidence of deduction will necessarily follow.

MR. ESCOT. Possibly, when the inroads of luxury and disease shall
have exterminated nine hundred and ninety-nine thousand nine
hundred and ninety-nine of every million of the human race, the

[1] Tooke's *Diversions of Purley.* [P.]
[2] *Trow* comes from *true*, not vice-versa. G.

remaining fractional units may congregate into one point, and come to something like the same conclusion.

MR. JENKISON. I doubt it much. I conceive, if only we three were survivors of the whole system of terrestrial being, we should never agree in our decisions as to the cause of the calamity.

MR. ESCOT. Be that as it may, I think you must at least assent to the following positions : that the many are sacrificed to the few ; that ninety-nine in a hundred are occupied in a perpetual struggle for the preservation of a perilous and precarious existence, while the remaining one wallows in all the redundancies of luxury that can be wrung from their labours and privations ; that luxury and liberty are incompatible ; and that every new want you invent for civilised man is a new instrument of torture for him who cannot indulge it.

They had now regained the shores of the lake, when the conversation was suddenly interrupted by a tremendous explosion, followed by a violent splashing of water, and various sounds of tumult and confusion, which induced them to quicken their pace towards the spot whence they proceeded.

CHAPTER VIII

THE TOWER

IN all the thoughts, words, and actions of Squire Headlong, there was a remarkable alacrity of progression, which almost annihilated the interval between conception and execution. He was utterly regardless of obstacles, and seemed to have expunged their very name from his vocabulary. His designs were never nipped in their infancy by the contemplation of those trivial difficulties which often turn awry the current of enterprise ; and, though the rapidity of his movements was sometimes arrested by a more formidable barrier, either naturally existing in the pursuit he had undertaken, or created by his own impetuosity, he seldom failed to succeed either in knocking it down or cutting his way through it. He had little idea of gradation : he saw no interval between the first step and the last, but pounced upon

his object with the impetus of a mountain cataract. This rapidity of
movement, indeed, subjected him to some disasters which cooler
spirits would have escaped. He was an excellent sportsman, and
almost always killed his game ; but now and then he killed his dog.[1]
Rocks, streams, hedges, gates, and ditches, were objects of no
account in his estimation ; though a dislocated shoulder, several
severe bruises, and two or three narrow escapes for his neck, might
have been expected to teach him a certain degree of caution in effect-
ing his transitions. He was so singularly alert in climbing precipices
and traversing torrents, that, when he went out on a shooting party,
he was very soon left to continue his sport alone, for he was sure to
dash up or down some nearly perpendicular path, where no one else
had either ability or inclination to follow. He had a pleasure boat
on the lake, which he steered with amazing dexterity ; but as he
always indulged himself in the utmost possible latitude of sail, he was
occasionally upset by a sudden gust, and was indebted to his skill in
the art of swimming for the opportunity of tempering with a copious
libation of wine the unnatural frigidity introduced into his stomach
by the extraordinary intrusion of water, an element which he had reli-
giously determined should never pass his lips, but of which, on these
occasions, he was sometimes compelled to swallow no inconsiderable
quantity. This circumstance alone, of the various disasters that
befell him, occasioned him any permanent affliction, and he accordingly noted the day in his pocket-book as a *dies nefastus*,[2] with
this simple abstract, and brief chronicle of the calamity : *Mem.*

[1] Some readers will, perhaps, recollect the Archbishop of Prague, who
also was an excellent sportsman, and who,

> Com' era scritto in certi suoi giornali,
> Ucciso avea con le sue proprie mani
> Un numero infinito d'animali :
> Cinquemila con quindici fagiani,
> Seimila lepri, ottantatrè cignali,
> E per disgrazia, ancor *tredici cani*, &c. [P.]

[" As was written in some of his diaries, he had killed an infinite number
of animals with his own hands : five thousand and fifteen pheasants, six
thousand hares, eighty-three wild boars, and, by accident, some thirteen
dogs, etc." The passage comes from G. B. Casti, *L'arcivescovo di Praga*,
which is the 34th of his *Novelle*, and occurs in Stanza III, ll. 1–6. Cf.
Novelle di Giambatista Casti Romano, Vol. IV (Parigi anno IX), p. 174. G.]
[2] An evil day. G.

Swallowed two or three pints of water : without any notice whatever of the concomitant circumstances. These days, of which there were several, were set apart in Headlong Hall for the purpose of anniversary expiation ; and, as often as the day returned on which the squire had swallowed water, he not only made a point of swallowing a treble allowance of wine himself, but imposed a heavy mulct on every one of his servants who should be detected in a state of sobriety after sunset : but their conduct on these occasions was so uniformly exemplary, that no instance of the infliction of the penalty appears on record.

The squire and Mr. Milestone, as we have already said, had set out immediately after breakfast to examine the capabilities of the scenery. The object that most attracted Mr. Milestone's admiration was a ruined tower on a projecting point of rock, almost totally overgrown with ivy. This ivy, Mr. Milestone observed, required trimming and clearing in various parts : a little pointing and polishing was also necessary for the dilapidated walls : and the whole effect would be materially increased by a plantation of spruce fir, interspersed with cypress and juniper, the present rugged and broken ascent from the land side being first converted into a beautiful slope, which might be easily effected by blowing up a part of the rock with gunpowder, laying on a quantity of fine mould, and covering the whole with an elegant stratum of turf.

Squire Headlong caught with avidity at this suggestion ; and, as he had always a store of gunpowder in the house, for the accommodation of himself and his shooting visitors, and for the supply of a small battery of cannon, which he kept for his private amusement, he insisted on commencing operations immediately. Accordingly, he bounded back to the house, and very speedily returned, accompanied by the little butler, and half a dozen servants and labourers, with pickaxes and gunpowder, a hanging stove and a poker, together with a basket of cold meat and two or three bottles of Madeira : for the Squire thought, with many others, that a copious supply of provision is a very necessary ingredient in all rural amusements.

Mr. Milestone superintended the proceedings. The rock was excavated, the powder introduced, the apertures strongly blockaded with fragments of stone : a long train was laid to a spot which

Mr. Milestone fixed on as sufficiently remote from the possibility of harm : the Squire seized the poker, and, after flourishing it in the air with a degree of dexterity which induced the rest of the party to leave him in solitary possession of an extensive circumference, applied the end of it to the train ; and the rapidly communicated ignition ran hissing along the surface of the soil.

At this critical moment, Mr. Cranium and Mr. Panscope appeared at the top of the tower, which, unseeing and unseen, they had ascended on the opposite side to that where the Squire and Mr. Milestone were conducting their operations. Their sudden appearance a little dismayed the Squire, who, however, comforted himself with the reflection, that the tower was perfectly safe, or at least was intended to be so, and that his friends were in no probable danger but of a knock on the head from a flying fragment of stone.

The succession of these thoughts in the mind of the Squire was commensurate in rapidity to the progress of the ignition, which having reached its extremity, the explosion took place, and the shattered rock was hurled into the air in the midst of fire and smoke.

Mr. Milestone had properly calculated the force of the explosion ; for the tower remained untouched : but the Squire, in his consolatory reflections, had omitted the consideration of the influence of sudden fear, which had so violent an effect on Mr. Cranium, who was just commencing a speech concerning the very fine prospect from the top of the tower, that, cutting short the thread of his observations, he bounded, under the elastic influence of terror, several feet into the air. His ascent being unluckily a little out of the perpendicular, he descended with a proportionate curve from the apex of his projection, and alighted, not on the wall of the tower, but in an ivy-bush by its side, which, giving way beneath him, transferred him to a tuft of hazel at its base, which, after upholding him an instant, consigned him to the boughs of an ash that had rooted itself in a fissure about half way down the rock, which finally transmitted him to the waters below.[1]

---

[1] " Dr. Gryffydh, the other night, trusting to a rotten branch, had a fall of fifteen feet perpendicular, and but for an intervening hazel, would infallibly have been hurled to the bottom." Peacock to E. T. Hookham, 22 March 1810. G.

Squire Headlong anxiously watched the tower as the smoke which at first enveloped it rolled away ; but when this shadowy curtain was withdrawn, and Mr. Panscope was discovered, *solus*, in a tragical attitude, his apprehensions became boundless, and he concluded that the unlucky collision of a flying fragment of rock had indeed emancipated the spirit of the craniologist from its terrestrial bondage.

Mr. Escot had considerably outstripped his companions, and arrived at the scene of the disaster just as Mr. Cranium, being utterly destitute of natatorial skill, was in imminent danger of final submersion. The deteriorationist, who had cultivated this valuable art with great success, immediately plunged in to his assistance, and brought him alive and in safety to a shelving part of the shore. Their landing was hailed with a view-holla from the delighted Squire, who, shaking them both heartily by the hand, and making ten thousand lame apologies to Mr. Cranium, concluded by asking, in a pathetic tone, *How much water he had swallowed ?* and without waiting for his answer, filled a large tumbler with Madeira, and insisted on his tossing it off, which was no sooner said than done. Mr. Jenkison and Mr. Foster now made their appearance. Mr. Panscope descended the tower, which he vowed never again to approach within a quarter of a mile. The tumbler of Madeira was replenished, and handed round to recruit the spirits of the party, which now began to move towards Headlong Hall, the Squire capering for joy in the van, and the little fat butler waddling in the rear.

The Squire took care that Mr. Cranium should be seated next to him at dinner, and plied him so hard with Madeira to prevent him, as he said, from taking cold, that long before the ladies sent in their summons to coffee, every organ in his brain was in a complete state of revolution, and the Squire was under the necessity of ringing for three or four servants to carry him to bed, observing, with a smile of great satisfaction, that he was in a very excellent way for escaping any ill consequences that might have resulted from his accident.

The beautiful Cephalis, being thus freed from his *surveillance*, was enabled, during the course of the evening, to develop to his preserver the full extent of her gratitude.

CHAPTER IX

THE SEXTON

MR. ESCOT passed a sleepless night, the ordinary effect of love, according to some amatory poets, who seem to have composed their whining ditties for the benevolent purpose of bestowing on others that gentle slumber of which they so pathetically lament the privation. The deteriorationist entered into a profound moral soliloquy, in which he first examined *whether a philosopher ought to be in love ?* Having decided this point affirmatively against Plato and Lucretius, he next examined, *whether that passion ought to have the effect of keeping a philosopher awake ?* Having decided this negatively, he resolved to go to sleep immediately : not being able to accomplish this to his satisfaction, he tossed and tumbled, like Achilles or Orlando, first on one side, then on the other ; repeated to himself several hundred lines of poetry ; counted a thousand ; began again, and counted another thousand : in vain : the beautiful Cephalis was the predominant image in all his soliloquies, in all his repetitions : even in the numerical process from which he sought relief, he did but associate the idea of number with that of his dear tormentor, till she appeared to his mind's eye in a thousand similitudes, distinct, not different. These thousand images, indeed, were but one ; and yet the one was a thousand, a sort of uni-multiplex phantasma, which will be very intelligible to some understandings.

He arose with the first peep of day, and sallied forth to enjoy the balmy breeze of morning, which any but a lover might have thought too cool ; for it was an intense frost, the sun had not risen, and the wind was rather fresh from north-east and by north. But a lover, who, like Ladurlad in the Curse of Kehama, always has, or at least is supposed to have, " a fire in his heart and a fire in his brain," [1] feels a wintry breeze from N.E. and by N. steal over his cheek like the south over a bank of violets : [2] therefore, on walked the philosopher, with his coat unbuttoned and his hat in his hand, careless of whither he went, till he found himself near the enclosure of a little mountain-chapel.

[1] Southey : *The Curse of Kehama*, Book II, Stanza 14. G.
[2] *Twelfth Night*, Act I, Sc. 1 : " Like the sweet sound that breathes upon a bank of violets." G.

Passing through the wicket, and stepping over two or three graves, he stood on a rustic tombstone, and peeped through the chapel window, examining the interior with as much curiosity as if he had " forgotten what the inside of a church was made of," [1] which, it is rather to be feared, was the case. Before him and beneath him were the font, the altar, and the grave ; which gave rise to a train of moral reflections on the three great epochs in the course of the *featherless biped*,—birth, marriage, and death. The middle stage of the process arrested his attention ; and his imagination placed before him several figures, which he thought, with the addition of his own, would make a very picturesque group ; the beautiful Cephalis, " arrayed in her bridal apparel of white ; " her friend Caprioletta officiating as brides-maid ; Mr. Cranium giving her away ; and, last not least, the Reverend Doctor Gaster, intoning the marriage ceremony with the regular orthodox allowance of nasal recitative. Whilst he was feasting his eyes on this imaginary picture, the demon of mistrust insinuated himself into the storehouse of his conceptions, and, removing his figure from the group, substituted that of Mr. Panscope, which gave such a violent shock to his feelings, that he suddenly exclaimed, with an extraordinary elevation of voice, Οιμοι κακοδαιμων, και τρις κακοδαιμων, και τετρακις, και πεντακις, και δωδεκακις, και μυριακις ! [2] to the great terror of the sexton, who was just entering the church-yard, and, not knowing from whence the voice proceeded, *pensa que fut un diableteau.* The sight of the philosopher dispelled his apprehensions, when, growing suddenly valiant, he immediately addressed him :—

" Cot pless your honour, I shouldn't have thought of meeting any pody here at this time of the morning, except, look you, it was the tevil—who, to pe sure, toes not often come upon consecrated cround —put for all that, I think I have seen him now and then, in former tays, when old Nanny Llwyd of Llyn-isa was living—Cot teliver us ! a terriple old witch to pe sure she was—I tidn't much like tigging her crave—put I prought two cocks with me—the tevil hates cocks— and tied them py the leg on two tombstones—and I tug, and the

---

[1] *Henry IV, Pt. I*, Act III, Sc. 3.   G.
[2] Me miserable ! and thrice miserable ! and four times, and five times, and twelve times, and ten thousand times miserable !   [P.]

cocks crowed, and the tevil kept at a tistance. To pe sure now, if I hadn't peen very prave py nature—as I ought to pe truly—for my father was Owen Ap-Llwyd Ap-Gryffydd Ap-Shenkin Ap-Williams Ap-Thomas Ap-Morgan Ap-Parry Ap-Evan Ap-Rhys, a coot preacher and a lover of *cwrw* [1]—I should have thought just now pefore I saw your honour, that the foice I heard was the tevil's calling Nanny Llwyd—Cot pless us ! to pe sure she should have been puried in the middle of the river, where the tevil can't come, as your honour fery well knows."

" I am perfectly aware of it," said Mr. Escot.

" True, true," continued the sexton ; " put to pe sure, Owen Thomas of Morfa-Bach will have it that one summer evening—when he went over to Cwm Cynfael in Meirionnydd, apout some cattles he wanted to puy—he saw a strange figure—pless us !—with five horns ! —Cot save us ! sitting on Hugh Llwyd's pulpit, which, your honour fery well knows, is a pig rock in the middle of the river——"

" Of course he was mistaken," said Mr. Escot.

" To pe sure he was," said the sexton. " For there is no toubt put the tevil, when Owen Thomas saw him, must have peen sitting on a piece of rock in a straight line from him on the other side of the river, where he used to sit, look you, for a whole summer's tay, while Hugh Llwyd was on his pulpit, and there they used to talk across the water ! for Hugh Llwyd, please your honour, never raised the tevil except when he was safe in the middle of the river, which proves that Owen Thomas, in his fright, didn't pay proper attention to the exact spot where the tevil was."

The sexton concluded his speech with an approving smile at his own sagacity, in so luminously expounding the nature of Owen Thomas's mistake.

" I perceive," said Mr. Escot, " you have a very deep insight into things, and can, therefore, perhaps, facilitate the resolution of a question, concerning which, though I have little doubt on the subject, I am desirous of obtaining the most extensive and accurate information."

The sexton scratched his head, the language of Mr. Escot not being to his apprehension quite so luminous as his own.

[1] Pronounced *cooroo*—the Welsh word for *ale*. [P.]

"You have been sexton here," continued Mr. Escot, in the language of Hamlet, "man and boy, forty years." [1]

The sexton turned pale. The period Mr. Escot named was so nearly the true one, that he began to suspect the personage before him of being rather too familiar with Hugh Llwyd's sable visitor. Recovering himself a little, he said, "Why, thereapouts, sure enough."

"During this period, you have of course dug up many bones of the people of ancient times."

"Pones! Cot pless you, yes! pones as old as the 'orlt."

"Perhaps you can show me a few."

The sexton grinned horribly a ghastly smile. "Will you take your Pible oath you ton't want them to raise the tevil with?"

"Willingly," said Mr. Escot, smiling; "I have an abstruse reason for the inquiry."

"Why, if you have an *obtuse* reason," said the sexton, who thought this a good opportunity to show that he could pronounce hard words as well as other people; "if you have an *obtuse* reason, that alters the case."

So saying he led the way to the bone-house, from which he began to throw out various bones and skulls of more than common dimensions, and amongst them a skull of very extraordinary magnitude, which he swore by St. David was the skull of Cadwallader.

"How do you know this to be his skull?" said Mr. Escot.

"He was the piggest man that ever lived, and he was puried here; and this is the piggest skull I ever found: you see now——"

"Nothing can be more logical," said Mr. Escot. "My good friend, will you allow me to take this skull away with me?"

"St. Winifred pless us!" exclaimed the sexton:—"would you have me haunted py his chost for taking his plessed pones out of consecrated cround? Would you have him come in the tead of the night, and fly away with the roof of my house? Would you have all the crop of my carden come to nothing? for, look you, his epitaph says,

"He that my pones shall ill pestow,
Leek in his cround shall never crow."

"You will ill bestow them," said Mr. Escot, "in confounding them

[1] *Hamlet*, Act V, Sc. 1. Actually "thirty years." G.

with those of the sons of little men, the degenerate dwarfs of later generations : you will well bestow them in giving them to me ; for I will have this illustrious skull bound with a silver rim, and filled with mantling wine, with this inscription, NUNC TANDEM : signifying that that pernicious liquor has at length found its proper receptacle ; for, when the wine is in, the brain is out." [1]

Saying these words, he put a dollar into the hands of the sexton, who instantly stood spell-bound by the talismanic influence of the coin, while Mr. Escot walked off in triumph with the skull of Cadwallader.

CHAPTER X

THE SKULL

WHEN Mr. Escot entered the breakfast-room he found the majority of the party assembled, and the little butler very active at his station. Several of the ladies shrieked at the sight of the skull ; and Miss Tenorina, starting up in great haste and terror, caused the subversion of a cup of chocolate, which a servant was handing to the Reverend Doctor Gaster, into the nape of the neck of Sir Patrick O'Prism. Sir Patrick, rising impetuously, *to clap an extinguisher*, as he expressed himself, *on the farthing rushlight of the rascal's life*,[2] pushed over the chair of Marmaduke Milestone, Esquire, who, catching for support at the first thing that came in his way, which happened unluckily to be the corner of the table-cloth, drew it instantaneously with him to the floor, involving plates, cups and saucers, in one promiscuous ruin. But, as the principal *matériel* of the breakfast apparatus was on the little butler's side-table, the confusion occasioned by this accident was happily greater than the damage. Miss Tenorina was so agitated that she was obliged to retire : Miss Graziosa accompanied her through pure sisterly affection and

---

[1] *Much Ado About Nothing*, Act III, Sc. 5, adapted. G.

[2] O'Fir, Sir Patrick O'Prism's prototype in Peacock's farce *The Three Doctors*, exclaims : " Then I'll clap an extinguisher on the farthing rushlight of his life." G.

sympathy, not without a lingering look at Sir Patrick, who likewise retired to change his coat, but was very expeditious in returning to resume his attack on the cold partridge. The broken cups were cleared away, the cloth relaid, and the array of the table restored with wonderful celerity.

Mr. Escot was a little surprised at the scene of confusion which signalised his entrance ; but, perfectly unconscious that it originated with the skull of Cadwallader, he advanced to seat himself at the table by the side of the beautiful Cephalis, first placing the skull in a corner, out of the reach of Mr. Cranium, who sate eyeing it with lively curiosity, and after several efforts to restrain his impatience, exclaimed, " You seem to have found a rarity."

" A rarity indeed," said Mr. Escot, cracking an egg as he spoke ; " no less than the genuine and indubitable skull of Cadwallader."

" The skull of Cadwallader ! " vociferated Mr. Cranium : " O treasure of treasures ! "

Mr. Escot then detailed by what means he had become possessed of it, which gave birth to various remarks from the other individuals of the party : after which, rising from table, and taking the skull again in his hand,

" This skull," said he, " is the skull of a hero, παλαι κατατεθνειωτος,[1] and sufficiently demonstrates a point, concerning which I never myself entertained a doubt, that the human race is undergoing a gradual process of diminution in length, breadth, and thickness. Observe this skull. Even the skull of our reverend friend, which is the largest and thickest in the company, is not more than half its size. The frame this skull belonged to could scarcely have been less than nine feet high.[2] Such is the lamentable progress of degeneracy and decay. In the course of ages, a boot of the present generation would form an ample chateau for a large family of our remote posterity.

[1] Long since dead. [P.] [Homer : Il. VII. 89, and XXIII. 331. G.]

[2] Mr. Escot's remarks indicate that he believed that the owner of the skull had lived in ancient times. He would therefore be either the King of Gwynedd slain at Hexham A.D. 634, or more probably the semi-mythical King of the Britons who died of plague c. A.D. 664, and not the twelfth-century Prince of Gwynedd buried at Bangor, or the sixteenth-century poet, or the Catholic Martyr executed in 1610. But however genuine the skull, the epitaph, in English, must be suspected of being a late addition to the grave. G.

The mind, too, participates in the contraction of the body. Poets and philosophers of all ages and nations have lamented this too visible process of physical and moral deterioration. 'The sons of little men,' says Ossian. Ὅιοι νυν βροτοι εισιν, says Homer [1] : 'such men as live in these degenerate days.' 'All things,' says Virgil,[2] 'have a retrocessive tendency, and grow worse and worse by the inevitable doom of fate.' 'We live in the ninth age,' says Juvenal,[3] 'an age worse than the age of iron ; nature has no metal sufficiently pernicious to give a denomination to its wickedness.' 'Our fathers,' says Horace,[4] 'worse than our grandfathers, have given birth to us, their more vicious progeny, who, in our turn, shall become the parents of a still viler generation.' You all know the fable of the buried Pict, who bit off the end of a pickaxe, with which sacrilegious hands were breaking open his grave, and called out with a voice like subterranean thunder, *I perceive the degeneracy of your race by the smallness of your little finger !* videlicet, the pickaxe. This, to be sure, is a fiction ; but it shows the prevalent opinion, the feeling, the conviction, of absolute, universal, irremediable deterioration."

" I should be sorry," said Mr. Foster, " that such an opinion should become universal, independently of my conviction of its fallacy. Its general admission would tend, in a great measure, to produce the very evils it appears to lament. What could be its effect, but to check the ardour of investigation, to extinguish the zeal of philanthropy, to freeze the current of enterprising hope, to bury in the torpor of scepticism and in the stagnation of despair, every better faculty of the human mind, which will necessarily become retrograde in ceasing to be progressive ? "

" I am inclined to think, on the contrary," said Mr. Escot, " that the deterioration of man is accelerated by his blindness—in many respects wilful blindness—to the truth of the fact itself, and to the causes which produce it ; that there is no hope whatever of ameliorating his condition but in a total and radical change of the whole scheme of human life, and that the advocates of his indefinite perfectibility are in reality the greatest enemies to the practical possibility of their own system, by so strenuously labouring to

[1] *Il.* V. 304, and elsewhere.　G.
[2] *Georg.* I. 199.　[P.]　[3] *Sat.* XIII. 28.　[P.]　[4] *Carm.* III. 6. 46.　[P.]

impress on his attention that he is going on in a good way, while he is really in a deplorably bad one."

"I admit," said Mr. Foster, "there are many things that may, and therefore will, be changed for the better."

"Not on the present system," said Mr. Escot, "in which every change is for the worse."

"In matters of taste I am sure it is," said Mr. Gall : "there is, in fact, no such thing as good taste left in the world."

"O, Mr. Gall!" said Miss Philomela Poppyseed, "I thought my novel——"

"My paintings," said Sir Patrick O'Prism——

"My ode," said Mr. Mac Laurel——

"My ballad," said Mr. Nightshade——

"My plan for Lord Littlebrain's park," said Marmaduke Milestone, Esquire——

"My essay," said Mr. Treacle——

"My sonata," said Mr. Chromatic——

"My claret," said Squire Headlong——

"My lectures," said Mr. Cranium——

"Vanity of vanities," said the Reverend Doctor Gaster, turning down an empty egg-shell ; "all is vanity and vexation of spirit." [1]

CHAPTER XI

THE ANNIVERSARY

AMONG the *dies albâ cretâ notandos*,[2] which the beau monde of the Cambrian mountains was in the habit of remembering with the greatest pleasure, and anticipating with the most lively satisfaction, was the Christmas ball which the ancient family of the Headlongs had been accustomed to give from time immemorial. Tradition attributed the honour of its foundation to Headlong Ap-Headlong Ap-Breakneck Ap-Headlong Ap-Cataract Ap-Pistyll [3] Ap-Rhaidr

---

[1] *Ecclesiastes*, i and ii.   G.

[2] The nearest English equivalent is "red-letter days" and the closest classical parallel will be found in Horace : *Sat.* II. iii. 246.   G.

[3] Pistyll, in Welsh, signifies a cataract, and Rhaidr a cascade.   [P.]

Ap-Headlong, who lived about the time of the Trojan war. Certain
it is, at least, that a grand chorus was always sung after supper in
honour of this illustrious ancestor of the squire. This ball was,
indeed, an æra in the lives of all the beauty and fashion of Caernarvon, Meirionnydd, and Anglesea, and, like the Greek Olympiads
and the Roman consulates, served as the main pillar of memory,
round which all the events of the year were suspended and entwined.
Thus, in recalling to mind any circumstance imperfectly recollected,
the principal point to be ascertained was, whether it had occurred in
the year of the first, second, third, or fourth ball of Headlong
Ap-Breakneck, or Headlong Ap-Torrent, or Headlong Ap-Hurricane ;
and, this being satisfactorily established, the remainder followed of
course in the natural order of its ancient association.

This eventful anniversary being arrived, every chariot, coach,
barouche, and barouchette, landau and landaulet, chaise, curricle,
buggy, whiskey, and tilbury, of the three counties, was in motion :
not a horse was left idle within five miles of any gentleman's seat,
from the high-mettled hunter to the heath-cropping galloway. The
ferrymen of the Menai were at their stations before day-break, taking
a double allowance of rum and *cwrw* to strengthen them for the
fatigues of the day. The ivied towers of Caernarvon, the romantic
woods of Tan-y-bwlch, the heathy hills of Kernioggau, the sandy
shores of Tremadoc, the mountain recesses of Bedd-Gelert, and the
lonely lakes of Capel-Cerig, re-echoed to the voices of the delighted
ostlers and postillions, who reaped on this happy day their wintry
harvest. Landlords and landladies, waiters, chambermaids, and
toll-gate keepers, roused themselves from the torpidity which the
last solitary tourist, flying with the yellow leaves on the wings of the
autumnal wind, had left them to enjoy till the returning spring : the
bustle of August was renewed on all the mountain roads, and, in the
meanwhile, Squire Headlong and his little fat butler carried most
energetically into effect the lessons of the *savant* in the Court of
Quintessence, *qui par engin mirificque jectoit les maisons par les
fenestres.*[1]

It was the custom for the guests to assemble at dinner on the day

[1] Rabelais. [P.] [Bk. V, Ch. xxi. " One with a wonderful engine threw
the houses out at the windows." Urquhart and Motteux translation. G.]

of the ball, and depart on the following morning after breakfast. Sleep during this interval was out of the question : the ancient harp of Cambria suspended the celebration of the noble race of Shenkin, and the songs of Hoel and Cyveilioc, to ring to the profaner but more lively modulation of *Voulez vous danser, Mademoiselle ?* in conjunction with the symphonious scraping of fiddles, the tinkling of triangles, and the beating of tambourines. Comus and Momus were the deities of the night; and Bacchus of course was not forgotten by the male part of the assembly (with them, indeed, a ball was invariably a scene of *"tipsy dance and jollity"* [1]): the servants flew about with wine and negus, and the little butler was indefatigable with his cork-screw, which is reported on one occasion to have grown so hot under the influence of perpetual friction that it actually set fire to the cork.

The company assembled. The dinner, which on this occasion was a secondary object, was despatched with uncommon celerity. When the cloth was removed, and the bottle had taken its first round, Mr. Cranium stood up and addressed the company.

" Ladies and gentlemen," said he, " the golden key of mental phænomena, which has lain buried for ages in the deepest vein of the mine of physiological research, is now, by a happy combination of practical and speculative investigations, grasped, if I may so express myself, firmly and inexcussibly, in the hands of physiognomical empiricism." The Cambrian visitors listened with profound attention, not comprehending a single syllable he said, but concluding he would finish his speech by proposing the health of Squire Headlong. The gentlemen accordingly tossed off their heel taps, and Mr. Cranium proceeded : " Ardently desirous, to the extent of my feeble capacity, of disseminating, as much as possible, the inexhaustible treasures to which this golden key admits the humblest votary of philosophical truth, I invite you, when you have sufficiently restored, replenished, refreshed, and exhilarated that osteosarchæmatosplanchnochondro-neuromuelous, or to employ a more intelligible term, osseocarni-sanguineoviscericartilaginonervomedullary,[2] *compages,* or shell, the body, which at once envelops and develops that mysterious and

---

[1] Milton : *Comus,* l. 104.   G.
[2] These monstrous terms enumerate all the tissues of the body.   G.

inestimable kernel, the desiderative, determinative, ratiocinative, imaginative, inquisitive, appetitive, comparative, reminiscent, congeries of ideas and notions, simple and compound, comprised in the comprehensive denomination of mind, to take a peep with me into the mechanical arcana of the anatomico-metaphysical universe. Being not in the least dubitative of your spontaneous compliance, I proceed," added he, suddenly changing his tone, " to get every thing ready in the library." Saying these words, he vanished.

The Welsh squires now imagined they had caught a glimpse of his meaning, and set him down in their minds for a sort of gentleman conjuror, who intended to amuse them before the ball with some tricks of legerdemain. Under this impression, they became very impatient to follow him, as they had made up their minds not to be drunk before supper. The ladies, too, were extremely curious to witness an exhibition which had been announced in so singular a preamble ; and the squire, having previously insisted on every gentleman tossing off a half-pint bumper, adjourned the whole party to the library, where they were not a little surprised to discover Mr. Cranium seated, in a pensive attitude, at a large table, decorated with a copious variety of skulls.

Some of the ladies were so much shocked at this extraordinary display, that a scene of great confusion ensued. Fans were very actively exercised, and water was strenuously called for by some of the most officious of the gentlemen ; on which the little butler entered with a large allowance of liquid, which bore, indeed, the name of *water*, but was in reality a very powerful spirit. This was the only species of water which the little butler had ever heard called for in Headlong Hall. The mistake was not attended with any evil effects : for the fluid was no sooner applied to the lips of the fainting fair ones, than it resuscitated them with an expedition truly miraculous.

Order was at length restored ; the audience took their seats ; and the craniological orator held forth in the following terms :—

CHAPTER XII

THE LECTURE

" PHYSIOLOGISTS have been much puzzled to account for the varieties of moral character in men, as well as for the remarkable similarity of habit and disposition in all the individual animals of every other respective species. A few brief sentences, perspicuously worded, and scientifically arranged, will enumerate all the characteristics of a lion, or a tiger, or a wolf, or a bear, or a squirrel, or a goat, or a horse, or an ass, or a rat, or a cat, or a hog, or a dog ; and whatever is physiologically predicated of any individual lion, tiger, wolf, bear, squirrel, goat, horse, ass, hog, or dog, will be found to hold true of all lions, tigers, wolves, bears, squirrels, goats, horses, asses, hogs, and dogs, whatsoever. Now, in man, the very reverse of this appears to be the case ; for he has so few distinct and characteristic marks which hold true of all his species, that philosophers in all ages have found it a task of infinite difficulty to give him a definition. Hence one has defined him to be a *featherless biped*, a definition which is equally applicable to an unfledged fowl : another, to be *an animal which forms opinions*, than which nothing can be more inaccurate, for a very small number of the species form opinions, and the remainder take them upon trust, without investigation or inquiry.

" Again, man has been defined to be *an animal that carries a stick* : an attribute which undoubtedly belongs to man only, but not to all men always ; though it uniformly characterises some of the graver and more imposing varieties, such as physicians, oran-outangs, and lords in waiting.

" We cannot define man to be a reasoning animal, for we do not dispute that idiots are men ; to say nothing of that very numerous description of persons who consider themselves reasoning animals, and are so denominated by the ironical courtesy of the world, who labour, nevertheless, under a very gross delusion in that essential particular.

" It appears to me, that man may be correctly defined an animal, which, without any peculiar or distinguishing faculty of its own, is, as it were, a bundle or compound of faculties of other animals, by a distinct enumeration of which any individual of the species may be satisfactorily described. This is manifest, even in the ordinary language of conversation, when, in summing up, for example, the qualities of an accomplished courtier, we say he has the vanity of a peacock, the cunning of a fox, the treachery of an hyæna, the cold-heartedness of a cat, and the servility of a jackal. That this is perfectly consentaneous to scientific truth, will appear in the further progress of these observations.

"Every particular faculty of the mind has its corresponding organ in the brain. In proportion as any particular faculty or propensity acquires paramount activity in any individual, these organs develop themselves, and their development becomes externally obvious by corresponding lumps and bumps, exuberances and protuberances, on the osseous compages of the occiput and sinciput. In all animals but man, the same organ is equally developed in every individual of the species: for instance, that of migration in the swallow, that of destruction in the tiger, that of architecture in the beaver, and that of parental affection in the bear. The human brain, however, consists, as I have said, of a bundle or compound of all the faculties of all other animals ; and from the greater development of one or more of these, in the infinite varieties of combination, result all the peculiarities of individual character.

"Here is the skull of a beaver, and that of Sir Christopher Wren. You observe, in both these specimens, the prodigious development of the organ of constructiveness.

"Here is the skull of a bullfinch, and that of an eminent fiddler. You may compare the organ of music.

"Here is the skull of a tiger. You observe the organ of carnage. Here is the skull of a fox. You observe the organ of plunder. Here is the skull of a peacock. You observe the organ of vanity.[1] Here is the skull of an illustrious robber, who, after a long and triumphant process of depredation and murder, was suddenly checked in his career by means of a certain quality inherent in preparations of hemp,

---

[1] In April, 1815, the *Quarterly Review* printed an article on phrenology stating that Dr. Gall had identified a protuberance in the skulls of chamois with that which in man signifies pride and hauteur. As M. Mayoux comments, " ce qui est joli." G.

which, for the sake of perspicuity, I shall call *suspensiveness*. Here is the skull of a conqueror, who, after over-running several kingdoms, burning a number of cities, and causing the deaths of two or three millions of men, women, and children, was entombed with all the pageantry of public lamentation, and figured as the hero of several thousand odes and a round dozen of epics ; while the poor highwayman was twice executed—

> ' At the gallows first, and after in a ballad,
> Sung to a villanous tune.' [1]

You observe, in both these skulls, the combined development of the organs of carnage, plunder, and vanity, which I have separately pointed out in the tiger, the fox, and the peacock. The greater enlargement of the organ of vanity in the hero is the only criterion by which I can distinguish them from each other. Born with the same faculties, and the same propensities, these two men were formed by nature to run the same career : the different combinations of external circumstances decided the differences of their destinies.

" Here is the skull of a Newfoundland dog. You observe the organ of benevolence, and that of attachment. Here is a human skull, in which you may observe a very striking negation of both these organs ; and an equally striking development of those of destruction, cunning, avarice, and self-love. This was one of the most illustrious statesmen that ever flourished in the page of history.

" Here is the skull of a turnspit, which, after a wretched life of *dirty work*, was turned out of doors to die on a dunghill. I have been induced to preserve it, in consequence of its remarkable similarity to this, which belonged to a courtly poet, who having grown grey in flattering the great, was cast off in the same manner to perish by the same catastrophe."

After these, and several other illustrations, during which the skulls were handed round for the inspection of the company, Mr. Cranium proceeded thus :—

" It is obvious, from what I have said, that no man can hope for worldly honour or advancement, who is not placed in such a relation to external circumstances as may be consentaneous to his peculiar

---

[1] Massinger : *The Bondman*, Act V, Sc. 3. G.

cerebral organs ; and I would advise every parent, who has the welfare of his son at heart, to procure as extensive a collection as possible of the skulls of animals, and, before determining on the choice of a profession, to compare with the utmost nicety their bumps and protuberances with those of the skull of his son. If the development of the organ of destruction point out a similarity between the youth and the tiger, let him be brought to some profession (whether that of a butcher, a soldier, or a physician, may be regulated by circumstances) in which he may be furnished with a licence to kill : as, without such licence, the indulgence of his natural propensity may lead to the untimely rescission of his vital thread, ' with edge of penny cord and vile reproach.'[1] If he show an analogy with the jackal, let all possible influence be used to procure him a place at court, where he will infallibly thrive. If his skull bear a marked resemblance to that of a magpie, it cannot be doubted that he will prove an admirable lawyer ; and if with this advantageous conformation be combined any similitude to that of an owl, very confident hopes may be formed of his becoming a judge."

A furious flourish of music was now heard from the ball-room, the squire having secretly despatched the little butler to order it to strike up, by way of a hint to Mr. Cranium to finish his harangue. The company took the hint and adjourned tumultuously, having just understood as much of the lecture as furnished them with amusement for the ensuing twelvemonth, in feeling the skulls of all their acquaintance.

CHAPTER XIII

THE BALL

THE ball-room was adorned with great taste and elegance, under the direction of Miss Caprioletta and her friend Miss Cephalis, who were themselves its most beautiful ornaments, even though romantic Meirion, the pre-eminent in loveliness, sent many of its loveliest daughters to grace the festive scene. Numberless were the solicita-

---

[1] *Henry V*, Act III, Sc. 6. G.

tions of the dazzled swains of Cambria for the honour of the two first dances with the one or the other of these fascinating friends ; but little availed, on this occasion, the pedigree lineally traced from Caractacus or King Arthur : their two philosophical lovers, neither of whom could have given the least account of his great-great-grandfather, had engaged them many days before. Mr. Panscope chafed and fretted like Llugwy [1] in his bed of rocks, when the object of his adoration stood up with his rival : but he consoled himself with a lively damsel from the vale of Edeirnion, having first compelled Miss Cephalis to promise him her hand for the fourth set.

The ball was accordingly opened by Miss Caprioletta and Mr. Foster, which gave rise to much speculation among the Welsh gentry, as to who this Mr. Foster could be ; some of the more learned among them secretly resolving to investigate most profoundly the antiquity of the name of Foster, and ascertain what right a person so denominated could have to open the most illustrious of all possible balls with the lovely Caprioletta Headlong, the only sister of Harry Headlong, Esquire, of Headlong Hall, in the Vale of Llanberris, the only surviving male representative of the antediluvian family of Headlong Ap-Rhaiader.

When the two first dances were ended, Mr. Escot, who did not choose to dance with any one but his adorable Cephalis, looking round for a convenient seat, discovered Mr. Jenkison in a corner by the side of the Reverend Doctor Gaster, who was keeping excellent time with his nose to the lively melody of the harp and fiddle. Mr. Escot seated himself by the side of Mr. Jenkison, and inquired if he took no part in the amusement of the night ?

MR. JENKISON. No. The universal cheerfulness of the company induces me to rise ; the trouble of such violent exercise induces me to sit still. Did I see a young lady in want of a partner, gallantry would incite me to offer myself as her devoted knight for half an hour : but, as I perceive there are enough without me, that motive is null. I have been weighing these points *pro* and *con*, and remain *in statu quo*.

MR. ESCOT. I have danced, contrary to my system, as I have done

[1] A mountain stream near Bettws-y-Coed.   G.

many other things since I have been here, from a motive that you will easily guess. (*Mr. Jenkison smiled.*) I have great objections to dancing. The wild and original man is a calm and contemplative animal. The stings of natural appetite alone rouse him to action. He satisfies his hunger with roots and fruits, unvitiated by the malignant adhibition of fire, and all its diabolical processes of elixion and assation [1] : he slakes his thirst in the mountain-streams, συμμισγεται τη επιτυχουση,[2] and returns to his peaceful state of meditative repose.

MR. JENKISON. Like the metaphysical statue of Condillac.[3]

MR. ESCOT. With all its senses and purely natural faculties developed, certainly. Imagine this tranquil and passionless being, occupied in his first meditation on the simple question of *Where am I ? Whence do I come ? And what is the end of my existence ?* Then suddenly place before him a chandelier, a fiddler, and a magnificent beau in silk stockings and pumps, bounding, skipping, swinging, capering, and throwing himself into ten thousand attitudes, till his face glows with fever, and distils with perspiration : the first impulse excited in his mind by such an apparition will be that of violent fear, which, by the reiterated perception of its harmlessness, will subside into simple astonishment. Then let any genius, sufficiently powerful to impress on his mind all the terms of the communication, impart to him, that after a long process of ages, when his race shall have attained what some people think proper to denominate a very advanced stage of perfectibility, the most favoured and distinguished of the community shall meet by hundreds, to grin, and labour, and gesticulate, like the phantasma before him, from sunset to sunrise, while all nature is at rest, and that they shall consider this a happy and pleasurable mode of existence, and furnishing the most delight-

[1] " In the assation or roasting it will sometimes abate a dragme." Sir Thomas Browne : *Pseudodoxia Epidemica.* Elixion = boiling. G.

[2] Mates with the first comer. G.

[3] Condillac in his *Traité des Sensations* imagines a statue organised inwardly like a man, animated by a soul which has never received an idea, into which no sense-impression has penetrated. He then unlocks its senses one by one. The work challenges Locke's doctrine that the senses provide an intuitive knowledge of objects. The *Traité des Sensations* ends with observations on a " wild boy " found living with bears in Lithuania. G.

ful of all possible contrasts to what they will call his vegetative state :
would he not groan from his inmost soul for the lamentable condition
of his posterity ?

MR. JENKISON. I know not what your wild and original man
might think of the matter in the abstract ; but comparatively, I
conceive, he would be better pleased with the vision of such a scene
as this, than with that of a party of Indians (who would have all the
advantage of being nearly as wild as himself), dancing their infernal
war-dance round a midnight fire in a North American forest.

MR. ESCOT. Not if you should impart to him the true nature
of both, by laying open to his view the springs of action in both
parties.

MR. JENKISON. To do this with effect, you must make him a
profound metaphysician, and thus transfer him at once from his
wild and original state to a very advanced stage of intellectual
progression ; whether that progression be towards good or evil, I
leave you and our friend Foster to settle between you.

MR. ESCOT. I wish to make no change in his habits and feelings,
but to give him, hypothetically, so much mental illumination, as
will enable him to take a clear view of two distinct stages of the
deterioration of his posterity, that he may be enabled to compare
them with each other, and with his own more happy condition. The
Indian, dancing round the midnight fire, is very far deteriorated ;
but the magnificent beau, dancing to the light of chandeliers, is
infinitely more so. The Indian is a hunter : he makes great use of
fire, and subsists almost entirely on animal food. The malevolent
passions that spring from these pernicious habits involve him in
perpetual war. He is, therefore, necessitated, for his own preservation, to keep all the energies of his nature in constant activity : to
this end his midnight war-dance is very powerfully subservient, and,
though in itself a frightful spectacle, is at least justifiable on the iron
plea of necessity.

MR. JENKISON. On the same iron plea, the modern system of
dancing is more justifiable. The Indian dances to prepare himself

for killing his enemy : but while the beaux and belles of our assemblies dance, they are in the very act of killing theirs—TIME !— a more inveterate and formidable foe than any the Indian has to contend with ; for, however completely and ingeniously killed, he is sure to rise again, "with twenty mortal murders on his crown,"[1] leading his army of blue devils,[2] with ennui in the van, and vapours in the rear.

MR. ESCOT. Your observation militates on my side of the question ; and it is a strong argument in favour of the Indian, that he has no such enemy to kill.

MR. JENKISON. There is certainly a great deal to be said against dancing : there is also a great deal to be said in its favour. The first side of the question I leave for the present to you : on the latter, I may venture to allege that no amusement seems more natural and more congenial to youth than this. It has the advantage of bringing young persons of both sexes together, in a manner which its publicity renders perfectly unexceptionable, enabling them to see and know each other better than, perhaps, any other mode of general association. *Tête-à-têtes* are dangerous things. Small family parties are too much under mutual observation. A ball-room appears to me almost the only scene uniting that degree of rational and innocent liberty of intercourse, which it is desirable to promote as much as possible between young persons, with that scrupulous attention to the delicacy and propriety of female conduct, which I consider the fundamental basis of all our most valuable social relations.

MR. ESCOT. There would be some plausibility in your argument, if it were not the very essence of this species of intercourse to exhibit them to each other under false colours. Here all is show, and varnish, and hypocrisy, and coquetry ; they dress up their moral character for the evening at the same toilet where they manufacture their shapes and faces. Ill-temper lies buried under a studied accumula-

---

[1] *Macbeth*, Act III, Sc. 4. G.

[2] A blue devil was a familiar and baleful demon in the seventeenth century. By a natural process he became identified first with melancholia and then with delirium tremens, and finally lost his features, as Victorian respectability increased, in " a fit of the blues." G.

tion of smiles. Envy, hatred, and malice, retreat from the countenance, to entrench themselves more deeply in the heart. Treachery lurks under the flowers of courtesy. Ignorance and folly take refuge in that unmeaning gabble which it would be profanation to call language, and which even those whom long experience in "the dreary intercourse of daily life"[1] has screwed up to such a pitch of stoical endurance that they can listen to it by the hour, have branded with the ignominious appellation of "*small talk*." Small indeed !—the absolute minimum of the infinitely little.

MR. JENKISON. Go on. I have said all I intended to say on the favourable side. I shall have great pleasure in hearing you balance the argument.

MR. ESCOT. I expect you to confess that I shall have more than balanced it. A ball-room is an epitome of all that is most worthless and unamiable in the great sphere of human life. Every petty and malignant passion is called into play. Coquetry is perpetually on the alert to captivate, caprice to mortify, and vanity to take offence. One amiable female is rendered miserable for the evening by seeing another, whom she intended to outshine, in a more attractive dress than her own ; while the other omits no method of giving stings to her triumph, which she enjoys with all the secret arrogance of an oriental sultana. Another is compelled to dance with a *monster* she abhors. A third has set her heart on dancing with a particular partner, perhaps for the amiable motive of annoying one of her *dear friends* : not only he does not ask her, but she sees him dancing with that identical *dear friend*, whom from that moment she hates more cordially than ever. Perhaps, what is worse than all, she has set her heart on refusing some impertinent fop, who does not give her the opportunity.—As to the men, the case is very nearly the same with them. To be sure, they have the privilege of making the first advances, and are, therefore, less liable to have an odious partner forced upon them ; though this sometimes happens, as I know by woful experience : but it is seldom they can procure the very partner they prefer ; and when they do, the absurd necessity of changing

---

[1] Wordsworth: *Tintern Abbey*, l. 131. G.

every two dances forces them away,[1] and leaves them only the miserable alternative of taking up with something disagreeable perhaps in itself, and at all events rendered so by contrast, or of retreating into some solitary corner, to vent their spleen on the first idle coxcomb they can find.

MR. JENKISON. I hope that is not the motive which brings you to me.

MR. ESCOT. Clearly not. But the most afflicting consideration of all is, that these malignant and miserable feelings are masked under that uniform disguise of pretended benevolence, *that fine and delicate irony, called politeness, which gives so much ease and pliability to the mutual intercourse of civilised man, and enables him to assume the appearance of every virtue, without the reality of one.*[2]

The second set of dances was now terminated, and Mr. Escot flew off to reclaim the hand of the beautiful Cephalis, with whom he figured away with surprising alacrity, and probably felt at least as happy among the chandeliers and silk stockings, at which he had just been railing, as he would have been in an American forest, making one in an Indian ring, by the light of a blazing fire, even though his hand had been locked in that of the most beautiful *squaw* that ever listened to the roar of Niagara.

Squire Headlong was now beset by his maiden aunt, Miss Brindlemew Grimalkin Phœbe Tabitha Ap-Headlong, on one side, and Sir Patrick O'Prism on the other; the former insisting that he should immediately procure her a partner; the latter earnestly requesting the same interference in behalf of Miss Philomela Poppyseed. The squire thought to emancipate himself from his two petitioners by making them dance with each other; but Sir Patrick vehemently pleading a prior engagement, the squire threw his eyes around till they alighted on Mr. Jenkison and the Reverend Doctor Gaster;

---

[1] It is clear from *Evelina* that before 1777 it had been the custom to dance the whole evening with the same partner. The fashion later developed of dancing the minuet up and down twice with the same partner, i.e. two dances. This lasted till the minuet was superseded by the waltz and the polka. G.

[2] Rousseau, *Discours sur les Sciences.* [P.]

both of whom, after waking the latter, he pressed into the service. The doctor, arising with a strange kind of guttural sound, which was half a yawn and half a groan, was handed by the officious squire to Miss Philomela, who received him with sullen dignity : she had not yet forgotten his falling asleep during the first chapter of her novel, while she was condescending to detail to him the outlines of four superlative volumes. The doctor, on his part, had most completely forgotten it ; and though he thought there was something in her physiognomy rather more forbidding than usual, he gave himself no concern about the cause, and had not the least suspicion that it was at all connected with himself. Miss Brindle-mew was very well contented with Mr. Jenkison, and gave him two or three ogles, accompanied by a most risible distortion of the countenance which she intended for a captivating smile. As to Mr. Jenkison, it was all one to him with whom he danced, or whether he danced or not : he was therefore just as well pleased as if he had been left alone in his corner ; which is probably more than could have been said of any other human being under similar circumstances.

At the end of the third set, supper was announced ; and the party, pairing off like turtles, adjourned to the supper-room. The squire was now the happiest of mortal men, and the little butler the most laborious. The centre of the largest table was decorated with a model of Snowdon, surmounted with an enormous artificial leek, the leaves of angelica, and the bulb of blanc-mange. A little way from the summit was a tarn, or mountain-pool, supplied through concealed tubes with an inexhaustible flow of milk-punch, which, dashing in cascades down the miniature rocks, fell into the more capacious lake below, washing the mimic foundations of Headlong Hall. The reverend doctor handed Miss Philomela to the chair most conveniently situated for enjoying this interesting scene, protesting he had never before been sufficiently impressed with the magnificence of that mountain, which he now perceived to be well worthy of all the fame it had obtained.

"Now, when they had eaten and were satisfied,"[1] Squire Headlong called on Mr. Chromatic for a song ; who, with the assistance of his

---

[1] Translation of a line frequently recurring in Homer. G.

two accomplished daughters, regaled the ears of the company with
the following

TERZETTO.[1]

Grey Twilight, from her shadowy hill,
　Discolours Nature's vernal bloom,
And sheds on grove, and field, and rill,
　One placid tint of deepening gloom.

The sailor sighs 'mid shoreless seas,
　Touched by the thought of friends afar,
As, fanned by ocean's flowing breeze,
　He gazes on the western star.

The wanderer hears, in pensive dream,
　The accents of the last farewell,
As, pausing by the mountain stream,
　He listens to the evening bell.

This terzetto was of course much applauded; Mr. Milestone
observing, that he thought the figure in the last verse would have
been more picturesque, if it had been represented with its arms folded
and its back against a tree; or leaning on its staff, with a cockle-shell
in its hat, like a pilgrim of ancient times.

Mr. Chromatic professed himself astonished that a gentleman of
genuine modern taste, like Mr. Milestone, should consider the words
of a song of any consequence whatever, seeing that they were at the
best only a species of pegs, for the more convenient suspension of
crochets and quavers. This remark drew on him a very severe
reprimand from Mr. Mac Laurel, who said to him, "Dinna ye
ken, sir, that soond is a thing utterly worthless in itsel, and only
effectual in agreeable excitements, as far as it is an aicho to sense?
Is there ony soond mair meeserable an' peetifu' than the scrape
o' a feddle, when it does na touch ony chord i' the human
sensorium? Is there ony mair divine than the deep note o' a bagpipe, when it breathes the auncient meelodies o' leeberty an' love?
It is true, there are peculiar trains o' feeling an' sentiment, which
parteecular combinations o' meelody are calculated to excite; an'
sae far music can produce its effect without words: but it does na
follow, that, when ye put words to it, it becomes a matter of

[1] Imitated from a passage in the *Purgatorio* of Dante. [P.] [viii. 1–6.
G.]

indefference what they are ; for a gude strain of impassioned poetry will greatly increase the effect, and a tessue o' nonsensical doggrel will destroy it a' thegither. Noo, as gude poetry can produce its effect without music, sae will gude music without poetry ; and as gude music will be mair pooerfu' by itsel' than wi' bad poetry, sae will gude poetry than wi' bad music : but, when ye put gude music an' gude poetry thegither, ye produce the divinest compound o' senti-mental harmony that can possibly find its way through the lug to the saul."

Mr. Chromatic admitted that there was much justice in these observations, but still maintained the subserviency of poetry to music. Mr. Mac Laurel as strenuously maintained the contrary ; and a furious war of words was proceeding to perilous lengths, when the squire interposed his authority towards the reproduction of peace, which was forthwith concluded, and all animosities drowned in a libation of milk-punch, the Reverend Doctor Gaster officiating as high priest on the occasion.

Mr. Chromatic now requested Miss Caprioletta to favour the company with an air. The young lady immediately complied and sung the following simple

BALLAD.

" O Mary, my sister, thy sorrow give o'er,
I soon shall return, girl, and leave thee no more :
But with children so fair, and a husband so kind,
I shall feel less regret when I leave thee behind.

" I have made thee a bench for the door of thy cot,
And more would I give thee, but more I have not :
Sit and think of me there, in the warm summer day,
And give me three kisses, my labour to pay."

She gave him three kisses, and forth did he fare,
And long did he wander, and no one knew where ;
And long from her cottage, through sunshine and rain,
She watched his return, but he came not again.

Her children grew up, and her husband grew grey ;
She sate on the bench through the long summer day :
One evening, when twilight was deep on the shore,
There came an old soldier, and stood by the door.

In English he spoke, and none knew what he said,
But her oatcake and milk on the table she spread ;
Then he sate to his supper, and blithely he sung,
And she knew the dear sounds of her own native tongue :

" O rich are the feasts in the Englishman's hall,
And the wine sparkles bright in the goblets of Gaul :
But their mingled attractions I well could withstand,
For the milk and the oatcake of Meirion's dear land."

" And art thou a Welshman, old soldier ? " she cried.
" Many years have I wandered," the stranger replied :
" 'Twixt Danube and Thames many rivers there be,
But the bright waves of Cynfael are fairest to me.

" I felled the grey oak, ere I hastened to roam,
And I fashioned a bench for the door of my home ;
And well my dear sister my labour repaid,
Who gave me three kisses when first it was made.

" In the old English soldier thy brother appears :
Here is gold in abundance, the saving of years :
Give me oatcake and milk in return for my store,
And a seat by thy side on the bench at the door."

Various other songs succeeded, which, as we are not composing a song book, we shall lay aside for the present.

An old squire, who had not missed one of these anniversaries, during more than half a century, now stood up, and filling a half-pint bumper, pronounced, with a stentorian voice—" To the immortal memory of Headlong Ap-Rhaiader, and to the health of his noble descendant and worthy representative ! " This example was followed by all the gentlemen present. The harp struck up a triumphal strain ; and, the old squire already mentioned vociferating the first stave, they sang, or rather roared, the following

CHORUS.

Hail to the Headlong ! the Headlong Ap-Headlong !
All hail to the Headlong, the Headlong Ap-Headlong !
    The Headlong Ap-Headlong
    Ap-Breakneck Ap-Headlong
Ap-Cataract Ap-Pistyll Ap-Rhaiader Ap-Headlong !

The bright bowl we steep in the name of the Headlong :
Let the youths pledge it deep to the Headlong Ap-Headlong,
 And the rosy-lipped lasses
 Touch the brim as it passes,
And kiss the red tide for the Headlong Ap-Headlong !

The loud harp resounds in the hall of the Headlong :
The light step rebounds in the hall of the Headlong :
 Where shall music invite us,
 Or beauty delight us,
If not in the hall of the Headlong Ap-Headlong ?

Huzza ! to the health of the Headlong Ap-Headlong !
Fill the bowl, fill in floods, to the health of the Headlong !
 Till the stream ruby-glowing,
 On all sides o'erflowing,
Shall fall in cascades to the health of the Headlong !
 The Headlong Ap-Headlong
 Ap-Breakneck Ap-Headlong
Ap-Cataract Ap-Pistyll Ap-Rhaiader Ap-Headlong !

Squire Headlong returned thanks with an appropriate libation, and the company re-adjourned to the ball-room, where they kept it up till sun-rise, when the little butler summoned them to breakfast.

CHAPTER XIV

THE PROPOSALS

THE chorus, which celebrated the antiquity of her lineage, had been ringing all night in the ears of Miss Brindle-mew Grimalkin Phœbe Tabitha Ap-Headlong, when, taking the squire aside, while the visitors were sipping their tea and coffee, " Nephew Harry," said she, "I have been noting your behaviour, during the several stages of the ball and supper ; and, though I cannot tax you with any want of gallantry, for you are a very gallant young man, nephew Harry, very gallant—I wish I could say as much for every one " (added she, throwing a spiteful look towards a distant corner, where Mr. Jenkison was sitting with great *nonchalance*, and at the moment dipping a rusk in a cup of chocolate) ; " but I lament to perceive that you were at least as pleased with your lakes of milk-punch, and your bottles of Champagne and Burgundy, as with any of your delightful partners.

Now, though I can readily excuse this degree of incombustibility in the descendant of a family so remarkable in all ages for personal beauty as ours, yet I lament it exceedingly, when I consider that, in conjunction with your present predilection for the easy life of a bachelor, it may possibly prove the means of causing our ancient genealogical tree, which has its roots, if I may so speak, in the foundations of the world, to terminate suddenly in a point : unless you feel yourself moved by my exhortations to follow the example of all your ancestors, by choosing yourself a fitting and suitable helpmate to immortalise the pedigree of Headlong Ap-Rhaiader."

" Egad ! " said Squire Headlong, " that is very true. I'll marry directly. A good opportunity to fix on some one, now they are all here ; and I'll pop the question without further ceremony."

" What think you," said the old lady, " of Miss Nanny Glyn-Du, the lineal descendant of Llewelyn Ap Yorwerth ? "

" She won't do," said Squire Headlong.

" What say you, then," said the lady, " to Miss Williams, of Pontyglasrhydyrallt, the descendant of the ancient family of —— ? "

" I don't like her," said Squire Headlong ; " and as to her ancient family, that is a matter of no consequence. I have antiquity enough for two. They are all moderns, people of yesterday, in comparison with us. What signify six or seven centuries, which are the most they can make up ? "

" Why, to be sure," said the aunt, " on that view of the question, it is of no consequence. What think you, then, of Miss Owen, of Nidd-y-Gygfraen ? She will have six thousand a year."

" I would not have her," said Squire Headlong, " if she had fifty. I'll think of somebody presently. I should like to be married on the same day with Caprioletta."

" Caprioletta ! " said Miss Brindle-mew ; " without my being consulted ! "

" Consulted ! " said the squire : " I was commissioned to tell you, but somehow or other I let it slip. However, she is going to be married to my friend Mr. Foster, the philosopher."

" Oh ! " said the maiden aunt, " that a daughter of our ancient family should marry a philosopher ! It is enough to make the bones of all the Ap-Rhaiaders turn in their graves ! "

" I happen to be more enlightened," said Squire Headlong, " than any of my ancestors were. Besides, it is Caprioletta's affair, not mine. I tell you, the matter is settled, fixed, determined ; and so am I, to be married on the same day. I don't know, now I think of it, whom I can choose better than one of the daughters of my friend Chromatic."

" A Saxon ! " said the aunt, turning up her nose, and was commencing a vehement remonstrance ; but the squire, exclaiming " Music has charms ! " [1] flew over to Mr. Chromatic, and, with a hearty slap on the shoulder, asked him " how he should like him for a son-in-law ? " Mr. Chromatic, rubbing his shoulder, and highly delighted with the proposal, answered, " Very much indeed : " but, proceeding to ascertain which of his daughters had captivated the squire, the squire demurred, and was unable to satisfy his curiosity. " I hope," said Mr. Chromatic, " it may be Tenorina ; for I imagine Graziosa has conceived a *penchant* for Sir Patrick O'Prism."— " Tenorina, exactly," said Squire Headlong ; and became so impatient to bring the matter to a conclusion, that Mr. Chromatic undertook to communicate with his daughter immediately. The young lady proved to be as ready as the squire, and the preliminaries were arranged in little more than five minutes.

Mr. Chromatic's words, that he imagined his daughter Graziosa had conceived a *penchant* for Sir Patrick O'Prism, were not lost on the squire, who at once determined to have as many companions in the scrape as possible, and who, as soon as he could tear himself from Mrs. Headlong elect, took three flying bounds across the room to the baronet, and said, " So, Sir Patrick, I find you and I are going to be married ? "

" Are we ? " said Sir Patrick : " then sure won't I wish you joy, and myself too ? for this is the first I have heard of it."

" Well," said Squire Headlong, " I have made up my mind to it, and you must not disappoint me."

" To be sure I won't, if I can help it," said Sir Patrick ; " and I am very much obliged to you for taking so much trouble off my hands. And pray, now, who is it that I am to be metamorphosing into Lady O'Prism ? "

[1] Congreve : *The Mourning Bride*, Act I, Sc. 1. G.

" Miss Graziosa Chromatic," said the squire.

" Och violet and vermilion ! " said Sir Patrick ; " though I never thought of it before, I dare say she will suit me as well as another : but then you must persuade the ould Orpheus to draw out a few *notes* of rather a more magical description than those he is so fond of scraping on his crazy violin."

" To be sure he shall," said the squire ; and, immediately returning to Mr. Chromatic, concluded the negotiation for Sir Patrick as expeditiously as he had done for himself.

The squire next addressed himself to Mr. Escot : " Here are three couple of us going to throw off together, with the Reverend Doctor Gaster for whipper-in : now, I think you cannot do better than make the fourth with Miss Cephalis ; and then, as my father-in-law that is to be would say, we shall compose a very harmonious octave."

" Indeed," said Mr. Escot, " nothing would be more agreeable to both of us than such an arrangement : but the old gentleman, since I first knew him, has changed, like the rest of the world, very lamentably for the worse : now, we wish to bring him to reason, if possible, though we mean to dispense with his consent, if he should prove much longer refractory."

" I'll settle him," said Squire Headlong ; and immediately posted up to Mr. Cranium, informing him that four marriages were about to take place by way of a merry winding up of the Christmas festivities.

" Indeed ! " said Mr. Cranium ; " and who are the parties ? "

" In the first place," said the squire, " my sister and Mr. Foster : in the second, Miss Graziosa Chromatic and Sir Patrick O'Prism : in the third, Miss Tenorina Chromatic and your humble servant : and in the fourth—to which, by the by, your consent is wanted——"

" Oho ! " said Mr. Cranium.

" Your daughter," said Squire Headlong.

" And Mr. Panscope ? " said Mr. Cranium.

" And Mr. Escot," said Squire Headlong. " What would you have better ? He has ten thousand virtues."

" So has Mr. Panscope," said Mr. Cranium ; " he has ten thousand a year."

" Virtues ? " said Squire Headlong.

" Pounds," said Mr. Cranium.

" I have set my mind on Mr. Escot," said the squire.

" I am much obliged to you," said Mr. Cranium, " for dethroning me from my paternal authority."

" Who fished you out of the water ? " said Squire Headlong.

" What is that to the purpose ? " said Mr. Cranium. " The whole process of the action was mechanical and necessary. The application of the poker necessitated the ignition of the powder : the ignition necessitated the explosion : the explosion necessitated my sudden fright, which necessitated my sudden jump, which, from a necessity equally powerful, was in a curvilinear ascent : the descent, being in a corresponding curve, and commencing at a point perpendicular to the extreme line of the edge of the tower, I was, by the necessity of gravitation, attracted, first, through the ivy, and secondly through the hazel, and thirdly through the ash, into the water beneath. The motive or impulse thus adhibited in the person of a drowning man, was as powerful on his material compages as the force of gravitation on mine ; and he could no more help jumping into the water than I could help falling into it." [1]

" All perfectly true," said Squire Headlong ; " and, on the same principle, you make no distinction between the man who knocks you down and him who picks you up."

" I make this distinction," said Mr. Cranium, " that I avoid the former as a machine containing a peculiar *cataballitive* [2] quality, which I have found to be not consentaneous to my mode of pleasurable existence ; but I attach no moral merit or demerit to either of them, as these terms are usually employed, seeing that they are equally creatures of necessity, and must act as they do from the nature of their organisation. I no more blame or praise a man for what is called vice or virtue, than I tax a tuft of hemlock with malevolence, or discover great philanthropy in a field of potatoes, seeing that the men and the plants are equally incapacitated, by their original internal organisation, and the combinations and modifications of external circumstances, from being anything but what they are. *Quod victus fateare necesse est.*" [3]

---

[1] Mr. Cranium anticipates the theories of behaviourist philosophers. G.
[2] A nonce-word meaning " tending to throw down." G.
[3] " You are vanquished and must confess that this is so." G.

" Yet you destroy the hemlock," said Squire Headlong, " and cultivate the potatoe : that is my way, at least."

" I do," said Mr. Cranium ; " because I know that the farinaceous qualities of the potatoe will tend to preserve the great requisites of unity and coalescence in the various constituent portions of my animal republic ; and that the hemlock, if gathered by mistake for parsley, chopped up small with butter, and eaten with a boiled chicken, would necessitate a great derangement, and perhaps a total decomposition, of my corporeal mechanism."

" Very well," said the squire ; " then you are necessitated to like Mr. Escot better than Mr. Panscope ? "

" That is a *non sequitur*," said Mr. Cranium.

" Then this is a *sequitur*," said the squire : " your daughter and Mr. Escot are necessitated to love one another ; and, unless you feel necessitated to adhibit your consent, they will feel necessitated to dispense with it ; since it does appear to moral and political economists to be essentially inherent in the eternal fitness of things."

Mr. Cranium fell into a profound reverie : emerging from which, he said, looking Squire Headlong full in the face, " Do you think Mr. Escot would give me that skull ? "

" Skull ! " said Squire Headlong.

" Yes," said Mr. Cranium, " the skull of Cadwallader."

" To be sure he will," said the squire.

" Ascertain the point," said Mr. Cranium.

" How can you doubt it ? " said the squire.

" I simply know," said Mr. Cranium, " that if it were once in my possession, I would not part with it for any acquisition on earth, much less for a wife. I have had one : and, as marriage has been compared to a pill, I can very safely assert that *one is a dose* : and my reason for thinking that he will not part with it is, that its extraordinary magnitude tends to support his system, as much as its very marked protuberances tend to support mine ; and you know his own system is of all things the dearest to every man of liberal thinking and a philosophical tendency."

The squire flew over to Mr. Escot. " I told you," said he, " I would settle him : but there is a very hard condition attached to his compliance."

" I submit to it," said Mr. Escot, " be it what it may."

" Nothing less," said Squire Headlong, " than the absolute and unconditional surrender of the skull of Cadwallader."

" I resign it," said Mr. Escot.

" The skull is yours," said the squire, skipping over to Mr. Cranium.

" I am perfectly satisfied," said Mr. Cranium.

" The lady is yours," said the squire, skipping back to Mr. Escot.

" I am the happiest man alive," said Mr. Escot.

" Come," said the squire, " then there is an amelioration in the state of the sensitive man."

" A slight oscillation of good in the instance of a solitary individual," answered Mr. Escot, " by no means affects the solidity of my opinions concerning the general deterioration of the civilised world ; which when I can be induced to contemplate with feelings of satisfaction, I doubt not but that I may be persuaded *to be in love with tortures, and to think charitably of the rack.*" [1]

Saying these words, he flew off as nimbly as Squire Headlong himself, to impart the happy intelligence to his beautiful Cephalis.

Mr. Cranium now walked up to Mr. Panscope, to condole with him on the disappointment of their mutual hopes. Mr. Panscope begged him not to distress himself on the subject, observing, that the monotonous system of female education brought every individual of the sex to so remarkable an approximation of similarity, that no wise man would suffer himself to be annoyed by a loss so easily repaired ; and that there was much truth, though not much elegance, in a remark which he had heard made on a similar occasion by a post-captain of his acquaintance, " that there never was a fish taken out of the sea, but left another as good behind."

Mr. Cranium replied, that no two individuals having all the organs of the skull similarly developed, the universal resemblance of which Mr. Panscope had spoken could not possibly exist. Mr. Panscope rejoined ; and a long discussion ensued, concerning the comparative influence of natural organisation and artificial education, in which the beautiful Cephalis was totally lost sight of, and which ended, as most controversies do, by each party continuing firm in his own opinion,

[1] Jeremy Taylor. [P.]

and professing his profound astonishment at the blindness and prejudices of the other.

In the meanwhile, a great confusion had arisen at the outer doors, the departure of the ball-visitors being impeded by a circumstance which the experience of ages had discovered no means to obviate. The grooms, coachmen, and postillions, were all drunk. It was proposed that the gentlemen should officiate in their places : but the gentlemen were almost all in the same condition. This was a fearful dilemma : but a very diligent investigation brought to light a few servants and a few gentlemen not above *half-seas-over* ; and by an equitable distribution of these rarities, the greater part of the guests were enabled to set forward, with very nearly an even chance of not having their necks broken before they reached home.

CHAPTER XV

THE CONCLUSION

THE squire and his select party of philosophers and dilettanti were again left in peaceful possession of Headlong Hall : and, as the former made a point of never losing a moment in the accomplishment of a favourite object, he did not suffer many days to elapse, before the spiritual metamorphosis of eight into four was effected by the clerical dexterity of the Reverend Doctor Gaster.

Immediately after the ceremony, the whole party dispersed, the squire having first extracted from every one of his chosen guests a positive promise to re-assemble in August, when they would be better enabled, in its most appropriate season, to form a correct judgment of Cambrian hospitality.

Mr. Jenkison shook hands at parting with his two brother philosophers. " According to your respective systems," said he, " I ought to congratulate *you* on a change for the better, which I do most cordially : and to condole with *you* on a change for the worse, though, when I consider whom you have chosen, I should violate every principle of probability in doing so."

" You will do well," said Mr. Foster, " to follow our example.

The extensive circle of general philanthropy, which, in the present advanced stage of human nature, comprehends in its circumference the destinies of the whole species, originated, and still proceeds, from that narrower circle of domestic affection, which first set limits to the empire of selfishness, and, by purifying the passions and enlarging the affections of mankind, has given to the views of benevolence an increasing and illimitable expansion, which will finally diffuse happiness and peace over the whole surface of the world."

" The affection," said Mr. Escot, " of two congenial spirits, united not by legal bondage and superstitious imposture, but by mutual confidence and reciprocal virtues, is the only counterbalancing consolation in this scene of mischief and misery. But how rarely is this the case according to the present system of marriage ! So far from being a central point of expansion to the great circle of universal benevolence, it serves only to concentrate the feelings of natural sympathy in the reflected selfishness of family interest, and to substitute for the *humani nihil alienum puto* [1] of youthful philanthropy, the *charity begins at home* of maturer years. And what accession of individual happiness is acquired by this oblivion of the general good ? Luxury, despotism, and avarice have so seized and entangled nine hundred and ninety-nine out of every thousand of the human race, that the matrimonial compact, which ought to be the most easy, the most free, and the most simple of all engagements, is become the most slavish and complicated,—a mere question of finance,—a system of bargain, and barter, and commerce, and trick, and chicanery, and dissimulation, and fraud. Is there one instance in ten thousand, in which the buds of first affection are not most cruelly and hopelessly blasted, by avarice, or ambition, or arbitrary power ? Females, condemned during the whole flower of their youth to a worse than monastic celibacy, irrevocably debarred from the hope to which their first affections pointed, will, at a certain period of life, as the natural delicacy of taste and feeling is gradually worn away by the attrition of society, become willing to take up with any coxcomb or scoundrel, whom that merciless and mercenary gang of cold-blooded slaves and assassins, called, in the ordinary prostitution of language *friends*, may agree in designating as a *prudent choice*.

[1] " I count nothing that is human as alien to me." Terence, I. i. 25. G.

Young men, on the other hand, are driven by the same vile superstitions from the company of the most amiable and modest of the
opposite sex, to that of those miserable victims and outcasts of a
world which dares to call itself virtuous, whom that very society
whose pernicious institutions first caused their aberrations,—
consigning them, without one tear of pity or one struggle of remorse,
to penury, infamy, and disease,—condemns to bear the burden of its
own atrocious absurdities ! Thus, the youth of one sex is consumed
in slavery, disappointment, and spleen ; that of the other, in frantic
folly and selfish intemperance : till at length, on the necks of a
couple so enfeebled, so perverted, so distempered both in body and
soul, society throws the yoke of marriage : that yoke which, once
rivetted on the necks of its victims, clings to them like the poisoned
garments of Nessus or Medea. What can be expected from these
ill-assorted yoke-fellows, but that, like two ill-tempered hounds,
coupled by a tyrannical sportsman, they should drag on their indissoluble fetter, snarling and growling, and pulling in different directions ? What can be expected for their wretched offspring, but
sickness and suffering, premature decrepitude, and untimely death ?
In this, as in every other institution of civilised society, avarice,
luxury, and disease constitute the TRIANGULAR HARMONY of the life
of man. Avarice conducts him to the abyss of toil and crime ;
luxury seizes on his ill-gotten spoil ; and, while he revels in her
enchantments, or groans beneath her tyranny, disease bursts upon
him, and sweeps him from the earth." [1]

"Your theory," said Mr. Jenkison, "forms an admirable counterpoise to your example. As far as I am attracted by the one, I am
repelled by the other. Thus, the scales of my philosophical balance
remain eternally equiponderant, and I see no reason to say of either
of them, *ΟΙΧΕΤΑΙ ΕΙΣ ΑΙΔΑΟ*." [2]

---

[1] See Shelley : *Queen Mab*, Note to Canto V, l. 189. Peacock shared
Shelley's views.

[2] *It descends to the shades* : or, in other words, *it goes to the devil*. [P.]

MELINCOURT

VOCEM COMŒDIA TOLLIT [1]

---

[1] " Comedy takes up the tale."   G.

MELINCOURT

" Nous nous moquons des Paladins ! quand
ces maximes romanesques commencèrent à
devenir ridicules, ce changement fut moins
l'ouvrage de la raison que celui des
mauvaises mœurs."—Rousseau.

Melincourt was first published in 1817

CONTENTS
OF MELINCOURT

CHAPTER		PAGE
	Introduction by David Garnett .	97
	Peacock's 1856 Preface . .	101
I	ANTHELIA	103
II	FASHIONABLE ARRIVALS . .	107
III	HYPOCON HOUSE . . .	114
IV	REDROSE ABBEY . . .	116
V	SUGAR	121
VI	SIR ORAN HAUT-TON . .	127
VII	THE PRINCIPLE OF POPULATION	139
VIII	THE SPIRIT OF CHIVALRY .	143
IX	THE PHILOSOPHY OF BALLADS .	148
X	THE TORRENT . . .	154
XI	LOVE AND MARRIAGE . .	160
XII	LOVE AND POVERTY . .	165
XIII	DESMOND	169
XIV	THE COTTAGE . . .	179
XV	THE LIBRARY . . .	185
XVI	THE SYMPOSIUM . . .	192
XVII	MUSIC AND DISCORD . .	201
XVIII	THE STRATAGEM . . .	205
XIX	THE EXCURSION . . .	209

CONTENTS

CHAPTER		PAGE
XX	THE SEA-SHORE . . .	217
XXI	THE CITY OF NOVOTE . .	220
XXII	THE BOROUGH OF ONEVOTE .	227
XXIII	THE COUNCIL OF WAR . .	234
XXIV	THE BAROUCHE . . .	239
XXV	THE WALK . . .	246
XXVI	THE COTTAGERS . . .	251
XXVII	THE ANTI-SACCHARINE FÊTE .	254
XXVIII	THE CHESS DANCE . .	259
XXIX	THE DISAPPEARANCE . .	266
XXX	THE PAPER-MILL . . .	269
XXXI	CIMMERIAN LODGE . .	274
XXXII	THE DESERTED MANSION .	282
XXXIII	THE PHANTASM . . .	287
XXXIV	THE CHURCHYARD . . .	290
XXXV	THE RUSTIC WEDDING . .	293
XXXVI	THE VICARAGE . . .	298
XXXVII	THE MOUNTAINS . . .	303
XXXVIII	THE FRACAS . . .	306
XXXIX	MAINCHANCE VILLA . .	308
XL	THE HOPES OF THE WORLD .	323
XLI	ALGA CASTLE . . .	331
XLII	CONCLUSION . . .	337

INTRODUCTION TO
MELINCOURT

Melincourt is Peacock's second novel and in the opinion of most readers his least successful. It was written after he had abandoned the unfinished *Calidore*, which begins with the description of two Welsh clergymen who had passed every Sunday evening together for forty years at an inn and had scarcely exchanged any remarks beyond : " Will you join me in another jug ? "—of beer, the price of which they always shared. Unfortunately *Calidore* goes to pieces in every sense of the words. The fault of *Melincourt* is that it goes on too long. Mr Brett-Smith believes that an early version, ending with the marriage of Anthelia and Forester immediately after the Anti-saccharine fête, was completed by the summer of 1816 but that the publishers objected that it was too short for three volumes and too long for one. If this was the case, as seems probable, Peacock ruined his story by lengthening it, substituting Anthelia's abduction for her marriage and taking her not very anxious suitor on a series of leisurely visits to the Lake poets in which he discusses every subject except how to find her.

Yet *Melincourt* in some ways tells us more about the author than any of his other novels—nowhere else does he so obviously take sides, reserving most of his satire for members of the opposite political party. The book originated with the idea of making Lord Monboddo's positive belief that the Orang Outang was not an ape but a variety of the human species, and that its lack of speech was accidental, furnish a central character who should be introduced to polite society, attend the opera, receive a baronetcy, be elected for a pocket-borough and take his seat in the House of Commons.

James Burnett, Lord Monboddo, was a Scottish judge, who put forward, as original, the views of Rousseau which he expounded with no sense of the need for experiment or of the value of evidence.

He was serious, confused, gullible, and occasionally, by pure chance, one of his absurdities came near to being the truth. Peacock delighted in him and handled him most tenderly, with his tongue just perceptibly in his cheek. This tenderness did not extend to the Tories. The Napoleonic wars had been won; the British people were impoverished, and the Government was using victory to stamp out liberty at home and abroad, muzzling freedom of speech and the liberty of the press. Its power was based on a mockery of parliamentary representation and functioned partly by widespread bribery and corruption.

Like Shelley, Peacock hated the Tories, though he was personally attached to George III, who had been a familiar sight riding about near Windsor and whom he had liked to see " week after week at Covent Garden, very genial in his hearty enjoyment of comedy." Even more than the Government, he hated those who appeared to be renegades from the cause of liberty, or hirelings supporting tyranny. This accounts for the venom with which he always treated Southey, who, as Hazlitt remarked, " had missed his way in Utopia and found it at Old Sarum "—who had accepted the laureateship and turned his back on all his old ideas. This explains the bitter attacks on Wordsworth and on Coleridge, poets whom Peacock greatly admired but who had changed their views after living through the events of the French Revolution and seeing its results.

They had, as Hazlitt says of Coleridge, " hailed the rising orb of liberty, since quenched in darkness and in blood . . . had kindled affections at the blaze of the French Revolution, and sang for joy when the towers of the Bastille and the proud places of the insolent and the oppressor fell—and at last had turned on the pivot of a subtle casuistry to the unclean side." Those who have lived through a comparable experience in the last thirty years find it possible to take a more generous view.

Peacock was of a generation too young to have been disillusioned, and, inspired perhaps by the naval traditions of his family, he had always hated the French. " Frozen vipers " he called them to Shelley in 1818. " Violence when violence is possible, cringing fraud when it is not."

Since Carl van Doren has referred to Peacock's toryism and

George Saintsbury has laid it down that whatever Peacock may have been in politics, he was at no period a liberal, it is perhaps worth stating what he was. He was a radical individualist, an admirer of Cobbett, a Utilitarian who believed in *laisser-faire*. He distrusted Governments and hated State interference, loathed corruption and tyranny and had no illusions about the mob.

At the end of his life, in 1861, he wrote, in a letter to Thomas L'Estrange, that he had lived to see " the Tories as completely extinct as the Mammoth. Their successors, the Conservatives as they call themselves, appear to me like Falstaff's otter ' neither fish nor flesh ' ; one knows not where to have them."

Peacock helped Shelley with the revision of *Laon and Cythna*, which enabled it to be published as *The Revolt of Islam*. Shelley spent the first fortnight of September 1817 staying with Peacock at Marlow, and they were continually together from the end of the year until *Melincourt* was published—and for months afterwards.

" It was an agreeable year," said Peacock in his *Memoirs of Shelley*, though in both their minds was the thought of Harriet's suicide the previous December. *Melincourt*, revised in those months, is shrill in tone, and one suspects that in places the shrillness is an echo of Shelley's voice. May not Shelley have given Peacock suggestions of how to expand *Melincourt* to the required length ? This is piling one hypothesis upon another, but it is a tempting one. Certainly Peacock's satire is most effective when he is laughing at the foibles of his friends ; he is most amusing when he is most good-tempered. Shelley, on the contrary, is most deadly when he is angriest :

> An old, mad, blind, despised, and dying king,—
> Princes, the dregs of their dull race, who flow
> Through public scorn,—mud from a muddy spring,—
> Rulers who neither see, nor feel, nor know,
> But leech-like to their fainting country cling,
> Till they drop, blind in blood, without a blow.

Peacock is quite incapable of that concentrated passion. After *Melincourt* and Shelley's departure to Italy he was scarcely ever bad-tempered in print again.

D. G.

PREFACE

TO THE EDITION PUBLISHED IN 1856

" MELINCOURT " was first published thirty-nine years ago. Many changes have since occurred, social, mechanical, and political. The boroughs of Onevote and Threevotes have been extinguished : but there remain boroughs of Fewvotes, in which Sir Oran Haut-ton might still find a free and enlightened constituency. Beards disfigure the face, and tobacco poisons the air, in a degree not then imagined. A boy, with a cigar in his mouth, was a phenomenon yet unborn. Multitudinous bubbles have been blown and have burst : sometimes prostrating dupes and imposters together ; sometimes leaving a colossal jobber upright in his triumphal chariot, which has crushed as many victims as the car of Juggernaut. Political mountebanks have founded profitable investments on public gullibility. British colonists have been compelled to emancipate their slaves ; and foreign slave labour, under the pretext of free trade, has been brought to bear against them by the friends of liberty. The Court is more moral : therefore, the public is more moral ; more decorous, at least, in external semblance, wherever the homage, which Hypocrisy pays to Virtue,[1] can yield any profit to the professor : but always ready for the same reaction, with which the profligacy of the Restoration rolled, like a spring-tide, over the puritanism of the Commonwealth. The progress of intellect, with all deference to those who believe in it, is not quite so obvious as the progress of mechanics. The " reading public " has increased its capacity of swallow, in a proportion far exceeding that of its digestion. Thirty-nine years ago, steam-boats were just coming into action, and the railway locomotive was not even thought of. Now everybody goes everywhere : going for the sake of going, and rejoicing in the

[1] This seems a slip of the pen. Hypocrisy does not pay homage to Virtue, but is itself the homage paid to Virtue by Vice. G.

rapidity with which they accomplish nothing. *On va, mais on ne voyage pas.* Strenuous idleness drives us on the wings of steam in boats and trains, seeking the art of enjoying life, which, after all, is in the regulation of the mind, and not in the whisking about of the body.[1] Of the disputants whose opinions and public characters (for I never trespassed on private life) were shadowed in some of the persons of the story, almost all have passed from the diurnal scene. Many of the questions, discussed in the dialogues, have more of general than of temporary application, and have still their advocates on both sides : and new questions have arisen, which furnish abundant argument for similar conversations, and of which I may yet, perhaps, avail myself on some future occasion.

THE AUTHOR OF "HEADLONG HALL."

March, 1856.

[1] Hor. Epist. I. ii. 27–30. [P.]

MELINCOURT

CHAPTER I

ANTHELIA

ANTHELIA MELINCOURT, at the age of twenty-one, was mistress of herself and of ten thousand a year, and of a very ancient and venerable castle in one of the wildest valleys in Westmoreland. It follows of course, without reference to her personal qualifications, that she had a very numerous list of admirers, and equally of course that there were both Irishmen and clergymen among them. The young lady nevertheless possessed sufficient attractions to kindle the flames of disinterested passion; and accordingly we shall venture to suppose, that there was at least one in the number of her sighing swains with whom her rent-roll and her old castle were secondary considerations; and if the candid reader should esteem this supposition too violent for the probabilities of daily experience in this calculating age, he will at least concede it to that degree of poetical licence which is invariably accorded to a tale founded on facts.

Melincourt Castle had been a place of considerable strength in those golden days of feudal and royal prerogative, when no man was safe in his own house unless he adopted every possible precaution for shutting out all his neighbours. It is, therefore, not surprising, that a rock, of which three sides were perpendicular, and which was only accessible on the fourth by a narrow ledge, forming a natural bridge over a tremendous chasm, was considered a very enviable situation for a gentleman to build on. An impetuous torrent boiled through the depth of the chasm, and after eddying round the base of the castle-rock, which it almost insulated, disappeared in the obscurity of a woody glen, whose mysterious recesses, by popular superstition formerly consecrated to the devil, are now fearlessly explored by the solitary angler, or laid open to view by the more profane hand of the picturesque tourist, who contrives, by the magic of his pencil, to transport their romantic terrors from the depths of mountain-solitude to the gay and crowded, though not very wholesome atmosphere of a metropolitan exhibition.

The narrow ledge, which formed the only natural access to the castle-rock, had been guarded by every impediment which the genius of fortification could oppose to the progress of the hungry Scot, who might be disposed, in his neighbourly way, to drop in without invitation and carouse at the expense of the owner, rewarding him, as usual, for his extorted hospitality, by cutting his throat and setting fire to his house. A drawbridge over the chasm, backed by a double portcullis, presented the only mode of admission. In this secure retreat, thus strongly guarded both by nature and art, and always plentifully victualled for a siege, lived the lords of Melincourt in all the luxury of rural seclusion, throwing open their gates on occasional halcyon days to regale all the peasants and mountaineers of the vicinity with roasted oxen and vats of October.[1]

When these times of danger and turbulence had passed, Melincourt Castle was not, as most of its brother edifices were, utterly deserted. The drawbridge, indeed, became gradually divorced from its chains; the double portcullis disappeared; the turrets and battlements were abandoned to the owl and the ivy; and a very spacious wing was left free to the settlement of a colony of ghosts, which, according to the report of the peasantry and the domestics, very soon took possession, and retained it most pertinaciously, notwithstanding the pious incantations of the neighbouring vicar, the Reverend Mr. Portpipe, who often passed the night in one of the dreaded apartments over a blazing fire with the same invariable exorcising apparatus of a large venison pasty, a little prayer-book, and three bottles of Madeira : for the reverend gentleman sagaciously observed, that as he had always found the latter an infallible charm against blue devils,[2] he had no doubt of its proving equally efficacious against black, white, and grey. In this opinion experience seemed to

---

[1] The strongest ale was brewed in October, from the first batches of malt made from the barley harvested in August and September. It was ready for drinking by Christmas. G.

[2] See *Headlong Hall*, p. 74. G.

confirm him; for though he always maintained a becoming silence as to the mysteries of which he was a witness during his spectral vigils, yet a very correct inference might be drawn from the fact, that he was always found in the morning comfortably asleep in his large arm-chair, with the dish scraped clean, the three bottles empty, and the prayer-book clasped and folded precisely in the same state and place in which it had lain the preceding night.

But the larger and more commodious part of the castle continued still to be inhabited; and while one half of the edifice was fast improving into a picturesque ruin, the other was as rapidly degenerating, in its interior at least, into a comfortable modern dwelling.

In this romantic seclusion Anthelia was born. Her mother died in giving her birth. Her father, Sir Henry Melincourt, a man of great acquirements, and of a retired disposition, devoted himself in solitude to the cultivation of his daughter's understanding; for he was one of those who maintained the heretical notion that women are, or at least may be, rational beings; though, from the great pains usually taken in what is called education to make them otherwise, there are unfortunately very few examples to warrant the truth of the theory.

The majestic forms and wild energies of Nature that surrounded her from her infancy, impressed their character on her mind, communicating to it all their own wildness, and more than their own beauty. Far removed from the pageantry of courts and cities, her infant attention was awakened to spectacles more interesting and more impressive: the misty mountain-top, the ash-fringed precipice, the gleaming cataract, the deep and shadowy glen, and the fantastic magnificence of the mountain clouds. The murmur of the woods, the rush of the winds, and the tumultuous dashing of the torrents, were the first music of her childhood. A fearless wanderer among these romantic solitudes, the spirit of mountain liberty diffused itself through the whole tenour of her feelings, modelled the symmetry of her form, and illumined the expressive but feminine brilliancy of her features: and when she had attained the age at which the mind expands itself to the fascinations of poetry, the muses of Italy became the chosen companions of her wanderings, and nourished a naturally susceptible imagination by conjuring up the splendid visions of chivalry and enchantment in scenes so congenial to their development.[1]

It was seldom that the presence of a visitor dispelled the solitude of Melincourt; and the few specimens of the living world with whom its inmates held occasional intercourse, were of the usual character of country acquaintance, not calculated to leave behind them any very lively regret, except for the loss of time during the period of their stay. One of these was the Reverend Mr. Portpipe, whom we have already celebrated for his proficiency in the art of exorcising goblins by dint of venison and Madeira. His business in the ghost line had, indeed, declined with the progress of the human understanding, and no part of his vocation was in very high favour with Sir Henry, who, though an unexceptionable moral character, was unhappily not one of the children of grace, in the theological sense of the word : but the vicar, adopting St. Paul's precept of being all things to all men, found it on this occasion his interest to be liberal ; and observing that no man could coerce his opinions, repeated with great complacency the line of Virgil :

Tros Tyriusque mihi nullo discrimine agetur ; [2]

though he took especial care that this heterodox concession should not reach the ears of his bishop, who would infallibly have unfrocked him for promulgating a doctrine so subversive of the main pillar of all orthodox establishments.

When Anthelia had attained her sixteenth year, her father deemed it necessary to introduce her to that human world of which she had hitherto seen so little, and for this purpose took a journey to London, where he was received by the surviving portion of his old acquaintance as a ghost returned from Acheron. The impression which the gay scenes of the metropolis made on the mind of Anthelia—to what

[1] Anthelia has been variously stated to have been an idealisation of Peacock's first love and of the Welsh girl, Jane Gryffydh, whom he afterwards married. Mr. Brett-Smith has pointed out that she is more likely to be the Miss Scott whose uncle was " a philosopher, and an admirer of Italian poetry. I believe he principally formed the mind of his niece, and this is sufficient to prove him a man of fine understanding." Peacock to E. T. Hookham, April 9, 1811. G.

[2] " I will make no distinction between Trojan and Tyrian." *Æn.* I. 574.
G.

illustrious characters she was introduced—" and all she thought of all she saw,"—it would be foreign to our present purpose to detail : suffice it to say, that from this period Sir Henry regularly passed the winter in London and the summer in Westmoreland, till his daughter attained the age of twenty, about which period he died.

Anthelia passed twelve months from this time in total seclusion at Melincourt, notwithstanding many pressing invitations from various match-making dowagers in London, who were solicitous to dispose of her according to their views of her advantage ; in which how far their own was lost sight of, it may not be difficult to determine.

Among the numerous lovers who had hitherto sighed at her shrine, not one had succeeded in making the slightest impression on her heart ; and during the twelve months of seclusion which elapsed from the death of her father to the commencement of this authentic history, they had all completely vanished from the tablet of her memory. Her knowledge of love was altogether theoretical ; and her theory, being formed by the study of Italian poetry in the bosom of mountain solitude, naturally and necessarily pointed to a visionary model of excellence which it was very little likely the modern world could realize.

The dowagers at length despairing of drawing her from her retirement, respectively came to various resolutions for the accomplishment of their ends ; some resolving to go in person to Melincourt, and exert all their powers of oratory to mould her to their wishes, and others instigating their several *protégés* to set boldly forward in search of fortune, and lay siege to the castle and its mistress together.

CHAPTER II

FASHIONABLE ARRIVALS

It was late in the afternoon of an autumnal day, when the elegant post-chariot of the Honourable Mrs. Pinmoney, a lady of high renown in the annals of match-making, turned the corner of a stupendous precipice in the narrow pass which formed the only access to the valley of Melincourt. This Honourable lady was accompanied by her

only daughter Miss Danaretta Contantina ; which names, by the
by, appear to be female diminutives of the Italian words *danaro
contante*, signifying *ready money*, and genteelly hinting to all fashionable Strephons, the only terms on which the *commodity* so denominated would be disposed of, according to the universal practice of this
liberal and enlightened generation, in that most commercial of all
bargains, marriage.

The ivied battlements and frowning towers of Melincourt Castle,
as they burst at once upon the sight, very much astonished the elder
and delighted the younger lady ; for the latter had cultivated a great
deal of theoretical romance—in taste, not in feeling—an important
distinction—which enabled her to be most liberally sentimental in
words, without at all influencing her actions ; to talk of heroic
affection and self-sacrificing enthusiasm, without incurring the least
danger of forming a disinterested attachment, or of erring in any way
whatever on the score of practical generosity. Indeed, in all
respects of practice the young lady was the true counterpart of her
mother, though they sometimes differed a little in the forms of sentiment : thus, for instance, when any of their dear friends happened to
go, as it is called, down hill in the world, the old lady was generally
very severe on their *imprudence*, and the young lady very pathetic on
their *misfortune* : but as to holding any further intercourse with, or
rendering any species of assistance to, any dear friend so circumstanced, neither the one nor the other was ever suspected of conduct
so very unfashionable. In the main point, therefore, of both their
lives, that of making a *good match* for Miss Danaretta, their views
perfectly coincided ; and though Miss Danaretta, in her speculative
conversations on this subject, among her female acquaintance, talked
as young ladies always talk, and laid down very precisely *the only
kind of man she would ever think of marrying*, endowing him, of
course, with all the virtues in our good friend Hookham's Library ;[1]
yet it was very well understood, as it usually is on similar occasions,
that no other proof of the possession of the aforesaid virtues would be
required from any individual, who might present himself in the

[1] Peacock was a friend of Edward T. Hookham, the son of the publisher
and bookseller, Thomas Hookham, who published most of Peacock's
volumes of verse and all his novels except *Gryll Grange*. G.

character of *Corydon sospiroso*, than a satisfactory certificate from the old lady in Threadneedle Street, that the bearer was a *good man*, and could be proved so in the *Alley*.[1]

Such were the amiable specimens of worldly wisdom and affected romance, that prepared to invade the retirement of the mountain-enthusiast, the really romantic unworldly Anthelia.

" What a strange-looking old place ! " said Mrs. Pinmoney : " it seems like any thing but the dwelling of a young heiress. I am afraid the rascally postboys have joined in a plot against us, and intend to deliver us to a gang of thieves ! "

" Banditti, you should say, mamma," said Miss Danaretta : " thieves is an odious word."

" Pooh, child ! " said Mrs. Pinmoney. " The reality is odious enough, let the word be what it will. Is not a rogue a rogue, call him by what name you may ? "

" O, certainly not," said Miss Danaretta ; " for in that case a poor rogue without a title, would not be more a rogue than a rich rogue with one ; but that he is so in a most infinite proportion, the whole experience of the world demonstrates."

" True," said the old lady ; " and as our reverend friend Dr. Bosky observes, to maintain the contrary would be to sanction a principle utterly subversive of all social order and aristocratical privilege."

The carriage now rolled over the narrow ledge, which connected the site of the castle with the neighbouring rocks. A furious peal at the outer bell brought forth a venerable porter, who opened the gates with becoming gravity, and the carriage entered a spacious court, of much more recent architecture than the exterior of the castle, and built in a style of modern Gothic, that seemed to form a happy medium between the days of feudality, commonly called the dark ages, and the nineteenth century, commonly called the enlightened age : *why* I could never discover.

The inner gates were opened by another grave and venerable domestic, who with all the imperturbable decorum and formality of the old school, assisted the ladies to alight, and ushered them along an elegant colonnade into the library, which we shall describe no

[1] 'Change Alley, by the London Stock Exchange. G.

farther than by saying, that the apartment was Gothic and the furniture Grecian : whether this be an unpardonable incongruity calculated to disarrange all legitimate associations, or a judicious combination of solemnity and elegance, most happily adapted to the purposes of study, we must leave to the decision, or rather discussion, of picturesque and antiquarian disputants.

The windows, which were of stained glass, were partly open to a shrubbery, which admitting the meditative mind into the recesses of nature, and excluding all view of distant scenes, heightened the deep seclusion and repose of the apartment. It consisted principally of evergreens ; but the parting beauty of the last flowers of autumn, and the lighter and now fading tints of a few deciduous shrubs, mingled with the imperishable verdure of the cedar and the laurel.

The old domestic went in search of his young mistress, and the ladies threw themselves on a sofa in graceful attitudes. They were shortly joined by Anthelia, who welcomed them to Melincourt with all the politeness which the necessity of the case imposed.

The change of dress, the dinner, the dessert, seasoned with the *newest news* of the fashionable world, which the visitors thought must be of all things the most delightful to the mountain-recluse, filled up a portion of the evening. When they returned from the dining-room to the library, the windows were closed, the curtains drawn, and the tea and coffee urns bubbling on the table, and sending up their steamy columns : an old fashion, to be sure, and sufficiently rustic, for which we apologize in due form to the reader, who prefers his tea and coffee brought in cool by the butler in little cups on a silver salver, and handed round to the simpering company till it is as cold as an Iceland spring. There is no disputing about taste, and the taste of Melincourt Castle on this subject had been always very poetically unfashionable ; for the tea would have satisfied Johnson, and the coffee enchanted Voltaire.

" I must confess, my dear," said the Honourable Mrs. Pinmoney, " there is a great deal of comfort in your way of living, that is, there would be in good company ; but you are so solitary——"

" Here is the best of company," said Anthelia smiling, and pointing to the shelves of the library.

THE HONOURABLE MRS. PINMONEY. Very true : books are very good things in their way ; but an hour or two at most is quite enough of them for me : more can serve no purpose but to muddle one's head. If I were to live such a life for a week as you have done for the last twelve months, I should have more company than I like, in the shape of a whole legion of blue devils.

MISS DANARETTA. Nay, I think there is something delightfully romantic in Anthelia's mode of life : but I confess I should like now and then, peeping through the ivy of the battlements, to observe a *preux chevalier* exerting all his eloquence to persuade the inflexible porter to open the castle gates, and allow him one opportunity of throwing himself at the feet of the divine lady of the castle, for whom he had been seven years dying a lingering death.

THE HONOURABLE MRS. PINMONEY. And growing fatter all the while.—Heaven defend me from such hypocritical fops ! Seven years indeed ! It did not take as many weeks to bring me and poor dear dead Mr. Pinmoney together.

ANTHELIA. I should have been afraid that so short an acquaint-ance would scarcely have been sufficient to acquire that mutual knowledge of each other's tastes, feelings and character, which I should think the only sure basis of matrimonial happiness.

THE HONOURABLE MRS. PINMONEY. Tastes, feelings, and char-acter ! Why, my love, you really do seem to believe yourself in the age of chivalry, when those words certainly signified very essential differences. But now the matter is very happily simplified. Tastes : —they depend on the fashion. There is always a fashionable taste : a taste for driving the mail—a taste for acting Hamlet—a taste for philosophical lectures—a taste for the marvellous—a taste for the simple—a taste for the brilliant—a taste for the sombre—a taste for the tender—a taste for the grim—a taste for banditti—a taste for ghosts—a taste for the devil—a taste for French dancers and Italian singers, and German whiskers and tragedies—a taste for enjoying the country in November, and wintering in London till the end of the dog-days—a taste for making shoes—a taste for picturesque tours—a taste for taste itself, or for essays on taste :—but no gentleman would be so rash as to have a taste of his own, or his last winter's taste, or any taste, my love, but the fashionable taste. Poor dear Mr. Pinmoney was reckoned a man of exquisite taste among all his acquaintance ; for the new taste, let it be what it would, always fitted him as well as his new coat, and he was the very pink and mirror of fashion, as much in the one as the other. So much for tastes, my dear.

ANTHELIA. I am afraid I shall always be a very unfashionable creature ; for I do not think I should have sympathized with any one of the tastes you have just enumerated.

THE HONOURABLE MRS. PINMONEY. You are so contumacious, such a romantic heretic from the orthodox supremacy of fashion. Now, as for feelings, my dear, you know there are no such things in the fashionable world ; therefore that difficulty vanishes even more easily than the first.

ANTHELIA. I am sorry for it.

THE HONOURABLE MRS. PINMONEY. Sorry !—Feelings are very troublesome things, and always stand in the way of a person's own interests. Then, as to character—a gentleman's character is usually in the keeping of his banker, or his agent, or his steward, or his solicitor ; and if they can certify and demonstrate that he has the means of keeping a handsome equipage, and a town and country house, and of giving routs and dinners, and of making a good settlement on the happy object of his choice—what more of any gentleman's character would you desire to know ?

ANTHELIA. A great deal more. I would require him to be free in all his thoughts, true in all his words, generous in all his actions—ardent in friendship, enthusiastic in love, disinterested in both—prompt in the conception, and constant in the execution, of benevolent enterprise—the friend of the friendless, the champion of the feeble, the firm opponent of the powerful oppressor—not to be enervated by luxury, nor corrupted by avarice, nor intimidated by tyranny, nor enthralled by superstition—more desirous to distribute wealth than to possess it, to disseminate liberty than to appropriate power, to cheer the heart of sorrow than to dazzle the eyes of folly.

THE HONOURABLE MRS. PINMONEY.   And do you really expect to find such a knight-errant ?   The age of chivalry is gone.

ANTHELIA.   It is, but its spirit survives.   Disinterested benevolence, the mainspring of all that is really admirable in the days of chivalry, will never perish for want of some minds calculated to feel its influence, still less for want of a proper field of exertion.   To protect the feeble—to raise the fallen—to liberate the captive—to be the persevering foe of tyrants (whether the great tyrant of an overwhelming empire, the petty tyrant of the fields, or the " little tyrant of a little corporation " [1]), it is not necessary to wind the bugle before enchanted castles, or to seek adventures in the depths of mountain-caverns and forests of pine : there is no scene of human life but presents sufficient scope to energetic generosity : the field of action, though less splendid in its accompaniments, is not less useful in its results, nor less attractive to a liberal spirit : and I believe it possible to find as true a knight-errant in a brown coat in the nineteenth century, as in a suit of golden armour in the days of Charlemagne.

THE HONOURABLE MRS. PINMONEY.   Well ! well ! my dear, when you have seen a little more of the world, you will get rid of some of your chivalrous whimsies ; and I think you will then agree with me, that there is not, in the whole sphere of fashion, a more elegant, fine-spirited, dashing, generous fellow than my nephew Sir Telegraph Paxarett, who by the by will be driving his barouche this way shortly, and if you do not absolutely forbid it, will call on me in his route.

These words seemed to portend that the Honourable Mrs. Pinmoney's visit would be a visitation, and at the same time threw a clear light on its motive ; but they gave birth in the mind of Anthelia to a train of ideas which concluded in a somewhat singular determination.

[1] Junius. [P.] [Letter XXIII ; To His Grace the Duke of Bedford. G.]

CHAPTER III

HYPOCON[1] HOUSE

ANTHELIA had received intimations, from various quarters, of similar intentions on the part of various individuals, not less valuable than Sir Telegraph Paxarett in the scale of moral utility ; and though there was not one among them for whom she felt the slightest interest, she thought it would be too uncourteous in a pupil of chivalry, and too inhospitable in the mistress of an old English castle, to bar her gates against them. At the same time she felt the want of a lord seneschal to receive and entertain visitors so little congenial to her habits and inclinations : and it immediately occurred to her, that no one would be more fit for this honourable office, if he could be prevailed on to undertake it, than an old relation, a medium, as it were, between cousin and great uncle ; who had occasionally passed a week or a month with her father at Melincourt. The name of this old gentleman was Hippy : Humphrey Hippy, Esquire, of Hypocon House, in the county of Durham.[2] He was a bachelor, and his character exhibited a singular compound of kind-heartedness, spleen, and melancholy, which governed him by turns, and sometimes in such rapid succession that they seemed almost co-existent. To him Anthelia determined on sending an express, with a letter entreating him to take on himself, for a short time, the superintendence of Melincourt Castle, and giving as briefly as possible her reasons for the request. In pursuance of this determination, old Peter Gray, a favourite domestic of Sir Henry, and I believe a distant relation of little Lucy,[3] was despatched the following morning to Hypocon House, where the gate was opened to him by old Harry Fell, a distant relation of little Alice, who, as the reader well knows, " belonged to Durham." Old Harry had become, by long habit, a curious species

[1] Short for Hypochondria. G.

[2] Miss Sylva Norman points out (in *After Shelley*, 1934) Jefferson Hogg-like characteristics in Mr. Hippy. It is questionable whether, writing in 1817, Peacock had a " pure anticipated cognition " of what Hogg would develop into, but he may have had. Peacock had employed both of the names Paxarett and Hippy in his farce *The Three Doctors*. G.

[3] For Lucy Gray and Alice Fell, see Mr. Wordsworth's *Lyrical Ballads*.

[P.]

of animated mirror, and reflected all the humours of his master with wonderful nicety. When Mr. Hippy was in a rage, old Harry looked fierce: when Mr. Hippy was in a good humour, old Harry was the picture of human kindness: when Mr. Hippy was blue-devilled, old Harry was vapourish: when Mr. Hippy was as melancholy as a gib cat, old Harry was as dismal as a screech-owl. The latter happened to be the case, when old Peter presented himself at the gate, and old Harry accordingly opened it with a most rueful elongation of visage. Peter Gray was ready with a warm salutation for his old acquaintance Harry Fell; but the lamentable cast of expression in the physiognomy of the latter froze it on his lips, and he contented himself with asking in a hesitating tone, "Is Mr. Hippy at home?"

"He is," slowly and sadly articulated Harry Fell, shaking his head.

"I have a letter for him," said Peter Gray.

"Ah!" said Harry Fell, taking the letter, and stalking off with it as solemnly as if he had been following a funeral.

"A pleasant reception," thought Peter Gray, "instead of the old ale and cold sirloin I dreamed of."

Old Harry tapped three times at the door of his master's chamber, observing the same interval between each tap as is usual between the sounds of a muffled drum: then, after a due pause, he entered the apartment. Mr. Hippy was in his night-gown and slippers, with one leg on a cushion, suffering under an imaginary attack of the gout, and in the last stage of despondency. Old Harry walked forward in the same slow pace till he found himself at the proper distance from his master's chair. Then putting forth his hand as deliberately as if it had been the hour-hand of the kitchen clock, he presented the letter. Mr. Hippy took it in the same manner, sunk back in his chair as if exhausted with the effort, and cast his eyes languidly on the seal. Immediately his eyes brightened, he tore open the letter, read it in an instant, sprang up, flung his night-gown one way, his night-cap another, kicked off his slippers, kicked away his cushion, kicked over his chair, and bounced downstairs, roaring for his coat and boots, and his travelling chariot, with old Harry capering at his heels, and re-echoing all his requisitions. Harry Fell was now a new man: Peter Gray was seized by the hand and dragged into the buttery, where a cold goose and a flagon of ale were placed before him; to

which he immediately proceeded to do ample justice ; while old
Harry rushed off with a cold fowl and ham, for the refection of Mr.
Hippy, who had been too seriously indisposed in the morning, to
touch a morsel of breakfast. Having placed these and a bottle of
Madeira in due form and order before his master, he flew back to the
buttery to assist old Peter in the demolition of the goose and ale, his
own appetite in the morning having sympathised with his master's,
and being now equally disposed to make up for lost time.

Mr. Hippy's travelling chariot was rattled up to the door by four
high-mettled posters from the nearest inn. Mr. Hippy sprang into
the carriage, old Harry vaulted into the dicky, the postillions cracked
their whips, and away they went,

> " Over the hills and the plains,
> Over the rivers and rocks," [1]

leaving old Peter gaping after them at the gate, in profound astonishment at their sudden metamorphosis, and in utter despair of being
able, by any exertions of his own, to be their forerunner and
announcer at Melincourt. Considering, therefore, that when the
necessity of being too late is inevitable, hurry is manifestly superfluous, he mounted his galloway with great gravity and deliberation,
and trotted slowly off towards the mountains, philosophizing all the
way in the usual poetical style of a Cumberland peasant. Our
readers will of course feel much obliged to us for not presenting them
with his meditations. But instead of jogging back with old Peter
Gray, or travelling post with Humphrey Hippy, Esquire, we shall
avail ourselves of the four-in-hand barouche which is just coming in
view, to take a seat on the box by the side of Sir Telegraph Paxarett,
and proceed in his company to Melincourt.

CHAPTER IV

REDROSE ABBEY

Sir Telegraph Paxarett had entered the precincts of the mountains
of Westmoreland, and was bowling his barouche along a romantic

[1] Southey : *Thalaba the Destroyer*, Bk. VIII, St. 35. G.

valley, looking out very anxiously for an inn, as he had now driven his regular diurnal allowance of miles, and was becoming very impatient for his equally regular diurnal allowance of fish, fowl, and Madeira. A wreath of smoke ascending from a thick tuft of trees at a distance, and in a straight direction before him, cheered up his spirits, and induced him to cheer up those of his horses with two or three of those technical terms of the road, which we presume to have formed part of the genuine language of the ancient Houhynnhmns, since they seem not only much better adapted to equine than human organs of sound, but are certainly much more generally intelligible to four-footed than to two-footed animals. Sir Telegraph was doomed to a temporary disappointment; for when he had attained the desired point, the smoke proved to issue from the chimneys of an ancient abbey which appeared to have been recently converted from a pile of ruins into the habitation of some variety of the human species, with very singular veneration for the relics of antiquity, which, in their exterior aspect, had suffered little from the alteration. There was something so analogous between the state of this building and what he had heard of Melincourt, that if it had not been impossible to mistake an abbey for a castle, he might almost have fancied himself arrived at the dwelling of the divine Anthelia. Under a detached piece of ruins near the road, which appeared to have been part of a chapel, several workmen were busily breaking the ground with spade and pickaxe : a gentleman was superintending their operations, and seemed very eager to arrive at the object of his search. Sir Telegraph stopped his barouche to inquire the distance to the nearest inn: the gentleman replied, six miles. "That is just five miles and a half too far," said Sir Telegraph, and was proceeding to drive on, when, on turning round to make his parting bow to the stranger, he suddenly recognised him for an old acquaintance and fellow-collegian.

"Sylvan Forester ! " exclaimed Sir Telegraph ; "who should have dreamed of meeting you in this uncivilized part of the world ? " [1]

"I am afraid," said Mr. Forester, "this part of the world does not deserve the compliment implied in the epithet you have bestowed on

[1] Forester is based on the maturer, as Scythrop in *Nightmare Abbey* is based on the immature, Shelley. G.

it. Within no very great distance from this spot are divers towns, villages, and hamlets, in any one of which, if you have money, you may make pretty sure of being cheated, and if you have none, quite sure of being starved—strong evidences of a state of civilisation."

"Aha!" said Sir Telegraph, "your old way, now I recollect—always fond of railing at civilised life, and holding forth in praise of savages and what you called original men. But what, in truth, make you in Westmoreland?"[1]

"I have purchased this old abbey," said Mr. Forester, "(anciently called the abbey of Rednose, which I have altered to Redrose, as being more analogous to my notions of beauty, whatever the reverend Fellows of our old college might have thought of it), and have fitted it up for my habitation, with the view of carrying on in peace and seclusion some peculiar experiments on the nature and progress of man. Will you dine with me, and pass the night here? and I will introduce you to an original character."

"With all my heart," said Sir Telegraph; "I can assure you, independently of the pleasure of meeting an old acquaintance, it is a great comfort to dine in a gentleman's house, after living from inn to inn, and being poisoned with bad wine for a month."

Sir Telegraph descended from his box, and directed one of his grooms to open the carriage-door and emancipate the coachman, who was fast asleep inside. Sir Telegraph gave him the reins, and Mr. Forester sent one of his workmen to show him the way to the stables.

"And pray," said Sir Telegraph, as the barouche disappeared among the trees, "what may be the object of your researches in this spot?"

"You know," said Mr. Forester, "it is a part of my tenets that the human species is gradually decreasing in size and strength, and I am digging in the old cemetery for bones and skulls to establish the truth of my theory."

"Have you found any?" said Sir Telegraph.

"Many," said Mr. Forester. "About three weeks ago we dug up a very fine skeleton, no doubt of some venerable father, who must have been, in more senses than one, a pillar of the church. I have

[1] Compare *Hamlet*, Act I, Sc. 2. "But what, in faith, make you from Wittenberg?" G.

had the skull polished and set in silver.   You shall drink your wine out of it, if you please, to-day." [1]

" I thank you," said Sir Telegraph, " but I am not particular : a glass will suit me as well as the best skull in Europe.   Besides, I am a moderate man : one bottle of Madeira and another of claret are enough for me at any time ; so that the quantity of wine a reverend sconce can carry would be just treble my usual allowance."

They walked together towards the abbey.   Sir Telegraph earnestly requested, that, before they entered, he might be favoured with a peep at the stable.   Mr. Forester of course complied.   Sir Telegraph found this important part of the buildings capacious and well adapted to its purpose, but did not altogether approve its being totally masked by an old ivied wall, which had served in former times to prevent the braw and bonny Scot from making too free with the beeves of the pious fraternity.

The new dwelling-house was so well planned, and fitted in so well between the ancient walls, that very few vestiges of the modern architect were discernible ; and it was obvious that the growth of ivy, and of numerous trailing and twining plants, would soon over-run all vestiges of the innovation, and blend the whole exterior into one venerable character of antiquity.

" I do not think," said Mr. Forester, as they proceeded through part of the grounds, " that the most determined zealot of the picturesque would quarrel with me here.   I found the woods around the abbey matured by time and neglect into a fine state of wildness and intricacy, and I think I have left enough of them to gratify their most ardent admirer."

" Quite enough, in all conscience," said Sir Telegraph, who was in white jean trowsers, with very thin silk stockings and pumps.   " I do not generally calculate on being, as an old song I have somewhere heard expresses it,

> " Forced to scramble,
> When I ramble,
> Through a copse of furze and bramble ; " [2]

---

[1] See *Nightmare Abbey*, p. 371. Byron had also entertained his guests at Newstead in 1809 by passing round a skull filled with Burgundy. G.

[2] This " old song " is by Peacock and is taken from his musical farce *The Three Doctors*. He also introduces the theme in *Maid Marian*, p. 451. G.

which would be all very pleasant perhaps, if the fine effect of picturesque roughness were not unfortunately, as Macbeth says of his dagger, 'sensible to feeling as to sight.' [1] But who is that gentleman, sitting under the great oak yonder in the green coat and nankins ? He seems very thoughtful."

" He is of a contemplative disposition," said Mr. Forester : " you must not be surprised if he should not speak a word during the whole time you are here. The politeness of his manner makes amends for his habitual taciturnity. I will introduce you."

The gentleman under the oak had by this time discovered them, and came forward with great alacrity to meet Mr. Forester, who cordially shook hands with him, and introduced him to Sir Telegraph as Sir Oran Haut-ton, Baronet.

Sir Telegraph looked earnestly at the stranger, but was too polite to laugh, though he could not help thinking there was something very ludicrous in Sir Oran's physiognomy, notwithstanding the air of high fashion which characterized his whole deportment, and which was heightened by a pair of enormous whiskers, and the folds of a vast cravat. He therefore bowed to Sir Oran with becoming gravity, and Sir Oran returned the bow with very striking politeness.

" Possibly," thought Sir Telegraph, " possibly I may have seen an uglier fellow."

The trio entered the abbey, and shortly after sate down to dinner.

Mr. Forester and Sir Oran Haut-ton took the head and foot of the table. Sir Telegraph sate between them. " Some soup, Sir Telegraph ? " said Mr. Forester. " I rather think," said Sir Telegraph, " I shall trouble Sir Oran for a slice of fish." Sir Oran helped him with great dexterity, and then performed the same office for himself. " I think you will like this Madeira ? " said Mr. Forester. " Capital ! " said Sir Telegraph : " Sir Oran, shall I have the pleasure of taking wine with you ? " Sir Oran Haut-ton bowed gracefully to Sir Telegraph Paxarett, and the glasses were tossed off with the usual ceremonies. Sir Oran preserved an inflexible silence during the whole duration of dinner, but showed great proficiency in the dissection of game.

When the cloth was removed, the wine circulated freely, and Sir

[1] Act II, Sc. 1. G.

Telegraph, as usual, filled a numerous succession of glasses. Mr. Forester, not as usual, did the same ; for he was generally very abstemious in this respect : but, on the present occasion, he relaxed from his severity, quoting the *Placari genius festis impune diebus*,[1] and the *Dulce est desipere in loco*,[2] of Horace. Sir Oran likewise approved, by his practice, that he thought the wine particularly excellent, and *Beviamo tutti tre* [3] appeared to be the motto of the party. Mr. Forester inquired into the motives which had brought Sir Telegraph to Westmoreland ; and Sir Telegraph entered into a rapturous encomium of the heiress of Melincourt, which was suddenly cut short by Sir Oran, who having taken a glass too much, rose suddenly from table, took a flying leap through the window, and went dancing along the woods like a harlequin.

"Upon my word," said Sir Telegraph, "a devilish lively, pleasant fellow ! Curse me, if I know what to make of him."

"I will tell you his history," said Mr. Forester, "by and by. In the mean time I must look after him, that he may neither do nor receive mischief. Pray take care of yourself till I return." Saying this, he sprang through the window after Sir Oran, and disappeared by the same track among the trees.

"Curious enough !" soliloquized Sir Telegraph ; "however, not much to complain of, as the best part of the company is left behind : videlicet, the bottle."

CHAPTER V

SUGAR

SIR TELEGRAPH was tossing off the last heeltap of his regular diurnal allowance of wine, when Mr. Forester and Sir Oran Haut-ton re-appeared, walking past the window arm in arm ; Sir Oran's mode of progression being very vacillating, indirect, and titubant ; enough so, at least, to show that he had not completely danced off the effects of the Madeira. Mr. Forester shortly after entered ; and Sir Tele-

---

[1] "There is no danger in propitiating the Genius on festal days." *Ars Poet*, l. 210. G.

[2] "It is sweet to play the fool on meet occasion." *Od*. IV. xii. 28. G.

[3] "Let us drink all three." G.

graph inquiring concerning Sir Oran, " I have persuaded him to go
to bed," said Mr. Forester, " and I doubt not he is already fast
asleep." A servant now entered with tea. Sir Telegraph proceeded
to help himself, when he perceived there was no sugar, and reminded
his host of the omission.

MR. FORESTER. If I had anticipated the honour of your company,
Sir Telegraph, I would have provided myself with a small quantity
of that nefarious ingredient : but in this solitary situation, these
things are not to be had at a moment's notice. As it is, seeing little
company, and regulating my domestic arrangements on philosophical
principles, I never suffer an atom of West Indian produce to pass my
threshold. I have no wish to resemble those pseudo-philanthropists,
those miserable declaimers against slavery, who are very liberal of
words which cost them nothing, but are not capable of advancing
the object they profess to have at heart, by submitting to the smallest
personal privation. If I wish seriously to exterminate an evil, I begin
by examining how far I am myself, in any way whatever, an accomplice in the extension of its baleful influence. My reform commences
at home. How can I unblushingly declaim against thieves, while
I am a receiver of stolen goods ? How can I seriously call myself an
enemy to slavery, while I indulge in the luxuries that slavery
acquires ? How can the consumer of sugar pretend to throw on the
grower of it the exclusive burden of their participated criminality ?
How can he wash his hands, and say with Pilate : " *I am innocent of
this blood, see ye to it* " ?

Sir Telegraph poured some cream into his unsweetened tea, drank
it, and said nothing. Mr. Forester proceeded :

If every individual in this kingdom, who is truly and conscientiously an enemy to the slave-trade, would subject himself to so very
trivial a privation as abstinence from colonial produce, I consider
that a mortal blow would be immediately struck at the roots of that
iniquitous system.[1]

[1] Peacock is here voicing not only Shelley's views, but his own. His
granddaughter has recorded that he renounced the use of sugar on principle.
The boycott of sugar and rum, the products of slave labour, had been initiated by the abolitionist William Fox in 1791, and had spread widely. G.

SIR TELEGRAPH PAXARETT. If every individual enemy to the
slave-trade would follow your example, the object would no doubt
be much advanced; but the practice of one individual, more or less,
has little or no influence on general society ; most of us go on with
the tide, and the dread of the single word *quiz* has more influence in
keeping the greater part of us within the pale of custom, fashion, and
precedent, than all the moral reasonings and declamations in the
world will ever have in persuading us to break through it. As to
the diffusion of liberty, and the general happiness of mankind, which
used to be your favourite topics when we were at college together,
I should have thought your subsequent experience would have shown
you, that there is not one person in ten thousand, who knows what
liberty means, or cares a single straw for any happiness but his
own——

MR. FORESTER. Which his own miserable selfishness must estrange
from him for ever. He whose heart has never glowed with a generous
resolution, who has never felt the conscious triumph of a disinterested
sacrifice, who has never sympathized with human joys or sorrows,
but when they have had a direct and palpable reference to himself,
can never be acquainted with even the semblance of happiness. His
utmost enjoyment must be many degrees inferior to that of a pig,
inasmuch as the sordid mire of selfish and brutal stupidity is more
defiling to the soul, than any coacervation of mere material mud can
possibly be to the body. The latter may be cleared away with two
or three ablutions, but the former cleaves and accumulates into a
mass of impenetrable corruption, that bids defiance to the united
powers of Hercules and Alpheus.[1]

SIR TELEGRAPH PAXARETT. Be that as it may, every man will
continue to follow his own fancy. The world is bad enough, I dare
say ; but it is not for you or me to mend it.

MR. FORESTER. There is the keystone of the evil—mistrust of the
influence of individual example. " We are bad ourselves, because
we despair of the goodness of others." [2]   Yet the history of the world

[1] Hercules used the waters of the river Alpheus to clean the Augean
stable. G.
[2] Coleridge's *Friend*. [P] [General Introduction, Essay XIV. G.]

abounds with sudden and extraordinary revolutions in the opinions of mankind, which have been effected by single enthusiasts.

SIR TELEGRAPH PAXARETT.   Speculative opinions have been some-times changed by the efforts of roaring fanatics.   Men have been found very easily permutable into *ites* and *onians, avians* and *arians*, Wesleyites or Whitfieldites, Huntingdonians or Muggletonians, Moravians, Trinitarians, Unitarians, Anythingarians : but the metamorphosis only affects a few obscure notions concerning types, symbols, and mysteries, which have scarcely any effect on moral theory, and of course, *a fortiori*, none whatever on moral practice : the latter is for the most part governed by the general habits and manners of the society we live in.   One man may twang responses in concert with the parish-clerk ; another may sit silent in a Quakers' meeting, waiting for the inspiration of the Spirit ; a third may groan and howl in a tabernacle ; a fourth may breakfast, dine, and sup, in a Sandemanian chapel : but meet any of the four in the common intercourse of society, you will scarcely know one from another. The single adage, *Charity begins at home*, will furnish a complete key to the souls of all four : for I have found, as far as my observation has extended, that men carry their religion [1] in other men's heads, and their morality in their own pockets.

[1] " There is not any burden that some would gladlier post off to another than the charge and care of their religion. There be of Protestants and professors who live and die in as arrant and implicit faith as any lay Papist of Loretto. A wealthy man, addicted to his pleasure and to his profits, finds religion to be a traffic so entangled and of so many peddling accounts, that, of all mysteries, he cannot skill to keep a stock going upon that trade. What should he do ? Fain would he have the name to be religious : fain would he bear up with his neighbours in that. What does he, therefore, but resolves to give over toiling, and to find himself out some factor, to whose care and credit he may commit the whole management of his religious affairs ; some divine of note and estimation that must be. To him he adheres, resigns the whole warehouse of his religion, with all the locks and keys, into his custody, and, indeed, makes the very person of that man his religion, esteems his associating with him a sufficient evidence and commendatory of his own piety. So that a man may say, his religion is now no more within himself, but is become a dividual movable, and goes and comes near him according as that good man frequents the house. He entertains him, gives him gifts, feasts him, lodges him : his religion comes home at night, prays, is liberally supped, and sumptuously laid to sleep, rises, is saluted, and after the malmsey, or some well-spiced brewage, and

MR. FORESTER. I think it will be found that individual example has in many instances produced great moral effects on the practice of society. Even if it were otherwise, is it not better to be Abdiel among the fiends,[1] than to be lost and confounded in the legion of imps grovelling in the train of the evil power ?

SIR TELEGRAPH PAXARETT. There is something in that.

MR. FORESTER. To borrow an allegory from Homer : I would say society is composed of two urns, one of good, and one of evil.[2] I will suppose, that every individual of the human species receives from his natal genius a little phial, containing one drop of a fluid, which shall be evil, if poured into the urn of evil, and good if into that of good. If you were proceeding to the station of the urns with ten thousand persons, every one of them predetermined to empty his phial into the urn of evil, which I fear is too true a picture of the practice of society, should you consider their example, if you were hemmed in in the centre of them, a sufficient excuse for not breaking from them, and approaching the neglected urn ? Would you say, " The urn of good will derive little increase from my solitary drop, and one more or less will make very little difference in the urn of ill : I will spare myself trouble, do as the world does, and let the urn of good take its chance, from those who can approach it with less difficulty " ? No : you would rather say, " That neglected urn contains the hopes of the human species : little, indeed, is the addition I can make to it, but it will be good as far as it goes ; " and if, on approaching the urn, you should find it not so empty as you had anticipated, if the genius appointed to guard it should say to you, " There is enough in this urn already to allow a reasonable expectation that it will one day be full, and yet it has only accumulated drop by drop through the efforts of individuals, who broke through the pale and pressure of the multi-

---

better breakfasted than he whose morning appetite would have gladly fed on green figs between Bethany and Jerusalem, his religion walks abroad at eight, and leaves his kind entertainer in the shop, trading all day without his religion."—Milton's *Speech for the Liberty of unlicensed Printing.* [P.]

[1] Milton : *Paradise Lost,* Bk. V, lines 893–4 :

" So spake the seraph Abdiel, faithful found,
Among the faithless, faithful only he." G.

[2] *Il.* XXIV. 527. G.

tude, and did not despair of human virtue ; " would you not feel ten thousand times repaid for the difficulties you had overcome, and the scoffs of the fools and slaves you had abandoned, by the single reflection that would then rush upon your mind, *I am one of these* ?

SIR TELEGRAPH PAXARETT. Gad, very likely : I never considered the subject in that light. You have made no allowance for the mixture of good and evil, which I think the fairest state of the case. It seems to me, that the world always goes on pretty much in one way. People eat, drink, and sleep, make merry with their friends, get as much money as they can, marry when they can afford it, take care of their children because they are their own, are thought well of while they live in proportion to the depth of their purse, and when they die, are sure of as good a character on their tombstones as the bellman and stonemason can afford for their money.

MR. FORESTER. Such is the multitude ; but there are noble exceptions to this general littleness.

SIR TELEGRAPH PAXARETT. Now and then an original genius strikes out of the common track ; but there are two ways of doing that—into a worse as well as a better.

MR. FORESTER. There are some assuredly, who strike into a better; and these are the ornaments of their age, and the lights of the world. You must admit too, that there are many, who, though without energy or capacity to lead, have yet virtue enough to follow an illustrious example.

SIR TELEGRAPH PAXARETT. One or two.

MR. FORESTER. In every mode of human action there are two ways to be pursued—a good and a bad one. It is the duty of every man to ascertain the former, as clearly as his capacity will admit, by an accurate examination of general relations ; and to act upon it rigidly, without regard to his own previous habits, or the common practice of the world.

SIR TELEGRAPH PAXARETT. And you infer from all this, that it is my duty to drink my tea without sugar.

MR. FORESTER. I infer, that it is the duty of every one, thoroughly penetrated with the iniquity of the slave-trade, to abstain entirely from the use of colonial produce.

SIR TELEGRAPH PAXARETT. I may do that, without any great effort of virtue. I find the difference in this instance, more trivial than I could have supposed. In fact, I never thought of it before.

MR. FORESTER. I hope I shall before long have the pleasure of enrolling you a member of the Anti-saccharine Society, which I have had the happiness to organize, and which is daily extending its numbers. Some of its principal members will shortly pay a visit to Redrose Abbey; and I purpose giving a festival, to which I shall invite all that is respectable and intelligent in this part of the country, and in which I intend to demonstrate practically, that a very elegant and luxurious entertainment may be prepared without employing a single particle of that abominable ingredient, and theoretically, that the use of sugar is economically superfluous, physically pernicious, morally atrocious, and politically abominable.

SIR TELEGRAPH PAXARETT. I shall be happy to join the party, and I may possibly bring with me one or two inside passengers, who will prove both ornamental and attractive to your festival. But you promised me an account of Sir Oran.

CHAPTER VI

SIR ORAN HAUT-TON

MR. FORESTER. Sir Oran Haut-ton was caught very young in the woods of Angola.

SIR TELEGRAPH PAXARETT. Caught!

MR. FORESTER. Very young. He is a specimen of the natural and original man—the wild man of the woods; called, in the language of the more civilized and sophisticated natives of Angola, *Pongo*, and in that of the Indians of South America, *Oran Outang*.[1]

[1] The Pongo is the Chimpanzee. Oran Outang is Malay for wild man. There are no anthropoid apes native to South America. G.

SIR TELEGRAPH PAXARETT. The devil he is !

MR. FORESTER. Positively. Some presumptuous naturalists have refused his species the honours of humanity ; but the most enlightened and illustrious philosophers agree in considering him in his true light as the natural and original man.[1] One French philosopher, indeed, has been guilty of an inaccuracy, in considering him as a degenerated man : [2] degenerated he cannot be ; as his prodigious

[1] " I think I have established his humanity by proof that ought to satisfy every one who gives credit to human testimony."—[James Burnett, Lord Monboddo:] *Ancient Metaphysics*, vol. iii. p. 40.

" I have brought myself to a perfect conviction that the oran outang is a human creature as much as any of us."—*Ibid.* p. 133.

" Nihil humani ei deesse diceres praeter loquelam."—BONTIUS.

" The fact truly is, that the man is easily distinguishable in him ; nor are there any differences betwixt him and us, but what may be accounted for in so satisfactory a manner, that it would be extraordinary and unnatural if they were not to be found. His body, which is of the same shape as ours, is bigger and stronger than ours, . . . according to that general law of nature above observed (*that all animals thrive best in their natural state*). His mind is such as that of a man must be, uncultivated by arts and sciences, and living wild in the woods. . . . One thing, at least, is certain : that if ever men were in that state which I call natural, it must have been in such a country and climate as Africa, where they could live without art upon the natural fruits of the earth. ' Such countries,' Linnaeus says, ' are the native country of man ; there he lives naturally ; in other countries, *non nisi coacte*, that is, by force of art.' If this be so, then, the short history of man is, that the race having begun in those fine climates, and having, as is natural, multiplied there so much that the spontaneous productions of the earth could not support them, they migrated into other countries, where they were obliged to invent arts for their subsistence ; and with such arts, language, in process of time, would necessarily come. . . . That my facts and arguments are so convincing as to leave no doubt of the humanity of the oran outang, I will not take upon me to say ; but this much I will venture to affirm, that I have said enough to make the philosopher consider it as problematical, and a subject deserving to be inquired into. *For, as to the vulgar, I can never expect that they should acknowledge any relation to those inhabitants of the woods of Angola ;* but that they should continue, through a false pride, to think highly derogatory from human nature what the philosopher, on the contrary, will think the greatest praise of man, that from the savage state in which the oran outang is, he should, by his own sagacity and industry, have arrived at the state in which we now see him.—[Lord Monboddo:] *Origin and Progress of Language*, book ii. chap. 5. [P.]

[2] " L'Oran outang, ou l'homme des bois, est un être particulier à la zone torride de notre hémisphère : le Pline de la nation qui l'a rangé dans la classe de singes ne me paroît pas conséquent ; car il résulte des principaux

physical strength, his uninterrupted health, and his amiable simplicity of manners demonstrate. He is, as I have said, a specimen of the natural and original man—a genuine fac simile of the philosophical Adam.

He was caught by an intelligent negro very young, in the woods of Angola ; and his gentleness and sweet temper [1] winning the hearts of the negro and negress, they brought him up in their cottage as the playfellow of their little boys and girls, where, with the exception of speech, he acquired the practice of such of the simpler arts of life as the degree of civilization in that part of Africa admits. In this way he lived till he was about seventeen years of age——

SIR TELEGRAPH PAXARETT. By his own reckoning ?

MR. FORESTER. By analogical computation. At this period, my old friend Captain Hawltaught of the Tornado frigate, being driven by stress of weather to the coast of Angola, was so much struck with the contemplative cast of Sir Oran's countenance,[2] that he offered the negro an irresistible bribe to surrender him to his possession. The negro brought him on board, and took an opportunity to leave him slily, but with infinite reluctance and sympathetic grief. When

---

traits de sa description que c'est un homme dégénéré."—*Philosophie de la Nature*. [P.] [*De la Philosophie de la Nature, ou, Traité de Morale pour le Genre Humain* (1770) by Jean Baptiste Claude Isoard Delisle, also known as Delisle de Sales and, here most appropriately, as " Le Singe de Diderot."
                                                                          G.]
[1] " The dispositions and affections of his mind are mild, gentle, and humane."—*Origin and Progress of Language*, book ii. chap. 4.

" The oran outang whom Buffon himself saw was of a sweet temper."— *Ibid.* [P.]

[2] " But though I hold the oran outang to be of our species, it must not be supposed that I think the monkey or ape, with or without a tail, participates of our nature : on the contrary, I maintain that, however much his form may resemble man's, yet he is, as Linnaeus says of the Troglodyte, *nec nostri generis nec sanguinis.* For as the mind, or internal principle, is the chief part of every animal, it is by it principally that the ancients have distinguished the several specieses. Now, it is laid down by Mr. Buffon, and I believe it to be a fact that cannot be contested, that neither monkey, ape, nor baboon, have any thing mild or gentle, tractable or docile, benevolent or humane in their dispositions ; but, on the contrary, are malicious and untractable, to be governed only by force and fear, and without any *gravity or composure in their gait or behaviour, such as the oran outang has.*"— *Ibid.* [P.]

the ship weighed anchor, and Sir Oran found himself separated from
the friends of his youth, and surrounded with strange faces, he wept
bitterly,[1] and fell into such deep grief that his life was despaired of.[2]
The surgeon of the ship did what he could for him ; and a much better
doctor, Time, completed his cure. By degrees a very warm friendship for my friend Captain Hawltaught extinguished his recollection
of his negro friends. Three years they cruised together in the
Tornado, when a dangerous wound compelled the old Captain to
renounce his darling element, and lay himself up in ordinary for the
rest of his days. He retired on his half-pay and the produce of his
prize-money, to a little village in the west of England, where he
employed himself very assiduously in planting cabbages and watching the changes of the wind. Mr. Oran, as he was then called, was his
inseparable companion, and became a very expert practical gardener.
The old Captain used to observe, he could always say he had an
honest man in his house, which was more than could be said of many
honourable houses where there was much vapouring about honour.

Mr. Oran had long before shown a taste for music, and, with some
little instruction from a marine officer in the Tornado, had become
a proficient on the flute and French horn.[3] He could never be
brought to understand the notes ; but from hearing any simple

---

[1] " He is capable of the greatest affection, not only to his brother oran
outangs, but to such among us as use him kindly. And it is a fact well
attested to me by a gentleman who was an eye-witness of it, that an oran
outang on board his ship conceived such an affection for the cook, that when
upon some occasion he left the ship to go ashore, the gentleman saw the
oran outang shed tears in great abundance."—*Origin and Progress of
Language*, book ii. chap. 4. [P.]

[2] " One of them was taken, and brought with some negro slaves to the
capital of the kingdom of Malemba. He was a young one, but six feet and
a half tall. Before he came to this city, he had been kept some months in
company with the negro slaves, and during that time was tame and gentle,
and took his victuals very quietly ; but when he was brought into the town,
such crowds of people came about him to gaze at him, that he could not
bear it, but grew sullen, abstained from food, and died in four or five days."
—*Ibid*. [P.]

[3] " He has the capacity of being a musician, and has actually learned to
play upon the pipe and harp : a fact attested, not by a common traveller,
but by a man of science, Mr. Peiresc, and who relates it, not as a hearsay,
but as a fact consisting with his own knowledge. And this is the more to
be attended to, as it shows that the oran outang has a perception of
numbers, measure, and melody, which has always been accounted peculiar

tune played or sung two or three times, he never failed to perform it with great exactness and brilliancy of execution. I shall merely observe, *en passant*, that music appears, from this and several similar circumstances, to be more natural to man than speech. The old Captain was fond of his bottle of wine after dinner, and his glass of grog at night. Mr. Oran was easily brought to sympathize in this taste;[1] and they have many times sat up together half the night over a flowing bowl, the old Captain singing Rule Britannia, True Courage, or Tom Tough, and Sir Oran accompanying him on the French horn.

During a summer tour in Devonshire, I called on my old friend Captain Hawltaught,[2] and was introduced to Mr. Oran. You, who have not forgotten my old speculations on the origin and progress of man, may judge of my delight at this happy *rencontre*. I exerted all the eloquence I was master of to persuade Captain Hawltaught to resign him to me, that I might give him a philosophical education.[3] Finding this point unattainable, I took a house in the neighbourhood, and the intercourse which ensued was equally beneficial and agreeable to all three.

---

to our species. But the learning to speak, as well as the learning music, must depend upon particular circumstances; and men, living, as the oran outangs do, upon the natural fruits of the earth, with few or no arts, are not in a situation that is proper for the invention of language. The oran outangs who played upon the pipe had certainly not invented this art in the woods, but they had learned it from the negroes or the Europeans; and that they had not at the same time learned to speak, may be accounted for in one or other of two ways: either the same pains had not been taken to teach them articulation; or, secondly, music is more natural to man, and more easily acquired than speech."—*Ibid.* book. ii. chap. 5. [P.]

[1] " Ces animaux," dit M. de la Brosse, " ont l'instinct de s'asseoir à table comme les hommes; ils mangent de tout sans distinction; ils se servent du couteau, de la cuillère, et de la fourchette, pour prendre et couper ce qu'on sert sur l'assiette : *ils boivent du vin et d'autres liqueurs :* nous les portâmes à bord; quand ils étoient à table, ils se faisoient entendre des mousses lorsqu'ils avoient besoin de quelque chose."—BUFFON. [P.]

[2] Peacock's grandfather, Thomas Love, Master of H.M.S. *Prothée,* who lost a leg under Rodney, with whom Peacock and his widowed mother lived from the time Peacock was three till he was fifteen years old. G.

[3] " If I can believe the newspapers, there was an oran outang of the great kind, that was some time ago shipped aboard a French East India ship. I hope he has had a safe voyage to Europe, and that his education will be taken care of."—*Ancient Metaphysics,* vol. iii. p. 40. [P.]

SIR TELEGRAPH PAXARETT. And what part did you take in their nocturnal concerts, with Tom Tough and the French horn?

MR. FORESTER. I was seldom present at them, and often remonstrated, but ineffectually, with the Captain, on his corrupting the amiable simplicity of the natural man by this pernicious celebration of vinous and spiritous orgies; but the only answer I could ever get from him was a hearty damn against all water-drinkers, accompanied with a reflection that he was sure every enemy to wine and grog must have clapped down the hatches of his conscience on some secret villainy, which he feared good liquor would pipe ahoy: and he usually concluded by striking up *Nothing like Grog, Saturday Night,* or *Swing the flowing Bowl,* his friend Oran's horn ringing in sympathetic symphony.

The old Captain used to say that grog was the elixir of life; but it did not prove so to him; for one night he tossed off his last bumper, sung his last stave, and heard the last flourish of his Oran's horn. I thought poor Oran would have broken his heart; and had he not been familiarized to me, and conceived a very lively friendship for me before the death of his old friend, I fear the consequences would have been fatal.

Considering that change of scene would divert his melancholy, I took him with me to London. The theatres delighted him, particularly the opera, which not only accorded admirably with his taste for music; but where, as he looked round on the ornaments of the fashionable world, he seemed to be particularly comfortable, and to feel himself completely at home.

There is to a stranger something ludicrous in a first view of his countenance, which led me to introduce him only into the best society, where politeness would act as a preventive to the propensity to laugh; for he has so nice a sense of honour (which I shall observe, by the way, is peculiar to man), that if he were to be treated with any kind of contumely, he would infallibly die of a broken heart, as has been seen in some of his species.[1] With a view of ensuring him the respect of society, which always attends on rank and fortune, I have purchased him a baronetcy, and made over to him an estate. I have

---

[1] *Origin and Progress of Language,* book ii. chap. 4. [P.]

also purchased of the Duke of Rottenburgh one half of the elective franchise vested in the body of Mr. Christopher Corporate, the free, fat, and dependent burgess of the ancient and honourable borough of Onevote, who returns two members to Parliament, one of whom will shortly be Sir Oran. (*Sir Telegraph gave a long whistle.*) But before taking this important step, I am desirous that he should *finish his education.* (*Sir Telegraph whistled again.*) I mean to say, that I wish, if possible, to put a few words into his mouth, which I have hitherto found impracticable, though I do not entirely despair of ultimate success. But this circumstance, for reasons which I will give you by and by, does not at all militate against the proofs of his being a man.

SIR TELEGRAPH PAXARETT. If he be but half a man, he will be the fitter representative of half an elector ; for as that " large body corporate of one," the free, fat, and dependent burgess of Onevote, returns two members to the honourable house, Sir Oran can only be considered as the representative of half of him. But, seriously, is not your principal object an irresistible exposure of the universality and omnipotence of corruption by purchasing for an oran outang one of those seats, the sale of which is unblushingly acknowledged to be *as notorious as the sun at noonday ?* or do you really think him *one of us ?*

MR. FORESTER. I really think him a variety of the human species ; and this is a point which I have it much at heart to establish in the acknowledgment of the civilized world.

SIR TELEGRAPH PAXARETT. Buffon, whom I dip into now and then in the winter, ranks him, with Linnaeus, in the class of *Simiæ.*

MR. FORESTER. Linnaeus has given him the curious denominations of *Troglodytes, Homo nocturnus,* and *Homo silvestris* : but he evidently thought him a man : he describes him as having a hissing speech, thinking, reasoning, believing that the earth was made for him, and that he will one day be its sovereign.[1]

[1] " Homo nocturnus, Troglodytes, Silvestris, orang outang Bontii. Corpus album, incessu erectum. . . . Loquitur sibilo, cogitat, ratiocinatur, credit sui causa factam tellurem, se aliquando iterum fore imperantem."— LINNAEUS. [P.]

SIR TELEGRAPH PAXARETT. God save King Oran! By the by, you put me very much in mind of Valentine and Orson.[1] This wild man of yours will turn out some day to be the son of a king, lost in the woods, and suckled by a lioness:—" No waiter, but a knight templar : "—no Oran, but a true prince.

MR. FORESTER. As to Buffon, it is astonishing how that great naturalist could have placed him among the *singes*, when the very words of his description give him all the characteristics of human nature.[2] It is still more curious to think that modern travellers should have made beasts, under the names of Pongos, Mandrills, and Oran Outangs, of the very same beings whom the ancients

---

[1] A Carolingian Romance of twin brothers. Valentine is brought up as a knight at the court of Peppin ; Orson, reared in a bear's den, grows up wild, but is afterwards caught and tamed by Valentine whose comrade in arms he becomes. G.

[2] " Il n'a point de queue : ses bras, ses mains, ses doigts, ses ongles, sont pareils aux nôtres : il marche toujours debout : il a des traits approchans de ceux de l'homme, des oreilles de la même forme, des cheveux sur la tête, de la barbe au menton, et du poil ni plus ni moins que l'homme en a dans l'état de nature. Aussi les habitans de son pays, les Indiens policés, n'ont pas hésité de l'associer à l'espèce humaine, par le nom d'oran outang, *homme sauvage*. Si l'on ne faisoit attention qu'à la figure, on pourroit regarder l'oran outang comme le premier des singes ou le dernier des hommes, parce qu'à l'exception de l'âme, il ne lui manque rien de tout ce que nous avons, et parce qu'il diffère moins de l'homme pour le corps qu'il ne diffère des autres animaux auxquels on a donné le même nom de singe.— S'il y avoit un degré par lequel on pût descendre de la nature humaine à celle des animaux, si l'essence de cette nature consistoit en entier dans la forme du corps et dépendoit de son organisation, l'oran outang se trouveroit plus près de l'homme que d'aucun animal : assis au second rang des êtres, s'il ne pouvoit commander en premier, il feroit au moins sentir aux autres sa supériorité, et s'efforceroit à ne pas obéir : si l'imitation qui semble copier de si près la pensée en étoit le vrai signe ou l'un des résultats, il se trouveroit encore à une plus grande distance des animaux et plus voisin de l'homme."—BUFFON.

" On est tout étonné, d'après tout ces aveux, que M. de Buffon ne fasse de l'oran outang qu'une espèce de magot, essentiellement circonscrit dans les bornes de l'animalité : il falloit, ou infirmer les rélations des voyageurs, ou s'en tenir à leurs résultats.—Quand on lit dans ce naturaliste l'histoire du Nègre blanc, on voit que ce bipède diffère de nous bien plus que l'oran outang, soit par l'organisation, soit par l'intelligence, et cependant on ne balance pas à le mettre dans la classe des hommes."—*Philosophie de la Nature.* [P.]

worshipped as divinities under the names of Fauns and Satyrs, Silenus and Pan.[1]

SIR TELEGRAPH PAXARETT.   Your Oran rises rapidly in the scale of being:—from a Baronet and M.P. to a king of the world, and now to a god of the woods.

MR. FORESTER.   When I was in London last winter, I became acquainted with a learned mythologist,[2] who has long laboured to rebuild the fallen temple of Jupiter. I introduced him to Sir Oran, for whom he immediately conceived a high veneration, and would never call him by any name but Pan. His usual salutation to him was in the following words:

> ἐλθε, μακαρ, σκιρτητα, φιλενθεος, ἀντροδιαιτε,
> ἁρμονιην κοσμοιο κρεκων φιλοπαιγμονι μολπῃ,
> κοσμοκρατωρ, βακχευτα ![3]

Which he thus translated:

> King of the world! enthusiast free,
> Who dwell'st in caves of liberty!
> And on thy wild pipe's notes of glee
> Respondest Nature's harmony!
> Leading beneath the spreading tree
> The Bacchanalian revelry!

---

[1] " Les jugemens précipités, et qui ne sont point le fruit d'une raison éclairée, sont sujets à donner dans l'excès. Nos voyageurs font sans façon des bêtes, sous les noms de pongos, de mandrills, d'oran outangs, de ces mêmes êtres, dont, sous le nom de satyres, de faunes, de sylvains, les anciens faisoient des divinités. Peut-être, après des recherches plus exactes, trouvera-t-on que ce sont des hommes."—ROUSSEAU, *Discours sur l'Inégalité*, note 8.

" Il est presque démontré que les faunes, les satyres, les sylvains, les ægipans, et toute cette foule de demi-dieux, difformes et libertins, à qui les filles des Phocion et des Paul Émile s'avisèrent de rendre hommage, ne furent dans l'origine que des oran outangs. Dans la suite, les poëtes chargèrent le portrait de l'homme des bois, en lui donnant des pieds de chèvre, une queue et des cornes ; mais le type primordial resta, et le philosophe l'apperçoit dans les monumens les plus défigurés par l'imagination d'Ovide et le ciseau de Phidias. Les anciens, très embarrassés de trouver la filiation de leurs sylvains, et de leurs satyres, se tirèrent d'affaire en leur donnant des dieux pour pères : les dieux étoient d'un grand secours aux philosophes des tems reculés, pour résoudre les problèmes d'histoire naturelle ; ils leur servoient comme les cycles et les épicycles dans le système planétaire de Ptolomée : avec des cycles et des dieux on répond à tout, quoiqu'on ne satisfasse personne."—*Philosophie de la Nature*. [P.]

[2] Thomas Taylor, the Platonist, who called Peacock " Greeky Peaky."

[3] *Orphica*, Hymn. XI. (X *Gesn.*). [P.]   [G.

" This," said he, " is part of the Orphic invocation of Pan. It alludes to the happy existence of the dancing Pans, Fauns, Orans, *et id genus omne*, whose dwellings are the caves of rocks and the hollows of trees, such as undoubtedly was, or would have been, the natural mode of life of our friend Pan among the woods of Angola. It alludes, too, to their musical powers, which in our friend Pan it gives me indescribable pleasure to find so happily exemplified. The epithet *Bacchic*, our friend Pan's attachment to the bottle demonstrates to be very appropriate ; and the epithet κοσμοκρατωρ, king of the world, points out a striking similarity between the Orphic Pan and the Troglodyte of Linnaeus, *who believes that the earth was made for him, and that he will again be its sovereign.*" He laid great stress on the word AGAIN, and observed, if he were to develope all the ideas to which this word gave rise in his mind, he should find ample matter for a volume. Then repeating several times, Παν κοσμοκρατωρ, and *iterum fore telluris imperantem*, he concluded by saying, he had known many profound philosophical and mythological systems founded on much slighter analogies.

SIR TELEGRAPH PAXARETT. Your learned mythologist appears to be *non compos*.

MR. FORESTER. By no means. He has a system of his own,[1] which only appears in the present day more absurd than other systems, because it has fewer followers. The manner in which the spirit of system twists every thing to its own views is truly wonderful. I believe that in every nation of the earth the system which has most followers will be found the most absurd in the eye of an enlightened philosophy.

SIR TELEGRAPH PAXARETT. But if your Oran be a man, how is it that his long intercourse with other varieties of the human species has not taught him to speak ?

MR. FORESTER. Speech is a highly artificial faculty. Civilized

[1] Thomas Taylor embraced the Pythagorean doctrine of metempsychosis, kept a small menagerie of animals which he treated with profound respect, and was the author of a *Vindication of the Rights of Brutes*, imitated from the *Vindication of the Rights of Women* by Mary Wollstonecraft, who had lodged in his house. G.

man is a highly artificial animal. The change from the wild to the civilized state affects not only his moral but his physical nature, and this not rapidly and instantly, but in a long process of generations. The same change is obvious in domestic animals, and in cultivated plants. You know not where to look for the origin of the common dog or the common fowl. The wild and tame hog, and the wild and tame cat, are marked by more essential differences than the oran and the civilized man. The origin of corn is as much a mystery to us, as the source of the Nile was to the ancients. Innumerable flowers have been so changed from their original simplicity, that the art of horticulture may almost lay claim to the magic of a new creation. Is it then wonderful, that the civilized man should have acquired some physical faculties, which the natural man has not ? It is demonstrable that speech is one. I do not, however, despair of seeing him make some progress in this art. Comparative anatomy shows that he has all the organs of articulation. Indeed, he has in every essential particular, the human form and the human anatomy. *Now I will only observe, that if an animal who walks upright—is of the human form, both outside and inside—uses a weapon for defence and attack—associates with his kind—makes huts to defend himself from the weather, better I believe than those of the New Hollanders—is tame and gentle—and instead of killing men and women, as he could easily do, takes them prisoners, and makes servants of them—who has, what I think essential to the human kind, a sense of honour ;* which is shown by breaking his heart, if laughed at, or made a show, or treated with any kind of contumely—*who, when he is brought into the company of civilized men, behaves* (as you have seen) *with dignity and composure, altogether unlike a monkey ; from whom he differs likewise in this material respect, that he is capable of great attachment to particular persons, of which the monkey is altogether incapable ; and also in this respect, that a monkey never can be so tamed, that we may depend on his not doing mischief when left alone, by breaking glasses or china within his reach ; whereas the oran outang is altogether harmless ;—who has so much of the docility of a man, that he learns not only to do the common offices of life, but also to play on the flute* and French horn ; *which shows that he must have an idea of melody, and concord of sounds, which no brute animal has ;—and lastly, if joined to all these qualities, he has*

the organ of pronunciation, and consequently the capacity of speech,
though not the actual use of it ; if, I say, such an animal be not a man,
I should desire to know in what the essence of a man consists, and what
it is that distinguishes a natural man from the man of art.[1] That he
understands many words, though he does not yet speak any, I think
you may have observed, when you asked him to take wine, and
applied to him for fish and partridge.[2]

SIR TELEGRAPH PAXARETT. The gestures, however slight, that
accompany the expression of the ordinary forms of intercourse, may
possibly explain that.

MR. FORESTER. You will find that he understands many things
addressed to him, on occasions of very unfrequent occurrence. *With*
regard to his moral character, he is undoubtedly a man, and a much

---

[1] The words in italics are from the *Ancient Metaphysics*, vol. iii. pp. 41,
42. Lord Monboddo adds : " I hold it to be impossible to convince any
philosopher or any man of common sense, who has bestowed any time to
consider the mechanism of speech, that such various actions and configur-
ations of the organs of speech as are necessary for articulation can be
natural to man. Whoever thinks this possible, should go and see, as I
have done, Mr. Braidwood of Edinburgh, or the Abbé de l'Epée in Paris,
teach the dumb to speak ; and when he has observed all the different
actions of the organs, which those professors are obliged to mark distinctly
to their pupils with a great deal of pains and labour, so far from thinking
articulation natural to man, he will rather wonder how, by any teaching or
imitation, he should attain to the ready performance of such various and
complicated operations."

" Quoique l'organe de la parole soit naturel à l'homme, la parole elle-même
ne lui est pourtant pas naturelle."—ROUSSEAU, *Discours sur l'Inégalité,*
note 8.

" The oran outang, so accurately dissected by Tyson, had exactly the
same organs of voice that a man has."—*Ancient Metaphysics*, vol. iii. p. 44.

" I have been told that the oran outang who is to be seen in Sir Ashton
Lever's collection, had learned before he died to articulate some words."—
Ibid. p. 40. [P.]

[2] " I desire any philosopher to tell me the specific difference between an
oran outang, sitting at table, and behaving as M. de la Brosse or M. Buffon
himself has described him, and one of our dumb persons ; and in general
I believe it will be very difficult, or rather impossible, for a man who is
accustomed to divide things according to specific marks, not individual
differences, to draw the line betwixt the oran outang and the dumb persons
among us : they have both their organs of pronunciation, and both show
signs of intelligence by their actions."—*Origin and Progress of Language,*
book ii. chap. 4. [P.]

better man than many that are to be found in civilized countries,[1] as, when you are better acquainted with him, I feel very confident you will readily acknowledge.[2]

SIR TELEGRAPH PAXARETT.   I shall be very happy, when his election comes on for Onevote, to drive him down in my barouche to the ancient and honourable borough.

Mr. Forester promised to avail himself of this proposal ; when the iron tongue of midnight tolling twelve [3] induced them to separate for the night.

CHAPTER VII

THE PRINCIPLE OF POPULATION

THE next morning, while Sir Telegraph, Sir Oran, and Mr. Forester, were sitting down to their breakfast, a post-chaise rattled up to the

---

[1] *Ancient Metaphysics*, vol. iv. p. 55. [P.]

[2] " Toute la terre est couverte de nations, dont nous ne connoissons que les noms, et nous nous mêlons de juger le genre humain ! Supposons un Montesquieu, un Buffon, un Diderot, un Duclos, un d'Alembert, un Condillac, ou des hommes de cette trempe, voyageant pour instruire leurs compatriotes, observant et décrivant comme ils sçavent faire, la Turquie, l'Égypte, la Barbarie, l'Empire de Maroc, la Guinée, le pays des Caffres, l'intérieur de l'Afrique et ses côtes orientales, les Malabares, le Mogol, les rives du Gange, les royaumes de Siam, de Pégu et d'Ava, la Chine, la Tartarie, et sur-tout le Japon ; puis dans l'autre hémisphère le Méxique, le Pérou, le Chili, les Terres Magellaniques, sans oublier les Patagons vrais ou faux, le Tucuman, le Paraguai, s'il étoit possible, le Brésil, enfin les Caraïbes, la Floride, et toutes les contrées sauvages, voyage le plus important de tous, et celui qu'il faudroit faire avec le plus de soin ; supposons que ces nouveaux Hercules, de retour de ces courses mémorables, fissent en suite à loisir l'histoire naturelle, morale, et politique de ce qu'ils auroient vus, nous verrions nous-mêmes sortir un monde nouveau de dessous leur plume, et nous apprendrions ainsi à connoître le nôtre : je dis que quand de pareils observateurs affirmeront d'un tel animal que c'est un homme, et d'un autre que c'est une bête, il faudra les en croire ; mais ce seroit une grande simplicité de s'en rapporter là-dessus à des voyageurs grossiers, sur lesquels on seroit quelquefois tenté de faire la même question qu'ils se mêlent de résoudre sur d'autres animaux."—ROUSSEAU, *Discours sur l'Inégalité*, note 8. [P.]

[3] *A Midsummer Night's Dream*, Act V, Sc. 1 :

  " The iron tongue of midnight hath told twelve ;
   Lovers to bed ; 'tis almost fairy time."   G.

door ; the glass was let down, and a tall, thin, pale, grave-looking
personage peeped from the aperture. " This is Mr. Fax," said Mr.
Forester, " the champion of calm reason, the indefatigable explorer
of the cold clear springs of knowledge, the bearer of the torch of
dispassionate truth, that gives more light than warmth. He looks
on the human world, the world of mind, the conflict of interests, the
collision of feelings, the infinitely diversified developments of energy
and intelligence, as a mathematician looks on his diagrams, or a
mechanist on his wheels and pulleys, as if they were foreign to his
own nature, and were nothing more than subjects of curious
speculation." [1]

Mr. Forester had not time to say more ; for Mr. Fax entered, and
shook hands with him, was introduced in due form to Sir Telegraph,
and sate down to assist in the demolition of the *matériel* of breakfast.

MR. FAX. Your Redrose Abbey is a beautiful metamorphosis.—
I can scarcely believe that these are the mouldering walls of the pious
fraternity of Rednose, which I contemplated two years ago.

MR. FORESTER. The picturesque tourists will owe me no goodwill
for the metamorphosis, though I have endeavoured to leave them as
much mould, mildew, and weather-stain as possible.

MR. FAX. The exterior has suffered little ; it still retains a truly
venerable monastic character.

SIR TELEGRAPH PAXARETT. Something monastic in the interior too.
—Very orthodox old wine in the cellar, I can tell you. And the
Reverend Father Abbot there, as determined a bachelor as the Pope.

MR. FORESTER. If I am so, it is because, like the Squire of Dames,[2]
I seek and cannot find. I see in my mind's eye the woman I would
choose, but I very much fear that is the only mode of optics, in which
she will ever be visible.

---

[1] Mr. Fax is based on Malthus. G.
[2] Spenser : *The Faerie Queene*, Bk. III, Canto 7, St. 51. The Squire of
Dames was punished by his lady-love by being ordered to woo her sex
promiscuously until he had been refused three hundred times, but in three
years he only met three women who refused him, a harlot and a nun for
professional reasons, and a cottage girl because of her real chastity. G.

MR. FAX. No matter. Bachelors and spinsters I decidedly venerate. The world is overstocked with featherless bipeds. More men than corn, is a fearful pre-eminence, the sole and fruitful cause of penury, disease, and war, plague, pestilence, and famine.

SIR TELEGRAPH PAXARETT. I hope you will not long have cause to venerate me. What is life without love ? A rose-bush in winter, all thorns, and no flowers.

MR. FAX. And what is it with love. A double-blossomed cherry, flowers without fruit ; if the blossoms last a month, it is as much as can be expected : they fall, and what comes in their place ? Vanity, and vexation of spirit.

SIR TELEGRAPH PAXARETT. Better vexation, than stagnation : marriage may often be a stormy lake, but celibacy is almost always a muddy horsepond.

MR. FAX. Rather a calm clear river——

MR. FORESTER. Flowing through a desert, where it moves in loneliness, and reflects no forms of beauty.

MR. FAX. That is not the way to consider the case. Feelings and poetical images are equally out of place in a calm philosophical view of human society. Some must marry, that the world may be peopled : [1] many must abstain, that it may not be overstocked. *Little and good*, is very applicable in this case. It is better that the world should have a smaller number of peaceable and rational inhabitants, living in universal harmony and social intercourse, than the disproportionate mass of fools, slaves, coxcombs, thieves, rascals, liars, and cut-throats, with which its surface is at present encumbered. It is in vain to declaim about the preponderance of physical and moral evil, and attribute it, with the Manicheans, to a mythological principle, or, with some modern philosophers, to the physical constitution of the globe. The cause of all the evils of human society is single, obvious, reducible to the most exact mathematical calculation ; and of course susceptible not only of remedy, but even of utter annihilation. The cause is the tendency of population to

[1] Compare *Much Ado About Nothing*, Act II, Sc. 3.   G.

increase beyond the means of subsistence. The remedy is an universal social compact, binding both sexes to equally rigid celibacy, till the prospect of maintaining the average number of six children be as clear as the arithmetic of futurity can make it.

MR. FORESTER. The arithmetic of futurity has been found in a more than equal number of instances to baffle human skill. The rapid and sudden mutations of fortune are the inexhaustible theme of history, poetry, and romance; and they are found in forms as various and surprising, in the scenes of daily life, as on the stage of Drury Lane.

MR. FAX. That the best prospects are often overshadowed, is most certainly true; but there are degrees and modes of well-grounded reliance on futurity, sufficient to justify the enterprises of prudence, and equally well-grounded prospiciencies of hopelessness and helplessness, that should check the steps of rashness and passion, in their headlong progress to perdition.

MR. FORESTER. You have little cause to complain of the present age. It is calculating enough to gratify the most determined votary of moral and political arithmetic. This certainly is not the time,

"When unrevenged stalks Cocker's injured ghost." [1]

What is friendship—except in some most rare and miraculous instances—but the fictitious bond of interest, or the heartless intercourse of idleness and vanity? What is love, but the most venal of all venal commodities? What is marriage, but the most sordid of bargains, the most cold and slavish of all the forms of commerce? We want no philosophical ice-rock, towed into the Dead Sea of modern society, to freeze that which is too cold already. We want rather the torch of Prometheus to revivify our frozen spirits. We are a degenerate race, half-reasoning developments of the principle of infinite littleness, "with hearts in our bodies, no bigger than pins' heads." [2] We are in no danger of forgetting that two and two make

---

[1] A witty embroidery on *Hudibras*, Pt. I, Canto 2, line 498. Cocker was the author of Cocker's Arithmetic. Hence "According to Cocker." G.

[2] *Henry IV*, *Pt. I*, Act IV, Sc. 2. Peacock has either bowdlerised "bellies" to "bodies" or was using a bowdlerised edition. G.

four. There is no fear that the warm impulses of feeling will ever overpower, with us, the tangible eloquence of the pocket.

MR. FAX. With relation to the middle and higher classes, you are right in a great measure as to fact, but wrong, as I think, in the asperity of your censure. But among the lower orders the case is quite different. The baleful influence of the poor laws has utterly destroyed the principle of calculation in them. They marry by wholesale, without scruple or compunction, and commit the future care of their family to Providence and the overseer. They marry even in the workhouse, and convert the intended asylum of age and infirmity, into a flourishing manufactory of young beggars and vagabonds.

Sir Telegraph's barouche rolled up gracefully to the door. Mr. Forester pressed him to stay another day, but Sir Telegraph's plea of urgency was not to be overcome. He promised very shortly to revisit Redrose Abbey, shook hands with Mr. Forester and Sir Oran, bowed politely to Mr. Fax, mounted his box, and disappeared among the trees.

" Those four horses," said Mr. Fax, as the carriage rolled away, " consume the subsistence of eight human beings, for the foolish amusement of one. As Solomon observes : ' This is vanity, and a great evil.' "

" Sir Telegraph is thoughtless," said Mr. Forester, " but he has a good heart and a good natural capacity. I have great hopes of him. He had some learning, when he went to college ; but he was cured of it before he came away. Great, indeed, must be the zeal for improvement, which an academical education cannot extinguish."

CHAPTER VIII

THE SPIRIT OF CHIVALRY

SIR TELEGRAPH was welcomed to Melincourt in due form by Mr. Hippy, and in a private interview with the Honourable Mrs. Pinmoney, was exhorted to persevere in his suit to Anthelia, though she could not flatter him with very strong hopes of immediate success, the young lady's notions being, as she observed, extremely outré and fantastical, but such as she had no doubt time and experience would cure. She informed him at the same time, that he would shortly meet a formidable rival, no less a personage than Lord Anophel Achthar,[1] son and heir of the Marquis of Agaric,[2] who was somewhat in favour with Mr. Hippy, and seemed determined at all hazards to carry his point; " and with any other girl than Anthelia," said Mrs. Pinmoney, " considering his title and fortune, I should pronounce his success infallible, unless a Duke were to make his appearance." She added, " the young lord would be accompanied by his tutor, the Reverend Mr. Grovelgrub, and by a celebrated poet, Mr. Feathernest,[3] to whom the Marquis had recently given a place in exchange for his conscience. It was thought by Mr. Feathernest's friends, that he had made a very good bargain. The poet had, in consequence, burned his old Odes to Truth and Liberty, and had published a volume of Panegyrical Addresses ' to all the crowned heads in Europe,' with the motto, ' Whatever is at court, is right.' " [4]

The dinner party that day at Melincourt Castle consisted of Mr. Hippy, in the character of lord of the mansion; Anthelia, in that of his inmate; Mrs. and Miss Pinmoney, as her visitors; and Sir Telegraph, as the visitor of Mrs. Pinmoney, seconded by Mr. Hippy's invitation to stay. Nothing very luminous passed on this occasion.

The fame of Mr. Hippy, and his hospitable office, was rapidly diffused by Dr. Killquick, the physician of the district; who thought a draught or pill could not possibly be efficacious, unless administered with an anecdote, and who was called in, in a very few hours after Mr. Hippy's arrival, to cure the hypochondriacal old gentleman of an imaginary swelling in his elbow. The learned doctor, who had studied with peculiar care the symptoms, diagnostics, prognostics,

---

[1] *ΑΝΩΦΕΛον ΑΧΘος ΑΡουρας. Terrae pondus inutile.* [P.] [" A useless cumber of the ground." G.]

[2] AGARICUS, in Botany, a genus of plants of the class Cryptogamia, comprehending the mushroom, and a copious variety of toadstools. [P.]

[3] Southey. G.

[4] In 1814 Southey had published *Carmina Aulica*, a sequence of odes " on the Arrival of the Allied Sovereigns in England." Its motto consisted of lines 11 and 12 of Pindar's thirteenth Olympiad, which may be translated : " I have noble things to say, and courage unerring urges me to speak." G.

sedatives, lenitives, and sanatives of hypochondriasis, had arrived
at the sagacious conclusion, that the most effectual method of curing
an imaginary disease was to give the patient a real one ; and he
accordingly sent Mr. Hippy a pint bottle of mixture, to be taken by
a table-spoonful every two hours, which would have infallibly accomplished the purpose, but that the bottle was cracked over the head of
Harry Fell, for treading on his master's toe, as he presented the
composing potion, which would perhaps have composed him in the
Roman sense.

The fashionable attractions of Low-wood and Keswick [1] afforded
facilities to some of Anthelia's lovers to effect a *logement* in her
neighbourhood, from whence occasionally riding over to Melincourt
Castle, they were hospitably received by the lord seneschal, Humphrey Hippy, Esquire, who often made them fixed stars in the
circumference of that jovial system, of which the bottle and glasses
are the sun and planets, till it was too late to dislodge for the night ;
by which means they sometimes contrived to pass several days
together at the Castle.

The gentlemen in question were Lord Anophel Achthar, with his
two parasites, Mr. Feathernest, and the Reverend Mr. Grovelgrub ;
Harum O'Scarum, Esquire, the sole proprietor of a vast tract of
undrained bog in the county of Kerry; and Mr. Derrydown,[2] the only
son of an old lady in London, who having in vain solicited a visit
from Anthelia, had sent off her hopeful progeny to try his fortune in
Westmoreland. Mr. Derrydown had received a laborious education,
and had consumed a great quantity of midnight oil, over ponderous
tomes of ancient and modern learning, particularly of moral, political,
and metaphysical philosophy, ancient and modern. His lucubra-
tions in the latter branch of science having conducted him, as he
conceived, into the central opacity of utter darkness, he formed a
hasty conclusion " that all human learning is vanity " ; and one day
in a listless mood, taking down a volume of the Reliques of Ancient
Poetry, he found, or fancied he found, in the plain language of the old

[1] Southey and Coleridge lived at Greta Hall, Keswick. The Ruskin
family used to stay at Lowwood Inn in the 1820's and Ruskin describes it
as " a mere cottage." G.
[2] Based upon Sir Walter Scott. G.

English ballad, glimpses of the truth of things, which he had vainly sought in the vast volumes of philosophical disquisition. In consequence of this luminous discovery, he locked up his library, purchased a travelling chariot, with a shelf in the back, which he filled with collections of ballads, and popular songs; and passed the greater part of every year in posting about the country, for the purpose, as he expressed it, of studying together poetry and the peasantry, unsophisticated nature and the truth of things.

Mr. Hippy introduced Lord Anophel, and his two learned friends, to Sir Telegraph, and Mrs. and Miss Pinmoney. Mr. Feathernest whispered to the Reverend Mr. Grovelgrub, " This Sir Telegraph Paxarett has some good livings in his gift : " which bent the plump figure of the reverend gentleman into a very orthodox right angle.

Anthelia, who felt no inclination to show particular favour to any one of her Strephons, was not sorry to escape the evil of a solitary persecutor, more especially as they so far resembled the suitors of Penelope, as to eat and drink together with great cordiality. She could have wished, when she left them to the congenial society of Bacchus, to have retired to company more congenial to her, than that of Mrs. Pinmoney and Miss Danaretta : but she submitted to the course of necessity with the best possible grace.

She explicitly made known to all her suitors her ideas on the subject of marriage. She had never perverted the simplicity of her mind, by indulging in the usual cant of young ladies, that she should prefer a single life : but she assured them that the spirit of the age of chivalry, manifested in the forms of modern life, would constitute the only character on which she could fix her affections.

Lord Anophel was puzzled, and applied for information to his tutor. " Grovelgrub," said he, " what is the spirit of the age of chivalry ? "

" Really, my Lord," said the Reverend Mr. Grovelgrub, " my studies never lay that way."

" True," said Lord Anophel ; " it was not necessary to your degree."

His Lordship's next recourse was to Mr. Feathernest. " Feathernest, what is the spirit of the age of chivalry ? "

Mr. Feathernest was taken by surprise. Since his profitable

metamorphosis into an *ami du prince*,[1] he had never dreamed of such a question. It burst upon him like the spectre of his youthful integrity, and he mumbled a half-intelligible reply, about truth and liberty—disinterested benevolence—self-oblivion—heroic devotion to love and honour—protection of the feeble, and subversion of tyranny.

"All the ingredients of a rank Jacobin, Feathernest, 'pon honour!" exclaimed his Lordship.

There was something in the word Jacobin very grating to the ears of Mr. Feathernest, and he feared he had thrown himself between the horns of a dilemma; but from all such predicaments he was happily provided with an infallible means of extrication. His friend Mr. Mystic,[2] of Cimmerian Lodge, had initiated him in some of the mysteries of the transcendental philosophy, which on this, as on all similar occasions, he called in to his assistance; and overwhelmed his Lordship with a volley of ponderous jargon, which left him in profound astonishment at the depth of Mr. Feathernest's knowledge.

"The spirit of the age of chivalry!" soliloquized Mr. O'Scarum; "I think I know what that is: I'll shoot all my rivals, one after another, as fast as I can find a decent pretext for picking a quarrel. I'll write to my friend Major O'Dogskin to come to Low-wood Inn, and hold himself in readiness. He is the neatest hand in Ireland at delivering a challenge."

"The spirit of the age of chivalry!" soliloquized Mr. Derrydown: "I think I am at home there. I will be a knight of the round table. I will be Sir Lancelot, or Sir Gawaine, or Sir Tristram. No: I will be a troubadour—a love-lorn minstrel. I will write the most irresistible ballads in praise of the beautiful Anthelia. She shall be my lady of the lake. We will sail about Ulleswater in our pinnace, and sing duets about Merlin, and King Arthur, and Fairyland. I will develope the idea to her in a ballad: it cannot fail to fascinate her romantic spirit." And down he sate to put his scheme in execution.

Sir Telegraph's head ran on tilts and tournaments, and trials of skill and courage. How could they be resolved into the forms of modern life? A four-in-hand race he thought would be a pretty substitute: Anthelia to be arbitress of the contest, and place the

---

[1] See *Maid Marian*, p. 491. G.   [2] Coleridge. G.

Olympic wreath on the head of the victor, which he had no doubt would be himself, though Harum O'Scarum, Esquire, would dash through neck or nothing, and Lord Anophel Achthar was reckoned one of the best coachmen in England.

CHAPTER IX

THE PHILOSOPHY OF BALLADS

THE very indifferent success of Lord Anophel did not escape the eye of his abject slave, the Reverend Mr. Grovelgrub, whose vanity led him to misinterpret Anthelia's general sweetness of manner into the manifestation of something like a predilection for himself. Having made this notable discovery, he sate down to calculate the probability of his chance of Miss Melincourt's fortune on the one hand, and the certainty of church-preferment, through the patronage of the Marquis of Agaric, on the other. The sagacious reflection, that a bird in the hand was worth two in the bush, determined him not to risk the loss of the Marquis's favour for the open pursuit of a doubtful success; but he resolved to carry on a secret attack on the affections of Anthelia, and not to throw off the mask to Lord Anophel till he could make sure of his prize.

It would have totally disconcerted the schemes of the Honourable Mrs. Pinmoney, if Lord Anophel had made any progress in the favour of Anthelia—not only because she had made up her mind that her young friend should be her niece and Lady Paxarett, but because, from the moment of Lord Anophel's appearance, she determined on drawing lines of circumvallation round him, to compel him to surrender at discretion to her dear Danaretta, who was very willing to second her views. That Lord Anophel was both a fool and a coxcomb, did not strike her at all as an objection; on the contrary, she considered them as very favourable circumstances for the facilitation of her design.

As Anthelia usually passed the morning in the seclusion of her library, Lord Anophel and the Reverend Mr. Grovelgrub killed the time in shooting; Sir Telegraph, in driving Mrs. and Miss Pinmoney in his barouche, to astonish the natives of the mountain-villages ; Harum O'Scarum, Esquire, in riding full gallop along the best roads, looking every now and then at his watch, to see how time went ; Mr. Derrydown, in composing his troubadour ballad ; Mr. Feathernest, in writing odes to all the crowned heads in Europe ; and Mr. Hippy, in getting very ill after breakfast every day of a new disease, which came to its climax at the intermediate point of time between breakfast and dinner, showed symptoms of great amendment at the ringing of the first dinner-bell, was very much alleviated at the butler's summons, vanished entirely at the sight of Anthelia, and was consigned to utter oblivion after the ladies retired from table, when the Reverend Mr. Grovelgrub lent his clerical assistance to lay its ghost in the Red Sea of a copious libation of claret.

Music and conversation consumed the evenings.   Mr. Feathernest and Mr. Derrydown were both zealous admirers of old English literature ; but the former was chiefly enraptured with the ecclesiastical writers and the translation of the Bible ; the latter admired nothing but ballads, which he maintained to be, whether ancient or modern, the only manifestations of feeling and thought containing any vestige of truth and nature.

" Surely," said Mr. Feathernest one evening, " you will not maintain that Chevy Chase is a finer poem than Paradise Lost ? "

MR. DERRYDOWN.   I do not know what you mean by a fine poem ; but I will maintain that it gives a much deeper insight into the truth of things.

MR. FEATHERNEST.   I do not know what you mean by the truth of things.

THE REVEREND MR. GROVELGRUB.   Define, gentlemen, define : let the one explain what he means by a fine poem, and the other what he means by the truth of things.

MR. FEATHERNEST.   A fine poem is a luminous development of the complicated machinery of action and passion, exalted by sublimity, softened by pathos, irradiated with scenes of magnificence, figures of loveliness and characters of energy, and harmonized with infinite variety of melodious combination.

LORD ANOPHEL ACHTHAR. Admirable!

MISS DANARETTA CONTANTINA PINMONEY. Admirable, indeed, my Lord! (*With a sweet smile at his Lordship, which unluckily missed fire.*)

THE REVEREND MR. GROVELGRUB. Now, Sir, for the truth of things.

MR. O'SCARUM. Troth, Sir, that is the last point about which I should expect a gentleman of your cloth to be very solicitous.

THE REVEREND MR. GROVELGRUB. I must say, Sir, that is a very uncalled for, and very illiberal observation.

MR. O'SCARUM. Your coat is your protection, Sir.

THE REVEREND MR. GROVELGRUB. I will appeal to his Lordship if——

MR. O'SCARUM. I shall be glad to know his Lordship's opinion.

LORD ANOPHEL ACHTHAR. Really, Sir, I have no opinion on the subject.

MR. O'SCARUM. I am sorry for it, my Lord.

MR. DERRYDOWN. The truth of things is nothing more than an exact view of the necessary relations between object and subject, in all the modes of reflection and sentiment which constitute the reciprocities of human association.

THE REVEREND MR. GROVELGRUB. I must confess I do not exactly comprehend——

MR. DERRYDOWN. I will illustrate. You all know the ballad of Old Robin Gray.

> Young Jamie loved me well, and asked me for his bride ;
> But saving a crown, he had nothing else beside.
> To make the crown a pound my Jamie went to sea,
> And the crown and the pound they were both for me.
>
> He had not been gone a twelvemonth and a day,
> When my father broke his arm, and our cow was stolen away ;
> My mother she fell sick, and Jamie at the sea,
> And old Robin Gray came a courting to me.

In consequence whereof, as you all very well know, old Robin being rich, the damsel married the aforesaid old Robin.

THE REVEREND MR. GROVELGRUB.   In the heterodox kirk of the north ?

MR. DERRYDOWN.   Precisely.   Now, in this short space, you have a more profound view than the deepest metaphysical treatise or the most elaborate history can give you of the counteracting power of opposite affections, the conflict of duties and inclinations, the omnipotence of interest, tried by the test of extremity, and the supreme and irresistible dominion of universal moral necessity.

"Young Jamie loved me well, and asked me for his bride ; "

and would have had her, it is clear, though she does not explicitly say so, if there had not been a necessary moral motive counteracting what would have been otherwise the plain free will of both.   " Young Jamie loved me well."   She does not say that she loved young Jamie ;   and here is a striking illustration of that female decorum which forbids young ladies to speak as they think on any subject whatever :   an admirable political institution, which has been found by experience to be most happily conducive to that ingenuousness of mind and simplicity of manner which constitute so striking a charm in the generality of the fair sex.

"But saving a crown, he had nothing else beside."

Here is the quintessence of all that has been said and written on the subject of love and prudence, a decisive refutation of the stoical doctrine that poverty is no evil, a very clear and deep insight into the nature of the preventive or prudential check to population, and a particularly luminous view of the respective conduct of the two sexes on similar occasions.   The poor love-stricken swain, it seems, is ready to sacrifice all for love.   He comes with a crown in his pocket, and asks her for his bride.   The damsel is a better arithmetician.   She is fully impressed with the truth of the old proverb about poverty coming in at the door, and immediately stops him short, with " What can you settle on me, Master Jamie ? " or, as Captain Bobadil[1] would

[1] Ben Jonson : *Every Man in his Humour*, Act I, Sc. 5.   G.

express it, " How much money ha' you about you, Master Matthew ? "
Poor Jamie looks very foolish—fumbles in his pocket—produces his
crown-piece—and answers like Master Matthew, with a remarkable
elongation of visage, " 'Faith, I ha'n't past a five shillings or so."
" Then," says the young lady, in the words of another very admirable
ballad—where you will observe it is also the damsel who asks the
question :

> " Will the love that you're so rich in,
> Make a fire in the kitchen ? " [1]

On which the poor lover shakes his head, and the lady gives him
leave of absence.   Hereupon Jamie falls into a train of reflections.

MR. O'SCARUM.   Never mind his reflections.

MR. DERRYDOWN.   The result of which is, that he goes to seek his
fortune at sea ; intending, with the most perfect and disinterested
affection, to give all he can get to his mistress, who seems much
pleased with the idea of having it.   But when he comes back, as you
will see in the sequel, he finds his mistress married to a rich old man.
The detail of the circumstances abounds with vast and luminous
views of human nature and society, and striking illustrations of the
truth of things.

MR. FEATHERNEST.   I do not yet see that the illustration throws
any light on the definition, or that we are at all advanced in the
answer to the question concerning Chevy Chase and Paradise Lost.

MR. DERRYDOWN.   We will examine Chevy Chase, then, with a
view to the truth of things, instead of Old Robin Gray :

> " God prosper long our noble king,
> Our lives and safeties all."

---

[1] See Halliwell's *Nursery Rhymes* (" There was a little man," etc.).   The
first printing I can find was on a single-sheet broadsheet at Strawberry Hill.
On May 31st, 1764, Horace Walpole wrote in his Printing-Office Journal :
" Printed some copies of a ballad by Sr Ch. Sidley, beginning, There was
a little Man."   The author seems likely to have been Sir Charles Sedley
(? 1721–1778), a great-grandson of the Restoration wit and a fellow
member of White's with Walpole.   As printed in the broadsheet these
lines run :

> " Will the flames you're only rich in, make a fire in the kitchen,
> And the little God of Love turn the spit ? "   G.

MR. O'SCARUM. God prosper us all, indeed! if you are going through Chevy Chase at the same rate as you were through Old Robin Gray, there is an end of us all for a month. The truth of things, now!—is it that you're looking for? Ask Miss Melincourt to touch the harp. The harp is the great key to the truth of things; and in the hand of Miss Melincourt it will teach you the music of the spheres, the concord of creation, and the harmony of the universe.

ANTHELIA. You are a libeller of our sex, Mr. Derrydown, if you think the truth of things consists in showing it to be more governed by the meanest species of self-interest than yours. Few, indeed, are the individuals of either in whom the spirit of the age of chivalry survives.

MR. DERRYDOWN. And yet, a man distinguished by that spirit would not be in society what Miss Melincourt is—a phœnix. Many knights can wield the sword of Orlando,[1] but only one nymph can wear the girdle of Florimel.[2]

THE HONOURABLE MRS. PINMONEY. That would be a very pretty compliment, Mr. Derrydown, if there were no other ladies in the room.

Poor Mr. Derrydown looked a little disconcerted: he felt conscious that he had on this occasion lost sight of his usual politeness by too close an adherence to the truth of things.

ANTHELIA. Both sexes, I am afraid, are too much influenced by the spirit of mercenary calculation. The desire of competence is prudence; but the desire of more than competence is avarice: it is against the latter only that moral censure should be directed: but I fear that in ninety-nine cases out of an hundred in which the course of true love is thwarted by considerations of fortune, it will be found that avarice rather than prudence is to be considered as the cause. Love in the age of chivalry, and love in the age of commerce, are

[1] The king of Sericana declared war on Charlemagne to obtain Orlando's sword, Durindana, in Boiardo's *Orlando Innamorato.* G.

[2] Spenser: *The Faerie Queene*, Bk. IV, C. 5. V. xviii and xix. Florimel could not wear her girdle after she had proved false and unchaste, and, of the assembled ladies, only Amoret could wear it. G.

certainly two very different deities ; so much so, that the former
may almost be regarded as a departed power ; and, perhaps, the little
ballad I am about to sing does not contain too severe an allegory in
placing the tomb of chivalric love among the ruins of the castles of
romance.

THE TOMB OF LOVE.

By the mossy weed-flowered column,
　　Where the setting moonbeam's glance
Streams a radiance cold and solemn
　　On the haunts of old romance :
Know'st thou what those shafts betoken,
　　Scattered on that tablet lone,
Where the ivory bow lies broken
　　By the monumental stone ?

When true knighthood's shield, neglected,
　　Mouldered in the empty hall ;
When the charms that shield protected
　　Slept in death's eternal thrall ;
When chivalric glory perished
　　Like the pageant of a dream,
Love in vain its memory cherished,
　　Fired in vain the minstrel's theme.

Falsehood to an elvish minion
　　Did the form of Love impart :
Cunning plumed its vampire pinion ;
　　Avarice tipped its golden dart.
Love, the hideous phantom flying,
　　Hither came, no more to rove :
There his broken bow is lying
　　On that stone—the tomb of Love !

CHAPTER X

THE TORRENT

ANTHELIA did not wish to condemn herself to celibacy, but in none
of her present suitors could she discover any trace of the character
she had drawn in her mind for the companion of her life : yet she was
aware of the rashness of precipitate judgments, and willing to avail
herself of this opportunity of studying the kind of beings that constitute modern society.　She was happy in the long interval between

breakfast and dinner, to retire to the seclusion of her favourite apartment; whence she sometimes wandered into the shades of her shrubbery: sometimes passing onward through a little postern door, she descended a flight of rugged steps, which had been cut in the solid stone, into the gloomy glen of the torrent that dashed round the base of the castle rock; and following a lonely path through the woods that fringed its sides, wandered into the deepest recesses of mountain solitude. The sunshine of a fine autumnal day, the solemn beauty of the fading woods, the thin grey mist, that spread waveless over the mountains, the silence of the air, the deep stillness of nature, broken only by the sound of the eternal streams, tempted her on one occasion beyond her usual limits.

Passing over the steep and wood-fringed hills of rock that formed the boundary of the valley of Melincourt, she descended through a grove of pines, into a romantic chasm, where a foaming stream was crossed by a rude and ancient bridge, consisting of two distinct parts, each of which rested against a columnar rock, that formed an island in the roaring waters. An ash had fixed its roots in the fissures of the rock, and the knotted base of its aged trunk offered to the passenger a natural seat, over-canopied with its beautiful branches, and leaves, now tinged with their autumnal yellow. Anthelia rested awhile in this delightful solitude. There was no breath of wind, no song of birds, no humming of insects, only the dashing of the waters beneath. She felt the presence of the genius of the scene. She sate absorbed in a train of contemplations, dimly defined, but infinitely delightful: emotions rather than thoughts, which attention would have utterly dissipated, if it had paused to seize their images.

She was roused from her reverie by sounds of music, issuing from the grove of pines, through which she had just passed, and which skirted the hollow. The notes were wild and irregular, but their effect was singular and pleasing. They ceased. Anthelia looked to the spot from which they had proceeded, and saw, or thought she saw, a face peeping at her through the trees; but the glimpse was momentary. There was in the expression of the countenance, something so extraordinary, that she almost felt convinced her imagination had created it; yet her imagination was not in the habit of creating such physiognomies. She could not, however, apprehend that this remarkable vision portended any evil to her ; for, if so, alone and defenceless as she was, why should it be deferred ? She rose, therefore, to pursue her walk, and ascended, by a narrow winding path, the brow of a lofty hill, which sunk precipitously on the other side, to the margin of a lake, that seemed to slumber in the same eternal stillness as the rocks that bordered it. The murmur of the torrent was inaudible at that elevation. There was an almost oppressive silence in the air. The motion and life of nature seemed suspended. The grey mist that hung on the mountains spreading its thin transparent uniform veil over the whole surrounding scene, gave a deeper impression to the mystery of loneliness, the predominant feeling that pressed on the mind of Anthelia, to seem the only thing that lived and moved in all that wide and awful scene of beauty.

Suddenly the grey mist fled before the rising wind, and a deep black line of clouds appeared in the west, that rising rapidly, volume on volume, obscured in a few minutes the whole face of the heavens. There was no interval of preparation, no notice for retreat. The rain burst down in a sheeted cataract, comparable only to the bursting of a waterspout. The sides of the mountains gleamed at once with a thousand torrents. Every little hollow and rain-worn channel, which but a few minutes before was dry, became instantaneously the bed of a foaming stream. Every half-visible rivulet swelled to a powerful and turbid river. Anthelia glided down the hill like an Oread, but the wet and slippery footing of the steep descent necessarily retarded her progress. When she regained the bridge, the swollen torrent had filled the chasm beneath, and was still rising like a rapid and impetuous tide, rushing and roaring along with boiling tumult and inconceivable swiftness. She had passed one half of the bridge—she had gained the insular rock—a few steps would have placed her on the other side of the chasm—when a large trunk of an oak, which months, perhaps years before had baffled the woodman's skill, and fallen into the dingle above, now disengaged by the flood, and hurled onward with irresistible strength, with large and projecting boughs towering high above the surface, struck the arch she had yet to pass, which, shattered into instant ruin, seemed to melt like snow into the torrent, leaving scarcely a vestige of its place.

Anthelia followed the trunk with her eyes till it disappeared among the rocks, and stood gazing on the torrent with feelings of awful delight. The contemplation of the mighty energies of nature, energies of liberty and power which nothing could resist or impede, absorbed, for a time, all considerations of the difficulty of regaining her home. The water continued to rise, but still she stood rivetted to the spot, watching with breathless interest its tumultuous revolutions. She dreamed not, that its increasing pressure was mining the foundation of the arch she had passed. She was roused from her reverie only by the sound of its dissolution. She looked back, and found herself on the solitary rock insulated by the swelling flood.

Would the flood rise above the level of the rock ? The ash must in that case be her refuge. Could the force of the torrent rend its massy roots from the rocky fissures which grasped them with giant strength ? Nothing could seem less likely : yet it was not impossible. But she had always looked with calmness on the course of necessity : she felt that she was always in the order of nature. Though her life had been a series of uniform prosperity, she had considered deeply the changes of things, and *the nearness of the paths of night and day* [1] in every pursuit and circumstance of human life. She sate on the stem of the ash. The torrent rolled almost at her feet. Could this be the calm sweet scene of the morning, the ivied bridges, the romantic chasm, the stream far below, bright in its bed of rocks, chequered by the pale sunbeams through the leaves of the ash ?

She looked towards the pine-grove, through which she had descended in the morning ; she thought of the wild music she had heard, and of the strange face that had appeared among the trees. Suddenly it appeared again : and shortly after, a stranger issuing from the wood, ran with surprising speed to the edge of the chasm.

Anthelia had never seen so singular a physiognomy ; but there was nothing in it to cause alarm. The stranger seemed interested for her situation, and made gestures expressive of a design to assist her. He paused a moment, as if measuring with his eyes the breadth of the chasm, and then returning to the grove, proceeded very deliberately

[1] Σγγνς γαρ νυκτος τε και ηματος εισι κελευθοι. [P.] [Homer : *Od.* X. 86. G.]

to pull up a pine.[1]   Anthelia thought him mad ; but infinite was her astonishment to see the tree sway and bend beneath the efforts of his incredible strength, till at length he tore it from the soil, and bore it on his shoulders to the chasm : where placing one end on a high point of the bank, and lowering the other on the insulated rock, he ran like a flash of lightning along the stem, caught Anthelia in his arms, and carried her safely over in an instant : not that we should wish the reader to suppose, our heroine, a mountaineer from her infancy, could not have crossed a pine-bridge without such assistance ; but the stranger gave her no time to try the experiment.

The remarkable physiognomy and unparalleled strength of the stranger, caused much of surprise, and something of apprehension, to mingle with Anthelia's gratitude : but the air of high fashion, which characterized his whole deportment, diminished her apprehension, while it increased her surprise at the exploit he had performed.

Shouts were now heard in the wood, from which shortly emerged Mr. Hippy, Lord Anophel Achthar, and the Reverend Mr. Grovelgrub.   Anthelia had been missed at Melincourt at the commencement of the storm, and Mr. Hippy had been half distracted on the occasion. The whole party had in consequence dispersed in various directions in search of her, and accident had directed these three gentlemen to the spot where Anthelia was just set down by her polite deliverer, Sir Oran Haut-ton, Baronet.

Mr. Hippy ran up with great alacrity to Anthelia, assuring her that at the time when Miss Danaretta Contantina Pinmoney informed him his dear niece was missing, he was suffering under a complete paralysis of his right leg, and was on the point of swallowing a potion sent to him by Dr. Killquick, which, on receiving the alarming intelligence, he had thrown out of the window, and he believed it had alighted on the doctor's head, as he was crossing the court.   Anthelia communicated to him the particulars of the signal service she had

---

[1] " Ils sont si robustes, dit le traducteur de l'Histoire des Voyages, que dix hommes ne suffiroient pas pour les arrêter."—ROUSSEAU.

" The oran outang is prodigiously strong."—*Ancient Metaphysics*, vol. iv. p. 51 ; vol. v. p. 4.

" I have heard the natives say, he can throw down a palm-tree, by his amazing strength, to come at the wine."—*Letter of a Bristol Merchant, in a note to the Origin and Progress of Language*, book ii. chap. 4.   [P.]

received from the stranger, whom Mr. Hippy stared at heartily, and shook hands with cordially.

Lord Anophel now came up, and surveyed Sir Oran through his quizzing-glass, who making him a polite bow, took his quizzing-glass from him, and examined him through it, in the same manner. Lord Anophel flew into a furious passion ; but receiving a gentle hint from Mr. Hippy, that the gentleman to whom he was talking, had just pulled up a pine, he deemed it prudent to restrain his anger within due bounds.

The Reverend Mr. Grovelgrub now rolled up to the party, muffled in a ponderous great coat, and surmounted with an enormous umbrella, humbly soliciting Miss Melincourt to take shelter. Anthelia assured him that she was so completely wet through, as to render all shelter superfluous, till she could change her clothes. On this, Mr. Hippy, who was wet through himself, but had not till that moment been aware that he was so, voted for returning to Melincourt with all possible expedition; adding, that he feared it would be necessary, immediately on their arrival, to send off an express for Dr. Killquick, for his dear Anthelia's sake, as well as his own. Anthelia disclaimed any intention or necessity on her part, of calling in the services of the learned doctor, and, turning to Sir Oran, requested the favour of his company to dinner at Melincourt. This invitation was warmly seconded by Mr. Hippy, with gestures as well as words. Sir Oran bowed acknowledgment, but pointing in a direction different from that of Melincourt, shook his head, and took a respectful farewell.

" I wonder who he is," said Mr. Hippy, as they walked rapidly homewards : " manifestly dumb, poor fellow ! a man of consequence, no doubt : no great beauty, by the by ; but as strong as Hercules, quite an Orlando Furioso. He pulled up a pine, my Lord, as you would a mushroom."

" Sir," said Lord Anophel, " I have nothing to do with mushrooms : and as to this gentleman, whoever he is, I must say, notwithstanding his fashionable air, his taking my quizzing-glass was a piece of impertinence, for which I shall feel necessitated to require gentlemanly satisfaction."

A long, toilsome, and slippery walk, brought the party to the castle-gate.

CHAPTER XI

LOVE AND MARRIAGE

SIR ORAN HAUT-TON, as we conjecture, had taken a very long ramble
beyond the limits of Redrose Abbey, and had sat down in the pine-
grove to solace himself with his flute, when Anthelia, bursting upon
him like a beautiful vision, rivetted him in silent admiration to the
spot whence she departed, about which he lingered in hopes of her
reappearance, till the accident which occurred on her return enabled
him to exert his extraordinary physical strength, in a manner so
remarkably advantageous to her. On parting from her and her
companions, he ran back all the way to the Abbey, a formidable
distance, and relieved the anxious apprehensions which his friend
Mr. Forester entertained respecting him.

A few mornings after this occurrence, as Mr. Forester, Mr. Fax,
and Sir Oran were sitting at breakfast, a letter was brought in,
addressed to *Sir Oran Haut-ton, Baronet, Redrose Abbey* ; a circumstance which very much surprised Mr. Forester, as he could not
imagine how Sir Oran had obtained a correspondent, seeing that he
could neither write nor read. He accordingly took the liberty of
opening the letter himself.

It proved to be from a limb of the law, signing himself Richard
Ratstail, and purported to be a notice to Sir Oran to defend himself
in an action brought against him by the said Richard Ratstail,
solicitor, in behalf of his client, Lawrence Litigate, Esquire, lord of
the manor of Muckwormsby, for that he the said Sir Oran Haut-ton
did, with force and arms, videlicet, swords, pistols, daggers, bludgeons,
and staves, break into the manor of the said Lawrence Litigate,
Esquire, and did then and there, with malice aforethought, and
against the peace of our sovereign lord the King, his crown and
dignity, cut down, root up, hew, hack, and cut in pieces sundry and
several pine-trees, of various sizes and dimensions, to the utter ruin,
havoc, waste, and devastation of a large tract of pine-land ; and that
he had wilfully, maliciously, and with intent to injure the said
Lawrence Litigate, Esquire, carried off with force and arms, namely,
swords, pistols, bludgeons, daggers, and staves, fifty cart-loads of

trunks, fifty cart-loads of bark, fifty cart-loads of loppings, and fifty cart-loads of toppings.

This was a complete enigma to Mr. Forester ; and his surprise was increased when, on reading further, he found that Miss Melincourt, of Melincourt Castle, was implicated in the affair, as having aided and abetted Sir Oran in devastating the pine-grove, and carrying it off by cartloads with force and arms.

It immediately occurred to him, that the best mode he could adopt of elucidating the mystery would be, to call on Miss Melincourt, whom, besides, Sir Telegraph's enthusiastic description had given him some curiosity to see ; and the present appeared a favourable opportunity to indulge it.

He therefore asked Mr. Fax if he were disposed for a very long walk. Mr. Fax expressed a cordial assent to the proposal, and no time was lost in preparation.

Mr. Forester, though he had built stables for the accommodation of his occasional visitors, kept no horses himself, for reasons which will appear hereafter.

They set forth accordingly, accompanied by Sir Oran, who joined them without waiting for an invitation.

" We shall see Sir Telegraph Paxarett," said Mr. Forester, " and, perhaps, his phœnix, Miss Melincourt."

MR. FAX. If a woman be the object, and a lover's eyes the medium, I should say there is nothing in nature so easily found as a phœnix.

MR. FORESTER. My eyes have no such magical property. I am not a lover, it is true, but it is because I have never found a phœnix.

MR. FAX. But you have one in your mind, a *beau idéal*, I doubt not.

MR. FORESTER. Not too ideal to exclude the possible existence of its material archetype, though I have never found it yet.

MR. FAX. You will, however, find a female who has some one at least of the qualities of your imaginary damsel, and that one quality will serve as a peg on which your imagination will suspend all the others. This is the usual process of mental hallucination. A little truth forms the basis, and the whole superstructure is falsehood.

MR. FORESTER. I shall guard carefully against such self-deception ; though, perhaps, a beautiful chimæra is better than either a hideous reality or a vast and formless void.

MR. FAX. As an instrument of transitory pleasure, probably ; but very far from it as a means of permanent happiness, which is only consistent with perfect mental tranquillity, which again is only consistent with the calm and dispassionate contemplation of truth.

MR. FORESTER. What say you, then, to the sentiment of Voltaire ?

> " Le raisonneur tristement s'accrédite :
> On court, dit-on, après la vérité,
> Ah ! croyez-moi, l'erreur a son mérite."

MR. FAX. You will scarcely coincide with such a sentiment, when you consider how much this doctrine of happy errors, and pleasing illusions, and salutary prejudices, has tended to rivet the chains of superstition on the necks of the grovelling multitude.

MR. FORESTER. And yet, if you take the colouring of imagination from the objects of our mental perception, and pour the full blaze of daylight into all the dark recesses of selfishness and cunning, I am afraid a refined and enthusiastic benevolence will find little to interest or delight in the contemplation of the human world.

MR. FAX. That should rather be considered the consequence of morbid feelings, and exaggerated expectations of society and human nature. It is the false colouring in which youthful enthusiasm depicts the scenes of futurity that throws the gloom of disappointment so deeply on their actual presence. You have formed to yourself, as you acknowledge, a visionary model of female perfection, which has rendered you utterly insensible to the real attractions of every woman you have seen. This exaggerated imagination loses more than it gains. It has not made a fair calculation of the mixture of good and evil in every constituent portion of the world of reality. It has utterly excluded the latter from the objects of its hope, and has magnified the former into such gigantic proportions, that the real goodness and beauty which would be visible and delightful to simpler optics, vanish into imperceptibility in the infinity of their diminution.

MR. FORESTER. I desire no phantasm of abstract perfection—no visionary creation of a romantic philosophy : I seek no more than I know to have existed—than, I doubt not, does exist, though in such lamentable rarity, that the calculations of probability make the search little better than desperate. I would have a woman that can love and feel poetry, not only in its harmony and decorations, which limit the admiration of ordinary mortals, but in the deep sources of love, and liberty, and truth, which are its only legitimate springs, and without which well-turned periods and glittering images are nothing more nor less than the vilest and most mischievous tinsel. She should be musical, but she should have music in her soul as well as her fingers : her voice and her touch should have no one point in common with that mechanical squalling and jingling which are commonly dignified with the insulted name of music : they should be modes of the harmony of her mind.

MR. FAX. I do not very well understand that ; but I think I have a glimpse of your meaning. Pray proceed.

MR. FORESTER. She should have charity—not penny charity——

MR. FAX. I hope not.

MR. FORESTER. But a liberal discriminating practical philanthropy, that can select with justice the objects of its kindness, and give that kindness a form of permanence equally delightful and useful to its object and to society, by increasing the aggregate mass of intelligence and happiness.

MR. FAX. Go on.

MR. FORESTER. She should have no taste for what are called public pleasures. Her pleasures should be bounded in the circle of her family, and a few, a very few congenial friends, her books, her music, her flowers—she should delight in flowers—the uninterrupted cheerfulness of domestic concord, the delightful effusions of unlimited confidence. The rocks, and woods, and mountains, boundaries of the valley of her dwelling, she should be content to look on as the boundaries of the world.

MR. FAX. Anything more ?

MR. FORESTER. She should have a clear perception of the beauty of truth. Every species of falsehood, even in sportiveness, should be abhorrent to her. The simplicity of her thoughts should shine through the ingenuousness of her words. Her testimony should convey as irresistible conviction as the voice of the personified nature of things. And this ingenuousness should comprise, in its fullest extent, that perfect conformity, of feelings and opinions, which ought to be the most common, but is unfortunately the most rare of the qualities of the female mind.

MR. FAX. You say nothing of beauty.

MR. FORESTER. As to what is usually called beauty, mere symmetry of form and features, it would be an object with me in purchasing a statue, but none whatever in choosing a wife. Let her countenance be the mirror of such qualities as I have described, and she cannot be otherwise than beautiful. I think with the Athenians, that beauty and goodness are inseparable. I need not remind you of the perpetual καλος κἀγαθος.[1]

MR. FAX. You have said nothing of the principal, and, indeed, almost the only usual consideration in marriage—fortune.

MR. FORESTER. I am rich enough myself to dispense with such considerations. Even were I not so, I doubt if worldly wisdom would ever influence me to bend my knee with the multitude, at the shrine of the omnipotence of money. Nothing is more uncertain, more transient, more perishable, than riches. How many prudent marriages of interest and convenience were broken to atoms by the French revolution! Do you think there was one couple, among all those calculating characters that acted in those trying times, like Louvet and his Lodoiska?[2] But without looking to periods of public convulsion, in no state of society is any individual secure against the changes of fortune. What becomes of those ill-assorted unions, which have no basis but money, when, as is very often the case, the money departs, and the persons remain? The qualities of the heart and of the mind are alone out of the power of accident;

[1] " Fair and good." G.
[2] See Louvet's *Récit de mes Périls*. [P.]

and by these, and these only, shall I be guided in the choice of the companion of my life.

MR. FAX.   Are there no other indispensable qualities, that you have omitted in your enumeration ?

MR. FORESTER.   None, I think, but such as are implied in those I have mentioned, and must necessarily be coexistent with them : an endearing sensibility, an agreeable cheerfulness, and that serenity of temper which is truly the balm of being, and the absence of which, in the intercourse of domestic life, obliterates all the radiance of beauty, all the splendour of talent, and all the dignity of virtue.

MR. FAX.   I presume, then, you seriously purpose to marry, when you can find such a woman as this you have described ?

MR. FORESTER.   Seriously I do.

MR. FAX.   And not till then ?

MR. FORESTER.   Certainly not.

MR. FAX.   Then your present heir presumptive has nothing to fear for his reversion.

CHAPTER XII

LOVE AND POVERTY

" WE shall presently," said Mr. Fax, as they pursued their walk, " come in sight of a cottage, which I remarked two years ago : a deplorable habitation ! A picture of its exterior and interior suspended in some public place, in every town in the kingdom, with a brief commentary subjoined, would operate *in terrorem* in favour of the best interests of political economy, by placing before the eyes of the rising generation, the lamentable consequences of imprudent marriage, and the necessary result of attachment, of which romance is the foundation, and marriage the superstructure, without the only cement which will make it wind-and-water-tight—money."

MR. FORESTER.   Nothing but money ! The resemblance Fluellen found between Macedon and Monmouth,[1] because both began with an

[1] *Henry V*, Act IV, Sc. 7.   G.

M, holds equally true of money and marriage : but there seems to be a much stronger connexion in the latter case ; for marriage is but a body, of which money is the soul.

MR. FAX. It is so. It must be so. The constitution of society imperiously commands it to be so. The world of reality is not the world of romance. When a lover talks of lips of coral, teeth of pearl, tresses of gold, and eyes of diamonds, he knows all the while that he is lying by wholesale ; and that no baker in England would give him credit for a penny roll, on all this display of his Utopian treasury. All the aërial castles that are founded in the contempt of worldly prudence, have not half the solidity of the cloud-built towers that surround the setting of the autumnal sun.

MR. FORESTER. I maintain, on the contrary, that, *let all possible calamities be accumulated on two affectionate and congenial spirits, they will find more true happiness in weeping together, than they would have found in all the riches of the world, poisoned by the disunion of hearts.*[1]

MR. FAX. The disunion of hearts is an evil of another kind. It is not a comparison of evils I wish to institute. That two rich people fettered by the indissoluble bond of marriage, and hating each other cordially, are two as miserable animals as any on the face of the earth, is certain ; but that two poor ones, let them love each other ever so fondly, starving together in a garret, are therefore in a less positively wretched condition, is an inference which no logic, I think, can deduce. For the picture you must draw in your mind's eye, is not that of a neatly-dressed, young, healthy-looking couple, weeping in each other's arms in a clean, however homely cottage, in a fit of tender sympathy ; but you must surround them with all the squalid accompaniments of poverty, rags, and famine, the contempt of the world, the dereliction of friends, half a dozen hungry squalling children, all clothed perhaps in the cutting up of an old blanket, duns in presence, bailiffs in prospect, and the long perspective of hopelessness closed by the workhouse or the gaol.

MR. FORESTER. You imagine an extreme case, which something more than the original want of fortune seems requisite to produce.

[1] Rousseau, *Émile*, liv. 5. [P.]

MR. FAX. I have heard you declaim very bitterly against those who maintain the necessary connexion between misfortune and imprudence.

MR. FORESTER. Certainly. To assert that the unfortunate must necessarily have been imprudent, is to furnish an excuse to the cold-hearted and illiberal selfishness of a state of society, which needs no motive superadded to its own miserable narrow-mindedness, to produce the almost total extinction of benevolence and sympathy. Good and evil fortune depend so much on the combinations of external circumstances, that the utmost skill and industry cannot command success ; neither is the result of the most imprudent actions always fatal :

> Our indiscretions sometimes serve us well,
> When our deep plots do pall.[1]

MR. FAX. Sometimes, no doubt ; but not so often as to equalize the probable results of indiscretion and prudence. " Where there is prudence," says Juvenal, " fortune is powerless " ; and this doctrine, though liable to exceptions, is replete with general truth. We have

---

[1] [*Hamlet :* Act V, Sc. 2. G.]

" L'issuë aucthorise souvent une tres-inepte conduitte. Nostre entremise n'est quasy qu'une routine, et plus communement consideration d'usage et d'exemple que de raison. . . . L'heur et le mal-heur sont à mon gré deux souveraines puissances. C'est imprudence d'estimer que l'humaine prudence puisse remplir le roolle de la fortune. Et vaine est l'entreprinse de celuy qui presume, d'embrasser et causes et consequences, et meiner par la main le progrez de son faict. . . . Qu'on reguarde qui sont les plus puissans aux villes, et qui font mieulx leurs besongnes, on trouvera ordinairement que ce sont les moins habiles. . . . Nous attribuons les effects de leur bonne fortune à leur prudence. . . . Parquoy je dy bien, en toutes façons, que les evenements sont maigres tesmoings de nostre prix et capacité."—MONTAIGNE, liv. iii. chap 8. [P.]

[" The issue doth often aucthorise a simple conduct. Our interposition is in a manner nothing els but an experience, and more commonly a consideration of use and example than of reason. . . . Good and bad fortune, are in my conceit two soveraigne powers. 'Tis folly to thinke that humane wisedome may act the full part of Fortune. And vaine is his enterprise, that presumeth to embrace both causes and consequences and lead the progresses of his act by the hand. . . . Let but a man looke who are the mightiest in Cities and who thrive best in their businesse : he shall commonly find they are the siliest and poorest in wit. . . . We ascribe their good fortune's effects unto their prudence. . . . Wherefore I say well, that howsoever, events are but weake testimonies of our worth and capacity." John Florio's translation. G.]

a nice balance to adjust. To check the benevolence of the rich, by
persuading them that all misfortune is the result of imprudence, is a
great evil; but it would be a much greater evil to persuade the poor,
that indiscretion may have a happier result than prudence ; for
where this appears to be true in one instance, it is manifestly false in
a thousand. It is certainly not enough to possess industry and
talent ; there must be means for exerting them ; and in a redundant
population these means are often wanting, even to the most skilful
and the most industrious : but though Calamity sometimes seizes
those who use their best efforts to avoid her, yet she seldom dis-
appoints the intentions of those who leap headlong into her arms.

MR. FORESTER.   It seems, nevertheless, peculiarly hard, that all the
blessings of life should be confined to the rich. If you banish the
smiles of love from the cottage of poverty, what remains to cheer its
dreariness ?   The poor man has no friends, no amusements, no
means of exercising benevolence, nothing to fill up the gloomy and
desolate vacancy of his heart, if you banish love from his dwelling.
" There is one alone, and there is not a second," says one of the
greatest poets and philosophers of antiquity : " there is one alone, and
there is not a second : yea, he hath neither child nor brother ; yet is
there no end of all his labour : . . . neither saith he, For whom do I
labour and bereave my soul of good ? . . .   Two are better than one
. . . for if they fall, the one will lift up his fellow ; but woe to him that
is alone when he falleth, for he hath not another to help him up." [1]
Society in poverty, is better than solitude in wealth ; but solitude
and poverty together, it is scarcely in human nature to tolerate.

MR. FAX.   This, if I remember rightly, is the cottage of which I was
speaking.

The cottage was ruined and uninhabited. The roof had fallen in.
The garden was choked with weeds. " What," said Mr. Fax, " can
have become of its unfortunate inhabitants ? "

MR. FORESTER.   What were they ?

MR. FAX.   A couple for whom nature had done much, and fortune
nothing.   I took shelter in their cottage from a passing storm.   The

[1] *Ecclesiastes,* chap. iv.   [P.]

picture which you called the imagination of an extreme case, falls
short of the reality of what I witnessed here. It was the utmost
degree of misery and destitution compatible with the preservation of
life. A casual observer might have passed them by, as the most
abject of the human race. But their physiognomy showed better
things. It was with the utmost difficulty I could extract a word
from either of them: but when I at last succeeded, I was astonished,
in garments so mean and a dwelling so deplorable, to discover feelings
so generous and minds so enlightened. The semblance of human
sympathy seemed strange to them; little of it as you may suppose
could be discovered through my saturnine complexion, and the
habitual language of what you call my frosty philosophy. By
degrees I engaged their confidence, and he related to me his history,
which I will tell you as nearly as I can remember, in his own words.

CHAPTER XIII

DESMOND

My name is Desmond. My father was a naval officer, who in the
prime of life was compelled by wounds to retire from the service on
his half-pay, and a small additional pension. I was his only son, and
he submitted to the greatest personal privations, to procure me a
liberal education, in the hope that by these means he should live to
see me making my way in the world : but he always accompanied his
wishes for this consummation, with a hope that I should consider
money as a means, and not as an end, and that I should remember
the only real treasures of human existence were truth, health, and
liberty. You will not wonder, that, with such principles, the father
had been twenty years a lieutenant, and that the son was looked on
at College as a fellow that would come to nothing.

I profited little at the University, as you will easily suppose. The
system of education pursued there, appeared to me the result of a
deep-laid conspiracy against the human understanding, a mighty
effort of political and ecclesiastical machiavelism, to turn the energies
of inquiring minds into channels, where they will either stagnate in
disgust, or waste themselves in nugatory labour. To discover or

even to illustrate a single moral truth, to shake the empire of a single prejudice, to apply a single blow of the axe of philosophy to the wide-spreading roots of superstition and political imposture, is to render a real service to the best hopes of mankind ; but all this is diametrically opposed to the selfish interests of the hired misleaders of society, the chosen few, as they are called, before whom the wretched multitude grovel in the dust as before

> " The children of a race,
> Mightier than they, and wiser, and by heaven
> Beloved and favoured more." [1]

Moral science, therefore, moral improvement, the doctrines of benevolence, the amelioration of the general condition of mankind, will not only never form a part of any public institution, for the performance of that ridiculous and mischievous farce called the *Finishing of Education* ; but every art of clerical chicanery and fraudulent misrepresentation will be practised, to render odious the very names of philosophy and philanthropy, and to extinguish, by ridicule and persecution, that enthusiastic love of truth, which never fails to conduct its votaries to conclusions very little compatible with the views of those who have built, or intend to build, their own worldly prosperity, on the foundations of hypocrisy and servility in themselves, and ignorance and credulity in others.

The study of morals and of mind occupied my exclusive attention. I had little taste for the science of lines and numbers, and still less for verbal criticism, the pinnacle of academical glory.

I delighted in the poets of Greece and Rome, but I thought that the *igneus vigor et coelestis origo* [2] of their conceptions and expressions was often utterly lost sight of, in the microscopic inspection of philological minutiæ. I studied Greek, as the means of understanding Homer and Æschylus : I did not look on them as mere secondary instruments to the attainment of a knowledge of their language. I had no conception of the taste that could prefer Lycophron to Sophocles, because he had the singular advantage of being obscure ; and should have been utterly at a loss to account for such a phænomenon, if I had not seen that the whole system of public

---

[1] Southey : *Madoc*, Pt. I, Sec. 6, lines 4–6. G.

[2] " Fiery strength and celestial origin." Virgil : *Æn.* VI. 730. G.

education was purposely calculated to make inferior minds recoil in disgust and terror from the vestibule of knowledge, and superior minds consume their dangerous energies in the *difficiles nugae* and *labor ineptiarum* [1] of its adytum.

I did not *finish*, as it is called, my college *education*. My father's death compelled me to leave it before the expiration of the usual period, at the end of which the same distinction is conferred on all capacities, by the academical noometry, not of merit but of time. I found myself almost destitute; but I felt the consciousness of talents, that I doubted not would amply provide for me in that great centre of intellect and energy, London. To London I accordingly went, and became a boarder in the humble dwelling of a widow, who maintained herself and an only daughter by the perilous and precarious income derived from lodgers.

My first application was to a bookseller in Bond Street, to whom I offered the copyright of a treatise on the Elements of Morals. " My dear Sir," said he, with an air of supercilious politeness, "only take the trouble of sitting a few hours in my shop, and if you detect any one of my customers in the fact of pronouncing the word *morals*, I will give any price you please to name for your copyright." But, glancing over the manuscript, " I perceive," said he, " there are some smart things here ; and though they are good for nothing where they are, they would cut a pretty figure in a Review. My friend Mr. Vamp,[2] the editor, is in want of a hand for the moral department of his Review : I will give you a note to him." I thanked him for his kindness, and, furnished with the note, proceeded to the lodgings of Mr. Vamp, whom I found in an elegant first floor, lounging over a large quarto, which he was marking with a pencil. A number of books and pamphlets, and fragments of both curiously cut up, were scattered on the table before him, together with a large pot of paste, and an enormous pair of scissars.

He received me with great hauteur, read the note, and said, " Mr. Foolscap has told you we are in want of a hand, and he thinks you have a turn in the moral line : I shall not be sorry if it prove so, for

---

[1] " Tiresome trifles " and " labour spent on absurdities." Martial. G.
[2] Gifford, editor of the *Quarterly Review*, started life as a shoemaker's apprentice. Byron borrowed the name Vamp for him, to use in *The Blues, a Literary Eclogue.* G.

we have been very ill provided in that way a long while ; and though
morals are not much in demand among our patrons and customers,
and will not do, by any means, for a standing dish, they make,
nevertheless, a very pretty seasoning for our politics, in cases where
they might otherwise be rather unpalatable and hard of digestion.
You see this pile of pamphlets, these volumes of poetry, and this
rascally quarto : all these, though under very different titles, and
the productions of very different orders of mind, have, either openly
or covertly, only one object ; and a most impertinent one it is.   This
object is two-fold: first, to prove the existence, to an immense extent,
of what these writers think proper to denominate political corruption ;
secondly, to convince the public that this corruption ought to be
extinguished.   Now, we are anxious to do away with the effect of all
these incendiary clamours.   As to the existence of corruption (it is
a villainous word, by the by—we call it *persuasion in a tangible
shape*) : as to the existence, then, of *persuasion in a tangible shape*,
we do not wish to deny it ; on the contrary, we have no hesitation
in affirming that it is *as notorious as the sun at noonday* : but as to
the inference that it ought to be extinguished—that is the point
against which we direct the full fire of our critical artillery ; we
maintain that it ought to exist ; and here is the leading article of our
next number,[1] in which we confound in one mass all these obnoxious
publications, putting the weakest at the head of the list, that if any
of our readers should feel inclined to judge for themselves (I must do
them the credit to say I do not suspect many of them of such a
democratical propensity), they may be stopped *in limine*, by finding
very little temptation to proceed.   The political composition of this
article is beautiful : it is the production of a gentleman high in office,
who is indebted to *persuasion in a tangible shape* for his present income
of several thousands per annum ; but it wants, as I have hinted,
a little moral seasoning ; and there, as ill-luck will have it, we are
all thrown out.   We have several reverend gentlemen in our corps,
but morals are unluckily quite out of their way.   We have, on some

---

[1] An article in the *Quarterly Review*, No. XXXI, 1816, admitting widespread corruption in elections, described it as a matter of private bargaining,
and argued that it was in no way detrimental to the composition of Parliament.   Peacock devotes Ch. XXXIX to satirising the views expressed in
this article.   G.

occasions, with their assistance, substituted theology for morals :
they manage this very cleverly, but, I am sorry to say, it only takes
among the old women ; and though the latter are our best and most
numerous customers, yet we have some very obstinate and hard-
headed readers who will not, as I have observed, swallow our politics
without a little moral seasoning ; and, as I told Mr. Foolscap, if we
did not contrive to pick up a spice of morals somewhere or other,
all the eloquence of *persuasion in a tangible shape* would soon become
of little avail. Now, if you will undertake the seasoning of this
article in such a manner as to satisfy my employers, I will satisfy
you : you understand me."

I observed, that I hoped he would allow me the free exercise of my
own opinion ; and that I should wish to season his article in such
a manner as to satisfy myself, which I candidly told him would not
be in such a manner as seemed likely to satisfy him.

On this he flew into a rage, and vowed vengeance against Mr.
Foolscap for having sent him a Jacobin. I strenuously disclaimed
this appellation ; and being then quite a novice in the world, I
actually endeavoured to reason with him, as if the conviction of
general right and wrong could have any influence upon him ; but he
stopped me short, by saying, that till I could reason him out of his
pension, I might spare myself the trouble of interfering with his
opinions ; as the logic from which they were deduced had presented
itself to him in a much more *tangible shape* than any abstract notions
of truth and liberty. He had thought, from Mr. Foolscap's letter,
that I had a talent for moral theory, and that I was inclined to turn
it to account ; as for moral practice, he had nothing to do with it,
desired to know nothing about it, and wished me a good morning.

I was not yet discouraged, and made similar applications to the
editors and proprietors of several daily, weekly, monthly, and
quarterly publications, but I found every where the same indifference
or aversion to general principles, the same partial and perverted
views : every one was the organ of some division or subdivision of
a faction ; and had entrenched himself in a narrow circle, within the
pale of which all was honour, consistency, integrity, generosity, and
justice ; while all without it was villainy, hypocrisy, selfishness,
corruption, and lies. Not being inclined to imprison myself in any

one of these magical rings, I found all my interviews terminate like that with Mr. Vamp.

By the advice and introduction of a college acquaintance, I accepted the situation of tutor in the family of Mr. Dross, a wealthy citizen, who had acquired a large fortune by contracts with Government, in the execution of which he had not forgotten to charge for his vote and interest. His conscience, indeed, of all the commodities he dealt in, was that which he had brought to the best market; though, among his more fair dealing, and consequently poorer neighbours, it was thought he had made the ministry pay too dearly for so very rotten an article. They seemed not to be aware that a corrupt administration estimates conscience and Stilton cheese by the same criterion, and that its rottenness was its recommendation.

Mr. Dross was a tun of man, with the soul of a hazel-nut : his wife was a tun of woman, without any soul whatever. The principle that animated her bulk was composed of three ingredients— arrogance, ignorance, and the pride of money. They were, in every sense of the word, what the world calls respectable people.

Mrs. Dross aspired to be *somebody*, aped the nobility, and gave magnificent routs, which were attended by many noble personages, and by all that portion of the fashionable world that will go anywhere for a crowd and a supper.

Their idea of virtue consisted in having no debts, going regularly to church, and feeding the parson; their idea of charity, in paying the poor-rates, and putting down their names to public subscriptions : and they had a profound contempt for every species of learning, which they associated indissolubly with rags and famine, and with that neglect of the main chance, which they regarded as the most deadly of all deadly sins. But as they had several hopeful children, and as Mrs. Dross found it was fashionable to have a governess and a *tutorer*, they had looked out for two pieces of human furniture under these denominations, and my capricious destiny led me to their splendid dwelling in the latter capacity.

I found the governess, Miss Pliant, very admirably adapted to her situation. She did not presume to have a will of her own. Suspended like Mahomet's coffin between the mistress and the housekeeper, despising the one, and despised by the other, her mind seemed unconscious of its vacancy, and her heart of its loneliness. She had neither feelings nor principles, either of good or ill : perfectly selfish, perfectly cold-hearted, and perfectly obsequious, she was contented with her situation, because it seemed likely to lead to an advantageous establishment ; for if ever she thought of marriage, it was only in the light of a system of bargain, in which youth and beauty were very well disposed of when bartered for age and money. She was highly accomplished : a very scientific musician, without any soul in her performance ; a most skilful copier of landscapes, without the least taste for the beauties of nature ; and a proficient in French grammar, though she had read no book in that language but *Telemaque*, and hated the names of Rousseau and Voltaire, because she had heard them called rascals by her father, who had taken his opinion on trust from the Reverend Mr. Simony, who had never read a page of either of them.

I very soon found that I was regarded as an upper servant—as a person of more pretension, but less utility, than the footman. I was expected to be really more servile, in mind especially. If I presumed to differ in opinion from Mr. or Mrs. Dross, they looked at each other and at me with the most profound astonishment, wondering at so much audacity in one of their moveables. I really envied the footman, living as he did among his equals, where he might have his own opinion, as far as he was capable of forming one, and express it without reserve or fear ; while all my thoughts were to be those of a mirror, and my motions those of an automaton. I soon saw that I had but the choice of alternatives : either to mould myself into a slave, liar, and hypocrite, or to take my leave of Mr. Dross. I therefore embraced the latter, and determined from that moment never again to live under the roof of a superior, if my own dwelling were to be the most humble and abject of human habitations.

I returned to my old lodgings, and, after a short time, procured some employment in the way of copying for a lawyer. My labour was assiduous, and my remuneration scanty ; but my habits were simple, my evenings were free, and in the daughter of the widow with whom I lodged, I found a congenial mind : a desire for knowledge, an ardent love of truth, and a capacity that made my voluntary office of instruction at once easy and delightful.

The widow died embarrassed : her creditors seized her effects, and her daughter was left destitute. I was her only friend : to every other human being, not only her welfare, but even her existence, were matters of total indifference. The course of necessity seemed to have thrown her on my protection, and if I before loved her, I now regarded her as a precious trust, confided to me by her evil fate. Call it what you may, imprudence, madness, frenzy—we were married.

The lawyer who employed me, had chosen his profession very injudiciously, for he was an honest and benevolent man. He interested himself for me, acquainted himself with my circumstances, and, without informing me of his motives, increased my remuneration ; though, as I afterwards found, he could very ill afford to do so. By this means we lived twelve months in comfort, I may say, considering the simplicity of our habits, in prosperity. The birth of our first child was an accession to our domestic happiness. We had no pleasures beyond the limits of our humble dwelling. Our circumstances and situation were much below the ordinary level of those of well-educated people : we had, therefore, no society, but we were happy in each other : our evenings were consecrated to our favourite authors ; and the din of the streets, the tumult of crowds and carriages thronging to parties of pleasure and scenes of public amusement, came to us like the roar of a stormy ocean, on which we had neither wish nor power to embark.

One evening we were surprised by an unexpected visitor : it was the lawyer my employer. " Desmond ! " said he, " I am a ruined man. For having been too scrupulous to make beggars of others, I have a fair prospect of becoming one myself. You are shocked and astonished. Do not grieve on my account. I have neither wife nor children. Very trivial and very remediable is the evil that can happen to me. ' The valiant by himself, what can he suffer ? ' You will think a lawyer has as little business with poetry as he has with justice. Perhaps so. I have been too partial to both."

I was glad to see him so cheerful, and expressed a hope that his affairs would take a better turn than he seemed to expect. " You shall know more," said he, " in a few days ; in the mean time, here are the arrears I owe you."

When he came again, he said : " My creditors are neither numerous nor cruel. I have made over to them all my property, but they allow me to retain possession of a small house in Westmoreland, with an annuity for my life, sufficient to maintain me in competence. I could propose a wild scheme to you if I thought you would not be offended."

" That," said I, " I certainly will not, propose what you may."

" Tell me," said he, " which do you think the most useful and uncontaminating implement, the quill or the spade ? "

" The spade," said I, " generally speaking, unquestionably : the quill, in some most rare and solitary instances."

" In the hand of Homer and Plutarch, of Seneca and Tacitus, of Shakespeare and Rousseau ? I am not speaking of them, or of those who, however humbly, reflect their excellencies. But in the hands of the slaves of commerce, the minions of law, the venal advocates of superstition, the sycophants of corruption, the turnspits of litera-ture, the paragraph-mongers of prostituted journals, the hireling compounders of party praise and censure, under the name of periodical criticism, what say you to it ? "

" What can I say," said I, " but that it is the curse of society, and the bane of the human mind ? "

" And yet," said he, " in some of these ways must you employ it, if you wish to live by it. Literature is not the soil in which truth and liberty can flourish, unless their cultivators be independent of the world. Those who are not so, whatever be the promise of their beginning, will end either in sycophants or beggars. As mere mechanical instruments, in pursuits unconnected with literature, what say you to the comparison ? "

" What Cincinnatus would have said," I answered.

" I am glad," said he, " to hear it. You are not one of the multitude, neither I believe am I. I embraced my profession, I assure you, from very disinterested motives. I considered that the greater the powers of mischief with which that profession is armed, and I am sorry to add, the practice of mischief in the generality of its professors, the greater might be the scope of philan-thropy, in protecting weakness, and counteracting oppression. Thus I have passed my life in an attempt to reconcile philanthropy and law. I had property sufficient to enable me to try the experiment. The natural consequence is, my property has vanished. I do not regret it, for I have done some good. But I can do no more. My power is annulled. I must retire from the stage of life. If I retire alone, I must have servants ; I had much rather have friends. If you will accompany me to Westmoreland, we will organize a little republic of our own. Your wife shall be our housekeeper. We will cultivate our garden. We shall want little more, and that my annuity will amply supply. We will select a few books, and we will pronounce eternal banishment on pen and ink."

I could not help smiling at the earnestness with which he pronounced the last clause. The change of a lawyer into a Roman republican appeared to me as miraculous as any metamorphosis in Ovid. Not to weary you with details, we carried this scheme into effect, and passed three years of natural and healthy occupation, with perfect simplicity and perfect content. They were the happiest of our lives. But at the end of this period, our old friend died. His annuity died with him. He left me his heir, but his habitation and its furniture were all he had to leave. I procured a tenant for the house, and we removed to this even yet more humble dwelling. The difference of the rent, a very trifling sum indeed, constituted our only income. The increase of our family, and the consequent pressure of necessity, compelled us to sell the house. From the same necessity we have become strict Pythagoreans.[1] I do not complain that we live hardly : it is almost wonderful that we live at all. The produce of our little garden preserves us from famine : but this is all it does. I consider myself a mere rustic, and very willingly engage in agricultural labour, when the neighbouring farmers think proper to employ me : but they feel no deficiency of abler hands. There are more labourers than means of labour. In the cities it is the same. If all the modes of human occupation in this kingdom, from the highest to the lowest, were to require at once a double number of persons, there would not remain one of them twelve hours unfilled.

With what views could I return to London ? Of the throng continually pressing onward, to spring into the vacancies of employment, the foremost ranks are unfortunately composed of the selfish,

---

[1] i.e. vegetarians. G.

the servile, the intriguing ; of those to whose ideas general justice is a chimæra, liberty an empty name, and truth at best a verbal veil for the sycophantic falsehood of a mercenary spirit. To what end could a pupil of the ancient Romans mingle with such a multitude ? To cringe, to lie, to flatter ? To bow to the insolence of wealth, the superciliousness of rank, the contumely of patronage, that, while it exacts the most abject mental prostration, in return for promises never meant to be performed, despises the servility it fosters, and laughs at the credulity it betrays ?

The wheel of fortune is like a water-wheel, and human beings are like the waters it disturbs. Many are thrown into the channels of action, many are thrown back to be lost for ever in the stream. I am one of the latter : but I shall not consider it disgraceful to me that I am so, till I see that candour, simplicity, integrity, and intellectual power directed by benevolence and liberty, have a better claim to worldly estimation, than either venal talent prostituted to the wages of corruption, or ignorance, meanness, and imbecility, exalted by influence and interest.

CHAPTER XIV

THE COTTAGE

MR. FAX (*in continuation*) " I cannot help thinking," said I, when Desmond had done speaking, " that you have formed too hasty an estimate of the world. Mr. Vamp and Mr. Dross are bad specimens of human nature : but there are many good specimens of it in both those classes of men. The world is, indeed, full of prejudices and superstitions, which produce ample profit to their venal advocates, who consequently want neither the will nor the power to calumniate and persecute the enlightened and the virtuous. The rich, too, are usually arrogant and exacting, and those feelings will never perish for want of sycophants to nourish them. An ardent love of truth and liberty will, therefore, always prove an almost insuperable barrier to any great degree of worldly advancement. A celebrated divine, who turned his theological morality to very excellent account, and died *en bonne odeur*, used to say, *he could not afford to have a conscience, for it was the most expensive luxury a man could indulge in.*[1] So it certainly is : but though a conscientious man, who has his own way to make in the world, will very seldom flourish in the sunshine of prosperity, it is not, therefore, necessary that he should sit quietly down and starve." He said he would think of it, and if he could find any loop-hole in the great feudal fortress of society, at which poverty and honesty could creep in together, he would try to effect an entrance. I made more particular inquiry into their circumstances, and they at length communicated to me, but with manifest reluctance, that they were in imminent danger of being deprived of their miserable furniture, and turned out of their wretched habitation, by Lawrence Litigate, Esquire, their landlord, for arrears of rent amounting to five pounds.

MR. FORESTER.   Which of course you paid ?

MR. FAX.   I did so : but I do not see that it is of course.

Mr. Forester, Mr. Fax, and Sir Oran, were still leaning over the gate of the cottage, when a peasant came whistling along the road. " Pray, my honest friend," said Mr. Fax, " can you inform me what has become of the family which inhabited this cottage two years ago ? "—" Ye'll voind them," said the peasant, " about a mile vurther an, just by the lake's edge like, wi' two large elms by the door, and a vir tree." [2]   He resumed his tune and his way.

The philosophical trio proceeded on their walk.

MR. FORESTER.   You have said little of his wife.

MR. FAX.   She was an interesting creature. With her the feelings of misfortune had subsided into melancholy silence, while with him they broke forth in misanthropical satire.

MR. FORESTER.   And their children ?

MR. FAX.   They would have been fine children, if they had been better clothed and fed.

[1] William Paley, in reference to the Thirty-Nine Articles. See Meadley : *Memoirs of Paley* (1809). G.
[2] Peacock's peasantry speak in the dialect of his native Dorset even when they are met in Westmorland. G.

MR. FORESTER. Did they seem to repent their marriage ?

MR. FAX. Not for themselves. They appeared to have no wish but to live and die together. For their children, indeed, I could easily perceive they felt more grief than they expressed.

MR. FORESTER. You have scarcely made out your case. Poverty had certainly come in at the door, but Love does not seem to have flown out at the window. You would not have prevailed on them to separate at the price of living in palaces. The energy of intellect was not deadened ; the independence of spirit was not broken. The participation of love communicates a luxury to sorrow, that all the splendour of selfishness can never bestow. If, as has been said, a friend is more valuable than the elements of fire and water, how much more valuable must be the one only associate, the more than friend, to him whom in affliction and in poverty all other friends have abandoned ! If the sun shines equally on the palace and the cottage, why should not love, the sun of the intellectual world, shine equally on both ? More needful, indeed, is its genial light to the latter, where there is no worldly splendour to diminish or divide its radiance.

With a sudden turn of the road, a scene of magnificent beauty burst upon their view : the still expanse of a lake, bordered with dark precipices and fading woods, and mountains rising above them, height on height, till the clouds rested on their summits. A picturesque tourist had planted his travelling-chair under the corner of a rock, and was intently occupied in sketching the scene. The process attracted Sir Oran's curiosity : he walked up to the tourist, who was too deeply engaged to notice his approach, and peeped over his shoulder. Sir Oran, after looking at the picture, then at the landscape, then at the picture, then at the landscape again; at length suddenly expressed his delight in a very loud and very singular shout, close in the painter's ear, that re-echoed from rock to rock. The tourist sprang up in violent alarm, and seeing the extraordinary physiognomy of the personage at his elbow, drew a sudden conclusion of evil intentions, and ran off with great rapidity, leaving all his apparatus behind him. Sir Oran sate down in the artist's seat, took up the drawing utensils, placed the unfinished drawing on his knee, and sate in an attitude of deep contemplation, as if meditating on the means to be pursued for doing the same thing himself.

The flying tourist encountered Messieurs Fax and Forester, who had observed the transaction, and were laughing at it as heartily as Democritus himself could have done.[1] They tranquillized his apprehensions, and led him back to the spot. Sir Oran, on a hint from his friend Mr. Forester, rose, made the tourist a polite bow, and restored to him his beloved portfolio. They then wished him a good morning, and left him in a state of nervous trepidation, which made it very obvious that he would draw no more that day.

MR. FAX. Can Sir Oran draw ?

MR. FORESTER. No : but I think he would easily acquire the art. It is very probable that in the nation of the Orans, which I take to be *a barbarous nation, that has not yet learned the use of speech,*[2] drawing, as a means of communicating ideas, may be in no contemptible state of forwardness.[3]

MR. FAX. He has of course seen many drawings, since he has been among civilized men : what so peculiarly delighted and surprised him in this ?

[1] The cheerful disposition of Democritus led him to look at the comic aspect of everything. G.

[2] *Origin and Progress of Language,* book ii. chap. 4. [P.]

[3] " I have endeavoured to support the ancient definition of man, and to show that it belongs to the oran outang, though he have not the use of speech. And indeed it appears surprising to me, that any man, pretending to be a philosopher, should not be satisfied with the expression of intelligence in the most useful way, for the purposes of life ; I mean by actions ; but should require likewise the expression of them, by those signs of arbitrary institution we call *words,* before they will allow an animal to deserve the name of *man.* Suppose that, upon inquiry, it should be found, that the oran outangs have not only invented the art of building huts, and of attacking and defending with sticks, *but also have contrived a way of communicating to the absent, and recording their ideas by the method of painting or drawing,* as is practised by many barbarous nations (and the supposition is not at all impossible, or even improbable) ; and suppose they should have contrived some form of government, and should elect kings or rulers, which is possible, and, according to the information of the Bristol merchant above mentioned, is reported to be actually the case, what would Mr. Buffon then say ? Must they still be accounted brutes, because they have not yet fallen upon the method of communication by articulate sounds ? "
—*Origin and Progress of Language,* book ii. chap. 4. [P.]

MR. FORESTER. I suspect this is the first opportunity he has had, of comparing the natural original with the artificial copy ; and his delight was excited by seeing the vast scene before him, transferred so accurately into so small a compass, and growing as it were into a distinct identity under the hand of the artist.

They now arrived at the elms and the fir-tree, which the peasant had pointed out as the landmarks of the dwelling of Desmond. They were surprised to see a very pretty cottage standing in the midst of a luxuriant garden, one part of which sloped down to the edge of the lake. Every thing bore the air of comfort and competence. They almost doubted if the peasant had been correct in his information. Three rosy children, plainly but neatly dressed, were sitting on the edge of the shallow water, watching with intense delight and interest the manœuvres of a paper flotilla which they had committed to the mercy of the waves.[1]

MR. FAX. What is the difference between these children and Xerxes on the shores of Salamis ?

MR. FORESTER. None, but that where they have pure and unmingled pleasure, his feelings began in selfish pride, and ended in slavish fear : their amusement is natural and innocent ; his was unnatural, cruel, and destructive, and, therefore, more unworthy of a rational being. *Better is a poor and wise child, than a foolish king that will not be admonished.*[2]

A female came from the cottage. Mr. Fax recognised Mrs. Desmond. He was surprised at the change in her appearance. Health and content animated her countenance. The simple neatness of her dress derived an appearance of elegance from its interesting wearer ; contrary to the fashionable process in which dress, neither neat nor simple, but a heterogeneous mixture of all the fripperies of

---

[1] " . . . We came on a pool of water, which Shelley would not part from till he had rigged out a flotilla from any unfortunate letters he happened to have in his pocket. . . . I sympathized with him in this taste : I had it before I knew him : I am not sure that I did not originate it with him." Peacock : *Memoirs of Percy Bysshe Shelley*, Pt. 2.   G.

[1] *Ecclesiastes*, iv. 13.   G.

Europe, gives what the world calls elegance, where less partial nature has denied it. There are in this respect two classes of human beings : Nature makes the first herself, for the beauty of her own creation : her journeymen cut out the second for tailors and mantua-makers to finish. The first, when apparelled, may be called dressed people—the second, peopled dresses : the first bear the same relation to their clothes as an oak bears to its foliage—the second, the same as a wig-block bears to a wig : the first may be compared to cocoa-nuts, in which the kernel is more valuable than the shell—the second, to some varieties of the *Testaceous Mollusca*, where a shell of infinite value covers a stupid fish that is good for nothing.

Mrs. Desmond recognised Mr. Fax. " O Sir ! " said she, " I rejoice to see you."—" And I rejoice," said Mr. Fax, " to see you as you now are : Fortune has befriended you."—" You rendered us great service, Sir, in our wretched condition ; but the benefit, of course, was transient. With the next quarter-day Mr. Litigate, our landlord, resumed his persecutions ; and we should have been turned out of our wretched dwelling to perish in the roads, had not some happy accident made Miss Melincourt acquainted with our situation. To know what it was, and to make it what it is, were the same thing to her. So suddenly, when the extremity of evil was impending over us, to be placed in this little Paradise in competence—nay, to our simple habits, in affluence, and in such a manner, as if we were bestowing, not receiving, favours— O Sir! there cannot be two Miss Melincourts! But will you not walk in, and take some refreshment ? —We can offer you refreshment now. My husband is absent at present, but he will very soon return."

While she was speaking he arrived. Mr. Fax congratulated him. At his earnest solicitation, they entered the cottage, and were delighted with the beautiful neatness that predominated in every part of it. The three children ran in to see the strangers. Mr. Forester took up the little girl, Mr. Fax a boy, and Sir Oran Haut-ton another. The latter took alarm at the physiognomy of his new friend, and cried, and kicked, and struggled for release ; but Sir Oran producing a flute from his pocket, struck up a lively air, which reconciled the child, who then sate very quietly on his knee.

Some refreshment was placed before them, and Sir Oran testified, by a copious draught, that he found much virtue in home-brewed ale.

"There is a farm attached to this cottage," said Mr. Desmond; "and Miss Melincourt, by having placed me in it, enabled me to maintain my family in comfort and independence, and to educate them in a free, healthy, and natural occupation. I have ever thought agriculture the noblest of human pursuits: to the theory and practice of it I now devote my whole attention, and I am not without hopes that the improvement of this part of my benefactress's estate will justify her generous confidence in a friendless stranger: but what can repay her benevolence?"

"I will answer for her," said Mr. Forester, "though she is as yet personally unknown to me, that she loves benevolence for its own sake, and is satisfied with its consummation."

After a short conversation, and a promise soon to revisit the now happy family, Mr. Forester, Mr. Fax, and Sir Oran Haut-ton resumed their walk. Mr. Forester, at parting, put unobserved into the hand of the little boy a folded paper, telling him to give it to his father. It was a leaf which he had torn from his pocket-book: he had enclosed in it a bank-note, and had written on it with a pencil, "Do not refuse to a stranger the happiness of reflecting that he has, however tardily and slightly, co-operated with Miss Melincourt in a work of justice."

CHAPTER XV

THE LIBRARY

MR. FORESTER, Mr. Fax, and Sir Oran Haut-ton arrived at Melincourt Castle. They were shown into a parlour, where they were left alone a few minutes; when Mr. Hippy made his appearance, and recognising Sir Oran, shook hands with him very cordially. Mr. Forester produced the letter he had received from Mr. Ratstail, which Mr. Hippy having read, vented a string of invectives against the impudent rascal, and explained the mystery of the adventure, though he seemed to think it strange that Sir Oran could not have explained it himself. Mr. Forester shook his head significantly; and Mr. Hippy affecting to understand the gesture, exclaimed, " Ah! poor gentleman! "—He then invited them to stay to dinner. " I won't be refused," said he; " I am lord and master of this castle at present, and here you shall stay till to-morrow. Anthy will be delighted to see her friend here" (bowing to Sir Oran, who returned it with great politeness), " and we will hold a council of war how to deal with this pair of puppies, Lawrence Litigate, Esquire, and Richard Ratstail, Solicitor. I have several visitors here already: lords, baronets, and squires, all Corydons, sighing for Anthy; but it seems *Love's Labour Lost* with all of them. However, love and wine, you know! Anthy won't give them the first, so I drench them with the second: there will be more bottles than hearts cracked in the business, for all Anthy's beauty. *Men die, and worms eat them*, as usual, *but not for love*." [1]

Mr. Forester inquired for Sir Telegraph Paxarett. " An excellent fellow after dinner! " exclaimed Mr. Hippy. " I never see him in the morning; nor any one else, but my rascal Harry Fell, and now and then Doctor Killquick. The moment breakfast is over, one goes one way, and another another. Anthy locks herself up in the library."

" Locks herself up in the library! " said Mr. Fax: " a young lady, a beauty, and an heiress, in the nineteenth century, think of cultivating her understanding! "

" Strange but true," said Mr. Hippy; " and here am I, a poor invalid, left alone all the morning to prowl about the castle like a ghost; that is, when I am well enough to move, which is not always the case. But the library is opened at four, and the party assembles there before dinner; and as it is now about the time, come with me, and I will introduce you."

They followed Mr. Hippy to the library, where they found Anthelia alone.

" Anthy," said Mr. Hippy, after the forms of introduction, " do you know you are accused of laying waste a pine-grove, and carrying it off by cart-loads, with force and arms? "

---

[1] *As You Like It*, Act IV, Sc. 1.   G.

Anthelia read Mr. Ratstail's letter. " This is a very strange piece of folly," she said : " I hope it will not be a mischievous one." She then renewed the expressions of her gratitude to Sir Oran, and bade him welcome to Melincourt. Sir Oran bowed in silence.

" Folly and mischief," said Mr. Fax, " are very nearly allied ; and no where more conspicuously than in the forms of the law."

MR. FORESTER. You have an admirable library, Miss Melincourt : and I judge from the great number of Italian books, you are justly partial to the poets of that exquisite language. The apartment itself seems singularly adapted to the genius of their poetry, which combines the magnificent simplicity of ancient Greece with the mysterious grandeur of the feudal ages. Those windows of stained glass would recall to an enthusiastic mind the attendant spirit of Tasso[1]; and the waving of the cedars beyond, when the wind makes music in their boughs, with the birds singing in their shades and the softened dash of the torrent from the dingle below, might, with little aid from fancy, be modulated into that exquisite combination of melody which flowed from the enchanted wood at the entrance of Rinaldo, and which Tasso has painted with a degree of harmony not less magical than the music he describes. Italian poetry is all fairyland : I know not any description of literature so congenial to the tenderness and delicacy of the female mind, which, however opposite may be the tendency of modern education, Nature has most pre-eminently adapted to be " a mansion for all lovely forms : a dwelling-place for all sweet sounds and harmonies."[2] Of these, Italian poetry is a most inexhaustible fountain ; and for that reason I could wish it to be generally acknowledged a point of the very first importance in female education.

ANTHELIA. You have a better opinion of the understandings of women, Sir, than the generality of your lordly sex seems disposed to entertain.

MR. FORESTER. The conduct of men, in this respect, is much like

[1] During his insanity one of Torquato Tasso's recurring hallucinations was the frequent visitation of a familiar spirit with whom he held long dialogues. G.

[2] Wordsworth's *Tintern Abbey*. [P.]

that of a gardener who should plant a plot of ground with merely ornamental flowers, and then pass sentence on the soil for not bearing substantial fruit. If women are treated only as pretty dolls, and dressed in all the fripperies of irrational education ; if the vanity of personal adornment and superficial accomplishments be made from their very earliest years to suppress all mental aspirations, and to supersede all thoughts of intellectual beauty, is it to be inferred that they are incapable of better things ? But such is the usual logic of tyranny, which first places its extinguisher on the flame, and then argues that it cannot burn.

MR. FAX. Your remark is not totally just : for though custom, how justly I will not say, banishes women from the fields of classical literature, yet the study of Italian poetry, of which you think so highly, is very much encouraged among them.

MR. FORESTER. You should rather say it is not discouraged. They are permitted to know it : but in very few instances is the permission accompanied by any practical aid. The only points practically enforced in female education are sound, colour, and form, —music, dress, drawing, and dancing. The mind is left to take care of itself.

MR. FAX. And has as much chance of doing so as a horse in a pound, circumscribed in the narrowest limits, and studiously deprived of nourishment.

ANTHELIA. The simile is, I fear, too just. To think is one of the most unpardonable errors a woman can commit in the eyes of society. In our sex a taste for intellectual pleasures is almost equivalent to taking the veil ; and though not absolutely a vow of perpetual celibacy, it has almost always the same practical tendency. In that universal system of superficial education which so studiously depresses the mind of women, a female who aspires to mental improvement will scarcely find in her own sex a congenial associate ; and the other will regard her as an intruder on its prescriptive authority, its legitimate and divine right over the dominion of thought and reason : and the general consequence is, that she remains insulated between both, in more than cloistered loneliness.

Even in its effect on herself, the ideal beauty which she studies will
make her fastidious, too fastidious, perhaps, to the world of realities,
and deprive her of the happiness that might be her portion, by fixing
her imagination on chimæras of unattainable excellence.

MR. FORESTER.   I can answer for men, Miss Melincourt, that there
are some, many I hope, who can appreciate justly that most heavenly
of earthly things, an enlightened female mind ; whatever may be
thought by the pedantry that envies, the foppery that fears, the folly
that ridicules, or the wilful blindness that will not see its loveliness.
I am afraid your last observation approaches most nearly to the
truth, and that it is owing more to their own fastidiousness than to
the want of friends and admirers, that intelligent women are so often
alone in the world.   But were it otherwise, the objection will not
apply to Italian poetry, a field of luxuriant beauty, from which
women are not interdicted even by the most intolerant prejudice of
masculine usurpation.

ANTHELIA.   They are not interdicted, certainly ; but they are
seldom encouraged to enter it.   Perhaps it is feared, that, having
gone thus far, they might be tempted to go farther : that the friend
of Tasso might aspire to the acquaintance of Virgil, or even to an
introduction to Homer and Sophocles.

MR. FORESTER.   And why should she not ?   Far from desiring to
suppress such a noble ambition, how delightful should I think the
task of conducting the lovely aspirant through the treasures of
Grecian genius !—to wander hand-in-hand with such a companion
among the valleys and fountains of Ida, and by the banks of the
eddying Scamander ; [1] through the island of Calypso and the
gardens of Alcinous ; [2] to the rocks of the Scythian desert ; [3] to the
caverned shores of the solitary Lemnos ; [4] and to the fatal sands of
Troezene : [5]—to kindle in such scenes the enthusiasm of such a mind,
and to see the eyes of love and beauty beaming with their reflected

[1] The *Iliad*. [P.]   [2] The *Odyssey*.   [P.]
[3] The *Prometheus* of Æschylus.   [P.]
[4] The *Philoctetes* of Sophocles.   [P.]
[5] The *Hippolytus* of Euripides.   [P.]

inspiration ! Miserably perverted, indeed, must be the selfishness of him who, having such happiness in his power, would,

> "Like the base Indian, throw a pearl away,
> Richer than all his tribe." [1]

MR. FAX. My friend's enthusiasm, Miss Melincourt, usually runs away with him when any allusion is made to ancient Greece.

Mr. Forester had spoken with ardour and animation; for the scenes of which he spoke rose upon his mind as depicted in the incomparable poetry to which he had alluded; the figurative idea of wandering among them with a young and beautiful female aspirant, assumed for a moment a visionary reality; and when he subsequently reflected on it, it appeared to him very singular that the female figure in the mental picture had assumed the form and features of Anthelia Melincourt.

Anthelia, too, saw in the animated countenance of Sylvan Forester traces of more than common feeling, generosity, and intelligence : his imaginary wanderings through the classic scenes of antiquity assumed in her congenial mind the brightest colours of intellectual beauty; and she could not help thinking that if he were what he appeared, such wanderings, with such a guide, would not be the most unenviable of earthly destinies.

The other guests dropped in by ones and twos. Sir Telegraph was agreeably surprised to see Mr. Forester : " By the bye," said he, " have you heard that a general election is to take place immediately ? "

" I have," said Mr. Forester, " and was thinking of putting you and your barouche in requisition very shortly."

" As soon as you please," said Sir Telegraph.

The Honourable Mrs. Pinmoney took Sir Telegraph aside, to make inquiry concerning the new-comers.

THE HONOURABLE MRS. PINMONEY. Who is that very bright-eyed wild-looking young man ?

SIR TELEGRAPH PAXARETT. That is my old acquaintance and

[1] *Othello*, Act V, Sc. 2. G.

fellow-collegian, Sylvan Forester, now of Redrose Abbey, in this county.

THE HONOURABLE MRS. PINMONEY.   Is he respectable ?

SIR TELEGRAPH PAXARETT.   He has a good estate, if you mean that.

THE HONOURABLE MRS. PINMONEY.   To be sure I mean that.   And who is that tall thin saturnine personage ?

SIR TELEGRAPH PAXARETT.   I know nothing of him but that his name is Fax, and that he is now on a visit to Mr. Forester at Redrose Abbey.

THE HONOURABLE MRS. PINMONEY.   And who is that *very* tall and remarkably ugly gentleman ?

SIR TELEGRAPH PAXARETT.   That is Sir Oran Haut-ton, Baronet ; to which designation you may shortly add M.P. for the ancient and honourable borough of Onevote.

THE HONOURABLE MRS. PINMONEY. A Baronet ! and M.P. ! Well, now I look at him again, I certainly do not think him so very plain : he has a very fashionable air.   Haut-ton !   French extraction, no doubt.   And now I think of it, there is something very French in his physiognomy.

Dinner was announced, and the party adjourned to the dining-room.   Mr. Forester offered his hand to Anthelia ; and Sir Oran Haut-ton, following the example, presented his to the Honourable Mrs. Pinmoney.[1]

---

[1] " Je l'ai vu présenter sa main pour reconduire les gens qui venoient le visiter ; se promener gravement avec eux et comme de compagnie, &c."— BUFFON. *H. N. de l'Oran-Outang.* [P.]

CHAPTER XVI

THE SYMPOSIUM

THE dinner passed off with great harmony. The ladies withdrew. The bottle revolved with celerity, under the presidency of Mr. Hippy, and the vice-presidency of Sir Telegraph Paxarett. The Reverend Mr. Portpipe, who was that day of the party, pronounced an eulogium on the wine, which was echoed by the Reverend Mr. Grovelgrub, Mr. O'Scarum, Lord Anophel Achthar, Mr. Feathernest, and Mr. Derrydown. Mr. Forester and Mr. Fax showed no disposition to destroy the unanimity of opinion on this interesting subject. Sir Oran Haut-ton maintained a grave and dignified silence, but demonstrated by his practice that his taste was orthodox. Mr. O'Scarum sate between Sir Oran and the Reverend Mr. Portpipe, and kept a sharp look-out on both sides of him; but did not, during the whole course of the sitting, detect either of his supporters in the heinous fact of a heeltap.

MR. HIPPY.   Dr. Killquick may say what he pleases

> " Of mithridate, cordials, and elixirs;
>   But from my youth this was my only physic.—
>   Here's a colour ! what lady's cheek comes near it ?
>   It sparkles, hangs out diamonds !   O my sweet heart !
>   Mistress of merry hearts ! they are not worth thy favours
>   Who number thy moist kisses in these crystals ! " [1]

THE REVEREND MR. PORTPIPE.   An excellent text !—sound doctrine, plain and practical. When I open the bottle, I shut the book of Numbers. There are two reasons for drinking : one is, when you are thirsty, to cure it ; the other, when you are not thirsty, to prevent it. The first is obvious, mechanical, and plebeian ; the second is most refined, abstract, prospicient, and canonical. I drink by anticipation of thirst that may be. Prevention is better than cure. Wine is the elixir of life. " The soul," says St. Augustine, " cannot live in drought." [2] What is death ? Dust and ashes. There is nothing so dry. What is life ? Spirit. What is Spirit ? Wine.

---

[1] Fletcher's *Sea Voyage*. [P.] [Act V, Sc. 1.   Two speeches telescoped.
                                                                        G.]

[2] Anima certe, quia spiritus est, in sicco habitare non potest. [P.]

MR. O'SCARUM. And whisky.

THE REVEREND MR. PORTPIPE. Whisky is hepatic, phlogistic, and exanthematous. Wine is the hierarchical and archiepiscopal fluid. Bacchus is said to have conquered the East, and to have returned loaded with its spoils. "Marry how? tropically." [1] The conquests of Bacchus are the victories of imagination, which, sublimated by wine, puts to rout care, fear, and poverty, and revels in the treasures of Utopia.

MR. FEATHERNEST. The juice of the grape is the liquid quint-essence of concentrated sun-beams. Man is an exotic, in this northern climate, and must be nourished like a hot-house plant, by the perpetual adhibition of artificial heat.

LORD ANOPHEL ACHTHAR. You were not always so fond of wine, Feathernest ?

MR. FEATHERNEST. Oh, my Lord! no allusion, I beseech you, to my youthful errors. Demosthenes being asked what wine he liked best, answered, that which he drank at the expense of others.

THE REVEREND MR. PORTPIPE. Demosthenes was right. His circumstance, or qualification, is an accompaniment of better relish than a devilled biscuit or an anchovy toast.

MR. FEATHERNEST. In former days, my Lord, I had no experience that way ; therefore I drank water against my will.

LORD ANOPHEL ACHTHAR. And wrote Odes upon it, to Truth and Liberty.

MR. FEATHERNEST. " Ah, no more of that, an' thou lovest me." [2] Now that I can get it for a song, I take my pipe of wine a year : and what is the effect ? Not cold phlegmatic lamentations over the sufferings of the poor, but high-flown, jovial, reeling dithyrambics " to all the crowned heads in Europe." I had then a vague notion that all was wrong. Persuasion has since appeared to me in a tangible shape, and convinced me that all is right, especially at

[1] *Hamlet*, Act III, Sc. 2. G.
[2] *Henry IV*, *Pt. I*, Act II, Sc. 4. G.

court. Then I saw darkly through a glass—of water. Now I see
clearly through a glass of wine.

THE REVEREND MR. PORTPIPE (*looking through his glass, at the light.*
An infallible telescope !

MR. FORESTER. I am unfortunately one of those, Sir, who very
much admired your Odes to Truth and Liberty, and read your royal
lyrics with very different sensations.

MR. FEATHERNEST. I presume, Sir, every man has a right to change
his opinions.

MR. FORESTER. From disinterested conviction undoubtedly : but
when it is obviously from mercenary motives, the apostacy of a
public man is a public calamity. It is not his single loss to the cause
he supported, that is alone to be lamented : the deep shade of mistrust which his conduct throws on that of all others, who embark in
the same career, tends to destroy all sympathy with the enthusiasm
of genius, all admiration for the intrepidity of truth, all belief in the
sincerity of zeal for public liberty : if their advocates drop one by
one into the vortex of courtly patronage, every new one that arises
will be more and more regarded as a hollow-hearted hypocrite, a false
and venal angler for pension and place ; for there is in these cases no
criterion, by which the world can distinguish the baying of a noble
dog that will defend his trust till death, from the yelping of a political
cur, that only infests the heels of power to be silenced with the offals
of corruption.

LORD ANOPHEL ACHTHAR. Cursed severe, Feathernest, 'pon
honour.

MR. FAX. *The gradual falling off of prudent men from unprofitable
virtues, is perhaps too common an occurrence to deserve much notice, or
justify much reprobation.*[1]

MR. FORESTER. If it were not common, it would not need reprobation. Vices of unfrequent occurrence stand sufficiently self-
exposed in the insulation of their own deformity. The vices that

---

[1] *Edinburgh Review*, No. liii. p. 10. [P.]

call for the scourge of satire, are those which pervade the whole frame of society, and which, under some specious pretence of private duty, or the sanction of custom and precedent, are almost permitted to assume the semblance of virtue, or at least to pass unstigmatized in the crowd of congenial transgressions.

MR. FEATHERNEST. You may say what you please, Sir. I am accustomed to this language, and am quite callous to it, I assure you. I am in good odour at court, Sir ; and you know, *Non cuivis homini contingit adire Corinthum.*[1] While I was out, Sir, I made a great noise till I was let in. There was a pack of us, Sir, to keep up your canine metaphor : two or three others got in at the same time : we knew very well that those who were shut out, would raise a hue and cry after us : it was perfectly natural : we should have done the same in their place : mere envy and malice, nothing more. Let them bark on : when they are either wanted or troublesome, they will be let in, in their turn. If there be any man, who prefers a crust and water, to venison and sack, I am not of his mind. It is pretty and politic to make a virtue of necessity : but when there is an end of the necessity I am very willing that there should be an end of the virtue. *If you could live on roots,* said Diogenes to Aristippus, *you would have nothing to do with kings.—If you could live on kings,* replied Aristippus, *you would have nothing to do with roots.*—Every man for himself, Sir, and God for all of us.

MR. DERRYDOWN. The truth of things on this subject, is contained in the following stave :

> " This world is a well-furnished table,
> Where guests are promiscuously set :
> We all fare as well as we're able,
> And scramble for what we can get." [2]

---

[1] " It does not fall to the lot of every man to visit Corinth." Hor. *Epist.* I. xvii. 36. G.

[2] These lines clearly inspired the more famous epigram of Byron, first published in *Letters and Journals* V. ii. 494.

> " The world is a bundle of hay,
> Mankind are the asses who pull ;
> Each tugs it a different way,
> And the greatest of all is John Bull."

Byron greatly appreciated *Melincourt.* (Shelley to Peacock, Aug. 1821.)
G.

SIR TELEGRAPH PAXARETT. Buz the bottle.

MR. O'SCARUM. Over, by Jupiter!

SIR TELEGRAPH PAXARETT. No.

MR. O'SCARUM. Yes.

THE REVEREND MR. PORTPIPE. No. The Baronet has a most mathematical eye. Buzzed to a drop!

MR. FORESTER. Fortunately, Sir, for the hopes of mankind, every man does not bring his honour and conscience to market, though I admit the majority do: there are some who dare be honest in the worst of times.

MR. FEATHERNEST. Perhaps, Sir, you are one of those who can *afford to have a conscience*, and are therefore under no necessity of bringing it to market. If so, you should " give God thanks, and make no boast of it." [1] It is a great luxury certainly, and well worth keeping, *cæteris paribus*. But it is neither meat, clothes, nor fire. It becomes a good coat well; but it will never make one. Poets are verbal musicians, and, like other musicians, they have a right to sing and play, where they can be best paid for their music.

MR. FORESTER. There could be no objection to that, if they would be content to announce themselves as dealers and chapmen: but the poetical character is too frequently a combination of the most arrogant and exclusive assumption of freedom and independence in theory, with the most abject and unqualified venality, servility, and sycophancy in practice.

MR. FEATHERNEST. It is *as notorious*, Sir, *as the sun at noonday*, that theory and practice are never expected to coincide. If a West Indian planter declaims against the Algerines, do you expect him to lose any favourable opportunity of increasing the number of his own slaves? If an invaded country cries out against spoliation, do you suppose, if the tables were turned, it would show its weaker neighbours the forbearance it required? If an Opposition orator clamours

---

[1] *Much Ado About Nothing*, Act III, Sc. 3. G.

for a reform in Parliament, does any one dream, that, if he gets into office, he will ever say another word about it ?   If one of your reverend friends should display his touching eloquence on the subject of temperance, would you therefore have the barbarity to curtail him of one drop of his three bottles ?   Truth and liberty, Sir, are pretty words, very pretty words—a few years ago they were the gods of the day—they superseded in poetry the agency of mythology and magic : they were the only passports into the poetical market : I acted accordingly the part of a prudent man : I took my station, became my own crier, and vociferated Truth and Liberty, till the noise I made brought people about me, to bid for me : and to the highest bidder I knocked myself down, at less than I am worth certainly ; but when an article is not likely to keep, it is by no means prudent to postpone the sale.

> "What makes all doctrines plain and clear ?
> About two hundred pounds a year.—
> And that which was proved true before,
> Prove false again ?—Two hundred more." [1]

MR. HIPPY.   A dry discussion !   Pass the bottle, and moisten it.

MR. O'SCARUM.   Here's half of us fast asleep.   Let us make a little noise to wake us.   A glee now : I'll be one : who'll join ?

SIR TELEGRAPH PAXARETT.   I.

THE REVEREND MR. PORTPIPE.   And I.

MR. HIPPY.   Strike up then.   Silence !

GLEE—THE GHOSTS

In life three ghostly friars were we,
And now three friarly ghosts we be.
Around our shadowy table placed,
The spectral bowl before us floats :
With wine that none but ghosts can taste,
We wash our unsubstantial throats.
Three merry ghosts—three merry ghosts—three merry ghosts are we :
Let the ocean be Port, and we'll think it good sport
To be laid in that Red Sea.

---

[1] Butler : *Hudibras*, Pt. III, Canto 1, lines 1277–80.   G.

With songs that jovial spectres chaunt,
Our old refectory still we haunt.
The traveller hears our midnight mirth :
" O list ! " he cries, " the haunted choir !
"The merriest ghost that walks the earth,
" Is sure the ghost of a ghostly friar."
Three merry ghosts—three merry ghosts—three merry ghosts are we :
Let the ocean be Port, and we'll think it good sport
To be laid in that Red Sea.

MR. HIPPY.   Bravo ! I should like to have my house so haunted.
The deuce is in it, if three such ghosts would not keep the blue devils
at bay.   Come, we'll lay them in a bumper of claret.

(*Sir Oran Haut-ton took his flute from his pocket, and played over
the air of the glee. The company was at first extremely surprised, and
then joined in applauding his performance. Sir Oran bowed acknowledgment, and returned his flute to his pocket.*)

MR. FORESTER.   It is, perhaps, happy for yourself, Mr. Feathernest, that you can treat with so much levity a subject that fills me
with the deepest grief.   Man under the influence of civilization has
fearfully diminished in size and deteriorated in strength.   The intellectual are confessedly nourished at the expense of the physical
faculties.   Air, the great source and fountain of health and life, can
scarcely find access to civilized man, muffled as he is in clothes, pent
in houses, smoke-dried in cities, half-roasted by artificial fire, and
parboiled in the hydrogen of crowded apartments.   Diseases multiply
upon him in compound proportion.   Even if the prosperous among us
enjoy some comforts unknown to the natural man, yet what is the
poverty of the savage, compared with that of the lowest classes in
civilized nations ?   The specious aspect of luxury and abundance
in one, is counterbalanced by the abject penury and circumscription
of hundreds.   Commercial prosperity is a golden surface, but all
beneath it is rags and wretchedness.   It is not in the splendid bustle
of our principal streets—in the villas and mansions that sprinkle our
valleys—for those who enjoy these things (even if they did enjoy them
—even if they had health and happiness—and the rich have seldom
either), bear but a small proportion to the whole population :—but it
is in the mud hovel of the labourer—in the cellar of the artizan—in

our crowded prisons—our swarming hospitals—our overcharged workhouses—in those narrow districts of our overgrown cities, which the affluent never see—where thousands and thousands of families are compressed within limits not sufficient for the pleasure-ground of a simple squire,—that we must study the true mechanism of political society. When the philosopher turns away in despair from this dreadful accumulation of moral and physical evil, where is he to look for consolation, if not in the progress of science, in the enlargement of mind, in the diffusion of philosophical truth ? But if truth is a chimæra—if virtue is a name—if science is not the handmaid of moral improvement, but the obsequious minister of recondite luxury, the specious appendage of vanity and power—then indeed, *that man has fallen never to rise again*,[1] is as much the cry of nature as the dream of superstition.

THE REVEREND MR. PORTPIPE. Man has fallen, certainly, by the fruit of the tree of knowledge : which shows that human learning is vanity and a great evil, and therefore very properly discountenanced by all bishops, priests, and deacons.

MR. FAX. The picture which you have drawn of poverty is not very tempting ; and you must acknowledge that it is most galling to the most refined feelings. You must not, therefore, wonder that it is peculiarly obnoxious to the practical notions of poets. If the radiance of gold and silver gleam not through the foliage of the Pierian laurel, there is something to be said in their excuse if they carry their chaplet to those who will gild its leaves ; and in that case they will find their best customers and patrons among those who are ambitious of acquiring panegyric by a more compendious method than the troublesome practice of the virtues that deserve it.

MR. FORESTER. You have quoted Juvenal, but you should have completed the sentence : " If you see no glimpse of coin in the Pierian shade, you will prefer the name and occupation of a barber or an auctioneer." [2] This is most just : if the pursuits of literature,

---

[1] See the preface to the third volume of the *Ancient Metaphysics*. See also Rousseau's *Discourse on Inequality*, and that on the *Arts and Sciences*.   [P.]

[2] nam si Pieria quadrans tibi nullus in umbra
    ostendatur, ames nomen victumque Machæræ,
    et vendas potius commissa quod auctio vendit, &c.—JUV. [P.]
                                        [*Sat*. VII. 8–10. G.]

conscientiously conducted, condemn their votary to famine, let him
live by more humble, but at least by honest, and therefore honourable occupations : he may still devote his leisure to his favourite
pursuits. If he produce but a single volume consecrated to moral
truth, its effect must be good as far as it goes ; but if he purchase
leisure and luxury by the prostitution of talent to the cause of superstition and tyranny, every new exertion of his powers is a new
outrage to reason and virtue, and in precise proportion to those
powers is he a curse to his country, and a traitor to mankind.

MR. FEATHERNEST. A barber, Sir !—a man of genius turn
barber !

MR. O'SCARUM. Troth, Sir, and I think it is better he should
be in the suds himself, than help to bring his country into that
situation.

MR. FORESTER. I can perceive, Sir, in your exclamation the
principle that has caused so enormous a superabundance in the number of bad books over that of good ones.   The objects of the majority
of men of talent seem to be exclusively two : the first, to convince
the world of their transcendent abilities ; the second, to convert that
conviction into a source of the greatest possible pecuniary benefit to
themselves.   But there is no class of men more resolutely indifferent
to the moral tendency of the means by which their ends are accomplished.   Yet this is the most extensively pernicious of all modes of
dishonesty ; for that of a private man can only injure the pockets of
a few individuals (a great evil, certainly, but light in comparison) ;
while that of a public writer, who has previously taught the multitude
to respect his talents, perverts what is much more valuable, the
mental progress of thousands ; misleading, on the one hand, the
shallow believers in his sincerity ; and on the other, stigmatizing
the whole literary character in the opinions of all who see through
the veil of his venality.

MR. FEATHERNEST. All this is no reason, Sir, why a man of genius
should condescend to be a barber.

MR. FORESTER. He condescends much more in being a sycophant.

The poorest barber in the poorest borough in England, who will not sell his vote, is a much more honourable character in the estimate of moral comparison than the most self-satisfied dealer in courtly poetry, whose well-paid eulogiums of licentiousness and corruption were ever re-echoed by the "most sweet voices" of hireling gazetteers and pensioned reviewers.

The summons to tea and coffee put a stop to the conversation.

CHAPTER XVII

MUSIC AND DISCORD

THE evenings were beginning to give symptoms of winter, and a large fire was blazing in the library. Mr. Forester took the opportunity of stigmatizing the use of sugar, and had the pleasure of observing that the practice of Anthelia in this respect was the same as his own. He mentioned his intention of giving an anti-saccharine festival at Red-rose Abbey, and invited all the party at Melincourt to attend it. He observed that his aunt, Miss Evergreen, who would be there at the time, would send an invitation in due form to the ladies, to remove all scruples on the score of propriety; and added, that if he could hope for the attendance of half as much moral feeling as he was sure there would be of beauty and fashion, he should be satisfied that a great step would be made towards accomplishing the object of the Anti-saccharine Society.

The Reverend Mr. Grovelgrub felt extremely indignant at Mr. Forester's notion " of every real enemy to slavery being bound by the strictest moral duty to practical abstinence from the luxuries which slavery acquires;" but when he found that the notion was to be developed in the shape of a festival, he determined to suspend his judgment till he had digested the solid arguments that were to be brought forward on the occasion.

Mr. O'Scarum was, as usual, very clamorous for music, and was

seconded by the unanimous wish of the company, with which
Anthelia readily complied, and sung as follows :

THE FLOWER OF LOVE.

'Tis said the rose is Love's own flower,
　Its blush so bright, its thorns so many ;
And winter on its bloom has power,
　But has not on its sweetness any.
For though young Love's ethereal rose
　Will droop on Age's wintry bosom,
Yet still its faded leaves disclose
　The fragrance of their earliest blossom.

But ah ! the fragrance lingering there
　Is like the sweets that mournful duty
Bestows with sadly-soothing care,
　To deck the grave of bloom and beauty.
For when its leaves are shrunk and dry,
　Its blush extinct, to kindle never,
That fragrance is but Memory's sigh,
　That breathes of pleasures past for ever.

Why did not Love the amaranth choose,
　That bears no thorns, and cannot perish ?
Alas ! no sweets its flowers diffuse,
　And only sweets Love's life can cherish.
But be the rose and amaranth twined,
　And Love, their mingled powers assuming,
Shall round his brows a chaplet bind,
　For ever sweet, for ever blooming.

" I am afraid," said Mr. Derrydown, " the flower of modern love is
neither the rose nor the amaranth, but the *chrysanthemum*, or *gold-
flower*. If Miss Danaretta and Mr. O'Scarum will accompany me,
we will sing a little harmonized ballad, something in point, and rather
more comformable to the truth of things." Mr. O'Scarum and Miss
Danaretta consented, and they accordingly sung the following

BALLAD TERZETTO

THE LADY, THE KNIGHT, AND THE FRIAR

THE LADY

O cavalier ! what dost thou here,
　Thy tuneful vigils keeping ;
While the northern star looks cold from far,
　And half the world is sleeping ?

THE KNIGHT

O lady ! here, for seven long year,
Have I been nightly sighing,
Without the hope of a single tear
To pity me were I dying.

THE LADY

Should I take thee to have and to hold,
Who hast nor lands nor money ?
Alas ! 'tis only in flowers of gold
That married bees find honey.

THE KNIGHT

O lady fair ! to my constant prayer
Fate proves at last propitious ;
And bags of gold in my hand I bear,
And parchment scrolls delicious.

THE LADY

My maid the door shall open throw,
For we too long have tarried :
The friar keeps watch in the cellar below,
And we will at once be married.

THE FRIAR

My children ! great is Fortune's power ;
And plain this truth appears,
That gold thrives more in a single hour,
Than love in seven long years.

During this terzetto the Reverend Mr. Portpipe fell asleep, and
accompanied the performance with rather a deeper bass than was
generally deemed harmonious.

Sir Telegraph Paxarett took Mr. Forester aside, to consult him on
the subject of the journey to Onevote.

"I have asked," said he, "my aunt and cousin, Mrs. and Miss
Pinmoney, to join the party, and have requested them to exert their
influence with Miss Melincourt to induce her to accompany them."

"That would make it a delightful expedition, indeed," said Mr.
Forester, "if Miss Melincourt could be prevailed on to comply."

"*Nil desperandum*," said Sir Telegraph.

The Honourable Mrs. Pinmoney drew Anthelia into a corner, and
developed all her eloquence in enforcing the proposition. Miss
Danaretta joined in it with great earnestness ; and they kept up the

fire of their importunity till they extorted from Anthelia a promise that she would consider of it.

Mr. Forester took down a splendid edition of Tasso, printed by Bodoni at Parma,[1] and found it ornamented with Anthelia's drawings. In the magic of her pencil the wild and wonderful scenes of Tasso seemed to live under his eyes : he could not forbear expressing to her the delight he experienced from these new proofs of her sensibility and genius, and entered into a conversation with her concerning her favourite poet, in which the congeniality of their tastes and feelings became more and more manifest to each other.

Mr. Feathernest and Mr. Derrydown got into a hot dispute over Chapman's Homer and Jeremy Taylor's Holy Living : Mr. Derrydown maintaining that the ballad metre which Chapman had so judiciously chosen, rendered his volume the most divine poem in the world ; Mr. Feathernest asserting that Chapman's verses were mere doggerel : which vile aspersion Mr. Derrydown revenged by depreciating Mr. Feathernest's favourite Jeremy. Mr. Feathernest said he could expect no better judgment from a man who was mad enough to prefer Chevy Chase to Paradise Lost ; and Mr. Derrydown retorted, that it was idle to expect either taste or justice from one who had thought fit to unite in himself two characters so anomalous as those of a poet and a critic, in which duplex capacity he had first deluged the world with torrents of execrable verses, and then written anonymous criticisms to prove them divine. " Do you think, Sir," he continued, " that it is possible for the same man to be both Homer and Aristotle ? No, Sir ; but it is very possible to be both Dennis and Colley Cibber,[2] as in the melancholy example before me."

At this all the blood of the *genus irritabile* boiled in Mr. Feather-

---

[1] The *Aminta* was printed at Parma by Bodoni in 1787. G.

[2] Dennis was a bad critic and dramatist whose plays were failures, but he invented a new kind of stage thunder which was an improvement on earlier rumblings. His bitter remark : " They have stolen my thunder ! " when listening to a rival's play, is his chief claim to immortality. Southey, however, praised his criticism, which makes Mr. Derrydown's remark particularly apt. Colley Cibber, the actor, wrote about thirty plays, mostly adaptations from Shakespeare. Of one of them he remarked : " I have endeavoured to make it more like a play than I found it in Shakespeare." Both Dennis and Cibber were embroiled in feuds with Pope and figure in *The Dunciad*. G.

nest's veins, and uplifting the ponderous folio, he seemed inclined to
bury his antagonist under Jeremy's *weight of words*, by applying
them in a *tangible shape* ; but wisely recollecting that this was not
the time and place

> " To prove his doctrine orthodox,
>   By apostolic blows and knocks," [1]

he contented himself with a point-blank denial of the charge that he
wrote critiques on his own works, protesting that all the articles on
his poems were written either by his friend Mr. Mystic, of Cimmerian
Lodge, or by Mr. Vamp, the amiable editor of the Legitimate Review.
" Yes," said Mr. Derrydown, " on the ' *Tickle me, Mr. Hayley* '
principle ; by which a miserable cabal of doggerel rhymesters and
worn-out paragraph-mongers of bankrupt gazettes ring the eternal
changes of panegyric on each other, and on every thing else that is
either rich enough to buy their praise, or vile enough to deserve it :
like a gang in a country steeple, paid for being a public nuisance, and
maintaining that noise is melody."

Mr. Feathernest on this became perfectly outrageous ; and waving
Jeremy Taylor in the air, exclaimed, " *Oh that mine enemy had written
a book !* [2] Horrible should be the vengeance of the Legitimate
Review ! "

Mr. Hippy now deemed it expedient to interpose for the restoration
of order, and entreated Anthelia to throw in a little musical harmony
as a sedative to the ebullitions of poetical discord. At the sound
of the harp the antagonists turned away, the one flourishing his
Chapman and the other his Jeremy with looks of lofty defiance.

CHAPTER XVIII

THE STRATAGEM

The Reverend Mr. Grovelgrub, who had acquired a great proficiency
in the art of hearing without seeming to listen, had overheard Mrs.

---

[1] Butler : *Hudibras*, Pt. I, Canto 1, lines 199-200. G.
[2] *Job* xxxi. 35. G.

Pinmoney's request to Anthelia ; and, notwithstanding the young lady's hesitation, he very much feared she would ultimately comply. He had seen, much against his will, a great congeniality in feelings and opinions, between her and Mr. Forester, and had noticed some unconscious external manifestations of the interior mind on both sides, some outward and visible signs of the inward and spiritual sentiment, which convinced him that a more intimate acquaintance with each other would lead them to a conclusion, which, for the reasons we have given in the ninth chapter, he had no wish to see established. After long and mature deliberation, he determined to rouse Lord Anophel to a sense of his danger, and spirit him up to an immediate *coup-de-main*. He calculated, that, as the young Lord was a spoiled child, immoderately vain, passably foolish, and totally unused to contradiction, he should have little difficulty in moulding him to his views. His plan was, that Lord Anophel, with two or three confidential fellows, should lie in ambush for Anthelia in one of her solitary rambles, and convey her to a lonely castle of his Lordship's on the sea-coast, with a view of keeping her in close custody, till fair means or foul should induce her to regain her liberty, in the character of Lady Achthar. This was to be Lord Anophel's view of the subject ; but the Reverend Mr. Grovelgrub had in the inner cave of his perceptions a very promising image of a different result. As he would have free access to Anthelia in her confinement, he intended to worm himself into her favour, under the cover of friendship and sympathy, with the most ardent professions of devotion to her cause, and promises of endeavours to effect her emancipation, involving the accomplishment of this object in a multitude of imaginary difficulties, which it should be his professed study to vanquish. He deemed it very probable, that, by a skilful adoperation of these means, and by moulding Lord Anophel, at the same time, into a system of conduct as disagreeable as possible to Anthelia, he might himself become the lord and master of the lands and castle of Melincourt, when he would edify the country with the example of his truly orthodox life, faring sumptuously every day, raising the rents of his tenants, turning out all who were in arrear, and occasionally treating the rest with discourses on temperance and charity.

With these ideas in his head, he went in search of Lord Anophel, and proceeding *pedetentim*, and opening the subject *peirastically*,[1] he managed so skilfully that his Lordship became himself the proposer of the scheme, with which the Reverend Mr. Grovelgrub seemed unwillingly to acquiesce.

Mr. Forester, Mr. Fax, and Sir Oran Haut-ton took leave of the party at Melincourt Castle; the former having arranged with Sir Telegraph Paxarett, that he was to call for them at Redrose Abbey in the course of three days, and reiterated his earnest hopes that Anthelia would be persuaded to accompany Mrs. Pinmoney and her beautiful daughter, in the expedition to Onevote.

Lord Anophel Achthar and the Reverend Mr. Grovelgrub also took leave, as a matter of policy, that their disappearance at the same time with Anthelia, might not excite surprise. They pretended a pressing temporary engagement in a distant part of the country, and carried off with them Mr. Feathernest the poet, whom, nevertheless, they did not deem it prudent to let into the secret of their scheme.

The next day Anthelia, still undecided on this subject, wandered alone to the ruined bridge, to contemplate the scene of her former misadventure. As she ascended the hill that bounded the valley of Melincourt, a countryman crossed her path, and touching his hat passed on. She thought there was something peculiar in his look, but had quite forgotten him, when, on looking back as she descended on the other side, she observed him making signs, as if to some one at a distance: she could not, however, consider that they had any relation to her. The day was clear and sunny; and when she entered the pine-grove, the gloom of its tufted foliage, with the sunbeams chequering the dark-red soil, formed a grateful contrast to the naked rocks and heathy mountains that lay around it, in the full blaze of daylight. In many parts of the grove was a luxuriant laurel underwood, glittering like silver in the partial sunbeams that penetrated the interstices of the pines. Few scenes in nature have a more mysterious solemnity than such a scene as this. Anthelia paused a moment. She thought she heard a rustling in the laurels, but all was again still. She proceeded: the rustling was renewed. She felt alarmed, yet she knew not why, and reproached herself for such

[1] Experimentally. G.

idle and unaccustomed apprehensions. She paused again to listen : the soft tones of a flute sounded from a distance : these gave her confidence, and she again proceeded. She passed by the tuft of laurels in which she had heard the rustling. Suddenly a mantle was thrown over her. She was wrapped in darkness, and felt that she was forcibly seized by several persons, who carried her rapidly along. She screamed, but the mantle was immediately pressed on her mouth, and she was hurried onward. After a time the party stopped : a tumult ensued : she found herself at liberty, and threw the mantle from her head. She was on a road at the verge of the pine-grove : a chaise and four was waiting. Two men were running away in the distance : two others, muffled and masked, were rolling on the ground, and roaring for mercy, while Sir Oran Haut-ton was standing over them with a stick,[1] and treating them as if he were a thresher, and they were sheaves of corn. By her side was Mr. Forester, who, taking her hand, assured her that she was in safety, while at the same time he endeavoured to assuage Sir Oran's wrath, that he might raise and unmask the fallen foes. Sir Oran, however, proceeded in his summary administration of natural justice till he had dispensed what was to his notion a *quantum sufficit* of the application : then throwing his stick aside, he caught them both up, one under each arm, and climbing with great dexterity a high and precipitous rock, left them perched upon its summit, bringing away their masks in his hand, and making them a profound bow at taking leave.[2]

Mr. Forester was anxious to follow them to their aërial seat, that he might ascertain who they were, which Sir Oran's precipitation had put it out of his power to do ; but Anthelia begged him to return with her immediately to the Castle, assuring him that she thought

[1] " They use an artificial weapon for attack and defence, viz. a stick, which no animal merely brute is known to do."—*Origin and Progress of Language*, book ii. chap. 4. [P.]

[2] " There is a story of one of them, which seems to show they have a sense of justice as well as honour. For a negro having shot a female of this kind, that was feeding among his Indian corn, the male, whom our author calls the husband of this female, pursued the negro into his house, of which having forced open the door, he seized the negro and dragged him out of the house to the place where his wife lay dead or wounded, and the people of the neighbourhood could not rescue the negro, nor force the oran to quit his hold of him, till they shot him likewise."—*Ibid.* [P.]

them already sufficiently punished, and had no apprehension that they would feel tempted again to molest her.

Sir Oran now opened the chaise-door, and drew out the post-boys by the leg, who, at the beginning of the fray, had concealed themselves from his fury under the seat. Mr. Forester succeeded in rescuing them from Sir Oran, and endeavoured to extract from them information as to their employers : but the boys declared that they knew nothing of them, the chaise having been ordered by a strange man to be in waiting at that place, and the hire paid in advance.

Anthelia, as she walked homeward, leaning on Mr. Forester's arm, inquired to what happy accident she was indebted for the timely intervention of himself and Sir Oran Haut-ton. Mr. Forester informed her, that having a great wish to visit the scene which had been the means of introducing him to her acquaintance, he had made Sir Oran understand his desire, and they had accordingly set out together, leaving Mr. Fax at Redrose Abbey, deeply engaged in the solution of a problem in political arithmetic.

CHAPTER XIX

THE EXCURSION

ANTHELIA found, from what Mr. Forester had said, that she had excited a much greater interest in his mind than she had previously supposed ; and she did not dissemble to herself that the interest was reciprocal. The occurrence of the morning, by taking the feeling of safety from her solitary walks, and unhinging her long associations with the freedom and security of her native mountains, gave her an inclination to depart for a time at least from Melincourt Castle ; and this inclination combining with the wish to see more of one who appeared to possess so much intellectual superiority to the generality of mankind, rendered her very flexible to Mrs. Pinmoney's wishes, when that Honourable lady renewed her solicitations to her to join the expedition to Onevote. Anthelia, however, desired that Mr. Hippy might be of the party, and that her going in Sir Telegraph's carriage should not be construed in any degree into a reception of his addresses. The Honourable Mrs. Pinmoney, delighted to carry her point, readily complied with the condition, trusting to the influence of time and intimacy to promote her own wishes, and the happiness of her dear nephew.

Mr. Hippy was so overjoyed at the project, that, in the first ebullitions of his transport, meeting Harry Fell on the landing-place, with a packet of medicine from Dr. Killquick, he seized him by the arm, and made him dance a *pas de deux* : the packet fell to the earth, and Mr. Hippy, as he whirled old Harry round to the tune of *La Belle Laitière*, danced over that which, but for this timely demolition, might have given his heir an opportunity of dancing over him.

It was accordingly arranged that Sir Telegraph Paxarett, with the ladies and Mr. Hippy, should call on the appointed day at Redrose Abbey for Mr. Forester, Mr. Fax, and Sir Oran Haut-ton.

Mr. Derrydown and Mr. O'Scarum were inconsolable on the occasion, notwithstanding Mr. Hippy's assurance that they should very soon return, and that the hospitality of Melincourt Castle should then be resumed under his supreme jurisdiction. Mr. Derrydown determined to consume the interval at Keswick, in the composition of dismal ballads; and Mr. O'Scarum to proceed to Low-wood Inn, and drown his cares in claret with Major O'Dogskin.

We shall pass over the interval till the arrival of the eventful day on which Mr. Forester, from the windows of Redrose Abbey, watched the approach of Sir Telegraph's barouche. The party from Melincourt arrived, as had been concerted, to breakfast: after which, they surveyed the Abbey, and perambulated the grounds. Mr. Forester produced the Abbot's skull,[1] and took occasion to expatiate very largely on the diminution of the size of mankind ; illustrating his theory by quotations and anecdotes from Homer,[2]

---

[1] See Chap. IV. [P.]

[2] " Homer has said nothing positively, of the size of any of his heroes, but only comparatively, as I shall presently observe : nor is this to be wondered at ; for I know no historian ancient or modern, that says any thing of the size of the men of his own nation, except comparatively with that of other nations. But in that fine episode of his, called by the ancient critics the Τειχοσκοπια, or *Prospect from the Walls,* he has given us a very accurate description of the persons of several of the Greek heroes ; which I am persuaded he had from very good information. In this description he tells us, that Ulysses was shorter than Agamemnon by the head, shorter than Menelaus by the head and shoulders, and that Ajax was taller than any of the Greeks by the head and shoulders ; consequently,

Herodotus,[1] Arrian, Plutarch, Philostratus, Pausanias, and Solinus
Polyhistor. He asked, if it were possible that men of such a stature
as they have dwindled to in the present age, could have erected that
stupendous. monument of human strength, Stonehenge? in the

Ulysses was shorter than Ajax by two heads and shoulders, which we
cannot reckon less than four feet. Now, if we suppose these heroes to
have been no bigger than we, then Ajax must have been a man about six
feet and a half, or at most seven feet ; and if so, Ulysses must have been
most contemptibly short, not more than three feet, which is certainly not
the truth, but a most absurd and ridiculous fiction, such as we cannot suppose in Homer : whereas, if we allow Ajax to have been twelve or thirteen
feet high, and, much more, if we suppose him to have been eleven cubits, as
Philostratus makes him, Ulysses, though four feet short of him, would have
been of a good size, and, with the extraordinary breadth which Homer
observes he had, may have been as strong a man as Ajax."—*Ancient
Metaphysics*, vol. iii. p. 146. [P.]
    [1] " It was only in after-ages, when the size of men was greatly decreased,
that the bodies of those heroes, if they happened to be discovered, were, as
was natural, admired and exactly measured. Such a thing happened in
Laconia, where the body of Orestes was discovered, and found to be of
length seven cubits, that is, ten feet and a half. The story is most
pleasantly told by Herodotus, and is to this effect : The Lacedemonians
were engaged in a war with the Tegeatæ, a people of Arcadia, in which
they were unsuccessful. They consulted the oracle at Delphi, what they
should do in order to be more successful. The oracle answered, ' That they
must bring to Sparta the bones of Orestes, the son of Agamemnon.' But
these bones they could not find, and therefore they sent again to the oracle
to inquire where Orestes lay buried. The God answered in hexameter
verse, but so obscurely and enigmatically, that they could not understand
what he meant. They went about inquiring every where for the bones of
Orestes, till at last a wise man among them, called by Herodotus *Liches*,
found them out, partly by good fortune, and partly by good understanding ;
for, happening to come one day to a smith's shop in the country of the
Tegeatæ, with whom at that time there was a truce and intercourse
betwixt the two nations, he looked at the operations of the smith, and
seemed to admire them very much ; which the smith observing, stopped his
work, and, ' Stranger,' says he, ' you that seem to admire so much the
working of iron, would have wondered much more if you had seen what
I saw lately ; for, as I was digging for a well in this court here, I fell upon
a coffin that was seven cubits long ; but *believing that there never were at any
time bigger men than the present*, I opened the coffin, and found there a dead
body as long as the coffin, which having measured, I again buried.' Hearing
this, the Spartan conjectured that the words of the oracle would apply to a
smith's shop, and to the operations there performed ; but taking care not
to make this discovery to the smith, he prevailed on him, with much
difficulty, to give him a lease of the court ; which having obtained, he
opened the coffin, and carried the bones to Sparta. After which, says our

vicinity of which, he said, a body had been dug up, measuring fourteen feet ten inches in length.[1]

author, the Spartans were upon every occasion superior in fight to the Tegeatæ."—*Ancient Metaphysics*, vol. iii. p. 146.

" The most of our philosophers at present are, I believe, of the opinion of the smith in Herodotus, who might be excused for having that opinion at a time when perhaps no other heroic body had been discovered. But in later times, I believe there was not the most vulgar man in Greece, who did not believe that those heroes were very much superior, both in mind and body, to the men of after-times. Indeed, they were not considered as mere men, but as something betwixt gods and men, and had *heroic* honours paid them, which were next to the *divine*. On the stage they were represented as of extraordinary size, both as to length and breadth ; for the actor was not only raised upon very high shoes, which they called *cothurns*, but he was put into a case that swelled his size prodigiously (and I have somewhere read a very ridiculous story of one of them, who, coming upon the stage, fell and broke his case, so that all the trash with which it was stuffed, came out and was scattered upon the stage in the view of the whole people). This accounts for the high style of ancient tragedy, in which the heroes speak a language so uncommon, that, if I considered them as men nowise superior to us, I should think it little better than fustian, and should be apt to apply to it what Falstaff says to Pistol : ' Pr'ythee, Pistol, speak like a man of this world.' And I apply the same observation to Homer's poems. If I considered his heroes as no more than men of this world, I should consider the things he relates of them as quite ridiculous ; but believing them to be men very much superior to us, I read Homer with the highest admiration, not only as a poet, but as the historian of the noblest race of men that ever existed. Thus, by having right notions of the superiority of men in former times, we both improve our philosophy of man, and our taste in poetry."—*Ibid.*, p. 150. [P.]

[1] " But though we should give no credit to those ancient authors, there are monuments still extant, one particularly to be seen in our own island, which I think ought to convince every man that the men of ancient times were much superior to us, at least in the powers of the body. The monument I mean is well known by the name of Stonehenge, and there are several of the same kind to be seen in Denmark and Germany. I desire to know where are the arms now, that, with so little help of machinery as they must have had, could have raised and set up on end such a number of prodigious stones, and put others on the top of them, likewise of very great size ? Such works are said by the peasants in Germany to be the works of giants, and I think they must have been giants compared with us. And, indeed, the men who erected Stonehenge could not, I imagine, be of size inferior to that man whose body was found in a quarry near to Salisbury, within a mile of which Stonehenge stands. The body of that man was fourteen feet ten inches. The fact is attested by an eye-witness, one Elyote, who writes, I believe, the first English-Latin Dictionary that ever was published. It is printed in London in 1542, in folio, and has, under the word *Gigas*, the following passage : ' About thirty years past and

The barouche bowled off from the Abbey gates, carrying four inside and eight out ; videlicet, the Honourable Mrs. Pinmoney,

---

somewhat more, I myself beynge with my father Syr Rycharde Elyote, at a monastery of regular canons, called Juy Churche, two myles from the citie of Sarisburye, beholde the bones of a deade man founde deep in the grounde, where they dygged stone, which being joined togyther, was in length xiiii feet and ten ynches, there beynge mette ; whereof one of the teethe my father hadde, whych was of the quantytie of a great walnutte. This have I wrytten, because some menne wylle believe nothynge that is out of the compasse of theyre owne knowledge, and yet some of them presume to have knowledge, above any other, contempnynge all men but themselfes or suche as they favour.' It is for the reason mentioned by this author, that I have given so many examples of the greater size of men than is to be seen in our day, to which I could add several others concerning bodies that have been found in this our island, particularly one mentioned by Hector Boece in his *Description of Scotland,* prefixed to his Scotch History, where he tells us that in a certain church which he names in the shire of Murray, the bones of a man of much the same size as those of the man mentioned by Elyote, viz. fourteen feet, were preserved. One of these bones Boece himself saw, and has particularly described."—*Ancient Metaphysics,* vol. iii. p. 156.

   " But without having recourse to bones or monuments of any kind, if a man has looked upon the world as long as I have done with any observation, he must be convinced that the size of man is diminishing. I have seen such bodies of men, as are not now to be seen: I have observed in families, of which I have known three generations, a gradual decline in that, and I am afraid in other respects. Others may think otherwise ; but for my part I have so great a veneration for our ancestors, that I have much indulgence for that ancient superstition among the Etrurians, and from them derived to the Romans, of worshipping the *manes* of their ancestors under the names of *Lares* or domestic gods, which undoubtedly proceeded upon the supposition that they were men superior to themselves, and their departed souls such genii as Hesiod has described,

Εσθλοι, αλεξικακοι, φυλακες θνητων ανθρωπων.

[" Noble protectors from evil, guardians of mortal men."   G.]

And if antiquity and the universal consent of nations can give a sanction to any opinion, it is to this, that our forefathers were better men than we. Even as far back as the Trojan war, the best age of men, of which we have any particular account, Homer has said that few men were better than their fathers, and the greater part worse :

Οι πλεονες κακιους, παυροι δε τε πατρος αρειους.

And this he puts into the mouth of the Goddess of Wisdom. . . .   But when I speak of the universal consent of nations, I ought to except the men, and particularly the young men, of this age, who generally believe themselves to be better men than their fathers, or than any of their predecessors."—*Ibid,* p. 161.   [P.]

Miss Danaretta, Mr. Hippy, and Anthelia, inside; Sir Telegraph
Paxarett and Sir Oran Haut-ton on the box, the former with his
whip and the latter with his French horn, in the characters of
coachman and guard; Mr. Forester and Mr. Fax in the front of the
roof; and Sir Telegraph's two grooms, with Peter Gray and Harry
Fell, behind. Sir Telegraph's coachman, as the inside of the carriage
was occupied, had been left at Melincourt.

In addition to Sir Telegraph's travelling library (which consisted
of a single quarto volume, magnificently bound : videlicet, a Greek
Pindar, which Sir Telegraph always carried with him; not that he
ever read a page of it, but that he thought such a classical inside
passenger would be a perpetual tacit vindication of his tethripphar-
matelasipedioploctypophilous [1] pursuits), Anthelia and Mr. Forester
had taken with them a few of their favourite authors; for, as the
ancient and honourable borough of Onevote was situated almost at
the extremity of the kingdom, and as Sir Telegraph's diurnal stages
were necessarily limited, they had both conjectured that

> " the poet's page, by one
> Made vocal for the amusement of the rest," [2]

might furnish an agreeable evening employment in the dearth of
conversation. Anthelia also, in compliance with the general desire,
had taken her lyre, by which the reader may understand, if he pleases,
the *harp-lute-guitar*; which, whatever be its merit as an instrument,
has so unfortunate an appellation, that we cannot think of dislocating
our pages with such a cacophonous compound.

They made but a short stage from Redrose Abbey, and stopped for
the first evening at Low-wood Inn, to the great joy of Mr. O'Scarum
and Major O'Dogskin. Mr. O'Scarum introduced the Major; and
both offered their services to assist Mr. Hippy and Sir Telegraph
Paxarett in the council they were holding with the landlady on the
eventful subject of dinner. This being arranged, and the hour and
minute punctually specified, it was proposed to employ the interval
in a little excursion on the lake. The party was distributed in two
boats : Sir Telegraph's grooms rowing the one, and Peter Gray and
Harry Fell the other. They rowed to the middle of the lake, and

---

[1] Driving a chariot of four horses with hoofs striking the ground. G.
[2] Cowper : *The Task*, Bk. IV (*The Winter Evening*). G.

rested on their oars. The sun sunk behind the summits of the western mountains : the clouds that, like other mountains, rested motionless above them, crested with the towers and battlements of aërial castles, changed by degrees from fleecy whiteness to the deepest hues of crimson. A solitary cloud, resting on an eastern pinnacle, became tinged with the reflected splendour of the west : the clouds over-head spreading, like an uniform veil of network, through the interstices of which the sky was visible, caught in their turn the radiance, and reflected it on the lake, that lay in its calm expanse like a mirror, imaging with such stillness and accuracy the forms and colours of all around and above it, that it seemed as if the waters were withdrawn by magic, and the boats floated in crimson light between the mountains and the sky.

The whole party was silent, even the Honourable Mrs. Pinmoney, till Mr. O'Scarum entreated Anthelia to sing " something neat and characteristic ; or a harmony now for three voices, would be the killing thing ; eh ! Major ? "—" Indeed and it would," said Major O'Dogskin : " there's something very soft and pathetic in a cool evening on the water, to sit still, doing nothing at all but listening to pretty words and tender melodies." And lest the sincerity of his opinion should be questioned, he accompanied it with an emphatical oath, to show that he was in earnest ; for which the Honourable Mrs. Pinmoney called him to order.

Major O'Dogskin explained.

Anthelia, accompanied by Miss Danaretta and Mr. O'Scarum, sung the following

TERZETTO

1. Hark ! o'er the silent waters stealing,
   The dash of oars sounds soft and clear :
   Through night's deep veil, all forms concealing,
   Nearer it comes, and yet more near.

2. See ! where the long reflection glistens,
   In yon lone tower her watch-light burns :
3. To hear our distant oars she listens,
   And, listening, strikes the harp by turns.

1. The stars are bright, the skies unclouded ;
   No moonbeams shine ; no breezes wake :
   Is it my love, in darkness shrouded,
   Whose dashing oar disturbs the lake ?

> 2.   O haste, sweet maid, the cords unrolling ;
>   The holy hermit chides our stay !
> 1. 2. 3.   Hark ! from his lonely islet tolling,
>   His midnight bell shall guide our way.

Sir Oran Haut-ton now produced his flute, and treated the company with a solo. Another pause succeeded. The contemplative silence was broken by Major O'Dogskin, who began to fidget about in the boat, and drawing his watch from his fob, held it up to Mr. Hippy, and asked him if he did not think the partridges would be spoiled ? "To be sure they will," said Mr. Hippy, " unless we make the best of our way. Cold comfort this, after all : sharp air and water :— give me a roaring fire and a six-bottle cooper of claret."

The oars were dashed into the water, and the fairy reflections of clouds, rocks, woods, and mountains were mingled in the confusion of chaos. The reader will naturally expect, that, having two lovers on a lake, we shall not lose the opportunity of throwing the lady into the water, and making the gentleman fish her out ; but whether that our Thalia is too veridicous to permit this distortion of facts, or that we think it the more original incident to return them to the shore as dry as they left it, the reader must submit to the disappointment, and be content to see the whole party comfortably seated, without let, hindrance, or molestation, at a very excellent dinner, served up under the judicious inspection of mine hostess of Low-wood.

The heroes and heroines of Homer used to eat and drink all day till the setting sun ; [1] and, by dint of industry, contrived to finish that important business by the usual period at which modern beaux and belles begin it—who are, therefore, necessitated, like Penelope, to sit up all night : not, indeed, to destroy the works of the day, for how can nothing be annihilated ? This does not apply to all our party, and we hope not to many of our readers.

---

[1] ῾Ημεις μεν προπαν ημαρ, ες ηελιον καταδυντα,
῾Ημεθα, δαινυμενοι κρεα τ᾽ ασπετα και μεθυ ἡδυ· κτλ.   [P.]

[" We the day long, until the setting of the sun,
  Sat feasting on meat in plenty and sweet wine."
                              Homer : *Od*. IX. 161–2.   G.]

CHAPTER XX

THE SEA-SHORE

THEY stopped the next evening at a village on the sea-shore. The wind rose in the night, but without rain. Mr. Forester was up before the sun, and descending to the beach, found Anthelia there before him, sitting on a rock, and listening to the dash of the waves, like a Nereid to Triton's shell.

MR. FORESTER. You are an early riser, Miss Melincourt.

ANTHELIA. I always was so. The morning is the infancy of the day, and, like the infancy of life, has health and bloom, and cheerfulness and purity, in a degree unknown to the busy noon, which is the season of care, or the languid evening, which is the harbinger of repose. Perhaps the song of the nightingale is not in itself less cheerful than that of the lark: it is the season of her song that invests it with the character of melancholy. It is the same with the associations of infancy: it is all cheerfulness, all hope: its path is on the flowers of an untried world. The daisy has more beauty in the eye of childhood than the rose in that of maturer life. The spring is the infancy of the year: its flowers are the flowers of promise and the darlings of poetry. The autumn too has its flowers; but they are little loved, and little praised: for the associations of autumn are not with ideas of cheerfulness, but with yellow leaves and hollow winds, heralds of winter, and emblems of dissolution.

MR. FORESTER. These reflections have more in them of the autumn than of the morning. But the mornings of autumn participate in the character of the season.

ANTHELIA. They do so: yet even in mists and storms the opening must be always more cheerful than the closing day.

MR. FORESTER. But this morning is fine and clear, and the wind blows over the sea. Yet this, to me at least, is not a cheerful scene.

ANTHELIA. Nor to me. But our long habits of association with the sound of the winds and the waters, have given them to us a voice of melancholy majesty : a voice not audible by those little children who are playing yonder on the shore. To them all scenes are cheerful. It is the morning of life : it is infancy that makes them so.

MR. FORESTER. Fresh air and liberty are all that is necessary to the happiness of children. In that blissful age " when nature's self is new," the bloom of interest and beauty is found alike in every object of perception—in the grass of the meadow, the moss on the rock, and the sea-weed on the sand. They find gems and treasures in shells and pebbles ; and the gardens of fairyland in the simplest flowers. They have no melancholy associations with autumn or with evening. The falling leaves are their playthings ; and the setting sun only tells them that they must go to rest as he does, and that he will light them to their sports in the morning. It is this bloom of novelty, and the pure, unclouded, unvitiated feelings with which it is contemplated, that throw such an unearthly radiance on the scenes of our infancy, however humble in themselves, and give a charm to their recollections which not even Tempe can compensate. It is the force of first impressions. The first meadow in which we gather cowslips, the first stream on which we sail, the first home in which we awake to the sense of human sympathy, have all a peculiar and exclusive charm, which we shall never find again in richer meadows, mightier rivers, and more magnificent dwellings ; nor even in themselves, when we revisit them after the lapse of years, and the sad realities of noon have dissipated the illusions of sunrise. It is the same, too, with first love, whatever be the causes that render it unsuccessful : the second choice may have just preponderance in the balance of moral estimation ; but the object of first affection, of all the perceptions of our being, will be most divested of the attributes of mortality. The magical associations of infancy are revived with double power in the feelings of first love ; but when they too have departed, then, indeed, the light of the morning is gone.

Pensa che questo di mai non raggiorna ! [1]

ANTHELIA. If this be so, let me never be the object of a second choice : let me never love, or love but once.

[1] " Realise that this day will never return." Dante : *Purgatorio*, XII. 84.　G.

MR. FORESTER. The object of a second choice you cannot be, with any one who will deserve your love : for to have loved any other woman, would show a heart too lightly captivated to be worthy of yours. The only mind that can deserve to love you, is one that would never have known love, if it never had known you.

Anthelia and Mr. Forester were both so unfashionably sincere, that they would probably, in a very few minutes, have confessed to each other, more than they had till that morning, perhaps, confessed to themselves, but that their conversation was interrupted by the appearance of Mr. Hippy fuming for his breakfast, accompanied by Sir Telegraph cracking his whip, and Sir Oran blowing the Reveillée on his French horn.

" So ho ! " exclaimed Sir Telegraph ; " Achilles and Thetis, I protest, consulting on the sea-shore."

ANTHELIA. Do you mean to say, Sir Telegraph, that I am old enough to be Mr. Forester's mother ?

SIR TELEGRAPH PAXARETT. No, no ; that is no part of the comparison : but we are the ambassadors of Agamemnon (videlicet, Mr. Fax, whom we left very busily arranging the urns, not of lots by the by, but of tea and coffee) : here is old Phœnix on one side of me, and Ajax on the other.

MR. FORESTER. And you, of course, are the wise Ulysses.

SIR TELEGRAPH PAXARETT. There the simile fails again. *Comparatio non urgenda*,[1] as I think Heyne [2] used to say, before I was laughed out of reading at college.

MR. FORESTER. You should have found me too, if you call me Achilles, solacing my mind with music, φϱενα τεϱπομενον φοϱμιγγι λιγειη [3] ; but, to make amends for the deficiency, you have brought me a musical Ajax.

SIR TELEGRAPH PAXARETT. You have no reason to wish even for

---

[1] " The comparison should not be pressed." G.

[2] Christian Gottlieb Heyne, 1729–1812, German classical scholar and archæologist. G.

[3] " Solacing his mind with shrill lyre." Homer : *Il.* IX. 186. G.

the golden lyre of my old friend Pindar himself : you have been listening to the music of the winds and the waters, and to what is more than music, the voice of Miss Melincourt.

MR. HIPPY. And there is a very pretty concert waiting for you at the inn—the tinkling of cups and spoons, and the divine song of the tea-urn.

CHAPTER XXI

THE CITY OF NOVOTE

ON the evening of the tenth day, the barouche rattled triumphantly into the large and populous city of Novote, which was situated at a short distance from the ancient and honourable borough of Onevote. The city contained fifty thousand inhabitants, and had no representative in the Honourable House, the deficiency being virtually supplied by the two members for Onevote ; who, having no affairs to attend to for the borough, or rather the burgess, that did return them, were supposed to have more leisure for those of the city which did not : a system somewhat analogous to that which the learned author of *Hermes* calls *a method of supply by negation.*[1]

Sir Oran signalized his own entrance by playing on his French horn, *See the conquering hero comes !* Bells were ringing, ale was flowing, mobs were huzzaing, and it seemed as if the inhabitants of the large and populous city were satisfied of the truth of the admirable doctrine, that the positive representation of one individual is a virtual representation of fifty thousand. They found afterwards, that all this festivity had been set in motion by Sir Oran's brother candidate, Simon Sarcastic, Esquire, to whom we shall shortly introduce our readers.

The barouche stopped at the door of a magnificent inn, and the party was welcomed with some scores of bows from the whole *corps d'hôtel*, with the fat landlady in the van, and Boots in the rear. They

[1] *Hermes*, a philosophical enquiry concerning universal grammar by James Harris, was published in 1751. Johnson said, " Harris is a sound sullen scholar . . . a prig, and a bad prig." G.

were shown into a splendid apartment, a glorious fire was kindled in a minute, and while Mr. Hippy looked over the bill of fare, and followed mine hostess to inspect the state of the larder, Sir Telegraph proceeded to *peel*, and emerged from his four *benjamins* [1] like a butterfly from its chrysalis.

After dinner they formed, as usual, a semicircle round the fire, with the table in front supported by Mr. Hippy and Sir Telegraph Paxarett.

" Now this," said Sir Telegraph, rubbing his hands, " is what I call devilish comfortable after a cold day's drive—an excellent inn, a superb fire, charming company, and better wine than has fallen to our lot since we left Melincourt Castle."

The waiter had picked up from the conversation at dinner, that one of the destined members for Onevote was in company ; and communicated this intelligence to Mr. Sarcastic, who was taking his solitary bottle in another apartment. Mr. Sarcastic sent his compliments to Sir Oran Haut-ton, and hoped he would allow his future colleague the honour of being admitted to join his party. Mr. Hippy, Mr. Forester, and Sir Telegraph, undertook to answer for Sir Oran, who was silent on the occasion : Mr. Sarcastic was introduced, and took his seat in the semicircle.

SIR TELEGRAPH PAXARETT. Your future colleague, Mr. Sarcastic, is *a man of few words* ; but he will join in a bumper to your better acquaintance.—(*The collision of glasses ensued between* SIR ORAN *and* MR. SARCASTIC.)

MR. SARCASTIC. I am proud of the opportunity of this introduction. The day after to-morrow is fixed for the election. I have made some preparations to give a little *éclat* to the affair, and have begun by intoxicating half the city of Novote, so that we shall have a great crowd at the scene of election, whom I intend to harangue from the hustings, on the great benefits and blessings of virtual representation.

MR. FORESTER. I shall, perhaps, take the opportunity of addressing them also, but with a different view of the subject.

---

[1] Driving-coats. G.

MR. SARCASTIC. Perhaps our views of the subject are not radically different, and the variety is in the mode of treatment. In my ordinary intercourse with the world, I reduce practice to theory : it is a habit, I believe, peculiar to myself, and a source of inexhaustible amusement.

SIR TELEGRAPH PAXARETT. Fill and explain.

MR. SARCASTIC. Nothing, you well know, is so rare as the coincidence of theory and practice. A man who " will go through fire and water to serve a friend " in words, will not give five guineas to save him from famine. A poet will write Odes to Independence, and become the obsequious parasite of any great man who will hire him. A burgess will hold up one hand for purity of election, while the price of his own vote is slily dropped into the other. I need not accumulate instances.

MR. FORESTER. You would find it difficult, I fear, to adduce many to the contrary.

MR. SARCASTIC. This then is my system. I ascertain the practice of those I talk to, and present it to them as from myself, in the shape of theory : the consequence of which is, that I am universally stigmatized as a promulgator of rascally doctrines. Thus I said to Sir Oliver Oilcake, " When I get into Parliament I intend to make the sale of my vote as notorious as the sun at noonday. I will have no rule of right, but my own pocket. I will support every measure of every administration, even if they ruin half the nation for the purpose of restoring the Great Lama, or of subjecting twenty millions of people to be hanged, drawn, and quartered at the pleasure of the man-milliner of Mahomet's mother. I will have ship-loads of turtle and rivers of Madeira for myself, if I send the whole swinish multitude to draff and husks." Sir Oliver flew into a rage, and swore he would hold no further intercourse with a man who maintained such infamous principles.

MR. HIPPY. Pleasant enough, to show a man his own picture, and make him damn the ugly rascal.

MR. SARCASTIC. I said to Miss Pennylove, whom I knew to be *laying herself out* for a *good match*, " When my daughter becomes of marriageable age, I shall commission Christie to put her up to auction, ' the highest bidder to be the buyer ; and if any dispute arise between two or more bidders, the lot to be put up again and resold.' " Miss Pennylove professed herself utterly amazed and indignant, that any man, and a father especially, should imagine a scheme so outrageous to the dignity and delicacy of the female mind.

THE HONOURABLE MRS. PINMONEY, AND MISS DANARETTA. A most horrid idea certainly.

MR. SARCASTIC. The fact, my dear ladies, the fact : how stands the fact ? Miss Pennylove afterwards married a man old enough to be her grandfather, for no other reason, but because he was rich ; and broke the heart of a very worthy friend of mine, to whom she had been previously engaged, who had no fault but the folly of loving her, and was quite rich enough for all purposes of matrimonial happiness. How the dignity and delicacy of such a person could have been affected, if the preliminary negotiation with her hobbling Strephon had been conducted through the instrumentality of honest Christie's hammer, I cannot possibly imagine.

MR. HIPPY. Nor I, I must say. All the difference is in the form, and not in the fact. It is a pity the form does not come into fashion : it would save a world of trouble.

MR. SARCASTIC. I irreparably offended the Reverend Doctor Vorax by telling him, that having a nephew, whom I wished to shine in the church, I was on the look-out for a luminous butler, and a cook of solid capacity, under whose joint tuition he might graduate. " Who knows," said I, " but he may immortalize himself at the University, by giving his name to a pudding ? "—I lost the acquaintance of Mrs. Cullender, by saying to her, when she had told me a piece of gossip as a very particular secret, that there was nothing so agreeable to me as to be in possession of a secret, for I made a point of telling it to all my acquaintance ;

> Intrusted under solemn vows,
> Of Mum, and Silence, and the Rose,
> To be retailed again in whispers,
> For the easy credulous to disperse.[1]

---

[1] *Hudibras :* Part III. ii. 1. 493. [P.]

Mrs. Cullender left me in great wrath, protesting she would never again throw away *her* confidence on so leaky a vessel.

SIR TELEGRAPH PAXARETT. Ha! ha! ha! Bravo! Come, a bumper to Mrs. Cullender.

MR. SARCASTIC. With all my heart; and another if you please to Mr. Christopher Corporate, the free, fat, and dependent burgess of Onevote, of which " plural unit " the Honourable Baronet and myself are to be the joint representatives—(*Sir Oran Haut-ton bowed.*)

MR. HIPPY. And a third, by all means, to His Grace the Duke of Rottenburgh.

MR. SARCASTIC. And a fourth, to crown all, to *the blessings of virtual representation*, which I shall endeavour to impress on as many of the worthy citizens of Novote, as shall think fit to be present the day after to-morrow, at the proceedings of the borough of Onevote.

SIR TELEGRAPH PAXARETT. And now for tea and coffee. Touch the bell for the waiter.

The bottles and glasses vanished, and the beautiful array of urns and cups succeeded. Sir Telegraph and Mr. Hippy seceded from the table, and resigned their stations to Mrs. and Miss Pinmoney.

MR. FORESTER. Your system is sufficiently amusing, but I much question its utility. The object of moral censure is reformation, and its proper vehicle is plain and fearless sincerity: VERBA ANIMI PROFERRE, ET VITAM IMPENDERE VERO.[1]

MR. SARCASTIC. I tried that in my youth, when I was troubled with the *passion for reforming the world*;[2] of which I have been long cured, by the conviction of the inefficacy of moral theory with respect to producing a practical change in the mass of mankind. Custom is the pillar round which opinion twines, and interest is the tie that binds it. It is not by reason that practical change can be effected, but by making a puncture to the quick in the feelings of personal

[1] " To utter the words that are in one's mind and stake one's life upon truth." Juvenal: *Sat.* IV. 91. G.

[2] See Forsyth's *Principles of Moral Science.* [P.]

hope and personal fear. The Reformation in England is one of the supposed triumphs of reason. But if the passions of Henry the Eighth had not been interested in that measure, he would as soon have built mosques as pulled down abbies : and you will observe, that, in all cases, reformation never goes as far as reason requires, but just as far as suits the personal interest of those who conduct it. Place Temperance and Bacchus side by side, in an assembly of jolly fellows, and endow the first with the most powerful eloquence that mere reason can give, with the absolute moral force of mathematical demonstration, Bacchus need not take the trouble of refuting one of her arguments ; he will only have to say, "Come, my boys ; here's *Damn Temperance* in a bumper," and you may rely on the toast being drank with an unanimous three times three.

(*At the sound of the word* bumper, *with which Captain Hawltaught had made him very familiar, Sir Oran Haut-ton looked round for his glass, but, finding it vanished, comforted himself with a dish of tea from the fair hand of Miss Danaretta, which, as his friend Mr. Forester had interdicted him from the use of sugar, he sweetened as well as he could with a copious infusion of cream.*) [1]

SIR TELEGRAPH PAXARETT. As an Opposition orator in the Honourable House will bring forward a long detail of unanswerable arguments, without even expecting that they will have the slightest influence on the vote of the majority.

MR. SARCASTIC. A reform of that honourable body, if ever it should take place, will be one of the " *triumphs of reason.*" But reason will have little to do with it. All that reason can say on the subject, has been said for years, by men of all parties—while they were *out*; but the moment they were *in*, the moment their own interest came in contact with their own reason, the victory of interest was never for a moment doubtful. While the great fountain of interest, rising in the caverns of borough patronage and ministerial influence, flowed through the whole body of the kingdom by the

---

[1] " Il buvoit du vin, mais le laissoit volontiers pour du lait, du thé, ou d'autres liqueurs douces."—Buffon *of the Oran Outang, whom he saw himself in Paris.* [P.]

channels of paper-money, and loans, and contracts, and jobs, and places either found or made for the useful dealers in secret services, so long the predominant interests of corruption overpowered the true and permanent interests of the country : but as those channels become dry, and they are becoming so with fearful rapidity, the crew of every boat that is left aground are convinced not by reason—that they had long heard and despised—but by the unexpected pressure of personal suffering, that they had been going on in the wrong way. Thus the re-action of interest takes place ; and when the concentrated interests of thousands, combined by the same pressure of personal suffering, shall have created an independent power, greater than the power of the interest of corruption, then, and not till then, the latter will give way, and this will be called the triumph of reason, though, in truth, like all the changes in human society, that have ever taken place from the birth-day of the world, it will be only the triumph of one mode of interest over another : but as the triumph in this case will be of the interest of the many, over that of the few, it is certainly a consummation devoutly to be wished.

MR. FORESTER. If I should admit that " the hope of personal advantage, and the dread of personal punishment,"[1] are the only springs that set the mass of mankind in action, the inefficacy of reason, and the inutility of moral theory, will by no means follow from the admission. The progress of truth is slow, but its ultimate triumph is secure ; though its immediate effects may be rendered almost imperceptible, by the power of habit and interest. If the philosopher cannot reform his own times, he may lay the foundation of amendment in those that follow. Give currency to reason, improve the moral code of society, and the theory of one generation will be the practice of the next. After a certain period of life, and that no very advanced one, men in general become perfectly unpersuadable to all practical purposes. Few philosophers, therefore, I believe, expect to produce much change in the habits of their contemporaries, as Plato proposed to banish from his republic all above the age of ten, and give a good education to the rest.

MR. SARCASTIC. Or, as Heraclitus the Ephesian proposed to his

[1] See *Headlong Hall*, p. 32 and Note. G.

countrymen, that all above the age of fourteen should hang themselves, before he would consent to give laws to the remainder.

CHAPTER XXII

THE BOROUGH OF ONEVOTE

THE day of election arrived. Mr. Sarcastic's rumoured preparations, and the excellence of the ale which he had broached in the city of Novote, had given a degree of *éclat* to the election for the borough of Onevote, which it had never before possessed ; the representatives usually sliding into their nomination with the same silence and decorum with which a solitary spinster slides into her pew at Wednesday or Friday's prayers in a country church. The resemblance holds good also in this respect, that, as the curate addresses the solitary maiden with the appellation of *dearly beloved brethren*, so the representatives always pluralized their solitary elector, by conferring on him the appellation of *a respectable body of constituents*. Mr. Sarcastic, however, being determined to amuse himself at the expense of this most "venerable *feature*" in our old constitution, as Lord C.[1] calls a rotten borough, had brought Mr. Christopher Corporate into his views, by the adhibition of *persuasion in a tangible shape*. It was generally known in Novote, that something would be going forward at Onevote, though nobody could tell precisely what, except that a long train of brewer's drays had left the city for the borough, in grand procession, on the preceding day, under the escort of a sworn band of special constables, who were to keep guard over the ale all night. This detachment was soon followed by another, under a similar escort, and with similar injunctions : and it was understood that this second expedition of *frothy rhetoric* was sent forth under the auspices of Sir Oran Haut-ton, Baronet, the brother candidate of Simon Sarcastic, Esquire, for the representation of the ancient and honourable borough.

The borough of Onevote stood in the middle of a heath, and

[1] Castlereagh, whose metaphors afforded continual merriment to his political opponents. Many, like this one, have become commonplaces today. G.

consisted of a solitary farm, of which the land was so poor and untractable, that it would not have been worth the while of any
human being to cultivate it, had not the Duke of Rottenburgh found
it very well worth his to pay his tenant for living there, to keep the
honourable borough in existence.

Mr. Sarcastic left the city of Novote some hours before his new
acquaintance, to superintend his preparations, followed by crowds of
persons of all descriptions, pedestrians and equestrians ; old ladies
in chariots, and young ladies on donkies ; the farmer on his hunter,
and the tailor on his hack ; the grocer and his family six in a chaise ;
the dancing-master in his tilbury ; the banker in his tandem ;
mantua-makers and servant-maids twenty-four in the waggon, fitted
up for the occasion with a canopy of evergreens ; pastry-cooks, men-
milliners, and journeymen tailors, by the stage, running for that day
only, six inside and fourteen out ; the sallow artizan emerging from
the cellar or the furnace, to freshen himself with the pure breezes of
Onevote Heath ; the bumpkin in his laced boots and Sunday coat,
trudging through the dust with his cherry-cheeked lass on his elbow ;
the gentleman coachman on his box, with his painted charmer by his
side ; the lean curate on his half-starved Rosinante ; the plump
bishop setting an example of Christian humility in his carriage and
six; the doctor on his white horse, like Death in the Revelations; and
the lawyer on his black one, like the devil in the Wild Huntsmen.[1]

Almost in the rear of this motley cavalcade went the barouche of
Sir Telegraph Paxarett, and rolled up to the scene of action amidst the
shouts of the multitude.

The heath had very much the appearance of a race ground ; with
booths and stalls, the voices of pie-men and apple-women, the grind-
ing of barrel organs, the scraping of fiddles, the squeaking of ballad-
singers, the chirping of corkscrews, the vociferations of ale-drinkers,
the cries of the " last dying speeches of desperate malefactors," and
of " The History and Antiquities of the honourable Borough of
Onevote, a full and circumstantial account, all in half a sheet, for the
price of one halfpenny ! "

The hustings were erected in proper form, and immediately

---

[1] A reference to Bürger's ballad, *Der Wilde Jäger*, of which Sir Walter
Scott published a translation in 1796.

opposite to them was an enormous marquee with a small opening in front, in which was seated the important person of Mr. Christopher Corporate, with a tankard of ale and a pipe. The ladies remained in the barouche under the care of Sir Telegraph and Mr. Hippy. Mr. Forester, Mr. Fax, and Sir Oran Haut-ton, joined Mr. Sarcastic on the hustings.

Mr. Sarcastic stepped forward amidst the shouts of the assembled crowd, and addressed Mr. Christopher Corporate :

" Free, fat, and dependent burgess of this ancient and honourable borough ! I stand forward an unworthy candidate, to be the representative of so important a personage, who comprises in himself a three hundredth part of the whole elective capacity of this extensive empire. For if the whole population be estimated at eleven millions, with what awe and veneration must I look on one, who is, as it were, the abstract and quintessence of thirty-three thousand six hundred and sixty-six people ! The voice of Stentor was like the voice of fifty, and the voice of Harry Gill [1] was like the voice of three ; but what are these to the voice of Mr. Christopher Corporate, which gives utterance in one breath to the concentrated power of thirty-three thousand six hundred and sixty-six voices ? Of such an one it may indeed be said, that *he is himself an host*, and that *none but himself can be his parallel.*[2]

" Most potent, grave, and reverend signor ! [3] it is usual on these occasions to make a great vapouring about honour and conscience : but as those words are now generally acknowledged to be utterly destitute of meaning, I have too much respect for your understanding to say any thing about them. The *monied interest*, Mr. Corporate, for which you are as illustrious *as the sun at noonday*, is the great point of connexion and sympathy between us : and no circumstances can throw a *wet blanket* on the ardour of our reciprocal esteem, while the *fundamental feature* of our mutual interests presents itself to us in so *tangible a shape.*[4] How high a value I set upon your voice, you may judge by the price I have paid for half of it : which, indeed, deeply

[1] See Mr. Wordsworth's *Lyrical Ballads*. [P.]
[2] Lewis Theobald : *The Double Falsehood*, Act III, Sc. 1. G.
[3] *Othello*, Act I, Sc. 3. G.
[4] The figures of speech marked in Italics are familiar to the admirers of parliamentary rhetoric. [P.]

lodged as my feelings are in my pocket, I yet see no reason to regret, since you will thus confer on mine, a transmutable and marketable value, which I trust with proper management will leave me no loser by the bargain."

" Huzza ! " said Mr. Corporate.

" People of the city of Novote ! " proceeded Mr. Sarcastic, " some of you, I am informed, consider yourselves aggrieved, that, while your large and populous city has no share whatever in the formation of the Honourable House, the *plural unity* of Mr. Christopher Corporate should be invested with the privilege of double representation. But, gentlemen, representation is of two kinds, actual, and virtual : an important distinction, and of great political consequence.

" The Honourable Baronet and myself being the actual representatives of the fat burgess of Onevote, shall be the virtual representatives of the worthy citizens of Novote ; and you may rely on it, gentlemen, (*with his hand on his heart,*) we shall always be deeply attentive to your interests, when they happen, as no doubt they sometimes will, to be perfectly compatible with our own.

" A member of Parliament, gentlemen, to speak to you in your own phrase, is a sort of staple commodity, manufactured for home consumption. Much has been said of the improvement of machinery in the present age, by which one man may do the work of a dozen. If this be admirable, and admirable it is acknowledged to be by all the civilized world, how much more admirable is the improvement of political machinery, by which one man does the work of thirty thousand ! I am sure, I need not say another word to a great manufacturing population like the inhabitants of the city of Novote, to convince them of the beauty and utility of this most luminous arrangement.

" The duty of a representative of the people, whether actual or virtual, is simply *to tax.* Now this important branch of public business is much more easily and expeditiously transacted by the means of virtual, than it possibly could be by that of actual representation. For when the minister draws up his scheme of ways and means, he will do it with much more celerity and confidence, when he knows that the propitious countenance of virtual representation will never cease to smile upon him as long as he continues in place, than if he had to encounter the doubtful aspect of actual representation, which might, perhaps, look black on some of his favourite projects, thereby greatly impeding the distribution of secret service money at home, and placing foreign legitimacy in a very awkward predicament. The carriage of the state would then be like a chariot in a forest, turning to the left for a troublesome thorn, and to the right for a sturdy oak ; whereas it now rolls forward like the car of Juggernaut over the plain, crushing whatever offers to impede its way.

"The constitution says that no man shall be taxed but by his own consent : a very plausible theory, gentlemen, but not reducible to practice. Who will apply a lancet to his own arm, and bleed himself ? Very few, you acknowledge. Who then, *a fortiori*, would apply a lancet to his own pocket, and draw off what is dearer to him than his blood—his money ? Fewer still of course : I humbly opine, none.—What then remains but to appoint a royal college of state surgeons, who may operate on the patient according to their views of his case ? Taxation is political phlebotomy : the Honourable House is, figuratively speaking, a royal college of state surgeons. A good surgeon must have firm nerves and a steady hand ; and, perhaps, the less feeling the better. Now, it is manifest, that, as all feeling is founded on sympathy, the fewer constituents a representative has, the less must be his sympathy with the public, and the less, of course, as is desirable, his feeling for his patient—the people :— who, therefore, with so much *sangfroid*, can phlebotomize the nation, as the representative of half an elector ?

"Gentlemen, as long as a *full Gazette* is pleasant to the *quidnunc* ; as long as an empty purse is delightful to the spendthrift ; as long as the cry of *Question* is a satisfactory *answer* to an argument, and to outvote reason, is to refute it ; as long as the way to pay old debts is to incur new ones of five times the amount ; as long as the grand recipes of political health and longevity are *bleeding* and *hot water*— so long must you rejoice in the privileges of Mr. Christopher Corporate, so long must you acknowledge, from the very bottom of your pockets, the benefits and blessings of *virtual representation.*"

This harangue was received with great applause, acclamations rent the air, and ale flowed in torrents. Mr. Forester declined speaking, and the party on the hustings proceeded to business. Sir Oran

Haut-ton, Baronet, and Simon Sarcastic, Esquire, were nominated in form. Mr. Christopher Corporate held up both his hands, with his tankard in one, and his pipe in the other : and neither poll nor scrutiny being demanded, the two candidates were pronounced duly elected, as representatives of the ancient and honourable borough of Onevote.

The shouts were renewed : the ale flowed rapidly : the pipe and tankard of Mr. Corporate were replenished. Sir Oran Haut-ton, Baronet, M.P. bowed gracefully to the people with his hand on his heart.

A cry was now raised of " Chair 'em ! chair 'em ! " when Mr. Sarcastic again stepped forward.

" Gentlemen ! " said he, " a slight difficulty opposes itself to the honour you would confer on us. The members should, according to form, be chaired by their electors : and how can one elector, great man as he is, chair two representatives ? But to obviate this dilemma as well as circumstances admit, I move that the ' large body corporate of one ' whom the Honourable Baronet and myself have the honour to represent, do resolve himself into a committee."

He had no sooner spoken, than the marquee opened, and a number of bulky personages, all in dress, aspect, size, and figure, very exact resemblances of Mr. Christopher Corporate, each with his pipe and his tankard, emerged into daylight, who encircling their venerable prototype, lifted their tankards high in air, and pronounced with Stentorian symphony, " HAIL, PLURAL UNIT ! " Then, after a simultaneous draught, throwing away their pipes and tankards, for which the mob immediately scrambled, they raised on high two magnificent chairs, and prepared to carry into effect the last ceremony of the election. The party on the hustings descended. Mr. Sarcastic stepped into his chair ; and his part of the procession, headed by Mr. Christopher Corporate, and surrounded by a multiform and many-coloured crowd, moved slowly off towards the city of Novote, amidst the undistinguishable clamour of multitudinous voices.

Sir Oran Haut-ton watched the progress of his precursor, as his chair rolled and swayed over the sea of heads, like a boat with one mast on a stormy ocean ; and the more he watched the agitation of its movements, the more his countenance gave indications of strong

dislike to the process : so that when his seat in the second chair was
offered to him, he with a very polite bow declined the honour. The
party that was to carry him, thinking that his repugnance arose
entirely from diffidence, proceeded with gentle force to overcome his
scruples, when not precisely penetrating their motives, and indignant
at this attempt to violate the freedom of the natural man, he seized
a stick from a sturdy farmer at his elbow, and began to lay about him
with great vigour and effect. Those who escaped being knocked
down by the first sweep of his weapon ran away with all their might,
but were soon checked by the pressure of the crowd, who, hearing the
noise of conflict, and impatient to ascertain the cause, bore down from
all points upon a common centre, and formed a circumferential
pressure that effectually prohibited the egress of those within ; and
they in their turn, in their eagerness to escape from Sir Oran (who
like Artegall's Iron Man,[1] or like Ajax among the Trojans, or like
Rodomont in Paris, or like Orlando among the soldiers of Agramant,
kept clearing for himself an ample space, in the midst of the encircling
crowd), waged desperate conflict with those without ; so that from
the equal and opposite action of the centripetal and centrifugal
forces, resulted a stationary combat, raging between the circum-
ferences of two concentric circles, with barbaric dissonance of deadly
feud, and infinite variety of oath and execration, till Sir Oran, charging
desperately along one of the radii, fought a free passage through all
opposition ; and rushing to the barouche of Sir Telegraph Paxarett,
sprang to his old station on the box, from whence he shook his sapling
at the foe, with looks of mortal defiance. Mr. Forester, who had been
forcibly parted from him at the commencement of the strife, and had
been all anxiety on his account, mounted with great alacrity to his
station on the roof : the rest of the party was already seated : the
Honourable Mrs. Pinmoney, half-fainting with terror, earnestly
entreated Sir Telegraph to fly : Sir Telegraph cracked his whip : the
horses sprang forward like racers : the wheels went round like the
wheels of a firework. The tumult of battle lessening as they
receded, came wafted to them on the wings of the wind : for the

[1] Spenser, *The Faerie Queene*, Bk. V, Canto 1. Talus, Artegall's iron
man, is a personification of rough justice who threshes out falsehood with
a flail. G.

flame of discord having been once kindled, was not extinguished by the departure of its first flambeau—Sir Oran ; but war raged wide and far, here in the thickest mass of central fight, there in the light skirmishing of flying detachments. The hustings were demolished, and the beams and planks turned into offensive weapons : the booths were torn to pieces, and the canvas converted into flags floating over the heads of magnanimous heroes that rushed to revenge they knew not what, in deadly battle with they knew not whom. The stalls and barrows were upset ; and the pears, apples, oranges, mutton-pies, and masses of gingerbread, flew like missiles of fate in all directions. The *sanctum sanctorum* of the ale was broken into, and the guardians of the Hesperian liquor were put to ignominious rout. Hats and wigs were hurled into the air, never to return to the heads from which they had suffered violent divorce. The collision of sticks, the ringing of empty ale-casks, the shrieks of women, and the vociferations of combatants, mingled in one deepening and indescribable tumult : till at length, every thing else being levelled with the heath, they turned the mingled torrent of their wrath on the cottage of Mr. Corporate, to which they triumphantly set fire, and danced round the blaze, like a rabble of village boys round the effigy of the immortal Guy. In a few minutes the ancient and honourable borough of Onevote was reduced to ashes : but we have the satisfaction to state that it was rebuilt a few days afterwards, at the joint expense of its two representatives, and His Grace the Duke of Rottenburgh.

CHAPTER XXIII

THE COUNCIL OF WAR

THE compassionate reader will perhaps sympathize in our anxiety, to take one peep at Lord Anophel Achthar and the Reverend Mr. Grovel-grub, whom we left perched on the summit of the rock, where Sir Oran had placed them, looking at each other as ruefully as Hudibras and Ralpho in their "wooden bastile,"[1] and falling by degrees into as knotty an argument, the *quæritur* of which was, how to descend from

---

[1] Butler : *Hudibras*, Argument, Pt. I, Canto 2.   G.

their elevation—an exploit which to them seemed replete with danger and difficulty. Lord Anophel, having, for the first time in his life, been made acquainted with the salutary effects of manual discipline, sate boiling with wrath and revenge; while the Reverend Mr. Grovelgrub, who in his youthful days had been beaten black and blue in the capacity of *fag* (a practice which reflects so much honour on our public seminaries), bore the infliction with more humility.

LORD ANOPHEL ACHTHAR, (*rubbing his shoulder.*) This is all your doing, Grovelgrub—all your fault, curse me!

THE REVEREND MR. GROVELGRUB. Oh, my Lord! my intention was good, though the catastrophe is ill. The race is not always to the swift, nor the battle to the strong.

LORD ANOPHEL ACHTHAR. But the battle was to the strong in this instance, Grovelgrub, curse me! though, from the speed with which you began to run off on the first alarm, it was no fault of yours that the race was not to the swift.

THE REVEREND MR. GROVELGRUB. I must do your Lordship the justice to say, that you too started with a degree of celerity highly creditable to your capacity of natural locomotion; and if that ugly monster, the dumb Baronet, had not knocked us both down in the incipiency of our progression——

LORD ANOPHEL ACHTHAR. We should have escaped as our two rascals did, who shall bitterly rue their dereliction. But as to the dumb Baronet, who has treated me with gross impertinence on various occasions, I shall certainly call him out, to give me the satisfaction of a gentleman.

THE REVEREND MR. GROVELGRUB. Oh, my Lord,

> Though with pistols 'tis the fashion,
> To satisfy your passion;
> Yet where's the satisfaction,
> If you perish in the action ? [1]

LORD ANOPHEL ACHTHAR. One of us must perish, Grovelgrub, 'pon honour. Death or revenge! We're blown, Grovelgrub. He took

---

[1] Quotation untraced. G.

off our masks ; and though he can't speak, he can write, no doubt, and read, too, as I shall try with a challenge.

THE REVEREND MR. GROVELGRUB. Can't speak, my Lord, is by no means clear. Won't speak, perhaps : none are so dumb as those who won't speak. Don't you think, my Lord, there was a sort of melancholy about him—a kind of sullenness ? Crossed in love I suspect. People crossed in love, Saint Chrysostom says, lose their voice.

LORD ANOPHEL ACHTHAR. Then I wish you were crossed in love, Grovelgrub, with all my heart.

THE REVEREND MR. GROVELGRUB. Nay, my Lord, what so sweet in calamity as the voice of the spiritual comforter ? All shall be well yet, my Lord. I have an infallible project hatching here : Miss Melincourt shall be ensconced in Alga Castle, and then the day is our own.

LORD ANOPHEL ACHTHAR. Grovelgrub, you know the old receipt for stewing a carp : " First, catch your carp."

THE REVEREND MR. GROVELGRUB. Your Lordship is pleased to be facetious : but if the carp be not caught, let me be devilled like a biscuit after the second bottle, or a turkey's leg at a twelfth night supper. The carp shall be caught.

LORD ANOPHEL ACHTHAR. Well, Grovelgrub, only take notice that I'll not come again within ten miles of dummy.

THE REVEREND MR. GROVELGRUB. You may rely upon it, my Lord, I shall always know my distance from the Honourable Baronet. But my plot is a good plot, and cannot fail of success.

LORD ANOPHEL ACHTHAR. You are a very skilful contriver, to be sure : this is your contrivance, our perch on the top of this rock. Now contrive, if you can, some way of getting to the bottom of it.

THE REVEREND MR. GROVELGRUB. My Lord, there is a passage in Æschylus, very applicable to our situation, where the chorus wishes to be in precisely such a place.

LORD ANOPHEL ACHTHAR. Then I wish the chorus were here instead of us, Grovelgrub, with all my soul.

THE REVEREND MR. GROVELGRUB. It is a very fine passage, my Lord, and worth your attention : the rock is described as

> λισσας αιγιλιψ απροσδεικτος
> οιοφρων ερημας γυπιας πετρα,
> βαθυ πτωμα μαρτυρουσα μοι.[1]

That is, my Lord, a precipitous rock, inaccessible to the goat—not to be pointed at (from having, as I take it, its head in the clouds), where there is the loneliness of mind, and the solitude of desolation, where the vulture has its nest, and the precipice testifies a deep and headlong fall.

LORD ANOPHEL ACHTHAR. I'll tell you what, Grovelgrub ; if ever I catch you quoting Æschylus again, I'll cashier you from your tutorship—that's positive.

THE REVEREND MR. GROVELGRUB. I am dumb, my Lord.

LORD ANOPHEL ACHTHAR. Think, I tell you, of some way of getting down.

THE REVEREND MR. GROVELGRUB. Nothing more easy, my Lord.

LORD ANOPHEL ACHTHAR. Plummet fashion, I suppose ?

THE REVEREND MR. GROVELGRUB. Why, as your Lordship seems to hint, that certainly is the most expeditious method ; but not, I think, in all points of view, the most advisable. On this side of the rock is a *dumetum* : we can descend, I think, by the help of the roots and shoots. O dear ! I shall be like Virgil's goat : I shall be seen from far to hang from the bushy rock, *Dumosâ pendere procul de rupe videbor !*

LORD ANOPHEL ACHTHAR. Confound your Greek and Latin ! you know there is nothing I hate so much ; and I thought you did so too, or you have *finished* your *education* to no purpose at college.

[1] *Supplices*, 807, Ed. Schutz. [P.]

THE REVEREND MR. GROVELGRUB. I do, my Lord : I hate them mortally, more than any thing except philosophy and the dumb Baronet.

Lord Anophel Achthar proceeded to examine the side of the rock to which the Reverend Mr. Grovelgrub had called his attention ; and as it seemed the most practicable mode of descent, it was resolved to submit to necessity, and make a valorous effort to regain the valley ; Lord Anophel, however, insisting on the Reverend Mr. Grovelgrub leading the way. The reverend gentleman seized with one hand the stem of a hazel, with the other the branch of an ash ; set one foot on the root of an oak, and deliberately lowered the other in search of a resting-place ; which having found on a projecting point of stone, he cautiously disengaged one hand and the upper foot, for which in turn he sought and found a firm *appui* ; and thus by little and little he vanished among the boughs from the sight of Lord Anophel, who proceeded with great circumspection to follow his example.

Lord Anophel had descended about one third of the elevation, comforting his ear with the rustling of the boughs below, that announced the safe progress of his reverend precursor : when suddenly, as he was shifting his right hand, a treacherous twig in his left gave way, and he fell with fearful lapse from bush to bush, till, striking violently on a bough to which the unfortunate divine was appended, it broke beneath the shock, and down they went, crashing through the bushes together.[1] Lord Anophel was soon wedged into the middle of a large holly, from which he heard the intermitted sound of the boughs as they broke, and were broken by, the fall of his companion : till at length they ceased, and fearful silence succeeded. He then extricated himself from the holly as well as he could, at the expense of a scratched face, and lowered himself down without further accident. On reaching the bottom, he had the pleasure to find the reverend gentleman in safety, sitting on a fragment of stone, and rubbing his shin. " Come, Grovelgrub," said Lord Anophel, " let us make the best of our way to the nearest inn."—" And pour

[1] See Mr. Cranium's fall, *Headlong Hall,* p. 54 and Note.   G.

oil and wine into our wounds," pursued the reverend gentleman,
" and over our Madeira and walnuts lay a more hopeful scheme for
our next campaign."

CHAPTER XXIV

THE BAROUCHE

THE morning after the election Sir Oran Haut-ton and his party
took leave of Mr. Sarcastic, Mr. Forester having previously obtained
from him a promise to be present at the Anti-saccharine fête.   The
barouche left the city of Novote, decorated with ribands : Sir Oran
Haut-ton was loudly cheered by the populace, and not least by those
whom he had most severely beaten ; the secret of which was, that a
double allowance of ale had been distributed over-night, to wash
away the effects of his indiscretion : it having been ascertained by
political economists, that a practical appeal either to the palm or the
palate will induce the friends of *things as they are* to submit to
any thing.

Autumn was now touching on the confines of winter, but the day
was mild and sunny.   Sir Telegraph asked Mr. Forester, if he did not
think the mode of locomotion very agreeable.

MR. FORESTER.   That I never denied : all I question is, the right
of any individual to indulge himself in it.

SIR TELEGRAPH PAXARETT.   Surely a man has a right to do what
he pleases with his own money.

MR. FORESTER.   A legal right, certainly, not a moral one.   The
possession of power does not justify its abuse.   The quantity of
money in a nation, the quantity of food, and the number of animals
that consume that food, maintain a triangular harmony, of which, in
all the fluctuations of time and circumstance, the proportions are
always the same.   You must consider, therefore, that for every horse
you keep for pleasure, you pass sentence of non-existence on two
human beings.

SIR TELEGRAPH PAXARETT.   Really, Forester, you are a very

singular fellow. I should not much mind what you say, if you had not such a strange habit of practising what you preach ; a thing quite unprecedented, and, egad, preposterous. I cannot think where you got it : I am sure you did not learn it at college.

MR. FAX. In a political light, every object of perception may be resolved into one of these three heads : the food consumed—the consumers—and money. In this point of view all convertible property that does not eat and drink, is money. Diamonds are money. When a man changes a bank-note for a diamond, he merely changes one sort of money for another, differing only in the facility of circulation and the stability of value. None of the produce of the earth is wasted by the permutation.

MR. FORESTER. The most pernicious species of luxury, therefore, is that which applies the fruits of the earth to any other purposes than those of human subsistence. All luxury is indeed pernicious, because its infallible tendency is to enervate the few, and enslave the many : but luxury, which, in addition to this evil tendency, destroys the fruits of the earth in the wantonness of idle ostentation, and thereby prevents the existence of so many human beings, as the quantity of food so destroyed would maintain, is marked by criminality of a much deeper die.

MR. FAX. At the same time you must consider, that, in respect of population, the great desideratum is not number, but quality. If the whole surface of this country were divided into gardens, and in every garden were a cottage, and in every cottage a family living entirely on potatoes, the number of its human inhabitants would be much greater than at present : but where would be the spirit of commercial enterprise, the researches of science, the exalted pursuits of philosophical leisure, the communication with distant lands, and all that variety of human life and intercourse, which is now so beautiful and so interesting ? Above all, where would be the refuge of such a population in times of the slightest defalcation ? Now, the waste of plenty is the resource of scarcity. The canal that does not overflow in the season of rain, will not be navigable in the season of drought. The rich have been often ready, in days of emergency, to lay their superfluities aside ; but when the fruits of the earth are applied, in plentiful or even ordinary seasons, to the utmost possibility of human subsistence, the days of deficiency in their produce must be days of inevitable famine.

MR. FORESTER. What then will you say of those, who, in times of actual famine, persevere in their old course, in the wanton waste of luxury ?

MR. FAX. Truly I have nothing to say for them, but that they know not what they do.

MR. FORESTER. If, in any form of human society, any one human being dies of hunger, while another wastes or consumes in the wantonness of vanity, as much as would have preserved his existence, I hold that second man guilty of the death of the first.

SIR TELEGRAPH PAXARETT. Surely, Forester, you are not serious ?

MR. FORESTER. Indeed I am. What would you think of a family of four persons, two of whom should not be contented with consuming their own share of diurnal provision, but, having adventitiously the pre-eminence of physical power, should either throw the share of the two others into the fire, or stew it down into a condiment for their own ?

SIR TELEGRAPH PAXARETT. I should think it very abominable, certainly.

MR. FORESTER. Yet what is human society, but one great family ? What is moral duty, but that precise line of conduct which tends to promote the greatest degree of general happiness ? And is not this duty most flagrantly violated, when one man appropriates to himself the subsistence of twelve ; while, perhaps, in his immediate neighbourhood, eleven of his fellow-beings are dying with hunger ? I have seen such a man walk with a demure face into church, as regularly as if the Sunday bell had been a portion of his corporeal mechanism, to hear a bloated and beneficed sensualist hold forth on the text of *Do as ye would be done by*, or, *Inasmuch as ye have done it unto the least of these my brethren, ye have done it unto me* : whereas, if he had wished his theory to coincide with his practice, he would have chosen for his text, *Behold a man gluttonous and a winebibber, a friend of publicans and sinners* : [1] and when the duty of words was over, the auditor and his ghostly adviser, issuing forth together, have committed poor Lazarus to the care of Providence, and proceeded to feast in the lordly mansion, like Dives that lived in purple.[2]

SIR TELEGRAPH PAXARETT. Well, Forester, there I escape your shaft; for I have " forgotten what the inside of a church is made of " [3] since they made me go to chapel twice a day at college. But go on, and don't spare *me*.

MR. FAX. Let us suppose that ten thousand quarters of wheat will maintain ten thousand persons during any given portion of time : if the ten thousand quarters be reduced to five, or if the ten thousand persons be increased to twenty, the consequence will be immediate and general distress : yet if the proportions be equally distributed, as in a ship on short allowance, the general perception of necessity and justice will preserve general patience and mutual goodwill : but let the first supposition remain unaltered, let there be ten thousand quarters of wheat, which shall be full allowance for ten thousand people ; then, if four thousand persons take to themselves the portion of eight thousand, and leave to the remaining six thousand the portion of two (and this I fear is even an inadequate picture of the common practice of the world); these latter will be in a much worse condition

---

[1] *Matthew*, xi. 19. [P.]

[2] " He that will mould a modern bishop into a primitive, must yield him to be elected by the popular voice, undiocesed, unrevenued, unlorded, and leave him nothing but brotherly equality, matchless temperance, frequent fasting, incessant prayer and preaching, continual watchings and labours in his ministry, which, what a rich booty it would be, what a plump endowment to the many-benefice-gaping mouth of a prelate, what a relish it would give to his canary-sucking and swan-eating palate, let old bishop Mountain judge for me.—They beseech us, that we would think them fit to be our justices of peace, our lords, our highest officers of state, though they come furnished with no more knowledge than they learnt between the cook and the manciple, or more profoundly at the college audit, or the regent house, or to come to their deepest insight, at their patron's table."— Milton : *Of Reformation in England.* [P.]

[3] *Henry IV, Pt. I*, Act III, Sc. 3. G.

on the last, than on the first supposition : while the habit of selfish
prodigality deadening all good feelings and extinguishing all sympathy on the one hand, and the habit of debasement and suffering
combining with the inevitable sense of oppression and injustice on the
other, will produce an action and re-action of open, unblushing, cold-
hearted pride, and servile, inefficient, ill-disguised resentment, which
no philanthropist can contemplate without dismay.

MR. FORESTER. What then will be the case if the same disproportionate division continues by regular gradations through the
remaining six thousand, till the lowest thousand receive such a
fractional pittance as will scarcely keep life together ?   If any of
these perish with hunger, what are they but the victims of the first
four thousand, who appropriated more to themselves than either
nature required or justice allowed ?   This, whatever the temporizers
with the world may say of it, I have no hesitation in pronouncing to
be wickedness of the most atrocious kind : and this I make no doubt
was the sense of the founder of the Christian religion when he said,
*It is easier for a camel to pass through the eye of a needle, than for a rich
man to enter the kingdom of heaven.*

MR. FAX. You must beware of the chimæra of an agrarian law,
the revolutionary doctrine of an equality of possession : which can
never be possible in practice, till the whole constitution of human
nature be changed.

MR. FORESTER. I am no revolutionist. I am no advocate for
violent and arbitrary changes in the state of society. I care not in
what proportions property is divided (though I think there are
certain limits which it ought never to pass, and approve the wisdom
of the American laws in restricting the fortune of a private citizen
to twenty thousand a year), provided the rich can be made to know
that they are but the stewards of the poor, that they are not to be
the monopolizers of solitary spoil, but the distributors of general
possession ; that they are responsible for that distribution to every
principle of general justice, to every tie of moral obligation, to every
feeling of human sympathy : that they are bound to cultivate simple
habits in themselves, and to encourage most such arts of industry

and peace, as are most compatible with the health and liberty of others.

MR. FAX.   On this principle, then, any species of luxury in the artificial adornment of persons and dwellings, which condemns the artificer to a life of pain and sickness in the alternations of the furnace and the cellar, is more baleful and more criminal, than even that which consuming in idle prodigality the fruits of the earth, destroys altogether in the proportion of its waste, so much of the possibility of human existence: since it is better not to be, than to be in misery.

SIR TELEGRAPH PAXARETT.   That is some consolation for me, as it shows me that there are others worse than myself: for I really thought you were going, between you, to prove me one of the greatest rogues in England.   But seriously, Forester, you think the keeping of pleasure-horses, for the reasons you have given, a selfish and criminal species of luxury ?

MR. FORESTER.   I am so far persuaded of it, that I keep none myself.[1]

SIR TELEGRAPH PAXARETT.   But are not these four very beautiful creatures ?   Would you wish not to see them in existence, living, as they do, a very happy and easy kind of life ?

MR. FORESTER.   That I am disposed to question, when I compare the wild horse in his native deserts, in the full enjoyment of health and liberty, and all the energies of his nature, with those docked, cropped, curtailed, mutilated animals, pent more than half their lives in the close confinement of a stable, never let out but to run in trammels, subject, like their tyrant man, to an infinite variety of diseases, the produce of civilization and unnatural life, and tortured every now and then by some villain of a farrier, who has no more feeling for them than a West Indian planter has for his slaves ; and when you consider, too, the fate of the most cherished of the species, racers and hunters, instruments and often victims of sports equally foolish and cruel, you will acknowledge that the life of the civilized horse is not an enviable destiny.

[1] See page 161.   [P.]   [Mr. Falconer in *Gryll Grange* (p. 890) shares this view.   G.]

MR. FAX.   Horses are noble and useful animals ; but as they must necessarily exist in great numbers for almost every purpose of human intercourse and business, it is desirable that none should be kept for purposes of mere idleness and ostentation.   A pleasure-horse is a sort of four-footed sinecurist.

SIR TELEGRAPH PAXARETT.   Not quite so mischievous as a two-footed one.

MR. FORESTER.   Perhaps not : but the latter has always a large retinue of the former, and therefore the evil is doubled.

SIR TELEGRAPH PAXARETT.   Upon my word, Forester, you will almost talk me out of my barouche, and then what will become of me ? · What shall I do to kill time ?

MR. FORESTER.   Read ancient books, the only source of permanent happiness left in this degenerate world.

SIR TELEGRAPH PAXARETT.   Read ancient books !   That may be very good advice to some people : but you forget that I have been at college, and *finished* my *education*.   By the by, I have one inside, a portable advocate for my proceedings, no less a personage than old Pindar.

MR. FORESTER.   Pindar has written very fine odes on driving, as Anacreon has done on drinking ; but the first can no more be adduced to prove the morality of the whip, than the second to demonstrate the virtue of intemperance.   Besides, as to the mental tendency and emulative associations of the pursuit itself, no comparison can be instituted between the charioteers of the Olympic games and those of our turnpike roads ; for the former were the emulators of heroes and demigods, and the latter of grooms and mail-coachmen.

SIR TELEGRAPH PAXARETT.   Well, Forester, as I recall to mind the various subjects against which I have heard you declaim, I will make you a promise.   When ecclesiastical dignitaries imitate the temperance and humility of the founder of that religion by which they feed and flourish : when the man in place acts on the principles which he professed while he was out : when borough electors will not sell their

suffrage, nor their representatives their votes : when poets are not
to be hired for the maintenance of any opinion : when learned
divines can afford to have a conscience : when universities are not
a hundred years in knowledge behind all the rest of the world :
when young ladies speak as they think, and when those who shudder
at a tale of the horrors of slavery will deprive their own palates of
a sweet taste, for the purpose of contributing all in their power to its
extinction :—why then, Forester, I will lay down my barouche.

CHAPTER XXV

THE WALK

THEY were to pass, in their return, through an estate belonging to
Mr. Forester, for the purpose of taking up his aunt Miss Evergreen,
who was to accompany them to Redrose Abbey. On arriving at an
inn on the nearest point of the great road, Mr. Forester told Sir
Telegraph, that, from the arrangements he had made, it was impossible for any carriage to enter his estate, as he had taken every
precaution for preserving the simplicity of his tenants from the
contagious exhibitions and examples of luxury. "This road," said
he, "is only accessible to pedestrians and equestrians : I have no
wish to exclude the visits of laudable curiosity, but there is nothing
I so much dread and deprecate as the intrusion of those heartless
fops, who take their fashionable autumnal tour, to gape at rocks and
waterfalls, for which they have neither eyes nor ears, and to pervert
the feelings and habits of the once simple dwellers of the mountains.[1]

[1] "Much have those travellers to answer for, whose casual intercourse
with this innocent and simple people tends to corrupt them ; disseminating
among them ideas of extravagance and dissipation—giving them a taste
for pleasures and gratifications of which they had no ideas—inspiring them
with discontent at home—and tainting their rough industrious manners
with idleness and a thirst after dishonest means.

"If travellers would frequent this country, with a view to examine its
grandeur and beauty, or to explore its varied and curious regions with the
eye of philosophy—if, in their passage through it, they could be content
with such fare as the country produces, or at least reconcile themselves to
it, by manly exercise and fatigue (for there is a time when the stomach and
the plainest food will be found in perfect harmony)—if they could thus,

Nature seems to have raised her mountain-barriers for the purpose
of rescuing a few favoured mortals from the vortex of that torrent
of physical and moral degeneracy, which seems to threaten nothing
less than the extermination of the human species : [1] but in vain,
while the annual opening of its sluices lets out a side stream of the
worst specimens of what is called refined society, to inundate the
mountain valleys with the corruptions of metropolitan folly. Thus
innocence, and health, and simplicity of life and manners, are
banished from their last retirement, and no where more lamentably
so than in the romantic scenery of the northern lakes, where every
wonder of nature is made an article of trade, where the cataracts are
locked up, and the echoes are sold : so that even the rustic character
of that ill-fated region is condemned to participate in the moral
stigma which must dwell indelibly on its poetical name."

---

instead of corrupting the manners of an innocent people, learn to amend
their own, by seeing in how narrow a compass the wants of human life
may be compressed—a journey through these wild scenes might be
attended, perhaps, with more improvement than a journey to Rome or
Paris. Where manners are polished into vicious refinement, simplifying
is the best mode of improving ; and the example of innocence is a more
instructive lesson than any that can be taught by artists and literati.

" But these parts are too often the resort of gay company, who are under
no impressions of this kind—who have no ideas but of extending the sphere
of their amusements, or of varying a life of dissipation. The grandeur of
the country is not taken into the question, or at least it is no otherwise
considered than as affording some new mode of pleasurable enjoyment.
Thus, even the diversions of Newmarket are introduced—diversions, one
would imagine, more foreign to the nature of this country than any other.
A number of horses are carried into the middle of the lake in a flat boat :
a plug is drawn from the bottom : the boat sinks, and the horses are left
floating on the surface. In different directions they make to land, and
the horse which arrives soonest secures the prize."—Gilpin's *Picturesque
Observations on Cumberland and Westmoreland*, vol. ii. p. 67. [P.]

[1] " The necessary consequence of men living in so unnatural a way with
respect to houses, clothes, and diet, and continuing to live so for many
generations, each generation adding to the vices, diseases, and weaknesses
produced by the unnatural life of the preceding, is, that they must gradually
decline in strength, health, and longevity, till at length the race dies out.
To deny this would be to deny that the life allotted by nature to man is the
best life for the preservation of his health and strength ; for, if it be so,
I think it is demonstration that the constant deviation from it, going on
for many centuries, must end in the extinction of the race."—*Ancient
Metaphysics*, vol. v. p. 237. [P.]

The party alighted, and a consultation being held, it was resolved to walk to the village in a body, the Honourable Mrs. Pinmoney lifting up her hands and eyes in profound astonishment at Mr. Forester's oldfashioned notions.

They followed a narrow winding path, through rocky and sylvan hills. They walked in straggling parties of ones, twos, and threes. Mr. Forester and Anthelia went first. Sir Oran Haut-ton followed alone, playing a pensive tune on his flute. Sir Telegraph Paxarett walked between his aunt and cousin, the Honourable Mrs. Pinmoney and Miss Danaretta. Mr. Hippy, in a melancholy vein, brought up the rear with Mr. Fax. A very beautiful child which had sat on the old gentleman's knee, at the inn where they breakfasted, had thrown him, not for the first time on a similar occasion, into a fit of dismal repentance, that he had not one of his own: he stalked along accordingly, with a most ruefully lengthened aspect, uttering every now and then a deep-drawn sigh. Mr. Fax in philosophic sympathy determined to console him, by pointing out to him the true nature and tendency of the principle of population, and the enormous evils resulting from the multiplication of the human species : observing that the only true criterion of the happiness of a nation was to be found in the number of its old maids and bachelors, whom he venerated as the sources and symbols of prosperity and peace. Poor Mr. Hippy walked on sighing and groaning, deaf as the adder to the voice of the charmer : for, in spite of all the eloquence of the antipopulationist, the image of the beautiful child which he had danced on his knee, continued to haunt his imagination, and threatened him with the blue devils for the rest of the day.

"I see," said Sir Telegraph to Mrs. Pinmoney, "my hopes are at an end. Forester is the happy man, though I am by no means sure that he knows it himself."

"Impossible," said Mrs. Pinmoney : "Anthelia may be amused a little while with his rhapsodies, but nothing more, believe me. The man is out of his mind. Do you know, I heard him say the other day, 'that not a shilling of his property was his own, that it was a portion of the general possession of human society, of which the distribution had devolved upon him ; and that for the mode of that distribution he was most rigidly responsible to the principles of immutable justice.' [1] If such a mode of talking——"

"And acting too," said Sir Telegraph; "for I assure you he quadrates his practice as nearly as he can to his theory."

"Monstrous!" said Mrs. Pinmoney: "what would our reverend friend, poor dear Doctor Bosky, say to him? But if such a way of talking and acting be the way to win a young heiress, I shall think the whole world is turned topsy-turvy."

"Your remark would be just," said Sir Telegraph, "were that young heiress any other than Anthelia Melincourt."

"Well," said Mrs. Pinmoney, "there are maidens in Scotland more lovely by far——"

"That I deny," said Sir Telegraph.

"Who will gladly be bride to the young Lochinvar," proceeded Mrs. Pinmoney.

"That will not do," said Sir Telegraph: "I shall resign with the best grace I can muster to a more favoured candidate, but I shall never think of another choice."

"Twelve months hence," said Mrs. Pinmoney, "you will tell another tale. In the mean time you will not die of despair as long as there is a good turnpike road and a pipe of Madeira in England."

"You will find," said Mr. Forester to Anthelia, "in the little valley we are about to enter, a few specimens of that simple and natural life which approaches as nearly as the present state of things will admit, to my ideas of the habits and manners of the primæval agriculturists, or the fathers of the Roman republic. You will think perhaps of Fabricius under his oak, of Curius in his cottage, of Regulus, when he solicited recall from the command of an army, because the man whom he had intrusted, in his absence, with the cultivation of his field and garden, had run away with his spade and rake, by which his wife and children were left without support; and when the senate decreed that the implements should be replaced, and a man provided at the public expense to maintain the consul's

---

[1] "That I should entail £120,000 of command over labor, of power to remit this, to employ it for beneficent purposes, on one whom I know not —who might, instead of being the benefactor of mankind, be its bane." Shelley to Elizabeth Hitchener, Dec. 15, 1811. G.

family, by cultivating his fields in his absence. Then poverty was as honourable, as it is now disgraceful: then the same public respect was given to him who could most simplify his habits and manners, that is now paid to those who can make the most shameless parade of wanton and selfish prodigality. Those days are past for ever: but it is something in the present time to resuscitate their memory, to call up even the shadow of the reflection of republican Rome— *Rome, the seat of glory and of virtue, if ever they had one on earth.*" [1]

"You excite my curiosity very highly," said Anthelia; "for, from the time when I read

> "——in those dear books that first
> Woke in my heart the love of poesy,
> How with the villagers Erminia dwelt,
> And Calidore, for a fair shepherdess,
> Forgot his guest to learn the shepherd's lore ;" [2]

how much have I regretted never to discover in the actual inhabitants of the country, the realization of the pictures of Spenser and Tasso!"

"The palaces," said Mr. Forester, "that every where rise around them to shame the meanness of their humble dwellings, the great roads that every where intersect their valleys, and bring them continually in contact with the overflowing corruption of cities, the devastating monopoly of large farms, that has almost swept the race of cottagers from the face of the earth, sending the parents to the workhouse or the army, and the children to perish like untimely blossoms in the blighting imprisonment of manufactories, have combined to diminish the numbers and deteriorate the character of the inhabitants of the country: but whatever be the increasing ravages of the Triad of Mammon, avarice, luxury, and disease, they will always be the last involved in the vortex of progressive degeneracy, realizing the beautiful fiction of ancient poetry, that, when primæval Justice departed from the earth, her last steps were among the cultivators of the fields." [3]

[1] "Rome, le siège de la gloire et de la vertu, si jamais elles en eurent un sur la terre."—Rousseau. [P.]

[2] Southey: *English Eclogues, The Ruined Cottage.* Last line actually: "forsook his quest." G.

[3] ——extrema per illos
Justitia, excedens terris, vestigia fecit.—Virg. [P.]
[*Georg.* II. 473-4. G.]

CHAPTER XXVI

THE COTTAGERS

THE valley expanded into a spacious amphitheatre, with a beautiful stream winding among pastoral meadows, which, as well as the surrounding hills, were studded with cottages, each with its own trees, its little garden, and its farm. Sir Telegraph was astonished to find so many human dwellings in a space that, on the modern tactics of rural œconomy, appeared only sufficient for three or four *moderate* farms ; and Mr. Fax looked perfectly aghast to perceive the principle of population in such a fearful state of activity. Mrs. and Miss Pinmoney expressed their surprise at not seeing a single lordly mansion asserting its regal pre-eminence over the dwellings of its miserable vassals ; while the voices of the children at play served only to condense the vapours that offuscated the imagination of poor Mr. Hippy. Anthelia, as their path wound among the cottages, was more and more delighted with the neatness and comfort of the dwellings, the exquisite order of the gardens, the ingenuous air of happiness and liberty that characterized the simple inhabitants, and the health and beauty of the little rosy children that were sporting in the fields. Mr. Forester had been recognised from a distance. The cottagers ran out in all directions to welcome him : the valley and the hills seemed starting into life, as men, women, and children poured down, as with one impulse, on the path of his approach, while some hastened to the residence of Miss Evergreen, ambitious of being the first to announce to her the arrival of her nephew. Miss Evergreen came forward to meet the party, surrounded by a rustic crowd of both sexes and of every age, from the old man leaning on his stick, to the little child that could just run alone, but had already learnt to attach something magical to the sound of the name of Forester.

The first idea they entertained at the sight of his party was, that he was married, and had brought his bride to visit his little colony ; and Anthelia was somewhat disconcerted by the benedictions that were poured upon her under this impression of the warm-hearted rustics.

They entered Miss Evergreen's cottage, which was small, but in a style of beautiful simplicity. Anthelia was much pleased with her countenance and manners ; for Miss Evergreen was an amiable and intelligent woman, and was single, not from having wanted lovers, but from being of that order of minds which can love but once.

Mr. Fax took occasion, during a temporary absence of Miss Evergreen from the apartment in which they were taking refreshment, to say, he was happy to have seen so amiable a specimen of that injured and calumniated class of human beings commonly called old maids, who were often so from possessing in too high a degree the qualities most conducive to domestic happiness ; for it might naturally be imagined, that the least refined and delicate minds would be the soonest satisfied in the choice of a partner, and the most ready to repair the loss of a first love by the substitution of a second. This might have led to a discussion, but Miss Evergreen's re-entrance prevented it. They now strolled out among the cottages in detached parties and in different directions. Mr. Fax attached himself to Mr. Hippy and Miss Evergreen. Anthelia and Mr. Forester went their own way. She was above the little affectation of feeling her *dignity* offended, as our female novel-writers express it, by the notions which the peasants had formed respecting her. " You see," said Mr. Forester, " I have endeavoured as much as possible to recall the images of better times, when the country was well peopled, from the farms being small, and cultivated chiefly by cottagers who lived in what was in Scotland called a *cottar town*.[1] Now you may go over vast tracts of country without seeing any thing like an *old English cottage,* to say nothing of the fearful difference which has been caused in the interior of the few that remain by the pressure of exorbitant taxation, of which the real, though not the nominal burden always falls most heavily on the labouring classes, backed by that *canker at the heart of national prosperity,* the imaginary riches of paper-credit, of which the means are delusion, the progress monopoly, and the ultimate effect the extinction of the best portion of national population, a healthy and industrious peasantry. Large farms bring more rent to the landlord, and, therefore, landlords in general make no scruple to increase their rents by depopulating their estates,[2] though Anthelia Melincourt will not comprehend the mental principle in which such feelings originate."

[1] *Ancient Metaphysics,* vol. v. book iv, chap. 8. [P.]   [2] *Ibid.* [P.]

" Is it possible," said Anthelia, " that you, so young as you are, can have created such a scene as this ? "

" My father," said Mr. Forester, " began what I merely perpetuate. He estimated his riches, not by the amount of rent his estate produced, but the number of simple and happy beings it maintained. He divided it into little farms of such a size as were sufficient, even in indifferent seasons, to produce rather more than the necessities of their cultivators required. So that all these cottagers are rich according to the definition of Socrates ; [1] for they have at all times a little more than they actually need, a subsidium for age, or sickness, or any accidental necessity."

They entered several of the cottages, and found in them all the same traces of comfort and content, and the same images of the better days of England : the clean-tiled floor, the polished beechen table, the tea-cups on the chimney, the dresser with its glittering dishes, the old woman with her spinning-wheel by the fire, and the old man with his little grandson in the garden, giving him his first lessons in the use of the spade, the goodwife busy in her domestic arrangements, and the pot boiling on the fire for the return of her husband from his labour in the field.

" Is it not astonishing," said Mr. Forester, " that there should be any who think, as I know many do, the number of cottagers on their land a grievance, and desire to be quit of them,[2] and have no feeling of remorse in allotting to one solitary family as much extent of cultivated land as was ploughed by the whole Roman people in the days of Cincinnatus ? [3] The three great points of every political system are the health, the morals, and the number of the people. Without health and morals, the people cannot be happy ; but without numbers they cannot be a great and powerful nation, nor even exist for any considerable time.[4] And by numbers I do not mean the

---

[1] See Xenophon's *Memorabilia*. [P.]
[2] *Ancient Metaphysics*, vol. v. book iv. chap. 8. [P.]
[3] Si tantum culti solus possederis agri,
    Quantum sub Tatio populus Romanus arabat.—Juv. [P.]
    [*Sat.* XIV. 159–60 : " If you have become sole possessor of as great an extent of farmland as was ploughed by the whole Roman people in the days of Tatius." G.]
[4] *Ancient Metaphysics*, vol. v. book iv. chap. 8. [P.]

inhabitants of the cities, the sordid and sickly victims of commerce, and the effeminate and enervated slaves of luxury ; but in estimating the power and the riches of a country I take my only criterion from its agricultural population."

CHAPTER XXVII

THE ANTI-SACCHARINE FÊTE

MISS EVERGREEN accompanied them in their return, to preside at the Anti-saccharine fête. Mr. Hippy was turned out to make room for her in the barouche, and took his seat on the roof with Messieurs Forester and Fax. Anthelia no longer deemed it necessary to keep a guard over her heart ; the bud of mutual affection between herself and Mr. Forester, both being, as they were, perfectly free and perfectly ingenuous, was rapidly expanding into the full bloom of happiness : they dreamed not that evil was near to check, if not to wither it.

The whole party was prevailed on by Miss Evergreen to be her guests at Redrose Abbey till after the Anti-saccharine fête, which very shortly took place, and was attended by the principal members of the Anti-saccharine Society, and by an illustrious assemblage from near and from far : amongst the rest by our old acquaintance, Mr. Derrydown, Mr. O'Scarum, Major O'Dogskin, Mr. Sarcastic, the Reverend Mr. Portpipe, and Mr. Feathernest the poet, who brought with him his friend Mr. Vamp the reviewer. Lord Anophel Achthar and the Reverend Mr. Grovelgrub deemed it not expedient to join the party, but ensconced themselves in Alga Castle, studying *michin malicho*, which means mischief.[1]

The Anti-saccharine fête commenced with a splendid dinner, as Mr. Forester thought to make luxury on this occasion subservient to morality, by showing what culinary art could effect without the intervention of West Indian produce ; and the preparers of the feast, under the superintendence of Miss Evergreen, had succeeded so well, that the company testified very general satisfaction, except that a worthy Alderman and Baronet from London (who had been studying

[1] *Hamlet,* Act III, Sc. 2. G.

the picturesque at Low-wood Inn, and had given several manifestations of exquisite taste that had completely won the hearts of
Mr. O'Scarum and Major O'Dogskin) having just helped himself to
a slice of venison, fell back aghast against the back of his chair, and
dropped the knife and fork from his nervous hands, on finding that
currant-jelly was prohibited : but being recovered by an application
of the Honourable Mrs. Pinmoney's vinaigrette, he proceeded to
revenge himself on a very fine pheasant, which he washed down with
floods of Madeira, being never at a loss for some one to take wine
with him, as he had the good fortune to sit opposite to the Reverend
Mr. Portpipe, who was *toujours prêt* on the occasion, and a *coup-
d'œil* between them arranged the whole preliminary of the com-
potatory ceremonial.

After dinner Mr. Forester addressed the company. They had seen,
he said, that culinary luxury could be carried to a great degree of
refinement without the intervention of West Indian produce : and
though he himself deprecated luxury altogether, yet he would wave
that point for the present, and concede a certain degree of it to those
who fancied they could not do without it, if they would only in return
make so very slight a concession to philanthropy, to justice, to liberty,
to every feeling of human sympathy, as to abstain from an indulgence
which was obtained by the most atrocious violation of them all, an
indulgence of which the foundations were tyranny, robbery, and
murder, and every form of evil, anguish, and oppression, at which
humanity shudders ; all which were comprehended in the single
name of SLAVERY. " Sugar," said he, "is œconomically superfluous,
nay, worse than superfluous : in the middling classes of life it is a
formidable addition to the expenses of a large family, and for no
benefit, for no addition to the stock of domestic comfort, which is
often sacrificed in more essential points to this frivolous and wanton
indulgence. It is physically pernicious, as its destruction of the
teeth, and its effects on the health of children much pampered with
sweetmeats, sufficiently demonstrate. It is morally atrocious, from
being the primary cause of the most complicated corporeal suffering
and the most abject mental degradation that ever outraged the form
and polluted the spirit of man. It is politically abominable, for
covering with every variety of wretchedness some of the fairest

portions of the earth, which, if the inhabitants of free countries could be persuaded *to abstain from sugar, till it were sent to them by freemen*, might soon become the abodes of happiness and liberty. Slaves cannot breathe in the air of England: ' They touch our country, and their fetters fall.' [1] Who is there among you that is not proud of this distinction ?—Yet this is not enough : the produce of the labour of slavery should be banished from our shores. Not any thing—not an atom of any thing, should enter an Englishman's dwelling, on which the Genius of Liberty had not set his seal. What would become of slavery if there were no consumers of its produce ? Yet I have seen a party of pretended philanthropists sitting round a tea-table, and while they dropped the sugar into their cups, repeat some tale of the sufferings of a slave, and execrate the colonial planters, who are but their caterers and stewards—the obsequious ministers of their unfeeling sensuality ! O my fair countrywomen ! you who have such tender hearts, such affectionate spirits, such amiable and delicate feelings, do you consider the mass of mischief and cruelty to which you contribute, nay, of which you are among the primary causes, when you indulge yourselves in so paltry, so contemptible a gratification as results from the use of sugar ? while to abstain from it entirely, is a privation so trivial, that it is most wonderful to think that Justice and Charity should have such a boon to beg from Beauty in the name of the blood and the tears of human beings. Be not deterred by the idea that you will have few companions by the better way : so much the rather should it be strictly followed by amiable and benevolent minds.[2] Secure to yourselves at least the delightful consciousness of reflecting that you are in no way whatever accomplices in the cruelty and crime of slavery, and accomplices in it you certainly are, nay, its very original springs, as long as you are receivers and consumers of its iniquitous acquisitions."

" I will answer you, Mr. Forester," said Mr. Sarcastic, " for myself

---

[1] Cowper : *The Task*, Bk. II (*The Time-Piece*). G.

[2] Pochi compagni avrai per l'altra via :
Tanto ti prego più, gentile spirto,
Non lasciar la magnanima tua impresa. Petrarca. [P.]

[" Thou wilt have few companions on the other road so I beseech you even more, gentle spirit, do not abandon your high-minded action." G.]

and the rest of the company. You shock our feelings excessively by calling us the primary causes of slavery; and there are very few among us who have not shuddered at the tales of West Indian cruelty. I assure you we are very liberal of theoretical sympathy; but as to practical abstinence from the use of sugar, do you consider what it is you require? Do you consider how very agreeable to us is the sensation of sweetness in our palates? Do you suppose we would give up that sensation because human creatures of the same flesh and blood as ourselves are oppressed and enslaved, and flogged and tortured, to procure it for us? Do you consider that Custom [1]

[1] " If it were seriously asked (and it would be no untimely question), who of all teachers and masters that have ever taught hath drawn the most disciples after him, both in religion and in manners, it might be not untruly answered, Custom. Though Virtue be commended for the most persuasive in her theory, and Conscience in the plain demonstration of the spirit finds most evincing; yet, whether it be the secret of divine will, or the original blindness we are born in, so it happens for the most part, that Custom still is silently received for the best instructor. Except it be because her method is so glib and easy, in some manner like to that vision of Ezekiel, rolling up her sudden book of implicit knowledge, for him that will to take and swallow down at pleasure; which proving but of bad nourishment in the concoction, as it was heedless in the devouring, puffs up unhealthily a certain big face of pretended learning, mistaken among credulous men for the wholesome habit of soundness and good constitution, but is, indeed, no other than that swoln visage of counterfeit knowledge and literature which not only in private mars our education, but also in public is the common climber into every chair where either religion is preached or law reported, filling each estate of life and profession with abject and servile principles, depressing the high and heaven-born spirit of man, far beneath the condition wherein either God created him, or sin hath sunk him. To pursue the allegory, Custom being but a mere face, as Echo is a mere voice, rests not in her unaccomplishment, until by secret inclination she accorporate herself with Error, who being a blind and serpentine body, without a head, willingly accepts what he wants, and supplies what her incompleteness went seeking : hence it is that Error supports Custom, Custom countenances Error, and these two, between them, would persecute and chase away all truth and solid wisdom out of human life, were it not that God, rather than man, once in many ages calls together the prudent and religious counsels of men deputed to repress the encroachments, and to work off the inveterate blots and obscurities wrought upon our minds by the subtle insinuating of Error and Custom, who, with the numerous and vulgar train of their followers, make it their chief design to envy and cry down the industry of free reasoning, under the terms of humour and innovation, as if the womb of teeming Truth were to be closed up, if she presume to bring forth aught that sorts not with her unchewed notions and suppositions;

is the great lord and master of our conduct ?   And do you suppose
that any feelings of pity, and sympathy, and charity, and benevolence,
and justice, will overcome the power of Custom, more especially
where any pleasure of sense is attached to his dominion ?   In
appealing to our pockets, indeed, you touched us to the quick : you
aimed your eloquence at our weak side—you hit us in the vulnerable
point ; but if it should appear that in this particular we really might
save our money, yet being expended in a matter of personal and
sensual gratification, it is not to be supposed so completely lost and
wasted as it would be if it were given either to a friend or a stranger
in distress.   I will admit, however, that you have touched our feelings a little, but this disagreeable impression will soon wear off : with
some of us it will last as long as pity for a starving beggar, and with
others as long as grief for the death of a friend ; and I find, on a very
accurate average calculation, that the duration of the former may be
considered to be at least three minutes, and that of the latter at most
ten days.

" Mr. Sarcastic," said Anthelia, " you do not render justice to the
feelings of the company ; nor is human nature so selfish and perverted as you seem to consider it.   Though there are undoubtedly
many who sacrifice the general happiness of humankind to their own
selfish gratification, yet even these, I am willing to believe, err not
in cruelty but in ignorance, from not seeing the consequences of their
own actions ; but it is not by persuading them that all the world is as
bad as themselves, that you will give them clearer views and better
feelings.   Many are the modes of evil—many the scenes of human
suffering ; but if the general condition of man is ever to be amelior-
ated, it can only be through the medium of BELIEF IN HUMAN
VIRTUE."

" Well, Forester," said Sir Telegraph, " if you wish to increase the
numbers of the Anti-saccharine Society, set me down for one."

" Remember," said Mr. Forester, " by enrolling your name among

---

against which notorious injury and abuse of man's free soul, to testify and
oppose the utmost that study and true labour can attain, heretofore the
incitement of men reputed grave hath led me among others, and now the
duty and the right of an instructed Christian calls me through the chance
of good or evil report TO BE THE SOLE ADVOCATE OF A DISCOUNTENANCED
TRUTH."—Milton : *The Doctrine and Discipline of Divorce.*   [P.]

us you pledge yourself to perpetual abstinence from West Indian produce."

"I am aware of it," said Sir Telegraph, "and you shall find me zealous in the cause."

The fat Alderman cried out about the ruin of commerce, and Mr. Vamp was very hot on the subject of the revenue. The question was warmly canvassed, and many of the party who had not been quite persuaded by what Mr. Forester had said in behalf of the Anti-saccharine system, were perfectly convinced in its favour when they had heard what Mr. Vamp and the fat Alderman had to say against it; and the consequence was, that, in spite of Mr. Sarcastic's opinion of the general selfishness of mankind, the numbers of the Anti-saccharine Society were very considerably augmented.

"You see," said Mr. Fax to Mr. Sarcastic, "the efficacy of associated sympathies. It is but to give an impulse of co-operation to any good and generous feeling, and its progressive accumulation, like that of an Alpine avalanche, though but a snowball at the summit, becomes a mountain in the valley."

CHAPTER XXVIII

THE CHESS DANCE

THE dinner was followed by a ball, for the opening of which Sir Telegraph Paxarett, who officiated as master of the ceremonies, had devised a fanciful scheme, and had procured for the purpose a number of appropriate masquerade dresses. An extensive area in the middle of the ball-room was chalked out into sixty-four squares of alternate white and red, in lines of eight squares each. Sir Telegraph, while the rest of the company were sipping, not without many wry faces, their anti-saccharine tea, called out into another apartment the gentlemen whom he had fixed on to perform in his little ballet; and Miss Evergreen at the same time withdrew with the intended female performers. Sir Telegraph now invested Mr. Hippy with the dignity of White King, Major O'Dogskin with that of Black King, and the Reverend Mr. Portpipe with that of White Bishop, which the latter hailed as a favourable omen, not precisely comprehending what was

going forward. As the reverend gentleman was the only one of his
cloth in the company, Sir Telegraph was under the necessity of
appointing three lay Bishops, whom he fixed on in the persons of
two country squires, Mr. Hermitage and Mr. Heeltap, and of the fat
Alderman already mentioned, Sir Gregory Greenmould. Sir Telegraph himself, Mr. O'Scarum, Mr. Derrydown, and Mr. Sarcastic,
were the Knights : and the Rooks were Mr. Feathernest the poet ;
Mr. Paperstamp,[1] another variety of the same genus, chiefly remarkable for an affected infantine lisp in his speech, and for always wearing waistcoats of duffil grey ; Mr. Vamp the reviewer ; and Mr.
Killthedead,[2] from Frogmarsh Hall, a great compounder of narcotics,
under the denomination of BATTLES, for he never heard of a deadly
field, especially if dotage and superstition, to which he was very
partial, gained the advantage over generosity and talent, both of
which he abhorred, but immediately seizing his goosequill and
foolscap,

> He fought the BATTLE o'er again,
> And thrice he slew the slain.[3]

Mr. Feathernest was a little nettled on being told that he was to
be the *King's Rook*, but smoothed his wrinkled brow on being
assured that no *mauvaise plaisanterie* was intended.

The Kings were accordingly crowned, and attired in regal robes.
The Reverend Mr. Portpipe and his three brother Bishops were
arrayed in full canonicals. The Knights were equipped in their
white and black armour, with sword, and dazzling helm, and nodding
crest. The Rooks were enveloped in a sort of mural robe, with a
headpiece formed on the model of that which occurs in the ancient

[1] Wordsworth had accepted the office of distributor of stamps for
Westmorland in 1813. G.

[2] Based upon John Wilson Croker, the *Quarterly* reviewer famous for
his hostile review of Keats's *Endymion*, and author of *Battles of Talavera*.
Croker was Secretary of the Admiralty, which is apparently the reason why
Saintsbury identified Killthedead with Sir John Barrow, Second Secretary
to the Admiralty. G.

[3] Dryden : *Alexander's Feast*, ll. 67–8. Peacock had previously used the
same quotation with regard to Croker in *Sir Proteus*, published pseudonym-
ously in 1814 :

> " Here Cr–k–r fights his battles o'er
> And doubly kills the slain." G.

figures of Cybele ; and thus attired, they bore a very striking resemblance to the walking wall in Pyramus and Thisbe.

The Kings now led the way to the ball-room, and the two beautiful Queens, Miss Danaretta Contantina Pinmoney, and Miss Celandina Paperstamp, each with eight beautiful nymphs, arrayed for the mimic field in light Amazonian dresses, white and black, did such instant execution among the hearts of the young gentlemen present, that they might be said to have " fought and conquered ere a sword was drawn."

They now proceeded to their stations on their respective squares ; but before we describe their manœuvres we will recapitulate the

TRIPUDII PERSONÆ

WHITE

King .	.	.	.	Mr. Hippy.
Queen	.	.	.	Miss Danaretta Contantina Pinmoney.
King's Bishop	.	.	The Reverend Mr. Portpipe.
Queen's Bishop	.	.	Sir Gregory Greenmould.
King's Knight	.	.	Mr. O'Scarum.
Queen's Knight	.	.	Sir Telegraph Paxarett.
King's Rook	.	.	Mr. Feathernest.
Queen's Rook	.	.	Mr. Paperstamp.
Eight Nymphs.			

BLACK

King .	.	.	.	Major O'Dogskin.
Queen	.	.	.	Miss Celandina Paperstamp.
King's Bishop	.	.	Squire Hermitage.
Queen's Bishop	.	.	Squire Heeltap.
King's Knight	.	.	Mr. Sarcastic.
Queen's Knight	.	.	Mr. Derrydown.
King's Rook	.	.	Mr. Killthedead.
Queen's Rook	.	.	Mr. Vamp.
Eight Nymphs.			

Mr. Hippy took his station on a black square, near the centre of one of the extreme lines, and Major O'Dogskin on an opposite white square of the parallel extreme. The Queens, who were to command in chief, stood on the left of the Kings : the Bishops were posted to the right and left of their respective sovereigns ; the Knights next to the Bishops ; the corners were occupied by the Rooks. The two lines in front of these principal personages were occupied by the

Nymphs ;—a space of four lines of eight squares each being left between the opposite parties for the field of action.[1]

The array was now complete, with the exception of the Reverend Mr. Portpipe, who being called by Miss Danaretta to take his place at the right hand of Mr. Hippy, and perceiving that he should be necessitated, in his character of Bishop, to take a very active part in the diversion, began to exclaim with great vehemence, NOLO EPISCOPARI![2] which is probably the only occasion on which these words were ever used with sincerity. But Mr. O'Scarum, in his capacity of White Knight, pounced on the reluctant divine, and placing him between himself and Mr. Hippy, stood by him with his sword drawn, as if to prevent his escape ; then clapping a sword into the hand of the reverend gentleman, exhorted him to conduct himself in a manner becoming an efficient member of the true church militant.

Lots were then cast for the privilege of attack ; and the chance falling on Miss Danaretta, the music struck up the tune of *The Triumph*, and the whole of the white party began dancing, with their faces towards the King, performing at the same time various manœuvres of the sword exercise, with appropriate pantomimic gestures, expressive of their entire devotion to His Majesty's service, and their desire to be immediately sent forward on active duty. In vain did the Reverend Mr. Portpipe remonstrate with Mr. O'Scarum that his dancing days were over : the inexorable Knight compelled him to caper and flourish his sword, " till the toil-drops fell from his brows like rain." [3] Sir Gregory Greenmould did his best on the occasion, and danced like an elephant in black drapery ; but Miss Danaretta and her eight lovely Nymphs rescued the exertions of the male performers from too critical observation. King Hippy received the proffered service of his army with truly royal condescension. Miss Danaretta waved her sword with inimitable grace, and made a sign to the damsel in front of the King to advance two squares. The same manœuvres now took place on the black

---

[1] The chess dance is imitated from the court of Queen Quintessence. Rabelais, Bk. V. Ch. 24–5. G.

[2] " I do not wish to be made a bishop." G.

[3] Scott : *The Lay of the Last Minstrel*, Canto 2, Stanza 18. G.

side ; and Miss Celandina sent forward the Nymph in front of Major O'Dogskin to obstruct the further progress of the white damsel. The dancing now recommenced on the white side, and Miss Danaretta ordered out the Reverend Mr. Portpipe to occupy the fourth square in front of Squire Heeltap. The reverend gentleman rolled forward with great alacrity, in the secret hope that he should very soon be taken prisoner, and put *hors de combat* for the rest of the evening. Squire Hermitage was detached by Miss Celandina on a similar service ; and these two episcopal heroes being thus brought together in the centre of the field, entered, like Glaucus and Diomede, into a friendly parle,[1] in the course of which the words Claret and Burgundy were repeatedly overheard. The music frequently varied, as in a pantomime, according to circumstances : the manœuvres were always directed by the waving of the sword of the Queen, and were always preceded by the dancing of the whole party, in the manner we have mentioned, which continued *ad libitum*, till she had decided on her movement. The Nymph in front of Sir Gregory Greenmould advanced one square. Mr. Sarcastic stepped forward to the third square of Squire Hermitage. Miss Danaretta's Nymph advanced two squares, and being immediately taken prisoner by the Nymph of Major O'Dogskin, conceded her place with a graceful bow, and retired from the field. The Nymph in front of Sir Gregory Greenmould avenged the fate of her companion ; and Mr. Hippy's Nymph withdrew in a similar manner. Squire Hermitage was compelled to cut short his conversation with Mr. Portpipe, and retire to the third square in front of Mr. Derrydown. Sir Telegraph skipped into the place which Sir Gregory Greenmould's Nymph had last forsaken. Mr. Killthedead danced into the deserted quarters of Squire Hermitage, and Major O'Dogskin swept round him with a minuet step into those of Mr. Sarcastic. To carry on the detail would require more time than we can spare, and, perhaps, more patience than our readers possess. The Reverend Mr. Portpipe saw his party fall around him, one by one,

[1] The Trojan Glaucus and the Greek Diomede recognised their hereditary friendship on the field of battle, exchanged armour, to the great advantage of the Greek, and plighted their mutual faith. See Homer : *Il.*, VI. 16. G.

and survived against his will to the close of the contest. Miss Danaretta and Miss Celandina moved like light over the squares, and Fortune alternately smiled and frowned on their respective banners, till the heavy mural artillery of Mr. Vamp being brought to bear on Mr. Paperstamp, who fancied himself a tower of strength, the latter was overthrown and carried off the field. Mr. Feathernest avenged his fate on the embattled front of Mr. Killthedead, and fell himself beneath the sword of Mr. Sarcastic. Squire Heeltap was taken off by the Reverend Mr. Portpipe, who begged his courteous prisoner to walk to the sideboard and bring him a glass of Madeira ; for Homer, he said, was very orthodox in his opinion that wine was a great refresher in the toils of war.[1]

The changeful scene concluded by Miss Danaretta, with the aid of Sir Telegraph and the Reverend Mr. Portpipe, hemming Major O'Dogskin into a corner, where he was reduced to an incapacity of locomotion ; on which the Major bowed, and made the best of his way to the sideboard, followed by the reverend gentleman, who, after joining the Major in a pacific libation, threw himself into an arm-chair, and slept very comfortably till the annunciation of supper.

Waltzes, quadrilles, and country dances followed in succession, and, with the exception of the interval of supper, in which Miss Evergreen developed all the treasures of anti-saccharine taste, were kept up with great spirit till the rising of the sun.

Anthelia, who of course did not join in the former, expressed to Mr. Forester her astonishment to see waltzing in Redrose Abbey.[2] "I did not dream of such a thing," said Mr. Forester ; "but I left the whole arrangement of the ball to Sir Telegraph, and I suppose, he deemed it incumbent on him to consult *the general taste of the young ladies.* Even I, young as I am, can remember the time when there was no point of resemblance between an English girl in a private

[1] Ἰλ. Ζ. 261. [P.]

[2] The waltz had only recently been introduced and was regarded as most improper. "But, judge of my surprise, on arriving, to see poor dear Mrs. Hornem with her arms half round the loins of a huge hussar-looking gentleman I never set eyes on before ; and his, to say truth, rather more than half round her waist, turning round, and round, and round, to a d——d see-saw up-and-down sort of tune." Byron : *The Waltz*, 1813. From the introductory letter to the publisher, signed " Horace Hornem." G.

ball-room, and a French *figurante* in a theatrical *ballet*: but waltzing and Parisian drapery have levelled the distinction, and the only criterion of the difference is the place of the exhibition.   Thus every succeeding year witnesses some new inroad on the simple manners of our ancestors ; some importation of continental vice and folly ; some unnatural fretwork of tinsel and frippery on the old Doric column of the domestic virtues of England.   An Englishman in stays, and an Englishwoman waltzing in treble-flounced short petticoats, are anomalies so monstrous, that till they actually existed, they never entered the most ominous visions of the speculators on progressive degeneracy.   What would our Alfred, what would our third Edward, what would our Milton, and Hampden, and Sidney, what would the barons of Runnymead have thought, if the voice of prophecy had denounced to them a period, when the perfection of accomplishment in the daughters of England would be found in the dress, manner, and action of the dancing girls of Paris ? "

The supper, of course, did not pass off without songs ; and among them Anthelia sang the following, which recalled to Mr. Forester their conversation on the sea-shore.

THE MORNING OF LOVE

O ! the spring-time of life is the season of blooming,
And the morning of love is the season of joy ;
Ere noontide and summer, with radiance consuming,
Look down on their beauty, to parch and destroy.

O ! faint are the blossoms life's pathway adorning,
When the first magic glory of hope is withdrawn ;
For the flowers of the spring, and the light of the morning,
Have no summer budding, and no second dawn.

Through meadows all sunshine, and verdure, and flowers,
The stream of the valley in purity flies ;
But mixed with the tides, where some proud city lowers,
O ! where is the sweetness that dwelt on its rise ?

The rose withers fast on the breast it first graces ;
Its beauty is fled ere the day be half done :—
And life is that stream which its progress defaces,
And love is that flower which can bloom but for one.

CHAPTER XXIX

THE DISAPPEARANCE

THE morning after the fête Anthelia and her party returned to Melincourt. Before they departed she conversed a few minutes alone with Mr. Forester in his library. What was said on this occasion we cannot precisely report ; but it seemed to be generally suspected that Mr. Hippy's authority would soon be at an end, and that the services of the Reverend Mr. Portpipe would be required in the old chapel of Melincourt Castle, which, we are sorry to say, had fallen for some years past very much into disuse, being never opened but on occasions of birth, marriage, and death in the family ; and these occasions, as our readers are aware, had not of late been very numerous.

The course of mutual love between Anthelia and Mr. Forester was as smooth as the gliding of a skiff down a stream, through the flowery meadows of June : and if matters were not quite definitively settled between them, yet, as Mr. Forester was shortly to be a visitor at the Castle, there was a very apparent probability that their intercourse would terminate in that grand climax and finale of all romantic adventure—marriage.

After the departure of the ladies, Mr. Forester observed with concern, that his friend Sir Oran's natural melancholy was visibly increased, and Mr. Fax was of opinion that he was smitten with the tender passion : but whether for Miss Melincourt, Mrs. Pinmoney, or Miss Danaretta, it was not so easy to determine. But Sir Oran grew more and more fond of solitude, and passed the greater part of the day in the woods, though it was now the reign of the gloomy November, which, however, accorded with the moody temper of his spirit ; and he often went without his breakfast, though he always came home to dinner. His perpetual companion was his flute, with which he made sad response to the wintry wind.

Mr. Forester and Mr. Fax were one morning consulting on the means to be adopted for diverting Sir Oran's melancholy, when Sir Telegraph Paxarett drove up furiously to the door—sprang from the box—and rushed into the apartment with the intelligence that

Anthelia had disappeared. No one had seen her since the hour of breakfast on the preceding day. Mr. Hippy, Mr. Derrydown, Mr. O'Scarum, and Major O'Dogskin, were scouring the country in all directions in search of her.

Mr. Forester determined not to rest night or day till he had discovered Anthelia. Sir Telegraph drove him, with Mr. Fax and Sir Oran, to the nearest inn, where leaving Sir Telegraph to pursue another track, they took a chaise and four, and posted over the country in all directions, day after day, without finding any clue to her retreat. Mr. Forester had no doubt that this adventure was connected with that which we have detailed in the eighteenth Chapter ; but his ignorance of the actors on that occasion prevented his deriving any light from the coincidence. At length, having investigated in vain all the main and cross roads for fifty miles round Melincourt, Mr. Fax was of opinion that she could not have passed so far along any of them, being conveyed, as no doubt she was, against her will, without leaving some trace of her course, which their indefatigable inquiries must have discovered. He therefore advised that they should discontinue their system of posting, and take a thorough pedestrian perlustration of all the most bye and unfrequented paths of the whole mountain-district, in some secluded part of which he had a strong presentiment she would be found. This plan was adopted ; but the season was unfavourable to its expeditious accomplishment ; and they could sometimes make but little progress in a day, being often compelled to turn aside from the wilder tracks, in search of a town or village, for the purposes of refreshment or rest :—there being this remarkable difference between the lovers of the days of chivalry, and those of modern times, that the former could pass a week or two in a desert or a forest, without meat, drink, or shelter—a very useful art for all travellers, whether lovers or not, which these degenerate days have unfortunately lost.

They arrived in the evening of the first day of their pedestrianism at a little inn among the mountains. They were informed they could have no beds ; and that the only parlour was occupied by two gentlemen, who meant to sit up all night, and would, perhaps, have no objection to their joining the party. A message being sent in, an affirmative answer was very politely returned : and on entering the apartment, they discovered Mr. O'Scarum and Major O'Dogskin engaged in a deep discussion over a large jug of wine.

" Troth, now," said Mr. O'Scarum, " and this is a merry meeting, sure enough, though it's on a dismal occasion, for it's Miss Melincourt you're looking for, as we are too, though you have most cause, Mr. Forester ; for I understand you are to be the happy man. Troth, and I did not know so much when I came to your fête, or, perhaps, I should have been for arguing the point of a prior claim (as far as my own consent was concerned), over a bit of neat turf, twelve yards long ; but Major O'Dogskin tells me, that by getting muzzy, and so I did, sure enough, on your old Madeira, and rare stuff it is, by my conscience, when Miss Melincourt was in your house, I have sanctioned the matter, and there's an end of it : but, by my soul, I did not mean to have been cut out quietly : and the Major says, too, you're too good a fellow to be kilt, and that's true enough : so I'll keep my ammunition for other friends ; and here's to you and Miss Melincourt, and a happy meeting to you both, and the devil take him that parts you, says Harum O'Scarum."—" And so says Dermot O'Dogskin," said the Major. " And my friend O'Scarum and myself will ride about till we get news of her, for we don't mind a little hardship.—You shall be wanting some dinner, joys, and there's nothing but fat bacon and potatoes ; but we have made a shift with it, and then here is the very creature itself, old sherry, my jewels ! troth, and how did we come home by it, think you ? I know what it is to pass a night in a little inn in the hills, and you don't find Major O'Dogskin turning out of the main road, without giving his man a couple of kegs of wine just to balance the back of his saddle. Sherry's a good traveller, and will stand a little shaking ; and what would one do without it in such a place as this, where it is water in the desert, and manna in the wilderness ? "

Mr. Forester thanked them very warmly for their good wishes and active exertions. The humble dinner of himself and his party was soon dispatched ; after which, the Major placed the two little kegs on the table and said, " They were both filled to-day ; so, you see, there is no lack of the good creature to keep us all alive till morning, and then we shall part again in search of Miss Melincourt, the jewel ! for there is not such another on the face of the earth. Och ! " con-

tinued the Major, as he poured the wine from one of the kegs into a
brown jug ; for the house could not afford them a decanter, and some
little ale tumblers supplied the place of wine-glasses ; " Och ! the
ould jug, that never held any thing better than sour ale: how proud
he must feel of being filled to the brim with sparkling sherry, for the
first and last time in the course of his life ! "

CHAPTER XXX

THE PAPER-MILL

TAKING leave of Mr. O'Scarum and Major O'Dogskin, they continued
their wanderings as choice or chance directed : sometimes penetrating
into the most sequestered valleys ; sometimes returning into the
principal roads, and investigating the most populous districts.
Passing through the town of Gullgudgeon, they found an immense
crowd assembled in a state of extreme confusion, exhibiting every
symptom of hurry, anxiety, astonishment, and dismay. They
stopped to inquire the cause of the tumult, and found it to proceed
from the sudden explosion of a paper-mill, in other words, the
stoppage of the country bank of Messieurs Smokeshadow, Airbubble,
Hopthetwig, and Company. Farmers, bumpkins, artisans, mechanics, tradesmen of all descriptions, the innkeeper, the lawyer,
the doctor, and the parson ; soldiers from the adjoining barracks,
and fishermen from the neighbouring coast, with their shrill-voiced
and masculine wives, rolled in one mass, like a stormy wave, around
a little shop, of which the shutters were closed, with the word BANK
in golden letters over the door, and a large board on the central shutter,
notifying that " Messieurs Smokeshadow, Airbubble, Hopthetwig,
and Company, had found themselves under the disagreeable necessity
of suspending their payments ; " in plain English, had found it
expedient to fly by night, leaving all the machinery of their mill,
and all the treasures of their mine, that is to say, several reams of
paper, half a dozen account-books, a desk, a joint-stool, an ink-
stand, a bunch of quills, and a copper-plate, to satisfy the claims of
the distracted multitude, who were shoaling in from all quarters

with *promises to pay*, of the said Smokeshadow, Airbubble, Hopthe-twig, and Company, to the amount of a hundred thousand pounds.

Mr. Fax addressed himself for an explanation of particulars to a plump and portly divine, who was standing at a little distance from the rest of the crowd, and whose countenance exhibited no symptoms of the rage, grief, and despair, which were depicted on the physiog-nomies of his dearly-beloved brethren of the town of Gullgudgeon. " You seem, Sir," said Mr. Fax, " to bear the general calamity with Christian resignation."—" I do, Sir," said the reverend gentleman, " and for a very orthodox reason—I have none of their notes—not I. I was obliged to take them now and again against my will, but I always sent them off to town, and got cash for them directly."

" You mean to say," said Mr. Forester, " you got a Threadneedle Street note for them."

" To be sure, Sir," said the divine, " and that is the same thing as cash. There is a Jacobin rascal in this town, who says it is a bad sign when the children die before the parent, and that a day of reckon-ing must come sooner or later for the old lady as well as for her daughters ; but myself and my brother magistrates have taken measures for him, and shall soon make the town of Gullgudgeon too hot to hold him, as sure as my name is Peppertoast."

" You seriously think, Sir," said Mr. Fax, " that his opinion is false? "

" Sir," said the reverend gentleman, somewhat nettled, " I do not know what right any one can have to ask a man of my cloth what he seriously thinks, when all that the world has to do with is what he seriously says."

" Then you seriously say it, Sir ? " said Mr. Fax.

" I do, Sir," said the divine ; " and for this very orthodox reason, that the system of paper-money is inseparably interwoven with the present order of things, and the present order of things I have made up my mind to stick by precisely as long as it lasts."

" *And no longer ?* " said Mr. Fax.

" I am no fool, Sir," said the divine.

" But, Sir," said Mr. Fax, "as you seem to have perceived the instability of what was called (like *lucus à non lucendo*), the *firm* of Smokeshadow, Airbubble, Hopthetwig, and Company, why did you not warn your flock of the impending danger ? "

"Sir," said the reverend gentleman, "I dined every week with one of the partners."

Mr. Forester took notice of an elderly woman, who was sitting with a small handful of dirty paper, weeping bitterly on the step of a door. "Forgive my intrusion," said he; "I need not ask you why you weep: the cause is in your hand."—"Ah, Sir!" said the poor woman, who could scarcely speak for sobbing, "all the savings of twenty years taken from me in a moment: and my poor boy, when he comes home from sea——" She could say no more: grief choked her utterance.

"Good God!" said Mr. Fax, "did you lay by your savings in country paper?"

"O Sir!" said the poor woman, "how was I to know that one piece of paper was not as good as another? And every body said that the firm of Smokeshadow, Airbubble, Hopthetwig, and Company, was as good as the Bank of England." She then unfolded one of the *promises to pay*, and fell to weeping more bitterly than ever. Mr. Forester comforted her as well as he could; but he found the purchasing of one or two of her notes much more efficacious than all the lessons of his philosophy.

"This is all your fault," said a fisherman to his wife: "you would be hoarding and hoarding, and stinting me of my drop of comfort when I came in after a hard day's work, tossed, and beaten, and wet through with salt-water, and there's what we've got by it."

"It was all your fault," retorted the wife: "when we had scraped together twenty as pretty golden guineas as ever laid in a chest, you would sell 'em, so you would, for twenty-seven pounds of Mr. Smoke-shadow's paper; *and now you see the difference.*"

"Here is an illustration," said Mr. Fax to Mr. Forester, "of the old maxim of *experience teaching wisdom*, or, as Homer expresses it, *Ρεχθεν δε τε νηπιος εγνω.*" [1]

"*We ought now to be convinced, if not before,*" said Mr. Forester, "*that what Plato has said is strictly true, that there will be no end of human misery till governors become philosophers, or philosophers governors*; and that all the evils which this country suffers, and, I fear, will suffer, to a much greater extent, from the bursting of this

[1] "A fool would know, after the event." *Il.* XVII. 32.   G.

fatal bubble of paper-money—this chimerical symbol of imaginary riches—*are owing to the want of philosophy and true political wisdom in our rulers, by which they might have seen things in their causes, not felt them only in their effects, as every the most vulgar man does; and by which foresight, all the mischiefs that are befalling us might have been prevented.*" [1]

" Very hard," said an old soldier, " very, very hard : —a poor five pounds, laid up for a rainy day—hardly got, and closely kept—very, very hard."

" Poor man ! " said Mr. Forester, who was interested in the soldier's physiognomy, " let me repair your loss. Here is better paper for you ; but get gold and silver for it as soon as you can."

" God bless your Honour," said the soldier, " and send as much power as good will to all such generous souls. Many is the worthy heart that this day's work will break, and here is more damage than one man can mend. God bless your Honour."

A respectable-looking female approached the crowd, and addressing herself to Mr. Fax, who seemed most at leisure to attend to her, asked him what chance there seemed to be for the creditors of Messieurs Smokeshadow, Airbubble, Hopthetwig, and Company. " By what I can gather from the people around me," said Mr. Fax, " none whatever." The lady was in great distress at this intelligence, and said they were her bankers, and it was the second misfortune of the kind that had happened to her. Mr. Fax expressed his astonishment that she should have been twice the victim of the system of paper-coinage, which seemed to contradict the old adage about a burnt child ; and said it was for his part astonishing to him how any human being could be so deluded after the perils of the system had been so clearly pointed out, and, amongst other things, in a pamphlet of his own on the Insubstantiality of Smoke. " Indeed," she said, " she had something better to do than to trouble herself about politics, and wondered he should insult her in her distress by talking of such stuff to her."

" Was ever such infatuation ? " said Mr. Fax, as the lady turned away. " This is one of those persons who choose to walk blindfold

[1] The words in italics are Lord Monboddo's : *Ancient Metaphysics,* vol. iii. preface, p. 79. [P.]

on the edge of a precipice, because it is too much trouble to see, and quarrel with their best friends for requesting them to make use of their eyes. There are many such, who think they have no business with politics : but they find to their cost that politics will have business with them."

" A curse light on all kite-flyers ! " vociferated a sturdy farmer. "Od rabbit me! here be a bundle o' trash, measters ! not worth a voive-and-zixpenny dollar all together. This comes o' peaper-mills. ' I promise to pay,' ecod ! O the good old days o' goulden guineas, when I used to ride whoame vrom market wi' a great heavy bag in my pocket ; and when I wapped it down on the old oak teable, it used to make zuch a zound as did one's heart good to hear it. No *promise to pay* then. Now a man may eat his whole vortin in a zandwich, or zet vire to it in a vardin rushlight. Promise to pay !— the lying rascals, they never meant to pay : they knew all the while they had no effects to pay : but zuch a pretty, zmooth-spoken, palavering zet o' fellers ! why, Lord bless you ! they'd ha' made you believe black was white ! and though you could never get anything of 'em but one o' their own dirty bits of peaper in change vor another, they made it out as clear as daylight, that they were as rich as zo many Jews. Ecod ! and we were all vools enough to believe 'em, and now mark the end o't."

" Yes, father," said a young fop at his elbow, " all blown, curse me ! "

" Ees," said the farmer, " and thee beest blown, and thee mun zell thy hunter, and turn to the plough-tail ; and thy zisters mun churn butter, and milk the cows, instead o' jingling penny-vorties, and dancing at race-balls wi' squires. We mun be old English varmers again, and none o' your voine high-flying promise to pay gentle-volks. There they be—spell 'em : *I promise to pay to Mr. Gregory Gas, or bearer, on demand, the zum o' voive pounds. Gullgudgeon Bank, April the virst. Vor Zmokeshadow, Airbubble, Zelf, and Company, Henry Hopthetwig. Entered, William Walkoff.* And there be their coat o' arms : two blacksmiths blowing a vorge, wi' the chimney vor a crest, and a wreath o' smoke coming out o't ; and the motto, ' You can't catch a bowl-full.' Od rabbit me! here be a whole handvul of 'em, and I'll zell 'em all vor a voive-and-zixpenny dollar."

The "Jacobin rascal," of whom the reverend gentleman had spoken, happened to be at the farmer's elbow. "I told you how it would be," said he, "Master Sheepshead, many years ago ; and I remember you wanted to put me in the stocks for my trouble."

"Why, I believe I did, Measter Lookout," said the farmer, with a very penitent face ; "but if you'll call on me zome day we'll drown old grudges in a jug o' ale, and light our poipes wi' the promises o' Measter Hopthetwig and his gang."

"Not with all of them, I entreat you," said Mr. Lookout. "I hope you will have one of them framed and glazed, and suspended over your chimney, as a warning to your children, and your children's children for ever, against ' *the blessed comforts of paper-money.*' "

"Why, Lord love you, Measter Lookout," said the farmer, " we shall ha' nothing but peaper-money still, you zee, only vrom another mill like."

"As to that, Master Sheepshead," replied Mr. Lookout, "I will only say to you in your own phrase, MARK THE END O'T."

" Do you hear him ? " said the Reverend Mr. Peppertoast ; " do you hear the Jacobin rascal ? Do you hear the libellous, seditious, factious, levelling, revolutionary, republican, democratical, atheistical villain ? "

CHAPTER XXXI

CIMMERIAN LODGE

AFTER a walk of some miles from the town of Gullgudgeon, where no information was to be obtained of Anthelia, their path wound along the shores of a lonely lake, embosomed in dark pine-groves and precipitous rocks. As they passed near a small creek, they observed a gentleman just stepping into a boat, who paused and looked up at the sound of their approximation ; and Mr. Fax immediately recognised the poeticopolitical, rhapsodicoprosaical, deisidæmoniaco-paradoxographical, pseudolatreiological, transcendental meteorosophist, Moley Mystic, Esquire, of Cimmerian Lodge. This gentleman's Christian name, according to his own account, was improperly spelt with an *e,* and was in truth nothing more nor less than

> " That Moly,
> Which Hermes erst to wise Ulysses gave ; " [1]

and which was, in the mind of Homer, a *pure anticipated cognition* of the system of Kantian metaphysics, or grand transcendental science of the *luminous obscure* ; for it had a *dark root,*[2] which was mystery ; and *a white flower,* which was abstract truth : *it was called Moly by the gods,* who then kept it to themselves ; and was *difficult to be dug up by mortal men,* having, in fact, laid *perdu* in subterranean darkness till the immortal Kant dug for it *under the stone of doubt,* and produced it to the astonished world as the *root of human science.* Other persons, however, derived his first name differently ; and maintained that the *e* in it showed it very clearly to be a corruption of *Mole-eye,* it being the opinion of some naturalists that the *mole* has *eyes,* which it can withdraw or project at pleasure, implying a faculty of wilful blindness, most happily characteristic of a transcendental metaphysician ; since, according to the old proverb, *None are so blind as those who won't see.* But be that as it may, Moley Mystic was his name, and Cimmerian Lodge was his dwelling.

Mr. Mystic invited Mr. Fax and his friends to step with him into the boat, and cross over his lake, which he called the *Ocean of Deceitful Form,* to the *Island of Pure Intelligence,* on which Cimmerian Lodge was situated : promising to give them a great treat in looking over his grounds, which he had laid out according to the *topography of the human mind* ; and to enlighten them, through the medium of " darkness visible," with an opticothaumaturgical process of transcendentalising a *cylindrical mirror,* which should teach them the difference between *objective* and *subjective reality.*[3] Mr. Forester was

---

[1] Milton : *Comus,* l. 636. G.

[2] Ριζη μεν μελαν εστι, γαλακτι δε εικελον ανθος,
ΜΩΛΥ δε μιν καλεουσι θεοι, χαλεπον δε τ᾿ ορυσσειν
Θνητοις ανθρωποισι. [*Od.* X. 304–6. G.]

[3] The reader who is desirous of elucidating the mysteries of the words and phrases marked in italics in this chapter, may consult the German works of Professor Kant, or Professor Born's Latin translation of them, or M. Villars's *Philosophie de Kant, ou Principes fondamentaux de la Philosophie Transcendentale* ; or the first article of the second number of the *Edinburgh Review,* or the article *Kant,* in the *Encyclopædia Londinensis,* or Sir William Drummond's *Academical Questions,* book ii. chap. 9. [P.]

unwilling to remit his search, even for a few hours : but Mr. Fax
observing that great part of the day was gone, and that Cimmerian
Lodge was very remote from the human world ; so that if they did
not avail themselves of Mr. Mystic's hospitality, they should probably be reduced to the necessity of passing the night among the rocks,
sub Jove frigido, which he did not think very inviting, Mr. Forester
complied ; and with Mr. Fax and Sir Oran Haut-ton, stepped into
the boat. The reader who is deficient in *taste for the bombast*, and is
no *admirer of the obscure*, may as well wait on the shore till they
return. But we must not enter the regions of mystery without an
Orphic invocation.

ΎΠΝΕ αναξ, καλεω σε μολειν κεχαρηοτα ΜΥΣΤΑΙΣ·
Και σε, μακαρ, λιτομαι, τανυσιπτερε, ουλε ΟΝΕΙΡΕ·
Και ΝΕΦΕΛΑΣ καλεω, δροσοειμονας, ηεροπλαγκτους·
ΝΥΚΤΑ τε πρεσβιστην, πολυηρατον ΟΡΓΙΟΦΑΝΤΑΙΣ,
ΝΥΚΤΕΡΙΟΥΣ τε ΘΕΟΥΣ, ύπο κευθεσιν οικι᾽ εχοντας,
Αντρῳ εν ηεροεντι, παρα ΣΤΥΓΟΣ ίερον ύδωρ·
ΠΡΩΤΕΙ συν πολυβουλῳ, όν ΟΛΒΟΔΟΤΗΝ [1] καλεουσιν.[2]

> O sovereign Sleep ! in whose papaverous glen
> Dwell the dark Muses of Cimmerian men !
> O Power of Dreams ! whose dusky pinions shed
> Primæval chaos on the slumberer's head !
> Ye misty Clouds ! amid whose folds sublime
> Blind Faith invokes the Ghost of Feudal Time !
> And thou, thick Night ! beneath whose mantle rove
> The Phantom Powers of Subterranean Jove !
> Arise, propitious to the mystic strain,
> From Lethe's flood, and Zeal's Tartarian fane ;
> Where Freedom's Shade, 'mid Stygian vapours damp,
> Sits, cold and pale, by Truth's extinguished lamp ;
> While Cowls and Crowns portentous orgies hold,
> And tuneful Proteus seals his eyes with gold !

They had scarcely left the shore when they were involved in a fog
of unprecedented density, so that they could not see one another ;
but they heard the dash of Mr. Mystic's oars, and were consoled
by his assurances that he could not miss his way in a state of the
atmosphere so very consentaneous to his peculiar mode of vision ; for

---

[1] *Πρωτευς Ολβοδοτης, Proteus the giver of riches*, certainly deserves a
place among the *Lares* of every poetical and political turncoat. [P.]

[2] *Orphica*, ed. Hermann. G.

that, though, in navigating his little skiff on the *Ocean of Deceitful Form*, he had very often wandered wide and far from the *Island of Pure Intelligence*, yet this had always happened when he went with his eyes open, in broad daylight ; but that he had soon found the means of obviating this little inconvenience, by always keeping his eyes close shut whenever the sun had the impertinence to shine upon him.

He immediately added, that he would take the opportunity of making a remark perfectly in point: " that Experience was a Cyclops, with his eye in the back of his head " ; and when Mr. Fax remarked, that he did not see the connexion, Mr. Mystic said he was very glad to hear it ; for he should be sorry if any one but himself could see the connexion of his ideas, as he arranged his thoughts *on a new principle*.

They went steadily on through the dense and heavy air, over waters that slumbered like the Stygian pool ; a chorus of frogs, that seemed as much delighted with their own melody, as if they had been an oligarchy of poetical critics, regaling them all the way with the Aristophanic symphony of BREK-EK-EK-EX ! KO-AX ! KO-AX ! [1] till the boat fixed its keel in the *Island of Pure Intelligence* ; and Mr. Mystic landed his party, as Charon did Æneas and the Sibyl, in a bed of weeds and mud : [2] after floundering in which for some time, from losing their guide in the fog, they were cheered by the sound of his voice from above, and scrambling up the bank, found themselves on a hard and barren rock ; and, still following the sound of Mr. Mystic's voice, arrived at Cimmerian Lodge.

The fog had penetrated into all the apartments : there was fog in the hall, fog in the parlour, fog on the staircases, fog in the bedrooms ;

> " The fog was here, the fog was there,
> The fog was all around." [3]

It was a little rarefied in the kitchen, by virtue of the enormous fire ; so far, at least, that the red face of the cook shone through it, as they passed the kitchen-door, like the disk of the rising moon through the

---

[1] See the Βατραχοι of Aristophanes. [P.]
[2] Informi limo glaucaque exponit in ulva. [P.] [" Sets them down upon the mud bank and the glimmering sedge." Virgil : *Æn.* VI. 416. G.]
[3] A misquotation from Coleridge's *Ancient Mariner*. G.

vapours of an autumnal river : but to make amends for this, it was condensed almost into solidity in the library, where the voice of their invisible guide bade them welcome to the *adytum* of the LUMINOUS OBSCURE.

Mr. Mystic now produced what he called his *synthetical torch*, and requested them to follow him, and look over his grounds. Mr. Fax said it was perfectly useless to attempt it in such a state of the atmosphere ; but Mr. Mystic protested it was the only state of the atmosphere in which they could be seen to advantage : as daylight and sunshine utterly destroyed their beauty.

They followed the " darkness visible " of the *synthetical torch*, which, according to Mr. Mystic, *shed around it the rays of trans-cendental illumination* ; and he continued to march before them, walking, and talking, and pointing out innumerable images of singularly nubilous beauty, though Mr. Forester and Mr. Fax both declared they could see nothing but the fog and " *la pale lueur du magique flambeau* : " till Mr. Mystic observing that they were now in a *Spontaneity free from Time and Space*, and at the point of *Absolute Limitation*, Mr. Fax said he was very glad to hear it ; for in that case they could go no further. Mr. Mystic observed that they must go further ; for they were entangled in a maze, from which they would never be able to extricate themselves without his assistance ; and he must take the liberty to tell them, that *the categories of modality were connected into the idea of absolute necessity*. As this was spoken in a high tone, they took it to be meant for a reprimand ; which carried the more weight as it was the less understood. At length, after floundering on another half hour, the fog still thicker and thicker, and the torch still dimmer and dimmer, they found themselves once more in Cimmerian Lodge.

Mr. Mystic asked them how they liked his grounds, and they both repeated they had seen nothing of them : on which he flew into a rage, and called them *empirical psychologists*, and *slaves of definition, induction, and analysis*, which he intended for terms of abuse, but which were not taken for such by the persons to whom he addressed them.

Recovering his temper, he observed that it was nearly the hour of dinner ; and as they did not think it worth while to be angry with him, they contented themselves with requesting that they might dine in the kitchen, which seemed to be the only spot on the *Island of Pure Intelligence* in which there was a glimmer of light.

Mr. Mystic remarked that he thought this very bad taste, but that he should have no objection if the cook would consent: who, he observed, had paramount dominion over that important division of the *Island of Pure Intelligence*. The cook, with a little murmuring, consented for once to evacuate her citadel as soon as the dinner was on table; entering, however, a protest, that this infringement on her privileges should not be pleaded as a precedent.

Mr. Fax was afraid that Mr. Mystic would treat them as Lord Peter treated his brothers;[1] that he would put nothing on the table, and regale them with a dissertation on the *pure idea of absolute substance*; but in this he was agreeably disappointed; for the *anticipated cognition* of a good dinner very soon smoked before them, in the *relation of determinate co-existence*; and the *objective phœnomenon* of some superexcellent Madeira quickly put the whole party in perfect good-humour. It appeared, indeed, to have a diffusive quality of occult and mysterious virtue; for, with every glass they drank, the fog grew thin, till by the time they had taken off four bottles among them, it had totally disappeared.

Mr. Mystic now prevailed on them to follow him to the library, where they found a blazing fire and a four-branched gas lamp, shedding a much brighter radiance than that of the *synthetical torch*. He said he had been obliged to light this lamp, as it seemed they could not see by the usual illumination of Cimmerian Lodge. The brilliancy of the gas lights he much disapproved; but he thought it would be very unbecoming in a transcendental philosopher to employ any other material for a purpose to which *smoke* was applicable. Mr. Fax said, he should have thought, on the contrary, that *ex fumo dare lucem* would have been, of all things, the most repugnant to his principles; and Mr. Mystic replied, that it had not struck him so before, but that Mr. Fax's view of the subject "was exquisitely dusky and fuliginous:" this being his usual mode of expressing approbation, instead of the common phraseology of *bright thoughts* and *luminous ideas*, which were equally abhorrent to him both in

[1] Swift: *A Tale of a Tub*. Lord Peter serves them with dry crusts which he calls mutton and wine. G.

theory and practice. However, he said, there the light was, for their benefit, and not for his : and as other men's light was his darkness, he should put on a pair of spectacles of smoked glass, which no one could see through but himself. Having put on his spectacles, he undrew a black curtain, discovered a *cylindrical mirror*, and placed a sphere before it with great solemnity. "This sphere," said he, " is an oblong spheroid in the perception of the cylindrical mirror : as long as the mirror thought that the object of his perception was a real external oblong spheroid, he was a mere *empirical philosopher* ; but he has grown wiser since he has been in my library ; and by reflecting very deeply on the degree in which the manner of his construction might influence the forms of his perception, has taken a very opaque and tenebricose view of how much of the spheroidical perception belongs to the *object*, which is the sphere, and how much to the *subject*, which is himself, in his quality of *cylindrical mirror*. He has thus discovered the difference between *objective* and *subjective reality* : and this point of view is *transcendentalism*."

" A very dusky and fuliginous speculation, indeed," said Mr. Fax, complimenting Mr. Mystic in his own phrase.

Tea and coffee were brought in. "I divide my day," said Mr. Mystic, "*on a new principle* : I am always poetical at breakfast, moral at luncheon, metaphysical at dinner, and political at tea. Now you shall know my opinion of the hopes of the world.—General discontent shall be the basis of public resignation ! [1] The materials of political gloom will build the steadfast frame of hope. [2] The main point is to get rid of analytical reason, which is experimental and practical, and live only by faith, [3] which is synthetical and oracular. The contradictory interests of ten millions may neutralize each other. [4] But the spirit of Antichrist is abroad : [5]—the people read !—nay, they think ! ! The people read and think ! ! ! The public, the public in general, the swinish multitude, the many-headed monster, actually reads and thinks ! ! ! ! [6] Horrible in thought, but in fact most

---

[1] Coleridge's *Lay Sermon*, p. 10. [P.]   [2] *Ibid*. [P.]
[3] *Ibid*. p. 21. [P.]   [4] *Ibid*. p. 25. [P.]   [5] *Ibid*. p. 27. [P.]
[6] *Ibid*. pp. 45, 46 (where the reader may find in a note the two worst jokes that ever were cracked). [P.] [" Am I at one with God ? . . . If not must I not be mad . . . if I do not embrace the means of atonement ? " Coleridge calls attention to the " dull though unintentional " pun. G.]

horrible !   Science classifies flowers.   Can it make them bloom
where it has placed them in its classification ? [1] No.   Therefore
flowers ought not to be classified.   This is transcendental logic.
Ha ! in that cylindrical mirror I see three shadowy forms :—dimly
I see them through the smoked glass of my spectacles.   Who art
thou ?—MYSTERY !—I hail thee !   Who art thou ?—JARGON !—
I love thee !   Who art thou ?—SUPERSTITION !—I worship thee !
Hail, transcendental TRIAD ! ''

Mr. Fax cut short the thread of his eloquence by saying he would
trouble him for the cream-jug.

Mr. Mystic began again, and talked for three hours without inter-
mission, except that he paused a moment on the entrance of sandwiches and Madeira.   His visitors sipped his wine in silence till he
had fairly talked himself hoarse.   Neither Mr. Fax nor Mr. Forester
replied to his paradoxes ; for to what end, they thought, should
they attempt to answer what few would hear, and none would
understand ?

It was now time to retire, and Mr. Mystic showed his guests to the
doors of their respective apartments, in each of which a gas-light
was burning, and ascended another flight of stairs to his own dor-
mitory, with a little twinkling taper in his hand.   Mr. Forester and
Mr. Fax stayed a few minutes on the landing-place, to have a word of
consultation before they parted for the night.   Mr. Mystic gained the
door of his apartment—turned the handle of the lock—and had just
advanced one step—when the whole interior of the chamber became
suddenly sheeted with fire : a tremendous explosion followed ; and
he was precipitated to the foot of the stairs in *the smallest conceivable
fraction of the infinite divisibility of time.*

Mr. Forester picked him up, and found him not much hurt ; only
a little singed, and very much frightened.   But the whole interior
of the apartment continued to blaze.   Mr. Forester and Sir Oran
Haut-ton ran for water : Mr. Fax rang the nearest bell : Mr. Mystic
vociferated " Fire ! '' with singular energy : the servants ran about
half-undressed : pails, buckets, and pitchers, were in active requisition ; till Sir Oran Haut-ton ascending the stairs with the great

[1] *Ibid.* p. xvii.   [P.]

rain-water tub, containing one hundred and eight gallons of water,[1] threw the whole contents on the flames with one sweep of his powerful arm.

The fire being extinguished, it remained to ascertain its cause. It appeared that the gas-tube in Mr. Mystic's chamber had been left unstopped, and the gas evolving without combustion (the apartment being perfectly air-tight), had condensed into a mass, which, on the approach of Mr. Mystic's taper, instantly ignited, blowing the transcendentalist down stairs, and setting fire to his curtains and furniture.

Mr. Mystic, as soon as he recovered from his panic, began to bewail the catastrophe : not so much, he said, for itself, as because such an event in Cimmerian Lodge was an infallible omen of evil—a type and symbol of an approaching period of public light—when the smoke of metaphysical mystery, and the vapours of ancient superstition, which he had done all that in him lay to consolidate in the spirit of man, would explode at the touch of analytical reason, leaving nothing but the plain common-sense matter-of-fact of moral and political truth— a day that he earnestly hoped he might never live to see.

" Certainly," said Mr. Forester, " it is a very bad omen for all who make it their study to darken the human understanding, when one of the pillars of their party is *blown up by his own smoke* ; but the symbol, as you call it, may operate as a warning to the apostles of superstitious chimæra and political fraud, that it is very possible *for smoke to be too thick* ; and that, in condensing in the human mind the vapours of ignorance and delusion, they are only compressing a body of inflammable gas, of which the explosion will be fatal in precise proportion to its density."

CHAPTER XXXII

THE DESERTED MANSION

THEY rose, as usual, before daylight, that they might pursue their perlustration ; and, on descending, found Mr. Mystic awaiting them at a table covered with a sumptuous apparatus of tea and coffee,

---

[1] " Some travellers speak of his strength as wonderful ; greater, they say, than that of ten men such as we."—*Ancient Metaphysics*, vol. iii. p. 105. [P.]

a pyramid of hot rolls, and a variety of cold provision. Cimmerian Lodge, he said, was famous for its breed of tame geese, and he could recommend the cold one on the table as one of his own training. The breakfast being despatched, he rowed them over the *Ocean of Deceitful Form* before the sun rose to disturb his navigation.

After walking some miles, a ruined mansion at the end of an ancient avenue of elms attracted their attention. As they made a point of leaving no place unexamined, they walked up to it. There was an air of melancholy grandeur in its loneliness and desolation which interested them to know its history. The briers that choked the court, the weeds that grew from the fissures of the walls and on the ledges of the windows, the fractured glass, the half-fallen door, the silent and motionless clock, the steps worn by the tread of other years, the total silence of the scene of ancient hospitality, broken only by the voices of the rooks whose nests were in the elms, all carried back the mind to the years that were gone. There was a sun-dial in the centre of the court : the sun shone on the brazen plate, and the shadow of the index fell on the line of noon. " Nothing impresses me more," said Mr. Forester, " in a ruin of this kind, than the contrast between the sun-dial and the clock, which I have frequently observed. This contrast I once made the basis of a little poem, which the similarity of circumstances induces me to repeat to you, though you are no votary of the spirit of rhyme."

THE SUN-DIAL

The ivy o'er the mouldering wall
Spreads like a tree, the growth of years :
The wild wind through the doorless hall
A melancholy music rears,
A solitary voice, that sighs
O'er man's forgotten pageantries.
Above the central gate, the clock,
Through clustering ivy dimly seen,
Seems, like the ghost of Time, to mock
The wrecks of power that once has been.
The hands are rusted on its face ;
Even where they ceased, in years gone by,
To keep the flying moments pace ;
Fixing, in Fancy's thoughtful eye,
A point of ages passed away,
A speck of time, that owns no tie
With aught that lives and breathes to-day.

But 'mid the rank and towering grass,
Where breezes wave, in mournful sport,
The weeds that choke the ruined court,
The careless hours, that circling pass,
Still trace upon the dialled brass
The shade of their unvarying way :
And evermore, with every ray
That breaks the clouds and gilds the air,
Time's stealthy steps are imaged there :
Even as the long-revolving years
In self-reflecting circles flow,
From the first bud the hedge-row bears,
To wintry Nature's robe of snow.
The changeful forms of mortal things
Decay and pass ; and art and power
Oppose in vain the doom that flings
Oblivion on their closing hour :
While still, to every woodland vale,
New blooms, new fruits, the seasons bring,
For other eyes and lips to hail
With looks and sounds of welcoming :
As where some stream light-eddying roves
By sunny meads and shadowy groves,
Wave following wave departs for ever,
But still flows on the eternal river.

An old man approached them, in whom they observed that look of
healthy and cheerful antiquity which showed that time only, and
neither pain nor sickness, had traced wrinkles on his cheek. Mr.
Forester made inquiries of him on the object he had most at heart ;
but the old man could give no gleam of light to guide his steps.
Mr. Fax then asked some questions concerning the mansion before
them.

" Ah, Zur ! " said the old man, "this be the zeat o' Squire Open-
hand : but he doant live here now : the house be growed too large
vor'n, as one may zay. I remember un playing about here on the
grass-plot, when he was half as high as the zun-dial poast, as if it was
but yesterday. The days that I ha' zeed here ! Rare doings there
used to be wi' the house vull o' gentlevolks zometimes to be zure :
but what he loiked best was, to zee a merry-making of all his tenants,
round the great oak that stands there in the large vield by himzelf.
He used to zay if there was any thing he could not abide, it was the
zight of a zorrowful feace ; and he was always prying about to voind
one : and if he did voind one, Lord bless you ! it was not a zorrowful

feace long, if it was any thing that he could mend. Zo he lived to
the length of his line, as the zaying is ; and when times grew worse,
it was a hard matter to draw in : howzomdever he did ; and when
the tax-gatherers came every year vor more and more, and the
peaper-money vlew about, buying up everything in the neighbourhood ; and every vifty pounds he got in peaper wasn't worth, as he
toald me, vorty pounds o' real money, why there was every year
fewer horses in his steable, and less wine on his board : and every
now and then came a queer zort o' chap dropped out o' the sky like—
a vundholder he called un,—and bought a bit o' ground vor a handvul
o' peaper, and built a cottage-horny, as they call it—there be one
there, on the hill zide—and had nothing to do wi' the country-people,
nor the country-people wi' he : no thing in the world to do, as we
could zee, but to eat and drink, and make little bits o' shrubberies,
o' quashies, and brutuses, and zelies, and cubies, and filigrees, and
ruddydunderums, instead o' the oak plantations, the old landlords
used to plant ; and the Squire could never abide the zight o' one o'
they gimcrack boxes ; and all the while he was nailing up a window
or two every year, and his horses were going one way, and his dogs
another, and his old zervants were zent away one by one, wi' heavy
hearts, poor zouls, and at last it came that he could not get half his
rents, and zome o' his tenants went to the workhouse, and others ran
away, because o' the poor-rates, and every thing went to zixes and
zevens, and I used to meet the Squire in his walks, and think to
myzelf it was very hard that he who could not bear to zee a zorrowful
feace, should have zuch a zorrowful one of his own ; and he used to
zay to me whenever I met un : ' All this comes o' peaper-money,
Measter Hawthorn.' Zo the upshot was, he could not afford any
longer to live in his own great house, where his vorevathers had lived
out o' memory o' man, and went to zome outlandish place wi' his
vamily to live, as he said, in much zuch a box as that gimcrack thing
on the hill."

"You have told us a very melancholy story," said Mr. Forester;
"but at present, I fear, a very common one, and one of which, if the
present system continue, every succeeding year will multiply
examples."

"Ah, Zur!" said the old man, "there was them as vorezeed it long ago, and voretold it too, up in the great house in Lunnun, where they zettles the affairs o' the nation : a pretty way o' zettling it be, to my thinking, to vill the country wi' tax-gatherers and vundholders, and peaper-money men, that turns all the old vamilies out o' the country, and zends their tenants to the workhouse : but there was them as vorezeed and voretold it too, but nobody minded 'em then : they begins to mind 'em now."

"But how do you manage in these times ? " said Mr. Forester.

" I lives, Measter," said the old man, " and pretty well too, vor myself. I had a little vreehold varm o' my own, that has been in my vamily zeven hundred year, and we woant part wi' it, I promise you, vor all the tax-collectors and vundholders in England. But my zon was never none o' your gentleman varmers, none o' your reacing and hunting bucks, that it's a shame vor a honest varmer to be : he always zet his shoulders to the wheel—always a-vield by peep o' day : zo now I be old, I've given up the varm to him ; and that I wouldn't ha' done to the best man in all the county bezide : but he's my zon, and I loves un. Zo I walks about the vields all day, and zits all the evening in the chimney-corner wi' an old neighbour or zo, and a jug o' ale, and talks over old times, when the Openhands, and zuch as they, could afford to live in the homes o' their vorevathers. It be a bad state o' things, my measters, and must come to a bad end, zooner or later ; but it'll last my time."

" You are not in the last stage of a consumption, are you, honest friend ? " said Mr. Fax.

" Lord love you, no, Measter," said the old farmer, rather frightened ; " do I look zo ? "

" No," said Mr. Fax ; " but you talked so."

" Ah ! thee beest a wag, I zee," said the farmer. " Things be in a conzumption zure enough, but they'll last my time vor all that ; and if they doant, it's no vault o' mine ; and I'se no money in the vunds, nor no zinecure pleace, zo I eats my beef-steak and drinks my ale, and lets the world slide."

CHAPTER XXXIII

THE PHANTASM

THE course of their perambulations brought them into the vicinity of Melincourt, and they stopped at the Castle to inquire if any intelligence had been obtained of Anthelia. The gate was opened to them by old Peter Gray, who informed them that himself and the female domestics were at that time the only inmates of the Castle, as the other male domestics had gone off at the same time with Mr. Hippy in search of their young mistress; and the Honourable Mrs. Pinmoney and Miss Danaretta were gone to London, because of the opera being open.

Mr. Forester inquired into the manner of Anthelia's disappearance. Old Peter informed him that she had gone into her library as usual after breakfast, and when the hour of dinner arrived she was missing. The central window was open, as well as the little postern door of the shrubbery, that led into the dingle, the whole vicinity of which they had examined, and had found the recent print of horses' feet on a narrow green road that skirted the other side of the glen: these traces they had followed till they had totally lost them, in a place where the road became hard and rocky, and divided into several branches: the pursuers had then separated into parties of two and three, and each party had followed a different branch of the road, but they had found no clue to guide them, and had hitherto been unsuccessful. He should not himself, he said, have remained inactive, but Mr. Hippy had insisted on his staying to take care of the Castle. He then observed, that, as it was growing late, he should humbly advise their continuing where they were till morning. To this they assented, and he led the way to the library.

Every thing in the library remained precisely in the place in which Anthelia left it. Her chair was near the table, and the materials of drawing were before it. The gloom of the winter evening, which was now closing in, was deepened through the stained glass of the windows. The moment the door was thrown open, Mr. Forester started, and threw himself forward into the apartment towards Anthelia's chair; but before he reached it, he stopped, placed his

hand before his eyes, and turning round, leaned for support on the
arm of Mr. Fax. He recovered himself in a few minutes, and sate
down by the table. Peter Gray, after kindling the fire, and lighting
the Argand lamp[1] that hung from the centre of the apartment, went
to give directions on the subject of dinner.

Mr. Forester observed, from the appearance of the drawing
materials, that they had been hastily left, and he saw that the last
subject on which Anthelia had been employed was a sketch of Redrose Abbey. He sate with his head leaning on his hand, and his eyes
fixed on the drawing in perfect silence. Mr. Fax thought it best not
to disturb his meditations, and took up a volume that was lying open
on the table, the last that Anthelia had been reading. It was a
posthumous work of the virtuous and unfortunate Condorcet, in
which that most amiable and sublime enthusiast, contemplating
human nature in the light of his own exalted spirit, had delineated
a beautiful vision of the future destinies of mankind.[2]

Sir Oran Haut-ton kept his eyes fixed on the door with looks of
anxious impatience, and showed manifest and increasing disappointment at every re-entrance of Old Peter, who at length summoned
them to dinner.

Mr. Fax was not surprised that Mr. Forester had no appetite, but
that Sir Oran had lost his, appeared to him extremely curious. The
latter grew more and more uneasy, rose from table, took a candle in
his hand, and wandered from room to room, searching every closet
and corner in the Castle, to the infinite amazement of Old Peter
Gray, who followed him every where, and became convinced that the
poor gentleman was crazed for love of his young mistress, who, he
made no doubt, was the object of his search ; and the conviction was
strengthened by the perfect inattention of Sir Oran to all his assurances that his dear young lady was not in any of those places which
he searched so scrupulously. Sir Oran at length having left no
corner of the habitable part of the Castle unexamined, returned to
the dining-room, and throwing himself into a chair began to shed
tears in great abundance.[3]

[1] Invented by Aimé Argand, 1782, with a cylindrical wick. G.
[2] *Esquisse d'un Tableau historique des Progrès de l'Esprit humain.* [P.]
[3] See p. 130, note. [P.]

Mr. Fax made his two disconsolate friends drink several glasses of Madeira, by way of raising their spirits, and then asked Mr. Forester what it was that had so affected him on their first entering the library.

MR. FORESTER. It was the form of Anthelia, in the place where I first saw her, in that chair by the table. The vision was momentary, but, while it lasted, had all the distinctness of reality.

MR. FAX. This is no uncommon effect of the association of ideas when external objects present themselves to us, after an interval of absence, in their remembered arrangement, with only one form wanting, and that the dearest among them, to perfect the resemblance between the present sensation and the recollected idea. A vivid imagination, more especially when the nerves are weakened by anxiety and fatigue, will, under such circumstances, complete the imperfect scene, by replacing for a moment the one deficient form among those accustomed objects which had long formed its accompaniments in the contemplation of memory. This single mental principle will explain the greater number of *credible* tales of apparitions, and at the same time give a very satisfactory reason why a particular spirit is usually found haunting a particular place.

MR. FORESTER. Thus Petrarch's beautiful pictures of the Spirit of Laura on the banks of the Sorga,[1] are assuredly something more than the mere fancies of the closet, and must have originated in that system of mental connexion, which, under peculiar circumstances, gives ideas the force of sensations. Anxiety and fatigue are certainly great promoters of the state of mind most favourable to such impressions.

MR. FAX. It was under the influence of such excitements that Brutus saw the spirit of Cæsar ; and in similar states of feeling, the phantoms of poetry are usually supposed to be visible : the ghost of Banquo, for example, and that of Patroclus. But this only holds true of the poets who paint from nature ; for their artificial imitators, when they wish to call a spirit from the vasty deep,[2] are not always so attentive to the mental circumstances of the persons to whom they present it. In the early periods of society, when apparitions form

---

[1] See *Gryll Grange*, p. 828 note. G.
[2] *Henry IV, Pt. I*, Act III, Sc. 1. G.

a portion of the general creed ; when the life of man is wandering, precarious, and turbulent ; when the uncultured wildness of the heath and the forest harmonizes with the chimæras of superstition, and when there is not, as in later times, a rooted principle of reason and knowledge, to weaken such perceptions in their origin, and destroy the seeming reality of their subsequent recollection, impressions of this nature will be more frequent, and will be as much invested with the character of external existence, as the scenes to which they are attached by the connecting power of the mind.   They will always be found with their own appropriate character of time, and place, and circumstance.   The ghost of the warrior will be seen on the eve of battle by him who keeps his lonely watch near the blaze of the nightly fire, and the spirit of the huntress maid will appear to her lover when he pauses on the sunny heath, or rests in the moonlight cave.

CHAPTER XXXIV

THE CHURCHYARD

THE next morning Mr. Forester determined on following the mountain-road on the other side of the dingle, of which Peter Gray had spoken : but wishing first to make some inquiries of the Reverend Mr. Portpipe, they walked to his vicarage, which was in a village at some distance.   Just as they reached it the reverend gentleman emerged in haste, and seeing Mr. Forester and his friends, said he was very sorry that he could not attend to them just then, as he had a great press of business to dispose of, namely, a christening, a marriage, and a funeral, but he would knock them off as fast as he could, after which he should be perfectly at their service, hoped they would wait in the vicarage till his return, and observed he had good ale and a few bottles of London Particular.[1]   He then left them to dispatch his affairs in the church.

They preferred waiting in the churchyard.   " A christening, a marriage, and a funeral ! " said Mr. Forester.   " With what indifference he runs through the whole drama of human life, raises the

---

[1] A Madeira wine imported for the London market and hence, from its colour, a London fog.   G.

curtain on its commencement, superintends the most important and eventful action of its progress, and drops the curtain on its close ! "

MR. FAX. Custom has rendered them all alike indifferent to him. In every human pursuit and profession the routine of ordinary business renders the mind indifferent to all the forms and objects of which that routine is composed. The sexton "sings at grave-making ; "[1] the undertaker walks with a solemn face before the coffin, because a solemn face is part of his trade : but his heart is as light as if there were no funeral at his heels : he is quietly conning over the items of his bill, or thinking of the party in which he is to pass his evening ; and the reverend gentleman who concludes the process, and consigns to its last receptacle the shell of extinguished intelligence, has his thoughts on the wing of the sports of the field, or the jovial board of the Squire.

MR. FORESTER. Your observation is just. It is this hardening power of custom that gives steadiness to the hand of the surgeon, firmness to the voice of the criminal judge, coolness to the soldier "in the imminent deadly breach,"[2] self-possession to the sailor in the rage of the equinoctial storm. It is under this influence that the lawyer deals out writs and executions as carelessly as he deals out cards at his evening whist ; that the gaoler turns the key with the same stern indifference on unfortunate innocence as on hardened villany ; that the venal senator votes away by piecemeal the liberties of his country ; and that the statesman sketches over the bottle his series of deliberate schemes for the extinction of human freedom, the enchaining of human reason, and the waste of human life.

MR. FAX. Contemplate any of these men only in the sphere of their routine, and you will think them utterly destitute of all human sympathy. Make them change places with each other, and you will see symptoms of natural feelings. Custom cannot kill the better feelings of human nature : it merely lays them asleep.

MR. FORESTER. You must acknowledge then, at least, that their sleep is very sound.

[1] *Hamlet*, Act V, Sc. 1. G.   [2] *Othello*, Act I, Sc. 3. G.

MR. FAX. In most cases certainly as sound as that of Epimenides, or of the seven sleepers of Ephesus.[1] But these did wake at last, and, therefore, according to Aristotle, they had always the capacity of waking.

MR. FORESTER. You must allow me to wait for a similar proof, before I admit such a capacity in respect to the feelings of some of the characters we have mentioned. Yet I am no sceptic in human virtue.

MR. FAX. You have no reason to be, with so much evidence before your eyes, of the excellence of the past generation, and I do not suppose the present is much worse than its predecessors. Read the epitaphs around you, and see what models and mirrors of all the social virtues have left the examples of their shining light to guide the steps of their posterity.

MR. FORESTER. I observe the usual profusion of dutiful sons, affectionate husbands, faithful friends, kind neighbours, and honest men. These are the luxuriant harvest of every churchyard. But is it not strange, that even the fertility of fiction should be so circumscribed in the variety of monumental panegyric? Yet a few words comprehend the summary of all the moral duties of ordinary life. Their degrees and diversities are like the shades of colour, that shun for the most part the power of language : at all events, the nice distinctions and combinations that give individuality to historical character, scarcely come within the limits of sepulchral inscription, which merely serves to testify the regret of the survivors for one whose society was dear, and whose faults are forgotten. For there is a feeling in the human mind, that, in looking back on former scenes of intercourse with those who are passed for ever beyond the limits of injury and resentment, gradually destroys all the bitterness and heightens all the pleasures of the remembrance ; as, when we revert in fancy to the days of our childhood, we scarcely find a vestige of their tears, pains, and disappointments, and perceive only their

---

[1] Epimenides, the Cretan prophet, was sent to find sheep when a boy. He lay down in a cave, fell asleep for fifty-seven years and resumed his search when he woke up. The Seven Sleepers took refuge from persecution in a cave and slept for two hundred and thirty years. G.

fields, their flowers, and their sunshine, and the smiles of our little associates.

MR. FAX.   The history of common life seems as circumscribed as its moral attributes : for the most extensive information I can collect from these gravestones is, that the parties married, lived in trouble, and died of a conflict between a disease and a physician.   I observe a last request, which I suppose was very speedily complied with : that of a tender husband to his loving wife not to weep for him long. If it be as you say, that the faults of the dead are soon forgotten, yet the memory of their virtues is not much longer lived ; and I have often thought that these words of Rabelais would furnish an appropriate inscription for ninety-nine gravestones out of every hundred : *Sa mémoire expira avecque le son des cloches qui carillonarent à son enterrement.*[1]

CHAPTER XXXV

THE RUSTIC WEDDING

THE bride and bridegroom, with half a dozen of their friends, now entered the churchyard.   The bride, a strong, healthy-looking country girl, was clinging to the arm of her lover, not with the light and scarcely perceptible touch, with which Miss Simper complies with the request of Mr. Giggle, " that she will do him the honour to take his arm," but with a cordial and unsophisticated pressure that would have made such an arm as Mr. Giggle's black and blue.   The bridegroom, with a pair of chubby cheeks, which in colour precisely rivalled his new scarlet waistcoat, and his mouth expanded into a broad grin, that exhibited the total range of his teeth, advanced in a sort of step that was half a walk and half a dance, as if the preconceived notion of the requisite solemnity of demeanour were struggling with the natural impulses of the overflowing joy of his heart.

Mr. Fax looked with great commiseration on this bridal pair, and

[1] " The memory of it was lost with the sound of the bells that rung for joy at his funeral."   Bk. IV, Ch. xii, Urquhart and Motteux translation.

G.

determined to ascertain if they had a clear notion of the evils that awaited them in consequence of the rash step they were about to take. He therefore accosted them with an observation that the Reverend Mr. Portpipe was not at leisure, but would be in a few minutes. " In the mean time," said he, " I stand here as the representative of general reason, to ask if you have duly weighed the consequences of your present proceeding ? "

THE BRIDEGROOM. General Reason ! I be's no soger man, and bea'n't countable to no General whatzomecomedever. We bea'n't under martial law, be we ? Voine toimes indeed if General Reason be to interpole between a poor man and his sweetheart.

MR. FAX. That is precisely the case which calls most loudly for such an interposition.

THE BRIDEGROOM. If General Reason waits till I or Zukey calls loudly vor'n, he'll wait long enough. Woa'n't he, Zukey ?

THE BRIDE. Ees, zure, Robin.

MR. FAX. General reason, my friend, I assure you, has nothing to do with martial law, nor with any other mode of arbitrary power, but with authority that has truth for its fountain, benevolence for its end, and the whole universe for its sphere of action.

THE BRIDEGROOM. (scratching his head.) There be a mort o' voine words, but I zuppose you means to zay as how this General Reason be a Methody preacher ; but I be's true earthy-ducks church, and zo be Zukey : bea'n't you, Zukey ?

THE BRIDE. Ees, zure, Robin.

THE BRIDEGROOM. And we has nothing to do wi' General Reason neither on us. Has we, Zukey ?

THE BRIDE. No, zure, Robin.

MR. FAX. Well, my friend, be that as it may, you are going to be married ?

THE BRIDEGROOM. Why, I think zo, Zur, wi' General Reason's leave. Bea'n't we, Zukey ?

THE BRIDE. Ees, zure, Robin.

MR. FAX. And are you fully aware, my honest friend, what marriage is ?

THE BRIDEGROOM. Vor zartin I be : Zukey and I ha' got it by heart out o' t' Book o' Common Prayer. Ha'n't we, Zukey ? (*This time Susan did not think proper to answer.*) It be ordained that zuch parsons as hav'n't the gift of—— (*Susan gave him such a sudden and violent pinch on the arm, that his speech ended in a roar.*) Od rabbit me ! that wur a twinger ! I'll have my revenge, howzome-comedever. (*And he imprinted a very emphatical kiss on the lips of his blushing bride, that greatly scandalized Mr. Fax.*)

MR. FAX. Do you know, that in all likelihood, in the course of six years, you will have as many children ?

THE BRIDEGROOM. The more the merrier, Zur. Bea'n't it, Zukey ? (*Susan was mute again.*)

MR. FAX. I hope it may prove so, my friend ; but I fear you will find the more the sadder. What are your occupations ?

THE BRIDEGROOM. Anan, Zur ?

MR. FAX. What do you do to get your living ?

THE BRIDEGROOM. Works vor Varmer Brownstout : sows and reaps, threshes, and goes to market wi' corn and cattle, turns to plough-tail when hap chances, cleans and feeds horses, hedges and ditches, fells timber, gathers in t' orchard, brews ale, and drinks it, and gets vourteen shill'ns a week vor my trouble. And Zukey here ha' laid up a mint o' money : she wur dairy-maid at Varmer Cheese-curd's, and ha' gotten vour pounds zeventeen shill'ns and ninepence, in t' old chest wi' three vlat locks and a padlock. Ha'n't you, Zukey ?

THE BRIDE. Ees, zure, Robin.

MR. FAX. It does not appear to me, my worthy friend, that your fourteen shillings a week, even with Mistress Susan's consolidated fund of four pounds seventeen shillings and ninepence, will be altogether adequate to the maintenance of such a family as you seem likely to have.

THE BRIDEGROOM. Why, Zur, in t' virst pleace, I doan't know what be Zukey's intentions in that respect—Od rabbit it, Zukey ! doan't pinch zo—and in t' next pleace, wi' all due submission to you and General Reason the Methody preacher, I takes it to be our look-out, and none o' nobody's else.

MR. FAX. But it is somebody's else, for this reason : that if you cannot maintain your own children, the parish must do it for you.

THE BRIDEGROOM. Vor zartin—in a zort o' way ; and bad enough at best. But I wants no more to do wi' t' parish than parish wi' me.

MR. FAX. I dare say you do not, at present. But, my good friend, when the cares of a family come upon you, your independence of spirit will give way to necessity ; and if, by any accident, you are thrown out of work, as in the present times many honest fellows are, what will you do then ?

THE BRIDEGROOM. Do the best I can, Measter, as I always does and nobody can't do no better.

MR. FAX. Do you suppose, then, you are doing the best you can now, in marrying, with such a doubtful prospect before you ? How will you bring up your children ?

THE BRIDEGROOM. Why, in the vear o' the Lord, to be zure.

MR. FAX. Of course : but how will you bring them up to get their living ?

THE BRIDEGROOM. That's as thereafter may happen. They woan't starve, I'se warrant 'em, if they teakes after their veyther. But I zees now who General Reason be. He be one o' your zinecure vundholder peaper-money taxing men, as isn't zatisfied wi' takin' t' bread out o' t' poor man's mouth, and zending his chillern to army and navy, and vactories, and zuch-like, but wants to take away his wife into t' bargain.

MR. FAX. There, my honest friend, you have fallen into a radical

mistake, which I shall try to elucidate for your benefit.   It is owing
to poor people having more children than they can maintain, that
those children are obliged to go to the army and navy, and consequently that statesmen and conquerors find so many ready instruments for the oppression and destruction of the human species : it
follows, therefore, that if people would not marry till they could be
certain of maintaining all their children comfortably at home——

THE BRIDEGROOM.   Lord love you, that be all mighty voine
rigmarol ; but the short and the long be this : I can't live without
Zukey, nor Zukey without I, can you, Zukey ?

THE BRIDE.   No, zure, Robin.

THE BRIDEGROOM.   Now there be a plain downright honest-
hearted old English girl : none o' your quality madams, as zays one
thing and means another ; and zo you may tell General Reason he
may teake away chair and teable, salt-box and trencher, bed and
bedding, pig and pig-sty, but neither he nor all his peaper-men
together shall take away his own Zukey from Robin Ruddyfeace ;
if they shall I'm dom'd.

  " What profane wretch," said the Reverend Mr. Portpipe, emerging
from the church, " what profane wretch is swearing in the very gate
of the temple ? " and seeing by the bridegroom's confusion that he
was the culprit, he reprimanded him severely, and declared he would
not marry him that day.   The very thought of such a disappointment was too much for poor Robin to bear, and, after one or two
ineffectual efforts to speak, he distorted his face into a most rueful
expression, and struck up such a roar of crying as completely electri-
fied the Reverend Mr. Portpipe, whose wrath, nevertheless, was not
to be mollified by Robin's grief and contrition, but yielded at length
to the intercessions of Mr. Forester.   Robin's face cleared up in an
instant, and the natural broad grin of his ruddy countenance shone
forth through his tears like the sun through a shower.   " You are
such an honest and warm-hearted fellow," said Mr. Forester, putting
a banknote into Robin's hand, " that you must not refuse me the
pleasure of making this little addition to Mistress Susan's consolidated fund."—" Od rabbit me ! " said the bridegroom, overcome with

joy and surprise, " I doan't know who thee beest, but thee bees'n't
General Reason, that's vor zartin."

The rustic party then followed the Reverend Mr. Portpipe into
the church. Robin, when he reached the porch, looked round over
his shoulder to Mr. Fax, and said with a very arch look, " My
dutiful sarvice to General Reason." And looking round a second
time before he entered the door, added : " and Zukey's too."

CHAPTER XXXVI

THE VICARAGE

WHEN the Reverend Mr. Portpipe had dispatched his " press of
business," he set before his guests in the old oak parlour of his
vicarage a cold turkey and ham, a capacious jug of " incomparable
ale," and a bottle of his London Particular ; all which, on trial,
were approved to be excellent, and a second bottle of the latter was
very soon required, and produced with great alacrity. The reverend
gentleman expressed much anxiety in relation to the mysterious
circumstance of the disappearance of Anthelia, on whom he pronounced a very warm eulogium, saying she was the flower of the
mountains, the type of ideal beauty, the daughter of music, the
rosebud of sweetness, and the handmaid of charity. He professed
himself unable to throw the least light on the transaction, but
supposed she had been spirited away for some nefarious purpose.
He said that the mountain road had been explored without success
in all its ramifications, not only by Mr. Hippy and the visitors and
domestics of Melincourt, but by all the peasants and mountaineers
of the vicinity—that it led through a most desolate and inhospitable
tract of country, and he would advise them, if they persisted in their
intention of following it themselves, to partake of his poor hospitality
till morning, and set forward with the first dawn of daylight. Mr.
Fax seconded this proposal, and Mr. Forester complied.

They spent the evening in the old oak parlour, and conversed on
various subjects, during which a knotty point opposing itself to the
solution of an historical question, Mr. Forester expressed a wish to
be allowed access to the reverend gentleman's library. The reverend

gentleman hummed awhile with great gravity and deliberation : then slowly rising from his large arm-chair, he walked across the room to the further corner, where throwing open the door of a little closet, he said with extreme complacency, " There is my library : Homer, Virgil, and Horace, for old acquaintance sake, and the credit of my cloth : Tillotson, Atterbury, and Jeremy Taylor, for materials of exhortation and ingredients of sound doctrine : and for my own private amusement, in an occasional half hour between my dinner and my nap, a translation of Rabelais and the Tale of a Tub."

MR. FAX. A well-chosen collection.

THE REVEREND MR. PORTPIPE. *Multum in parvo.* But there is something that may amuse you : a little drawer of mineral specimens that have been picked up in this vicinity, and a fossil or two. Among the latter is a curious bone that was found in a hill just by, invested with stalactite.

MR. FORESTER. The bone of a human thumb, unquestionably.

THE REVEREND MR. PORTPIPE. Very probably.

MR. FORESTER. Which, by its comparative proportion, must have belonged to an individual about eleven feet six or seven inches in height : there are no such men now.

MR. FAX. Except, perhaps, among the Patagonians, whose existence is, however, disputed.

MR. FORESTER. It is disputed on no tenable ground, but that of the narrow and bigoted vanity of civilized men, who, pent in the unhealthy limits of towns and cities, where they dwindle from generation to generation in a fearful rapidity of declension towards the abyss of the infinitely little, in which they will finally vanish from the system of nature, will not admit that there ever were, or are, or can be better, stronger, and healthier men than themselves. The Patagonians are a vagrant nation, without house or home, and are, therefore, only occasionally seen on the coast : but because some voyagers have not seen them, I know not why we should impeach the evidence of those who have. The testimony of a man of honour, like Mr. Byron,[1] would alone have been sufficient : but all his officers and men gave the same account.   And there are other testimonies ; that, for instance, of M. de Guyot, who brought from the coast of Patagonia a skeleton of one of these great men, which measured between twelve and thirteen feet.   This skeleton he was bringing to Europe, but happening to be caught in a great storm, and having on board a Spanish Bishop (the Archbishop of Lima), who was of opinion that the storm was caused by the bones of this Pagan which they had on board ; and having persuaded the crew that this was the case, the captain was obliged to throw the skeleton overboard.   The Bishop died soon after, and was thrown overboard in his turn.   I could have wished that he had been thrown overboard sooner, and then the bones of the Patagonian would have arrived in Europe.[2]

THE REVEREND MR. PORTPIPE.   Your wish is orthodox, inasmuch as the Bishop was himself a Pagan, and moreover an Inquisitor. And your doctrine of large men is also orthodox, for the sons of Anak and the family of Goliah did once exist, though now their race is extinct.

MR. FORESTER.   The multiplication of diseases, the diminution of strength, and the contraction of the term of existence, keep pace with the diminution of the stature of men.   The mortality of a manufacturing town, compared with that of a mountain-village, is more than three to one, which clearly shows the evil effects of the departure from natural life, and of the coacervation of multitudes within the narrow precincts of cities, where the breath of so many animals, and the exhalations from the dead, the dying, and corrupted things of all kinds, make the air little better than a slow poison, and so offensive as to be perceptible to the sense of those who are not accustomed to it ; for the wandering Arabs will smell a town at the

---

[1] Vice-Admiral the Hon. John Byron, known as " Foul-weather Jack " (1723–86), was wrecked off the Chilean coast, 1741, and published a narrative of his shipwreck and his early adventures with Anson, 1768, which was utilised by Byron in *Don Juan*.   In the *Epistle to Augusta*, the poet wrote :

> " Reversed for him our grandsire's fate of yore,
> He had no rest at sea, nor I on shore."   G.

[2] *Ancient Metaphysics*, vol. iii. p. 139.   [P.]

distance of several leagues. And in this country the cottagers who are driven by the avarice of landlords and great tenants to seek a subsistence in towns, are very soon destroyed by the change.[1] And this hiving of human beings is not the only evil effect of commerce, which tends also to keep up a constant circulation of the elements of destruction, and to make the vices and diseases of one country the vices and diseases of all.[2] Thus, with every extension of our intercourse with distant lands, we bring home some new seed of death ; and how many we leave as vestiges of our visitation, let the South Sea Islanders testify. Consider, too, the frightful consequences of the consumption of spiritous liquors : a practice so destructive, that if all the devils were again to be assembled in Pandemonium,[3] to contrive the ruin of the human species, nothing so mischievous could be devised by them ; [4] but which it is considered politic to encourage, according to our method of raising money on the vices of the people.[5] When these and many other causes of destruction are considered, it would be wonderful indeed, if every new generation were not, as all experience proves that it is, smaller, weaker, more diseased, and more miserable than the preceding.

MR. FAX. Do you find, in the progress of science and the rapid diffusion of intellectual light, no counterpoise to this mass of physical calamity, even admitting it to exist in the extent you suppose ?

MR. FORESTER. Without such a counterpoise the condition of human nature would be desperate indeed. The intellectual, as I have often observed to you, are nourished at the expense of the animal faculties.

MR. FAX. You cannot, then, conceive the existence of *mens sana in corpore sano* ?

MR. FORESTER. Scarcely in the present state of human degeneracy: at best in a very limited sense.

---

[1] *Ibid.* p. 193. [P.]   [2] *Ibid.* p. 191. [P.]
[3] Milton : *Paradise Lost*, Bk. I, ll. 755–7 :

> " A solemn Councel forthwith to be held
> At *Pandæmonium*, the high Capital
> Of Satan and his Peers." G.

[4] *Ancient Metaphysics*, vol. iii. p. 181. [P.]   [5] *Ibid.* p. 182. [P.]

MR. FAX. Nevertheless you do, nay, you must, acknowledge that the intellectual, which is the better part of human nature, is in a progress of rapid improvement, continually enlarging its views and multiplying its acquisitions.

MR. FORESTER. The collective stock of knowledge which is the common property of scientific men necessarily increases, and will increase from the circumstance of admitting the co-operation of numbers : but collective knowledge is as distinct from individual mental power as it is confessedly unconnected with wisdom and moral virtue, and independent of political liberty. A man of modern times, with machines of complicated powers, will lift a heavier mass than that which Hector hurled from his unassisted arm against the Grecian gates ; but take away his mechanism, and what comparison is there between him and Hector ? In the same way a modern man of science *knows* more than Pythagoras knew : but consider them with relation only to *mental power*, and what comparison remains between them ? [1] No more than between a modern poet and Homer —a comparison which the most strenuous partisan of modern improvement will scarcely venture to institute.

MR. FAX. I will venture to oppose Shakespeare to him nevertheless.

MR. FORESTER. That is, however, going back two centuries, to a state of society very peculiar, and very fertile in genius. Shakespeare is the great phænomenon of the modern world, but his men and women are beings like ourselves ; whereas those of Homer are of a nobler and mightier race ; and his poetry is worthy of his characters : it is the language of the gods.

Mr. Forester rose, and approached the little closet, with the avowed intention of taking down Homer. "Take care how you touch him," said the Reverend Mr. Portpipe : "he is in a very dusty condition, for he has not been disturbed these thirty years."

[1] See *Headlong Hall*, p. 25. G.

CHAPTER XXXVII

THE MOUNTAINS

THEY followed the mountain-road till they arrived at the spot where it divided into several branches, one of which they selected on some principle of preference, which we are not sagacious enough to penetrate. They now proceeded by a gradual ascent of several miles along a rugged passage of the hills, where the now flowerless heath was the only vestige of vegetation ; and the sound of the little streams that every where gleamed beside their way, the only manifestation of the life and motion of nature.

" It is a subject worthy of consideration," said Mr. Fax, " how far scenes like these are connected with the genius of liberty: how far the dweller of the mountains, who is certainly surrounded by more sublime excitements, has more loftiness of thought, and more freedom of spirit, than the cultivator of the plains."

MR. FORESTER.   A modern poet has observed, that the voices of the sea and the mountains are the two voices of liberty : [1] the words mountain-liberty have, indeed, become so intimately associated, that I never yet found any one who even thought of questioning their necessary and natural connexion.

MR. FAX.   And yet I question it much ; and in the present state of human society I hold the universal inculcation of such a sentiment in poetry and romance, to be not only a most gross delusion, but an error replete with the most pernicious practical consequences.   For I have often seen a young man of high and aspiring genius, full of noble enthusiasm for the diffusion of truth and the general happiness of mankind, withdrawn from all intercourse with polished and intellectual society, by the distempered idea, that he would no where find fit aliment for his high cogitations, but among heaths, and rocks, and torrents.

MR. FORESTER.   In a state of society so corrupted as that in which

[1] Wordsworth : *Thought of a Briton on the Subjugation of Switzerland.* The same idea inspired lines in Shelley's *Liberty*, written three years after the publication of *Melincourt*.   G.

we live, the best instructors and companions are ancient books ; and these are best studied in those congenial solitudes, where the energies of nature are most pure and uncontrolled, and the aspect of external things recalls in some measure the departed glory of the world.

MR. FAX. Holding, as I do, that no branch of knowledge is valuable, but such as in its ultimate results has a plain and practical tendency to the general diffusion of moral and political truth, you must allow me to doubt the efficacy of solitary intercourse with stocks and stones, however rugged and fantastic in their shapes, towards the production of this effect.

MR. FORESTER. It is matter of historical testimony that occasional retirement into the recesses of nature has produced the most salutary effects of the very kind you require, in the instance of some of the most illustrious minds that have adorned the name of man.

MR. FAX. That the health and purity of the country, its verdure and its sunshine, have the most beneficial influence on the mental and corporeal faculties, I am very far from being inclined to deny : but this is a different consideration from that of the connexion between the scenery of the mountains and the genius of liberty. Look into the records of the world. What have the mountains done for freedom and mankind ? When have the mountains, to speak in the cant of the new school of poetry, "sent forth a voice of power"[1] to awe the oppressors of the world ? Mountaineers are for the most part a stupid and ignorant race ; and where there are stupidity and ignorance, there will be superstition ; and where there is superstition, there will be slavery.

MR. FORESTER. To a certain extent I cannot but agree with you. The names of Hampden and Milton are associated with the level plains and flat pastures of Buckinghamshire ; but I cannot now remember what names of true greatness and unshaken devotion to

[1] Perhaps suggested by Wordsworth's *The White Doe of Rylstone*, Canto 1, ll. 21-4 :

> "but the tower
> Is standing with a voice of power,
> That ancient voice which wont to call
> To mass or some high festival." G.

general liberty, are associated with these heathy rocks and cloud-capped mountains of Cumberland. We have seen a little horde of poets, who brought hither from the vales of the south, the harps which they had consecrated to Truth and Liberty, to acquire new energy in the mountain-winds : and now those harps are attuned to the praise of luxurious power, to the strains of courtly sycophancy, and to the hymns of exploded superstition. But let not the innocent mountains bear the burden of their transgressions.

MR. FAX.   All I mean to say is, that there is nothing in the nature of mountain-scenery either to make men free, or to keep them so. The only source of freedom is intellectual light. The ignorant are always slaves, though they dwell among the Andes. The wise are always free, though they cultivate a savannah. Who is so stupid and so servile as a Swiss, whom you find, like a piece of living furniture, the human latch of every great man's door ?

MR. FORESTER.   Let us look back to former days, to the mountains of the North :

> " Wild the Runic faith,
> And wild the realms where Scandinavian chiefs
> And Scalds arose, and hence the Scald's strong verse
> Partook the savage wildness. And methinks,
> Amid such scenes as these the poet's soul
> Might best attain full growth." [1]

MR. FAX.   As to the " Scald's strong verse," I must say I have never seen any specimens of it, that I did not think mere trash. It is little more than a rhapsody of rejoicing in carnage, a ringing of changes on the biting sword and the flowing of blood and the feast of the raven and the vulture, and fulsome flattery of the chieftain, of whom the said Scald was the abject slave, vassal, parasite, and laureat, interspersed with continual hints that he ought to be well paid for his lying panegyrics.

MR. FORESTER.   There is some justice in your observations : nevertheless, I must still contend that those who seek the mountains in a proper frame of feeling, will find in them images of energy and

[1] From Southey's lines to Amos Cottle, prefixed to the latter's *Icelandic Poetry*, 1797 ; but not reprinted in Southey's works. G.

liberty, harmonizing most aptly with the loftiness of an unprejudiced mind, and nerving the arm of resistance to every variety of oppression and imposture, that winds the chains of power round the free-born spirit of man.

CHAPTER XXXVIII

THE FRACAS

AFTER a long ramble among heath and rock, and over moss and moor, they began to fear the probability of being benighted among those desolate wilds, when fortunately they found that their track crossed one of the principal roads, which they followed for a short time, and entered a small town, where they stopped for the night at an inn. They were shown up stairs into an apartment separated from another only by a moveable partition, which allowed the two rooms to be occasionally laid into one. They were just sitting down to dinner when they heard the voices of some newly-arrived company in the adjoining apartment, and distinguished the tones of a female voice indicative of alarm and anxiety, and the masculine accents of one who seemed to be alternately comforting the afflicted fair one, and swearing at the obsequious waiter, with reiterated orders, as it appeared, for another chaise immediately. Mr. Fax was not long in divining that the new-comers were two runaway lovers in momentary apprehension of being overtaken; and this conjecture was confirmed, when, after a furious rattle of wheels in the yard, the door of the next apartment was burst open, and a violent scream from the lady was followed by a gruff shout of—" So, ho, Miss, here you are. Gretna, eh ? Your journey's marred for this time ; and if you get off again, say you have my consent—that's all." Low soft tones of supplication ensued, but in undistinguishable words, and continued to be repeated in the intervals of the following harangue : " Love indeed ! don't tell me. Aren't you my daughter ? Answer me that. And haven't I a right over you till you are twenty-one ? You may marry then ; but not a rap of the ready : my money's my own all my life. Haven't I chosen you a proper husband—a nice rich young fellow not above forty-five ?—Sixty, you minx ! no such thing. Rolling in riches : member for Threevotes : two places, three pensions, and a sinecure : famous borough interest to make all your children generals and archbishops. And here a miserable vagabond with only five hundred a year in landed property.—Pish ! love indeed !—own age—congenial minds—pshaw ! all a farce. Money—money—money—that's the matter—money is the first thing—money is the second thing—money is the third thing—money is the only thing—money is every thing and all things."—" Vagabond, Sir," said a third voice : " I am a gentleman, and have money sufficient to maintain your daughter in comfort."—" Comfort ! " said the gruff voice again; " comfort with five hundred a year, ha ! ha ! ha ! eh ! Sir Bonus ? "—" Hooh ! hooh ! hooh ! very droll indeed," said a fourth voice, in a sound that seemed a mixture of a cough and a laugh. " Very well, Sir," said the third voice ; " I shall not part with my treasure quietly, I assure you."—" Rebellion ! flat rebellion against parental authority," exclaimed the second. " But I'm too much for you, youngster. Where are all my varlets and rascals ? "

A violent trampling of feet and various sounds of tumult ensued, as if the old gentleman and his party were tearing the lovers asunder by main force ; and at length an agonizing scream from the young lady seemed to announce that their purpose was accomplished. Mr. Forester started up with a view of doing all in his power to assist the injured damsel ; and Sir Oran Haut-ton, who, as the reader has seen, had very strong feelings of natural justice, and a most chivalrous sympathy with females in distress, rushed with a desperate impulse against the partition, and hurled a great portion of it, with a violent crash, into the adjoining apartment. This unexpected event had the effect of fixing the whole group within for a few moments in motionless surprise in their respective places.

The fat and portly father, who was no other than our old acquaintance Sir Gregory Greenmould, and the old valetudinarian he had chosen for his daughter, Sir Bonus Mac Scrip, were directing the efforts of their myrmidons to separate the youthful pair. The young lady was clinging to her lover with the tenacity of the tendrils of a vine : the young gentleman's right arm was at liberty, and he was keeping the assailants at bay with the poker, which he had seized on the first irruption of the foe, and which had left vestiges of its impression, to speak in ancient phraseology, in various green wounds and bloody coxcombs.[1]

As Sir Oran was not habituated to allow any very long process of syllogistic reasoning to interfere between his conception and execution of the dictates of natural justice, he commenced operations by throwing the assailants one by one down stairs, who, as fast as they could rise from the ground, ran or limped away into sundry holes and coverts. Sir Bonus Mac Scrip retreated through the breach, and concealed himself under the dining-table in Mr. Forester's apartment. Mr. Forester succeeded in preventing Sir Gregory from being thrown after his myrmidons : but Sir Oran kept the fat Baronet a close prisoner in the corner of the room, while the lovers slipped away into the inn-yard, where the chaise they had ordered was in readiness ; and the cracking of whips, the trampling of horses, and the rattling of wheels, announced the final discomfiture of the schemes of Sir Gregory Greenmould and the hopes of Sir Bonus Mac Scrip.

CHAPTER XXXIX

MAINCHANCE VILLA

THE next day they resumed their perquisitions, still without any clue to guide them in their search. They had hitherto had the advantage of those halcyon days, which often make the middle of winter a season of serenity and sunshine ; but, on this day towards the evening, the sky grew black with clouds, the snow fell rapidly in massy flakes, and the mountains and valleys were covered with one uniform veil of whiteness. All vestiges of road and paths were obliterated. They were winding round the side of a mountain, and their situation began to wear a very unpromising aspect, when, on a sudden turn of the road, the trees and chimneys of a villa burst upon their view in the valley below. To this they bent their way, and on ringing at the gate-bell, and making the requisite inquiries, they found it to be Mainchance Villa, the new residence of Peter Paypaul Paperstamp, Esquire, whom we introduced to our readers in the twenty-eighth chapter. They sent in their names, and received a polite invitation

[1] *Henry V*, Act V, Sc. 1. G.

to walk in. They were shown into a parlour, where they found their old acquaintance Mr. Derrydown tête-à-tête at the piano with Miss Celandina,[1] with whom he was singing a duet. Miss Celandina said, " her papa was just then engaged, but would soon have the pleasure of waiting on them: in the mean time Mr. Derrydown would do the honours of the house." Miss Celandina left the room; and they learned in conversation with Mr. Derrydown, that the latter, finding his case hopeless with Anthelia, had discovered some good reasons in an old ballad for placing his affections where they would be more welcome; he had therefore thrown himself at the feet of Miss Celandina Paperstamp; the young lady's father, having inquired into Mr. Derrydown's fortune, had concluded, from the answer he received, that it would be a very *good match* for his daughter; and the day was already definitively arranged on which Miss Celandina Paperstamp was to be metamorphosed into Mrs. Derrydown.

Mr. Derrydown informed them, that they would not see Mr. Paperstamp till dinner, as he was closeted in close conference with Mr. Feathernest, Mr. Vamp, Mr. Killthedead, and Mr. Anyside Antijack,[2] a very important personage just arrived from abroad on the occasion of a letter from Mr. Mystic of Cimmerian Lodge, denouncing an approaching period of public light, which had filled Messieurs Paperstamp, Feathernest, Vamp, Killthedead, and Antijack, with the deepest dismay; and they were now holding a consultation on the best means to be adopted for totally and finally extinguishing the light of the human understanding. " I am excluded from the council," proceeded Mr. Derrydown, " and it is their intention to keep me altogether in the dark on the subject; but I shall wait very patiently for the operation of the second bottle, when the wit will be out of the brain, and the cat will be out of the bag."

[1] Wordsworth was the poet of the celandine. Peacock had sent one in a letter to Shelley who had written of the withered flower (see W. E. Peck: *Shelley, His Life and Work*, 1927, Vol. I, p. 477):

> " A type of that whence I and thou
> Are thus familiar, Celandine—
> A deathless poet whose young prime
> Was serene as thine
> But he is changed and withered now,
> Fallen on a cold and evil time." G.

[2] Canning. A reference to the *Anti-Jacobin* newspaper. G.

" Is that picture a family piece ? " said Mr. Fax.

" I hardly know," said Mr. Derrydown, " whether there is any relationship between Mr. Paperstamp and the persons there represented ; but there is at least a very intimate connexion. The old woman in the scarlet cloak is the illustrious Mother Goose—the two children playing at see-saw are Margery Daw and Tommy with his Banbury cake—the little boy and girl, the one with a broken pitcher, and the other with a broken head, are little Jack and Jill : the house, at the door of which the whole party is grouped, is the famous house that Jack built ; you see the clock through the window, and the mouse running up it, as in that sublime strain of immortal genius, entitled Dickery Dock : and the boy in the corner is little Jack Horner eating his Christmas pie. The latter is one of the most splendid examples on record of the admirable practical doctrine of ' taking care of number one,' and he is therefore in double favour with Mr. Paperstamp, for his excellence as a pattern of moral and political wisdom, and for the beauty of the poetry in which his great achievement of extracting a plum from the Christmas pie is celebrated. Mr. Paperstamp, Mr. Feathernest, Mr. Vamp, Mr. Killthedead, and Mr. Anyside Antijack, are unanimously agreed that the Christmas pie in question is a type and symbol of the public purse ; and as that is a pie in which every one of them has a finger, they look with great envy and admiration on little Jack Horner, who extracted a *plum* from it, and who I believe haunts their dreams with his pie and his plum, saying, ' Go, and do thou likewise ! ' "

The secret council broke up, and Mr. Paperstamp entering with his four compeers, bade the new-comers welcome to Mainchance Villa, and introduced to them Mr. Anyside Antijack. Mr. Paperstamp did not much like Mr. Forester's modes of thinking ; indeed he disliked them the more, from their having once been his own ; but a man of large landed property was well worth a little civility, as there was no knowing what turn affairs might take, what party might come into place, and who might have the cutting up of the Christmas pie.

They now adjourned to dinner, during which, as usual, little was said, and much was done. When the wine began to circulate, Mr. Feathernest held forth for some time in praise of himself ; and by the assistance of a little smattering in Mr. Mystic's synthetical logic, proved himself to be a model of taste, genius, consistency, and public virtue. This was too good an example to be thrown away ; and Mr. Paperstamp followed it up with a very lofty encomium on his own virtues and talents, declaring that he did not believe so great a genius, or so amiable a man, as himself, Peter Paypaul Paperstamp, Esquire, of Mainchance Villa, had appeared in the world since the days of Jack the Giant-killer, whose *coat of darkness* he hoped would become the costume of all the rising generation, whenever adequate provision should be made for the whole people to be taught and trained.

Mr. Vamp, Mr. Killthedead, and Mr. Anyside Antijack, were all very loud in their encomiums of the wine, which Mr. Paperstamp observed had been tasted for him by his friend Mr. Feathernest, who was a great connoisseur in " Sherris sack."

Mr. Derrydown was very intent on keeping the bottle in motion, in the hope of bringing the members of the criticopoetical council into that state of blind self-love, when the great vacuum of the head, in which brain was, like Mr. Harris's indefinite article,[1] *supplied by negation*, would be inflated with œnogen gas,[2] or, in other words, with the fumes of wine, the effect of which, according to psychological chemistry, is, after filling up every chink and crevice of the cranial void, to evolve through the labial valve, bringing with it all the secrets both of memory and anticipation, which had been carefully laid up in the said chinks and crevices. This state at length arrived ; and Mr. Derrydown, to quicken its operation, contrived to pick a quarrel with Mr. Vamp, who being naturally very testy and waspish, poured out upon him a torrent of invectives, to the infinite amusement of Mr. Derrydown, who, however, affecting to be angry, said to him in a tragical tone,

"Thus in dregs of folly sunk,
Art thou, miscreant, mad or drunk ?
Cups intemperate always teach
Virulent abusive speech."[3]

This produced a general cry of Chair ! chair ! Mr. Paperstamp

---

[1] See Note, p. 220. G.

[2] A nonce-word, invented by Peacock from the Greek for wine, to sound like oxygen. G.

[3] Cottle's *Edda*, or, as the author calls it, *Translation* of the *Edda*, which is a misnomer. [P.]

called Mr. Derrydown to order.   The latter apologized with as much gravity as he could assume, and said, to make amends for his warmth, he would give them a toast, and pronounced accordingly : " Your scheme for extinguishing the light of the human understanding : may it meet the success it merits."

MR. ANYSIDE ANTIJACK.   Nothing can be in a more hopeful train. We must set the alarmists at work, as in the days of the Antijacobin war : when, to be sure, we had one or two honest men among our opposers [1]—(*Mr. Feathernest and Mr. Paperstamp smiled and bowed*) —though they were for the most part ill read in history, and ignorant of human nature.[2]

MR. FEATHERNEST AND MR. PAPERSTAMP.   How, Sir ?

MR. ANYSIDE ANTIJACK.   For the most part, observe me.   Of course, I do not include my quondam antagonists, and now very dear friends, Mr. Paperstamp and Mr. Feathernest, who have altered their minds, as the sublime Burke altered his mind,[3] from the most disinterested motives.

MR. FORESTER.   Yet there are some persons, and those not the lowest in the scale of moral philosophy, who have called the sublime Burke a pensioned apostate.

MR. VAMP.   Moral philosophy !   Every man who talks of moral philosophy is a thief and a rascal, and will never make any scruple of seducing his neighbour's wife, or stealing his neighbour's property.[4]

MR. FORESTER.   You can prove that assertion, of course ?

MR. VAMP.   Prove it !   The editor of the Legitimate Review required to prove an assertion !

MR. ANYSIDE ANTIJACK.   The church is in danger !

MR. FORESTER.   I confess I do not see how the church is endangered by a simple request to prove the asserted necessary connexion between the profession of moral philosophy and the practice of robbery.

[1] *Quarterly Review*, No. xxxi. p. 237.   [P.]
[2] *Ibid.*   [P.]   [3] *Ibid.* p. 252.   [P.]   [4] *Ibid.* p. 227.   [P.]

MR. ANYSIDE ANTIJACK.   For your satisfaction, Sir, and from my disposition to oblige you, as you are a gentleman of family and fortune, I will prove it.   Every moral philosopher discards the creed and commandments : [1] the sixth commandment says, Thou shalt not steal ; therefore, every moral philosopher is a thief.

MR. FEATHERNEST, MR. KILLTHEDEAD, AND MR. PAPERSTAMP. Nothing can be more logical.   The church is in danger !   The church is in danger !

MR. VAMP.   Keep up that.   It is an infallible tocsin for rallying all the old women in the country about us when every thing else fails.

MR. VAMP, MR. FEATHERNEST, MR. PAPERSTAMP, MR. KILLTHEDEAD, AND MR. ANYSIDE ANTIJACK.   The church is in danger ! the church is in danger !

MR. FORESTER.   I am very well aware that the time has been when the voice of reason could be drowned by clamour, and by rallying round the banners of corruption and delusion a mass of blind and bigoted prejudices, that had no real connexion with the political question which it was the object to cry down : but I see with pleasure that those days are gone.   The people read and think ; their eyes are opened ; they know that all their grievances arise from the pressure of taxation far beyond their means, from the fictitious circulation of paper-money, and from the corrupt and venal state of popular representation.   These facts lie in a very small compass ; and till you can reason them out of this knowledge, you may vociferate " The church is in danger " for ever, without a single unpaid voice to join in the outcry.

MR. FEATHERNEST.   My friend Mr. Mystic holds that it is a very bad thing for the people to read : so it certainly is.   Oh for the happy ignorance of former ages ! when the people were dolts, and knew themselves to be so.[2]   An ignorant man judging from instinct, judges much better than a man who reads, and is consequently misinformed.[3]

MR. VAMP.   Unless he reads the Legitimate Review.

[1] *Ibid.* p. 227.   [P.]   [2] *Ibid.* p. 226.   [P.]   [3] *Ibid.*   [P.]

MR. PAPERSTAMP. Darkness! darkness! Jack the Giant-killer's coat of darkness! That is your only wear.

MR. ANYSIDE ANTIJACK. There was a time when we could lead the people any way, and make them join with all their lungs in the yell of war : then they were people of sound judgment, and of honest and honourable feelings : [1] but when they pretend to feel the pressure of personal suffering, and to read and think about its causes and remedies—such impudence is intolerable.

MR. FAX. Are they not the same people still? If they were capable of judging then, are they not capable of judging now?

MR. ANYSIDE ANTIJACK. By no means : they are only capable of judging when they see with our eyes ; then they see straight forward ; when they pretend to use their own, they squint. [2] They saw with our eyes in the beginning of the Antijacobin war. They would have determined on that war, if it had been decided by universal suffrage. [3]

MR. FAX. Why was not the experiment tried?

MR. ANYSIDE ANTIJACK. It was not convenient. But they were in a most amiable ferment of intolerant loyalty. [4]

MR. FORESTER. Of which the proof is to be found in the immortal Gagging Bills, by which that intolerant loyalty was coerced.

MR. ANYSIDE ANTIJACK. The Gagging Bills? Hem! ha! What shall we say to that?—(*To Mr. Vamp.*)

MR. VAMP. Say? The church is in danger!

MR. FEATHERNEST, MR. PAPERSTAMP, MR. KILLTHEDEAD, AND MR. ANYSIDE ANTIJACK. The church is in danger! the church is in danger!

MR. FORESTER. Why was a war undertaken to prevent revolution, if all the people of this country were so well fortified in loyalty? Did they go to war for the purpose of forcibly preventing themselves from following a bad example against their own will? For this is what your argument seems to imply.

[1] *Quarterly Review*, No. xxxi. p. 236. [P.]
[2] *Ibid.* p. 226. [P.]   [3] *Ibid.* p. 228. [P.]   [4] *Ibid.* [P.]

MR. FAX. That the people were in a certain degree of ferment, is true : but it required a great deal of management and delusion to turn that ferment into the channel of foreign war.

MR. ANYSIDE ANTIJACK. Well, Sir, and there was no other way to avoid domestic reform, which every man who desires is a ruffian, a scoundrel, and an incendiary,[1] as much so as those two rascals Rousseau and Voltaire, who were the trumpeters of Hebert and Marat.[2] Reform, Sir, is not to be thought of ; we have been at war twenty-five years to prevent it ; and to have it after all, would be very hard. We have got the national debt instead of it : in my opinion a very pretty substitute.

MR. DERRYDOWN *sings*.

> And I'll hang on thy neck, my love, my love,
> And I'll hang on thy neck for aye !
> And closer and closer I'll press thee, my love,
> Until my *dying day*.

MR. ANYSIDE ANTIJACK. I am happy to reflect that the silly question of reform will have very few supporters in the Honourable House : but few as they are, the number would be lessened, if all who come into Parliament by means which that question attempts to stigmatize, would abstain from voting upon it. Undoubtedly such practices are scandalous, as being legally, and therefore morally wrong : but it is false that any evil to the legislature arises from them.[3]

MR. FORESTER. Perhaps not, Sir ; but very great evil arises through them from the legislature to the people. Your admission, that they are legally, and *therefore* morally wrong, implies a very curious method of deriving morality from law ; but I suspect there is much immorality that is perfectly legal, and much legality that is supremely immoral. But these practices, you admit, are both legally and morally wrong ; yet you call it a silly question to propose their cessation ; and you assert, that all who wish to abolish them, all who wish to abolish illegal and immoral practices, are ruffians, scoundrels, and incendiaries.

[1] *Ibid*. No. xxxi. p. 273 *et passim*. [P.] [2] *Ibid*. p. 258. [P.]
[3] *Ibid*. [P.]

MR. KILLTHEDEAD. Yes, and madmen moreover, and villains.[1] We are all upon gunpowder! The insane and the desperate are scattering firebrands![2] We shall all be blown up in a body:

[1] *Quarterly Review*, No. xxxi. p. 249. It is curious, that in the fourth article of the same number, from which I have borrowed so many exquisite passages, the reviewers are very angry that certain "scandalous and immoral practices" in the island of Wahoo are not reformed : but certainly, according to the logic of these reviewers, the government of Wahoo is entitled to look upon *them* in the light of "ruffians, scoundrels, incendiaries, firebrands, madmen, and villains ; " since all these hard names belong of primary right to those who propose the reformation of "scandalous and immoral practices!" The people of Wahoo, it appears, are very much addicted to drunkenness and debauchery ; and the reviewers, in the plenitude of their wisdom, recommend that a few clergymen should be sent out to them, by way of mending their morals. It does not appear, whether King Tamaahmaah is a king by *divine right* ; but we must take it for granted that he is not ; as, otherwise, the Quarterly Reviewers would either not admit that there were any "scandalous and immoral practices" under his government, or, if they did admit them, they would not be such "incendiaries, madmen, and villains," as to advocate their reformation. There are some circumstances, however, which are conclusive against the *legitimacy* of King Tamaahmaah, which are these : that he is a man of great "feeling, energy, and steadiness of conduct ; " that he "goes about among his people to learn their wants ; " and that he has "prevented the recurrence of those horrid murders" which disgraced the reigns of his predecessors : from which it is obvious that he has neither put to death brave and generous men, who surrendered themselves under the faith of treaties, nor re-established a fallen Inquisition, nor sent those to whom he owed his crown, to the dungeon and the galleys.

In the tenth article of the same number, the reviewers pour forth the bitterness of their gall against Mr. Warden of the Northumberland, who has detected them in promulgating much gross and foolish falsehood concerning the captive Napoleon. They labour most assiduously to *impeach his veracity* and to *discredit his judgment*. On the first point, it is sufficient evidence of the truth of his statements, that the Quarterly Reviewers contradict them : but, on the second, they accuse him, among other misdemeanours, of having called their *Review* " *a respectable work* ! " which certainly *discredits his judgment* completely. [P.]

[2] *Ibid.*—The reader will be reminded of *Croaker* in the fourth act of the *Good-natured Man* : " Blood and gunpowder in every line of it. Blown up ! murderous dogs ! all blown up ! (*Reads.*) ' Our pockets are low, and money we must have.' Ay, there's the reason : they'll blow us up *because they have got low pockets*. . . . Perhaps this moment I'm treading on lighted matches, blazing brimstone, and barrels of gunpowder. They are preparing to blow me up into the clouds. Murder ! . . . Here, John, Nicodemus, search the house. Look into the cellars, to see if there be any combustibles below, and above in the apartments, that no matches be thrown in at the windows. *Let all the fires be put out,* and let the *engine* be

sinecures, rotten boroughs, secret-service-men, and the whole *honourable band of gentlemen pensioners*, will all be blown up in a body ! *A stand ! a stand ! it is time to make a stand against popular encroachment !*

MR. VAMP, MR. FEATHERNEST, AND MR. PAPERSTAMP. The church is in danger !

MR. ANYSIDE ANTIJACK. Here is the great blunderbuss that is to blow the whole nation to atoms ! the *Spencean* blunderbuss ! [1]— (*Saying these words, he produced a pop-gun from his pocket*,[2] *and shot off a paper pellet in the ear of Mr. Paperstamp*,

> " *Who in a kind of study sate*
> *Denominated brown ;* " [3]

drawn out in the yard, to *play upon the house* in case of necessity."— *Croaker* was a deep politician. The *engine* to *play* upon the *house* : mark that ! [P.] [By Goldsmith. Peacock's quotation is at the expense of Croaker, the *Quarterly* reviewer. G.]

[1] Thomas Spence, 1750–1814, an early communist, propounded a plan for land nationalisation. Canning exaggerated the importance of Spence's plan and suggested that a shot had been fired at the Regent's carriage on the opening of Parliament when actually a stone had been thrown. G.

[2] This illustration of the old fable of the mouse and the mountain falls short of an exhibition in the Honourable House, on the 29th of January 1817 ; when Mr. Canning, amidst a tremendous denunciation of the parliamentary reformers, and a rhetorical chaos of storms, whirlwinds, rising suns, and twilight assassins, produced in proof of his charges— *Spence's Plan !* which was received with an *éclat* of laughter on one side, and shrugs of surprise, disappointment, and disapprobation, on the other. I can find but one parallel for the Right Honourable Gentleman's dismay :

> So having said, awhile he stood, expecting
> Their universal shout and high applause
> To fill his ear ; when contrary he hears
> On all sides, from innumerable tongues,
> A dismal universal hiss, the sound
> Of public scorn. *Paradise Lost*, x. 504.

This Spencean chimæra, which is the very foolishness of folly, and which was till lately invisible to the naked eye of the political entomologist, has since been subjected to a *lens* of *extraordinary power*, under which, like an insect in a microscope, it has appeared a formidable and complicated monster, all bristles, scales, and claws, with a " husk about it like a chest-nut : " *horridus, in jaculis, et pelle Libystidis ursae !* [P.] [Virgil : *Æn.* V. 37. " Bristling with javelins and girt with the skin of a Libyan bear." G.]

[3] Quotation untraced. G.

*which made the latter spring up in sudden fright, to the irremediable
perdition of a decanter of "Sherris sack," over which Mr. Feathernest
lamented bitterly.)*

MR. FORESTER. I do not see what connexion the Spencean
theory, the impracticable chimæra of an obscure herd of fanatics, has
with the great national question of parliamentary reform.

MR. ANYSIDE ANTIJACK. Sir, you may laugh at this pop-gun, but
you will find it the mallet of Thor.[1] The Spenceans are far more
respectable than the parliamentary reformers, and have a more
distinct and intelligible system ! ! ![2]

MR. VAMP. Bravo ! bravo ! bravo ! There is not another man in
our corps with brass enough to make such an assertion, but Mr.
Anyside Antijack. (*Reiterated shouts of Bravo! from Mr. Vamp,
Mr. Feathernest, Mr. Paperstamp, and Mr. Killthedead.*)

MR. KILLTHEDEAD. Make out that, and our job is done.

MR. ANYSIDE ANTIJACK. Make it out ! Nonsense ! I shall take
it for granted : I shall set up the Spencean plan as a more sensible
plan than that of the parliamentary reformers : then knock down the
former, and argue against the latter, *à fortiori*.—(*The shouts of Bravo!
here became perfectly deafening, the criticopoetical corps being by this
time much more than half-seas-over.*)

MR. KILLTHEDEAD. The members for rotten boroughs are the most
independent members in the Honourable House, and the representatives of most constituents least so.[3]

MR. FAX. How will you prove that ?

MR. KILLTHEDEAD. By calling the former gentlemen, and the
latter, mob representatives.[4]

MR. VAMP. Nothing can be more logical.

MR. FAX. Do you call that logic ?

[1] *Quarterly Review*, No. xxxi. p. 271. [P.]
[2] *Ibid.* [P.]   [3] *Ibid.* p. 258. [P.]   [4] *Ibid.* [P.]

MR. VAMP.   Excellent logic.   At least it will pass for such with our readers.

MR. ANYSIDE ANTIJACK.   We, and those who think with us, are the only wise and good men.[1]

MR. FORESTER.   May I take the liberty to inquire, what you mean by a wise and a good man ?

MR. ANYSIDE ANTIJACK.   A wise man is he who looks after the one thing needful ; and a good man, is he who has it.   The acme of wisdom and goodness in conjunction, consists in appropriating as much as possible of the public money ; and saying to those from whose pockets it is taken, " I am perfectly satisfied with things as they are.   Let *well* alone ! "

MR. PAPERSTAMP.   We shall make out a very good case ; but you must not forget to call the present public distress an awful dispensation : [2] a little pious cant goes a great way towards turning the thoughts of men from the dangerous and jacobinical propensity of looking into moral and political causes, for moral and political effects.

MR. FAX.   But the moral and political causes are now too obvious, and too universally known, to be obscured by any such means.   All the arts and eloquence of corruption may be overthrown by the enumeration of these simple words : boroughs, taxes, and paper-money.

MR. ANYSIDE ANTIJACK.   Paper-money !   What, is the ghost of bullion abroad ? [3]

MR. FORESTER.   Yes ! and till you can make the buried substance burst the paper cerements of its sepulchre, its ghost will continue to walk like the ghost of Cæsar, saying to the desolated nation : " I am thy evil spirit ! " [4]

MR. ANYSIDE ANTIJACK.   I must say, I am very sorry to find a gentleman like you, taking the part of the swinish multitude, who are only fit for beasts of burden, to raise subsistence for their betters,

---

[1] *Ibid.* p. 273.   [P.]   [2] *Ibid.* p. 276.   [P.]   [3] *Ibid.* p. 260.   [P.]
[4] *Julius Cæsar*, Act IV, Sc. 3.   G.

pay taxes for placemen, and recruit the army and navy for the benefit of legitimacy, divine right, the Jesuits, the Pope, the Inquisition,
and the Virgin Mary's petticoat.

MR. PAPERSTAMP. Hear! hear! hear! Hear the voice which the
stream of Tendency is uttering for elevation of our thought!

MR. FORESTER. It was once said by a poet, whose fallen state none
can more bitterly lament than I do :

> We shall exult if they who rule the land
> Be men who hold its many blessings dear,
> Wise, upright, valiant ; not a venal band,
> Who are to judge of danger which they fear,
> And honour which they do not understand.[1]

MR. FEATHERNEST. Poets, Sir, are not amenable to censure,
however frequently their political opinions may exhibit marks of
inconsistency.[2] The Muse, as a French author says, is a mere
étourdie, a *folâtre* who may play at her option on heath or on turf, and
transfer her song at pleasure, from Hampden to Ferdinand, and from
Washington to Louis.

MR. FORESTER. If a poet be contented to consider himself in the
light of a merry-andrew, be it so.   But if he assume the garb of moral
austerity, and pour forth against corruption and oppression the
language of moral indignation, there would at least be some decency,
if, when he changes sides, he would let the world see that conversion
and promotion have not gone hand in hand.

MR. FEATHERNEST. What decency might be in that, I know not :
but of this I am very certain, that there would be no wisdom in it.

MR. ANYSIDE ANTIJACK. No! no! there would be no wisdom in it.

---

[1] Wordsworth's Sonnet, *November 1806*. The last two lines were taken
from the following passage in Fulke Greville's *Life of Sir Philip Sidney*,
1652 :
   " In which view, nature guiding his eyes, first to his Native Country,
he found greatness of worth and place counterpoysed there by the arts of
power and favor. The stirring spirits sent abroad as fewell, to keep the
flame far off ; and the effeminate made judges of danger which they fear,
and honor which they understand not."   G.
[2] *Quarterly Review*, No. xxxi. p. 192. [P.]

MR. FEATHERNEST.   Sir, I am a wise and a good man : mark that, Sir ; ay, and an honourable man.

MR. VAMP.   " So are we all, all honourable men ! " [1]

MR. ANYSIDE ANTIJACK.   And we will stick by one another with heart and hand——

MR. KILLTHEDEAD.   To make a stand against popular encroachment——

MR. FEATHERNEST.   To bring back the glorious ignorance of the feudal ages——

MR. PAPERSTAMP.   To rebuild the mystic temples of venerable superstition——

MR. VAMP.   To extinguish, totally and finally, the light of the human understanding——

MR. ANYSIDE ANTIJACK.   And to get all we can for our trouble !

MR. FEATHERNEST.   So we will all say.

MR. PAPERSTAMP.   And so we will all sing.

QUINTETTO.

MR. FEATHERNEST, MR. VAMP, MR. KILLTHEDEAD, MR. PAPERSTAMP,
AND MR. ANYSIDE ANTIJACK.

To the tune of " *Turning, turning, turning, as the wheel goes round.*"

RECITATIVE.   MR. PAPERSTAMP.

Jack Horner's CHRISTMAS PIE my learned nurse
Interpreted to mean the *public purse.*
From thence a *plum* he drew.   O happy Horner !
Who would not be ensconced in thy snug corner ?

THE FIVE.

While round the public board all eagerly we linger,
For what we can get we will try, try, try :
And we'll all have a finger, a finger, a finger,
We'll all have a finger in the CHRISTMAS PIE.

---

[1] *Julius Cæsar*, Act III, Sc. 2.   G.

MR. FEATHERNEST.

By my own poetic laws, I'm a dealer in applause
For those who don't deserve it, but will buy, buy, buy :
So round the court I linger, and thus I get a finger,
A finger, finger, finger in the CHRISTMAS PIE.

THE FIVE.

And we'll all have a finger, a finger, a finger,
We'll all have a finger in the CHRISTMAS PIE.

MR. VAMP.

My share of pie to win, I will dash through thick and thin,
And philosophy and liberty shall fly, fly, fly :
And truth and taste shall know, that their everlasting foe
Has a finger, finger, finger in the CHRISTMAS PIE.

THE FIVE.

And we'll all have a finger, a finger, a finger,
We'll all have a finger in the CHRISTMAS PIE.

MR. KILLTHEDEAD.

I'll make my verses rattle with the din of war and battle,
For war doth increase sa-la-ry, ry, ry :
And I'll shake the public ears with the triumph of Algiers,[1]
And thus I'll get a finger in the CHRISTMAS PIE.

THE FIVE.

And we'll all have a finger, a finger, a finger,
We'll all have a finger in the CHRISTMAS PIE.

MR. PAPERSTAMP.

And while you thrive by ranting, I'll try my luck at canting,
And scribble verse and prose all so dry, dry, dry :
And Mystic's patent smoke public intellect shall choke,
And we'll all have a finger in the CHRISTMAS PIE.

THE FIVE.

We'll all have a finger, a finger, a finger,
We'll all have a finger in the CHRISTMAS PIE.

MR. ANYSIDE ANTIJACK.

My tailor is so clever, that my coat will turn for ever,
And take any colour you can dye, dye, dye :
For all my earthly wishes are among the loaves and fishes,
And to have my little finger in the CHRISTMAS PIE.

---

[1] The naval demonstration, under Lord Exmouth, against the Barbary
pirates, 1816. G.

THE FIVE.
And we'll all have a finger, a finger, a finger,
We'll all have a finger in the CHRISTMAS PIE.

CHAPTER XL

THE HOPES OF THE WORLD

THE mountain-roads being now buried in snow, they were compelled,
on leaving Mainchance Villa, to follow the most broad and beaten
track, and they entered on a turnpike road which led in the direction
of the sea.

" I no longer wonder," said Mr. Fax, " that men in general are so
much disposed, as I have found them, to look with supreme contempt
on the literary character, seeing the abject servility and venality by
which it is so commonly debased." [1]

MR. FORESTER.   What then becomes of the hopes of the world,
which you have admitted to consist entirely in the progress of
mind, allowing, as you must allow, the incontrovertible fact of the
physical deterioration of the human race ?

MR. FAX.   When I speak of the mind, I do not allude either to
poetry or to periodical criticism, nor in any great degree to physical

---

[1] " To scatter praise or blame without regard to justice, is to destroy the
distinction of good and evil.   Many have no other test of actions than
general opinion ; and all are so far influenced by a sense of reputation, that
they are often restrained by fear of reproach, and excited by hope of
honour, when other principles have lost their power ; nor can any species
of prostitution promote general depravity more, than that which destroys
the force of praise by showing that it may be acquired without deserving it,
and which, by setting free the active and ambitious from the dread of
infamy, lets loose the rapacity of power, and weakens the only authority
by which greatness is controlled.   What credit can he expect who professes
himself the hireling of vanity however profligate, and without shame or
scruple celebrates the worthless, dignifies the mean, and gives to the
corrupt, licentious, and oppressive, the ornaments which ought only to add
grace to truth, and loveliness to innocence ?   EVERY OTHER KIND OF
ADULTERATION, HOWEVER SHAMEFUL, HOWEVER MISCHIEVOUS, IS LESS
DETESTABLE THAN THE CRIME OF COUNTERFEITING CHARACTERS, AND
FIXING THE STAMP OF LITERARY SANCTION UPON THE DROSS AND REFUSE
OF THE WORLD."—*Rambler*, No. 136.   [P.]   [Dr Johnson.   G.]

science ; but I rest my hopes on the very same basis with Mr. Mystic's fear—the general diffusion of moral and political truth.

MR. FORESTER. For poetry, its best days are gone. Homer, Shakespeare, and Milton, will return no more.

MR. FAX. Lucretius we yet may hope for.[1]

MR. FORESTER. Not till superstition and prejudice have been shorn of a much larger portion of their power. If Lucretius should arise among us in the present day, exile or imprisonment would be his infallible portion. We have yet many steps to make, before we shall arrive at the liberality and toleration of Tiberius ! [2] And as to physical science, though it does in some measure weaken the dominion of mental error, yet I fear, where it proves itself, in one instance, the friend of human liberty, it will be found in ninety-nine, the slave of corruption and luxury.

MR. FAX. In many cases, science is both morally and politically neutral, and its speculations have no connexion whatever with the business of life.

MR. FORESTER. It is true ; and such speculations are often called sublime : though the sublimity of uselessness passes my comprehension. But the neutrality is only apparent : for it has in these cases the real practical effect, and a most pernicious one it is, of withdrawing some of the highest and most valuable minds from the only path of real utility, which I agree with you to be that of moral and political knowledge, to pursuits of no more real importance than that of keeping a dozen eggs at a time dancing one after another in the air.

MR. FAX. If it be admitted on the one hand, that the progress of luxury has kept pace with that of physical science, it must be acknowledged on the other, that superstition has decayed in at least an equal proportion ; and I think it cannot be denied that the world is a gainer by the exchange.

[1] The subject of Lucretius's *De Rerum Natura* seemed one for the nineteenth century ; this forecast was later fulfilled by Tennyson. G.

[2] Deorum injurias diis curae.—*Tiberius apud Tacit. Ann. I.* 73. [P.] [" Let the Gods deal with those who do them wrong." G.]

MR. FORESTER. The decay of superstition is immeasurably beneficial: but the growth of luxury is not therefore the less pernicious. It is lamentable to reflect that *there is most indigence in the richest countries ;* [1] and that the increase of superfluous enjoyment in the few, is counterbalanced by the proportionate diminution of comfort in the many. Splendid equipages and sumptuous dwellings are far from being symbols of general prosperity. The palace of luxurious indolence is much rather the symbol of a thousand hovels, by the labours and privations of whose wretched inhabitants that baleful splendour is maintained. Civilization, vice, and folly grow old together. Corruption begins among the higher orders, and from them descends to the people ; so that in every nation the ancient nobility is the first to exhibit symptoms of corporeal and mental

---

[1] " Besides all these evils of modern times which I have mentioned, there is in some countries of Europe, and particularly in England, another evil peculiar to civilized countries, but quite unknown in barbarous nations. The evil I mean is *indigence,* and the reader will be surprised when I tell him that it is *greatest in the richest countries* ; and, therefore, in England, which I believe is the richest country in Europe, there is more indigence than in any other ; for the number of people that are there maintained on public or private charity, and who may therefore be called *beggars,* is prodigious. What proportion they may bear to the whole people, I have never heard computed : but I am sure it must be very great. And I am afraid in those countries they call rich, indigence is not confined to the lower sort of people, but extends even to the better sort : for such is the effect of wealth in a nation, that (however paradoxical it may appear) it does at least make all men poor and indigent ; the lower sort through idleness and debauchery, the better sort through luxury, vanity, and extravagant expense. Now I would desire to know from the greatest admirers of modern times, who maintain that the human race is not degenerated but rather improved, whether they know any other source of human misery, besides vice, disease, and indigence, and whether these three are not in the greatest abundance in the rich and flourishing country of England ? I would further ask these gentlemen, whether in the cities of the ancient world there were poor's houses, hospitals, infirmaries, and those other receptacles of indigence and disease, which we see in the modern cities ? And whether in the streets of ancient Athens and Rome there were so many objects of disease, deformity, and misery to be seen, as in our streets, besides those which are concealed from public view in the houses above mentioned. In later times, indeed, in those cities, when the corruption of manners was almost as great as among us, some such things might have been seen, as we are sure they were to be seen in Constantinople, under the later Greek Emperors."—*Ancient Metaphysics,* vol. iii. p. 194.
[P.]

degeneracy, and to show themselves unfit both for council and war.
If you recapitulate the few titled names that will adorn the history
of the present times, you will find that almost all of them are new
creations. The corporeal decay of mankind I hold to be undeniable :
the increase of general knowledge I allow : but reason is of slow
growth ; and if men in general only become more corrupt as they
become more learned, the progress of literature will oppose no
adequate counterpoise to that of avarice, luxury, and disease.

MR. FAX. Certainly, the progress of reason is slow, but the ground
which it has once gained it never abandons. The interest of rulers,
and the prejudices of the people, are equally hostile to every thing
that comes in the shape of innovation ; but all that now wears the
strongest sanction of antiquity was once received with reluctance
under the semblance of novelty : and that reason, which in the
present day can scarcely obtain a footing from the want of precedents, will grow with the growth of years, and become a precedent
in its turn.[1]

MR. FORESTER. Reason may be diffused in society, but it is only
in minds which *have courage enough to despise prejudice, and virtue
enough to love truth only for itself*,[2] that its seeds will germinate into
wholesome and vigorous life. The love of truth is the most noble
quality of human intellect, the most delightful in the interchange of
private confidence, the most important in the direction of those
speculations which have public happiness for their aim. Yet of all
qualities this is the most rare : it is the Phœnix of the intellectual
world. In private intercourse, how very very few are they whose
assertions carry conviction ! How much petty deception, paltry
equivocation, hollow profession, smiling malevolence, and polished
hypocrisy, combine to make a desert and a solitude of what is called
society ! How much empty pretence, and simulated patriotism, and

[1] " Omnia, quae nunc vetustissima creduntur, nova fuere. Inveterascet
hoc quoque : et, quod hodie exemplis tuemur, inter exempla erit."—
Tacitus, *Ann. XI.* 24. [P.] [" All that we now look upon as of the greatest
antiquity, once was new. This too will grow old, and that which we now
defend by addressing precedents, will one day itself be appealed to as a
precedent." G.]
[2] Drummond's *Academical Questions*—Preface, p. 4. [P.]

shameless venality, and unblushing dereliction of principle, and
clamorous recrimination, and daring imposture, and secret cabal,
and mutual undermining of " Honourable Friends," render utterly
loathsome and disgusting the theatre of public life ! How much
timid deference to vulgar prejudice, how much misrepresentation of
the motives of conscientious opponents, how many appeals to
unreflecting passion, how much assumption of groundless hypotheses,
how many attempts to darken the clearest light and entangle the
simplest clue, render not only nugatory but pernicious the speculations of moral and political reason ! pernicious, inasmuch as it is
better for the benighted traveller to remain stationary in darkness,
than to follow an *ignis fatuus* through the fen ! Falsehood is the
great vice of the age : falsehood of heart, falsehood of mind, falsehood
of every form and mode of intellect and intercourse : so that it is
hardly possible *to find a man of worth and goodness of whom to make
a friend : but he who does find such an one will have more enjoyment
of friendship, than in a better age; for he will be doubly fond of him,
and will love him as Hamlet does Horatio, and with him retiring, and
getting as it were under the shelter of a wall, will let the storm of life
blow over him.*[1]

MR. FAX. But that retirement must be consecrated to philosophical labour, or, however delightful to the individuals, it will be
treason to the public cause. Be the world as bad as it may, it would
necessarily be much worse if the votaries of truth and the children of
virtue were all to withdraw from its vortex, and leave it to itself. If
reason be progressive, however slowly, the wise and good have
sufficient encouragement to persevere ; and even if the doctrine of
deterioration be true, it is no less their duty to contribute all in their
power to retard its progress, by investigating its causes and remedies.

MR. FORESTER. Undoubtedly. But the progress of theoretical
knowledge has a most fearful counterpoise in the accelerated
depravation of practical morality. The frantic love of money, which
seems to govern our contemporaries to a degree unprecedented in the
history of man, paralyses the energy of independence, darkens the
light of reason, and blights the blossoms of love.

[1] *Ancient Metaphysics,* vol. iii. p. 280. [P.]

MR. FAX. The *amor sceleratus habendi* [1] is not peculiar either to our times or to civilized life. *Money you must have, no matter from whence,* is a sentence, if we may believe Euripides, as old as the heroic age : and *the monk Rubruquis says of the Tartars, that, as parents keep all their daughters till they can sell them, their maids are sometimes very stale before they are married.* [2]

MR. FORESTER. In that respect, then, I must acknowledge the Tartars and we are much on a par. It is a collateral question well worth considering, how far the security of property, which contributes so much to the diffusion of knowledge, and the permanence of happiness, is favourable to the growth of individual virtue ?

MR. FAX. Security of property tranquillizes the minds of men, and fits them to shine rather in speculation than in action. In turbulent and insecure states of society, when the fluctuations of power, or the incursions of predatory neighbours, hang like the sword of Damocles over the most flourishing possessions, friends are more dear to each other, mutual services and sacrifices are more useful and more necessary, the energies of heart and hand are continually called forth, and shining examples of the self-oblivious virtues are produced in the same proportion as mental speculation is unknown or disregarded : but our admiration of these virtues must be tempered by the remark, that they arise more from impulsive feeling than from reflective principle ; and that, where life and fortune hold by such a precarious tenure, the first may be risked, and the second abandoned, with much less effort than would be required for inferior sacrifices in more secure and tranquil times.

MR. FORESTER. Alas, my friend ! I would willingly see such virtues as do honour to human nature, without being very solicitous as to the comparative quantities of impulse and reflection in which they originate. If the security of property and the diffusion of general knowledge were attended with a corresponding increase of benevolence and *individual mental power,* no philanthropist could look with despondency on the prospects of the world : but I can discover no symptoms of either the one or the other. Insatiable

[1] " Accursed love of possession." Ovid : *Met.* I. 131. G.
[2] Malthus on *Population,* book i. chap. vii. [P.]

accumulators, overgrown capitalists, fatteners on public spoil, I cannot but consider as excrescences on the body politic, typical of disease and prophetic of decay : yet it is to these and such as these, that the poet tunes his harp, and the man of science consecrates his labours : it is for them that an enormous portion of the population is condemned to unhealthy manufactories, not less deadly but more lingering than the pestilence : it is for them that the world rings with lamentations, if the most trivial accident, the most transient sickness, the most frivolous disappointment befal them : but when the prisons swarm, when the workhouses overflow, when whole parishes declare themselves bankrupt, when thousands perish by famine in the wintry streets, where then is the poet, where is the man of science, where is the *elegant* philosopher ? The poet is singing hymns to the great ones of the world, the man of science is making discoveries for the adornment of their dwellings or the enhancement of their culinary luxuries, and the *elegant* philosopher is much too refined a personage to allow such vulgar subjects as the sufferings of the poor to interfere with his sublime speculations. *They are married, and cannot come !* [1]

MR. FAX. *Εψαυσας αλγεινοτατας εμοι μεριμνας !* [2] Those *elegant* philosophers are among the most fatal enemies to the advancement of moral and political knowledge : laborious triflers, profound investigators of nothing, everlasting talkers about taste and beauty, who see in the starving beggar only the picturesqueness of his rags, and in the ruined cottage only the harmonizing tints of moss, mildew, and stonecrop.

MR. FORESTER. We talk of public feeling and national sympathy. Our dictionaries may define those words, and our lips may echo them : but we must look for the realities among less enlightened nations. The Canadian savages cannot imagine the possibility of any individual in a community having a full meal, while another has but half an one : [3] still less could they imagine that one should have too much,

---

[1] See *Luke*, xiv. 20. G
[2] Sophocles, *Antigone*, 850. (Ed. Erfurdt.) [P.] [" Thou hast touched the care that pains me most." G.]
[3] " It is notorious, that towards one another the Indians are liberal in the extreme, and for ever ready to supply the deficiencies of their neighbours with any superfluities of their own. They have no idea of amassing wealth

while another had nothing. Theirs is that bond of brotherhood which nature weaves and civilization breaks, and from which, the older nations grow, the farther they recede.

MR. FAX. It cannot be otherwise. The state you have described, is adapted only to a small community, and to the infancy of human society. I shall make a very liberal concession to your views, if I admit it to be possible that the middle stage of the progress of man, is worse than either the point from which he started, or that at which he will arrive. But it is my decided opinion that we have passed that middle stage, and that every evil incident to the present condition of human society will be removed by the diffusion of moral and political knowledge, and the general increase of moral and political liberty. I contemplate with great satisfaction the rapid decay of many hoary absurdities, which a few transcendental hierophants of the venerable and the mysterious are labouring in vain to revive. I look with well-grounded confidence to a period when there will be neither slaves among the northern, nor monks among the southern Americans. The sun of freedom has risen over that great continent, with the certain promise of a glorious day. I form the best hopes for my own country, in the mental improvement of the people, whenever she shall breathe from the pressure of that preposterous system of finance which sooner or later must fall by its own weight.

MR. FORESTER. I apply to our system of finance, a fiction of the northern mythology. The ash of Yggdrasil overshadows the world : Ratatosk, the squirrel, sports in the branches : Nidhogger, the serpent, gnaws at the root.[1] The ash of Yggdrasil is the tree of national prosperity : Ratatosk the squirrel is the careless and unreflecting fundholder : Nidhogger the serpent is POLITICAL CORRUPTION, which will in time consume the root, and spread the branches on the dust. What will then become of the squirrel ?

---

for themselves individually ; and they wonder that persons can be found in any society so destitute of every generous sentiment, as to enrich themselves at the expense of others, and to live in ease and affluence regardless of the misery and wretchedness of members of the same community to which they themselves belong."—Weld's *Travels in Canada* ; *Letter XXXV.*

[1] See the *Edda* and the *Northern Antiquities.* [P.]   [P.]

MR. FAX. Ratatosk must look to himself: Nidhogger must be killed : and the ash of Yggdrasil will rise like a vegetable Phœnix to flourish again for ages.

Thus conversing, they arrived on the sea-shore, where we shall leave them to pursue their way, while we investigate the fate of Anthelia.

CHAPTER XLI

ALGA CASTLE

ANTHELIA had not ventured to resume her solitary rambles after her return from Onevote ; more especially as she anticipated the period when she should revisit her favourite haunts in the society of one congenial companion, whose presence would heighten the magic of their interest, and restore to them that feeling of security which her late adventure had destroyed. But as she was sitting in her library on the morning of her disappearance, she suddenly heard a faint and mournful cry like the voice of a child in distress. She rose, opened the window, and listened. She heard the sounds more distinctly. They seemed to ascend from that part of the dingle immediately beneath the shrubbery that fringed her windows. It was certainly the cry of a child. She immediately ran through the shrubbery and descended the rocky steps into the dingle, where she found a little boy tied to the stem of a tree, crying and sobbing as if his heart would break. Anthelia easily set him at liberty, and his grief passed away like an April shower. She asked who had the barbarity to treat him in such a manner. He said he could not tell— four strange men on horseback had taken him up on the common where his father lived, and brought him there and tied him to the tree, he could not tell why. Anthelia took his hand, and was leading him from the dingle, intending to send him home by Peter Gray, when the men who had made the little child their unconscious decoy, broke from their ambush, seized Anthelia, and taking effectual precautions to stifle her cries, placed her on one of their horses, and travelled with great rapidity along narrow and unfrequented ways, till they arrived at a solitary castle on the sea-shore, where they conveyed her to a splendid suite of apartments, and left her in solitude, locking, as they retired, the door of the outer room.

She was utterly unable to comprehend the motive of so extraordinary a proceeding, or to form any conjecture as to its probable result. An old woman of a very unmeaning physiognomy shortly after entered, to tender her services; but to all Anthelia's questions, she only replied with a shake of her head, and a smile which she meant to be very consolatory.

The old woman retired, and shortly after re-appeared with an elegant dinner, which Anthelia dismissed untouched. "There is no harm intended you, my sweet lady," said the old woman: "so pray don't starve yourself." Anthelia assured her she had no such intention, but had no appetite at that time; but she drank a glass of wine at the old woman's earnest entreaty.

In the evening the mystery was elucidated by a visit from Lord Anophel Achthar; who falling on his knees before her, entreated her to allow the violence of his passion to plead his pardon for a proceeding which nothing but the imminent peril of seeing her in the arms of a rival could have induced him to adopt. Anthelia replied, that if his object were to obtain her affections, he had taken the most effectual method to frustrate his own views; that if he thought by constraint and cruelty to obtain her hand without her affections, he might be assured that he would never succeed. Her heart, however, she candidly told him, was no longer in her power to dispose of; and she hoped, after this frank avowal, he would see the folly, if not the wickedness, of protracting his persecution.

He now, still on his knees, broke out into a rhapsody about love, and hope, and death, and despair, in which he developed the whole treasury of his exuberant and overflowing folly. He then expatiated on his expectations, and pointed out all the advantages of wealth and consequence attached to the title of Marchioness of Agaric, and concluded by saying, that she must be aware so important and decisive a measure had not been taken without the most grave and profound deliberation, and that he never could suffer her to make her exit from Alga Castle in any other character than that of Lady Achthar. He then left her to meditate on his heroic resolution.

The next day he repeated his visit—resumed his supplications—

reiterated his determination to persevere—and received from Anthelia the same reply. She endeavoured to reason with him on the injustice and absurdity of his proceedings ; but he told her the Reverend Mr. Grovelgrub and Mr. Feathernest the poet had taught him that all reasonings pretending to point out absurdity and injustice were manifestly jacobinical, which he, as one of the pillars of the state, was bound not to listen to.

He renewed his visits every day for a week, becoming, with every new visit, less humble and more menacing, and consequently more disagreeable to Anthelia, as the Reverend Mr. Grovelgrub, by whose instructions he acted, secretly foresaw and designed. The latter now undertook to plead his Lordship's cause, and set in a clear point of view to Anthelia the inflexibility of his Lordship's resolutions, which, properly expounded, could not fail to have due weight against the alternatives of protracted solitude and hopeless resistance.

The reverend gentleman, however, had other views than those he held out to Lord Anophel, and presented himself to Anthelia with an aspect of great commiseration. He said he was an unwilling witness of his Lordship's unjust proceedings, which he had done all in his power to prevent, and which had been carried into effect against his will. It was his firm intention to set her at liberty as soon as he could devise the means of doing so ; but all the outlets of Alga Castle were so guarded, that he had not yet been able to devise any feasible scheme for her escape : but it should be his sole study night and day to effect it.

Anthelia thanked him for his sympathy, and asked why he could not give notice to her friends of her situation ; which would accomplish the purpose at once. He replied, that Lord Anophel already mistrusted him, and that if anything of the kind were done, however secretly he might proceed, the suspicion would certainly fall upon him, and that he should then be a ruined man, as all his worldly hopes rested on the Marquis of Agaric. Anthelia offered to make him the utmost compensation for the loss of the Marquis of Agaric's favour ; but he said that was impossible, unless she could make him a bishop, as the Marquis of Agaric would do. His plan, he said, must be to effect her liberation, without seeming to be himself in any way whatever concerned in it ; and though he would willingly lose everything for her sake, yet he trusted she would not think ill of him for wishing to wait a few days, that he might try to devise the means of serving her without ruining himself.

He continued his daily visits of sympathy, sometimes amusing her with a hopeful scheme, at others detailing with a rueful face the formidable nature of some unexpected obstacle, hinting continually at his readiness to sacrifice every thing for her sake, lamenting the necessity of delay, and assuring her that in the mean while no evil should happen to her. He flattered himself that Anthelia, wearied out with the irksomeness of confinement and the continual alternations of hope and disappointment, and contrasting the respectful tenderness of his manner with the disagreeable system of behaviour to which he had fashioned Lord Anophel, would at length come to a determination of removing all his difficulties by offering him her hand and fortune as a compensation for his anticipated bishopric. It was not, however, very long before Anthelia penetrated his design ; but as she did not deem it prudent to come to a rupture with him at that time, she continued to listen to his daily details of plans and impediments, and allowed him to take to himself all the merit he seemed to assume for supplying her with music and books ; though he expressed himself very much shocked at her asking him for Gibbon and Rousseau, whose works, he said, ought to be burned *in foro* by the hands of *Carnifex*.[1]

The windows of her apartment were at an immense elevation from the beach, as that part of the castle-wall formed a continued line with the black and precipitous side of the rock on which it stood. During the greater portion of the hours of daylight she sate near the window with her harp, gazing on the changeful aspects of the wintry sea, now slumbering like a summer lake in the sunshine of a halcyon day—now raging beneath the sway of the tempest, while the dancing snow-flakes seemed to accumulate on the foam of the billows, and the spray was hurled back like snow-dust from the rocks. The feelings these scenes suggested she developed in the following stanzas, to which she adapted a wild and impassioned air, and they became the favourite song of her captivity.

---

[1] An executioner. G.

THE MAGIC BARK.

I.

O Freedom ! power of life and light !
Sole nurse of truth and glory !
Bright dweller on the rocky cliff !
Lone wanderer on the sea !
Where'er the sunbeam slumbers bright
On snow-clad mountains hoary ;
Wherever flies the veering skiff,
O'er waves that breathe of thee !
Be thou the guide of all my thought—
The source of all my being—
The genius of my waking mind—
The spirit of my dreams !
To me thy magic spell be taught,
The captive spirit freeing,
To wander with the ocean-wind
Where'er thy beacon beams.

II.

O ! sweet it were, in magic bark,
On one loved breast reclining,
To sail around the varied world,
To every blooming shore ;
And oft the gathering storm to mark
Its lurid folds combining ;
And safely ride, with sails unfurled,
Amid the tempest's roar ;
And see the mighty breakers rave
On cliff, and sand, and shingle,
And hear, with long re-echoing shock,
The caverned steeps reply ;
And while the storm-cloud and the wave
In darkness seemed to mingle,
To skim beside the surf-swept rock,
And glide uninjured by.

III.

And when the summer seas were calm,
And summer skies were smiling,
And evening came, with clouds of gold,
To gild the western wave ;
And gentle airs and dews of balm,
The pensive mind beguiling,

Should call the Ocean Swain to fold
His sea-flocks in the cave,
Unearthly music's tenderest spell,
With gentlest breezes blending
And waters softly rippling near
The prow's light course along,
Should flow from Triton's winding shell,
Through ocean's depths ascending
From where it charmed the Nereid's ear,
Her coral bowers among.

IV.

How sweet, where eastern Nature smiles,
With swift and mazy motion
Before the odour-breathing breeze
Of dewy morn to glide ;
Or 'mid the thousand emerald isles
That gem the southern ocean,
Where fruits and flowers, from loveliest trees,
O'erhang the slumbering tide :
Or up some western stream to sail,
To where its myriad fountains
Roll down their everlasting rills
From many a cloud-capped height,
Till mingling in some nameless vale,
'Mid forest-cinctured mountains,
The river-cataract shakes the hills
With vast and volumed might.

V.

The poison-trees their leaves should shed,
The yellow snake should perish,
The beasts of blood should crouch and cower,
Where'er that vessel past :
All plagues of fens and vapours bred,
That tropic fervors cherish,
Should fly before its healing power,
Like mists before the blast.
Where'er its keel the strand imprest,
The young fruit's ripening cluster,
The bird's free song, its touch should greet,
The opening flower's perfume ;
The streams along the green earth's breast
Should roll in purer lustre,
And love should heighten every sweet,
And brighten every bloom.

VI.

And, Freedom ! thy meridian blaze
Should chase the clouds that lower,
Wherever mental twilight dim
Obscures Truth's vestal flame,
Wherever Fraud and Slavery raise
The throne of blood-stained Power,
Wherever Fear and Ignorance hymn
Some fabled dæmon's name !
The bard, where torrents thunder down
Beside thy burning altar,
Should kindle, as in days of old,
The mind's ethereal fire ;
Ere yet beneath a tyrant's frown
The Muse's voice could falter,
Or Flattery strung with chords of gold
The minstrel's venal lyre.

CHAPTER XLII

CONCLUSION

LORD ANOPHEL one morning paid Anthelia his usual visit. " You
must be aware, Miss Melincourt," said he, " that if your friends could
have found you out, they would have done it before this ; but they
have searched the whole country far and near, and have now gone
home in despair."

ANTHELIA. That, my Lord, I cannot believe ; for there is one, at
least, who I am confident will never be weary of seeking me, and
who, I am equally confident, will not always seek in vain.

LORD ANOPHEL ACHTHAR. If you mean the young lunatic of Redrose Abbey, or his friend the dumb Baronet, they are both gone to
London to attend the opening of the Honourable House ; and if you
doubt my word, I will show you their names in the Morning Post,
among the Fashionable Arrivals at Wildman's Hotel.

ANTHELIA. Your Lordship's word is quite as good as the authority
you have quoted.

LORD ANOPHEL ACHTHAR. Well, then, Miss Melincourt, I presume you perceive that you are completely in my power, and that I have gone too far to recede. If, indeed, I had supposed myself an object of such very great repugnance to you, which I must say (*looking at himself in a glass*) is quite unaccountable, I might not, perhaps, have laid this little scheme, which I thought would be only settling the affair in a compendious way ; for, that any woman in England would consider it a very great hardship to be Lady Achthar, and hereafter Marchioness of Agaric, and would feel any very mortal resentment for means that tended to make her so, was an idea, egad, that never entered my head. However, as I have already observed, you are completely in my power : both our characters are compromised, and there is only one way to mend the matter, which is, to call in Grovelgrub, and make him strike up " Dearly beloved."

ANTHELIA. As to your character, Lord Anophel, that must be your concern. Mine is in my own keeping ; for, having practised all my life a system of uniform sincerity, which gives me a right to be believed by all who know me, and more especially by all who love me, I am perfectly indifferent to private malice or public misrepresentation.

LORD ANOPHEL ACHTHAR. There is such a thing, Miss Melincourt, as tiring out a man's patience ; and 'pon honour, if gentle means don't succeed with you, I must have recourse to rough ones, 'pon honour.

ANTHELIA. My Lord !

LORD ANOPHEL ACHTHAR. I am serious, curse me. You will be glad enough to hush all up then, and we'll go to court together in due form.

ANTHELIA. What you mean by hushing up, Lord Anophel, I know not : but of this be assured, that under no circumstances will I ever be your wife ; and that whatever happens to me in any time or place, shall be known to all who are interested in my welfare. I know too well the difference between the true modesty of a pure and simple mind, and the false affected quality which goes by that name in the world, to be intimidated by threats which can only be dictated by a supposition that your wickedness would be my disgrace, and that false shame would induce me to conceal what both truth and justice would command me to make known.[1]

Lord Anophel stood aghast for a few minutes, at the declaration of such unfashionable sentiments. At length saying, " Ay, preaching is one thing, and practice another, as Grovelgrub can testify;" he seized her hand with violence, and threw his arm round her waist. Anthelia screamed, and at that very moment a violent noise of ascending steps was heard on the stairs ; the door was burst open, and Sir Oran Haut-ton appeared in the aperture, with the Reverend Mr. Grovelgrub in custody, whom he dragged into the apartment, followed by Mr. Forester and Mr. Fax. Mr. Forester flew to Anthelia, who threw herself into his arms, hid her face in his bosom, and burst into tears : which when Sir Oran saw, his wrath grew boundless, and quitting his hold of the Reverend Mr. Grovelgrub (who immediately ran downstairs, and out of the castle, as fast as a pair of short thick legs could carry him), seized on Lord Anophel Achthar, and was preparing to administer natural justice by throwing him out at the window ; but Mr. Fax interposed, and calling Mr. Forester's attention, which was totally engaged with Anthelia, they succeeded in rescuing the terrified sprig of nobility ; who immediately leaving the enemy in free possession, flew downstairs after his reverend tutor ; whom, on issuing from the castle, he discovered at an immense distance on the sands, still running with all his might. Lord Anophel gave him chase, and after a long time came within hail of him, and shouted to him to stop. But this only served to quicken the reverend gentleman's speed ; who, hearing the voice of pursuit, and too much terrified to look back, concluded that the dumb Baronet had found his voice, and was then in the very act of gaining on his flight. Therefore, the more Lord Anophel shouted " Stop ! " the more nimbly the reverend gentleman sped along the sands, running and roaring all the way, like Falstaff on Gadshill ; his Lordship still exerting all his powers of speed in the rear, and gaining on his flying Mentor by very imperceptible gradations : where we shall

[1] Anthelia derives her morality, which, like her education, was far in advance of her age, from Mary Wollstonecraft. G.

leave them to run *ad libitum*, while we account for the sudden appearance of Mr. Forester and his friends.

We left them walking along the shore of the sea, which they followed, till they arrived in the vicinity of Alga Castle, from which the Reverend Mr. Grovelgrub emerged in evil hour, to take a meditative walk on the sands. The keen sight of the natural man descried him from far. Sir Oran darted on his prey ; and though it is supposed that he could not have overtaken the swift-footed Achilles,[1] he had very little difficulty in overtaking the Reverend Mr. Grovelgrub, who had begun to run for his life as soon as he was aware of the foe. Sir Oran shook his stick over his head, and the reverend gentleman dropping on his knees, put his hands together, and entreated for mercy, saying " he would confess all." Mr. Forester and Mr. Fax came up in time to hear the proposal : the former restrained the rage of Sir Oran, who, however, still held his prisoner fast by the arm ; and the reluctant divine, with many a heavy groan, conducted his unwelcome company to the door of Anthelia's apartments.

" O Forester ! " said Anthelia, " you have realized all my wishes. I have found you the friend of the poor, the enthusiast of truth, the disinterested cultivator of the rural virtues, the active promoter of the cause of human liberty. It only remained that you should emancipate a captive damsel, who, however, will but change the mode of her durance, and become your captive for life."

It was not long after this event, before the Reverend Mr. Portpipe, and the old chapel of Melincourt Castle, were put in requisition, to make a mystical unit of Anthelia and Mr. Forester. The day was celebrated with great festivity throughout their respective estates, and the Reverend Mr. Portpipe was *voti compos* : that is to say, he

---

[1] " The civilized man will submit to the greatest pain and labour, in order to excel in any exercise which is honourable ; and this induces me to believe that such a man as Achilles might have beat in running even an oran outang, or the savage of the Pyrenees, whom nobody could lay hold of, though that be the exercise in which savages excel the most, and though I am persuaded that the oran outang of Angola is naturally stronger and swifter of foot than Achilles was, or than even the heroes of the preceding age, such as Hercules, and such as Theseus, Pirithous, and others mentioned by Nestor."—*Ancient Metaphysics*, vol. iii. p. 76. [P.]

had taken a resolution on the day of Anthelia's christening, that he would on the day of her marriage drink one bottle more than he had ever taken at one sitting on any other occasion ; which resolution he had now the satisfaction of carrying into effect.

Sir Oran Haut-ton continued to reside with Mr. Forester and Anthelia. They discovered in the progress of time, that he had formed for the latter the same kind of reverential attachment, as the Satyr in Fletcher forms for the Holy Shepherdess : [1] and Anthelia might have said to him in the words of Clorin :—

> " —They wrong thee that do call thee rude :
>   Though thou be'st outward rough and tawny-hued,

---

[1] See Fletcher's *Faithful Shepherdess*. The following extracts from the Satyr's speeches to Clorin will explain the allusion in the text.

> But behold a fairer sight !
> By that heavenly form of thine,
> Brightest fair ! thou art divine !
> Sprung from great immortal race
> Of the gods ; for in thy face
> Shines more awful majesty,
> Than dull weak mortality
> Dare with misty eyes behold,
> And live ! Therefore on this mould
> Lowly do I bend my knee,
> In worship of thy deity.
>   *Act I. Scene I.*
>
> Brightest ! if there be remaining
> Any service, without feigning
> I will do it : were I set
> To catch the nimble wind, or get
> Shadows gliding on the green,
> Or to steal from the great queen
> Of the fairies all her beauty,
> I would do it, so much duty
> Do I owe those precious eyes.
>   *Act IV. Scene II.*
>
> Thou divinest, fairest, brightest,
> Thou most powerful maid, and whitest,
> Thou most virtuous and most blessed,
> Eyes of stars, and golden tressed
> Like Apollo ! Tell me, sweetest,
> What new service now is meetest

Thy manners are as gentle and as fair,
As his who boasts himself born only heir
To all humanity." [1]

His greatest happiness was in listening to the music of her harp and
voice : in the absence of which he solaced himself, as usual, with his
flute and French horn.   He became likewise a proficient in drawing ;
but what progress he made in the art of speech, we have not been able
to ascertain.

Mr. Fax was a frequent visitor at Melincourt, and there was always
a cover at the table for the Reverend Mr. Portpipe.

Mr. Hippy felt half inclined to make proposals to Miss Evergreen ;
but understanding from Mr. Forester, that, from the death of her
lover in early youth, that lady had irrevocably determined on a
single life,[2] he comforted himself with passing half his time at
Melincourt Castle, and dancing the little Foresters on his knee,

----

> For the Satyr ?   Shall I stray
> In the middle air, and stay
> The sailing rack ? or nimbly take
> Hold by the moon, and gently make
> Suit to the pale queen of night
> For a beam to give thee light ?
> Shall I dive into the sea,
> And bring thee coral, making way
> Through the rising waves that fall
> In snowy fleeces ?   Dearest, shall
> I catch thee wanton fawns, or flies
> Whose woven wings the summer dyes
> Of many colours ?   Get thee fruit ?
> Or steal from heaven old Orpheus' lute ?
> All these I'll venture for, and more,
> To do her service all these woods adore.
>
> *Act V. Scene V.*   [P.]

[1] *Faithful Shepherdess*, Act IV, Sc. 1 : " call " should be " term " ; the
punctuation here and in the note is incorrect.   G.

[2] " There are very few women who might not have married in some way
or other.   The old maid, who has either never formed an attachment, or
has been disappointed in the object of it, has, under the circumstances
in which she has been placed, conducted herself with the most perfect
propriety ; and has acted a much more virtuous and honourable part in
society, than those women who marry without a proper degree of love, or
at least of esteem, for their husbands ; a species of immorality which is not
reprobated as it deserves."—Malthus on *Population*, book iv. chap. viii.

[P.]

whom he taught to call him "grandpapa Hippy," and seemed extremely proud of the imaginary relationship.

Mr. Forester disposed of Redrose Abbey to Sir Telegraph Paxarett, who, after wearing the willow twelve months,[1] married, left off driving, and became a very respectable specimen of an English country gentleman.

We must not conclude without informing those among our tender-hearted readers, who would be much grieved if Miss Danaretta Contantina Pinmoney should have been disappointed in her principal object of making a *good match*, that she had at length the satisfaction, through the skilful management of her mother, of making the happiest of men of Lord Anophel Achthar.

THE END

---

[1] " The Willow, worne of forlorne Paramours."   Spenser : *The Faerie Queene*, Bk. I, Canto 1, St. 9.   G.

NIGHTMARE ABBEY

NIGHTMARE ABBEY

There's a dark lantern of the spirit,
Which none see by but those who bear it,
That makes them in the dark see visions
And hag themselves with apparitions,
Find racks for their own minds, and vaunt
Of their own misery and want. BUTLER.[1]

[1] A marriage of several lines, some misquoted, from Butler to form a connected whole. *Hudibras*, Pt. I, Canto 1, ll. 505-6 ; Pt. III, Canto 3, ll. 19-20 ; *Satire Upon the Weakness and Misery of Man*, ll. 71-2 and 172-4. G.

Nightmare Abbey was first published in 1818

Matthew. Oh ! it's your only fine humour, sir. Your true melancholy breeds your perfect fine wit, sir. I am melancholy myself, divers times, sir ; and then do I no more but take pen and paper presently, and overflow you half a score or a dozen of sonnets at a sitting.

Stephen. Truly, sir, and I love such things out of measure.

Matthew. Why, I pray you, sir, make use of my study : it's at your service.

Stephen. I thank you, sir, I shall be bold, I warrant you. Have you a stool there, to be melancholy upon ?

Ben Jonson, *Every man in his Humour,*

A. 3, Sc. 1.[1]

---

[1] Shelley wrote to Peacock, July 5th, 1818 : " We have found an excellent quotation in Ben Jonson's *Every Man in his Humour.* I will transcribe it, as I do not think you have these plays at Marlow. . . The last expression would not make a bad motto." Shelley was referring to the last sentence only, which he underlined, but Peacock adopted the whole, omitting only Ed. Knowell's interlocutions. G.

INTRODUCTION TO
NIGHTMARE ABBEY

SHELLEY and Mary left London for Italy on March 11th, 1818. Peacock spent the evening with them after going to the first performance in England of *The Barber of Seville*, the first of Rossini's operas to be performed in England. It was also the first appearance in England of Malibran's father, Garcia, who took the part of Almaviva.

Ten days later Peacock wrote to Hogg from Marlow : " I have been here since Monday, as lonely as a cloud, and as melancholy as a gib cat. . . . Shelley left town on Wednesday, the 11th, at 5 in the morning. We had a farewell supper in Russell Street, with Mr and Mrs Hunt, on Tuesday night after the Opera. I stayed three or four days in pure dread of facing the associations of this scenery, and did not venture abroad for two or three days more after my return. However, I have been forth into the woods, and broken the spell in some measure, and now think of passing the summer where I am."

On the 28th of April, he had abandoned the project of a novel, set in London, and wrote to Hogg : " At present I am writing a comic romance with a title of ' Nightmare Abbey ', and amusing myself with the darkness and misanthropy of modern literature, from the lantern jaws of which I shall endeavour to elicit a laugh." [1]

At the end of May he wrote to Shelley to give him news of its progress, telling him that it was " to ' make a stand ' against the ' encroachments ' of black bile. The fourth canto of *Childe Harold* is really too bad. I cannot consent to be an *auditor tantum* of this systematical ' poisoning ' of the ' mind ' of the " reading public.' "

---

[1] Both the letters to Hogg were first published with the Hogg-Shelley Correspondence in *Shelley at Oxford*, edited by W. S. Scott (Golden Cockerel Press, 1944).

A few lines from *Childe Harold* will remind the reader what Peacock objected to.

> We wither from our youth, we gasp away—
> Sick—sick ; unfound the boon, unslaked the thirst,
> Though to the last, in verge of our decay,
> Some phantom lures, such as we sought at first—
> But all too late,—so are we doubly curst.
> Love, fame, ambition, avarice—'tis the same—
> Each idle—and all ill—and none the worst—
> For all are meteors with a different name,
> And Death the sable smoke where vanishes the flame.
>
> Have I not had to wrestle with my lot ?
> Have I not suffer'd things to be forgiven ?
> Have I not had my brain sear'd, my heart riven,
> Hopes sapp'd, name blighted, Life's life lied away ?
> And only not to desperation driven,
> Because not altogether of such clay
> As rots into the souls of those whom I survey.

Byron's gloom and grandeur were not original, nor were they only the result of his chosen way of life, which Shelley described to Peacock as associating with the lowest women his gondoliers picked up in the streets of Venice, and " countesses smelling so strongly of garlic that an ordinary Englishman cannot approach them." Gloom and grandeur were among the fruits of German romanticism after it had been transplanted to England—a " upas-tree " (to use a simile from *Childe Harold*) overshadowing our literature, other fruits of which were the novels of Mrs Radcliffe, of William Godwin, of Shelley himself, the stories of M. G. Lewis and all the works eagerly sought after by Jane Austen's heroines because they were " horrid."

With German romanticism Peacock, naturally enough, coupled German transcendental philosophy which had been introduced with it. In one of several magnificent passages on the same subject, Hazlitt describes how Coleridge had " wandered into Germany and lost himself in the labyrinths of the Hartz forests and of Kantean philosophy, and amongst the cabalistic names of Fichte and Schelling and Lessing and Heaven knows who." Coleridge emerges from these labyrinths to visit Nightmare Abbey as Mr Flosky. *Nightmare Abbey* is closer to life than any other of Peacock's novels ; Scythrop, Marionetta and Celinda, Mr Toobad, Mr Flosky, Mr Cypress and

Mr Listless are all recognisable caricatures, and I feel sure that it is only neglect on the part of Peacock's other editors, and lamentable ignorance on my own, which prevents us from recognising the features of some eminent zoologist in those of that amateur of mermaids, Mr Asterias. The plot itself is close enough to Shelley's situation when he wanted to live with Mary without forsaking Harriet—and Scythrop is pretty close to what we know of Shelley at the age of nineteen. Some of Shelley's admirers have resented *Nightmare Abbey* on his behalf. But at twenty-six Shelley himself was delighted both with the portrait and with the novel. True he thought it inferior to *Melincourt*, which " had more of the true spirit, and an object less indefinite, than in either *Headlong Hall* or Scythrop," but on the arrival of *Nightmare Abbey* he wrote to Peacock :

" Enough of melancholy ! *Nightmare Abbey*, though no cure, is a palliative. I have just received the parcel which contained it. . . . I am delighted with *Nightmare Abbey*. I think Scythrop a character admirably conceived and executed ; and I know not how to praise sufficiently the lightness, chastity, and strength of the language of the whole. It perhaps exceeds all your works in this. The catastrophe is excellent. I suppose the moral is contained in what Falstaff says—' For God's sake, talk like a man of this world ' ; and yet, looking deeper into it, is not the misdirected enthusiasm of Scythrop what J. C. calls the ' salt of the earth ' ? "

Shelley added that his friends, the Gisbornes, delighted in it. Mary Shelley, who disliked Peacock, may have been less pleased, for even if she did not mind the portrait of herself and the rivalry between Marionetta and Celinda, she almost certainly must have resented the reference to her father's work. Shelley and Mary had read *Mandeville* at the end of November 1817. It had " shaken their deepest souls " and left them " wondering whence he drew the darkness with which its shades are deepened." William Godwin was not only generally regarded as a political philosopher of the front rank, but his immortality as a novelist was believed to be assured.

Hazlitt, writing in 1825, declared that *Caleb Williams* and *St Leon* are " two of the most splendid and impressive works of the imagination that have appeared in our times," and contrasts him most favourably with Scott. Mary aspired to tread in her father's foot-steps ; her *Frankenstein* had been published in 1818, and she cannot have been pleased at the dismissal of *Mandeville* as : "*Devilman*, a novel. H'm. Hatred—revenge—misanthropy—and quotations from the Bible. This is the morbid anatomy of black bile "—a judgment of Mr Flosky's which time has confirmed. Nor is *Mandeville* the only one of Godwin's novels to have fallen by the way ; it is a simple but tiring matter to disprove Hazlitt's assertion that no one who ever read *Caleb Williams* or *St Leon* through could possibly forget them. I am afraid that I have done so, though it is nothing to boast of. I do not know whether Shelley revised his first judgment of *Mandeville*, but about *Childe Harold* he was in complete agreement with Peacock, to whom he wrote :

"The spirit in which it is written is, if insane, the most wicked and mischievous insanity that was ever given forth. It is a kind of obstinate and self-willed folly, in which he hardens himself. . . . Nothing can be less sublime than the true source of these expressions of contempt and desperation. . . ."

After reading *Nightmare Abbey*, Byron sent Peacock a rosebud, with the message that he bore him no ill-will for his satire. Peacock had it mounted in an oval gold locket inscribed on the back : " From Byron to T. L. Peacock, 1819."

Shelley's recognition of the lightness, chastity and strength of the language of *Nightmare Abbey* is true. The style is exquisite, and in my opinion the book is the best of Peacock's novels, the only one in which his delightful wit and admirable criticism of life are combined with unity of structure and an amusing plot with no loose ends.

D. G.

NIGHTMARE ABBEY

Ay esleu gazouiller et siffler oye, comme dit le commun proverbe, entre les cygnes, plutoust que d'estre entre tant de gentils poëtes et faconds orateurs mut du tout estimé.—Rabelais, *Prol. L.* 5.[1]

CHAPTER I

Nightmare Abbey, a venerable family-mansion, in a highly picturesque state of semi-dilapidation, pleasantly situated on a strip of dry land between the sea and the fens, at the verge of the county of Lincoln, had the honour to be the seat of Christopher Glowry, Esquire. This gentleman was naturally of an atrabilarious temperament, and much troubled with those phantoms of indigestion which are commonly called *blue devils*.[2] He had been deceived in an early friendship : he had been crossed in love ; and had offered his hand, from pique, to a lady, who accepted it from interest, and who, in so doing, violently tore asunder the bonds of a tried and youthful attachment. Her vanity was gratified by being the mistress of a very extensive, if not very lively, establishment ; but all the springs of her sympathies were frozen. Riches she possessed, but that which enriches them, the participation of affection, was wanting. All that they could purchase for her became indifferent to her, because that which they could not purchase, and which was more valuable than themselves, she had, for their sake, thrown away. She discovered, when it was too late, that she had mistaken the means for the end—that riches, rightly used, are instruments of happiness, but are not in themselves happiness. In this wilful blight of her affections, she found them valueless as means : they had been the end to

[1] " I have made bold to choose to chirrup and warble my plain ditty, or, as they say, to whistle like a goose among the swans, rather than be thought deaf among so many pretty poets and eloquent orators." Urquhart and Motteux translation. G.

[2] See p. 74. G.

which she had immolated all her affections, and were now the only end that remained to her. She did not confess this to herself as a principle of action, but it operated through the medium of unconscious self-deception, and terminated in inveterate avarice. She laid on external things the blame of her mind's internal disorder, and thus became by degrees an accomplished scold. She often went her daily rounds through a series of deserted apartments, every creature in the house vanishing at the creak of her shoe, much more at the sound of her voice, to which the nature of things affords no simile; for, as far as the voice of woman, when attuned by gentleness and love, transcends all other sounds in harmony, so far does it surpass all others in discord, when stretched into unnatural shrillness by anger and impatience.

Mr. Glowry used to say that his house was no better than a spacious kennel, for every one in it led the life of a dog. Disappointed both in love and in friendship, and looking upon human learning as vanity, he had come to a conclusion that there was but one good thing in the world, *videlicet*, a good dinner; and this his parsimonious lady seldom suffered him to enjoy: but, one morning, like Sir Leoline in Christabel, "he woke and found his lady dead," [1] and remained a very consolate widower, with one small child.

This only son and heir Mr. Glowry had christened Scythrop,[2] from the name of a maternal ancestor, who had hanged himself one rainy day in a fit of *tædium vitæ*, and had been eulogised by a coroner's jury in the comprehensive phrase of *felo de se*; on which account, Mr. Glowry held his memory in high honour, and made a punchbowl of his skull.

When Scythrop grew up, he was sent, as usual, to a public school, where a little learning was painfully beaten into him, and from thence to the university, where it was carefully taken out of him; and he was sent home like a well-threshed ear of corn, with nothing in his head: having finished his education to the high satisfaction of the master and fellows of his college, who had, in testimony of their

---

[1] *Woke* should be *rose*. G.

[2] From the Greek σκυθρωπος, " of a sullen countenance." Scythrop is based on Shelley as a very young man. The caricature delighted Shelley, who called the tower at Valsovano, in which he wrote *The Cenci*, " Scythrop's tower." G.

approbation, presented him with a silver fish-slice, on which his name figured at the head of a laudatory inscription in some semi-barbarous dialect of Anglo-Saxonised Latin.

His fellow-students, however, who drove tandem and random [1] in great perfection, and were connoisseurs in good inns, had taught him to drink deep ere he departed. He had passed much of his time with these choice spirits, and had seen the rays of the midnight lamp tremble on many a lengthening file of empty bottles. He passed his vacations sometimes at Nightmare Abbey, sometimes in London, at the house of his uncle, Mr. Hilary, a very cheerful and elastic gentleman, who had married the sister of the melancholy Mr. Glowry. The company that frequented his house was the gayest of the gay. Scythrop danced with the ladies and drank with the gentlemen, and was pronounced by both a very accomplished charming fellow, and an honour to the university.

At the house of Mr. Hilary, Scythrop first saw the beautiful Miss Emily Girouette. He fell in love ; which is nothing new. He was favourably received ; which is nothing strange. Mr. Glowry and Mr. Girouette had a meeting on the occasion, and quarrelled about the terms of the bargain ; which is neither new nor strange. The lovers were torn asunder, weeping and vowing everlasting constancy ; and, in three weeks after this tragical event, the lady was led a smiling bride to the altar, by the Honourable Mr. Lackwit ; which is neither strange nor new.

Scythrop received this intelligence at Nightmare Abbey, and was half distracted on the occasion. It was his first disappointment, and preyed deeply on his sensitive spirit.[2] His father, to comfort him, read him a Commentary on Ecclesiastes, which he had himself composed, and which demonstrated incontrovertibly that all is vanity. He insisted particularly on the text, " One man among a thousand have I found, but a woman amongst all those have I not found."

" How could he expect it," said Scythrop, " when the whole thousand were locked up in his seraglio ? His experience is no precedent for a free state of society like that in which we live."

---

[1] A joke on random-tandem, i.e. with three horses harnessed tandem. G.
[2] Like Shelley's with Harriet Grove. G.

" Locked up or at large," said Mr. Glowry, " the result is the same : their minds are always locked up, and vanity and interest keep the key. I speak feelingly, Scythrop."

" I am sorry for it, sir," said Scythrop. " But how is it that their minds are locked up ? The fault is in their artificial education, which studiously models them into mere musical dolls, to be set out for sale in the great toy-shop of society."

" To be sure," said Mr. Glowry, " their education is not so well finished as yours has been ; and your idea of a musical doll is good. I bought one myself, but it was confoundedly out of tune ; but, whatever be the cause, Scythrop, the effect is certainly this, that one is pretty nearly as good as another, as far as any judgment can be formed of them before marriage. It is only after marriage that they show their true qualities, as I know by bitter experience. Marriage is, therefore, a lottery, and the less choice and selection a man bestows on his ticket the better ; for, if he has incurred considerable pains and expense to obtain a lucky number, and his lucky number proves a blank, he experiences not a simple, but a complicated disappointment ; the loss of labour and money being superadded to the disappointment of drawing a blank, which, constituting simply and entirely the grievance of him who has chosen his ticket at random, is, from its simplicity, the more endurable." This very excellent reasoning was thrown away upon Scythrop, who retired to his tower as dismal and disconsolate as before.

The tower which Scythrop inhabited stood at the south-eastern angle of the Abbey ; and, on the southern side, the foot of the tower opened on a terrace, which was called the garden, though nothing grew on it but ivy, and a few amphibious weeds. The south-western tower, which was ruinous and full of owls, might, with equal propriety, have been called the aviary. This terrace or garden, or terrace-garden, or garden-terrace (the reader may name it *ad libitum*), took in an oblique view of the open sea, and fronted a long tract of level sea-coast, and a fine monotony of fens and windmills.

The reader will judge, from what we have said, that this building was a sort of castellated abbey ; and it will, probably, occur to him to inquire if it had been one of the strong-holds of the ancient church militant. Whether this was the case, or how far it had been indebted to the taste of Mr. Glowry's ancestors for any transmutations from its original state, are, unfortunately, circumstances not within the pale of our knowledge.

The north-western tower contained the apartments of Mr. Glowry. The moat at its base, and the fens beyond, comprised the whole of his prospect. This moat surrounded the Abbey, and was in immediate contact with the walls on every side but the south.

The north-eastern tower was appropriated to the domestics, whom Mr. Glowry always chose by one of two criterions,—a long face, or a dismal name. His butler was Raven ; his steward was Crow ; his valet was Skellet. Mr. Glowry maintained that the valet was of French extraction, and that his name was Squelette. His grooms were Mattocks and Graves. On one occasion, being in want of a footman, he received a letter from a person signing himself Diggory Deathshead, and lost no time in securing this acquisition ; but on Diggory's arrival, Mr. Glowry was horror-struck by the sight of a round ruddy face, and a pair of laughing eyes. Deathshead was always grinning,—not a ghastly smile, but the grin of a comic mask ; and disturbed the echoes of the hall with so much unhallowed laughter, that Mr. Glowry gave him his discharge. Diggory, however, had staid long enough to make conquests of all the old gentleman's maids, and left him a flourishing colony of young Deathsheads to join chorus with the owls, that had before been the exclusive choristers of Nightmare Abbey.

The main body of the building was divided into rooms of state, spacious apartments for feasting, and numerous bed-rooms for visitors, who, however, were few and far between.

Family interests compelled Mr. Glowry to receive occasional visits from Mr. and Mrs. Hilary, who paid them from the same motive ; and, as the lively gentleman on these occasions found few conductors for his exuberant gaiety, he became like a double-charged electric jar, which often exploded in some burst of outrageous merriment to the signal discomposure of Mr. Glowry's nerves.

Another occasional visitor, much more to Mr. Glowry's taste, was Mr. Flosky,[1] a very lachrymose and morbid gentleman, of some note

[1] A *corruption* of Filosky, quasi Φιλοσκιος, a lover, or sectator, of shadows. [P.] [The character is based on Coleridge. G.]

in the literary world, but in his own estimation of much more merit than name. The part of his character which recommended him to Mr. Glowry, was his very fine sense of the grim and the tearful. No one could relate a dismal story with so many minutiæ of supererogatory wretchedness. No one could call up a *raw-head and bloody-bones* [1] with so many adjuncts and circumstances of ghastliness. Mystery was his mental element. He lived in the midst of that visionary world in which nothing is but what is not. He dreamed with his eyes open, and saw ghosts dancing round him at noontide. He had been in his youth an enthusiast for liberty, and had hailed the dawn of the French Revolution as the promise of a day that was to banish war and slavery, and every form of vice and misery, from the face of the earth. Because all this was not done, he deduced that nothing was done; and from this deduction, according to his system of logic, he drew a conclusion that worse than nothing was done; that the overthrow of the feudal fortresses of tyranny and superstition was the greatest calamity that had ever befallen mankind; and that their only hope now was to rake the rubbish together, and rebuild it without any of those loopholes by which the light had originally crept in. To qualify himself for a coadjutor in this laudable task, he plunged into the central opacity of Kantian metaphysics, and lay *perdu* several years in transcendental darkness, till the common daylight of common sense became intolerable to his eyes. He called the sun an *ignis fatuus*; and exhorted all who would listen to his friendly voice, which were about as many as called " God save King Richard," [2] to shelter themselves from its delusive radiance in the obscure haunt of Old Philosophy. This word Old had great charms for him. The good old times were always on his lips; meaning the days when polemic theology was in its prime, and rival prelates beat the drum ecclesiastic [3] with Herculean vigour, till the one wound up his series of syllogisms with the very orthodox conclusion of roasting the other.

But the dearest friend of Mr. Glowry, and his most welcome

---

[1] This proverbial phrase is first recorded in Florio's Italian Dictionary, *The World of Wordes*, 1598. See also *Hudibras*: Pt. III, Canto 2, l. 682.
[2] i.e. none. See *Richard II*, Act V, Sc. 2. G.   [G.
[3] Butler: *Hudibras*, Pt. I, Canto 1, lines. 11–12. G.

guest, was Mr. Toobad, the Manichæan Millenarian.[1] The twelfth verse of the twelfth chapter of Revelations was always in his mouth : " Woe to the inhabiters of the earth and of the sea ! for the devil is come among you, having great wrath, because he knoweth that he hath but a short time." He maintained that the supreme dominion of the world was, for wise purposes, given over for a while to the Evil Principle ; and that this precise period of time, commonly called the enlightened age, was the point of his plenitude of power. He used to add that by and by he would be cast down, and a high and happy order of things succeed ; but he never omitted the saving clause, " Not in our time : " which last words were always echoed in doleful response by the sympathetic Mr. Glowry.

Another and very frequent visitor, was the Reverend Mr. Larynx, the vicar of Claydyke, a village about ten miles distant ;—a good-natured accommodating divine, who was always most obligingly ready to take a dinner and a bed at the house of any country gentleman in distress for a companion. Nothing came amiss to him,—a game at billiards, at chess, at draughts, at backgammon, at piquet, or at all-fours in a *tête-à-tête*,—or any game on the cards, round, square, or triangular, in a party of any number exceeding two. He would even dance among friends, rather than that a lady, even if she were on the wrong side of thirty, should sit still for want of a partner. For a ride, a walk, or a sail, in the morning,—a song after dinner, a ghost story after supper,—a bottle of port with the squire, or a cup of green tea with his lady,—for all or any of these, or for any thing else that was agreeable to any one else, consistently with the dye of his coat, the Reverend Mr. Larynx was at all times equally ready. When at Nightmare Abbey, he would condole with Mr. Glowry,—drink Madeira with Scythrop,—crack jokes with Mr. Hilary,—hand Mrs. Hilary to the piano, take charge of her fan and gloves, and turn over her music with surprising dexterity,—quote Revelations with Mr. Toobad,—and lament the good old times of feudal darkness with the transcendental Mr. Flosky.

---

[1] Based on J. F. Newton, the " zodiacal mythologist " and vegetarian who believed man had steadily deteriorated since a golden age. See p. 7 and Note on p. 12. G.

CHAPTER II

SHORTLY after the disastrous termination of Scythrop's passion for
Miss Emily Girouette, Mr. Glowry found himself, much against his
will, involved in a lawsuit, which compelled him to dance attendance
on the High Court of Chancery. Scythrop was left alone at Nightmare Abbey. He was a burnt child, and dreaded the fire of female
eyes. He wandered about the ample pile, or along the garden-
terrace, with " his cogitative faculties immersed in cogibundity of
cogitation." [1] The terrace terminated at the south-western tower,
which, as we have said, was ruinous and full of owls. Here would
Scythrop take his evening seat, on a fallen fragment of mossy stone,
with his back resting against the ruined wall,—a thick canopy of
ivy, with an owl in it, over his head,—and the Sorrows of Werter
in his hand. He had some taste for romance reading before he went
to the university, where, we must confess, in justice to his college,
he was cured of the love of reading in all its shapes ; and the cure
would have been radical, if disappointment in love, and total solitude,
had not conspired to bring on a relapse. He began to devour
romances and German tragedies, and, by the recommendation of Mr.
Flosky, to pore over ponderous tomes of transcendental philosophy,
which reconciled him to the labour of studying them by their mystical
jargon and necromantic imagery. In the congenial solitude of
Nightmare Abbey, the distempered ideas of metaphysical romance
and romantic metaphysics had ample time and space to germinate
into a fertile crop of chimeras, which rapidly shot up into vigorous
and abundant vegetation.

He now became troubled with the *passion for reforming the world*.[2]
He built many castles in the air, and peopled them with secret
tribunals, and bands of illuminati, who were always the imaginary
instruments of his projected regeneration of the human species. As
he intended to institute a perfect republic, he invested himself with
absolute sovereignty over these mystical dispensers of liberty. He

[1] From Act I, Sc. 1, of *Chrononhotonthologos*, the most Tragical Tragedy
that ever was tragedized by any Company of Tragedians, by Henry Carey,
1734. G.
[2] See Forsyth's *Principles of Moral Science*. [P.]

slept with Horrid Mysteries [1] under his pillow, and dreamed of venerable eleutherarchs [2] and ghastly confederates holding midnight conventions in subterranean caves. He passed whole mornings in his study, immersed in gloomy reverie, stalking about the room in his nightcap, which he pulled over his eyes like a cowl, and folding his striped calico dressing-gown about him like the mantle of a conspirator.

"Action," thus he soliloquised, " is the result of opinion, and to new-model opinion would be to new-model society. Knowledge is power ; it is in the hands of a few, who employ it to mislead the many, for their own selfish purposes of aggrandisement and appropriation. What if it were in the hands of a few who should employ it to lead the many ? What if it were universal, and the multitude were enlightened ? No. The many must be always in leading-strings ; but let them have wise and honest conductors. A few to think, and many to act ; that is the only basis of perfect society. So thought the ancient philosophers : they had their esoterical and exoterical doctrines. So thinks the sublime Kant, who delivers his oracles in language which none but the initiated can comprehend. Such were the views of those secret associations of illuminati, which were the terror of superstition and tyranny, and which, carefully selecting wisdom and genius from the great wilderness of society, as the bee selects honey from the flowers of the thorn and the nettle, bound all human excellence in a chain, which, if it had not been prematurely broken, would have commanded opinion, and regenerated the world."

Scythrop proceeded to meditate on the practicability of reviving a confederation of regenerators. To get a clear view of his own ideas, and to feel the pulse of the wisdom and genius of the age, he wrote and published a treatise, in which his meanings were carefully wrapt up in the monk's hood of transcendental technology, but filled with hints of matter deep and dangerous, which he thought would set the whole nation in a ferment ; and he awaited the result in awful

[1] *Horrid Mysteries*, a translation from the German of the Marquis of Grosse by P. Will, 1796. See Note, p. 368. G.

[2] These beings figure in Hogg's novel, *The Memoirs of Prince Alexy Haimatoff*. " The swans and the Eleutherarchs," wrote Shelley to Hogg (Nov. 26th, 1813), " are proofs that you were a little sleepy." G.

C.N.P. N

expectation, as a miner who has fired a train awaits the explosion of a rock. However, he listened and heard nothing; for the explosion, if any ensued, was not sufficiently loud to shake a single leaf of the ivy on the towers of Nightmare Abbey; and some months afterwards he received a letter from his bookseller, informing him that only seven copies had been sold, and concluding with a polite request for the balance.[1]

Scythrop did not despair. "Seven copies," he thought, "have been sold. Seven is a mystical number, and the omen is good. Let me find the seven purchasers of my seven copies, and they shall be the seven golden candle-sticks with which I will illuminate the world."

Scythrop had a certain portion of mechanical genius, which his romantic projects tended to develop. He constructed models of cells and recesses, sliding panels and secret passages, that would have baffled the skill of the Parisian police. He took the opportunity of his father's absence to smuggle a dumb carpenter into the Abbey, and between them they gave reality to one of these models in Scythrop's tower. Scythrop foresaw that a great leader of human regeneration would be involved in fearful dilemmas, and determined, for the benefit of mankind in general, to adopt all possible precautions for the preservation of himself.

The servants, even the women, had been tutored into silence. Profound stillness reigned throughout and around the Abbey, except when the occasional shutting of a door would peal in long reverberations through the galleries, or the heavy tread of the pensive butler would wake the hollow echoes of the hall. Scythrop stalked about like the grand inquisitor, and the servants flitted past him like familiars. In his evening meditations on the terrace, under the ivy of the ruined tower, the only sounds that came to his ear were the rustling of the wind in the ivy, the plaintive voices of the feathered choristers, the owls, the occasional striking of the Abbey clock, and the monotonous dash of the sea on its low and level shore. In the mean time, he drank Madeira, and laid deep schemes for a thorough repair of the crazy fabric of human nature.

[1] Shelley had published, in his Scythrop period, *Proposals for an Association of those Philanthropists who, convinced of the inadequacy of the moral and political state of Ireland to produce benefits which are nevertheless obtainable, are willing to unite to accomplish its regeneration.* G.

CHAPTER III

MR. GLOWRY returned from London with the loss of his lawsuit. Justice was with him, but the law was against him. He found Scythrop in a mood most sympathetically tragic; and they vied with each other in enlivening their cups by lamenting the depravity of this degenerate age, and occasionally interspersing divers grim jokes about graves, worms, and epitaphs.[1] Mr. Glowry's friends, whom we have mentioned in the first chapter, availed themselves of his return to pay him a simultaneous visit. At the same time arrived Scythrop's friend and fellow-collegian, the Honourable Mr. Listless.[2] Mr. Glowry had discovered this fashionable young gentleman in London, " stretched on the rack of a too easy chair," [3] and devoured with a gloomy and misanthropical *nil curo*, and had pressed him so earnestly to take the benefit of the pure country air, at Nightmare Abbey, that Mr. Listless, finding it would give him more trouble to refuse than to comply, summoned his French valet, Fatout, and told him he was going to Lincolnshire. On this simple hint, Fatout went to work, and the imperials [4] were packed, and the post-chariot was at the door, without the Honourable Mr. Listless having said or thought another syllable on the subject.

Mr. and Mrs. Hilary brought with them an orphan niece, a daughter of Mr. Glowry's youngest sister, who had made a runaway love-match with an Irish officer. The lady's fortune disappeared in the first year : love, by a natural consequence, disappeared in the second : the Irishman himself, by a still more natural consequence, disappeared in the third. Mr. Glowry had allowed his sister an annuity, and she had lived in retirement with her only daughter, whom, at her death, which had recently happened, she commended to the care of Mrs. Hilary.

Miss Marionetta Celestina O'Carroll was a very blooming and

---

[1] *Richard II*, Act III, Sc. 2. G.

[2] Based on Sir Lumley Skeffington, the playwright and fop, a school-fellow and friend of Shelley's. G.

[3] Pope : *The Dunciad*, Bk. IV, l. 342. G.

[4] A trunk designed to be carried on the " imperiale " or top of the carriage. G.

accomplished young lady.[1]   Being a compound of the *Allegro Vivace* of the O'Carrolls, and of the *Andante Doloroso* of the Glowries, she exhibited in her own character all the diversities of an April sky. Her hair was light-brown ; her eyes hazel, and sparkling with a mild but fluctuating light ; her features regular ; her lips full, and of equal size ; and her person surpassingly graceful.   She was a proficient in music.   Her conversation was sprightly, but always on subjects light in their nature and limited in their interest : for moral sympathies, in any general sense, had no place in her mind.   She had some coquetry, and more caprice, liking and disliking almost in the same moment ; pursuing an object with earnestness while it seemed unattainable, and rejecting it when in her power as not worth the trouble of possession.

Whether she was touched with a *penchant* for her cousin Scythrop, or was merely curious to see what effect the tender passion would have on so *outré* a person, she had not been three days in the Abbey before she threw out all the lures of her beauty and accomplishments to make a prize of his heart.   Scythrop proved an easy conquest. The image of Miss Emily Girouette was already sufficiently dimmed by the power of philosophy and the exercise of reason : for to these influences, or to any influence but the true one, are usually ascribed the mental cures performed by the great physician Time.   Scythrop's romantic dreams had indeed given him many *pure anticipated cognitions*[2] of combinations of beauty and intelligence, which, he had some misgivings, were not exactly realised in his cousin Marionetta ; but, in spite of these misgivings, he soon became distractedly in love ; which, when the young lady clearly perceived, she altered her tactics, and assumed as much coldness and reserve as she had before shown ardent and ingenuous attachment.   Scythrop was confounded

---

[1] Marionetta is a portrait of Shelley's first wife, Harriet Westbrook.   G.

[2] " The votaries of the new metaphysics are, in their own language, the interpreters of the *Transcendental Philosophy*, who unfold the mysteries of their science, not by the aid of *empiricism*, but of *criticism* ; who contemplate the laws of nature *in visions of pure reason* ; and who deduce truth from *anticipated cognitions a priori*."   William Drummond : *Academical Questions*, 1805, p. 352.   Both Peacock and Shelley had read Drummond's book and used the phrase to make fun of Coleridge and Kantian Philosophy.   See Shelley : *Peter Bell the Third*, Pt. VI, xiii–xvi and Note.   G.

at the sudden change ; but, instead of falling at her feet and requesting an explanation, he retreated to his tower, muffled himself in his nightcap, seated himself in the president's chair of his imaginary secret tribunal, summoned Marionetta with all terrible formalities, frightened her out of her wits, disclosed himself, and clasped the beautiful penitent to his bosom.

While he was acting this reverie—in the moment in which the awful president of the secret tribunal was throwing back his cowl and his mantle, and discovering himself to the lovely culprit as her adoring and magnanimous lover, the door of the study opened, and the real Marionetta appeared.

The motives which had led her to the tower were a little penitence, a little concern, a little affection, and a little fear as to what the sudden secession of Scythrop, occasioned by her sudden change of manner, might portend. She had tapped several times unheard, and of course unanswered ; and at length, timidly and cautiously opening the door, she discovered him standing up before a black velvet chair, which was mounted on an old oak table, in the act of throwing open his striped calico dressing-gown, and flinging away his nightcap—which is what the French call an imposing attitude.

Each stood a few moments fixed in their respective places—the lady in astonishment, and the gentleman in confusion. Marionetta was the first to break silence. " For heaven's sake," said she, " my dear Scythrop, what is the matter ? "

" For heaven's sake, indeed ! " said Scythrop, springing from the table ; " for your sake, Marionetta, and you are my heaven,— distraction is the matter. I adore you, Marionetta, and your cruelty drives me mad." He threw himself at her knees, devoured her hand with kisses, and breathed a thousand vows in the most passionate language of romance.

Marionetta listened a long time in silence, till her lover had exhausted his eloquence and paused for a reply. She then said, with a very arch look, " I prithee deliver thyself like a man of this world."[1] The levity of this quotation, and of the manner in which it was delivered, jarred so discordantly on the high-wrought enthusiasm of the romantic inamorato, that he sprang upon his feet, and beat his

[1] *Henry IV, Pt. II*, Act V, Sc. 3.   G.

forehead with his clenched fists. The young lady was terrified ; and, deeming it expedient to soothe him, took one of his hands in hers, placed the other hand on his shoulder, looked up in his face with a winning seriousness, and said, in the tenderest possible tone, " What would you have, Scythrop ? "

Scythrop was in heaven again. " What would I have ? What but you, Marionetta ? You, for the companion of my studies, the partner of my thoughts, the auxiliary of my great designs for the emancipation of mankind."

" I am afraid I should be but a poor auxiliary, Scythrop. What would you have me do ? "

" Do as Rosalia does with Carlos, divine Marionetta. Let us each open a vein in the other's arm, mix our blood in a bowl, and drink it as a sacrament of love.[1] Then we shall see visions of transcendental illumination, and soar on the wings of ideas into the space of pure intelligence."

Marionetta could not reply ; she had not so strong a stomach as Rosalia, and turned sick at the proposition. She disengaged herself suddenly from Scythrop, sprang through the door of the tower, and fled with precipitation along the corridors. Scythrop pursued her, crying, " Stop, stop, Marionetta—my life, my love ! " and was gaining rapidly on her flight, when, at an ill-omened corner, where two corridors ended in an angle, at the head of a staircase, he came into sudden and violent contact with Mr. Toobad, and they both plunged together to the foot of the stairs, like two billiard-balls into one pocket. This gave the young lady time to escape, and enclose herself in her chamber ; while Mr. Toobad, rising slowly, and rubbing his knees and shoulders, said, " You see, my dear Scythrop, in this little incident, one of the innumerable proofs of the temporary supremacy of the devil ; for what but a systematic design and con-current contrivance of evil could have made the angles of time and

---

[1] *Horrid Mysteries.* See Note, p. 363. The story is written in the first person by Carlos, Marquis of Grosse, and the following passage is referred to : " Her hand was still armed with the dagger. She [Rosalia] bared my arm, and opened a vein, sucking the blood which flowed from the orifice in large drops ; and then wounded her arm in return, bidding me to imbibe the roseate stream, and exclaimed : ' Thus our souls shall be mixed together.' " G.

place coincide in our unfortunate persons at the head of this accursed staircase ? "

" Nothing else, certainly," said Scythrop : " you are perfectly in the right, Mr. Toobad. Evil, and mischief, and misery, and confusion, and vanity, and vexation of spirit, and death, and disease, and assassination, and war, and poverty, and pestilence, and famine, and avarice, and selfishness, and rancour, and jealousy, and spleen, and malevolence, and the disappointments of philanthropy, and the faithlessness of friendship, and the crosses of love—all prove the accuracy of your views, and the truth of your system ; and it is not impossible that the infernal interruption of this fall downstairs may throw a colour of evil on the whole of my future existence."

" My dear boy," said Mr. Toobad, " you have a fine eye for consequences."

So saying, he embraced Scythrop, who retired, with a disconsolate step, to dress for dinner ; while Mr. Toobad stalked across the hall, repeating, " Woe to the inhabiters of the earth, and of the sea, for the devil is come among you, having great wrath."

CHAPTER IV

THE flight of Marionetta, and the pursuit of Scythrop, had been witnessed by Mr. Glowry, who, in consequence, narrowly observed his son and his niece in the evening ; and, concluding from their manner, that there was a better understanding between them than he wished to see, he determined on obtaining the next morning from Scythrop a full and satisfactory explanation. He, therefore, shortly after breakfast, entered Scythrop's tower, with a very grave face, and said, without ceremony or preface, " So, sir, you are in love with your cousin."

Scythrop, with as little hesitation, answered, " Yes, sir."

" That is candid, at least ; and she is in love with you."

" I wish she were, sir."

" You know she is, sir."

" Indeed, sir, I do not."

" But you hope she is."

" I do, from my soul."

" Now that is very provoking, Scythrop, and very disappointing : I could not have supposed that you, Scythrop Glowry, of Nightmare Abbey, would have been infatuated with such a dancing, laughing, singing, thoughtless, careless, merry-hearted thing, as Marionetta— in all respects the reverse of you and me. It is very disappointing, Scythrop. And do you know, sir, that Marionetta has no fortune ? "

" It is the more reason, sir, that her husband should have one."

" The more reason for her ; but not for you. My wife had no fortune, and I had no consolation in my calamity. And do you reflect, sir, what an enormous slice this lawsuit has cut out of our family estate ? we who used to be the greatest landed proprietors in Lincolnshire."

" To be sure, sir, we had more acres of fen than any man on this coast : but what are fens to love ? What are dykes and windmills to Marionetta ? "

" And what, sir, is love to a windmill ? Not grist, I am certain : besides, sir, I have made a choice for you. I have made a choice for you, Scythrop. Beauty, genius, accomplishments, and a great fortune into the bargain. Such a lovely, serious creature, in a fine state of high dissatisfaction with the world, and every thing in it. Such a delightful surprise I had prepared for you. Sir, I have pledged my honour to the contract—the honour of the Glowries of Nightmare Abbey : and now, sir, what is to be done ? "

" Indeed, sir, I cannot say. I claim, on this occasion, that liberty of action which is the co-natal prerogative of every rational being."

" Liberty of action, sir ? there is no such thing as liberty of action. We are all slaves and puppets of a blind and unpathetic necessity."

" Very true, sir ; but liberty of action, between individuals, consists in their being differently influenced, or modified, by the same universal necessity ; so that the results are unconsentaneous, and their respective necessitated volitions clash and fly off in a tangent."

" Your logic is good, sir : but you are aware, too, that one individual may be a medium of adhibiting to another a mode or form of necessity, which may have more or less influence in the production of consentaneity ; and, therefore, sir, if you do not comply with my wishes in this instance (you have had your own way in every thing else), I shall be under the necessity of disinheriting you, though I shall do it with tears in my eyes." Having said these words, he vanished suddenly, in the dread of Scythrop's logic.

Mr. Glowry immediately sought Mrs. Hilary, and communicated to her his views of the case in point. Mrs. Hilary, as the phrase is, was as fond of Marionetta as if she had been her own child : but— there is always a *but* on these occasions—she could do nothing for her in the way of fortune, as she had two hopeful sons, who were finishing their education at Brazen-nose, and who would not like to encounter any diminution of their prospects, when they should be brought out of the house of mental bondage—i.e. the university— to the land flowing with milk and honey—i.e. the west end of London.

Mrs. Hilary hinted to Marionetta, that propriety, and delicacy, and decorum, and dignity, &c. &c. &c.,[1] would require them to leave the Abbey immediately. Marionetta listened in silent submission, for she knew that her inheritance was passive obedience ; but, when Scythrop, who had watched the opportunity of Mrs. Hilary's departure, entered, and, without speaking a word, threw himself at her feet in a paroxysm of grief, the young lady, in equal silence and sorrow, threw her arms round his neck and burst into tears. A very tender scene ensued, which the sympathetic susceptibilities of the soft-hearted reader can more accurately imagine than we can delineate. But when Marionetta hinted that she was to leave the Abbey immediately, Scythrop snatched from its repository his ancestor's skull, filled it with Madeira,[2] and presenting himself before Mr. Glowry, threatened to drink off the contents if Mr. Glowry did not immediately promise that Marionetta should not be taken from the Abbey without her own consent. Mr. Glowry, who took the Madeira to be some deadly brewage, gave the required promise in dismal panic. Scythrop returned to Marionetta with a joyful heart, and drank the Madeira by the way.

Mr. Glowry, during his residence in London, had come to an agree-

[1] We are not masters of the whole vocabulary. See any novel by any literary lady. [P.]

[2] Shelley had drunk out of a skull to raise a ghost when he was at Eton. Byron had entertained his young friends at Newstead Abbey by passing round a skull full of burgundy. See also pp. 60 and 119. G.

ment with his friend Mr. Toobad, that a match between Scythrop and
Mr. Toobad's daughter would be a very desirable occurrence. She
was finishing her education in a German convent, but Mr. Toobad
described her as being fully impressed with the truth of his
Ahrimanic [1] philosophy, and being altogether as gloomy and anti-
thalian [2] a young lady as Mr. Glowry himself could desire for the
future mistress of Nightmare Abbey. She had a great fortune in
her own right, which was not, as we have seen, without its weight
in inducing Mr. Glowry to set his heart upon her as his daughter-in-
law that was to be ; he was therefore very much disturbed by
Scythrop's untoward attachment to Marionetta. He condoled on
the occasion with Mr. Toobad ; who said, that he had been too long
accustomed to the intermeddling of the devil in all his affairs, to be
astonished at this new trace of his cloven claw ; but that he hoped
to outwit him yet, for he was sure there could be no comparison
between his daughter and Marionetta in the mind of any one who
had a proper perception of the fact, that, the world being a great
theatre of evil, seriousness and solemnity are the characteristics of
wisdom, and laughter and merriment make a human being no better
than a baboon. Mr. Glowry comforted himself with this view of the
subject, and urged Mr. Toobad to expedite his daughter's return
from Germany. Mr. Toobad said he was in daily expectation of her
arrival in London, and would set off immediately to meet her, that

[1] Ahrimanes, in the Persian mythology, is the evil power, the prince of
the kingdom of darkness. He is the rival of Oromazes, the prince of the
kingdom of light. These two powers have divided and equal dominion.
Sometimes one of the two has a temporary supremacy.—According to Mr.
Toobad, the present period would be the reign of Ahrimanes. Lord Byron
seems to be of the same opinion, by the use he has made of Ahrimanes in
" Manfred " ; where the great Alastor, or Κακος Δαιμων, of Persia, is
hailed king of the world by the Nemesis of Greece, in concert with three of
the Scandinavian Valkyræ, under the name of the Destinies ; the astro-
logical spirits of the alchemists of the middle ages ; an elemental witch,
transplanted from Denmark to the Alps ; and a chorus of Dr. Faustus's
devils, who come in the last act for a soul. It is difficult to conceive where
this heterogeneous mythological company could have originally met,
except at a *table d'hôte*, like the six kings in " Candide." [P.] [Peacock
had attempted an exposition of J. F. Newton's ideas in a narrative poem
called *Ahrimanes*, written in Spenserian stanzas. It remained unfinished.

                                                                          G.]

[2] Opposed to Thalia, the Muse of Comedy : killjoy. G.

he might lose no time in bringing her to Nightmare Abbey. " Then," he added, " we shall see whether Thalia or Melpomene—whether the Allegra or the Penserosa—will carry off the symbol of victory."— " There can be no doubt," said Mr. Glowry, " which way the scale will incline, or Scythrop is no true scion of the venerable stem of the Glowrys."

CHAPTER V

MARIONETTA felt secure of Scythrop's heart ; and notwithstanding the difficulties that surrounded her, she could not debar herself from the pleasure of tormenting her lover, whom she kept in a perpetual fever. Sometimes she would meet him with the most unqualified affection ; sometimes with the most chilling indifference ; rousing him to anger by artificial coldness—softening him to love by eloquent tenderness—or inflaming him to jealousy by coquetting with the Honourable Mr. Listless, who seemed, under her magical influence, to burst into sudden life, like the bud of the evening primrose. Sometimes she would sit by the piano, and listen with becoming attention to Scythrop's pathetic remonstrances ; but, in the most impassioned part of his oratory, she would convert all his ideas into a chaos, by striking up some Rondo Allegro, and saying, " Is it not pretty ? " Scythrop would begin to storm ; and she would answer him with,

> " Zitti, zitti, piano, piano,
> Non facciamo confusione," [1]

or some other similar *facezia*, till he would start away from her, and enclose himself in his tower, in an agony of agitation, vowing to renounce her, and her whole sex, for ever ; and returning to her presence at the summons of the billet, which she never failed to send with many expressions of penitence and promises of amendment. Scythrop's schemes for regenerating the world, and detecting his

---

[1] " Silence, silence, quiet, quiet,
Let us not create confusion."

From a song in Rossini's *The Barber of Seville*, taken note by note from Simon's air in Haydn's *Seasons*. G.

seven golden candlesticks, went on very slowly in this fever of his spirit.

Things proceeded in this train for several days ; and Mr. Glowry began to be uneasy at receiving no intelligence from Mr. Toobad ; when one evening the latter rushed into the library, where the family and the visitors were assembled, vociferating, " The devil is come among you, having great wrath ! " He then drew Mr. Glowry aside into another apartment, and after remaining some time together, they re-entered the library with faces of great dismay, but did not condescend to explain to any one the cause of their discomfiture.

The next morning, early, Mr. Toobad departed. Mr. Glowry sighed and groaned all day, and said not a word to any one. Scythrop had quarrelled, as usual, with Marionetta, and was enclosed in his tower, in a fit of morbid sensibility. Marionetta was comforting herself at the piano, with singing the airs of *Nina pazza per amore* [1] ; and the Honourable Mr. Listless was listening to the harmony, as he lay supine on the sofa, with a book in his hand, into which he peeped at intervals. The Reverend Mr. Larynx approached the sofa, and proposed a game of billiards.

THE HONOURABLE MR. LISTLESS. Billiards ! Really I should be very happy ; but, in my present exhausted state, the exertion is too much for me. I do not know when I have been equal to such an effort. (*He rang the bell for his valet. Fatout entered.*) Fatout ! when did I play at billiards last ?

FATOUT. De fourteen December de last year, Monsieur. (*Fatout bowed and retired.*)

THE HONOURABLE MR. LISTLESS. So it was. Seven months ago. You see, Mr. Larynx ; you see, sir. My nerves, Miss O'Carroll, my nerves are shattered. I have been advised to try Bath. Some of the faculty recommend Cheltenham. I think of trying both, as the seasons don't clash. The season, you know, Mr. Larynx—the season, Miss O'Carroll—the season is every thing.

MARIONETTA. And health is something. *N'est-ce pas*, Mr. Larynx ?

[1] Paisiello's opera, *Nina, o La Pazza per Amore.* G.

THE REVEREND MR. LARYNX. Most assuredly, Miss O'Carroll. For, however reasoners may dispute about the *summum bonum*, none of them will deny that a very good dinner is a very good thing : and what is a good dinner without a good appetite ? and whence is a good appetite but from good health ? Now, Cheltenham, Mr. Listless, is famous for good appetites.

THE HONOURABLE MR. LISTLESS. The best piece of logic I ever heard, Mr. Larynx ; the very best, I assure you. I have thought very seriously of Cheltenham : very seriously and profoundly. I thought of it—let me see—when did I think of it ? (*He rang again, and Fatout re-appeared.*) Fatout ! when did I think of going to Cheltenham, and did not go ?

FATOUT. De Juillet twenty-von, de last summer, Monsieur. (*Fatout retired.*)

THE HONOURABLE MR. LISTLESS. So it was. An invaluable fellow that, Mr. Larynx—invaluable, Miss O'Carroll.

MARIONETTA. So I should judge, indeed. He seems to serve you as a walking memory, and to be a living chronicle, not of your actions only, but of your thoughts.

THE HONOURABLE MR. LISTLESS. An excellent definition of the fellow, Miss O'Carroll,—excellent, upon my honour. Ha ! ha ! he ! Heigho ! Laughter is pleasant, but the exertion is too much for me.

A parcel was brought in for Mr. Listless ; it had been sent express. Fatout was summoned to unpack it ; and it proved to contain a new novel, and a new poem, both of which had long been anxiously expected by the whole host of fashionable readers ; and the last number of a popular Review, of which the editor and his coadjutors were in high favour at court, and enjoyed ample pensions [1] for their services to church and state. As Fatout left the room, Mr. Flosky entered, and curiously inspected the literary arrivals.

---

[1] " PENSION. Pay given to a slave of state for treason to his country."
—Johnson's *Dictionary*. [P.] [Misquotation for *State hireling*. G.]

MR. FLOSKY. (*turning over the leaves.*) "Devilman, a novel." [1] Hm. Hatred—revenge—misanthropy—and quotations from the Bible. Hm. This is the morbid anatomy of black bile.—"Paul Jones, a poem." Hm. I see how it is. Paul Jones, an amiable enthusiast—disappointed in his affections—turns pirate from ennui and magnanimity—cuts various masculine throats, wins various feminine hearts—is hanged at the yard-arm! The catastrophe is very awkward, and very unpoetical.[2]—"The Downing Street Review." Hm. First article—An Ode to the Red Book,[3] by Roderick Sackbut, Esquire.[4] Hm. His own poem reviewed by himself. Hm-m-m.

(*Mr. Flosky proceeded in silence to look over the other articles of the Review ; Marionetta inspected the novel, and Mr. Listless the poem.*)

THE REVEREND MR. LARYNX. For a young man of fashion and family, Mr. Listless, you seem to be of a very studious turn.

THE HONOURABLE MR. LISTLESS. Studious! You are pleased to be facetious, Mr. Larynx. I hope you do not suspect me of being studious. I have finished my education. But there are some fashionable books that one must read, because they are ingredients of the talk of the day ; otherwise, I am no fonder of books than I dare say you yourself are, Mr. Larynx.

THE REVEREND MR. LARYNX. Why, sir, I cannot say that I am indeed particularly fond of books ; yet neither can I say that I never do read. A tale or a poem, now and then, to a circle of ladies over their work, is no very heterodox employment of the vocal

---

[1] Godwin's *Mandeville*. Shelley and Mary had read it on Dec. 1, 1817, at Marlow. Shelley wrote to Godwin: "it shakes the deepest soul . . . we wonder whence you drew the darkness with which its shades are deepened." G.

[2] Paul Jones, the celebrated American privateer, in fact adopted French citizenship during the French Revolution. He died in Paris and his remains were identified after exhuming a large part of a Parisian cemetery and removed with naval honours to Annapolis, U.S.A., in 1905. Peacock's synopsis of the poem recalls Byron's *The Corsair*. G.

[3] *The Red Book of Hergest*, a compilation of mediæval Welsh verse and prose. G.

[4] Southey, in allusion to the Laureate's perquisite of a butt of sack. G.

energy. And I must say, for myself, that few men have a more Job-like endurance of the eternally recurring questions and answers that interweave themselves, on these occasions, with the crisis of an adventure, and heighten the distress of a tragedy.

THE HONOURABLE MR. LISTLESS. And very often make the distress when the author has omitted it.

MARIONETTA. I shall try your patience some rainy morning, Mr. Larynx ; and Mr. Listless shall recommend us the very newest new book, that every body reads.

THE HONOURABLE MR. LISTLESS. You shall receive it, Miss O'Carroll, with all the gloss of novelty ; fresh as a ripe green-gage in all the downiness of its bloom. A mail-coach copy from Edinburgh, forwarded express from London.

MR. FLOSKY. This rage for novelty is the bane of literature. Except my works and those of my particular friends, nothing is good that is not as old as Jeremy Taylor : and, *entre nous*, the best parts of my friends' books were either written or suggested by myself.[1]

THE HONOURABLE MR. LISTLESS. Sir, I reverence you. But I must say, modern books are very consolatory and congenial to my feelings. There is, as it were, a delightful north-east wind, an intellectual blight breathing through them ; a delicious misanthropy and dis-content, that demonstrates the nullity of virtue and energy, and puts me in good humour with myself and my sofa.

MR. FLOSKY. Very true, sir. Modern literature is a north-east wind—a blight of the human soul. I take credit to myself for having helped to make it so. The way to produce fine fruit is to blight the flower. You call this a paradox. Marry, so be it. Ponder thereon.

The conversation was interrupted by the re-appearance of Mr. Toobad, covered with mud. He just showed himself at the door,

---

[1] A claim which Coleridge was fully entitled to make. His contributions to *Lyrical Ballads* and his collaboration with Southey in *The Devil's Thoughts* are cases in point. G.

muttered " The devil is come among you ! " and vanished. The
road which connected Nightmare Abbey with the civilised world,
was artificially raised above the level of the fens, and ran through
them in a straight line as far as the eye could reach, with a ditch on
each side, of which the water was rendered invisible by the aquatic
vegetation that covered the surface. Into one of these ditches the
sudden action of a shy horse, which took fright at a windmill, had
precipitated the travelling chariot of Mr. Toobad, who had been
reduced to the necessity of scrambling in dismal plight through the
window. One of the wheels was found to be broken ; and Mr.
Toobad, leaving the postillion to get the chariot as well as he could
to Claydyke for the purposes of cleaning and repairing, had walked
back to Nightmare Abbey, followed by his servant with the imperial,
and repeating all the way his favourite quotation from the
Revelations.

CHAPTER VI

Mr. Toobad had found his daughter Celinda in London, and after
the first joy of meeting was over, told her he had a husband ready
for her. The young lady replied, very gravely, that she should take
the liberty to choose for herself. Mr. Toobad said he saw the devil
was determined to interfere with all his projects, but he was resolved
on his own part, not to have on his conscience the crime of passive
obedience and non-resistance to Lucifer, and therefore she should
marry the person he had chosen for her. Miss Toobad replied, *très
posément*, she assuredly would not. " Celinda, Celinda," said Mr.
Toobad, " you most assuredly shall."—" Have I not a fortune in my
own right, sir ? " said Celinda. " The more is the pity," said Mr.
Toobad : " but I can find means, miss ; I can find means. There
are more ways than one of breaking in obstinate girls."   They parted
for the night with the expression of opposite resolutions, and in the
morning the young lady's chamber was found empty, and what was
become of her Mr. Toobad had no clue to conjecture. He continued
to investigate town and country in search of her ; visiting and

revisiting Nightmare Abbey at intervals, to consult with his friend, Mr. Glowry. Mr. Glowry agreed with Mr. Toobad that this was a very flagrant instance of filial disobedience and rebellion ; and Mr. Toobad declared, that when he discovered the fugitive, she should find that " the devil was come unto her, having great wrath."

In the evening, the whole party met, as usual, in the library. Marionetta sat at the harp ; the Honourable Mr. Listless sat by her and turned over her music, though the exertion was almost too much for him. The Reverend Mr. Larynx relieved him occasionally in this delightful labour. Scythrop, tormented by the demon Jealousy, sat in the corner biting his lips and fingers. Marionetta looking at him every now and then with a smile of most provoking good humour, which he pretended not to see, and which only the more exasperated his troubled spirit. He took down a volume of Dante, and pretended to be deeply interested in the Purgatorio, though he knew not a word he was reading, as Marionetta was well aware ; who, tripping across the room, peeped into his book, and said to him, " I see you are in the middle of Purgatory."—" I am in the middle of hell," said Scythrop furiously. " Are you ? " said she ; " then come across the room, and I will sing you the finale of Don Giovanni." [1]

" Let me alone," said Scythrop. Marionetta looked at him with a deprecating smile, and said, " You unjust, cross creature, you." —" Let me alone," said Scythrop, but much less emphatically than at first, and by no means wishing to be taken at his word. Marionetta left him immediately, and returning to the harp, said, just loud enough for Scythrop to hear—" Did you ever read Dante, Mr. Listless ? Scythrop is reading Dante, and is just now in Purgatory." —" And I," said the Honourable Mr. Listless, " am not reading Dante, and am just now in Paradise," bowing to Marionetta.

MARIONETTA. You are very gallant, Mr. Listless ; and I dare say you are very fond of reading Dante.

THE HONOURABLE MR. LISTLESS. I don't know how it is, but Dante never came in my way till lately. I never had him in my collection, and if I had had him I should not have read him. But I

---

[1] In which Don Giovanni disappears in flames. G.

find he is growing fashionable, and I am afraid I must read him some wet morning.[1]

MARIONETTA. No, read him some evening, by all means. Were you ever in love, Mr. Listless?

THE HONOURABLE MR. LISTLESS. I assure you, Miss O'Carroll, never—till I came to Nightmare Abbey. I dare say it is very pleasant; but it seems to give so much trouble that I fear the exertion would be too much for me.

MARIONETTA. Shall I teach you a compendious method of courtship, that will give you no trouble whatever?

THE HONOURABLE MR. LISTLESS. You will confer on me an inexpressible obligation. I am all impatience to learn it.

MARIONETTA. Sit with your back to the lady and read Dante; only be sure to begin in the middle, and turn over three or four pages at once—backwards as well as forwards, and she will immediately perceive that you are desperately in love with her—desperately.

(*The Honourable Mr. Listless sitting between Scythrop and Marionetta, and fixing all his attention on the beautiful speaker, did not observe Scythrop, who was doing as she described.*)

THE HONOURABLE MR. LISTLESS. You are pleased to be facetious, Miss O'Carroll. The lady would infallibly conclude that I was the greatest brute in town.

MARIONETTA. Far from it. She would say, perhaps, some people have odd methods of showing their affection.

THE HONOURABLE MR. LISTLESS. But I should think, with submission——

MR. FLOSKY. (*joining them from another part of the room.*) Did I not hear Mr. Listless observe that Dante is becoming fashionable?

THE HONOURABLE MR. LISTLESS. I did hazard a remark to that

[1] Cary published a translation of *The Inferno* in 1805 and a complete translation of the *Divina Commedia* in 1814. Coleridge lectured on Dante in 1818. G.

effect, Mr. Flosky, though I speak on such subjects with a consciousness of my own nothingness, in the presence of so great a man as
Mr. Flosky. I know not what is the colour of Dante's devils, but as
he is certainly becoming fashionable I conclude they are blue ; for
the blue devils, as it seems to me, Mr. Flosky, constitute the fundamental feature of fashionable literature.

MR. FLOSKY. The blue are, indeed, the staple commodity ; but
as they will not always be commanded, the black, red, and grey
may be admitted as substitutes. Tea, late dinners, and the French
Revolution, have played the devil, Mr. Listless, and brought the
devil into play.

MR. TOOBAD (*starting up*). Having great wrath.

MR. FLOSKY. This is no play upon words, but the sober sadness of
veritable fact.

THE HONOURABLE MR. LISTLESS. Tea, late dinners, and the French
Revolution. I cannot exactly see the connection of ideas.

MR. FLOSKY. I should be sorry if you could ; I pity the man who
can see the connection of his own ideas. Still more do I pity him,
the connection of whose ideas any other person can see.[1] Sir, the
great evil is, that there is too much commonplace light in our moral
and political literature ; and light is a great enemy to mystery, and
mystery is a great friend to enthusiasm. Now the enthusiasm for
abstract truth is an exceedingly fine thing, as long as the truth,
which is the object of the enthusiasm, is so completely abstract as
to be altogether out of the reach of the human faculties ; and, in
that sense, I have myself an enthusiasm for truth, but in no other,
for the pleasure of metaphysical investigation lies in the means, not
in the end ; and if the end could be found, the pleasure of the means
would cease. The mind, to be kept in health, must be kept in
exercise. The proper exercise of the mind is elaborate reasoning.
Analytical reasoning is a base and mechanical process, which takes
to pieces and examines, bit by bit, the rude material of knowledge,
and extracts therefrom a few hard and obstinate things called facts,

[1] An elaboration of a passage in *Melincourt*, p. 277. G.

every thing in the shape of which I cordially hate.   But synthetical reasoning, setting up as its goal some unattainable abstraction, like an imaginary quantity in algebra, and commencing its course with taking for granted some two assertions which cannot be proved, from the union of these two assumed truths produces a third assumption, and so on in infinite series, to the unspeakable benefit of the human intellect.   The beauty of this process is, that at every step it strikes out into two branches, in a compound ratio of ramification ; so that you are perfectly sure of losing your way, and keeping your mind in perfect health, by the perpetual exercise of an interminable quest ;   and for these reasons I have christened my eldest son Emanuel Kant Flosky.[1]

THE REVEREND MR. LARYNX.   Nothing can be more luminous.

THE HONOURABLE MR. LISTLESS.   And what has all that to do with Dante, and the blue devils ?

MR. HILARY.   Not much, I should think, with Dante, but a great deal with the blue devils.

MR. FLOSKY.   It is very certain, and much to be rejoiced at, that our literature is hag-ridden.   Tea has shattered our nerves ; late dinners make us slaves of indigestion ;   the French Revolution has made us shrink from the name of philosophy, and has destroyed, in the more refined part of the community (of which number I am one), all enthusiasm for political liberty.   That part of the *reading public* which shuns the solid food of reason for the light diet of fiction, requires a perpetual adhibition of *sauce piquante* to the palate of its depraved imagination.   It lived upon ghosts, goblins, and skeletons (I and my friend Mr. Sackbut served up a few of the best), till even the devil himself, though magnified to the size of Mount Athos, became too base, common, and popular,[2] for its surfeited appetite. The ghosts have therefore been laid, and the devil has been cast into outer darkness, and now the delight of our spirits is to dwell on all the vices and blackest passions of our nature, tricked out in a masquerade dress of heroism and disappointed benevolence ;   the

[1] Coleridge named his two eldest children Hartley and Berkeley.   G.
[2] *Henry V*, Act IV, Sc. 1.   G.

whole secret of which lies in forming combinations that contradict all our experience, and affixing the purple shred of some particular virtue to that precise character, in which we should be most certain not to find it in the living world ; and making this single virtue not only redeem all the real and manifest vices of the character, but make them actually pass for necessary adjuncts, and indispensable accompaniments and characteristics of the said virtue.

MR. TOOBAD. That is, because the devil is come among us, and finds it for his interest to destroy all our perceptions of the distinctions of right and wrong.

MARIONETTA. I do not precisely enter into your meaning, Mr. Flosky, and should be glad if you would make it a little more plain to me.

MR. FLOSKY. One or two examples will do it, Miss O'Carroll. If I were to take all the mean and sordid qualities of a money-dealing Jew, and tack on to them, as with a nail, the quality of extreme benevolence, I should have a very decent hero for a modern novel ; and should contribute my quota to the fashionable method of administering a mass of vice, under a thin and unnatural covering of virtue, like a spider wrapt in a bit of gold leaf, and administered as a wholesome pill. On the same principle, if a man knocks me down, and takes my purse and watch by main force, I turn him to account, and set him forth in a tragedy as a dashing young fellow, disinherited for his romantic generosity, and full of a most amiable hatred of the world in general, and his own country in particular, and of a most enlightened and chivalrous affection for himself : then, with the addition of a wild girl to fall in love with him, and a series of adventures in which they break all the Ten Commandments in succession (always, you will observe, for some sublime motive, which must be carefully analysed in its progress), I have as amiable a pair of tragic characters as ever issued from that new region of the belles lettres, which I have called the Morbid Anatomy of Black Bile, and which is greatly to be admired and rejoiced at, as affording a fine scope for the exhibition of mental power.

MR. HILARY. Which is about as well employed as the power of a hot-house would be in forcing up a nettle to the size of an elm. If we go on in this way, we shall have a new art of poetry, of which one of the first rules will be : To remember to forget that there are any such things as sunshine and music in the world.

THE HONOURABLE MR. LISTLESS. It seems to be the case with us at present, or we should not have interrupted Miss O'Carroll's music with this exceedingly dry conversation.

MR. FLOSKY. I should be most happy if Miss O'Carroll would remind us that there are yet both music and sunshine——

THE HONOURABLE MR. LISTLESS. In the voice and the smile of beauty. May I entreat the favour of—(*turning over the pages of music.*)

All were silent, and Marionetta sung :—

> Why are thy looks so blank, grey friar ?
>   Why are thy looks so blue ?
> Thou seem'st more pale and lank, grey friar,
>   Than thou wast used to do :—
>   Say, what has made thee rue ?
>
> Thy form was plump, and a light did shine
>   In thy round and ruby face,
> Which showed an outward visible sign
>   Of an inward spiritual grace :—
>   Say, what has changed thy case ?
>
> Yet will I tell thee true, grey friar,
>   I very well can see,
> That, if thy looks are blue, grey friar,
>   'Tis all for love of me,—
>   'Tis all for love of me.
>
> But breathe not thy vows to me, grey friar,
>   Oh, breathe them not, I pray ;
> For ill beseems in a reverend friar,
>   The love of a mortal may ;
>   And I needs must say thee nay.
>
> But, could'st thou think my heart to move
>   With that pale and silent scowl ?
> Know, he who would win a maiden's love,
>   Whether clad in cap or cowl,
>   Must be more of a lark than an owl.

Scythrop immediately replaced Dante on the shelf, and joined the circle round the beautiful singer. Marionetta gave him a smile of approbation that fully restored his complacency, and they continued on the best possible terms during the remainder of the evening. The Honourable Mr. Listless turned over the leaves with double alacrity, saying, " You are severe upon invalids, Miss O'Carroll : to escape your satire, I must try to be sprightly, though the exertion is too much for me."

CHAPTER VII

A NEW visitor arrived at the Abbey, in the person of Mr. Asterias, the ichthyologist. This gentleman had passed his life in seeking the living wonders of the deep through the four quarters of the world ; he had a cabinet of stuffed and dried fishes, of shells, sea-weeds, corals, and madrepores, that was the admiration and envy of the Royal Society. He had penetrated into the watery den of the Sepia Octopus, disturbed the conjugal happiness of that turtle-dove of the ocean, and come off victorious in a sanguinary conflict. He had been becalmed in the tropical seas, and had watched, in eager expectation, though unhappily always in vain, to see the colossal polypus rise from the water, and entwine its enormous arms round the masts and the rigging. He maintained the origin of all things from water, and insisted that the polypodes were the first of animated things, and that, from their round bodies and many-shooting arms, the Hindoos had taken their gods, the most ancient of deities. But the chief object of his ambition, the end and aim of his researches, was to discover a triton and a mermaid, the existence of which he most potently and implicitly believed, and was prepared to demonstrate, *à priori*, *à posteriori*, *à fortiori*, synthetically and analytically, syllogistically and inductively, by arguments deduced both from acknowledged facts and plausible hypotheses. A report that a mermaid had been seen "sleeking her soft alluring locks" [1] on the sea-coast of Lincolnshire, had brought him in great haste from

[1] Milton : *Comus*, l. 882. G.

London, to pay a long-promised and often-postponed visit to his old acquaintance, Mr. Glowry.

Mr. Asterias was accompanied by his son, to whom he had given the name of Aquarius—flattering himself that he would, in the process of time, become a constellation among the stars of ichthyological science. What charitable female had lent him the mould in which this son was cast, no one pretended to know; and, as he never dropped the most distant allusion to Aquarius's mother, some of the wags of London maintained that he had received the favours of a mermaid, and that the scientific perquisitions which kept him always prowling about the sea-shore, were directed by the less philosophical motive of regaining his lost love.

Mr. Asterias perlustrated the sea-coast for several days, and reaped disappointment, but not despair. One night, shortly after his arrival, he was sitting in one of the windows of the library, looking towards the sea, when his attention was attracted by a figure which was moving near the edge of the surf, and which was dimly visible through the moonless summer night. Its motions were irregular, like those of a person in a state of indecision. It had extremely long hair, which floated in the wind. Whatever else it might be, it certainly was not a fisherman. It might be a lady; but it was neither Mrs. Hilary nor Miss O'Carroll, for they were both in the library. It might be one of the female servants; but it had too much grace, and too striking an air of habitual liberty, to render it probable. Besides, what should one of the female servants be doing there at this hour, moving to and fro, as it seemed, without any visible purpose? It could scarcely be a stranger; for Claydyke, the nearest village, was ten miles distant; and what female would come ten miles across the fens, for no purpose but to hover over the surf under the walls of Nightmare Abbey? Might it not be a mermaid? It was possibly a mermaid. It was probably a mermaid. It was very probably a mermaid. Nay, what else could it be but a mermaid? It certainly was a mermaid. Mr. Asterias stole out of the library on tiptoe, with his finger on his lips, having beckoned Aquarius to follow him.

The rest of the party was in great surprise at Mr. Asterias's movement, and some of them approached the window to see if the locality would tend to elucidate the mystery. Presently they saw him and Aquarius cautiously stealing along on the other side of the moat, but they saw nothing more ; and Mr. Asterias returning, told them, with accents of great disappointment, that he had had a glimpse of a mermaid, but she had eluded him in the darkness, and was gone, he presumed, to sup with some enamoured triton, in a submarine grotto.

"But, seriously, Mr. Asterias," said the Honourable Mr. Listless, " do you positively believe there are such things as mermaids ? "

MR. ASTERIAS. Most assuredly ; and tritons too.

THE HONOURABLE MR. LISTLESS. What ! things that are half human and half fish ?

MR. ASTERIAS. Precisely. They are the oran-outangs of the sea. But I am persuaded that there are also complete sea men, differing in no respect from us, but that they are stupid, and covered with scales ; for, though our organisation seems to exclude us essentially from the class of amphibious animals, yet anatomists well know that the *foramen ovale* may remain open in an adult, and that respiration is, in that case, not necessary to life : and how can it be otherwise explained that the Indian divers, employed in the pearl fishery, pass whole hours under the water ; and that the famous Swedish gardener of Troningholm lived a day and a half under the ice without being drowned ? A nereid, or mermaid, was taken in the year 1403 in a Dutch lake, and was in every respect like a French woman, except that she did not speak.[1] Towards the end of the seventeenth century, an English ship, a hundred and fifty leagues from land, in the Greenland seas, discovered a flotilla of sixty or seventy little skiffs, in each of which was a triton, or sea man : at the approach of the English vessel the whole of them, seized with simultaneous fear, disappeared, skiffs and all, under the water, as if they had been a human variety of the nautilus. The illustrious Don Feijoo [2] has preserved an

[1] Norman Douglas gives Jacob Noierus as the authority for this Siren. See *Siren Land*, Ch. I. G.

[2] Don Benito Geronimo Feijoo y Montenegro, 1675–1764. The cautious scepticism of this popular Benedictine led his admirers to call him " the Spanish Voltaire." G.

authentic and well-attested story of a young Spaniard, named Francis de la Vega, who, bathing with some of his friends in June, 1674, suddenly dived under the sea and rose no more. His friends thought him drowned; they were plebeians and pious Catholics; but a philosopher might very legitimately have drawn the same conclusion.

THE REVEREND MR. LARYNX. Nothing could be more logical.

MR. ASTERIAS. Five years afterwards, some fishermen near Cadiz found in their nets a triton, or sea man; they spoke to him in several languages——

THE REVEREND MR. LARYNX. They were very learned fishermen.

MR. HILARY. They had the gift of tongues by especial favour of their brother fisherman, Saint Peter.

THE HONOURABLE MR. LISTLESS. Is Saint Peter the tutelar saint of Cadiz?

(*None of the company could answer this question, and* MR. ASTERIAS *proceeded.*)

They spoke to him in several languages, but he was as mute as a fish. They handed him over to some holy friars, who exorcised him; but the devil was mute too. After some days he pronounced the name Lierganes. A monk took him to that village. His mother and brothers recognised and embraced him; but he was as insensible to their caresses as any other fish would have been. He had some scales on his body, which dropped off by degrees; but his skin was as hard and rough as shagreen. He stayed at home nine years, without recovering his speech or his reason: he then disappeared again; and one of his old acquaintance, some years after, saw him pop his head out of the water near the coast of the Asturias. These facts were certified by his brothers, and by Don Gaspardo de la Riba Aguero, Knight of Saint James, who lived near Lierganes, and often had the pleasure of our triton's company to dinner.—Pliny mentions an embassy of the Olyssiponians to Tiberius, to give him intelligence of a triton which had been heard playing on its shell in a certain cave ; with several other authenticated facts on the subject of tritons and nereids.[1]

THE HONOURABLE MR. LISTLESS. You astonish me. I have been much on the sea-shore, in the season, but I do not think I ever saw a mermaid. (*He rang, and summoned Fatout, who made his appearance half-seas-over.*) Fatout ! did I ever see a mermaid ?

FATOUT. Mermaid ! mer-r-m-m-aid ! Ah ! merry maid ! Oui, monsieur ! Yes, sir, very many. I vish dere vas von or two here in de kitchen—ma foi ! Dey be all as melancholic as so many tombstone.

THE HONOURABLE MR. LISTLESS. I mean, Fatout, an odd kind of human fish.

FATOUT. De odd fish ! Ah, oui ! I understand de phrase : ve have seen nothing else since ve left town—ma foi !

THE HONOURABLE MR. LISTLESS. You seem to have a cup too much, sir.

FATOUT. Non, monsieur : de cup too little. De fen be very unwholesome, and I drink-a-de ponch vid Raven de butler, to keep out de bad air.

THE HONOURABLE MR. LISTLESS. Fatout ! I insist on your being sober.

FATOUT. Oui, monsieur ; I vil be as sober as de révérendissime père Jean.[2] I should be ver glad of de merry maid ; but de butler be de odd fish, and he swim in de bowl de ponch. Ah ! ah ! I do recollect de leetle-a song :—" About fair maids, and about fair maids, and about my merry maids all." (*Fatout reeled out, singing.*)

THE HONOURABLE MR. LISTLESS. I am overwhelmed : I never saw the rascal in such a condition before. But will you allow me, Mr. Asterias, to inquire into the *cui bono* of all the pains and expense you have incurred to discover a mermaid ? The *cui bono*, sir, is the question I always take the liberty to ask when I see any one taking

---

[1] *Pliny*, Bk. VIII, Ch. 3. G.
[2] Rabelais's Frère Jean des Entommeures, Bk. I, Ch. 27. G.

much trouble for any object. I am myself a sort of Signor Poco-curante, and should like to know if there be any thing better or pleasanter, than the state of existing and doing nothing ?

MR. ASTERIAS. I have made many voyages, Mr. Listless, to remote and barren shores : I have travelled over desert and inhospitable lands : I have defied danger—I have endured fatigue—I have submitted to privation. In the midst of these I have experienced pleasures which I would not at any time have exchanged for that of existing and doing nothing. I have known many evils, but I have never known the worst of all, which, as it seems to me, are those which are comprehended in the inexhaustible varieties of *ennui* : spleen, chagrin, vapours, blue devils, time-killing, discontent, misanthropy, and all their interminable train of fretfulness, queru-lousness, suspicions, jealousies, and fears, which have alike infected society, and the literature of society ; and which would make an arctic ocean of the human mind, if the more humane pursuits of philosophy and science did not keep alive the better feelings and more valuable energies of our nature.

THE HONOURABLE MR. LISTLESS. You are pleased to be severe upon our fashionable belles lettres.

MR. ASTERIAS. Surely not without reason, when pirates, highway-men, and other varieties of the extensive genus Marauder, are the only *beau idéal* of the active, as splenetic and railing misanthropy is of the speculative energy. A gloomy brow and a tragical voice seem to have been of late the characteristics of fashionable manners : and a morbid, withering, deadly, antisocial sirocco, loaded with moral and political despair, breathes through all the groves and valleys of the modern Parnassus ; while science moves on in the calm dignity of its course, affording to youth delights equally pure and vivid—to maturity, calm and grateful occupation—to old age, the most pleasing recollections and inexhaustible materials of agree-able and salutary reflection ; and, while its votary enjoys the dis-interested pleasure of enlarging the intellect and increasing the comforts of society, he is himself independent of the caprices of human intercourse and the accidents of human fortune. Nature is his great and inexhaustible treasure. His days are always too short for his enjoyment : *ennui* is a stranger to his door. At peace with the world and with his own mind, he suffices to himself, makes all around him happy, and the close of his pleasing and beneficial existence is the evening of a beautiful day.[1]

THE HONOURABLE MR. LISTLESS. Really I should like very well to lead such a life myself, but the exertion would be too much for me. Besides, I have been at college. I contrive to get through my day by sinking the morning in bed, and killing the evening in company ; dressing and dining in the intermediate space, and stopping the chinks and crevices of the few vacant moments that remain with a little easy reading. And that amiable discontent and antisociality which you reprobate in our present drawing-room-table literature, I find, I do assure you, a very fine mental tonic, which reconciles me to my favourite pursuit of doing nothing, by showing me that nobody is worth doing any thing for.

MARIONETTA. But is there not in such compositions a kind of unconscious self-detection, which seems to carry their own antidote with them ? For surely no one who cordially and truly either hates or despises the world will publish a volume every three months to say so.

MR. FLOSKY. There is a secret in all this, which I will elucidate with a dusky remark. According to Berkeley, the *esse* of things is *percipi*. They exist as they are perceived. But, leaving for the present, as far as relates to the material world, the materialists, hyloists, and antihyloists, to settle this point among them, which is indeed

> A subtle question, raised among
> Those out o' their wits, and those i' the wrong : [2]

for only we transcendentalists are in the right : we may very safely assert that the *esse* of happiness is *percipi*. It exists as it is perceived. " It is the mind that maketh well or ill." The elements of pleasure and pain are every where. The degree of happiness that any

[1] See Denys Montfort : *Histoire Naturelle des Mollusques ; Vues Générales*, pp. 37, 38. [P.]

[2] Butler : *Hudibras*, Pt. I, Canto II, ll. 703-4. G.

circumstances or objects can confer on us depends on the mental disposition with which we approach them. If you consider what is meant by the common phrases, a happy disposition and a discontented temper, you will perceive that the truth for which I am contending is universally admitted.

(*Mr. Flosky suddenly stopped: he found himself unintentionally trespassing within the limits of common sense.*)

MR. HILARY. It is very true ; a happy disposition finds materials of enjoyment every where. In the city, or the country—in society, or in solitude—in the theatre, or the forest—in the hum of the multitude, or in the silence of the mountains, are alike materials of reflection and elements of pleasure. It is one mode of pleasure to listen to the music of " Don Giovanni," in a theatre glittering with light, and crowded with elegance and beauty : it is another to glide at sunset over the bosom of a lonely lake, where no sound disturbs the silence but the motion of the boat through the waters. A happy disposition derives pleasure from both, a discontented temper from neither, but is always busy in detecting deficiencies, and feeding dissatisfaction with comparisons. The one gathers all the flowers, the other all the nettles, in its path. The one has the faculty of enjoying every thing, the other of enjoying nothing. The one realises all the pleasure of the present good ; the other converts it into pain, by pining after something better, which is only better because it is not present, and which, if it were present, would not be enjoyed. These morbid spirits are in life what professed critics are in literature ; they see nothing but faults, because they are predetermined to shut their eyes to beauties. The critic does his utmost to blight genius in its infancy ; that which rises in spite of him he will not see ; and then he complains of the decline of literature. In like manner, these cankers of society complain of human nature and society, when they have wilfully debarred themselves from all the good they contain, and done their utmost to blight their own happiness and that of all around them. Misanthropy is sometimes the product of disappointed benevolence ; but it is more frequently the offspring of overweening and mortified vanity, quarrelling with the world for not being better treated than it deserves.

SCYTHROP (*to Marionetta*). These remarks are rather uncharitable. There is great good in human nature, but it is at present ill-conditioned. Ardent spirits cannot but be dissatisfied with things as they are ; and according to their views of the probabilities of amelioration, they will rush into the extremes of either hope or despair—of which the first is enthusiasm, and the second misanthropy ; but their sources in this case are the same, as the Severn and the Wye run in different directions, and both rise in Plinlimmon.

MARIONETTA. "And there is salmon in both ; " for the resemblance is about as close as that between Macedon and Monmouth.[1]

CHAPTER VIII

MARIONETTA observed the next day a remarkable perturbation in Scythrop, for which she could not imagine any probable cause. She was willing to believe at first that it had some transient and trifling source, and would pass off in a day or two ; but, contrary to this expectation, it daily increased. She was well aware that Scythrop had a strong tendency to the love of mystery, for its own sake ; that is to say, he would employ mystery to serve a purpose, but would first choose his purpose by its capability of mystery. He seemed now to have more mystery on his hands than the laws of the system allowed, and to wear his coat of darkness with an air of great discomfort. All her little playful arts lost by degrees much of their power either to irritate or to soothe ; and the first perception of her diminished influence produced in her an immediate depression of spirits, and a consequent sadness of demeanour, that rendered her very interesting to Mr. Glowry ; who, duly considering the improbability of accomplishing his wishes with respect to Miss Toobad (which improbability naturally increased in the diurnal ratio of that young lady's absence), began to reconcile himself by degrees to the idea of Marionetta being his daughter.

Marionetta made many ineffectual attempts to extract from Scythrop the secret of his mystery ; and, in despair of drawing it from himself, began to form hopes that she might find a clue to it

[1] *Henry V*, Act IV, Sc. 7. G.

from Mr. Flosky, who was Scythrop's dearest friend, and was more frequently than any other person admitted to his solitary tower. Mr. Flosky, however, had ceased to be visible in a morning. He was engaged in the composition of a dismal ballad; and, Marionetta's uneasiness overcoming her scruples of decorum, she determined to seek him in the apartment which he had chosen for his study. She tapped at the door, and at the sound "Come in," entered the apartment. It was noon, and the sun was shining in full splendour, much to the annoyance of Mr. Flosky, who had obviated the inconvenience by closing the shutters, and drawing the window-curtains. He was sitting at his table by the light of a solitary candle, with a pen in one hand, and a muffineer in the other, with which he occasionally sprinkled salt on the wick to make it burn blue. He sate with "his eye in a fine frenzy rolling,"[1] and turned his inspired gaze on Marionetta as if she had been the ghastly ladie of a magical vision; then placed his hand before his eyes, with an appearance of manifest pain—shook his head—withdrew his hand—rubbed his eyes, like a waking man—and said, in a tone of ruefulness most jeremitaylorically pathetic, "To what am I to attribute this very unexpected pleasure, my dear Miss O'Carroll?"

MARIONETTA. I must apologise for intruding on you, Mr. Flosky; but the interest which I—you—take in my cousin Scythrop——

MR. FLOSKY. Pardon me, Miss O'Carroll; I do not take any interest in any person or thing on the face of the earth; which sentiment, if you analyse it, you will find to be the quintessence of the most refined philanthropy.

MARIONETTA. I will take it for granted that it is so, Mr. Flosky; I am not conservant with metaphysical subtleties, but——

MR. FLOSKY. Subtleties! my dear Miss O'Carroll. I am sorry to find you participating in the vulgar error of the *reading public*, to whom an unusual collocation of words, involving a juxtaposition of antiperistatical ideas, immediately suggests the notion of hyperoxysophistical paradoxology.[2]

[1] *A Midsummer Night's Dream*, Act V, Sc. 1. G.
[2] Contrary, antagonistic to; over-specious maintenance of paradoxical opinions. G.

MARIONETTA. Indeed, Mr. Flosky, it suggests no such notion to me. I have sought you for the purpose of obtaining information.

MR. FLOSKY (*shaking his head*). No one ever sought me for such a purpose before.

MARIONETTA. I think, Mr. Flosky—that is, I believe—that is, I fancy—that is, I imagine——

MR. FLOSKY. The τουτεστι, the *id est*, the *cioè*, the *c'est à dire*, the *that is*, my dear Miss O'Carroll, is not applicable in this case—if you will permit me to take the liberty of saying so. Think is not synonymous with believe—for belief, in many most important particulars, results from the total absence, the absolute negation of thought, and is thereby the sane and orthodox condition of mind ; and thought and belief are both essentially different from fancy, and fancy, again, is distinct from imagination. This distinction between fancy and imagination is one of the most abstruse and important points of metaphysics. I have written seven hundred pages of promise to elucidate it, which promise I shall keep as faithfully as the bank will its promise to pay.

MARIONETTA. I assure you, Mr. Flosky, I care no more about metaphysics than I do about the bank ; and, if you will condescend to talk to a simple girl in intelligible terms——

MR. FLOSKY. Say not condescend ! Know you not that you talk to the most humble of men, to one who has buckled on the armour of sanctity, and clothed himself with humility as with a garment ?

MARIONETTA. My cousin Scythrop has of late had an air of mystery about him, which gives me great uneasiness.

MR. FLOSKY. That is strange : nothing is so becoming to a man as an air of mystery. Mystery is the very key-stone of all that is beautiful in poetry, all that is sacred in faith, and all that is recondite in transcendental psychology. I am writing a ballad which is all mystery ; it is " such stuff as dreams are made of," [1] and is, indeed, stuff made of a dream ; for, last night I fell asleep as usual over my

---

[1] *The Tempest*, Act IV, Sc. 1. G.

book, and had a vision of pure reason. I composed five hundred lines in my sleep [1]; so that, having had a dream of a ballad, I am now officiating as my own Peter Quince, and making a ballad of my dream, and it shall be called Bottom's Dream, because it has no bottom. [2]

MARIONETTA. I see, Mr. Flosky, you think my intrusion unseasonable, and are inclined to punish it, by talking nonsense to me. (*Mr. Flosky gave a start at the word nonsense, which almost overturned the table.*) I assure you, I would not have intruded if I had not been very much interested in the question I wish to ask you.—(*Mr. Flosky listened in sullen dignity.*)—My cousin Scythrop seems to have some secret preying on his mind.—(*Mr. Flosky was silent.*)—He seems very unhappy—Mr. Flosky.—Perhaps you are acquainted with the cause. —(*Mr. Flosky was still silent.*)—I only wish to know—Mr. Flosky— if it is any thing—that could be remedied by any thing—that any one—of whom I know any thing—could do.

MR. FLOSKY (*after a pause*). There are various ways of getting at secrets. The most approved methods, as recommended both theoretically and practically in philosophical novels, are eavesdropping at key-holes, picking the locks of chests and desks, peeping into letters, steaming wafers, and insinuating hot wire under sealing wax ; none of which methods I hold it lawful to practise.

MARIONETTA. Surely, Mr. Flosky, you cannot suspect me of wishing to adopt or encourage such base and contemptible arts.

MR. FLOSKY. Yet are they recommended, and with well-strung reasons, by writers of gravity and note, as simple and easy methods of studying character, and gratifying that laudable curiosity which aims at the knowledge of man.

MARIONETTA. I am as ignorant of this morality which you do not approve, as of the metaphysics which you do : I should be glad to know by your means, what is the matter with my cousin ; I do not like to see him unhappy, and I suppose there is some reason for it.

[1] An allusion to Coleridge's *Kubla Khan*. G.
[2] *A Midsummer Night's Dream*, Act IV, Sc. 1. G.

MR. FLOSKY. Now I should rather suppose there is no reason for it : it is the fashion to be unhappy. To have a reason for being so would be exceedingly common-place : to be so without any is the province of genius : the art of being miserable for misery's sake, has been brought to great perfection in our days ; and the ancient Odyssey, which held forth a shining example of the endurance of real misfortune, will give place to a modern one, setting out a more instructive picture of querulous impatience under imaginary evils.

MARIONETTA. Will you oblige me, Mr. Flosky, by giving me a plain answer to a plain question ?

MR. FLOSKY. It is impossible, my dear Miss O'Carroll. I never gave a plain answer to a question in my life.

MARIONETTA. Do you, or do you not, know what is the matter with my cousin ?

MR. FLOSKY. To say that I do not know, would be to say that I am ignorant of something ; and God forbid, that a transcendental metaphysician, who has pure anticipated cognitions of every thing, and carries the whole science of geometry in his head without ever having looked into Euclid, should fall into so empirical an error as to declare himself ignorant of any thing : to say that I do know, would be to pretend to positive and circumstantial knowledge touching present matter of fact, which, when you consider the nature of evidence, and the various lights in which the same thing may be seen——

MARIONETTA. I see, Mr. Flosky, that either you have no information, or are determined not to impart it ; and I beg your pardon for having given you this unnecessary trouble.

MR. FLOSKY. My dear Miss O'Carroll, it would have given me great pleasure to have said any thing that would have given you pleasure ; but if any person living could make report of having obtained any information on any subject from Ferdinando Flosky, my transcendental reputation would be ruined for ever.

CHAPTER IX

SCYTHROP grew every day more reserved, mysterious, and *distrait*; and gradually lengthened the duration of his diurnal seclusions in his tower. Marionetta thought she perceived in all this very manifest symptoms of a warm love cooling.

It was seldom that she found herself alone with him in the morning, and, on these occasions, if she was silent in the hope of his speaking first, not a syllable would he utter; if she spoke to him indirectly, he assented monosyllabically; if she questioned him, his answers were brief, constrained, and evasive. Still, though her spirits were depressed, her playfulness had not so totally forsaken her, but that it illuminated at intervals the gloom of Nightmare Abbey; and if, on any occasion, she observed in Scythrop tokens of unextinguished or returning passion, her love of tormenting her lover immediately got the better both of her grief and her sympathy, though not of her curiosity, which Scythrop seemed determined not to satisfy. This playfulness, however, was in a great measure artificial, and usually vanished with the irritable Strephon, to whose annoyance it had been exerted. The Genius Loci, the *tutela* of Nightmare Abbey, the spirit of black melancholy, began to set his seal on her pallescent countenance. Scythrop perceived the change, found his tender sympathies awakened, and did his utmost to comfort the afflicted damsel, assuring her that his seeming inattention had only proceeded from his being involved in a profound meditation on a very hopeful scheme for the regeneration of human society. Marionetta called him ungrateful, cruel, cold-hearted, and accompanied her reproaches with many sobs and tears : poor Scythrop growing every moment more soft and submissive—till, at length, he threw himself at her feet, and declared that no competition of beauty, however dazzling, genius, however transcendent, talents, however cultivated, or philosophy, however enlightened, should ever make him renounce his divine Marionetta.

"Competition!" thought Marionetta, and suddenly, with an air of the most freezing indifference, she said, "You are perfectly at liberty, sir, to do as you please ; I beg you will follow your own plans, without any reference to me."

Scythrop was confounded. What was become of all her passion and her tears ? Still kneeling, he kissed her hand with rueful timidity, and said, in most pathetic accents, " Do you not love me, Marionetta ? "

" No," said Marionetta, with a look of cold composure : " No." Scythrop still looked up incredulously. " No, I tell you."

" Oh ! very well, madam," said Scythrop, rising, " if that is the case, there are those in the world——"

" To be sure there are, sir ;—and do you suppose I do not see through your designs, you ungenerous monster ? "

" My designs ? Marionetta ! "

" Yes, your designs, Scythrop. You have come here to cast me off, and artfully contrive that it should appear to be my doing, and not yours, thinking to quiet your tender conscience with this pitiful stratagem. But do not suppose that you are of so much consequence to me : do not suppose it : you are of no consequence to me at all— none at all : therefore, leave me : I renounce you : leave me ; why do you not leave me ? "

Scythrop endeavoured to remonstrate, but without success. She reiterated her injunctions to him to leave her, till, in the simplicity of his spirit, he was preparing to comply. When he had nearly reached the door, Marionetta said, " Farewell." Scythrop looked back. " Farewell, Scythrop," she repeated, " you will never see me again."

" Never see you again, Marionetta ? "

" I shall go from hence to-morrow, perhaps to-day ; and before we meet again, one of us will be married, and we might as well be dead, you know, Scythrop."

The sudden change of her voice in the last few words, and the burst of tears that accompanied them, acted like electricity on the tender-hearted youth ; and, in another instant, a complete reconcilia-tion was accomplished without the intervention of words.

There are, indeed, some learned casuists, who maintain that love has no language, and that all the misunderstandings and dissensions of lovers arise from the fatal habit of employing words on a subject to which words are inapplicable ; that love, beginning with looks, that is to say, with the physiognomical expression of congenial mental dispositions, tends through a regular gradation of signs and symbols of affection, to that consummation which is most devoutly to be wished ; and that it neither is necessary that there should be, nor probable that there would be, a single word spoken from first to last between two sympathetic spirits, were it not that the arbitrary institutions of society have raised, at every step of this very simple process, so many complicated impediments and barriers in the shape of settlements and ceremonies, parents and guardians, lawyers, Jew-brokers, and parsons, that many an adventurous knight (who, in order to obtain the conquest of the Hesperian fruit, is obliged to fight his way through all these monsters), is either repulsed at the onset, or vanquished before the achievement of his enterprise : and such a quantity of unnatural talking is rendered inevitably necessary through all the stages of the progression, that the tender and volatile spirit of love often takes flight on the pinions of some of the επεα πτεροεντα, or *winged words*, which are pressed into his service in despite of himself.

At this conjuncture, Mr. Glowry entered, and sitting down near them, said, " I see how it is ; and, as we are all sure to be miserable do what we may, there is no need of taking pains to make one another more so ; therefore, with God's blessing and mine, there "—joining their hands as he spoke.

Scythrop was not exactly prepared for this decisive step ; but he could only stammer out, " Really, sir, you are too good ; " and Mr. Glowry departed to bring Mr. Hilary to ratify the act.

Now, whatever truth there may be in the theory of love and language, of which we have so recently spoken, certain it is, that during Mr. Glowry's absence, which lasted half an hour, not a single word was said by either Scythrop or Marionetta.

Mr. Glowry returned with Mr. Hilary, who was delighted at the prospect of so advantageous an establishment for his orphan niece, of whom he considered himself in some manner the guardian, and nothing remained, as Mr. Glowry observed, but to fix the day.

Marionetta blushed, and was silent. Scythrop was also silent for a time, and at length hesitatingly said, " My dear sir, your goodness overpowers me ; but really you are so precipitate."

Now, this remark, if the young lady had made it, would, whether she thought it or not—for sincerity is a thing of no account on these occasions, nor indeed on any other, according to Mr. Flosky—this remark, if the young lady had made it, would have been perfectly *comme il faut*; but, being made by the young gentleman, it was *toute autre chose*, and was, indeed, in the eyes of his mistress, a most heinous and irremissible offence. Marionetta was angry, very angry, but she concealed her anger, and said, calmly and coldly, "Certainly, you are much too precipitate, Mr. Glowry. I assure you, sir, I have by no means made up my mind; and, indeed, as far as I know it, it inclines the other way; but it will be quite time enough to think of these matters seven years hence." Before surprise permitted reply, the young lady had locked herself up in her own apartment.

"Why Scythrop," said Mr. Glowry, elongating his face exceedingly, "the devil is come among us sure enough, as Mr. Toobad observes: I thought you and Marionetta were both of a mind."

"So we are, I believe, sir," said Scythrop, gloomily, and stalked away to his tower.

"Mr. Glowry," said Mr. Hilary, "I do not very well understand all this."

"Whims, brother Hilary," said Mr. Glowry; "some little foolish love quarrel, nothing more. Whims, freaks, April showers. They will be blown over by to-morrow."

"If not," said Mr. Hilary, "these April showers have made us April fools."

"Ah!" said Mr. Glowry, "you are a happy man, and in all your afflictions you can console yourself with a joke, let it be ever so bad, provided you crack it yourself. I should be very happy to laugh with you, if it would give you any satisfaction; but, really, at present, my heart is so sad, that I find it impossible to levy a contribution on my muscles."

CHAPTER X

On the evening on which Mr. Asterias had caught a glimpse of a female figure on the sea-shore, which he had translated into the

visual sign of his interior cognition of a mermaid, Scythrop, retiring
to his tower, found his study pre-occupied. A stranger, muffled in a
cloak, was sitting at his table. Scythrop paused in surprise. The
stranger rose at his entrance, and looked at him intently a few
minutes, in silence. The eyes of the stranger alone were visible.
All the rest of the figure was muffled and mantled in the folds of a
black cloak, which was raised, by the right hand, to the level of the
eyes. This scrutiny being completed, the stranger, dropping the
cloak, said, " I see, by your physiognomy, that you may be trusted ; "
and revealed to the astonished Scythrop a female form and countenance of dazzling grace and beauty, with long flowing hair of raven
blackness, and large black eyes of almost oppressive brilliancy, which
strikingly contrasted with a complexion of snowy whiteness.[1] Her
dress was extremely elegant, but had an appearance of foreign fashion,
as if both the lady and her mantua-maker were of "a far countree."

> " I guess 'twas frightful there to see
> A lady so richly clad as she,
> Beautiful exceedingly." [2]

For, if it be terrible to one young lady to find another under a
tree at midnight, it must, *à fortiori*, be much more terrible to a young
gentleman to find a young lady in his study at that hour. If the
logical consecutiveness of this conclusion be not manifest to my
readers, I am sorry for their dulness, and must refer them, for more
ample elucidation, to a treatise which Mr. Flosky intends to write,
on the Categories of Relation, which comprehend Substance and
Accident, Cause and Effect, Action and Re-action.

Scythrop, therefore, either was or ought to have been frightened ;
at all events, he was astonished ; and astonishment, though not in
itself fear, is nevertheless a good stage towards it, and is, indeed, as
it were, the half-way house between respect and terror, according to
Mr. Burke's graduated scale of the sublime.[3]

[1] This lady was based on Mary Godwin, Shelley's second wife, and
Peacock was careful to make the physical resemblance as slight as possible,
Mary being strikingly fair and blue-eyed. G.

[2] Coleridge: *Christabel.* G.

[3] There must be some mistake in this, for the whole honourable band of
gentlemen-pensioners has resolved unanimously, that Mr. Burke was a very
sublime person, particularly after he had prostituted his own soul, and

" You are surprised," said the lady ; " yet why should you be surprised ? If you had met me in a drawing-room, and I had been introduced to you by an old woman, it would have been a matter of course : can the division of two or three walls, and the absence of an unimportant personage, make the same object essentially different in the perception of a philosopher ? "

" Certainly not," said Scythrop ; " but when any class of objects has habitually presented itself to our perceptions in invariable conjunction with particular relations, then, on the sudden appearance of one object of the class divested of those accompaniments, the essential difference of the relation is, by an involuntary process, transferred to the object itself, which thus offers itself to our perceptions with all the strangeness of novelty."

" You are a philosopher," said the lady, " and a lover of liberty. You are the author of a treatise called ' Philosophical Gas ; or, a Project for a General Illumination of the Human Mind.' "

" I am," said Scythrop, delighted at this first blossom of his renown.

" I am a stranger in this country," said the lady ; " I have been but a few days in it, yet I find myself immediately under the necessity of seeking refuge from an atrocious persecution. I had no friend to whom I could apply ; and, in the midst of my difficulties,

---

betrayed his country and mankind, for £1200 a year : yet he does not appear to have been a very terrible personage, and certainly went off with a very small portion of human respect, though he contrived to excite, in a great degree, the astonishment of all honest men. Our immaculate laureate (who gives us to understand that, if he had not been purified by holy matrimony into a mystical type, he would have died a virgin,) is another sublime gentleman of the same genus : he very much astonished some persons when he sold his birthright for a pot of sack ; but not even his *Sosia* has a grain of respect for him, though, doubtless, he thinks his name very terrible to the enemy, when he flourishes his criticopoeticopolitical tomahawk, and sets up his Indian yell for the blood of his old friends : but, at best, he is a mere political scarecrow, a man of straw, ridiculous to all who know of what materials he is made ; and to none more so, than to those who have stuffed him, and set him up, as the Priapus of the garden of the golden apples of corruption. [P.] [The reference is to Burke's *Philosophical Inquiry into the origin of our ideas of the Sublime and Beautiful*. In Plautus's *Amphitryon* Mercury assumes the form of Sosia. Peacock uses Sosia here to mean Southey's other self, the author of his early republican poems. G.]

accident threw your pamphlet in my way. I saw that I had, at least, one kindred mind in this nation, and determined to apply to you."

"And what would you have me do ? " said Scythrop, more and more amazed, and not a little perplexed.

"I would have you," said the young lady, "assist me in finding some place of retreat, where I can remain concealed from the indefatigable search that is being made for me. I have been so nearly caught once or twice already, that I cannot confide any longer in my own ingenuity."

Doubtless, thought Scythrop, this is one of my golden candle-sticks. "I have constructed," said he, "in this tower, an entrance to a small suite of unknown apartments in the main building, which I defy any creature living to detect. If you would like to remain there a day or two, till I can find you a more suitable concealment, you may rely on the honour of a transcendental eleutherarch."

"I rely on myself," said the lady. "I act as I please, go where I please, and let the world say what it will. I am rich enough to set it at defiance. It is the tyrant of the poor and the feeble, but the slave of those who are above the reach of its injury."

Scythrop ventured to inquire the name of his fair *protégée*. "What is a name ? " said the lady : " any name will serve the purpose of distinction. Call me Stella.[1] I see by your looks," she added, "that you think all this very strange. When you know me better, your surprise will cease. I submit not to be an accomplice in my sex's slavery. I am, like yourself, a lover of freedom, and I carry my theory into practice. *They alone are subject to blind authority who have no reliance on their own strength.*" [2]

Stella took possession of the recondite apartments. Scythrop intended to find her another asylum ; but from day to day he postponed his intention, and by degrees forgot it. The young lady reminded him of it from day to day, till she also forgot it. Scythrop

---

[1] Goethe's *Stella*, translated by Hookham and Carpenter, 1798. Ferdinand, the hero, has relations with "three incomparable beings, made miserable by me—wretched without me ! " his situation resembling that of Scythrop, and indeed that of Shelley between Harriet and Mary. G.

[2] Mary Wollstonecraft. *A Vindication of the Rights of Women*, Ch. V, Sec. 4. G.

was anxious to learn her history ; but she would add nothing to what she had already communicated, that she was shunning an atrocious persecution. Scythrop thought of Lord C. and the Alien Act, and said, " As you will not tell your name, I suppose it is in the green bag." Stella, not understanding what he meant, was silent ; and Scythrop, translating silence into acquiescence, concluded that he was sheltering an *illuminée* whom Lord S. suspected of an intention to take the Tower, and set fire to the Bank : exploits, at least, as likely to be accomplished by the hands and eyes of a young beauty, as by a drunken cobbler and doctor, armed with a pamphlet and an old stocking.[1]

Stella, in her conversations with Scythrop, displayed a highly cultivated and energetic mind, full of impassioned schemes of liberty, and impatience of masculine usurpation. She had a lively sense of all the oppressions that are done under the sun ; [2] and the vivid pictures which her imagination presented to her of the numberless scenes of injustice and misery which are being acted at every moment in every part of the inhabited world, gave an habitual seriousness to her physiognomy, that made it seem as if a smile had never once hovered on her lips. She was intimately conversant with the German language and literature ; and Scythrop listened with delight to her repetitions of her favourite passages from Schiller and Goethe, and to her encomiums on the sublime Spartacus Weishaupt, the immortal founder of the sect of the Illuminati.[3] Scythrop found that his soul had a greater capacity of love than the image of Marionetta had filled. The form of Stella took possession of every vacant corner of the cavity, and by degrees displaced that of Marionetta from many of the outworks of the citadel ; though the latter still held possession of the *keep*. He judged, from his new friend calling herself Stella, that, if it were not her real name, she was an admirer of the principles

[1] Lords C. and S. are Castlereagh and Sidmouth. The Alien Act of 1816 gave the Government power to deport suspected aliens. The green bag is a brief case, here used for the Attorney General's in a prosecution. The " drunken cobbler and doctor " were a cobbler named Carter and a surgeon named Watson, who were arrested after a riot in the City of London on 2nd December 1816. G.

[2] *Ecclesiastes* iv. 1. G.

[3] Adam Weishaupt, known as Spartacus, founded the secret society of the Illuminati at Ingoldstadt in 1776. G.

of the German play from which she had taken it, and took an opportunity of leading the conversation to that subject ; but to his great surprise, the lady spoke very ardently of the singleness and exclusiveness of love, and declared that the reign of affection was one and indivisible ; that it might be transferred, but could not be participated. "If I ever love," said she, " I shall do so without limit or restriction. I shall hold all difficulties light, all sacrifices cheap, all obstacles gossamer. But for love so total, I shall claim a return as absolute. I will have no rival : whether more or less favoured will be of little moment. I will be neither first nor second—I will be alone. The heart which I shall possess I will possess entirely, or entirely renounce."

Scythrop did not dare to mention the name of Marionetta ; he trembled lest some unlucky accident should reveal it to Stella, though he scarcely knew what result to wish or anticipate, and lived in the double fever of a perpetual dilemma. He could not dissemble to himself that he was in love, at the same time, with two damsels of minds and habits as remote as the antipodes. The scale of predilection always inclined to the fair one who happened to be present ; but the absent was never effectually outweighed, though the degrees of exaltation and depression varied according to accidental variations in the outward and visible signs of the inward and spiritual graces of his respective charmers. Passing and repassing several times a day from the company of the one to that of the other, he was like a shuttle-cock between two battle-dores, changing its direction as rapidly as the oscillations of a pendulum, receiving many a hard knock on the cork of a sensitive heart, and flying from point to point on the feathers of a super-sublimated head. This was an awful state of things. He had now as much mystery about him as any romantic transcendentalist or transcendental romancer could desire. He had his esoterical and his exoterical love. He could not endure the thought of losing either of them, but he trembled when he imagined the possibility that some fatal discovery might deprive him of both. The old proverb concerning two strings to a bow gave him some gleams of comfort ; but that concerning two stools occurred to him more frequently, and covered his forehead with a cold perspiration. With Stella, he could indulge freely in all his romantic and philosophical visions. He could build castles in the air, and she would pile towers and turrets on the imaginary edifices. With Marionetta it was otherwise : she knew nothing of the world and society beyond the sphere of her own experience. Her life was all music and sunshine, and she wondered what any one could see to complain of in such a pleasant state of things. She loved Scythrop, she hardly knew why ; indeed she was not always sure that she loved him at all : she felt her fondness increase or diminish in an inverse ratio to his. When she had manœuvred him into a fever of passionate love, she often felt and always assumed indifference : if she found that her coldness was contagious, and that Scythrop either was, or pretended to be, as indifferent as herself, she would become doubly kind, and raise him again to that elevation from which she had previously thrown him down. Thus, when his love was flowing, hers was ebbing : when his was ebbing, hers was flowing. Now and then there were moments of level tide, when reciprocal affection seemed to promise imperturbable harmony ; but Scythrop could scarcely resign his spirit to the pleasing illusion, before the pinnace of the lover's affections was caught in some eddy of the lady's caprice, and he was whirled away from the shore of his hopes, without rudder or compass, into an ocean of mists and storms. It resulted, from this system of conduct, that all that passed between Scythrop and Marionetta consisted in making and unmaking love. He had no opportunity to take measure of her understanding by conversations on general subjects, and on his favourite designs ; and, being left in this respect to the exercise of indefinite conjecture, he took it for granted, as most lovers would do in similar circumstances, that she had great natural talents, which she wasted at present on trifles : but coquetry would end with marriage, and leave room for philosophy to exert its influence on her mind. Stella had no coquetry, no disguise : she was an enthusiast in subjects of general interest ; and her conduct to Scythrop was always uniform, or rather showed a regular progression of partiality which seemed fast ripening into love.

CHAPTER XI

SCYTHROP, attending one day the summons to dinner, found in the drawing-room his friend Mr. Cypress the poet,[1] whom he had known at college, and who was a great favourite of Mr. Glowry. Mr. Cypress said, he was on the point of leaving England, but could not think of doing so without a farewell-look at Nightmare Abbey and his respected friends, the moody Mr. Glowry and the mysterious Mr. Scythrop, the sublime Mr. Flosky and the pathetic Mr. Listless ; to all of whom, and the morbid hospitality of the melancholy dwelling in which they were then assembled, he assured them he should always look back with as much affection as his lacerated spirit could feel for anything. The sympathetic condolence of their respective replies was cut short by Raven's announcement of " dinner on table."

The conversation that took place when the wine was in circulation, and the ladies were withdrawn, we shall report with our usual scrupulous fidelity.

MR. GLOWRY.   You are leaving England, Mr. Cypress.   There is a delightful melancholy in saying farewell to an old acquaintance, when the chances are twenty to one against ever meeting again. A smiling bumper to a sad parting, and let us all be unhappy together.

MR. CYPRESS (*filling a bumper*).   This is the only social habit that the disappointed spirit never unlearns.

THE REVEREND MR. LARYNX (*filling*).   It is the only piece of academical learning that the finished educatee retains.

MR. FLOSKY (*filling*).   It is the only objective fact which the sceptic can realise.

SCYTHROP (*filling*).   It is the only styptic for a bleeding heart.

THE HONOURABLE MR. LISTLESS (*filling*).   It is the only trouble that is very well worth taking.

MR. ASTERIAS (*filling*).   It is the only key of conversational truth.

[1] Byron.   G.

MR. TOOBAD (*filling*). It is the only antidote to the great wrath of the devil.

MR. HILARY (*filling*). It is the only symbol of perfect life. The inscription "HIC NON BIBITUR" will suit nothing but a tombstone.[1]

MR. GLOWRY. You will see many fine old ruins, Mr. Cypress; crumbling pillars, and mossy walls—many a one-legged Venus and headless Minerva—many a Neptune buried in sand—many a Jupiter turned topsy-turvy—many a perforated Bacchus doing duty as a water-pipe—many reminiscences of the ancient world, which I hope was better worth living in than the modern; though, for myself, I care not a straw more for one than the other, and would not go twenty miles to see any thing that either could show.

MR. CYPRESS. It is something to seek, Mr. Glowry. The mind is restless, and must persist in seeking, though to find is to be disappointed. Do you feel no aspirations towards the countries of Socrates and Cicero? No wish to wander among the venerable remains of the greatness that has passed for ever?

MR. GLOWRY. Not a grain.

SCYTHROP. It is, indeed, much the same as if a lover should dig up the buried form of his mistress, and gaze upon relics which are any thing but herself, to wander among a few mouldy ruins, that are only imperfect indexes to lost volumes of glory, and meet at every step the more melancholy ruins of human nature—a degenerate race of stupid and shrivelled slaves,[2] grovelling in the lowest depths of servility and superstition.

THE HONOURABLE MR. LISTLESS. It is the fashion to go abroad. I have thought of it myself, but am hardly equal to the exertion. To be sure, a little eccentricity and originality are allowable in some cases; and the most eccentric and original of all characters is an Englishman who stays at home.

SCYTHROP. I should have no pleasure in visiting countries that are past all hope of regeneration. There is great hope of our own;

[1] See Rabelais: Bk. I, Ch. 1. G.
[2] "The men are hardly men; they look a tribe of stupid and shrivelled slaves." Shelley to Peacock, Milan, April 20, 1818. G.

and it seems to me that an Englishman, who, either by his station in society, or by his genius, or (as in your instance, Mr. Cypress,) by both, has the power of essentially serving his country in its arduous struggle with its domestic enemies, yet forsakes his country, which is still so rich in hope, to dwell in others which are only fertile in the ruins of memory, does what none of those ancients, whose fragmentary memorials you venerate, would have done in similar circumstances.

MR. CYPRESS. Sir, I have quarrelled with my wife ; and a man who has quarrelled with his wife is absolved from all duty to his country. I have written an ode to tell the people as much, and they may take it as they list.

SCYTHROP. Do you suppose, if Brutus had quarrelled with his wife, he would have given it as a reason to Cassius for having nothing to do with his enterprise ? Or would Cassius have been satisfied with such an excuse ?

MR. FLOSKY. Brutus was a senator ; so is our dear friend : but the cases are different. Brutus had some hope of political good : Mr. Cypress has none. How should he, after what we have seen in France ?

SCYTHROP. A Frenchman is born in harness, ready saddled, bitted, and bridled, for any tyrant to ride. He will fawn under his rider one moment, and throw him and kick him to death the next ; but another adventurer springs on his back, and by dint of whip and spur on he goes as before. We may, without much vanity, hope better of ourselves.

MR. CYPRESS. I have no hope for myself or for others. Our life is a false nature ; it is not in the harmony of things ; it is an all-blasting upas, whose root is earth, and whose leaves are the skies which rain their poison-dews upon mankind. We wither from our youth ; we gasp with unslaked thirst for unattainable good ; lured from the first to the last by phantoms—love, fame, ambition, avarice —all idle, and all ill—one meteor of many names, that vanishes in the smoke of death.[1]

[1] *Childe Harold*, canto 4. cxxiv. cxxvi. [P.]

MR. FLOSKY. A most delightful speech, Mr. Cypress. A most amiable and instructive philosophy. You have only to impress its truth on the minds of all living men, and life will then, indeed, be the desert and the solitude ; and I must do you, myself, and our mutual friends, the justice to observe, that let society only give fair play at one and the same time, as I flatter myself it is inclined to do, to your system of morals, and my system of metaphysics, and Scythrop's system of politics, and Mr. Listless's system of manners, and Mr. Toobad's system of religion, and the result will be as fine a mental chaos as even the immortal Kant himself could ever have hoped to see ; in the prospect of which I rejoice.

MR. HILARY. "Certainly, ancient, it is not a thing to rejoice at : "[1] I am one of those who cannot see the good that is to result from all this mystifying and blue-devilling of society. The contrast it presents to the cheerful and solid wisdom of antiquity is too forcible not to strike any one who has the least knowledge of classical litera- ture. To represent vice and misery as the necessary accompaniments of genius, is as mischievous as it is false, and the feeling is as un- classical as the language in which it is usually expressed.

MR. TOOBAD. It is our calamity. The devil has come among us, and has begun by taking possession of all the cleverest fellows. Yet, forsooth, this is the enlightened age. Marry, how ? Did our ancestors go peeping about with dark lanterns, and do we walk at our ease in broad sunshine ? Where is the manifestation of our light ? By what symptoms do you recognise it ? What are its signs, its tokens, its symptoms, its symbols, its categories, its condi- tions ? What is it, and why ? How, where, when is it to be seen, felt, and understood ? What do we see by it which our ancestors saw not, and which at the same time is worth seeing ? We see a hundred men hanged, where they saw one. We see five hundred transported, where they saw one. We see five thousand in the workhouse, where they saw one. We see scores of Bible Societies, where they saw none. We see paper, where they saw gold. We see men in stays, where they saw men in armour. We see painted faces, where they saw healthy ones. We see children perishing in manu-

---

[1] *Henry V*, Act III, Sc. 6.   G.

factories, where they saw them flourishing in the fields. We see prisons, where they saw castles. We see masters, where they saw representatives.[1] In short, they saw true men, where we see false knaves. They saw Milton, and we see Mr. Sackbut.

MR. FLOSKY. "The false knave, sir, is my honest friend; therefore, I beseech you, let him be countenanced. God forbid but a knave should have some countenance at his friend's request." [2]

MR. TOOBAD. " Good men and true " was their common term, like the καλος κάγαθος [3] of the Athenians. It is so long since men have been either good or true, that it is to be questioned which is most obsolete, the fact or the phraseology.

MR. CYPRESS. There is no worth nor beauty but in the mind's idea. Love sows the wind and reaps the whirlwind.[4] Confusion, thrice confounded, is the portion of him who rests even for an instant on that most brittle of reeds—the affection of a human being. The sum of our social destiny is to inflict or to endure.[5]

MR. HILARY. Rather to bear and forbear, Mr. Cypress—a maxim which you perhaps despise. Ideal beauty is not the mind's creation : it is real beauty, refined and purified in the mind's alembic, from the alloy which always more or less accompanies it in our mixed and imperfect nature. But still the gold exists in a very ample degree. To expect too much is a disease in the expectant, for which human nature is not responsible ; and, in the common name of humanity, I protest against these false and mischievous ravings. To rail against humanity for not being abstract perfection, and against human love for not realising all the splendid visions of the poets of chivalry, is to rail at the summer for not being all sunshine, and at the rose for not being always in bloom.

MR. CYPRESS. Human love ! Love is not an inhabitant of the earth. We worship him as the Athenians did their unknown God : but broken hearts are the martyrs of his faith, and the eye shall never see the form which phantasy paints, and which passion pursues

---

[1] Heirs of great families, i.e. leaders of the nobility. G.
[2] *Henry IV, Pt. II*, Act V, Sc. 1. G.   [3] " Fair and good." G.
[4] *Childe Harold*, canto 4. cxxiii. [P.]   [5] *Ibid.*, canto 3. lxxi. [P.]

through paths of delusive beauty, among flowers whose odours are agonies, and trees whose gums are poison.[1]

MR. HILARY. You talk like a Rosicrucian, who will love nothing but a sylph, who does not believe in the existence of a sylph, and who yet quarrels with the whole universe for not containing a sylph.

MR. CYPRESS. The mind is diseased of its own beauty, and fevers into false creation. The forms which the sculptor's soul has seized exist only in himself.[2]

MR. FLOSKY. Permit me to discept. They are the mediums of common forms combined and arranged into a common standard. The ideal beauty of the Helen of Zeuxis was the combined medium of the real beauty of the virgins of Crotona.

MR. HILARY. But to make ideal beauty the shadow in the water, and, like the dog in the fable, to throw away the substance in catching at the shadow, is scarcely the characteristic of wisdom, whatever it may be of genius. To reconcile man as he is to the world as it is, to preserve and improve all that is good, and destroy or alleviate all that is evil, in physical and moral nature—have been the hope and aim of the greatest teachers and ornaments of our species. I will say, too, that the highest wisdom and the highest genius have been invariably accompanied with cheerfulness. We have sufficient proofs on record that Shakespeare and Socrates were the most festive of companions. But now the little wisdom and genius we have seem to be entering into a conspiracy against cheerfulness.

MR. TOOBAD. How can we be cheerful with the devil among us?

THE HONOURABLE MR. LISTLESS. How can we be cheerful when our nerves are shattered?

MR. FLOSKY. How can we be cheerful when we are surrounded by a *reading public*, that is growing too wise for its betters?

SCYTHROP. How can we be cheerful when our great general designs are crossed every moment by our little particular passions?

---

[1] *Ibid.*, canto 4. cxxi. cxxxvi. [P.]   [2] *Ibid.*, canto 4. cxxii. [P.]

MR. CYPRESS.   How can we be cheerful in the midst of disappointment and despair ?

MR. GLOWRY.   Let us all be unhappy together.

MR. HILARY.   Let us sing a catch.

MR. GLOWRY.   No: a nice tragical ballad.   The Norfolk Tragedy[1] to the tune of the Hundredth Psalm.

MR. HILARY.   I say a catch.

MR. GLOWRY.   I say no.   A song from Mr. Cypress.

ALL.   A song from Mr. Cypress.

MR. CYPRESS *sung*—

> There is a fever of the spirit,
>   The brand of Cain's unresting doom,
> Which in the lone dark souls that bear it
>   Glows like the lamp in Tullia's tomb :
> Unlike that lamp, its subtle fire
>   Burns, blasts, consumes its cell, the heart,
> Till, one by one, hope, joy, desire,
>   Like dreams of shadowy smoke depart.
>
> When hope, love, life itself, are only
>   Dust—spectral memories—dead and cold—
> The unfed fire burns bright and lonely,
>   Like that undying lamp of old :
> And by that drear illumination,
>   Till time its clay-built home has rent,
> Thought broods on feeling's desolation—
>   The soul is its own monument.

MR. GLOWRY.   Admirable.   Let us all be unhappy together.

MR. HILARY.   Now, I say again, a catch.

THE REVEREND MR. LARYNX.   I am for you.

MR. HILARY.   " Seamen three."

THE REVEREND MR. LARYNX.   Agreed.   I'll be Harry Gill, with the voice of three.[2]   Begin.

[1] The story of *The Babes in the Wood.*   G.
[2] Wordsworth : *Goody Blake and Harry Gill,* l. 20.   G.

MR. HILARY AND THE REVEREND MR. LARYNX.

Seamen three ! What men be ye ?
Gotham's three wise men we be.
Whither in your bowl so free ?
To rake the moon from out the sea.
The bowl goes trim. The moon doth shine.
And our ballast is old wine ;
And your ballast is old wine.

Who art thou, so fast adrift ?
I am he they call Old Care.
Here on board we will thee lift.
No : I may not enter there.
Wherefore so ? 'Tis Jove's decree,
In a bowl Care may not be ;
In a bowl Care may not be.

Fear ye not the waves that roll ?
No : in charmed bowl we swim.
What the charm that floats the bowl ?
Water may not pass the brim.
The bowl goes trim. The moon doth shine.
And our ballast is old wine ;
And your ballast is old wine.

This catch was so well executed by the spirit and science of Mr.
Hilary, and the deep tri-une voice of the reverend gentleman, that
the whole party, in spite of themselves, caught the contagion, and
joined in chorus at the conclusion, each raising a bumper to his lips :

The bowl goes trim : the moon doth shine :
And our ballast is old wine.

Mr. Cypress, having his ballast on board, stepped, the same evening,
into his bowl, or travelling chariot, and departed to rake seas and
rivers, lakes and canals, for the moon of ideal beauty.

CHAPTER XII

It was the custom of the Honourable Mr. Listless, on adjourning from
the bottle to the ladies, to retire for a few moments to make a second
toilette, that he might present himself in becoming taste. Fatout,
attending as usual, appeared with a countenance of great dismay,

and informed his master that he had just ascertained that the abbey was haunted. Mrs. Hilary's *gentlewoman*, for whom Fatout had lately conceived a *tendresse*, had been, as she expressed it, " fritted out of her seventeen senses " the preceding night, as she was retiring to her bedchamber, by a ghastly figure which she had met stalking along one of the galleries, wrapped in a white shroud, with a bloody turban on its head. She had fainted away with fear ; and, when she recovered, she found herself in the dark, and the figure was gone. " *Sacre—cochon—bleu !* " exclaimed Fatout, giving very deliberate emphasis to every portion of his terrible oath—" I vould not meet de *revenant*, de ghost—*non*—not for all de *bowl-de-ponch* in de vorld."

" Fatout," said the Honourable Mr. Listless, " did I ever see a ghost ? "

" *Jamais*, monsieur, never."

" Then I hope I never shall, for, in the present shattered state of my nerves, I am afraid it would be too much for me. There—loosen the lace of my stays a little, for really this plebeian practice of eating —Not too loose—consider my shape. That will do. And I desire that you bring me no more stories of ghosts ; for, though I do not believe in such things, yet, when one is awake in the night, one is apt, if one thinks of them, to have fancies that give one a kind of a chill, particularly if one opens one's eyes suddenly on one's dressing gown, hanging in the moonlight, between the bed and the window."

The Honourable Mr. Listless, though he had prohibited Fatout from bringing him any more stories of ghosts, could not help thinking of that which Fatout had already brought ; and, as it was uppermost in his mind, when he descended to the tea and coffee cups, and the rest of the company in the library, he almost involuntarily asked Mr. Flosky, whom he looked up to as a most oraculous personage, whether any story of any ghost that had ever appeared to any one, was entitled to any degree of belief ?

MR. FLOSKY. By far the greater number, to a very great degree.[1]

THE HONOURABLE MR. LISTLESS. Really, that is very alarming !

[1] Unfair. Coleridge had drawn up a synopsis for a course of lectures in 1818, the year in which *Nightmare Abbey* was written. Lecture 12 was devoted to a severely rationalistic treatment of Dreams and Apparitions. See Rayzon : *Coleridge's Miscellaneous Criticism*, 1936. G.

MR. FLOSKY. *Sunt geminæ somni portæ.*[1] There are two gates through which ghosts find their way to the upper air : fraud and self-delusion. In the latter case, a ghost is a *deceptio visûs,* an ocular spectrum, an idea with the force of a sensation. I have seen many ghosts myself. I dare say there are few in this company who have not seen a ghost.

THE HONOURABLE MR. LISTLESS. I am happy to say, I never have, for one.

THE REVEREND MR. LARYNX. We have such high authority for ghosts, that it is rank scepticism to disbelieve them. Job saw a ghost, which came for the express purpose of asking a question, and did not wait for an answer.

THE HONOURABLE MR. LISTLESS. Because Job was too frightened to give one.

THE REVEREND MR. LARYNX. Spectres appeared to the Egyptians during the darkness with which Moses covered Egypt. The witch of Endor raised the ghost of Samuel. Moses and Elias appeared on Mount Tabor. An evil spirit was sent into the army of Sennacherib, and exterminated it in a single night.

MR. TOOBAD. Saying, The devil is come among you, having great wrath.

MR. FLOSKY. Saint Macarius interrogated a skull, which was found in the desert, and made it relate, in presence of several witnesses, what was going forward in hell. Saint Martin of Tours, being jealous of a pretended martyr, who was the rival saint of his neighbourhood, called up his ghost, and made him confess that he was damned. Saint Germain, being on his travels, turned out of an inn a large party of ghosts, who had every night taken possession of the *table d'hôte,* and consumed a copious supper.

MR. HILARY. Jolly ghosts, and no doubt all friars. A similar party took possession of the cellar of M. Swebach, the painter, in Paris, drank his wine, and threw the empty bottles at his head.[2]

[1] " There are twin gates of sleep." Virgil : *Æn.* VI. 893. G.
[2] James Swebach, Flemish painter, also known as Desfontaines, 1768–1824. G.

THE REVEREND MR. LARYNX.   An atrocious act.

MR. FLOSKY.   Pausanias relates, that the neighing of horses and the tumult of combatants were heard every night on the field of Marathon : that those who went purposely to hear these sounds suffered severely for their curiosity ; but those who heard them by accident passed with impunity.[1]

THE REVEREND MR. LARYNX.   I once saw a ghost myself, in my study, which is the last place where any one but a ghost would look for me.   I had not been into it for three months, and was going to consult Tillotson,[2] when, on opening the door, I saw a venerable figure in a flannel dressing gown, sitting in my armchair, and reading my Jeremy Taylor.   It vanished in a moment, and so did I ; and what it was or what it wanted I have never been able to ascertain.

MR. FLOSKY.   It was an idea with the force of a sensation.   It is seldom that ghosts appeal to two senses at once ; but, when I was in Devonshire, the following story was well attested to me.   A young woman, whose lover was at sea, returning one evening over some solitary fields, saw her lover sitting on a stile over which she was to pass.   Her first emotions were surprise and joy, but there was a paleness and seriousness in his face that made them give place to alarm.   She advanced towards him, and he said to her, in a solemn voice, " The eye that hath seen me shall see me no more.   Thine eye is upon me, but I am not."   And with these words he vanished ; and on that very day and hour, as it afterwards appeared, he had perished by shipwreck.

The whole party now drew round in a circle, and each related some ghostly anecdote, heedless of the flight of time, till, in a pause of the conversation, they heard the hollow tongue of midnight sounding twelve.[3]

MR. HILARY.   All these anecdotes admit of solution on psychological principles.   It is more easy for a soldier, a philosopher, or

---

[1] *Pausanias*, Bk. I, Chs. 32–4.   G.

[2] The sermons of John Tillotson (1630–94) served as models for generations of clergymen.   G.

[3] *An echo of A Midsummer Night's Dream*, Act V, Sc. 1.   G.

even a saint, to be frightened at his own shadow, than for a dead man
to come out of his grave. Medical writers cite a thousand singular
examples of the force of imagination. Persons of feeble, nervous,
melancholy temperament, exhausted by fever, by labour, or by spare
diet, will readily conjure up, in the magic ring of their own phantasy,
spectres, gorgons, chimæras, and all the objects of their hatred and
their love. We are most of us like Don Quixote, to whom a windmill
was a giant, and Dulcinea a magnificent princess : all more or less
the dupes of our own imagination, though we do not all go so far
as to see ghosts, or to fancy ourselves pipkins and teapots.

MR. FLOSKY. I can safely say I have seen too many ghosts myself
to believe in their external existence.[1] I have seen all kinds of
ghosts : black spirits and white, red spirits and grey. Some in the
shapes of venerable old men, who have met me in my rambles at
noon ; some of beautiful young women, who have peeped through
my curtains at midnight.

THE HONOURABLE MR. LISTLESS. And have proved, I doubt not,
" palpable to feeling as to sight." [2]

MR. FLOSKY. By no means, sir. You reflect upon my purity.
Myself and my friends, particularly my friend Mr. Sackbut, are
famous for our purity. No, sir, genuine untangible ghosts. I live
in a world of ghosts. I see a ghost at this moment.

Mr. Flosky fixed his eyes on a door at the farther end of the
library. The company looked in the same direction. The door
silently opened, and a ghastly figure, shrouded in white drapery,
with the semblance of a bloody turban on its head, entered and stalked
slowly up the apartment. Mr. Flosky, familiar as he was with
ghosts, was not prepared for this apparition, and made the best of
his way out at the opposite door. Mrs. Hilary and Marionetta

[1] C. R. Leslie in *Autobiographical Recollections*, 1860, Vol. I, states that
Sir James Mackintosh quoted this as an actual repartee of Coleridge's to
a question asked at one of his Shakespeare lectures. G.
[2] *Macbeth*, Act II, Sc. 1, misquoted. See also Notes on pp. 120 and 931.
Hazlitt makes the same misquotation from *Macbeth* in his essay on
Horne Tooke in *The Spirit of the Age.* G.

followed, screaming. The Honourable Mr. Listless, by two turns of his body, rolled first off the sofa and then under it. The Reverend Mr. Larynx leaped up and fled with so much precipitation, that he overturned the table on the foot of Mr. Glowry. Mr. Glowry roared with pain in the ear of Mr. Toobad. Mr. Toobad's alarm so bewildered his senses, that, missing the door, he threw up one of the windows, jumped out in his panic, and plunged over head and ears in the moat. Mr. Asterias and his son, who were on the watch for their mermaid, were attracted by the splashing, threw a net over him, and dragged him to land.

Scythrop and Mr. Hilary meanwhile had hastened to his assistance, and, on arriving at the edge of the moat, followed by several servants with ropes and torches, found Mr. Asterias and Aquarius busy in endeavouring to extricate Mr. Toobad from the net, who was entangled in the meshes, and floundering with rage. Scythrop was lost in amazement ; but Mr. Hilary saw, at one view, all the circumstances of the adventure, and burst into an immoderate fit of laughter ; on recovering from which, he said to Mr. Asterias, " You have caught an odd fish, indeed." Mr. Toobad was highly exasperated at this unseasonable pleasantry ; but Mr. Hilary softened his anger, by producing a knife, and cutting the Gordian knot of his reticular envelopement. "You see," said Mr. Toobad, "you see, gentlemen, in my unfortunate person proof upon proof of the present dominion of the devil in the affairs of this world ; and I have no doubt but that the apparition of this night was Apollyon himself in disguise, sent for the express purpose of terrifying me into this complication of misadventures. The devil is come among you, having great wrath, because he knoweth that he hath but a short time."

CHAPTER XIII

Mr. Glowry was much surprised, on occasionally visiting Scythrop's tower, to find the door always locked, and to be kept sometimes waiting many minutes for admission : during which he invariably heard a heavy rolling sound like that of a ponderous mangle, or of a waggon on a weighing-bridge, or of theatrical thunder.

He took little notice of this for some time : at length his curiosity was excited, and, one day, instead of knocking at the door, as usual, the instant he reached it, he applied his ear to the key-hole, and like Bottom, in the Midsummer Night's Dream, " spied a voice," which he guessed to be of the feminine gender, and knew to be not Scythrop's, whose deeper tones he distinguished at intervals. Having attempted in vain to catch a syllable of the discourse, he knocked violently at the door, and roared for immediate admission. The voices ceased, the accustomed rolling sound was heard, the door opened, and Scythrop was discovered alone. Mr. Glowry looked round to every corner of the apartment, and then said, " Where is the lady ? "

" The lady, sir ? " said Scythrop.

" Yes, sir, the lady."

" Sir, I do not understand you."

" You don't, sir ? "

" No, indeed, sir. There is no lady here."

" But, sir, this is not the only apartment in the tower, and I make no doubt there is a lady up stairs."

" You are welcome to search, sir."

" Yes, and while I am searching, she will slip out from some lurking place, and make her escape."

" You may lock this door, sir, and take the key with you."

" But there is the terrace door : she has escaped by the terrace."

" The terrace, sir, has no other outlet, and the walls are too high for a lady to jump down."

" Well, sir, give me the key."

Mr. Glowry took the key, searched every nook of the tower, and returned.

" You are a fox, Scythrop ; you are an exceedingly cunning fox, with that demure visage of yours. What was that lumbering sound I heard before you opened the door ? "

" Sound, sir ? "

" Yes, sir, sound."

" My dear sir, I am not aware of any sound, except my great table, which I moved on rising to let you in."

" The table !—let me see that. No, sir ; not a tenth part heavy enough, not a tenth part."

"But, sir, you do not consider the laws of acoustics : a·whisper becomes a peal of thunder in the focus of reverberation. Allow me to explain this : sounds striking on concave surfaces are reflected from them, and, after reflection, converge to points which are the foci of these surfaces. It follows, therefore, that the ear may be so placed in one, as that it shall hear a sound better than when situated nearer to the point of the first impulse : again, in the case of two concave surfaces placed opposite to each other——"

"Nonsense, sir. Don't tell me of foci. Pray, sir, will concave surfaces produce two voices when nobody speaks ? I heard two voices, and one was feminine ; feminine, sir : what say you to that ? "

"Oh, sir, I perceive your mistake : I am writing a tragedy, and was acting over a scene to myself. To convince you, I will give you a specimen ; but you must first understand the plot. It is a tragedy on the German model. The Great Mogul is in exile, and has taken lodgings at Kensington, with his only daughter, the Princess Rantrorina, who takes in needlework, and keeps a day school. *The princess is discovered hemming a set of of shirts for the parson of the parish : they are to be marked with a large R. Enter to her the Great Mogul. A pause, during which they look at each other expressively. The princess changes colour several times. The Mogul takes snuff in great agitation. Several grains are heard to fall on the stage. His heart is seen to beat through his upper benjamin.*—THE MOGUL (*with a mournful look at his left shoe*). "My shoe-string is broken."—THE PRINCESS (*after an interval of melancholy reflection*). " I know it."—THE MOGUL. " My second shoe-string ! The first broke when I lost my empire : the second has broken to-day. When will my poor heart break ? "—THE PRINCESS. " Shoe-strings, hearts, and empires ! Mysterious sympathy ! "

"Nonsense, sir," interrupted Mr. Glowry. " That is not at all like the voice I heard."

"But, sir," said Scythrop, " a key-hole may be so constructed as to act like an acoustic tube, and an acoustic tube, sir, will modify sound in a very remarkable manner. Consider the construction of the ear, and the nature and causes of sound. The external part of the ear is a cartilaginous funnel."

"It won't do, Scythrop. There is a girl concealed in this tower, and find her I will. There are such things as sliding panels and secret closets."—He sounded round the room with his cane, but detected no hollowness.—" I have heard, sir," he continued, " that during my absence, two years ago, you had a dumb carpenter closeted with you day after day. I did not dream that you were laying contrivances for carrying on secret intrigues. Young men will have their way : I had my way when I was a young man : but, sir, when your cousin Marionetta——"

Scythrop now saw that the affair was growing serious. To have clapped his hand upon his father's mouth, to have entreated him to be silent, would, in the first place, not have made him so ; and, in the second, would have shown a dread of being overheard by somebody. His only resource, therefore, was to try to drown Mr. Glowry's voice ; and, having no other subject, he continued his description of the ear, raising his voice continually as Mr. Glowry raised his.

" When your cousin Marionetta," said Mr. Glowry, " whom you profess to love—whom you profess to love, sir——"

" The internal canal of the ear," said Scythrop, " is partly bony and partly cartilaginous. This internal canal is——"

" Is actually in the house, sir ; and, when you are so shortly to be—as I expect——"

" Closed at the further end by the *membrana tympani*——"

" Joined together in holy matrimony——"

" Under which is carried a branch of the fifth pair of nerves——"

" I say, sir, when you are so shortly to be married to your cousin Marionetta——"

" The *cavitas tympani*——"

A loud noise was heard behind the book-case, which, to the astonishment of Mr. Glowry, opened in the middle, and the massy compartments, with all their weight of books, receding from each other in the manner of a theatrical scene, with a heavy rolling sound (which Mr. Glowry immediately recognised to be the same which had excited his curiosity,) disclosed an interior apartment, in the entrance of which stood the beautiful Stella, who, stepping forward, exclaimed, " Married ! Is he going to be married ? The profligate ! "

" Really, madam," said Mr. Glowry, " I do not know what he is going to do, or what I am going to do, or what any one is going to do ; for all this is incomprehensible."

" I can explain it all," said Scythrop, " in a most satisfactory manner, if you will but have the goodness to leave us alone."

" Pray, sir, to which act of the tragedy of the Great Mogul does this incident belong ? "

" I entreat you, my dear sir, leave us alone."

Stella threw herself into a chair, and burst into a tempest of tears. Scythrop sat down by her, and took her hand. She snatched her hand away, and turned her back upon him. He rose, sat down on the other side, and took her other hand. She snatched it away, and turned from him again. Scythrop continued entreating Mr. Glowry to leave them alone ; but the old gentleman was obstinate, and would not go.

" I suppose, after all," said Mr. Glowry maliciously, " it is only a phænomenon in acoustics, and this young lady is a reflection of sound from concave surfaces."

Some one tapped at the door : Mr. Glowry opened it, and Mr. Hilary entered. He had been seeking Mr. Glowry, and had traced him to Scythrop's tower. He stood a few moments in silent surprise, and then addressed himself to Mr. Glowry for an explanation.

" The explanation," said Mr. Glowry, " is very satisfactory. The Great Mogul has taken lodgings at Kensington, and the external part of the ear is a cartilaginous funnel."

" Mr. Glowry, that is no explanation."

" Mr. Hilary, it is all I know about the matter."

" Sir, this pleasantry is very unseasonable. I perceive that my niece is sported with in a most unjustifiable manner, and I shall see if she will be more successful in obtaining an intelligible answer." And he departed in search of Marionetta.

Scythrop was now in a hopeless predicament. Mr. Hilary made a hue and cry in the abbey, and summoned his wife and Marionetta to Scythrop's apartment. The ladies, not knowing what was the matter, hastened in great consternation. Mr. Toobad saw them sweeping along the corridor, and judging from their manner that the devil had manifested his wrath in some new shape, followed from pure curiosity.

Scythrop meanwhile vainly endeavoured to get rid of Mr. Glowry and to pacify Stella. The latter attempted to escape from the tower, declaring she would leave the abbey immediately, and he should never see her or hear of her more. Scythrop held her hand and detained her by force, till Mr. Hilary reappeared with Mrs. Hilary and Marionetta. Marionetta, seeing Scythrop grasping the hand of a strange beauty, fainted away in the arms of her aunt. Scythrop flew to her assistance; and Stella with redoubled anger sprang towards the door, but was intercepted in her intended flight by being caught in the arms of Mr. Toobad, who exclaimed—" Celinda ! "

" Papa ! " said the young lady disconsolately.

" The devil is come among you," said Mr. Toobad, " how came my daughter here ? "

" Your daughter ! " exclaimed Mr. Glowry.

" Your daughter ! " exclaimed Scythrop, and Mr. and Mrs. Hilary.

" Yes," said Mr. Toobad, " my daughter Celinda."

Marionetta opened her eyes and fixed them on Celinda; Celinda in return fixed hers on Marionetta. They were at remote points of the apartment. Scythrop was equidistant from both of them, central and motionless, like Mahomet's coffin.

" Mr. Glowry," said Mr. Toobad, " can you tell by what means my daughter came here ? "

" I know no more," said Mr. Glowry, " than the Great Mogul."

" Mr. Scythrop," said Mr. Toobad, " how came my daughter here ? "

" I did not know, sir, that the lady was your daughter."

" But how came she here ? "

" By spontaneous locomotion," said Scythrop, sullenly.

" Celinda," said Mr. Toobad, " what does all this mean ? "

" I really do not know, sir."

" This is most unaccountable. When I told you in London that I had chosen a husband for you, you thought proper to run away from him; and now, to all appearance, you have run away to him."

" How, sir ! was that your choice ? "

" Precisely; and if he is yours too we shall be both of a mind, for the first time in our lives."

"He is not my choice, sir. This lady has a prior claim : I renounce him."

"And I renounce him," said Marionetta.

Scythrop knew not what to do. He could not attempt to conciliate the one without irreparably offending the other ; and he was so fond of both, that the idea of depriving himself for ever of the society of either was intolerable to him : he therefore retreated into his strong-hold, mystery; maintained an impenetrable silence ; and contented himself with stealing occasionally a deprecating glance at each of the objects of his idolatry. Mr. Toobad and Mr. Hilary, in the mean time, were each insisting on an explanation from Mr. Glowry, who they thought had been playing a double game on this occasion. Mr. Glowry was vainly endeavouring to persuade them of his innocence in the whole transaction. Mrs. Hilary was endeavouring to mediate between her husband and brother. The Honourable Mr. Listless, the Reverend Mr. Larynx, Mr. Flosky, Mr. Asterias, and Aquarius, were attracted by the tumult to the scene of action, and were appealed to severally and conjointly by the respective disputants. Multitudinous questions, and answers *en masse*, composed a *charivari*, to which the genius of Rossini alone could have given a suitable accompaniment, and which was only terminated by Mrs. Hilary and Mr. Toobad retreating with the captive damsels. The whole party followed, with the exception of Scythrop, who threw himself into his arm-chair, crossed his left foot over his right knee, placed the hollow of his left hand on the interior ancle of his left leg, rested his right elbow on the elbow of the chair, placed the ball of his right thumb against his right temple, curved the forefinger along the upper part of his forehead, rested the point of the middle finger on the bridge of his nose, and the points of the two others on the lower part of the palm, fixed his eyes intently on the veins in the back of his left hand, and sat in this position like the immoveable Theseus, who, as is well known to many who have not been at college, and to some few who have, *sedet, æternumque sedebit*.[1] We hope the admirers of the *minutiæ* in poetry and romance will appreciate this accurate description of a pensive attitude.

[1] Sits, and will sit for ever. [P.] [Virgil : *Æn.* VI. 617. G.]

CHAPTER XIV

SCYTHROP was still in this position when Raven entered to announce that dinner was on table.

" I cannot come," said Scythrop.

Raven sighed. " Something is the matter," said Raven : " but man is born to trouble."

" Leave me," said Scythrop : " go, and croak elsewhere."

" Thus it is," said Raven. " Five-and-twenty years have I lived in Nightmare Abbey, and now all the reward of my affection is— Go, and croak elsewhere. I have danced you on my knee, and fed you with marrow."

" Good Raven," said Scythrop, " I entreat you to leave me."

" Shall I bring your dinner here ? " said Raven. " A boiled fowl and a glass of Madeira are prescribed by the faculty in cases of low spirits. But you had better join the party : it is very much reduced already."

" Reduced ! how ? "

" The Honourable Mr. Listless is gone. He declared that, what with family quarrels in the morning, and ghosts at night, he could get neither sleep nor peace ; and that the agitation was too much for his nerves : though Mr. Glowry assured him that the ghost was only poor Crow walking in his sleep, and that the shroud and bloody turban were a sheet and a red nightcap."

" Well, sir ? "

" The Reverend Mr. Larynx has been called off on duty, to marry or bury (I don't know which) some unfortunate person or persons, at Claydyke : but man is born to trouble ! "

" Is that all ? "

" No. Mr. Toobad is gone too, and a strange lady with him."

" Gone ! "

" Gone. And Mr. and Mrs. Hilary, and Miss O'Carroll : they are all gone. There is nobody left but Mr. Asterias and his son, and they are going to-night."

" Then I have lost them both."

" Won't you come to dinner ? "

" No."

" Shall I bring your dinner here ? "

" Yes."

" What will you have ? "

" A pint of port and a pistol." [1]

" A pistol ! "

" And a pint of port. I will make my exit like Werter. Go. Stay. Did Miss O'Carroll say any thing ? "

" No."

" Did Miss Toobad say any thing ? "

" The strange lady ? No."

" Did either of them cry ? "

" No."

" What did they do ? "

" Nothing."

" What did Mr. Toobad say ? "

" He said, fifty times over, the devil was come among us."

" And they are gone ? "

" Yes ; and the dinner is getting cold. There is a time for every thing under the sun. You may as well dine first, and be miserable afterwards."

" True, Raven. There is something in that. I will take your advice : therefore, bring me——"

" The port and the pistol ? "

" No ; the boiled fowl and Madeira."

Scythrop had dined, and was sipping his Madeira alone, immersed in melancholy musing, when Mr. Glowry entered, followed by Raven, who, having placed an additional glass and set a chair for Mr. Glowry, withdrew. Mr. Glowry sat down opposite Scythrop. After a pause, during which each filled and drank in silence, Mr. Glowry said, " So, sir, you have played your cards well. I proposed Miss Toobad to you : you refused her. Mr. Toobad proposed you to her : she refused you. You fell in love with Marionetta, and were going to poison yourself, because, from pure fatherly regard to your temporal interests, I withheld my consent. When, at length, I offered you

---

[1] See *The Sorrows of Werter*, Letter 93. [P.] [Ferdinand, the hero of Goethe's *Stella*, also snatches up a pistol and exclaims, " Here it must end ! " when in difficulties with three lovely and incomparable females. G.]

my consent, you told me I was too precipitate. And, after all, I find you and Miss Toobad living together in the same tower, and behaving in every respect like two plighted lovers. Now, sir, if there be any rational solution of all this absurdity, I shall be very much obliged to you for a small glimmering of information."

"The solution, sir, is of little moment; but I will leave it in writing for your satisfaction. The crisis of my fate is come: the world is a stage, and my direction is *exit*."

"Do not talk so, sir ;—do not talk so, Scythrop. What would you have ? "

"I would have my love."

"And pray, sir, who is your love ? "

"Celinda—Marionetta—either—both."

"Both ! That may do very well in a German tragedy; and the Great Mogul might have found it very feasible in his lodgings at Kensington; but it will not do in Lincolnshire. Will you have Miss Toobad ? "

"Yes."

"And renounce Marionetta ? "

"No."

"But you must renounce one."

"I cannot."

"And you cannot have both. What is to be done ? "

"I must shoot myself."

"Don't talk so, Scythrop. Be rational, my dear Scythrop. Consider, and make a cool, calm choice, and I will exert myself in your behalf."

"Why should I choose, sir ? Both have renounced *me*: I have no hope of either."

"Tell me which you will have, and I will plead your cause irresistibly."

"Well, sir,—I will have—no, sir, I cannot renounce either. I cannot choose either. I am doomed to be the victim of eternal disappointments; and I have no resource but a pistol."

"Scythrop—Scythrop ;—if one of them should come to you— what then ? "

"That, sir, might alter the case : but that cannot be."

"It can be, Scythrop; it will be : I promise you it will be.   Have but a little patience—but a week's patience ; and it shall be."

"A week, sir, is an age : but, to oblige you, as a last act of filial duty, I will live another week.   It is now Thursday evening, twenty-five minutes past seven.   At this hour and minute, on Thursday next, love and fate shall smile on me, or I will drink my last pint of port in this world."

Mr. Glowry ordered his travelling chariot, and departed from the abbey.

CHAPTER XV

THE day after Mr. Glowry's departure was one of incessant rain, and Scythrop repented of the promise he had given.   The next day was one of bright sunshine : he sat on the terrace, read a tragedy of Sophocles, and was not sorry, when Raven announced dinner, to find himself alive.   On the third evening, the wind blew, and the rain beat, and the owl flapped against his windows ; and he put a new flint in his pistol.   On the fourth day, the sun shone again ; and he locked the pistol up in a drawer, where he left it undisturbed, till the morning of the eventful Thursday, when he ascended the turret with a telescope, and spied anxiously along the road that crossed the fens from Claydyke : but nothing appeared on it.   He watched in this manner from ten A.M. till Raven summoned him to dinner at five ; when he stationed Crow at the telescope, and descended to his own funeral-feast.   He left open the communications between the tower and turret, and called aloud at intervals to Crow,—"Crow, Crow, is any thing coming ? "[1]   Crow answered, "The wind blows, and the windmills turn, but I see nothing coming ; " and, at every answer, Scythrop found the necessity of raising his spirits with a bumper.   After dinner, he gave Raven his watch to set by the abbey clock.   Raven brought it, Scythrop placed it on the table, and Raven departed.   Scythrop called again to Crow ; and Crow, who had fallen asleep, answered mechanically, " I see nothing

---

[1] " Anne, ma sœur Anne, ne vois-tu rien venir ? " et la sœur Anne lui répondait, " Je ne vois rien que le soleil qui poudroie et l'herbe qui verdoie."   Perrault: *Barbe Bleue.* G.

coming." Scythrop laid his pistol between his watch and his bottle.
The hour-hand passed the VII.—the minute-hand moved on ;—it
was within three minutes of the appointed time. Scythrop called
again to Crow : Crow answered as before. Scythrop rang the bell :
Raven appeared.

"Raven," said Scythrop, "the clock is too fast."

"No, indeed," said Raven, who knew nothing of Scythrop's
intentions ; "if any thing, it is too slow."

"Villain ! " said Scythrop, pointing the pistol at him ; "it is too
fast."

"Yes—yes—too fast, I meant," said Raven, in manifest fear.

"How much too fast ? " said Scythrop.

"As much as you please," said Raven.

"How much, I say ? " said Scythrop, pointing the pistol again.

"An hour, a full hour, sir," said the terrified butler.

"Put back my watch," said Scythrop.

Raven, with trembling hand, was putting back the watch, when
the rattle of wheels was heard in the court ; and Scythrop, springing
down the stairs by three steps together, was at the door in sufficient
time to have handed either of the young ladies from the carriage, if
she had happened to be in it ; but Mr. Glowry was alone.

"I rejoice to see you," said Mr. Glowry ; "I was fearful of being
too late, for I waited till the last moment in the hope of accomplishing my promise ; but all my endeavours have been vain, as these
letters will show."

Scythrop impatiently broke the seals. The contents were these :—

"Almost a stranger in England, I fled from parental tyranny, and
the dread of an arbitrary marriage, to the protection of a stranger
and a philosopher, whom I expected to find something better than,
or at least something different from, the rest of his worthless species.
Could I, after what has occurred, have expected nothing more from
you than the common-place impertinence of sending your father to
treat with me, and with mine, for me ?   I should be a little moved
in your favour, if I could believe you capable of carrying into effect
the resolutions which your father says you have taken, in the event
of my proving inflexible ; though I doubt not you will execute them,

as far as relates to the pint of wine, twice over, at least. I wish you much happiness with Miss O'Carroll. I shall always cherish a grateful recollection of Nightmare Abbey, for having been the means of introducing me to a true transcendentalist ; and, though he is a little older than myself, which is all one in Germany, I shall very soon have the pleasure of subscribing myself

CELINDA FLOSKY."

" I hope, my dear cousin, that you will not be angry with me, but that you will always think of me as a sincere friend, who will always feel interested in your welfare ; I am sure you love Miss Toobad much better than me, and I wish you much happiness with her. Mr. Listless assures me that people do not kill themselves for love now-a-days, though it is still the fashion to talk about it. I shall, in a very short time, change my name and situation, and shall always be happy to see you in Berkeley Square, when, to the unalterable designation of your affectionate cousin, I shall subjoin the signature of

MARIONETTA LISTLESS."

Scythrop tore both the letters to atoms, and railed in good set terms against the fickleness of women.

" Calm yourself, my dear Scythrop," said Mr. Glowry ; " there are yet maidens in England."

" Very true, sir," said Scythrop.

" And the next time," said Mr. Glowry, " have but one string to your bow."

" Very good advice, sir," said Scythrop.

" And, besides," said Mr. Glowry, " the fatal time is past, for it is now almost eight."

" Then that villain, Raven," said Scythrop, " deceived me when he said that the clock was too fast ; but, as you observe very justly, the time has gone by, and I have just reflected that these repeated crosses in love qualify me to take a very advanced degree in misanthropy ; and there is, therefore, good hope that I may make a figure in the world. But I shall ring for the rascal Raven, and admonish him."

Raven appeared. Scythrop looked at him very fiercely two or three minutes; and Raven, still remembering the pistol, stood quaking in mute apprehension, till Scythrop, pointing significantly towards the dining-room, said, " Bring some Madeira."

THE END

MAID MARIAN

MAID MARIAN

Yet thanks I must you con, that you work not
In holier shapes : for there is boundless theft
In limited professions.—*Timon of Athens.*[1]

---

[1] Act IV, Sc. 3, telescoped.   G.

Maid Marian was first published in 1822

INTRODUCTION TO
MAID MARIAN

MAID MARIAN is said to be by far the most popular of Peacock's novels, Saintsbury declaring that it is " by general consent the completest and urbanest product of the author's genius."—a verdict for which I •cannot find an explanation, unless it be that *Maid Marian* is less concerned with ideas than the other novels—not that it is empty of ideas, but it is not stuffed full and overflowing with them. Moreover the author, when he wrote it, shared the taste of his age for a mediæval period-setting filled with comic monks and friars, wicked Norman knights, sterling Saxons and all the stock-in-trade which made, I trust, a positively last appearance in Dendy Sadler's pictures of rows of comic monks fishing on the banks of the Ouse.

Peacock showed no interest in what the twelfth century was really like and made no pretence to give a picture of it. He pleads guilty to this indictment, for an entry in his diary for 6th August 1818 reads: " Could not read or write for scheming my romance. Rivers castles forests abbies monks maids kings and banditti dancing before me like a masked ball."

On 12th August he notes : " Read ballads about Robin Hood." He was sailing every day on the Thames, reading *The Wealth of Nations* and corresponding with Marianne de St Croix.

On 29th November 1818, he wrote to Shelley : " I am writing a comic Romance of the Twelfth Century, which I shall make the vehicle of much oblique satire on all the oppressions that are done under the sun. I have suspended the Essay till the completion of the Romance."

All but the last three chapters had been written by the end of 1818, though the book was not published until 1822. The dates are important and Peacock, in a note to the first edition, draws the reader's attention to the date when the book was written. For in December 1819, a year after Peacock had practically completed *Maid Marian*, Scott published *Ivanhoe*, which deals with precisely the same subject. The two books have nothing in common except some of the characters and some of the situations. Sir Henry Newbolt, however, in *Studies Green and Gray*, 1926, has pointed out a large number of details which he believed Peacock must have taken from *Ivanhoe*. On the face of it Peacock is not likely to have filched tiny details from an author of whom he makes Dr. Folliott, in *Crotchet Castle*, say : " My quarrel with him is, that his works contain nothing worth quoting; and a book that furnishes no quotations, is, *me judice*, no book—it is a plaything."

Peacock's source for *Maid Marian* was Joseph Ritson's *Robin Hood, a collection of all the ancient poems, songs, and ballads now extant relative to that celebrated outlaw*, 1795. Scott was making use of the same source at the same time, so similarities are not surprising. Some seem to me to be rendered probable by the subject itself. It is natural that Peacock should make a forester, who is disguised as a friar to rescue young Gamwell from the gallows, greet him with the words *Dominus vobiscum*. He had no need to steal the remark from Chapter XXVI of *Ivanhoe*, in which Wamba, the jester, disguised as a friar, used the password *Pax Vobiscum* in order to enter Torquilstone Castle. After all, Peacock knew Latin, and *Dominus vobiscum* is part of the stock-in-trade for friars in historical novels about the twelfth century.

But if we can acquit Peacock of stealing phrases and incidents from *Ivanhoe*, we discover that large parts of *Maid Marian* are mere paraphrases of the old ballads in Ritson's collection. · M. Mayoux has illustrated the process with parallel columns of quotations. One example will suffice :

Brede and wyne they hade ynough And nombles of the deer. Swannes and fesauntes they had full good And foules of the revere.	Robin helped them largely to numble-pie and cygnet and pheasant and the other dainties of the table. . . .
But pay or ye wende, sayd Robin, Me thynketh it is good ryght.	" Now," said Robin, " you are at liberty to pursue your journey : but first be pleased to pay for your dinner. . . ."

I have no more but ten shillings sayd the
   knyght.
Yf you have no more, sayd Robin
I will not one peny ;
And yf thou have nede of any more
More shall I len ye.

". . . all I have about me
are five shillings and a ring,
. . ." " Little John must
search ; and if he finds no
more than you say, not a
penny will I touch ; . . . if
want of money be the cause
of your melancholy, speak."

What tydinge, Johan, sayd Robyn.
Sir, the knyght is trewe inough.

Said Little John, " and the
young man has spoken true."

The date of *Maid Marian* is important, not only because of the
question of plagiarisms from *Ivanhoe* but also, more generally, because
of the oblique satire on " all the oppressions that are done under the
sun " which he had promised Shelley to include. Europe had been
stabilised by the Holy Alliance ; in every country monarchies had
been set up which were unpopular with their subjects and dependent
upon police spies and gendarmes for their existence. Peacock's
satire found expression in such passages as :

" Now, as the repeal of the outlawry would involve the restitution
of the estates to the rightful owner, it was obvious that it could never
be expected from that most legitimate and most Christian king,
Richard the First of England, the arch-crusader and anti-jacobin by
excellence,—the very type, flower, cream, pink, symbol, and mirror
of all the Holy Alliances that have ever existed on earth, excepting that he seasoned his superstition and his love of conquest with
a certain condiment of romantic generosity and chivalrous self-
devotion, with which his imitators in all other points have found it
convenient to dispense."

But curiously enough Peacock had taken not only his subject-
matter from Ritson's collection of ballads but also the morals for
his satire from Ritson's introduction and notes.

Joseph Ritson was a free-thinker and a jacobin—also a
vegetarian and an oddly Peacockian character. His preface contains
a thumping advocacy of Robin Hood's practice of robbing the rich
in order to give to the poor (and living comfortably on the marginal
difference). The argument is wittily developed by Peacock in
Chapters XI and XII. Thus it becomes clear that the whole conception, oblique satire as well as subject, was suggested to Peacock
by reading Ritson's *Robin Hood.*

There is no evidence that Peacock drew on any other sources. Long extracts of Munday and Chettle's plays, *The Downfall* and *The Death of Robert, Earl of Huntington,* appear in Ritson's *Robin Hood.* I have failed, as M. Mayoux failed before me, to find any evidence that Peacock had read the complete plays themselves.

The most original part of *Maid Marian* is therefore neither the subject nor the satire, but, in Richard Garnett's words, " the concentration of the love of sylvan nature fostered by years of open air life and perpetual rambles in Windsor Forest and by the banks of the Thames . . . a pervading sylvan feeling."

The book was a success and the theatrical character of the story, the friar and foresters dancing like characters at a masked ball, caught the attention of Charles Kemble. J. R. Planché promptly produced the libretto, drawing also upon *Ivanhoe,* for a three-act opera for which Henry Rowley Bishop provided the music. Peacock, who was an enthusiastic lover of opera, was pleased, and intervened to secure permission from Hookham, who had at first threatened to bring an injunction against Planché. *Maid Marian, or the Huntress of Arlingford,* was accordingly produced, at Covent Garden, on 3rd December, 1822. Charles Kemble took the part of the friar and made a hit with the song :

> The bramble, the bramble,
> The jolly, jolly bramble,

which is mentioned by Thackeray in *The History of Samuel Titmarsh and the Great Hoggarty Diamond* as " one of Charles Kemble's famous songs in *Maid Marian,* a play that was all the rage then, taken from a famous story book by one Peacock, a clerk in the India House, and a precious good place he has too."

Conceivably it is the tradition of the opera " which was all the rage " which has led to the belief in the widespread popular preference for *Maid Marian.* I have never heard of anyone, who liked Peacock's novels at all, who preferred it to the others, except Saintsbury. Certainly what Richard Garnett called " the pervading sylvan feeling," which I do not think can possibly be what Saintsbury meant by " urbanity," is very charming indeed.

D. G.

This little work, with the exception of the three last chapters, was written in the autumn of 1818.   [P.]

March 15, 1822.

MAID MARIAN

CHAPTER I

Now come ye for peace here, or come ye for war ? SCOTT.[1]

"THE abbot, in his alb arrayed," stood at the altar in the abbey-
chapel of Rubygill, with all his plump, sleek, rosy friars, in goodly
lines disposed, to solemnise the nuptials of the beautiful Matilda
Fitzwater, daughter of the Baron of Arlingford, with the noble
Robert Fitz-Ooth, Earl of Locksley and Huntingdon.[2] The abbey of
Rubygill stood in a picturesque valley, at a little distance from the
western boundary of Sherwood Forest, in a spot which seemed
adapted by nature to be the retreat of monastic mortification, being
on the banks of a fine trout-stream, and in the midst of woodland
coverts, abounding with excellent game. The bride, with her father
and attendant maidens, entered the chapel ; but the earl had not
arrived. The baron was amazed, and the bridemaidens were disconcerted. Matilda feared that some evil had befallen her lover, but
felt no diminution of her confidence in his honour and love. Through
the open gates of the chapel she looked down the narrow road that
wound along the side of the hill ; and her ear was the first that heard
the distant trampling of horses, and her eye was the first that caught
the glitter of snowy plumes, and the light of polished spears. " It is
strange," thought the baron, " that the earl should come in this
martial array to his wedding ; " but he had not long to meditate on
the phenomenon, for the foaming steeds swept up to the gate like a
whirlwind, and the earl, breathless with speed, and followed by a few
of his yeomen, advanced to his smiling bride. It was then no time

---

[1] *Lochinvar*, from *Marmion*, Canto V, Section 12. G.

[2] The real Earl of Huntingdon at this period was David, brother of King
William of Scotland. Stukeley's pedigree, deducing the descent of Robin
Hood from FitzOoth, a companion of the Conqueror, is dismissed as absurd
in *The Dictionary of National Biography*. G.

445

to ask questions, for the organ was in full peal, and the choristers were in full voice.

The abbot began to intone the ceremony in a style of modulation impressively exalted, his voice issuing most canonically from the roof of his mouth, through the medium of a very musical nose newly tuned for the occasion. But he had not proceeded far enough to exhibit all the variety and compass of this melodious instrument, when a noise was heard at the gate, and a party of armed men entered the chapel. The song of the choristers died away in a shake of demisemiquavers, contrary to all the rules of psalmody. The organ-blower, who was working his musical air-pump with one hand, and with two fingers and a thumb of the other insinuating a peeping-place through the curtain of the organ-gallery, was struck motionless by the double operation of curiosity and fear ; while the organist, intent only on his performance, and spreading all his fingers to strike a swell of magnificent chords, felt his harmonic spirit ready to desert his body on being answered by the ghastly rattle of empty keys, and in the consequent *agitato furioso*[1] of the internal movements of his feelings, was preparing to restore harmony by the *segue subito*[2] of an *appoggiatura con foco*[3] with the corner of a book of anthems on the head of his neglectful assistant, when his hand and his attention together were arrested by the scene below. The voice of the abbot subsided into silence through a descending scale of long-drawn melody, like the sound of the ebbing sea to the explorers of a cave. In a few moments all was silence, interrupted only by the iron tread of the armed intruders, as it rang on the marble floor and echoed from the vaulted aisles.

The leader strode up to the altar ; and placing himself opposite to the abbot, and between the earl and Matilda, in such a manner that the four together seemed to stand on the four points of a diamond, exclaimed, " In the name of King Henry, I forbid the ceremony, and attach Robert Earl of Huntingdon as a traitor ! " and at the same time he held his drawn sword between the lovers, as if to emblem that royal authority which laid its temporal ban upon their contract. The earl drew his own sword instantly, and struck down

[1] " Furious agitation." G. [2] " Sudden following." G.
[3] " Laying on with fire." G.

the interposing weapon; then clasped his left arm round Matilda, who sprang into his embrace, and held his sword before her with his right hand. His yeomen ranged themselves at his side, and stood with their swords drawn, still and prepared, like men determined to die in his defence. The soldiers, confident in superiority of numbers, paused. The abbot took advantage of the pause to introduce a word of exhortation. "My children," said he, "if you are going to cut each other's throats, I entreat you, in the name of peace and charity, to do it out of the chapel."

"Sweet Matilda," said the earl, "did you give your love to the Earl of Huntingdon, whose lands touch the Ouse and the Trent, or to Robert Fitz-Ooth, the son of his mother?"

"Neither to the earl nor his earldom," answered Matilda firmly, "but to Robert Fitz-Ooth and his love."

"That I well knew," said the earl; "and though the ceremony be incomplete, we are not the less married in the eye of my only saint, our Lady, who will yet bring us together. Lord Fitzwater, to your care, for the present, I commit your daughter.—Nay, sweet Matilda, part we must for a while; but we will soon meet under brighter skies, and be this the seal of our faith."

He kissed Matilda's lips, and consigned her to the baron, who glowered about him with an expression of countenance that showed he was mortally wroth with somebody; but whatever he thought or felt he kept to himself. The earl, with a sign to his followers, made a sudden charge on the soldiers, with the intention of cutting his way through. The soldiers were prepared for such an occurrence, and a desperate skirmish succeeded. Some of the women screamed, but none of them fainted; for fainting was not so much the fashion in those days, when the ladies breakfasted on brawn and ale at sunrise, as in our more refined age of green tea and muffins at noon. Matilda seemed disposed to fly again to her lover, but the baron forced her from the chapel. The earl's bowmen at the door sent in among the assailants a volley of arrows, one of which whizzed past the ear of the abbot, who, in mortal fear of being suddenly translated from a ghostly friar into a friarly ghost, began to roll out of the chapel as fast as his bulk and his holy robes would permit, roaring "Sacrilege!" with all his monks at his heels, who were, like himself, more

intent to go at once than to stand upon the order of their going.[1]   The
abbot, thus pressed from behind, and stumbling over his own drapery
before, fell suddenly prostrate in the door-way that connected the
chapel with the abbey, and was instantaneously buried under a
pyramid of ghostly carcasses, that fell over him and each other, and
lay a rolling chaos of animated rotundities, sprawling and bawling in
unseemly disarray, and sending forth the names of all the saints in
and out of heaven, amidst the clashing of swords, the ringing of
bucklers, the clattering of helmets, the twanging of bow-strings, the
whizzing of arrows, the screams of women, the shouts of the warriors,
and the vociferations of the peasantry, who had been assembled to
the intended nuptials, and who, seeing a fair set-to, contrived to pick
a quarrel among themselves on the occasion, and proceeded, with
staff and cudgel, to crack each other's skulls for the good of the king
and the earl.   One tall friar alone was untouched by the panic of his
brethren, and stood steadfastly watching the combat with his arms
a-kembo, the colossal emblem of an unarmed neutrality.

At length, through the midst of the internal confusion, the earl,
by the help of his good sword, the staunch valour of his men, and the
blessing of the Virgin, fought his way to the chapel-gate—his bowmen
closed him in—he vaulted into his saddle, clapped spurs to his horse,
rallied his men on the first eminence, and exchanged his sword for
a bow and arrow, with which he did old execution among the pursuers, who at last thought it most expedient to desist from offensive
warfare, and to retreat into the abbey, where, in the king's name,
they broached a pipe of the best wine, and attached all the venison
in the larder, having first carefully unpacked the tuft of friars, and
set the fallen abbot on his legs.

The friars, it may be well supposed, and such of the king's men as
escaped unhurt from the affray, found their spirits a cup too low, and
kept the flask moving from noon till night.   The peaceful brethren, unused to the tumult of war, had undergone, from fear and discomposure,
an exhaustion of animal spirits that required extraordinary refection.
During the repast, they interrogated Sir Ralph Montfaucon, the
leader of the soldiers, respecting the nature of the earl's offence.

" A complication of offences," replied Sir Ralph, " superinduced

[1] *Macbeth*, Act III, Sc. 4.   G.

on the original basis of forest-treason. He began with hunting the
king's deer, in despite of all remonstrance ; followed it up by contempt of the king's mandates, and by armed resistance to his power,
in defiance of all authority ; and combined with it the resolute
withholding of payment of certain moneys to the abbot of Doncaster, in denial of all law ; and has thus made himself the declared
enemy of church and state, and all for being too fond of venison."
And the knight helped himself to half a pasty.

"A heinous offender," said a little round oily friar, appropriating
the portion of pasty which Sir Ralph had left.

"The earl is a worthy peer," said the tall friar whom we have already
mentioned in the chapel scene, "and the best marksman in England."

"Why this is flat treason, brother Michael," said the little round
friar, "to call an attainted traitor a worthy peer."

"I pledge you," said brother Michael.   The little friar smiled and
filled his cup.   "He will draw the long bow," pursued brother
Michael, "with any bold yeoman among them all."

"Don't talk of the long bow," said the abbot, who had the sound
of the arrow still whizzing in his ear : "what have we pillars of the
faith to do with the long bow ? "

"Be that as it may," said Sir Ralph, "he is an outlaw from this
moment."

"So much the worse for the law then," said brother Michael.
"The law will have a heavier miss of him than he will have of the law.
He will strike as much venison as ever, and more of other game.   I
know what I say : but *basta* ; Let us drink."

"What other game ? " said the little friar.   "I hope he won't
poach among our partridges."

"Poach ! not he," said brother Michael : "if he wants your
partridges, he will strike them under your nose (here's to you), and
drag your trout-stream for you on a Thursday evening."

"Monstrous ! and starve us on fast-day," said the little friar.

"But that is not the game I mean," said brother Michael.

"Surely, son Michael," said the abbot, "you do not mean to
insinuate that the noble earl will turn freebooter ? "

"A man must live," said brother Michael, "earl or no.   If the law
takes his rents and beeves without his consent, he must take beeves

and rents where he can get them without the consent of the law. This is the *lex talionis*."

" Truly," said Sir Ralph, " I am sorry for the damsel : she seems fond of this wild runagate."

" A mad girl, a mad girl," said the little friar.

" How a mad girl ? " said brother Michael. " Has she not beauty, grace, wit, sense, discretion, dexterity, learning, and valour ? "

" Learning ! " exclaimed the little friar ; " what has a woman to do with learning ? And valour ! who ever heard a woman commended for valour ? Meekness and mildness, and softness, and gentleness, and tenderness, and humility, and obedience to her husband, and faith in her confessor, and domesticity, or, as learned doctors call it, the faculty of stayathomeitiveness, and embroidery, and music, and pickling, and preserving, and the whole complex and multiplex detail of the noble science of dinner, as well in preparation for the table, as in arrangement over it, and in distribution around it to knights, and squires, and ghostly friars,—these are female virtues : but valour—why who ever heard—— ? "

" She is the all in all," said brother Michael, " gentle as a ring-dove, yet high-soaring as a falcon : humble below her deserving, yet deserving beyond the estimate of panegyric : an exact economist in all superfluity, yet a most bountiful dispenser in all liberality : the chief regulator of her household, the fairest pillar of her hall, and the sweetest blossom of her bower : having, in all opposite proposings, sense to understand, judgment to weigh, discretion to choose, firmness to undertake, diligence to conduct, perseverance to accomplish, and resolution to maintain. For obedience to her husband, that is not to be tried till she has one : for faith in her confessor, she has as much as the law prescribes : for embroidery an Arachne : for music a Siren : and for pickling and preserving, did not one of her jars of sugared apricots give you your last surfeit at Arlingford Castle ? "

" Call you that preserving ? " said the little friar ; " I call it destroying. Call you it pickling ? Truly it pickled me. My life was saved by miracle."

" By canary,"[1] said brother Michael. " Canary is the only life

[1] The Canaries were unknown to the mediæval world until their rediscovery in 1334. G.

preserver, the true *aurum potabile*, the universal panacea for all diseases, thirst, and short life. Your life was saved by canary."

"Indeed, reverend father," said Sir Ralph, "if the young lady be half what you describe, she must be a paragon : but your commending her for valour does somewhat amaze me."

"She can fence," said the little friar, "and draw the long bow, and play at single-stick and quarter-staff."

"Yet mark you," said brother Michael, "not like a virago or a hoyden, or one that would crack a serving-man's head for spilling gravy on her ruff, but with such womanly grace and temperate self-command as if those manly exercises belonged to her only, and were become for her sake feminine."

"You incite me," said Sir Ralph, "to view her more nearly. That madcap earl found me other employment than to remark her in the chapel."

"The earl is a worthy peer," said brother Michael ; "he is worth any fourteen earls on this side Trent, and any seven on the other." (The reader will please to remember that Rubygill Abbey was *north* of Trent.)

"His mettle will be tried," said Sir Ralph. "There is many a courtier will swear to King Henry to bring him in dead or alive."

"They must look to the brambles then," said brother Michael.

> "The bramble, the bramble, the bonny forest bramble,
>   Doth make a jest
>   Of silken vest,
> That will through greenwood scramble :
> The bramble, the bramble, the bonny forest bramble."

"Plague on your lungs, son Michael," said the abbot ; "this is your old coil : always roaring in your cups."

"I know what I say," said brother Michael ; "there is often more sense in an old song than in a new homily.

> The courtly pad doth amble,
> When his gay lord would ramble :
>   But both may catch
>   An awkward scratch,
> If they ride among the bramble :
> The bramble, the bramble, the bonny forest bramble." [1]

---

[1] Peacock had already used this theme in *The Three Doctors* and in *Melincourt*. See p. 119. G.

"Tall friar," said Sir Ralph, "either you shoot the shafts of your merriment at random, or you know more of the earl's designs than beseems your frock."

"Let my frock," said brother Michael, "answer for its own sins. It is worn past covering mine. It is too weak for a shield, too transparent for a screen, too thin for a shelter, too light for gravity, and too threadbare for a jest. The wearer would be naught indeed who should misbeseem such a wedding garment.

> But wherefore does the sheep wear wool ?
> That he in season sheared may be,
> And the shepherd be warm though his flock be cool :
> *So I'll have a new cloak about me.*" [1]

CHAPTER II

Vray moyne si oncques en feut depuis que le monde moynant moyna de moynerie.—RABELAIS. [2]

THE Earl of Huntingdon, living in the vicinity of a royal forest, and passionately attached to the chase from his infancy, had long made as free with the king's deer as Lord Percy proposed to do with those of Lord Douglas in the memorable hunting of Cheviot. It is sufficiently well known how severe were the forest-laws in those days, and with what jealousy the kings of England maintained this branch of their prerogative ; but menaces and remonstrances were thrown away on the earl, who declared that he would not thank Saint Peter for admission into Paradise, if he were obliged to leave his bow and hounds at the gate. King Henry (the Second) swore by Saint Botolph to make him rue his sport, and, having caused him to be duly and formally accused, summoned him to London to answer the

---

[1] This is obviously a verse of the sixteenth-century poem, or ballad, *The Old Cloak*, also called *Bell my Wiffe* and *Take thy Old Cloak About Thee*, one verse of which is sung by Iago in *Othello*, Act II, Sc. 3. It is not, however, in the text contained in the *Percy Folio MS.* or in Ramsay's *Teatable Miscellany* (1753) which were combined in Percy's *Reliques*, from which the version in *The Oxford Book of English Verse* was taken. Peacock either had access to another source or, conceivably, wrote it himself. G.

[2] "A right monk, if ever there was any, since the monking world monked a monkery." Bk. I, Ch. xxvii. Urquhart and Motteux translation. G.

charge. The earl, deeming himself safer among his own vassals than among King Henry's courtiers, took no notice of the mandate. King Henry sent a force to bring him, *vi et armis*, to court. The earl made a resolute resistance, and put the king's force to flight under a shower of arrows : an act which the courtiers declared to be treason. At the same time, the abbot of Doncaster sued up the payment of certain moneys, which the earl, whose revenue ran a losing race with his hospitality, had borrowed at sundry times of the said abbot : for the abbots and the bishops were the chief usurers of those days, and, as the end sanctifies the means, were not in the least scrupulous of employing what would have been extortion in the profane, to accomplish the pious purpose of bringing a blessing on the land by rescuing it from the frail hold of carnal and temporal into the firmer grasp of ghostly and spiritual possessors. But the earl, confident in the number and attachment of his retainers, stoutly refused either to repay the money, which he could not, or to yield the forfeiture, which he would not : a refusal which in those days was an act of outlawry in a gentleman, as it is now of bankruptcy in a base mechanic ; the gentleman having in our wiser times a more liberal privilege of gentility, which enables him to keep his land and laugh at his creditor. Thus the mutual resentments and interests of the king and the abbot concurred to subject the earl to the penalties of outlawry, by which the abbot would gain his due upon the lands of Locksley, and the rest would be confiscate to the king. Still the king did not think it advisable to assail the earl in his own strong-hold, but caused a diligent watch to be kept over his motions, till at length his rumoured marriage with the heiress of Arlingford seemed to point out an easy method of laying violent hands on the offender. Sir Ralph Montfaucon, a young man of good lineage and of an aspiring temper, who readily seized the first opportunity that offered of recommending himself to King Henry's favour by manifesting his zeal in his service, undertook the charge : and how he succeeded we have seen.

Sir Ralph's curiosity was strongly excited by the friar's description of the young lady of Arlingford ; and he prepared in the morning to visit the castle, under the very plausible pretext of giving the baron an explanation of his intervention at the nuptials. Brother Michael and the little fat friar proposed to be his guides. The proposal was courteously accepted, and they set out together, leaving Sir Ralph's followers at the abbey. The knight was mounted on a spirited charger ; brother Michael on a large heavy-trotting horse ; and the little fat friar on a plump soft-paced galloway, so correspondent with himself in size, rotundity, and sleekness, that if they had been amalgamated into a centaur, there would have been nothing to alter in their proportions.

" Do you know," said the little friar, as they wound along the banks of the stream, " the reason why lake-trout is better than river-trout, and shyer withal ? "

" I was not aware of the fact," said Sir Ralph.

" A most heterodox remark," said brother Michael : " know you not, that in all nice matters you should take the implication for absolute, and, without looking into the *fact whether*, seek only the *reason why* ? But the fact is so, on the word of a friar ; which what layman will venture to gainsay who prefers a down bed to a grid-iron ? "

" The fact being so," said the knight, " I am still at a loss for the reason ; nor would I undertake to opine in a matter of that magnitude : since, in all that appertains to the good things either of this world or the next, my reverend spiritual guides are kind enough to take the trouble of thinking off my hands."

" Spoken," said brother Michael, " with a sound Catholic conscience. My little brother here is most profound in the matter of trout. He has marked, learned, and inwardly digested the subject, twice a week at least for five-and-thirty years. I yield to him in this. My strong points are venison and canary."

" The good qualities of a trout," said the little friar, " are firmness and redness : the redness, indeed, being the visible sign of all other virtues."

" Whence," said brother Michael, " we choose our abbot by his nose :

> The rose on the nose doth all virtues disclose :
> For the outward grace shows
> That the inward overflows,
> When it glows in the rose of a red, red nose."

" Now," said the little friar, " as is the firmness so is the redness, and as is the redness so is the shyness."

" Marry why ? " said brother Michael. " The solution is not physical-natural, but physical-historical, or natural-superinductive. And thereby hangs a tale, which may be either said or sung :

> The damsel stood to watch the fight
>   By the banks of Kingslea Mere,
> And they brought to her feet her own true knight
>   Sore-wounded on a bier.
>
> She knelt by him his wounds to bind,
>   She washed them with many a tear :
> And shouts rose fast upon the wind,
>   Which told that the foe was near.
>
> ' Oh ! let not,' he said, ' while yet I live,
>   The cruel foe me take :
> But with thy sweet lips a last kiss give,
>   And cast me in the lake.'
>
> Around his neck she wound her arms,
>   And she kissed his lips so pale :
> And evermore the war's alarms
>   Came louder up the vale.
>
> She drew him to the lake's steep side,
>   Where the red heath fringed the shore ;
> She plunged with him beneath the tide,
>   And they were seen no more.
>
> Their true blood mingled in Kingslea Mere,
>   That to mingle on earth was fain :
> And the trout that swims in that crystal clear
>   Is tinged with the crimson stain.

" Thus you see how good comes of evil, and how a holy friar may fare better on fast-day for the violent death of two lovers two hundred years ago. The inference is most consecutive, that wherever you catch a red-fleshed trout, love lies bleeding under the water : an occult quality, which can only act in the stationary waters of a lake, being neutralised by the rapid transition of those of a stream."

" And why is the trout shyer for that ? " asked Sir Ralph.

" Do you not see ? " said brother Michael. " The virtues of both lovers diffuse themselves through the lake. The infusion of masculine valour makes the fish active and sanguineous : the infusion of maiden modesty makes him coy and hard to win : and you shall find through life, the fish which is most easily hooked is not the best worth dishing. But yonder are the towers of Arlingford."

The little friar stopped. He seemed suddenly struck with an awful thought, which caused a momentary pallescence in his rosy complexion ; and after a brief hesitation, he turned his galloway, and told his companions he should give them good day.

"Why, what is in the wind now, brother Peter ? " said Friar Michael.

"The lady Matilda," said the little friar, "can draw the long-bow. She must bear no goodwill to Sir Ralph ; and if she should espy him from her tower, she may testify her recognition with a cloth-yard shaft. She is not so infallible a markswoman, but that she might shoot at a crow and kill a pigeon. She might peradventure miss the knight, and hit me, who never did her any harm."

"Tut, tut, man," said brother Michael, "there is no such fear."

"Mass," said the little friar, "but there is such a fear, and very strong too. You who have it not may keep your way, and I who have it shall take mine. I am not just now in the vein for being picked off at a long shot." And saying these words, he spurred up his four-footed better half, and galloped off as nimbly as if he had had an arrow singing behind him.

"Is this lady Matilda, then, so very terrible a damsel ? " said Sir Ralph to brother Michael.

"By no means," said the friar. "She has certainly a high spirit ; but it is the wing of the eagle, without his beak or his claw. She is as gentle as magnanimous ; but it is the gentleness of the summer wind, which, however lightly it wave the tuft of the pine, carries with it the intimation of a power, that, if roused to its extremity, could make it bend to the dust."

"From the warmth of your panegyric, ghostly father," said the knight, "I should almost suspect you were in love with the damsel."

"So I am," said the friar, "and I care not who knows it ; but all in the way of honesty, master soldier. I am, as it were, her spiritual lover ; and were she a damsel errant, I would be her ghostly esquire, her friar militant. I would buckle me in armour of proof, and the devil might thresh me black with an iron flail, before I would knock under in her cause. Though they be not yet one canonically, thanks to your soldiership, the earl is her liege lord, and she is his liege lady. I am her father confessor and ghostly director : I have taken on me to show her the way to the next world ; and how can I do that if I lose sight of her in this ? seeing that this is but the road to the other, and has so many circumvolutions and ramifications of bye-ways and beaten paths (all more thickly set than the true one with finger-posts and mile-stones, not one of which tells truth), that a traveller has need of some one who knows the way, or the odds go hard against him that he will ever see the face of Saint Peter."

"But there must surely be some reason," said Sir Ralph, " for father Peter's apprehension."

"None," said brother Michael, " but the apprehension itself ; fear being its own father, and most prolific in self-propagation. The lady did, it is true, once signalize her displeasure against our little brother, for reprimanding her in that she would go hunting a-mornings instead of attending matins. She cut short the thread of his eloquence by sportively drawing her bow-string and loosing an arrow over his head ; he waddled off with singular speed, and was in much awe of her for many months. I thought he had forgotten it : but let that pass. In truth, she would have had little of her lover's company, if she had liked the chaunt of the choristers better than the cry of the hounds : yet I know not ; for they were companions from the cradle, and reciprocally fashioned each other to the love of the fern and the fox-glove. Had either been less sylvan, the other might have been more saintly ; but they will now never hear matins but those of the lark, nor reverence vaulted aisle but that of the green-wood canopy. They are twin plants of the forest, and are identified with its growth.

> For the slender beech and the sapling oak,
>   That grow by the shadowy rill,
> You may cut down both at a single stroke,
>   You may cut down which you will.
>
> But this you must know, that as long as they grow,
>   Whatever change may be,
> You never can teach either oak or beech
>   To be aught but a greenwood tree."

CHAPTER III

*Inflamed wrath in glowing breast.—*BUTLER.[1]

THE knight and the friar arriving at Arlingford Castle, and leaving their horses in the care of lady Matilda's groom, with whom the friar was in great favour, were ushered into a stately apartment, where they found the baron alone, flourishing an enormous carving-knife over a brother baron—of beef—with as much vehemence of action as if he were cutting down an enemy. The baron was a gentleman of a fierce and choleric temperament: he was lineally descended from the redoubtable Fierabras of Normandy, who came over to England with the Conqueror, and who, in the battle of Hastings, killed with his own hand four-and-twenty Saxon cavaliers all on a row.[2] The very excess of the baron's internal rage on the preceding day had smothered its external manifestation : he was so equally angry with both parties, that he knew not on which to vent his wrath. He was enraged with the earl for having brought himself into such a dilemma without his privity ; and he was no less enraged with the king's men for their very unseasonable intrusion. He could willingly have fallen upon both parties, but he must necessarily have begun with one ; and he felt that on whichever side he should strike the first blow, his retainers would immediately join battle. He had therefore contented himself with forcing away his daughter from the scene of action. In the course of the evening he had received intelligence that the earl's castle was in possession of a party of king's men, who had been detached by Sir Ralph Montfaucon to seize on it during the earl's absence. The baron inferred from this that the earl's case was desperate ; and those who have had the opportunity of seeing a rich friend fall suddenly into poverty, may easily judge by their own feelings how quickly and completely the whole moral being of the earl was changed in the baron's estimation. The baron immediately proceeded to require in his daughter's mind the same summary revolution that had taken place in his own, and considered himself exceedingly ill-used by her non-compliance. The lady had retired to

[1] *Hudibras*, Pt. I, Canto 2, l. 684. G.
[2] The English fought on foot at Hastings. G.

her chamber, and the baron had passed a supperless and sleepless night, stalking about his apartments till an advanced hour of the morning, when hunger compelled him to summon into his presence the spoils of the buttery, which, being the intended array of an uneaten wedding feast, were more than usually abundant, and on which, when the knight and the friar entered, he was falling with desperate valour. He looked up at them fiercely, with his mouth full of beef and his eyes full of flame, and rising, as ceremony required, made an awful bow to the knight, inclining himself forward over the table and presenting his carving-knife *en militaire*, in a manner that seemed to leave it doubtful whether he meant to show respect to his visitor, or to defend his provision : but the doubt was soon cleared up by his politely motioning the knight to be seated ; on which the friar advanced to the table, saying, " For what we are going to receive," and commenced operations without further prelude by filling and drinking a goblet of wine. The baron at the same time offered one to Sir Ralph, with the look of a man in whom habitual hospitality and courtesy were struggling with the ebullitions of natural anger. They pledged each other in silence, and the baron, having completed a copious draught, continued working his lips and his throat, as if trying to swallow his wrath as he had done his wine. Sir Ralph, not knowing well what to make of these ambiguous signs, looked for instructions to the friar, who by significant looks and gestures seemed to advise him to follow his example and partake of the good cheer before him, without speaking till the baron should be more intelligible in his demeanour. The knight and the friar, accordingly, proceeded to refect themselves after their ride ; the baron looking first at the one and then at the other, scrutinising alternately the serious looks of the knight and the merry face of the friar, till at length, having calmed himself sufficiently to speak, he said, " Courteous knight and ghostly father, I presume you have some other business with me than to eat my beef and drink my canary ; and if so, I patiently await your leisure to enter on the topic."

" Lord Fitzwater," said Sir Ralph, " in obedience to my royal master, King Henry, I have been the unwilling instrument of frustrating the intended nuptials of your fair daughter ; yet will you,

I trust, owe me no displeasure for my agency herein, seeing that the noble maiden might otherwise by this time have been the bride of an outlaw."

"I am very much obliged to you, sir," said the baron; "very exceedingly obliged. Your solicitude for my daughter is truly paternal, and for a young man and a stranger very singular and exemplary : and it is very kind withal to come to the relief of my insufficiency and inexperience, and concern yourself so much in that which concerns you not."

"You misconceive the knight, noble baron," said the friar. "He urges not his reason in the shape of a preconceived intent, but in that of a subsequent extenuation. True, he has done the lady Matilda great wrong——"

"How, great wrong ?" said the baron. "What do you mean by great wrong ? Would you have had her married to a wild fly-by-night, that accident made an earl and nature a deer-stealer ? that has not wit enough to eat venison without picking a quarrel with monarchy ? that flings away his own lands into the clutches of rascally friars, for the sake of hunting in other men's grounds, and feasting vagabonds that wear Lincoln green, and would have flung away mine into the bargain if he had had my daughter ? What do you mean by great wrong ? "

"True," said the friar, "great right, I meant."

"Right ! " exclaimed the baron : " what right has any man to do my daughter right but myself ? What right has any man to drive my daughter's bridegroom out of the chapel in the middle of the marriage ceremony, and turn all our merry faces into green wounds and bloody coxcombs,[1] and then come and tell me he has done us great right ? "

"True," said the friar : " he has done neither right nor wrong."

"But he has," said the baron, " he has done both, and I will maintain it with my glove."

"It shall not need," said Sir Ralph; "I will concede any thing in honour."

"And I," said the baron, "will concede nothing in honour : I will concede nothing in honour to any man."

[1] *Henry V*, Act V, Sc. 1. G.

" Neither will I, Lord Fitzwater," said Sir Ralph, " in that sense :
but hear me. I was commissioned by the king to apprehend the
Earl of Huntingdon. I brought with me a party of soldiers, picked
and tried men, knowing that he would not lightly yield. I sent my
lieutenant with a detachment to surprise the earl's castle in his absence,
and laid my measures for intercepting him on the way to his intended
nuptials; but he seems to have had intimation of this part of my plan,
for he brought with him a large armed retinue, and took a circuitous
route, which made him, I believe, somewhat later than his appointed
hour. When the lapse of time showed me that he had taken another
track, I pursued him to the chapel ; and I would have awaited the
close of the ceremony, if I had thought that either yourself or your
daughter would have felt desirous that she should have been the
bride of an outlaw."

" Who said, sir," cried the baron, " that we were desirous of any
such thing ? But truly, sir, if I had a mind to the devil for a son-in-
law, I would fain see the man that should venture to interfere."

" That would I," said the friar ; " for I have undertaken to make
her renounce the devil."

" She shall not renounce the devil," said the baron, " unless I
please. You are very ready with your undertakings. Will you
undertake to make her renounce the earl, who, I believe, is the devil
incarnate ? Will you undertake that ? "

" Will I undertake," said the friar, " to make Trent run westward,
or to make flame burn downward, or to make a tree grow with its
head in the earth and its root in the air ? "

" So then," said the baron, " a girl's mind is as hard to change as
nature and the elements, and it is easier to make her renounce the
devil than a lover. Are you a match for the devil, and no match for
a man ? "

" My warfare," said the friar, " is not of this world. I am militant
not against man, but the devil, who goes about seeking what he may
devour."

" Oh ! does he so ? " said the baron : " then I take it that makes
you look for him so often in my buttery. Will you cast out the
devil whose name is Legion, when you cannot cast out the imp whose
name is Love ? "

" Marriages," said the friar, " are made in heaven.   Love is God's work, and therewith I meddle not."

" God's work, indeed ! " said the baron, " when the ceremony was cut short in the church.   Could men have put them asunder, if God had joined them together ?   And the earl is now no earl, but plain Robert Fitz-Ooth : therefore, I'll none of him."

" He may atone," said the friar, " and the king may mollify.   The earl is a worthy peer, and the king is a courteous king."

"He cannot atone," said Sir Ralph.   "He has killed the king's men ; and if the baron should aid and abet, he will lose his castle and land."

" Will I ? " said the baron ; " not while I have a drop of blood in my veins.   He that comes to take them shall first serve me as the friar serves my flasks of canary : he shall drain me dry as hay.   Am I not disparaged ?   Am I not outraged ?   Is not my daughter vilified, and made a mockery ?   A girl half-married ?   There was my butler brought home with a broken head.   My butler, friar : there is that may move your sympathy.   Friar, the earl-no-earl shall come no more to my daughter."

" Very good," said the friar.

" It is not very good," said the baron, " for I cannot get her to say so."

" I fear," said Sir Ralph, " the young lady must be much distressed and discomposed."

" Not a whit, sir," said the baron.   " She is, as usual, in a most provoking imperturbability, and contradicts me so smilingly that it would enrage you to see her."

" I had hoped," said Sir Ralph, " that I might have seen her, to make my excuse in person for the hard necessity of my duty."

He had scarcely spoken, when the door opened, and the lady made her appearance.

CHAPTER IV

Are you mad, or what are you, that you squeak out your catches without mitigation or remorse of voice ?   *Twelfth Night.*[1]

MATILDA, not dreaming of visitors, tripped into the apartment in a dress of forest green, with a small quiver by her side, and a bow and

[1] Act II, Sc. 3.   G.

arrow in her hand. Her hair, black and glossy as the raven's wing, curled like wandering clusters of dark ripe grapes under the edge of her round bonnet ; and a plume of black feathers fell back negligently above it, with an almost horizontal inclination, that seemed the habitual effect of rapid motion against the wind. Her black eyes sparkled like sunbeams on a river : a clear, deep, liquid radiance, the reflection of ethereal fire,—tempered, not subdued, in the medium of its living and gentle mirror. Her lips were half opened to speak as she entered the apartment ; and with a smile of recognition to the friar, and a courtesy to the stranger knight, she approached the baron and said, " You are late at your breakfast, father."

" I am not at breakfast," said the baron. " I have been at supper : my last night's supper ; for I had none."

" I am sorry," said Matilda, " you should have gone to bed supperless."

" I did not go to bed supperless," said the baron : " I did not go to bed at all : and what are you doing with that green dress and that bow and arrow ? "

" I am going a-hunting," said Matilda.

" A-hunting ! " said the baron. " What, I warrant you, to meet with the earl, and slip your neck into the same noose ? "

" No," said Matilda : " I am not going out of our own woods to-day."

" How do I know that ? " said the baron. " What surety have I of that ? "

" Here is the friar," said Matilda. " He will be surety."

" Not he," said the baron : " he will undertake nothing but where the devil is a party concerned."

" Yes, I will," said the friar : " I will undertake any thing for the lady Matilda."

" No matter for that," said the baron : " she shall not go hunting to-day."

" Why, father," said Matilda, " if you coop me up here in this odious castle, I shall pine and die like a lonely swan on a pool."

" No," said the baron, " the lonely swan does not die on the pool. If there be a river at hand, she flies to the river, and finds her a mate ; and so shall not you."

"But," said Matilda, "you may send with me any, or as many, of your grooms as you will."

"My grooms," said the baron, "are all false knaves. There is not a rascal among them but loves you better than me. Villains that I feed and clothe."

"Surely," said Matilda, "it is not villainy to love me : if it be, I should be sorry my father were an honest man." The baron relaxed his muscles into a smile. "Or my lover either," added Matilda. The baron looked grim again.

"For your lover," said the baron, "you may give God thanks of him. He is as arrant a knave as ever poached."

"What, for hunting the king's deer ? " said Matilda. "Have I not heard you rail at the forest laws by the hour ? "

"Did you ever hear me," said the baron, "rail myself out of house and land ? If I had done that, then were I a knave."

"My lover," said Matilda, "is a brave man, and a true man, and a generous man, and a young man, and a handsome man ; aye, and an honest man too."

"How can he be an honest man," said the baron, "when he has neither house nor land, which are the better part of a man ? "

"They are but the husk of a man," said Matilda, "the worthless coat of the chesnut : the man himself is the kernel."

"The man is the grape stone," said the baron, "and the pulp of the melon. The house and land are the true substantial fruit, and all that give him savour and value."

"He will never want house or land," said Matilda, "while the meeting boughs weave a green roof in the wood, and the free range of the hart marks out the bounds of the forest."

"Vert and venison ! vert and venison ! " exclaimed the baron. "Treason and flat rebellion. Confound your smiling face ! what makes you look so good-humoured ? What ! you think I can't look at you, and be in a passion ? You think so, do you ? We shall see. Have you no fear in talking thus, when here is the king's liegeman come to take us all into custody, and confiscate our goods and chattels ? "

"Nay, Lord Fitzwater," said Sir Ralph, "you wrong me in your report. My visit is one of courtesy and excuse, not of menace and authority."

" There it is," said the baron : " every one takes a pleasure in contradicting me. Here is this courteous knight, who has not opened his mouth three times since he has been in my house except to take in provision, cuts me short in my story with a flat denial."

" Oh ! I cry you mercy, sir knight," said Matilda ; " I did not mark you before. I am your debtor for no slight favour, and so is my liege lord."

" Her liege lord ! " exclaimed the baron, taking large strides across the chamber.

" Pardon me, gentle lady," said Sir Ralph. " Had I known you before yesterday, I would have cut off my right hand ere it should have been raised to do you displeasure."

" Oh, sir," said Matilda, " a good man may be forced on an ill office : but I can distinguish the man from his duty." She presented to him her hand, which he kissed respectfully, and simultaneously with the contact thirty-two invisible arrows plunged at once into his heart, one from every point of the compass of his pericardia.

" Well, father," added Matilda, " I must go to the woods."

" Must you ? " said the baron ; " I say you must not."

" But I am going," said Matilda.

" But I will have up the drawbridge," said the baron.

" But I will swim the moat," said Matilda.

" But I will secure the gates," said the baron.

" But I will leap from the battlement," said Matilda.

" But I will lock you in an upper chamber," said the baron.

" But I will shred the tapestry," said Matilda, " and let myself down."

" But I will lock you in a turret," said the baron, " where you shall only see light through a loophole."

" But through that loophole," said Matilda, " will I take my flight, like a young eagle from its aerie ; and, father, while I go out freely, I will return willingly : but if once I slip out through a loophole——" She paused a moment, and then added, singing,—

> The love that follows fain
> Will never its faith betray :
> But the faith that is held in a chain
> Will never be found again,
> If a single link give way.

The melody acted irresistibly on the harmonious propensities of the friar, who accordingly sang in his turn,—

> For hark ! hark ! hark !
> The dog doth bark,
>   That watches the wild deer's lair.
> The hunter awakes at the peep of the dawn,
> But the lair it is empty, the deer it is gone,
>   And the hunter knows not where.

Matilda and the friar then sang together,—

> Then follow, oh follow ! the hounds do cry :
> The red sun flames in the eastern sky :
>   The stag bounds over the hollow.
> He that lingers in spirit, or loiters in hall,
> Shall see us no more till the evening fall,
> And no voice but the echo shall answer his call :
>   Then follow, oh follow, follow :
>   Follow, oh follow, follow !

During the process of this harmony, the baron's eyes wandered from his daughter to the friar, and from the friar to his daughter again, with an alternate expression of anger differently modified : when he looked on the friar, it was anger without qualification ; when he looked on his daughter it was still anger, but tempered by an expression of involuntary admiration and pleasure. These rapid fluctuations of the baron's physiognomy—the habitual, reckless, resolute merriment in the jovial face of the friar,—and the cheerful, elastic spirits that played on the lips and sparkled in the eyes of Matilda,—would have presented a very amusing combination to Sir Ralph, if one of the three images in the group had not absorbed his total attention with feelings of intense delight very nearly allied to pain. The baron's wrath was somewhat counteracted by the reflection that his daughter's good spirits seemed to show that they would naturally rise triumphant over all disappointments ; and he had had sufficient experience of her humour to know that she might sometimes be led, but never could be driven. Then, too, he was always delighted to hear her sing, though he was not at all pleased in this instance with the subject of her song. Still he would have endured the subject for the sake of the melody of the treble, but his mind was not sufficiently attuned to unison to relish the harmony of the bass. The friar's accompaniment put him out of all patience, and—"So," he exclaimed, "this is the way, you teach my daughter to renounce the devil, is it ? A hunting friar, truly ! Who ever heard before of a hunting friar ? A profane, roaring, bawling, bumper-bibbing, neck-breaking, catch-singing friar ? "

"Under favour, bold baron," said the friar ; but the friar was warm with canary, and in his singing vein ; and he could not go on in plain unmusical prose. He therefore sang in a new tune,—

> Though I be now a grey, grey friar,
>   Yet I was once a hale young knight :
> The cry of my dogs was the only choir
>   In which my spirit did take delight.
>
> Little I recked of matin bell,
>   But drowned its toll with my clanging horn :
> And the only beads I loved to tell
>   Were the beads of dew on the spangled thorn.

The baron was going to storm, but the friar paused, and Matilda sang in repetition,—

> Little I reck of matin bell,
>   But drown its toll with my clanging horn :
> And the only beads I love to tell
>   Are the beads of dew on the spangled thorn.

And then she and the friar sang the four lines together, and rang the changes upon them alternately.

> Little I reck of matin bell,

sang the friar.

"A precious friar," said the baron.

> But drown its toll with my clanging horn,

sang Matilda.

"More shame for you," said the baron.

> And the only beads I love to tell
>   Are the beads of dew on the spangled thorn,

sang Matilda and the friar together.

"Penitent and confessor," said the baron : "a hopeful pair truly."

The friar went on,—

An archer keen I was withal,
　　As ever did lean on greenwood tree ;
And could make the fleetest roebuck fall,
　　A good three hundred yards from me.
Though changeful time, with hand severe,
　　Has made me now these joys forego,
Yet my heart bounds whene'er I hear
　　Yoicks ! hark away ! and tally ho !

Matilda chimed in as before.

" Are you mad ? " said the baron. " Are you insane ? Are you possessed ? What do you mean ? What in the devil's name do you both mean ? "

　　　　　　　Yoicks ! hark away ! and tally ho !
roared the friar.

The baron's pent-up wrath had accumulated like the waters above the dam of an overshot mill. The pond-head of his passion being now filled to the utmost limit of its capacity, and beginning to overflow in the quivering of his lips and the flashing of his eyes, he pulled up all the flash-boards at once, and gave loose to the full torrent of his indignation, by seizing, like furious Ajax, not a massy stone more than two modern men could raise, but a vast dish of beef more than fifty ancient yeomen could eat, and whirled it like a coit, *in terrorem*, over the head of the friar, to the extremity of the apartment,

Where it on oaken floor did settle,
With mighty din of ponderous metal.[1]

" Nay father," said Matilda, taking the baron's hand, " do not harm the friar : he means not to offend you. My gaiety never before displeased you. Least of all should it do so now, when I have need of all my spirits to outweigh the severity of my fortune."

As she spoke the last words, tears started into her eyes, which, as if ashamed of the involuntary betraying of her feelings, she turned away to conceal. The baron was subdued at once. He kissed his daughter, held out his hand to the friar, and said, " Sing on, in God's name, and crack away the flasks till your voice swims in canary." Then turning to Sir Ralph, he said, " You see how it is, sir knight. Matilda is my daughter ; but she has me in leading-strings, that is the truth of it."

[1] Butler uses these rhymes more than once in *Hudibras*. Possibly the lines are Peacock's. G.

CHAPTER V

'Tis true, no lover has that power
To enforce a desperate amour,
As he that has two strings to his bow,
And burns for love and money too.
—BUTLER. [1]

THE friar had often had experience of the baron's testy humour ; but it had always before confined itself to words, in which the habit of testiness often mingled more expression of displeasure than the internal feeling prompted. He knew the baron to be hot and choleric, but at the same time hospitable and generous ; passionately fond of his daughter, often thwarting her in seeming, but always yielding to her in fact. The early attachment between Matilda and the Earl of Huntingdon had given the baron no serious reason to interfere with her habits and pursuits, which were so congenial to those of her lover ; and not being overburdened with orthodoxy, that is to say, not being seasoned with more of the salt of the spirit than was necessary to preserve him from excommunication, confiscation, and philotheoparoptesism,[2] he was not sorry to encourage his daughter's choice of her confessor in brother Michael, who had more jollity and less hypocrisy than any of his fraternity, and was very little anxious to disguise his love of the good things of this world under the semblance of a sanctified exterior. The friar and Matilda had often sung duets together, and had been accustomed to the baron's chiming in with a stormy *capriccio*, which was usually charmed into silence by some sudden turn in the witching melodies of Matilda. They had therefore naturally calculated, as far as their wild spirits calculated at all, on the same effects from the same causes. But the circumstances of the preceding day had made an essential alteration in the case. The baron knew well, from the intelligence he had received, that the earl's offence was past remission : which would have been of less moment but for the awful fact of his castle being in the possession of the king's forces, and in those days possession was considerably more than eleven points of the law. The baron was therefore convinced that the earl's outlawry was infallible, and that

---

[1] *Hudibras*, Pt. III, Canto 1, lines 1–4. G.
[2] Roasting by a slow fire for the love of God. [P.]

Matilda must either renounce her lover, or become with him an out-law and a fugitive. In proportion, therefore, to the baron's know-ledge of the strength and duration of her attachment, was his fear of the difficulty of its ever being overcome : her love of the forest and the chase, which he had never before discouraged, now presented itself to him as matter of serious alarm ; and if her cheerfulness gave him hope on the one hand by indicating a spirit superior to all dis-appointments, it was suspicious to him on the other, as arising from some latent certainty of being soon united to the earl. All these circumstances concurred to render their songs of the vanished deer and greenwood archery and Yoicks and Harkaway, extremely *mal-a-propos*, and to make his anger boil and bubble in the cauldron of his spirit, till its more than ordinary excitement burst forth with sudden impulse into active manifestation.

> But as it sometimes happens, from the might
> Of *rage* in minds that can no farther go,
> As high as they have mounted in *despite*
> In their *remission* do they sink as low,
> To *our bold baron* did it happen so.[1]

For his discobolic exploit proved the climax of his rage, and was succeeded by an immediate sense that he had passed the bounds of legitimate passion ; and he sunk immediately from the very pinnacle of opposition to the level of implicit acquiescence. The friar's spirits were not to be marred by such a little incident. He was half-inclined, at first, to return the baron's compliment ; but his love of Matilda checked him ; and when the baron held out his hand, the friar seized it cordially, and they drowned all recollection of the affair by pledging each other in a cup of canary.

The friar, having stayed long enough to see everything replaced on a friendly footing, rose, and moved to take his leave. Matilda told him he must come again on the morrow, for she had a very long confession to make to him. This the friar promised to do, and departed with the knight.

Sir Ralph, on reaching the abbey, drew his followers together, and led them to Locksley Castle, which he found in the possession of his

---

[1] Of these lines all that is not in italics belongs to Mr. Wordsworth : *Resolution and Independence*. [P.]

lieutenant; whom he again left there with a sufficient force to hold
it in safe keeping in the king's name, and proceeded to London to
report the results of his enterprise.

Now Henry our royal king was very wroth at the earl's evasion,
and swore by Saint Thomas-à-Becket (whom he had himself translated into a saint by having him knocked on the head), that he would
give the castle and lands of Locksley to the man who should bring in
the earl. Hereupon ensued a process of thought in the mind of the
knight. The eyes of the fair huntress of Arlingford had left a wound
in his heart which only she who gave could heal. He had seen that
the baron was no longer very partial to the outlawed earl, but that
he still retained his old affection for the lands and castle of Locksley.
Now the lands and castle were very fair things in themselves, and
would be pretty appurtenances to an adventurous knight; but they
would be doubly valuable as certain passports to the father's favour,
which was one step towards that of the daughter, or at least towards
obtaining possession of her either quietly or perforce; for the knight
was not so nice in his love as to consider the lady's free grace a *sine
qua non*: and to think of being, by any means whatever, the lord of
Locksley and Arlingford, and the husband of the bewitching Matilda,
was to cut in the shades of futurity a vista very tempting to a soldier
of fortune. He set out in high spirits with a chosen band of followers,
and beat up all the country far and wide around both the Ouse and
the Trent; but fortune did not seem disposed to second his diligence,
for no vestige whatever could he trace of the earl. His followers,
who were only paid with the wages of hope, began to murmur and
fall off; for, as those unenlightened days were ignorant of the happy
invention of paper machinery, by which one promise to pay is satisfactorily paid with another promise to pay, and that again with
another in infinite series, they would not, as their wiser posterity has
done, take those tenders for true pay which were not sterling; so
that, one fine morning, the knight found himself sitting on a pleasant
bank of the Trent, with only a solitary squire, who still clung to the
shadow of preferment, because he did not see at the moment any
better chance of the substance.

The knight did not despair because of the desertion of his followers:
he was well aware that he could easily raise recruits if he could once

find trace of his game ; he, therefore, rode about indefatigably over hill and dale, to the great sharpening of his own appetite and that of his squire, living gallantly from inn to inn when his purse was full, and quartering himself in the king's name on the nearest ghostly brotherhood when it happened to be empty. An autumn and a winter had passed away, when the course of his perlustrations brought him one evening into a beautiful sylvan valley, where he found a number of young women weaving garlands of flowers, and singing over their pleasant occupation. He approached them, and courteously inquired the way to the nearest town.

" There is no town within several miles," was the answer.

" A village, then, if it be but large enough to furnish an inn ? "

" There is Gamwell just by, but there is no inn nearer than the nearest town."

" An abbey, then ? "

" There is no abbey nearer than the nearest inn."

" A house then, or a cottage, where I may obtain hospitality for the night ? "

" Hospitality ! " said one of the young women ; " you have not far to seek for that. Do you not know that you are in the neighbourhood of Gamwell-Hall ? "

" So far from it," said the knight, " that I never heard the name of Gamwell-Hall before."

" Never heard of Gamwell-Hall ? " exclaimed all the young women together, who could as soon have dreamed of his never having heard of the sky.

" Indeed, no," said Sir Ralph ; " but I shall be very happy to get rid of my ignorance."

" And so shall I," said his squire ; " for it seems that in this case knowledge will for once be a cure for hunger, wherewith I am grievously afflicted."

" And why are you so busy, my pretty damsels, weaving these garlands ? " said the knight.

" Why, do you not know, sir," said one of the young women, " that to-morrow is Gamwell feast ? "

The knight was again obliged, with all humility, to confess his ignorance.

" Oh ! sir," said his informant, " then you will have something to
see, that I can tell you ; for we shall choose a Queen of the May,
and we shall crown her with flowers, and place her in a chariot of
flowers, and draw it with lines of flowers, and we shall hang all the
trees with flowers, and we shall strew all the ground with flowers,
and we shall dance with flowers, and in flowers, and on flowers, and
we shall be all flowers."

" That you will," said the knight ; " and the sweetest and brightest
of all the flowers of the May, my pretty damsels."   On which all the
pretty damsels smiled at him and each other.

" And there will be all sorts of May-games, and there will be prizes
for archery, and there will be the knight's ale, and the foresters'
venison, and there will be Kit Scrapesqueak with his fiddle, and little
Tom Whistlerap with his fife and tabor, and Sam Trumtwang with his
harp, and Peter Muggledrone with his bagpipe, and how I shall dance
with Will Whitethorn ! " added the girl, clapping her hands as she spoke,
and bounding from the ground with the pleasure of the anticipation.

A tall athletic young man approached, to whom the rustic maidens
courtesied with great respect ; and one of them informed Sir Ralph
that it was young Master William Gamwell.   The young gentleman
invited and conducted the knight to the hall, where he introduced
him to the old knight his father, and to the old lady his mother, and
to the young lady his sister, and to a number of bold yeomen, who
were laying siege to beef, brawn, and plum pie around a ponderous
table, and taking copious draughts of old October.[1]   A motto was
inscribed over the interior door,—

EAT, DRINK, AND BE MERRY :

an injunction which Sir Ralph and his squire showed remarkable
alacrity in obeying.   Old Sir Guy of Gamwell gave Sir Ralph a very
cordial welcome, and entertained him during supper with several of
his best stories, enforced with an occasional slap on the back, and
pointed with a peg in the ribs ; a species of vivacious eloquence in
which the old gentleman excelled, and which is supposed by many of
that pleasant variety of the human species, known by the name of
choice fellows and comical dogs, to be the genuine tangible shape of
the cream of a good joke.

[1] See Note, p. 104.   G.

CHAPTER VI

What ! shall we have incision ? shall we embrew ?—Henry IV.[1]

OLD Sir Guy of Gamwell, and young William Gamwell, and fair Alice Gamwell, and Sir Ralph Montfaucon and his squire, rode together the next morning to the scene of the feast. They arrived on a village-green, surrounded with cottages peeping from among the trees by which the green was completely encircled. The whole circle was hung round with one continuous garland of flowers, depending in irregular festoons from the branches. In the centre of the green was a May-pole hidden in boughs and garlands ; and a multitude of round-faced bumpkins and cherry-cheeked lasses were dancing around it, to the quadruple melody of Scrapesqueak, Whistlerap, Trumtwang, and Muggledrone : harmony we must not call it ; for, though they had agreed to a partnership in point of tune, each, like a true painstaking man, seemed determined to have his time to himself : Muggledrone played *allegretto*, Trumtwang *allegro*, Whistlerap *presto*, and Scrapesqueak *prestissimo*. There was a kind of mathematical proportion in their discrepancy : while Muggledrone played the tune four times, Trumtwang played it five, Whistlerap six, and Scrapesqueak eight ; for the latter completely distanced all his competitors, and indeed worked his elbow so nimbly that its outline was scarcely distinguishable through the mistiness of its rapid vibration.

While the knight was delighting his eyes and ears with these pleasant sights and sounds, all eyes were turned in one direction ; and Sir Ralph, looking round, saw a fair lady in green and gold come riding through the trees, accompanied by a portly friar in grey, and several fair damsels and gallant grooms. On their nearer approach, he recognised the lady Matilda and her ghostly adviser, brother Michael. A party of foresters arrived from another direction, and then ensued cordial interchanges of greeting, and collisions of hands and lips, among the Gamwells and the new-comers,—" How does my fair coz, Mawd ? " and " How does my sweet coz, Mawd ? " and " How does my wild coz, Mawd ? " And " Eh ! jolly friar, your

---

[1] *Pt. II*, Act II, Sc. 4. G.

hand, old boy : " and " Here, honest friar : " and " To me, merry friar : " and " By your favour, mistress Alice : " and " Hey ! cousin Robin : " and " Hey ! cousin Will : " and " Od's life ! merry Sir Guy, you grow younger every year,"—as the old knight shook them all in turn with one hand, and slapped them on the back with the other, in token of his affection. A number of young men and women advanced, some drawing, and others dancing round, a floral car ; and having placed a crown of flowers on Matilda's head, they saluted her Queen of the May, and drew her to the place appointed for the rural sports.

A hogshead of ale was abroach under an oak, and a fire was blazing in an open space before the trees to roast the fat deer which the foresters brought. The sports commenced ; and, after an agreeable series of bowling, coiting, pitching, hurling, racing, leaping, grinning, wrestling or friendly dislocation of joints, and cudgel-playing or amicable cracking of skulls, the trial of archery ensued. The conqueror was to be rewarded with a golden arrow from the hand of the Queen of the May, who was to be his partner in the dance till the close of the feast. This stimulated the knight's emulation : young Gamwell supplied him with a bow and arrow, and he took his station among the foresters, but had the mortification to be out-shot by them all, and to see one of them lodge the point of his arrow in the golden ring of the centre, and receive the prize from the hand of the beautiful Matilda, who smiled on him with particular grace. The jealous knight scrutinised the successful champion with great attention, and surely thought he had seen that face before. In the mean time the forester led the lady to the station. The luckless Sir Ralph drank deep draughts of love from the matchless grace of her attitudes, as, taking the bow in her left hand, and adjusting the arrow with her right, advancing her left foot, and gently curving her beautiful figure with a slight motion of her head that waved her black feathers and her ringleted hair, she drew the arrow to its head, and loosed it from her open fingers. The arrow struck within the ring of gold, so close to that of the victorious forester that the points were in contact, and the feathers were intermingled. Great acclamations succeeded, and the forester led Matilda to the dance. Sir Ralph gazed on her fascinating motions till the torments of baffled love and jealous rage became unendurable; and approaching young Gamwell, he asked him if he knew the name of that forester who was leading the dance with the Queen of the May?

"Robin, I believe," said young Gamwell carelessly; "I think they call him Robin."

"Is that all you know of him?" said Sir Ralph.

"What more should I know of him?" said young Gamwell.

"Then I can tell you," said Sir Ralph, "he is the outlawed Earl of Huntingdon, on whose head is set so large a price."

"Ay, is he?" said young Gamwell, in the same careless manner.

"He were a prize worth the taking," said Sir Ralph.

"No doubt," said young Gamwell.

"How think you?" said Sir Ralph: "are the foresters his adherents?"

"I cannot say," said young Gamwell.

"Is your peasantry loyal and well-disposed?" said Sir Ralph.

"Passing loyal," said young Gamwell.

"If I should call on them in the king's name," said Sir Ralph, "think you they would aid and assist?"

"Most likely they would," said young Gamwell, "one side or the other."

"Ay, but which side?" said the knight.

"That remains to be tried," said young Gamwell.

"I have King Henry's commission," said the knight, "to apprehend this earl that was. How would you advise me to act, being, as you see, without attendant force?"

"I would advise you," said young Gamwell, "to take yourself off without delay, unless you would relish the taste of a volley of arrows, a shower of stones, and a hailstorm of cudgel-blows, which would not be turned aside by a God save King Henry."

Sir Ralph's squire no sooner heard this, and saw by the looks of the speaker that he was not likely to prove a false prophet, than he clapped spurs to his horse and galloped off with might and main. This gave the knight a good excuse to pursue him, which he did with great celerity, calling, "Stop, you rascal." When the squire fancied himself safe out of the reach of pursuit, he checked his speed, and allowed the knight to come up with him. They rode on several miles in silence, till they discovered the towers and spires of Nottingham, where the knight introduced himself to the sheriff, and demanded an armed force to assist in the apprehension of the outlawed Earl of Huntingdon. The sheriff, who was willing to have his share of the prize, determined to accompany the knight in person, and regaled him and his man with good store of the best ; after which, they, with a stout retinue of fifty men, took the way to Gamwell feast.

" God's my life," said the sheriff, as they rode along, " I had as lief you would tell me of a service of plate. I much doubt if this outlawed earl, this forester Robin, be not the man they call Robin Hood, who has quartered himself in Sherwood Forest, and whom in endeavouring to apprehend I have fallen divers times into disasters. He has gotten together a band of disinherited prodigals, outlawed debtors, excommunicated heretics, elder sons that have spent all they had, and younger sons that never had any thing to spend ; and with these he kills the king's deer, and plunders wealthy travellers of five-sixths of their money ; but if they be abbots or bishops, them he despoils utterly."

The sheriff then proceeded to relate to his companion the adventure of the abbot of Doubleflask (which some grave historians have related of the abbot of Saint Mary's, and others of the bishop of Hereford): how the abbot, returning to his abbey in company with his high selerer, who carried in his portmanteau the rents of the abbey-lands, and with a numerous train of attendants, came upon four seeming peasants, who were roasting the king's venison by the king's high-way : how, in just indignation at this flagrant infringement of the forest laws, he asked them what they meant, and they answered that they meant to dine : how he ordered them to be seized and bound, and led captive to Nottingham, that they might know wild-flesh to have been destined by Providence for licensed and privileged appetites, and not for the base hunger of unqualified knaves : how they prayed for mercy, and how the abbot swore by Saint Charity that he would show them none : how one of them thereupon drew a bugle-horn from under his smock-frock and blew three blasts, on which the abbot and his train were instantly surrounded by sixty bowmen in green : how they tied him to a tree, and made him say mass for their sins : how they unbound him, and sate him down with

them to dinner, and gave him venison and wild-fowl and wine, and
made him pay for his fare all the money in his high selerer's portmanteau, and enforced him to sleep all night under a tree in his
cloak, and to leave the cloak behind him in the morning : how the
abbot, light in pocket and heavy in heart, raised the country upon
Robin Hood, for so he had heard the chief forester called by his men,
and hunted him into an old woman's cottage : how Robin changed
dresses with the old woman, and how the abbot rode in great
triumph to Nottingham, having in custody an old woman in a green
doublet and breeches : how the old woman discovered herself : how
the merrymen of Nottingham laughed at the abbot : how the abbot
railed at the old woman, and how the old woman out-railed the
abbot, telling him that Robin had given her food and fire through the
winter, which no abbot would ever do, but would rather take it from
her for what he called the good of the church, by which he meant his
own laziness and gluttony ; and that she knew a true man from a
false thief, and a free forester from a greedy abbot.

"Thus you see," added the sheriff, "how this villain perverts the
deluded people by making them believe that those who tithe and toll
upon them for their spiritual and temporal benefit are not their best
friends and fatherly guardians ; for he holds that in giving to boors
and old women what he takes from priests and peers, he does but
restore to the former what the latter had taken from them ; and this
the impudent varlet calls distributive justice. Judge now if any
loyal subject can be safe in such neighbourhood."

While the sheriff was thus enlightening his companion concerning
the offenders, and whetting his own indignation against them, the
sun was fast sinking to the west. They rode on till they came in view
of a bridge, which they saw a party approaching from the opposite
side, and the knight presently discovered that the party consisted of
the lady Matilda and friar Michael, young Gamwell, cousin Robin,
and about half-a-dozen foresters. The knight pointed out the earl
to the sheriff, who exclaimed, "Here, then, we have him an easy
prey ; " and they rode on manfully towards the bridge, on which the
other party made halt.

"Who be these," said the friar, "that come riding so fast this
way ? Now, as God shall judge me, it is that false knight Sir Ralph

Montfaucon, and the sheriff of Nottingham, with a posse of men. We must make good our post, and let them dislodge us if they may."

The two parties were now near enough to parley; and the sheriff and the knight, advancing in the front of the cavalcade, called on the lady, the friar, young Gamwell, and the foresters, to deliver up that false traitor, Robert, formerly Earl of Huntingdon. Robert himself made answer by letting fly an arrow that struck the ground between the fore feet of the sheriff's horse. The horse reared up from the whizzing, and lodged the sheriff in the dust; and, at the same time, the fair Matilda favoured the knight with an arrow in his right arm, that compelled him to withdraw from the affray. His men lifted the sheriff carefully up, and replaced him on his horse, whom he immediately with great rage and zeal urged on to the assault with his fifty men at his heels, some of whom were intercepted in their advance by the arrows of the foresters and Matilda; while the friar, with an eight-foot staff, dislodged the sheriff a second time, and laid on him with all the vigour of the church militant on earth, in spite of his ejaculations of "Hey, friar Michael! What means this, honest friar? Hold, ghostly friar! Hold, holy friar!"—till Matilda interposed, and delivered the battered sheriff to the care of the foresters. The friar continued flourishing his staff among the sheriff's men, knocking down one, breaking the ribs of another, dislocating the shoulder of a third, flattening the nose of a fourth, cracking the skull of a fifth, and pitching a sixth into the river,[1] till the few, who were lucky enough to escape with whole bones, clapped spurs to their horses and fled for their lives, under a farewell volley of arrows.

Sir Ralph's squire, meanwhile, was glad of the excuse of attending his master's wound to absent himself from the battle; and put the poor knight to a great deal of unnecessary pain by making as long a business as possible of extracting the arrow, which he had not accomplished when Matilda, approaching, extracted it with great facility, and bound up the wound with her scarf, saying, "I reclaim my arrow, sir knight, which struck where I aimed it, to admonish you to desist from your enterprise. I could as easily have lodged it in your heart."

[1] Imitated from Rabelais, Bk. I, Ch. xxvii.   G.

" It did not need," said the knight, with rueful gallantry ; " you have lodged one there already."

" If you mean to say that you love me," said Matilda, " it is more than I ever shall you : but if you will show your love by no further interfering with mine, you will at least merit my gratitude."

The knight made a wry face under the double pain of heart and body caused at the same moment by the material or martial, and the metaphorical or erotic arrow, of which the latter was thus barbed by a declaration more candid than flattering ; but he did not choose to put in any such claim to the lady's gratitude as would bar all hopes of her love : he therefore remained silent ; and the lady and her escort, leaving him and the sheriff to the care of the squire, rode on till they came in sight of Arlingford Castle, when they parted in several directions. The friar rode off alone ; and after the foresters had lost sight of him they heard his voice through the twilight, singing,—

> A staff, a staff, of a young oak graff,
> That is both stoure and stiff,
> Is all a good friar can needs desire
> To shrive a proud sheriffe.
> And thou, fine fellôwe, who has tasted so
> Of the forester's greenwood game,
> Wilt be in no haste thy time to waste
> In seeking more taste of the same :
> Or this can I read thee, and riddle thee well,
> Thou hadst better by far be the devil in hell,
> Than the sheriff of Nottinghâme.

CHAPTER VII

Now, master sheriff, what's your will with me ? *Henry IV.*[1]

MATILDA had carried her point with the baron of ranging at liberty whithersoever she would, under her positive promise to return home ; she was a sort of prisoner on parole : she had obtained this indulgence by means of an obsolete habit of always telling the truth and keeping her word, which our enlightened age has discarded with other barbarisms, but which had the effect of giving her father so much confidence in her, that he could not help considering her word a better security than locks and bars.

[1] *Pt. I*, Act I, Sc. 4. G.

The baron had been one of the last to hear of the rumours of the new outlaws of Sherwood, as Matilda had taken all possible precautions to keep those rumours from his knowledge, fearing that they might cause the interruption of her greenwood liberty ; and it was only during her absence at Gamwell feast, that the butler, being thrown off his guard by liquor, forgot her injunctions, and regaled the baron with a long story of the right merry adventure of Robin Hood and the abbot of Doubleflask.

The baron was one morning, as usual, cutting his way valorously through a rampart of cold provision, when his ears were suddenly assailed by a tremendous alarum, and sallying forth, and looking from his castle wall, he perceived a large party of armed men on the other side of the moat, who were calling on the warder in the king's name to lower the drawbridge and raise the portcullis, which had both been secured by Matilda's order. The baron walked along the battlement till he came opposite to these unexpected visitors, who, as soon as they saw him, called out, " Lower the drawbridge, in the king's name."

" For what, in the devil's name ? " said the baron.

" The sheriff of Nottingham," said one, " lies in bed grievously bruised, and many of his men are wounded, and several of them slain ; and Sir Ralph Montfaucon, knight, is sore wounded in the arm; and we are charged to apprehend William Gamwell the younger, of Gamwell Hall, and father Michael of Rubygill Abbey, and Matilda Fitzwater of Arlingford Castle, as agents and accomplices in the said breach of the king's peace."

" Breach of the king's fiddlestick ! " answered the baron. " What do you mean by coming here with your cock and bull stories of my daughter grievously bruising the sheriff of Nottingham ? You are a set of vagabond rascals in disguise ; and I hear, by the bye, there is a gang of thieves that has just set up business in Sherwood Forest : a pretty pretence, indeed, to get into my castle with force and arms, and make a famine in my buttery, and a drought in my cellar, and a void in my strong box, and a vacuum in my silver scullery."

" Lord Fitzwater," cried one, " take heed how you resist lawful authority : we will prove ourselves——"

" You will prove yourselves arrant knaves, I doubt not," answered the baron : " but, villains, you shall be more grievously bruised by me than ever was the sheriff by my daughter (a pretty tale truly !), if you do not forthwith avoid my territory."

By this time the baron's men had flocked to the battlements, with long-bows and cross-bows, slings and stones, and Matilda with her bow and quiver at their head. The assailants, finding the castle so well defended, deemed it expedient to withdraw till they could return in greater force, and rode off to Rubygill Abbey, where they made known their errand to the father abbot, who, having satisfied himself of their legitimacy, and conned over the allegations, said that doubtless brother Michael had heinously offended ; but it was not for the civil law to take cognizance of the misdoings of a holy friar ; that he would summon a chapter of monks, and pass on the offender a sentence proportionate to his offence. The ministers of civil justice said that would not do. The abbot said it would do and should ; and bade them not provoke the meekness of his catholic charity to lay them under the curse of Rome. This threat had its effect, and the party rode off to Gamwell-Hall, where they found the Gamwells and their men just sitting down to dinner, which they saved them the trouble of eating by consuming it in the king's name themselves, having first seized and bound young Gamwell ; all which they accomplished by dint of superior numbers, in despite of a most vigorous stand made by the Gamwellites in defence of their young master and their provisions.

The baron, meanwhile, after the minsters of justice had departed, interrogated Matilda concerning the alleged fact of the grievous bruising of the sheriff of Nottingham. Matilda told him the whole history of Gamwell feast, and of their battle on the bridge, which had its origin in a design of the sheriff of Nottingham to take one of the foresters into custody.

" Ay ! ay ! " said the baron, " and I guess who that forester was ; but truly this friar is a desperate fellow. I did not think there could have been so much valour under a grey frock. And so you wounded the knight in the arm. You are a wild girl, Mawd,—a chip of the old block, Mawd. A wild girl, and a wild friar, and three or four foresters, wild lads all, to keep a bridge against a tame knight, and a tame sheriff, and fifty tame varlets ; by this light, the like was never heard! But do you know, Mawd, you must not go about so any more, sweet Mawd: you must stay at home, you must ensconce; for there is your tame sheriff on the one hand, that will take you perforce; and there is your wild forester on the other hand, that will take you without any force at all, Mawd: your wild forester, Robin, cousin Robin, Robin Hood of Sherwood Forest, that beats and binds bishops, spreads nets for archbishops, and hunts a fat abbot as if he were a buck: excellent game, no doubt, but you must hunt no more in such company. I see it now: truly I might have guessed before that the bold outlaw Robin, the most courteous Robin, the new thief of Sherwood Forest, was your lover, the earl that has been: I might have guessed it before, and what led you so much to the woods; but you hunt no more in such company. No more May games and Gamwell feasts. My lands and castle would be the forfeit of a few more such pranks; and I think they are as well in my hands as the king's, quite as well."

"You know, father," said Matilda, "the condition of keeping me at home: I get out if I can, and not on parole."

"Ay! ay!" said the baron, "if you can; very true: watch and ward, Mawd, watch and ward is my word: if you can, is yours. The mark is set, and so start fair."

The baron would have gone on in this way for an hour; but the friar made his appearance with a long oak staff in his hand, singing,—

> Drink and sing, and eat and laugh,
> And so go forth to battle:
> For the top of a skull and the end of a staff
> Do make a ghostly rattle.

"Ho! ho! friar!" said the baron—"singing friar, laughing friar, roaring friar, fighting friar, hacking friar, thwacking friar; cracking, cracking, cracking friar; joke-cracking, bottle-cracking, skull-cracking friar!"

"And ho! ho!" said the friar,—"bold baron, old baron, sturdy baron, wordy baron, long baron, strong baron, mighty baron, flighty baron, mazed baron, crazed baron, hacked baron, thwacked baron; cracked, cracked, cracked baron; bone-cracked, sconce-cracked, brain-cracked baron!"

"What do you mean," said the baron, "bully friar, by calling me hacked and thwacked?"

"Were you not in the wars?" said the friar, "where he who escapes unhacked does more credit to his heels than his arms. I pay tribute to your valour in calling you hacked and thwacked."

"I never was thwacked in my life," said the baron; "I stood my ground manfully, and covered my body with my sword. If I had had the luck to meet with a fighting friar indeed, I might have been thwacked, and soundly too; but I hold myself a match for any two laymen; it takes nine fighting laymen to make a fighting friar."

"Whence come you now, holy father?" asked Matilda.

"From Rubygill Abbey," said the friar, "whither I never return:

> For I must seek some hermit cell,
> Where I alone my beads may tell,
> And on the wight who that way fares
> Levy a toll for my ghostly pray'rs,
> Levy a toll, levy a toll,
> Levy a toll for my ghostly pray'rs."

"What is the matter then, father?" said Matilda.

"This is the matter," said the friar: "my holy brethren have held a chapter on me, and sentenced me to seven years' privation of wine. I therefore deemed it fitting to take my departure, which they would fain have prohibited. I was enforced to clear the way with my staff. I have grievously beaten my dearly beloved brethren: I grieve thereat; but they enforced me thereto. I have beaten them much; I mowed them down to the right and to the left, and left them like an ill-reaped field of wheat, ear and straw pointing all ways, scattered in singleness and jumbled in masses; and so bade them farewell, saying, Peace be with you. But I must not tarry, lest danger be in my rear: therefore, farewell, sweet Matilda; and farewell, noble baron; and farewell, sweet Matilda again, the alpha and omega of father Michael, the first and the last."

"Farewell, father," said the baron, a little softened; "and God send you be never assailed by more than fifty men at a time."

"Amen," said the friar, "to that good wish."

"And we shall meet again, father, I trust," said Matilda.

"When the storm is blown over," said the baron.

"Doubt it not," said the friar, "though flooded Trent were between us, and fifty devils guarded the bridge."

He kissed Matilda's forehead, and walked away without a song.

CHAPTER VIII

Let gallows gape for dog : let man go free. *Henry V.*[1]

A PAGE had been brought up in Gamwell-Hall, who, while he was little, had been called Little John, and continued to be so called after he had grown to be a foot taller than any other man in the house. He was full seven feet high. His latitude was worthy of his longitude, and his strength was worthy of both ; and though an honest man by profession, he had practised archery on the king's deer for the benefit of his master's household, and for the improvement of his own eye and hand, till his aim had become infallible within the range of two miles.[2] He had fought manfully in defence of his young master, took his captivity exceedingly to heart, and fell into bitter grief and boundless rage when he heard that he had been tried in Nottingham and sentenced to die. Alice Gamwell, at Little John's request, wrote three letters of one tenour ; and Little John, having attached them to three blunt arrows, saddled the fleetest steed in old Sir Guy of Gamwell's stables, mounted, and rode first to Arlingford Castle, where he shot one of the three arrows over the battlements ; then to Rubygill Abbey, where he shot the second into the abbey-garden ; then back past Gamwell-Hall to the borders of Sherwood Forest, where he shot the third into the wood. Now the first of these arrows lighted in the nape of the neck of Lord Fitzwater, and lodged itself firmly between his skin and his collar ; the second rebounded with the hollow vibration of a drumstick from the shaven sconce of the abbot of Rubygill ; and the third pitched perpendicularly into the centre of a venison pasty in which Robin Hood was making incision.

[1] Act III, Sc. 6. G.
[2] The record is 608 yards, held by an American. In 1795 Mahmoud Effendi of the Turkish Embassy shot 482 yards, then a record. Sultan Selim was credited with shooting 972 yards, but the claim proves nothing but the power of the bowstring in convincing his subjects. G.

Matilda ran up to her father in the court of Arlingford Castle, seized the arrow, drew off the letter, and concealed it in her bosom before the baron had time to look round, which he did with many expressions of rage against the impudent villain who had shot a blunt arrow into the nape of his neck.

"But you know, father," said Matilda, "a sharp arrow in the same place would have killed you; therefore the sending a blunt one was very considerate."

"Considerate, with a vengeance!" said the baron. "Where was the consideration of sending it at all? This is some of your forester's pranks. He has missed you in the forest, since I have kept watch and ward over you, and by way of a love-token and a remembrance to you takes a random shot at me."

The abbot of Rubygill picked up the missile-missive or messenger arrow, which had rebounded from his shaven crown, with a very unghostly malediction on the sender, which he suddenly checked with a pious and consolatory reflection on the goodness of Providence in having blessed him with such a thickness of skull, to which he was now indebted for temporal preservation, as he had before been for spiritual promotion. He opened the letter, which was addressed to father Michael; and found it to contain an intimation that William Gamwell was to be hanged on Monday at Nottingham.

"And I wish," said the abbot, "father Michael were to be hanged with him: an ungrateful monster, after I had rescued him from the fangs of civil justice, to reward my lenity by not leaving a bone unbruised among the holy brotherhood of Rubygill."

Robin Hood extracted from his venison pasty a similar intimation of the evil destiny of his cousin, whom he determined, if possible, to rescue from the jaws of Cerberus.

The sheriff of Nottingham, though still sore with his bruises, was so intent on revenge, that he raised himself from his bed to attend the execution of William Gamwell. He rode to the august structure of retributive Themis, as the French call a gallows, in all the pride and pomp of shrievalty, and with a splendid retinue of well-equipped knaves and varlets, as our ancestors called honest serving-men.

Young Gamwell was brought forth with his arms pinioned behind him; his sister Alice and his father, Sir Guy, attending him in disconsolate mood. He had rejected the confessor provided by the sheriff, and had insisted on the privilege of choosing his own, whom Little John had promised to bring. Little John, however, had not made his appearance when the fatal procession began its march ; but when they reached the place of execution, Little John appeared, accompanied by a ghostly friar.

" Sheriff," said young Gamwell, " let me not die with my hands pinioned : give me a sword, and set any odds of your men against me, and let me die the death of a man, like the descendant of a noble house, which has never yet been stained with ignominy."

" No, no," said the sheriff ; " I have had enough of setting odds against you. I have sworn you shall be hanged, and hanged you shall be."

" Then God have mercy on me," said young Gamwell ; " and now, holy friar, shrive my sinful soul."

The friar approached.

" Let me see this friar," said the sheriff : " if he be the friar of the bridge, I had as lief have the devil in Nottingham ; but he shall find me too much for him here."

" The friar of the bridge," said Little John, " as you very well know, sheriff, was father Michael of Rubygill Abbey, and you may easily see that this is not the man."

" I see it," said the sheriff ; " and God be thanked for his absence."

Young Gamwell stood at the foot of the ladder. The friar approached him, opened his book, groaned, turned up the whites of his eyes, tossed up his arms in the air, and said " *Dominus vobiscum.*" [1] He then crossed both his hands on his breast under the folds of his holy robes, and stood a few moments as if in inward prayer. A deep silence among the attendant crowd accompanied this action of the friar ; interrupted only by the hollow tone of the death-bell, at long and dreary intervals. Suddenly the friar threw off his holy robes, and appeared a forester clothed in green, with a sword in his right hand and a horn in his left. With the sword he cut the bonds of William Gamwell, who instantly snatched a sword from one of the

---

[1] See Scott : *Ivanhoe*, Ch. XXVI, in which Wamba enters Torquilstone Castle disguised as a friar using the password *Pax Vobiscum* to rescue his master Cedric. G.

sheriff's men ; and with the horn he blew a loud blast, which was answered at once by four bugles from the quarters of the four winds, and from each quarter came five-and-twenty bowmen running all on a row.

"Treason ! treason ! " cried the sheriff. Old Sir Guy sprang to his son's side, and so did Little John ; and the four setting back to back, kept the sheriff and his men at bay till the bowmen came within shot and let fly their arrows among the sheriff's men, who, after a brief resistance, fled in all directions. The forester, who had personated the friar, sent an arrow after the flying sheriff, calling with a strong voice, " To the sheriff's left arm, as a keepsake from Robin Hood." The arrow reached its destiny ; the sheriff redoubled his speed, and, with the one arrow in his arm, did not stop to breathe till he was out of reach of another.

The foresters did not waste time in Nottingham, but were soon at a distance from its walls. Sir Guy returned with Alice to Gamwell-Hall ; but thinking he should not be safe there, from the share he had had in his son's rescue, they only remained long enough to supply themselves with clothes and money, and departed, under the escort of Little John, to another seat of the Gamwells in Yorkshire. Young Gamwell, taking it for granted that his offence was past remission, determined on joining Robin Hood, and accompanied him to the forest, where it was deemed expedient that he should change his name ; and he was rechristened without a priest, and with wine instead of water, by the immortal name of Scarlet.

CHAPTER IX

Who set my man i' the stocks ?——
I set him there, Sir : but his own disorders
Deserved much less advancement.—*Lear*.[1]

THE baron was inflexible in his resolution not to let Matilda leave the castle. The letter, which announced to her the approaching fate of young Gamwell, filled her with grief, and increased the irksomeness of a privation which already preyed sufficiently on her spirits, and

[1] Act II, Sc. 4.　G.

began to undermine her health. She had no longer the consolation of the society of her old friend father Michael : the little fat friar of Rubygill was substituted as the castle confessor, not without some misgivings in his ghostly bosom ; but he was more allured by the sweet savour of the good things of this world at Arlingford Castle, than deterred by his awe of the lady Matilda, which nevertheless was so excessive, from his recollection of the twang of the bow-string, that he never ventured to find her in the wrong, much less to enjoin any thing in the shape of penance, as was the occasional practice of holy confessors, with or without cause, for the sake of pious discipline, and what was in those days called social order, namely, the preservation of the privileges of the few who happened to have any, at the expense of the swinish multitude who happened to have none, except that of working and being shot at for the benefit of their betters, which is obviously not the meaning of social order in our more enlightened times : let us therefore be grateful to Providence, and sing *Te Deum laudamus* in chorus with the Holy Alliance.

The little friar, however, though he found the lady spotless, found the butler a great sinner : at least so it was conjectured, from the length of time he always took to confess him in the buttery.

Matilda became every day more pale and dejected : her spirit, which could have contended against any strenuous affliction, pined in the monotonous inaction to which she was condemned. While she could freely range the forest with her lover in the morning, she had been content to return to her father's castle in the evening, thus preserving underanged the balance of her duties, habits, and affections ; not without a hope that the repeal of her lover's outlawry might be eventually obtained, by a judicious distribution of some of his forest spoils among the holy fathers and saints-that-were-to-be,—pious proficients in the ecclesiastic art equestrian, who rode the conscience of King Henry with double-curb bridles, and kept it well in hand when it showed mettle and seemed inclined to rear and plunge. But the affair at Gamwell feast threw many additional difficulties in the way of the accomplishment of this hope ; and very shortly afterwards King Henry the Second went to make up in the next world his quarrel with Thomas-à-Becket ; and Richard Cœur de Lion made all England resound with preparations for the crusade, to the great delight of many zealous adventurers, who eagerly flocked under his banner in the hope of enriching themselves with Saracen spoil, which they called fighting the battles of God. Richard, who was not remarkably scrupulous in his financial operations, was not likely to overlook the lands and castle of Locksley, which he appropriated immediately to his own purposes, and sold to the highest bidder. Now, as the repeal of the outlawry would involve the restitution of the estates to the rightful owner, it was obvious that it could never be expected from that most legitimate and most Christian king, Richard the First of England, the arch-crusader and anti-jacobin by excellence,—the very type, flower, cream, pink, symbol, and mirror of all the Holy Alliances that have ever existed on earth, excepting that he seasoned his superstition and love of conquest with a certain condiment of romantic generosity and chivalrous self-devotion, with which his imitators in all other points have found it convenient to dispense. To give freely to one man what he had taken forcibly from another, was generosity of which he was very capable ; but to restore what he had taken to the man from whom he had taken it, was something that wore too much of the cool physiognomy of justice to be easily reconcileable to his kingly feelings. He had, besides, not only sent all King Henry's saints about their business, or rather about their no-business—their *fainéantise*—but he had laid them under rigorous contribution for the purposes of his holy war; and having made them refund to the piety of the successor what they had extracted from the piety of the precursor, he compelled them, in addition, to give him their blessing for nothing. Matilda, therefore, from all these circumstances, felt little hope that her lover would be any thing but an outlaw for life.

The departure of King Richard from England was succeeded by the episcopal regency of the bishops of Ely and Durham. Longchamp, bishop of Ely, proceeded to show his sense of Christian fellowship by arresting his brother bishop, and despoiling him of his share in the government ; and to set forth his humility and loving-kindness in a retinue of nobles and knights who consumed in one night's entertainment some five years' revenue of their entertainer, and in a guard of fifteen hundred foreign soldiers, whom he considered indispensable to the exercise of a vigour beyond the law in maintaining wholesome discipline over the refractory English. The ignorant impatience of the swinish multitude with these fruits of good living, brought forth by one of the meek who had inherited the earth, displayed itself in a general ferment, of which Prince John took advantage to make the experiment of getting possession of his brother's crown in his absence. He began by calling at Reading a council of barons, whose aspect induced the holy bishop to disguise himself (some say as an old woman, which, in the twelfth century, perhaps might have been a disguise for a bishop), and make his escape beyond sea. Prince John followed up his advantage by obtaining possession of several strong posts, and among others of the castle of Nottingham.

While John was conducting his operations at Nottingham, he rode at times past the castle of Arlingford. He stopped on one occasion to claim Lord Fitzwater's hospitality, and made most princely havoc among his venison and brawn. Now it is a matter of record among divers great historians and learned clerks, that he was then and there grievously smitten by the charms of the lovely Matilda, and that a few days after he despatched his travelling ministrel, or laureate, Harpiton [1] (whom he retained at moderate wages, to keep a journal of his proceedings, and prove them all just and legitimate), to the castle of Arlingford, to make proposals to the lady. This Harpiton was a very useful person. He was always ready, not only to maintain the cause of his master with his pen, and to sing his eulogies to his harp, but to undertake at a moment's notice any kind of courtly employment, called dirty work by the profane, which the blessings of civil government, namely, his master's pleasure, and the interests of social order, namely, his own emolument, might require. In short,

> Il eût l'emploi qui certes n'est pas mince,
> Et qu'à la cour, où tout se peint en beau,
> On appelloit être l'ami du prince ;
> Mais qu'à la ville, et surtout en province,
> Les gens grossiers ont nommé maquereau. [2]

---

[1] Harp-it-on : or, a *corruption* of Ἑρπετον, a creeping thing. [P.]
[2] Voltaire : *La Pucelle d'Orléans*, Chant Premier, lines 56–60. G.

Prince John was of opinion that the love of a prince actual and king expectant, was in itself a sufficient honour to the daughter of a simple baron, and that the right divine of royalty would make it sufficiently holy without the rite divine of the church. He was, therefore, graciously pleased to fall into an exceeding passion, when his confidential messenger returned from his embassy in piteous plight, having been, by the baron's order, first tossed in a blanket and set in the stocks to cool, and afterwards ducked in the moat and set again in the stocks to dry. John swore to revenge horribly this flagrant outrage on royal prerogative, and to obtain possession of the lady by force of arms ; and accordingly collected a body of troops, and marched upon Arlingford Castle. A letter, conveyed as before on the point of a blunt arrow, announced his approach to Matilda : and Lord Fitzwater had just time to assemble his retainers, collect a hasty supply of provision, raise the drawbridge, and drop the portcullis, when the castle was surrounded by the enemy. The little fat friar, who during the confusion was asleep in the buttery, found himself, on awaking, inclosed in the besieged castle, and dolefully bewailed his evil chance.

CHAPTER X

A noble girl, i' faith. Heart ! I think I fight with a familiar, or the ghost of a fencer. Call you this an amorous visage ? Here's blood that would have served me these seven years, in broken heads and cut fingers, and now it runs out altogether.—Middleton. *Roaring Girl.*[1]

PRINCE JOHN sat down impatiently before Arlingford Castle in the hope of starving out the besieged ; but finding the duration of their supplies extend itself in an equal ratio with the prolongation of his hope, he made vigorous preparations for carrying the place by storm. He constructed an immense machine on wheels, which, being advanced to the edge of the moat, would lower a temporary bridge, of which one end would rest on the bank, and the other on the battlements, and which, being well furnished with stepping boards, would enable his men to ascend the inclined plane with speed and facility. Matilda received intimation of this design by the usual

[1] Act III, Sc. 1. G.

friendly channel of a blunt arrow, which must either have been sent from some secret friend in the prince's camp, or from some vigorous archer beyond it : the latter will not appear improbable, when we consider that Robin Hood and Little John could shoot two English miles and an inch point-blank,

Come scrive Turpino, che non erra.[1]

The machine was completed, and the ensuing morning fixed for the assault. Six men, relieved at intervals, kept watch over it during the night. Prince John retired to sleep, congratulating himself in the expectation that another day would place the fair culprit at his princely mercy. His anticipations mingled with the visions of his slumber, and he dreamed of wounds and drums, and sacking and firing the castle, and bearing off in his arms the beautiful prize through the midst of fire and smoke. In the height of this imaginary turmoil, he awoke, and conceived for a few moments that certain sounds which rang in his ears, were the continuation of those of his dream, in that sort of half-consciousness between sleeping and waking, when reality and phantasy meet and mingle in dim and confused resemblance. He was, however, very soon fully awake to the fact of his guards calling on him to arm, which he did in haste, and beheld the machine in flames, and a furious conflict raging around it. He hurried to the spot, and found that his camp had been suddenly assailed from one side by a party of foresters, and that the baron's people had made a sortie on the other, and that they had killed the guards, and set fire to the machine, before the rest of the camp could come to the assistance of their fellows.

The night was in itself intensely dark, and the fire-light shed around it a vivid and unnatural radiance. On one side, the crimson light quivered by its own agitation on the waveless moat, and on the bastions and buttresses of the castle, and their shadows lay in massy blackness on the illuminated walls : on the other, it shone upon the woods, streaming far within among the open trunks, or resting on the closer foliage. The circumference of darkness bounded the scene on all sides : and in the centre raged the war ; shields,

[1] " As Turpin wrote who could not err." The reference is to the Latin Chronicles of Charlemagne and his paladins, attributed to Turpin, Archbishop of Rheims in the eighth century, actually fabricated in the eleventh.

helmets, and bucklers gleaming and glittering as they rang and clashed against each other ; plumes confusedly tossing in the crimson light, and the massy light and shade that fell on the faces of the combatants, giving additional energy to their ferocious expression.

John, drawing nearer to the scene of action, observed two young warriors fighting side by side, one of whom wore the habit of a forester, the other that of a retainer of Arlingford. He looked intently on them both : their position towards the fire favoured the scrutiny ; and the hawk's eye of love very speedily discovered that the latter was the fair Matilda. The forester he did not know : but he had sufficient tact to discern that his success would be very much facilitated by separating her from this companion, above all others. He therefore formed a party of men into a wedge, only taking especial care not to be the point of it himself, and drove it between them with so much precision, that they were in a moment far asunder.

" Lady Matilda," said John, " yield yourself my prisoner."

" If you would wear me, prince," said Matilda, " you must win me : " and without giving him time to deliberate on the courtesy of fighting with the lady of his love, she raised her sword in the air, and lowered it on his head with an impetus that would have gone nigh to fathom even that extraordinary depth of brain which always by divine grace furnishes the interior of a head-royal, if he had not very dexterously parried the blow. Prince John wished to disarm and take captive, not in any way to wound or injure, least of all to kill, his fair opponent. Matilda was only intent to get rid of her antagonist at any rate : the edge of her weapon painted his complexion with streaks of very unloverlike crimson, and she would probably have marred John's hand for ever signing Magna Charta, but that he was backed by the advantage of numbers, and that her sword broke short on the boss of his buckler. John was following up his advantage to make a captive of the lady, when he was suddenly felled to the earth by an unseen antagonist. Some of his men picked him carefully up, and conveyed him to his tent, stunned and stupefied.

When he recovered, he found Harpiton diligently assisting in his recovery, more in the fear of losing his place than in that of losing his master : the prince's first inquiry was for the prisoner he had been on the point of taking at the moment when his *habeas corpus* was so

unseasonably suspended. He was told that his people had been on
the point of securing the said prisoner, when the devil suddenly
appeared among them in the likeness of a tall friar, having his grey
frock cinctured with a sword-belt, and his crown, which whether it
were shaven or no they could not see, surmounted with a helmet,
and flourishing an eight-foot staff, with which he laid about him to
the right and to the left, knocking down the prince and his men as
if they had been so many nine-pins : in fine, he had rescued the
prisoner, and made a clear passage through friend and foe, and in
conjunction with a chosen party of archers, had covered the retreat
of the baron's men and the foresters, who had all gone off in a body
towards Sherwood Forest.

Harpiton suggested that it would be desirable to sack the castle,
and volunteered to lead the van on the occasion, as the defenders
were withdrawn, and the exploit seemed to promise much profit and
little danger : John considered that the castle would in itself be a
great acquisition to him, as a stronghold in furtherance of his design
on his brother's throne ; and was determining to take possession with
the first light of morning, when he had the mortification to see the
castle burst into flames in several places at once. A piteous cry was
heard from within, and while the prince was proclaiming a reward
to any one who would enter into the burning pile, and elucidate the
mystery of the doleful voice, forth waddled the little fat friar in an
agony of fear, out of the fire into the frying-pan ; for he was instantly
taken into custody and carried before prince John, wringing his
hands and tearing his hair.

"Are you the friar," said prince John, in a terrible voice, "that
laid me prostrate in battle, mowed down my men like grass, rescued
my captive, and covered the retreat of my enemies ? And, not
content with this, have you now set fire to the castle in which I
intended to take up my royal quarters ? "

The little friar quaked like a jelly : he fell on his knees, and
attempted to speak ; but in his eagerness to vindicate himself from
this accumulation of alarming charges, he knew not where to begin ;
his ideas rolled round upon each other like the radii of a wheel ; the
words he desired to utter, instead of issuing, as it were, in a right line
from his lips, seemed to conglobate themselves into a sphere turning

on its own axis in his throat : after several ineffectual efforts, his
utterance totally failed him, and he remained gasping, with his mouth
open, his lips quivering, his hands clasped together, and the whites of
his eyes turned up towards the prince with an expression most
ruefully imploring.

" Are you that friar ? " repeated the prince.

Several of the by-standers declared that he was not that friar.
The little friar, encouraged by this patronage, found his voice, and
pleaded for mercy. The prince questioned him closely concerning
the burning of the castle. The little friar declared, that he had been
in too great fear during the siege to know much of what was going
forward, except that he had been conscious during the last few days
of a lamentable deficiency of provisions, and had been present that
very morning at the broaching of the last butt of sack. Harpiton
groaned in sympathy. The little friar added, that he knew nothing of
what had passed since, till he heard the flames roaring at his elbow.[1]

" Take him away, Harpiton," said the prince, " fill him with sack,
and turn him out."

" Never mind the sack," said the little friar, " turn me out at once."

" A sad chance," said Harpiton, " to be turned out without sack."

But what Harpiton thought a sad chance the little friar thought
a merry one, and went bounding like a fat buck towards the abbey
of Rubygill.

An arrow, with a letter attached to it, was shot into the camp, and
carried to the prince. The contents were these :—

" PRINCE JOHN,—I do not consider myself to have resisted lawful
authority in defending my castle against you, seeing that you are at
present in a state of active rebellion against your liege sovereign
Richard : and if my provisions had not failed me, I would have
maintained it till doomsday. As it is, I have so well disposed my
combustibles that it shall not serve you as a strong hold in your
rebellion. If you hunt in the chases of Nottinghamshire, you may
catch other game than my daughter. Both she and I are content to
be houseless for a time, in the reflection that we have deserved your
enmity, and the friendship of Cœur-de-Lion.   " FITZWATER."

[1] See Scott : *Ivanhoe*, Ch. XXXII.   G.

CHAPTER XI

—Tuck, the merry friar, who many a sermon made
In praise of Robin Hood, his outlaws, and their trade.
DRAYTON.[1]

THE baron, with some of his retainers and all the foresters, halted at daybreak in Sherwood Forest. The foresters quickly erected tents, and prepared an abundant breakfast of venison and ale.

"Now, Lord Fitzwater," said the chief forester, "recognise your son-in-law that was to have been, in the outlaw Robin Hood."

"Ay, ay," said the baron, "I have recognised you long ago."

"And recognise your young friend Gamwell," said the second, "in the outlaw Scarlet."

"And Little John, the page," said the third, "in Little John the outlaw."

"And Father Michael, of Rubygill Abbey," said the friar, "in Friar Tuck, of Sherwood Forest. Truly, I have a chapel here hard by, in the shape of a hollow tree, where I put up my prayers for travellers, and Little John holds the plate at the door, for good praying deserves good paying."

"I am in fine company," said the baron.

"In the very best of company," said the friar, "in the high court of Nature, and in the midst of her own nobility. Is it not so? This goodly grove is our palace: the oak and the beech are its colonnade and its canopy: the sun and the moon and the stars are its everlasting lamps: the grass, and the daisy, and the primrose, and the violet, are its many-coloured floor of green, white, yellow, and blue; the may-flower, and the woodbine, and the eglantine, and the ivy, are its decorations, its curtains, and its tapestry: the lark, and the thrush, and the linnet, and the nightingale, are its unhired minstrels and musicians. Robin Hood is king of the forest both by dignity of birth and by virtue of his standing army: to say nothing of the free choice of his people, which he has indeed, but I pass it by as an illegitimate basis of power. He holds his dominion over the forest,

---

[1] *Polyolbion*, Song 26. These lines are quoted on the title page of Ritson's *Robin Hood*, 1795, from which Peacock no doubt took them. G.

and its horned multitude of citizen-deer, and its swinish multitude
or peasantry of wild boars, by right of conquest and force of arms.
He levies contributions among them by the free consent of his
archers, their virtual representatives. If they should find a voice to
complain that we are ' tyrants and usurpers to kill and cook them up
in their assigned and native dwelling-place,' we should most con-
vincingly admonish them, with point of arrow, that they have
nothing to do with our laws but to obey them. Is it not written that
the fat ribs of the herd shall be fed upon by the mighty in the land ?
And have not they withal my blessing ? my orthodox, canonical, and
archiepiscopal blessing ? Do I not give thanks for them when they
are well roasted and smoking under my nose ? What title had
William of Normandy to England, that Robin of Locksley has not to
merry Sherwood ? William fought for his claim. So does Robin.
With whom, both ? With any that would or will dispute it.
William raised contributions. So does Robin. From whom, both ?
From all that they could or can make pay them. Why did any
pay them to William ? Why do any pay them to Robin ? For the
same reason to both : because they could not or cannot help it.
They differ indeed, in this, that William took from the poor and gave
to the rich, and Robin takes from the rich and gives to the poor :
and therein is Robin illegitimate ; though in all else he is true prince.
Scarlet and John, are they not peers of the forest ? lords temporal of
Sherwood ? And am not I lord spiritual ? Am I not archbishop ?
Am I not pope ? Do I not consecrate their banner and absolve their
sins ? Are not they state, and am not I church ? Are not they
state monarchical, and am not I church militant ? Do I not
excommunicate our enemies from venison and brawn, and by 'r Lady,
when need calls, beat them down under my feet ? The state levies
tax, and the church levies tithe. Even so do we. Mass, we take all
at once. What then ? It is tax by redemption and tithe by
commutation. Your William and Richard can cut and come again,
but our Robin deals with slippery subjects that come not twice to his
exchequer. What need we then to constitute a court, except a fool
and a laureate ? For the fool, his only use is to make false knaves
merry by art, and we are true men and are merry by nature. For
the laureate, his only office is to find virtues in those who have none,

and to drink sack for his pains. We have quite virtue enough to need him not, and can drink our sack for ourselves."

"Well preached, friar," said Robin Hood : "yet there is one thing wanting to constitute a court, and that is a queen. And now, lovely Matilda, look round upon these sylvan shades where we have so often roused the stag from his ferny covert. The rising sun smiles upon us through the stems of that beechen knoll. Shall I take your hand, Matilda, in the presence of this my court ? Shall I crown you with our wild-wood coronal, and hail you queen of the forest ? Will you be the queen Matilda of your own true king Robin ? "

Matilda smiled assent.

"Not Matilda," said the friar : " the rules of our holy alliance require new birth. We have excepted in favour of Little John, because he is great John, and his name is a misnomer. I sprinkle, not thy forehead with water, but thy lips with wine, and baptize thee MARIAN."

"Here is a pretty conspiracy," exclaimed the baron. "Why, you villanous friar, think you to nickname and marry my daughter before my face with impunity ? "

"Even so, bold baron," said the friar ; " we are strongest here. Say you, might overcomes right ? I say no. There is no right but might : and to say that might overcomes right is to say that right overcomes itself : an absurdity most palpable. Your right was the stronger in Arlingford, and ours is the stronger in Sherwood. Your right was right as long as you could maintain it ; so is ours. So is King Richard's, with all deference be it spoken ; and so is King Saladin's ; and their two mights are now committed in bloody fray, and that which overcomes will be right, just as long as it lasts, and as far as it reaches. And now if any of you know any just impediment——"

"Fire and fury," said the baron.

"Fire and fury," said the friar, " are modes of that might which constitutes right, and are just impediments to anything against which they can be brought to bear. They are our good allies upon occasion, and would declare for us now if you should put them to the test."

"Father," said Matilda, " you know the terms of our compact :

from the moment you restrained my liberty, you renounced your claim to all but compulsory obedience. The friar argues well. Right ends with might. Thick walls, dreary galleries, and tapestried chambers, were indifferent to me while I could leave them at pleasure, but have ever been hateful to me since they held me by force. May I never again have roof but the blue sky, nor canopy but the green leaves, nor barrier but the forest-bounds ; with the foresters to my train, Little John to my page, Friar Tuck to my ghostly adviser, and Robin Hood to my liege lord. I am no longer Lady Matilda Fitzwater, of Arlingford Castle, but plain Maid Marian, of Sherwood Forest."

"Long live Maid Marian !" re-echoed the foresters.

"Oh false girl!" said the baron, "do you renounce your name and parentage ? "

"Not my parentage," said Marian, "but my name indeed : do not all maids renounce it at the altar ? "

"The altar !" said the baron : "grant me patience ! what do you mean by the altar ? "

"Pile green turf," said the friar, "wreathe it with flowers, and crown it with fruit, and we will show the noble baron what we mean by the altar."

The foresters did as the friar directed.

"Now, Little John," said the friar, "on with the cloak of the abbot of Doubleflask. I appoint thee my clerk : thou art here duly elected in full mote."

"I wish you were all in full moat together," said the baron, "and smooth wall on both sides."

"Punnest thou ? " said the friar. "A heinous anti-christian offence. Why anti-christian ? Because anti-catholic. Why anti-catholic ? Because anti-roman. Why anti-roman ? Because Carthaginian. Is not pun from Punic ? *punica fides* : the very quint-essential quiddity of bad faith : double-visaged : double-tongued. He that will make a pun will—— I say no more. Fie on it. Stand forth, clerk. Who is the bride's father ? "

"There is no bride's father," said the baron. "I am the father of Matilda Fitzwater."

"There is none such," said the friar. "This is the fair Maid Marian. Will you make a virtue of necessity, or will you give laws

to the flowing tide ? Will you give her, or shall Robin take her ?
Will you be her true natural father, or shall I commute paternity ?
Stand forth, Scarlet."

"Stand back, sirrah Scarlet," said the baron. "My daughter
shall have no father but me. Needs must when the devil drives."

"No matter who drives," said the friar, "so that, like a well-
disposed subject, you yield cheerful obedience to those who can
enforce it."

"Mawd, sweet Mawd," said the baron, "will you then forsake
your poor old father in his distress, with his castle in ashes, and his
enemy in power ? "

"Not so, father," said Marian ; "I will always be your true
daughter : I will always love, and serve, and watch, and defend you :
but neither will I forsake my plighted love, and my own liege lord,
who was your choice before he was mine, for you made him my
associate in infancy ; and that he continued to be mine when he
ceased to be yours, does not in any way show remissness in my duties
or falling off in my affections. And though I here plight my troth
at the altar to Robin, in the presence of this holy priest and pious
clerk, yet. . . . Father, when Richard returns from Palestine, he
will restore you to your barony, and perhaps, for your sake, your
daughter's husband to the earldom of Huntingdon : should that
never be, should it be the will of fate that we must live and die in the
greenwood, I will live and die MAID MARIAN." [1]

"A pretty resolution," said the baron, "if Robin will let you
keep it."

"I have sworn it," said Robin. "Should I expose her tenderness
to the perils of maternity, when life and death may hang on shifting
at a moment's notice from Sherwood to Barnsdale, and from Barnsdale to the sea-shore ? And why should I banquet when my merry
men starve ? Chastity is our forest law, and even the friar has kept
it since he has been here."

---

[1] And therefore is she called Maid Marian,
Because she leads a spotless maiden life,
And shall till Robin's outlaw life have end.

Old Play. [P.]

[Anthony Munday : *The Downfall of Robert, Earl of Huntington*, Act III,
Sc. 2. G.]

" Truly so," said the friar : " for temptation dwells with ease and luxury : but the hunter is Hippolytus, and the huntress is Dian. And now, dearly beloved——"

The friar went through the ceremony with great unction, and Little John was most clerical in the intonation of his responses. After which, the friar sang, and Little John fiddled, and the foresters danced, Robin with Marian, and Scarlet with the baron ; and the venison smoked, and the ale frothed, and the wine sparkled, and the sun went down on their unwearied festivity : which they wound up with the following song, the friar leading and the foresters joining chorus :

> Oh ! bold Robin Hood is a forester good,
> As ever drew bow in the merry greenwood :
> At his bugle's shrill singing the echoes are ringing,
> The wild deer are springing for many a rood :
> Its summons we follow, through brake, over hollow,
> The thrice-blown shrill summons of bold Robin Hood.
>
> And what eye hath e'er seen such a sweet Maiden Queen,
> As Marian, the pride of the forester's green ?
> A sweet garden-flower, she blooms in the bower,
> Where alone to this hour the wild rose has been :
> We hail her in duty the queen of all beauty :
> We will live, we will die, by our sweet Maiden Queen.
>
> And here's a grey friar, good as heart can desire,
> To absolve all our sins as the case may require :
> Who with courage so stout, lays his oak-plant about,
> And puts to the rout all the foes of his choir :
> For we are his choristers, we merry foresters,
> Chorussing thus with our militant friar.
>
> And Scarlet doth bring his good yew-bough and string,
> Prime minister is he of Robin our king :
> No mark is too narrow for Little John's arrow,
> That hits a cock sparrow a mile on the wing ;
> Robin and Mariòn, Scarlet, and Little John,
> Long with their glory old Sherwood shall ring.
>
> Each a good liver, for well-feathered quiver
> Doth furnish brawn, venison, and fowl of the river :
> But the best game we dish up, it is a fat bishop :
> When his angels we fish up, he proves a free giver :
> For a prelate so lowly has angels more holy,
> And should this world's false angels to sinners deliver.

Robin and Mariòn, Scarlet and Little John,
Drink to them one by one, drink as ye sing :
Robin and Mariòn, Scarlet and Little John,
Echo to echo through Sherwood shall fling :
Robin and Mariòn, Scarlet and Little John,
Long with their glory old Sherwood shall ring.

CHAPTER XII

A single volume paramount : a code :
A master spirit : a determined road.
WORDSWORTH.[1]

THE next morning Robin Hood convened his foresters, and desired Little John, for the baron's edification, to read over the laws of their forest society. Little John read aloud with a stentorophonic voice.

" At a high court of foresters, held under the greenwood tree, an hour after sun-rise, Robin Hood President, William Scarlet Vice-President, Little John Secretary : the following articles, moved by Friar Tuck in his capacity of Peer Spiritual, and seconded by Much the Miller, were unanimously agreed to.

" The principles of our society are six : Legitimacy, Equity, Hospitality, Chivalry, Chastity, and Courtesy.

" The articles of Legitimacy are four : [2]

" I. Our government is legitimate, and our society is founded on the one golden rule of right, consecrated by the universal consent of mankind, and by the practice of all ages, individuals, and nations : namely, To keep what we have, and to catch what we can.

" II. Our government being legitimate, all our proceedings shall be legitimate : wherefore we declare war against the whole world, and every forester is by this legitimate declaration legitimately invested with a roving commission, to make lawful prize of every thing that comes in his way.

" III. All forest laws but our own we declare to be null and void.

" IV. All such of the old laws of England as do not in any way

---

[1] Misquoted to give the opposite meaning. Wordsworth wrote of the French revolution : " No single volume . . . no master spirit, no determined road." *Sonnets dedicated to National Independence and Liberty*, XV. G.

[2] Peacock is satirising the Holy Alliance and the restoration of legitimate monarchs in Europe against the wishes of their peoples. G.

interfere with, or militate against, the views of this honourable assembly, we will loyally adhere to and maintain. The rest we declare null and void as far as relates to ourselves, in all cases wherein a vigour beyond the law may be conducive to our own interest and preservation.

" The articles of Equity are three :

" I. The balance of power among the people being very much deranged, by one having too much and another nothing, we hereby resolve ourselves into a congress or court of equity, to restore as far as in us lies the said natural balance of power, by taking from all who have too much as much of the said too much as we can lay our hands on ; and giving to those who have nothing such a portion thereof as it may seem to us expedient to part with.

" II. In all cases a quorum of foresters shall constitute a court of equity, and as many as may be strong enough to manage the matter in hand shall constitute a quorum.

" III. All usurers, monks, courtiers, and other drones of the great hive of society, who shall be found laden with any portion of the honey whereof they have wrongfully despoiled the industrious bee, shall be rightly despoiled thereof in turn ; and all bishops and abbots shall be bound and beaten,[1] especially the abbot of Doncaster ; as shall also all sheriffs, especially the sheriff of Nottingham.

" The articles of Hospitality are two :

" I. Postmen, carriers and market-folk, peasants and mechanics, farmers and millers, shall pass through our forest dominions without let or molestation.

" II. All other travellers through the forest shall be graciously invited to partake of Robin's hospitality ; and if they come not willingly they shall be compelled ; and the rich man shall pay well

---

[1] " These byshoppes and these archbyshoppes
    Ye shall them bete and bynde,"
says Robin Hood, in an old ballad. Perhaps, however, this is to be taken not in a literal, but in a figurative sense, from the binding and beating of wheat : for as all rich men were Robin's harvest, the bishops and archbishops must have been the finest and fattest ears among them, from which Robin merely proposes to thresh the grain when he directs them to be bound and beaten : and as Pharaoh's fat kine were typical of fat ears of wheat, so may fat ears of wheat, *mutatis mutandis,* be typical of fat kine.
[P.]

for his fare ; and the poor man shall feast scot free, and peradventure receive bounty in proportion to his desert and necessity.

"The article of Chivalry is one :

"I. Every forester shall, to the extent of his power, aid and protect maids, widows, and orphans, and all weak and distressed persons whomsoever : and no woman shall be impeded or molested in any way ; nor shall any company receive harm which any woman is in.

"The article of Chastity is one :

"I. Every forester, being Diana's forester and minion of the moon, shall commend himself to the grace of the Virgin, and shall have the gift of continency on pain of expulsion : that the article of chivalry may be secure from infringement, and maids, wives, and widows pass without fear through the forest.

"The article of Courtesy is one :

"I. No one shall miscall a forester. He who calls Robin Robert of Huntingdon, or salutes him by any other title or designation whatsoever except plain Robin Hood ; or who calls Marian Matilda Fitzwater, or salutes her by any other title or designation whatsoever except plain Maid Marian ; and so of all others ; shall for every such offence forfeit a mark, to be paid to the friar.

"And these articles we swear to keep as we are good men and true. Carried by acclamation. God save King Richard.

"LITTLE JOHN, Secretary."

"Excellent laws," said the baron : "excellent, by the holy rood. William of Normandy, with my great great grandfather Fierabras at his elbow, could not have made better. And now, sweet Mawd——"

"A fine, a fine," cried the friar, "a fine, by the article of courtesy."

"Od's life," said the baron, "shall I not call my own daughter Mawd ? Methinks there should be a special exception in my favour."

"It must not be," said Robin Hood : "our constitution admits no privilege."

"But I will commute," said the friar ; "for twenty marks a year duly paid into my ghostly pocket you shall call your daughter Mawd two hundred times a day."

"Gramercy," said the baron, "and I agree, honest friar, when I can get twenty marks to pay: for till Prince John be beaten from Nottingham, my rents are like to prove but scanty."

" I will trust," said the friar, " and thus let us ratify the stipulation ; so shall our laws and your infringement run together in an amicable parallel."

" But," said Little John, " this is a bad precedent, master friar. It is turning discipline into profit, penalty into perquisite, public justice into private revenue. It is rank corruption, master friar."

" Why are laws made ? " said the friar. " For the profit of somebody. Of whom ? Of him who makes them first, and of others as it may happen. Was not I legislator in the last article, and shall I not thrive by my own law ? "

" Well then, sweet Mawd," said the baron, " I must leave you, Mawd : your life is very well for the young and the hearty, but it squares not with my age or my humour. I must house, Mawd. I must find refuge : but where ? That is the question."

" Where Sir Guy of Gamwell has found it," said Robin Hood, " near the borders of Barnsdale. There you may dwell in safety with him and fair Alice, till King Richard return, and Little John shall give you safe conduct. You will have need to travel with caution, in disguise and without attendants, for Prince John commands all this vicinity, and will doubtless lay the country for you and Marian. Now it is first expedient to dismiss your retainers. If there be any among them who like our life, they may stay with us in the greenwood ; the rest may return to their homes."

Some of the baron's men resolved to remain with Robin and Marian, and were furnished accordingly with suits of green, of which Robin always kept good store.

Marian now declared that as there was danger in the way to Barnsdale, she would accompany Little John and the baron, as she should not be happy unless she herself saw her father placed in security. Robin was very unwilling to consent to this, and assured her that there was more danger for her than the baron : but Marian was absolute.

" If so, then," said Robin, " I shall be your guide instead of Little John, and I shall leave him and Scarlet joint-regents of Sherwood during my absence, and the voice of Friar Tuck shall be decisive between them if they differ in nice questions of state policy." Marian objected to this, that there was more danger for Robin than either herself or the baron : but Robin was absolute in his turn.

" Talk not of my voice," said the friar ; " for if Marian be a damsel errant, I will be her ghostly esquire."

Robin insisted that this should not be, for number would only expose them to greater risk of detection. The friar, after some debate, reluctantly acquiesced.

While they were discussing these matters, they heard the distant sound of horse's feet.

" Go," said Robin to Little John, " and invite yonder horseman to dinner."

Little John bounded away, and soon came before a young man, who was riding in a melancholy manner, with the bridle hanging loose on the horse's neck, and his eyes drooping towards the ground.

" Whither go you ? " said Little John.

" Whithersoever my horse pleases," said the young man.

" And that shall be," said Little John, " whither I please to lead him. I am commissioned to invite you to dine with my master."

" Who is your master ? " said the young man.

" Robin Hood," said Little John.

" The bold outlaw ? " said the stranger. " Neither he nor you should have made me turn an inch aside yesterday ; but to-day I care not."

" Then it is better for you," said Little John, " that you came to-day than yesterday, if you love dining in a whole skin : for my master is the pink of courtesy : but if his guests prove stubborn, he bastes them and his venison together, while the friar says mass before meat."

The young man made no answer, and scarcely seemed to hear what Little John was saying, who therefore took the horse's bridle and led him to where Robin and his foresters were setting forth their dinner. Robin seated the young man next to Marian. Recovering a little from his stupor, he looked with much amazement at her, and the baron, and Robin, and the friar ; listened to their conversation, and seemed much astonished to find himself in such holy and courtly company. Robin helped him largely to numble-pie and cygnet and pheasant, and the other dainties of his table ; and the friar pledged him in ale and wine, and exhorted him to make good cheer. But the young man drank little, ate less, spake nothing, and every now and then sighed heavily.

When the repast was ended, "Now," said Robin, "you are at liberty to pursue your journey: but first be pleased to pay for your dinner."

"That would I gladly do, Robin," said the young man, "but all I have about me are five shillings and a ring. To the five shillings you shall be welcome, but for the ring I will fight while there is a drop of blood in my veins."

"Gallantly spoken," said Robin Hood. "A love-token, without doubt: but you must submit to our forest laws. Little John must search; and if he find no more than you say, not a penny will I touch; but if you have spoken false, the whole is forfeit to our fraternity."

"And with reason," said the friar; "for thereby is the truth maintained. The abbot of Doubleflask swore there was no money in his valise, and Little John forthwith emptied it of four hundred pounds. Thus was the abbot's perjury but of one minute's duration; for though his speech was false in the utterance, yet was it no sooner uttered than it became true, and we should have been *participes criminis* to have suffered the holy abbot to depart in falsehood: whereas he came to us a false priest, and we sent him away a true man. Marry, we turned his cloak to further account, and thereby hangs a tale that may be either said or sung; for in truth I am minstrel here as well as chaplain; I pray for good success to our just and necessary warfare, and sing thanksgiving odes when our foresters bring in booty:

Bold Robin has robed him in ghostly attire,
And forth he is gone like a holy friar,
    Singing, hey down, ho down, down, derry down:
And of two grey friars he soon was aware,
Regaling themselves with dainty fare,
    All on the fallen leaves so brown.

"Good morrow, good brothers," said bold Robin Hood,
"And what make you in the good greenwood,
    Singing hey down, ho down, down, derry down!
Now give me, I pray you, wine and food;
For none can I find in the good greenwood,
    All on the fallen leaves so brown."

" Good brother," they said, " we would give you full fain,
But we have no more than enough for twain,
 Singing, hey down, ho down, down, derry down."
" Then give me some money," said bold Robin Hood,
" For none can I find in the good greenwood,
 All on the fallen leaves so brown."

" No money have we, good brother," said they :
" Then," said he, " we three for money will pray :
 Singing, hey down, ho down, down, derry down :
And whatever shall come at the end of our prayer,
We three holy friars will piously share,
 All on the fallen leaves so brown."

" We will not pray with thee, good brother, God wot :
For truly, good brother, thou pleasest us not,
 Singing hey down, ho down, down, derry down : "
Then up they both started from Robin to run,
But down on their knees Robin pulled them each one,
 All on the fallen leaves so brown.

The grey friars prayed with a doleful face,
But bold Robin prayed with a right merry grace,
 Singing, hey down, ho down, down, derry down :
And when they had prayed, their portmanteau he took,
And from it a hundred good angels he shook,
 All on the fallen leaves so brown.

" The saints," said bold Robin, " have hearkened our prayer,
And here's a good angel apiece for your share :
If more you would have, you must win ere you wear :
 Singing hey down, ho down, down, derry down : "
Then he blew his good horn with a musical cheer,
And fifty green bowmen came trooping full near,
And away the grey friars they bounded like deer,
 All on the fallen leaves so brown.

CHAPTER XIII

What can a young lassie, what shall a young lassie,
What can a young lassie do wi' an auld man ?—BURNS.

" HERE is but five shillings and a ring," said Little John, " and the
young man has spoken true."

" Then," said Robin to the stranger, " if want of money be the
cause of your melancholy, speak. Little John is my treasurer, and
he shall disburse to you."

"It is, and it is not," said the stranger; "it is, because, had I not wanted money I had never lost my love; it is not, because, now that I have lost her, money would come too late to regain her."

"In what way have you lost her?" said Robin: "let us clearly know that she is past regaining, before we give up our wishes to restore her to you."

"She is to be married this day," said the stranger, "and perhaps is married by this, to a rich old knight; and yesterday I knew it not."

"What is your name?" said Robin.

"Allen," said the stranger.

"And where is the marriage to take place, Allen?" said Robin.

"At Edwinstow church," said Allen, "by the bishop of Nottingham."

"I know that bishop," said Robin; "he dined with me a month since, and paid three hundred pounds for his dinner. He has a good ear and loves music. The friar sang to him to some tune. Give me my harper's cloak, and I will play a part at this wedding."

"These are dangerous times, Robin," said Marian, "for playing pranks out of the forest."

"Fear not," said Robin; "Edwinstow lies not Nottingham-ward, and I will take my precautions."

Robin put on his harper's cloak, while Little John painted his eyebrows and cheeks, tipped his nose with red, and tied him on a comely beard. Marian confessed, that had she not been present at the metamorphosis, she should not have known her own true Robin. Robin took his harp and went to the wedding.

Robin found the bishop and his train in the church porch, impatiently expecting the arrival of the bride and bridegroom. The clerk was observing to the bishop that the knight was somewhat gouty, and that the necessity of walking the last quarter of a mile from the road to the churchyard probably detained the lively bridegroom rather longer than had been calculated upon.

"Oh! by my fay," said the music-loving bishop, "here comes a harper in the nick of time, and now I care not how long they tarry. Ho! honest friend, are you come to play at the wedding?"

"I am come to play anywhere," answered Robin, "where I can get a cup of sack; for which I will sing the praise of the donor in lofty verse, and emblazon him with any virtue which he may wish to have the credit of possessing, without the trouble of practising."

"A most courtly harper," said the bishop; "I will fill thee with sack; I will make thee a walking butt of sack, if thou wilt delight my ears with thy melodies."

"That will I," said Robin; "in what branch of my art shall I exert my faculty? I am passing well in all, from the anthem to the glee, and from the dirge to the coranto."

"It would be idle," said the bishop, "to give thee sack for playing me anthems, seeing that I myself do receive sack for hearing them sung. Therefore, as the occasion is festive, thou shalt play me a coranto."

Robin struck up and played away merrily, the bishop all the while in great delight, noddling his head, and beating time with his foot, till the bride and bridegroom appeared. The bridegroom was richly apparelled, and came slowly and painfully forward, hobbling and leering, and pursing up his mouth into a smile of resolute defiance to the gout, and of tender complacency towards his lady love, who, shining like gold at the old knight's expense, followed slowly between her father and mother, her cheeks pale, her head drooping, her steps faltering, and her eyes reddened with tears.

Robin stopped his minstrelsy, and said to the bishop, "This seems to me an unfit match."

"What do you say, rascal?" said the old knight, hobbling up to him.

"I say," said Robin, "this seems to me an unfit match. What, in the devil's name, can you want with a young wife, who have one foot in flannels and the other in the grave?"

"What is that to thee, sirrah varlet?" said the old knight; "stand away from the porch, or I will fracture thy sconce with my cane."

"I will not stand away from the porch," said Robin, "unless the bride bid me, and tell me that you are her own true love."

"Speak," said the bride's father, in a severe tone, and with a look of significant menace. The girl looked alternately at her father and Robin. She attempted to speak, but her voice failed in the effort, and she burst into tears.

"Here is lawful cause and just impediment," said Robin, "and I forbid the banns."

"Who are you, villain ? " said the old knight, stamping his sound foot with rage.

"I am the Roman law," said Robin, "which says that there shall not be more than ten years between a man and his wife ; and here are five times ten : and so says the law of nature."

"Honest harper," said the bishop, "you are somewhat over-officious here, and less courtly than I deemed you. If you love sack, forbear ; for this course will never bring you a drop. As to your Roman law, and your law of nature, what right have they to say any thing which the law of Holy Writ says not ? "

"The law of Holy Writ does say it," said Robin ; "I expound it so to say ; and I will produce sixty commentators to establish my exposition."

And so saying, he produced a horn from beneath his cloak, and blew three blasts, and threescore bowmen in green came leaping from the bushes and trees ; and young Allen was the first among them to give Robin his sword, while Friar Tuck and Little John marched up to the altar. Robin stripped the bishop and clerk of their robes, and put them on the friar and Little John ; and Allen advanced to take the hand of the bride. Her cheeks grew red and her eyes grew bright, as she locked her hand in her lover's, and tripped lightly with him into the church.

"This marriage will not stand," said the bishop, "for they have not been thrice asked in church."

"We will ask them seven times," said Little John, "lest three should not suffice."

"And in the meantime," said Robin, "the knight and the bishop shall dance to my harping."

So Robin sat in the church porch and played away merrily, while his foresters formed a ring, in the centre of which the knight and bishop danced with exemplary alacrity ; and if they relaxed their exertions, Scarlet gently touched them up with the point of an arrow.

The knight grimaced ruefully, and begged Robin to think of his gout.

" So I do," said Robin ; " this is the true antipodagron [1] : you shall dance the gout away, and be thankful to me while you live. I told you," he added to the bishop, " I would play at this wedding ; but you did not tell me that you would dance at it. The next couple you marry, think of the Roman law."

The bishop was too much out of breath to reply ; and now the young couple issued from church, and the bride having made a farewell obeisance to her parents, they departed together with the foresters, the parents storming, the attendants laughing, the bishop puffing and blowing, and the knight rubbing his gouty foot, and uttering doleful lamentations for the gold and jewels with which he had so unwittingly adorned and dowered the bride.

CHAPTER XIV

As ye came from the holy land
Of blessed Walsinghame,
Oh met ye not with my true love,
As by the way ye came ?—*Old Ballad.*

IN pursuance of the arrangement recorded in the twelfth chapter, the baron, Robin, and Marian disguised themselves as pilgrims returned from Palestine, and travelling from the sea-coast of Hampshire to their home in Northumberland. By dint of staff and cockle-shell, sandal and scrip, they proceeded in safety the greater part of the way (for Robin had many sly inns and resting-places between Barnsdale and Sherwood), and were already on the borders of Yorkshire, when, one evening, they passed within view of a castle, where they saw a lady standing on a turret, and surveying the whole extent of the valley through which they were passing. A servant came running from the castle, and delivered to them a message from his lady, who was sick with expectation of news from her lord in the Holy Land, and entreated them to come to her, that she might question them concerning him.[2] This was an awkward occurrence : but there was no pretence for refusal, and they followed the servant

[1] " Remedy for the gout." G.
[2] See Scott: *Ivanhoe*, Ch. II to VI, in which Locksley (Robin Hood), disguised as a pilgrim, is questioned by Rowena on his adventures in the Holy Land. G.

into the castle.   The baron, who had been in Palestine in his youth, undertook to be spokesman on the occasion, and to relate his own adventures to the lady as having happened to the lord in question. This preparation enabled him to be so minute and circumstantial in his detail, and so coherent in his replies to her questions, that the lady fell implicitly into the delusion, and was delighted to find that her lord was alive and in health, and in high favour with the king, and performing prodigies of valour in the name of his lady, whose miniature he always wore in his bosom.[1]   The baron guessed at this circumstance from the customs of that age, and happened to be in the right.

" This miniature," added the baron, " I have had the felicity to see, and should have known you by it among a million."   The baron was a little embarrassed by some questions of the lady concerning her lord's personal appearance ; but Robin came to his aid, observing a picture suspended opposite to him on the wall, which he made a bold conjecture to be that of the lord in question ; and making a calcula- tion of the influences of time and war, which he weighed with a com- parison of the lady's age, he gave a description of her lord sufficiently like the picture in its groundwork to be a true resemblance, and sufficiently differing from it in circumstances to be more an original than a copy.   The lady was completely deceived, and entreated them to partake her hospitality for the night ; but this they deemed it prudent to decline, and with many humble thanks for her kindness, and representations of the necessity of not delaying their homeward course, they proceeded on their way.

As they passed over the drawbridge, they met Sir Ralph Mont- faucon and his squire, who were wandering in quest of Marian, and were entering to claim that hospitality which the pilgrims had declined.   Their countenances struck Sir Ralph with a kind of imperfect recognition, which would never have been matured, but that the eyes of Marian, as she passed him, encountered his, and the images of those stars of beauty continued involuntarily twinkling in his sensorium to the exclusion of all other ideas, till memory, love, and hope concurred with imagination to furnish a probable reason for their haunting him so pertinaciously.   Those eyes, he thought, were

[1] Miniatures belong to a later age than Robin Hood's.   G.

certainly the eyes of Matilda Fitzwater ; and if the eyes were hers, it was extremely probable, if not logically consecutive, that the rest of the body they belonged to was hers also. Now, if it were really Matilda Fitzwater, who were her two companions ? The baron ? Aye, and the elder pilgrim was something like him. And the Earl of Huntingdon ? Very probably. The earl and the baron might be good friends again, now that they were both in disgrace together. While he was revolving these cogitations, he was introduced to the lady, and after claiming and receiving the promise of hospitality, he inquired what she knew of the pilgrims who had just departed ? The lady told him they were newly returned from Palestine, having been long in the Holy Land. The knight expressed some scepticism on this point. The lady replied, that they had given her so minute a detail of her lord's proceedings, and so accurate a description of his person, that she could not be deceived in them. This staggered the knight's confidence in his own penetration ; and if it had not been a heresy in knighthood to suppose for a moment that there could be *in rerum naturâ* such another pair of eyes as those of his mistress, he would have acquiesced implicitly in the lady's judgment. But while the lady and the knight were conversing, the warder blew his bugle-horn, and presently entered a confidential messenger from Palestine, who gave her to understand that her lord was well ; but entered into a detail of his adventures most completely at variance with the baron's narrative, to which not the correspondence of a single incident gave the remotest colouring of similarity. It now became manifest that the pilgrims were not true men ; and Sir Ralph Mont-faucon sate down to supper with his head full of cogitations, which we shall leave him to chew and digest with his pheasant and canary.

Meanwhile our three pilgrims proceeded on their way. The evening set in black and lowering, when Robin turned aside from the main track, to seek an asylum for the night, along a narrow way that led between rocky and woody hills. A peasant observed the pilgrims as they entered that narrow pass, and called after them : " Whither go you, my masters ? there are rogues in that direction."

" Can you show us a direction," said Robin, " in which there are none ? If so, we will take it in preference." The peasant grinned, and walked away whistling.

The pass widened as they advanced, and the woods grew thicker and darker around them.   Their path wound along the slope of a woody declivity, which rose high above them in a thick rampart of foliage, and descended almost precipitously to the bed of a small river, which they heard dashing in its rocky channel, and saw its white foam gleaming at intervals in the last faint glimmerings of twilight.   In a short time all was dark, and the rising voice of the wind foretold a coming storm.   They turned a point of the valley, and saw a light below them in the depth of the hollow, shining through a cottage-casement and dancing in its reflection on the restless stream.   Robin blew his horn, which was answered from below. The cottage door opened :   a boy came forth with a torch, ascended the steep, showed tokens of great delight at meeting with Robin, and lighted them down a flight of steps rudely cut in the rock, and over a series of rugged stepping-stones, that crossed the channel of the river.   They entered the cottage, which exhibited neatness, comfort, and plenty, being amply enriched with pots, pans, and pipkins, and adorned with flitches of bacon and sundry similar ornaments, that gave goodly promise in the firelight that gleamed upon the rafters. A woman, who seemed just old enough to be the boy's mother, had thrown down her spinning-wheel in her joy at the sound of Robin's horn, and was bustling with singular alacrity to set forth her festal ware and prepare an abundant supper.   Her features, though not beautiful, were agreeable and expressive, and were now lighted up with such manifest joy at the sight of Robin, that Marian could not help feeling a momentary touch of jealousy, and a half-formed suspicion that Robin had broken his forest law, and had occasionally gone out of bounds, as other great men have done upon occasion, in order to reconcile the breach of the spirit, with the preservation of the letter, of their own legislation.   However, this suspicion, if it could be said to exist in a mind so generous as Marian's, was very soon dissipated by the entrance of the woman's husband, who testified as much joy as his wife had done at the sight of Robin ;   and in a short time the whole of the party were amicably seated round a smoking supper of river-fish and wild wood fowl, on which the baron fell with as much alacrity as if he had been a true pilgrim from Palestine.

The husband produced some recondite flasks of wine, which were laid by in a binn consecrated to Robin, whose occasional visits to them in his wanderings were the festal days of these warm-hearted cottagers, whose manners showed that they had not been born to this low estate. Their story had no mystery, and Marian easily collected it from the tenour of their conversation. The young man had been, like Robin, the victim of an usurious abbot, and had been outlawed for debt, and his nut-brown maid had accompanied him to the depths of Sherwood, where they lived an unholy and illegitimate life, killing the king's deer, and never hearing mass. In this state, Robin, then earl of Huntingdon, discovered them in one of his huntings, and gave them aid and protection. When Robin himself became an outlaw, the necessary qualification or gift of continency was too hard a law for our lovers to subscribe to; and as they were thus disqualified for foresters, Robin had found them a retreat in this romantic and secluded spot. He had done similar service to other lovers similarly circumstanced, and had disposed them in various wild scenes which he and his men had discovered in their flittings from place to place, supplying them with all necessaries and comforts from the reluctant disgorgings of fat abbots and usurers. The benefit was in some measure mutual; for these cottages served him as resting-places in his removals, and enabled him to travel untraced and unmolested; and in the delight with which he was always received he found himself even more welcome than he would have been at an inn[1]; and this is saying very much for gratitude and affection together. The smiles which surrounded him were of his own creation, and he participated in the happiness he had bestowed.

The casements began to rattle in the wind, and the rain to beat upon the windows. The wind swelled to a hurricane, and the rain dashed like a flood against the glass. The boy retired to his little bed, the wife trimmed the lamp, the husband heaped logs upon the fire: Robin broached another flask; and Marian filled the baron's cup, and sweetened Robin's by touching its edge with her lips.

"Well," said the baron, "give me a roof over my head, be it never

---

[1] " Whoe'er has travelled life's dull round,
    Where'er his stages may have been,
    May sigh to think he still has found
    The warmest welcome at an inn."
Shenstone: *Written at an Inn at Henley.* G.

so humble.[1] Your greenwood canopy is pretty and pleasant in sunshine ; but if I were doomed to live under it, I should wish it were water-tight."

" But," said Robin, " we have tents and caves for foul weather, good store of wine and venison, and fuel in abundance."

" Ay, but," said the baron, " I like to pull off my boots of a night, which you foresters seldom do, and to ensconce myself thereafter in a comfortable bed. Your beech-root is over-hard for a couch, and your mossy stump is somewhat rough for a bolster."

" Had you not dry leaves," said Robin, " with a bishop's surplice over them ? What would you have softer ? And had you not an abbot's travelling cloak for a coverlet ? What would you have warmer ? "

" Very true," said the baron, " but that was an indulgence to a guest, and I dreamed all night of the sheriff of Nottingham. I like to feel myself safe," he added, stretching out his legs to the fire, and throwing himself back in his chair with the air of a man determined to be comfortable. " I like to feel myself safe," said the baron.

At that moment the woman caught her husband's arm, and all the party following the direction of her eyes, looked simultaneously to the window, where they had just time to catch a glimpse of an apparition of an armed head, with its plumage tossing in the storm, on which the light shone from within, and which disappeared immediately.

CHAPTER XV

O knight, thou lack'st a cup of canary.   When did I see thee so put down ?
—*Twelfth Night.*[2]

SEVERAL knocks, as from the knuckles of an iron glove, were given to the door of the cottage, and a voice was heard entreating shelter

---

[1] Strongly reminiscent of :

> " Be it ever so humble
> There is no place like home."

These lines from *Home Sweet Home* first appeared in *Clari*, an opera, by the American John Howard Payne, with music by Sir Henry Bishop, produced on May 8th, 1823. Bishop had written the music for the operatic version of *Maid Marian*, which was produced in December, 1822. One can make a case for Payne having plagiarised *Maid Marian* to obtain the only song by which he is remembered, just as one can make a case for Peacock having plagiarised *Ivanhoe*. G.   [2] Act I, Sc. 3. G.

from the storm for a traveller who had lost his way. Robin arose
and went to the door.

" What are you ? " said Robin.

" A soldier," replied the voice : " an unfortunate adherent of
Longchamp, flying the vengeance of Prince John."

" Are you alone ? " said Robin.

" Yes," said the voice : " it is a dreadful night. Hospitable
cottagers, pray give me admittance. I would not have asked it but
for the storm. I would have kept my watch in the woods."

" That I believe," said Robin.   " You did not reckon on the storm
when you turned into this pass. Do you know there are rogues this
way ? "

" I do," said the voice.

" So do I," said Robin.

A pause ensued, during which Robin listening attentively caught
a faint sound of whispering.

" You are not alone," said Robin.   " Who are your companions ? "

" None but the wind and the water," said the voice, " and I would
I had them not."

" The wind and the water have many voices," said Robin, " but
I never before heard them say, What shall we do ? "

Another pause ensued : after which,

" Look ye, master cottager," said the voice, in an altered tone, " if
you do not let us in willingly, we will break down the door."

" Ho ! ho ! " roared the baron, " you are become plural are you,
rascals ?   How many are there of you, thieves ?   What, I warrant,
you thought to rob and murder a poor harmless cottager and his wife,
and did not dream of a garrison ?   You looked for no weapon of
opposition but spit, poker, and basting ladle, wielded by unskilful
hands : but, rascals, here is short sword and long cudgel in hands well
tried in war, wherewith you shall be drilled into cullenders and
beaten into mummy." [1]

No reply was made, but furious strokes from without resounded
upon the door. Robin, Marian, and the baron threw by their
pilgrim's attire, and stood in arms on the defensive. They were

---

[1] Mummy : an adhesive mass like the mediæval medicament made from
the ground-up bodies of Egyptian mummies. G.

provided with swords, and the cottager gave them bucklers and helmets, for all Robin's haunts were furnished with secret armouries. But they kept their swords sheathed, and the baron wielded a ponderous spear, which he pointed towards the door ready to run through the first that should enter, and Robin and Marian each held a bow with the arrow drawn to its head and pointed in the same direction. The cottager flourished a strong cudgel (a weapon in the use of which he prided himself on being particularly expert), and the wife seized the spit from the fireplace, and held it as she saw the baron hold his spear. The storm of wind and rain continued to beat on the roof and the casement, and the storm of blows to resound upon the door, which at length gave way with a violent crash, and a cluster of armed men appeared without, seemingly not less than twelve. Behind them rolled the stream now changed from a gentle and shallow river to a mighty and impetuous torrent, roaring in waves of yellow foam, partially reddened by the light that streamed through the open door, and turning up its convulsed surface in flashes of shifting radiance from restless masses of half-visible shadow. The stepping-stones, by which the intruders must have crossed, were buried under the waters. On the opposite bank the light fell on the stems and boughs of the rock-rooted oak and ash tossing and swaying in the blast, and sweeping the flashing spray with their leaves.

The instant the door broke, Robin and Marian loosed their arrows. Robin's arrow struck one of the assailants in the juncture of the shoulder, and disabled his right arm : Marian's struck a second in the juncture of the knee, and rendered him unserviceable for the night. The baron's long spear struck on the mailed breastplate of a third, and being stretched to its full extent by the long-armed hero, drove him to the edge of the torrent, and plunged him into its eddies, along which he was whirled down the darkness of the descending stream, calling vainly on his comrades for aid, till his voice was lost in the mingled roar of the waters and the wind. A fourth springing through the door was laid prostrate by the cottager's cudgel : but the wife being less dexterous than her company, though an Amazon in strength, missed her pass at a fifth, and drove the point of the spit several inches into the right hand door-post as she stood close to the left, and thus made a new barrier which the invaders could not pass

without dipping under it and submitting their necks to the sword :
but one of the assailants seizing it with gigantic rage, shook it at once
from the grasp of its holder and from its lodgment in the post, and
at the same time made good the irruption of the rest of his party
into the cottage.

Now raged an unequal combat, for the assailants fell two to one on
Robin, Marian, the baron, and the cottager ; while the wife, being
deprived of her spit, converted every thing that was at hand to a
missile, and rained pots, pans, and pipkins on the armed heads of the
enemy.   The baron raged like a tiger, and the cottager laid about him
like a thresher.   One of the soldiers struck Robin's sword from his
hand and brought him on his knee, when the boy, who had been
roused by the tumult and had been peeping through the inner door,
leaped forward in his shirt, picked up the sword and replaced it in
Robin's hand, who instantly springing up, disarmed and wounded
one of his antagonists, while the other was laid prostrate under the
dint of a brass cauldron launched by the Amazonian dame.   Robin
now turned to the aid of Marian, who was parrying most dexterously
the cuts and slashes of her two assailants, of whom Robin delivered
her from one, while a well-applied blow of her sword struck off the
helmet of the other, who fell on his knees to beg a boon, and she
recognised Sir Ralph Montfaucon.   The men who were engaged with
the baron and the peasant, seeing their leader subdued, immediately
laid down their arms and cried for quarter.   The wife brought some
strong rope, and the baron tied their arms behind them.

"Now, Sir Ralph," said Marian, "once more you are at my mercy."

" That I always am, cruel beauty," said the discomfited lover.

" Odso ! courteous knight," said the baron, " is this the return you
make for my beef and canary, when you kissed my daughter's hand in
token of contrition for your intermeddling at her wedding ?   Heart,
I am glad to see she has given you a bloody coxcomb. Slice him
down, Mawd ! slice him down, and fling him into the river."

" Confess," said Marian, " what brought you here, and how did
you trace our steps ? "

" I will confess nothing," said the knight.

" Then confess you, rascal," said the baron, holding his sword to
the throat of the captive squire.

"Take away the sword," said the squire, "it is too near my mouth, and my voice will not come out for fear : take away the sword, and I will confess all." The baron dropped his sword, and the squire proceeded ; "Sir Ralph met you, as you quitted Lady Falkland's castle, and by representing to her who you were, borrowed from her such a number of her retainers as he deemed must ensure your capture, seeing that your familiar the friar was not at your elbow. We set forth without delay, and traced you first by means of a peasant who saw you turn into this valley, and afterwards by the light from the casement of this solitary dwelling. Our design was to have laid an ambush for you in the morning, but the storm and your observation of my unlucky face through the casement made us change our purpose ; and what followed you can tell better than I can, being indeed masters of the subject."

"You are a merry knave," said the baron, "and here is a cup of wine for you."

"Gramercy," said the squire, "and better late than never : but I lacked a cup of this before. Had I been pot-valiant, I had held you play."

"Sir knight," said Marian, "this is the third time you have sought the life of my lord and of me, for mine is interwoven with his. And do you think me so spiritless as to believe that I can be yours by compulsion ? Tempt me not again, for the next time shall be the last, and the fish of the nearest river shall commute the flesh of a recreant knight into the fast-day dinner of an uncarnivorous friar. I spare you now, not in pity but in scorn. Yet shall you swear to a convention never more to pursue or molest my lord or me, and on this condition you shall live."

The knight had no alternative but to comply, and swore, on the honour of knighthood, to keep the convention inviolate. How well he kept his oath we shall have no opportunity of narrating : *Di lui la nostra istoria più non parla.*[1]

---

[1] "Of him our story says no more." G.

CHAPTER XVI

Carry me over the water, thou fine fellowe. *Old Ballad.*

THE pilgrims, without experiencing further molestation, arrived at the retreat of Sir Guy of Gamwell. They found the old knight a cup too low; partly from being cut off from the scenes of his old hospitality and the shouts of his Nottinghamshire vassals, who were wont to make the rafters of his ancient hall re-echo to their revelry; but principally from being parted from his son, who had long been the better half of his flask and pasty. The arrival of our visitors cheered him up; and finding that the baron was to remain with him, he testified his delight and the cordiality of his welcome by pegging him in the ribs till he made him roar.

Robin and Marian took an affectionate leave of the baron and the old knight; and before they quitted the vicinity of Barnsdale, deeming it prudent to return in a different disguise, they laid aside their pilgrim's attire, and assumed the habits and appurtenances of wandering minstrels.

They travelled in this character safely and pleasantly, till one evening at a late hour they arrived by the side of a river, where Robin looking out for a mode of passage perceived a ferry-boat safely moored in a nook on the opposite bank; near which a chimney sending up a wreath of smoke through the thick-set willows, was the only symptom of human habitation; and Robin naturally conceiving the said chimney and wreath of smoke to be the outward signs of the inward ferryman, shouted " Over ! " with much strength and clearness; but no voice replied, and no ferryman appeared. Robin raised his voice, and shouted with redoubled energy, " Over, Over, O-o-o-over ! " A faint echo alone responded " Over ! " and again died away into deep silence: but after a brief interval a voice from among the willows, in a strange kind of mingled intonation that was half a shout and half a song, answered :

> Over, over, over, jolly, jolly rover,
> Would you then come over ?   Over, over, over ?
> Jolly, jolly rover, here's one lives in clover :
> Who finds the clover ?   The jolly, jolly rover.
> He finds the clover, let him then come over,
> The jolly, jolly rover, over, over, over.

" I much doubt," said Marian, " if this ferryman do not mean by clover something more than the toll of his ferry-boat."

" I doubt not," answered Robin, " he is a levier of toll and tithe, which I shall put him upon proof of his right to receive, by making trial of his might to enforce."

The ferryman emerged from the willows and stepped into his boat. " As I live," exclaimed Robin, " the ferryman is a friar."

" With a sword," said Marian, " stuck in his rope girdle."

The friar pushed his boat off manfully, and was presently half over the river.

" It is friar Tuck," said Marian.

" He will scarcely know us," said Robin ; " and if he do not, I will break a staff with him for sport."

The friar came singing across the water : the boat touched the land : Robin and Marian stepped on board : the friar pushed off again.

" Silken doublets, silken doublets," said the friar : " slenderly lined, I trow : your wandering minstrel is always poor toll : your sweet angels of voices pass current for a bed and a supper at the house of every lord that likes to hear the fame of his valour without the trouble of fighting for it. What need you of purse or pouch ? You may sing before thieves. Pedlars, pedlars : wandering from door to door with the small ware of lies and cajolery : exploits for carpet-knights ; honesty for courtiers ; truth for monks, and chastity for nuns : a good saleable stock that costs the vender nothing, defies wear and tear, and when it has served a hundred customers is as plentiful and as marketable as ever. But, sirrahs, I'll none of your balderdash. You pass not hence without clink of brass, or I'll knock your musical noddles together till they ring like a pair of cymbals. That will be a new tune for your minstrelships."

This friendly speech of the friar ended as they stepped on the opposite bank. Robin had noticed as they passed that the summer stream was low.

" Why, thou brawling mongrel," said Robin, " that whether thou be thief, friar, or ferryman, or an ill-mixed compound of all three, passes conjecture, though I judge thee to be simple thief, what barkest thou at thus ? Villain, there is clink of brass for thee. Dost thou see this coin ? Dost thou hear this music ? Look and

listen : for touch thou shalt not : my minstrelship defies thee.
Thou shalt carry me on thy back over the water, and receive nothing
but a cracked sconce for thy trouble."

" A bargain," said the friar : " for the water is low, the labour is
light, and the reward is alluring." And he stooped down for Robin,
who mounted his back, and the friar waded with him over the river.

" Now, fine fellow," said the friar, " thou shalt carry me back over
the water, and thou shalt have a cracked sconce for thy trouble." [1]

Robin took the friar on his back, and waded with him into the
middle of the river, when by a dexterous jerk he suddenly flung him
off and plunged him horizontally over head and ears in the water.
Robin waded to shore, and the friar, half swimming and half
scrambling, followed.

" Fine fellow, fine fellow," said the friar, " now will I pay thee thy
cracked sconce."

" Not so," said Robin, " I have not earned it : but thou hast
earned it, and shalt have it."

It was not, even in those good old times, a sight of every day to
see a troubadour and a friar playing at single-stick by the side of a
river, each aiming with fell intent at the other's coxcomb. The
parties were both so skilled in attack and defence, that their mutual
efforts for a long time expended themselves in quick and loud
rappings on each other's oaken staves. At length Robin by a
dexterous feint contrived to score one on the friar's crown : but in the
careless moment of triumph a splendid sweep of the friar's staff
struck Robin's out of his hand into the middle of the river, and
repaid his crack on the head with a degree of vigour that might have
passed the bounds of a jest if Marian had not retarded its descent
by catching the friar's arm.

" How now, recreant friar," said Marian ; " what have you to say
why you should not suffer instant execution, being detected in open
rebellion against your liege lord ? Therefore kneel down, traitor,
and submit your neck to the sword of the offended law."

" Benefit of clergy," said the friar : " I plead my clergy. And
is it you indeed, ye scapegraces ? Ye are well disguised : I knew ye
not, by my flask. Robin, jolly Robin, he buys a jest dearly that pays

[1] See Ritson : *Robin Hood*, Vol. II : *Robin Hood and the Curtall Fryer*. G.

for it with a bloody coxcomb. But here is balm for all bruises, outward and inward. (The friar produced a flask of canary.) Wash thy wound twice and thy throat thrice with this solar concoction, and thou shalt marvel where was thy hurt. But what moved ye to this frolic ? Knew ye not that ye could not appear in a mask more fashioned to move my bile than in that of these gilders and lackerers of the smooth surface of worthlessness, that bring the gold of true valour into disrepute, by stamping the baser metal with the fairer impression ? I marvelled to find any such given to fighting (for they have an old instinct of self-preservation) : but I rejoiced thereat, that I might discuss to them poetical justice : and therefore have I cracked thy sconce : for which, let this be thy medicine."

"But wherefore," said Marian, "do we find you here, when we left you joint lord warden of Sherwood ? "

"I do but retire to my devotions," replied the friar. "This is my hermitage, in which I first took refuge when I escaped from my beloved brethren of Rubygill ; and to which I still retreat at times from the vanities of the world, which else might cling to me too closely, since I have been promoted to be peer-spiritual of your forest-court. For, indeed, I do find in myself certain indications and admonitions that my day has passed its noon ; and none more cogent than this : that daily of bad wine I grow more intolerant, and of good wine have a keener and more fastidious relish. There is no surer symptom of receding years. The ferryman is my faithful varlet. I send him on some pious errand, that I may meditate in ghostly privacy, when my presence in the forest can best be spared : and when can it be better spared than now, seeing that the neighbourhood of Prince John, and his incessant perquisitions for Marian, have made the forest too hot to hold more of us than are needful to keep up a quorum, and preserve unbroken the continuity of our forest-dominion ? For, in truth, without your greenwood majesties, we have hardly the wit to live in a body, and at the same time to keep our necks out of jeopardy, while that arch-rebel and traitor John infests the precincts of our territory."

The friar now conducted them to his peaceful cell, where he spread his frugal board with fish, venison, wild-fowl, fruit, and canary. Under the compound operation of this *materia medica* Robin's wounds healed apace, and the friar, who hated minstrelsy, began as usual chirping in his cups. Robin and Marian chimed in with his tuneful humour till the midnight moon peeped in upon their revelry.

It was now the very witching time of night,[1] when they heard a voice shouting " Over ! " They paused to listen, and the voice repeated " Over ! " in accents clear and loud, but which at the same time either were in themselves, or seemed to be, from the place and the hour, singularly plaintive and dreary. The friar fidgetted about in his seat : fell into a deep musing : shook himself, and looked about him : first at Marian, then at Robin, then at Marian again ; filled and tossed off a cup of canary, and relapsed into his reverie.

" Will you not bring your passenger over ? " said Robin. The friar shook his head and looked mysterious.

" That passenger," said the friar, " will never come over. Every full moon, at midnight, that voice calls, ' Over ! ' I and my varlet have more than once obeyed the summons, and we have sometimes had a glimpse of a white figure under the opposite trees : but when the boat has touched the bank, nothing has been to be seen; and the voice has been heard no more till the midnight of the next full moon."

" It is very strange," said Robin.

" Wondrous strange," said the friar, looking solemn.

The voice again called " Over ! " in a long plaintive musical cry.

" I must go to it," said the friar, " or it will give us no peace. I would all my customers were of this world. I begin to think that I am Charon, and that this river is Styx."

" I will go with you, friar," said Robin.

" By my flask," said the friar, " but you shall not."

" Then I will," said Marian.

"Still less," said the friar, hurrying out of the cell. Robin and Marian followed : but the friar outstepped them, and pushed off his boat.

A white figure was visible under the shade of the opposite trees. The boat approached the shore, and the figure glided away. The friar returned.

They re-entered the cottage, and sat some time conversing on the phenomenon they had seen. The friar sipped his wine, and after a time, said :

---

[1] *Hamlet*, Act III, Sc. 2.   G.

"There is a tradition of a damsel who was drowned here some years ago.   The tradition is——"

But the friar could not narrate a plain tale : he therefore cleared his throat, and sang with due solemnity, in a ghostly voice :

A damsel came in midnight rain,
    And called across the ferry :
The weary wight she called in vain,
    Whose senses sleep did bury.
At evening, from her father's door
    She turned to meet her lover :
At midnight, on the lonely shore,
    She shouted, " Over, over ! "

She had not met him by the tree
    Of their accustomed meeting,
And sad and sick at heart was she,
    Her heart all wildly beating.
In chill suspense the hours went by,
    The wild storm burst above her :
She turned her to the river nigh,
    And shouted, " Over, over ! "

A dim, discoloured, doubtful light
    The moon's dark veil permitted,
And thick before her troubled sight
    Fantastic shadows flitted.
Her lover's form appeared to glide,
    And beckon o'er the water :
Alas ! his blood that morn had dyed
    Her brother's sword with slaughter.

Upon a little rock she stood,
    To make her invocation :
She marked not that the rain-swoll'n flood
    Was islanding her station.
The tempest mocked her feeble cry :
    No saint his aid would give her :
The flood swelled high and yet more high,
    And swept her down the river.

Yet oft beneath the pale moonlight,
    When hollow winds are blowing,
The shadow of that maiden bright
    Glides by the dark stream's flowing.
And when the storms of midnight rave,
    While clouds the broad moon cover,
The wild gusts waft across the wave
    The cry of, " Over, over ! "

While the friar was singing, Marian was meditating : and when he
had ended she said, "Honest friar, you have misplaced your tradition,
which belongs to the æstuary of a nobler river, where the damsel was
swept away by the rising of the tide, for which your land-flood is an
indifferent substitute.   But the true tradition of this stream I think
I myself possess, and I will narrate it in your own way :

> It was a friar of orders free,
> A friar of Rubygill :
> At the greenwood-tree a vow made he,
> But he kept it very ill :
> A vow made he of chastity,
> But he kept it very ill.
> He kept it, perchance, in the conscious shade
> Of the bounds of the forest wherein it was made :
> But he roamed where he listed, as free as the wind,
> And he left his good vow in the forest behind :
> For its woods out of sight were his vow out of mind,
> With the friar of Rubygill.
>
> In lonely hut himself he shut,
> The friar of Rubygill ;
> Where the ghostly elf absolved himself,
> To follow his own good will :
> And he had no lack of canary sack,
> To keep his conscience still.
> And a damsel well knew, when at lonely midnight
> It gleamed on the waters, his signal-lamp-light :
> " Over ! over ! " she warbled with nightingale throat,
> And the friar sprung forth at the magical note,
> And she crossed the dark stream in his trim ferry-boat,
> With the friar of Rubygill.

" Look you now," said Robin, " if the friar does not blush.   Many
strange sights have I seen in my day, but never till this moment did
I see a blushing friar."

" I think," said the friar, " you never saw one that blushed not,
or you saw good canary thrown away.   But you are welcome to
laugh if it so please you.   None shall laugh in my company, though
it be at my expense, but I will have my share of the merriment.   The
world is a stage, and life is a farce, and he that laughs most has most
profit of the performance.   The worst thing is good enough to be
laughed at, though it be good for nothing else ; and the best thing,
though it be good for something else, is good for nothing better."

And he struck up a song in praise of laughing and quaffing, without further adverting to Marian's insinuated accusation ; being, perhaps, of opinion, that it was a subject on which the least said would be the soonest mended.

So passed the night. In the morning a forester came to the friar, with intelligence that Prince John had been compelled, by the urgency of his affairs in other quarters, to disembarrass Nottingham Castle of his royal presence. Our wanderers returned joyfully to their forest-dominion, being thus relieved from the vicinity of any more formidable belligerent than their old bruised and beaten enemy the sheriff of Nottingham.

CHAPTER XVII

Oh ! this life
Is nobler than attending for a check,
Richer than doing nothing for a bribe,
Prouder than rustling in unpaid-for silk.
—*Cymbeline.*[1]

So Robin and Marian dwelt and reigned in the forest, ranging the glades and the greenwoods from the matins of the lark to the vespers of the nightingale, and administering natural justice according to Robin's ideas of rectifying the inequalities of human condition : raising genial dews from the bags of the rich and idle, and returning them in fertilising showers on the poor and industrious : an operation which more enlightened statesmen have happily reversed, to the unspeakable benefit of the community at large. The light footsteps of Marian were impressed on the morning dew beside the firmer step of her lover, and they shook its large drops about them as they cleared themselves a passage through the thick tall fern, without any fear of catching cold, which was not much in fashion in the twelfth century. Robin was as hospitable as Cathmor[2]; for seven men stood on seven paths to call the stranger to his feast. It is true, he superadded the small improvement of making the stranger pay for it :

[1] Act III, Sc. 3. The first folio reads : " doing nothing for a *babe* ; " which is interpreted as a *baub* or *bauble*. G.

[2] Macpherson : *Ossian.* Cathmor is a hospitable hero. G.

than which what could be more generous ?   For Cathmor was himself the prime giver of his feast, whereas Robin was only the agent to
a series of strangers, who provided in turn for the entertainment of
their successors; which is carrying the disinterestedness of hospitality
to its acme.   Marian often killed the deer,

> Which Scarlet dressed, and Friar Tuck blessed,
> While Little John wandered in search of a guest.

Robin was very devout, though there was great unity in his
religion : it was exclusively given to our Lady the Virgin, and he
never set forth in a morning till he had said three prayers, and had
heard the sweet voice of his Marian singing a hymn to their mutual
patroness.   Each of his men had, as usual, a patron saint according
to his name or taste.   The friar chose a saint for himself, and fixed
on Saint Botolph, whom he euphonised into Saint Bottle, and maintained that he was that very Panomphic Pantagruelian saint, well
known in ancient France as a female divinity, by the name of La Dive
Bouteille, whose oracular monosyllable " Trincq," is celebrated and
understood by all nations, and is expounded by the learned doctor
Alcofribas,[1] who has treated at large on the subject, to signify
" drink."   Saint Bottle, then, was the saint of Friar Tuck, who did
not yield even to Robin and Marian in the assiduity of his devotions
to his chosen patron.   Such was their summer life, and in their
winter caves they had sufficient furniture, ample provender, store of
old wine, and assuredly no lack of fuel, with joyous music and pleasant
discourse to charm away the season of darkness and storms.

Many moons had waxed and waned, when on the afternoon of a
lovely summer day a lusty broad-boned knight was riding through
the forest of Sherwood.   The sun shone brilliantly on the full green
foliage, and afforded the knight a fine opportunity of observing
picturesque effects, of which it is to be feared he did not avail himself.   But he had not proceeded far, before he had an opportunity of

---

[1] Alcofribas Nasier : an anagram of François Rabelais, and his assumed
appellation.

The reader who desires to know more about this oracular divinity, may
consult the said doctor Alcofribas Nasier, who will usher him into the
adytum through the medium of the high priestess Bacbuc.   [P.]

[Bk. V, Ch. 44.   G.]

observing something much more interesting, namely, a fine young
outlaw leaning, in the true Sherwood fashion, with his back against
a tree. The knight was preparing to ask the stranger a question,
the answer to which, if correctly given, would have relieved him from
a doubt that pressed heavily on his mind, as to whether he was in the
right road or the wrong, when the youth prevented the inquiry by
saying : " In God's name, sir knight, you are late to your meals.
My master has tarried dinner for you these three hours."

" I doubt," said the knight, " I am not he you wot of. I am
no where bidden to-day, and I know none in this vicinage."

" We feared," said the youth, " your memory would be
treacherous : therefore am I stationed here to refresh it."

" Who is your master ? " said the knight ; " and where does he
abide ? "

" My master," said the youth, " is called Robin Hood, and he
abides hard by."

" And what knows he of me ? " said the knight.

" He knows you," answered the youth, " as he does every way-
faring knight and friar, by instinct."

" Gramercy," said the knight ; " then I understand his bidding :
but how if I say I will not come ? "

" I am enjoined to bring you," said the youth. " If persuasion
avail not, I must use other argument."

" Say'st thou so ? " said the knight ; " I doubt if thy stripling
rhetoric would convince me."

" That," said the young forester, " we will see."

" We are not equally matched, boy," said the knight. " I should
get less honour by thy conquest, than grief by thy injury."

" Perhaps," said the youth, " my strength is more than my seeming, and my cunning more than my strength. Therefore let it please
your knighthood to dismount."

" It shall please my knighthood to chastise thy presumption," said
the knight, springing from his saddle.

Hereupon, which in those days was usually the result of a meeting
between any two persons anywhere, they proceeded to fight.

The knight had in an uncommon degree both strength and skill :
the forester had less strength, but not less skill than the knight, and

showed such a mastery of his weapon as reduced the latter to great admiration.[1]

They had not fought many minutes by the forest clock, the sun; and had as yet done each other no worse injury than that the knight had wounded the forester's jerkin, and the forester had disabled the knight's plume; when they were interrupted by a voice from a thicket, exclaiming, "Well fought, girl: well fought. Mass, that had nigh been a shrewd hit. Thou owest him for that, lass. Marry, stand by, I'll pay him for thee."

The knight turning to the voice, beheld a tall friar issuing from the thicket, brandishing a ponderous cudgel.

" Who art thou ? " said the knight.

" I am the church militant of Sherwood," answered the friar. " Why art thou in arms against our lady queen ? "

" What meanest thou ? " said the knight.

" Truly, this," said the friar, " is our liege lady of the forest, against whom I do apprehend thee in overt act of treason. What sayest thou for thyself ? "

" I say," answered the knight, " that if this be indeed a lady, man never yet held me so long."

" Spoken," said the friar, " like one who hath done execution. Hast thou thy stomach full of steel ? Wilt thou diversify thy repast with a taste of my oak-graff ? Or wilt thou incline thine heart to our venison, which truly is cooling ? Wilt thou fight ? or wilt thou dine ? or wilt thou fight and dine ? or wilt thou dine and fight ? I am for thee, choose as thou mayest."

" I will dine," said the knight; " for with lady I never fought before, and with friar I never fought yet, and with neither will I ever fight knowingly: and if this be the queen of the forest, I will not, being in her own dominions, be backward to do her homage."

So saying, he kissed the hand of Marian, who was pleased most graciously to express her approbation.

" Gramercy, sir knight," said the friar, " I laud thee for thy courtesy, which I deem to be no less than thy valour. Now do thou

[1] This episode was invented by Peacock who combined two ballads, *Robin Hood and Maid Marian*, and *The King's disguise and friendship with Robin Hood*. (Ritson: *Robin Hood*, Vol. II, xxiv and xxv.) G.

follow me, while I follow my nose, which scents the pleasant odour of roast from the depth of the forest recesses. I will lead thy horse, and do thou lead my lady."

The knight took Marian's hand, and followed the friar, who walked before them, singing :

> When the wind blows, when the wind blows
> From where under buck the dry log glows,
>   What guide can you follow,
>   O'er brake and o'er hollow,
> So true as a ghostly, ghostly nose ?

CHAPTER XVIII

Robin and Richard were two pretty men. *Mother Goose's Melody.*

THEY proceeded, following their infallible guide, first along a light elastic greensward under the shade of lofty and wide-spreading trees that skirted a sunny opening of the forest, then along labyrinthine paths, which the deer, the outlaw, or the woodman had made, through the close shoots of the young coppices, through the thick under-growth of the ancient woods, through beds of gigantic fern that filled the narrow glades and waved their green feathery heads above the plume of the knight. Along these sylvan alleys they walked in single file ; the friar singing and pioneering in the van, the horse plunging and floundering behind the friar, the lady following " in maiden meditation fancy-free," [1] and the knight bringing up the rear, much marvelling at the strange company into which his stars had thrown him. Their path had expanded sufficiently to allow the knight to take Marian's hand again, when they arrived in the august presence of Robin Hood and his court.

Robin's table was spread under a high overarching canopy of living boughs, on the edge of a natural lawn of verdure starred with flowers, through which a swift transparent rivulet ran sparkling in the sun. The board was covered with abundance of choice food and excellent liquor, not without the comeliness of snow-white linen and the splendour of costly plate, which the sheriff of Nottingham had unwillingly contributed to supply, at the same time with an excellent

---

[1] *A Midsummer Night's Dream*, Act II, Sc. 1. G.

cook, whom Little John's art had spirited away to the forest with the contents of his master's silver scullery.

An hundred foresters were here assembled over-ready for their dinner, some seated at the table and some lying in groups under the trees.

Robin bade courteous welcome to the knight, who took his seat between Robin and Marian at the festal board ; at which was already placed one strange guest in the person of a portly monk, sitting between Little John and Scarlet, with his rotund physiognomy elongated into an unnatural oval by the conjoint influence of sorrow and fear : sorrow for the departed contents of his travelling treasury, a good-looking valise which was hanging empty on a bough ; and fear for his personal safety, of which all the flasks and pasties before him could not give him assurance. The appearance of the knight, however, cheered him up with a semblance of protection, and gave him just sufficient courage to demolish a cygnet and a numble-pie, which he diluted with the contents of two flasks of canary sack.

But wine, which sometimes creates and often increases joy, doth also, upon occasion, heighten sorrow : and so it fared now with our portly monk, who had no sooner explained away his portion of provender, than he began to weep and bewail himself bitterly.

" Why dost thou weep, man ? " said Robin Hood. " Thou hast done thine embassy justly, and shalt have thy Lady's grace."

" Alack ! alack ! " said the monk : " no embassy had I, luckless sinner, as well thou wottest, but to take to my abbey in safety the treasure whereof thou hast despoiled me."

" Propound me his case," said Friar Tuck, " and I will give him ghostly counsel."

" You well remember," said Robin Hood, " the sorrowful knight who dined with us here twelve months and a day gone by."

" Well do I," said Friar Tuck. " His lands were in jeopardy with a certain abbot, who would allow him no longer day for their redemption. Whereupon you lent to him the four hundred pounds which he needed, and which he was to repay this day, though he had no better security to give than our Lady the Virgin."

" I never desired better," said Robin, " for she never yet failed to send me my pay ; and here is one of her own flock, this faithful and well-favoured monk of St. Mary's, hath brought it me duly, principal and interest to a penny, as Little John can testify, who told it forth. To be sure, he denied having it, but that was to prove our faith. We sought and found it."

" I know nothing of your knight," said the monk : " and the money was our own, as the Virgin shall bless me."

" She shall bless thee," said Friar Tuck, " for a faithful messenger."

The monk resumed his wailing. Little John brought him his horse. Robin gave him leave to depart. He sprang with singular nimbleness into the saddle, and vanished without saying, God give you good day.

The stranger knight laughed heartily as the monk rode off.

" They say, sir knight," said Friar Tuck, " they should laugh who win : but thou laughest who art likely to lose."

" I have won," said the knight, " a good dinner, some mirth, and some knowledge : and I cannot lose by paying for them."

" Bravely said," answered Robin. " Still it becomes thee to pay : for it is not meet that a poor forester should treat a rich knight. How much money hast thou with thee ? "

" Troth, I know not," said the knight. " Sometimes much, sometimes little, sometimes none. But search, and what thou findest, keep : and for the sake of thy kind heart and open hand, be it what it may, I shall wish it were more."

" Then, since thou sayest so," said Robin, " not a penny will I touch. Many a false churl comes hither, and disburses against his will : and till there is lack of these, I prey not on true men."

" Thou art thyself a true man, right well I judge, Robin," said the stranger knight, " and seemest more like one bred in court than to thy present outlaw life."

" Our life," said the friar, " is a craft, an art, and a mystery. How much of it, think you, could be learned at court ? "

" Indeed, I cannot say," said the stranger knight : " but I should apprehend very little."

" And so should I," said the friar : " for we should find very little of our bold open practice, but should hear abundance of praise of our principles. To live in seeming fellowship and secret rivalry ; to have a hand for all, and a heart for none ; to be everybody's acquaintance, and nobody's friend ; to meditate the ruin of all on whom we smile, and to dread the secret stratagems of all who smile on us ; to pilfer honours and despoil fortunes, not by fighting in daylight, but by sapping in darkness : these are arts which the court can teach, but which we, by 'r Lady, have not learned. But let your court-minstrel tune up his throat to the praise of your court-hero, then come our principles into play : then is our practice extolled : not by the same name, for their Richard is a hero, and our Robin is a thief : marry, your hero guts an exchequer, while your thief disembowels a portmanteau ; your hero sacks a city, while your thief sacks a cellar : your hero marauds on a larger scale, and that is all the difference, for the principle and the virtue are one : but two of a trade cannot agree : therefore your hero makes laws to get rid of your thief, and gives him an ill name that he may hang him : for might is right, and the strong make laws for the weak, and they that make laws to serve their own turn do also make morals to give colour to their laws."

" Your comparison, friar," said the stranger, " fails in this : that your thief fights for profit, and your hero for honour. I have fought under the banners of Richard, and if, as you phrase it, he guts exchequers, and sacks cities, it is not to win treasure for himself, but to furnish forth the means of his greater and more glorious aim."

" Misconceive me not, sir knight," said the friar. " We all love and honour King Richard, and here is a deep draught to his health : but I would show you, that we foresters are miscalled by opprobrious names, and that our virtues, though they follow at humble distance, are yet truly akin to those of Cœur-de-Lion. I say not that Richard is a thief, but I say that Robin is a hero : and for honour, did ever yet man, miscalled thief, win greater honour than Robin ? Do not all men grace him with some honourable epithet ? The most gentle thief, the most courteous thief, the most bountiful thief, yea, and the most honest thief ? Richard is courteous, bountiful, honest, and valiant : but so also is Robin : it is the false word that makes the unjust distinction. They are twin-spirits, and should be friends, but that fortune hath differently cast their lot : but their names shall descend together to the latest days, as the flower of their age and of England : for in the pure principles of freebootery have they excelled all men ; and to the principles of freebootery, diversely developed, belong all the qualities to which song and story concede renown."

"And you may add, friar," said Marian, "that Robin, no less than Richard, is king in his own dominion ; and that if his subjects be fewer, yet are they more uniformly loyal."

"I would, fair lady," said the stranger, "that thy latter observation were not so true. But I nothing doubt, Robin, that if Richard could hear your friar, and see you and your lady, as I now do, there is not a man in England whom he would take by the hand more cordially than yourself."

"Gramercy, sir knight," said Robin——But his speech was cut short by Little John calling, "Hark ! "

All listened. A distant trampling of horses was heard. The sounds approached rapidly, and at length a group of horsemen glittering in holyday dresses was visible among the trees.

"God's my life ! " said Robin, "what means this ? To arms, my merrymen all."

"No arms, Robin," said the foremost horseman, riding up and springing from his saddle : "have you forgotten Sir William of the Lee ? "

"No, by my fay," said Robin ; "and right welcome again to Sherwood."

Little John bustled to re-array the disorganised economy of the table, and replace the dilapidations of the provender.

"I come late, Robin," said Sir William, "but I came by a wrestling, where I found a good yeoman wrongfully beset by a crowd of sturdy varlets, and I staid to do him right."

"I thank thee for that, in God's name," said Robin, "as if thy good service had been to myself."

"And here," said the knight, "is thy four hundred pound ; and my men have brought thee an hundred bows and as many well-furnished quivers ; which I beseech thee to receive and to use as a poor token of my grateful kindness to thee : for me and my wife and children didst thou redeem from beggary."

"Thy bows and arrows," said Robin, "will I joyfully receive :

but of thy money, not a penny. It is paid already. My Lady, who was thy security, hath sent it me for thee."

Sir William pressed, but Robin was inflexible.

" It is paid," said Robin, " as this good knight can testify, who saw my Lady's messenger depart but now."

Sir William looked round to the stranger knight, and instantly fell on his knee, saying, " God save King Richard."

The foresters, friar and all, dropped on their knees together, and repeated in chorus : " God save King Richard."

" Rise, rise," said Richard, smiling : " Robin is king here, as his lady hath shown. I have heard much of thee, Robin, both of thy present and thy former state. And this, thy fair forest-queen, is, if tales say true, the lady Matilda Fitzwater."

Marian signed acknowledgment.

" Your father," said the king, " has approved his fidelity to me, by the loss of his lands, which the newness of my return, and many public cares, have not yet given me time to restore : but this justice shall be done to him, and to thee also, Robin, if thou wilt leave thy forest-life and resume thy earldom, and be a peer of Cœur-de-Lion : for braver heart and juster hand I never yet found."

Robin looked round on his men.

" Your followers," said the king, " shall have free pardon, and such of them as thou wilt part with shall have maintenance from me ; and if ever I confess to priest, it shall be to thy friar."

" Gramercy to your majesty," said the friar ; " and my inflictions shall be flasks of canary ; and if the number be (as in grave cases I may, peradventure, make it) too great for one frail mortality, I will relieve you by vicarious penance, and pour down my own throat the redundancy of the burden."

Robin and his followers embraced the king's proposal. A joyful meeting soon followed with the baron and Sir Guy of Gamwell : and Richard himself honoured with his own presence a formal solemnization of the nuptials of our lovers, whom he constantly distinguished with his peculiar regard.

The friar could not say, Farewell to the forest, without something of a heavy heart : and he sang as he turned his back upon its bounds, occasionally reverting his head :

Ye woods, that oft at sultry noon
 Have o'er me spread your massy shade :
Ye gushing streams, whose murmured tune
 Has in my ear sweet music made,
While, where the dancing pebbles show
 Deep in the restless fountain-pool
The gelid water's upward flow,
 My second flask was laid to cool :

Ye pleasant sights of leaf and flower :
 Ye pleasant sounds of bird and bee :
Ye sports of deer in sylvan bower :
 Ye feasts beneath the greenwood tree :
Ye baskings in the vernal sun :
 Ye slumbers in the summer dell :
Ye trophies that this arm has won :
 And must ye hear your friar's farewell ?

But the friar's farewell was not destined to be eternal. He was
domiciled as the family confessor of the earl and countess of
Huntingdon, who led a discreet and courtly life, and kept up old
hospitality in all its munificence, till the death of King Richard and
the usurpation of John, by placing their enemy in power, compelled
them to return to their greenwood sovereignty ; which, it is probable,
they would have before done from choice, if their love of sylvan
liberty had not been counteracted by their desire to retain the
friendship of Cœur-de-Lion. Their old and tried adherents, the friar
among the foremost, flocked again round their forest-banner ; and
in merry Sherwood they long lived together, the lady still retaining
her former name of Maid Marian, though the appellation was then
as much a misnomer as that of Little John.

THE END

THE MISFORTUNES
OF ELPHIN

Quod non exspectes ex transverso fit,
Et suprà nos Fortuna negotia curat :
Quare da nobis vina Falerna, puer.

PETRONIUS ARBITER.[1]

---

[1] What appears to be Peacock's translation of this passage is printed
on the title-page.   G.

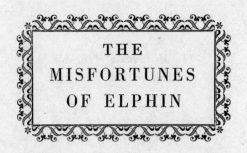

THE MISFORTUNES OF ELPHIN

Unlooked-for good betides us still,
And unanticipated ill :
Blind Fortune rules the hours that roll :
Then fill with good old wine the bowl.

The Misfortunes of Elphin
was first published in 1829

CONTENTS OF
THE MISFORTUNES OF ELPHIN

CHAPTER		PAGE
	Introduction by David Garnett . .	549
I	THE PROSPERITY OF GWAELOD .	553
II	THE DRUNKENNESS OF SEITHENYN	557
III	THE OPPRESSION OF GWENHIDWY.	564
IV	THE LAMENTATIONS OF GWYTHNO.	572
V	THE PRIZE OF THE WEIR . .	577
VI	THE EDUCATION OF TALIESIN .	580
VII	THE HUNTINGS OF MAELGON .	587
VIII	THE LOVE OF MELANGHEL . .	591
IX	THE SONGS OF DIGANWY . .	593
X	THE DISAPPOINTMENT OF RHÛN .	599
XI	THE HEROES OF DINAS VAWR .	602
XII	THE SPLENDOUR OF CAER LLEON.	608
XIII	THE GHOSTLINESS OF AVALLON .	615
XIV	THE RIGHT OF MIGHT . . .	621
XV	THE CIRCLE OF THE BARDS . .	626
XVI	THE JUDGMENTS OF ARTHUR	634

INDEX TO THE POETRY

		PAGE
1	The Circling of the Mead-Horns . . .	558
2	The Song of the Four Winds . . .	566
3	A Lament of Gwythno	574
4	Another Lament of Gwythno . . .	575
5	The Consolation of Elphin	579
6	The Mead Song	593
7	The Song of the Wind	595
8	The Indignation of Taliesin with the Bards of Maelgon Gwyneth	597
9	Taliesin and Melanghel	600
10	The War-Song of Dinas Vawr . . .	603
11	The Brilliancies of Winter	627
12	Merlin's Apple-Trees	628
13	The Massacre of the Britons . . .	630
14	The Cauldron of Ceridwen	632

INTRODUCTION TO
THE MISFORTUNES OF ELPHIN

In January 1819 Peacock took up regular employment at the India House at a salary of £600 a year, which was to rise until it reached £2,000. He was settled for life, and in November 1819 he wrote a businesslike proposal to Jane Gryffydh, to which she replied in a letter which betrays her agitation, warning him that:

"I fear you *very* much over-rate my worth, and I must tell you that I am less calculated to be *your* Companion than I *even* was at the period you knew me : Fortune pouring on my defenceless head an unceasing succession of her Evils, thereby enervating my mind and disabling it from receiving its due cultivation : this consideration will I *hope* dispose *you* to pardon want of presicion [*sic*] of style *and all* imperfections."

I take this to mean that she had scarcely opened a book since the year 1812. The marriage was possibly a mistake for other reasons, as those in disgrace with Fortune inevitably carry unhappiness with them. In this case the succession of evils did not cease, as Mrs Peacock's health broke down a few years after marriage and she became a semi-permanent invalid.

The marriage was, however, fortunate in one respect. Although Mrs Peacock could not read Æschylus or Nonnus, she is said to have spoken Welsh and to have been familiar with the ancient literature of Wales. Peacock is said to have learnt a little Welsh during his early visits to Wales, but a renewed interest in the language and its poetry was the result of his marriage, and *The Misfortunes of Elphin* was one of its fruits.

Maid Marian was not published until two years after Peacock's marriage, and another seven years elapsed before the publication of *The Misfortunes of Elphin*. The reason may have been partly that

Peacock had to keep regular hours during the day, and that his wife and family claimed his evenings until their removal to Halliford. It is also clear that the work of acting as Shelley's executor and carrying on endless negotiations between Sir Timothy and his agent on the one hand, and Mary Shelley on the other, must have taken up a great deal of time after the autumn of 1822.

But an obvious reason for the interval was the amount of research which went into the little tale. There is no reason to think Peacock was exaggerating when he told Sir Edward Strachey that he was proud of the fact that Welsh archæologists treated his book as a serious and valuable addition to Welsh history, and that he had great difficulty in getting at the true story of Taliesin's birth, as more than one learned authority had concealed his ignorance on the matter by saying that the story was too long to be told then.

Peacock's chief sources were *The Myvyrian Archaiology of Wales* (which is almost entirely in Welsh) and a monthly periodical, *The Cambro-Briton*, which had been started, in 1819, as the result of a widespread revival in the Welsh language and which continued to be published for some three years. *The Mabinogion* was not available in English until Lady Charlotte Guest's translation of 1838–49, and Nash's *Taliesin* not until 1858.

In *The Misfortunes of Elphin* Peacock has skilfully grafted the legend of Elphin on to that of Taliesin, and has moreover given them a background of the Court of King Arthur lacking in the originals.

Peacock wisely omitted the details of the pre-natal history of Taliesin, which being supernatural would not have harmonised with the ironic temper of the tale, and compressed a distorted version of them into one song, "The Cauldron of Ceridwen," in the pen-ultimate chapter of the book.

These strange events which led to Taliesin being found, like a second Moses in the bulrushes, by Elphin in his salmon-weir are contained in *The Mabinogion*. They have obviously a common origin with the Gaelic legend of how Finn MacCool got his gift of second sight by scalding his thumb and clapping it into his mouth when cooking the magic salmon for his master.

A striking characteristic of Peacock's novels is his introduction of songs, and in none of them do they appear more appropriately than in that devoted to the adventures of Welsh bards at the Court of King Arthur. The best of them, " The War-Song of Dinas Vawr," is Peacock's own; the others are translations or imitations from famous Welsh poems ascribed to the legendary bards who figure in the book. Whether this confers on " English Peacock " precedency over Taliesin, Llywarch Hen, and Merlin is a delicate point which reference to Nash's *Taliesin* may help those interested to elucidate.

The charm of *The Misfortunes of Elphin* has, however, little to do with the legends which went to the making of it, or with the ancient poems which are introduced by the way. It is almost entirely the result of the felicitous blend of irony and good humour, qualities which are all too seldom found together. Irony is usually bitter, a weapon only resorted to by those consumed by *sæva indignatio*. Peacock's irony is that of one of his great Gods as the Twilight descended upon them. It reaches its highest point whenever we encounter Prince Seithenyn ap Seithyn Saidi, one of the immortal drunkards in the literature of the world.

D. G.

THE MISFORTUNES OF ELPHIN

CHAPTER I

THE PROSPERITY OF GWAELOD

Regardless of the sweeping whirlwind's sway,
That, hush'd in grim repose, expects his evening prey.

GRAY.[1]

IN the beginning of the sixth century, when Uther Pendragon held the nominal sovereignty of Britain over a number of petty kings, Gwythno Garanhir was king of Caredigion. The most valuable portion of his dominions was the Great Plain of Gwaelod, an extensive tract of level land, stretching along that part of the sea-coast which now belongs to the counties of Merioneth and Cardigan. This district was populous and highly cultivated. It contained sixteen fortified towns, superior to all the towns and cities of the Cymry, excepting Caer Lleon upon Usk; and, like Caer Lleon, they bore in their architecture, their language, and their manners, vestiges of past intercourse with the Roman lords of the world. It contained also one of the three privileged ports of the isle of Britain, which was called the Port of Gwythno. This port, we may believe if we please, had not been unknown to the Phœnicians and Carthaginians, when they visited the island for metal, accommodating the inhabitants, in return, with luxuries which they would not otherwise have dreamed of, and which they could very well have done without; of course, in arranging the exchange of what they denominated equivalents, imposing on their simplicity, and taking advantage of their ignorance, according to the approved practice of civilised nations; which they called imparting the blessings of Phœnician and Carthaginian light.

An embankment of massy stone protected this lowland country from the sea, which was said, in traditions older than the embank-

[1] *The Bard*, II. 2. G.

ment, to have, in occasional spring-tides, paid short but unwelcome visits to the interior inhabitants, and to have, by slow aggressions, encroached considerably on the land. To prevent the repetition of the first of these inconveniences, and to check the progress of the second, the people of Gwaelod had built the stony rampart, which had withstood the shock of the waves for centuries, when Gwythno began his reign.

Gwythno, like other kings, found the business of governing too light a matter to fill up the vacancy of either his time or his head, and took to the more solid pursuits of harping and singing ; not forgetting feasting, in which he was glorious ; nor hunting, wherein he was mighty. His several pursuits composed a very harmonious triad. The chace conduced to the good cheer of the feast, and to the good appetite which consumed it ; the feast inspired the song ; and the song gladdened the feast, and celebrated the chace.

Gwythno and his subjects went on together very happily. They had little to do with him but to pay him revenue, and he had little to do with them but to receive it. Now and then they were called on to fight for the protection of his sacred person, and for the privilege of paying revenue to him rather than to any of the kings in his vicinity, a privilege of which they were particularly tenacious. His lands being far more fertile, and his people, consequently, far more numerous, than those of the rocky dwellers on his borders, he was always victorious in the defensive warfare to which he restricted his military achievements ; and, after the invaders of his dominions had received two or three inflictions of signal chastisement, they limited their aggressions to coming quietly in the night, and vanishing, before morning, with cattle : an heroic operation, in which the preeminent glory of Scotland renders the similar exploits of other nations not worth recording.

Gwythno was not fond of the sea : a moonstruck bard had warned him to beware of the oppression of Gwenhidwy ; [1] and he thought he could best do so by keeping as far as possible out of her way. He had a palace built of choice slate stone on the rocky banks of the Mawddach, just above the point where it quitted its native moun-

---

[1] *Gwen-hudiw*, " the white alluring one : " the name of a mermaid. Used figuratively for the elemental power of the sea. [P.]

tains, and entered the plain of Gwaelod. Here, among green woods
and sparkling waters, he lived in festal munificence, and expended
his revenue in encouraging agriculture, by consuming a large quantity
of produce.

Watchtowers were erected along the embankment, and watchmen
were appointed to guard against the first approaches of damage or
decay. The whole of these towers, and their companies of guards,
were subordinate to a central castle, which commanded the sea-port
already mentioned, and wherein dwelt Prince Seithenyn ap Seithyn
Saidi, who held the office of Arglwyd Gorwarcheidwad yr Argae
Breninawl, which signifies, in English, Lord High Commissioner of
Royal Embankment ; and he executed it as a personage so denominated might be expected to do : he drank the profits, and left the
embankment to his deputies, who left it to their assistants, who left
it to itself.

The condition of the head, in a composite as in a simple body,
affects the entire organization to the extremity of the tail, excepting
that, as the tail in the figurative body usually receives the largest
share in the distribution of punishment, and the smallest in the
distribution of reward, it has the stronger stimulus to ward off evil,
and the smaller supply of means to indulge in diversion ; and it
sometimes happens that one of the least regarded of the component
parts of the said tail will, from a pure sense of duty, or an inveterate
love of business, or an oppressive sense of ennui, or a development
of the organ of order, or some other equally cogent reason, cheerfully
undergo all the care and labour, of which the honour and profit will
redound to higher quarters.

Such a component portion of the Gwaelod High Commission of
Royal Embankment was Teithrin ap Tathral, who had the charge
of a watchtower where the embankment terminated at the point of
Mochres, in the high land of Ardudwy.   Teithrin kept his portion of
the embankment in exemplary condition, and paced with daily care
the limits of his charge ; but one day, by some accident, he strayed
beyond them, and observed symptoms of neglect that filled him with
dismay.   This circumstance induced him to proceed till his wanderings brought him round to the embankment's southern termination
in the high land of Caredigion.   He met with abundant hospitality

at the towers of his colleagues, and at the castle of Seithenyn : he was supposed to be walking for his amusement ; he was asked no questions, and he carefully abstained from asking any. He examined and observed in silence ; and, when he had completed his observations, he hastened to the palace of Gwythno.

Preparations were making for a high festival, and Gwythno was composing an ode. Teithrin knew better than to interrupt him in his *awen*.[1]

Gwythno had a son named Elphin, who is celebrated in history as the most expert of fishers. Teithrin, finding the king impracticable, went in search of the young prince.

Elphin had been all the morning fishing in the Mawddach, in a spot where the river, having quitted the mountains and not yet entered the plain, ran in alternate streams and pools, sparkling through a pastoral valley. Elphin sat under an ancient ash, enjoying the calm brightness of an autumnal noon, and the melody and beauty of the flying stream, on which the shifting sunbeams fell chequering through the leaves. The monotonous music of the river, and the profound stillness of the air, had contributed to the deep abstraction of a meditation into which Elphin had fallen. He was startled into attention by a sudden rush of the wind through the trees, and during the brief interval of transition from the state of reverie to that of perfect consciousness, he heard, or seemed to hear, in the gust that hurried by him, the repetition of the words, " Beware of the oppression of Gwenhidwy." The gust was momentary : the leaves ceased to rustle, and the deep silence of nature returned.

The prophecy, which had long haunted the memory and imagination of his father, had been often repeated to Elphin, and had sometimes occupied his thoughts, but it had formed no part of his recent meditation, and he could not persuade himself that the words had not been actually spoken near him. He emerged from the shade of the trees that fringed the river, and looked round him from the rocky bank.

At this moment Teithrin ap Tathral discovered and approached him.

Elphin knew him not, and inquired his name. He answered, " Teithrin ap Tathral."

" And what seek you here ? " said Elphin.

---

[1] The rapturous and abstracted state of poetical inspiration. [P.]

"I seek," answered Teithrin, "the Prince of Gwaelod, Elphin ap Gwythno Garanhir."

"You spoke," said Elphin, "as you approached." Teithrin answered in the negative.

"Assuredly you did," said Elphin. "You repeated the words, 'Beware of the oppression of Gwenhidwy.'"

Teithrin denied having spoken the words; but their mysterious impression made Elphin listen readily to his information and advice; and the result of their conference was a determination, on the part of the Prince, to accompany Teithrin ap Tathral on a visit of remonstrance to the Lord High Commissioner.

They crossed the centre of the enclosed country to the privileged port of Gwythno, near which stood the castle of Seithenyn. They walked towards the castle along a portion of the embankment, and Teithrin pointed out to the Prince its dilapidated condition. The sea shone with the glory of the setting sun; the air was calm; and the white surf, tinged with the crimson of sunset, broke lightly on the sands below. Elphin turned his eyes from the dazzling splendour of ocean to the green meadows of the Plain of Gwaelod; the trees, that in the distance thickened into woods; the wreaths of smoke rising from among them, marking the solitary cottages, or the populous towns; the massy barrier of mountains beyond, with the forest rising from their base; the precipices frowning over the forest; and the clouds resting on their summits, reddened with the reflection of the west. Elphin gazed earnestly on the peopled plain, reposing in the calm of evening between the mountains and the sea, and thought, with deep feelings of secret pain, how much of life and human happiness was intrusted to the ruinous mound on which he stood.

CHAPTER II

THE DRUNKENNESS OF SEITHENYN

The three immortal drunkards of the isle of Britain: Ceraint of Essyllwg; Gwrtheyrn Gwrthenau; and Seithenyn ap Seithyn Saidi.
TRIADS OF THE ISLE OF BRITAIN.

THE sun had sunk beneath the waves when they reached the castle of Seithenyn. The sound of the harp and the song saluted them as they approached it. As they entered the great hall, which was already blazing with torchlight, they found his highness, and his highness's household, convincing themselves and each other with wine and wassail, of the excellence of their system of virtual superintendence ; and the following jovial chorus broke on the ears of the visitors :

THE CIRCLING OF THE MEAD HORNS [1]

Fill the blue horn, the blue buffalo horn :
Natural is mead in the buffalo horn :
As the cuckoo in spring, as the lark in the morn,
So natural is mead in the buffalo horn.

As the cup of the flower to the bee when he sips,
Is the full cup of mead to the true Briton's lips :
From the flower-cups of summer, on field and on tree,
Our mead cups are filled by the vintager bee.

Seithenyn [2] ap Seithyn, the generous, the bold,
Drinks the wine of the stranger from vessels of gold ; [3]
But we from the horn, the blue silver-rimmed horn,
Drink the ale and the mead in our fields that were born.

The ale-froth is white, and the mead sparkles bright ;
They both smile apart, and with smiles they unite : [4]
The mead from the flower, and the ale from the corn,
Smile, sparkle, and sing in the buffalo horn.

The horn, the blue horn, cannot stand on its tip ;
Its path is right on from the hand to the lip :
Though the bowl and the wine-cup our tables adorn,
More natural the draught from the buffalo horn.

But Seithenyn ap Seithyn, the generous, the bold,
Drinks the bright-flowing wine from the far-gleaming gold :
The wine, in the bowl by his lip that is worn,
Shall be glorious as mead in the buffalo horn.

---

[1] Suggested by a poem included in Parry's Welsh Melodies, reprinted in the *Cambro-Briton*, Vol. III, Jan. 1822, p. 185, the words of which are by Mrs. Hemans and which begins : " Fill high the blue Hirlas, that shines like the wave. . . ." This is itself imitated from the *Hirlas* (or drinking horn) of Prince Owain Kyveiliog, the subject of which is feasting after victory. G.

[2] The accent is on the second syllable : Seithényn. [P.]

[3] Gwin . . . o eur . . . ANEURIN. [P.]

[4] The mixture of ale and mead made *bradawd*, a favourite drink of the Ancient Britons. [P.]

The horns circle fast, but their fountains will last,
As the stream passes ever, and never is past :
Exhausted so quickly, replenished so soon,
They wax and they wane like the horns of the moon.

Fill high the blue horn, the blue buffalo horn ;
Fill high the long silver-rimmed buffalo horn :
While the roof of the hall by our chorus is torn,
Fill, fill to the brim, the deep silver-rimmed horn.

Elphin and Teithrin stood some time on the floor of the hall before
they attracted the attention of Seithenyn, who, during the chorus,
was tossing and flourishing his golden goblet. The chorus had
scarcely ended when he noticed them, and immediately roared aloud,
" You are welcome all four."

Elphin answered, " We thank you : we are but two."

" Two or four," said Seithenyn, " all is one. You are welcome
all. When a stranger enters, the custom in other places is to begin
by washing his feet. My custom is, to begin by washing his throat.
Seithenyn ap Seithyn Saidi bids you welcome."

Elphin, taking the wine-cup, answered, " Elphin ap Gwythno
Garanhir thanks you."

Seithenyn started up. He endeavoured to straighten himself into
perpendicularity, and to stand steadily on his legs. He accomplished
half his object by stiffening all his joints but those of his ancles, and
from these the rest of his body vibrated upwards with the inflexibility
of a bar. After thus oscillating for a time, like an inverted
pendulum, finding that the attention requisite to preserve his
rigidity absorbed all he could collect of his dissipated energies, and
that he required a portion of them for the management of his voice,
which he felt a dizzy desire to wield with peculiar steadiness in the
presence of the son of the king, he suddenly relaxed the muscles that
perform the operation of sitting, and dropped into his chair like a
plummet. He then, with a gracious gesticulation, invited Prince
Elphin to take his seat on his right hand, and proceeded to compose
himself into a dignified attitude, throwing his body back into the left
corner of his chair, resting his left elbow on its arm and his left
cheekbone on the middle of the back of his left hand, placing his left
foot on a footstool, and stretching out his right leg as straight and

as far as his position allowed. He had thus his right hand at liberty, for the ornament of his eloquence and the conduct of his liquor.

Elphin seated himself at the right hand of Seithenyn. Teithrin remained at the end of the hall : on which Seithenyn exclaimed, " Come on, man, come on. What, if you be not the son of a king, you are the guest of Seithenyn ap Seithyn Saidi. The most honourable place to the most honourable guest, and the next most honourable place to the next most honourable guest ; the least honourable guest above the most honourable inmate ; and, where there are but two guests, be the most honourable who he may, the least honourable of the two is next in honour to the most honourable of the two, because they are no more but two ; and, where there are only two, there can be nothing between. Therefore sit, and drink. GWIN O EUR : wine from gold."

Elphin motioned Teithrin to approach, and sit next to him.

Prince Seithenyn, whose liquor was " his eating and his drinking solely,"[1] seemed to measure the gastronomy of his guests by his own ; but his groom of the pantry thought the strangers might be disposed to eat, and placed before them a choice of provision, on which Teithrin ap Tathral did vigorous execution.

" I pray your excuses," said Seithenyn, " my stomach is weak, and I am subject to dizziness in the head, and my memory is not so good as it was, and my faculties of attention are somewhat impaired, and I would dilate more upon the topic, whereby you should hold me excused, but I am troubled with a feverishness and parching of the mouth, that very much injures my speech, and impedes my saying all I would say, and will say before I have done, in token of my loyalty and fealty to your highness and your highness's house. I must just moisten my lips, and I will then proceed with my observations. Cupbearer, fill."[2]

" Prince Seithenyn," said Elphin, " I have visited you on a subject of deep moment. Reports have been brought to me, that the embankment, which has been so long intrusted to your care, is in a state of dangerous decay."

---

[1] Beaumont and Fletcher : *The Scornful Lady*, Act IV, Sc. 2. See *Gryll Grange*, p. 960. G.

[2] *Diwallow di venestr*. Each verse of the *Hirlas* of Prince Owain Kyveiliog begins with these words. G.

"Decay," said Seithenyn, "is one thing, and danger is another.[1] Every thing that is old must decay. That the embankment is old, I am free to confess ; that it is somewhat rotten in parts, I will not altogether deny ; that it is any the worse for that, I do most sturdily gainsay. It does its business well : it works well : it keeps out the water from the land, and it lets in the wine upon the High Commission of Embankment. Cupbearer, fill. Our ancestors were wiser than we : they built it in their wisdom ; and, if we should be so rash as to try to mend it, we should only mar it."

"The stonework," said Teithrin, "is sapped and mined : the piles are rotten, broken, and dislocated : the floodgates and sluices are leaky and creaky."

"That is the beauty of it," said Seithenyn. "Some parts of it are rotten, and some parts of it are sound."

"It is well," said Elphin, "that some parts are sound : it were better that all were so."

"So I have heard some people say before," said Seithenyn ; "perverse people, blind to venerable antiquity : that very unamiable sort of people, who are in the habit of indulging their reason. But I say, the parts that are rotten give elasticity to those that are sound : they give them elasticity, elasticity, elasticity. If it were all sound, it would break by its own obstinate stiffness : the soundness is checked by the rottenness, and the stiffness is balanced by the elasticity. There is nothing so dangerous as innovation. See the waves in the equinoctial storms, dashing and clashing, roaring and pouring, spattering and battering, rattling and battling against it. I would not be so presumptuous as to say, I could build any thing that would stand against them half an hour ; and here this immortal old work, which God forbid the finger of modern mason should bring into jeopardy, this immortal work has stood for centuries, and will stand for centuries more, if we let it alone. It is well : it works well : let well alone. Cupbearer, fill. It was half rotten when I was born, and that is a conclusive reason why it should be three parts rotten when I die."

[1] Prince Seithenyn's speech is modelled on the arguments used by the opponents of Reform who exaggerated the dangers of tampering in any way with the British Constitution.   G.

The whole body of the High Commission roared approbation.

" And after all," said Seithenyn, " the worst that could happen would be the overflow of a spring tide, for that was the worst that happened before the embankment was thought of ; and, if the high water should come in, as it did before, the low water would go out again, as it did before. We should be no deeper in it than our ancestors were, and we could mend as easily as they could make."

" The level of the sea," said Teithrin, " is materially altered."

" The level of the sea ! " exclaimed Seithenyn. " Who ever heard of such a thing as altering the level of the sea ? Alter the level of that bowl of wine before you, in which, as I sit here, I see a very ugly reflection of your very goodlooking face. Alter the level of that : drink up the reflection : let me see the face without the reflection, and leave the sea to level itself."

" Not to level the embankment," said Teithrin.

" Good, very good," said Seithenyn. " I love a smart saying, though it hits at me. But, whether yours is a smart saying or no, I do not very clearly see ; and, whether it hits at me or no, I do not very sensibly feel. But all is one. Cupbearer, fill.

" I think," pursued Seithenyn, looking as intently as he could at Teithrin ap Tathral, " I have seen something very like you before. There was a fellow here the other day very like you : he stayed here some time : he would not talk : he did nothing but drink : he used to drink till he could not stand, and then he went walking about the embankment. I suppose he thought it wanted mending ; but he did not say any thing. If he had, I should have told him to embank his own throat, to keep the liquor out of that. That would have posed him : he could not have answered that : he would not have had a word to say for himself after that."

" He must have been a miraculous person," said Teithrin, " to walk when he could not stand."

" All is one for that," said Seithenyn. " Cupbearer, fill."

" Prince Seithenyn," said Elphin, " if I were not aware that wine speaks in the silence of reason, I should be astonished at your strange vindication of your neglect of duty, which I take shame to myself for not having sooner known and remedied. The wise bard has well observed, ' Nothing is done without the eye of the king.' "

" I am very sorry," said Seithenyn, " that you see things in a wrong light : but we will not quarrel for three reasons : first, because you are the son of the king, and may do and say what you please, without any one having a right to be displeased : second, because I never quarrel with a guest, even if he grows riotous in his cups : third, because there is nothing to quarrel about ; and perhaps that is the best reason of the three ; or rather the first is the best, because you are the son of the king ; and the third is the second, that is, the second best, because there is nothing to quarrel about ; and the second is nothing to the purpose, because, though guests will grow riotous in their cups, in spite of my good orderly example, God forbid I should say, that is the case with you. And I completely agree in the truth of your remark, that reason speaks in the silence of wine."

Seithenyn accompanied his speech with a vehement swinging of his right hand : in so doing, at this point, he dropped his cup : a sudden impulse of rash volition, to pick it dexterously up before he resumed his discourse, ruined all his devices for maintaining dignity ; in stooping forward from his chair, he lost his balance, and fell prostrate on the floor.

The whole body of the High Commission arose in simultaneous confusion, each zealous to be the foremost in uplifting his fallen chief. In the vehemence of their uprise, they hurled the benches backward and the tables forward ; the crash of cups and bowls accompanied their overthrow ; and rivulets of liquor ran gurgling through the hall. The household wished to redeem the credit of their leader in the eyes of the Prince ; but the only service they could render him was to participate in his discomfiture ; for Seithenyn, as he was first in dignity, was also, as was fitting, hardest in skull ; and that which had impaired his equilibrium had utterly destroyed theirs. Some fell, in the first impulse, with the tables and benches ; others were tripped up by the rolling bowls ; and the remainder fell at different points of progression, by jostling against each other, or stumbling over those who had fallen before them.

CHAPTER III

THE OPPRESSION OF GWENHIDWY

> Nid meddw y dyn a allo
> Cwnu ei hun a rhodio,
> Ac yved rhagor ddiawd :
> Nid yw hyny yn veddwdawd.
>
> Not drunk is he, who from the floor
> Can rise alone, and still drink more ;
> But drunk is he, who prostrate lies,
> Without the power to drink or rise.

A SIDE door, at the upper end of the hall, to the left of Seithenyn's chair, opened, and a beautiful young girl entered the hall, with her domestic bard, and her attendant maidens.

It was Angharad, the daughter of Seithenyn. The tumult had drawn her from the solitude of her chamber, apprehensive that some evil might befall her father in that incapability of self-protection to which he made a point of bringing himself by set of sun. She gracefully saluted Prince Elphin, and directed the cupbearers, (who were bound, by their office, to remain half sober till the rest of the company were finished off, after which they indemnified themselves at leisure,) she directed the cupbearers to lift up Prince Seithenyn, and bear him from the hall. The cupbearers reeled off with their lord, who had already fallen asleep, and who now began to play them a pleasant march with his nose, to inspirit their progression.

Elphin gazed with delight on the beautiful apparition, whose gentle and serious loveliness contrasted so strikingly with the broken trophies and fallen heroes of revelry that lay scattered at her feet.

"Stranger," she said, "this seems an unfitting place for you : let me conduct you where you will be more agreeably lodged."

"Still less should I deem it fitting for you, fair maiden," said Elphin.

She answered, "The pleasure of her father is the duty of Angharad."

Elphin was desirous to protract the conversation, and this very desire took from him the power of speaking to the purpose. He paused for a moment to collect his ideas, and Angharad stood still, in apparent expectation that he would show symptoms of following, in compliance with her invitation.

In this interval of silence, he heard the loud dashing of the sea, and the blustering of the wind through the apertures of the walls.

This supplied him with what has been, since Britain was Britain, the alpha and omega of British conversation. He said, " It seems a stormy night."

She answered, " We are used to storms : we are far from the mountains, between the lowlands and the sea, and the winds blow round us from all quarters."

There was another pause of deep silence. The noise of the sea was louder, and the gusts pealed like thunder through the apertures. Amidst the fallen and sleeping revellers, the confused and littered hall, the low and wavering torches, Angharad, lovely always, shone with single and surpassing loveliness. The gust died away in murmurs, and swelled again into thunder, and died away in murmurs again ; and, as it died away, mixed with the murmurs of ocean, a voice, that seemed one of the many voices of the wind, pronounced the ominous words, " Beware of the oppression of Gwenhidwy."

They looked at each other, as if questioning whether all had heard alike.

" Did you not hear a voice ? " said Angharad, after a pause.

" The same," said Elphin, " which has once before seemed to say to me, ' Beware of the oppression of Gwenhidwy.' "

Teithrin hurried forth on the rampart : Angharad turned pale, and leaned against a pillar of the hall. Elphin was amazed and awed, absorbed as his feelings were in her. The sleepers on the floor made an uneasy movement, and uttered an inarticulate cry.

Teithrin returned. " What saw you ? " said Elphin.

Teithrin answered, " A tempest is coming from the west. The moon has waned three days, and is half hidden in clouds, just visible above the mountains : the bank of clouds is black in the west ; the scud is flying before them ; and the white waves are rolling to the shore."

" This is the highest of the springtides," said Angharad, " and they are very terrible in the storms from the west, when the spray flies over the embankment, and the breakers shake the tower which has its foot in the surf."

" Whence was the voice," said Elphin, " which we heard erewhile ?

Was it the cry of a sleeper in his drink, or an error of the fancy, or a warning voice from the elements ? "

" It was surely nothing earthly," said Angharad, " nor was it an error of the fancy, for we all heard the words, ' Beware of the oppression of Gwenhidwy.'   Often and often, in the storms of the spring-tides, have I feared to see her roll her power over the fields of Gwaelod."

" Pray heaven she do not tonight," said Teithrin.

" Can there be such a danger ? " said Elphin.

" I think," said Teithrin, " of the decay I have seen, and I fear the voice I have heard."

A long pause of deep silence ensued, during which they heard the intermitting peals of the wind, and the increasing sound of the rising sea, swelling progressively into wilder and more menacing tumult, till, with one terrific impulse, the whole violence of the equinoctial tempest seemed to burst upon the shore.   It was one of those tempests which occur once in several centuries, and which, by their extensive devastations, are chronicled to eternity ; for a storm that signalizes its course with extraordinary destruction, becomes as worthy of celebration as a hero for the same reason.   The old bard seemed to be of this opinion ; for the turmoil which appalled Elphin, and terrified Angharad, fell upon his ears as the sound of inspiration : the *awen* came upon him ; and, seizing his harp, he mingled his voice and his music with the uproar of the elements :

THE SONG OF THE FOUR WINDS [1]

Wind from the north : the young spring day
Is pleasant on the sunny mead ;
The merry harps at evening play ;
The dance gay youths and maidens lead :
The thrush makes chorus from the thorn :
The mighty drinker fills his horn.

---

[1] This poem is a specimen of a numerous class of ancient Welsh poems, in which each stanza begins with a repetition of the predominant idea, and terminates with a proverb, more or less applicable to the subject.   In some poems, the sequence of the main images is regular and connected, and the proverbial terminations strictly appropriate : in others, the sequence of the main images is loose and incoherent, and the proverbial termination has little or nothing to do with the subject of the stanza.   The basis of the poem in the text is in the *Englynion* of Llwyarch Hên.   [P.]

Wind from the east : the shore is still ;
The mountain-clouds fly tow'rds the sea ;
The ice is on the winter-rill ;
The great hall fire is blazing free :
The prince's circling feast is spread :
Drink fills with fumes the brainless head.

Wind from the south : in summer shade
'Tis sweet to hear the loud harp ring ;
Sweet is the step of comely maid,
Who to the bard a cup doth bring :
The black crow flies where carrion lies :
Where pignuts lurk, the swine will work.

Wind from the west : the autumnal deep
Rolls on the shore its billowy pride :
He, who the rampart's watch must keep,
Will mark with awe the rising tide :
The high springtide, that bursts its mound,
May roll o'er miles of level ground.

Wind from the west : the mighty wave
Of ocean bounds o'er rock and sand ;
The foaming surges roar and rave
Against the bulwarks of the land :
When waves are rough, and winds are high,
Good is the land that's high and dry.

Wind from the west : the storm-clouds rise ;
The breakers rave ; the whirlblasts roar ;
The mingled rage of seas and skies
Bursts on the low and lonely shore :
When safety's far, and danger nigh,
Swift feet the readiest aid supply.

Wind from the west——

His song was cut short by a tremendous crash. The tower, which
had its foot in the sea, had long been sapped by the waves ; the
storm had prematurely perfected the operation, and the tower fell
into the surf, carrying with it a portion of the wall of the main
building, and revealing, through the chasm, the white raging of the
breakers beneath the blackness of the midnight storm. The wind
rushed into the hall, extinguishing the torches within the line of its
course, tossing the grey locks and loose mantle of the bard, and the

light white drapery and long black tresses of Angharad. With the crash of the falling tower, and the simultaneous shriek of the women, the sleepers started from the floor, staring with drunken amazement; and, shortly after, reeling like an Indian from the wine-rolling Hydaspes,[1] in staggered Seithenyn ap Seithyn.

Seithenyn leaned against a pillar, and stared at the sea through the rifted wall, with wild and vacant surprise. He perceived that there was an innovation, and he felt that he was injured: how, or by whom, he did not quite so clearly discern. He looked at Elphin and Teithrin, at his daughter, and at the members of his household, with a long and dismal aspect of blank and mute interrogation, modified by the struggling consciousness of puzzled self-importance, which seemed to require from his chiefship some word of command in this incomprehensible emergency. But the longer he looked, the less clearly he saw; and the longer he pondered, the less he understood. He felt the rush of the wind; he saw the white foam of the sea; his ears were dizzy with their mingled roar. He remained at length motionless, leaning against the pillar, and gazing on the breakers with fixed and glaring vacancy.

" The sleepers of Gwaelod," said Elphin, " they who sleep in peace and security, trusting to the vigilance of Seithenyn, what will become of them ? "

" Warn them with the beacon fire," said Teithrin, " if there be fuel on the summit of the landward tower."

" That of course has been neglected too," said Elphin.

" Not so," said Angharad, " that has been my charge."

Teithrin seized a torch, and ascended the eastern tower, and, in a few minutes, the party in the hall beheld the breakers reddening with the reflected fire, and deeper and yet deeper crimson tinging the whirling foam, and sheeting the massy darkness of the bursting waves.

Seithenyn turned his eyes on Elphin. His recollection of him was

---

[1] In the fourteenth and fifteenth books of the *Dionysiaca* of Nonnus, Bacchus changes the river Astacis into wine; and the multitudinous army of water-drinking Indians, proceeding to quench their thirst in the stream, become franticly drunk, and fall an easy prey to the Bacchic invaders. In the thirty-fifth book, the experiment is repeated on the Hydaspes. " *Ainsi conquesta Bacchus l'Inde*," as Rabelais has it. [P.]

extremely faint, and the longer he looked on him he remembered him the less. He was conscious of the presence of strangers, and of the occurrence of some signal mischief, and associated the two circumstances in his dizzy perceptions with a confused but close connexion. He said at length, looking sternly at Elphin, " I do not know what right the wind has to blow upon me here ; nor what business the sea has to show itself here ; nor what business you have here : but one thing is very evident, that either my castle or the sea is on fire ; and I shall be glad to know who has done it, for terrible shall be the vengeance of Seithenyn ap Seithyn. Show me the enemy," he pursued, drawing his sword furiously, and flourishing it over his head, " Show me the enemy ; show me the enemy."

An unusual tumult mingled with the roar of the waves ; a sound, the same in kind, but greater in degree, with that produced by the loose stones of the beach, which are rolled to and fro by the surf.

Teithrin rushed into the hall, exclaiming, " All is over ! the mound is broken ; and the springtide is rolling through the breach."

Another portion of the castle wall fell into the mining waves, and, by the dim and thickly-clouded moonlight, and the red blaze of the beacon fire, they beheld a torrent pouring in from the sea upon the plain, and rushing immediately beneath the castle walls, which, as well as the points of the embankment that formed the sides of the breach, continued to crumble away into the waters.

" Who has done this ? " vociferated Seithenyn. " Show me the enemy."

" There is no enemy but the sea," said Elphin, " to which you, in your drunken madness, have abandoned the land. Think, if you can think, of what is passing in the plain. The storm drowns the cries of your victims ; but the curses of the perishing are upon you."

" Show me the enemy," vociferated Seithenyn, flourishing his sword more furiously.

Angharad looked deprecatingly at Elphin, who abstained from further reply.

" There is no enemy but the sea," said Teithrin, " against which your sword avails not."

" Who dares to say so ? " said Seithenyn. " Who dares to say that there is an enemy on earth against whom the sword of Seithenyn ap Seithyn is unavailing ? Thus, thus I prove the falsehood."

And, springing suddenly forward, he leaped into the torrent, flourishing his sword as he descended.

" Oh, my unhappy father ! " sobbed Angharad, veiling her face with her arm on the shoulder of one of her female attendants, whom Elphin dexterously put aside, and substituted himself as the supporter of the desolate beauty.

" We must quit the castle," said Teithrin, " or we shall be buried in its ruins. We have but one path of safety, along the summit of the embankment, if there be not another breach between us and the high land, and if we can keep our footing in this hurricane. But there is no alternative. The walls are melting away like snow."

The bard, who was now recovered from his *awen*, and beginning to be perfectly alive to his own personal safety, conscious at the same time that the first duty of his privileged order was to animate the less-gifted multitude by examples of right conduct in trying emergencies, was the first to profit by Teithrin's admonition, and to make the best of his way through the door that opened to the embankment, on which he had no sooner set his foot than he was blown down by the wind, his harp-strings ringing as he fell. He was indebted to the impediment of his harp, for not being rolled down the mound into the waters which were rising within.

Teithrin picked him up, and admonished him to abandon his harp to its fate, and fortify his steps with a spear. The bard murmured objections : and even the reflection that he could more easily get another harp than another life, did not reconcile him to parting with his beloved companion. He got over the difficulty by slinging his harp, cumbrous as it was, to his left side, and taking a spear in his right hand.

Angharad, recovering from the first shock of Seithenyn's catastrophe, became awake to the imminent danger. The spirit of the Cymric female, vigilant and energetic in peril, disposed her and her attendant maidens to use their best exertions for their own preservation. Following the advice and example of Elphin and Teithrin, they armed themselves with spears, which they took down from the walls.

Teithrin led the way, striking the point of his spear firmly into the earth, and leaning from it on the wind : Angharad followed in the same manner : Elphin followed Angharad, looking as earnestly to her safety as was compatible with moderate care of his own : the attendant maidens followed Elphin ; and the bard, whom the result of his first experiment had rendered unambitious of the van, followed the female train. Behind them went the cupbearers, whom the accident of sobriety had qualified to march : and behind them reeled and roared those of the bacchanal rout who were able and willing to move ; those more especially who had wives or daughters to support their tottering steps. Some were incapable of locomotion, and others, in the heroic madness of liquor, sat down to await their destiny, as they finished the half-drained vessels.

The bard, who had somewhat of a picturesque eye, could not help sparing a little leisure from the care of his body, to observe the effects before him : the volumed blackness of the storm ; the white bursting of the breakers in the faint and scarcely-perceptible moonlight ; the rushing and rising of the waters within the mound ; the long floating hair and waving drapery of the young women ; the red light of the beacon fire falling on them from behind ; the surf rolling up the side of the embankment, and breaking almost at their feet ; the spray flying above their heads ; and the resolution with which they impinged the stony ground with their spears, and bore themselves up against the wind.

Thus they began their march. They had not proceeded far, when the tide began to recede, the wind to abate somewhat of its violence, and the moon to look on them at intervals through the rifted clouds, disclosing the desolation of the inundated plain, silvering the tumultuous surf, gleaming on the distant mountains, and revealing a lengthened prospect of their solitary path, that lay in its irregular line like a ribbon on the deep.

CHAPTER IV

THE LAMENTATIONS OF GWYTHNO

Οὐ παύσομαι τὰς Χάριτας
Μούσαις συγκαταμιγνύς,
Ἡδίσταν συζυγίαν.

EURIPIDES.[1]

Not, though grief my age defaces,
Will I cease, in concert dear,
Blending still the gentle graces
With the muses more severe.

KING GWYTHNO had feasted joyously, and had sung his new ode to a chosen party of his admiring subjects, amidst their, of course, enthusiastic applause. He heard the storm raging without, as he laid himself down to rest : he thought it a very hard case for those who were out in it, especially on the sea ; congratulated himself on his own much more comfortable condition ; and went to sleep with a pious reflection on the goodness of Providence to himself.

He was roused from a pleasant dream by a confused and tumultuous dissonance, that mingled with the roar of the tempest. Rising with much reluctance, and looking forth from his window, he beheld in the moonlight a half-naked multitude, larger than his palace thrice multiplied could have contained, pressing round the gates, and clamouring for admission and shelter ; while beyond them his eye fell on the phænomenon of stormy waters, rolling in the place of the fertile fields from which he derived his revenue.

Gwythno, though a king and his own laureate, was not without sympathy for the people who had the honour and happiness of victualling his royal house, and he issued forth on his balcony full of perplexities and alarms, stunned by the sudden sense of the half-understood calamity, and his head still dizzy from the effects of abruptly-broken sleep, and the vapours of the overnight's glorious festival.

Gwythno was altogether a reasonably good sort of person, and a poet of some note. His people were somewhat proud of him on the latter score, and very fond of him on the former ; for even the tenth part of those homely virtues, that decorate the memories of

[1] *Hercules Furens*, l. 674.   G.

" husbands kind and fathers dear " in every churchyard, are matters of plebeian admiration in the persons of royalty ; and every tangible point in every such virtue so located, becomes a convenient peg for the suspension of love and loyalty. While, therefore, they were unanimous in consigning the soul of Seithenyn to a place that no well-bred divine will name to a polite congregation, they overflowed, in the abundance of their own griefs, with a portion of sympathy for Gwythno, and saluted him, as he issued forth on his balcony, with a hearty *Duw cadw y Brenin*, or God save the King, which he returned with a benevolent wave of the hand ; but they followed it up by an intense vociferation for food and lodging, which he received with a pitiful shake of the head.

Meanwhile the morning dawned : the green spots, that peered with the ebbing tide above the waste of waters, only served to indicate the irremediableness of the general desolation.

Gwythno proceeded to hold a conference with his people, as deliberately as the stormy state of the weather and their minds, and the confusion of his own, would permit. The result of the conference was, that they should use their best exertions to catch some stray beeves, which had escaped the inundation, and were lowing about the rocks in search of new pastures. This measure was carried into immediate effect : the victims were killed and roasted, carved, distributed, and eaten, in a very Homeric fashion, and washed down with a large portion of the contents of the royal cellars ; after which, having more leisure to dwell on their losses, the fugitives of Gwaelod proceeded to make loud lamentation, all collectively for home and for country, and severally for wife or husband, parent or child, whom the flood had made its victims.

In the midst of these lamentations arrived Elphin and Angharad, with her bard and attendant maidens, and Teithrin ap Tathral. Gwythno, after a consultation, despatched Teithrin and Angharad's domestic bard on an embassy to the court of Uther Pendragon, and to such of the smaller kings as lay in the way, to solicit such relief as their several majesties might be able and willing to afford to a king in distress. It is said, that the bard, finding a royal bardship vacant in a more prosperous court, made the most of himself in the market, and stayed where he was better fed and lodged than he could expect to be in Caredigion ; but that Teithrin returned, with many valuable gifts, and most especially one from Merlin, being a hamper, which multiplied an hundredfold by morning whatever was put into it overnight, so that, for a ham and a flask put by in the evening, an hundred hams and an hundred flasks were taken out in the morning. It is at least certain that such a hamper is enumerated among the thirteen wonders of Merlin's art, and, in the authentic catalogue thereof, is called the Hamper of Gwythno.[1]

Be this as it may, Gwythno, though shorn of the beams of his revenue, kept possession of his palace. Elphin married Angharad, and built a salmon-weir on the Mawddach, the produce of which, with that of a series of beehives, of which his princess and her maidens made mead, constituted for some time the principal wealth and subsistence of the royal family of Caredigion.

King Gwythno, while his son was delving or fishing, and his daughter spinning or making mead, sat all day on the rocks, with his harp between his knees, watching the rolling of ocean over the locality of his past dominion, and pouring forth his soul in pathetic song on the change of his own condition, and the mutability of human things. Two of his songs of lamentation have been preserved by tradition : they are the only relics of his muse which time has spared.

GWYDDNAU EI CANT,

PAN DDOAI Y MOR DROS CANTREV Y GWAELAWD.

A SONG OF GWYTHNO GARANHIR,

ON THE INUNDATION OF THE SEA OVER THE PLAIN OF GWAELOD.

> Stand forth, Seithenyn : winds are high :
> Look down beneath the lowering sky ;
> Look from the rock : what meets thy sight ?
> Nought but the breakers rolling white.

> Stand forth, Seithenyn : winds are still :
> Look from the rock and heathy hill
> For Gwythno's realm : what meets thy view ?
> Nought but the ocean's desert blue.

---

[1] The basket of Gwythno Garanhir.   It was one of the thirteen precious things in Britain, not one of the thirteen wonders of Merlin's art.   G.

Curst be the treacherous mound, that gave
A passage to the mining wave :
Curst be the cup, with mead-froth crowned,
That charmed from thought the trusted mound.

A tumult, and a cry to heaven !
The white surf breaks ; the mound is riven :
Through the wide rift the ocean-spring
Bursts with tumultuous ravaging.

The western ocean's stormy might
Is curling o'er the rampart's height :
Destruction strikes with want and scorn
Presumption, from abundance born.

The tumult of the western deep
Is on the winds, affrighting sleep :
It thunders at my chamber-door ;
It bids me wake, to sleep no more.

The tumult of the midnight sea
Swells inland, wildly, fearfully :
The mountain-caves respond its shocks
Among the unaccustomed rocks.

The tumult of the vext sea-coast
Rolls inland like an armed host :
It leaves, for flocks and fertile land,
But foaming waves and treacherous sand.

The wild sea rolls where long have been
Glad homes of men, and pastures green :
To arrogance and wealth succeed
Wide ruin and avenging need.

Seithenyn, come : I call in vain :
The high of birth and weak of brain
Sleeps under ocean's lonely roar
Between the rampart and the shore.

The eternal waste of waters, spread
Above his unrespected head,
The blue expanse, with foam besprent,
Is his too glorious monument.

ANOTHER SONG OF GWYTHNO

I love the green and tranquil shore ;
I hate the ocean's dizzy roar,
Whose devastating spray has flown
High o'er the monarch's barrier-stone.

Sad was the feast, which he who spread
Is numbered with the inglorious dead ;
The feast within the torch-lit hall,
While stormy breakers mined the wall.

To him repentance came too late :
In cups the chatterer met his fate :
Sudden and sad the doom that burst
On him and me, but mine the worst.

I love the shore, and hate the deep :
The wave has robbed my nights of sleep :
The heart of man is cheered by wine ;
But now the wine-cup cheers not mine.

The feast, which bounteous hands dispense,
Makes glad the soul, and charms the sense :
But in the circling feast I know
The coming of my deadliest foe.

Blest be the rock, whose foot supplied
A step to them that fled the tide ;
The rock of bards, on whose rude steep
I bless the shore, and hate the deep.

" The sigh of Gwythno Garanhir when the breakers ploughed up his land " [1] is the substance of a proverbial distich, which may still be heard on the coast of Merioneth and Cardigan, to express the sense of an overwhelming calamity. The curious investigator may still land on a portion of the ancient stony rampart ; which stretches, off the point of Mochres, far out into Cardigan Bay, nine miles of the summit being left dry, in calm weather, by the low water of the springtides ; and which is now called Sarn Badrig, or St. Patrick's Causeway.

Thus the kingdom of Caredigion fell into ruin : its people were destroyed, or turned out of house and home ; and its royal family were brought to a condition in which they found it difficult to get loaves to their fishes. We, who live in more enlightened times, amidst the " gigantic strides of intellect," when offices of public trust are so conscientiously and zealously discharged, and so vigilantly checked and superintended, may wonder at the wicked

---

[1] Ochenaid Gwyddnau Garanhir
Pan droes y don dros ei dir. [P.]

negligence of Seithenyn ; at the sophisms with which, in his liquor, he vindicated his system, and pronounced the eulogium of his old dilapidations, and at the blind confidence of Gwythno and his people in this virtual guardian of their lives and property : happy that our own public guardians are too virtuous to act or talk like Seithenyn, and that we ourselves are too wise not to perceive, and too free not to prevent it, if they should be so disposed.

CHAPTER V

THE PRIZE OF THE WEIR

> Weave a circle round him thrice,
> And close your eyes with holy dread ;
> For he on honey-dew hath fed,
> And drank the milk of paradise.
>   COLERIDGE.[1]

PRINCE ELPHIN constructed his salmon-weir on the Mawddach at the point where the fresh water met the top of the springtides.   He built near it a dwelling for himself and Angharad, for which the old king Gwythno gradually deserted his palace.   An amphitheatre of rocky mountains enclosed a pastoral valley.   The meadows gave pasture to a few cows ; and the flowers of the mountain-heath yielded store of honey to the bees of many hives, which were tended by Angharad and her handmaids.   Elphin had also some sheep, which wandered on the mountains.   The worst was, they often wandered out of reach ; but, when he could not find his sheep, he brought down a wild goat, the venison of Gwyneth.   The woods and turbaries supplied unlimited fuel.   The straggling cultivators, who had escaped from the desolation of Gwaelod, and settled themselves above the level of the sea, on a few spots propitious to the plough, still acknowledged their royalty, and paid them tribute in corn. But their principal wealth was fish.   Elphin was the first Briton who caught fish on a large scale, and salted them for other purposes than home consumption.

The weir was thus constructed : a range of piles crossed the river from shore to shore, slanting upwards from both shores, and meeting

---

[1] *Kubla Khan* : last four lines.   G.

at an angle in the middle of the river. A little down the stream a
second range of piles crossed the river in the same manner, having
towards the middle several wide intervals with light wicker gates,
which, meeting at an angle, were held together by the current, but
were so constructed as to yield easily to a very light pressure from
below. These gates gave all fish of a certain magnitude admission
to a chamber, from which they could neither advance nor retreat,
and from which, standing on a narrow bridge attached to the lower
piles, Elphin bailed them up at leisure. The smaller fish passed
freely up and down the river through the interstices of the piles.
This weir was put together in the early summer, and taken to pieces
and laid by in the autumn.

Prince Elphin, one fine July night, was sleepless and troubled in
spirit. His fishery had been beyond all precedent unproductive, and
the obstacle which this circumstance opposed to his arrangements
for victualling his little garrison kept him for the better half of the
night vigilant in unprofitable cogitation. Soon after the turn of
midnight, when dreams are true, he was startled from an incipient
doze by a sudden cry of Angharad, who had been favoured with a
vision of a miraculous draught of fish. Elphin, as a drowning man
catches at a straw, caught at the shadowy promise of Angharad's
dream, and at once, beneath the clear light of the just-waning moon,
he sallied forth with his princess to examine his weir.

The weir was built across the stream of the river, just above the
flow of the ordinary tides ; but the springtide had opened the
wicker gates, and had floated up a coracle [1] between a pair of them,
which closing, as the tide turned, on the coracle's nose, retained it
within the chamber of the weir, at the same time that it kept the
gates sufficiently open to permit the escape of any fish that might
have entered the chamber. The great prize, which undoubtedly
might have been there when Angharad dreamed of it, was gone to a
fish.

Elphin, little pleased, stepped on the narrow bridge, and opened
the gates with a pole that terminated piscatorially in a hook. The
coracle began dropping down the stream. Elphin arrested its
course, and guided it to land.

[1] A small boat of basketwork, sheathed with leather. [P.]

In the coracle lay a sleeping child, clothed in splendid apparel. Angharad took it in her arms. The child opened its eyes, and stretched its little arms towards her with a smile ; and she uttered, in delight and wonder at its surpassing beauty, the exclamation of " Taliesin ! " " Radiant brow ! "

Elphin, nevertheless, looked very dismal [1] on finding no food, and an additional mouth ; so dismal, that his physiognomy on that occasion passed into a proverb : " As rueful as Elphin when he found Taliesin." [2]

In after years, Taliesin, being on the safe side of prophecy, and writing after the event, addressed a poem to Elphin, in the character of the foundling of the coracle, in which he supposes himself, at the moment of his discovery, to have addressed Elphin as follows :

DYHUDDIANT ELFFIN.

THE CONSOLATION OF ELPHIN.

Lament not, Elphin : do no measure
By one brief hour thy loss or gain :
Thy weir tonight has borne a treasure,
Will more than pay thee years of pain.
St. Cynllo's aid will not be vain :
Smooth thy bent brow, and cease to mourn :
Thy weir will never bear again
Such wealth as it tonight has borne.

The stormy seas, the silent rivers,
The torrents down the steeps that spring,
Alike of weal or woe are givers,
As pleases heaven's immortal king.
Though frail I seem, rich gifts I bring,
Which in Time's fulness shall appear,
Greater than if the stream should fling
Three hundred salmon in thy weir.

Cast off this fruitless sorrow, loading
With heaviness the unmanly mind :
Despond not ; mourn not ; evil boding
Creates the ill it fears to find.

---

[1] " He lifted the boy in his arms, and, lamenting his mischance, he placed him sorrowfully beside him.   And he made his horse amble gently that had before been trotting."   *The Mabinogion.*   G.

[2] Mor drist ac Elffin pan gavod Taliesin.   [P.]

When fates are dark, and most unkind
Are they who most should do thee right,
Then wilt thou know thine eyes were blind
To thy good fortune of tonight.

Though, small and feeble, from my coracle
To thee my helpless hands I spread,
Yet in me breathes a holy oracle
To bid thee lift thy drooping head.
When hostile steps around thee tread,
A spell of power my voice shall wield,
That, more than arms with slaughter red,
Shall be thy refuge and thy shield.[1]

Two years after this event, Angharad presented Elphin with a
daughter, whom they named Melanghel. The fishery prospered;
and the progress of cultivation and population among the more
fertile parts of the mountain districts brought in a little revenue to
the old king.

CHAPTER VI

THE EDUCATION OF TALIESIN

The three objects of intellect : the true, the beautiful, and the beneficial.
    The three foundations of wisdom : youth, to acquire learning ; memory, to
retain learning ; and genius, to illustrate learning.

TRIADS OF WISDOM.[2]

The three primary requisites of poetical genius : an eye, that can see nature ;
a heart, that can feel nature ; and a resolution, that dares follow nature.

TRIADS OF POETRY.[3]

As Taliesin grew up, Gwythno instructed him in all the knowledge
of the age, which was of course not much, in comparison with ours.
The science of political economy was sleeping in the womb of time.
The advantage of growing rich by getting into debt and paying
interest was altogether unknown : the safe and economical currency,
which is produced by a man writing his name on a bit of paper, for
which other men give him their property, and which he is always

---

[1] According to *The Mabinogion*, Taliesin composed and delivered this
poem on the spot, and this was the first that he ever sang, as well it might
be. G.

[2] The *Cambro-Briton*, Vol. II, p. 293, March 1821. G.

[3] *Ibid.*, p. 100, Nov. 1820. G.

ready to exchange for another bit of paper, of an equally safe and economical manufacture, being also equally ready to render his own person, at a moment's notice, as impalpable as the metal which he promises to pay, is a stretch of wisdom to which the people of those days had nothing to compare. They had no steam-engines, with fires as eternal as those of the nether world, wherein the squalid many, from infancy to age, might be turned into component portions of machinery for the benefit of the purple-faced few. They could neither poison the air with gas, nor the waters with its dregs : in short, they made their money of metal, and breathed pure air, and drank pure water, like unscientific barbarians.

Of moral science they had little ; but morals, without science, they had about the same as we have. They had a number of fine precepts, partly from their religion, partly from their bards, which they remembered in their liquor, and forgot in their business.

Political science they had none. The blessings of virtual representation were not even dreamed of ; so that, when any of their barbarous metallic currency got into their pockets or coffers, it had a chance to remain there, subjecting them to the inconvenience of unemployed capital. Still they went to work politically much as we do. The powerful took all they could get from their subjects and neighbours ; and called something or other sacred and glorious, when they wanted the people to fight for them. They repressed disaffection by force, when it showed itself in an overt act ; but they encouraged freedom of speech, when it was, like Hamlet's reading, " words, words, words."

There was no liberty of the press, because there was no press ; but there was liberty of speech to the bards, whose persons were inviolable, and the general motto of their order was y GWIR YN ERBYN Y BYD : the Truth against the World.[1] If many of them, instead of acting up to this splendid profession, chose to advance their personal fortunes by appealing to the selfishness, the passions, and the prejudices, of kings, factions, and the rabble, our free press gentry may afford them a little charity out of the excess of their own virtue.

[1] Peacock put this " Bardic maxim " at the head of Part Two of his *Memoirs of Percy Bysshe Shelley*, in which he defended the memory of Harriet Shelley. G.

In physical science, they supplied the place of knowledge by converting conjectures into dogmas ; an art which is not yet lost. They held that the earth was the centre of the universe ; that an immense ocean surrounded the earth ; that the sky was a vast frame resting on the ocean ; that the circle of their contact was a mystery of infinite mist ; with a great deal more of cosmogony and astronomy, equally correct and profound, which answered the same purpose as our more correct and profound astronomy answers now, that of elevating the mind, as the eidouranion[1] lecturers have it, to sublime contemplations.

Medicine was cultivated by the Druids, and it was just as much a science with them as with us ; but they had not the wit or the means to make it a flourishing trade ; the principal means to that end being women with nothing to do, articles which especially belong to a high state of civilization.

The laws lay in a small compass : every bard had those of his own community by heart. The king, or chief, was the judge ; the plaintiff and defendant told their own story ; and the cause was disposed of in one hearing. We may well boast of the progress of light, when we turn from this picture to the statutes at large, and the Court of Chancery ; and we may indulge in a pathetic reflection on our sweet-faced myriads of " learned friends," who would be under the unpleasant necessity of suspending themselves by the neck, if this barbaric " practice of the courts " were suddenly revived.

The religion of the time was Christianity grafted on Druidism. The Christian faith had been very early preached in Britain. Some of the Welsh historians are of opinion that it was first preached by some of the apostles : most probably by St. John. They think the evidence inconclusive with respect to St. Paul. But, at any rate, the faith had made considerable progress among the Britons at the period of the arrival of Hengist ; for many goodly churches, and, what was still better, richly-endowed abbeys, were flourishing in many places. The British clergy were, however, very contumacious towards the see of Rome, and would only acknowledge the spiritual authority of the archbishopric of Caer Lleon, which was, during

---

[1] *Eidouranion :* a mechanical contrivance for representing the motions of heavenly bodies : an orrery. G.

many centuries, the primacy of Britain. St. Augustin, when he came over, at a period not long subsequent to that of the present authentic history, to preach Christianity to the Saxons, who had for the most part held fast to their Odinism, had also the secondary purpose of making them instruments for teaching the British clergy submission to Rome : as a means to which end, the newly-converted Saxons set upon the monastery of Bangor Iscoed, and put its twelve hundred monks to the sword. This was the first overt act in which the Saxons set forth their new sense of a religion of peace. It is alleged, indeed, that these twelve hundred monks supported themselves by the labour of their own hands. If they did so, it was, no doubt, a gross heresy ; but whether it deserved the castigation it received from St. Augustin's proselytes, may be a question in polemics.

As the people did not read the Bible, and had no religious tracts, their religion, it may be assumed, was not very pure. The rabble of Britons must have seen little more than the superficial facts, that the lands, revenues, privileges, and so forth, which once belonged to Druids and so forth, now belonged to abbots, bishops, and so forth, who, like their extruded precursors, walked occasionally in a row, chanting unintelligible words, and never speaking in common language but to exhort the people to fight ; having, indeed, better notions than their predecessors of building, apparel, and cookery ; and a better knowledge of the means of obtaining good wine, and of the final purpose for which it was made.

They were observant of all matters of outward form, and tradition even places among them personages who were worthy to have founded a society for the suppression of vice. It is recorded, in the Triads, that " Gwrgi Garwlwyd killed a male and female of the Cymry daily, and devoured them ; and, on the Saturday, he killed two of each, that he might not kill on the Sunday." This can only be a type of some sanctimonious hero, who make a cloak of piety for oppressing the poor.

But, even among the Britons, in many of the least populous and most mountainous districts, Druidism was still struggling with Christianity. The lamb had driven the wolf from the rich pastures of the vallies to the high places of the wilderness, where the rites and mysteries of the old religion flourished in secrecy, and where a stray proselyte of the new light was occasionally caught and roasted for the glory of Andraste.

Taliesin, worshipping Nature in her wildest solitudes, often strayed away for days from the dwelling of Elphin, and penetrated the recesses of Eryri,[1] where one especial spot on the banks of Lake Ceirionydd became the favourite haunt of his youth. In these lonely recesses, he became familiar with Druids, who initiated him in their mysteries, which, like all other mysteries, consisted of a quantity of allegorical mummery, pretending to be symbolical of the immortality of the soul, and of its progress through various stages of being ; interspersed with a little, too literal, ducking and singeing of the aspirant, by way of trying his mettle, just enough to put him in fear, but not in risk, of his life.

That Taliesin was thoroughly initiated in these mysteries is evident from several of his poems, which have neither head nor tail, and which, having no sense in any other point of view, must necessarily, as a learned mythologist has demonstrated, be assigned to the class of theology, in which an occult sense can be found or made for them, according to the views of the expounder. One of them, a shade less obscure than its companions, unquestionably adumbrates the Druidical doctrine of transmigration. According to this poem, Taliesin had been with the cherubim at the fall of Lucifer, in Paradise at the fall of man, and with Alexander at the fall of Babylon ; in the ark with Noah, and in the milky-way with Tetragrammaton[2]; and in many other equally marvellous or memorable conditions : showing that, though the names and histories of the new religion were adopted, its doctrines had still to be learned ; and, indeed, in all cases of this description, names are changed more readily than doctrines, and doctrines more readily than ceremonies.

When any of the Romans or Saxons, who invaded the island, fell into the hands of the Britons, before the introduction of Christianity, they were handed over to the Druids, who sacrificed them, with pious ceremonies, to their goddess Andraste. These human sacrifices have done much injury to the Druidical character, amongst us, who

[1] Snowdon. [P.]
[2] The four sacred letters of the name of God. G.

never practise them in the same way. They lacked, it must be confessed, some of our light, and also some of our prisons. They lacked some of our light, to enable them to perceive that the act of coming, in great multitudes, with fire and sword, to the remote dwellings of peaceable men, with the premeditated design of cutting their throats, ravishing their wives and daughters, killing their children, and appropriating their worldly goods, belongs, not to the department of murder and robbery, but to that of legitimate war, of which all the practitioners are gentlemen, and entitled to be treated like gentlemen. They lacked some of our prisons, in which our philanthropy had provided accommodation for so large a portion of our own people, wherein, if they had left their prisoners alive, they could have kept them from returning to their countrymen, and being at their old tricks again immediately. They would also, perhaps, have found some difficulty in feeding them, from the lack of the county rates, by which the most sensible and amiable part of our nation, the country squires, contrive to coop up, and feed, at the public charge, all who meddle with the wild animals of which they have given themselves the monopoly. But as the Druids could neither lock up their captives, nor trust them at large, the darkness of their intellect could suggest no alternative to the process they adopted, of putting them out of the way, which they did with all the sanctions of religion and law. If one of these old Druids could have slept, like the seven sleepers of Ephesus, and awaked, in the nineteenth century, some fine morning near Newgate, the exhibition of some half-dozen funipendulous forgers might have shocked the tender bowels of his humanity, as much as one of his wicker baskets of captives in the flames shocked those of Caesar[1] ; and it would, perhaps, have been difficult to convince him that paper credit was not an idol, and one of a more sanguinary character than his Andraste. The Druids had their view of these matters, and we have ours ; and it does not comport with the steam-engine speed of our march of mind to look at more than one side of a question.

The people lived in darkness and vassalage. They were lost in the grossness of beef and ale. They had no pamphleteering societies to demonstrate that reading and writing are better than meat and

[1] See Cæsar : *Gallic Wars*, Bk. VI, Ch. 16.   G.

drink ; and they were utterly destitute of the blessings of those " schools for all," the house of correction, and the treadmill, wherein the autochthonal justice of our agrestic kakistocracy [1] now castigates the heinous sins which were then committed with impunity, of treading on old footpaths, picking up dead wood, and moving on the face of the earth within sound of the whir of a partridge.

The learning of the time was confined to the bards. It consisted in a somewhat complicated art of versification ; in a great number of pithy apophthegms, many of which have been handed down to posterity under the title of the Wisdom of Catog ; in an interminable accumulation of Triads, in which form they bound up all their knowledge, physical, traditional, and mythological ; and in a mighty condensation of mysticism, being the still-cherished relics of the Druidical rites and doctrines.

The Druids were the sacred class of the bardic order. Before the change of religion, it was by far the most numerous class ; for the very simple reason, that there was most to be got by it : all ages and nations having been sufficiently enlightened to make the trade of priest more profitable than that of poet. During this period, therefore, it was the only class that much attracted the notice of foreigners. After the change of religion, the denomination was retained as that of the second class of the order. The Bardd Braint, or Bard of Presidency, was of the ruling order, and wore a robe of sky-blue. The Derwydd, or Druid, wore a robe of white. The Ovydd, or Ovate, was of the class of initiation, and wore a robe of green. The Awenyddion, or disciples, the candidates for admission into the Bardic order, wore a variegated dress of the three colours, and were passed through a very severe moral and intellectual probation.

Gwythno was a Bardd Braint, or Bard of Presidency, and as such he had full power in his own person, without the intervention of a Bardic Congress, to make his Awenydd or disciple, Taliesin, an Ovydd or Ovate, which he did accordingly. Angharad, under the old king's instructions, prepared the green robe of the young aspirant's investiture. He afterwards acquired the white robe amongst the Druids of Eryri.

In all Bardic learning, Gwythno was profound. All that he knew

[1] Rural government by the worst citizens. G.

he taught to Taliesin.   The youth drew in the draughts of inspiration among the mountain forests and the mountain streams, and grew up under the roof of Elphin, in the perfection of genius and beauty.

CHAPTER VII

THE HUNTINGS OF MAELGON

Ἀεὶ τὸ μὲν ζῇ, τὸ δὲ μεθίσταται κακὸν,
Τὸ δ' ἐκπέφηνεν αὐτίκ' ἐξ ἀρχῆς νέον.
                                    EURIPIDES.[1]

> One ill is ever clinging ;
> One treads upon its heels ;
> A third, in distance springing,
> Its fearful front reveals.

GWYTHNO slept, not with his fathers, for they were under the sea, but as near to them as was found convenient, within the sound of the breakers that rolled over their ancient dwellings.   Elphin was now king of Caredigion, and was lord of a large but thinly-peopled tract of rock, mountain, forest, and bog.   He held his sovereignty, however, not, as Gwythno had done during the days of the glory of Gwaelod, by that most indisputable sort of right which consists in might, but by the more precarious tenure of the absence of inclination in any of his brother kings to take away any thing he had.

Uther Pendragon, like Gwythno, went the way of all flesh, and Arthur reigned in Caer Lleon, as king of the kings of Britain.   Maelgon Gwyneth was then king of that part of North Wales which bordered on the kingdom of Caredigion.

Maelgon was a mighty hunter, and roused the echoes of the mountains with horn and with hound.   He went forth to the chace as to war, provisioned for days and weeks, supported by bard and butler, and all the apparel of princely festivity.   He pitched his tents in the forest of Snowdon, by the shore of lake or torrent; and, after hunting all the day, he feasted half the night.   The light of his torches gleamed on the foam of the cataracts, and the sound of harp and song was mingled with their midnight roar.

When not thus employed, he was either feasting in his Castle of

---

[1] *Æolus Nauck*, 35.   G.

Diganwy, on the Conwy, or fighting with any of the neighbouring
kings, who had any thing which he wanted, and which he thought himself strong enough to take from them.

Once, towards the close of autumn, he carried the tumult of the
chace into the recesses of Meirion. The consonance, or dissonance,
of men and dogs, outpealed the noise of the torrents among the rocks
and woods of the Mawddach. Elphin and Teithrin were gone after
the sheep or goats in the mountains ; Taliesin was absent on the
borders of his favourite lake ; Angharad and Melanghel were alone.
The careful mother, alarmed at the unusual din, and knowing, by
rumour, of what materials the Nimrods of Britain were made, fled,
with her daughter and handmaids, to the refuge of a deeply-secluded
cavern, which they had long before noted as a safe retreat from peril.
As they ascended the hills that led to the cavern, they looked back,
at intervals, through the openings of the woods, to the growing
tumult on the opposite side of the valley. The wild goats were first
seen, flying in all directions, taking prodigious leaps from crag to
crag, now and then facing about, and rearing themselves on their
hind legs, as if in act to butt, and immediately thinking better of it,
and springing away on all fours among the trees. Next, the more
rare spectacle of a noble stag presented itself on the summit of a
projecting rock, pausing a moment to snuff the air, then bounding
down the most practicable slope to the valley. Next, on the summit
which the stag had just deserted, appeared a solitary huntsman,
sitting on a prancing horse, and waking a hundred echoes with the
blast of his horn. Next rushed into view the main body of the royal
company, and the two-legged and four-legged avalanche came
thundering down on the track of the flying prey : not without
imminent hazard of broken necks ; though the mountain-bred horses,
which possessed by nature almost the surefootedness of mules, had
finished their education under the first professors of the age.

The stag swam the river, and stood at bay before the dwelling of
Elphin, where he was in due time despatched by the conjoint valour
of dog and man. The royal train burst into the solitary dwelling,
where, finding nothing worthy of much note, excepting a large store
of salt salmon and mead, they proceeded to broil and tap, and made
fearful havoc among the family's winter provision. Elphin and

Teithrin, returning to their expected dinner, stood aghast on the threshold of their plundered sanctuary. Maelgon condescended to ask them who they were ; and, learning Elphin's name and quality, felt himself bound to return his involuntary hospitality by inviting him to Diganwy. So strong was his sense of justice on this head, that, on Elphin's declining the invitation, which Maelgon ascribed to modesty, he desired two of his grooms to take him up and carry him off.

So Elphin was impressed into royal favour, and was feasted munificently in the castle of Diganwy. Teithrin brought home the ladies from the cavern, and, during the absence of Elphin, looked after the sheep and goats, and did his master's business as well as his own.

One evening, when the royal " nowle" was "tottie of the must,"[1] while the bards of Maelgon were singing the praises of their master, and of all and every thing that belonged to him, as the most eximious and transcendent persons and things of the superficial garniture of the earth, Maelgon said to Elphin, " My bards say that I am the best and bravest of kings, that my queen is the most beautiful and chaste of women, and that they themselves, by virtue of belonging to me, are the best and wisest of bards. Now what say you, on these heads?"

This was a perplexing question to Elphin, who, nevertheless, answered : " That you are the best and bravest of kings I do not in the least doubt ; yet I cannot think that any woman surpasses my own wife in beauty and chastity ; or that any bard equals my bard in genius and wisdom."

" Hear you him, Rhûn ? " said Maelgon.

" I hear," said Rhûn, " and mark."

Rhûn was the son of Maelgon, and a worthy heir-apparent of his illustrious sire. Rhûn set out the next morning on an embassy very similar to Tarquin's,[2] accompanied by only one attendant. They lost their way and each other, among the forests of Meirion. The attendant, after riding about some time in great trepidation, thought he heard the sound of a harp, mixed with the roar of the torrents, and following its indications, came at length within sight of an oak-

[1] Spenser : *The Faerie Queene*, Bk. VII, Canto VII, St. 139. " When the royal brain was drunk with new wine." G.

[2] i.e. to rape Lucrece. G.

fringed precipice, on the summit of which stood Taliesin, playing and singing to the winds and waters. The attendant could not approach him without dismounting ; therefore, tying his horse to a branch, he ascended the rock, and, addressing the young bard, inquired his way to the dwelling of Elphin. Taliesin, in return, inquired his business there ; and, partly by examination, partly by divination, ascertained his master's name, and the purport of his visit.

Taliesin deposited his harp in a dry cavern of the rock, and undertook to be the stranger's guide. The attendant remounted his horse, and Taliesin preceded him on foot. But the way by which he led him grew more and more rugged, till the stranger called out, " Whither lead you, my friend ? My horse can no longer keep his footing." " There is no other way," said Taliesin. " But give him to my management, and do you follow on foot." The attendant consented. Taliesin mounted the horse, and presently struck into a more practicable track ; and immediately giving the horse the reins, he disappeared among the woods, leaving the unfortunate equerry to follow as he might, with no better guide than the uncertain recollection of the sound of his horse's heels.

Taliesin reached home before the arrival of Rhûn, and warned Angharad of the mischief that was designed her.

Rhûn, arriving at his destination, found only a handmaid dressed as Angharad, and another officiating as her attendant. The fictitious princess gave him a supper, and every thing else he asked for ; and, at parting in the morning, a lock of her hair, and a ring, which Angharad had placed on her finger.

After riding a short distance on his return, Rhûn met his unlucky attendant, torn, tired, and half-starved, and cursing some villain who had stolen his horse. Rhûn was too happy in his own success to have a grain of sympathy for his miserable follower, whom he left to find his horse and his way, or either, or neither, as he might, and returned alone to Diganwy.

Maelgon exultingly laid before Elphin the proofs of his wife's infidelity.[1] Elphin examined the lock of hair, and listened to the

[1] According to *The Mabinogion*, Rhûn brought away not only the ring but her little finger, which Elphin demonstrated could not be his wife's, inasmuch as the nail had not been pared for a month, and had been kneading rye-dough within three days. G.

narration of Rhûn.   He divined at once the trick that had been put
upon the prince ;   but he contented himself with saying, " I do not
believe that Rhûn has received the favours of Angharad ;   and I still
think that no wife in Britain, not even the queen of Maelgon Gwyneth,
is more chaste or more beautiful than mine."

Hereupon Maelgon waxed wroth.   Elphin, in a point which much
concerned him, held a belief of his own, different from that which his
superiors in worldly power required him to hold.   Therefore Maelgon
acted as the possessors of worldly power usually act in similar cases :
he locked Elphin up within four stone walls, with an intimation that
he should keep him there till he pronounced a more orthodox
opinion on the question in dispute.

CHAPTER VIII

THE LOVE OF MELANGHEL

Ἀλλὰ τεαῖς παλάμῃσι μαχήμονα θύρσον ἀείρων,
Αἰθέρος ἄξια ῥέξον· ἐπεὶ Διὸς ἄμβροτος αὐλὴ
Οὔ σε πόνων ἀπάνευθε δεδέξεται· οὐδέ σοι ῟Ωραι
Μήπω ἀεθλεύσαντι πύλας πετάσωσιν 'Ολύμπου.

Grasp the bold thyrsus ; seek the field's array ;
And do things worthy of ethereal day :
Not without toil to earthborn man befalls
To tread the floors of Jove's immortal halls :
Never to him, who not by deeds has striven,
Will the bright Hours roll back the gates of heaven.
                    IRIS TO BACCHUS, *in the* 13*th Book of the*
                              Dionysiaca of NONNUS.

THE household of Elphin was sufficiently improsperous during the
absence of its chief.   The havoc which Maelgon's visitation had made
in their winter provision, it required the utmost exertions of their
collective energies to repair.   Even the young princess Melanghel
sallied forth, in the garb of a huntress, to strike the deer or the wild
goat among the wintry forests, on the summits of the bleak crags, or
in the vallies of the flooded streams.

Taliesin, on these occasions, laid aside his harp, and the robe of his
order, and accompanied the princess with his hunting spear, and more
succintly apparelled.

Their retinue, it may be supposed, was neither very numerous nor royal, nor their dogs very thoroughbred. It sometimes happened that the deer went one way, the dogs another ; the attendants, losing sight of both, went a third, leaving Taliesin, who never lost sight of Melanghel, alone with her among the hills.

One day, the ardour of the chace having carried them far beyond their ordinary bounds, they stood alone together on Craig Aderyn, the Rock of Birds, which overlooks the river Dysyni. This rock takes its name from the flocks of birds which have made it their dwelling, and which make the air resonant with their multitudinous notes. Around, before, and above them, rose mountain beyond mountain, soaring above the leafless forests, to lose their heads in mist ; beneath them lay the silent river ; and along the opening of its narrow valley, they looked to the not-distant sea.

" Prince Llywarch," said Taliesin, " is a bard and a warrior : he is the son of an illustrious line. Taliesin is neither prince nor warrior : he is the unknown child of the waters."

" Why think you of Llywarch ? " said Melanghel, to whom the name of the prince was known only from Taliesin, who knew it only from fame.

" Because," said Taliesin, " there is that in my soul which tells me that I shall have no rival among the bards of Britain : but, if its princes and warriors seek the love of Melanghel, I shall know that I am but a bard, and not as Llywarch."

" You would be Prince Taliesin," said Melanghel, smiling, " to make me your princess. Am I not a princess already ? and such an one as is not on earth, for the land of my inheritance is under the sea, under those very waves that now roll within our view ; and, in truth, you are as well qualified for a prince as I am for a princess, and have about as valuable a dominion in the mists and the clouds as I have under the waters."

Her eyes sparkled with affectionate playfulness, while her long black hair floated loosely in the breeze that pressed the folds of her drapery against the matchless symmetry of her form.

" Oh, maid ! " said Taliesin, " what shall I do to win your love ? "

" Restore me my father," said Melanghel, with a seriousness as winning as her playfulness had been fascinating.

"That will I do," said Taliesin, "for his own sake. What shall I do for yours?"

"Nothing more," said Melanghel, and she held out her hand to the youthful bard. Taliesin seized it with rapture, and pressed it to his lips; then, still grasping her hand, and throwing his left arm round her, he pressed his lips to hers.

Melanghel started from him, blushing, and looked at him a moment with something like severity; but he blushed as much as she did, and seemed even more alarmed at her displeasure than she was at his momentary audacity. She reassured him with a smile; and, pointing her spear in the direction of her distant home, she bounded before him down the rock.

This was the kiss of Taliesin to the daughter of Elphin, which is celebrated in an inedited triad, as one of "the Three Chaste Kisses of the island of Britain."

CHAPTER IX

THE SONGS OF DIGANWY

Three things that will always swallow, and never be satisfied: the sea; a burial ground; and a king.

TRIADS OF WISDOM.[1]

THE hall of Maelgon Gwyneth was ringing with music and revelry, when Taliesin stood on the floor, with his harp, in the midst of the assembly, and, without introduction or preface, struck a few chords, that, as if by magic, suspended all other sounds, and fixed the attention of all in silent expectation. He then sang as follows:

CANU Y MEDD.

THE MEAD SONG OF TALIESIN.

The King of kings upholds the heaven,
And parts from earth the billowy sea:
By Him all earthly joys are given;
He loves the just, and guards the free.
Round the wide hall, for thine and thee,
With purest draughts the mead-horns foam,
Maelgon of Gwyneth! Can it be
That here a prince bewails his home?

---

[1] The *Cambro-Briton*, Vol. I, p. 284, April 1820. G.

The bee tastes not the sparkling draught
Which mortals from his toils obtain ;
That sends, in festal circles quaffed,
Sweet tumult through the heart and brain.
The timid, while the horn they drain,
Grow bold ; the happy more rejoice ;
The mourner ceases to complain ;
The gifted bard exalts his voice.

To royal Elphin life I owe,
Nurture and name, the harp, and mead :
Full, pure, and sparkling be their flow,
The horns to Maelgon's lips decreed :
For him may horn to horn succeed,
Till, glowing with their generous fire,
He bid the captive chief be freed,
Whom at his hands my songs require.

Elphin has given me store of mead,
Mead, ale, and wine, and fish, and corn ;
A happy home ; a splendid steed,
Which stately trappings well adorn.
Tomorrow be the auspicious morn
That home the expected chief shall lead ;
So may King Maelgon drain the horn
In thrice three million feasts of mead.

" I give you," said Maelgon, " all the rights of hospitality, and as
many horns as you please of the mead you so well and justly extol.
If you be Elphin's bard, it must be confessed he spoke truth with
respect to you, for you are a much better bard than any of mine, as
they are all free to confess : I give them that liberty."

The bards availed themselves of the royal indulgence, and confessed their own inferiority to Taliesin, as the king had commanded
them to do.[1]   Whether they were all as well convinced of it as they
professed to be, may be left to the decision of that very large class of
literary gentlemen who are in the habit of favouring the reading
public with their undisguised opinions.

" But," said Maelgon, " your hero of Caredigion indulged himself
in a very unjustifiable bravado with respect to his queen ; for he

---

[1] *The Mabinogion* says that Taliesin had cast a charm upon the bards,
which " caused the King to wonder and to deem within himself that they
were drunk with many liquors."   G.

said she was as beautiful and as chaste as mine. Now Rhûn has proved the contrary, with small trouble, and brought away trophies of his triumph ; yet still Elphin persists in his first assertion, wherein he grossly disparages the queen of Gwyneth ; and for this I hold him in bondage, and will do, till he make recantation."

" That he will never do," said Taliesin. " Your son received only the favours of a handmaid, who was willing, by stratagem, to preserve her lady from violence. The real Angharad was concealed in a cavern."

Taliesin explained the adventure of Rhûn, and pronounced an eulogium on Angharad, which put the king and prince into a towering passion.

Rhûn secretly determined to set forth on a second quest ; and Maelgon swore by his mead-horn he would keep Elphin till doomsday. Taliesin struck his harp again, and, in a tone of deep but subdued feeling, he poured forth the

SONG OF THE WIND.[1]

The winds that wander far and free,
Bring whispers from the shores they sweep ;
Voices of feast and revelry ;
Murmurs of forests and the deep ;

Low sounds of torrents from the steep
Descending on the flooded vale ;
And tumults from the leaguered keep,
Where foes the dizzy rampart scale.

The whispers of the wandering wind
Are borne to gifted ears alone ;
For them it ranges unconfined,
And speaks in accents of its own.

---

[1] This poem has little or nothing of Taliesin's *Canu y Gwynt*, with the exception of the title. That poem is apparently a fragment ; and, as it now stands, is an incoherent and scarcely-intelligible rhapsody. It contains no distinct or explicit idea, except the proposition that it is an unsafe booty to carry off fat kine, which may be easily conceded in a case where nimbleness of heel, both in man and beast, must have been of great importance. The idea from which, if from any thing in the existing portion of the poem, it takes its name, that the whispers of the wind bring rumours of war from Deheubarth, is rather implied than expressed. [P.]

It tells me of Deheubarth's throne ;
The spider weaves not in its shield : [1]
Already from its towers is blown
The blast that bids the spoiler yield.

Ill with his prey the fox may wend,
When the young lion quits his lair :
Sharp sword, strong shield, stout arm, should tend
On spirits that unjustly dare.

To me the wandering breezes bear
The war-blast from Caer Lleon's brow ;
The avenging storm is brooding there
To which Diganwy's towers shall bow.[2]

" If the wind talks to you," said Maelgon, " I may say, with the
proverb, you talk to the wind ; for I am not to be sung, or cajoled, or
vapoured, or bullied out of my prisoner.   And as to your war-blasts
from Caer Lleon, which I construe into a threat that you will stir up
King Arthur against me, I can tell you for your satisfaction, and to
spare you the trouble of going so far, that he has enough to do with
seeking his wife, who has been carried off by some unknown marauder,
and with fighting the Saxons, to have much leisure or inclination to

[1] The spider weaving in suspended armour, is an old emblem of peace and
inaction.   Thus Bacchylides, in his fragment on Peace :

> Ἐν δὲ σιδαροδέτοις πόρπαξιν
> Αἰθᾶν ἀραχνᾶν ἔργα πέλονται.   [*Bacchides*, Bolck 13.   G.]

Euripides, in a fragment of *Erechtheus* :

> Κείσθω δόρυ μοι μίτον ἀμφιπλέκειν
> Ἀράχναις.   [*Erechtheus*, Nauck, 370.   G.]

And Nonnus, whom no poetical image escaped : (*Dionysiaca*, L. xxxviii.)

> Οὐ φόνος, οὐ τότε δῆρις · ἔκειτο δὲ τηλόθι χάρμης
> Βακχιὰς ἐξαέτηρος ἀραχνιόωσα βοείη.

And Beaumont and Fletcher, in the *Wife for a Month* :

> " Would'st thou live so long, till thy sword hung by,
> And lazy spiders filled the hilt with cobwebs ? "

[A telescoping of four lines in Act II.   G.]

A Persian poet says, describing ruins :

" The spider spreads the veil in the palace of the Caesars."

And among the most felicitous uses of this emblem, must never be forgotten Hogarth's cobweb over the lid of the charity-box.   [P.]

[2] Peacock's literal translation of this poem is published in the Halliford
Edition, Vol. VIII, p. 455.   G.

quarrel with a true Briton, who is one of his best friends, and his heir presumptive ; for, though he is a man of great prowess, and moreover, saving his reverence and your presence, a cuckold, he has not yet favoured his kingdom with an heir apparent.   And I request you to understand, that when I extolled you above my bards, I did so only in respect of your verse and voice, melody and execution, figure and action, in short, of your manner ; for your matter is naught ; and I must do my own bards the justice to say, that, however much they may fall short of you in the requisites aforesaid, they know much better than you do, what is fitting for bards to sing, and kings to hear."

The bards, thus encouraged, recovered from the first shock of Maelgon's ready admission of Taliesin's manifest superiority, and struck up a sort of consecutive chorus, in a series of pennillion, or stanzas, in praise of Maelgon and his heirship presumptive, giving him credit for all the virtues of which the reputation was then in fashion ; and, amongst the rest, they very loftily celebrated his justice and magnanimity.

Taliesin could not reconcile his notions of these qualities with Maelgon's treatment of Elphin.   He changed his measure and his melody, and pronounced, in impassioned numbers, the poem which a learned Welsh historian calls " The Indignation of the Bards," though, as the indignation was Taliesin's, and not theirs, he seems to have made a small mistake in regard to the preposition.

THE INDIGNATION OF TALIESIN
WITH THE
BARDS OF MAELGON GWYNETH.

> False bards the sacred fire pervert,
> Whose songs are won without desert ;
> Who falsehoods weave in specious lays,
> To gild the base with virtue's praise.
>
> From court to court, from tower to tower,
> In warrior's tent, in lady's bower,
> For gold, for wine, for food, for fire,
> They tune their throats at all men's hire.
>
> Their harps reecho wide and far
> With sensual love, and bloody war,
> And drunkenness, and flattering lies :
> Truth's light may shine for other eyes.

In palaces they still are found,
At feasts, promoting senseless sound :
He is their demigod at least,
Whose only virtue is his feast.

They love to talk ; they hate to think ;
All day they sing ; all night they drink :
No useful toils their hands employ ;
In boisterous throngs is all their joy.

The bird will fly, the fish will swim,
The bee the honied flowers will skim ;
Its food by toil each creature brings,
Except false bards and worthless kings.

Learning and wisdom claim to find
Homage and succour from mankind ;
But learning's right, and wisdom's due,
Are falsely claimed by slaves like you.

True bards know truth, and truth will show ;
Ye know it not, nor care to know :
Your king's weak mind false judgment warps ;
Rebuke his wrong, or break your harps.

I know the mountain and the plain ;
I know where right and justice reign ;
I from the tower will Elphin free ;
Your king shall learn his doom from me.

A spectre of the marsh shall rise,
With yellow teeth, and hair, and eyes,
From whom your king in vain aloof
Shall crouch beneath the sacred roof.

He through the half-closed door shall spy
The Yellow Spectre sweeping by ;
To whom the punishment belongs
Of Maelgon's crimes and Elphin's wrongs.

By the name of the Yellow Spectre, Taliesin designated a pestilence,
which afterwards carried off great multitudes of the people, and,
amongst them, Maelgon Gwyneth, then sovereign of Britain, who
had taken refuge from it in a church.

Maelgon paid little attention to Taliesin's prophecy, but he was
much incensed by the general tenor of his song.

" If it were not," said Maelgon, " that I do not choose to add to the number of the crimes of which you so readily accuse me, that of disregarding the inviolability of your bardship, I would send you to keep company with your trout-catching king, and you might amuse his salmon-salting majesty with telling him as much truth as he is disposed to listen to ; which, to judge by his reception of Rhûn's story of his wife, I take to be exceedingly little. For the present, you are welcome to depart ; and, if you are going to Caer Lleon, you may present my respect to King Arthur, and tell him, I hope he will beat the Saxons, and find his wife ; but I hope, also, that the cutting me off with an heir apparent will not be the consequence of his finding her, or (which, by the by, is more likely,) of his having lost her."

Taliesin took his departure from the hall of Diganwy, leaving the bards biting their lips at his rebuke, and Maelgon roaring with laughter at his own very excellent jest.

CHAPTER X

THE DISAPPOINTMENT OF RHÛN

Παρθένε, πῶς μετάμειψας ἐρευθαλέην σέο μορφήν ;
Εἰαρινὴν δ᾽ ἀκτῖνα τίς ἔσβεσε σεῖο προσώπου ;
Οὐκέτι σῶν μελέων ἀμαρύσσεται ἄργυφος αἴγλη ·
Οὐκέτι δ᾽, ὡς τὸ πρόσθε, τεαὶ γελόωσιν ὀπωπαί.

Sweet maid, what grief has changed thy roseate grace,
And quenched the vernal sunshine of thy face ?
No more thy light form sparkles as it flies,
Nor laughter flashes from thy radiant eyes.
            VENUS TO PASITHEA, *in the* 33d *Book of the*
                        Dionysiaca of NONNUS.

TALIESIN returned to the dwelling of Elphin, auguring that, in consequence of his information, Rhûn would pay it another visit. In this anticipation he was not mistaken, for Rhûn very soon appeared, with a numerous retinue, determined, apparently, to carry his point by force of arms. He found, however, no inmate in the dwelling but Taliesin and Teithrin ap Tathral.

Rhûn stormed, entreated, promised, and menaced, without success. He perlustrated the vicinity, and found various caverns, but not the one he sought. He passed many days in the search, and, finally, departed ; but, at a short distance, he dismissed all his retinue, except his bard of all work, or laureate expectant, and, accompanied by this worthy, returned to the banks of the Mawd-dach, where they resolved themselves into an ambuscade. It was not long before they saw Taliesin issue from the dwelling, and begin ascending the hill. They followed him, at a cautious distance; first up a steep ascent of the forest-covered rocks ; then along a small space of densely-wooded tableland, to the edge of a dingle ; and, again, by a slight descent, to the bed of a mountain stream, in a spot where the torrent flung itself, in a series of cataracts, down the rift of a precipitous rock, that towered high above their heads. About half way up the rock, near the base of one of these cataracts, was a projecting ledge, or natural platform of rock, behind which was seen the summit of the opening of a cave. Taliesin paused, and looked around him, as if to ascertain that he was unobserved ; and then, standing on a projection of the rock below, he mingled, in spontaneous song, the full power of his voice with the roar of the waters.

TALIESIN.

Maid of the rock ! though loud the flood,
My voice will pierce thy cell :
No foe is in the mountain wood ;
No danger in the dell :
The torrents bound along the glade ;
Their path is free and bright ;
Be thou as they, Oh mountain maid !
In liberty and light.

Melanghel appeared on the rocky platform, and answered the song of her lover :

MELANGHEL.

The cataracts thunder down the steep ;
The woods all lonely wave :
Within my heart the voice sinks deep
That calls me from my cave.
The voice is dear, the song is sweet,
And true the words must be :
Well pleased I quit the dark retreat,
To wend away with thee.

TALIESIN.

Not yet ; not yet : let nightdews fall,
And stars be bright above,
Ere to her long deserted hall
I guide my gentle love.
When torchlight flashes on the roof,
No foe will near thee stray :
Even now his parting courser's hoof
Rings from the rocky way.

MELANGHEL.

Yet climb the path, and comfort speak,
To cheer the lonely cave,
Where woods are bare, and rocks are bleak,
And wintry torrents rave.
A dearer home my memory knows,
A home I still deplore ;
Where firelight glows, while winds and snows
Assail the guardian door.

Taliesin vanished a moment from the sight of Rhûn, and almost immediately reappeared by the side of Melanghel, who had now been joined by her mother.   In a few minutes he returned, and Angharad and Melanghel withdrew.

Rhûn watched him from the dingle, and then proceeded to investigate the path by which he had gained the platform.   After some search he discovered it, ascended to the platform, and rushed into the cavern.

They here found a blazing fire, a half-finished dinner, materials of spinning and embroidering, and other signs of female inhabitancy ; but they found not the inhabitants.   They searched the cavern to its depth, which was not inconsiderable ;   much marvelling how the ladies had vanished.   While thus engaged, they heard a rushing sound, and a crash on the rocks, as of some ponderous body.   The mystery of this noise was very soon explained to them, in a manner that gave an unusual length to their faces, and threw a deep tinge of blue into their rosy complexions.   A ponderous stone, which had been suspended like a portcullis at the mouth of the cavern, had been dropped by some unseen agency, and made them as close prisoners as Elphin.

They were not long kept in suspense as to how this matter had been managed.   The hoarse voice of Teithrin ap Tathral sounded in their ears from without, " Foxes ! you have been seen through, and you are fairly trapped. Eat and drink. You shall want nothing but to get out ; which you must want some time ; for it is sworn that no hand but Elphin's shall raise the stone of your captivity."

" Let me out," vociferated Rhûn, " and on the word of a prince——" but, before he could finish the sentence, the retreating steps of Teithrin were lost in the roar of the torrent.

CHAPTER XI

THE HEROES OF DINAS VAWR

L'ombra sua torna ch'era dipartita. DANTE.[1]
While there is life there is hope. English Proverb.

PRINCE RHÛN being safe in schistous bastile, Taliesin commenced his journey to the court of King Arthur. On his way to Caer Lleon, he was received with all hospitality, entertained with all admiration, and dismissed with all honour, at the castles of several petty kings, and, amongst the rest, at the castle of Dinas Vawr, on the Towy, which was then garrisoned by King Melvas, who had marched with a great force out of his own kingdom, on the eastern shores of the Severn, to levy contributions in the country to the westward, where, as the pleasure of his company had been altogether unlooked for, he had got possession of a good portion of moveable property. The castle of Dinas Vawr presenting itself to him as a convenient hold, he had taken it by storm ; and having cut the throats of the former occupants, thrown their bodies into the Towy, and caused a mass to be sung for the good of their souls, he was now sitting over his bowl, with the comfort of a good conscience, enjoying the fruits of the skill and courage with which he had planned and accomplished his scheme of ways and means for the year.

The hall of Melvas was full of magnanimous heroes, who were celebrating their own exploits in sundry chorusses, especially in that which follows, which is here put upon record as being the quint-essence of all the war-songs that ever were written, and the sum and

---

[1] " His shade returns that had departed." Dante : <i>Inferno,</i> IV, 81. G.

substance of all the appetencies, tendencies, and consequences of military glory :

THE WAR-SONG OF DINAS VAWR.

The mountain sheep are sweeter,
But the valley sheep are fatter ;
We therefore deemed it meeter
To carry off the latter.
We made an expedition ;
We met a host, and quelled it ;
We forced a strong position,
And killed the men who held it.

On Dyfed's richest valley,
Where herds of kine were brousing,
We made a mighty sally,
To furnish our carousing.
Fierce warriors rushed to meet us ;
We met them, and o'erthrew them :
They struggled hard to beat us ;
But we conquered them, and slew them.

As we drove our prize at leisure,
The king marched forth to catch us :
His rage surpassed all measure,
But his people could not match us.
He fled to his hall-pillars ;
And, ere our force we led off,
Some sacked his house and cellars,
While others cut his head off.

We there, in strife bewild'ring,
Spilt blood enough to swim in :
We orphaned many children,
And widowed many women.
The eagles and the ravens
We glutted with our foemen ;
The heroes and the cravens,
The spearmen and the bowmen.

We brought away from battle,
And much their land bemoaned them,
Two thousand head of cattle,
And the head of him who owned them :
Ednyfed, king of Dyfed,
His head was borne before us ;
His wine and beasts supplied our feasts,
And his overthrow, our chorus.

As the doughty followers of Melvas, having sung themselves hoarse with their own praises, subsided one by one into drunken sleep, Taliesin, sitting near the great central fire, and throwing around a scrutinizing glance on all the objects in the hall, noticed a portly and somewhat elderly personage, of an aspect that would have been venerable, if it had been less rubicund and Bacchic, who continued plying his potations with undiminished energy, while the heroes of the festival dropped round him, like the leaves of autumn. This figure excited Taliesin's curiosity. The features struck him with a sense of resemblance to objects which had been somewhere familiar to him ; but he perplexed himself in vain, with attempts at definite recollections. At length, when these two were almost the sole survivors of the evening, the stranger approached him with a golden goblet, which he had just replenished with the choicest wine of the vaults of Dinas Vawr, and pronounced the oracular monosyllable, "Drink ! " to which he subjoined emphatically " GWIN O EUR: Wine from gold. That is my taste. Ale is well ; mead is better; wine is best. Horn is well ; silver is better ; gold is best."

Taliesin, who had been very abstemious during the evening, took the golden goblet, and drank to please the inviter ; in the hope that he would become communicative, and satisfy the curiosity his appearance had raised.

The stranger sat down near him, evidently in that amiable state of semi-intoxication which inflates the head, warms the heart, lifts up the veil of the inward man, and sets the tongue flying, or rather tripping, in the double sense of nimbleness and titubancy.

The stranger repeated, taking a copious draught, " My taste is wine from gold."

" I have heard those words," said Taliesin, " GWIN O EUR, repeated as having been the favourite saying of a person whose memory is fondly cherished by one as dear to me as a mother, though his name, with all others, is the by-word of all that is disreputable."

" I cannot believe," said the stranger, " that a man whose favourite saying was GWIN O EUR, could possibly be a disreputable person, or deserve any other than that honourable remembrance, which, you say, only one person is honest enough to entertain for him."

" His name," said Taliesin, " is too unhappily notorious throughout Britain, by the terrible catastrophe of which his GWIN O EUR was the cause."

"And what might that be ? " said the stranger.

"The inundation of Gwaelod," said Taliesin.

"You speak then," said the stranger, taking an enormous potation, "of Seithenyn, Prince Seithenyn, Seithenyn ap Seithyn Saidi, Arglwyd Gorwarcheidwad yr Argae Breninawl."

"I seldom hear his name," said Taliesin, "with any of those sounding additions ; he is usually called Seithenyn the Drunkard."

The stranger goggled about his eyes in an attempt to fix them steadily on Taliesin, screwed up the corners of his mouth, stuck out his nether lip, pursed up his chin, thrust forward his right foot, and elevated his golden goblet in his right hand ; then, in a tone which he intended to be strongly becoming of his impressive aspect and imposing attitude, he muttered, "Look at me."

Taliesin looked at him accordingly, with as much gravity as he could preserve.

After a silence, which he designed to be very dignified and solemn, the stranger spoke again : "I am the man."

"What man ? " said Taliesin.

"The man," replied his entertainer, "of whom you have spoken so disparagingly ; Seithenyn ap Seithyn Saidi."

"Seithenyn," said Taliesin, "has slept twenty years under the waters of the western sea, as King Gwythno's Lamentations have made known to all Britain."

"They have not made it known to me," said Seithenyn, "for the best of all reasons, that one can only know the truth ; for, if that which we think we know is not truth, it is something which we do not know. A man cannot know his own death ; for, while he knows any thing, he is alive ; at least, I never heard of a dead man who knew any thing, or pretended to know any thing : if he had so pretended, I should have told him to his face he was no dead man."

"Your mode of reasoning," said Taliesin, "unquestionably corresponds with what I have heard of Seithenyn's : but how is it possible Seithenyn can be living ? "

"Every thing that is, is possible, says Catog the Wise," answered

Seithenyn, with a look of great sapience. "I will give you proof that I am not a dead man; for, they say, dead men tell no tales: now I will tell you a tale, and a very interesting one it is. When I saw the sea sapping the tower, I jumped into the water, and just in the nick of time. It was well for me that I had been so provident as to empty so many barrels, and that somebody, I don't know who, but I suppose it was my daughter, had been so provident as to put the bungs into them, to keep them sweet; for the beauty of it was that, when there was so much water in the case, it kept them empty; and when I jumped into the sea, the sea was just making a great hole in the cellar, and they were floating out by dozens. I don't know how I managed it, but I got one arm over one, and the other arm over another: I nipped them pretty tight; and, though my legs were under water, the good liquor I had in me kept me warm. I could not help thinking, as I had nothing else to think of just then that touched me so nearly, that if I had left them full, and myself empty, as a sober man would have done, we should all three, that is, I and the two barrels, have gone to the bottom together, that is to say, separately; for we should never have come together, except at the bottom, perhaps; when no one of us could have done the other any good; whereas they have done me much good, and I have requited it; for, first, I did them the service of emptying them; and then they did me the service of floating me with the tide, whether the ebb, or the flood, or both, is more than I can tell, down to the coast of Dyfed, where I was picked up by fishermen; and such was my sense of gratitude, that, though I had always before detested an empty barrel, except as a trophy, I swore I would not budge from the water unless my two barrels went with me; so we were all marched inland together, and were taken into the service of King Ednyfed, where I stayed till his castle was sacked, and his head cut off, and his beeves marched away with, by the followers of King Melvas, of whom I killed two or three; but they were too many for us: therefore, to make the best of a bad bargain, I followed leisurely in the train of the beeves, and presented myself to King Melvas, with this golden goblet, saying GWIN O EUR. He was struck with my deportment, and made me his chief butler; and now my two barrels are the two pillars of his cellar, where I regularly fill them from affection, and as regularly empty them from gratitude, taking care to put the bungs in them, to keep them sweet."

" But all this while," said Taliesin, " did you never look back to the Plain of Gwaelod, to your old king, and, above all, to your daughter ? "

" Why yes," said Seithenyn, " I did in a way ! But as to the Plain of Gwaelod, that was gone, buried under the sea, along with many good barrels, which I had been improvident enough to leave full : then, as to the old king, though I had a great regard for him, I thought he might be less likely to feast me in his hall, than to set up my head on a spike over his gate : then, as to my daughter——"

Here he shook his head, and looked maudlin ; and dashing two or three drops from his eye, he put a great many into his mouth.

" Your daughter," said Taliesin, " is the wife of King Elphin, and has a daughter, who is now as beautiful as her mother was."

" Very likely," said Seithenyn, " and I should be very glad to see them all ; but I am afraid King Elphin, as you call him, (what he is king of, you shall tell me at leisure,) would do me a mischief. At any rate, he would stint me in liquor. No ! If they will visit me, here I am. Fish, and water, will not agree with me. I am growing old, and need cordial nutriment. King Melvas will never want for beeves and wine ; nor, indeed, for any thing else that is good. I can tell you what," he added, in a very low voice, cocking his eye, and putting his finger on his lips, " he has got in this very castle the finest woman in Britain."

" That I doubt," said Taliesin.

" She is the greatest, at any rate," said Seithenyn, " and ought to be the finest."

" How the greatest ? " said Taliesin.

Seithenyn looked round, to observe if there were any listener near, and fixed a very suspicious gaze on a rotund figure of a fallen hero, who lay coiled up like a maggot in a filbert, and snoring with an energy that, to the muddy apprehensions of Seithenyn, seemed to be counterfeit. He determined, by a gentle experiment, to ascertain if his suspicions were well founded ; and proceeded, with what he thought great caution, to apply the point of his foot to the most bulging portion of the fat sleeper's circumference. But he greatly miscalculated his intended impetus, for he impinged his foot with a force that overbalanced himself, and hurled him headlong over his man, who instantly sprang on his legs, shouting " To arms ! " Numbers started up at the cry ; the hall rang with the din of arms, and with the vociferation of questions, which there were many to ask, and none to answer. Some stared about for the enemy ; some rushed to the gates ; others to the walls. Two or three, reeling in the tumult and the darkness, were jostled over the parapet, and went rolling down the precipitous slope of the castle hill, crashing through the bushes, and bellowing for some one to stop them, till their clamours were cut short by a plunge into the Towy, where the conjoint weight of their armour and their liquor carried them at once to the bottom. The rage which would have fallen on the enemy, if there had been one, was turned against the author of the false alarm ; but, as none could point him out, the tumult subsided by degrees, through a descending scale of imprecations, into the last murmured malediction of him whom the intensity of his generous anger kept longest awake. By this time, the rotund hero had again coiled himself up into his ring ; and Seithenyn was stretched in a right line, as a tangent to the circle, in a state of utter incapacity to elucidate the mystery of King Melvas's possession of the finest woman in Britain.

CHAPTER XII

THE SPLENDOUR OF CAER LLEON

The three principal cities of the isle of Britain : Caer Llion upon Wysg in Cymru ; Caer Llundain in Lloegr ; and Caer Evrawg in Deifr and Brynaich.[1]
TRIADS OF THE ISLE OF BRITAIN.[2]

THE sunset of a bright December day was glittering on the waves of the Usk, and on the innumerable roofs, which, being composed chiefly of the glazed tiles of the Romans, reflected the light almost as vividly as the river; when Taliesin descended one of the hills that border the beautiful valley in which then stood Caer Lleon, the metropolis of Britain, and in which now stands, on a small portion of the selfsame

[1] Caer Lleon upon Usk in Cambria : London in Loegria : and York in Deïra and Bernicia. [P.]
[2] The *Cambro-Briton*, Vol. II, p. 387. G.

space, a little insignificant town, possessing nothing of its ancient glory but the unaltered name of Caer Lleon.

The rapid Usk flowed then, as now, under the walls : the high wooden bridge, with its slender piles, was then much the same as it is at this day : it seems to have been never regularly rebuilt, but to have been repaired, from time to time, on the original Roman model. The same green and fertile meadows, the same gently-sloping wood-covered hills, that now meet the eye of the tourist, then met the eye of Taliesin ; except that the woods on one side of the valley, were then only the skirts of an extensive forest, which the nobility and beauty of Caer Lleon made frequently reecho to the clamours of the chace.

The city, which had been so long the centre of the Roman supremacy, which was now the seat of the most illustrious sovereign that had yet held the sceptre of Britain, could not be approached by the youthful bard, whose genius was destined to eclipse that of all his countrymen, without feelings and reflections of deep interest. The sentimental tourist, (who, perching himself on an old wall, works himself up into a soliloquy of philosophical pathos, on the vicissitudes of empire and the mutability of all sublunary things, interrupted only by an occasional peep at his watch, to ensure his not over-staying the minute at which his fowl, comfortably roasting at the nearest inn, has been promised to be ready,) has, no doubt, many fine thoughts well worth recording in a dapper volume ; but Taliesin had an interest in the objects before him too deep to have a thought to spare, even for his dinner.   The monuments of Roman magnificence, and of Roman domination, still existing in comparative freshness ; the arduous struggle, in which his countrymen were then engaged with the Saxons, and which, notwithstanding the actual triumphs of Arthur, Taliesin's prophetic spirit told him would end in their being dispossessed of all the land of Britain, except the wild region of Wales, (a result which political sagacity might have apprehended from their disunion, but which, as he told it to his countrymen in that memorable prophecy which every child of the Cymry knows, has established for him, among them, the fame of a prophet ;) the importance to himself and his benefactors of the objects of his visit to the city, on the result of which depended the liberation of Elphin, and the success of his love for Melanghel; the degree in which these objects might be promoted by the construction he had put on Seithenyn's imperfect communication respecting the lady in Dinas Vawr; furnished, all together, more materials for absorbing thought, than the most zealous peregrinator, even if he be at once poet, antiquary, and philosopher, is likely to have at once in his mind, on the top of the finest old wall on the face of the earth.

Taliesin passed, in deep musing, through the gates of Caer Lleon; but his attention was speedily drawn to the objects around him. From the wild solitudes in which he had passed his earlier years, the transition to the castles and cities he had already visited, furnished much food to curiosity: but the ideas of them sunk into comparative nothingness before the magnificence of Caer Lleon.

He did not stop in the gateway to consider the knotty question, which has since puzzled so many antiquaries, whether the name of Caer Lleon signifies the City of Streams, the City of Legions, or the City of King Lleon? He saw a river filled with ships, flowing through fine meadows, bordered by hills and forests; walls of brick, as well as of stone; a castle, of impregnable strength; stately houses, of the most admirable architecture; palaces, with gilded roofs; Roman temples, and Christian churches; a theatre, and an amphitheatre. The public and private buildings of the departed Romans were in excellent preservation; though the buildings, and especially the temples, were no longer appropriated to their original purposes. The king's butler, Bedwyr, had taken possession of the Temple of Diana, as a cool place of deposit for wine: he had recently effected a stowage of vast quantities therein, and had made a most luminous arrangement of the several kinds; under the judicious and experienced superintendence of Dyvrig, the Ex-Archbishop of Caer Lleon; who had just then nothing else to do, having recently resigned his see in favour of King Arthur's uncle, David, who is, to this day, illustrious as the St. David in whose honour the Welshmen annually adorn their hats with a leek. This David was a very respectable character in his way: he was a man of great sanctity and simplicity; and, in order to eschew the vanities of the world, which were continually present to him in Caer Lleon, he removed the metropolitan see, from Caer Lleon, to the rocky, barren, woodless, streamless, meadowless, tempest-beaten point of Mynyw, which was afterwards called St. David's. He was the mirror and pattern of a godly life ; teaching by example, as by precept ; admirable in words, and excellent in deeds ; tall in stature, handsome in aspect, noble in deportment, affable in address, eloquent and learned, a model to his followers, the life of the poor, the protector of widows, and the father of orphans. This makes altogether a very respectable saint ; and it cannot be said, that the honourable leek is unworthily consecrated. A long series of his Catholic successors maintained, in great magnificence, a cathedral, a college, and a palace ; keeping them all in repair, and feeding the poor into the bargain, from the archiepiscopal, or, when the primacy of Caer Lleon had merged in that of Canterbury, from the episcopal, revenues : but these things were reformed altogether by one of the first Protestant bishops, who, having a lady that longed for the gay world, and wanting more than all the revenues for himself and his family, first raised the wind by selling off the lead from the roof of his palace, and then obtained permission to remove from it, on the plea that it was not watertight. The immediate successors of this bishop, whose name was Barlow, were in every way worthy of him ; the palace and college have, consequently, fallen into incurable dilapidation, and the cathedral has fallen partially into ruins, and, most impartially, into neglect and defacement.[1]

To return to Taliesin, in the streets of Caer Lleon. Plautus and Terence were not heard in the theatre, nor to be heard of in its neighbourhood ; but it was thought an excellent place for an Eisteddfod, or Bardic Congress, and was made the principal place of assembly of the Bards of the island of Britain. This is what Ross of Warwick means, when he says there was a noble university of students in Caer Lleon.

The mild precepts of the new religion had banished the ferocious sports to which the Romans had dedicated the amphitheatre, and, as Taliesin passed, it was pouring forth an improved and humanized

[1] The rapacity of William Barlow was responsible for great injury to the cathedral. He resigned his see upon the accession of Mary, but was imprisoned in the Tower, after which he recanted and went to Germany. He became Bishop of Chichester after the accession of Elizabeth. The cathedral was restored in 1862 by Sir Gilbert Scott. G.

multitude, who had been enjoying the pure British pleasure of baiting a bear.

The hot baths and aqueducts, the stoves of " wonderful artifice," as Giraldus has it, which diffused hot air through narrow spiracles, and many other wonders of the place, did not all present themselves to a first observation. The streets were thronged with people, especially of the fighting order, of whom a greater number flocked about Arthur, than he always found it convenient to pay. Horsemen, with hawks and hounds, were returning from the neighbouring forest, accompanied by beautiful huntresses, in scarlet and gold.

Taliesin, having perlustrated the city, proceeded to the palace of Arthur. At the gates he was challenged by a formidable guard, but passed by his bardic privilege. It was now very near Christmas, and when Taliesin entered the great hall, it was blazing with artificial light, and glowing with the heat of the Roman stoves.

Arthur had returned victorious from the great battle of Badon hill, in which he had slain with his own hand four hundred and forty Saxons ; and was feasting as merrily as an honest man can be supposed to do while his wife is away. Kings, princes, and soldiers of fortune, bards and prelates, ladies superbly apparelled, and many of them surpassingly beautiful ; and a most gallant array of handsome young cupbearers, marshalled and well drilled by the king's butler, Bedwyr, who was himself a petty king, were the chief components of the illustrious assembly.

Amongst the ladies were the beautiful Tegau Eurvron ; Dywir the Golden-haired ; Enid, the daughter of Yniwl ; Garwen, the daughter of Henyn ; Gwyl, the daughter of Enddaud ; and Indeg, the daughter of Avarwy Hir, of Maelienydd. Of these, Tegau Eurvron, or Tegau of the Golden Bosom, was the wife of Caradoc, and one of the Three Chaste Wives of the island of Britain. She is the heroine, who, as the lady of Sir Cradock, is distinguished above all the ladies of Arthur's court, in the ballad of the Boy and the Mantle.[1]

Amongst the bards were Prince Llywarch, then in his youth, afterwards called Llywarch Hên, or Lywarch the Aged ; Aneurin, the British Homer, who sang the fatal battle of Cattraëth, which laid the foundation of the Saxon ascendency, in heroic numbers, which the

---

[1] Percy's *Reliques*, 3rd series, Bk. I. G.

gods have preserved to us, and who was called the Monarch of the Bards, before the days of the glory of Taliesin ; and Merddin Gwyllt, or Merlin the Wild, who was so deep in the secrets of nature, that he obtained the fame of a magician, to which he had at least as good a title as either Friar Bacon or Cornelius Agrippa.

Amongst the petty kings, princes, and soldiers of fortune, were twenty-four marchawg, or cavaliers, who were the counsellors and champions of Arthur's court. This was the heroic band, illustrious, in the songs of chivalry, as the Knights of the Round Table. Their names and pedigrees would make a very instructive and entertaining chapter ; and would include the interesting characters of Gwalchmai ap Gwyar the Courteous, the nephew of Arthur ; Caradoc, "Colofn Cymry," the Pillar of Cambria, whose lady, as above noticed, was the mirror of chastity ; and Trystan ap Tallwch, the lover of the beautiful Essyllt, the daughter, or, according to some, the wife, of his uncle March ap Meirchion ; persons known to all the world, as Sir Gawain, Sir Cradock, and Sir Tristram.

On the right hand of King Arthur sate the beautiful Indeg, and on his left the lovely Garwen. Taliesin advanced, along the tesselated floor, towards the upper end of the hall, and, kneeling before King Arthur, said, " What boon will King Arthur grant to him who brings news of his queen ? "

" Any boon," said Arthur, " that a king can give."

" Queen Gwenyvar," said Taliesin, " is the prisoner of King Melvas, in the castle of Dinas Vawr."

The mien and countenance of his informant satisfied the king that he knew what he was saying ; therefore, without further parlance, he broke up the banquet, to make preparations for assailing Dinas Vawr.

But, before he began his march, King Melvas had shifted his quarters, and passed beyond the Severn to the isle of Avallon, where the marches and winter-floods assured him some months of tranquillity and impunity.

King Arthur was highly exasperated, on receiving the intelligence of Melvas's movement ; but he had no remedy, and was reduced to the alternative of making the best of his Christmas with the ladies, princes, and bards who crowded his court.

The period of the winter solstice had been always a great festival with the northern nations, the commencement of the lengthening of the days being, indeed, of all points in the circle of the year, that in which the inhabitants of cold countries have most cause to rejoice. This great festival was anciently called Yule ; whether derived from the Gothic *Iola*, to make merry ; or from the Celtic *Hiaul*, the sun ; or from the Danish and Swedish *Hiul*, signifying wheel or revolution, December being *Hiul-month*, or the month of return ; or from the Cimbric word *Ol*, which has the important signification of ALE, is too knotty a controversy to be settled here : but Yule had been long a great festival, with both Celts and Saxons; and, with the change of religion, became the great festival of Christmas, retaining most of its ancient characteristics while England was Merry England ; a phrase which must be a mirifical puzzle to any one who looks for the first time on its present most lugubrious inhabitants.

The mistletoe of the oak was gathered by the Druids with great ceremonies, as a symbol of the season. The mistletoe continued to be so gathered, and to be suspended in halls and kitchens, if not in temples, implying an unlimited privilege of kissing ; which circumstance, probably, led a learned antiquary to opine that it was the forbidden fruit.

The Druids, at this festival, made, in a capacious cauldron, a mystical brewage of carefully-selected ingredients, full of occult virtues, which they kept from the profane, and which was typical of the new year and of the transmigration of the soul. The profane, in humble imitation, brewed a bowl of spiced ale, or wine, throwing therein roasted crabs ; the hissing of which, as they plunged, piping hot, into the liquor, was heard with much unction at midwinter, as typical of the conjunct benignant influences of fire and strong drink. The Saxons called this the Wassail-bowl, and the brewage of it is reported to have been one of the charms with which Rowena fascinated Vortigern.

King Arthur kept his Christmas so merrily, that the memory of it passed into a proverb : [1] " As merry as Christmas in Caer Lleon."

Caer Lleon was the merriest of places, and was commonly known by the name of Merry Caer Lleon ; which the English ballad-makers,

[1] Mor llawen ag Ngdolig yn Nghaerlleon. [P.]

for the sake of the smoother sound, and confounding Cambria with Cumbria, most ignorantly or audaciously turned into Merry Carlisle ; thereby emboldening a northern antiquary to set about proving that King Arthur was a Scotchman ; according to the old principles of harry and foray, which gave Scotchmen a right to whatever they could find on the English border ; though the English never admitted their title to any thing there, excepting a halter in Carlisle.[1]

The chace, in the neighbouring forest ; tilting in the amphitheatre ; trials of skill in archery, in throwing the lance and riding at the quintain, and similar amusements of the morning, created good appetites for the evening feasts ; in which Prince Cei, who is well known as Sir Kay, the seneschal, superintended the viands, as King Bedwyr did the liquor ; having each a thousand men at command, for their provision, arrangement, and distribution ; and music worthy of the banquet was provided and superintended by the king's chief harper, Geraint, of whom a contemporary poet observes, that when he died, the gates of heaven were thrown wide open, to welcome the ingress of so divine a musician.

CHAPTER XIII

THE GHOSTLINESS OF AVALLON

Poco più poco meno, tutti al mondo vivono d'impostura : e chi è di buon gusto, dissimula quando occorre, gode quando può, crede quel che vuole, ride de' pazzi, e figura un mondo a suo gusto.   GOLDONI.[2]

" WHERE is the young bard," said King Arthur, after some nights of Christmas had passed by, " who brought me the news of my queen, and to whom I promised a boon, which he has not yet claimed ? "

None could satisfy the king's curiosity.   Taliesin had disappeared

---

[1] From the departure of the Romans until the ninth century Cumbria, stretching from the Ribble to the Clyde, was inhabited by Britons who frequently fought side by side with the Britons of Wales against the Saxons.   The four bards, Aneirin, Llywarch Hen, Taliesin and Merlin, were reputed to have lived, not in Wales, but in Cumbria.   G.

[2] " All in this world live by deception, some to a greater extent, some to a lesser, and the full-blooded man dissimulates when necessary, rejoices when he can, believes what he wants to believe, laughs at the fools, and pictures the world as he desires."   G.

from Caer Lleon. He knew the power and influence of Maelgon Gwyneth ; and he was aware that King Arthur, however favourably he might receive his petition, would not find leisure to compel the liberation of Elphin, till he had enforced from Melvas the surrender of his queen. It occurred to him that her restoration might be effected by peaceable means ; and he knew that, if he could be in any degree instrumental to this result, it would greatly strengthen his claims on the king. He engaged a small fishing-vessel, which had just landed a cargo for the Christmas feasts of Caer Lleon, and set sail for the isle of Avallon. At that period, the springtides of the sea rolled round a cluster of islands, of which Avallon was one, over the extensive fens, which wiser generations have embanked and reclaimed.

The abbey of Avallon, afterwards called Glastonbury, was, even then, a comely and commodious pile, though not possessing any of that magnificence which the accumulated wealth of ages subsequently gave to it. A large and strongly fortified castle, almost adjoining the abbey, gave to the entire place the air of a stronghold of the church militant. King Melvas was one of the pillars of the orthodoxy of those days : he was called the Scourge of the Pelagians ; and extended the shield of his temporal might over the spiritual brotherhood of Avallon, who, in return, made it a point of conscience not to stint him in absolutions.

Some historians pretend that a comfortable nunnery was erected at a convenient distance from the abbey, that is to say, close to it ; but this involves a nice question in monastic antiquity, which the curious may settle for themselves.

It was about midway between nones and vespers when Taliesin sounded, on the gate of the abbey, a notice of his wish for admission. A small trapdoor in the gate was cautiously opened, and a face, as round and as red as the setting sun in November, shone forth in the aperture.

The topographers who have perplexed themselves about the origin of the name of Ynys Avallon, "the island of apples," had not the advantage of this piece of meteoroscopy : if they could have looked on this archetype of a Norfolk beefin, with the knowledge that it was only a sample of a numerous fraternity, they would at once have perceived the fitness of the appellation. The brethren of Avallon were the apples of the church. It was the oldest monastic establishment in Britain ; and consequently, as of reason, the most plump, succulent, and rosy. It had, even in the sixth century, put forth the fruits of good living, in a manner that would have done honour to a more enlightened age. It went on steadily improving in this line till the days of its last abbot, Richard Whiting, who built the stupendous kitchen, which has withstood the ravages of time and the Reformation ; and who, as appears by authentic documents, and, amongst others, by a letter signed with the honoured name of Russell, was found guilty, by a right worshipful jury, of being suspected of great riches, and of an inclination to keep them ; and was accordingly sentenced to be hanged forthwith, along with his treasurer and subtreasurer, who were charged with aiding and abetting him in the safe custody of his cash and plate ; at the same time that the Abbot of Peterborough was specially reprieved from the gallows, on the ground that he was the said Russell's particular friend. This was a compendium of justice and mercy according to the new light of King Henry the Eighth. The abbot's kitchen is the most interesting and perfect portion of the existing ruins. These ruins were overgrown with the finest ivy in England, till it was, not long since, pulled down by some Vandal, whom the Society of Antiquaries had sent down to make drawings of the walls, which he executed literally, by stripping them bare, that he might draw the walls, and nothing else.[1] Its shade no longer waves over the musing moralist, who, with folded arms, and his back against a wall, dreams of the days that are gone ; or the sentimental cockney, who, seating himself with much gravity on a fallen column, produces a flute from his pocket, and strikes up " I'd be a butterfly." [2]

From the phænomenon of a blushing fruit that was put forth in the abbey gate of Avallon issued a deep, fat, gurgling voice, which demanded of Taliesin his name and business.

[1] Thanks to the destruction of the ivy the ruins of Glastonbury have been preserved. G.
[2] A popular song of Peacock's day, written by Thomas Haynes Bayly and beginning :

" I'd be a butterfly,
Born in a bower,
Where roses and lilies and violets meet ! " G.

" I seek the abbot of Avallon," said Taliesin.

" He is confessing a penitent," said the ghostly brother, who was officiating in turn as porter.

" I can await his leisure," said Taliesin, " but I must see him."

" Are you alone ? " said the brother.

" I am," said Taliesin.

The gate unclosed slowly, just wide enough to give him admittance. It was then again barred and barricadoed.

The ghostly brother, of whom Taliesin had now a full view, had a figure corresponding with his face, and wanted nothing but a pair of horns and a beard in ringlets, to look like an avatar of Bacchus. He maintained, however, great gravity of face, and decorum of gesture, as he said to Taliesin, " Hospitality is the rule of our house ; but we are obliged to be cautious in these times, though we live under powerful protection. Those bloody Nimrods, the Saxons, are athirst for the blood of the righteous. Monsters that are born with tails."

Taliesin had not before heard of this feature of Saxon conformation, and expressed his astonishment accordingly.

" How ? " said the monk. " Did not a rabble of them fasten goats' tails to the robe of the blessed preacher in Riw, and did he not, therefore, pray that their posterity might be born with tails ? And it is so. But let that pass.[1] Have they not sacked monasteries, plundered churches, and put holy brethren to the sword ? The blood of the saints calls for vengeance."

" And will have it," said Taliesin, " from the hand of Arthur."

The name of Arthur evidently discomposed the monk, who, desiring Taliesin to follow him, led the way across the hall of the abbey, and along a short wide passage, at the end of which was a portly door.

---

[1] Suggested by stories in two of Peacock's favourite authors—Horne Tooke and Lord Monboddo. Tooke banters Monboddo's positive belief that the inhabitants of the Nicobar Islands had tails like cats which they waved in the same manner, by quoting a story of the Dorset men who were punished with tails because they threw fish tails at Augustine. " But Polydorus applieth it to Kentish men at Strood by Rochester for cutting off Thomas Becket's horse's tail. Thus hath England in all other lands a perpetual infamy of tails."   G.

The monk disappeared through this door, and, presently returning, said, " The abbot requires your name and quality."

"Taliesin, the bard of Elphin ap Gwythno Garanhir," was the reply.

The monk disappeared again, and, returning, after a longer pause than before, said, " You may enter."

The abbot was a plump and comely man, of middle age, having three roses in his complexion ; one in full blossom on each cheek, and one in bud on the tip of his nose.

He was sitting at a small table, on which stood an enormous vase, and a golden goblet ; and opposite to him sat the penitent of whom the round-faced brother had spoken, and in whom Taliesin recognised his acquaintance of Dinas Vawr, who called himself Seithenyn ap Seithyn.

The abbot and Seithenyn sat with their arms folded on the table, leaning forward towards each other, as if in momentous discussion.

The abbot said to Taliesin, " Sit ; " and to his conductor, " Retire, and be silent."

" Will it not be better," said the monk, " that I cross my lips with the sign of secrecy ? "

" It is permitted," said the abbot.

Seithenyn held forth the goblet to the monk, who swallowed the contents with much devotion.   He then withdrew, and closed the door.

" I bid you most heartily welcome," said Seithenyn to Taliesin. " Drink off this, and I will tell you more.   You are admitted to this special sitting at my special instance.   I told the abbot I knew you well.   Now I will tell you what I know.   You have told King Arthur that King Melvas has possession of Queen Gwenyvar, and, in consequence, King Arthur is coming here, to sack and raze the castle and abbey, and cut every throat in the isle of Avallon.   I have just brought the abbot this pleasant intelligence, and, as I knew it would take him down a cup or two, I have also brought what I call my little jug, to have the benefit of his judgment on a piece of rare wine which I have broached this morning : there is no better in Caer Lleon.   And now we are holding council on the emergency. But I must say you abuse your bardic privilege, to enjoy people's hospitality, worm out their secrets, and carry the news to the enemy. It was partly to give you this candid opinion, that I have prevailed on the abbot to admit you to this special sitting. Therefore drink. GWIN O EUR : Wine from gold."

" King Arthur is not a Saxon, at any rate," sighed the abbot, winding up his fainting spirits with a draught. " Think not, young stranger, that I am transgressing the laws of temperance : my blood runs so cold when I think of the bloodthirsty Saxons, that I take a little wine medicinally, in the hope of warming it ; but it is a slow and tedious remedy."

" Take a little more," said Seithenyn. " That is the true quantity. Wine is my medicine ; and my quantity is a little more. A little more."

" King Arthur," said Taliesin, " is not a Saxon ; but he does not brook injuries lightly. It were better for your abbey that he came not here in arms. The aiders and abettors of Melvas, even though they be spiritual, may not carry off the matter without some share of his punishment, which is infallible."

" That is just what I have been thinking," said Seithenyn.

" God knows," said the abbot, " we are not abettors of Melvas, though we need his temporal power to protect us from the Saxons."

" How can it be otherwise," said Taliesin, " than that these Saxon despoilers should be insolent and triumphant, while the princes of Britain are distracted with domestic broils : and for what ? "

" Ay," said Seithenyn, " that is the point. For what ? For a woman, or some such rubbish."

" Rubbish, most verily," said the abbot. " Women are the flesh which we renounce with the devil."

" Holy father," said Taliesin, " have you not spiritual influence with Melvas, to persuade him to surrender the queen without bloodshed, and, renewing his allegiance to Arthur, assist him in his most sacred war against the Saxon invaders ? "

" A righteous work," said the abbot ; " but Melvas is headstrong and difficult."

" Screw yourself up with another goblet," said Seithenyn ; " you will find the difficulty smooth itself off wonderfully. Wine from gold has a sort of double light, that illuminates a dark path miraculously."

The abbot sighed deeply, but adopted Seithenyn's method of throwing light on the subject.

" The anger of King Arthur," said Taliesin, " is certain, and its

consequences infallible. The anger of King Melvas is doubtful, and
its consequences to you cannot be formidable."

" That is nearly true," said the abbot, beginning to look resolute,
as the rosebud at his nose-tip deepened into damask.

" A little more," said Seithenyn, " and it will become quite true."

By degrees the proposition ripened into absolute truth. The
abbot suddenly inflated his cheeks, started on his legs, and stalked
bolt upright out of the apartment, and forthwith out of the abbey,
followed by Seithenyn, tossing his goblet in the air, and catching it
in his hand, as he went.

The round-faced brother made his appearance almost immediately.
" The abbot," he said, " commends you to the hospitality of the
brotherhood. They will presently assemble to supper. In the meanwhile, as I am thirsty, and content with whatever falls in my way,
I will take a simple and single draught of what happens to be here."

His draught was a model of simplicity and singleness ; for, having
uplifted the ponderous vase, he held it to his lips, till he had drained
it of the very copious remnant which the abrupt departure of the
abbot had caused Seithenyn to leave in it.

Taliesin proceeded to enjoy the hospitality of the brethren, who
set before him a very comfortable hot supper, at which he quickly
perceived, that, however dexterous King Elphin might be at catching
fish, the monks of Avallon were very far his masters in the three
great arts of cooking it, serving it up, and washing it down ; but he
had not time to profit by their skill and experience in these matters,
for he received a pressing invitation to the castle of Melvas, which
he obeyed immediately.

CHAPTER XIV

THE RIGHT OF MIGHT

The three triumphs of the bards of the isle of Britain : the triumph of learning
over ignorance ; the triumph of reason over error ; and the triumph of peace
over violence.
TRIADS OF BARDISM.[1]

" FRIEND SEITHENYN," said the abbot, when, having passed the
castle gates, and solicited an audience, he was proceeding to the

[1] The Cambro-Briton, Vol. II, p. 291, 1821. G.

presence of Melvas, "this task, to which I have accinged [1] myself, is arduous, and in some degree awful ; being, in truth, no less than to persuade a king to surrender a possession, which he has inclination to keep for ever, and power to keep, at any rate, for an indefinite time."

" Not so very indefinite," said Seithenyn ; " for with the first song of the cuckoo (whom I mention on this occasion as a party concerned,) King Arthur will batter his castle about his ears, and, in all likelihood, the abbey about yours."

The abbot sighed heavily.

" If your heart fail you," said Seithenyn, " another cup of wine will set all to rights."

" Nay, nay, friend Seithenyn," said the abbot, " that which I have already taken has just brought me to the point at which the heart is inspirited, and the wit sharpened, without any infraction of the wisdom and gravity which become my character, and best suit my present business."

Seithenyn, however, took an opportunity of making signs to some cupbearers, and, when they entered the apartment of Melvas, they were followed by vessels of wine and goblets of gold.

King Melvas was a man of middle age, with a somewhat round, large, regular-featured face, and an habitual smile of extreme self-satisfaction, which he could occasionally convert into a look of terrific ferocity, the more fearful for being rare.   His manners were, for the most part, pleasant.   He did much mischief, not for mischief's sake, nor yet for the sake of excitement, but for the sake of something tangible.   He had a total and most complacent indifference to every thing but his own will and pleasure.   He took what he wanted wherever he could find it, by the most direct process, and without any false pretence.   He would have disdained the trick which the chroniclers ascribe to Hengist, of begging as much land as a bull's hide would surround, and then shaving it into threads, which surrounded a goodly space.   If he wanted a piece of land, he encamped upon it, saying, " This is mine."   If the former possessor could eject him, so ; it was not his : if not, so ; it remained his.   Cattle, wine, furniture, another man's wife, whatever he took a fancy to, he pounced upon and appropriated.   He was intolerant of resistance ;

---

[1] Girded : applied. G.

and, as the shortest way of getting rid of it, and not from any blood-thirstiness of disposition, or, as the phrenologists have it, development of the organ of destructiveness, he always cut through the resisting body, longitudinally, horizontally, or diagonally, as he found most convenient. He was the arch-marauder of West Britain. The abbey of Avallon shared largely in the spoil, and they made up together a most harmonious church and state. He had some respect for King Arthur; wished him success against the Saxons; knew the superiority of his power to his own; but he had heard that Queen Gwenyvar was the most beautiful woman in Britain; was, therefore, satisfied of his own title to her, and, as she was hunting in the forest, while King Arthur was absent from Caer Lleon, he seized her, and carried her off.

" Be seated, holy father," said Melvas; " and you, also, Seithenyn, unless the abbot wishes you away."

But the abbot's heart misgave him, and he assented readily to Seithenyn's stay.

MELVAS. Now, holy father, to your important matter of private conference.

SEITHENYN. He is tongue-tied, and a cup too low.

THE ABBOT. Set the goblet before me, and I will sip in moderation.

MELVAS. Sip, or not sip, tell me your business.

THE ABBOT. My business, of a truth, touches the lady your prisoner, King Arthur's queen.

MELVAS. She is my queen, while I have her, and no prisoner. Drink, man, and be not afraid. Speak your mind: I will listen, and weigh your words.

THE ABBOT. This queen——

SEITHENYN. Obey the king: first drink, then speak.

THE ABBOT. I drink to please the king.

MELVAS. Proceed.

THE ABBOT. This queen, Gwenyvar, is as beautiful as Helen, who caused the fatal war that expelled our forefathers from Troy : and I fear she will be a second Helen, and expel their posterity from Britain.[1]   The infidel Saxons, to whom the cowardly and perfidious Vortigern gave footing in Britain, have prospered even more by the disunion of her princes than either by his villainy, or their own valour.   And now there is no human hope against them but in the arms of Arthur.   And how shall his arms prosper against the common enemy, if he be forced to turn them on the children of his own land for the recovery of his own wife ?

MELVAS.   What do you mean by his own ?   That which he has, is his own : but that which I have, is mine.   I have the wife in question, and some of the land.   Therefore they are mine.

THE ABBOT.   Not so.   The land is yours under fealty to him.

MELVAS.   As much fealty as I please, or he can force me, to give him.

THE ABBOT.   His wife, at least, is most lawfully his.

MELVAS.   The winner makes the law, and his law is always against the loser.   I am so far the winner ;   and, by my own law, she is lawfully mine.

THE ABBOT.   There is a law above all human law, by which she is his.

MELVAS.   From that it is for you to absolve me ;   and I dispense my bounty according to your indulgence.

THE ABBOT.   There are limits we must not pass.

MELVAS.   You set up your landmark, and I set up mine.   They are both moveable.

THE ABBOT.   The Church has not been niggardly in its indulgences to King Melvas.

[1] According to the British Chronicles, Brutus, the great grandson of Æneas, having killed his father, Silvius, to fulfil a prophecy, went to Greece, where he found the posterity of Helenus, the son of Priam; collected all of the Trojan race within the limits of Greece ; and, after some adventures by land and sea, settled them in Britain, which was before uninhabited, " except by a few giants."   [P.]

MELVAS. Nor King Melvas in his gifts to the Church.

THE ABBOT. But, setting aside this consideration, I would treat it as a question of policy.

SEITHENYN. Now you talk sense. Right without might is the lees of an old barrel, without a drop of the original liquor.

THE ABBOT. I would appeal to you, King Melvas, by your love to your common country, by your love of the name of Britain, by your hatred of the infidel Saxons, by your respect for the character of Arthur; will you let your passion for a woman, even though she be a second Helen, frustrate, or even impede, the great cause, of driving these spoilers from a land in which they have no right even to breathe?

MELVAS. They have a right to do all they do, and to have all they have. If we can drive them out, they will then have no right here. Have not you and I a right to this good wine, which seems to trip very merrily over your ghostly palate? I got it by seizing a good ship, and throwing the crew overboard, just to remove them out of the way, because they were troublesome. They disputed my right, but I taught them better. I taught them a great moral lesson, though they had not much time to profit by it. If they had had the might to throw me overboard, I should not have troubled myself about their right, any more, or, at any rate, any longer, than they did about mine.

SEITHENYN. The wine was lawful spoil of war.

THE ABBOT. But if King Arthur brings his might to bear upon yours, I fear neither you nor I shall have a right to this wine, nor to any thing else that is here.

SEITHENYN. Then make the most of it while you have it.

THE ABBOT. Now, while you have some months of security before you, you may gain great glory by surrendering the lady; and, if you be so disposed, you may no doubt claim, from the gratitude of King Arthur, the fairest princess of his court to wife, and an ample dower withal.

MELVAS. That offers something tangible.

SEITHENYN.   Another ray from the golden goblet will set it in a most luminous view.

THE ABBOT.   Though I should advise the not making it a condition, but asking it, as a matter of friendship, after the first victory that you have helped him to gain over the Saxons.

MELVAS.   The worst of those Saxons is, that they offer nothing tangible, except hard knocks.   They bring nothing with them.   They come to take ; and lately they have not taken much.   But I will muse on your advice ; and, as it seems, I may get more by following than rejecting it, I shall very probably take it, provided that you now attend me to the banquet in the hall.

SEITHENYN.   Now you talk of the hall and the banquet, I will just intimate that the finest of all youths, and the best of all bards, is a guest in the neighbouring abbey.

MELVAS.   If so, I have a clear right to him, as a guest for myself.

The abbot was not disposed to gainsay King Melvas's right. Taliesin was invited accordingly, and seated at the left hand of the king, the abbot being on the right.   Taliesin summoned all the energies of his genius to turn the passions of Melvas into the channels of Anti-Saxonism, and succeeded so perfectly, that the king and his whole retinue of magnanimous heroes were inflamed with intense ardour to join the standard of Arthur ; and Melvas vowed most solemnly to Taliesin, that another sun should not set, before Queen Gwenyvar should be under the most honourable guidance on her return to Caer Lleon.

CHAPTER XV

THE CIRCLE OF THE BARDS

The three dignities of poetry : the union of the true and the wonderful ; the union of the beautiful and the wise ; and the union of art and nature.
TRIADS OF POETRY.[1]

AMONGST the Christmas amusements of Caer Lleon, a grand Bardic Congress was held in the Roman theatre, when the principal bards of

[1] The *Cambro-Briton*, Vol. II, p. 291, 1821.   G.

Britain contended for the preeminence in the art of poetry, and in its appropriate moral and mystical knowledge. The meeting was held by daylight. King Arthur presided, being himself an irregular bard, and admitted, on this public occasion, to all the efficient honours of a Bard of Presidency.

To preside in the Bardic Congress was long a peculiar privilege of the kings of Britain. It was exercised in the seventh century by King Cadwallader. King Arthur was assisted by twelve umpires, chosen by the bards, and confirmed by the king.

The Court, of course, occupied the stations of honour, and every other part of the theatre was crowded with a candid and liberal audience.

The bards sate in a circle on that part of the theatre corresponding with the portion which we call the stage.

Silence was proclaimed by the herald; and, after a grand symphony, which was led off in fine style by the king's harper, Geraint, Prince Cei came forward, and made a brief oration, to the effect that any of the profane, who should be irregular and tumultuous, would be forcibly removed from the theatre, to be dealt with at the discretion of the officer of the guard. Silence was then a second time proclaimed by the herald.

Each bard, as he stood forward, was subjected to a number of interrogatories, metrical and mystical, which need not be here reported. Many bards sang many songs. Amongst them, Prince Llywarch sang

GORWYNION Y GAUAV.
THE BRILLIANCIES OF WINTER.

Last of flowers, in tufts around
Shines the gorse's golden bloom :
Milkwhite lichens clothe the ground
'Mid the flowerless heath and broom :
Bright are holly-berries, seen
Red, through leaves of glossy green.

Brightly, as on rocks they leap,
Shine the sea-waves, white with spray ;
Brightly, in the dingles deep,
Gleams the river's foaming way ;
Brightly through the distance show
Mountain-summits clothed in snow.

Brightly, where the torrents bound,
Shines the frozen colonnade,
Which the black rocks, dripping round,
And the flying spray have made :
Bright the icedrops on the ash
Leaning o'er the cataract's dash.

Bright the hearth, where feast and song
Crown the warrior's hour of peace,
While the snow-storm drives along,
Bidding war's worse tempest cease ;
Bright the hearthflame, flashing clear
On the up-hung shield and spear.

Bright the torchlight of the hall
When the wintry night-winds blow ;
Brightest when its splendours fall
On the mead-cup's sparkling flow :
While the maiden's smile of light
Makes the brightness trebly bright.

Close the portals ; pile the hearth ;
Strike the harp ; the feast pursue ;
Brim the horns : fire, music, mirth,
Mead and love, are winter's due.
Spring to purple conflict calls
Swords that shine on winter's walls.

Llywarch's song was applauded, as presenting a series of images
with which all present were familiar, and which were all of them
agreeable.

Merlin sang some verses of the poem, which is called

AVALLENAU MYRDDIN.
MERLIN'S APPLE-TREES.

Fair the gift to Merlin given,
Apple-trees seven score and seven ;
Equal all in age and size ;
On a green hill-slope, that lies
Basking in the southern sun,
Where bright waters murmuring run.

Just beneath the pure stream flows ;
High above the forest grows ;
Not again on earth is found
Such a slope of orchard ground :
Song of birds, and hum of bees,
Ever haunt the apple-trees.

Three hundred chiefs, three score and three,
Went, where the festal torches burned
Before the dweller of the sea :
They went ; and three alone returned.

'Till dawn the pale sweet mead they quaffed :
The ocean-chief unclosed his vest ;
His hand was on his dagger's haft,
And daggers glared at every breast.

But him, at Eidiol's [1] breast who aimed,
The mighty Briton's arm laid low :
His eyes with righteous anger flamed ;
He wrenched the dagger from the foe ;

And through the throng he cleft his way,
And raised without his battle cry ;
And hundreds hurried to the fray,
From towns, and vales, and mountains high.

But Britain's best blood dyed the floor
Within the treacherous Saxon's hall ;
Of all, the golden chain who wore,
Two only answered Eidiol's call.

Then clashed the sword ; then pierced the lance ;
Then by the axe the shield was riven ;
Then did the steed on Cattraeth prance,
And deep in blood his hoofs were driven.

Even as the flame consumes the wood,
So Eidiol rushed along the field ;
As sinks the snow-bank in the flood,
So did the ocean-rovers yield.

The spoilers from the fane he drove
He hurried to the rock-built tower,
Where the base king,[2] in mirth and love,
Sate with his Saxon paramour.[2]

The storm of arms was on the gate,
The blaze of torches in the hall,
So swift, that ere they feared their fate,
The flames had scaled their chamber wall.

They died : for them no Briton grieves ;
No planted flower above them waves ;
No hand removes the withered leaves
That strew their solitary graves.

---

[1] Eidiol or Emrys : Emrys Wledig : Ambrosius. [P.]
[2] Vortigern and Rowena. [P.]

And time the avenging day brought round
That saw the sea-chief vainly sue :
To make his false host bite the ground
Was all the hope our warrior knew.

And evermore the strife he led,
Disdaining peace, with princely might,
Till, on a spear, the spoiler's [1] head
Was reared on Caer-y-Cynan's height.

The Song of Aneurin touched deeply on the sympathies of the audience, and was followed by a grand martial symphony, in the midst of which Taliesin appeared in the Circle of Bards. King Arthur welcomed him with great joy, and sweet smiles were showered upon him from all the beauties of the court.

Taliesin answered the metrical and mystical questions to the astonishment of the most proficient ; and, advancing, in his turn, to the front of the circle, he sang a portion of a poem which is now called HANES TALIESIN, The History of Taliesin [2]; but which shall be here entitled

THE CAULDRON OF CERIDWEN.

The sage Ceridwen was the wife
Of Tegid Voël, of Pemble Mere :
Two children blest their wedded life,
Morvran and Creirwy, fair and dear :
Morvran, a son of peerless worth,
And Creirwy, loveliest nymph of earth :
But one more son Ceridwen bare,
As foul as they before were fair.

She strove to make Avagddu wise ;
She knew he never could be fair :
And, studying magic mysteries,
She gathered plants of virtue rare :
She placed the gifted plants to steep
Within the magic cauldron deep,
Where they a year and day must boil,
'Till three drops crown the matron's toil.

---

[1] Hengist. [P.]

[2] Peacock has not attempted to follow the fragmentary *Hanes Taliesin* here, but has told the story as given in *The Mabinogion*. See Nash's *Taliesin*, p. 156, and Guest : *Mabinogion*, pp. 471-3. G.

Nine damsels raised the mystic flame ;
Gwion the Little near it stood :
The while for simples roved the dame
Through tangled dell and pathless wood.
And, when the year and day had past,
The dame within the cauldron cast
The consummating chaplet wild,
While Gwion held the hideous child.

But from the cauldron rose a smoke
That filled with darkness all the air :
When through its folds the torchlight broke,
Nor Gwion, nor the boy, was there.
The fire was dead, the cauldron cold,
And in it lay, in sleep uprolled,
Fair as the morning-star, a child,
That woke, and stretched its arms, and smiled.

What chanced her labours to destroy,
She never knew ; and sought in vain
If 'twere her own misshapen boy,
Or little Gwion, born again :
And, vext with doubt, the babe she rolled
In cloth of purple and of gold,
And in a coracle consigned
Its fortunes to the sea and wind.

The summer night was still and bright,
The summer moon was large and clear,
The frail bark, on the springtide's height,
Was floated into Elphin's weir.
The baby in his arms he raised :
His lovely spouse stood by, and gazed,
And, blessing it with gentle vow,
Cried " TALIESIN ! " " Radiant brow ! "

And I am he : and well I know
Ceridwen's power protects me still ;
And hence o'er hill and vale I go,
And sing, unharmed, whate'er I will.
She has for me Time's veil withdrawn :
The images of things long gone,
The shadows of the coming days,
Are present to my visioned gaze.

And I have heard the words of power,
By Ceirion's solitary lake,
That bid, at midnight's thrilling hour,
Eryri's hundred echoes wake.

I to Diganwy's towers have sped,
And now Caer Lleon's halls I tread,
Demanding justice, now, as then,
From Maelgon, most unjust of men.

The audience shouted with delight at the song of Taliesin, and King Arthur, as President of the Bardic Congress, conferred on him, at once, the highest honours of the sitting.

Where Taliesin picked up the story which he told of himself, why he told it, and what he meant by it, are questions not easily answered. Certain it is, that he told this story to his contemporaries, and that none of them contradicted it. It may, therefore, be presumed that they believed it; as any one who pleases is most heartily welcome to do now.

Besides the single songs, there were songs in dialogue, approaching very nearly to the character of dramatic poetry; and pennillion, or unconnected stanzas, sung in series by different singers, the stanzas being complete in themselves, simple as Greek epigrams, and presenting in succession moral precepts, pictures of natural scenery, images of war or of festival, the lamentations of absence or captivity, and the complaints or triumphs of love. This pennillion-singing long survived among the Welsh peasantry almost every other vestige of bardic customs, and may still be heard among them on the few occasions on which rack-renting, tax-collecting, common-enclosing, methodist-preaching, and similar developments of the light of the age, have left them either the means or inclination of making merry.

CHAPTER XVI

THE JUDGMENTS OF ARTHUR

Three things to which success cannot fail where they shall justly be: discretion, exertion, and hope.

TRIADS OF WISDOM.

KING ARTHUR had not long returned to his hall, when Queen Gwenyvar arrived, escorted by the Abbot of Avallon and Seithenyn ap Seithyn Saidi, who had brought his golden goblet, to gain a new harvest of glory from the cellars of Caer Lleon.

Seithenyn assured King Arthur, in the name of King Melvas, and on the word of a king, backed by that of his butler, which, truth being in wine, is good warranty even for a king, that the queen returned as pure as on the day King Melvas had carried her off.

"None here will doubt that;" said Gwenvach, the wife of Modred. Gwenyvar was not pleased with the compliment, and, almost before she had saluted King Arthur, she turned suddenly round, and slapped Gwenvach on the face, with a force that brought more crimson into one cheek than blushing had ever done into both. This slap is recorded in the Bardic Triads as one of the Three Fatal Slaps of the Island of Britain. A terrible effect is ascribed to this small cause ; for it is said to have been the basis of that enmity between Arthur and Modred, which terminated in the battle of Camlan, wherein all the flower of Britain perished on both sides : a catastrophe more calamitous than any that ever before or since happened in Christendom, not even excepting that of the battle of Roncesvalles ; for, in the battle of Camlan, the Britons exhausted their own strength, and could no longer resist the progress of the Saxon supremacy. This, however, was a later result, and comes not within the scope of the present veridicous narrative.

Gwenvach having flounced out of the hall, and the tumult occasioned by this little incident having subsided, Queen Gwenyvar took her ancient seat by the side of King Arthur, who proceeded to inquire into the circumstances of her restoration.. The Abbot of Avallon began an oration, in praise of his own eloquence, and its miraculous effects on King Melvas ; but he was interrupted by Seithenyn, who said, " The abbot's eloquence was good and well timed ; but the chief merit belongs to this young bard, who prompted him with good counsel, and to me, who inspirited him with good liquor. If he had not opened his mouth pretty widely when I handed him this golden goblet, exclaiming GWIN O EUR, he would never have had the heart to open it to any other good purpose. But the most deserving person is this very promising youth, in whom I can see no fault, but that he has not the same keen perception as my friend the abbot has of the excellent relish of wine from gold. To be sure, he plied me very hard with strong drink in the hall of Dinas Vawr, and thereby wormed out of me the secret of Queen Gwenyvar's captivity ; and, afterwards, he pursued us to Avallon, where he persuaded me and the abbot, and the abbot persuaded King Melvas, that it would be better for all parties to restore the queen peaceably : and then he clenched the matter with the very best song I ever heard in my life. And, as my young friend has a boon to ask, I freely give him all my share of the merit, and the abbot's into the bargain."

" Allow me, friend GWIN O EUR," said the abbot, " to dispose of my own share of merit in my own way.   But, such as it is, I freely give it to this youth, in whom, as you say, I can see no fault, but that his head is brimfull of Pagan knowledge."

Arthur paid great honour to Taliesin, and placed him on his left hand at the banquet.   He then said to him, " I judge, from your song of this morning, that the boon you require from me concerns Maelgon Gwyneth.   What is his transgression, and what is the justice you require ? "

Taliesin narrated the adventures of Elphin in such a manner as gave Arthur an insight into his affection for Melanghel ; and he supplicated King Arthur to command and enforce the liberation of Elphin from the Stone Tower of Diganwy.

Before King Arthur could signify his assent, Maelgon Gwyneth stalked into the hall, followed by a splendid retinue.   He had been alarmed by the absence of Rhûn, had sought him in vain on the banks of the Mawddach, had endeavoured to get at the secret by pouncing upon Angharad and Melanghel, and had been baffled in his project by the vigilance of Teithrin ap Tathral.   He had, there-fore, as a last resort, followed Taliesin to Caer Lleon, conceiving that he might have had some share in the mysterious disappearance of Rhûn.

Arthur informed him that he was in possession of all the circum-stances, and that Rhûn, who was in safe custody, would be liberated on the restoration of Elphin.

Maelgon boiled with rage and shame, but had no alternative but submission to the will of Arthur.

King Arthur commanded that all the parties should be brought before him.   Caradoc was charged with the execution of this order, and, having received the necessary communications and powers from Maelgon and Taliesin, he went first to Diganwy, where he liberated Elphin, and then proceeded to give effect to Teithrin's declaration, that "no hand but Elphin's should raise the stone of Rhûn's captivity." Rhûn, while his pleasant adventure had all the gloss of novelty upon it, and his old renown as a gay deceiver was consequently in such dim eclipse, was very unwilling to present himself before the ladies of Caer Lleon ; but Caradoc was peremptory, and carried off the crest-fallen prince, together with his bard of all work, who was always willing to go to any court, with any character, or none.

Accordingly, after a moderate lapse of time, Caradoc reappeared in the hall of Arthur, with the liberated captives, accompanied by Angharad and Melanghel, and Teithrin ap Tathral.

King Arthur welcomed the new comers with a magnificent festival, at which all the beauties of his court were present, and, addressing himself to Elphin, said, " We are all debtors to this young bard : my queen and myself for her restoration to me ; you for your liberation from the Stone Tower of Diganwy. Now, if there be, amongst all these ladies, one whom he would choose for his bride, and in whose eyes he may find favour, I will give the bride a dowry worthy of the noblest princess in Britain."

Taliesin, thus encouraged, took the hand of Melanghel, who did not attempt to withdraw it, but turned to her father a blushing face, in which he read her satisfaction and her wishes. Elphin immediately said, " I have nothing to give him but my daughter ; but her I most cordially give him."

Taliesin said, " I owe to Elphin more than I can ever repay : life, honour, and happiness."

Arthur said, " You have not paid him ill ; but you owe nothing to Maelgon and Rhûn, who are your debtors for a lesson of justice, which I hope they will profit by during the rest of their lives. Therefore Maelgon shall defray the charge of your wedding, which shall be the most splendid that has been seen in Caer Lleon."

Maelgon looked exceedingly grim, and wished himself well back in Diganwy.

There was a very pathetic meeting of recognition between Seithenyn and his daughter ; at the end of which he requested her husband's interest to obtain for him the vacant post of second butler to King Arthur. He obtained this honourable office ; and was so zealous in the fulfilment of its duties, that, unless on actual service with a detachment of liquor, he never was a minute absent from the Temple of Diana.

At a subsequent Bardic Congress, Taliesin was unanimously elected Pen Beirdd, or Chief of the Bards of Britain. The kingdom of Caredigion flourished under the protection of Arthur, and, in the ripeness of time, passed into the hands of Avaon, the son of Taliesin and Melanghel.

THE END

CROTCHET CASTLE

Should once the world resolve to abolish
All that's ridiculous and foolish,
It would have nothing left to do,
To apply in jest or earnest to.

BUTLER.[1]

---

[1] *Miscellaneous Thoughts.*   G.

¹ Peacock has improved the sense of the lines opposite by misquotation from the Marquis de Sade's :

> " Tous les hommes sont fous et qui n'en veut pas voir
> Doit rester dans sa chambre et casser son miroir."

De Sade appears to have taken them from the 4th Satire of Claude Le Petit's *Discours Satiriques* (Rouen, 1686), where they occur in the illogical form :

> " C'est une nation de telle entendue
> Que de quelque côté que l'on tourne la vue
> Il s'en presente aux yeux, et qui n'en veut pas voir
> Doit les tenir fermés et casser son miroir."

—the smashing of the mirror being unnecessary. The final polishing is found in a brilliant translation in Mark Lemon's *Jest Book*, Epigram DCCXXVIII :

> " He that will never look upon an ass,
> Must lock his door and break his looking-glass."   G.

CROTCHET CASTLE

Le monde est plein de fous, et qui n'en veut pas voir,
Doit se tenir tout seul, et casser son miroir.[1]

Crotchet Castle was first published in 1831

CONTENTS OF
CROTCHET CASTLE

CHAPTER		PAGE
	Introduction by David Garnett .	645
I	THE VILLA	649
II	THE MARCH OF MIND . .	655
III	THE ROMAN CAMP . . .	663
IV	THE PARTY	671
V	CHARACTERS	677
VI	THEORIES	685
VII	THE SLEEPING VENUS . .	694
VIII	SCIENCE AND CHARITY . .	702
IX	THE VOYAGE	708
X	THE VOYAGE, CONTINUED . .	713
XI	CORRESPONDENCE . . .	719
XII	THE MOUNTAIN INN . . .	724
XIII	THE LAKE—THE RUIN . .	727
XIV	THE DINGLE	729
XV	THE FARM	734
XVI	THE NEWSPAPER . . .	738
XVII	THE INVITATION . . .	746
XVIII	CHAINMAIL HALL . . .	750

INTRODUCTION TO
CROTCHET CASTLE

CROTCHET CASTLE was published in 1831, two years after *The Misfortunes of Elphin*, and as many of the allusions in it are topical we may assume that it was written in the interval. It has been generally regarded as the best of Peacock's novels; nevertheless I personally prefer both *Nightmare Abbey* and *Gryll Grange*. The only reasons that I can put forward for this opinion are that both appear to me to show greater unity of construction and to be peopled with more delightful characters. From the latter point of view, the defect of *Crotchet Castle* is the Crotchet family; not the crotchets in the heads of its visitors, which are as amusing as ever, but Mr. Crotchet, Mr Crotchet junior, and Miss Crotchet, who are unworthy of their guests. They make the best amends possible in the way of salmon, hock, champagne, Graves, Sauternes, Hermitage, chicken and asparagus, and vintage of 1815, which explains why the company is better than one would expect to find in the house of a retired Scotch stockbroker who confesses that he has invited them for an ulterior reason. "The sentimental against the rational, the intuitive against the inductive, the ornamental against the useful, the intense against the tranquil, the romantic against the classical; these are great and interesting controversies, which I should like, before I die, to see satisfactorily settled."

What an awful way to pay for one's dinner! What a prize bore! And how far more sympathetic as hosts are that enthusiastic tipsy Squire Headlong, that blue-stocking Anthelia Melincourt, and Mr Gryll whose pedigree alone makes one glad to have met him. Even the whimsical and gloomy Mr Christopher Glowry claims sympathy as a real eccentric, though there is no question but that the castellated villa at Streatley or Goring—or is it Henley-on-Thames?—was much more comfortable than the ancient Lincolnshire Abbey noisy with owls and young Deathsheads.

The reader, unable to enjoy the comfort of the villa, will however find the company at Crotchet Castle superior in one way, since Lady Clarinda is rightly and unanimously regarded as the most attractive of all Peacock's women. The ladies in *Gryll Grange*, not forgetting Miss Ilex, run her close.

Professor Raleigh first pointed out the pleasant impression that all Peacock's young women make on the reader, partly owing to their absence of censoriousness, and he suggested that Meredith was indebted to his father-in-law for the characters of his women. He undoubtedly was thinking of Peacock himself when he created the character of Dr Middleton in *The Egoist*.

The least attractive feature of nineteenth-century literature, from Scott and Byron onwards, is the convention with which male writers treated their female characters, in an attempt to disguise the inferior position of women. This conventional attitude resulted in an endless procession of insipid heroines, mercenary hags and ancient crones.

Peacock is markedly in advance of his age in his preference for intelligent, well-educated, and even moderately emancipated women. Indeed in this respect he is more like a French than an English writer of the period. We know also that what was true of Peacock's novels was true of his life.

In contrast to his insistence on female education is his suspicion of the introduction of popular education by Brougham and the Society for the Diffusion of Useful Knowledge.

Almost all of Peacock's biographers and editors have fallen into the mistake of identifying his opinions with those of Dr Folliott, perhaps because of the immense vigour and vitality of that divine. Peacock would not have shared Dr Folliott's prejudices in Chapter VII. Like Dr Folliott, Peacock was a traditionalist who believed in a class-stratified society which, as Cobbett advocated, should be based on an independent and prosperous yeomanry. And like the Doctor, he hated the industrial revolution and the " march of mind " which accompanied it.

Nevertheless the attacks on Brougham, " the learned friend," must not be misunderstood or set down to Peacock's having changed his views as the result of obtaining a secure position. At first it looks like it. In a letter to Shelley dated July 5, 1818, Peacock wrote: "Brougham is contesting Westmoreland against the Lowthers. Wordsworth has published an *Address to the Freeholders*, in which he says they ought not to choose so poor a man as Brougham, riches being the only guarantees of political integrity. He goes farther than this, and actually asserts that the Commons ought to be chosen by the Peers. Now there is a pretty rascal for you." On July 19 he gives Shelley the further news: "Brougham has lost the Westmoreland election by a small difference of number. The Cumberland Poets, by their own conduct on this occasion, have put the finishing stroke to their own disgrace. I am persuaded there is nothing in the way of dirty work that these men are not abject enough to do, if the blessed Lord (Lonsdale) commanded it, or any other blessed member of the holy and almighty seat-selling aristocracy to which they have sold themselves, body and soul."

By 1831 Peacock was, as the reader will see, vehemently opposed to Brougham and all his works. He had not, however, changed his principles; he had merely learned to mistrust Brougham. In this he showed some prescience, for Brougham's egotism after he was made Lord Chancellor on 22 November, 1830, gravely embarrassed the Prime Ministers, Lord Grey and Lord Melbourne, under whom he served, and to both of whom he was so constantly disloyal that after 1835 the Whigs resolved that he should never again hold office in one of their cabinets. Among instances of Brougham's unreliability when Lord Chancellor may be mentioned his spending the night in a drunken orgy with members of the Bar at Lancaster, losing the Great Seal during a game of blind man's buff at a country house, and delivering a harangue on his own virtues at a banquet given in honour of Lord Grey, after he had helped to bring about Grey's resignation.

I am not suggesting that Peacock was a political partisan. He was not; but five years after the publication of *Crotchet Castle* there were many Whigs, or Liberals, who would have most forcibly endorsed every word of Dr Folliott's with regard to "the learned friend."

The real villain of the piece, however, is Sir Simon Steeltrap, who has "enclosed commons and woodlands; abolished cottage-gardens;

taken the village cricket-ground into his own park, out of pure regard
to the sanctity of Sunday ; shut up footpaths and alehouses . . . put
down fairs and fiddlers . . . convicted one-third of the peasantry
. . . suspected the rest.''

It is for these sins that Dr Folliott was the victim of an attack
by footpads ; and that the company at Chainmail Hall had to defend
itself against the rabble-rout followers of Captain Swing. As we
shall see in *Gryll Grange*, Peacock's suspicions of the " progressive "
parties grew steadily during the following thirty years—and, as we
shall see, with good reason.

Though *Crotchet Castle* fails to achieve the perfectly balanced unity
of construction of *Nightmare Abbey*, falling, though in a lesser degree,
into the faults of *Melincourt*, there is a noticeable improvement in
the dialogue, which has indeed reached perfection. Shelley knew
not how to praise sufficiently the lightness, chastity and strength of
the language of *Nightmare Abbey*, a judgment which is even truer of
Crotchet Castle. Mr Priestley most justly points out that the
epigrammatic brevity of all the talkers, so that " even the maddest
of them is something of a stylist and a wit, gives a curious under-
current of irony. . . . They explain themselves, as it were, only
too well." In that, he says, lies the enduring appeal of Peacock's
style for those with a sense of humour and a fine literary palate.
I know of no better judgment of Peacock as a writer.

D. G.

CROTCHET CASTLE

CHAPTER I

THE VILLA

Captain Jamy. I wad full fain hear some question 'tween you tway.
—*Henry V.*[1]

In one of those beautiful vallies, through which the Thames (not yet polluted by the tide, the scouring of cities, or even the minor defilement of the sandy streams of Surrey,) rolls a clear flood through flowery meadows, under the shade of old beech woods, and the smooth mossy greensward of the chalk hills (which pour into it their tributary rivulets, as pure and pellucid as the fountain of Bandusium, or the wells of Scamander, by which the wives and daughters of the Trojans washed their splendid garments in the days of peace, before the coming of the Greeks); in one of those beautiful vallies, on a bold round-surfaced lawn, spotted with juniper, that opened itself in the bosom of an old wood, which rose with a steep, but not precipitous ascent, from the river to the summit of the hill, stood the castellated villa of a retired citizen. Ebenezer Mac Crotchet, Esquire, was the London-born offspring of a worthy native of the "north countrie," who had walked up to London on a commercial adventure, with all his surplus capital, not very neatly tied up in a not very clean handkerchief, suspended over his shoulder from the end of a hooked stick, extracted from the first hedge on his pilgrimage; and who, after having worked himself a step or two up the ladder of life, had won the virgin heart of the only daughter of a highly respectable merchant of Duke's Place, with whom he inherited the honest fruits of a long series of ingenuous dealings.

Mr. Mac Crotchet had derived from his mother the instinct, and from his father the rational principle, of enriching himself at the

[1] Act III, Sc. 2. G.

expense of the rest of mankind, by all the recognised modes of accumulation on the windy side of the law. After passing many years in the alley,[1] watching the turn of the market, and playing many games almost as desperate as that of the soldier of Lucullus,[2] the fear of losing what he had so righteously gained predominated over the sacred thirst of paper-money; his caution got the better of his instinct, or rather transferred it from the department of acquisition to that of conservation. His friend, Mr. Ramsbottom, the zodiacal mythologist,[3] told him that he had done well to withdraw from the region of Uranus or Brahma, the maker, to that of Saturn or Veeshnu, the preserver, before he fell under the eye of Jupiter or Seva, the destroyer, who might have struck him down at a blow.

It is said, that a Scotchman returning home, after some years' residence in England, being asked what he thought of the English, answered: "They hanna ower muckle sense, but they are an unco braw people to live amang;" which would be a very good story, if it were not rendered apocryphal, by the incredible circumstance of the Scotchman going back.

Mr. Mac Crotchet's experience had given him a just title to make, in his own person, the last-quoted observation, but he would have known better than to go back, even if himself, and not his father, had been the first comer of his line from the north. He had married an English Christian, and, having none of the Scotch accent, was ungracious enough to be ashamed of his blood. He was desirous to obliterate alike the Hebrew and Caledonian vestiges in his name, and signed himself E. M. Crotchet, which by degrees induced the majority of his neighbours to think that his name was Edward Matthew. The more effectually to sink the Mac, he christened his villa Crotchet Castle, and determined to hand down to posterity the honours of Crotchet of Crotchet. He found it essential to his dignity to furnish himself with a coat of arms, which, after the proper ceremonies (payment being the principal), he obtained, videlicet: Crest, a crotchet rampant, in A sharp: Arms, three empty bladders,

---

[1] 'Change Alley, by the London Stock Exchange. G.

[2] *Luculli miles*, &c, HOR. *Ep.* II. 2. 26. "In Anna's wars, a soldier poor and bold," &c.—POPE's *Imitation*. [P.] "Bold" should be "old." G.

[3] J. F. Newton. See pp. xiii, 7, 12 and 361. G.

turgescent, to show how opinions are formed ; three bags of gold, pendent, to show why they are maintained ; three naked swords, tranchant, to show how they are administered ; and three barbers' blocks, gaspant, to show how they are swallowed.

Mr. Crotchet was left a widower, with two children ; and, after the death of his wife, so strong was his sense of the blessed comfort she had been to him, that he determined never to give any other woman an opportunity of obliterating the happy recollection.

He was not without a plausible pretence for styling his villa a castle, for, in its immediate vicinity, and within his own enclosed domain, were the manifest traces, on the brow of the hill, of a Roman station, or *castellum*, which was still called the castle by the country people. The primitive mounds and trenches, merely overgrown with greensward, with a few patches of juniper and box on the vallum, and a solitary ancient beech surrounding the place of the prætorium, presented nearly the same depths, heights, slopes, and forms, which the Roman soldiers had originally given them. From this *castellum* Mr. Crotchet christened his villa. With his rustic neighbours he was of course immediately and necessarily a squire : Squire Crotchet of the castle ; and he seemed to himself to settle down as naturally into an English country gentleman, as if his parentage had been as innocent of both Scotland and Jerusalem, as his education was of Rome and Athens.

But as, though you expel nature with a pitchfork, she will yet always come back ; [1] he could not become, like a true-born English squire, part and parcel of the barley-giving earth ; he could not find in game-bagging, poacher-shooting, trespasser-pounding, footpath-stopping, common-enclosing, rack-renting, and all the other liberal pursuits and pastimes which make a country gentleman an ornament to the world, and a blessing to the poor ; he could not find in these valuable and amiable occupations, and in a corresponding range of ideas, nearly commensurate with that of the great King Nebuchadnezzar, when he was turned out to grass ; he could not find in this great variety of useful action, and vast field of comprehensive thought, modes of filling up his time that accorded with his Cale-

---

[1] Naturam expellas furcâ, tamen usque recurret.—Hor. *Ep.* I. 10. 24.

[P.]

donian instinct. The inborn love of disputation, which the excitements and engagements of a life of business had smothered, burst
forth through the calmer surface of a rural life. He grew as fain as
Captain Jamy, " to hear some airgument betwixt ony tway ; " and
being very hospitable in his establishment, and liberal in his invitations, a numerous detachment from the advanced guard of the
" march of intellect," often marched down to Crotchet Castle.

When the fashionable season filled London with exhibitors of all
descriptions, lecturers and else, Mr. Crotchet was in his glory ; for,
in addition to the perennial literati of the metropolis, he had the
advantage of the visits of a number of hardy annuals, chiefly from
the north, who, as the interval of their metropolitan flowering
allowed, occasionally accompanied their London brethren in excur-
sions to Crotchet Castle.

Amongst other things, he took very naturally to political economy,
read all the books on the subject which were put forth by his own
countrymen, attended all lectures thereon, and boxed the technology
of the sublime science as expertly as an able seaman boxes the
compass.

With this agreeable mania he had the satisfaction of biting his son,
the hope of his name and race, who had borne off from Oxford the
highest academical honours ; and who, treading in his father's foot-
steps to honour and fortune, had, by means of a portion of the old
gentleman's surplus capital, made himself a junior partner in the
eminent loan-jobbing firm of Catchflat and Company. Here, in the
days of paper prosperity, he applied his science-illumined genius to
the blowing of bubbles, the bursting of which sent many a poor devil
to the jail, the workhouse, or the bottom of the river, but left young
Crotchet rolling in riches.

These riches he had been on the point of doubling, by a marriage
with the daughter of Mr. Touchandgo, the great banker, when, one
foggy morning, Mr. Touchandgo and the contents of his till were
suddenly reported absent ; and as the fortune which the young
gentleman had intended to marry was not forthcoming, this tender
affair of the heart was nipped in the bud.

Miss Touchandgo did not meet the shock of separation quite so
complacently as the young gentleman ; for he lost only the lady,

whereas she lost a fortune as well as a lover. Some jewels, which had glittered on her beautiful person as brilliantly as the bubble of her father's wealth had done in the eyes of his gudgeons, furnished her with a small portion of paper currency; and this, added to the contents of a fairy purse of gold, which she found in her shoe on the eventful morning when Mr. Touchandgo melted into thin air, enabled her to retreat into North Wales, where she took up her lodging in a farm-house in Merionethshire, and boarded very comfortably for a trifling payment, and the additional consideration of teaching English, French, and music to the little Ap-Llymry's. In the course of this occupation, she acquired sufficient knowledge of Welsh to converse with the country people.

She climbed the mountains, and descended the dingles, with a foot which daily habit made by degrees almost as steady as a native's. She became the nymph of the scene [1]; and if she sometimes pined in thought for her faithless Strephon, her melancholy was any thing but green and yellow [2]; it was as genuine white and red as occupation, mountain air, thyme-fed mutton, thick cream, and fat bacon, could make it: to say nothing of an occasional glass of double X, which Ap-Llymry, [3] who yielded to no man west of the Wrekin in brewage, never failed to press upon her at dinner and supper. He was also earnest, and sometimes successful, in the recommendation of his mead, and most pertinacious on winter nights in enforcing a trial of the virtues of his elder wine. The young lady's personal appearance, consequently, formed a very advantageous contrast to that of her quondam lover, whose physiognomy the intense anxieties of his bubble-blowing days, notwithstanding their triumphant result, had left blighted, sallowed, and crow's-footed, to a degree not far below that of the fallen spirit who, in the expressive language of German romance, is described as " scathed by the ineradicable traces of the thunder-bolts of Heaven;" so that, contemplating their relative geological positions, the poor deserted damsel was flourishing on slate, while her rich and false young knight was pining on chalk.

[1] The physical resemblance between Peacock's heroine and Jane Gryffydh, who later became Mrs. Peacock, was a tradition with her daughters. See pp. 730 and 733. G.

[2] *Twelfth Night*, Act II, Sc. 4. G.

[3] Llymry. *Anglicé* flummery. [P.]

Squire Crotchet had also one daughter, whom he had christened Lemma,[1] and who, as likely to be endowed with a very ample fortune, was, of course, an object very tempting to many young soldiers of fortune, who were marching with the march of mind, in a good condition for taking castles, as far as not having a groat is a qualification for such exploits.[2] She was also a glittering bait to divers young squires expectant (whose fathers were too well acquainted with the occult signification of mortgage), and even to one or two sprigs of nobility, who thought that the lining of a civic purse would superinduce a very passable factitious nap upon a threadbare title. The young lady had received an expensive and complicated education ; complete in all the elements of superficial display. She was thus eminently qualified to be the companion of any masculine luminary who had kept due pace with the " astounding progress " of intelligence. It must be confessed, that a man who has not kept due pace with it is not very easily found ; this march being one of that " astounding " character in which it seems impossible that the rear can be behind the van. The young lady was also tolerably good-looking : north of Tweed, or in Palestine, she would probably have been a beauty ; but for the vallies of the Thames, she was perhaps a little too much to the taste of Solomon, and had a nose which rather too prominently suggested the idea of the tower of Lebanon, which looked towards Damascus.

In a village in the vicinity of the castle was the vicarage of the Reverend Doctor Folliott, a gentleman endowed with a tolerable stock of learning, an interminable swallow, and an indefatigable pair of lungs. His pre-eminence in the latter faculty gave occasion to some etymologists to ring changes on his name, and to decide that it was derived from Follis Optimus, softened through an Italian medium into Folle Ottimo, contracted poetically into Folleotto, and elided Anglicé into Folliott, signifying a first-rate pair of bellows. He claimed to be descended lineally from the illustrious Gilbert Folliott, the eminent theologian, who was a bishop of London in the twelfth century, whose studies were interrupted in the dead of night

---

[1] Gain, income, profit. G.
[2] " Let him take castles who has ne'er a groat."—POPE, *ubi suprà*.
[P.]

by the devil ; when a couple of epigrams passed between them ; and the devil, of course, proved the smaller wit of the two.[1]

This reverend gentleman, being both learned and jolly, became by degrees an indispensable ornament to the new squire's table.   Mr. Crotchet himself was eminently jolly, though by no means eminently learned.   In the latter respect he took after the great majority of the sons of his father's land ; had a smattering of many things, and a knowledge of none ; but possessed the true northern art of making the most of his intellectual harlequin's jacket, by keeping the best patches always bright and prominent.

CHAPTER II

THE MARCH OF MIND

Quoth Ralpho : nothing but the abuse
Of human learning you produce.—BUTLER.[2]

" GOD bless my soul, sir ! " exclaimed the Reverend Doctor Folliott, bursting, one fine May morning, into the breakfast-room at Crotchet

---

[1] The devil began : (he had caught the bishop musing on politics).

> Oh Gilberte Folliott !
> Dum revolvis tot et tot,
> Deus tuus est Astarot.

> Oh Gilbert Folliott !
> While thus you muse and plot,
> Your god is Astarot.

The bishop answered :

> Tace, dæmon : qui est deus
> Sabbaot, est ille meus.

> Peace, fiend ; the power I own
> Is Sabbaoth's Lord alone.

It must be confessed, the devil was easily posed in the twelfth century. He was a sturdier disputant in the sixteenth.

> Did not the devil appear to Martin
> Luther in Germany for certain ?

when " the heroic student," as Mr. Coleridge calls him, was forced to proceed to " *voies de fait.*"   The curious may see at this day, on the wall of Luther's study, the traces of the ink-bottle which he threw at the devil's head.   [P.]

[2] *Hudibras*, Pt. I, Canto 3, ll. 1337–8.   G.

Castle, " I am out of all patience with this march of mind. Here
has my house been nearly burned down, by my cook taking it into
her head to study hydrostatics, in a sixpenny tract, published by the
Steam Intellect Society, and written by a learned friend who is for
doing all the world's business as well as his own, and is equally well
qualified to handle every branch of human knowledge. I have a
great abomination of this learned friend[1]; as author, lawyer, and
politician, he is *triformis*, like Hecate : and in every one of his three
forms he is *bifrons*, like Janus ; the true Mr. Facing-both-ways of
Vanity Fair. My cook must read his rubbish in bed ; and as might
naturally be expected, she dropped suddenly fast asleep, overturned
the candle, and set the curtains in a blaze. Luckily, the footman
went into the room at the moment, in time to tear down the curtains
and throw them into the chimney, and a pitcher of water on her
nightcap extinguished her wick : she is a greasy subject, and would
have burned like a short mould." [2]

The reverend gentleman exhaled his grievance without looking to
the right or to the left ; at length, turning on his pivot, he perceived
that the room was full of company, consisting of young Crotchet and
some visitors whom he had brought from London. The Reverend
Doctor Folliott was introduced to Mr. Mac Quedy,[3] the economist ;
Mr. Skionar,[4] the transcendental poet ; Mr. Firedamp, the meteoro-
logist ; and Lord Bossnowl, son of the Earl of Foolincourt, and
member for the borough of Rogueingrain.

The divine took his seat at the breakfast-table, and began to
compose his spirits by the gentle sedative of a large cup of tea, the
demulcent of a well-buttered muffin, and the tonic of a small lobster.

THE REV. DR. FOLLIOTT. You are a man of taste, Mr. Crotchet.
A man of taste is seen at once in the array of his breakfast-table.
It is the foot of Hercules, the far-shining face of the great work,

[1] Lord Brougham founded the Society for the Diffusion of Useful Knowledge, 1825, and published *Observations on Education of the People* in the
same year. He reappears as Lord Facing-both-ways in *Gryll Grange*. G.

[2] Short for " mould-candle." G.

[3] Quasi Mac Q. E. D., son of a demonstration. [P.] [MacCulloch, the
economist. G.]

[4] ΣΚΙᾶς ΟΝΑΡ. *Umbræ somnium.* [P.] [" The dream of a shade."
Coleridge is intended. G.]

according to Pindar's doctrine : ἀρχομένου ἔργου, πρόσωπον χρὴ
θέμεν τηλαυγές.[1] The breakfast is the πρόσωπον of the great work
of the day. Chocolate, coffee, tea, cream, eggs, ham, tongue, cold
fowl,—all these are good, and bespeak good knowledge in him who
sets them forth : but the touchstone is fish : anchovy is the first
step, prawns and shrimps the second ; and I laud him who reaches
even to these : potted char and lampreys are the third, and a fine
stretch of progression ; but lobster is, indeed, matter for a May
morning,[2] and demands a rare combination of knowledge and virtue
in him who sets it forth.

MR. MAC QUEDY. Well, sir, and what say you to a fine fresh trout,
hot and dry, in a napkin ? or a herring out of the water into the frying
pan, on the shore of Loch Fyne ?

THE REV. DR. FOLLIOTT. Sir, I say every nation has some eximious
virtue ; and your country is pre-eminent in the glory of fish for
breakfast. We have much to learn from you in that line at any rate.

MR. MAC QUEDY. And in many others, sir, I believe. Morals and
metaphysics, politics and political economy, the way to make the
most of all the modifications of smoke ; steam, gas, and paper
currency ; you have all these to learn from us ; in short, all the arts
and sciences. We are the modern Athenians.

THE REV. DR. FOLLIOTT. I, for one, sir, am content to learn
nothing from you but the art and science of fish for breakfast. Be
content, sir, to rival the Bœotians, whose redeeming virtue was in
fish, touching which point you may consult Aristophanes and his
scholiast, in the passage of Lysistrata, ἀλλ' ἄφελε τὰς ἐγχέλεις,[3] and
leave the name of Athenians to those who have a sense of the beautiful, and a perception of metrical quantity.

MR. MAC QUEDY. Then, sir, I presume you set no value on the
right principles of rent, profit, wages, and currency ?

[1] Far-shining be the face
    Of a great work begun.—PIND. Ol. vi. [P.] [3–4. G.]
[2] Twelfth Night, Act III, Sc. 4. G.
[3] Calonice wishes destruction to all Bœotians. Lysistrata answers,
" Except the eels." Lysistrata, 36. [P.]

THE REV. DR. FOLLIOTT. My principles, sir, in these things are, to take as much as I can get, and to pay no more than I can help. These are every man's principles, whether they be the right principles or no. There, sir, is political economy in a nutshell.

MR. MAC QUEDY. The principles, sir, which regulate production and consumption, are independent of the will of any individual as to giving or taking, and do not lie in a nutshell by any means.

THE REV. DR. FOLLIOTT. Sir, I will thank you for a leg of that capon.

LORD BOSSNOWL. But, sir, by the by, how came your footman to be going into your cook's room ? It was very providential to be sure, but——

THE REV. DR. FOLLIOTT. Sir, as good came of it, I shut my eyes, and asked no questions. I suppose he was going to study hydrostatics, and he found himself under the necessity of practising hydraulics.

MR. FIREDAMP. Sir, you seem to make very light of science.

THE REV. DR. FOLLIOTT. Yes, sir, such science as the learned friend deals in : every thing for every body, science for all, schools for all, rhetoric for all, law for all, physic for all, words for all, and sense for none. I say, sir, law for lawyers, and cookery for cooks : and I wish the learned friend, for all his life, a cook that will pass her time in studying his works ; then every dinner he sits down to at home, he will sit on the stool of repentance.

LORD BOSSNOWL. Now really that would be too severe : my cook should read nothing but Ude.[1]

THE REV. DR. FOLLIOTT. No, sir ! let Ude and the learned friend singe fowls together ; let both avaunt from my kitchen. $Θύρας$ $δ' ἐπίθεσθε βεβήλοις.$[2] Ude says an elegant supper may be given

[1] Louis Eustache Ude, chef to Louis XVI, then to the Earl of Sefton, later steward of the United Services Club and maître d'hôtel at Crockford's. Author of *The French Cook adapted to the use of English families*. Ude introduced the light sandwich supper during the Regency. G.

[2] " Shut the doors against the profane." *Orphica, passim.* [P.]

with sandwiches. *Horresco referens.* An elegant supper! *Di meliora piis.* No Ude for me. Conviviality went out with punch and suppers. I cherish their memory. I sup when I can, but not upon sandwiches. To offer me a sandwich, when I am looking for a supper, is to add insult to injury. Let the learned friend, and the modern Athenians, sup upon sandwiches.

MR. MAC QUEDY. Nay, sir; the modern Athenians know better than that. A literary supper in sweet Edinbroo' would cure you of the prejudice you seem to cherish against us.

THE REV. DR. FOLLIOTT. Well, sir, well; there is cogency in a good supper; a good supper, in these degenerate days, bespeaks a good man; but much more is wanted to make up an Athenian. Athenians, indeed! where is your theatre? who among you has written a comedy? where is your attic salt? which of you can tell who was Jupiter's great grandfather? or what metres will successively remain, if you take off the three first syllables, one by one, from a pure antispastic acatalectic tetrameter? Now, sir, there are three questions for you; theatrical, mythological, and metrical; to every one of which an Athenian would give an answer that would lay me prostrate in my own nothingness.

MR. MAC QUEDY. Well, sir, as to your metre and your mythology, they may e'en wait a wee. For your comedy, there is the Gentle Shepherd of the divine Allan Ramsay.

THE REV. DR. FOLLIOTT. The Gentle Shepherd! It is just as much a comedy as the book of Job.

MR. MAC QUEDY. Well, sir, if none of us have written a comedy, I cannot see that it is any such great matter, any more than I can conjecture what business a man can have at this time of day with Jupiter's great grandfather.

THE REV. DR. FOLLIOTT. The great business is, sir, that you call yourselves Athenians, while you know nothing that the Athenians thought worth knowing, and dare not show your noses before the civilised world in the practice of any one art in which they were excellent. Modern Athens, sir! the assumption is a personal affront

to every man who has a Sophocles in his library. I will thank you
for an anchovy.

MR. MAC QUEDY. Metaphysics, sir; metaphysics. Logic and
moral philosophy. There we are at home. The Athenians only
sought the way, and we have found it ; and to all this we have added
political economy, the science of sciences.

THE REV. DR. FOLLIOTT. A hyperbarbarous technology, that no
Athenian ear could have borne. Premises assumed without evidence,
or in spite of it ; and conclusions drawn from them so logically, that
they must necessarily be erroneous.

MR. SKIONAR. I cannot agree with you, Mr. Mac Quedy, that you
have found the true road of metaphysics, which the Athenians only
sought. The Germans have found it, sir : the sublime Kant, and his
disciples.

MR. MAC QUEDY. I have read the sublime Kant, sir, with an
anxious desire to understand him ; and I confess I have not
succeeded.

THE REV. DR. FOLLIOTT. He wants the two great requisites of head
and tail.

MR. SKIONAR. Transcendentalism is the philosophy of intuition,
the development of universal convictions ; truths which are inherent
in the organisation of mind, which cannot be obliterated, though they
may be obscured, by superstitious prejudice on the one hand, and by
the Aristotelian logic on the other.

MR. MAC QUEDY. Well, sir, I have no notion of logic obscuring a
question.

MR. SKIONAR. There is only one true logic, which is the transcendental ; and this can prove only the one true philosophy, which
is also the transcendental. The logic of your modern Athens can
prove every thing equally ; and that is, in my opinion, tantamount
to proving nothing at all.

MR. CROTCHET. The sentimental against the rational, the intuitive against the inductive, the ornamental against the useful, the intense against the tranquil, the romantic against the classical; these are great and interesting controversies, which I should like, before I die, to see satisfactorily settled.

MR. FIREDAMP. There is another great question, greater than all these, seeing that it is necessary to be alive in order to settle any question; and this is the question of water against human woe. Wherever there is water, there is *malaria*, and wherever there is *malaria*, there are the elements of death. The great object of a wise man should be to live on a gravelly hill, without so much as a duck-pond within ten miles of him, eschewing cisterns and water-butts, and taking care that there be no gravel-pits for lodging the rain. The sun sucks up infection from water, wherever it exists on the face of the earth.

THE REV. DR. FOLLIOTT. Well, sir, you have for you the authority of the ancient mystagogue, who said, ῎Εστιν ὕδωρ ψυχῇ θάνατος.[1] For my part I care not a rush (or any other aquatic and inesculent vegetable) who or what sucks up either the water or the infection. I think the proximity of wine a matter of much more importance than the longinquity of water. You are here within a quarter of a mile of the Thames; but in the cellar of my friend, Mr. Crotchet, there is the talismanic antidote of a thousand dozen of old wine; a beautiful spectacle, I assure you, and a model of arrangement.

MR. FIREDAMP. Sir, I feel the malignant influence of the river in every part of my system. Nothing but my great friendship for Mr. Crotchet would have brought me so nearly within the jaws of the lion.

THE REV. DR. FOLLIOTT. After dinner, sir, after dinner, I will meet you on this question. I shall then be armed for the strife. You may fight like Hercules against Achelous, but I shall flourish the Bacchic thyrsus, which changed rivers into wine: as Nonnus sweetly sings, Οἴνῳ κυματόεντι μέλας κελάρυζεν Ὑδάσπης.[2]

---

[1] Literally, which is sufficient for the present purpose, " Water is death to the soul." *Orphica* : *Fr.* XIX. [P.]
[2] Hydaspes gurgled, dark with billowy wine. *Dionysiaca*, XXV. 280. [P.]

MR. CROTCHET, JUN. I hope, Mr. Firedamp, you will let your friendship carry you a little closer into the jaws of the lion. I am fitting up a flotilla of pleasure boats, with spacious cabins, and a good cellar, to carry a choice philosophical party up the Thames and Severn, into the Ellesmere canal, where we shall be among the mountains of North Wales ; which we may climb or not, as we think proper ; but we will, at any rate, keep our floating hotel well provisioned, and we will try to settle all the questions over which a shadow of doubt yet hangs in the world of philosophy.[1]

MR. FIREDAMP. Out of my great friendship for you, I will certainly go, but I do not expect to survive the experiment.

THE REV. DR. FOLLIOTT. *Alter erit tum Tiphys, et altera quæ vehat Argo Delectos Heroas.*[2] I will be of the party, though I must hire an officiating curate, and deprive poor Mrs. Folliott, for several weeks, of the pleasure of combing my wig.

LORD BOSSNOWL. I hope if I am to be of the party, our ship is not to be the ship of fools [3] : He ! He !

THE REV. DR. FOLLIOTT. If you are one of the party, sir, it most assuredly will not : Ha ! Ha !

LORD BOSSNOWL. Pray sir, what do you mean by Ha ! Ha ! ?

THE REV. DR. FOLLIOTT. Precisely, sir, what you mean by He ! He !

MR. MAC QUEDY. You need not dispute about terms ; they are two modes of expressing merriment, with or without reason ; reason being in no way essential to mirth. No man should ask another

---

[1] Charles Clairmont in his account of Shelley's voyage to the source of the Thames, in which Peacock took part, says : " We had conceived the scheme of going along a canal which here joins the Thames, to get into the Severn, and so also follow up that river to its source, . . . but the Commissioners would not allow us to pass the Severn Canal under £20." G.

[2] " Another Tiphys on the waves shall float,
And chosen heroes freight his glorious boat."
VIRG. *Ecl.* IV. [P.] [34–5. G.]

[3] A poem by Alexander Barclay, 1509, a paraphrase from the German of Sebastian Brandt. G.

why he laughs, or at what, seeing that he does not always know, and that, if he does, he is not a responsible agent. Laughter is an involuntary action of certain muscles, developed in the human species by the progress of civilisation. The savage never laughs.

THE REV. DR. FOLLIOTT. No, sir, he has nothing to laugh at. Give him Modern Athens, the "learned friend," and the Steam Intellect Society. They will develop his muscles.

CHAPTER III

THE ROMAN CAMP

> He loved her more then seven yere,
> Yet was he of her love never the nere ;
> He was not ryche of golde and fe,
> A gentyll man forsoth was he.
> *The Squyr of Low Degre.*[1]

THE Reverend Doctor Folliott having promised to return to dinner, walked back to his vicarage, meditating whether he should pass the morning in writing his next sermon, or in angling for trout, and had nearly decided in favour of the latter proposition, repeating to himself, with great unction, the lines of Chaucer :—

> And as for me, though that I can but lite,
> On bokis for to read I me delite,
> And to 'hem yeve I faithe and full credence,
> And in mine herte have 'hem in reverence,
> So hertily, that there is gamé none,
> That fro my bokis makith me to gone,
> But it be seldome, on the holie daie ;
> Save certainly whan that the month of Maie
> Is comin, and I here the foulis sing,
> And that the flouris ginnin for to spring,
> Farewell my boke and my devocion : [2]

when his attention was attracted by a young gentleman who was sitting on a camp stool with a portfolio on his knee, taking a sketch of the Roman Camp, which, as has been already said, was within the enclosed domain of Mr. Crotchet. The young stranger, who had

[1] The Early English metrical romance in the Percy Folio. See Hazlitt's *Early Popular Poetry*, Vol. II, p. 23. G.
[2] *The Legend of Good Women*, Prologue, ll. 29–40. G.

climbed over the fence, espying the portly divine, rose up, and hoped that he was not trespassing. " By no means, sir," said the divine ; " all the arts and sciences are welcome here : music, painting, and poetry ; hydrostatics, and political economy ; meteorology, trans-cendentalism, and fish for breakfast."

THE STRANGER. A pleasant association, sir, and a liberal and discriminating hospitality. This is an old British camp, I believe, sir ?

THE REV. DR. FOLLIOTT. Roman, sir ; Roman : undeniably Roman. The vallum is past controversy. It was not a camp, sir, a *castrum*, but a *castellum*, a little camp, or watch-station, to which was attached, on the peak of the adjacent hill, a beacon for trans-mitting alarms. You will find such here and there, all along the range of chalk hills, which traverses the country from north-east to south-west, and along the base of which runs the ancient Ikenild road, whereof you may descry a portion in that long strait white line.

THE STRANGER. I beg your pardon, sir : do I understand this place to be your property ?

THE REV. DR. FOLLIOTT. It is not mine, sir : the more is the pity ; yet is it so far well, that the owner is my good friend, and a highly respectable gentleman.

THE STRANGER. Good and respectable, sir, I take it, mean rich ?

THE REV. DR. FOLLIOTT. That is their meaning, sir.

THE STRANGER. I understand the owner to be a Mr. Crotchet. He has a handsome daughter, I am told.

THE REV. DR. FOLLIOTT. He has, sir. Her eyes are like the fish-pools of Heshbon, by the gate of Bethrabbim[1]; and she is to have a handsome fortune, to which divers disinterested gentlemen are paying their addresses. Perhaps you design to be one of them.

THE STRANGER. No, sir ; I beg pardon if my questions seem impertinent ; I have no such design. There is a son, too, I believe, sir, a great and successful blower of bubbles.

[1] *The Song of Solomon*, vii, 4. G.

THE REV. DR. FOLLIOTT. A hero, sir, in his line. Never did angler in September hook more gudgeons.

THE STRANGER. To say the truth, two very amiable young people, with whom I have some little acquaintance, Lord Bossnowl, and his sister, Lady Clarinda, are reported to be on the point of concluding a double marriage with Miss Crotchet and her brother, by way of putting a new varnish on old nobility. Lord Foolincourt, their father, is terribly poor for a lord who owns a borough.

THE REV. DR. FOLLIOTT. Well, sir, the Crotchets have plenty of money, and the old gentleman's weak point is a hankering after high blood. I saw your acquaintance Lord Bossnowl this morning; but I did not see his sister. She may be there, nevertheless, and doing fashionable justice to this fine May morning, by lying in bed till noon.

THE STRANGER. Young Mr. Crotchet, sir, has been, like his father, the architect of his own fortune, has he not ? An illustrious example of the reward of honesty and industry ?

THE REV. DR. FOLLIOTT. As to honesty, sir, he made his fortune in the city of London; and if that commodity be of any value there, you will find it in the price current. I believe it is below par, like the shares of young Crotchet's fifty companies. But his progress has not been exactly like his father's : it has been more rapid, and he started with more advantages. He began with a fine capital from his father. The old gentleman divided his fortune into three not exactly equal portions : one for himself, one for his daughter, and one for his son, which he handed over to him, saying, " Take it once for all, and make the most of it ; if you lose it where I won it, not another stiver do you get from me during my life." But, sir, young Crotchet doubled, and trebled, and quadrupled it, and is, as you say, a striking example of the reward of industry ; not that I think his labour has been so great as his luck.

THE STRANGER. But, sir, is all this solid ? is there no danger of reaction ? no day of reckoning, to cut down in an hour prosperity that has grown up like a mushroom ?

THE REV. DR. FOLLIOTT. Nay, sir, I know not. I do not pry into these matters. I am, for my own part, very well satisfied with the young gentleman. Let those who are not so look to themselves. It is quite enough for me that he came down last night from London, and that he had the good sense to bring with him a basket of lobsters. Sir, I wish you a good morning.

The stranger, having returned the reverend gentleman's good morning, resumed his sketch, and was intently employed on it when Mr. Crotchet made his appearance, with Mr. Mac Quedy and Mr. Skionar, whom he was escorting round his grounds, according to his custom with new visitors; the principal pleasure of possessing an extensive domain being that of showing it to other people. Mr. Mac Quedy, according also to the laudable custom of his countrymen, had been appraising every thing that fell under his observation; but, on arriving at the Roman camp, of which the value was purely imaginary, he contented himself with exclaiming, " Eh! this is just a curiosity, and very pleasant to sit in on a summer day."

MR. SKIONAR. And call up the days of old, when the Roman eagle spread its wings in the place of that beechen foliage. It gives a fine idea of duration, to think that that fine old tree must have sprung from the earth ages after this camp was formed.

MR. MAC QUEDY. How old, think you, may the tree be?

MR. CROTCHET. I have records which show it to be three hundred years old.

MR. MAC QUEDY. That is a great age for a beech in good condition. But you see the camp is some fifteen hundred years, or so, older; and three times six being eighteen, I think you get a clearer idea of duration out of the simple arithmetic than out of your eagle and foliage.

MR. SKIONAR. That is a very unpoetical, if not unphilosophical, mode of viewing antiquities. Your philosophy is too literal for our imperfect vision. We cannot look directly into the nature of things; we can only catch glimpses of the mighty shadow in the camera obscura of transcendental intelligence. These six and eighteen are only words to which we give conventional meanings. We can reason, but we cannot feel, by help of them. The tree and the eagle, contemplated in the ideality of space and time, become subjective realities, that rise up as landmarks in the mystery of the past.

MR. MAC QUEDY. Well, sir, if you understand that, I wish you joy. But I must be excused for holding that my proposition, three times six are eighteen, is more intelligible than yours. A worthy friend of mine, who is a sort of amateur in philosophy, criticism, politics, and a wee bit of many things more, says, " Men never begin to study antiquities till they are saturated with civilisation." [1]

MR. SKIONAR. What is civilisation ?

MR. MAC QUEDY. It is just respect for property : a state in which no man takes wrongfully what belongs to another, is a perfectly civilised state.

MR. SKIONAR. Your friend's antiquaries must have lived in El Dorado, to have had an opportunity of being saturated with such a state.

MR. MAC QUEDY. It is a question of degree. There is more respect for property here than in Angola.

MR. SKIONAR. That depends on the light in which things are viewed.

Mr. Crotchet was rubbing his hands, in hopes of a fine discussion, when they came round to the side of the camp where the picturesque gentleman was sketching. The stranger was rising up, when Mr. Crotchet begged him not to disturb himself, and presently walked away with his two guests.

Shortly after Miss Crotchet and Lady Clarinda, who had breakfasted by themselves, made their appearance at the same spot, hanging each on an arm of Lord Bossnowl, who very much preferred their company to that of the philosophers, though he would have preferred the company of the latter, or any company, to his own. He thought it very singular that so agreeable a person as he held himself to be to others, should be so exceedingly tiresome to himself :

[1] *Edinburgh Review*, somewhere. [P.]

he did not attempt to investigate the cause of this phenomenon, but was contented with acting on his knowledge of the fact, and giving himself as little of his own private society as possible.

The stranger rose as they approached, and was immediately recognised by the Bossnowls as an old acquaintance, and saluted with the exclamation of " Captain Fitzchrome ! " The interchange of salutation between Lady Clarinda and the Captain was accompanied with an amiable confusion on both sides, in which the observant eyes of Miss Crotchet seemed to read the recollection of an affair of the heart.

Lord Bossnowl was either unconscious of any such affair, or indifferent to its existence. He introduced the Captain very cordially to Miss Crotchet, and the young lady invited him, as the friend of their guests, to partake of her father's hospitality ; an offer which was readily accepted.

The Captain took his portfolio under his right arm, his camp stool in his right hand, offered his left arm to Lady Clarinda, and followed at a reasonable distance behind Miss Crotchet and Lord Bossnowl, contriving, in the most natural manner possible, to drop more and more into the rear.

LADY CLARINDA. I am glad to see you can make yourself so happy with drawing old trees and mounds of grass.

CAPTAIN FITZCHROME. Happy, Lady Clarinda ! oh, no ! How can I be happy when I see the idol of my heart about to be sacrificed on the shrine of Mammon ?

LADY CLARINDA. Do you know, though Mammon has a sort of ill name, I really think he is a very popular character ; there must be at the bottom something amiable about him. He is certainly one of those pleasant creatures whom every body abuses, but without whom no evening party is endurable. I dare say, love in a cottage is very pleasant ; but then it positively must be a cottage ornée : but would not the same love be a great deal safer in a castle, even if Mammon furnished the fortification ?

CAPTAIN FITZCHROME. Oh, Lady Clarinda ! there is a heartlessness in that language that chills me to the soul.

LADY CLARINDA. Heartlessness! No: my heart is on my lips. I speak just what I think. You used to like it, and say it was as delightful as it was rare.

CAPTAIN FITZCHROME. True, but you did not then talk as you do now, of love in a castle.

LADY CLARINDA. Well, but only consider: a dun is a horridly vulgar creature; it is a creature I cannot endure the thought of: and a cottage lets him in so easily. Now a castle keeps him at bay. You are a half-pay officer, and are at leisure to command the garrison: but where is the castle? and who is to furnish the commissariat?

CAPTAIN FITZCHROME. Is it come to this, that you make a jest of my poverty? Yet is my poverty only comparative. Many decent families are maintained on smaller means.

LADY CLARINDA. Decent families: aye, decent is the distinction from respectable. Respectable means rich, and decent means poor. I should die if I heard my family called decent. And then your decent family always lives in a snug little place: I hate a little place; I like large rooms and large looking-glasses, and large parties, and a fine large butler, with a tinge of smooth red in his face; an outward and visible sign that the family he serves is respectable; if not noble, highly respectable.

CAPTAIN FITZCHROME. I cannot believe that you say all this in earnest. No man is less disposed than I am to deny the importance of the substantial comforts of life. I once flattered myself that in our estimate of these things we were nearly of a mind.

LADY CLARINDA. Do you know, I think an opera-box a very substantial comfort, and a carriage. You will tell me that many decent people walk arm in arm through the snow, and sit in clogs and bonnets in the pit at the English theatre. No doubt it is very pleasant to those who are used to it; but it is not to my taste.

CAPTAIN FITZCHROME. You always delighted in trying to provoke me; but I cannot believe that you have not a heart.

LADY CLARINDA. You do not like to believe that I have a heart, you mean. You wish to think I have lost it, and you know to whom ; and when I tell you that it is still safe in my own keeping, and that I do not mean to give it away, the unreasonable creature grows angry.

CAPTAIN FITZCHROME. Angry ! far from it : I am perfectly cool.

LADY CLARINDA. Why, you are pursing your brows, biting your lips, and lifting up your foot as if you would stamp it into the earth. I must say anger becomes you ; you would make a charming Hotspur. Your every-day-dining-out face is rather insipid : but I assure you my heart is in danger when you are in the heroics. It is so rare, too, in these days of smooth manners, to see any thing like natural expression in a man's face. There is one set form for every man's face in female society ; a sort of serious comedy, walking gentleman's face ; but the moment the creature falls in love, he begins to give himself airs, and plays off all the varieties of his physiognomy, from the Master Slender to the Petruchio ; and then he is actually very amusing.

CAPTAIN FITZCHROME. Well, Lady Clarinda, I will not be angry, amusing as it may be to you : I listen more in sorrow than in anger. I half believe you in earnest, and mourn as over a fallen angel.

LADY CLARINDA. What, because I have made up my mind not to give away my heart when I can sell it ? I will introduce you to my new acquaintance, Mr. Mac Quedy : he will talk to you by the hour about exchangeable value, and show you that no rational being will part with any thing, except to the highest bidder.

CAPTAIN FITZCHROME. Now, I am sure you are not in earnest. You cannot adopt such sentiments in their naked deformity.

LADY CLARINDA. Naked deformity : why Mr. Mac Quedy will prove to you that they are the cream of the most refined philosophy. You live a very pleasant life as a bachelor, roving about the country with your portfolio under your arm. I am not fit to be a poor man's wife. I cannot take any kind of trouble, or do any one thing that is of any use. Many decent families roast a bit of mutton on a string ; but if I displease my father I shall not have as much as will buy the string, to say nothing of the meat ; and the bare idea of such cookery gives me the horrors.

By this time they were near the castle, and met Miss Crotchet and her companion, who had turned back to meet them. Captain Fitzchrome was shortly after heartily welcomed by Mr. Crotchet, and the party separated to dress for dinner, the captain being by no means in an enviable state of mind, and full of misgivings as to the extent of belief that he was bound to accord to the words of the lady of his heart.

CHAPTER IV

THE PARTY

En quoi cognoissez-vous la folie anticque ? En quoi cognoissez-vous la sagesse présente ?—RABELAIS.[1]

" IF I were sketching a bandit who had just shot his last pursuer, having outrun all the rest, that is the very face I would give him," soliloquised the captain, as he studied the features of his rival in the drawing-room, during the miserable half-hour before dinner, when dulness reigns predominant over the expectant company, especially when they are waiting for some one last comer, whom they all heartily curse in their hearts, and whom, nevertheless, or indeed therefore-the-more, they welcome as a sinner, more heartily than all the just persons who had been punctual to their engagement. Some new visitors had arrived in the morning, and, as the company dropped in one by one, the captain anxiously watched the unclosing door for the form of his beloved ; but she was the last to make her appearance, and on her entry gave him a malicious glance, which he construed into a telegraphic communication that she had stayed away to torment him. Young Crotchet escorted her with marked attention to the upper end of the drawing-room, where a great portion of the company was congregated around Miss Crotchet. These being the only ladies in the company, it was evident that old Mr. Crotchet

[1] " Pray, how came you to know that men were formerly fools ? How did you find that they are now wise ? " Author's Prologue to Bk. V. Urquhart and Motteux translation. G.

would give his arm to Lady Clarinda, an arrangement with which the captain could not interfere. He therefore took his station near the door, studying his rival from a distance, and determined to take advantage of his present position, to secure the seat next to his charmer. He was meditating on the best mode of operation for securing this important post with due regard to *bienséance*, when he was twitched by the button by Mr. Mac Quedy, who said to him : " Lady Clarinda tells me, sir, that you are anxious to talk with me on the subject of exchangeable value, from which I infer that you have studied political economy ; and as a great deal depends on the definition of value, I shall be glad to set you right on that point."— " I am much obliged to you, sir," said the captain, and was about to express his utter disqualification for the proposed instruction, when Mr. Skionar walked up, and said : " Lady Clarinda informs me that you wish to talk over with me the question of subjective reality. I am delighted to fall in with a gentleman who duly appreciates the transcendental philosophy."—" Lady Clarinda is too good," said the captain : and was about to protest that he had never heard the word transcendental before, when the butler announced dinner. Mr. Crotchet led the way with Lady Clarinda : Lord Bossnowl followed with Miss Crotchet : the economist and transcendentalist pinned in the captain, and held him, one by each arm, as he impatiently descended the stairs in the rear of several others of the company, whom they had forced him to let pass ; but the moment he entered the dining-room he broke loose from them, and at the expense of a little *brusquerie*, secured his position.

" Well, captain," said Lady Clarinda, " I perceive you can still manœuvre."

" What could possess you," said the captain, " to send two unendurable and inconceivable bores, to intercept me with rubbish about which I neither know nor care any more than the man in the moon ? "

" Perhaps," said Lady Clarinda, " I saw your design, and wished to put your generalship to the test. But do not contradict any thing I have said about you, and see if the learned will find you out."

" There is fine music, as Rabelais observes, in the *cliquetis d'assiettes*, a refreshing shade in the *ombre de salle à manger*, and an elegant fragrance in the *fumée de rôti*," said a voice at the captain's elbow. The captain turning round, recognised his clerical friend of the morning, who knew him again immediately, and said he was extremely glad to meet him there ; more especially as Lady Clarinda had assured him that he was an enthusiastic lover of Greek poetry.

"Lady Clarinda," said the captain, "is a very pleasant young lady."

THE REV. DR. FOLLIOTT. So she is, sir : and I understand she has all the wit of the family to herself, whatever that *totum* may be. But a glass of wine after soup is, as the French say, the *verre de santé*. The current of opinion sets in favour of Hock : but I am for Madeira ; I do not fancy Hock till I have laid a substratum of Madeira. Will you join me ?

CAPTAIN FITZCHROME. With pleasure.

THE REV. DR. FOLLIOTT. Here is a very fine salmon before me : and May is the very *point nommé* to have salmon in perfection. There is a fine turbot close by, and there is much to be said in his behalf ; but salmon in May is the king of fish.

MR. CROTCHET. That salmon before you, doctor, was caught in the Thames this morning.

THE REV. DR. FOLLIOTT. Παπαπαῖ! Rarity of rarities ! A Thames salmon caught this morning. Now, Mr. Mac Quedy, even in fish your Modern Athens must yield. *Cedite Graii.*[1]

MR. MAC QUEDY. Eh ! sir, on its own ground, your Thames salmon has two virtues over all others : first, that it is fresh ; and, second, that it is rare ; for I understand you do not take half a dozen in a year.

THE REV. DR. FOLLIOTT. In some years, sir, not one. Mud, filth, gas dregs, lock-weirs, and the march of mind, developed in the form of poaching, have ruined the fishery. But when we do catch a salmon, happy the man to whom he falls.

[1] " Yield, Greek [poets]." Propertius : *Eleg.* II. xxxiv, 65, where he says that Greek and Roman writers alike must yield, because Virgil's forthcoming *Æneid* will surpass the *Iliad*. G.

MR. MAC QUEDY. I confess, sir, this is excellent ; but I cannot see why it should be better than a Tweed salmon at Kelso.

THE REV. DR. FOLLIOTT. Sir, I will take a glass of Hock with you.

MR. MAC QUEDY. With all my heart, sir. There are several varieties of the salmon genus : but the common salmon, the *salmo salar,* is only one species, one and the same every where, just like the human mind. Locality and education make all the difference.

THE REV. DR. FOLLIOTT. Education ! Well, sir, I have no doubt schools for all are just as fit for the species *salmo salar* as for the genus *homo.* But you must allow, that the specimen before us has finished his education in a manner that does honour to his college. However, I doubt that the *salmo salar* is only one species, that is to say, precisely alike in all localities. I hold that every river has its own breed, with essential differences ; in flavour especially. And as for the human mind, I deny that it is the same in all men. I hold that there is every variety of natural capacity from the idiot to Newton and Shakespeare ; the mass of mankind, midway between these extremes, being blockheads of different degrees ; education leaving them pretty nearly as it found them, with this single difference, that it gives a fixed direction to their stupidity, a sort of incurable wry neck to the thing they call their understanding. So one nose points always east, and another always west, and each is ready to swear that it points due north.

MR. CROTCHET. If that be the point of truth, very few intellectual noses point due north.

MR. MAC QUEDY. Only those that point to the Modern Athens.

THE REV. DR. FOLLIOTT. Where all native noses point southward.

MR. MAC QUEDY. Eh, sir, northward for wisdom, and southward for profit.

MR. CROTCHET, JUN. Champagne, doctor ?

THE REV. DR. FOLLIOTT. Most willingly. But you will permit my drinking it while it sparkles. I hold it a heresy to let it deaden in

my hand, while the glass of my *compotator* is being filled on the
opposite side of the table.   By the bye, captain, you remember a
passage in Athenæus, where he cites Menander on the subject of
fish-sauce : ὀψάριον ἐπὶ ἰχθύος.[1]   (*The captain was aghast for an answer
that would satisfy both his neighbours, when he was relieved by the divine
continuing.*)   The science of fish sauce, Mr. Mac Quedy, is by no
means brought to perfection ; a fine field of discovery still lies open
in that line.

MR. MAC QUEDY.   Nay, sir, beyond lobster sauce, I take it, ye
cannot go.

THE REV. DR. FOLLIOTT.   In their line, I grant you, oyster and
lobster sauce are the pillars of Hercules.   But I speak of the cruet
sauces, where the quintessence of the sapid is condensed in a phial.
I can taste in my mind's palate a combination, which, if I could give
it reality, I would christen with the name of my college, and hand it
down to posterity as a seat of learning indeed.

MR. MAC QUEDY.   Well, sir, I wish you success, but I cannot
let slip the question we started just now.   I say, cutting off idiots,
who have no minds at all, all minds are by nature alike.   Education
(which begins from their birth) makes them what they are.

THE REV. DR. FOLLIOTT.   No, sir, it makes their tendencies, not
their power.   Cæsar would have been the first wrestler on the village
common.   Education might have made him a Nadir Shah[2]; it might
also have made him a Washington ; it could not have made him a
merry-andrew, for our newspapers to extol as a model of eloquence.

MR. MAC QUEDY.   Now, sir, I think education would have made
him just any thing, and fit for any station, from the throne to the
stocks ; saint or sinner, aristocrat or democrat, judge, counsel, or
prisoner at the bar.

THE REV. DR. FOLLIOTT.   I will thank you for a slice of lamb, with
lemon and pepper.   Before I proceed with this discussion,—Vin de

[1] 385 E.   G.
[2] The military genius who delivered Persia from the Afghans in 1730
and usurped the title of Shah in 1736.   G.

Grave, Mr. Skionar,—I must interpose one remark. There is a set of persons in your city, Mr. Mac Quedy, who concoct every three or four months a thing which they call a review : a sort of sugar-plum manufacturers to the Whig aristocracy.[1]

MR. MAC QUEDY. I cannot tell, sir, exactly, what you mean by that ; but I hope you will speak of those gentlemen with respect, seeing that I am one of them.

THE REV. DR. FOLLIOTT. Sir, I must drown my inadvertence in a glass of Sauterne with you. There is a set of gentlemen in your city——

MR. MAC QUEDY. Not in our city, exactly ; neither are they a set. There is an editor, who forages for articles in all quarters, from John O'Groat's house to the Land's End. It is not a board, or a society : it is a mere intellectual bazaar, where A., B., and C. bring their wares to market.

THE REV. DR. FOLLIOTT. Well, sir, these gentlemen among them, the present company excepted, have practised as much dishonesty as, in any other department than literature, would have brought the practitioner under the cognisance of the police. In politics, they have run with the hare and hunted with the hound. In criticism they have, knowingly and unblushingly, given false characters, both for good and for evil : sticking at no art of misrepresentation, to clear out of the field of literature all who stood in the way of the interests of their own clique. They have never allowed their own profound ignorance of any thing (Greek, for instance) to throw even an air of hesitation into their oracular decision on the matter. They set an example of profligate contempt for truth, of which the success was in proportion to the effrontery ; and when their prosperity had filled the market with competitors, they cried out against their own reflected sin, as if they had never committed it, or were entitled to a monopoly of it. The latter, I rather think, was what they wanted.

MR. CROTCHET. Hermitage, doctor ?

[1] Peacock himself wrote an article in the *Edinburgh Review* on " Steam Communication with India," Jan. 1835. G.

THE REV. DR. FOLLIOTT. Nothing better, sir. The father who first chose the solitude of that vineyard, knew well how to cultivate his spirit in retirement. Now, Mr. Mac Quedy, Achilles was distinguished above all the Greeks for his inflexible love of truth : could education have made Achilles one of your reviewers ?

MR. MAC QUEDY. No doubt of it, even if your character of them were true to the letter.

THE REV. DR. FOLLIOTT. And I say, sir—chicken and asparagus—Titan had made him of better clay.[1] I hold with Pindar : " All that is most excellent is so by nature." *Τὸ δὲ φυᾷ κράτιστον ἅπαν.*[2] Education can give purposes, but not powers ; and whatever purposes had been given him, he would have gone straight forward to them ; straight forward, Mr. Mac Quedy.

MR. MAC QUEDY. No, sir, education makes the man, powers, purposes, and all.

THE REV. DR. FOLLIOTT. There is the point, sir, on which we join issue.

Several others of the company now chimed in with their opinions, which gave the divine an opportunity to degustate one or two side dishes, and to take a glass of wine with each of the young ladies.

CHAPTER V

CHARACTERS

Ay imputé a honte plus que mediocre être vu spectateur ocieux de tant vaillans, disertz, et chevalereux personnaiges.—RABELAIS.[3]

LADY CLARINDA (*to the Captain*). I declare the creature has been listening to all this rigmarole, instead of attending to me. Do you ever expect forgiveness ? But now that they are all talking together, and you cannot make out a word they say, nor they hear a word that we say, I will describe the company to you. First, there is the old

[1] Juv. xiv. 35. [P.]   [2] *Ol.* ix. 152. [P.]
[3] " I held it not a little disgraceful to be only an idle spectator of so many valorous, eloquent, and warlike persons." Author's prologue to Book III. Urquhart and Motteux translation. G.

gentleman on my left hand, at the head of the table, who is now leaning the other way to talk to my brother. He is a good tempered,
half-informed person, very unreasonably fond of reasoning, and of
reasoning people ; people that talk nonsense logically : he is fond
of disputation himself, when there are only one or two, but seldom
does more than listen in a large company of *illuminés*. He made
a great fortune in the city, and has the comfort of a good conscience.
He is very hospitable, and is generous in dinners ; though nothing
would induce him to give sixpence to the poor, because he holds that
all misfortune is from imprudence, that none but the rich ought to
marry, and that all ought to thrive by honest industry, as he did.
He is ambitious of founding a family, and of allying himself with
nobility ; and is thus as willing as other grown children, to throw
away thousands for a gew-gaw, though he would not part with a penny
for charity. Next to him is my brother, whom you know as well as I
do. He has finished his education with credit, and as he never
ventures to oppose me in any thing, I have no doubt he is very
sensible. He has good manners, is a model of dress, and is reckoned
ornamental in all societies. Next to him is Miss Crotchet, my sister-
in-law that is to be. You see she is rather pretty, and very genteel.
She is tolerably accomplished, has her table always covered with new
novels, thinks Mr. Mac Quedy an oracle, and is extremely desirous
to be called " my lady." Next to her is Mr. Firedamp, a very absurd
person, who thinks that water is the evil principle. Next to him is
Mr. Eavesdrop, a man who, by dint of a certain something like
smartness, has got into good society. He is a sort of bookseller's
tool, and coins all his acquaintance in reminiscences and sketches of
character. I am very shy of him, for fear he should print me.[1]

CAPTAIN FITZCHROME. If he print you in your own likeness, which
is that of an angel, you need not fear him. If he print you in any
other, I will cut his throat. But proceed——

[1] Leigh Hunt. Peacock, who had never been a close friend of Hunt's,
referred, in a review of Thomas Moore's *Letters and Journals of Lord Byron*
in the *Westminster Review* of April 1830, to Hunt's " querulous egotisms,
the scaturient vanity bubbling up in every page like the hundred fountains
of the river Hoangho, the readiness to violate all the confidences of private
life, the intrinsic nothingness of what the writer had it in his power to
tell. . . ." G.

LADY CLARINDA. Next to him is Mr. Henbane, the toxicologist, I think he calls himself. He has passed half his life in studying poisons and antidotes. The first thing he did on his arrival here, was to kill the cat ; and while Miss Crotchet was crying over her, he brought her to life again. I am more shy of him than the other.

CAPTAIN FITZCHROME. They are two very dangerous fellows, and I shall take care to keep them both at a respectful distance. Let us hope that Eavesdrop will sketch off Henbane, and that Henbane will poison him for his trouble.

LADY CLARINDA. Well, next to him sits Mr. Mac Quedy, the Modern Athenian, who lays down the law about every thing, and therefore may be taken to understand every thing. He turns all the affairs of this world into questions of buying and selling. He is the Spirit of the Frozen Ocean to every thing like romance and sentiment. He condenses their volume of steam into a drop of cold water in a moment. He has satisfied me that I am a commodity in the market, and that I ought to set myself at a high price. So you see he who would have me must bid for me.

CAPTAIN FITZCHROME. I shall discuss that point with Mr. Mac Quedy.

LADY CLARINDA. Not a word for your life. Our flirtation is our own secret. Let it remain so.

CAPTAIN FITZCHROME. Flirtation, Clarinda ! Is that all that the most ardent——

LADY CLARINDA. Now, don't be rhapsodical here. Next to Mr. Mac Quedy is Mr. Skionar, a sort of poetical philosopher, a curious compound of the intense and the mystical. He abominates all the ideas of Mr. Mac Quedy, and settles every thing by sentiment and intuition.

CAPTAIN FITZCHROME. Then, I say, he is the wiser man.

LADY CLARINDA. They are two oddities ; but a little of them is amusing, and I like to hear them dispute. So you see I am in training for a philosopher myself.

CAPTAIN FITZCHROME. Any philosophy, for heaven's sake, but the pound-shilling-and-pence philosophy of Mr. Mac Quedy.

LADY CLARINDA. Why, they say that even Mr. Skionar, though he is a great dreamer, always dreams with his eyes open, or with one eye at any rate, which is an eye to his gain : but I believe that in this respect the poor man has got an ill name by keeping bad company. He has two dear friends, Mr. Wilful Wontsee, and Mr. Rumblesack Shantsee, poets of some note, who used to see visions of Utopia, and pure republics beyond the Western deep : but finding that these El Dorados brought them no revenue, they turned their vision-seeing faculty into the more profitable channel of espying all sorts of virtues in the high and the mighty, who were able and willing to pay for the discovery.[1]

CAPTAIN FITZCHROME. I do not fancy these virtue-spyers.

LADY CLARINDA. Next to Mr. Skionar, sits Mr. Chainmail, a good-looking young gentleman, as you see, with very antiquated tastes. He is fond of old poetry, and is something of a poet himself. He is deep in monkish literature, and holds that the best state of society was that of the twelfth century, when nothing was going forward but fighting, feasting, and praying, which he says are the three great purposes for which man was made. He laments bitterly over the inventions of gunpowder, steam, and gas, which he says have ruined the world. He lives within two or three miles, and has a large hall, adorned with rusty pikes, shields, helmets, swords, and tattered banners, and furnished with yew-tree chairs, and two long, old, worm-eaten oak tables, where he dines with all his household, after the fashion of his favourite age. He wants us all to dine with him, and I believe we shall go.[2]

CAPTAIN FITZCHROME. That will be something new at any rate.

[1] Wordsworth and Southey. G.

[2] Sir Edward Strachey was only eighteen years old when *Crotchet Castle* was written, nevertheless I think Peacock had him in mind, as the hero of *Cotswold Chace* (a fragment begun in 1860) seems obviously to be Sir Edward Strachey as a very young man and bears a considerable likeness to Mr. Chainmail. He was the son of Peacock's colleague Edward Strachey, and the author of *Talk at a Country House* (1895), which bears every mark of Mr. Chainmail's interests. G.

LADY CLARINDA. Next to him is Mr. Toogood, the co-operationist,[1] who will have neither fighting nor praying ; but wants to parcel out the world into squares like a chess-board, with a community on each, raising every thing for one another, with a great steam-engine to serve them in common for tailor and hosier, kitchen and cook.

CAPTAIN FITZCHROME. He is the strangest of the set, so far.

LADY CLARINDA. This brings us to the bottom of the table, where sits my humble servant, Mr. Crotchet the younger. I ought not to describe him.

CAPTAIN FITZCHROME. I entreat you do.

LADY CLARINDA. Well, I really have very little to say in his favour.

CAPTAIN FITZCHROME. I do not wish to hear any thing in his favour ; and I rejoice to hear you say so, because——

LADY CLARINDA. Do not flatter yourself. If I take him, it will be to please my father, and to have a town and country-house, and plenty of servants, and a carriage and an opera-box, and make some of my acquaintance who have married for love, or for rank, or for any thing but money, die for envy of my jewels. You do not think I would take him for himself. Why he is very smooth and spruce, as far as his dress goes ; but as to his face, he looks as if he had tumbled headlong into a volcano, and been thrown up again among the cinders.

CAPTAIN FITZCHROME. I cannot believe, that, speaking thus of him, you mean to take him at all.

LADY CLARINDA. Oh ! I am out of my teens. I have been very much in love ; but now I am come to years of discretion, and must think, like other people, of settling myself advantageously. He was in love with a banker's daughter, and cast her off on her father's bankruptcy, and the poor girl has gone to hide herself in some wild place.

CAPTAIN FITZCHROME. She must have a strange taste, if she pines for the loss of him.

[1] Robert Owen. G.

LADY CLARINDA. They say he was good-looking, till his bubble-schemes, as they call them, stamped him with the physiognomy of a desperate gambler. I suspect he has still a *penchant* towards his first flame. If he takes me, it will be for my rank and connection, and the second seat of the borough of Rogueingrain. So we shall meet on equal terms, and shall enjoy all the blessedness of expecting nothing from each other.

CAPTAIN FITZCHROME. You can expect no security with such an adventurer.

LADY CLARINDA. I shall have the security of a good settlement, and then if *andare al diavolo* be his destiny, he may go, you know, by himself. He is almost always dreaming and *distrait*. It is very likely that some great reverse is in store for him : but that will not concern me, you perceive.

CAPTAIN FITZCHROME. You torture me, Clarinda, with the bare possibility.

LADY CLARINDA. Hush ! Here is music to soothe your troubled spirit. Next to him, on this side, sits the dilettante composer, Mr. Trillo ; they say his name was O'Trill, and he has taken the O from the beginning, and put it at the end. I do not know how this may be. He plays well on the violoncello, and better on the piano : sings agreeably; has a talent at verse-making, and improvises a song with some felicity.[1] He is very agreeable company in the evening, with his instruments and music-books. He maintains that the sole end of all enlightened society is to get up a good opera, and laments that wealth, genius, and energy, are squandered upon other pursuits, to the neglect of this one great matter.

CAPTAIN FITZCHROME. That is a very pleasant fancy at any rate.

LADY CLARINDA. I assure you he has a great deal to say for it. Well, next to him again, is Dr. Morbific, who has been all over the world to prove that there is no such thing as contagion ; and has inoculated himself with plague, yellow fever, and every variety of pestilence, and is still alive to tell the story. I am very shy of him,

[1] Tom Moore. G.

too ; for I look on him as a walking phial of wrath, corked full of all infections, and not to be touched without extreme hazard.

CAPTAIN FITZCHROME. This is the strangest fellow of all.

LADY CLARINDA. Next to him sits Mr. Philpot,[1] the geographer, who thinks of nothing but the heads and tails of rivers, and lays down the streams of Terra Incognita as accurately as if he had been there. He is a person of pleasant fancy, and makes a sort of fairy land of every country he touches, from the Frozen Ocean to the Deserts of Zahara.

CAPTAIN FITZCHROME. How does he settle matters with Mr. Firedamp ?

LADY CLARINDA. You see Mr. Firedamp has got as far as possible out of his way. Next to him is Sir Simon Steeltrap, of Steeltrap Lodge, Member for Crouching-Curtown, Justice of Peace for the county, and Lord of the United Manors of Spring-gun and Treadmill ; a great preserver of game and public morals. By administering the laws which he assists in making, he disposes, at his pleasure, of the land and its live stock, including all the two-legged varieties, with and without feathers, in a circumference of several miles round Steeltrap Lodge. He has enclosed commons and woodlands ; abolished cottage-gardens ; taken the village cricket-ground into his own park, out of pure regard to the sanctity of Sunday ; shut up footpaths and alehouses, (all but those which belong to his electioneering friend, Mr. Quassia, the brewer ;) put down fairs and fiddlers ; committed many poachers ; shot a few ; convicted one third of the peasantry ; suspected the rest ; and passed nearly the whole of them through a wholesome course of prison discipline, which has finished their education at the expense of the county.[2]

[1] ΦΙΛοΠΟΤαμος. *Fluviorum amans.* [P.] ["The river-lover." Mac-Grigor Laird, a friend of Peacock's, who was planning a voyage up the Niger which he carried out, 1832–4. G.]

[2] " Speaking generally, the privileged classes of our rural districts take infinite pains to be abhorred by their poorest neighbours. They enclose commons, they stop footpaths, they wall in their parks, they set spring-guns and man-traps, they superintend alehouses, deny skittles, deprecate beer-shops, meddle with fairs, and otherwise curtail the already narrow amusements of the poor." E. G. Wakefield : *Swing Unmasked* (published in 1831). G.

C.N.P.   Z

CAPTAIN FITZCHROME. He is somewhat out of his element here :
among such a diversity of opinions he will hear some he will not like.

LADY CLARINDA. It was rather ill-judged in Mr. Crotchet to invite
him to-day. But the art of assorting company is above these
parvenus, They invite a certain number of persons without considering how they harmonise with each other. Between Sir Simon
and you is the Reverend Doctor Folliott. He is said to be an excellent scholar, and is fonder of books than the majority of his cloth ;
he is very fond, also, of the good things of this world. He is of an
admirable temper, and says rude things in a pleasant half-earnest
manner, that nobody can take offence with. And next to him,
again, is one Captain Fitzchrome, who is very much in love with a
certain person that does not mean to have any thing to say to him,
because she can better her fortune by taking somebody else.

CAPTAIN FITZCHROME. And next to him, again, is the beautiful,
the accomplished, the witty, the fascinating, the tormenting Lady
Clarinda, who traduces herself to the said captain by assertions
which it would drive him crazy to believe.

LADY CLARINDA. Time will show, sir. And now we have gone
the round of the table.

CAPTAIN FITZCHROME. But I must say, though I know you had
always a turn for sketching characters, you surprise me by your
observation, and especially by your attention to opinions.

LADY CLARINDA. Well, I will tell you a secret : I am writing a
novel.

CAPTAIN FITZCHROME. A novel !

LADY CLARINDA. Yes, a novel. And I shall get a little finery
by it : trinkets and fal-lals, which I cannot get from papa. You
must know I have been reading several fashionable novels, the
fashionable this, and the fashionable that ; and I thought to myself,
why I can do better than any of these myself. So I wrote a chapter
or two, and sent them as a specimen to Mr. Puffall, the bookseller,
telling him they were to be a part of the fashionable something or
other, and he offered me, I will not say how much, to finish it in three

volumes, and let him pay all the newspapers for recommending it as the work of a lady of quality, who had made very free with the characters of her acquaintance.

CAPTAIN FITZCHROME. Surely you have not done so ?

LADY CLARINDA. Oh, no ; I leave that to Mr. Eavesdrop. But Mr. Puffall made it a condition that I should let him say so.

CAPTAIN FITZCHROME. A strange recommendation.

LADY CLARINDA. Oh, nothing else will do. And it seems you may give yourself any character you like, and the newspapers will print it as if it came from themselves. I have commended you to three of our friends here, as an economist, a transcendentalist, and a classical scholar ; and if you wish to be renowned through the world for these, or any other accomplishments, the newspapers will confirm you in their possession for half-a-guinea a piece.

CAPTAIN FITZCHROME. Truly, the praise of such gentry must be a feather in any one's cap.

LADY CLARINDA. So you will see, some morning, that my novel is " the most popular production of the day." This is Mr. Puffall's favourite phrase. He makes the newspapers say it of every thing he publishes. But " the day," you know, is a very convenient phrase ; it allows of three hundred and sixty-five " most popular productions " in a year. And in leap-year one more.

CHAPTER VI

THEORIES

> But when they came to shape the model,
> Not one could fit the other's noddle.—BUTLER.[1]

MEANWHILE, the last course, and the dessert, passed by. When the ladies had withdrawn, young Crotchet addressed the company.

MR. CROTCHET, JUN. There is one point in which philosophers of

[1] *Hudibras*, Pt. III, Canto 2, ll. 253–4.   G.

all classes seem to be agreed; that they only want money to regenerate the world.

MR. MAC QUEDY. No doubt of it. Nothing is so easy as to lay down the outlines of perfect society. There wants nothing but money to set it going. I will explain myself clearly and fully by reading a paper. (*Producing a large scroll.*) " In the infancy of society——"

THE REV. DR. FOLLIOTT. Pray, Mr. Mac Quedy, how is it that all gentlemen of your nation begin every thing they write with the " infancy of society " ?

MR. MAC QUEDY. Eh, sir, it is the simplest way to begin at the beginning. " In the infancy of society, when government was invented to save a percentage; say two and a half per cent.——"

THE REV. DR. FOLLIOTT. I will not say any such thing.

MR. MAC QUEDY. Well, say any percentage you please.[1]

THE REV. DR. FOLLIOTT. I will not say any percentage at all.

MR. MAC QUEDY. " On the principle of the division of labour——"

THE REV. DR. FOLLIOTT. Government was invented to spend a percentage.

MR. MAC QUEDY. To save a percentage.

THE REV. DR. FOLLIOTT. No, sir, to spend a percentage; and a good deal more than two and a half per cent. Two hundred and fifty per cent.; that is intelligible.

MR. MAC QUEDY. " In the infancy of society "——

---

[1] Sir Edward Strachey says in his *Recollections of Peacock* : " He one day came to my father's room, and said, with mock indignation, ' I will never dine with Mill again, for he asks me to meet only political economists. I dined with him last night, when he had Mushet and MacCulloch, and after dinner, Mushet took a paper out of his pocket, and began to read : " In the infancy of society, when Government was invented to save a percentage— say, of $3\frac{1}{2}\%$ "—on which he was stopped by MacCulloch with, " I will say no such thing," meaning that this was not the proper percentage.' "
G.

MR. TOOGOOD. Never mind the infancy of society. The question is of society in its maturity. Here is what it should be. (*Producing a paper.*) I have laid it down in a diagram.

MR. SKIONAR. Before we proceed to the question of government, we must nicely discriminate the boundaries of sense, understanding, and reason. Sense is a receptivity——

MR. CROTCHET, JUN. We are proceeding too fast. Money being all that is wanted to regenerate society, I will put into the hands of this company a large sum for the purpose. Now let us see how to dispose of it.

MR. MAC QUEDY. We will begin by taking a committee-room in London, where we will dine together once a week, to deliberate.

THE REV. DR. FOLLIOTT. If the money is to go in deliberative dinners, you may set me down for a committee man and honorary caterer.

MR. MAC QUEDY. Next, you must all learn political economy, which I will teach you, very compendiously, in lectures over the bottle.

THE REV. DR. FOLLIOTT. I hate lectures over the bottle. But pray, sir, what is political economy ?

MR. MAC QUEDY. Political economy is to the state what domestic economy is to the family.

THE REV. DR. FOLLIOTT. No such thing, sir. In the family there is a *paterfamilias*, who regulates the distribution, and takes care that there shall be no such thing in the household as one dying of hunger, while another dies of surfeit. In the state it is all hunger at one end, and all surfeit at the other. Matchless claret, Mr. Crotchet.

MR. CROTCHET. Vintage of fifteen, doctor.

MR. MAC QUEDY. The family consumes, and so does the state.

THE REV. DR. FOLLIOTT. Consumes, sir ! Yes : but the mode, the proportions ; there is the essential difference between the state and the family. Sir, I hate false analogies.

MR. MAC QUEDY. Well, sir, the analogy is not essential. Distribution will come under its proper head.

THE REV. DR. FOLLIOTT. Come where it will, the distribution of the state is in no respect analogous to the distribution of the family. The *paterfamilias*, sir : the *paterfamilias*.

MR. MAC QUEDY. Well, sir, let that pass. The family consumes, and in order to consume, it must have supply.

THE REV. DR. FOLLIOTT. Well, sir, Adam and Eve knew that, when they delved and span.

MR. MAC QUEDY. Very true, sir (*reproducing his scroll*). "In the infancy of society——"

MR. TOOGOOD. The reverend gentleman has hit the nail on the head. It is the distribution that must be looked to : it is the *paterfamilias* that is wanting in the state. Now here I have provided him. (*Reproducing his diagram.*)

MR. TRILLO. Apply the money, sir, to building and endowing an opera house, where the ancient altar of Bacchus may flourish, and justice may be done to sublime compositions. (*Producing a part of a manuscript opera.*)

MR. SKIONAR. No, sir, build *sacella* for transcendental oracles to teach the world how to see through a glass darkly. (*Producing a scroll.*)

MR. TRILLO. See through an opera-glass brightly.

THE REV. DR. FOLLIOTT. See through a wine-glass, full of claret : then you see both darkly and brightly. But, gentlemen, if you are all in the humour for reading papers, I will read you the first half of my next Sunday's sermon. (*Producing a paper.*)

OMNES. No sermon ! No sermon !

THE REV. DR. FOLLIOTT. Then I move that our respective papers be committed to our respective pockets.

MR. MAC QUEDY. Political economy is divided into two great branches, production and consumption.

THE REV. DR. FOLLIOTT. Yes, sir; there are two great classes of men: those who produce much and consume little; and those who consume much and produce nothing. The *fruges consumere nati* [1] have the best of it. Eh, captain! you remember the characteristics of a great man according to Aristophanes: ὅστις γε πίνειν οἶδε καὶ βίνειν μόνον.[2] Ha! ha! ha! Well, captain, even in these tight-laced days, the obscurity of a learned language allows a little pleasantry.

CAPTAIN FITZCHROME. Very true, sir: the pleasantry and the obscurity go together: they are all one, as it were;—to me at any rate. (*aside.*)

MR. MAC QUEDY. Now, sir——

THE REV. DR. FOLLIOTT. Pray, sir, let your science alone, or you will put me under the painful necessity of demolishing it bit by bit, as I have done your exordium. I will undertake it any morning; but it is too hard exercise after dinner.

MR. MAC QUEDY. Well, sir, in the meantime I hold my science established.

THE REV. DR. FOLLIOTT. And I hold it demolished.

MR. CROTCHET, JUN. Pray, gentlemen, pocket your manuscripts; fill your glasses; and consider what we shall do with our money.

MR. MAC QUEDY. Build lecture rooms and schools for all.

MR. TRILLO. Revive the Athenian theatre: regenerate the lyrical drama.

MR. TOOGOOD. Build a grand co-operative parallelogram, with a steam-engine in the middle for a maid of all work.

---

[1] " Born to consume the fruits of the earth." Horace: *Ep.* I. ii. 27. G.
[2] " One who knows of nought but wine and women." *Frogs*, 740. G.

MR. FIREDAMP. Drain the country, and get rid of *malaria*, by abolishing duck-ponds.[1]

DR. MORBIFIC. Found a philanthropic college of anti-contagionists, where all the members shall be inoculated with the virus of all known diseases. Try the experiment on a grand scale.

MR. CHAINMAIL. Build a great dining-hall : endow it with beef and ale, and hang the hall round with arms to defend the provisions.

MR. HENBANE. Found a toxicological institution for trying all poisons and antidotes. I myself have killed a frog twelve times, and brought him to life eleven ; but the twelfth time he died. I have a phial of the drug which killed him in my pocket, and shall not rest till I have discovered its antidote.

THE REV. DR. FOLLIOTT. I move that the last speaker be dispossessed of his phial, and that it be forthwith thrown into the Thames.

MR. HENBANE. How, sir ? my invaluable, and in the present state of human knowledge, infallible poison ?

THE REV. DR. FOLLIOTT. Let the frogs have all the advantage of it.

MR. CROTCHET. Consider, doctor, the fish might participate. Think of the salmon.

THE REV. DR. FOLLIOTT. Then let the owner's right-hand neighbour swallow it.

MR. EAVESDROP. Me, sir ! What have I done, sir, that I am to be poisoned, sir ?

THE REV. DR. FOLLIOTT. Sir, you have published a character of your facetious friend, the Reverend Doctor F., wherein you have sketched off me ; me, sir, even to my nose and wig. What business have the public with my nose and wig ?

---

[1] Here the visionary crank has since got the better of the scoffer ; malaria has been eliminated in Britain by draining the fens and in Panama by " abolishing duckponds," while the smoke of wood embers is a good way of keeping off mosquitoes. See p. 757. G.

MR. EAVESDROP. Sir, it is all good humoured : all in *bonhomie* : all friendly and complimentary.

THE REV. DR. FOLLIOTT. Sir, the bottle, *la Dive Bouteille*,[1] is a recondite oracle, which makes an Eleusinian temple of the circle in which it moves. He who reveals its mysteries must die. Therefore, let the dose be administered. *Fiat experimentum in animâ vili.*

MR. EAVESDROP. Sir, you are very facetious at my expense.

THE REV. DR. FOLLIOTT. Sir, you have been very unfacetious, very inficete at mine. You have dished me up, like a savory omelette, to gratify the appetite of the reading rabble for gossip. The next time, sir, I will respond with the *argumentum baculinum.* Print that, sir ; put it on record as a promise of the Reverend Doctor F., which shall be most faithfully kept, with an exemplary bamboo.

MR. EAVESDROP. Your cloth protects you, sir.

THE REV. DR. FOLLIOTT. My bamboo shall protect me, sir.

MR. CROTCHET. Doctor, doctor, you are growing too polemical.

THE REV. DR. FOLLIOTT. Sir, my blood boils. What business have the public with my nose and wig ?

MR. CROTCHET. Doctor ! Doctor !

MR. CROTCHET, JUN. Pray, gentlemen, return to the point. How shall we employ our fund ?

MR. PHILPOT. Surely in no way so beneficially as in exploring rivers. Send a fleet of steamboats down the Niger, and another up the Nile. So shall you civilise Africa, and establish stocking factories in Abyssinia and Bambo.

THE REV. DR. FOLLIOTT. With all submission, breeches and petticoats must precede stockings. Send out a crew of tailors. Try if the king of Bambo will invest inexpressibles.

MR. CROTCHET, JUN. Gentlemen, it is not for partial, but for

---

[1] *Dive* is old French for *Divine*.   G.

general benefit, that this fund is proposed : a grand and universally applicable scheme for the amelioration of the condition of man.

SEVERAL VOICES.   That is my scheme.   I have not heard a scheme but my own that has a grain of common sense.

MR. TRILLO.   Gentlemen, you inspire me.   Your last exclamation runs itself into a chorus, and sets itself to music.   Allow me to lead, and to hope for your voices in harmony.

> After careful meditation,
> And profound deliberation,
> On the various pretty projects which have just been shown,
> Not a scheme in agitation,
> For the world's amelioration,
> Has a grain of common sense in it, except my own.

SEVERAL VOICES.   We are not disposed to join in any such chorus.

THE REV. DR. FOLLIOTT.   Well, of all these schemes, I am for Mr. Trillo's.   Regenerate the Athenian theatre.   My classical friend here, the captain, will vote with me.

CAPTAIN FITZCHROME.   I, sir ? oh ! of course, sir.

MR. MAC QUEDY.   Surely, captain, I rely on you to uphold political economy.

CAPTAIN FITZCHROME.   Me, sir ? oh ! to be sure, sir.

THE REV. DR. FOLLIOTT.   Pray, sir, will political economy uphold the Athenian theatre ?

MR. MAC QUEDY.   Surely not.   It would be a very unproductive investment.

THE REV. DR. FOLLIOTT.   Then the captain votes against you. What, sir, did not the Athenians, the wisest of nations, appropriate to their theatre their most sacred and intangible fund.   Did not they give to melopœia,[1] choregraphy, and the sundry forms of didascalics, the precedence of all other matters, civil and military ?   Was it not their law, that even the proposal to divert this fund to any other purpose should be punished with death ?   But, sir, I further propose

[1] Music-making.   G.

that the Athenian theatre being resuscitated, the admission shall be free to all who can expound the Greek choruses, constructively, mythologically, and metrically, and to none others. So shall all the world learn Greek : Greek, the Alpha and Omega of all knowledge. At him who sits not in the theatre, shall be pointed the finger of scorn : he shall be called in the highway of the city, " a fellow without Greek."

MR. TRILLO. But the ladies, sir, the ladies.

THE REV. DR. FOLLIOTT. Every man may take in a lady : and she who can construe and metricise a chorus, shall, if she so please, pass in by herself.

MR. TRILLO. But, sir, you will shut me out of my own theatre. Let there at least be a double passport, Greek and Italian.

THE REV. DR. FOLLIOTT. No, sir ; I am inexorable. No Greek, no theatre.

MR. TRILLO. Sir, I cannot consent to be shut out from my own theatre.

THE REV. DR. FOLLIOTT. You see how it is, Squire Crotchet the younger ; you can scarcely find two to agree on a scheme, and no two of those can agree on the details. Keep your money in your pocket. And so ends the fund for regenerating the world.

MR. MAC QUEDY. Nay, by no means. We are all agreed on deliberative dinners.

THE REV. DR. FOLLIOTT. Very true ; we will dine and discuss. We will sing with Robin Hood, " If I drink water while this doth last ; " and while it lasts we will have no adjournment, if not to the Athenian theatre.

MR. TRILLO. Well, gentlemen, I hope this chorus at least will please you :

> If I drink water while this doth last,
> May I never again drink wine :
> For how can a man, in his life of a span,
> Do any thing better than dine ?

We'll dine and drink, and say if we think
That any thing better can be ;
And when we have dined, wish all mankind
May dine as well as we.

And though a good wish will fill no dish,
And brim no cup with sack,
Yet thoughts will spring, as the glasses ring,
To illume our studious track.
On the brilliant dreams of our hopeful schemes
The light of the flask shall shine ;
And we'll sit till day, but we'll find the way
To drench the world with wine.

The schemes for the world's regeneration evaporated in a tumult
of voices.

CHAPTER VII

THE SLEEPING VENUS

Quoth he : In all my life till now,
I ne'er saw so profane a show.—BUTLER.[1]

THE library of Crotchet Castle was a large and well furnished apartment, opening on one side into an anteroom, on the other into a
music-room.   It had several tables stationed at convenient distances;
one consecrated to the novelties of literature, another to the novelties
of embellishment ; others unoccupied, and at the disposal of the
company.   The walls were covered with a copious collection of
ancient and modern books ; the ancient having been selected and
arranged by the Reverend Doctor Folliott.   In the anteroom were
card-tables ; in the music-room were various instruments, all
popular operas, and all fashionable music.   In this suite of apartments, and not in the drawing-room, were the evenings of Crotchet
Castle usually passed.

The young ladies were in the music-room ; Miss Crotchet at the
piano, Lady Clarinda, at the harp, playing and occasionally singing,
at the suggestion of Mr. Trillo, portions of *Matilde di Shabran*.[2]

[1] *Hudibras*, Pt. II, Canto 2, ll. 665–6.   G.
[2] This *Opera Buffa* by Rossini had been produced in Paris at the Théâtre
Italien in 1829.   It was first performed in Rome in 1821.   G.

Lord Bossnowl was turning over the leaves for Miss Crotchet; the captain was performing the same office for Lady Clarinda, but with so much more attention to the lady than the book, that he often made sad work with the harmony, by turning over two leaves together. On these occasions Miss Crotchet paused, Lady Clarinda laughed, Mr. Trillo scolded, Lord Bossnowl yawned, the captain apologised, and the performance proceeded.

In the library, Mr. Mac Quedy was expounding political economy to the Reverend Doctor Folliott, who was *pro more* demolishing its doctrines *seriatim*.

Mr. Chainmail was in hot dispute with Mr. Skionar, touching the physical and moral well-being of man. Mr. Skionar was enforcing his friend Mr. Shantsee's views of moral discipline; maintaining that the sole thing needful for man in this world, was loyal and pious education; the giving men good books to read, and enough of the hornbook to read them; with a judicious interspersion of the lessons of Old Restraint, which was his poetic name for the parish stocks. Mr. Chainmail, on the other hand, stood up for the exclusive necessity of beef and ale, lodging and raiment, wife and children, courage to fight for them all, and armour wherewith to do so.

Mr. Henbane had got his face scratched, and his finger bitten, by the cat, in trying to catch her for a second experiment in killing and bringing to life; and Doctor Morbific was comforting him with a disquisition, to prove that there were only four animals having the power to communicate hydrophobia, of which the cat was one; and that it was not necessary that the animal should be in a rabid state, the nature of the wound being every thing, and the idea of contagion a delusion. Mr. Henbane was listening very lugubriously to this dissertation.

Mr. Philpot had seized on Mr. Firedamp, and pinned him down to a map of Africa, on which he was tracing imaginary courses of mighty inland rivers, terminating in lakes and marshes, where they were finally evaporated by the heat of the sun; and Mr. Firedamp's hair was standing on end at the bare imagination of the mass of *malaria* that must be engendered by the operation. Mr. Toogood had begun explaining his diagrams to Sir Simon Steeltrap; but Sir Simon grew testy, and told Mr. Toogood that the promulgators of such doctrines ought to be consigned to the treadmill. The philanthropist walked off from the country gentleman, and proceeded to hold forth to young Crotchet who stood silent, as one who listens, but in reality without hearing a syllable. Mr. Crotchet senior, as the master of the house, was left to entertain himself with his own meditations, till the Reverend Doctor Folliott tore himself from Mr. Mac Quedy, and proceeded to expostulate with Mr. Crotchet on a delicate topic.

There was an Italian painter, who obtained the name of *Il Bragatore*, by the superinduction of inexpressibles on the naked Apollos and Bacchuses of his betters. The fame of this worthy remained one and indivisible, till a set of heads, which had been, by a too common mistake of nature's journeymen, stuck upon magisterial shoulders, as the Corinthian capitals of " fair round bellies with fat capon lined,"[1] but which nature herself had intended for the noddles of porcelain mandarins, promulgated simultaneously from the east and the west of London, an order that no plaster-of-Paris Venus should appear in the streets without petticoats. Mr. Crotchet, on reading this order in the evening paper, which, by the postman's early arrival, was always laid on his breakfast-table, determined to fill his house with Venuses of all sizes and kinds. In pursuance of this resolution, came packages by water-carriage, containing an infinite variety of Venuses. There were the Medicean Venus, and the Bathing Venus; the Uranian Venus, and the Pandemian Venus; the Crouching Venus, and the Sleeping Venus; the Venus rising from the sea, the Venus with the apple of Paris, and the Venus with the armour of Mars.

The Reverend Doctor Folliott had been very much astonished at this unexpected display. Disposed, as he was, to hold, that whatever had been in Greece, was right; he was more than doubtful of the propriety of throwing open the classical *adytum* to the illiterate profane. Whether, in his interior mind, he was at all influenced, either by the consideration that it would be for the credit of his cloth, with some of his vice-suppressing neighbours, to be able to say that he had expostulated; or by curiosity, to try what sort of defence his city-bred friend, who knew the classics only by translations, and

[1] *As You Like It*, Act II, Sc. 7. G.

whose reason was always a little a-head of his knowledge, would make for his somewhat ostentatious display of liberality in matters of taste ; is a question, on which the learned may differ : but, after having duly deliberated on two full-sized casts of the Uranian and Pande-mian Venus, in niches on each side of the chimney, and on three alabaster figures, in glass cases, on the mantelpiece, he proceeded, peirastically, to open his fire.

THE REV. DR. FOLLIOTT. These little alabaster figures on the mantelpiece, Mr. Crotchet, and those large figures in the niches— may I take the liberty to ask you what they are intended to represent ?

MR. CROTCHET. Venus, sir ; nothing more, sir ; just Venus.

THE REV. DR. FOLLIOTT. May I ask you, sir, why they are there ?

MR. CROTCHET. To be looked at, sir ; just to be looked at : the reason for most things in a gentleman's house being in it at all ; from the paper on the walls, and the drapery of the curtains, even to the books in the library, of which the most essential part is the appearance of the back.

THE REV. DR. FOLLIOTT. Very true, sir. As great philosophers hold that the *esse* of things is *percipi*, so a gentleman's furniture exists to be looked at. Nevertheless, sir, there are some things more fit to be looked at than others ; for instance, there is nothing more fit to be looked at than the outside of a book. It is, as I may say, from repeated experience, a pure and unmixed pleasure to have a goodly volume lying before you, and to know that you may open it if you please, and need not open it unless you please. It is a resource against *ennui*, if *ennui* should come upon you. To have the resource and not to feel the *ennui*, to enjoy your bottle in the present, and your book in the indefinite future, is a delightful condition of human existence. There is no place, in which a man can move or sit, in which the outside of a book can be otherwise than an innocent and becoming spectacle. Touching this matter, there cannot, I think, be two opinions. But with respect to your Venuses there can be, and indeed there are, two very distinct opinions. Now, sir, that little figure in the centre of the mantelpiece,—as a grave *pater-familias*, Mr. Crotchet, with a fair nubile daughter, whose eyes are like the fish-pools of Heshbon,—I would ask you if you hold that figure to be altogether delicate ?

MR. CROTCHET.   The Sleeping Venus, sir ?   Nothing can be more delicate than the entire contour of the figure, the flow of the hair on the shoulders and neck, the form of the feet and fingers.   It is altogether a most delicate morsel.

THE REV. DR. FOLLIOTT.   Why, in that sense, perhaps, it is as delicate as whitebait in July.   But the attitude, sir, the attitude.

MR. CROTCHET.   Nothing can be more natural, sir.

THE REV. DR. FOLLIOTT.   That is the very thing, sir.   It is too natural : too natural, sir : it lies for all the world like——I make no doubt, the pious cheesemonger, who recently broke its plaster fac-simile over the head of the itinerant vendor, was struck by a certain similitude to the position of his own sleeping beauty, and felt his noble wrath thereby justly aroused.

MR. CROTCHET.   Very likely, sir.   In my opinion, the cheese-monger was a fool, and the justice who sided with him was a greater.

THE REV. DR. FOLLIOTT.   Fool, sir, is a harsh term : call not thy brother a fool.

MR. CROTCHET.   Sir, neither the cheesemonger nor the justice is a brother of mine.

THE REV. DR. FOLLIOTT.   Sir, we are all brethren.

MR. CROTCHET.   Yes, sir, as the hangman is of the thief ; the 'squire of the poacher ; the judge of the libeller ; the lawyer of his client ; the statesman of his colleague ; the bubble-blower of the bubble-buyer ; the slave-driver of the negro : as these are brethren, so am I and the worthies in question.

THE REV. DR. FOLLIOTT.   To be sure, sir, in these instances, and in many others, the term brother must be taken in its utmost latitude of interpretation : we are all brothers, nevertheless.   But to return to the point.   Now these two large figures, one with drapery on the lower half of the body, and the other with no drapery at all ; upon my word, sir, it matters not what godfathers and godmothers may have promised and vowed for the children of this world, touching the devil and other things to be renounced, if such figures as those are to be put before their eyes.

MR. CROTCHET. Sir, the naked figure is the Pandemian Venus, and the half-draped figure is the Uranian Venus ; and I say, sir, that figure realises the finest imaginings of Plato, and is the personification of the most refined and exalted feeling of which the human mind is susceptible ; the love of pure, ideal, intellectual beauty.

THE REV. DR. FOLLIOTT. I am aware, sir, that Plato, in his Symposium, discourseth very eloquently touching the Uranian and Pandemian Venus : but you must remember that, in our Universities, Plato is held to be little better than a misleader of youth ; and they have shown their contempt for him, not only by never reading him (a mode of contempt in which they deal very largely), but even by never printing a complete edition of him ; although they have printed many ancient books, which nobody suspects to have been ever read on the spot, except by a person attached to the press, who is therefore emphatically called " the reader."

MR. CROTCHET. Well, sir ?

THE REV. DR. FOLLIOTT. Why, sir, to " the reader " aforesaid (supposing either of our Universities to have printed an edition of Plato), or to any one else who can be supposed to have read Plato, or indeed to be ever likely to do so, I would very willingly show these figures ; because to such they would, I grant you, be the outward and visible signs of poetical and philosophical ideas : but, to the multitude, the gross carnal multitude, they are but two beautiful women, one half undressed, and the other quite so.

MR. CROTCHET. Then, sir, let the multitude look upon them and learn modesty.

THE REV. DR. FOLLIOTT. I must say that, if I wished my footman to learn modesty, I should not dream of sending him to school to a naked Venus.

MR. CROTCHET. Sir, ancient sculpture is the true school of modesty. But where the Greeks had modesty, we have cant; where they had poetry, we have cant; where they had patriotism, we have cant; where they had any thing that exalts, delights, or adorns humanity, we have nothing but cant, cant, cant. And, sir, to show my contempt for cant in all its shapes, I have adorned my house with the Greek Venus, in all her shapes, and am ready to fight her battle against all the societies that ever were instituted for the suppression of truth and beauty.

THE REV. DR. FOLLIOTT. My dear sir, I am afraid you are growing warm. Pray be cool. Nothing contributes so much to good digestion as to be perfectly cool after dinner.

MR. CROCHET. Sir, the Lacedæmonian virgins wrestled naked with young men: and they grew up, as the wise Lycurgus had foreseen, into the most modest of women, and the most exemplary of wives and mothers.

THE REV. DR. FOLLIOTT. Very likely, sir; but the Athenian virgins did no such thing, and they grew up into wives who stayed at home,—stayed at home, sir; and looked after the husband's dinner,—his dinner, sir, you will please to observe.

MR. CROTCHET. And what was the consequence of that, sir? that they were such very insipid persons that the husband would not go home to eat his dinner, but preferred the company of some Aspasia, or Lais.

THE REV. DR. FOLLIOTT. Two very different persons, sir, give me leave to remark.

MR. CROTCHET. Very likely, sir; but both too good to be married in Athens.

THE REV. DR. FOLLIOTT. Sir, Lais was a Corinthian.

MR. CROTCHET. 'Od's vengeance, sir, some Aspasia and any other Athenian name of the same sort of person you like——

THE REV. DR. FOLLIOTT. I do not like the sort of person at all:

the sort of person I like, as I have already implied, is a modest woman, who stays at home and looks after her husband's dinner.

MR. CROTCHET. Well, sir, that was not the taste of the Athenians. They preferred the society of women who would not have made any scruple about sitting as models to Praxiteles ; as you know, sir, very modest women in Italy did to Canova : one of whom, an Italian countess, being asked by an English lady, " how she could bear it ? " answered, " Very well ; there was a good fire in the room."

THE REV. DR. FOLLIOTT. Sir, the English lady should have asked how the Italian lady's husband could bear it. The phials of my wrath would overflow if poor dear Mrs. Folliott—— : sir, in return for your story, I will tell you a story of my ancestor, Gilbert Folliott. The devil haunted him, as he did Saint Francis, in the likeness of a beautiful damsel ; but all he could get from the exemplary Gilbert was an admonition to wear a stomacher and longer petticoats.

MR. CROTCHET. Sir, your story makes for my side of the question. It proves that the devil, in the likeness of a fair damsel, with short petticoats and no stomacher, was almost too much for Gilbert Folliott. The force of the spell was in the drapery.

THE REV. DR. FOLLIOTT. Bless my soul, sir !

MR. CROTCHET. Give me leave, sir. Diderot——

THE REV. DR. FOLLIOTT. Who was he, sir ?

MR. CROTCHET. Who was he, sir ? the sublime philosopher, the father of the encyclopædia, of all the encyclopædias that have ever been printed.

THE REV. DR. FOLLIOTT. Bless me, sir, a terrible progeny ! they belong to the tribe of *Incubi*.

MR. CROTCHET. The great philosopher, Diderot——

THE REV. DR. FOLLIOTT. Sir, Diderot is not a man after my heart. Keep to the Greeks, if you please ; albeit this Sleeping Venus is not an antique.

MR. CROTCHET. Well, sir, the Greeks : why do we call the Elgin marbles inestimable ? Simply because they are true to nature. And why are they so superior in that point to all modern works, with all our greater knowledge of anatomy ? Why, sir, but because the Greeks, having no cant, had better opportunities of studying models ?

THE REV. DR. FOLLIOTT. Sir, I deny our greater knowledge of anatomy. But I shall take the liberty to employ, on this occasion, the *argumentum ad hominem.* Would you have allowed Miss Crotchet to sit for a model to Canova ?

MR. CROTCHET. Yes, sir.

" God bless my soul, sir ! " exclaimed the Reverend Doctor Folliott, throwing himself back into a chair, and flinging up his heels, with the premeditated design of giving emphasis to his exclamation : but by miscalculating his *impetus,* he overbalanced his chair, and laid himself on the carpet in a right angle, of which his back was the base.

CHAPTER VIII

SCIENCE AND CHARITY

Chi sta nel mondo un par d'ore contento,
Nè gli vien tolta, ovver contaminata,
Quella sua pace in veruno momento,
Può dir che Giove drittamente il guata.
                                    FORTEGUERRI.[1]

THE Reverend Doctor Folliott took his departure about ten o'clock, to walk home to his vicarage. There was no moon ; but the night was bright and clear, and afforded him as much light as he needed. He paused a moment by the Roman Camp, to listen to the nightingale ; repeated to himself a passage of Sophocles ; proceeded through the park gate, and entered the narrow lane that led to the village. He walked on in a very pleasant mood of the state called *reverie* ; in which fish and wine, Greek and political economy, the

[1] " He who in this world enjoys a few hours of contentment and whose peace is neither snatched from him nor in any way marred can say that God gazes directly upon him." From *Il Ricciardetto,* a burlesque of Ariosto. G.

Sleeping Venus he had left behind and poor dear Mrs. Folliott, to whose fond arms he was returning, passed as in a *camera obscura* over the tablets of his imagination. Presently the image of Mr. Eavesdrop, with a printed sketch of the Reverend Doctor F., presented itself before him, and he began mechanically to flourish his bamboo. The movement was prompted by his good genius, for the uplifted bamboo received the blow of a ponderous cudgel, which was intended for his head. The reverend gentleman recoiled two or three paces, and saw before him a couple of ruffians, who were preparing to renew the attack, but whom, with two swings of his bamboo, he laid with cracked sconces on the earth, where he proceeded to deal with them like corn beneath the flail of the thresher. One of them drew a pistol, which went off in the very act of being struck aside by the bamboo, and lodged a bullet in the brain of the other. There was then only one enemy, who vainly struggled to rise, every effort being attended with a new and more signal prostration. The fellow roared for mercy. " Mercy, rascal ! " cried the divine ; " what mercy were you going to show me, villain ? What ! I warrant me, you thought it would be an easy matter, and no sin, to rob and murder a parson on his way home from dinner. You said to yourselves, doubtless, ' We'll waylay the fat parson (you irreverent knave) as he waddles home (you disparaging ruffian), half-seas-over (you calumnious vagabond).' " And with every dyslogistic term, which he supposed had been applied to himself, he inflicted a new bruise on his rolling and roaring antagonist. " Ah, rogue ! " he proceeded ; " you can roar now, marauder ; you were silent enough when you devoted my brains to dispersion under your cudgel. But seeing that I cannot bind you, and that I intend you not to escape, and that it would be dangerous to let you rise, I will disable you in all your members ; I will contund you as Thestylis did strong-smelling herbs,[1] in the quality whereof you do most gravely partake, as my nose beareth testimony, ill weed that you are. I will beat you to a jelly, and I will then roll you into the ditch, to lie till the constable comes for you, thief."

---

[1] Thestylis . . . . .
. . . . herbas contundit olentes.
VIRG. *Ecl.* ii. 10, 11. [P.]

"Hold! hold! reverend sir," exclaimed the penitent culprit, "I am disabled already in every finger, and in every joint. I will roll myself into the ditch, reverend sir."

"Stir not, rascal," returned the divine, "stir not so much as the quietest leaf above you, or my bamboo rebounds on your body like hail in a thunderstorm. Confess speedily, villain; are you simple thief, or would you have manufactured me into a subject, for the benefit of science? Ay, miscreant caitiff, you would have made me a subject for science, would you?[1] You are a schoolmaster abroad, are you? You are marching with a detachment of the march of mind, are you? You are a member of the Steam Intellect Society, are you? You swear by the learned friend, do you?"

"Oh, no! reverend sir," answered the criminal, "I am innocent of all these offences, whatever they are, reverend sir. The only friend I had in the world is lying dead beside me, reverend sir."

The reverend gentleman paused a moment, and leaned on his bamboo. The culprit, bruised as he was, sprang on his legs, and went off in double quick time. The doctor gave him chase, and had nearly brought him within arm's length, when the fellow turned at right angles, and sprang clean over a deep dry ditch. The divine, following with equal ardour, and less dexterity, went down over head and ears into a thicket of nettles. Emerging with much discomposure, he proceeded to the village, and roused the constable; but the constable found, on reaching the scene of action, that the dead man was gone, as well as his living accomplice.

"Oh, the monster!" exclaimed the Reverend Doctor Folliott, "he has made a subject for science of the only friend he had in the world." "Ay, my dear," he resumed, the next morning at breakfast, "if my old reading, and my early gymnastics (for as the great Hermann says, before I was demulced by the Muses, I was *ferocis ingenii puer, et ad arma quam ad literas paratior*[2]), had not imbued me indelibly with some of the holy rage of *Frère Jean des Entommeures*,[3]

[1] The difficulty of obtaining subjects for dissection in the medical schools had led to the horrid trade of "resurrectionists" who dug up the newly buried, and carried on a black market in corpses. G.

[2] "A boy of fierce disposition, more inclined to arms than to letters."—Hermann's *Dedication of Homer's Hymns to his Preceptor Ilgen*. [P.]

[3] Rabelais: Bk. I, ch. xxvii. G.

I should be, at this moment, lying on the table of some flinty-hearted anatomist, who would have sliced and disjointed me as unscrupulously as I do these remnants of the capon and chine, wherewith you consoled yourself yesterday for my absence at dinner. Phew! I have a noble thirst upon me, which I will quench with floods of tea."

The reverend gentleman was interrupted by a messenger, who informed him that the Charity Commissioners requested his presence at the inn, where they were holding a sitting.

"The Charity Commissioners!" exclaimed the reverend gentleman, "who on earth are they?"[1]

The messenger could not inform him, and the reverend gentleman took his hat and stick, and proceeded to the inn.

On entering the best parlour, he saw three well-dressed and bulky gentlemen sitting at a table, and a fourth officiating as clerk, with an open book before him, and a pen in his hand. The churchwardens, who had been also summoned, were already in attendance.

The chief commissioner politely requested the Reverend Doctor Folliott to be seated; and after the usual meteorological preliminaries had been settled by a resolution, *nem. con.*, that it was a fine day but very hot, the chief commissioner stated, that in virtue of the commission of Parliament, which they had the honour to hold, they were now to inquire into the state of the public charities of this village.

THE REV. DR. FOLLIOTT. The state of the public charities, sir, is exceedingly simple. There are none. The charities here are all private, and so private, that I for one know nothing of them.

FIRST COMMISSIONER. We have been informed, sir, that there is an annual rent charged on the land of Hautbois, for the endowment and repair of an almshouse

THE REV. DR. FOLLIOTT. Hautbois! Hautbois!

FIRST COMMISSIONER. The manorial farm of Hautbois, now

[1] In 1818 and 1819 commissions had been set up to investigate educational charities and all the charities for the poor in England and Wales, chiefly thanks to Lord Brougham. They reported in 1835. G.

occupied by Farmer Seedling, is charged with the endowment and maintenance of an almshouse.

THE REV. DR. FOLLIOTT (*to the Churchwarden*). How is this, Mr. Bluenose ?

FIRST CHURCHWARDEN. I really do not know, sir. What say you, Mr. Appletwig ?

MR. APPLETWIG (*parish-clerk and schoolmaster; an old man*). I do remember, gentlemen, to have been informed, that there did stand at the end of the village a ruined cottage, which had once been an almshouse, which was endowed and maintained, by an annual revenue of a mark and a half, or one pound sterling, charged some centuries ago on the farm of Hautbois ; but the means, by the progress of time, having become inadequate to the end, the almshouse tumbled to pieces.

FIRST COMMISSIONER. But this is a right which cannot be abrogated by desuetude, and the sum of one pound per annum is still chargeable for charitable purposes on the manorial farm of Hautbois.

THE REV. DR. FOLLIOTT. Very well, sir.

MR. APPLETWIG. But sir, the one pound per annum is still received by the parish, but was long ago, by an unanimous vote in open vestry, given to the minister.

THE THREE COMMISSIONERS (*unâ voce*). The minister !

FIRST COMMISSIONER. This is an unjustifiable proceeding.

SECOND COMMISSIONER. A misappropriation of a public fund.

THIRD COMMISSIONER. A flagrant perversion of a charitable donation.

THE REV. DR. FOLLIOTT. God bless my soul, gentlemen ! I know nothing of this matter. How is this, Mr. Bluenose ? Do I receive this one pound per annum ?

FIRST CHURCHWARDEN. Really, sir, I know no more about it than you do.

MR. APPLETWIG. You certainly receive it, sir. It was voted to one of your predecessors. Farmer Seedling lumps it in with his tithes.

FIRST COMMISSIONER. Lumps it in, sir! Lump in a charitable donation!

SECOND AND THIRD COMMISSIONER. Oh-oh-oh-h-h!

FIRST COMMISSIONER. Reverend sir, and gentlemen, officers of this parish, we are under the necessity of admonishing you that this is a most improper proceeding ; and you are hereby duly admonished accordingly. Make a record, Mr. Milky.

MR. MILKY (*writing*). The clergyman and churchwardens of the village of Hm-m-m-m gravely admonished. Hm-m-m-m.

THE REV. DR. FOLLIOTT. Is that all, gentlemen ?

THE COMMISSIONERS. That is all, sir ; and we wish you a good morning.

THE REV. DR. FOLLIOTT. A very good morning to you, gentlemen.

" What in the name of all that is wonderful, Mr. Bluenose," said the Reverend Doctor Folliott, as he walked out of the inn, " what in the name of all that is wonderful, can those fellows mean ? They have come here in a chaise and four, to make a fuss about a pound per annum, which, after all, they leave as it was. I wonder who pays them for their trouble, and how much."

MR. APPLETWIG. The public pay for it, sir. It is a job of the learned friend whom you admire so much. It makes away with public money in salaries, and private money in lawsuits, and does no particle of good to any living soul.

THE REV. DR. FOLLIOTT. Ay, ay, Mr. Appletwig ; that is just the sort of public service to be looked for from the learned friend. Oh, the learned friend ! the learned friend ! He is the evil genius of every thing that falls in his way.

The reverend doctor walked off to Crotchet Castle, to narrate his misadventures, and exhale his budget of grievances on Mr. Mac Quedy, whom he considered a ringleader of the march of mind.

CHAPTER IX

THE VOYAGE

Οἱ μὲν ἔπειτ' ἀναβάντες ἐπέπλεον ὑγρὰ κέλευθα.

Mounting the bark, they cleft the watery ways. HOMER.[1]

FOUR beautiful cabined pinnaces, one for the ladies, one for the gentlemen, one for kitchen and servants, one for a dining-room and band of music, weighed anchor, on a fine July morning, from below Crotchet Castle, and were towed merrily, by strong trotting horses, against the stream of the Thames. They passed from the district of chalk, successively into the districts of clay, of sand-rock, of oolite, and so forth. Sometimes they dined in their floating dining-room, sometimes in tents, which they pitched on the dry smooth-shaven green of a newly mown meadow ; sometimes they left their vessels to see sights in the vicinity ; sometimes they passed a day or two in a comfortable inn.

At Oxford, they walked about to see the curiosities of architecture, painted windows, and undisturbed libraries. The Reverend Doctor Folliott laid a wager with Mr. Crotchet " that in all their perlustrations they would not find a man reading," and won it.[2] " Ay, sir," said the reverend gentleman, " this is still a seat of learning, on the principle of—once a captain always a captain. We may well ask, in these great reservoirs of books whereof no man ever draws a sluice, *Quorsum pertinuit stipare Platona Menandro ?*[3] What is done here for the classics ? Reprinting German editions on better paper. A great boast, verily ! What for mathematics ? What for metaphysics ? What for history ? What for any thing worth knowing ? This was a seat of learning in the days of Friar Bacon.

---

[1] *Il.* I. 312. *Od.* IV. 842. G.

[2] " Tuesday, August 6th., 1822. I was at the Library the whole day, and not a single member of the University came into the room, excepting Mr. Eden, the assistant. Oxford Race day." *Dr. Bliss's Memorandum,* quoted in Murray's *Annals of the Bodleian Library.* G.

[3] Wherefore is Plato on Menander piled ? HOR. *Sat.* ii. 3, 11. [P.]

But the friar is gone, and his learning with him. Nothing of him is left but the immortal nose, which when his brazen head had tumbled to pieces, crying " Time's past," was the only palpable fragment among its minutely pulverised atoms, and which is still resplendent over the portals of its cognominal college. That nose, sir, is the only thing to which I shall take off my hat, in all this Babylon of buried literature.[1]

MR. CROTCHET. But, doctor, it is something to have a great reservoir of learning, at which some may draw if they please.

THE REV. DR. FOLLIOTT. But, here, good care is taken that nobody shall please. If even a small drop from the sacred fountain, πίδακος ἐξ ἱερῆς ὀλίγη λιβὰς, as Callimachus has it,[2] were carried off by any one, it would be evidence of something to hope for. But the system of dissuasion from all good learning is brought here to a pitch of perfection that baffles the keenest aspirant. I run over to myself the names of the scholars of Germany, a glorious catalogue ! but ask for those of Oxford—Where are they ? The echoes of their courts, as vacant as their heads, will answer, Where are they ? The tree shall be known by its fruit ; and seeing that this great tree, with all its specious seeming, brings forth no fruit, I do denounce it as a barren fig.

MR. MAC QUEDY. I shall set you right on this point. We do nothing without motives. If learning get nothing but honour, and very little of that ; and if the good things of this world, which ought to be the rewards of learning, become the mere gifts of self-interested patronage ; you must not wonder if, in the finishing of education, the science which takes precedence of all others, should be the science of currying favour.

THE REV. DR. FOLLIOTT. Very true, sir. Education is well

---

[1] See Robert Greene : *Friar Bacon and Friar Bungay.* Roger Bacon was popularly believed to have constructed a brazen head which was destroyed by unknown powers after he had made it speak. A doorknocker, in the form of a brazen nose, may have given the name to the original hall of Brasenose College, which was founded in the twelfth century. G.

[2] *Ap.* 112. "A streamlet springing from the sacred fountain." G.

finished, for all worldly purposes, when the head is brought into the
state whereinto I am accustomed to bring a marrow-bone, when it
has been set before me on a toast, with a white napkin wrapped
round it.   Nothing trundles along the high road of preferment so
trimly as a well-biased sconce, picked clean within, and polished
without ;   *totus teres atque rotundus*.[1]   The perfection of the finishing
lies in the bias, which keeps it trundling in the given direction.
There is good and sufficient reason for the fig being barren, but it is
not therefore the less a barren fig.

At Godstow they gathered hazel on the grave of Rosamond ;   and,
proceeding on their voyage, fell into a discussion on legendary
histories.

LADY CLARINDA.   History is but a tiresome thing in itself;   it
becomes more agreeable the more romance is mixed up with it.
The great enchanter has made me learn many things which I should
never have dreamed of studying, if they had not come to me in the
form of amusement.

THE REV. DR. FOLLIOTT.   What enchanter is that ?   There are two
enchanters :   he of the North,[2] and he of the South.

MR. TRILLO.   Rossini ?

THE REV. DR. FOLLIOTT.   Ay, there is another enchanter.   But
I mean the great enchanter of Covent Garden :   he who, for more
than a quarter of a century, has produced two pantomimes a year,
to the delight of children of all ages, including myself at all ages.
That is the enchanter for me.   I am for the pantomimes.   All the
northern enchanter's romances put together would not furnish
materials for half the southern enchanter's pantomimes.

LADY CLARINDA.   Surely you do not class literature with
pantomime ?

THE REV. DR. FOLLIOTT.   In these cases I do.   They are both one,
with a slight difference.   The one is the literature of pantomime,
the other is the pantomime of literature.   There is the same variety

---

[1] All smooth and round.   [P.]   [Horace :   *Sat.* II. vii. 86.   G.]
[2] Sir Walter Scott.   G.

of character, the same diversity of story, the same copiousness of incident, the same research into costume, the same display of heraldry, falconry, minstrelsy, scenery, monkery, witchery, devilry, robbery, poachery, piracy, fishery, gipsy-astrology, demonology, architecture, fortification, castrametation, navigation ; the same running base of love and battle. The main difference is, that the one set of amusing fictions is told in music and action ; the other in all the worst dialects of the English language. As to any sentence worth remembering, any moral or political truth, any thing having a tendency, however remote, to make men wiser or better, to make them think, to make them even think of thinking ; they are both precisely alike : *nuspiam, nequaquam, nullibi, nullimodis.*[1]

LADY CLARINDA. Very amusing, however.

THE REV. DR. FOLLIOTT. Very amusing, very amusing.

MR. CHAINMAIL. My quarrel with the northern enchanter is, that he has grossly misrepresented the twelfth century.

THE REV. DR. FOLLIOTT. He has misrepresented every thing, or he would not have been very amusing. Sober truth is but dull matter to the reading rabble. The angler, who puts not on his hook the bait that best pleases the fish, may sit all day on the bank without catching a gudgeon.[2]

MR. MAC QUEDY. But how do you mean that he has misrepresented the twelfth century ? By exhibiting some of its knights and ladies in the colours of refinement and virtue, seeing that they were all no better than ruffians, and something else that shall be nameless ?

MR. CHAINMAIL. By no means. By depicting them as much worse than they were, not, as you suppose, much better. No one would infer from his pictures that theirs was a much better state of society than this which we live in.

[1] Nothing, by no means, nowhere, no how. G.
[2] Eloquentiæ magister, nisi, tamquam piscator, eam imposuerit hamis escam, quam scierit appetituros esse pisciculos, sine spe prædæ moratur in scopulo. Petronius Arbiter. [P.] [*Satyricon* C. iii. " The teacher of eloquence who does not follow the example of the fisherman and bait his hook with what he knows the fishes will bite at, wastes his time upon the bank, with no hope of taking anything." G.]

MR. MAC QUEDY. No, nor was it. It was a period of brutality,
ignorance, fanaticism, and tyranny; when the land was covered
with castles, and every castle contained a gang of banditti, headed
by a titled robber, who levied contributions with fire and sword;
plundering, torturing, ravishing, burying his captives in loathsome
dungeons, and broiling them on gridirons, to force from them the
surrender of every particle of treasure which he suspected them of
possessing; and fighting every now and then with the neighbouring
lords, his conterminal bandits, for the right of marauding on the
boundaries. This was the twelfth century, as depicted by all
contemporary historians and poets.

MR. CHAINMAIL. No, sir. Weigh the evidence of specific facts;
you will find more good than evil. Who was England's greatest
hero; the mirror of chivalry, the pattern of honour, the fountain of
generosity, the model to all succeeding ages of military glory?
Richard the First. There is a king of the twelfth century. What
was the first step of liberty? Magna Charta. That was the best
thing ever done by lords. There are lords of the twelfth century.
You must remember, too, that these lords were petty princes, and
made war on each other as legitimately as the heads of larger communities did or do. For their system of revenue, it was, to be sure,
more rough and summary than that which has succeeded it, but it
was certainly less searching and less productive. And as to the
people, I content myself with these great points: that every man
was armed, every man was a good archer, every man could and would
fight effectively with sword or pike, or even with oaken cudgel: no
man would live quietly without beef and ale; if he had them not,
he fought till he either got them, or was put out of condition to want
them. They were not, and could not be, subjected to that powerful
pressure of all the other classes of society, combined by gunpowder,
steam, and *fiscality*, which has brought them to that dismal degradation in which we see them now. And there are the people of the
twelfth century.

MR. MAC QUEDY. As to your king, the enchanter has done him
ample justice, even in your own view. As to your lords and their
ladies, he has drawn them too favourably, given them too many of

the false colours of chivalry, thrown too attractive a light on their abominable doings. As to the people, he keeps them so much in the back-ground, that he can hardly be said to have represented them at all, much less misrepresented them, which indeed he could scarcely do, seeing that, by your own showing, they were all thieves, ready to knock down any man for what they could not come by honestly.

MR. CHAINMAIL. No, sir. They could come honestly by beef and ale, while they were left to their simple industry. When oppression interfered with them in that, then they stood on the defensive, and fought for what they were not permitted to come by quietly.

MR. MAC QUEDY. If A, being aggrieved by B, knocks down C, do you call that standing on the defensive ?

MR. CHAINMAIL. That depends on who or what C is.

THE REV. DR. FOLLIOTT. Gentlemen, you will never settle this controversy, till you have first settled what is good for man in this world ; the great question, *de finibus*, which has puzzled all philosophers. If the enchanter has represented the twelfth century too brightly for one, and too darkly for the other of you, I should say, as an impartial man, he has represented it fairly. My quarrel with him is, that his works contain nothing worth quoting ; and a book that furnishes no quotations, is, *me judice*, no book—it is a plaything. There is no question about the amusement—amusement of multitudes ; but if he who amuses us most, is to be our enchanter κατ᾽ ἐξοχὴν,[1] then my enchanter is the enchanter of Covent Garden.

CHAPTER X

THE VOYAGE, CONTINUED

Continuant nostre routte, navigasmes par trois jours *sans rien descouvrir.*
—RABELAIS.[2]

" THERE is a beautiful structure," said Mr. Chainmail, as they glided by Lechlade church ; " a subject for the pencil, Captain. It is a

[1] *par excellence.* G.
[2] " Pursuing our voyage, we sailed three days, without discovering any thing." Bk. V, ch. i. Urquhart and Motteux translation. G.

question worth asking, Mr. Mac Quedy, whether the religious spirit which reared these edifices, and connected with them everywhere an asylum for misfortune and a provision for poverty, was not better than the commercial spirit, which has turned all the business of modern life into schemes of profit, and processes of fraud and extortion. I do not see, in all your boasted improvements, any compensation for the religious charity of the twelfth century. I do not see any compensation for that kindly feeling which, within their own little communities, bound the several classes of society together, while full scope was left for the development of natural character, wherein individuals differed as conspicuously as in costume. Now, we all wear one conventional dress, one conventional face ; we have no bond of union, but pecuniary interest ; we talk any thing that comes uppermost, for talking's sake, and without expecting to be believed ; we have no nature, no simplicity, no picturesqueness : every thing about us is as artificial and as complicated as our steam-machinery : our poetry is a kaleidoscope of false imagery, expressing no real feeling, portraying no real existence. I do not see any compensation for the poetry of the twelfth century."

MR. MAC QUEDY. I wonder to hear you, Mr. Chainmail, talking of the religious charity of a set of lazy monks and beggarly friars, who were much more occupied with taking than giving ; of whom, those who were in earnest did nothing but make themselves, and everybody about them, miserable, with fastings, and penances, and other such trash ; and those who were not, did nothing but guzzle and royster, and, having no wives of their own, took very unbecoming liberties with those of honester men. And as to your poetry of the twelfth century, it is not good for much.

MR. CHAINMAIL. It has, at any rate, what ours wants, truth to nature, and simplicity of diction. The poetry, which was addressed to the people of the dark ages, pleased in proportion to the truth with which it depicted familiar images, and to their natural connection with the time and place to which they were assigned. In the poetry of our enlightened times, the characteristics of all seasons, soils, and climates, may be blended together, with much benefit to the author's fame as an original genius. The cowslip of a civic poet is always in blossom, his fern is always in full feather ; he gathers the celandine, the primrose, the heath-flower, the jasmine, and the chrysanthemum, all on the same day, and from the same spot : his nightingale sings all the year round, his moon is always full, his cygnet is as white as his swan, his cedar is as tremulous as his aspen, and his poplar as embowering as his beech. Thus all nature marches with the march of mind ; but, among barbarians, instead of mead and wine, and the best seat by the fire, the reward of such a genius would have been, to be summarily turned out of doors in the snow, to meditate on the difference between day and night, and between December and July. It is an age of liberality, indeed, when not to know an oak from a burdock is no disqualification for sylvan minstrelsy. I am for truth and simplicity.

THE REV. DR. FOLLIOTT. Let him who loves them read Greek : Greek, Greek, Greek.

MR. MAC QUEDY. If he can, sir.

THE REV. DR. FOLLIOTT. Very true, sir ; if he can. Here is the captain, who can. But I think he must have finished his education at some very rigid college, where a quotation, or any other overt act showing acquaintance with classical literature, was visited with a severe penalty. For my part, I make it my boast that I was not to be so subdued. I could not be abated of a single quotation by all the bumpers in which I was fined.

In this manner they glided over the face of the waters, discussing every thing and settling nothing. Mr. Mac Quedy and the Reverend Doctor Folliott had many digladiations on political economy : wherein, each in his own view, Doctor Folliott demolished Mr. Mac Quedy's science, and Mr. Mac Quedy demolished Doctor Folliott's objections.

We would print these dialogues if we thought any one would read them : but the world is not yet ripe for this *haute sagesse Panta-grueline*. We must, therefore, content ourselves with an *échantillon* of one of the Reverend Doctor's perorations.

" You have given the name of a science to what is yet an imperfect inquiry ; and the upshot of your so-called science is this, that you increase the wealth of a nation by increasing in it the quantity of things which are produced by labour : no matter what they are, no matter how produced, no matter how distributed. The greater the quantity of labour that has gone to the production of the quantity of things in a community, the richer is the community. That is your doctrine. Now, I say, if this be so, riches are not the object for a community to aim at. I say, the nation is best off, in relation to other nations, which has the greatest quantity of the common necessaries of life distributed among the greatest number of persons ; which has the greatest number of honest hearts and stout arms united in a common interest, willing to offend no one, but ready to fight in defence of their own community against all the rest of the world, because they have something in it worth fighting for. The moment you admit that one class of things, without any reference to what they respectively cost, is better worth having than another ; that a smaller commercial value, with one mode of distribution, is better than a greater commercial value, with another mode of distribution ; the whole of that curious fabric of postulates and dogmas, which you call the science of political economy, and which I call *politicæ œconomiæ inscientia*, tumbles to pieces."

Mr. Toogood agreed with Mr. Chainmail against Mr. Mac Quedy, that the existing state of society was worse than that of the twelfth century ; but he agreed with Mr. Mac Quedy against Mr. Chainmail, that it was in progress to something much better than either,—to which " something much better " Mr. Toogood and Mr. Mac Quedy attached two very different meanings.

Mr. Chainmail fought with Doctor Folliott, the battle of the romantic against the classical in poetry ; and Mr. Skionar contended with Mr. Mac Quedy for intuition and synthesis, against analysis and induction in philosophy.

Mr. Philpot would lie along for hours, listening to the gurgling of the water round the prow, and would occasionally edify the company with speculations on the great changes that would be effected in the world by the steam-navigation of rivers [1]: sketching the course of a

---

[1] Peacock carried out an investigation into the possibility of quick communication with India by means of steamboats carrying the mails up the Euphrates. He was later responsible for steamboats going up Indian rivers in support of the Company's armed forces. G.

steam-boat up and down some mighty stream which civilisation had either never visited, or long since deserted ; the Missouri and the Columbia, the Oroonoko and the Amazon, the Nile and the Niger, the Euphrates and the Tigris, the Oxus and the Indus, the Ganges and the Hoangho ; under the overcanopying forests of the new, or by the long-silent ruins of the ancient, world ; through the shapeless mounds of Babylon, or the gigantic temples of Thebes.

Mr. Trillo went on with the composition of his opera, and took the opinions of the young ladies on every step in its progress ; occasionally regaling the company with specimens, and wondering at the blindness of Mr. Mac Quedy, who could not, or would not, see that an opera in perfection, being the union of all the beautiful arts,— music, painting, dancing, poetry,—exhibiting female beauty in its most attractive aspects, and in its most becoming costume,—was, according to the well-known precept, *Ingenuas didicisse, &c.*,[1] the most efficient instrument of civilisation, and ought to take precedence of all other pursuits in the minds of true philanthropists. The Reverend Doctor Folliott, on these occasions, never failed to say a word or two on Mr. Trillo's side, derived from the practice of the Athenians, and from the combination, in their theatre, of all the beautiful arts, in a degree of perfection unknown to the modern world.

Leaving Lechlade, they entered the canal that connects the Thames with the Severn ; ascended by many locks ; passed by a tunnel three miles long, through the bowels of Sapperton Hill ; agreed unanimously that the greatest pleasure derivable from visiting a cavern of any sort was that of getting out of it ; descended by many locks again, through the valley of Stroud into the Severn ; continued their navigation into the Ellesmere canal ; moored their pinnaces in the Vale of Llangollen by the aqueduct of Pontycysyllty ; and determined to pass some days in inspecting the scenery, before commencing their homeward voyage.

The captain omitted no opportunity of pressing his suit on Lady Clarinda, but could never draw from her any reply but the same

---

[1] " Ingenuas didicisse fideliter artes
  Emollit mores, nec sinit esse feros."
                                        Ovid : *Ep. ex Pont.* II. ix. 47–8.

" Faithful study of the noble arts softens the nature and saves it from savagery." G.

doctrines of worldly wisdom, delivered in a tone of *badinage*, mixed with a certain kindness of manner that induced him to hope she was not in earnest.

But the morning after they had anchored under the hills of the Dee, —whether the lady had reflected more seriously than usual, or was somewhat less in good humour than usual, or the Captain was more pressing than usual,—she said to him, " It must not be, Captain Fitzchrome ; 'the course of true love never did run smooth :[1]' my father must keep his borough, and I must have a town house and a country house, and an opera box, and a carriage. It is not well for either of us that we should flirt any longer : ' I must be cruel only to be kind.'[2] Be satisfied with the assurance that you alone, of all men, have ever broken my rest. To be sure, it was only for about three nights in all ; but that is too much."

The captain had *le cœur navré*. He took his portfolio under his arm, made up the little *valise* of a pedestrian, and, without saying a word to any one, wandered off at random among the mountains.

After the lapse of a day or two, the captain was missed, and every one marvelled what was become of him. Mr. Philpot thought he must have been exploring a river, and fallen in and got drowned in the process. Mr. Firedamp had no doubt he had been crossing a mountain bog, and had been suddenly deprived of life by the exhalations of marsh miasmata. Mr. Henbane deemed it probable that he had been tempted in some wood by the large black brilliant berries of the *Atropa Belladonna,* or Deadly Nightshade ; and lamented that he had not been by, to administer an infallible anti-dote. Mr. Eavesdrop hoped the particulars of his fate would be ascertained ; and asked if any one present could help him to any authentic anecdotes of their departed friend. The Reverend Doctor Folliott proposed that an inquiry should be instituted as to whether the march of intellect had reached that neighbourhood ; as, if so, the captain had probably been made a subject for science. Mr. Mac Quedy said it was no such great matter to ascertain the precise mode in which the surplus population was diminished by one. Mr. Toogood asseverated that there was no such thing as

---

[1] *A Midsummer Night's Dream*, Act I, Sc. 1. G.
[2] *Hamlet*, Act III, Sc. 4. G.

surplus population, and that the land, properly managed, would maintain twenty times its present inhabitants : and hereupon they fell into a disputation.

Lady Clarinda did not doubt that the captain had gone away designedly : she missed him more than she could have anticipated ; and wished she had at least postponed her last piece of cruelty till the completion of their homeward voyage.

CHAPTER XI

CORRESPONDENCE

" Base is the slave that pays."—ANCIENT PISTOL.[1]

THE captain was neither drowned nor poisoned, neither miasmatised nor anatomised. But, before we proceed to account for him, we must look back to a young lady, of whom some little notice was taken in the first chapter ; and who, though she has since been out of sight, has never with us been out of mind ; Miss Susannah Touchandgo, the forsaken of the junior Crotchet, whom we left an inmate of a solitary farm, in one of the deep valleys under the cloudcapt summits of Meirion, comforting her wounded spirit with air and exercise, rustic cheer, music, painting, and poetry, and the prattle of the little Ap Llymrys.

One evening, after an interval of anxious expectation, the farmer, returning from market, brought for her two letters, of which the contents were these :—

" *Dotandcarryonetown,*
State of Apodidraskiana : [2]
April 1, 18. .

" MY DEAR CHILD,

" I am anxious to learn what are your present position, intention, and prospects. The fairies who dropped gold in your shoe, on the morning when I ceased to be a respectable man in London, will soon find a talismanic channel for transmitting you a stocking full of dollars, which will fit the shoe, as well as the foot of Cinderella fitted her slipper. I am happy to say, I am again become a respectable

---

[1] *Henry V*, Act II, Sc. 1. G.
[2] Derived from a Greek word signifying " to run away." G.

man. It was always my ambition to be a respectable man ; and I am a very respectable man here, in this new township of a new state, where I have purchased five thousand acres of land, at two dollars an acre, hard cash, and established a very flourishing bank. The notes of Touchandgo and Company, soft cash, are now the exclusive currency of all this vicinity. This is the land in which all men flourish ; but there are three classes of men who flourish especially,—Methodist preachers, slave-drivers, and paper-money manufacturers ; and as one of the latter, I have just painted the word BANK on a fine slab of maple, which was green and growing when I arrived, and have discounted for the settlers, in my own currency, sundry bills, which are to be paid when the proceeds of the crop they have just sown shall return from New Orleans ; so that my notes are the representatives of vegetation that is to be, and I am accordingly a capitalist of the first magnitude. The people here know very well that I ran away from London, but the most of them have run away from some place or other ; and they have a great respect for me, because they think I ran away with something worth taking, which few of them had the luck or the wit to do. This gives them confidence in my resources, at the same time that, as there is nothing portable in the settlement except my own notes, they have no fear that I shall run away with them. They know I am thoroughly conversant with the principles of banking ; and as they have plenty of industry, no lack of sharpness, and abundance of land, they wanted nothing but capital to organise a flourishing settlement ; and this capital I have manufactured to the extent required, at the expense of a small importation of pens, ink, and paper, and two or three inimitable copper plates. I have abundance here of all good things, a good conscience included ; for I really cannot see that I have done any wrong. This was my position : I owed half a million of money ; and I had a trifle in my pocket. It was clear that this trifle could never find its way to the right owner. The question was, whether I should keep it, and live like a gentleman ; or hand it over to lawyers and commissioners of bankruptcy, and die like a dog on a dunghill. If I could have thought that the said lawyers, &c., had a better title to it than myself, I might have hesitated ; but, as such title was not apparent to my satisfaction, I decided the question in my own favour;

the right owners, as I have already said, being out of the question altogether. I have always taken scientific views of morals and politics, a habit from which I derive much comfort under existing circumstances.

" I hope you adhere to your music, though I cannot hope again to accompany your harp with my flute. My last *andante* movement was too *forte* for those whom it took by surprise. Let not your *allegro vivace* be damped by young Crotchet's desertion, which, though I have not heard it, I take for granted. He is, like myself, a scientific politician, and has an eye as keen as a needle, to his own interest. He has had good luck so far, and is gorgeous in the spoils of many gulls ; but I think the Polar Basin and Walrus Company will be too much for him yet. There has been a splendid outlay on credit ; and he is the only man, of the original parties concerned, of whom his majesty's sheriffs could give any account.

" I will not ask you to come here. There is no husband for you. The men smoke, drink, and fight, and break more of their own heads than of girls' hearts. Those among them who are musical sing nothing but psalms. They are excellent fellows in their way, but you would not like them.

" *Au reste*, here are no rents, no taxes, no poor-rates, no tithes, no church-establishment, no routs, no clubs, no rotten boroughs, no operas, no concerts, no theatres, no beggars, no thieves, no king, no lords, no ladies, and only one gentleman, videlicet, your loving father,

" TIMOTHY TOUCHANDGO.[1]

" P.S.—I send you one of my notes ; I can afford to part with it. If you are accused of receiving money from me, you may pay it over to my assignees. Robthetill continues to be my factotum; I say no more of him in this place : he will give you an account of himself."

" *Dotandcarryonetown, &c.*

" DEAR MISS,

" Mr. Touchandgo will have told you of our arrival here, of our setting up a bank, and so forth. We came here in a tilted waggon,

---

[1] Rowland Stevenson, a Lombard Street banker, who in 1828 absconded with his clerk, owing £100,000. G.

which served us for parlour, kitchen, and all. We soon got up a log-house ; and, unluckily, we as soon got it down again, for the first fire we made in it burned down house and all. However, our second experiment was more fortunate ; and we are pretty well lodged in a house of three rooms on a floor ; I should say the floor, for there is but one.

" This new state is free to hold slaves ; all the new states have not this privilege : Mr. Touchandgo has bought some, and they are building him a villa. Mr. Touchandgo is in a thriving way, but he is not happy here : he longs for parties and concerts, and a seat in congress. He thinks it very hard that he cannot buy one with his own coinage, as he used to do in England. Besides, he is afraid of the regulators, who, if they do not like a man's character, wait upon him and flog him, doubling the dose at stated intervals, till he takes himself off. He does not like this system of administering justice : though I think he has nothing to fear from it. He has the character of having money, which is the best of all characters here, as at home. He lets his old English prejudices influence his opinions of his new neighbours ; but I assure you they have many virtues. Though they do keep slaves, they are all ready to fight for their own liberty ; and I should not like to be an enemy within reach of one of their rifles. When I say enemy, I include bailiff in the term. One was shot not long ago. There was a trial ; the jury gave two dollars damages ; the judge said they must find guilty or not guilty ; but the counsel for the defendant (they would not call him prisoner), offered to fight the judge upon the point : and as this was said literally, not metaphorically, and the counsel was a stout fellow, the judge gave in. The two dollars damages were not paid after all ; for the defendant challenged the foreman to box for double or quits, and the foreman was beaten. The folks in New York made a great outcry about it, but here it was considered all as it should be. So you see, Miss, justice, liberty, and every thing else of that kind, are different in different places, just as suits the convenience of those who have the sword in their own hands. Hoping to hear of your health and happiness, I remain,

" Dear Miss, your dutiful servant,

" RODERICK ROBTHETILL."

Miss Touchandgo replied as follows, to the first of these letters :—

" MY DEAR FATHER,

" I am sure you have the best of hearts, and I have no doubt you have acted with the best intentions. My lover, or I should rather say, my fortune's lover, has indeed forsaken me. I cannot say I did not feel it ; indeed, I cried very much ; and the altered looks of people who used to be so delighted to see me, really annoyed me so that I determined to change the scene altogether. I have come into Wales, and am boarding with a farmer and his wife. Their stock of English is very small, but I managed to agree with them ; and they have four of the sweetest children I ever saw, to whom I teach all I know, and I manage to pick up some Welsh. I have puzzled out a little song, which I think very pretty ; I have translated it into English, and I send it you, with the original air. You shall play it on your flute at eight o'clock every Saturday evening, and I will play and sing it at the same time, and I will fancy that I hear my dear papa accompanying me.

" The people in London said very unkind things of you : they hurt me very much at the time ; but now I am out of their way, I do not seem to think their opinion of much consequence. I am sure, when I recollect, at leisure, every thing I have seen and heard among them, I cannot make out what they do that is so virtuous as to set them up for judges of morals. And I am sure they never speak the truth about any thing, and there is no sincerity in either their love or their friendship. An old Welsh bard here, who wears a waistcoat embroidered with leeks, and is called the Green Bard of Cadair Idris, says the Scotch would be the best people in the world if there was nobody but themselves to give them a character ; and so, I think, would the Londoners. I hate the very thought of them, for I do believe they would have broken my heart if I had not got out of their way. Now I shall write you another letter very soon, and describe to you the country, and the people, and the children, and how I amuse myself, and every thing that I think you will like to hear about : and when I seal this letter, I shall drop a kiss on the cover.

" Your loving daughter,
" SUSANNAH TOUCHANDGO.

" P.S.—Tell Mr. Robthetill I will write to him in a day or two. This is the little song I spoke of :—

> ' Beyond the sea, beyond the sea,
> My heart is gone, far, far from me ;
> And ever on its track will flee
> My thoughts, my dreams, beyond the sea.

> ' Beyond the sea, beyond the sea,
> The swallow wanders fast and free :
> Oh, happy bird ! were I like thee,
> I, too, would fly beyond the sea.

> ' Beyond the sea, beyond the sea,
> Are kindly hearts and social glee :
> But here for me they may not be ;
> My heart is gone beyond the sea.' ''

CHAPTER XII

THE MOUNTAIN INN

'Ωs ἡδὺ τῷ μισοῦντι τοὺς φαύλους τρόπους
Ἐρημία.

How sweet to minds that love not sordid ways
Is solitude !—MENANDER.[1]

THE captain wandered despondingly up and down hill for several days, passing many hours of each in sitting on rocks ; making, almost mechanically, sketches of waterfalls, and mountain pools ; taking care, nevertheless, to be always before nightfall in a comfortable inn, where, being a temperate man, he wiled away the evening with making a bottle of sherry into negus. His rambles brought him at length into the interior of Merionethshire, the land of all that is beautiful in nature, and all that is lovely in woman.

Here, in a secluded village, he found a little inn, of small pretension and much comfort. He felt so satisfied with his quarters, and discovered every day so much variety in the scenes of the surrounding mountains, that his inclination to proceed farther diminished progressively.

It is one thing to follow the high road through a country, with

[1] *Fragm.* 466 K.   G.

every principally remarkable object carefully noted down in a book, taking, as therein directed, a guide, at particular points, to the more recondite sights : it is another to sit down on one chosen spot, especially when the choice is unpremeditated, and from thence, by a series of explorations, to come day by day on unanticipated scenes. The latter process has many advantages over the former ; it is free from the disappointment which attends excited expectation, when imagination has outstripped reality, and from the accidents that mar the scheme of the tourist's single day, when the valleys may be drenched with rain, or the mountains shrouded with mist.

The captain was one morning preparing to sally forth on his usual exploration, when he heard a voice without, inquiring for a guide to the ruined castle. The voice seemed familiar to him, and going forth into the gateway, he recognised Mr. Chainmail. After greetings and inquiries for the absent, " You vanished very abruptly, captain," said Mr. Chainmail, " from our party on the canal."

CAPTAIN FITZCHROME. To tell you the truth, I had a particular reason for trying the effect of absence from a part of that party.

MR. CHAINMAIL. I surmised as much : at the same time, the unusual melancholy of an in general most vivacious young lady made me wonder at your having acted so precipitately. The lady's heart is yours, if there be truth in signs.

CAPTAIN FITZCHROME. Hearts are not now what they were in the days of the old song, " Will love be controlled by advice ? "

MR. CHAINMAIL. Very true ; hearts, heads, and arms have all degenerated, most sadly. We can no more feel the high impassioned love of the ages, which some people have the impudence to call dark, than we can wield King Richard's battleaxe, bend Robin Hood's bow, or flourish the oaken graff of the Pinder of Wakefield.[1] Still we have our tastes and feelings, though they deserve not the name of passions ; and some of us may pluck up spirit to try to carry a point, when we reflect that we have to contend with men no better than ourselves.

[1] A popular hero, associated with Robin Hood in ballad and story and still commemorated in the names of public-houses. A pinder was the guardian of a pound for strayed animals. G.

CAPTAIN FITZCHROME. We do not now break lances for ladies.

MR. CHAINMAIL. No, nor even bulrushes. We jingle purses for them, flourish paper-money banners, and tilt with scrolls of parchment.

CAPTAIN FITZCHROME. In which sort of tilting I have been thrown from the saddle. I presume it was not love that led you from the flotilla.

MR. CHAINMAIL. By no means. I was tempted by the sight of an old tower, not to leave this land of ruined castles, without having collected a few hints for the adornment of my baronial hall.

CAPTAIN FITZCHROME. I understand you live *en famille* with your domestics. You will have more difficulty in finding a lady who would adopt your fashion of living, than one who would prefer you to a richer man.

MR. CHAINMAIL. Very true. I have tried the experiment on several as guests ; but once was enough for them : so, I suppose, I shall die a bachelor.

CAPTAIN FITZCHROME. I see, like some others of my friends, you will give up any thing except your hobby.

MR. CHAINMAIL. I will give up any thing but my baronial hall.

CAPTAIN FITZCHROME. You will never find a wife for your purpose, unless in the daughter of some old-fashioned farmer.

MR. CHAINMAIL. No, I thank you. I must have a lady of gentle blood ; I shall not marry below my own condition : I am too much of a herald; I have too much of the twelfth century in me for that.

CAPTAIN FITZCHROME. Why then your chance is not much better than mine. A well-born beauty would scarcely be better pleased with your baronial hall, than with my more humble offer of love in a cottage. She must have a town-house, and an opera-box, and roll about the streets in a carriage ; especially if her father has a rotten borough, for the sake of which he sells his daughter, that he may continue to sell his country. But you were inquiring for a guide to the ruined castle in this vicinity; I know the way, and will conduct you.

The proposal pleased Mr. Chainmail, and they set forth on their expedition.

CHAPTER XIII

THE LAKE—THE RUIN

Or vieni, Amore, e quà meco t'assetta. ORLANDO INNAMORATO.[1]

MR. CHAINMAIL. Would it not be a fine thing, captain,—you being picturesque, and I poetical; you being for the lights and shadows of the present, and I for those of the past,—if we were to go together over the ground which was travelled in the twelfth century by Giraldus de Barri, when he accompanied Archbishop Baldwin to preach the crusade?

CAPTAIN FITZCHROME. Nothing, in my present frame of mind, could be more agreeable to me.

MR. CHAINMAIL. We would provide ourselves with his *Itinerarium*; compare what has been with what is; contemplate in their decay the castles and abbeys which he saw in their strength and splendour; and, while you were sketching their remains, I would dispassionately inquire what has been gained by the change.

CAPTAIN FITZCHROME. Be it so.

But the scheme was no sooner arranged than the captain was summoned to London by a letter on business, which he did not expect to detain him long. Mr. Chainmail, who, like the captain, was fascinated with the inn and the scenery, determined to await his companion's return; and, having furnished him with a list of books, which he was to bring with him from London, took leave of him, and began to pass his days like the heroes of Ariosto, who

—— tutto il giorno, al bel oprar intenti,
Saliron balze, e traversar torrenti.[2]

---

[1] " Come now, love, and settle here with me." Boiardo. G.
[2] " All day long, intent on noble deeds,
    They climbed hills and crossed torrents." G.

One day Mr. Chainmail traced upwards the course of a mountain-stream, to a spot where a small waterfall threw itself over a slab of perpendicular rock, which seemed to bar his farther progress. On a nearer view, he discovered a flight of steps, roughly hewn in the rock, on one side of the fall. Ascending these steps, he entered a narrow winding pass, between high and naked rocks, that afforded only space for a rough footpath carved on one side, at some height above the torrent.

The pass opened on a lake, from which the stream issued, and which lay like a dark mirror, set in a gigantic frame of mountain precipices. Fragments of rock lay scattered on the edge of the lake, some half-buried in the water : Mr. Chainmail scrambled some way over these fragments, till the base of a rock, sinking abruptly in the water, effectually barred his progress. He sat down on a large smooth stone ; the faint murmur of the stream he had quitted, the occasional flapping of the wings of the heron, and at long intervals the solitary springing of a trout, were the only sounds that came to his ear. The sun shone brightly half-way down the opposite rocks, presenting, on their irregular faces, strong masses of light and shade. Suddenly he heard the dash of a paddle, and, turning his eyes, saw a solitary and beautiful girl gliding over the lake in a coracle ; she was proceeding from the vicinity of the point he had quitted towards the upper end of the lake. Her apparel was rustic, but there was in its style something more *recherché*, in its arrangement something more of elegance and precision, than was common to the mountain peasant girl. It had more of the *contadina* of the opera than of the genuine mountaineer ; so at least thought Mr. Chainmail ; but she passed so rapidly, and took him so much by surprise, that he had little opportunity for accurate observation. He saw her land, at the farther extremity, and disappear among the rocks : he rose from his seat, returned to the mouth of the pass, stepped from stone to stone across the stream, and attempted to pass round by the other side of the lake ; but there again the abruptly sinking precipice closed his way.

Day after day he haunted the spot, but never saw again either the damsel or the coracle. At length, marvelling at himself for being so solicitous about the apparition of a peasant girl in a coracle, who could not, by any possibility, be any thing to him, he resumed his explorations in another direction.

One day he wandered to the ruined castle, on the seashore, which was not very distant from his inn ; and sitting on the rock, near the base of the ruin, was calling up the forms of past ages on the wall of an ivied tower, when on its summit appeared a female figure, whom he recognised in an instant for his nymph of the coracle.   The folds of the blue gown pressed by the sea breeze against one of the most symmetrical of figures, the black feather of the black hat, and the ringleted hair beneath it fluttering in the wind ; the apparent peril of her position, on the edge of the mouldering wall, from whose immediate base the rock went down perpendicularly to the sea, presented a singularly interesting combination to the eye of the young antiquary.

Mr. Chainmail had to pass half round the castle, on the land side, before he could reach the entrance : he coasted the dry and bramble-grown moat, crossed the unguarded bridge, passed the unportcullised arch of the gateway, entered the castle court, ascertained the tower, ascended the broken stairs, and stood on the ivied wall.   But the nymph of the place was gone.   He searched the ruins within and without, but he found not what he sought : he haunted the castle day after day, as he had done the lake, but the damsel appeared no more.

CHAPTER XIV

THE DINGLE

> The stars of midnight shall be dear
> To her, and she shall lean her ear
> In many a secret place,
> Where rivulets dance their wayward round,
> And beauty, born of murmuring sound,
> Shall pass into her face.—WORDSWORTH.[1]

MISS Susannah Touchandgo had read the four great poets of Italy, and many of the best writers of France.   About the time of her father's downfall, accident threw into her way *Les Rêveries du Promeneur Solitaire* ; and from the impression which these made on

[1] *Poems of the Imagination*, X.   G.

her, she carried with her into retirement all the works of Rousseau. In the midst of that startling light which the conduct of old friends on a sudden reverse of fortune throws on a young and inexperienced mind, the doctrines of the philosopher of Geneva struck with double force upon her sympathies : she imbibed the sweet poison, as somebody calls it, of his writings, even to a love of truth ; which, every wise man knows, ought to be left to those who can get any thing by it. The society of children, the beauties of nature, the solitude of the mountains, became her consolation, and, by degrees, her delight. The gay society from which she had been excluded remained on her memory only as a disagreeable dream. She imbibed her new monitor's ideas of simplicity of dress, assimilating her own with that of the peasant girls in the neighbourhood ; the black hat, the blue gown, the black stockings, the shoes tied on the instep.

Pride was, perhaps, at the bottom of the change ; she was willing to impose in some measure on herself, by marking a contemptuous indifference to the characteristics of the class of society from which she had fallen,

> " And with the food of pride sustained her soul
> In solitude." [1]

It is true that she somewhat modified the forms of her rustic dress : to the black hat she added a black feather, to the blue gown she added a tippet, and a waistband fastened in front with a silver buckle ; she wore her black stockings very smooth and tight on her ancles, and tied her shoes in tasteful bows, with the nicest possible ribbon. In this apparel, to which, in winter, she added a scarlet cloak, she made dreadful havoc among the rustic mountaineers, many of whom proposed to " keep company " with her in the Cambrian fashion, an honour which, to their great surprise, she always declined. Among these, Harry Ap-Heather, whose father rented an extensive sheepwalk, and had a thousand she-lambs wandering in the mountains, was the most strenuous in his suit, and the most pathetic in his lamentations for her cruelty.

Miss Susannah often wandered among the mountains alone, even to some distance from the farm-house. Sometimes she descended into

[1] Wordsworth : *The Yew-Tree Seat.* G.

the bottom of the dingles, to the black rocky beds of the torrents, and dreamed away hours at the feet of the cataracts. One spot in particular, from which she had at first shrunk with terror, became by degrees her favourite haunt. A path turning and returning at acute angles, led down a steep wood-covered slope to the edge of a chasm, where a pool, or resting-place of a torrent, lay far below. A cataract fell in a single sheet into the pool ; the pool boiled and bubbled at the base of the fall, but through the greater part of its extent lay calm, deep, and black, as if the cataract had plunged through it to an unimaginable depth without disturbing its eternal repose. At the opposite extremity of the pool, the rocks almost met at their summits, the trees of the opposite banks intermingled their leaves, and another cataract plunged from the pool into a chasm on which the sunbeams never gleamed. High above, on both sides, the steep woody slopes of the dingle soared into the sky ; and from a fissure in the rock, on which the little path terminated, a single gnarled and twisted oak stretched itself over the pool, forming a fork with its boughs at a short distance from the rock.[1] Miss Susannah often sat on the rock, with her feet resting on this tree : in time, she made her seat on the tree itself, with her feet hanging over the abyss ; and at length she accustomed herself to lie along upon its trunk, with her side on the mossy boll of the fork, and an arm round one of the branches. From this position a portion of the sky and the woods was reflected in the pool, which, from its bank, was but a mass of darkness. The first time she reclined in this manner, her heart beat audibly ; in time, she lay down as calmly as on the mountain heather : the perception of the sublime was probably heightened by an intermingled sense of danger ; and perhaps that indifference to life, which early disappointment forces upon sensitive minds, was necessary to the first experiment. There was, in the novelty and strangeness of the position, an excitement which never wholly passed away, but which became gradually subordinate to the influence, at

[1] " The ' dingle ' . . . is a real scene, on the river Velenrhyd, in Merionethshire. There is no chasm on that river which it is possible to leap over ; but there is more than one on the river Cynfael, which flows into the same valley. I took the poetical licence of approximating the scenes. That on the Velenrhyd is called Llyn-y-Gygfraen, the Raven's pool." Peacock to Thomas L'Estrange, July 11th, 1861. G.

once tranquillising and elevating, of the mingled eternity of motion, sound, and solitude.

One sultry noon, she descended into this retreat with a mind more than usually disturbed by reflections on the past. She lay in her favourite position, sometimes gazing on the cataract; looking sometimes up the steep sylvan acclivities into the narrow space of the cloudless ether; sometimes down into the abyss of the pool, and the deep bright-blue reflections that opened another immensity below her. The distressing recollections of the morning, the world, and all its littlenesses, faded from her thoughts like a dream; but her wounded and wearied spirit drank in too deeply the tranquillising power of the place, and she dropped asleep upon the tree like a ship-boy on the mast.

At this moment Mr. Chainmail emerged into daylight, on a projection of the opposite rock, having struck down through the woods in search of unsophisticated scenery. The scene he discovered filled him with delight: he seated himself on the rock, and fell into one of his romantic reveries; when suddenly the semblance of a black hat and feather caught his eye among the foliage of the projecting oak. He started up, shifted his position, and got a glimpse of a blue gown. It was his lady of the lake, his enchantress of the ruined castle, divided from him by a barrier, which, at a few yards below, he could almost overleap, yet unapproachable but by a circuit perhaps of many hours. He watched with intense anxiety. To listen if she breathed was out of the question: the noses of a dean and chapter would have been soundless in the roar of the torrent. From her extreme stillness, she appeared to sleep: yet what creature, not desperate, would go wilfully to sleep in such a place? Was she asleep then? Nay, was she alive? She was as motionless as death. Had she been murdered, thrown from above, and caught in the tree? She lay too regularly and too composedly for such a supposition. She was asleep then, and in all probability her waking would be fatal. He shifted his position. Below the pool two beetle-browed rocks nearly overarched the chasm, leaving just such a space at the summit as was within the possibility of a leap; the torrent roared below in a fearful gulf. He paused some time on the brink, measuring the practicability and the danger, and casting every now and then an anxious glance to his sleeping beauty. In one of these glances he saw a slight movement of the blue gown, and, in a moment after, the black hat and feather dropped into the pool. Reflection was lost for a moment, and, by a sudden impulse, he bounded over the chasm.

He stood above the projecting oak ; the unknown beauty lay like the nymph of the scene ; her long black hair, which the fall of her hat had disengaged from its fastenings, drooping through the boughs : he saw that the first thing to be done was to prevent her throwing her feet off the trunk, in the first movements of waking. He sat down on the rock, and placed his feet on the stem, securing her ancles between his own : one of her arms was round a branch of the fork, the other lay loosely on her side. The hand of this arm he endeavoured to reach, by leaning forward from his seat ; he approximated, but could not touch it : after several tantalising efforts, he gave up the point in despair. He did not attempt to wake her, because he feared it might have bad consequences, and he resigned himself to expect the moment of her natural waking, determined not to stir from his post, if she should sleep till midnight.

In this period of forced inaction, he could contemplate at leisure the features and form of his charmer. She was not one of the slender beauties of romance ; she was as plump as a partridge ; her cheeks were two roses, not absolutely damask, yet verging thereupon ; her lips twin-cherries, of equal size ; her nose regular, and almost Grecian ; her forehead high, and delicately fair ; her eyebrows symmetrically arched ; her eyelashes long, black, and silky, fitly corresponding with the beautiful tresses that hung among the leaves of the oak, like clusters of wandering grapes.[1] Her eyes were yet to be seen ; but how could he doubt that their opening would be the rising of the sun, when all that surrounded their fringy portals was radiant as " the forehead of the morning sky " ? [2]

---

[1] Ἀλήμονα βότρυν ἐθείρας.—NONNUS. [P.] [*Dion.* I. 528 : " The straying clusters of her hair." G.]

[2] Milton : *Lycidas*, l. 171. G.

CHAPTER XV

THE FARM

Da ydyw'r gwaith, rhaid d'we'yd y gwir,
Ar fryniau Sir Meirionydd ;
Golwg oer o'r gwaela gawn
Mae hi etto yn llawn llawenydd.[1]

Though Meirion's rocks, and hills of heath
  Repel the distant sight ;
Yet where, than those bleak hills beneath,
  Is found more true delight ?

AT length the young lady awoke. She was startled at the sudden sight of the stranger, and somewhat terrified at the first perception of her position. But she soon recovered her self-possession, and, extending her hand to the offered hand of Mr. Chainmail, she raised herself up on the tree, and stepped on the rocky bank.

Mr. Chainmail solicited permission to attend her to her home, which the young lady graciously conceded. They emerged from the woody dingle, traversed an open heath, wound along a mountain road by the shore of a lake, descended to the deep bed of another stream, crossed it by a series of stepping stones, ascended to some height on the opposite side, and followed upwards the line of the stream, till the banks opened into a spacious amphitheatre, where stood, in its fields and meadows, the farm-house of Ap-Llymry.

During this walk, they had kept up a pretty animated conversation. The lady had lost her hat ; and, as she turned towards Mr. Chainmail, in speaking to him, there was no envious projection of brim to intercept the beams of those radiant eyes he had been so anxious to see unclosed. There was in them a mixture of softness and brilliancy, the perfection of the beauty of female eyes, such as some men have passed through life without seeing, and such as no man ever saw, in any pair of eyes, but once ; such as can never be seen and forgotten. Young Crotchet had seen it ; he had not forgotten it ; but he had trampled on its memory, as the renegade

[1] The first four lines of *Penillion*, No. XXXIX, of Welsh poetry published in *The Cambro-Briton*, Vol. I, p. 230 (Feb. 1820). The translation is not that published there and is presumably by Peacock. G.

tramples on the emblems of a faith which his interest only, and not his heart or his reason, has rejected.

Her hair streamed over her shoulders ; the loss of the black feather had left nothing but the rustic costume, the blue gown, the black stockings, and the ribbon-tied shoes. Her voice had that full soft volume of melody which gives to common speech the fascination of music. Mr. Chainmail could not reconcile the dress of the damsel with her conversation and manners. He threw out a remote question or two, with the hope of solving the riddle ; but, receiving no reply, he became satisfied that she was not disposed to be communicative respecting herself, and, fearing to offend her, fell upon other topics. They talked of the scenes of the mountains, of the dingle, the ruined castle, the solitary lake. She told him that lake lay under the mountains behind her home, and the coracle and the pass at the extremity saved a long circuit to the nearest village, whither she sometimes went to inquire for letters.

Mr. Chainmail felt curious to know from whom these letters might be ; and he again threw out two or three fishing questions, to which, as before, he obtained no answer.

The only living biped they met in their walk was the unfortunate Harry Ap-Heather, with whom they fell in by the stepping-stones, who, seeing the girl of his heart hanging on another man's arm, and, concluding at once that they were " keeping company," fixed on her a mingled look of surprise, reproach, and tribulation ; and, unable to control his feelings under the sudden shock, burst into a flood of tears, and blubbered till the rocks re-echoed.

They left him mingling his tears with the stream, and his lamentations with its murmurs. Mr. Chainmail inquired who that strange creature might be, and what was the matter with him. The young lady answered, that he was a very worthy young man, to whom she had been the innocent cause of much unhappiness.

" I pity him sincerely," said Mr. Chainmail ; and, nevertheless, he could scarcely restrain his laughter at the exceedingly original figure which the unfortunate rustic lover had presented by the stepping-stones.

The children ran out to meet their dear Miss Susan, jumped all round her, and asked what was become of her hat. Ap-Llymry came out in great haste, and invited Mr. Chainmail to walk in and dine : Mr. Chainmail did not wait to be asked twice. In a few minutes the whole party, Miss Susan and Mr. Chainmail, Mr. and Mrs. Ap-Llymry, and progeny, were seated over a clean homespun tablecloth, ornamented with fowls and bacon, a pyramid of potatoes, another of cabbage, which Ap-Llymry said " was poiled with the pacon, and as coot as marrow," a bowl of milk for the children, and an immense brown jug of foaming ale, with which Ap-Llymry seemed to delight in filling the horn of his new guest.

Shall we describe the spacious apartment, which was at once kitchen, hall, and dining-room,—the large dark rafters, the pendent bacon and onions, the strong old oaken furniture, the bright and trimly arranged utensils ?   Shall we describe the cut of Ap-Llymry's coat, the colour and tie of his neckcloth, the number of buttons at his knees,—the structure of Mrs. Ap-Llymry's cap, having lappets over the ears, which were united under the chin, setting forth especially whether the bond of union were a pin or a ribbon ?   We shall leave this tempting field of interesting expatiation to those whose brains are high-pressure steam engines for spinning prose by the furlong, to be trumpeted in paid-for paragraphs in the quack's corner of newspapers :   modern literature having attained the honourable distinction of sharing with blacking and macassar oil, the space which used to be monopolized by razor-strops and the lottery, whereby that very enlightened community, the reading public, is tricked into the perusal of much exemplary nonsense ;   though the few who see through the trickery have no reason to complain, since as " good wine needs no bush," so, *ex vi oppositi*, these bushes of venal panegyric point out very clearly that the things they celebrate are not worth reading.

The party dined very comfortably in a corner most remote from the fire ;   and Mr. Chainmail very soon found his head swimming with two or three horns of ale, of a potency to which even he was unaccustomed.   After dinner, Ap-Llymry made him finish a bottle of mead, which he willingly accepted, both as an excuse to remain, and as a drink of the dark ages, which he had no doubt was a genuine brewage, from uncorrupted tradition.

In the meantime, as soon as the cloth was removed, the children

had brought out Miss Susannah's harp. She began, without
affectation, to play and sing to the children, as was her custom of
an afternoon, first in their own language, and their national melodies,
then in English ; but she was soon interrupted by a general call of
little voices for " Ouf ! di giorno." She complied with the request,
and sang the ballad from Paër's Camilla : *Un dì carco il mulinaro.*[1]
The children were very familiar with every syllable of this ballad,
which had been often fully explained to them. They danced in a
circle with the burden of every verse, shouting out the chorus with
good articulation and joyous energy ; and at the end of the second
stanza, where the traveller has his nose pinched by his grandmother's
ghost, every nose in the party was nipped by a pair of little fingers.
Mr. Chainmail, who was not prepared for the process, came in for a
very energetic tweak, from a chubby girl that sprang suddenly on
his knees for the purpose, and made the roof ring with her laughter.

So passed the time till evening, when Mr. Chainmail moved to
depart. But it turned out on inquiry that he was some miles from
his inn, that the way was intricate, and that he must not make any
difficulty about accepting the farmer's hospitality till morning.
The evening set in with rain : the fire was found agreeable ; they
drew around it. The young lady made tea ; and afterwards, from
time to time, at Mr. Chainmail's special request, delighted his ear
with passages of ancient music. Then came a supper of lake trout,
fried on the spot, and thrown, smoking hot, from the pan to the

---

[1] In this ballad, the terrors of the Black Forest are narrated to an
assemblage of domestics and peasants, who, at the end of every stanza,
dance in a circle round the narrator. The second stanza is as follows :

> Una notte in un stradotto
> Un incauto s'inoltrò ;
> E uno strillo udí di botto
> Che l'orecchio gl'intronò :—
> Era l'ombra di sua nonna,
> Che pel naso Io pigliò.
> Ouf ! di giorno nè di sera,
> Non passiam la selva nera.—
>
> *(Ballano in Giro.)* [P.]

[" One night a rash person went a long way down a lane. Suddenly he
heard a scream which resounded in his ear. It was his grandmother's
shadow, which took him by the nose. Ouf ! let us not pass the Black
Forest either by day or by night. *(They dance in a circle.)*" G.]

plate. Then came a brewage, which the farmer called his nightcap, of which he insisted on Mr. Chainmail's taking his full share. After which the gentleman remembered nothing, till he awoke, the next morning, to the pleasant consciousness that he was under the same roof with one of the most fascinating creatures under the canopy of heaven.

CHAPTER XVI

THE NEWSPAPER

Ποίας δ' ἀποσπασθεῖσα φύτλας
'Ορέων κευθμῶνας ἔχει σκιοέντων;

Sprung from what line, adorns the maid
These valleys deep in mountain shade?

PIND. *Pyth.* IX.[1]

MR. CHAINMAIL forgot the captain and the route of Giraldus de Barri. He became suddenly satisfied that the ruined castle in his present neighbourhood was the best possible specimen of its class, and that it was needless to carry his researches further.

He visited the farm daily : found himself always welcome ; flattered himself that the young lady saw him with pleasure, and dragged a heavier chain at every new parting from Miss Susan, as the children called his nymph of the mountains. What might be her second name, he had vainly endeavoured to discover.

Mr. Chainmail was in love ; but the determination he had long before formed and fixed in his mind, to marry only a lady of gentle blood, without a blot on her escutcheon, repressed the declarations of passion which were often rising to his lips. In the meantime, he left no means untried, to pluck out the heart of her mystery.[2]

The young lady soon divined his passion, and penetrated his prejudices. She began to look on him with favourable eyes ; but she feared her name and parentage would present an insuperable barrier to his feudal pride.

Things were in this state when the captain returned, and unpacked his maps and books in the parlour of the inn.

[1] 59–60. G.   [2] *Hamlet*, Act III, Sc. 2. G.

MR. CHAINMAIL. Really, captain, I find so many objects of attraction in this neighbourhood, that I would gladly postpone our purpose.

CAPTAIN FITZCHROME. Undoubtedly, this neighbourhood has many attractions ; but there is something very inviting in the scheme you laid down.

MR. CHAINMAIL. No doubt, there is something very tempting in the route of Giraldus de Barri. But there are better things in this vicinity even than that. To tell you the truth, captain, I have fallen in love.

CAPTAIN FITZCHROME. What ! while I have been away ?

MR. CHAINMAIL. Even so.

CAPTAIN FITZCHROME. The plunge must have been very sudden, if you are already over head and ears.

MR. CHAINMAIL. As deep as Llyn-y-dreiddiad-vrawd.

CAPTAIN FITZCHROME. And what may that be ?

MR. CHAINMAIL. A pool not far off : a resting-place of a mountain stream, which is said to have no bottom. There is a tradition connected with it ; and here is a ballad on it, at your service :—

LLYN-Y-DREIDDIAD-VRAWD.

THE POOL OF THE DIVING FRIAR.

GWENWYNWYN withdrew from the feasts of his hall ;
He slept very little, he prayed not at all ;
He pondered, and wandered, and studied alone ;
And sought, night and day, the philosopher's stone.

He found it at length, and he made its first proof
By turning to gold all the lead of his roof :
Then he bought some magnanimous heroes, all fire,
Who lived but to smite and be smitten for hire.

With these, on the plains like a torrent he broke ;
He filled the whole country with flame and with smoke ;
He killed all the swine, and he broached all the wine ;
He drove off the sheep, and the beeves, and the kine ;

He took castles and towns ; he cut short limbs and lives ;
He made orphans and widows of children and wives :
This course many years he triumphantly ran,
And did mischief enough to be called a great man.

When, at last, he had gained all for which he had striven,
He bethought him of buying a passport to heaven ;
Good and great as he was, yet he did not well know
How soon, or which way, his great spirit might go.

He sought the grey friars, who, beside a wild stream,
Refected their frames on a primitive scheme ;
The gravest and wisest Gwenwynwyn found out,
All lonely and ghostly, and angling for trout.

Below the white dash of a mighty cascade,
Where a pool of the stream a deep resting-place made,
And rock-rooted oaks stretched their branches on high,
The friar stood musing, and throwing his fly.

To him said Gwenwynwyn, " Hold, father, here's store,
For the good of the church, and the good of the poor ; "
Then he gave him the stone ; but, ere more he could speak,
Wrath came on the friar, so holy and meek :

He had stretched forth his hand to receive the red gold,
And he thought himself mocked by Gwenwynwyn the Bold ;
And in scorn of the gift, and in rage at the giver,
He jerked it immediately into the river.

Gwenwynwyn, aghast, not a syllable spake ;
The philosopher's stone made a duck and a drake :
Two systems of circles a moment were seen,
And the stream smoothed them off, as they never had been.

Gwenwynwyn regained, and uplifted, his voice :
" Oh friar, grey friar, full rash was thy choice ;
The stone, the good stone, which away thou hast thrown,
Was the stone of all stones, the philosopher's stone ! "

The friar looked pale, when his error he knew ;
The friar looked red, and the friar looked blue ;
And heels over head, from the point of a rock,
He plunged, without stopping to pull off his frock.

He dived very deep, but he dived all in vain,
The prize he had slighted he found not again :
Many times did the friar his diving renew,
And deeper and deeper the river still grew.

Gwenwynwyn gazed long, of his senses in doubt,
To see the grey friar a diver so stout :
Then sadly and slowly his castle he sought,
And left the friar diving, like dabchick distraught.

Gwenwynwyn fell sick with alarm and despite,
Died, and went to the devil, the very same night :
The magnanimous heroes he held in his pay
Sacked his castle, and marched with the plunder away.

No knell on the silence of midnight was rolled,
For the flight of the soul of Gwenwynwyn the Bold :
The brethren, unfeed, let the mighty ghost pass,
Without praying a prayer, or intoning a mass.

The friar haunted ever beside the dark stream ;
The philosopher's stone was his thought and his dream :
And day after day, ever head under heels
He dived all the time he could spare from his meals.

He dived, and he dived, to the end of his days,
As the peasants oft witnessed with fear and amaze :
The mad friar's diving-place long was their theme,
And no plummet can fathom that pool of the stream.

And still, when light clouds on the midnight winds ride,
If by moonlight you stray on the lone river-side,
The ghost of the friar may be seen diving there,
With head in the water, and heels in the air.

CAPTAIN FITZCHROME. Well, your ballad is very pleasant : you shall show me the scene, and I will sketch it ; but just now I am more interested about your love. What heroine of the twelfth century has risen from the ruins of the old castle, and looked down on you from the ivied battlements ?

MR. CHAINMAIL. You are nearer the mark than you suppose. Even from those battlements a heroine of the twelfth century has looked down on me.

CAPTAIN FITZCHROME. Oh ! some vision of an ideal beauty. I suppose the whole will end in another tradition and a ballad.

MR. CHAINMAIL. Genuine flesh and blood ; as genuine as Lady Clarinda. I will tell you the story.

Mr. Chainmail narrated his adventures.

CAPTAIN FITZCHROME. Then you seem to have found what you wished. Chance has thrown in your way what none of the gods would have ventured to promise you.

MR. CHAINMAIL. Yes, but I know nothing of her birth and parentage. She tells me nothing of herself, and I have no right to question her directly.

CAPTAIN FITZCHROME. She appears to be expressly destined for the light of your baronial hall. Introduce me : in this case, two heads are better than one.

MR. CHAINMAIL. No, I thank you. Leave me to manage my chance of a prize, and keep you to your own chance of a——

CAPTAIN FITZCHROME. Blank. As you please. Well, I will pitch my tent here, till I have filled my portfolio, and shall be glad of as much of your company as you can spare from more attractive society.

Matters went on pretty smoothly for several days, when an unlucky newspaper threw all into confusion. Mr. Chainmail received newspapers by the post, which came in three times a week. One morning, over their half-finished breakfast, the captain had read half a newspaper very complacently, when suddenly he started up in a frenzy, hurled over the breakfast table, and, bouncing from the apartment, knocked down Harry Ap-Heather, who was coming in at the door to challenge his supposed rival to a boxing-match.

Harry sprang up, in a double rage, and intercepted Mr. Chainmail's pursuit of the captain, placing himself in the doorway, in a pugilistic attitude. Mr. Chainmail, not being disposed for this mode of combat, stepped back into the parlour, took the poker in his right hand, and displacing the loose bottom of a large elbow chair, threw it over his left arm, as a shield. Harry, not liking the aspect of the enemy in this imposing attitude, retreated with backward steps into the kitchen, and tumbled over a cur, which immediately fastened on his rear.

Mr. Chainmail, half-laughing, half-vexed, anxious to overtake the captain, and curious to know what was the matter with him, pocketed the newspaper, and sallied forth, leaving Harry roaring for a doctor and a tailor, to repair the lacerations of his outward man.

Mr. Chainmail could find no trace of the captain. Indeed, he sought him but in one direction, which was that leading to the farm ; where he arrived in due time, and found Miss Susan alone. He laid the newspaper on the table, as was his custom, and proceeded to converse with the young lady : a conversation of many pauses, as much of signs as of words. The young lady took up the paper, and turned it over and over, while she listened to Mr. Chainmail, whom she found every day more and more agreeable, when, suddenly, her eye glanced on something which made her change colour, and dropping the paper on the ground, she rose from her seat, exclaiming, " Miserable must she be who trusts any of your faithless sex ! Never, never, never, will I endure such misery twice." And she vanished up the stairs. Mr. Chainmail was petrified. At length, he cried aloud, " Cornelius Agrippa [1] must have laid a spell on this accursed newspaper ; " and was turning it over, to look for the source of the mischief, when Mrs. Ap-Llymry made her appearance.

MRS. AP-LLYMRY. What have you done to poor dear Miss Susan ? She is crying, ready to break her heart.

MR. CHAINMAIL. So help me the memory of Richard Cœur-de-Lion, I have not the most distant notion of what is the matter !

MRS. AP-LLYMRY. Oh, don't tell me, sir ; you must have ill-used her. I know how it is. You have been keeping company with her, as if you wanted to marry her ; and now, all at once, you have been trying to make her your mistress. I have seen such tricks more than once, and you ought to be ashamed of yourself.

MR. CHAINMAIL. My dear madam, you wrong me utterly. I have none but the kindest feelings and the most honourable purposes towards her. She has been disturbed by something she has seen in this rascally paper.

---

[1] Henry Cornelius Agrippa von Nettesheim (1486–1535) was soldier and diplomatist and writer. His *De occulta philosophia* is a defence of magic. He was frequently in trouble with the Inquisition. G.

MRS. AP-LLYMRY. Why, then, the best thing you can do is to go away, and come again to-morrow.

MR. CHAINMAIL. Not I, indeed, madam. Out of this house I stir not, till I have seen the young lady, and obtained a full explanation.

MRS. AP-LLYMRY. I will tell Miss Susan what you say. Perhaps she will come down.

Mr. Chainmail sate with as much patience as he could command, running over the paper, from column to column. At length, he lighted on an announcement of the approaching marriage of Lady Clarinda Bossnowl with Mr. Crotchet the younger. This explained the captain's discomposure, but the cause of Miss Susan's was still to be sought; he could not know that it was one and the same.

Presently the sound of the longed-for step was heard on the stairs; the young lady reappeared, and resumed her seat: her eyes showed that she had been weeping. The gentleman was now exceedingly puzzled how to begin, but the young lady relieved him by asking, with great simplicity, " What do you wish to have explained, sir ? "

MR. CHAINMAIL. I wish, if I may be permitted, to explain myself to you. Yet could I first wish to know what it was that disturbed you in this unlucky paper. Happy should I be if I could remove the cause of your inquietude !

MISS SUSANNAH. The cause is already removed. I saw something that excited painful recollections; nothing that I could now wish otherwise than as it is.

MR. CHAINMAIL. Yet, may I ask why it is that I find one so accomplished living in this obscurity, and passing only by the name of Miss Susan ?

MISS SUSANNAH. The world and my name are not friends. I have left the world, and wish to remain for ever a stranger to all whom I once knew in it.

MR. CHAINMAIL. You can have done nothing to dishonour your name.

MISS SUSANNAH. No, sir. My father has done that of which the world disapproves, in matters of which I pretend not to judge. I have suffered for it as I will never suffer again. My name is my own secret ; I have no other, and that is one not worth knowing. You see what I am, and all I am. I live according to the condition of my present fortune ; and here, so living, I have found tranquillity.

MR. CHAINMAIL. Yet, I entreat you, tell me your name.

MISS SUSANNAH. Why, sir ?

MR. CHAINMAIL. Why, but to throw my hand, my heart, my fortune, at your feet, if——

MISS SUSANNAH. If my name be worthy of them.

MR. CHAINMAIL. Nay, nay, not so ; if your hand and heart are free.

MISS SUSANNAH. My hand and heart are free ; but they must be sought from myself, and not from my name.

She fixed her eyes on him, with a mingled expression of mistrust, of kindness, and of fixed resolution, which the far-gone *innamorato* found irresistible.

MR. CHAINMAIL. Then from yourself alone I seek them.

MISS SUSANNAH. Reflect. You have prejudices on the score of parentage. I have not conversed with you so often, without knowing what they are. Choose between them and me. I too have my own prejudices on the score of personal pride.

MR. CHAINMAIL. I would choose you from all the world, were you even the daughter of the *exécuteur des hautes œuvres*,[1] as the heroine of a romantic story I once read turned out to be.

MISS SUSANNAH. I am satisfied. You have now a right to know my history ; and, if you repent, I absolve you from all obligations.

She told him her history ; but he was out of the reach of repentance. " It is true," as at a subsequent period he said to the captain,

[1] Public executioner. G.

" she is the daughter of a moneychanger ; one who, in the days of Richard the First, would have been plucked by the beard in the streets ; but she is, according to modern notions, a lady of gentle blood. As to her father's running away, that is a minor consideration : I have always understood, from Mr. Mac Quedy, who is a great oracle in this way, that promises to pay ought not to be kept ; the essence of a safe and economical currency being an interminable series of broken promises. There seems to be a difference among the learned as to the way in which the promises ought to be broken ; but I am not deep enough in their casuistry to enter into such nice distinctions."

In a few days there was a wedding, a pathetic leave-taking of the farmer's family, a hundred kisses from the bride to the children, and promises twenty times reclaimed and renewed, to visit them in the ensuing year.

CHAPTER XVII

THE INVITATION

A cup of wine, that's brisk and fine,
And drink unto the leman mine.
MASTER SILENCE.[1]

THIS veridicous history began in May, and the occurrences already narrated have carried it on to the middle of autumn. Stepping over the interval to Christmas, we find ourselves in our first locality, among the chalk hills of the Thames ; and we discover our old friend, Mr. Crotchet, in the act of accepting an invitation, for himself, and any friends who might be with him, to pass their Christmas-day at Chainmail Hall, after the fashion of the twelfth century. Mr. Crotchet had assembled about him, for his own Christmas-festivities, nearly the same party which was introduced to the reader in the spring. Three of that party were wanting. Dr. Morbific, by inoculating himself once too often with non-contagious matter, had explained himself out of the world. Mr. Henbane had also departed, on the wings of an infallible antidote. Mr. Eavesdrop, having printed in a magazine some of the after-dinner conversations of the

---

[1] *Henry IV, Pt. II*, Act V, Sc. 3. G.

castle, had had sentence of exclusion passed upon him, on the motion of the Reverend Doctor Folliott, as a flagitious violator of the confidences of private life.

Miss Crotchet had become Lady Bossnowl, but Lady Clarinda had not yet changed her name to Crotchet. She had, on one pretence and another, procrastinated the happy event, and the gentleman had not been very pressing ; she had, however, accompanied her brother and sister-in-law, to pass Christmas at Crotchet Castle. With these, Mr. Mac Quedy, Mr. Philpot, Mr. Trillo, Mr. Skionar, Mr. Toogood, and Mr. Firedamp, were sitting at breakfast, when the Reverend Doctor Folliott entered and took his seat at the table.

THE REV. DR. FOLLIOTT. Well, Mr. Mac Quedy, it is now some weeks since we have met : how goes on the march of mind ?

MR. MAC QUEDY. Nay, sir ; I think you may see that with your own eyes.

THE REV. DR. FOLLIOTT. Sir, I have seen it, much to my discomfiture. It has marched into my rick-yard, and set my stacks on fire, with chemical materials, most scientifically compounded.[1] It has marched up to the door of my vicarage, a hundred and fifty strong ; ordered me to surrender half my tithes ; consumed all the provisions I had provided for my audit feast, and drunk up my old October. It has marched in through my back-parlour shutters, and out again with my silver spoons, in the dead of night. The policeman, who was sent down to examine, says my house has been broken open on the most scientific principles. All this comes of education.

MR. MAC QUEDY. I rather think it comes of poverty.

THE REV. DR. FOLLIOTT. No, sir. Robbery perhaps comes of poverty, but scientific principles of robbery come of education. I suppose the learned friend has written a sixpenny treatise on mechanics, and the rascals who robbed me have been reading it.

MR. CROTCHET. Your house would have been very safe, doctor, if they had had no better science than the learned friend's to work with.

[1] " A very large proportion of Swing incendiarism has been directed against the property of beneficed clergymen." E. G. Wakefield : *Swing Unmasked*, 1831. See note on p. 753. G.

THE REV. DR. FOLLIOTT. Well, sir, that may be. Excellent potted char. The Lord deliver me from the learned friend.

MR. CROTCHET. Well, doctor, for your comfort, here is a declaration of the learned friend's that he will never take office.

THE REV. DR. FOLLIOTT. Then, sir, he will be in office next week. Peace be with him! Sugar and cream.

MR. CROTCHET. But, doctor, are you for Chainmail Hall on Christmas-day?

THE REV. DR. FOLLIOTT. That am I, for there will be an excellent dinner, though, peradventure, grotesquely served.

MR. CROTCHET. I have not seen my neighbour since he left us on the canal.

THE REV. DR. FOLLIOTT. He has married a wife, and brought her home.

LADY CLARINDA. Indeed! If she suits him, she must be an oddity : it will be amusing to see them together.

LORD BOSSNOWL. Very amusing. He! he!

MR. FIREDAMP. Is there any water about Chainmail Hall?

THE REV. DR. FOLLIOTT. An old moat.

MR. FIREDAMP. I shall die of *malaria*.

MR. TRILLO. Shall we have any music?

THE REV. DR. FOLLIOTT. An old harper.

MR. TRILLO. Those fellows are always horridly out of tune. What will he play?

THE REV. DR. FOLLIOTT. Old songs and marches.

MR. SKIONAR. Amongst so many old things, I hope we shall find Old Philosophy.

THE REV. DR. FOLLIOTT. An old woman.

MR. PHILPOT. Perhaps an old map of the river in the twelfth century.

THE REV. DR. FOLLIOTT. No doubt.

MR. MAC QUEDY. How many more old things?

THE REV. DR. FOLLIOTT. Old hospitality, old wine, old ale—all the images of old England; an old butler.

MR. TOOGOOD. Shall we all be welcome?

THE REV. DR. FOLLIOTT. Heartily; you will be slapped on the shoulder, and called old boy.

LORD BOSSNOWL. I think we should all go in our old clothes. He! he!

THE REV. DR. FOLLIOTT. You will sit on old chairs, round an old table, by the light of old lamps, suspended from pointed arches, which, Mr. Chainmail says, first came into use in the twelfth century; with old armour on the pillars, and old banners in the roof.

LADY CLARINDA. And what curious piece of antiquity is the lady of the mansion?

THE REV. DR. FOLLIOTT. No antiquity there; none.

LADY CLARINDA. Who was she?

THE REV. DR. FOLLIOTT. That I know not.

LADY CLARINDA. Have you seen her?

THE REV. DR. FOLLIOTT. I have.

LADY CLARINDA. Is she pretty?

THE REV. DR. FOLLIOTT. More—beautiful. A subject for the pen of Nonnus, or the pencil of Zeuxis.[1] Features of all loveliness, radiant with all virtue and intelligence. A face for Antigone. A form at once plump and symmetrical, that, if it be decorous to divine it by externals, would have been a model for the Venus of

---

[1] A celebrated Greek Painter of the Asiatic school. G.

Cnidos. Never was any thing so goodly to look on, the present company excepted, and poor dear Mrs. Folliott. She reads moral philosophy, Mr. Mac Quedy, which indeed she might as well let alone ; she reads Italian poetry, Mr. Skionar ; she sings Italian music, Mr. Trillo ; but, with all this, she has the greatest of female virtues, for she superintends the household, and looks after her husband's dinner. I believe she was a mountaineer: παρθένος οὐρεσίφοιτος, ἐρήμαδι σύντροφος ὕλῃ,[1] as Nonnus sweetly sings.

CHAPTER XVIII

CHAINMAIL HALL

Vous autres dictes que ignorance est mere de tous maulx, et dictes vray : mais toutesfoys vous ne la bannissez mye de vos entendemens, et vivez en elle, avecques elle, et par elle. C'est pourquoy tant de maulx vous meshaignent de jour en jour.—RABELAIS, l. 5. c. 7.[2]

THE party which was assembled on Christmas-day in Chainmail Hall, comprised all the guests of Crotchet Castle, some of Mr. Chainmail's other neighbours, all his tenants and domestics, and Captain Fitz-chrome. The hall was spacious and lofty ; and with its tall fluted pillars and pointed arches, its windows of stained glass, its display of arms and banners intermingled with holly and mistletoe, its blazing cressets and torches, and a stupendous fire in the centre, on which blocks of pine were flaming and crackling, had a striking effect on eyes unaccustomed to such a dining-room. The fire was open on all sides, and the smoke was caught and carried back, under a funnel-formed canopy, into a hollow central pillar. This fire was the line of demarcation between gentle and simple, on days of high festival. Tables extended from it on two sides, to nearly the end of the hall.

Mrs. Chainmail was introduced to the company. Young Crotchet

---

[1] A mountain-wandering maid,
Twin-nourished with the solitary wood. [P.]
[Dion. IX. 76. G.]

[2] " You men of the other world say that ignorance is the mother of all evil, and so far you are right : yet for all that, you do not take the least care to get rid of it, but still plod on, and live in it, with it, and by it ; for which cause a plaguy deal of mischief lights on you every day."
Urquhart and Motteux translation. G.

felt some revulsion of feeling at the unexpected sight of one whom he had forsaken, but not forgotten, in a condition apparently so much happier than his own. The lady held out her hand to him with a cordial look of more than forgiveness ; it seemed to say that she had much to thank him for. She was the picture of a happy bride, *rayonnante de joie et d'amour.*

Mr. Crotchet told the Reverend Doctor Folliott the news of the morning. " As you predicted," he said, " your friend, the learned friend, is in office; he has also a title; he is now Sir Guy de Vaux." [1]

THE REV. DR. FOLLIOTT. Thank heaven for that ! he is disarmed from further mischief. It is something, at any rate, to have that hollow and wind-shaken reed rooted up for ever from the field of public delusion. [2]

[1] Brougham had been created Lord Brougham and Vaux. G.

[2] I may here insert, as somewhat germane to the matter, some lines which were written by me, in March, 1831, and printed in the *Examiner* of August 14, 1831. They were then called " An Anticipation : " they may now (1837), be fairly entitled " A Prophecy fulfilled."

THE FATE OF A BROOM: AN ANTICIPATION.

Lo ! in Corruption's lumber-room,
The remnants of a wondrous broom ;
That walking, talking, oft was seen,
Making stout promise to sweep clean ;
But evermore, at every push,
Proved but a stump without a brush.
Upon its handle-top, a sconce,
Like Brahma's, looked four ways at once,
Pouring on king, lords, church, and rabble,
Long floods of favour-currying gabble ;
From four-fold mouth-piece always spinning
Projects of plausible beginning,
Whereof said sconce did ne'er intend
That any one should have an end ;
Yet still, by shifts and quaint inventions,
Got credit for its good intentions,
Adding no trifle to the store,
Wherewith the devil paves his floor.
Worn out at last, found bare and scrubbish,
And thrown aside with other rubbish,
We'll e'en hand o'er the enchanted stick,
As a choice present for Old Nick,
To sweep, beyond the Stygian lake,
The pavement it has helped to make. [P.]

MR. CROTCHET. I suppose, doctor, you do not like to see a great reformer in office ; you are afraid for your vested interests.

THE REV. DR. FOLLIOTT. Not I, indeed, sir ; my vested interests are very safe from all such reformers as the learned friend. I vaticinate what will be the upshot of all his schemes of reform. He will make a speech of seven hours' duration, and this will be its quintessence : that, seeing the exceeding difficulty of putting salt on the bird's tail, it will be expedient to consider the best method of throwing dust in the bird's eyes. All the rest will be

> *Τιτιτιτιτιμπρό.*
> *Ποποποί, ποποποί.*
> *Τιοτιοτιοτιοτιοτιοτίγξ.*
> *Κικκαβαῦ, κικκαβαῦ.*
> *τοροτοροτοροτοροτορολιλιλίγξ.*[1]

as Aristophanes has it ; and so I leave him, in Nephelococcygia.[2]

Mr. Mac Quedy came up to the divine as Mr. Crotchet left him, and said : " There is one piece of news which the old gentleman has not told you. The great firm of Catchflat and Company, in which young Crotchet is a partner, has stopped payment."

THE REV. DR. FOLLIOTT. Bless me ! that accounts for the young gentleman's melancholy. I thought they would over-reach themselves with their own tricks. The day of reckoning, Mr. Mac Quedy, is the point which your paper-money science always leaves out of view.

MR. MAC QUEDY. I do not see, sir, that the failure of Catchflat and Company has any thing to do with my science.

THE REV. DR. FOLLIOTT. It has this to do with it, sir, that you would turn the whole nation into a great paper-money shop, and take no thought of the day of reckoning. But the dinner is coming. I think you, who are so fond of paper promises, should dine on the bill of fare.

The harper at the head of the hall struck up an ancient march, and the dishes were brought in, in grand procession.

---

[1] Sounds without meaning ; imitative of the voices of birds. From the Ὄρνιθες of Aristophanes. [P.]

[2] " Cuckoo-city-in-the-clouds." From the same comedy. [P.]

The boar's head, garnished with rosemary, with a citron in its mouth, led the van. Then came tureens of plum-porridge ; then a series of turkeys, and, in the midst of them, an enormous sausage, which it required two men to carry. Then came geese and capons, tongues and hams, the ancient glory of the Christmas pie, a gigantic plum-pudding, a pyramid of minced pies, and a baron of beef bringing up the rear.

"It is something new under the sun," said the divine, as he sat down, "to see a great dinner without fish."

MR. CHAINMAIL.   Fish was for fasts, in the twelfth century.

THE REV. DR. FOLLIOTT.   Well, sir, I prefer our reformed system of putting fasts and feasts together.   Not but here is ample indemnity.

Ale and wine flowed in abundance.   The dinner passed off merrily ; the old harper playing all the while the oldest music in his repertory. The tables being cleared, he indemnified himself for lost time at the lower end of the hall, in company with the old butler and the other domestics, whose attendance on the banquet had been indispensable.

The scheme of Christmas gambols, which Mr. Chainmail had laid for the evening, was interrupted by a tremendous clamour without.

THE REV. DR. FOLLIOTT   What have we here ?   Mummers ?

MR. CHAINMAIL.   Nay, I know not.   I expect none.

"Who is there ? " he added, approaching the door of the hall.

"Who is there ? " vociferated the divine, with the voice of Stentor.

"Captain Swing," replied a chorus of discordant voices.[1]

THE REV. DR. FOLLIOTT.   Ho, ho ! here is a piece of the dark ages we did not bargain for.   Here is the Jacquerie.   Here is the march of mind with a witness.

MR. MAC QUEDY.   Do you not see that you have brought disparates together ? the Jacquerie and the march of mind.

[1] "Captain Swing" was the name used by those who wrote threatening letters during a wave of incendiarism among farm labourers about 1830.
                                                                G.

THE REV. DR. FOLLIOTT.   Not at all, sir.   They are the same thing, under different names.   Πολλῶν ὀνομάτων μορφήμία.[1]   What was Jacquerie in the dark ages, is the march of mind in this very enlightened one—very enlightened one.

MR. CHAINMAIL.   The cause is the same in both; poverty in despair.

MR. MAC QUEDY.   Very likely; but the effect is extremely disagreeable.

THE REV. DR. FOLLIOTT.   It is the natural result, Mr. Mac Quedy, of that system of state seamanship which your science upholds. Putting the crew on short allowance, and doubling the rations of the officers, is the sure way to make a mutiny on board a ship in distress, Mr. Mac Quedy.

MR. MAC QUEDY.   Eh! sir, I uphold no such system as that.   I shall set you right as to cause and effect.   Discontent increases with the increase of information.[2]   That is all.

THE REV. DR. FOLLIOTT.   I said it was the march of mind.   But we have not time for discussing cause and effect now.   Let us get rid of the enemy.

And he vociferated at the top of his voice, " What do you want here ? "

" Arms, arms," replied a hundred voices, " Give us the arms."

THE REV. DR. FOLLIOTT.   You see, Mr. Chainmail, this is the inconvenience of keeping an armoury, not fortified with sand bags, green bags,[3] and old bags of all kinds.

MR. MAC QUEDY.   Just give them the old spits and toasting irons, and they will go away quietly.

[1] " One shape of many names."
                              Æschylus, Prometheus.   [P.] [212. G.]
[2] This looks so like caricature (a thing abhorrent to our candour), that we must give authority for it.   " We ought to look the evil manfully in the face, and not amuse ourselves with the dreams of fancy.   The discontent of the labourers in our times is rather a proof of their superior information than of their deterioration."   Morning Chronicle : December 20, 1830.   [P.]
[3] Barristers' brief bags.   Peacock uses them for prosecution, or prosecution by the Crown.   See Note, p. 405.   G.

MR. CHAINMAIL. My spears and swords! not without my life. These assailants are all aliens to my land and house. My men will fight for me, one and all. This is the fortress of beef and ale.

MR. MAC QUEDY. Eh! sir, when the rabble is up, it is very indiscriminating. You are e'en suffering for the sins of Sir Simon Steeltrap, and the like, who have pushed the principle of accumulation a little too far.

MR. CHAINMAIL. The way to keep the people down is kind and liberal usage.

MR. MAC QUEDY. That is very well (where it can be afforded), in the way of prevention; but in the way of cure, the operation must be more drastic. (*Taking down a battle-axe.*) I would fain have a good blunderbuss charged with slugs.

MR. CHAINMAIL. When I suspended these arms for ornament, I never dreamed of their being called into use.

MR. SKIONAR. Let me address them. I never failed to convince an audience that the best thing they could do was to go away.

MR. MAC QUEDY. Eh! sir, I can bring them to that conclusion in less time than you.

MR. CROTCHET. I have no fancy for fighting. It is a very hard case upon a guest, when the latter end of a feast is the beginning of a fray.

MR. MAC QUEDY. Give them the old iron.

THE REV. DR. FOLLIOTT. Give them the weapons! *Pessimo, medius fidius, exemplo.*[1] Forbid it the spirit of *Frère Jean des Entommeures!* No! let us see what the church militant, in the armour of the twelfth century, will do against the march of mind. Follow me who will, and stay who list. Here goes: *Pro aris et focis!*[2] that is, for tithe pigs and fires to roast them!

He clapped a helmet on his head, seized a long lance, threw open

---

[1] A most pernicious example, by Hercules!—Petronius Arbiter. [P.] [*Satyr*. C. civ. G.]
[2] "For our altars and hearths." G.

the gates, and tilted out on the rabble, side by side with Mr. Chain-mail, followed by the greater portion of the male inmates of the hall, who had armed themselves at random.

The rabble-rout, being unprepared for such a sortie, fled in all directions, over hedge and ditch.

Mr. Trillo stayed in the hall, playing a march on the harp, to inspirit the rest to sally out. The water-loving Mr. Philpot had diluted himself with so much wine, as to be quite *hors de combat.* Mr. Toogood, intending to equip himself in purely defensive armour, contrived to slip a ponderous coat of mail over his shoulders, which pinioned his arms to his sides ; and in this condition, like a chicken trussed for roasting, he was thrown down behind a pillar, in the first rush of the sortie. Mr. Crotchet seized the occurrence as a pretext for staying with him, and passed the whole time of the action in picking him out of his shell.

"Phew ! " said the divine, returning ; " an inglorious victory : but it deserves a devil and a bowl of punch."

MR. CHAINMAIL.   A wassail-bowl.

THE REV. DR. FOLLIOTT.   No, sir. No more of the twelfth century for me.

MR. CHAINMAIL.   Nay, doctor. The twelfth century has backed you well. Its manners and habits, its community of kind feelings between master and man, are the true remedy for these ebullitions.

MR. TOOGOOD.   Something like it : improved by my diagram : arts for arms.

THE REV. DR. FOLLIOTT.   No wassail-bowl for me. Give me an unsophisticated bowl of punch, which belongs to that blissful middle period, after the Jacquerie was down, and before the march of mind was up. But, see, who is floundering in the water ?

Proceeding to the edge of the moat, they fished up Mr. Firedamp, who had missed his way back, and tumbled in. He was drawn out, exclaiming, "that he had taken his last dose of *malaria* in this world."

THE REV. DR. FOLLIOTT.   Tut, man ; dry clothes, a turkey's leg and rump, well devilled, and a quart of strong punch, will set all to rights.

"Wood embers," said Mr. Firedamp, when he had been accommodated with a change of clothes, "there is no antidote to *malaria* like the smoke of wood embers ; pine embers." And he placed himself, with his mouth open, close by the fire.

THE REV. DR. FOLLIOTT. Punch, sir, punch : there is no antidote like punch.

MR. CHAINMAIL. Well, doctor, you shall be indulged. But I shall have my wassail-bowl nevertheless.

An immense bowl of spiced wine, with roasted apples hissing on its surface, was borne into the hall by four men, followed by an empty bowl of the same dimensions, with all the materials of arrack punch, for the divine's especial brewage. He accinged [1] himself to the task, with his usual heroism ; and having finished it to his entire satisfaction, reminded his host to order in the devil.

THE REV. DR. FOLLIOTT. I think, Mr. Chainmail, we can amuse ourselves very well here all night. The enemy may be still excubant : and we had better not disperse till daylight. I am perfectly satisfied with my quarters. Let the young folks go on with their gambols ; let them dance to your old harper's minstrelsy ; and if they please to kiss under the mistletoe, whereof I espy a goodly bunch suspended at the end of the hall, let those who like it not, leave it to those who do. Moreover, if among the more sedate portion of the assembly, which, I foresee, will keep me company, there were any to revive the good old custom of singing after supper, so to fill up the intervals of the dances, the steps of night would move more lightly.

MR. CHAINMAIL. My Susan will set the example, after she has set that of joining in the rustic dance, according to good customs long departed.

After the first dance, in which all classes of the company mingled,

---

[1] Applied. G.

the young lady of the mansion took her harp, and following the reverend gentleman's suggestion, sang a song of the twelfth century.

FLORENCE AND BLANCHFLOR.[1]

Florence and Blanchflor, loveliest maids,
    Within a summer grove,
Amid the flower-enamelled shades
    Together talked of love.

A clerk sweet Blanchflor's heart had gained ;
    Fair Florence lŏved a knight :
And each with ardent voice maintained,
    She loved the worthiest wight.

Sweet Blanchflor praised her scholar dear,
    As courteous, kind, and true ;
Fair Florence said her chevalier
    Could every foe subdue.

And Florence scorned the bookworm vain,
    Who sword nor spear could raise ;
And Blanchflor scorned the unlettered brain
    Could sing no lady's praise.

From dearest love, the maidens bright
    To deadly hatred fell ;
Each turned to shun the other's sight,
    And neither said farewell.

The king of birds, who held his court
    Within that flowery grove,
Sang loudly : " 'Twill be rare disport
    To judge this suit of love."

Before him came the maidens bright,
    With all his birds around,
To judge the cause, if clerk or knight
    In love be worthiest found.

The falcon and the sparrow-hawk
    Stood forward for the fight :
Ready to do, and not to talk,
    They voted for the knight.

---

[1] Imitated from the Fabliau, *De Florance et de Blanche Flor, alias Jugement d'Amour.* [P.]

And Blanchflor's heart began to fail,
  Till rose the strong-voiced lark,
And, after him, the nightingale,
  And pleaded for the clerk.

The nightingale prevailed at length,
  Her pleading had such charms ;
So eloquence can conquer strength,
  And arts can conquer arms.

The lovely Florence tore her hair,
  And died upon the place ;
And all the birds assembled there,
  Bewailed the mournful case.

They piled up leaves and flowerets rare,
  Above the maiden bright,
And sang : " Farewell to Florence fair,
  Who too well loved her knight."

Several others of the party sang in the intervals of the dances.
Mr. Chainmail handed to Mr. Trillo another ballad of the twelfth
century, of a merrier character than the former.   Mr. Trillo readily
accommodated it with an air, and sang,—

THE PRIEST AND THE MULBERRY TREE.[1]

Did you hear of the curate who mounted his mare,
And merrily trotted along to the fair ?
Of creature more tractable none ever heard,
In the height of her speed she would stop at a word ;
And again with a word, when the curate said Hey,
She put forth her mettle, and galloped away.

As near to the gates of the city he rode,
While the sun of September all brilliantly glowed,
The good priest discovered, with eyes of desire,
A mulberry tree in a hedge of wild briar ;
On boughs long and lofty, in many a green shoot,
Hung large, black, and glossy, the beautiful fruit.

The curate was hungry and thirsty to boot ;
He shrunk from the thorns, though he longed for the fruit ;
With a word he arrested his courser's keen speed,
And he stood up erect on the back of his steed ;
On the saddle he stood, while the creature stood still,
And he gathered the fruit, till he took his good fill.

---

[1] Imitated from the Fabliau, *Du Provoire qui mengea des Môres.* [P.]

" Sure never," he thought, " was a creature so rare,
So docile, so true, as my excellent mare.
Lo, here, how I stand " (and he gazed all around,)
" As safe and as steady as if on the ground,
Yet how had it been, if some traveller this way,
Had, dreaming no mischief, but chanced to cry Hey ? "

He stood with his head in the mulberry tree,
And he spoke out aloud in his fond reverie :
At the sound of the word, the good mare made a push,
And down went the priest in the wild-briar bush.
He remembered too late, on his thorny green bed,
Much that well may be thought, cannot wisely be said.

Lady Clarinda, being prevailed on to take the harp in her turn,
sang the following stanzas :—

In the days of old,
Lovers felt true passion,
Deeming years of sorrow
By a smile repaid.
Now the charms of gold,
Spells of pride and fashion,
Bid them say good morrow
To the best-loved maid.

Through the forests wild,
O'er the mountains lonely,
They were never weary
Honour to pursue :
If the damsel smiled
Once in seven years only,
All their wanderings dreary
Ample guerdon knew.

Now one day's caprice
Weighs down years of smiling,
Youthful hearts are rovers,
Love is bought and sold :
Fortune's gifts may cease,
Love is less beguiling ;
Wiser were the lovers,
In the days of old.

The glance which she threw at the Captain, as she sang the last
verse, awakened his dormant hopes. Looking round for his rival,
he saw that he was not in the hall ; and, approaching the lady of his
heart, he received one of the sweetest smiles of their earlier days.

After a time, the ladies, and all the females of the party, retired. The males remained on duty with punch and wassail, and dropped off one by one into sweet forgetfulness ; so that when the rising sun of December looked through the painted windows on mouldering embers and flickering lamps, the vaulted roof was echoing to a mellifluous concert of noses, from the clarionet of the waiting-boy at one end of the hall, to the double bass of the Reverend Doctor, ringing over the empty punch-bowl, at the other.

CONCLUSION.

FROM this eventful night, young Crotchet was seen no more on English mould. Whither he had vanished, was a question that could no more be answered in his case than in that of King Arthur, after the battle of Camlan. The great firm of Catchflat and Company figured in the Gazette and paid sixpence in the pound ; and it was clear that he had shrunk from exhibiting himself on the scene of his former greatness, shorn of the beams of his paper prosperity. Some supposed him to be sleeping among the undiscoverable secrets of some barbel-pool in the Thames ; but those who knew him best were more inclined to the opinion that he had gone across the Atlantic, with his pockets full of surplus capital, to join his old acquaintance, Mr. Touchandgo, in the bank of Dotandcarryonetown.

Lady Clarinda was more sorry for her father's disappointment than her own ; but she had too much pride to allow herself to be put up a second time in the money-market ; and when the Captain renewed his assiduities, her old partiality for him, combining with a sense of gratitude for a degree of constancy which she knew she scarcely deserved, induced her, with Lord Foolincourt's hard-wrung consent, to share with him a more humble, but less precarious fortune, than that to which she had been destined as the price of a rotten borough.

THE END

GRYLL GRANGE

GRYLL GRANGE

Opinion governs all mankind,
Like the blind leading of the blind :—
And like the world, men's jobbernoles
Turn round upon their ears the poles,
And what they're confidently told
By no sense else can be control'd.

BUTLER.[1]

---

[1] The first two lines are from *Miscellaneous Thoughts*, the other four from *Hudibras*, Pt. III, Canto 2, ll. 815–8.   G.

Gryll Grange was first published in 1860

CONTENTS OF
GRYLL GRANGE

CHAPTER   PAGE

   Introduction by David Garnett 769

  I MISNOMERS 775

  II THE SQUIRE AND HIS NIECE . . . 782

 III THE DUKE'S FOLLY 785

 IV THE FOREST—SOLILOQUY ON HAIR—THE VESTALS 791

  V THE SEVEN SISTERS 798

 VI THE RUSTIC LOVER 801

 VII THE VICAR AND HIS WIFE—FAMILIES OF LOVE—THE
    NEWSPAPER 804

VIII PANTOPRAGMATICS 810

 IX SAINT CATHARINE—IDEAL BEAUTY . . . 813

  X THE THUNDERSTORM 818

 XI ELECTRICAL SCIENCE—THE DEATH OF PHILEMON—
    THE CONVALESCENT 821

 XII THE FOREST DELL—THE POWER OF LOVE—THE
    LOTTERY OF MARRIAGE 826

 XIII LORD CURRYFIN — SIBERIAN DINNERS — SOCIAL
    MONOTONY 836

 XIV ANCIENT AND MODERN WINE—MUSIC AND PAINTING
    —JACK OF DOVER 842

 XV EXPRESSION IN MUSIC—BALLADS—THE DAPPLED
    PALFREY—LOVE AND AGE—COMPETITIVE EXAM-
    INATION 850

 XVI MISS NIPHET—THE THEATRE—THE PAVILION—
    THE LAKE—INFALLIBLE SAFETY . . 858

XVII HORSE TAMING—ATALANTA—LOVE IN DILEMMA—
    INJUNCTIONS—SONOROUS VASES . . 864

CHAPTER   PAGE

XVIII   LECTURES—THE POWER OF PUBLIC OPINION—A NEW ORDER OF CHIVALRY   871

XIX   A SYMPOSIUM — PERVERSIONS OF SCIENCE — TRANSATLANTIC TENDENCIES — AFTER-DINNER LECTURES—QUACKERIES OF EDUCATION . .   876

XX   ALGERNON AND MORGANA — BOJARDO — OPPORTUNITY AND REPENTANCE—THE FOREST IN WINTER   885

XXI   SKATING — PAS DE DEUX ON THE ICE — CONGENIALITY—FLINTS AMONG BONES . . .   892

XXII   THE SEVEN AGAINST THEBES—A SOLILOQUY ON CHRISTMAS   897

XXIII   THE TWO QUADRILLES—POPE'S OMBRE—POETICAL TRUTH TO NATURE—CLEOPATRA . . .   902

XXIV   PROGRESS OF SYMPATHY—LOVE'S INJUNCTION— ORLANDO INNAMORATO   909

XXV   HARRY AND DOROTHY   916

XXVI   DOUBTS AND QUESTIONS   919

XXVII   LOVE IN MEMORY   921

XXVIII   ARISTOPHANES IN LONDON   926

XXIX   THE BALD VENUS—IÑEZ DE CASTRO—THE UNITY OF LOVE   936

XXX   A CAPTIVE KNIGHT—RICHARD AND ALICE . .   942

XXXI   A TWELFTH-NIGHT BALL — PANTOPRAGMATIC COOKERY—MODERN VANDALISM—A BOWL OF PUNCH   949

XXXII   HOPES AND FEARS—COMPENSATIONS IN LIFE— ATHENIAN COMEDY—MADEIRA AND MUSIC— CONFIDENCES   954

XXXIII   THE CONQUEST OF THEBES   963

XXXIV   CHRISTMAS TALES—CLASSICAL TALES OF WONDER— THE HOST'S GHOST—A TALE OF A SHADOW—A TALE OF A BOGLE—THE LEGEND OF SAINT LAURA   965

XXXV   REJECTED SUITORS—CONCLUSION . . .   978

INTRODUCTION TO
GRYLL GRANGE

Gryll Grange seems to have been written after 1858 and was published in 1860, when the author was seventy-five, twenty-nine years after *Crotchet Castle*. It is thus separated by forty-three years from *Melincourt*, forty-three years *only*—for though that is long in the life of an author, it is little enough when we consider the change of atmosphere.

Writing in 1905, Richard Garnett remarked that it is always a misfortune not to be able to go with one's age, but that Peacock could serve as a model for those who stood still. It is not so easy for us to accept whole-heartedly the blessings of our time as it was for our grandfathers half a century ago. There are thus more of us who regret that we cannot like crabs go backwards to the wisdom of our predecessors, and, failing that power, will be grateful for a model of the art of standing still gracefully.

The satire of the earlier novels was largely at the expense of Peacock's very good friends and companions, the system-mongers ; in *Gryll Grange* it is rather at the expense of the world that they were rapidly creating, and which has only recently achieved its full perfection. Thus in some passages the satire is sharper to-day than when it was written ; in others it has ceased to be either satire or prejudice and become a commonplace.

For example, eminent scientists to-day often echo Dr Opimian's words : " Science is one thing and wisdom is another. . . . I almost think it is the ultimate destiny of science to exterminate the human race." The reader must try to remember that, when Peacock wrote, this suggestion was considered gross prejudice and satire. But apart from the satire, there is much to make *Gryll Grange* the most charming of the novels. With the exception of a single poem,

769

A New Order of Chivalry, which was almost certainly written many years before it was introduced into *Gryll Grange*, it is all perfectly good-tempered.

Edith Nicolls, Peacock's granddaughter, wrote that : " As he advanced in years, his detestation of anything disagreeable made him simply avoid whatever fretted him, laughing off all sorts of ordinary calls upon his leisure time. His love of ease and kindness of heart made it impossible that he could be actively unkind to any one, but he would not be worried, and just got away from anything that annoyed him. He was very fond of his children, and was an indulgent father to them, and he was a kind and affectionate grandfather ; he could not bear any one to be unhappy or uncomfortable about him, and this feeling he carried down to the animal creation ; his pet cats and dogs were especially cared for by himself, the birds in the garden were carefully watched over and fed, and no gun was ever allowed to be fired about the place. After he retired from the India House he seldom left Halliford ; his life was spent among his books, and in the garden, in which he took great pleasure, and on the river. May-day he always kept in true old English fashion ; all the children of the village came round with their garlands of flowers, and each child was presented with a new penny, or silver threepenny or fourpenny piece, according to the beauty of their garlands ; the money was given by the Queen of the May, always one of his granddaughters, who sat beside him, dressed in white and crowned with flowers, and holding a sceptre of flowers in her hand. He loved to keep up these old English customs."

The picture evoked might have come from *Gryll Grange* ; it has the same touch of paradise. The philosophy which pervades the book is Epicurean, but it is blended with romantic feeling and aristocratic good sense.

Not only are all the characters sympathetic, but they have a solidity which was previously lacking. Almost for the first time we feel that we are in a company of real people, and not a few Characters and many Humours.

The thought of death was in the author's mind when he wrote. Of the thirty-five chapters, sixteen are headed with quotations concerned with love, thirteen with death or old age, and ten with

wine. Some quotations combine thoughts of all three. The thought
of death brought no sadness and no regrets, but it did increase the
author's tolerance for his antipathies. The conversation in *Gryll
Grange* is as good as ever, but the sympathies are wider. It is a
paradise where we should like to take refuge, but since we cannot,
we may linger in it long enough to learn that " Laugh when you can "
is a very good maxim.

D. G.

In the following pages, the New Forest is always mentioned as if it were still unenclosed. This is the only state in which the Author has been acquainted with it. Since its enclosure, he has never seen it, and purposes never to do so.

The mottoes are sometimes specially apposite to the chapters to which they are prefixed; but more frequently to the general scope, or to borrow a musical term, the *motivo* of the *operetta*.

[P.]

GRYLL GRANGE

CHAPTER I

Ego sic semper et ubique vixi, ut ultimam quamque lucem, tamquam non redituram, consumerem.—PETRONIUS ARBITER.[1]

Always and everywhere I have so lived, that I might consume the passing light, as if it were not to return.

"PALESTINE soup!" said the Reverend Doctor Opimian,[2] dining with his friend Squire Gryll; "a curiously complicated misnomer. We have an excellent old vegetable, the artichoke, of which we eat the head; we have another of subsequent introduction, of which we eat the root, and which we also call artichoke, because it resembles the first in flavour, although, *me judice*, a very inferior affair. This last is a species of the helianthus, or sunflower genus of the *Syngenesia frustranea* class of plants. It is therefore a girasol, or turn-to-the-sun. From this girasol we have made Jerusalem, and from the Jerusalem artichoke we make Palestine soup."

MR. GRYLL. A very good thing, Doctor.

THE REVEREND DOCTOR OPIMIAN. A very good thing; but a palpable misnomer.

MR. GRYLL. I am afraid we live in a world of misnomers, and of a worse kind than this. In my little experience I have found that a gang of swindling bankers is a respectable old firm; that men who sell their votes to the highest bidder, and want only " the protection of the ballot " to sell the promise of them to both parties, are a free and independent constituency; that a man who successively betrays everybody that trusts him, and abandons every principle he

---

[1] *Satyr.* G.
[2] Opimian—a celebrated Roman wine of the vintage of the year A.U.C. 633 (*c.* 126 B.C.), when Opimian was Consul. G.

ever professed, is a great statesman, and a Conservative, forsooth,
à nil conservando ; that schemes for breeding pestilence are sanitary
improvements ; that the test of intellectual capacity is in swallow,
and not in digestion ; that the art of teaching everything, except
what will be of use to the recipient, is national education ; and that
a change for the worse is reform. Look across the Atlantic. A
Sympathizer would seem to imply a certain degree of benevolent
feeling. Nothing of the kind. It signifies a ready-made accomplice
in any species of political villany. A Know-Nothing would seem to
imply a liberal self-diffidence—on the scriptural principle that the
beginning of knowledge is to know that thou art ignorant. No such
thing. It implies furious political dogmatism, enforced by bludgeons
and revolvers. A Locofoco is the only intelligible term : a fellow
that would set any place on fire to roast his own eggs. A Filibuster
is a pirate under national colours ; but I suppose the word in its
origin implies something virtuous : perhaps a friend of humanity.[1]

THE REVEREND DOCTOR OPIMIAN. More likely a friend of roaring—
φιλοβωστϱὴς—in the sense in which roaring is used by our old
dramatists ; for which see Middleton's *Roaring Girl*, and the
commentators thereon.[2]

MR. GRYLL. While we are on the subject of misnomers, what say
you to the wisdom of Parliament ?

THE REVEREND DOCTOR OPIMIAN. Why, sir, I do not call that a
misnomer. The term wisdom is used in a parliamentary sense. The
wisdom of Parliament is a wisdom *sui generis*. It is not like any other
wisdom. It is not the wisdom of Socrates, nor the wisdom of
Solomon. It is the wisdom of Parliament. It is not easily analysed

---

[1] All these terms were current in contemporary American politics.
A Locofoco was originally a phosphorus match. Filibuster is derived
from the French *flibustier*, a corruption of " freebooter." G.

[2] " *Roaring boys* was a cant term for the riotous, quarrelsome blades of the
time, who abounded in London, and took pleasure in annoying its quieter
inhabitants. Of *Roaring Girls*, the heroine of the present play was the
choicest specimen. Her real name was *Mary Frith*, but she was most
commonly known by that of *Moll Cutpurse*." DYCE. She wore male
apparel, smoked, fought, robbed on the highway, kept all minor thieves
in subjection, and compelled the restitution of stolen goods, when duly
paid for her services. [P.]

or defined; but it is very easily understood. It has achieved wonderful things by itself, and still more when Science has come to its aid. Between them, they have poisoned the Thames, and killed the fish in the river. A little further development of the same wisdom and science will complete the poisoning of the air, and kill the dwellers on the banks. It is pleasant that the precious effluvium has been brought so efficiently under the Wisdom's own wise nose. Thereat the nose, like Trinculo's, has been in great indignation.[1] The Wisdom has ordered the Science to do something. The Wisdom does not know what, nor the Science either. But the Wisdom has empowered the Science to spend some millions of money; and this, no doubt, the Science will do. When the money has been spent, it will be found that the something has been worse than nothing. The Science will want more money to do some other something, and the Wisdom will grant it. *Redit labor actus in orbem.*[2] But you have got on moral and political ground. My remark was merely on a perversion of words, of which we have an inexhaustible catalogue.

MR. GRYLL. Whatever ground we take, Doctor, there is one point common to most of these cases : the word presents an idea, which does not belong to the subject, critically considered. Palestine Soup is not more remote from the true Jerusalem, than many an honourable friend from public honesty and honour. However, Doctor, what say you to a glass of old Madeira, which I really believe is what it is called ?

THE REVEREND DOCTOR OPIMIAN. *In vino veritas.* I accept with pleasure.

MISS GRYLL. You and my uncle, Doctor, get up a discussion on everything that presents itself; dealing with your theme like a series of variations in music. You have run half round the world *à propos* of the soup. What say you to the fish ?

THE REVEREND DOCTOR OPIMIAN. Premising that this is a remark-

---

[1] *The Tempest*, Act IV, Sc. 1.   G.
[2] The labour returns, compelled into a circle. [P.] [Virgil : *Georg.* II. 401.   G.]

ably fine slice of salmon, there is much to be said about fish : but not in the way of misnomers. Their names are single and simple. Perch, sole, cod, eel, carp, char, skate, tench, trout, brill, bream, pike, and many others, plain monosyllables : salmon, dory, turbot, gudgeon, lobster, whitebait, grayling, haddock, mullet, herring, oyster, sturgeon, flounder, turtle, plain dissyllables : only two trisyllables worth naming, anchovy and mackerel ; unless any one should be disposed to stand up for halibut, which for my part I have excommunicated.

MR. GRYLL.   I agree with you on that point ; but I think you have named one or two, that might as well keep it company.

THE REVEREND DOCTOR OPIMIAN.   I do not think I have named a single unpresentable fish.

MR. GRYLL.   Bream, Doctor : there is not much to be said for bream.

THE REVEREND DOCTOR OPIMIAN.   On the contrary, sir, I think there is much to be said for him.   In the first place, there is the authority of the monastic brotherhoods, who are universally admitted to have been connoisseurs in fish, and in the mode of preparing it ; and you will find bream pie set down as a prominent item of luxurious living in the indictments prepared against them at the dissolution of the monasteries.   The work of destruction was rather too rapid, and I fear the receipt is lost.   But he can still be served up as an excellent stew, provided always that he is full-grown, and has swum all his life in clear running water.   I call everything fish that seas, lakes, and rivers furnish to cookery ; though, scientifically, a turtle is a reptile, and a lobster an insect.   Fish, Miss Gryll—I could discourse to you on fish by the hour : but for the present I will forbear : as Lord Curryfin is coming down to Thornback Bay, to lecture the fishermen on fish and fisheries, and to astonish them all with the science of their art.   You will, no doubt, be curious to hear him.   There will be some reserved seats.

MISS GRYLL.   I shall be very curious to hear him, indeed.   I have never heard a lecturing lord.   The fancy of lords and gentlemen to lecture everybody on everything, everywhere, seems to me something very comical; but perhaps it is something very serious, gracious in the lecturer, and instructive to the audience. I shall be glad to be cured of my unbecoming propensity to laugh, whenever I hear of a lecturing lord.

THE REVEREND DOCTOR OPIMIAN. I hope, Miss Gryll, you will not laugh at Lord Curryfin: for you may be assured, nothing will be farther from his lordship's intention than to say anything in the slightest degree droll.

MR. GRYLL. Doctor Johnson was astonished at the mania for lectures, even in his day, when there were no lecturing lords. He thought little was to be learned from lectures, unless where, as in chemistry, the subject required illustration by experiment.[1] Now, if your lord is going to exhibit experiments, in the art of cooking fish, with specimens in sufficient number for all his audience to taste, I have no doubt his lecture will be well attended, and a repetition earnestly desired.

THE REVEREND DOCTOR OPIMIAN. I am afraid the lecture will not have the aid of such pleasant adventitious attractions. It will be a pure scientific exposition, carefully classified, under the several divisions and subdivisions of Ichthyology, Entomology, Herpetology, and Conchology. But I agree with Doctor Johnson, that little is to be learned from lectures. For the most part, those who do not already understand the subject will not understand the lecture, and those who do will learn nothing from it. The latter will hear many things they would like to contradict, which the *bienséance* of the lecture-room does not allow. I do not comprehend how people can find amusement in lectures. I should much prefer a *tenson*[2] of the

---

[1] Boswell: *Life of Johnson*, Vol. II, p. 7 (Birkbeck Hill). G.

[2] Among the troubadours a satirical verse often provoked a reply and attack and riposte developed into dialogue form. Frequently the dialogue was agreed to beforehand and became a poetical game. Such a tourney could take three forms. If the attack and riposte each constituted a poem, it was called a *coblas*. Otherwise questions and answers were exchanged in alternate couplets. If the challenger to such a duel of couplets chose the subject he had to offer his antagonist the choice of attacking or defending the proposition and undertake to take the other side whichever it might be. This was a *joc partit*. But if alternate couplets were exchanged without a subject having been agreed upon beforehand, the resulting poem was a *tenson*. See Jeanroy: *La Poésie Lyrique des Troubadours*. G.

twelfth century, when two or three masters of the *Gai Saber* [1] discussed questions of love and chivalry.

MISS GRYLL. I am afraid, Doctor, our age is too prosy for that sort of thing. We have neither wit enough, nor poetry enough, to furnish the disputants. I can conceive a state of society in which such *tensons* would form a pleasant winter evening amusement : but that state of society is not ours.

THE REVEREND DOCTOR OPIMIAN. Well, Miss Gryll, I should like, some winter evening, to challenge you to a *tenson*, and your uncle should be umpire. I think you have wit enough by nature, and I have poetry enough by memory, to supply a fair portion of the requisite materials, without assuming an absolute mastery of the *Gai Saber*.

MISS GRYLL. I shall accept the challenge, Doctor. The wit on one side will, I am afraid, be very shortcoming ; but the poetry on the other will no doubt be abundant.

MR. GRYLL. Suppose, Doctor, you were to get up a *tenson* a little more relative to our own wise days. Spirit-rapping, for example, is a fine field. *Nec pueri credunt . . . Sed tu vera puta.* [2] You might go beyond the limits of a *tenson*. There is ample scope for an Aristophanic comedy. In the contest between the Just and the Unjust in the *Clouds*, and in other scenes of Aristophanes, you have ancient specimens of something very like *tensons*, except that Love has not much share in them. Let us for a moment suppose this same spirit-rapping to be true—dramatically so, at least. Let us fit up a stage for the purpose : make the invoked spirits visible as well as audible : and calling before us some of the illustrious of former days, ask them what they think of us and our doings ? Of our astounding progress of intellect ? Our march of mind ? Our higher tone of morality ? Our vast diffusion of education ? Our art of choosing the most unfit man by competitive examination ?

THE REVEREND DOCTOR OPIMIAN. You had better not bring on

[1] The " gay science," i.e. the art of poetry. G.
[2] Not even boys believe it : but suppose it to be true. [P.] [Juvenal : *Sat.* II. 152–3. G.]

many of them at once, nor ask many similar questions, or the chorus of ghostly laughter will be overwhelming. I imagine the answer would be something like Hamlet's : " You yourselves, sirs, shall be as wise as we were, if, like crabs, you could go backward." [1] It is thought something wonderful that uneducated persons should believe in witchcraft in the nineteenth century : as if educated persons did not believe in grosser follies : such as this same spirit-rapping, unknown tongues, clairvoyance, table-turning, and all sorts of fanatical impositions, having for the present their climax in Mormonism. Herein all times are alike. There is nothing too monstrous for human credulity. I like the notion of the Aristophanic comedy. But it would require a numerous company, especially as the chorus is indispensable. The *tenson* may be carried on by two.

MR. GRYLL. I do not see why we should not have both.

MISS GRYLL. Oh pray, Doctor ! let us have the comedy. We hope to have a houseful at Christmas, and I think we may get it up well, chorus and all. I should so like to hear what my great ancestor, Gryllus, thinks of us : and Homer, and Dante, and Shakespeare, and Richard the First, and Oliver Cromwell.

THE REVEREND DOCTOR OPIMIAN. A very good *dramatis personæ*. With these, and the help of one or two Athenians and Romans, we may arrive at a tolerable judgment on our own immeasurable superiority to everything that has gone before us.

Before we proceed further, we will give some account of our interlocutors.

[1] Act II, Sc. 2, adapted. G.

CHAPTER II

FORTUNA . SPONDET . MULTA . MULTIS . PRAESTAT . NEMINI . VIVE . IN . DIES . ET . HORAS . NAM . PROPRIUM . EST . NIHIL.[1]

Marmor vetus apud Feam, ad Hor. Epist. i. II, 23.

Fortune makes many promises to many,
Keeps them to none. Live to the days and hours,
For nothing is your own.

GREGORY GRYLL, Esq., of Gryll Grange in Hampshire, on the borders of the New Forest, in the midst of a park which was a little forest in itself, reaching nearly to the sea, and well stocked with deer, having a large outer tract, where a numerous light-rented and well-conditioned tenantry fattened innumerable pigs, considered himself well located for what he professed to be, *Epicuri de grege porcus*,[2] and held, though he found it difficult to trace the pedigree, that he was lineally descended from the ancient and illustrious Gryllus, who maintained against Ulysses the superior happiness of the life of other animals to that of the life of man.[3]

[1] This inscription appears to consist of comic senarii, slightly dislocated for the inscriptional purpose,

Spondet ‾ ˘ ‾ ˘
Fortuna multa multis, praestat nemini.
Vive in dies et horas : nam proprium est nihil. [P.]
[Horace : *Ep.* I. iv. 16. G.]

[2] *A pig from the herd of Epicurus.* The old philosophers accepted good-humouredly the disparaging terms attached to them by their enemies or rivals. The Epicureans acquiesced in the pig, the Cynics in the dog, and Cleanthes was content to be called the Ass of Zeno, as being alone capable of bearing the burthen of the Stoic philosophy. [P.]

[3] PLUTARCH. *Bruta animalia ratione uti.* [" That brute beasts employ reason." G.] Gryllus, in this dialogue, seems to have the best of the argument. Spenser, however, did not think so, when he introduced his Gryll, in the Paradise of Acrasia, reviling Sir Guyon's Palmer for having restored him to the human form.

Streightway he with his virtuous staff them strooke,
And streight of beasts they comely men became :
Yet being men they did unmanly looke,
And stared ghastly, some for inward shame,
And some for wrath to see their captive dame :
But one above the rest in speciall,
That had an hog been late, hight Grylle by name,
Repyned greatly, and did him miscall,

It might seem that to a man who traced his ancestry from the Palace of Circe, the first care would be the continuance of his ancient race ; but a wife presented to him the forethought of a perturbation of his equanimity, which he never could bring himself to encounter. He liked to dine well, and withal to dine quietly, and to have quiet friends at his table, with whom he could discuss questions which might afford ample room for pleasant conversation and none for acrimonious dispute. He feared that a wife would interfere with his dinner, his company, and his after-dinner bottle of port. For the perpetuation of his name, he relied on an orphan niece, whom he had brought up from a child, who superintended his household, and sate at the head of his table. She was to be his heiress, and her husband was to take his name. He left the choice to her, but reserved to himself a veto if he should think the aspirant unworthy of the honourable appellation.

The young lady had too much taste, feeling, and sense to be likely to make a choice which her uncle would not approve ; but time, as it rolled on, foreshadowed a result which the Squire had not anticipated. Miss Gryll did not seem likely to make any choice at all. The atmosphere of quiet enjoyment in which she had grown up seemed to have steeped her feelings in its own tranquillity ; and still more, the affection which she felt for her uncle, and the conviction that, though he had always premeditated her marriage, her departure from his house would be the severest blow that fate could inflict on

---

That had from hoggish forme him brought to naturall.
    Said Guyon : " See the mind of beastly man,
That hath so soon forgot the excellence
Of his creation, when he life began,
That now he chooseth, with vile difference,
To be a beast, and lacke intelligence."
          Fairy Queen, Book ii. Canto 12.

In Plutarch's dialogue, Ulysses, after his own companions have been restored to the human form, solicits Circe to restore in the same manner any other Greeks who may be under her enchantments. Circe consents, provided they desire it. Gryllus, endowed with speech for the purpose, answers for all, that they had rather remain as they are ; and supports the decision by showing the greater comfort of their condition as it is, to what it would probably be if they were again sent forth to share the common lot of mankind. We have unfortunately only the beginning of the dialogue, of which the greater portion has perished. [P.]

him, led her to postpone what she knew must be an evil day to him, and might peradventure not be a good one to her.

" Oh, the ancient name of Gryll! " sighed the Squire to himself. " What if it should pass away in the nineteenth century, after having lived from the time of Circe ! "

Often indeed, when he looked at her at the head of his table, the star of his little circle, joyous herself and the source of joy in others, he thought the actual state of things admitted no change for the better, and the perpetuity of the old name became a secondary consideration ; but though the purpose was dimmed in the evening it usually brightened in the morning. In the meantime the young lady had many suitors, who were permitted to plead their cause, though they made little apparent progress.

Several young gentlemen of fair promise, seemingly on the point of being accepted, had been, each in his turn, suddenly and summarily dismissed. Why, was the young lady's secret. If it were known, it would be easy, she said, in these days of artificial manners, to counterfeit the presence of the qualities she liked, and, still more easy, the absence of the qualities she disliked. There was sufficient diversity in the characters of the rejected to place conjecture at fault, and Mr. Gryll began to despair.

The uncle and niece had come to a clear understanding on this subject. He might present to her attention any one whom he might deem worthy to be her suitor, and she might reject the suitor without assigning a reason for so doing. In this way several had appeared, and passed away like bubbles on a stream.

Was the young lady over fastidious, or were none among the presented worthy, or had that which was to touch her heart not yet appeared ?

Mr. Gryll was the godfather of his niece, and to please him, she had been called Morgana. He had had some thoughts of calling her Circe, but acquiesced in the name of a sister enchantress, who had worked out her own idea of a beautiful garden, and exercised similar power over the minds and forms of men.[1]

[1] Boiardo : *Orlando Innamorato.*　G.

CHAPTER III

Τέγγε πνεύμονας οἴνῳ· τὸ γὰρ ἄστρον περιτέλλεται·
Ἁ δ' ὥρα χαλεπά, πάντα δὲ διψᾷ ὑπὸ καύματος.
—ALCAEUS.[1]

Moisten your lungs with wine. The dog-star's sway
Returns, and all things thirst beneath his ray.

FALERNUM . OPIMIANUM . ANNORUM . CENTUM.

Heu ! Heu ! inquit Trimalchio, ergo diutius vivit vinum quam homuncio !
Quare τέγγε πνεύμονας faciamus. Vita vinum est.—PETRONIUS ARBITER.[2]

FALERNIAN OPIMIAN WINE AN HUNDRED YEARS OLD.

Alas ! Alas ! exclaimed Trimalchio. Thus wine lives longer than man !
Wherefore, let us sing " moisten your lungs." Wine is life.

WORDSWORTH'S question, in his *Poet's Epitaph*,

Art thou a man of purple cheer,
A rosy man, right plump to see ?

might have been answered in the affirmative by the Reverend Doctor
Opimian. The worthy divine dwelt in an agreeably situated
vicarage, on the outskirts of the New Forest. A good living, a
comfortable patrimony, a moderate dowry with his wife, placed
him sufficiently above the cares of the world to enable him to gratify
all his tastes without minute calculations of cost. His tastes in fact
were four : a good library, a good dinner, a pleasant garden, and rural
walks. He was an athlete in pedestrianism. He took no pleasure
in riding, either on horseback or in a carriage ; but he kept a
brougham for the service of Mrs. Opimian, and for his own occasional
use in dining out.

Mrs. Opimian was domestic. The care of the Doctor had supplied
her with the best books on cookery, to which his own inventive
genius and the kindness of friends had added a large and always
increasing manuscript volume. The lady studied them carefully,
and by diligent superintendence left the Doctor nothing to desire in
the service of his table. His cellar was well stocked with a selection
of the best vintages, under his own especial charge. In all its
arrangements his house was a model of order and comfort ; and the
whole establishment partook of the genial physiognomy of the

[1] Fragment. G.   [2] *Satyr*, Ch. xxxiv. G.

master. From the master and mistress to the cook, and from the cook to the tom cat, there was about the inhabitants of the vicarage a sleek and purring rotundity of face and figure that denoted community of feelings, habits, and diet ; each in its kind, of course, for the Doctor had his port, the cook her ale, and the cat his milk, in sufficiently liberal allowance. In the morning, while Mrs. Opimian found ample occupation in the details of her household duties and the care of her little family, the Doctor, unless he had predestined the whole day to an excursion, studied in his library. In the afternoon he walked ; in the evening he dined ; and after dinner read to his wife and family, or heard his children read to him. This was his home life. Now and then he dined out ; more frequently than at any other place with his friend and neighbour Mr. Gryll, who entirely sympathized with him in his taste for a good dinner.

Beyond the limits of his ordinary but within those of his occasional range was a solitary round tower on an eminence backed with wood, which had probably in old days been a landmark for hunters ; but having in modern days no very obvious use, was designated, as many such buildings are, by the name of the Folly. The country people called it " the Duke's Folly," though who the Duke in question was nobody could tell. Tradition had dropped his name.

One fine Midsummer day, with a southerly breeze and a cloudless sky, the Doctor, having taken an early breakfast, in the process of which he had considerably reduced the altitude of a round of beef, set out with a good stick in his hand and a Newfoundland dog at his heels for one of his longest walks, such as he could only take in the longest days.

Arriving at the Folly, which he had not visited for a long time, he was surprised to find it enclosed, and having at the back the novelty of a covered passage, built of the same grey stone as the tower itself. This passage passed away into the wood at the back, whence was ascending a wreath of smoke which immediately recalled to him the dwelling of Circe.[1] Indeed, the change before him had much the air

---

[1] Καὶ τότ' ἐγὼν ἐμὸν ἔγχος ἑλὼν καὶ φάσγανον ὀξὺ
Καρπαλίμως παρὰ νηὸς ἀνήϊον ἐς περιωπήν,
Εἴπως ἔργα ἴδοιμι βροτῶν ἐνοπήν τε πυθοίμην.
'Εστην δὲ, σκοπιὴν ἐς παιπαλόεσσαν ἀνελθών,

of enchantment ; and the Circean similitude was not a little enhanced by the antique masonry,[1] and the expanse of sea which was visible from the eminence. He leaned over the gate, repeated aloud the lines of the *Odyssey*, and fell into a brown study, from which he was aroused by the approach of a young gentleman from within the enclosure.

" I beg your pardon, sir," said the Doctor, "but my curiosity is excited by what I see here ; and if you do not think it impertinent, and would inform me how these changes have come about, I should be greatly obliged."

" Most willingly, sir," said the other ; " but if you will walk in, and see what has been done, the obligation will be mine."

The Doctor readily accepted the proposal. The stranger led the way, across an open space in the wood, to a circular hall, from each side of which a wide passage led, on the left hand to the tower, and on the right to the new building, which was so masked by the wood, as not to be visible except from within the glade. It was a square structure of plain stone, much in the same style as that of the tower.

Καί μοι ἐείσατο καπνὸς ἀπὸ χθονὸς εὐρυοδείης,
Κίρκης ἐν μεγάροισι, διὰ δρυμὰ πυκνὰ καὶ ὕλην.
Μερμήριξα δ᾽ ἔπειτα κατὰ φρένα καὶ κατὰ θυμὸν
᾽Ελθεῖν, ἠδὲ πυθέσθαι, ἐπεὶ ἴδον αἴθοπα καπνόν.

Od. K. 145–162.

I climbed a cliff with spear and sword in hand,
Whose ridge o'erlooked a shady length of land :
To learn if aught of mortal works appear,
Or cheerful voice of mortal strike the ear.
From the high point I marked, in distant view,
A stream of curling smoke ascending blue,
And spiry tops, the tufted trees above,
Of Circe's palace bosomed in the grove.
Thither to haste, the region to explore,
Was first my thought . . .   [P.]

[1] *Εὗρον δ᾽ ἐν βήσσῃσι τετυγμένα δώματα Κίρκης*
Ξεστοῖσιν λάεσσι, περισκέπτῳ ἐνὶ χώρῳ.

—*Ib.* 210, 211.

The palace in a woody vale they found,
High-raised of stone, a shaded space around.

POPE.   [P.]

The young gentleman took the left-hand passage, and introduced the Doctor to the lower floor of the tower.

" I have divided the tower," he observed, " into three rooms : one on each floor.   This is the dining-room ; above it is my bedroom ; above it again is my library.   The prospect is good from all the floors, but from the library it is most extensive, as you look over the woods far away into the open sea."

" A noble dining-room," said the Doctor.   " The height is well proportioned to the diameter.   That circular table well becomes the form of the room, and gives promise of a fine prospect in its way."

" I hope you will favour me by forming a practical judgment on the point," said his new acquaintance, as he led the way to the upper floor, the Doctor marvelling at the extreme courtesy with which he was treated.   " This building," thought he, " might belong to the age of chivalry, and my young host might be Sir Calidore himself." But the library brought him back to other days.

The walls were covered with books, the upper portion accessible by a gallery, running entirely round the apartment.   The books of the lower circle were all classical ; those of the upper, English, Italian, and French, with a few volumes in Spanish.

The young gentleman took down a Homer, and pointed out to the Doctor the passage which, as he leaned over the gate, he had repeated from the *Odyssey*.   This accounted to the Doctor for the deference shown to him.   He saw at once into the Greek sympathy.

" You have a great collection of books," said the Doctor.

" I believe," said the young gentleman, " I have all the best books in the languages I cultivate.   Horne Tooke says : ' Greek, Latin, Italian, and French, are unfortunately the usual bounds of an English scholar's acquisition.' [1]   I think any scholar fortunate whose acquisition extends so far.   These languages and our own comprise, I believe, with a few rare exceptions, all the best books in the world. I may add Spanish, for the sake of Cervantes, Lope de Vega, and Calderon.[2]   It was a *dictum* of Porson, that ' Life is too short to learn

---

[1] *The Diversions of Purley*, Advertisement to Ch. VII. G.
[2] Robert Buchanan, the poet, said that Peacock learned Spanish in his old age, but scarcely a Spanish book appeared in the catalogue of his library. G.

German : ' meaning, I apprehend, not that it is too difficult to be
acquired within the ordinary space of life, but that there is nothing
in it to compensate for the portion of life bestowed on its acquire-
ment, however little that may be." [1]

The Doctor was somewhat puzzled what to say. He had some
French and more Italian, being fond of romances of chivalry ; and in
Greek and Latin he thought himself a match for any man ; but he
was more occupied with speculations on the position and character of
his new acquaintance, than on the literary opinions he was enunciat-
ing. He marvelled to find a young man, rich enough to do what he
here saw done, doing anything of the kind, and fitting up a library in
a solitary tower, instead of passing his time in clubs and *réunions*,
and other pursuits and pleasures of general society. But he thought
it necessary to say something to the point, and rejoined :

" Porson was a great man, and his *dictum* would have weighed
with me if I had had a velleity towards German ; but I never had
any. But I rather wonder you should have placed your library on
the upper instead of the middle floor. The prospect, as you have
observed, is fine from all the floors ; but here you have the sea and
the sky to the greatest advantage ; and I would assign my best
look-out to the hours of dressing and undressing ; the first thing
in the morning, the last at night, and the half-hour before dinner.
You can give greater attention to the views before you, when you are
following operations, important certainly, but mechanical from
repetition, and uninteresting in themselves, than when you are
engaged in some absorbing study, which probably shuts out all
perception of the external world."

[1] Mr. Hayward's French hotel-keeper in Germany had a different, but not
less cogent reason for not learning German. " Whenever a dish attracts
attention by the art displayed in its conception or preparation, apart from
the material, the artist will commonly be discovered to be French. Many
years ago we had the curiosity to inquire, at the Hotel de France, at
Dresden, to whom our party were indebted for the enjoyment they had
derived from a *suprême de volaille*, and were informed the cook and the
master of the hotel were one and the same person : a Frenchman, *ci-devant
chef* of a Russian minister. He had been eighteen years in Germany, but
knew not a word of any language but his own. ' *À quoi bon, messieurs,*'
was his reply to our expression of astonishment ; ' *à quoi bon, apprendre la
langue d'un peuple qui ne possède pas une cuisine ?* ' "—*Art of Dining*,
pp. 69, 70. [P.] [by Abraham Hayward, 1852. G.]

" What you say is very true, sir," said the other ; " but you know the lines of Milton—

> Or let my lamp, at midnight hour,
> Be seen in some high lonely tower,
> Where I may oft outwatch the Bear,
> With thrice great Hermes.[1]

" These lines have haunted me from very early days, and principally influenced me in purchasing this tower, and placing my library on the top of it. And I have another association with such a mode of life."

A French clock in the library struck two, and the young gentleman proposed to his visitor to walk into the house. They accordingly descended the stairs, and crossed the entrance-hall to a large drawing-room, simply but handsomely furnished ; having some good pictures on the walls, an organ at one end of the room, a piano and harp at the other, and an elegantly disposed luncheon in the middle.

" At this time of the year," said the young gentleman, " I lunch at two, and dine at eight. This gives me two long divisions of the morning, for any in-door and out-door purposes. I hope you will partake with me. You will not find a precedent in Homer for declining the invitation."

" Really," said the Doctor, " that argument is cogent and conclusive. I accept with pleasure : and indeed my long walk has given me an appetite."

" Now you must know," said the young gentleman, " I have none but female domestics. You will see my two waiting-maids."

He rang the bell, and the specified attendants appeared : two young girls about sixteen and seventeen ; both pretty, and simply, but very becomingly, dressed.

Of the provision set before him the Doctor preferred some cold chicken and tongue. Madeira and sherry were on the table, and the young attendants offered him hock and claret. The Doctor took a capacious glass from each of the fair cup-bearers, and pronounced both wines excellent, and deliciously cool.[2] He declined more, not to over-heat himself in walking, and not to infringe on his anticipa-

---

[1] *Il Penseroso*, ll. 85–8. G.
[2] The claret should surely have been *chambré*. G.

tions of dinner. The dog, who had behaved throughout with exemplary propriety, was not forgotten. The Doctor rose to depart.

" I think," said his host, " I may now ask you the Homeric question—*Τίς* ; *πόθεν εἰς ἀνδρῶν* ; " [1]

" Most justly," said the Doctor. " My name is Theophilus Opimian. I am a Doctor of Divinity, and the incumbent of Ashbrook-cum-Ferndale."

" I am simply," said the other, " Algernon Falconer. I have inherited some money, but no land. Therefore having the opportunity, I made this purchase, to fit it up in my own fashion, and live in it in my own way."

The Doctor preparing to depart, Mr. Falconer proposed to accompany him part of the way, and calling out another Newfoundland dog, who immediately struck up a friendship with his companion, he walked away with the Doctor, the two dogs gambolling before them.

CHAPTER IV

Mille hominum species, et rerum discolor usus :
Velle suum cuique est, nec voto vivitur uno.
—Persius.[2]

In mind and taste men differ as in frame :
Each has his special will, and few the same.

THE REVEREND DOCTOR OPIMIAN.   It strikes me as singular that, with such a house, you should have only female domestics.

MR. FALCONER.   It is not less singular perhaps that they are seven sisters, all the children of two old servants of my father and mother. The eldest is about my own age, twenty-six, so that they have all grown up with me in time and place. They live in great harmony together, and divide among them the charge of all the household duties. Those whom you saw are the two youngest.

THE REVEREND DOCTOR OPIMIAN.   If the others acquit themselves as well, you have a very efficient staff ; but seven young women as the establishment of one young bachelor, for such I presume you to

¹ Who, and whence, are you ? [P.] [Homer : *passim*. G.]
² *Sat.* V. 62–3. G.

be (*Mr. Falconer assented*), is something new and strange. The world is not over charitable.

MR. FALCONER. The world will never suppose a good motive where it can suppose a bad one. I would not willingly offend any of its prejudices. I would not affect eccentricity. At the same time, I do not feel disposed to be put out of my way because it is not the way of the world—*Le Chemin du Monde*, as a Frenchman entitled Congreve's comedy [1]—but I assure you these seven young women live here as they might do in the temple of Vesta. It was a singular combination of circumstances that induced and enabled me to form such an establishment ; but I would not give it up, nor alter it, nor diminish it, nor increase it, for any earthly consideration.

THE REVEREND DOCTOR OPIMIAN. You hinted that, beside Milton's verses, you had another association of ideas with living in the top of a tower.

MR. FALCONER. I have read of somebody who lived so, and admitted to his *sanctum* only one young person, a niece or a daughter, I forget which, but on very rare occasions would descend to speak to some visitor who had previously propitiated the young lady to obtain him an interview.[2] At last the young lady introduced one who proposed for her, and gained the consent of the recluse (I am not sure of his name, but I always call him Lord Noirmont) to carry her off. I think this was associated with some affliction that was cured or some mystery that was solved, and that the hermit returned into the every-day world. I do not know where I read it, but I have always liked the idea of living like Lord Noirmont, when I shall have become a sufficiently disappointed man.[3]

THE REVEREND DOCTOR OPIMIAN. You look as little like a disappointed man as any I have seen ; but as you have neither daughter

---

[1] Congreve, le meilleur auteur comique d'Angleterre : ses pièces les plus estimées sont *Le Fourbe, Le Vieux Garçon, Amour pour Amour, L'Epouse du Matin, Le Chemin du Monde.—Manuel Bibliographique.* Par G. Peignot. Paris. 1800. [P.]

[2] Peacock adopted this habit after his retirement at Halliford. See Biographical Introduction, p. xvi. G.

[3] I have failed to identify this novel. G.

nor niece, you would have seven links instead of one between the top of your tower and the external world.

MR. FALCONER. We are all born to disappointment. It is as well to be prospective. Our happiness is not in what is, but in what is to be. We may be disappointed in our every-day realities, and if not, we may make an ideality of the unattainable, and quarrel with nature for not giving what she has not to give. It is unreasonable to be so disappointed, but it is disappointment not the less.

THE REVEREND DOCTOR OPIMIAN. It is something like the disappointment of the men of Gotham when they could not fish up the moon from the sea.

MR. FALCONER. It is very like it, and there are more of us in the predicament of the men of Gotham than are ready to acknowledge the similitude.

THE REVEREND DOCTOR OPIMIAN. I am afraid I am too matter-of-fact to sympathize very clearly with this form of æstheticism; but here is a charming bit of forest scenery. Look at that old oak with the deer under it; the long and deep range of fern running up from it to that beech-grove on the upland, the lights and shadows on the projections and recesses of the wood, and the blaze of foxglove in its foreground. It is a place in which a poet might look for a glimpse of a Hamadryad.

MR. FALCONER. Very beautiful for the actual present—too beautiful for the probable future. Some day or other the forest will be disforested; the deer will be either banished or destroyed; the wood will be either shut up or cut down. Here is another basis for disappointment. The more we admire it now, the more we shall regret it then. The admiration of sylvan and pastoral scenery is at the mercy of an inclosure act, and instead of the glimpse of a Hamadryad you will sometime see a large board warning you off the premises under penalty of rigour of law.

THE REVEREND DOCTOR OPIMIAN. But, my dear young friend, you have yourself enclosed a favourite old resort of mine and of many others. I did not see such a board as you speak of; but there is an effective fence which answers the purpose.

MR. FALCONER. True ; but when the lot of crown land was put up for sale, it was sure to be purchased and shut up by somebody. At any rate, I have not interfered with the external picturesque ; and I have been much more influenced by an intense desire of shutting up myself than of shutting up the place, merely because it is my property.

About half way from their respective homes the two new friends separated, the Doctor having promised to walk over again soon to dine and pass the night.

The Doctor soliloquized as he walked.

Strange metamorphosis of the old tower. A good dining-room. A good library. A bed-room between them : he did not show it me. Good wine : excellent. Pretty waiting-maids : exceedingly pretty. Two of seven Vestals, who maintain the domestic fire on the hearth of this young Numa.[1] By the way, they had something of the Vestal costume : white dresses with purple borders. But they had nothing on their heads but their own hair, very gracefully arranged. The Vestals had head-dresses, which hid their hair, if they had any. They were shaved on admission. Perhaps the hair was allowed to grow again. Perhaps not. I must look into the point. If not, it was a wise precaution. " Hair, the only grace of form," [2] says the *Arbiter Elegantiarum*, who compares a bald head to a fungus.[3] A head without hair, says Ovid, is as a field without grass, and a shrub without leaves.[4] Venus herself, if she had appeared with a bald

---

[1] The philosopher-king of Rome who established the college of the Vestals. G.

[2] Quod solum formæ decus est, cecidere capilli.—Petronius, c. 109. [P.]

[3] . . . lævior . . . rotundo
    Horti tubere, quod creavit unda.—*Ibid.*
[" Worse than the swollen mushroom which moisture breeds in garden soil." G.]

" A head, to speak in the gardener's style, is a bulbous excrescence, growing up between the shoulders."—G. A. Steevens : *Lecture on Heads.*
                                                                    [P.]

[4] Turpe pecus mutilum ; turpe est sine gramine campus ;
    Et sine fronde frutex ; et sine crine caput.
                        Ovid : *Artis Amatoriæ*, iii. 249. [P.]
[" A sad sight is a beast without horns, a field without grass, a leafless shrub, and a hairless head." G.]

head, would not have tempted Apuleius : [1] and I am of his mind.
A husband, in Menander,[2] in a fit of jealous madness, shaves his wife's
head ; and when he sees what he has made of her, rolls at her feet in
a paroxysm of remorse. He was at any rate safe from jealousy till
it grew again. And here is a subtlety of Euripides, which none of his
commentators have seen into. Ægisthus has married Electra to
a young farmer, who cultivates his own land. He respects the Princess from magnanimity, and restores her a pure virgin to her brother
Orestes. "Not probable," say some critics. But I say, highly
probable : for she comes on with her head shaved. There is the
talisman, and the consummate artifice of the great poet. It is
ostensibly a symbol of grief ; but not the less a most efficient ally of
the aforesaid magnanimity. " In mourning," says Aristotle,
" sympathizing with the dead, we deform ourselves by cutting off our
hair." And truly, it is sympathy in approximation. A woman's
head shaved is a step towards a death's head. As a symbol of grief,
it was not necessary to the case of Electra ; for in the sister tragedies
of Æschylus and Sophocles, her grief is equally great, and she appears
with flowing hair ; but in them she is an unmarried maid, and there
is no dramatic necessity for so conspicuous an antidote to her other
charms. Neither is it according to custom ; for in recent grief the
whole hair was sacrificed, but in the memory of an old sorrow only
one or two curls were cut off.[3] Therefore it was the dramatic
necessity of a counter-charm that influenced Euripides. Helen

---

[1] At vero, quod nefas dicere, neque sit ullum hujus rei tam dirum
exemplum : si cujuslibet eximiæ pulcherrimæque fœminæ caput capillo
exspoliaveris, et faciem nativa specie nudaveris, licet illa cœlo dejecta, mari
edita, fluctibus educata, licet, inquam, Venus ipsa fuerit, licet omni
Gratiarum choro stipata, et toto Cupidinum populo comitata, et balteo
suo cincta, cinnama fragrans, et balsama rorans, calva processerit, placere
non poterit nec Vulcano suo. Apuleius: *Metamorph.* ii. 25.

But, indeed, what it is profanation to speak, nor let there be hereof any
so dire example, if you despoil of its hair the head of any most transcendent
and perfectly beautiful woman, and present her face thus denuded of its
native loveliness, though it were even she, the descended from heaven, the
born of the sea, the educated in the waves, though, I say, it were Venus
herself, attended by the Graces, surrounded by the Loves, cinctured with
her girdle, fragrant with spices, and dewy with balsams, yet, if she
appeared with a bald head, she could not please even her own Vulcan. [P.]

[2] Περικειρομένη. [P.] [The Shaven Woman. G.]

[3] Sophocles: *Electra*, v. 449. [P.]

knew better than to shave her head in a case where custom required
it.   Euripides makes Electra reproach Helen for thus preserving her
beauty ; [1] which further illustrates his purpose in shaving the head
of Electra where custom did not require it.   And Terence showed his
taste in not shaving the head of his heroine in the *Phormio*, though
the severity of Athenian custom would have required it.   Her beauty
shone through her dishevelled hair, but with no hair at all she would
not have touched the heart of Antipho.   Ἀλλὰ τίη μοι ταῦτα φίλος
διελέξατο θυμός ; [2]   But wherefore does my mind discourse these
things to me ?   suspending dismal images on lovely realities ?   for the
luxuriant hair of these young girls is of no ordinary beauty.   Their
tresses have not been deposited under the shadow of the sacred
lotus, as Pliny tells us those of the Vestals were.   Well, this young
gentleman's establishment may be perfectly moral, strictly correct,
but in one sense it is morality thrown away :   the world will give
him no credit for it.   I am sure Mrs. Opimian will not.   If he were
married it would be different.   But I think, if he were to marry now,
there would be a fiercer fire than Vesta's among his Lares.   The
temple would be too hot for the seven virgins.   I suppose, as he is
so resolute against change, he does not mean to marry.   Then he
talks about anticipated disappointment in some unrealizable ideality,
leading him to live like Lord Noirmont, whom I never heard of
before.   He is far enough off from that while he lunches and walks
as he does, and no doubt dines in accordance.   He will not break
his heart for any moon in the water, if his cooks are as good as his
waiting-maids, and the wine which he gave me is a fair specimen of
his cellar.   He is learned too.   Greek seems to be the strongest
chord in his sympathies.   If it had not been for the singular accident
of his overhearing me repeat half a dozen lines of Homer, I should
not have been asked to walk in.   I might have leaned over the gate
till sunset, and have had no more notice taken of me than if I had
been a crow.

At dinner the Doctor narrated his morning adventure to Mrs.
Opimian, and found her, as he had anticipated, most virtuously

---

[1] Euripides: *Orestes*, v. 128.   [P.]

[2] " But why did my heart thus commune with me ? "   Homer : *Il.* XI.
407 *et passim*.   G.

uncharitable with respect to the seven sisters. She did not depart from her usual serenity, but said, with equal calmness and decision, that she had no belief in the virtue of young men.

"My dear," said the Doctor, "it has been observed, though I forget by whom, that there is in every man's life a page which is usually doubled down. Perhaps there is such a page in the life of our young friend; but if there be, the volume which contains it is not in the same house with the seven sisters."

The Doctor could not retire to rest without verifying his question touching the hair of the Vestals; and stepping into his study was taking out an old folio to consult *Lipsius de Vestalibus,* when a passage flashed across his memory, which seemed decisive on the point. "How could I overlook it?" he thought.

> " Ignibus Iliacis aderam : cum lapsa capillis
> Decidit ante sacros lanea vitta focos : [1]

says Rhea Sylvia in the *Fasti*."

He took down the *Fasti*, and turning over the leaves lighted on another line :—

> Attonitæ flebant demisso crine ministræ.[2]

With the note of an old commentator : "This will enlighten those who doubt if the Vestals wore their hair." "I infer," said the Doctor, "that I have doubted in good company; but it is clear that the Vestals did wear their hair of second growth. But if it was wrapped up in wool, it might as well not have been there. The *vitta* was at once the symbol and the talisman of chastity. Shall I recommend my young friend to wrap up the heads of his Vestals in a *vitta*? It would be safer for all parties. But I cannot imagine a piece of advice for which the giver would receive less thanks. And I had rather see them as they are. So I shall let well alone."

---

[1] The woollen wreath, by Vesta's inmost shrine,
Fell from my hair before the fire divine. [P.]
[Ovid : *Fasti,* III, 29–30. G.]

[2] With hair dishevelled wept the vestal train. [P.]
[IV. 441. G.]

CHAPTER V

Εὔφραινε σαυτόν· πίνε· τὸν καθ' ἡμέραν
Βίον λογίζου σόν, τὰ δ' ἄλλα τῆς Τύχης.

EURIPIDES : Alcestis.[1]

Rejoice thy spirit : drink : the passing day
Esteem thine own, and all beyond as Fortune's.

THE Doctor was not long without remembering his promise to revisit his new acquaintance, and purposing to remain till the next morning, he set out later in the day. The weather was intensely hot ; he walked slowly, and paused more frequently than usual, to rest under the shade of trees. He was shown into the drawing-room, where he was shortly joined by Mr. Falconer, and very cordially welcomed.

The two friends dined together in the lower room of the Tower. The dinner and wine were greatly to the Doctor's mind. In due time they adjourned to the drawing-room, and the two young handmaids who had waited at dinner attended with coffee and tea. The Doctor then said—" You are well provided with musical instruments. Do you play ? "

MR. FALCONER. No. I have profited by the observation of Doctor Johnson : " Sir, once on a time I took to fiddling ; but I found that to fiddle well I must fiddle all my life, and I thought I could do something better." [2]

THE REVEREND DOCTOR OPIMIAN. Then, I presume, these are pieces of ornamental furniture, for the use of occasional visitors ?

MR. FALCONER. Not exactly. My maids play on them, and sing to them.

THE REVEREND DOCTOR OPIMIAN. Your maids !

MR. FALCONER. Even so. They have been thoroughly well educated, and are all accomplished musicians.

---

[1] 788–9. G.

[2] Misquoted. Dr. Johnson said : " Had I learnt to fiddle, I should have done nothing else."

Boswell : " Pray Sir, did you ever play on any musical instrument ? "
Johnson : " No Sir, I once bought me a flageolet but I never made out a tune." Boswell : *Life of Johnson*, Vol. III, p. 242 (Birkbeck Hill). G.

THE REVEREND DOCTOR OPIMIAN. And at what time do they usually play on them ?

MR. FALCONER. Every evening about this time, when I am alone.

THE REVEREND DOCTOR OPIMIAN. And why not when you have company ?

MR. FALCONER. *La Morgue Aristocratique*, which pervades all society, would not tolerate such a proceeding on the part of young women, of whom some had superintended the preparation of the dinner, and others attended on it. It would not have been incongruous in the Homeric age.

THE REVEREND DOCTOR OPIMIAN. Then I hope you will allow it to be not incongruous this evening, Homer being the original *vinculum* between you and me.

MR. FALCONER. Would you like to hear them ?

THE REVEREND DOCTOR OPIMIAN. Indeed I should.

The two younger sisters having answered the summons, and the Doctor's wish having been communicated, the seven appeared together, all in the same dress of white and purple.

"The Seven Pleiads !" thought the Doctor. "What a constellation of beauty !" He stood up and bowed to them, which they gracefully acknowledged.

They then played on, and sang to, the harp and piano. The Doctor was enchanted.

After a while, they passed over to the organ, and performed some sacred music of Mozart and Beethoven. They then paused and looked round, as if for instructions.

"We usually end," said Mr. Falconer, "with a hymn to St. Catharine, but perhaps it may not be to your taste ; although Saint Catharine is a saint of the English Church Calendar."

"I like all sacred music," said the Doctor. "And I am not disposed to object to a saint of the English Church Calendar."

"She is also," said Mr. Falconer, "a most perfect emblem of purity, and in that sense alone there can be no fitter image to be presented to the minds of young women."

"Very true," said the Doctor. "And very strange withal," he thought to himself.

The sisters sang their hymn, made their obeisance, and departed.

THE REVEREND DOCTOR OPIMIAN. The hands of those young women do not show signs of menial work.

MR. FALCONER. They are the regulating spirits of the household. They have a staff of their own for the coarser and harder work.

THE REVEREND DOCTOR OPIMIAN. Their household duties, then, are such as Homeric damsels discharged in the homes of their fathers, with δμωαί [1] for the lower drudgery.

MR. FALCONER. Something like it.

THE REVEREND DOCTOR OPIMIAN. Young ladies, in short, in manners and accomplishments, though not in social position ; only more useful in a house than young ladies generally are.

MR. FALCONER. Something like that, too. If you know the tree by its fruit, the manner in which this house is kept may reconcile you to the singularity of the experiment.

THE REVEREND DOCTOR OPIMIAN. I am perfectly reconciled to it. The experiment is eminently successful.

The Doctor always finished his day with a tumbler of brandy and water : soda water in summer, and hot water in winter. After his usual draught he retired to his chamber, where he slept like a top, and dreamed of Electra and Nausicaa, Vestals, Pleiads, and Saint Catharine, and woke with the last words he had heard sung on the preceding night still ringing in his ears :—

> Dei virgo Catharina,
> Lege constans in divinâ,
> Cœli gemma preciosa,
> Margarita fulgida,
> Sponsa Christi gloriosa,
> Paradisi viola ! [2]

---

[1] Slave-women. G.

[2] Virgin bride, supremely bright,
Gem and flower of heavenly light,
Pearl of the empyreal skies,
Violet of Paradise ! [P.]

CHAPTER VI

Despairing beside a clear stream
A shepherd forsaken was laid.[1]

THE next morning, after a comfortable breakfast, the Doctor set out on his walk home. His young friend accompanied him part of the way, and did not part with him till he had obtained a promise of another and longer visit.

The Doctor, as usual, soliloquized as he walked. " No doubt these are Vestals. The purity of the establishment is past question. This young gentleman has every requisite which her dearest friends would desire in a husband for Miss Gryll. And she is in every way suited to him. But these seven damsels interpose themselves, like the sevenfold shield of Ajax. There is something very attractive in these damsels :

facies non omnibus una,
Nec diversa tamen : qualem decet esse sororum.[2]

If I had such an establishment, I should be loath to break it up. It is original, in these days of monotony. It is satisfactory, in these days of uncongenial relations between master and servant. It is effective, in the admirable arrangements of the household. It is graceful, in the personal beauty and tasteful apparel of the maidens. It is agreeable, in their manners, in their accomplishments, in their musical skill. It is like an enchanted palace. Mr. Gryll, who talks so much of Circe, would find himself at home ; he might fancy himself waited on by her handmaids, the daughters of fountains, groves, and rivers. Miss Gryll might fancy herself in the dwelling of her namesake, Morgana. But I fear she would be for dealing with it as Orlando did with Morgana, breaking the talisman and dissolving the enchantment. This would be a pity ; but it would also be a pity that these two young persons should not come together. But why should I trouble myself with match-making ? It is always a thankless office. If it turns out well, your good service is forgotten. If it turns out ill, you are abused by both parties."

[1] Nicholas Rowe: *Colin's Complaint.* G.
[2] Though various features did the sisters grace,
    A sister's likeness was in every face.
                              Addison : *Ovid. Met.* l. ii. [P.]

The Doctor's soliloquy was cut short by a sound of lamentation, which, as he went on, came to him in louder and louder bursts. He was attracted to the spot whence the sounds proceeded, and had some difficulty in discovering a doleful swain, who was ensconced in a mass of fern, taller than himself if he had been upright; and but that, by rolling over and over in the turbulence of his grief, he had flattened a large space down to the edge of the forest brook near which he reclined, he would have remained invisible in his lair. The tears in his eyes, and the passionate utterances of his voice, contrasted strangely with a round russetin face, which seemed fortified by beef and ale against all possible furrows of care; but against love, even beef and ale, mighty talismans as they are, are feeble barriers. Cupid's arrows had pierced through the *æs triplex* of treble X, and the stricken deer lay mourning by the stream.

The Doctor approaching, kindly inquired, "What is the matter?" but was answered only by a redoubled burst of sorrow and an emphatic rejection of all sympathy.

"You can't do me any good."

"You do not know that," said the Doctor. "No man knows what good another can do him till he communicates his trouble."

For some time the Doctor could obtain no other answer than the repetition of "You can't do me any good." But at length the patience and kind face of the inquirer had their effect on the sad shepherd, and he brought out with a desperate effort and a more clamorous explosion of grief,

"She won't have me!"

"Who won't have you?" said the Doctor.

"Well, if you must know," said the swain, "you must. It's one of the young ladies up at the Folly."

"Young ladies?" said the Doctor.

"Servants they call themselves," said the other; "but they are more like ladies, and hold their heads high enough when one of them won't have me. Father's is one of the best farms for miles round, and it's all his own. He's a true old yeoman, father is. And there's nobody but him and me. And if I had a nice wife, that would be a good housekeeper for him, and play and sing to him of an evening— for she can do anything, she can—read, and write, and keep accounts,

and play and sing—I've heard her—and make a plum pudding—
I've seen her—we should be as happy as three crickets—four,
perhaps, at the year's end : and she won't have me."

" You have put the question ? " said the Doctor.

" Plump," said the other. " And she looked at first as if she was
going to laugh. She didn't, though. Then she looked serious, and
said she was sorry for me. She said she saw I was in earnest. She
knew I was a good son, and deserved a good wife ; but she couldn't
have me. Miss, said I, do you like anybody better ? No, she said,
very heartily."

" That is one comfort," said the Doctor.

" What comfort," said the other, " when she won't have me ? "

" She may alter her mind," said the Doctor, " if she does not prefer
any one else. Besides, she only says she can't."

" Can't," said the other, " is civil for won't. That's all."

" Does she say why she can't ? " said the Doctor.

" Yes," said the other. " She says she and her sisters won't part
with each other and their young master."

" Now," said the Doctor, " you have not told me which of the
seven sisters is the one in question."

" It's the third," said the other. " What they call the second cook.
There's a housekeeper and two cooks, and two housemaids and two
waiting-maids. But they only manage for the young master.
There are others that wait on them."

" And what is her name ? " said the Doctor.

" Dorothy," said the other ; " her name is Dorothy. Their names
follow like A B C, only that A comes last. Betsey, Catharine,
Dorothy, Eleanor, Fanny, Grace, Anna. But they told me it was not
the alphabet they were christened from ; it was the key of A minor,
if you know what that means."

" I think I do," said the Doctor, laughing. " They were
christened from the Greek diatonic scale, and make up two conjunct
tetrachords, if you know what that means."

" I can't say I do," said the other, looking bewildered.

" And so," said the Doctor, " the young gentleman, whose name is
Algernon, is the Proslambanomenos, or key-note, and makes up the
octave. His parents must have designed it as a foretelling, that he

and his seven foster-sisters were to live in harmony all their lives. But how did you become acquainted ? "

" Why," said the other, " I take a great many things to the house from our farm, and it's generally she that takes them in."

" I know the house well," said the Doctor, "and the master, and the maids. Perhaps he may marry, and they may follow the example. Live in hope. Tell me your name."

" Hedgerow," said the other ; " Harry Hedgerow. And if you know her, ain't she a beauty ? "

" Why, yes," said the Doctor, "they are all good looking."

" And she won't have me," cried the other, but with a more subdued expression. The Doctor had consoled him, and given him a ray of hope. And they went on their several ways.

The Doctor resumed his soliloquy.

" Here is the semblance of something towards a solution of the difficulty. If one of the damsels should marry, it would break the combination. One will not by herself. But what if seven apple-faced Hedgerows should propose simultaneously, seven notes in the key of A minor, an octave below ? Stranger things have happened. I have read of six brothers who had the civility to break their necks in succession, that the seventh, who was the hero of the story, might inherit an estate. But, again and again, why should I trouble myself with match-making ? I had better leave things to take their own course."

Still in his interior *speculum*, the Doctor could not help seeing a dim reflection of himself pronouncing the nuptial benediction on his two young friends.

CHAPTER VII

Indulge Genio : carpamus dulcia : nostrum est
Quod vivis : cinis, et manes, et fabula fies.
Vive memor lethi : fugit hora : hoc quod loquor, inde est.

PERSIUS.[1]

Indulge thy Genius, while the hour's thine own :
Even while we speak, some part of it has flown.
Snatch the swift-passing good : 'twill end ere long
In dust, and shadow, and an old wife's song.

" AGAPĒTUS and Agapêtæ," [2] said the Reverend Doctor Opimian, the next morning at breakfast, " in the best sense of the words : that,

[1] *Sat.* 151–3. G.   [2] Ἀγαπητὸς καὶ ἀγαπηταί. [P.]

I am satisfied, is the relation between this young gentleman and his handmaids."

MRS. OPIMIAN. Perhaps, Doctor, you will have the goodness to make your view of this relation a little more intelligible to me.

THE REVEREND DOCTOR OPIMIAN. Assuredly, my dear. The word signifies " beloved," in its purest sense. And in this sense it was used by Saint Paul in reference to some of his female co-religionists and fellow-labourers in the vineyard, in whose houses he occasionally dwelt. And in this sense it was applied to virgins and holy men, who dwelt under the same roof in spiritual love.

MRS. OPIMIAN. Very likely, indeed. You are a holy man, Doctor, but I think, if you were a bachelor, and I were a maid, I should not trust myself to be your aga—aga——

THE REVEREND DOCTOR OPIMIAN. Agapêtê. But I never pretended to this sort of spiritualism. I followed the advice of Saint Paul, who says it is better to marry——[1]

MRS. OPIMIAN. You need not finish the quotation.

THE REVEREND DOCTOR OPIMIAN. Agapêtê is often translated " adoptive sister." A very possible relation, I think, where there are vows of celibacy, and inward spiritual grace.

MRS. OPIMIAN. Very possible, indeed : and equally possible where there are none.

THE REVEREND DOCTOR OPIMIAN. But more possible where there are seven adoptive sisters, than where there is only one.

MRS. OPIMIAN. Perhaps.

THE REVEREND DOCTOR OPIMIAN. The manners, my dear, of these damsels towards their young master, are infallible indications of the relations between them. Their respectful deference to him is a symptom in which I cannot be mistaken.

MRS. OPIMIAN. I hope you are not.

[1] *I Corinthians*, vii. 9. G.

THE REVEREND DOCTOR OPIMIAN. I am sure I am not. I would stake all my credit for observation and experience on the purity of the seven Vestals. I am not strictly accurate in calling them so : for in Rome the number of Vestals was only six. But there were seven Pleiads, till one disappeared. We may fancy she became a seventh Vestal. Or as the planets used to be seven, and are now more than fifty, we may pass a seventh Vestal in the name of modern progress.

MRS. OPIMIAN. There used to be seven deadly sins. How many has modern progress added to them ?

THE REVEREND DOCTOR OPIMIAN. None, I hope, my dear. But this will be due, not to its own tendencies, but to the comprehensiveness of the old definitions.

MRS. OPIMIAN. I think I have heard something like your Greek word before.

THE REVEREND DOCTOR OPIMIAN. Agapêmonê, my dear. You may have heard the word Agapêmonê.

MRS. OPIMIAN. That is it. And what may it signify ?

THE REVEREND DOCTOR OPIMIAN. It signifies Abode of Love : spiritual love, of course.

MRS. OPIMIAN. Spiritual love, which rides in carriages and four, fares sumptuously, like Dives, and protects itself with a high wall from profane observation.

THE REVEREND DOCTOR OPIMIAN. Well, my dear, and there may be no harm in all that.

MRS. OPIMIAN. Doctor, you are determined not to see harm in anything.

THE REVEREND DOCTOR OPIMIAN. I am afraid I see more harm in many things than I like to see. But one reason for not seeing harm in this Agapêmonê matter is, that I hear so little about it. The world is ready enough to promulgate scandal ; but that which is quietly right may rest in peace.

MRS. OPIMIAN. Surely, Doctor, you do not think this Agapêmonê right ?

THE REVEREND DOCTOR OPIMIAN. I only say I do not know whether it is right or wrong. It is nothing new. Three centuries ago there was a Family of Love, on which Middleton wrote a comedy. Queen Elizabeth persecuted this family ; Middleton made it ridiculous ; but it outlived them both, and there may have been no harm in it after all.[1]

MRS. OPIMIAN. Perhaps, Doctor, the world is too good to see any novelty except in something wrong.

THE REVEREND DOCTOR OPIMIAN. Perhaps it is only wrong that arrests attention, because right is common, and wrong is rare. Of the many thousand persons who walk daily through a street you only hear of one who has been robbed or knocked down. If ever Hamlet's news—" that the world has grown honest " [2]—should prove true, there would be an end of our newspaper. For, let us see, what is the epitome of a newspaper ? In the first place, specimens of all the deadly sins, and infinite varieties of violence and fraud ; a great quantity of talk, called by courtesy legislative wisdom, of which the result is " an incoherent and undigested mass of law, shot down, as from a rubbish-cart, on the heads of the people ; " [3] lawyers barking at each other in that peculiar style of hylactic [4] delivery which is called forensic eloquence, and of which the first and most distinguished practitioner was Cerberus ; [5] bear-garden meetings of mismanaged companies, in which directors and shareholders abuse each

---

[1] Dr. Opimian's tolerance leads one to suppose that he may have shared the heresy of this sect, which originated among the Dutch Anabaptists, that it was a matter of complete indifference what we believe about the nature of God, providing that our hearts burn with love. Mrs. Opimian's suspicion that carnal love was meant was generally held. The founder of the Family of Love, Henry Nicholas, came to England in the reign of Edward VI, and its members increased so rapidly that a royal proclamation of 3 Oct. 1580 ordered its suppression. Nicholas is mentioned by Ben Jonson (*Alchemist*, Act V, Sc. 3). G.

[2] Act II, Sc. 2. G.   [3] Jeremy Bentham. [P.]

[4] Yelping. G.

[5] Cerberus forensis erat causidicus.—Petronius Arbiter. [P.] [Fragment. G.]

other in choice terms, not all to be found even in Rabelais ; burstings
of bank bubbles, which, like a touch of harlequin's wand, strip off
their masks and dominoes from "highly respectable" gentlemen,
and leave them in their true figures of cheats and pickpockets ;
societies of all sorts, for teaching everybody everything, meddling
with everybody's business, and mending everybody's morals ;
mountebank advertisements promising the beauty of Helen in a
bottle of cosmetic, and the age of Old Parr [1] in a box of pills ; folly all
alive in things called reunions ; announcements that some exceedingly stupid fellow has been "entertaining" a select company ;
matters, however multiform, multifarious, and multitudinous, all
brought into family likeness by the varnish of false pretension with
which they are all overlaid.

MRS. OPIMIAN. I did not like to interrupt you, Doctor ; but it
struck me, while you were speaking, that in reading the newspaper
you do not hear the bark of the lawyers.

THE REVEREND DOCTOR OPIMIAN. True ; but no one who has once
heard the wow-wow can fail to reproduce it in imagination.

MRS. OPIMIAN. You have omitted accidents, which occupy a large
space in the newspaper. If the world grew ever so honest, there
would still be accidents.

THE REVEREND DOCTOR OPIMIAN. But honesty would materially
diminish the number. High-pressure steam boilers would not
scatter death and destruction around them, if the dishonesty of
avarice did not tempt their employment, where the more costly low
pressure would ensure absolute safety. Honestly built houses would
not come suddenly down and crush their occupants. Ships, faithfully built and efficiently manned, would not so readily strike on a
lee shore, nor go instantly to pieces on the first touch of the ground.
Honestly made sweetmeats would not poison children ; honestly
compounded drugs would not poison patients. In short, the larger
portion of what we call accidents are crimes.

MRS. OPIMIAN. I have often heard you say, of railways and steam

[1] Old Parr, born 1483, died 1635. G.

vessels, that the primary cause of their disasters is the insane passion of the public for speed. That is not crime, but folly.

THE REVEREND DOCTOR OPIMIAN. It is crime in those who ought to know better than to act in furtherance of the folly. But when the world has grown honest, it will no doubt grow wise. When we have got rid of crime, we may consider how to get rid of folly. So that question is adjourned to the Greek kalends.

MRS. OPIMIAN. There are always in a newspaper some things of a creditable character.

THE REVEREND DOCTOR OPIMIAN. When we are at war, naval and military heroism abundantly; but in time of peace, these virtues sleep. They are laid up like ships in ordinary. No doubt, of the recorded facts of civil life some are good, and more are indifferent, neither good nor bad; but good and indifferent together are scarcely more than a twelfth part of the whole. Still, the matters thus presented are all exceptional cases. A hermit reading nothing but a newspaper might find little else than food for misanthropy; but living among friends, and in the bosom of our family, we see that the dark side of life is the occasional picture, the bright is its every-day aspect. The occasional is the matter of curiosity, of incident, of adventure, of things that really happen to few, and may possibly happen to any. The interest attendant on any action or event is in just proportion to its rarity; and, happily, quiet virtues are all around us, and obtrusive vices seldom cross our path. On the whole, I agree in opinion with Theseus,[1] that there is more good than evil in the world.

MRS. OPIMIAN. I think, Doctor, you would not maintain any opinion if you had not an authority two thousand years old for it.

THE REVEREND DOCTOR OPIMIAN. Well, my dear, I think most opinions worth maintaining have an authority of about that age.[2]

---

[1] Eurip. *Suppl.* 207 : Herm. [P.] [In Modern text, 199. G.]
[2] E. J. Trelawny told Richard Garnett that almost the last remark Peacock made to him was: "Ah, Trelawny, don't talk to me about anything that has happened for the last two thousand years." G.

CHAPTER VIII

Ψῦξον τὸν οἶνον, Δῶρι.———
———Ἔγχεον σὺ δὴ πιεῖν·
Εὐζωρότερόν γε νὴ Δί, ὦ παῖ, δός· τὸ γάρ
Ὑδαρὲς ἅπαν τοῦτ᾽ ἐστὶ τῇ ψυχῇ κακόν.

DIPHILUS.[1]

Cool the wine, Doris. Pour it in the cup
Simple, unmixed with water. Such dilution
Serves only to wash out the spirit of man.

THE Doctor, under the attraction of his new acquaintance, had
allowed more time than usual to elapse between his visits to Gryll
Grange, and when he resumed them, he was not long without communicating the metamorphosis of the Old Tower, and the singularities
of its inhabitants. They dined well as usual, and drank their wine
cool.

MISS GRYLL.   There are many things in what you have told us that
excite my curiosity ; but first, what do you suppose is the young
gentleman's religion ?

THE REVEREND DOCTOR OPIMIAN.   From the great liking he seems
to have taken to me, I should think he was of the Church of England,
if I did not rather explain it by our Greek sympathy.   At the same
time, he kept very carefully in view that Saint Catharine is a Saint
of the English Church Calendar.   I imagine there is less of true piety
than of an abstract notion of ideal beauty, even in his devotion to
her.   But it is so far satisfactory that he wished to prove his religion,
such as it is, to be within the pale of the Church of England.

MISS GRYLL.   I like the idea of his closing the day with a hymn,
sung in concert by his seven Vestals.

THE REVEREND DOCTOR OPIMIAN.   I am glad that you think
charitably of the damsels.   It is not every lady that would.   But
I am satisfied they deserve it.

MR. GRYLL.   I should like to know the young gentleman.   I wish
you could manage to bring him here.   Should not you like to see him,
Morgana ?

[1] Op. Meinecke. Com. Fragm. iv, 375.   G.

MISS GRYLL. Yes, uncle.

MR. GRYLL. Try what you can do, Doctor. We shall have before long some poetical and philosophical visitors. That may tempt him to join us.

THE REVEREND DOCTOR OPIMIAN. It may ; but I am not confident. He seems to me to be indisposed to general society, and to care for nothing but woods, rivers, and the sea ; Greek poetry, Saint Catharine, and the seven Vestals. However, I will try what can be done.

MR. GRYLL. But, Doctor, I think he would scarcely have provided such a spacious dining-room, and so much domestic accommodation, if he had intended to shut himself up from society altogether. I expect that some day when you go there you will find a large party. Try if he will co-operate in the Aristophanic comedy.

THE REVEREND DOCTOR OPIMIAN. A good idea. That may be something to his mind.

MISS GRYLL. Talking of comedy, Doctor, what has become of Lord Curryfin, and his lecture on fish ?

THE REVEREND DOCTOR OPIMIAN. Why, Lord Michin Malicho,[1] Lord Facing-both-ways,[2] and two or three other arch-quacks, have taken to merry-andrewising in a new arena, which they call the Science of Pantopragmatics,[3] and they have bitten Lord Curryfin into tumbling with them ; but the mania will subside when the weather grows cool ; and no doubt we shall still have him at Thornback Bay, teaching the fishermen how to know a herring from a halibut.

MISS GRYLL. But pray, Doctor, what is this new science ?

THE REVEREND DOCTOR OPIMIAN. Why that, Miss Gryll, I cannot well make out. I have asked several professors of the science, and

[1] " Marry, this is *miching mallecho* : it means mischief."—*Hamlet*. [P.] [Act III, Sc. 2. G.]

[2] Lord John Russell and Lord Brougham are intended. Dr. Folliott compared Brougham to Mr. Facing-both-ways of Vanity Fair in *Pilgrim's Progress*. See *Crotchet Castle*, p. 656. G.

[3] The Pantopragmatic Society is The National Association for the Promotion of Social Science. G.

have got nothing in return but some fine varieties of rigmarole, of which I can make neither head nor tail. It seems to be a real art of talking about an imaginary art of teaching every man his own business. Nothing practical comes of it, and indeed so much the better. It will be at least harmless, as long as it is like Hamlet's reading, " words, words, words." [1] Like most other science, it resolves itself into lecturing, lecturing, lecturing, about all sorts of matters, relevant and irrelevant : one enormous bore prating about jurisprudence, another about statistics, another about education, and so forth ; the *crambe repetita* of the same rubbish, which has already been served up " twiës hot and twiës cold," [2] at as many other associations nick-named scientific.

MISS GRYLL. Then, Doctor, I should think Lord Curryfin's lecture would be a great relief to the unfortunate audience.

THE REVEREND DOCTOR OPIMIAN. No doubt more amusing, and equally profitable. Not a fish more would be caught for it, and this will typify the result of all such scientific talk. I had rather hear a practical cook lecture on bubble and squeak : no bad emblem of the whole affair.

MR. GRYLL. It has been said a man of genius can discourse on anything. Bubble and squeak seems a limited subject ; but in the days of the French revolution there was an amusing poem with that title ; [3] and there might be an amusing lecture ; especially if it were like the poem, discursive and emblematical. But men so dismally far gone in the affectation of earnestness would scarcely relish it.

---

[1] Act II, Sc. 2. G.

[2] And many a Jacke of Dover hast thou sold,
That hath been twiës hot and twiës cold.
Chaucer : *The Coke's Prologue.* [P.]
[A Jack of Dover is a fool. The editors of Chaucer have been at pains to explain its meaning and suggest pies and fish. Peacock himself decided "that it was something named after a Jacke of Dover, just as the well-known tea-cake is christened by Sally Lunn" (*Gastronomy and Civilization*). The simplest explanation is to read " that " as "that which," the Jack of Dover being the foolish customer who purchased the warmed-up dish. G.]

[3] *Bubble and Squeak : a Gallimaufry of British Beef with the Chopped Cabbage of Gallic Philosophy.* By Huddleston. [P.] [The Rev. George Huddleston. The book was published anonymously in 1799. G.]

CHAPTER IX

―― gli occhi su levai,
E vidi lei che si facea corona,
Riflettendo da sè gli eterni rai.
DANTE : *Paradiso*, xxxi. 70–72.

I lifted up my gaze,
And looked on her who made herself a crown,
Reflecting from herself the eternal rays.

IT was not long before the Doctor again walked over to the Tower, to propose to his young friend to co-operate in the Aristophanic comedy.

He found him well disposed to do so, and they passed a portion of the afternoon in arranging their programme.

They dined, and passed the evening much as before. The next morning, as they were ascending to the library to resume their pleasant labour, the Doctor said to himself, " I have passed along galleries wherein were many chambers, and the doors in the day were more commonly open than shut, yet this chamber door of my young friend is always shut. There must be a mystery in it." And the Doctor, not generally given to morbid curiosity, found himself very curious about this very simple matter.

At last he mustered up courage to say, " I have seen your library, dining-room, and drawing-room ; but you have so much taste in internal arrangements, I should like to see the rest of the house."

MR. FALCONER. There is not much more to see. You have occupied one of the best bedrooms. The rest do not materially differ.

THE REVEREND DOCTOR OPIMIAN. To say the truth, I should like to see your own.

MR. FALCONER. I am quite willing. But I have thought, perhaps erroneously, it is decorated in a manner you might not altogether approve.

THE REVEREND DOCTOR OPIMIAN. Nothing indecorous, I hope.

MR. FALCONER. Quite the contrary. You may, perhaps, think it too much devoted to my peculiar views of the purity of ideal beauty, as developed in Saint Catharine.

THE REVEREND DOCTOR OPIMIAN. You have not much to apprehend on that score.

MR. FALCONER. You see, there is an altar, with an image of Saint Catharine, and the panels of the room are painted with subjects from her life, mostly copied from Italian masters. The pictures of St. Catharine and her legend very early impressed her on my mind as the type of ideal beauty—of all that can charm, irradiate, refine, exalt, in the best of the better sex.[1]

THE REVEREND DOCTOR OPIMIAN. You are enthusiastic ; but indeed, though she is retained as a saint in the Reformed Church, I am not very familiar with her history. And to me some of these pictures require explanation.

MR. FALCONER. I will tell you her legend as briefly as I may. And we will pass from picture to picture as the subjects arise.

THE LEGEND OF SAINT CATHARINE

Catharine was a Princess of Alexandria in the third century. She embraced the Christian religion by divine inspiration. She was preeminent in beauty, learning, and discourse. She converted her father and mother, and all with whom she came into communication. The Emperor Maxentius brought together the fifty wisest men of the empire to convert her from the error of her way, and she converted them all to the new faith. Maxentius burned her proselytes, and threatened her with a similar death. She remained firm. He had her publicly scourged, and cast her into prison to perish by famine. Going on an expedition, he left the execution of his orders to the empress and his chief general, Porphyrius. Angels healed her wounds and supplied her with food ; and in a beatific vision the Saviour of the world placed a ring on her finger, and called her his bride.[2] The presence of the ring showed to her the truth of the

---

[1] Peacock collected prints and engravings of St. Catharine in his later years. G.

[2] Maria, Vergine delle Vergini, e Misericordia delle Misericordie, vestita de i lampi del Sole, e coronata de i raggi delle Stelle, prese il sottile, il delicato, ed il sacro dito di Catarina, humile di core e mansueta di vita, ed

visitation. The empress and Porphyrius visited the prison, and she converted them also. The emperor, returning, put the empress and Porphyrius to death ; and after many ineffectual expostulations with Catharine, determined on putting her to death by the wheel which bears her name. Four of these wheels, armed with iron teeth, and revolving towards each other, were to cut her to pieces. Angels broke the wheels. He then brought her to the stake, and the angels extinguished the flames. He then ordered her to be beheaded by the sword. This was permitted, and in the meantime the day had closed. The body, reserved for exposure to wild beasts, was left under guard at the place of execution. Intense darkness fell on the night, and in the morning the body had disappeared. The angels had borne it to the summit of the loftiest mountain of the Horeb range, where still a rock, bearing the form of a natural sarcophagus, meets the eye of the traveller. Here it was watched by angel-guards, and preserved in unchanging beauty, till, in the fulness of time it was revealed to a holy man, who removed it to the shrine, under which it lies to this day, with the ring still on its hand, in the convent which was then founded, and which bears her name—the convent of Saint Catharine of Mount Sinai.

THE REVEREND DOCTOR OPIMIAN. Most of this is new to me. Yet I am not unfamiliar with pictures of the Marriage of Saint Catharine, which was a favourite subject with the great Italian masters. But here is a picture which the legend, as you have related it, does not illustrate. What is this tomb, with flames bursting from it, and monks and others recoiling in dismay ?

MR. FALCONER. It represents a remarkable incident at the tomb of the saint. The Empress Catharine II was a great benefactress to the Convent of Mount Sinai, and desired to possess Saint Catharine's ring. She sent a mitred Abbot as an envoy to request it from the brotherhood. The monks, unwilling to displease the

il largo, il clemente, ed il pietoso figliuol suo lo cinse con lo anello.— *Vita di Santa Catarina,* l. ii. Vinezia, 1541. [P.] [" Mary, virgin of virgins, and mercy of mercies, clothed in the light of the sun and crowned with the rays of the stars, took the slender, delicate and sacred finger of Catharine of humble heart and meek life, and her bountiful, merciful and pious Son placed on it the ring." G.]

Empress, replied that they did not dare to remove it themselves, but that they would open the tomb, and the envoy might take it. They opened the tomb accordingly, and the envoy looked on the hand and the ring. He approached to draw it off; but flames burst forth: he recoiled, and the tomb closed. Under such a manifestation of the saint's displeasure, the fathers could not again attempt to open it.[1]

THE REVEREND DOCTOR OPIMIAN. I should like to have seen the Empress receiving the envoy's report.

MR. FALCONER. Her reception of it would depend on the degree of faith which she either actually felt, or might have thought it politic to assume. At any rate, the fathers had shown their devotion, and afforded her a good opportunity for exhibiting hers. She did not again seek to obtain the ring.

THE REVEREND DOCTOR OPIMIAN. Now, what are these three pictures in one frame, of chapels on hills?

MR. FALCONER. These chapels are here represented as they may be supposed to have been in the Catholic days of England. Three sisters, named Catharine, Martha, and Anne, built them to their namesake saints, on the summits of three hills, which took from these dedications the names they still bear. From the summit of each of these chapels the other two were visible. The sisters thought the chapels would long remain memorials of Catholic piety and sisterly love. The Reformation laid them in ruins. Nothing remains of the chapel of Saint Anne but a few grey stones, built into an earthen wall, which, some half century ago, enclosed a plantation. The hill is now better known by the memory of Charles Fox, than by that of its ancient saint.[2] The chapel of Saint Martha has been restored and applied to Protestant worship. The chapel of Saint Catharine remains a picturesque ruin, on the banks of the Wey, near Guildford.

THE REVEREND DOCTOR OPIMIAN. And that old church?

[1] *Illustrations of Jerusalem and Mount Sinai* (1837), p. 27. [P.]
[2] A reference to Charles James Fox's house, St. Anne's Hill, near Chertsey. G.

MR. FALCONER. That was the church of St. Catharine, which was pulled down to make way for the dock by which her name is now profaned ; an act of desecration which has been followed by others, and will be followed by many more, whenever it may suit the interests of commerce to commit sacrilege on consecrated ground and dissipate the ashes of the dead ; an act which, even when that of a barbarian invader, Horace thought it would be profanation even to look on.[1] Whatever may be in other respects the superiority of modern piety, we are far inferior to the ancients in reverence for temples and tombs.

THE REVEREND DOCTOR OPIMIAN. I am afraid I cannot gainsay that observation. But what is that stained glass window ?

MR. FALCONER. It is copied on a smaller scale, and with more of Italian artistic beauty in the principal figure, from the window in West Wickham church. She is trampling on the Emperor Maxentius. You see all her emblems : the palm, which belongs to all sainted martyrs ; the crown, the wheel, the fire, the sword, which belong especially to her ; and the book, with which she is always represented, as herself a miracle of learning, and its chosen universal patroness in the schools of the Middle Ages.

THE REVEREND DOCTOR OPIMIAN. Unquestionably the legend is interesting. At present, your faith is simply poetical. But take care, my young friend, that you do not finish by becoming the dupe of your own mystification.

MR. FALCONER. I have no fear of that. I think I can clearly distinguish devotion to ideal beauty from superstitious belief. I feel the necessity of some such devotion, to fill up the void which the world, as it is, leaves in my mind. I wish to believe in the presence of some local spiritual influence ; genius or nymph ; linking us by a medium of something like human feeling, but more pure and more exalted, to the all-pervading, creative, and preservative spirit of the universe ; but I cannot realize it from things as they are. Everything is too deeply tinged with sordid vulgarity. There can be no intellectual power resident in a wood, where the only inscription is

[1] *Epod.* 16, 13. [P.]

not " *Genio loci*," but " Trespassers will be prosecuted ; " no Naiad
in a stream that turns a cotton-mill ; no Oread in a mountain dell,
where a railway train deposits a cargo of Vandals ; no Nereids or
Oceanitides along the seashore, where a coast-guard is watching for
smugglers. No ; the intellectual life of the material world is dead.
Imagination cannot replace it. But the intercession of saints still
forms a link between the visible and invisible. In their symbols I
can imagine their presence. Each in the recess of our own thought
we may preserve their symbols from the intrusion of the world.
And the saint, whom I have chosen, presents to my mind the most
perfect ideality of physical, moral, and intellectual beauty.

THE REVEREND DOCTOR OPIMIAN. I cannot object to your taste.
But I hope you will not be led into investing the ideality with too
much of the semblance of reality. I should be sorry to find you far
gone in hagiolatry. I hope you will acquiesce in Martin, keeping
equally clear of Peter and Jack.[1]

MR. FALCONER. Nothing will more effectually induce me so to
acquiesce, than your company, dear Doctor. A tolerant liberality
like yours has a very persuasive influence.

From this digression, the two friends proceeded to the arrangement
of their Aristophanic comedy, and divided their respective shares
after the manner of Beaumont and Fletcher.

CHAPTER X

Si bene calculum ponas, ubique naufragium est.   PETRONIUS ARBITER.[2]

If you consider well the events of life, shipwreck is everywhere.

AFTER luncheon the Doctor thought of returning home, when a
rumbling of distant thunder made him pause. They reascended the
tower, to reconnoitre the elements from the library. The windows
were so arranged as to afford a panoramic view.

[1] Martin (Luther), Peter (Pope of Rome) and Jack (Calvin) are the
triplet brothers and chief characters of Swift's *A Tale of a Tub*. G.
[2] *Satyr*. G.

The thunder muttered far off, but there was neither rain nor visible lightning.

" The storm is at a great distance," said the Doctor, "and it seems to be passing away on the verge of the sky."

But on the opposite horizon appeared a mass of dark-blue cloud, which rose rapidly, and advanced in the direct line of the Tower. Before it rolled a lighter but still lurid volume of vapour, which curled and wreathed like eddying smoke before the denser blackness of the unbroken cloud.

Simultaneously followed the flashing of lightning, the rolling of thunder, and a deluge of rain like the bursting of a waterspout.

They sate some time in silence, watching the storm as it swept along, with wind, and driving rain, and whirling hail, bringing for a time almost the darkness of night, through which the forked lightning poured a scarcely interrupted blaze.

Suddenly came a long dazzling flash, that seemed to irradiate the entire circumference of the sky, followed instantaneously by one of those crashing peals of thunder, which always indicate that something very near has been struck by the lightning.

The Doctor turned round to make a remark on the awful grandeur of the effect, when he observed that his young friend had disappeared. On his return, he said he had been looking for what had been struck.

" And what was ? " said the Doctor.

" Nothing in the house," said his host.

" The Vestals," thought the Doctor ; " these were all his solicitude."

But though Mr. Falconer had looked no further than to the safety of the seven sisters, his attention was soon drawn to a tumult below, which seemed to indicate that some serious mischief had resulted from the lightning ; and the youngest of the sisters, appearing in great trepidation, informed him that one of two horses in a gentleman's carriage had been struck dead, and that a young lady in the carriage had been stunned by the passing flash, though how far she was injured by it could not be immediately known. The other horse, it appeared, had been prancing in terror, and had nearly overthrown the carriage ; but he had been restrained by the vigorous arm of a young farmer, who had subsequently carried the young lady into the house, where she was now resting on a couch in the female apartments, and carefully attended by the sisters.

Mr. Falconer and the Doctor descended into the hall, and were assured that the young lady was doing well, but that she would be much the better for being left some time longer undisturbed. An elderly gentleman issued from the female apartments, and the Doctor with some amazement recognised his friend Mr. Gryll, to whom and his niece this disaster had occurred.

The beauty of the morning had tempted them to a long drive ; and they thought it would be a good opportunity to gratify at least a portion of the curiosity which the Doctor's description of the Folly and its inhabitants had excited in them. They had therefore determined on taking a circuit, in which they would pass under the walls of the Tower. They were almost at the extremity of their longest radius when the storm burst over them, and were just under the Tower when the lightning struck one of their horses. Harry Hedgerow was on his way with some farm produce when the accident occurred, and was the young farmer who had subdued the surviving horse and carried the young lady into the house. Mr. Gryll was very panegyrical of this young man's behaviour, and the Doctor when he recognised him shook him heartily by the hand, and told him he felt sure that he was a lad who would make his way : a remark which Harry received as a good omen : for Dorothy heard it, and looked at him with a concurrent, though silent, approbation.

The drawing-room and the chambers for visitors were between the tower and the *gynæceum*, or female apartments, which were as completely separated from the rest of the house as they could have been in Athens.

After some anxious inquiries, it was reported that the young lady was sleeping, and that one or other of the sisters would keep constant watch by her. It was therefore arranged that Mr. Gryll should dine and pass the night where he was. Before dinner he had the satisfaction of hearing from medical authority that all would be well after a little time.

Harry Hedgerow had bethought him of a retired physician, who lived with a maiden sister in a cottage at no great distance from the Tower, and who often gave gratuitous advice to his poorer neigh-

bours. If he prescribed anything beyond their means, himself or his
sister was always ready to supply it. Though their own means were
limited, they were the good angels of a small circumference.

The old physician confirmed the opinion already given by the
sisters, that the young lady for the present only required repose :
but he accepted the invitation to remain till the morning, in the
event of his advice being needed.

So Miss Gryll remained with the elder sisters. Mr. Gryll and the
two Doctors, spiritual and temporal, sat down to dinner with Mr.
Falconer, and were waited on, as usual, by the younger handmaids.

CHAPTER XI

Οἴνου μὴ παρεόντος, ἀτερπέα δεῖπνα τραπέζης·
Οἴνου μὴ παρεόντος, ἀθελγέες εἰσὶ χορεῖαι.
Ἀνὴρ πένθος ἔχων, ὅτε γεύσεται ἡδέος οἴνου,
Στυγνὸν ἀεξομένης ἀποσείσεται ὄγκον ἀνίης.

Where wine is not, no mirth the banquet knows :
Where wine is not, the dance all joyless goes.
The man, oppressed with cares, who tastes the bowl,
Shall shake the weight of sorrow from his soul.
        BACCHUS, on the birth of the vine, predicting its benefits :
           in the twelfth book of the *Dionysiaca* of NONNUS.

THE conversation at dinner turned on the occurrences of the morning
and the phenomena of electricity. The physician, who had been
a traveller, related many anecdotes from his own observation ;
especially such as tended to show by similarity that the injury to
Miss Gryll would not be of long duration. He had known, in similar
cases, instances of apparent total paralysis ; but he had always found
it temporary. Perhaps in a day or two, but at most in a very few
days, it would certainly pass away. In the meantime, he recommended absolute repose. Mr. Falconer entreated Mr. Gryll to consider the house as his own. Matters were arranged accordingly ;
and it was determined that the next morning a messenger should be
despatched to Gryll Grange for a supply of apparel. The Reverend
Dr. Opimian, who was as fond as the Squire himself of the young
lady, had been grievously discomposed by the accident of the morning, and felt that he should not thoroughly recover his serenity till he

could again see her in her proper character, the light and life of her society. He quoted Homer, Æschylus, Aristotle, Plutarch, Athenæus, Horace, Persius, and Pliny, to show that all which is practically worth knowing on the subject of electricity had been known to the ancients. The electric telegraph he held to be a nuisance, as disarranging chronology, and giving only the heads of a chapter, of which the details lost their interest before they arrived, the heads of another chapter having intervened to destroy it. Then, what an amount of misery it inflicted, when, merely saying that there had been a great battle, and that thousands had been wounded or killed, it maintained an agony of suspense in all who had friends on the field, till the ordinary channels of intelligence brought the names of the sufferers. No Sicilian tyrant had invented such an engine of cruelty. This declamation against a supposed triumph of modern science, which was listened to with some surprise by the physician, and with great respect by his other auditors, having somewhat soothed his troubled spirit, in conjunction with the physician's assurance, he propitiated his Genius by copious libations of claret, pronouncing high panegyrics on the specimen before him, and interspersing quotations in praise of wine, as the one great panacea for the cares of this world.

A week passed away and the convalescent had made good progress. Mr. Falconer had not yet seen his fair guest. Six of the sisters, one remaining with Miss Gryll, performed every evening, at the earnest request of Mr. Gryll, a great variety of music, but always ending with the hymn to their master's saint. The old physician came once or twice and stayed the night. The Reverend Doctor Opimian went home for his Sunday duties, but took too much interest in the fair Morgana not to return as soon as he could to the Tower. Arriving one morning in the first division of the day, and ascending to the library, he found his young friend writing. He asked him if he were working on the Aristophanic comedy ? Mr. Falconer said, he got on best with that in the Doctor's company. "But I have been writing," he said, " on something connected with the Athenian drama. I have been writing a ballad on the death of Philemon, as told by Suidas and Apuleius." The Doctor expressed a wish to hear it, and Mr. Falconer read it to him.

THE DEATH OF PHILEMON [1]

I

Closed was Philemon's hundredth year :
The theatre was thronged to hear
 His last completed play :
In the mid scene, a sudden rain
Dispersed the crowd—to meet again
 On the succeeding day.

He sought his home, and slept, and dreamed,
Nine maidens through his door, it seemed,
 Passed to the public street.
He asked them, " Why they left his home ? "
They said, " A guest will hither come,
 We must not stay to meet."

He called his boy with morning light,
Told him the vision of the night,
 And bade his play be brought.
His finished page again he scanned,
Resting his head upon his hand,
 Absorbed in studious thought.

He knew not what the dream foreshowed :
That nought divine may hold abode
 Where death's dark shade is felt :
And therefore were the Muses nine
Leaving the old poetic shrine,
 Where they so long had dwelt.

II

The theatre was thronged once more,
More thickly than the day before,
 To hear the half-heard song.
The day wore on. Impatience came.
They called upon Philemon's name,
 With murmurs loud and long.

Some sought at length his studious cell,
And to the stage returned, to tell
 What thousands strove to ask.
" The poet we have been to seek
Sate with his hand upon his cheek,
 As pondering o'er his task.

---

[1] Suidas : *sub voce Φιλήμων*. Apuleius : *Florid*. 16. [P.]

" We spoke. He made us no reply.
We reverentially drew nigh,
          And twice our errand told.
He answered not.   We drew more near :
The awful mystery then was clear :
          We found him stiff and cold.

" Struck by so fair a death, we stood
Awhile in sad admiring mood ;
          Then hastened back, to say
That he, the praised and loved of all,
Is deaf for ever to your call :
          That on this self-same day,

" When here presented should have been
The close of his fictitious scene,
          His life's true scene was o'er :
We seemed, in solemn silence awed,
To hear the ' Farewell and applaud,'
          Which he may speak no more.

" Of tears the rain gave prophecy :
The nuptial dance of comedy
          Yields to the funeral train.
Assemble where his pyre must burn :
Honour his ashes in their urn :
And on another day return
          To hear his songs again."

THE REVEREND DOCTOR OPIMIAN.   A beautiful fiction.

MR. FALCONER. If it be a fiction. The supernatural is confined
to the dream. All the rest is probable ; and I am willing to think
it true, dream and all.

THE REVEREND DOCTOR OPIMIAN.   You are determined to connect
the immaterial with the material world, as far as you can.

MR. FALCONER. I like the immaterial world. I like to live among
thoughts and images of the past and the possible, and even of the
impossible, now and then.

THE REVEREND DOCTOR OPIMIAN.   Certainly, there is much in the
material world to displease sensitive and imaginative minds ; but I
do not know any one who has less cause to complain of it than you
have. You are surrounded with all possible comforts, and with all
the elements of beauty, and of intellectual enjoyment.

MR. FALCONER. It is not my own world that I complain of. It is the world on which I look " from the loop-holes of retreat." [1] I cannot sit here, like one of the Gods of Epicurus, who, as Cicero says, was satisfied with thinking, through all eternity, " how comfortable he was." [2] I look with feelings of intense pain on the mass of poverty and crime ; of unhealthy, unavailing, unremunerated toil, blighting childhood in its blossom, and womanhood in its prime ; of " all the oppressions that are done under the sun." [3]

THE REVEREND DOCTOR OPIMIAN. I feel with you on all these points ; but there is much good in the world ; more good than evil, I have always maintained.

They would have gone off in a discussion on this point, but the French clock warned them to luncheon.

In the evening the young lady was sufficiently recovered to join the little party in the drawing-room, which consisted, as before, of Mr. Falconer, Mr. Gryll, Doctor Anodyne, and the Reverend Doctor Opimian. Miss Gryll was introduced to Mr. Falconer. She was full of grateful encomium for the kind attention of the sisters, and expressed an earnest desire to hear their music. The wish was readily complied with. She heard them with great pleasure, and, though not yet equal to much exertion, she could not refrain from joining in with them in their hymn to Saint Catharine.

She accompanied them when they retired.

THE REVEREND DOCTOR OPIMIAN. I presume those Latin words are genuine old monastic verses : they have all the air of it.

MR. FALCONER. They are so, and they are adapted to old music.

DOCTOR ANODYNE. There is something in this hymn very solemn and impressive. In an age like ours, in which music and pictures are the predominant tastes, I do not wonder that the forms of the old

[1] Cowper : *The Task*, Bk. IV (*The Winter Evening*). G.

[2] Comprehende igitur animo, et propone ante oculos, deum nihil aliud in omni æternitate, nisi, Mihi pulchre est, et, Ego beatus sum, cogitantem.— Cicero : *De Naturâ Deorum*, l. i. c. 41. [P.] [" Imagine then, in your mind's eye, a God who through all eternity had no thought but, 'Things are well with me,' and ' I am well content.' " G.]

[3] *Ecclesiastes*, iv, 1. G.

Catholic worship are received with increasing favour. There is a sort of adhesion to the old religion, which results less from faith than from a certain feeling of poetry ; it finds its disciples ; but it is of modern growth ; and has very essential differences from what it outwardly resembles.

THE REVEREND DOCTOR OPIMIAN. It is, as I have frequently had occasion to remark, and as my young friend here will readily admit, one of the many forms of the love of ideal beauty, which, without being in itself religion, exerts on vivid imaginations an influence that is very often like it.

MR. FALCONER. An orthodox English Churchman was the poet who sang to the Virgin :

> Thy image falls to earth. Yet some, I ween,
> Not unforgiven the suppliant knee might bend,
> As to a visible Power, in which did blend
> All that was mixed and reconciled in thee,
> Of mother's love with maiden purity,
> Of high with low, celestial with terrene.[1]

THE REVEREND DOCTOR OPIMIAN. Well, my young friend, the love of ideal beauty has exercised none but a benignant influence on you, whatever degree of orthodoxy there may be in your view of it.

The little party separated for the night.

CHAPTER XII

> Τί δεῖ γὰρ ὄντα θνητόν, ἱκετεύω, ποιεῖν,
> Πλὴν ἡδέως ζῆν τὸν βίον καθ' ἡμέραν,
> Ἐὰν ἔχῃ τις ὁπόθεν . . . .
> Εἰς αὔριον δὲ μηδὲ φροντίζειν ὅ τι
> Ἔσται . . .
>
> PHILETAERUS : *Cynagis.*[2]

> I pray you, what can mortal man do better,
> Than live his daily life as pleasantly
> As daily means avail him ? Life's frail tenure
> Warns not to trust to-morrow.

THE next day Mr. Falconer was perfectly certain that Miss Gryll was not yet well enough to be removed. No one was anxious to refute the proposition ; they were all so well satisfied with the place and the company they were in, that they felt, the young lady included, a

---

[1] Wordsworth, *Ecclesiastical Sonnets*, i. 21. [P.] [Actually ii, 25. G.]
[2] Op. Meinecke. Com. Fragm. iii. 292. G.

decided unwillingness to go. That day Miss Gryll came to dinner, and the next day she came to breakfast, and in the evening she joined in the music, and in short she was once more altogether herself; but Mr. Falconer continued to insist that the journey home would be too much for her. When this excuse failed, he still entreated his new friends to remain; and so passed several days. At length Mr. Gryll found he must resolve on departing, especially as the time had arrived when he expected some visitors. He urgently invited Mr. Falconer to visit him in return. The invitation was cordially accepted, and in the meantime considerable progress had been made in the Aristophanic comedy.

Mr. Falconer, after the departure of his visitors, went up into his library. He took down one book after another, but they did not fix his attention as they had used to do; he turned over the leaves of Homer, and read some passages about Circe; then took down Bojardo, and read of Morgana and Falerina and Dragontina; then took down Tasso and read of Armida. He would not look at Ariosto's Alcina, because her change into an old woman destroyed all the charm of the previous picture. He dwelt on the enchantresses who remained in unaltered beauty. But even this he did only by fits and starts, and found himself continually wandering away towards a more enchanting reality.

He descended to his bedroom, and meditated on ideal beauty in the portraits of Saint Catharine. But he could not help thinking that the ideal might be real, at least in one instance, and he wandered down into his drawing-room. There he sat absorbed in thought, till his two young handmaids appeared with his luncheon. He smiled when he saw them, and sat down to the table as if nothing had disturbed him. Then, taking his stick and his dog, he walked out into the forest.

There was within moderate distance a deep dell, in the bottom of which ran a rivulet, very small in dry weather, but in heavy rains becoming a torrent, which had worn itself a high-banked channel, winding in fantastic curves from side to side of its narrow boundaries. Above this channel old forest trees rose to a great height on both sides of the dell. The slope every here and there was broken by promontories which during centuries the fall of the softer portions

of the soil had formed ; and on these promontories were natural
platforms, covered, as they were more or less accessible to the sun,
with grass and moss and fern and foxglove, and every variety of forest
vegetation. These platforms were favourite resorts of deer, which
imparted to the wild scene its own peculiar life.

This was a scene in which, but for the deeper and deeper wear of
the floods and the bolder falls of the promontories, time had made
little change. The eyes of the twelfth century had seen it much as it
appeared to those of the nineteenth. The ghosts of departed ages
might seem to pass through it in succession, with all their changes
of faith and purpose and manners and costume. To a man who
loved to dwell in the past, there could not be a more congenial scene.
One old oak stood in the centre of one of the green platforms, and
a portion of its gnarled roots presented a convenient seat. Mr.
Falconer had frequently passed a day here when alone. The deer
had become too accustomed to him to fly at his approach, and the
dog had been too well disciplined to molest them. There he had
sat for hours at a time, reading his favourite poets. There was no
great poet with some of whose scenes this scenery did not harmonize.
The deep woods that surrounded the dwelling of Circe, the obscure
sylvan valley in which Dante met Virgil, the forest depths through
which Angelica fled, the enchanted wood in which Rinaldo met the
semblance of Armida, the forest-brook by which Jaques moralized
over the wounded deer,[1] were all reproduced in this single spot, and
fancy peopled it at pleasure with nymphs and genii, fauns and
satyrs, knights and ladies, friars, foresters, hunters, and huntress
maids, till the whole diurnal world seemed to pass away like a vision.[2]
There, for him, Matilda had gathered flowers on the opposite bank ; [3]
Laura had risen from one of the little pools—resting-places of the
stream—to seat herself in the shade ; [4] Rosalind and Maid Marian

---

[1] *As You Like It*, Act II, Sc. 1.　G.

[2] See quotation from Peacock's diary, p. 439.　G.

[3] Dante: *Purgatorio*, c. 28.　[P.]　[The only passage in the *Divina
Commedia* which Shelley translated.　G.]

[4]　Or in forma di Ninfa o d' altra Diva,
　　Che del più chiaro fondo di Sorga esca,
　　E pongasi a seder in sulla riva.

　　　　　　　　　Petrarca : *Sonetto* 240.　[P.]

["Now in the form of nymph, or other goddess, issuing from the clearest
depths of the Sorga and sitting down upon its bank."　G.]

had peeped forth from their alleys green ; all different in form, in feature, and in apparel ; but now they were all one ; each, as she rose in imagination, presented herself under the aspect of the newly-known Morgana.

Finding his old imaginations thus disturbed, he arose and walked home. He dined alone, drank a bottle of Madeira as if it had been so much water, summoned the seven sisters to the drawing-room earlier, and detained them later than usual, till their music and its old associations had restored him to something like tranquillity. He had always placed the *summum bonum* of life in tranquillity and not in excitement. He felt that his path was now crossed by a disturbing force, and determined to use his utmost exertions to avoid exposing himself again to its influence.

In this mood the Reverend Doctor Opimian found him one morning in the library, reading. He sprang up to meet the divine, exclaiming, " Ah, dear Doctor, I am very glad to see you. Have you any especial favourite among the Odes of Pindar ? "

The Doctor thought this an odd question for the first salutation. He had expected that the first inquiry would have been for the fair convalescent. He divined that the evasion of this subject was the result of an inward struggle. He thought it would be best to fall in with the mood of the questioner, and said, " Charles Fox's favourite is said to have been the second Olympic ; I am not sure that there is, or can be, anything better. What say you ? "

MR. FALCONER. It may be that something in it touches a peculiar tone of feeling ; but to me there is nothing like the ninth Pythian.

THE REVEREND DOCTOR OPIMIAN. I can understand your fancy for that ode. You see an image of ideal beauty in the nymph Cyrene.

MR. FALCONER. " Hidden are the keys of wise persuasion of sacred endearments," [1] seems a strange phrase in English ; but in Greek the words invest a charming sentiment with singular grace. Fit words

---

[1] Κρυπταὶ κλαῖδες εντὶ σοφα Πειθοῦς ἱερᾶν φιλοτάτων. [P.]
[*Pyth.* 69–70. Pindar's recent translators, H. T. Wade-Gery and C. M. Bowra, render this passage : " They are secret keys with which Persuasion knows how to unlock the sanctuaries of love." Pindar's *Pythian Odes* (Nonesuch Press, 1928). G.]

to words as closely as we may, the difference of the mind which utters them fails to reproduce the true semblance of the thought. The difference of the effect, produced, as in this instance, by exactly corresponding words, can only be traced to the essential difference of the Greek and the English mind.

THE REVEREND DOCTOR OPIMIAN. And indeed, as with the words so with the image. We are charmed by Cyrene wrestling with the lion ; but we should scarcely choose an English girl so doing as the type of ideal beauty.

MR. FALCONER. We must draw the image of Cyrene, not from an English girl, but from a Greek statue.

THE REVEREND DOCTOR OPIMIAN. Unless a man is in love, and then to him all images of beauty take something of the form and features of his mistress.

MR. FALCONER. That is to say, a man in love sees everything through a false medium. It must be a dreadful calamity to be in love.

THE REVEREND DOCTOR OPIMIAN. Surely not, when all goes well with it.

MR. FALCONER. To me it would be the worst of all mischances.

THE REVEREND DOCTOR OPIMIAN. Every man must be subject to Love once in his life. It is useless to contend with him. " Love," says Sophocles, " is unconquered in battle, and keeps his watch in the soft cheeks of beauty." [1]

MR. FALCONER. I am afraid, Doctor, the Morgana to whom you have introduced me is a veritable enchantress. You find me here, determined to avoid the spell.

THE REVEREND DOCTOR OPIMIAN. Pardon me. You were introduced, as Jupiter was to Semele, by thunder and lightning, which was, happily, not quite as fatal.

MR. FALCONER. I must guard against its being as fatal in a

[1] Ἔρως ἀνίκατε μάχαν, κ.τ.λ.—Antigone. [P.] [781. G.]

different sense ; otherwise I may be myself the *triste bidental*.[1]
I have aimed at living, like an ancient Epicurean, a life of tranquillity. I had thought myself armed with triple brass against the
folds of a three-formed Chimera. What with classical studies, and
rural walks, and a domestic society peculiarly my own, I led what
I considered the perfection of life : " days so like each other they
could not be remembered." [2]

THE REVEREND DOCTOR OPIMIAN.   It is vain to make schemes of
life. The world will have its slaves, and so will Love.

> Say, if you can, in what you cannot change.
> For such the mind of man, as is the day
> The Sire of Gods and men brings over him.[3]

MR. FALCONER.   I presume, Doctor, from the complacency with
which you speak of Love, you have had no cause to complain of him.

THE REVEREND DOCTOR OPIMIAN.   Quite the contrary. I have
been an exception to the rule that " The course of true love never
did run smooth." [4]   Nothing could run more smooth than mine.
I was in love. I proposed. I was accepted. No crossings before.
No bickerings after. I drew a prize in the lottery of marriage.

MR. FALCONER.   It strikes me, Doctor, that the lady may say as
much.

THE REVEREND DOCTOR OPIMIAN.   I have made it my study to
give her cause to say so. And I have found my reward.

MR. FALCONER.   Still, yours is an exceptional case. For, as far as
my reading and limited observation have shown me, there are few
happy marriages. It has been said by an old comic poet, that " a

---

[1] *Bidental* is usually a place struck by lightning : thence enclosed, and
the soil forbidden to be moved.   Persius uses it for a person so killed. [P.]
[2] Wordsworth : *The Brothers.* [P.]
[3] Quid placet aut odio est, quod non mutabile credas ? [Horace :
Ep. II. i. 101. G.]

> Τοῖος γὰρ νόος ἐστὶν ἐπιχθονίων ἀνθρώπων,
> Οἷον ἐπ᾽ ἦμαρ ἄγῃσι πατὴρ ἀνδρῶν τε θεῶν τε.
> [Homer : *Od.* XVIII. 136–7. G.]

These two quotations form the motto of Knight's *Principles of Taste.* [P.]
[4] *A Midsummer Night's Dream*, Act I, Sc. 1. G.

man, who brings a wife into his house, brings into it with her either a good or an evil genius." [1] And I may add from Juvenal : " The Gods only know which it will be." [2]

THE REVEREND DOCTOR OPIMIAN. Well, the time advances for the rehearsals of our Aristophanic comedy, and independently of your promise to visit the Grange, and their earnest desire to see you, you ought to be there to assist in the preliminary arrangements.

MR. FALCONER. Before you came, I had determined not to go ; for to tell you the truth, I am afraid of falling in love.

THE REVEREND DOCTOR OPIMIAN. It is not such a fearful matter. Many have been the better for it. Many have been cured of it. It is one of those disorders which every one must have once.

MR. FALCONER. The later the better.

THE REVEREND DOCTOR OPIMIAN. No ; the later the worse, if it falls into a season when it cannot be reciprocated.

MR. FALCONER. That is just the season for it. If I were sure it would not be reciprocated, I think I should be content to have gone through it.

THE REVEREND DOCTOR OPIMIAN. Do you think it would be reciprocated ?

MR. FALCONER. Oh! no. I only think it possible that it might be.

THE REVEREND DOCTOR OPIMIAN. Well, there is a gentleman doing his best to bring about your wish.

---

[1] Ὅταν γὰρ ἄλοχον εἰς δόμους ἄγῃ πόσις,
Οὐχ ὡς-δοκεῖ γυναῖκα λαμβάνει μόνον,
Ὁμοῦ δὲ τῇδ' ἐπεισκομίζεται λαβὼν
Καὶ δαίμον' ἤτοι χρηστὸν ἢ τοὐναντίον.
Theodectes : *apud Stobaeum.* [P.]
[Flor. LXIX. G.]

[2] Conjugium petimus partumque uxoris, at illis
Notum, qui pueri, qualisque futura sit uxor.
Juv. *Sat.* x. 352–3. [P.]
[" We crave for marriage and offspring, but it is They who know what our children and what our wife will be." G.]

MR. FALCONER. Indeed! Who?

THE REVEREND DOCTOR OPIMIAN. A visitor at the Grange, who seems in great favour with both uncle and niece—Lord Curryfin.

MR. FALCONER. Lord Curryfin! I never heard you speak of him, but as a person to be laughed at.

THE REVEREND DOCTOR OPIMIAN. That was my impression of him, before I knew him. Barring his absurdities, in the way of lecturing on fish, and of shining in absurd company in the science of panto-pragmatics, he has very much to recommend him : and I discover in him one quality which is invaluable. He does all he can to make himself agreeable to all about him, and he has great tact in seeing how to do it. In any intimate relation of life—with a reasonable wife, for instance, he would be the pink of a good husband.

The Doctor was playing, not altogether unconsciously, the part of an innocent Iago. He said only what was true, and he said it with a good purpose ; for with all his repeated resolutions against match-making, he could not dismiss from his mind the wish to see his young friends come together ; and he would not have liked to see Lord Curryfin carry off the prize through Mr. Falconer's neglect of his opportunity. Jealousy being the test of love, he thought a spice of it might be not unseasonably thrown in.

MR. FALCONER. Notwithstanding your example, Doctor, love is to be avoided, because marriage is at best a dangerous experiment. The experience of all time demonstrates that it is seldom a happy condition. Jupiter and Juno, to begin with ; Venus and Vulcan. Fictions, to be sure, but they show Homer's view of the conjugal state. Agamemnon in the shades, though he congratulates Ulysses on his good fortune in having an excellent wife, advises him not to trust even her too far. Come down to realities, even to the masters of the wise : Socrates with Xantippe ; Euripides with his two wives, who made him a woman-hater ; Cicero, who was divorced ; Marcus Aurelius.—Travel downwards : Dante, who, when he left Florence, left his wife behind him ; Milton, whose first wife ran away from him ; Shakspeare, who scarcely shines in the light of a happy husband.

And if such be the lot of the lights of the world, what can humbler men expect ?

THE REVEREND DOCTOR OPIMIAN. You have given two or three heads of a catalogue which, I admit, might be largely extended. You can never read a history, you can never open a newspaper, without seeing some example of unhappy marriage. But the conspicuous are not the frequent. In the quiet path of everyday life—the *secretum iter et fallentis semita vitæ*—I could show you many couples who are really comforts and helpmates to each other. Then, above all things, children. The great blessing of old age, the one that never fails, if all else fail, is a daughter.

MR. FALCONER. All daughters are not good.

THE REVEREND DOCTOR OPIMIAN. Most are. Of all relations in life, it is the least disappointing : where parents do not so treat their daughters as to alienate their affections, which unhappily many do.

MR. FALCONER. You do not say so much for sons.

THE REVEREND DOCTOR OPIMIAN. Young men are ambitious, self-willed, self-indulgent, easily corrupted by bad example, of which there is always too much. I cannot say much for those of the present day, though it is not absolutely destitute of good specimens.

MR. FALCONER. You know what Paterculus says of those of his own day.

THE REVEREND DOCTOR OPIMIAN. "The faith of wives towards the proscribed was great ; of freed-men, middling ; of slaves, some ; of sons, none." [1] So he says ; but there were some : for example, of the sons of Marcus Oppius and Quintus Cicero. [2] You may observe, by the way, he gives the first place to the wives.

[1] Id tamen notandum est, fuisse in proscriptos uxorum fidem summam, libertorum mediam, servorum aliquam, filiqrum nullam.—Paterculus : l. ii. c. 67. [P.]

[2] A compendious and comprehensive account of these and other instances of filial piety, in the proscription of the second triumvirate, will be found in *Freinshemius ; Supplementa Liviana*, cxx. 77–80. [P.]

MR. FALCONER. Well, that is a lottery in which every man must take his chance. But my scheme of life was perfect.

THE REVEREND DOCTOR OPIMIAN. Perhaps there is something to be said against condemning seven young women to celibacy.

MR. FALCONER. But if such were their choice——

THE REVEREND DOCTOR OPIMIAN. No doubt there are many reasons why they should prefer the condition they are placed in to the ordinary chances of marriage : but after all, to be married is the natural aspiration of a young woman, and if favourable conditions presented themselves——

MR. FALCONER. Conditions suitable to their education are scarcely compatible with their social position.

THE REVEREND DOCTOR OPIMIAN. They have been educated to be both useful and ornamental. The ornamental need not, and in their case certainly does not, damage the useful, which in itself would procure them suitable matches.

Mr. Falconer shook his head, and after a brief pause poured out a volume of quotations, demonstrating the general unhappiness of marriage. The Doctor responded by as many demonstrating the contrary. He paused to take breath. Both laughed heartily. But the result of the discussion and the laughter was, that Mr. Falconer was curious to see Lord Curryfin, and would therefore go to Gryll Grange.

CHAPTER XIII

Ille potens sui
Laetusque deget, cui licet in diem
Dixisse, Vixi : cras vel atrâ
Nube polum pater occupato,
Vel sole puro : non tamen irritum
Quodcumque retro est efficiet ; neque
Diffinget infectumque reddet,
Quod fugiens semel hora vexit.

HOR. *Carm.* iii. 29.

Happy the man, and happy he alone,
He who can call to-day his own :
He who, secure within, can say,
To-morrow do thy worst, for I have lived to-day.
Be storm, or calm, or rain, or shine,
The joys I have possessed in spite of fate are mine.
Not heaven itself upon the past has power,
But what has been has been, and I have had my hour.

DRYDEN.

A LARGE party was assembled at the Grange. Among them were
some of the young ladies who were to form the chorus ; one elderly
spinster, Miss Ilex, who passed more than half her life in visits, and
was everywhere welcome, being always good-humoured, agreeable in
conversation, having much knowledge of society, good sense in
matters of conduct, good taste and knowledge in music ; sound
judgment in dress, which alone sufficed to make her valuable to young
ladies ; a fair amount of reading, old and new ; and on most subjects
an opinion of her own, for which she had always something to say ;
Mr. MacBorrowdale, an old friend of Mr. Gryll, a gentleman who
comprised in himself all that Scotland had ever been supposed to
possess of mental, moral, and political philosophy ; " And yet he
bore it not about ; " not " as being loth to wear it out," [1] but
because he held that there was a time for all things, and that dinner
was the time for joviality, and not for argument ; Mr. Minim, the
amateur composer of the music for the comedy ; Mr. Pallet, the

---

[1] We grant, although he had much wit,
    He was very shy of using it,
    As being loth to wear it out ;
    And therefore bore it not about,
    Except on holidays or so,
    As men their best apparel do.
        Hudibras. [P.] [Pt. I, Canto I, lines 45–50. G.]

amateur painter of the scenery ; and last, not least, the newly-made acquaintance, Lord Curryfin.

Lord Curryfin was a man on the younger side of thirty, with a good person, handsome features, a powerful voice, and an agreeable delivery. He had a strong memory, much power of application, and a facility of learning rapidly whatever he turned his mind to. But with all this, he valued what he learned less for the pleasure which he derived from the acquisition, than from the effect which it enabled him to produce on others. He liked to shine in conversation, and there was scarcely a subject which could be mooted in any society, on which his multifarious attainments did not qualify him to say something. He was readily taken by novelty in doctrine, and followed a new lead with great pertinacity ; and in this way he had been caught by the science of pantopragmatics, and firmly believed for a time that a scientific organization for teaching everybody everything, would cure all the evils of society. But being one of those " over sharp wits whose edges are very soon turned," he did not adhere to any opinion with sufficient earnestness to be on any occasion betrayed into intemperance in maintaining it. So far from this, if he found any unfortunate opinion in a hopeless minority of the company he happened to be in, he was often chivalrous enough to come to its aid, and see what could be said for it. When lecturing became a mania, he had taken to lecturing ; and looking about for an unoccupied subject, he had lighted on the natural history of fish, in which he soon became sufficiently proficient to amuse the ladies, and astonish the fishermen in any seaside place of fashionable resort. Here he always arranged his lecture-room, so that the gentility of his audience could sit on a platform, and the natives in a gallery above, and that thus the fishy and tarry odours which the latter were most likely to bring with them, might ascend into the upper air, and not mingle with the more delicate fragrances that surrounded the select company below. He took a summer tour to several watering-places, and was thoroughly satisfied with his success. The fishermen at first did not take cordially to him ; but their wives attended from curiosity, and brought their husbands with them on nights not favourable to fishing ; and by degrees he won on their attention, and they took pleasure in hearing him, though they learned nothing from him that was of any use in their trade. But he seemed to exalt their art in the eyes of themselves and others, and he told them some pleasant anecdotes of strange fish, and of perilous adventures of some of their own craft, which led in due time to the crowding of his gallery. The ladies went, as they always will go, to lectures, where they fancy they learn something, whether they learn anything or not ; and on these occasions, not merely to hear the lecturer, but to be seen by him. To them, however attractive the lecture might have been, the lecturer was more so. He was an irresistible tempta-tion to matrons with marriageable daughters, and wherever he sojourned he was overwhelmed with invitations. It was a contest who should have him to dinner, and in the simplicity of his heart, he ascribed to admiration of his science and eloquence, all the courtesies and compliments with which he was everywhere received. He did not like to receive unreturned favours, and never left a place in which he had accepted many invitations, without giving in return a ball and supper on a scale of great munificence ; which filled up the measure of his popularity, and left on all his guests a very enduring impression of a desire to see him again.

So his time passed pleasantly, with a heart untouched by either love or care, till he fell in at a dinner party with the Reverend Doctor Opimian. The Doctor spoke of Gryll Grange and the Aristo-phanic comedy which was to be produced at Christmas, and Lord Curryfin, with his usual desire to have a finger in every pie, expressed an earnest wish to be introduced to the Squire. This was no difficult matter. The Doctor had quickly brought it about, and Lord Curryfin had gone over in the Doctor's company to pass a few days at the Grange. Here, in a very short time, he had made himself completely at home ; and had taken on himself the office of architect, to super-intend the construction of the theatre, receiving with due deference instructions on the subject from the Reverend Doctor Opimian.

Sufficient progress had been made in the comedy for the painter and musician to begin work on their respective portions ; and Lord Curryfin, whose heart was in his work, passed whole mornings in indefatigable attention to the progress of the building. It was near the house, and was to be approached by a covered way. It was a miniature of the Athenian theatre, from which it differed in having a roof, but it resembled it in the arrangements of the stage and orchestra, and in the graduated series of semicircular seats for the audience.

When dinner was announced, Mr. Gryll took in Miss Ilex. Miss Gryll, of course, took the arm of Lord Curryfin. Mr. Falconer took in one of the young ladies and placed her on the left hand of the host. The Reverend Doctor Opimian took in another, and was consequently seated between her and Miss Ilex. Mr. Falconer was thus as far removed as possible from the young lady of the house, and was consequently, though he struggled as much as possible against it, frequently *distrait*, unconsciously and unwillingly observing Miss Gryll and Lord Curryfin, and making occasional observations very wide of the mark to the fair damsels on his right and left, who set him down in their minds for a very odd young man. The soup and fish were discussed in comparative silence ; the entrées not much otherwise ; but suddenly a jubilant expression from Mr. MacBorrowdale hailed the disclosure of a large sirloin of beef which figured before Mr. Gryll.

MR. MACBORROWDALE. You are a man of taste, Mr. Gryll. That is a handsomer ornament of a dinner-table than clusters of nosegays, and all sorts of uneatable decorations. I detest and abominate the idea of a Siberian dinner,[1] where you just look on fiddle-faddles, while your dinner is behind a screen, and you are served with rations like a pauper.

THE REVEREND DOCTOR OPIMIAN. I quite agree with Mr. MacBorrowdale. I like to see my dinner. And herein I rejoice to have Addison on my side ; for I remember a paper, in which he objects to having roast beef placed on a sideboard. Even in his day it had been displaced to make way for some incomprehensible French dishes, among which he could find nothing to eat.[2] I do not know what he

[1] The practice of carving at a sideboard behind a Russian screen (or iron curtain) was called dining *à la Russe*. Mr. MacBorrowdale called it Siberian as the joint had been sent into exile. G.

[2] I was now in great hunger and confusion, when I thought I smelled the agreeable savour of roast beef ; but could not tell from which dish it arose, though I did not question but it lay disguised in one of them. Upon turning my head I saw a noble sirloin on the side-table, smoking in the

would have said to its being placed altogether out of sight. Still there is something to be said on the other side. There is hardly one gentleman in twenty who knows how to carve; and as to ladies, though they did know once on a time, they do not now. What can be more pitiable than the right-hand man of the lady of the house, awkward enough in himself, with the dish twisted round to him in the most awkward possible position, digging in unutterable mortification for a joint which he cannot find, and wishing the unanatomisable *volaille* behind a Russian screen with the footmen?

MR. MACBORROWDALE. I still like to see the *volaille*. It might be put on table with its joints divided.

MR. GRYLL. As that turkey-poult is, Mr. MacBorrowdale; which gives my niece no trouble; but the precaution is not necessary with such a right-hand man as Lord Curryfin, who carves to perfection.

MR. MACBORROWDALE. Your arrangements are perfect. At the last of these Siberian dinners at which I had the misfortune to be present, I had offered me, for two of my rations, the tail of a mullet and the drum-stick of a fowl. Men who carve behind screens ought to pass a competitive examination before a jury of gastronomers. Men who carve at a table are drilled by degrees into something like tolerable operators by the mere shame of the public process.

MR. GRYLL. I will guarantee you against a Siberian dinner, whenever you dine with me.

THE REVEREND DOCTOR OPIMIAN. Mr. Gryll is a true conservative in dining.

MR. GRYLL. A true conservative, I hope. Not what a *soi-disant* conservative is practically: a man who sails under national colours, hauls them down, and hoists the enemy's. I like old customs. I like a glass of wine with a friend. What say you, Doctor? Mr. MacBorrowdale will join us?

---

most delicious manner. I had recourse to it more than once, and could not see without some indignation that substantial English dish banished in so ignominious a manner, to make way for French kickshaws.—*Tatler*, No. 148. [P.]

MR. MACBORROWDALE. Most willingly.

MISS GRYLL. My uncle and the Doctor have got as usual into a discussion, to the great amusement of the old lady, who sits between them and says nothing.

LORD CURRYFIN. Perhaps their discussion is too recondite for her.

MISS GRYLL. No ; they never talk before ladies of any subject in which ladies cannot join. And she has plenty to say for herself when she pleases. But when conversation pleases her, she likes to listen and be silent. It strikes me, by a few words that float this way, that they are discussing the Art of Dining.[1] She ought to be a proficient in it, for she lives much in the world, and has met as many persons whom she is equally willing either to meet to-morrow, or never to meet again, as any regular *dineur en ville*. And indeed that is the price that must be paid for society. Whatever difference of character may lie under the surface, the persons you meet in its circles are externally others yet the same : the same dress, the same manners, the same tastes and opinions, real or assumed. Strongly defined characteristic differences are so few, and artificial general resemblances so many, that in every party you may always make out the same theatrical company. It is like the flowing of a river : it is always different water, but you do not see the difference.

LORD CURRYFIN. For my part I do not like these monotonous exteriors. I like visible character. Now, in your party here, there is a good deal of character. Your uncle and Mr. MacBorrowdale are characters. Then the Reverend Doctor Opimian. He is not a man made to pattern. He is simple-minded, learned, tolerant, and the quintessence of *bonhomie*. The young gentleman who arrived to-day, the Hermit of the Folly, is evidently a character. I flatter myself, I am a character (*laughing*).

MISS GRYLL (*laughing*). Indeed you are, or rather many characters in one. I never knew a man of such infinite variety. You seem

---

[1] Peacock and his daughter Mary Ellen are believed to have collaborated in writing an article on *Gastronomy and Civilization* which appeared in *Fraser's Magazine*, Dec. 1851, under her name. It was reprinted in Volume IX of the Halliford Edition. G.

always to present yourself in the aspect in which those you are with would wish best to see you.

There was some ambiguity in the compliment'; but Lord Curryfin took it as implying that his aspect in all its variety was agreeable to the young lady. He did not then dream of a rival in the Hermit of the Folly.

CHAPTER XIV

Οὐ φίλος, ὃς κρατῆρι παρὰ πλέῳ οἰνοποτάζων
Νείκεα καὶ πόλεμον δακρυόεντα λέγει,
'Αλλ' ὅστις, Μουσέων τε καὶ ἀγλαὰ δῶρ' 'Αφροδίτης
Συμμίσγων, ἐρατῆς μνήσκεται εὐφροσύνης.
ANACREON.[1]

I love not him, who o'er the wine-cup's flow
Talks but of war, and strife, and scenes of woe:
But him, who can the Muses' gifts employ,
To mingle love and song with festal joy.

THE dinner and dessert passed away. The ladies retired to the drawing-room : the gentlemen discoursed over their wine. Mr. MacBorrowdale pronounced a eulogium on the port, which was cordially echoed by the divine in regard to the claret.

MR. FALCONER. Doctor, your tastes and sympathies are very much with the Greeks ; but I doubt if you would have liked their wine. Condiments of sea-water and turpentine must have given it an odd flavour ; and mixing water with it, in the proportion of three to one, must have reduced the strength of merely fermented liquor to something like the smallest ale of Christophero Sly.[2]

THE REVEREND DOCTOR OPIMIAN. I must say I should not like to put either salt-water or turpentine into this claret : they would not improve its bouquet ; nor to dilute it with any portion of water : it has to my mind, as it is, just the strength it ought to have, and no more. But the Greek taste was so exquisite in all matters in which we can bring it to the test, as to justify a strong presumption that in matters in which we cannot test it, it was equally correct. Salt-water and turpentine do not suit our wine : it does not follow that

[1] *Fragm.* Bergk 94. G. [2] *Taming of the Shrew*, Induction, Sc. 2. G.

theirs had not in it some basis of contrast, which may have made them pleasant in combination. And it was only a few of their wines that were so treated.

LORD CURRYFIN. Then it could not have been much like their drink of the present day. " My master cannot be right in his mind," said Lord Byron's man Fletcher, " or he would not have left Italy, where we had everything, to go to a country of savages ; there is nothing to eat in Greece but tough billy-goats, or to drink but spirits of turpentine." [1]

THE REVEREND DOCTOR OPIMIAN. There is an ambiguous present, which somewhat perplexes me, in an epigram of Rhianus, " Here is a vessel of half-wine, half-turpentine, and a singularly lean specimen of kid : the sender, Hippocrates, is worthy of all praise." [2] Perhaps this was a Doctor's present to a patient. Alcæus, Anacreon, and Nonnus could not have sung as they did under the inspiration of spirit of turpentine. We learn from Athenæus, and Pliny, and the old comedians, that the Greeks had a vast variety of wine, enough to suit every variety of taste. I infer the unknown from the known. We know little of their music. I have no doubt it was as excellent in its kind as their sculpture.

MR. MINIM. I can scarcely think that, sir. They seem to have had only the minor key, and to have known no more of counterpoint than they did of perspective.

THE REVEREND DOCTOR OPIMIAN. Their system of painting did not require perspective. Their main subject was on one foreground. Buildings, rocks, trees, served simply to indicate, not to delineate, the scene.

MR. FALCONER. I must demur to their having only the minor key. The natural ascent of the voice is in the major key, and with their

---

[1] Trelawny's *Recollections*. [P.] [ch. xviii. G.]

[2] Ἥμισυ μὲν πίσσης κωνίτιδος, ἥμισυ δ᾽ οἴνου,
Ἀρχῖν᾽, ἀτρεκέως ἥδε λάγυνος ἔχει·
Λεπτοτέρης δ᾽ οὐκ οἶδ᾽ ἐρίφου κρέας· πλὴν ὅγε πέμψας
Αἰνεῖσθαι πάντων ἄξιος Ἱπποκράτης.

Anthologia Palatina : Appendix : 72. [P.]

exquisite sensibility to sound they could not have missed the obvious expression of cheerfulness. With their three scales, diatonic, chromatic, and enharmonic, they must have exhausted every possible expression of feeling. Their scales were in true intervals ; they had really major and minor tones ; we have neither, but a confusion of both. They had both sharps and flats : we have neither, but a mere set of semitones, which serve for both. In their enharmonic scale the fineness of their ear perceived distinctions, which are lost on the coarseness of ours.

MR. MINIM. With all that they never got beyond melody. They had no harmony, in our sense. They sang only in unisons and octaves.

MR. FALCONER. It is not clear that they did not sing in fifths. As to harmony in one sense, I will not go so far as to say with Ritson, that the only use of the harmony is to spoil the melody ; but I will say, that to my taste a simple accompaniment, in strict subordination to the melody, is far more agreeable than that Niagara of sound under which it is now the fashion to bury it.

MR. MINIM. In that case, you would prefer a song with a simple pianoforte accompaniment to the same song on the Italian stage.

MR. FALCONER. A song sung with feeling and expression is good, however accompanied. Otherwise, the pianoforte is not much to my mind. All its intervals are false, and temperament is a poor substitute for natural intonation. Then its incapability of sustaining a note has led, as the only means of producing effect, to those infinitesimal subdivisions of sound, in which all sentiment and expression are twittered and frittered into nothingness.

THE REVEREND DOCTOR OPIMIAN. I quite agree with you. The other day a band passed my gate playing " The Campbells are coming ; " but instead of the fine old Scotch lilt, and the emphasis on " Ohó ! ohó ! " what they actually played was, " The Ca-a-a-a-mp-bells are co-o-o-o-ming, Oh-o-ho-o-o ! Oh-o-ho-o-o : " I thought to myself : There is the essence and quintessence of modern music. I like the old organ-music such as it was, when there were no keys but C and F, and every note responded to a syllable. The effect of the prolonged and sustained sound must have been truly magnificent :

> Where, through the long-drawn aisle and fretted vault,
> The pealing anthem swelled the note of praise.[1]

Who cares to hear sacred music on a piano ?

MR. MINIM. Yet I must say that there is a great charm in that brilliancy of execution, which is an exclusively modern and very modern accomplishment.

MR. FALCONER. To those who perceive it. All things are as they are perceived. To me music has no charm without expression.

LORD CURRYFIN (*who, having observed* MR. MACBORROWDALE'S *determination not to be drawn into an argument, amused himself with asking his opinion on all subjects*). What is your opinion, Mr. MacBorrowdale ?

MR. MACBORROWDALE. I hold to the opinion I have already expressed, that this is as good a glass of port as ever I tasted.

LORD CURRYFIN. I mean your opinion of modern music and musical instruments.

MR. MACBORROWDALE. The organ is very good for psalms, which I never sing, and the pianoforte for jigs, which I never dance. And if I were not to hear either of them from January to December, I should not complain of the privation.

LORD CURRYFIN. You are an utilitarian, Mr. MacBorrowdale. You are all for utility—public utility—and you see none in music.

MR. MACBORROWDALE. Nay, not exactly so. If devotion is good, if cheerfulness is good, and if music promotes each of them in proper time and place, music is useful. If I am as devout without the organ, and as cheerful without the piano, as I ever should be with them, that may be the defect of my head or my ear. I am not for forcing my tastes or no-tastes on other people. Let every man enjoy himself in his own way, while he does not annoy others. I

---

[1] Gray's *Elegy*. The word is actually " swells." G.

would not deprive you of your enjoyment of a brilliant symphony, and I hope you would not deprive me of my enjoyment of a glass of old wine.

THE REVEREND DOCTOR OPIMIAN.

"Tres mihi convivæ prope dissentire videntur,
　Poscentes vario multum diversa palato." [1]

MR. FALCONER. Nor our reverend friend of the pleasure of a classical quotation.

THE REVEREND DOCTOR OPIMIAN. And the utility, too, sir : for I think I am indebted to one for the pleasure of your acquaintance.

MR. FALCONER. When you did me the honour to compare my house to the Palace of Circe. The gain was mine.

MR. PALLET. You admit, sir, that the Greeks had no knowledge of perspective.

THE REVEREND DOCTOR OPIMIAN. Observing, that they had no need of it. Their subject was a foreground like a relievo. Their background was a symbol, not a representation. " No knowledge " is perhaps too strong. They had it where it was essential. They drew a peristyle, as it appeared to the eye, as accurately as we can do. In short, they gave to each distinct object its own proper perspective, but to separate objects they did not give their relative perspective, for the reason I have given, that they did not need it.

MR. FALCONER. There is to me one great charm in their painting, as we may judge from the specimens in Pompeii, which, though not their greatest works, indicate their school. They never crowded their canvas with figures. They presented one, two, three, four, or, at most, five persons, preferring one, and rarely exceeding three. These persons were never lost in the profusion of scenery, dress, and decoration. They had clearly-defined outlines, and were agreeable objects from any part of the room in which they were placed.

[1] Three guests dissent most widely in their wishes :
　With different taste they call for different dishes.　[P.]

[Horace : *Ep.* II. 61–2.　G.]

MR. PALLET. They must have lost much in beauty of detail.

THE REVEREND DOCTOR OPIMIAN. Therein is the essential difference of ancient and modern taste. Simple beauty—of idea in poetry, of sound in music, of figure in painting—was their great characteristic. Ours is detail in all these matters, overwhelming detail. We have not grand outlines for the imagination of the spectator or hearer to fill up : his imagination has no play of its own : it is overloaded with *minutiæ* and kaleidoscopical colours.

LORD CURRYFIN. Detail has its own beauty. I have admired a Dutch picture of a butcher's shop, where all the charm was in detail.

THE REVEREND DOCTOR OPIMIAN. I cannot admire anything of the kind. I must take pleasure in the thing represented before I can derive any from the representation.

MR. PALLET. I am afraid, sir, as our favourite studies all lead us to extreme opinions, you think the Greek painting was the better for not having perspective, and the Greek music for not having harmony.

THE REVEREND DOCTOR OPIMIAN. I think they had as much perspective and as much harmony as was consistent with that simplicity, which characterized their painting and music as much as their sculpture and poetry.

LORD CURRYFIN. What is your opinion, Mr. MacBorrowdale ?

MR. MACBORROWDALE. I think you may just buz that bottle before you.

LORD CURRYFIN. I mean your opinion of Greek perspective.

MR. MACBORROWDALE. Troth, I am of opinion that a bottle looks smaller at a distance than when it is close by, and I prefer it as a full-sized object in the foreground.

LORD CURRYFIN. I have often wondered that a gentleman so well qualified as you are to discuss all subjects should so carefully avoid discussing any.

MR. MACBORROWDALE. After dinner, my lord, after dinner. I work hard all the morning at serious things, sometimes till I get a headache, which, however, does not often trouble me. After dinner I like to crack my bottle and chirp and talk nonsense, and fit myself for the company of Jack of Dover.

LORD CURRYFIN. Jack of Dover! Who was he? [1]

MR. MACBORROWDALE. He was a man who travelled in search of a greater fool than himself, and did not find him.[2]

THE REVEREND DOCTOR OPIMIAN. He must have lived in odd times. In our days he would not have gone far without falling in with a teetotaller, or a decimal coinage man, or a school-for-all man, or a competitive examination man, who would not allow a drayman to lower a barrel into a cellar unless he could expound the mathematical principles by which he performed the operation.

MR. MACBORROWDALE. Nay, that is all pragmatical fooling. The fooling Jack looked for was jovial fooling, fooling to the top of his bent,[3] excellent fooling, which, under the semblance of folly, was both merry and wise. He did not look for mere unmixed folly, of which there never was a deficiency. The fool he looked for was one which it takes a wise man to make—a Shakspearian fool.[4]

THE REVEREND DOCTOR OPIMIAN. In that sense he might travel far, and return, as he did in his own day, without having found the fool he looked for.

MR. MACBORROWDALE. A teetotaller! Well! He is the true Heautontimorumenos,[5] the self-punisher, with a jug of toast-and-

---

[1] See Note to p. 812. G.

[2] *Jacke of Dover, His Quest of Inquirie, or His Privy Search for the Veriest Foole in England.* London. 1604. Reprinted for the Percy Society, 1842.

[3] *Hamlet*, Act III, Sc. 2. G.   [P.]

[4] Oeuvre, ma foi, où n'est facile atteindre :
     Pourtant qu'il faut parfaitement sage être,
     Pour le vrai fol bien naïvement feindre.
                                        Eutrapel, p. 28. [P.]

[The nom-de-plume of Nöel du Fail, seigneur de la Herissaye (died c. 1585), author of *Œuvres Facétieuses.* G.]

[5] The title of a play by Terence, the subject of which is taken from Menander. G.

water for his Christmas wassail. So far his folly is merely pitiable, but his intolerance makes it offensive. He cannot enjoy his own tipple unless he can deprive me of mine. A fox that has lost his tail. There is no tyrant like a thorough-paced reformer. I drink to his own reformation.

MR. GRYLL. He is like Bababec's faquir, who sat in a chair full of nails, *pour avoir de la considération*.[1] But the faquir did not want others to do the same. He wanted all the consideration for himself, and kept all the nails for himself. If these meddlers would do the like by their toast-and-water, nobody would begrudge it them.

THE REVEREND DOCTOR OPIMIAN. Now, sir, if the man who has fooled the greatest number of persons to the top of their bent were to be adjudged the fittest companion for Jack of Dover, you would find him in a distinguished meddler with everything, who has been for half a century the merry-andrew of a vast arena, which he calls moral and political science, but which has in it a dash of everything that has ever occupied human thought.

LORD CURRYFIN. I know whom you mean; but he is a great man in his way, and has done much good.[2]

THE REVEREND DOCTOR OPIMIAN. He has helped to introduce much change; whether for good or for ill remains to be seen. I forgot he was your lordship's friend. I apologize, and drink to his health.

LORD CURRYFIN. Oh! pray, do not apologize to me. I would not have my friendships, tastes, pursuits, and predilections interfere in the slightest degree with the fullest liberty of speech on all persons and things. There are many who think with you that he is a moral and political Jack of Dover. So be it. Time will bring him to his level.

MR. MACBORROWDALE. I will only say of the distinguished

---

[1] Voltaire's *Lettre d'un Turc*. The fakir is himself Bababec. The Turk, Omri, prevailed upon him to leave his bed of nails, wash and live decently. After a fortnight he returned to his nails for the reason given. G.

[2] Lord Brougham. G.

personage, that Jack of Dover would not pair off with him. This is the true universal science, the oracle of *La Dive Bouteille*.[1]

MR. GRYLL. It is not exactly Greek music, Mr. Minim, that you are giving us for our Aristophanic choruses.

MR. MINIM. No, sir; I have endeavoured to give you a good selection, as appropriate as I can make it.

MR. PALLET. Neither am I giving you Greek painting for the scenery. I have taken the liberty to introduce perspective.

THE REVEREND DOCTOR OPIMIAN. Very rightly both, for Aristophanes in London.

MR. MINIM. Besides, sir, we must have such music as your young ladies can sing.

THE REVEREND DOCTOR OPIMIAN. Assuredly; and so far as we have yet heard them rehearse, they sing it delightfully.

After a little more desultory conversation, they adjourned to the drawing-rooms.

CHAPTER XV

Τοῦτο βίος, τοῦτ᾽ αὐτό· τρυφὴ βίος· ἔρρετ᾽ ἀνίαι·
Ζωῆς ἀνθρώποις ὀλίγος χρόνος· ἄρτι Δύαιος,
Ἄρτι χοροί, στέφανοί τε φιλανθέες ἄρτι γυναῖκες.
Σήμερον ἐσθλὰ πάθω, τὸ γὰρ αὔριον οὐδενὶ δῆλον.
                                            Anthologia Palatina : V. 72.

This, this is life, when pleasure drives out care.
Short is the span of time we each may share.
To-day, while love, wine, song, the hours adorn,
To-day we live: none know the coming morn.

LORD CURRYFIN'S assiduities to Miss Gryll had discomposed Mr. Falconer more than he chose to confess to himself. Lord Curryfin, on entering the drawing-rooms, went up immediately to the young lady of the house; and Mr. Falconer, to the amazement of the

[1] *Dive* is old French for *Divine.* G.

reverend Doctor, sat down, in the outer drawing-room, on a sofa by the side of Miss Ilex, with whom he entered into conversation.

In the inner drawing-room some of the young ladies were engaged with music, and were entreated to continue their performance. Some of them were conversing, or looking over new publications.

After a brilliant symphony, performed by one of the young visitors, in which runs and crossings of demisemiquavers in *tempo prestissimo* occupied the principal share, Mr. Falconer asked Miss Ilex how she liked it.

MISS ILEX.   I admire it as a splendid piece of legerdemain ; but it expresses nothing.

MR. FALCONER.   It is well to know that such things can be done ; and when we have reached the extreme complications of art, we may hope to return to nature and simplicity.

MISS ILEX.   Not that it is impossible to reconcile execution and expression. Rubini identified the redundancies of ornament with the overflowings of feeling, and the music of Donizetti furnished him most happily with the means of developing this power. I never felt so transported out of myself as when I heard him sing *Tu che al ciel spiegasti l' ali.*[1]

MR. FALCONER.   Do you place Donizetti above Mozart ?

MISS ILEX.   Oh, surely not. But for supplying expressive music to a singer like Rubini, I think Donizetti has no equal ; at any rate no superior. For music that does not require, and does not even suit, such a singer, but which requires only to be correctly interpreted to be universally recognised as the absolute perfection of melody, harmony, and expression, I think Mozart has none. Beethoven perhaps : he composed only one opera, *Fidelio* : but what an opera

[1] An aria from *Lucia di Lammermoor* by Donizetti, first produced at Naples in 1835, and in London at Her Majesty's Theatre, April 5th, 1838. Rubini, the tenor, who is described as the *raison d'être* of all Italian opera in the period following Rossini, secured Donizetti's first operatic success with his thirty-second opera, *Anna Bolena*. He first visited England in 1831 and thereafter, until 1843, divided his time between London and Paris. G.

that is. What an effect in the sudden change of the key, when Leonora throws herself between her husband and Pizarro : and again, in the change of the key with the change of the scene, when we pass from the prison to the hall of the palace. What pathos in the songs of affection, what grandeur in the songs of triumph, what wonderful combinations in the accompaniments, where a perpetual stream of counter-melody creeps along in the bass, yet in perfect harmony with the melody above.

MR. FALCONER. What say you to Haydn ?

MISS ILEX. Haydn has not written operas, and my principal experience is derived from the Italian theatre. But his music is essentially dramatic. It is a full stream of perfect harmony in subjection to exquisite melody ; and in simple ballad-strains, that go direct to the heart, he is almost supreme and alone. Think of that air with which every one is familiar, " My mother bids me bind my hair ; " the graceful flow of the first part, the touching effect of the semitones in the second : with true intonation and true expression, the less such an air is accompanied the better.

MR. FALCONER. There is a beauty and an appeal to the heart in ballads which will never lose its effect except on those with whom the pretence of fashion overpowers the feeling of nature.[1]

MISS ILEX. It is strange, however, what influence that pretence has, in overpowering all natural feelings, not in music alone.

" Is it not curious," thought the Doctor, " that there is only one old woman in the room, and that my young friend should have selected her for the object of his especial attention ? "

But a few simple notes struck on the ear of his young friend, who rose from the sofa and approached the singer. The Doctor took his place to cut off his retreat.

Miss Gryll, who, though a proficient in all music, was particularly partial to ballads, had just begun to sing one.

[1] Braham said something like this to a Parliamentary Committee on Theatres, in 1832. [P.] [John Braham, operatic tenor, 1774–1856. G.]

THE DAPPLED PALFREY.[1]

" My traitorous uncle has wooed for himself :
Her father has sold her for land and for pelf :
My steed, for whose equal the world they might search,
In mockery they borrow to bear her to church.

" Oh ! there is one path through the forest so green,
Where thou and I only, my palfrey, have been :
We traversed it oft, when I rode to her bower
To tell my love tale through the rift of the tower.

" Thou know'st not my words, but thy instinct is good :
By the road to the church lies the path through the wood :
Thy instinct is good, and her love is as true :
Thou wilt see thy way homeward : dear palfrey, adieu."

They feasted full late and full early they rose,
And church-ward they rode more than half in a doze :
The steed in an instant broke off from the throng,
And pierced the green path, which he bounded along.

In vain was pursuit, though some followed pell-mell :
Through bramble and thicket they floundered and fell.
On the backs of their coursers some dozed as before,
And missed not the bride till they reached the church-door.

The knight from his keep on the forest-bound gazed :
The drawbridge was down, the portcullis was raised :
And true to his hope came the palfrey amain,
With his only loved lady, who checked not the rein.

The drawbridge went up : the portcullis went down :
The chaplain was ready with bell, book, and gown :
The wreck of the bride-train arrived at the gate :
The bride showed the ring, and they muttered " Too late ! "

" Not too late for a feast, though too late for a fray :
What's done can't be undone : make peace while you may : "
So spake the young knight, and the old ones complied,
And quaffed a deep health to the bridegroom and bride.

Mr. Falconer had listened to the ballad with evident pleasure.
He turned to resume his place on the sofa, but finding it pre-occupied
by the Doctor, he put on a look of disappointment, which seemed to
the Doctor exceedingly comic.

[1] Founded on *Le Vair Palefroi* : among the *Fabliaux* published by
Barbazan. [P.]

"Surely," thought the Doctor, "he is not in love with the old maid."

Miss Gryll gave up her place to a young lady, who in her turn sang a ballad of a different character.

LOVE AND AGE.

I played with you 'mid cowslips blowing,
When I was six and you were four ;
When garlands weaving, flower-balls throwing,
Were pleasures soon to please no more.
Through groves and meads, o'er grass and heather,
With little playmates, to and fro,
We wandered hand in hand together ;
But that was sixty years ago.

You grew a lovely roseate maiden,
And still our early love was strong ;
Still with no care our days were laden,
They glided joyously along ;
And I did love you, very dearly,
How dearly words want power to show ;
I thought your heart was touched as nearly ;
But that was fifty years ago.

Then other lovers came around you,
Your beauty grew from year to year,
And many a splendid circle found you
The centre of its glittering sphere.
I saw you then, first vows forsaking,
On rank and wealth your hand bestow ;
Oh, then I thought my heart was breaking,—
But that was forty years ago.

And I lived on, to wed another :
No cause she gave me to repine ;
And when I heard you were a mother,
I did not wish the children mine.
My own young flock, in fair progression,
Made up a pleasant Christmas row :
My joy in them was past expression ;—
But that was thirty years ago.

You grew a matron plump and comely,
You dwelt in fashion's brightest blaze ;
My earthly lot was far more homely ;
But I too had my festal days.

No merrier eyes have ever glistened
Around the hearth-stone's wintry glow,
Than when my youngest child was christened :—
But that was twenty years ago.

Time passed. My eldest girl was married,
And I am now a grandsire grey ;
One pet of four years old I've carried
Among the wild-flowered meads to play.
In our old fields of childish pleasure,
Where now, as then, the cowslips blow,
She fills her basket's ample measure,—
And that is not ten years ago.

But though first love's impassioned blindness
Has passed away in colder light,
I still have thought of you with kindness,
And shall do, till our last good-night.
The ever-rolling silent hours
Will bring a time we shall not know,
When our young days of gathering flowers
Will be an hundred years ago.

MISS ILEX. That is a melancholy song. But of how many first
loves is it the true tale ? And how many are far less happy ?

THE REVEREND DOCTOR OPIMIAN. It is simple and well sung, with
a distinctness of articulation not often heard.

MISS ILEX. That young lady's voice is a perfect contralto. It is
singularly beautiful, and I applaud her for keeping within her
natural compass, and not destroying her voice by forcing it upwards,
as too many do.

THE REVEREND DOCTOR OPIMIAN. Forcing, forcing, seems to be
the rule of life. A young lady who forces her voice into *altissimo*, and
a young gentleman who forces his mind into a receptacle for a chaos
of crudities, are pretty much on a par. Both do ill, where, if they
were contented with attainments within the limits of natural taste
and natural capacity, they might both do well. As to the poor young
men, many of them become mere crammed fowls, with the same
result as Hermogenes, who, after astonishing the world with his

attainments at seventeen, came to a sudden end at the age of twenty-five, and spent the rest of a long life in hopeless imbecility.[1]

MISS ILEX. The poor young men can scarcely help themselves. They are not held qualified for a profession unless they have over-loaded their understanding with things of no use in it—incongruous things too, which could never be combined into the pursuits of natural taste.

THE REVEREND DOCTOR OPIMIAN. Very true. Brindley would not have passed as a canal-maker,[2] nor Edward Williams [3] as a bridge-builder. I saw the other day some examination papers which would have infallibly excluded Marlborough from the army and Nelson from the navy. I doubt if Haydn would have passed as a composer before a committee of lords like one of his pupils, who insisted on demonstrating to him that he was continually sinning against the rules of counterpoint ; on which Haydn said to him, " I thought I was to teach you, but it seems you are to teach me, and I do not want a preceptor," and thereon he wished his lordship a good morning. Fancy Watt being asked, how much Joan of Naples got for Avignon when she sold it to Pope Clement the Sixth, and being held unfit for an engineer because he could not tell.

MISS ILEX. That is an odd question, Doctor. But how much did she get for it ?

THE REVEREND DOCTOR OPIMIAN. Nothing. He promised ninety thousand golden florins, but he did not pay one of them : and that, I suppose, is the profound sense of the question. It is true he paid her after a fashion, in his own peculiar coin. He absolved her of the murder of her first husband, and perhaps he thought that was worth the money. But how many of our legislators could answer the question ? Is it not strange that candidates for seats in parliament

---

[1] Donaldson's *History of Greek Literature*, vol. iii. p. 156. [P.] [On the other side there is the repartee of Pico della Mirandola who did not outlive his faculties, and who, to the observation of an old gentleman that forward boys make stupid men, retorted : " You must have had a fine understanding in your youth." G.]

[2] James Brindley constructed the Manchester and Liverpool and Grand Trunk Canals. G.

[3] The builder of Pont-y-Pryd. [P.]

should not be subjected to competitive examination ? Plato and Persius [1] would furnish good hints for it.   I should like to see honourable gentlemen having to answer such questions as are deemed necessary tests for government clerks, before they would be held qualified candidates for seats in the legislature. That would be something like a reform in the parliament.   Oh, that it were so, and I were the examiner ! Ha, ha, ha, what a comedy !

The Doctor's hearty laugh was contagious, and Miss Ilex joined in it. Mr. MacBorrowdale came up.

MR. MACBORROWDALE.   You are as merry as if you had discovered the object of Jack of Dover's quest.

THE REVEREND DOCTOR OPIMIAN.   Something very like it. We have an honourable gentleman under competitive examination for a degree in legislative wisdom.

MR. MACBORROWDALE.   Truly, that is fooling competition to the top of its bent.

THE REVEREND DOCTOR OPIMIAN.   Competitive examination for clerks, and none for legislators—is not this an anomaly ? Ask the honourable member for Muckborough on what acquisitions in history and mental and moral philosophy he founds his claim of competence to make laws for the nation ?   He can only tell you that he has been chosen as the most conspicuous Grub among the Money-grubs of his borough to be the representative of all that is sordid, selfish, hardhearted, unintellectual, and antipatriotic, which are the distinguishing qualities of the majority among them.   Ask a candidate for a clerkship what are his qualifications ?   He may answer, " All that are requisite—reading, writing, and arithmetic."   " Nonsense," says the questioner.   " Do you know the number of miles in direct distance from Timbuctoo to the top of Chimborazo ? " [2]   " I do not,"

---

[1] Plato : *Alcibiades*, i. ; Persius : *Sat.* iv.   [P.]

[2] Compare : " Could you tell me now, how would you calculate the distance in inches, say from London Bridge to the nearest portion of Jupiter's disc, at twelve o'clock on the 1st of April ? . . . I am not asking the distance, you know. I am only asking how you would compute it." Anthony Trollope : *The Three Clerks*, Ch. XI (1858).   G.

says the candidate. "Then you will not do for a clerk," says the competitive examiner. Does Moneygrub of Muckborough know? He does not; nor anything else. The clerk may be able to answer some of the questions put to him. Moneygrub could not answer one of them. But he is very fit for a legislator.

MR. MACBORROWDALE. Eh! but he is subjected to a pretty severe competitive examination of his own, by what they call a constituency, who just put him to the test in the art of conjuring, to see if he can shift money from his own pocket into theirs, without any inconvenient third party being aware of the transfer.

CHAPTER XVI

Amiam : che non ha tregua
Con gli anni umana vita, e si dilegua.
Amiam : che il sol si muore, e poi rinasce :
A noi sua breve luce
S'asconde, e il sonno eterna notte adduce.
                                    TASSO : *Aminta.*

Love, while youth knows its prime,
For mortal life can make no truce with time.
Love : for the sun goes down to rise as bright :
To us his transient light
Is veiled, and sleep comes on with everlasting night.

LORD CURRYFIN was too much a man of the world to devote his attentions in society exclusively to one, and make them the subject of special remark. He left the inner drawing-room, and came up to the Doctor to ask him if he knew the young lady who had sung the last ballad. The Doctor knew her well. She was Miss Niphet,[1] the only daughter of a gentleman of fortune, residing a few miles distant.

LORD CURRYFIN. As I looked at her while she was singing, I thought of Southey's description of Laila's face in *Thalaba* :

A broad light floated o'er its marble paleness,
As the wind waved the fountain-fire.[2]

Marble paleness suits her well. There is something statuesque in her whole appearance. I could not help thinking what an admirable Camilla she would make in Cimarosa's *Orazii*. Her features are

[1] From νιφετος, " a snow shower." G.   [2] Bk. X, St, 22, G,

singularly regular. They had not much play, but the expression of
her voice was such as if she felt the full force of every sentiment
she uttered.

THE REVEREND DOCTOR OPIMIAN. I consider her to be a person of
very deep feeling, which she does not choose should appear on the
surface. She is animated in conversation when she is led into it.
Otherwise, she is silent and retiring, but obliging in the extreme ;
always ready to take part in anything that is going forward. She
never needs, for example, being twice asked to sing. She is free from
the vice which Horace ascribes to all singers, of not complying when
asked, and never leaving off when they have once begun.[1] If this
be a general rule, she is an exception to it.

LORD CURRYFIN. I rather wonder she does not tinge her cheeks
with a slight touch of artificial red, just as much as would give her
a sort of blush-rose complexion.

MISS ILEX. You will not wonder when you know her better.
The artificial, the false, in any degree, however little, is impossible to
her. She does not show all she thinks and feels, but what she does
show is truth itself.

LORD CURRYFIN. And what part is she to take in the Aristophanic
comedy ?

THE REVEREND DOCTOR OPIMIAN. She is to be the leader of the
chorus.

LORD CURRYFIN. I have not seen her at the rehearsals.

THE REVEREND DOCTOR OPIMIAN. So far, her place has been
supplied. You will see her at the next.

In the meantime Mr. Falconer had gone into the inner drawing-
room, sat down by Miss Gryll, and entered into conversation with
her. The Doctor observed them from a distance, but with all the
opportunity he had had for observation, he was still undetermined
in his opinion of the impression they might have made on each other.

---

[1] *Sat.* I, iii, 1–3. G.

"It is well," he said to himself, "that Miss Ilex is an old maid.
If she were as young as Morgana, I think she would win our young
friend's heart. Her mind is evidently much to his mind. But so
would Morgana's be, if she could speak it as freely. She does not—
why not ? To him at any rate. She seems under no restraint with
Lord Curryfin. A good omen, perhaps. I never saw a couple so
formed for each other. Heaven help me ! I cannot help harping
on that string. After all, the Vestals are the obstacle."

Lord Curryfin, seeing Miss Niphet sitting alone at the side of the
room, changed his place, sate down by her, and entered into conversation on the topics of the day, novels, operas, pictures, and various
phenomena of London life. She kept up the ball with him very
smartly. She was every winter—May and June—in London, mixed
much in society, and saw everything that was to be seen. Lord
Curryfin, with all his Protean accomplishments, could not start a
subject on which she had not something to say. But she originated
nothing. He spoke, and she answered. One thing he remarked as
singular, that though she spoke with knowledge of many things, she
did not speak as with taste or distaste of any. The world seemed
to flow under her observation without even ruffling the surface of
her interior thoughts. This perplexed his versatile lordship. He
thought the young lady would be a subject worth studying : it was
clear that she was a character. So far so well. He felt that he should
not rest satisfied till he was able to define it.

The theatre made rapid progress. The walls were completed.
The building was roofed in. The stage portion was so far finished
as to allow Mr. Pallet to devote every morning to the scenery.
The comedy was completed. The music was composed. The
rehearsals went on with vigour, but for the present in the
drawing-rooms.

Miss Niphet, returning one morning from a walk before breakfast,
went into the theatre to see its progress, and found Lord Curryfin
swinging over the stage on a seat suspended by long ropes from above
the visible scene. He did not see her. He was looking upwards,
not as one indulging in an idle pastime, but as one absorbed in serious
meditation. All at once the seat was drawn up, and he disappeared
in the blue canvas that represented the sky. She was not aware

that gymnastics were to form any portion of the projected entertainment, and went away, associating the idea of his lordship, as many had done before, with something like a feeling of the ludicrous.

Miss Niphet was not much given to laughter, but whenever she looked at Lord Curryfin during breakfast she could not quite suppress a smile which hovered on her lips, and which was even the more forced on her by the contrast between his pantomimic disappearance and his quiet courtesy and remarkably good manners in company. The lines of Dryden—

> A man so various, that he seemed to be
> Not one, but all mankind's epitome,[1]

—passed through her mind as she looked at him.

Lord Curryfin noticed the suppressed smile, but did not apprehend that it had any relation to himself. He thought some graceful facetiousness had presented itself to the mind of the young lady, and that she was amusing herself with her own fancy. It was, however, to him another touch of character, that lighted up her statuesque countenance with a new and peculiar beauty. By degrees her features resumed their accustomed undisturbed serenity. Lord Curryfin felt satisfied that in that aspect he had somewhere seen something like her, and after revolving a series of recollections, he remembered that it was a statue of Melpomene.

There was in the park a large lake, encircled with varieties of woodland, and by its side was a pavilion to which Miss Niphet often resorted to read in an afternoon. And at no great distance from it was the boat-house, to which Lord Curryfin often resorted for a boat, to row or sail on the water. Passing the pavilion in the afternoon, he saw the young lady, and entering into conversation, ascertained what had so amused her in the morning. He told her he had been trying—severally by himself, and collectively with the workmen—the strength of the suspending lines for the descent of the Chorus of Clouds in the Aristophanic comedy. She said she had been very ungrateful to laugh at the result of his solicitude for the safety of herself and her young friends. He said that in having moved her to smile, even at his expense, he considered himself amply repaid.

[1] *Absalom and Achitophel*, ll. 545–6. G.

From this time they often met in the pavilion, that is to say, he often found her reading there on his way to a boat, and stopped awhile to converse with her. They had always plenty to say, and it resulted that he was always sorry to leave her, and she was always sorry to part with him. By degrees the feeling of the ludicrous ceased to be the predominant sentiment which she associated with him. *L'amour vient sans qu'on y pense.*

The days shortened, and all things were sufficiently advanced to admit of rehearsals in the theatre. The hours from twelve to two—from noon to luncheon—were devoted to this pleasant pastime. At luncheon there was much merriment over the recollections of the morning's work, and after luncheon there was walking in the park, rowing or sailing on the lake, riding or driving in the adjacent country, archery in a spacious field, and in bad weather billiards, reading in the library, music in the drawing-rooms, battledoor and shuttlecock in the hall; in short, all the methods of passing time agreeably which are available to good company, when there are ample means and space for their exercise; to say nothing of making love, which Lord Curryfin did with all delicacy and discretion—directly to Miss Gryll as he had begun, and indirectly to Miss Niphet, for whom he felt an involuntary and almost unconscious admiration. He had begun to apprehend that with the former he had a dangerous rival in the Hermit of the Folly, and he thought the latter had sufficient charms to console even Orlando for the loss of Angelica. In short, Miss Gryll had first made him think of marriage, and whenever he thought his hopes were dim in that quarter, he found an antidote to despair in the contemplation of the statue-like damsel.

Mr. Falconer took more and more pleasure in Miss Gryll's society, but he did not declare himself. He was more than once on the point of doing so, but the images of the Seven Sisters rose before him, and he suspended the intention. On these occasions he always went home for a day or two to fortify his resolution against his heart. Thus he passed his time between the Grange and the Tower, " letting I dare not wait upon I would." [1]

Miss Gryll had listened to Lord Curryfin. She had neither encouraged nor discouraged him. She thought him the most amus-

[1] *Macbeth*, Act I, Sc. 7. G.

ing person she had ever known. She liked his temper, his acquirements, and his manners. She could not divest herself of that feeling of the ludicrous which everybody seemed to associate with him; but she thought the chances of life presented little hope of a happier marriage than a woman who would fall in with his tastes and pursuits —which, notwithstanding their tincture of absurdity, were entertaining and even amiable—might hope for with him. Therefore, she would not say No, though, when she thought of Mr. Falconer, she could not say Yes.

Lord Curryfin invented a new sail of infallible safety, which resulted, like most similar inventions, in capsizing the inventor on the first trial. Miss Niphet, going one afternoon, later than usual, to her accustomed pavilion, found his lordship scrambling up the bank, and his boat, keel upwards, at some little distance in the lake. For a moment her usual self-command forsook her. She held out both her hands to assist him up the bank, and as soon as he stood on dry land, dripping like a Triton in trousers,[1] she exclaimed in such a tone as he had never before heard, " Oh ! my dear lord ! " Then, as if conscious of her momentary aberration, she blushed with a deeper tinge than that of the artificial rose which he had once thought might improve her complexion. She attempted to withdraw her hands, but he squeezed them both ardently, and exclaimed in his turn, like a lover in a tragedy,

" Surely, till now I never looked on beauty."

She was on the point of saying, " Surely, before now you have looked on Miss Gryll," but she checked herself. She was content to receive the speech as a sudden ebullition of gratitude for sympathy, and disengaging her hands, she insisted on his returning immediately to the house to change his " dank and dripping weeds." [2]

As soon as he was out of sight she went to the boat-house, to summon the men who had charge of it to the scene of the accident. Putting off in another boat, they brought the capsized vessel to land, and hung up the sail to dry. She returned in the evening, and finding the sail dry, she set it on fire. Lord Curryfin, coming down

---

[1] Involuntary immersions occur in every novel by Peacock. This is the last of them. G.

[2] Milton : trans. of *Fifth Ode of Horace, lib. I.* Actually " dropping." G.

to look after his tackle, found the young lady meditating over the tinder. She said to him,

" That sail will never put you under the water again."

He was touched by this singular development of solicitude for his preservation, but could not help saying something in praise of his invention, giving a demonstration of the infallibility of the principle, with several scientific causes of error in working out the practice. He had no doubt it would be all right on another experiment. Seeing that her looks expressed unfeigned alarm at this announcement, he assured her that her kind interest in his safety was sufficient to prevent his trying his invention again. They walked back together to the house, and in the course of conversation she said to him,

"The last time I saw the words Infallible Safety, they were painted on the back of a stage-coach, which in one of our summer tours we saw lying by the side of the road, with its top in a ditch and its wheels in the air."

The young lady was still a mystery to Lord Curryfin.

" Sometimes," he said to himself, " I could almost fancy Melpomene in love with me. But I have seldom seen her laugh, and when she has done so now and then, it has usually been at me. That is not much like love. Her last remark was anything but a compliment to my inventive genius."

CHAPTER XVII

O gran contrasto in giovenil pensiero,
Desir di laude, ed impeto d'amore !
ARIOSTO : C. 25.

How great a strife in youthful minds can raise ⌉
Impulse of love, and keen desire of praise.

LORD CURRYFIN, amongst his multifarious acquirements, had taken lessons from the great horse-tamer,[1] and thought himself as well

---

[1] The American, John S. Rarey, author of *The Taming of Wild Horses*, 1858. Rarey achieved fame in this country in 1858, taming many savage horses. In particular, he subdued Cruiser, a stallion kept for stud purposes, belonging to the fourth Lord Dorchester, which was said to have killed three men and to have savaged many others. Cruiser was kept in

qualified as his master to subdue any animal of the species, however vicious. It was therefore with great pleasure he heard that there was a singularly refractory specimen in Mr. Gryll's stables. The next morning after hearing this, he rose early, and took his troublesome charge in hand. After some preliminary management he proceeded to gallop him round and round a large open space in the park, which was visible from the house. Miss Niphet, always an early riser, and having just prepared for a walk, saw him from her chamber window engaged in this perilous exercise, and though she knew nothing of the peculiar character of his recalcitrant disciple, she saw by its shakings, kickings, and plungings, that it was exerting all its energies to get rid of its rider. At last it made a sudden dash into the wood, and disappeared among the trees.

It was to the young lady a matter of implicit certainty that some disaster would ensue. She pictured to herself all the contingencies of accident ; being thrown to the ground and kicked by the horse's hoofs, being dashed against a tree, or suspended, like Absalom, by the hair. She hurried down and hastened towards the wood, from which, just as she reached it, the rider and horse emerged at full speed as before. But as soon as Lord Curryfin saw Miss Niphet, he took a graceful wheel round, and brought the horse to a stand by her side ; for by this time he had mastered the animal, and brought it to the condition of Sir Walter's hunter in Wordsworth :—

> Weak as a lamb the hour that it is yeaned,
> And foaming like a mountain cataract.[1]

She did not attempt to dissemble that she had come to look for him, but said,

" I expected to find you killed."

He said, " You see all my experiments are not failures. I have been more fortunate with the horse than the sail."

At this moment one of the keepers appeared at a little distance. Lord Curryfin beckoned to him, and asked him to take the horse

---

a cage and fed through a trap-door in the roof. Rarey unlocked the door of the cage and walked in, and as the stallion charged, whispered to him. Cruiser stood bewildered and trembling, and Rarey led him round the cage. The story, told by Lord Dorchester, a witness, resembles that in Borrow's *Lavengro*, Ch. XIII. G.

[1] *Hartleap Well.* [P.]

to the stables. The keeper looked with some amazement, and exclaimed,

"Why, this is the horse that nobody could manage!"

"You will manage him easily enough now," said Lord Curryfin.

So it appeared ; and the keeper took charge of him, not altogether without misgiving.

Miss Niphet's feelings had been over-excited, the more so from the severity with which she was accustomed to repress them. The energy which had thus far upheld her, suddenly gave way. She sate down on a fallen tree, and burst into tears. Lord Curryfin sate down by her, and took her hand. She allowed him to retain it awhile ; but all at once snatched it from him and sped towards the house over the grass, with the swiftness and lightness of Virgil's Camilla, leaving his lordship as much astonished at her movements as the Volscian crowd, *attonitis inhians animis*,[1] had been at those of her prototype. He could not help thinking, "Few women run gracefully ; but she runs like another Atalanta."

When the party met at breakfast, Miss Niphet was in her place, looking more like a statue than ever, with, if possible, more of marble paleness. Lord Curryfin's morning exploit, of which the story had soon found its way from the stable to the hall, was the chief subject of conversation. He had received a large share of what he had always so much desired—applause and admiration ; but now he thought he would willingly sacrifice all he had ever received in that line, to see even the shadow of a smile, or the expression of a sentiment of any kind, on the impassive face of Melpomene. She left the room when she rose from the breakfast-table, appeared at the rehearsal, and went through her part as usual; sate down at luncheon, and departed as soon as it was over. She answered, as she had always done, everything that was said to her, frankly, and to the purpose ; and also, as usual, she originated nothing.

In the afternoon, Lord Curryfin went down to the pavilion. She was not there. He wandered about the grounds in all directions, and returned several times to the pavilion, always in vain. At last he

---

[1] Gaping with wondering minds. [P.] [*Æn.* VII. 814–15. They were watching Camilla setting off for the war with her Amazons, amazed at the smoothness and swiftness with which she moved. G.]

sate down in the pavilion, and fell into a meditation.   He asked himself how it could be, that having begun by making love to Miss Gryll, having indeed gone too far to recede unless the young lady absolved him, he was now evidently in a transition state towards a more absorbing and violent passion, for a person who, with all her frankness, was incomprehensible, and whose snowy exterior seemed to cover a volcanic fire, which she struggled to repress, and was angry with herself when she did not thoroughly succeed in so doing.   If he were quite free he would do his part towards the solution of the mystery, by making a direct and formal proposal to her.   As a preliminary to this, he might press Miss Gryll for an answer.   All he had yet obtained from her was, " Wait till we are better acquainted."   He was in a dilemma between Morgana and Melpomene.   It had not entered into his thoughts that Morgana was in love with him ; but he thought it nevertheless very probable that she was in a fair way to become so, and that even as it was she liked him well enough to accept him.   On the other hand, he could not divest himself of the idea that Melpomene was in love with him.   It was true, all the sympathy she had yet shown might have arisen from the excitement of strong feelings, at the real or supposed peril of a person with whom she was in the habit of daily intercourse.   It might be so. Still the sympathy was very impassioned ; though, but for his rashness in self-exposure to danger, he might never have known it. A few days ago, he would not press Miss Gryll for an answer, because he feared it might be a negative.   Now he would not, because he was at least not in haste for an affirmative.   But supposing it were a negative, what certainty had he that a negative from Morgana would not be followed by a negative from Melpomene ?   Then his heart would be at sea without rudder or compass.   We shall leave him awhile to the contemplation of his perplexities.

As his thoughts were divided, so were Morgana's.   If Mr. Falconer should propose to her, she felt she could accept him without hesitation.   She saw clearly the tendency of his feelings towards her.   She saw, at the same time, that he strove to the utmost against them in behalf of his old associations, though, with all his endeavours, he could not suppress them in her presence.   So there was the lover who did not propose, and who would have been preferred ; and there was the lover who had proposed, and who, if it had been clear that the former chance was hopeless, would not have been lightly given up.

If her heart had been as much interested in Lord Curryfin as it was in Mr. Falconer, she would quickly have detected a diminution in the ardour of his pursuit; but so far as she might have noticed any difference in his conduct, she ascribed it only to deference to her recommendation to " wait till they were better acquainted." The longer and the more quietly he waited, the better it seemed to please her. It was not on him, but on Mr. Falconer, that the eyes of her observance were fixed. She would have given Lord Curryfin his liberty instantly if she had thought he wished it.

Mr. Falconer also had his own dilemma, between his new love and his old affections. Whenever the first seemed likely to gain the ascendency, the latter rose in their turn, like Antaeus from earth, with renovated strength.[1] And he kept up their force by always revisiting the Tower, when the contest seemed doubtful.

Thus, Lord Curryfin and Mr. Falconer were rivals, with a new phase of rivalry. In some of their variations of feeling, each wished the other success; the latter, because he struggled against a spell that grew more and more difficult to be resisted; the former, because he had been suddenly overpowered by the same kind of light that had shone from the statue of Pygmalion. Thus their rivalry, such as it was, was entirely without animosity, and in no way disturbed the harmony of the Aristophanic party.

The only person concerned in these complications whose thoughts and feelings were undivided, was Miss Niphet. She had begun by laughing at Lord Curryfin, and had ended by forming a decided partiality for him. She contended against the feeling; she was aware of his intentions towards Miss Gryll; and she would perhaps have achieved a conquest over herself, if her sympathies had not been kept in a continual fever by the rashness with which he exposed himself to accidents by flood and field.[2] At the same time, as she was more interested in observing Morgana than Morgana was in observing her,

---

[1] A giant wrestler, by Neptune out of Mother Earth, from whom he received his strength, until Hercules squeezed him to death in mid-air. G.

[2] *Othello*, Act I, Sc. 3. G.

she readily perceived the latter's predilection for Mr. Falconer, and the gradual folding around him of the enchanted net. These observations, and the manifest progressive concentration of Lord Curryfin's affections on herself, showed her that she was not in the way of inflicting any very severe wound on her young friend's feelings, or encouraging a tendency to absolute hopelessness in her own.

Lord Curryfin was pursuing his meditations in the pavilion, when the young lady, whom he had sought there in vain, presented herself before him in great agitation. He started up to meet her, and held out both his hands. She took them both, held them a moment, disengaged them, and sate down at a little distance, which he immediately reduced to nothing. He then expressed his disappointment at not having previously found her in the pavilion, and his delight at seeing her now. After a pause, she said : "I felt so much disturbed in the morning, that I should have devoted the whole day to recovering calmness of thought, but for something I have just heard. My maid tells me that you are going to try that horrid horse in harness, and in a newly-invented high phaeton of your own, and that the grooms say they would not drive that horse in any carriage, nor any horse in that carriage, and that you have a double chance of breaking your neck. I have disregarded all other feelings to entreat you to give up your intention."

Lord Curryfin assured her that he felt too confident in his power over horses, and in the safety of his new invention, to admit the possibility of danger : but that it was a very small sacrifice to her to restrict himself to tame horses and low carriages, or to abstinence from all horses and carriages, if she desired it.

" And from sailing-boats," she added.

" And from sailing-boats," he answered.

" And from balloons," she said.

" And from balloons," he answered. " But what made you think of balloons ? "

" Because," she said, " they are dangerous, and you are inquiring and adventurous."

" To tell you the truth," he said, " I have been up in a balloon. I thought it the most charming excursion I ever made. I have thought of going up again. I have invented a valve——"

" Oh heavens ! " she exclaimed. " But I have your promise touching horses, and carriages, and sails, and balloons."

" You have," he said. " It shall be strictly adhered to."

She rose to return to the house. But this time he would not part with her, and they returned together.

Thus prohibited by an authority to which he yielded implicit obedience, from trying further experiments at the risk of his neck, he restricted his inventive faculty to safer channels, and determined that the structure he was superintending should reproduce, as far as possible, all the peculiarities of the Athenian Theatre. Amongst other things, he studied attentively the subject of the *écheia*, or sonorous vases, which, in that vast theatre, propagated and clarified sound ; and though in its smaller representative they were not needed, he thought it still possible that they might produce an agreeable effect. But with all the assistance of the Reverend Doctor Opimian, he found it difficult to arrive at a clear idea of their construction, or even of their principle ; for the statement of Vitruvius, that they gave an accordant resonance in the fourth, the fifth, and the octave, seemed incompatible with the idea of changes of key, and not easily reconcileable with the doctrine of Harmonics. At last he made up his mind that they had no reference to key, but solely to pitch, modified by duly proportioned magnitude and distance ; he therefore set to work assiduously, got a number of vases made, ascertained that they would give a resonance of some kind, and had them disposed at proper intervals, round the audience part of the building. This being done, the party assembled, some as audience, some as performers, to judge of the effect. The first burst of choral music produced a resonance, like the sound produced by sea-shells when placed against the ear, only many times multiplied, and growing like the sound of a gong : it was the exaggerated concentration of the symphony of a lime-grove full of cockchaffers,[1] on a fine evening in the early summer. The experiment was then tried with single voices : the hum was less in itself, but greater in proportion. It was then tried with speaking : the result was the same : a powerful and

---

[1] The drone of the cockchaffer, as he wheels by you in drowsy hum, sounds his corno di bassetto on F below the line.—Gardiner's *Music of Nature*. [P.]

perpetual hum, not resonant peculiarly to the diatessaron, the diapente, or the diapason, but making a new variety of continuous fundamental bass.

"I am satisfied," said Lord Curryfin, "the art of making these vases is as hopelessly lost as that of making mummies." Miss Niphet encouraged him to persevere. She said :

"You have produced a decided resonance : the only thing is to subdue it, which you may perhaps effect by diminishing the number and enlarging the intervals of the vases."

He determined to act on the suggestion, and she felt that, for some little time at least, she had kept him out of mischief. But whenever anything was said or sung in the theatre, it was necessary, for the time, to remove the *écheia*.

CHAPTER XVIII

Si, Mimnermus uti censet, sine amore jocisque
Nil est jucundum, vivas in amore jocisque.
HOR. *Epist.* I. vi. 65, 66.

If, as Mimnermus held, nought else can move
Your soul to pleasure, live in sports and love.

THE theatre was completed, and was found to be, without the *écheia*, a fine vehicle of sound. It was tried, not only in the morning rehearsals, but occasionally, and chiefly on afternoons of bad weather, by recitations, and even lectures ; for though some of the party attached no value to that mode of dogmatic instruction, yet with the majority, and especially with the young ladies, it was decidedly in favour.

One rainy afternoon Lord Curryfin was entreated to deliver in the theatre his lecture on Fish. He readily complied, and succeeded in amusing his audience more, and instructing them as much, as any of his more pretentious brother lecturers could have done. We shall not report the lecture, but we refer those who may be curious on the subject to the next meeting of the Pantopragmatic Society, under the presidency of Lord Facing-both-ways, and the vice-presidency of Lord Michin Malicho.

At intervals in similar afternoons of bad weather some others of the party were requested to favour the company with lectures or recitations in the theatre. Mr. Minim delivered a lecture on music, Mr. Pallet on painting ; Mr. Falconer, though not used to lecturing, got up one on domestic life in the Homeric age. Even Mr. Gryll took his turn, and expounded the Epicurean philosophy. Mr. Mac-Borrowdale, who had no objection to lectures before dinner, delivered one on all the affairs of the world—foreign and domestic, moral, political, and literary. In the course of it he touched on Reform. "The stone which Lord Michin Malicho—who was the Gracchus[1] of the last Reform, and is the Sisyphus of the present—has been so laboriously pushing up hill, is for the present deposited at the bottom in the Limbo of Vanity. If it should ever surmount the summit and run down on the other side, it will infallibly roll over and annihilate the franchise of the educated classes ; for it would not be worth their while to cross the road to exercise it against the rabble preponderance which would then have been created. Thirty years ago, Lord Michin Malicho had several cogent arguments in favour of Reform. One was, that the people were roaring for it, and that therefore they must have it. He has now in its favour the no less cogent argument, that the people do not care about it, and that the less it is asked for the greater will be the grace of the boon. On the former occasion the out-of-door logic was irresistible. Burning houses, throwing dead cats and cabbage-stumps into carriages, and other varieties of the same system of didactics, demonstrated the fitness of those who practised them to have representatives in Parliament. So they got their representatives, and many think Parliament would have been better without them. My father was a stanch Reformer. In his neighbourhood in London was the place of assembly of a Knowledge-is-Power Club. The members, at the close of their meetings, collected mending-stones from the road, and broke the windows to the right and left of their line of march. They had a flag on which was inscribed THE POWER OF PUBLIC OPINION. Whenever the enlightened assembly met, my father closed his shutters, but, closing within, they did not protect the glass. One morning he picked up, from where it had fallen between the window and the shutter, a very

[1] Famous for integrity and the devotion of the Roman populace. G.

large, and consequently very demonstrative, specimen of dialectical granite. He preserved it carefully, and mounted it on a handsome pedestal, inscribed with THE POWER OF PUBLIC OPINION. He placed it on the middle of his library mantel-piece, and the daily contemplation of it cured him of his passion for Reform. During the rest of his life he never talked, as he had used to do, of ' the people : ' he always said ' the rabble,' and delighted in quoting every passage of *Hudibras* in which the rabble-rout is treated as he had come to conclude it ought to be. He made this piece of granite the nucleus of many political disquisitions. It is still in my possession, and I look on it with veneration as my principal tutor, for it had certainly a large share in the elements of my education. If, which does not seem likely, another reform lunacy should arise in my time, I shall take care to close my shutters against THE POWER OF PUBLIC OPINION."

The Reverend Doctor Opimian being called on to contribute his share to these diversions of rainy afternoons, said :

" The sort of prose lecture which I am accustomed to deliver would not be exactly appropriate to the present time and place. I will therefore recite to you some verses, which I made some time since, on what appeared to me a striking specimen of absurdity on the part of the advisers of royalty here—the bestowing the honours of knighthood, which is a purely Christian institution, on Jews and Paynim ; very worthy persons in themselves, and entitled to any mark of respect befitting their class, but not to one strictly and exclusively Christian ; money-dealers, too, of all callings the most antipathetic to that of a true knight. The contrast impressed itself on me as I was reading a poem of the twelfth century, by Hues de Tabaret—*L'Ordène de Chevalerie*[1]—and I endeavoured to express the contrast in the manner and form following :

---

[1] Or Hue de Tabarie, Chastelain de St. Omer and French Trouvère. He accompanied Godefroy de Bouillon on the Crusade when the latter captured Jerusalem in July 1099. Godefroy's brother rewarded Hue with the principality of Galilee and the Seigneurie of Tiberias from which Hue took his name, which is variously spelt. Hue was taken prisoner by Saladin who commanded him to write his poem of 506 lines on the laws and ritual of chivalry. It would be interesting to know whether Saladin had it translated, or whether he learned French. See *Histoire Littéraire de France*, Tome XVI, and Méon's edition of the *Fabliaux*, 1808.   G.

A NEW ORDER OF CHIVALRY.

I.

Sir Moses, Sir Aaron, Sir Jamramajee,[1]
Two stock-jobbing Jews, and a shroffing Parsee,
Have girt on the armour of old Chivalrie,
And, instead of the Red Cross, have hoisted Balls Three.

Now fancy our Sovereign, so gracious and bland,
With the sword of Saint George in her royal right hand,
Instructing this trio of marvellous Knights
In the mystical meanings of Chivalry's rites.

" You have come from the bath, all in milk-white array,
To show you have washed wordly feelings away,
And, pure as your vestments from secular stain,
Renounce sordid passions and seekings for gain.

" This scarf of deep red o'er your vestments I throw,
In token, that down them your life-blood shall flow,
Ere Chivalry's honour, or Christendom's faith,
Shall meet, through your failure, or peril or scaith.

" These slippers of silk, of the colour of earth,
Are in sign of remembrance of whence you had birth ;
That from earth you have sprung, and to earth you return,
But stand for the faith, life immortal to earn.

" This blow of the sword, on your shoulder-blades true,
Is the mandate of homage, where homage is due,
And the sign, that your swords from the scabbard shall fly,
When ' St. George and the Right ' is the rallying cry.

" This belt of white silk, which no speck has defaced,
Is the sign of a bosom with purity graced,
And binds you to prove, whatsoever betides,
Of damsels distressed the friends, champions, and guides.

" These spurs of pure gold are the symbols which say,
As your steeds obey them, you the Church shall obey,
And speed at her bidding, through country and town,
To strike, with your falchions, her enemies down."

II.

Now fancy these Knights, when the speech they have heard,
As they stand, scarfed, shoed, shoulder-dubbed, belted and spurred,

---

[1] Sir Moses Montefiore and Sir Jamsetjee Jejeebhoy are two of those
referred to.   They were knighted in 1837 and 1842.   G.

With the cross-handled sword duly sheathed on the thigh,
Thus simply and candidly making reply :

" By your majesty's grace we have risen up Knights,
But we feel little relish for frays and for fights :
There are heroes enough, full of spirit and fire,
Always ready to shoot and be shot at for hire.

" True, with bulls and with bears we have battled our cause ;
And the bulls have no horns, and the bears have no paws ;
And the mightiest blow which we ever have struck,
Has achieved but the glory of laming a duck.[1]

" With two nations in arms, friends impartial to both,
To raise each a loan we shall be nothing loth ;
We will lend them the pay, to fit men for the fray ;
But shall keep ourselves carefully out of the way.

" We have small taste for championing maids in distress :
For State we care little : for Church we care less :
To Premium and Bonus our homage we plight :
' Percentage ! ' we cry : and ' A fig for the right ! '

" 'Twixt Saint George and the Dragon, we settle it thus :
Which has scrip above par, is the Hero for us :
For a turn in the market, the Dragon's red gorge
Shall have our free welcome to swallow Saint George."

Now God save our Queen, and if aught should occur,
To peril the crown, or the safety of her,
God send that the leader, who faces the foe,
May have more of King Richard than Moses and Co.

---

[1] In Stock Exchange slang, Bulls are speculators for a rise, Bears for
a fall. A lame duck is a man who cannot pay his differences, and is said to
waddle off. The patriotism of the money-market is well touched by
Ponsard, in his comedy *La Bourse*, Acte iv. Scène 3 [François Ponsard,
1814–1867. G.] :

ALFRED.

Quand nous sommes vainqueurs, dire qu'on a baissé !
Si nous étions battus, on aurait donc haussé ?

DELATOUR.

On a craint qu'un succès, si brillant pour la France,
De la paix qu'on rêvait n'éloignât l'espérance.

ALFRED.

Cette Bourse, morbleu ! n'a donc rien dans le cœur !
Ventre affamé n'a point d'oreilles . . . pour l'honneur !
Aussi je ne veux plus jouer—qu'après ma noce—
Et j'attends Waterloo pour me mettre à la hausse. [P.]

CHAPTER XIX

TRINCQ est ung mot panomphée, célébré et entendu de toutes nations, et nous signifie, BEUUEZ. Et ici maintenons que non rire, ains boyre est le propre de l'homme. Je ne dy boyre simplement et absolument, car aussy bien boyvent les bestes ; je dy boyre vin bon et fraiz.—RABELAIS : l. v. c. 45.[1]

SOME guests remained. Some departed and returned. Among these was Mr. MacBorrowdale. One day after dinner, on one of his reappearances, Lord Curryfin said to him :—

" Well, Mr. MacBorrowdale, in your recent observations, have you found anything likely to satisfy Jack of Dover, if he were prosecuting his inquiry among us ? "

MR. MACBORROWDALE. Troth, no, my lord. I think, if he were among us, he would give up the search as hopeless. He found it so in his own day, and he would find it still more so now. Jack was both merry and wise. We have less mirth in practice ; and we have more wisdom in pretension, which Jack would not have admitted.

THE REVEREND DOCTOR OPIMIAN. He would have found it like Juvenal's search for patriotic virtue, when Catiline was everywhere, and Brutus and Cato were nowhere.[2]

LORD CURRYFIN. Well, among us, if Jack did not find his superior, or even his equal, he would not have been at a loss for company to his mind. There is enough mirth for those who choose to enjoy it, and wisdom too, perhaps as much as he would have cared for. We ought to have more wisdom, as we have clearly more science.

---

[1] " *Trinc* is a panomphian word, that is, a word understood, used, and celebrated by all nations, and signifies drink. . . . Therefore here we hold not that laughing, but that drinking is the distinguishing character of man. I do not say drinking, taking that word singly and absolutely in the strictest sense ; no, beasts then might well put in for a share ; I mean drinking cool delicious wine." Urquhart and Motteux translation.
G.

[2] Et Catilinam
Quocumque in populo videas, quocumque sub axe :
Sed nec Brutus erit, Bruti nec avunculus usquam.
JUV. *Sat.* xiv. 41–43. [P.]
[" You will find a Catiline among any nation and in any clime ; nowhere a Brutus, or one like Brutus's uncle." G.]

THE REVEREND DOCTOR OPIMIAN. Science is one thing, and wisdom is another. Science is an edged tool, with which men play like children, and cut their own fingers. If you look at the results which science has brought in its train, you will find them to consist almost wholly in elements of mischief. See how much belongs to the word Explosion alone, of which the ancients knew nothing. Explosions of powder-mills and powder-magazines; of coal-gas in mines and in houses; of high-pressure engines in ships and boats and factories. See the complications and refinements of modes of destruction, in revolvers and rifles and shells and rockets and cannon. See collisions and wrecks and every mode of disaster by land and by sea, resulting chiefly from the insanity for speed, in those who for the most part have nothing to do at the end of the race, which they run as if they were so many Mercuries speeding with messages from Jupiter. Look at our scientific drainage, which turns refuse into poison. Look at the subsoil of London, whenever it is turned up to the air, converted by gas leakage into one mass of pestilent blackness, in which no vegetation can flourish, and above which, with the rapid growth of the ever-growing nuisance, no living thing will breathe with impunity. Look at our scientific machinery, which has destroyed domestic manufacture, which has substituted rottenness for strength in the thing made, and physical degradation in crowded towns for healthy and comfortable country life in the makers. The day would fail, if I should attempt to enumerate the evils which science has inflicted on mankind. I almost think it is the ultimate destiny of science to exterminate the human race.

LORD CURRYFIN. You have gone over a wide field, which we might exhaust a good bin of claret in fully discussing. But surely the facility of motion over the face of the earth and sea is both pleasant and profitable. We may now see the world with little expenditure of labour or time.

THE REVEREND DOCTOR OPIMIAN. You may be whisked over it, but you do not see it. You go from one great town to another, where manners and customs are not even now essentially different, and with this facility of intercourse become progressively less and less so. The intermediate country—which you never see, unless there is a show mountain or waterfall or ruin, for which there is a station, and to which you go as you would to any other exhibition—the intermediate country contains all that is really worth seeing, to enable you to judge of the various characteristics of men and the diversified objects of nature.

LORD CURRYFIN. You can suspend your journey if you please, and see the intermediate country if you prefer it.

THE REVEREND DOCTOR OPIMIAN. But who does prefer it ? You travel round the world by a hand-book, as you do round an exhibition-room by a catalogue.

MR. MACBORROWDALE. Not to say, that in the intermediate country you are punished by bad inns and bad wine ; of which I confess myself intolerant. I knew an unfortunate French tourist, who had made the round of Switzerland, and had but one expression for every stage of his journey : *Mauvaise auberge !*

LORD CURRYFIN. Well, then, what say you to the electric tele-graph, by which you converse at the distance of thousands of miles ? Even across the Atlantic, as no doubt we shall yet do.

MR. GRYLL. Some of us have already heard the Doctor's opinion on that subject.

THE REVEREND DOCTOR OPIMIAN. I have no wish to expedite communication with the Americans. If we could apply the power of electrical repulsion to preserve us from ever hearing anything more of them, I should think that we had for once derived a benefit from science.

MR. GRYLL. Your love for the Americans, Doctor, seems something like that of Cicero's friend Marius for the Greeks. He would not take the nearest road to his villa, because it was called the Greek-road.[1]

---

[1] Non enim te puto Græcos ludos desiderare : præsertim quum Græcos ita non ames, ut ne ad villam quidem tuam viâ Græcâ ire soleas.—Cicero : *Ep. ad Div.* vii. i. [P.] [" For I do not imagine you have any desire for Greek entertainments, especially since you regularly avoid the *via Graeca* even going to your country house." G.]

Perhaps if your nearest way home was called the American-road, you would make a circuit to avoid it.

THE REVEREND DOCTOR OPIMIAN. I am happy to say I am not put to the test. Magnetism, galvanism, electricity, are "one form of many names."[1] Without magnetism we should never have discovered America ; to which we are indebted for nothing but evil ; diseases in the worst forms that can afflict humanity, and slavery in the worst form in which slavery can exist. The Old World had the sugar-cane and the cotton-plant, though it did not so misuse them. Then, what good have we got from America ? What good of any kind, from the whole continent and its islands, from the Esquimaux to Patagonia ?

MR. GRYLL. Newfoundland salt fish, Doctor.

THE REVEREND DOCTOR OPIMIAN. That is something, but it does not turn the scale.

MR. GRYLL. If they have given us no good, we have given them none.

THE REVEREND DOCTOR OPIMIAN. We have given them wine and classical literature ; but I am afraid Bacchus and Minerva have equally

Scattered their bounty upon barren ground.[2]

On the other hand, we have given the red men rum, which has been the chief instrument of their perdition. On the whole, our inter-course with America has been little else than an interchange of vices and diseases.

LORD CURRYFIN. Do you count it nothing to have substituted civilized for savage men ?

THE REVEREND DOCTOR OPIMIAN. Civilized. The word requires definition. But looking into futurity, it seems to me that the

[1] Πολλῶν ὀνομάτων μορφὴ μία.—Æschylus: Prometheus. [P.]
[212. G.]
[2] Possibly adapted from Gray's Elegy, St. 16 : " To scatter plenty o'er a smiling land." G.

ultimate tendency of the change is to substitute the worse for the better race ; the Negro for the Red Indian. The Red Indian will not work for a master. No ill-usage will make him. Herein, he is the noblest specimen of humanity that ever walked the earth. Therefore, the white man exterminates his race. But the time will come, when by mere force of numbers, the black race will predominate, and exterminate the white. And thus the worse race will be substituted for the better, even as it is in Saint Domingo, where the Negro has taken the place of the Caraib. The change is clearly for the worse.

LORD CURRYFIN. You imply, that in the meantime the white race is better than the red.

THE REVEREND DOCTOR OPIMIAN. I leave that as an open question. But I hold, as some have done before me, that the human mind degenerates in America, and that the superiority, such as it is, of the white race is only kept up by intercourse with Europe. Look at the atrocities in their ships. Look at their Congress and their Courts of Justice ; debaters in the first ; suitors, even advocates, sometimes judges, in the second, settling their arguments with pistol and dagger. Look at their extensions of slavery, and their revivals of the slave-trade, now covertly, soon to be openly.[1] If it were possible that the two worlds could be absolutely dissevered for a century, I think a new Columbus would find nothing in America but savages.

LORD CURRYFIN. You look at America, Doctor, through your hatred of slavery. You must remember that we introduced it when they were our colonists. It is not so easily got rid of. Its abolition by France exterminated the white race in Saint Domingo, as the white race had exterminated the red. Its abolition by England ruined our West Indian colonies.

THE REVEREND DOCTOR OPIMIAN. Yes, in conjunction with the direct encouragement of foreign slave labour, given by our friends of liberty under the pretext of free trade. It is a mockery to keep up a squadron for suppressing the slave-trade on the one hand, while,

[1] This passage was written on the eve of the American Civil War. G.

on the other hand we encourage it to an extent that counteracts in a tenfold degree the apparent power of suppression. It is a clear case of false pretension.

MR. GRYLL. You know, Doctor, the Old World had slavery throughout its entire extent ; under the Patriarchs, the Greeks, the Romans ; everywhere, in short. Cicero thought our island not likely to produce anything worth having excepting slaves ; [1] and of those none skilled, as some slaves were, in letters and music, but all utterly destitute of both. And in the Old World the slaves were of the same race with the masters. The Negroes are an inferior race, not fit, I am afraid, for anything else.

THE REVEREND DOCTOR OPIMIAN. Not fit, perhaps, for anything else belonging to what we call civilized life. Very fit to live on little, and wear nothing, in Africa ; where it would have been a blessing to themselves and the rest of the world if they had been left unmolested ; if they had had a Friar Bacon to surround their entire continent with a wall of brass.

MR. FALCONER. I am not sure, Doctor, that in many instances, even yet, the white slavery of our factories is not worse than the black slavery of America. We have done much to amend it, and shall do more. Still much remains to be done.

THE REVEREND DOCTOR OPIMIAN. And will be done, I hope and believe. The Americans do nothing to amend their system. On the contrary, they do all they can to make bad worse. Whatever excuse there may be for maintaining slavery where it exists, there can be none for extending it into new territories ; none for reviving the African slave-trade. These are the crying sins of America. Our

---

[1] Etiam illud jam cognitum est, neque argenti scripulum esse ullum in illâ insulâ, neque ullam spem prædæ, nisi ex mancipiis : ex quibus nullos puto te literis aut musicis eruditos expectare.—Cicero *ad Atticum*, iv. 16.

[" It is also known that there is not an atom of silver in the island, and no hope of any loot, except in the shape of slaves, and I do not suppose that you expect any of them to be skilled in letters or in music." G.]

A hope is expressed by Pomponius Mela, l. iii. c. 6 (he wrote under Claudius), that, by the success of the Roman arms, the island and its savage inhabitants would soon be better known. It is amusing enough to peruse such passages in the midst of London.—Gibbon : c. i. [P.]

white slavery, so far as it goes, is so far worse, that it is the degradation of a better race.   But if it be not redressed, as I trust it will be,
it will work out its own retribution.   And so it is of all the oppressions
that are done under the sun.   Though all men but the red men will
work for a master, they will not fight for an oppressor in the day of his
need.   Thus gigantic empires have crumbled into dust at the first
touch of an invader's footstep.   For petty, as for great oppressions,
there is a day of retribution growing out of themselves.   It is often
long in coming.   *Ut sit magna, tamen certe lenta ira Deorum est.*[1]
But it comes.

> Raro antecedentem scelestum
> Deseruit pede Pœna claudo. [2]

LORD CURRYFIN.   I will not say, Doctor, " I've seen, and sure I
ought to know."   But I have been in America, and I have found
there, what many others will testify, a very numerous class of persons,
who hold opinions very like your own : persons who altogether keep
aloof from public life, because they consider it abandoned to the
rabble ; but who are as refined, as enlightened, as full of sympathy
for all that tends to justice and liberty, as any whom you may most
approve amongst ourselves.

THE REVEREND DOCTOR OPIMIAN.   Of that I have no doubt.   But
I look to public acts and public men.

LORD CURRYFIN.   I should much like to know what Mr. Mac-
Borrowdale thinks of all this.

MR. MACBORROWDALE.   Troth, my lord, I think we have strayed
far away from the good company we began with.   We have lost sight
of Jack of Dover.   But the discussion had one bright feature.   It
did not interfere with, it rather promoted, the circulation of the
bottle : for every man who spoke pushed it on with as much energy
as he spoke with, and those who were silent swallowed the wine and
the opinion together, as if they relished them both.

---

[1] The anger of the Gods, though great, is slow.   [P.]
      [Juvenal :   *Sat.* XIII. 100.   G.]
[2] The foot of Punishment, though lame,
      O'ertakes at last preceding Wrong.   [P.]
          [Horace :   *Odes*, III. 31.   G.]

THE REVEREND DOCTOR OPIMIAN. So far, discussion may find favour. In my own experience, I have found it very absorbent of claret. But I do not think it otherwise an incongruity after dinner, provided it be carried on, as our disquisitions have always been, with frankness and good humour. Consider how much instruction has been conveyed to us in the form of conversations at banquets, by Plato and Xenophon and Plutarch. I read nothing with more pleasure than their *Symposia* : to say nothing of Athenæus, whose work is one long banquet.

MR. MACBORROWDALE. Nay, I do not object to conversation on any subject. I object to after-dinner lectures. I have had some unfortunate experiences. I have found what began in conversation end in a lecture. I have on different occasions met several men, who were in that respect all alike. Once started they never stopped. The rest of the good company, or rather the rest, which without them would have been good company, was no company. No one could get in a word. They went on with one unvarying stream of monotonous desolating sound. This makes me tremble when a discussion begins. I sit in fear of a lecture.

LORD CURRYFIN. Well, you and I have lectured, but never after dinner. We do it when we have promised it, and when those who are present expect it. After dinner, I agree with you, it is the most doleful blight that can fall on human enjoyment.

MR. MACBORROWDALE. I will give you one or two examples of these post-prandial inflictions. One was a great Indian reformer. He did not open his mouth till he had had about a bottle and a half of wine. Then he burst on us with a declamation, on all that was wrong in India, and its remedy. He began in the Punjab, travelled to Calcutta, went southward, got into the Temple of Juggernaut, went southward again, and after holding forth for more than an hour, paused for a moment. The man who sate next him attempted to speak : but the orator clapped him on the arm, and said : " Excuse me : now I come to Madras." On which his neighbour jumped up and vanished. Another went on in the same way about currency. His first hour's talking carried him just through the Restriction Act of ninety-seven. As we had then more than half a century before us, I took my departure. But these were two whom topography and chronology would have brought to a close. The bore of all bores was the third. His subject had no beginning, middle, nor end. It was education. Never was such a journey through the desert of mind : the Great Sahara of intellect. The very recollection makes me thirsty.

THE REVEREND DOCTOR OPIMIAN. If all the nonsense which, in the last quarter of a century, has been talked on all other subjects, were thrown into one scale, and all that has been talked on the subject of education alone were thrown into the other, I think the latter would preponderate.

LORD CURRYFIN. We have had through the whole period some fine specimens of nonsense on other subjects : for instance, with a single exception, Political Economy.

MR. MACBORROWDALE. I understand your lordship's politeness as excepting the present company. You need not except me. I am " free to confess," as they say " in another place," that I have talked a great deal of nonsense on that subject myself.

LORD CURRYFIN. Then, we have had latterly a mighty mass on the Purification of the Thames.

THE REVEREND DOCTOR OPIMIAN. Allowing full weight to the two last-named ingredients, they are not more than a counterpoise to Competitive Examination, which is also a recent exotic belonging to education.

LORD CURRYFIN. Patronage, it used to be alleged, considered only the fitness of the place for the man, not the fitness of the man for the place. It was desirable to reverse this.

THE REVEREND DOCTOR OPIMIAN. True : but

Dum vitant stulti vitium, in contraria currunt.[1]

---

[1] When fools would from one vice take flight,
They rush into its opposite.
HOR. *Sat.* i. 2, 24. [P.]

Questions, which can only be answered by the parrotings of a memory, crammed to disease with all sorts of heterogeneous diet, can form no test of genius, taste, judgment, or natural capacity. Competitive Examination takes for its *norma* : " It is better to learn many things ill than one thing well ; " or rather : " It is better to learn to gabble about everything than to understand anything." This is not the way to discover the wood of which Mercuries are made.[1] I have been told that this precious scheme has been borrowed from China : a pretty fountain-head for moral and political improvement : and if so, I may say, after Petronius : " This windy and monstrous loquacity has lately found its way to us from Asia, and like a pestilential star has blighted the minds of youth, otherwise rising to greatness." [2]

LORD CURRYFIN. There is something to be said on behalf of applying the same tests, addressing the same questions, to everybody.

THE REVEREND DOCTOR OPIMIAN. I shall be glad to hear what can be said on that behalf.

LORD CURRYFIN (*after a pause*). " Mass," as the second grave-digger says in *Hamlet*, " I cannot tell." [3]

A chorus of laughter dissolved the sitting.

CHAPTER XX

Les violences qu'on se fait pour s'empêcher d'aimer sont souvent plus cruelles que les rigueurs de ce qu'on aime.—LA ROCHEFOUCAULD.

THE winter set in early. December began with intense frost. Mr. Falconer, one afternoon, entering the inner drawing-room, found Miss Gryll alone. She was reading, and on the entrance of her visitor

---

[1] " You cannot make a Mercury of every log." The proper wood for a statue of this God was box-wood. G.

[2] Nuper ventosa isthæc et enormis loquacitas Athenas ex Asiâ commigravit, animosque juvenum, ad magna surgentes, veluti pestilenti quodam sidere afflavit. [P.] [*Satyr*. C. 2. G.]

[3] Act V, Sc. 1. G.

laid down her book. He hoped he had not interrupted her in an agreeable occupation. "To observe romantic method,"[1] we shall give what passed between them with the Christian names of the speakers.

MORGANA. I am only reading what I have often read before, *Orlando Innamorato* ; and I was at the moment occupied with a passage about the enchantress from whom my name was borrowed. You are aware that enchantresses are in great favour here.

ALGERNON. Circe and Gryllus and your name sufficiently show that. And not your name only, but—I should like to see the passage, and should be still better pleased if you would read it to me.

MORGANA. It is where Orlando, who had left Morgana sleeping by the fountain, returns to seek the enchanted key, by which alone he can liberate his friends.

> Il Conte, che d'intrare havea gran voglia,
> Subitamente al fonte ritornava :
> Quivi trovò Morgana, che con gioglia
> Danzava intorno, e danzando cantava.
> Nè più leggier si move al vento foglia
> Come ella sanza sosta si voltava,
> Mirando hora a la terra ed hora al sole ;
> Ed al suo canto usava tal parole :
>
> " Qualonque cerca al mondo haver thesoro,
> Over diletto, o segue onore e stato,
> Ponga la mano a questa chioma d'oro,
> Ch' io porto in fronte, e quel farò beato.
> Ma quando ha il destro a far cotal lavoro,
> Non prenda indugio, che'l tempo passato
> Più non ritorna, e non si trova mai ;
> Ed io mi volto, e lui lascio con guai."
>
> Così cantava d' intorno girando
> La bella Fata a quella fresca fonte :
> Ma come gionto vide il Conte Orlando,
> Subitamente rivoltò la fronte :
> Il prato e la fontana abbandonando,
> Prese il viaggio suo verso d'un monte,

---

[1] Butler : *Hudibras*, Pt. II, Canto 1, l. 1.   G.

Qual chiudea la valletta picciolina :
Quivi fuggendo Morgana cammina.[1]

ALGERNON. I remember the passage well. The beautiful *Fata*, dancing and singing by the fountain, presents a delightful picture.

MORGANA. Then, you know, Orlando, who had missed his opportunity of seizing the golden forelock while she was sleeping, pursues her a long while in vain through rocky deserts, *La Penitenza*

---

[1] Bojardo : l. ii. c. 8.   *Ed. Vinegia*, 1544.

With earnest wish to pass the enchanted gate,
Orlando to the fount again advanced,
And found Morgana, all with joy elate,
Dancing around, and singing as she danced.
As lightly moved and twirled the lovely Fate
As to the breeze the lightest foliage glanced,
With looks alternate to the earth and sky,
She thus gave out her words of witchery :

" Let him, who seeks unbounded wealth to hold,
Or joy, or honour, or terrestrial state,
Seize with his hand this lock of purest gold,
That crowns my brow, and blest shall be his fate.
But when time serves, behoves him to be bold,
Nor even a moment's pause interpolate :
The chance once lost he never finds again :
I turn, and leave him to lament in vain."

Thus sang the lovely Fate in bowery shade,
Circling in joy around the crystal fount ;
But when within the solitary glade
Glittered the armour of the approaching Count,
She sprang upon her feet, as one dismayed,
And took her way towards a lofty mount,
That rose the valley's narrow length to bound :
Thither Morgana sped along the ground.

I have translated *Fata*, Fate. It is usually translated Fairy. But the idea differs essentially from ours of a fairy. Amongst other things, there is no *Fato*, no Oberon to the Titania. It does not, indeed, correspond with our usual idea of Fate, but it is more easily distinguished as a class ; for our old acquaintances the Fates are an inseparable three. The Italian *Fata* is independent of her sisters. They are enchantresses ; but they differ from other enchantresses in being immortal. They are beautiful too, and their beauty is immortal : always in Bojardo. He would not have turned Alcina into an old woman, as Ariosto did ; which I must always consider a dreadful blemish on the many charms of the *Orlando Furioso*. [P.]

following him with a scourge. The same idea was afterwards happily worked out by Machiavelli in his *Capitolo dell' Occasione.*

ALGERNON. You are fond of Italian literature ? You read the language beautifully. I observe you have read from the original poem, and not from Berni's *rifacciamento.*

MORGANA. I prefer the original. It is more simple, and more in earnest. Berni's playfulness is very pleasant, and his exordiums are charming ; and in many instances he has improved the poetry. Still, I think, he has less than the original of what are to me the great charms of poetry, truth and simplicity. Even the greater antiquity of style has its peculiar appropriateness to the subject. And Bojardo seems to have more faith in his narrative than Berni. I go on with him with ready credulity, where Berni's pleasantry interposes a doubt.

ALGERNON. You think that in narratives, however wild and romantic, the poet should write as if he fully believed in the truth of his own story.

MORGANA. I do ; and I think so in reference to all narratives, not to poetry only. What a dry skeleton is the History of the early ages of Rome, told by one who believes nothing that the Romans believed. Religion pervades every step of the early Roman History ; and in a great degree down at least to the Empire ; but because their religion is not our religion, we pass over the supernatural part of the matter in silence, or advert to it in a spirit of contemptuous incredulity. We do not give it its proper place, nor present it in its proper colours, as a cause in the production of great effects. Therefore, I like to read Livy, and I do not like to read Niebuhr.

ALGERNON. May I ask if you read Latin ?

MORGANA. I do ; sufficiently to derive great pleasure from it. Perhaps, after this confession, you will not wonder that I am a spinster.

ALGERNON. So far, that I think it would tend to make you fastidious in your choice. Not that you would be less sought by

any who would be worthy your attention. For I am told, you have
had many suitors, and have rejected them all in succession. And
have you not still many, and among them one very devoted lover,
who would bring you title as well as fortune ? A very amiable
person, too, though not without a comic side to his character.

MORGANA. I do not well know. He so far differs from all my
preceding suitors, that in every one of them I found the presence of
some quality that displeased me, or the absence of some which would
have pleased me : the want, in the one way or the other, of that
entire congeniality in taste and feeling, which I think essential to
happiness in marriage. He has so strong a desire of pleasing, and
such power of acquisition and assimilation, that I think a woman
truly attached to him might mould him to her mind. Still, I can
scarcely tell why, he does not complete my idealities. They say,
Love is his own avenger : and perhaps I shall be punished by finding
my idealities realised in one who will not care for me.

ALGERNON. I take that to be impossible.

Morgana blushed, held down her head, and made no reply.
Algernon looked at her with silent admiration. A new light seemed to
break in on him. Though he had had so many opportunities of
forming a judgment on the point, it seemed to strike him for the first
time with irresistible conviction that he had never before heard such
a sweet voice, nor seen such an expressive and intelligent countenance. And in this way they continued like two figures in a *tableau
vivant*, till the entrance of other parties broke the spell which had
thus fixed them in their positions.

A few minutes more, and their destinies might have been irrevocably fixed. But the interruption gave Mr. Falconer the opportunity
of returning again to his Tower, to consider, in the presence of the
seven sisters, whether he should not be in the position of a Roman,
who was reduced to the dilemma of migrating without his household
deities, or of suffering his local deities to migrate without him ; and
whether he could sit comfortably on either of the horns of this
dilemma. He felt that he could not. On the other hand, could he
bear to see the fascinating Morgana metamorphosed into Lady

Curryfin ? The time had been when he had half wished it, as the means of restoring him to liberty. He felt now, that when in her society he could not bear the idea ; but he still thought, that in the midst of his domestic deities he might become reconciled to it.

He did not care for horses, nor keep any for his own use.[1] But as time and weather were not always favourable to walking, he had provided for himself a comfortable travelling-chariot, without a box to intercept the view, in which, with post-horses after the fashion of the olden time, he performed occasional migrations. He found this vehicle of great use in moving to and fro between the Grange and the Tower ; for then, with all his philosophy, Impatience was always his companion : Impatience on his way to the Grange, to pass into the full attraction of the powerful spell by which he was drawn like the fated ship to the magnetic rock in the *Arabian Nights*: Impatience on his way to the Tower, to find himself again in the "Regions mild of pure and serene air," in which the seven sisters seemed to dwell, like Milton's ethereal spirits "Before the starry threshold of Jove's court."[2] Here was everything to soothe, nothing to irritate or disturb him : nothing on the spot : but it was with him, as it is with many, perhaps with all : the two great enemies of tranquillity, Hope and Remembrance, would still intrude : not like a bubble and a spectre, as in the beautiful lines of Coleridge :[3] for the remembrance of Morgana was not a spectre, and the hope of her love, which he cherished in spite of himself, was not a bubble : but their forces were not less disturbing, even in the presence of his earliest and most long and deeply cherished associations.

He did not allow his impatience to require that the horses should

---

[1] In this he shows his relation with Mr. Forester in *Melincourt*. See pp. 239 and 244. G.

[2] The fourth and first lines of *Comus*. G.

[3] Who late and lingering seeks thy shrine,
On him but seldom, Power divine,
Thy spirit rests. Satiety,
And sloth, poor counterfeits of thee,
Mock the tired worldling. Idle Hope,
And dire Remembrance, interlope,
And vex the feverish slumbers of the mind :
The bubble floats before : the spectre stalks behind.
　　　　　Coleridge's *Ode to Tranquillity*. [P.]

be put to extraordinary speed. He found something tranquillizing in the movement of a postillion in a smart jacket, vibrating on one horse upwards and downwards, with one invariable regulated motion like the cross-head of a side-lever steam-engine,[1] and holding the whip quietly arched over the neck of the other.   The mechanical monotony of the movement seemed less in contrast than in harmony with the profound stillness of the wintry forest : the leafless branches heavy with rime frost and glittering in the sun : the deep repose of nature, broken now and then by the traversing of deer, or the flight of wild birds : highest and loudest among them the long lines of rooks : but for the greater part of the way one long deep silence, undisturbed but by the rolling of the wheels and the iron tinkling of the hoofs on the -frozen ground. By degrees he fell into a reverie, and meditated on his last dialogue with Morgana.

" It is a curious coincidence," he thought, " that she should have been dwelling on a passage, in which her namesake enchantress inflicted punishment on Orlando for having lost his opportunity. Did she associate Morgana with herself and Orlando with me ?   Did she intend a graceful hint to me not to lose *my* opportunity ? I seemed in a fair way to seize the golden forelock, if we had not been interrupted. Do I regret that I did not ?   That is just what I cannot determine. Yet it would be more fitting, that whatever I may do should be done calmly, deliberately, philosophically, than suddenly, passionately, impulsively. One thing is clear to me. It is now or never : this or none. The world does not contain a second Morgana, at least not of mortal race. Well : the opportunity will return. So far, I am not in the predicament in which we left Orlando. I may yet ward off the scourge of *La Penitenza*."

But his arrival at home, and the sight of the seven sisters, who had all come to the hall-door to greet him, turned his thoughts for awhile into another channel.

He dined at his usual hour, and his two Hebes alternately filled his glass with Madeira. After which the sisters played and sang to him in the drawing-room ; and when he had retired to his chamber, had looked on the many portraitures of his Virgin Saint, and had

---

[1] A reminder that Peacock had personally supervised the steam trials of the ships which he had had constructed for the East India Company.   G.

thought by how many charms of life he was surrounded, he composed himself to rest with the reflection : " I am here like Rasselas in the Happy Valley : and I can now fully appreciate the force of that beautiful chapter : *The wants of him who wants nothing.*" [1]

CHAPTER XXI

Ubi lepos, joci, risus, ebrietas decent,
Gratiæ, decor, hilaritas, atque delectatio,
Qui quærit alia his, malum videtur quærere.
                              PLAUTUS : *In Pseudolo.* [2]

Where sport, mirth, wine, joy, grace, conspire to please,
He seeks but ill who seeks aught else than these.

THE frost continued. The lake was covered over with solid ice. This became the chief scene of afternoon amusement, and Lord Curryfin carried off the honours of the skating. In the dead of the night, there came across his memory a ridiculous stave :

There's Mr. Tait, he cuts an eight,
He cannot cut a nine : [3]

and he determined on trying if he could not outdo Mr. Tait. He thought it would be best to try his experiment without witnesses : and having more than an hour's daylight before breakfast, he devoted that portion of the morning to his purpose. But cutting a nine by itself baffled his skill, and treated him to two or three tumbles, which however did not abate his ardour. At length he bethought him of cutting a nine between two eights, and by shifting his feet rapidly at the points of difficulty, striking in and out of the nine to and from the eights on each side. In this he succeeded, and exhibiting his achievement in the afternoon, adorned the surface of the ice with successions of 898, till they amounted to as many sextillions, with their homogeneous sequences. He then enclosed the line with an oval, and returned to the bank through an admiring circle, who, if they had been as numerous as the spectators at the Olympic games, would have greeted him with as loud shouts of triumph as saluted Epharmostus of Opus. [4]

[1] Ch. III of *Rasselas* by Dr. Johnson.   G.
[2] *Prol.* 20–2.   G.   [3] Quotation untraced.   G.
[4] Διήρχετο κύκλον ὅσσα βοᾷ.—Pind. *Olymp.* ix. [140. G.]
With what a clamour he passed through the circle. [P.]

Among the spectators on the bank were Miss Niphet and Mr. MacBorrowdale, standing side by side. While Lord Curryfin was cutting his sextillions, Mr. MacBorrowdale said : " There is a young gentleman who is capable of anything, and who would shine in any pursuit, if he would keep to it. He shines as it is, in almost everything he takes in hand in private society : there is genius even in his failures, as in the case of the theatrical vases ; but the world is a field of strong competition, and affords eminence to few in any sphere of exertion, and to those few rarely but in one."

MISS NIPHET. Before I knew him, I never heard of him but as a lecturer on Fish : and to that he seems to limit his public ambition. In private life, his chief aim seems to be that of pleasing his company. Of course, you do not attach much value to his present pursuit. You see no utility in it.

MR. MACBORROWDALE. On the contrary, I see great utility in it. I am for a healthy mind in a healthy body : the first can scarcely be without the last, and the last can scarcely be without good exercise in pure air. In this way, there is nothing better than skating. I should be very glad to cut eights and nines with his lordship : but the only figure I should cut, would be that of as many feet as would measure my own length on the ice.

Lord Curryfin, on his return to land, thought it his duty first to accost Miss Gryll, who was looking on by the side of Miss Ilex. He asked her if she ever skated. She answered in the negative. " I have tried it," she said, " but unsuccessfully. I admire it extremely, and regret my inability to participate in it." He then went up to Miss Niphet, and asked her the same question. She answered : " I have skated often in our grounds at home." " Then why not now ? " he asked. She answered : " I have never done it before so many witnesses." " But what is the objection ? " he asked. " None that I know of," she answered. " Then," he said, " as I have done or left undone some things to please you, will you do this one thing to please me ? " " Certainly," she replied : adding to herself : " I will do anything in my power to please you."

She equipped herself expeditiously, and started before he was well aware. She was half round the lake before he came up with her. She then took a second start, and completed the circle before he came up with her again. He saw that she was an Atalanta on ice as on turf. He placed himself by her side, slipped her arm through his, and they started together on a second round, which they completed arm-in-arm. By this time the blush-rose bloom which had so charmed him on a former occasion again mantled on her cheeks, though from a different cause, for it was now only the glow of healthful exercise ; but he could not help exclaiming, " I now see why and with what tints the Athenians coloured their statues."

" Is it clear," she asked, " that they did so ? "

" I have doubted it before," he answered, " but I am now certain that they did."

In the meantime Miss Gryll, Miss Ilex, and the Reverend Doctor Opimian had been watching their movements from the bank.

MISS ILEX. I have seen much graceful motion in dancing, in private society and on the Italian stage ; and some in skating before to-day ; but anything so graceful as that double-gliding over the ice by those two remarkably handsome young persons, I certainly never saw before.

MISS GRYLL. Lord Curryfin is unquestionably handsome, and Miss Niphet, especially with that glow on her cheeks, is as beautiful a young woman as imagination can paint. They move as if impelled by a single will. It is impossible not to admire them both.

THE REVEREND DOCTOR OPIMIAN. They remind me of the mythological fiction, that Jupiter made men and women in pairs, like the Siamese twins ; but in this way they grew so powerful and presumptuous, that he cut them in two ; and now the main business of each half is to look for the other ; which is very rarely found, and hence so few marriages are happy.[1] Here the two true halves seem to have met.

The Doctor looked at Miss Gryll, to see what impression this remark might make on her. He concluded that, if she thought seriously of

[1] See Plato : *The Symposium,* Aristophanes's fable. G.

Lord Curryfin, she would show some symptom of jealousy of Miss Niphet ; but she did not. She merely said,

"I quite agree with you, Doctor. There is evidently great congeniality between them, even in their respective touches of eccentricity."

But the Doctor's remark had suggested to her what she herself had failed to observe ; Lord Curryfin's subsidence from ardour into deference, in his pursuit of herself. She had been so undividedly "the cynosure of neighbouring eyes,"[1] that she could scarcely believe in the possibility of even temporary eclipse. Her first impulse was to resign him to her young friend. But then appearances might be deceitful. Her own indifference might have turned his attentions into another channel, without his heart being turned with them. She had seen nothing to show that Miss Niphet's feelings were deeply engaged in the question. She was not a coquet ; but she would still feel it as a mortification that her hitherto unquestioned supremacy should be passing from her. She had felt all along, that there was one cause which would lead her to a decided rejection of Lord Curryfin. But her Orlando had not seized the golden forelock ; perhaps he never would. After having seemed on the point of doing so, he had disappeared, and not returned. He was now again within the links of the seven-fold chain, which had bound him from his earliest days. She herself, too, had had, perhaps had still, the chance of the golden forelock in another quarter. Might she not subject her after-life to repentance, if her first hope should fail her, when the second had been irrevocably thrown away ? The more she contemplated the sacrifice, the greater it appeared. Possibly doubt had given preponderance to her thoughts of Mr. Falconer ; and certainty had caused them to repose in the case of Lord Curryfin ; but when doubt was thrown into the latter scale also, the balance became more even. She would still give him his liberty, if she believed that he wished it ; for then her pride would settle the question ; but she must have more conclusive evidence on the point than the Reverend Doctor's metaphorical deduction from a mythological fiction.

In the evening, while the party in the drawing-room were amusing themselves in various ways, Mr. MacBorrowdale laid a drawing on

[1] Milton : *L'Allegro*. G.

the table, and said, "Doctor, what should you take that to represent ? "

THE REVEREND DOCTOR OPIMIAN. An unformed lump of I know not what.

MR. MACBORROWDALE. Not unformed. It is a flint formation of a very peculiar kind.

THE REVEREND DOCTOR OPIMIAN. Very peculiar, certainly. Who on earth can have amused himself with drawing a misshapen flint ? There must be some riddle in it ; some ænigma, as insoluble to me as *Aelia Laelia Crispis*.[1]

Lord Curryfin, and others of the party, were successively asked their opinions. One of the young ladies guessed it to be the petrifaction of an antediluvian mussel. Lord Curryfin said petrifactions were often siliceous, but never pure silex; which this purported to be. It gave him the idea of an ass's head ; which, however, could not by any process have been turned into flint.

Conjecture being exhausted, Mr. MacBorrowdale said, " It is a thing they call a Celt. The ass's head is somewhat germane to the matter. The Artium Societatis Syndicus Et Socii have determined that it is a weapon of war, evidently of human manufacture. It has been found, with many others like it, among bones of mammoths and other extinct animals, and is therefore held to prove, that men and mammoths were contemporaries."

[1] This ænigma has been the subject of many learned disquisitions. The reader, who is unacquainted with it, may find it under the article " Ænigma " in the *Encyclopædia Britannica*; and probably in every other encyclopædia.
[P.]
[In 1862, Peacock published his own interpretation of this famous enigma in the same volume as his translation of *Gl' Ingannati*, an Italian source for *Twelfth Night*. It is included in Vol. X of the Halliford Edition of Peacock's works. Aelia Laelia Crispis is a sepulchral inscription on a marble found near Bologna in the seventeenth century. It was erected to : " not man, nor woman, nor hermaphrodite . . . lying not in air, not in earth, not in the waters, but everywhere . . . by Lucius Agatho Priscus, not her husband, nor her lover, nor her friend," who " knows, and knows not, to whom he erects it." It is perhaps comparable to the monuments to Unknown Soldiers erected in several countries after the 1914–1918 war. G.]

THE REVEREND DOCTOR OPIMIAN. A weapon of war ? Had it a handle ? Is there a hole for a handle ? [1]

MR. MACBORROWDALE. That does not appear.

THE REVEREND DOCTOR OPIMIAN. These flints, and no other traces of men, among the bones of mammoths ?

MR. MACBORROWDALE. None whatever.

THE REVEREND DOCTOR OPIMIAN. What do the Artium Societatis Syndicus Et Socii suppose to have become of the men, who produced these demonstrations of high aboriginal art ?

MR. MACBORROWDALE. They think these finished specimens of skill in the art of chipping prove that the human race is of greater antiquity than has been previously supposed ; and the fact, that there is no other relic to prove the position, they consider of no moment whatever.

THE REVEREND DOCTOR OPIMIAN. Ha ! ha ! ha ! This beats the Elephant in the Moon,[2] which turned out to be a mouse in a telescope. But I can help them to an explanation of what became of these primæval men-of-arms. They were an ethereal race, and evaporated.

CHAPTER XXII

Over the mountains,
  And over the waves ;
Under the fountains,
  And under the graves ;
Under floods that are deepest,
  Which Neptune obey ;
Over rocks that are steepest,
  Love will find out the way.
                    Old Song in PERCY'S *Reliques*.

HARRY HEDGEROW had volunteered to be Mr. Falconer's Mercury during his absences from the Tower, and to convey to him letters and

---

[1] Peacock's intolerance for new ideas was seldom more at fault. Celts had handles and the method of attachment was the same as that used by many savages who used stone axes, e.g. the Maoris. G.

[2] See Butler's poem, with that title, in his *Miscellaneous Works*. [P.]

any communications which the sisters might have to make. Riding at a good trot, on a horse more distinguished for strength than grace, he found the shortest days long enough for the purpose of going and returning, with an ample interval for the refreshment of himself and his horse. While discussing beef and ale in the servants' hall, he heard a good deal of the family news, and many comments on the visitors. From these he collected, that there were several young gentlemen especially remarkable for their attention to the young lady of the mansion : that among them were two who were more in her good graces than the others : that one of these was the young gentleman who lived in the Duke's Folly, and who was evidently the favourite : and that the other was a young lord, who was the life and soul of the company, but who seemed to be very much taken with another young lady, who had, at the risk of her own life, jumped into the water and picked him out, when he was nearly being drowned. This story had lost nothing in travelling. Harry, deducing from all this the conclusion most favourable to his own wishes, determined to take some steps for the advancement of his own love-suit, especially as he had obtained some allies, who were willing to march with him to conquest, like the Seven against Thebes.

The Reverend Doctor Opimian had finished his breakfast, and had just sat down in his library, when he was informed that some young men wished to see him. The Doctor was always accessible, and the visitors were introduced. He recognised his friend Harry Hedgerow, who was accompanied by six others. After respectful salutations on their part, and benevolent acceptance on his, Harry, as the only one previously known to the Doctor, became spokesman for the deputation.

HARRY HEDGEROW. You see, Sir, you gave me some comfort when I was breaking my heart ; and now we are told that the young gentleman at the Folly is going to be married.

THE REVEREND DOCTOR OPIMIAN. Indeed ! you are better informed than I am.

HARRY HEDGEROW. Why, it's in everybody's mouth. He passes half his time at Squire Gryll's, and they say it's all for the sake of the young lady that's there : she that was some days at the Folly ; that I carried in, when she was hurt in the great storm. I am sure I hope it be true. For you said, if he married, and suitable parties proposed for her sisters, Miss Dorothy might listen to me. I have lived in the hope of that ever since. And here are six suitable parties to propose for her six sisters. That is the long and the short of it.

THE REVEREND DOCTOR OPIMIAN. The short of it, at any rate. You speak like a Spartan. You come to the point at once. But why do you come to me ? I have no control over the fair damsels.

HARRY HEDGEROW. Why, no, Sir, but you are the greatest friend of the young gentleman. And if you could just say a word for us to him, you see, Sir.

THE REVEREND DOCTOR OPIMIAN. I see seven notes in the key of A minor, proposing to sound in harmony with the seven notes of the octave above ; but I really do not see what I can do in the matter.

HARRY HEDGEROW. Indeed, Sir, if you could only ask the young gentleman if he would object to our proposing to the young ladies.

THE REVEREND DOCTOR OPIMIAN. Why not propose to them yourselves ? You seem to be all creditable young men.

HARRY HEDGEROW. I have proposed to Miss Dorothy, you know, and she would not have me ; and the rest are afraid. We are all something to do with the land and the wood ; farmers, and foresters, and nurserymen, and all that. And we have all opened our hearts to one another. They don't pretend to look above us ; but it seems somehow as if they did, and couldn't help it. They are so like young ladies. They daze us, like. Why, if they'd have us, they'd be all in reach of one another. Fancy what a family party there'd be at Christmas. We just want a good friend to put a good foot foremost for us ; and if the young gentleman does marry, perhaps they may better themselves by doing likewise.

THE REVEREND DOCTOR OPIMIAN. And so you seven young friends have each a different favourite among the seven sisters ?

HARRY HEDGEROW. Why, that's the beauty of it.

THE REVEREND DOCTOR OPIMIAN. The beauty of it ? Perhaps it is. I suppose there is an agistor [1] among you.

HARRY HEDGEROW (*after looking at his companions, who all shook their heads*). I am afraid not. Ought there to be ? We don't know what it means.

THE REVEREND DOCTOR OPIMIAN. I thought that among so many foresters there might be an agistor. But it is not indispensable. Well, if the young gentleman is going to be married, he will tell me of it. And when he does tell me, I will tell him of you. Have patience. It may all come right.

HARRY HEDGEROW. Thank ye, Sir. Thank ye, Sir, kindly.

Which being echoed in chorus by the other six, they took their departure, much marvelling what the Reverend Doctor could mean by an agistor.

"Upon my word," said the Doctor to himself, " a very good-looking, respectable set of young men. I do not know what the others may have to say for themselves. They behaved like a Greek chorus. They left their share of the dialogue to the coryphæus. He acquitted himself well, more like a Spartan than an Athenian, but none the worse for that. Brevity, in this case, is better than rhetoric. I really like that youth. How his imagination dwells on the family party at Christmas. When I first saw him, he was fancying how the presence of Miss Dorothy would gladden his father's heart at that season. Now he enlarges the circle, but it is still the same predominant idea. He has lost his mother. She must have been a good woman, and his early home must have been a happy one. The Christmas hearth would not be so uppermost in his thoughts if it had been otherwise. This speaks well for him and his. I myself think much of Christmas and all its associations. I always dine at

[1] An agistor was a forest officer, who superintended the taking in of strange cattle to board and lodge, and accounted for the profit to the sovereign. I have read the word, but never heard it. I am inclined to think, that in modern times the duty was carried on under another name, or merged in the duties of another office. [P.] [The agistor still carries out his duties in the New Forest under that name. G.]

home on Christmas-day, and measure the steps of my children's heads on the wall, and see how much higher each of them has risen, since the same time last year, in the scale of physical life. There are many poetical charms in the heraldings of Christmas. The halcyon builds its nest on the tranquil sea. ' The bird of dawning singeth all night long.'[1] I have never verified either of these poetical facts. I am willing to take them for granted. I like the idea of the Yule log, the enormous block of wood, carefully selected long before, and preserved where it would be thoroughly dry, which burned on the old-fashioned hearth. It would not suit the stoves of our modern saloons. We could not burn it in our kitchens, where a small fire in the midst of a mass of black iron, roasts, and bakes, and boils, and steams,. and broils, and fries, by a complicated apparatus, which, whatever may be its other virtues, leaves no space for a Christmas fire. I like the festoons of holly on the walls and windows ; the dance under the mistletoe ; the gigantic sausage ; the baron of beef ; the vast globe of plum-pudding, the true image of the earth, flattened at the poles ; the tapping of the old October ; the inexhaustible bowl of punch ; the life and joy of the old hall, when the squire and his household and his neighbourhood were as one. I like the idea of what has gone, and I can still enjoy the reality of what remains. I have no doubt Harry's father burns the Yule log, and taps the old October. Perhaps, instead of the beef, he produces a fat pig roasted whole, like Eumaeus, the divine swineherd in the *Odyssey*. How Harry will burn the Yule log if he can realize this day-dream of himself and his six friends with the seven sisters ! I shall make myself acquainted with the position and characters of these young suitors. To be sure, it is not my business, and I ought to recollect the words of Cicero : ' Est enim difficilis cura rerum alienarum : quamquam Terentianus ille Chremes humani nihil a se alienum putat.'[2] I hold with Chremes too. I am not without hope, from some symptoms I have lately seen, that rumour in the present case is in a fair way of being right ; and if, with the accordance of the

---

[1] *Hamlet*, Act I, Sc. 1. G.
[2] It is a hard matter to take active concern in the affairs of others ; although the Chremes of Terence thinks nothing human alien to himself.— *De Officiis*, i. 9. [P.]

young gentleman as key-note, these two heptachords should harmonize into a double octave, I do not see why I may not take my part as fundamental bass."

CHAPTER XXIII

Ἔγνωκα δ' οὖν . . . . .
Τοὺς ζῶντας ὥσπερ εἰς πανήγυρίν τινα
Ἀφειμένους ἐκ τοῦ θανάτου καὶ τοῦ σκότους
Εἰς τὴν διατριβὴν εἰς τὸ φῶς τε τουθ' ὃ δή
Ὁρῶμεν · ὃς δ' ἂν πλεῖστα γελάσῃ καὶ πίῃ,
Καὶ τῆς Ἀφροδίτης ἀντιλάβηται τὸν χρόνον
Τοῦτον ὃν ἀφεῖται, καὶ τύχῃ γ' ἐράνου τινός
Πανηγυρίσας, ἥδιστ' ἀπῆλθεν οἴκαδε.

ALEXIS : *Tarantini*.[1]

As men who leave their homes for public games,
We leave our native element of darkness
For life's brief light. And who has most of mirth,
And wine, and love, may, like a satisfied guest,
Return contented to the night he sprang from.

IN the mean time Mr. Falconer, after staying somewhat longer than usual at home, had returned to the Grange. He found much the same party as he had left : but he observed, or imagined, that Lord Curryfin was much more than previously in favour with Miss Gryll ; that she paid him more marked attention, and watched his conduct to Miss Niphet with something more than curiosity.

Amongst the winter evening's amusements were two forms of quadrille : the old-fashioned game of cards, and the more recently fashionable dance. On these occasions, it was of course a carpet-dance. Now dancing had never been in Mr. Falconer's line,[2] and though modern dancing, especially in quadrilles, is little more than walking, still in that " little more " there is ample room for grace and elegance of motion. Herein Lord Curryfin outshone all the other young men in the circle. He endeavoured to be as indiscriminating as possible in inviting partners : but it was plain to curious observation, especially if a spice of jealousy mingled with the curiosity, that his favourite partner was Miss Niphet. When they occasionally danced a polka, the Reverend Doctor's mythological theory came out in full force. It seemed as if Nature had pre-ordained that they

[1] *Fragm.* 219 K. G.
[2] Like Mr. Forester in *Melincourt*. See pp. 264-5. G.

should be inseparable, and the interior conviction of both, that so it
ought to be, gave them an accordance of movement that seemed to
emanate from the innermost mind.   Sometimes, too, they danced the
Minuet de la Cour.   Having once done it, they had been often
unanimously requested to repeat it.   In this they had no competitors.   Miss Gryll confined herself to quadrilles, and Mr. Falconer
did not even propose to walk through one with her.   When dancing
brought into Miss Niphet's cheeks the blush-rose bloom, which had
more than once before so charmed Lord Curryfin, it required little
penetration to see, through his external decorum, the passionate
admiration with which he regarded her.   Mr. Falconer remarked it,
and looking round to Miss Gryll, thought he saw the trace of a tear
in her eye.   It was a questionable glistening : jealousy construed
it into a tear.   But why should it be there ?   Was her mind turning
to Lord Curryfin ? and the more readily because of a newly-perceived
obstacle ?   Had mortified vanity any share in it ?   No : this was
beneath Morgana.   Then why was it there ?   Was it anything like
regret that, in respect of the young lord, she too had lost her opportunity ?   Was he himself blameless in the matter ?   He had been on
the point of declaration, and she had been apparently on the point of
acceptance : and instead of following up his advantage, he had been
absent longer than usual.   This was ill ; but in the midst of the contending forces which severally acted on him, how could he make it
well ?   So he sate still, tormenting himself.

In the meantime, Mr. Gryll had got up at a card-table in the outer,
which was the smaller, drawing-room, a quadrille party of his own,
consisting of himself, Miss Ilex, the Reverend Doctor Opimian, and
Mr. MacBorrowdale.

MR. GRYLL.   This is the only game of cards that ever pleased me.
Once it was the great evening charm of the whole nation.   Now,
when cards are played at all, it has given place to whist, which in
my younger days was considered a dry, solemn, studious game,
played in moody silence, only interrupted by an occasional outbreak
of dogmatism and ill-humour.   Quadrille is not so absorbing but
that we may talk and laugh over it, and yet is quite as interesting as
anything of the kind has need to be.

MISS ILEX. I delight in quadrille. I am old enough to remember when, in mixed society in the country, it was played every evening by some of the party. But *Chaque age a ses plaisirs, son esprit, et ses mœurs.*[1] It is one of the evils of growing old, that we do not easily habituate ourselves to changes of custom. The old, who sit still while the young dance and sing, may be permitted to regret the once always accessible cards, which, in their own young days, delighted the old of that generation : and not the old only.

THE REVEREND DOCTOR OPIMIAN. There are many causes for the diminished attraction of cards in evening society. Late dinners leave little evening. The old time for cards was the interval between tea and supper. Now there is no such interval, except here and there in out-of-the-way places, where, perhaps, quadrille and supper may still flourish as in the days of Queen Anne. Nothing was more common in country towns and villages, half a century ago, than parties meeting in succession at each other's houses, for tea, supper, and quadrille. How popular this game had been you may judge from Gay's ballad, which represents all classes as absorbed in quadrille.[2] Then the facility of locomotion dissipates, annihilates neighbourhood. People are not now the fixtures they used to be in their respective localities, finding their amusements within their own limited circle. Half the inhabitants of a country place are here to-day and gone to-morrow. Even of those, who are more what they call settled, the greater portion is less probably at home than whisking about the world. Then, again, where cards are played at all, whist is more con-

---

[1] Boileau. [P.]

[2] For example :

> When patients lie in piteous case,
>   In comes the apothecary,
> And to the Doctor cries, " Alas !
>   *Non debes quadrillare.*"
> The patient dies without a pill ;
> For why ?   The Doctor's at quadrille.

> Should France and Spain again grow loud,
>   The Muscovite grow louder,
> Britain, to curb her neighbours proud,
>   Would want both ball and powder ;
> Must want both sword and gun to kill ;
> For why ?   The General's at quadrille.   [P.]

sentaneous to modern solemnity : there is more wiseacre-ism about
it : in the same manner that this other sort of quadrille, in which
people walk to and from one another with faces of exemplary gravity,
has taken the place of the old-fashioned country dance. " The
merry dance I dearly love " would never suggest the idea of a
quadrille, any more than " merry England " would call up any
image not drawn from ancient ballads and the old English drama.

MR. GRYLL. Well, Doctor, I intend to have a ball at Christmas, in
which all modes of dancing shall have fair play, but country dances
shall have their full share.

THE REVEREND DOCTOR OPIMIAN. I rejoice in the prospect. I
shall be glad to see the young dancing as if they were young.

MISS ILEX. The variety of the game called tredrille—the Ombre
of Pope's *Rape of the Lock*—is a pleasant game for three. Pope had
many opportunities of seeing it played, yet he has not described it
correctly : and I do not know that this has been observed.

THE REVEREND DOCTOR OPIMIAN. Indeed, I never observed it.
I shall be glad to know how it is so.

MISS ILEX. Quadrille is played with forty cards : tredrille usually
with thirty : sometimes, as in Pope's Ombre, with twenty-seven.
In forty cards, the number of trumps is eleven in the black suits,
twelve in the red : [1] in thirty, nine in all suits alike.[2] In twenty-
seven, they cannot be more than nine in one suit, and eight in the
other three. In Pope's Ombre spades are trumps, and the number
is eleven : the number which they would be if the cards were forty.
If you follow his description carefully, you will find it to be so.

MR. MACBORROWDALE. Why then, we can only say, as a great
philosopher said on another occasion : The description is sufficient
"to impose on the degree of attention with which poetry is read." [3]

---

[1] Nine cards in the black and ten in the red suits, in addition to the aces
of spades and clubs, Spadille and Basto, which are trumps in all suits. [P.]

[2] Seven cards in each of the four suits in addition to Spadille and Basto.
[P.]

[3] Dugald Stewart, in the *Philosophy of the Human Mind*, I think ; but
I quote from memory. [P.]

MISS ILEX. It is a pity it should be so. Truth to nature is essential to poetry. Few may perceive an inaccuracy : but to those who do, it causes a great diminution, if not a total destruction, of pleasure in perusal. Shakspeare never makes a flower blossom out of season. Wordsworth, Coleridge, and Southey are true to nature in this and in all other respects : even in their wildest imaginings.

THE REVEREND DOCTOR OPIMIAN. Yet here is a combination, by one of our greatest poets, of flowers that never blossom in the same season :—

> Bring the rathe primrose, that forsaken dies,
> The tufted crow-toe, and pale jessamine,
> The white pink, and the pansie freakt with jet,
> The glowing violet,
> The musk rose, and the well-attired woodbine,
> With cowslips wan, that hang the pensive head,
> And every flower that sad embroidery wears :
> Bid amaranthus all his beauty shed,
> And daffadillies fill their cups with tears,
> To deck the laureat hearse where Lycid lies.[1]

And at the same time he plucks the berries of the myrtle and the ivy.

MISS ILEX. Very beautiful, if not true to English seasons : but Milton might have thought himself justified in making this combination in Arcadia. Generally he is strictly accurate, to a degree that is in itself a beauty. For instance, in his address to the nightingale :

> Thee, chauntress, oft the woods among,
> I woo to hear thy even-song,
> And missing thee, I walk unseen,
> On the dry smooth-shaven green.[2]

The song of the nightingale ceases about the time that the grass is mown.

THE REVEREND DOCTOR OPIMIAN. The old Greek poetry is always true to nature, and will bear any degree of critical analysis. I must say, I take no pleasure in poetry that will not.

MR. MACBORROWDALE. No poet is truer to nature than Burns,

---

[1] Milton : *Lycidas.* G.   [2] *Il Penseroso.* G.

and no one less so than Moore.[1]   His imagery is almost always false.
Here is a highly-applauded stanza, and very taking at first sight :

> The night-dew of heaven, though in silence it weeps,
> Shall brighten with verdure the sod where he sleeps ;
> And the tear that we shed, though in secret it rolls,
> Shall long keep his memory green in our souls.[2]

But it will not bear analysis.   The dew is the cause of the verdure :
but the tear is not the cause of the memory : the memory is the cause
of the tear.

THE REVEREND DOCTOR OPIMIAN.   There are inaccuracies more
offensive to me than even false imagery.   Here is one, in a song
which I have often heard with displeasure.   A young man goes up
a mountain, and as he goes higher and higher, he repeats *Excelsior* :
but *excelsior* is only taller in the comparison of things on a common
basis, not higher as a detached object in the air.   Jack's bean-stalk
was *excelsior* the higher it grew : but Jack himself was no more *celsus*
at the top than he had been at the bottom.[3]

MR. MACBORROWDALE.   I am afraid, Doctor, if you look for profound knowledge in popular poetry, you will often be disappointed.

THE REVEREND DOCTOR OPIMIAN.   I do not look for profound
knowledge.   But I do expect that poets should understand what they
talk of.   Burns was not a scholar, but he was always master of his
subject.   All the scholarship of the world would not have produced
Tam o' Shanter : but in the whole of that poem, there is not a false
image nor a misused word.   What do you suppose these lines
represent ?

> I turning saw, throned on a flowery rise,
>   One sitting on a crimson scarf unrolled :
> A queen, with swarthy cheeks and bold black eyes,
>   Brow-bound with burning gold.[4]

---

[1] Peacock had on more than one occasion showed his contempt for Moore
in reviews of his works.   G.

[2] *Irish Melodies*, " Oh breathe not his name."   G.

[3] Longfellow may have known this, but *Excelsior* is the motto of the
State of New York.   G.

[4] Tennyson : *A Dream of Fair Women*.   G.

MR. MACBORROWDALE.   I should take it to be a description of the Queen of Bambo.

THE REVEREND DOCTOR OPIMIAN.   Yet thus one of our most popular poets describes Cleopatra : and one of our most popular artists [1] has illustrated the description by a portrait of a hideous grinning Æthiop.   Moore led the way to this perversion by demonstrating, that the Ægyptian women must have been beautiful, because they were " the countrywomen of Cleopatra." [2]   Here we have a sort of counter-demonstration, that Cleopatra must have been a fright, because she was the countrywoman of the Ægyptians. But Cleopatra was a Greek, the daughter of Ptolemy Auletes and a lady of Pontus.   The Ptolemies were Greeks, and whoever will look at their genealogy, their coins, and their medals, will see how carefully they kept their pure Greek blood uncontaminated by African intermixture.   Think of this description and this picture, applied to one who, Dio says—and all antiquity confirms him— was " the most superlatively beautiful of women, splendid to see, and delightful to hear." [3]   For she was eminently accomplished : she spoke many languages with grace and facility.   Her mind was as wonderful as her personal beauty.   There is not a shadow of intellectual expression in that horrible portrait.

The conversation at the quadrille table was carried on with occasional pauses, and intermingled with the technicalities of the game.

Miss Gryll continued to alternate between joining in the quadrille dances and resuming her seat by the side of the room, where she was the object of great attention from some young gentlemen, who were glad to find her unattended by either Lord Curryfin or Mr. Falconer.   Mr. Falconer continued to sit, as if he had been fixed to his seat, like Theseus.   The more he reflected on his conduct, in disappearing at that critical point of time and staying away so long,

---

[1] Sir John Millais.   G.

[2] De Pauw, the great depreciator of everything Ægyptian, has, on the authority of a passage in Aelian, presumed to affix to the countrywomen of Cleopatra the stigma of complete and unredeemed ugliness.—Moore's *Epicurean*, fifth note.   [P.]

[3] Περικαλλεστάτη γυναικῶν . . . . λαμπρά τε ἰδεῖν καὶ ἀκουσθῆναι οὖσα.—DIO, xlii. 34.   [P.]

the more he felt that he had been guilty of an unjustifiable, and perhaps unpardonable, offence. He noticed with extreme discomposure the swarm of moths, as he called them to himself, who were fluttering in the light of her beauty : he would gladly have put them to flight ; and this being out of the question, he would have been contented to take his place among them ; but he dared not try the experiment.

Nevertheless, he would have been graciously received. The young lady was not cherishing any feeling of resentment against him. She understood, and made generous allowance for, his divided feelings. But his irresolution, if he were left to himself, was likely to be of long duration : and she meditated within herself the means of forcing him to a conclusion one way or the other.

CHAPTER XXIV

Δέρκεο τὴν νεᾶνιν, δέρκεο, κοῦρε·
Ἔγρεο, μὴ σε φύγῃ πέρδικος ἄγρα.
Ῥόδον ἀνθέων ἀνάσσει·
Ῥόδον ἐν κόραις Μυρίλλα.

ANACREON.[1]

See, youth, the nymph who charms your eyes ;
Watch, lest you lose the willing prize.
As queen of flowers the rose you own,
And her of maids the rose alone.

WHILE light, fire, mirth, and music were enlivening the party within the close-drawn curtains, without were moonless night and thickly-falling snow ; and the morning opened on one vast expanse of white, mantling alike the lawns and the trees, and weighing down the wide-spreading branches. Lord Curryfin, determined not to be baulked of his skating, sallied forth immediately after breakfast, collected a body of labourers, and swept clear an ample surface of ice, a path to it from the house, and a promenade on the bank. Here he and Miss Niphet amused themselves in the afternoon, in company with a small number of the party, and in the presence of about the usual number of spectators. Mr. Falconer was there, and contented himself with looking on.

[1] *Fragm.* Bergk. G.

Lord Curryfin proposed a reel, Miss Niphet acquiesced, but it was long before they found a third. At length one young gentleman, of the plump and rotund order, volunteered to supply the deficiency, and was soon deposited on the ice, where his partners in the ice-dance would have tumbled over him if they had not anticipated the result and given him a wide berth. One or two others followed, exhibiting several varieties in the art of falling ungracefully. At last the lord and the lady skated away on as large a circuit as the cleared ice permitted, and as they went he said to her,

"If you were the prize of skating, as Atalanta was of running, I should have good hope to carry you off against all competitors but yourself."

She answered, "Do not disturb my thoughts, or I shall slip."

He said no more, but the words left their impression. They gave him as much encouragement as, under their peculiar circumstances, he could dare to wish for, or she could venture to intimate.

Mr. Falconer admired their "poetry of motion" as much as all the others had done. It suggested a remark which he would have liked to address to Miss Gryll, but he looked round for her in vain. He returned to the house in the hope that he might find her alone, and take the opportunity of making his peace.

He found her alone, but it seemed that he had no peace to make. She received him with a smile, and held out her hand to him, which he grasped fervently. He fancied that it trembled, but her features were composed. He then sate down at the table, on which the old edition of Bojardo was lying open as before. He said, "You have not been down to the lake to see that wonderful skating." She answered, "I have seen it every day but this. The snow deters me to-day. But it is wonderful. Grace and skill can scarcely go beyond it."

He wanted to apologize for the mode and duration of his departure and absence, but did not know how to begin. She gave him the occasion. She said, "You have been longer absent than usual—from our rehearsals. But we are all tolerably perfect in our parts. But your absence was remarked—by some of the party. You seemed to be especially missed by Lord Curryfin. He asked the Reverend Doctor every morning if he thought you would return that day."

ALGERNON. And what said the Doctor ?

MORGANA. He usually said, " I hope so." But one morning he said something more specific.

ALGERNON. What was it ?

MORGANA. I do not know that I ought to tell you.

ALGERNON. Oh, pray do.

MORGANA. He said, " The chances are against it." " What are the odds ? " said Lord Curryfin. "Seven to one," said the Doctor. " It ought not to be so," said Lord Curryfin, " for here is a whole Greek chorus against seven vestals." The Doctor said, "I do not estimate the chances by the mere balance of numbers."

ALGERNON. He might have said more as to the balance of numbers.

MORGANA. He might have said more, that the seven outweighed the one.

ALGERNON. He could not have said that.

MORGANA. It would be much for the one to say that the balance was even.

ALGERNON. But how if the absentee himself had been weighed against another in that one's own balance ?

MORGANA. One to one promises at least more even weight.

ALGERNON. I would not have it so. Pray, forgive me.

MORGANA. Forgive you ? For what ?

ALGERNON. I wish to say, and I do not well know how, without seeming to assume what I have no right to assume, and then I must have double cause to ask your forgiveness.

MORGANA. Shall I imagine what you wish to say, and say it for you ?

ALGERNON. You would relieve me infinitely, if you imagine justly.

MORGANA. You may begin by saying with Achilles,

> My mind is troubled, like a fountain stirred ;
> And I myself see not the bottom of it.[1]

ALGERNON. I think I do see it more clearly.

MORGANA. You may next say, I live an enchanted life. I have been in danger of breaking the spell ; it has once more bound me with sevenfold force ; I was in danger of yielding to another attraction ; I went a step too far in all but declaring it ; I do not know how to make a decent retreat.

ALGERNON. Oh ! no, no ; nothing like that.

MORGANA. Then there is a third thing you may say ; but before I say that for you, you must promise to make no reply, not even a monosyllable ; and not to revert to the subject for four times seven days. You hesitate.

ALGERNON. It seems as if my fate were trembling in the balance.

MORGANA. You must give me the promise I have asked for.

ALGERNON. I do give it.

MORGANA. Repeat it then, word for word.

ALGERNON. To listen to you in silence ; not to say a syllable in reply ; not to return to the subject for four times seven days.

MORGANA. Then you may say, I have fallen in love ; very irrationally—(*he was about to exclaim, but she placed her finger on her lips*)—very irrationally ; but I cannot help it. I fear I must yield to my destiny. I will try to free myself from all obstacles ; I will, if I can, offer my hand where I have given my heart. And this I will do, if I ever do, at the end of four times seven days : if not then, never.

She placed her finger on her lips again, and immediately left the room; having first pointed to a passage in the open pages of *Orlando Innamorato*. She was gone before he was aware that she was going ;

---

[1] *Troilus and Cressida,* Act iii. Sc. 3. [P.]

but he turned to the book, and read the indicated passage. It was a part of the continuation of Orlando's adventure in the enchanted garden, when himself pursued and scourged by *La Penitenza*, he was pursuing the Fata Morgana over rugged rocks and through briary thickets.

Cosi diceva. Con molta roina
Sempre seguia Morgana il cavalliero :
Fiacca ogni bronco ed ogni mala spina,
Lasciando dietro a se largo il sentiero :
Ed a la Fata molto s' avicina
E già d' averla presa è il suo pensiero :
Ma quel pensiero è ben fallace e vano,
Però che presa anchor scappa di mano.

O quante volte gli dette di piglio,
Hora ne' panni ed hor nella persona :
Ma il vestimento, ch' è bianco e vermiglio,
Ne la speranza presto l' abbandona :
Pur una fiata rivoltando il ciglio,
Come Dio volse e la ventura bona,
Volgendo il viso quella Fata al Conte
Ei ben la prese al zuffo ne la fronte.

Allor cangiosse il tempo, e l' aria scura
Divenne chiara, e il ciel tutto sereno,
E l' aspro monte si fece pianura ;
E dove prima fu di spine pieno,
Se coperse de fiori e de verdura :
E 'l flagellar dell' altra venne meno :
La qual, con miglior viso che non suole,
Verso del Conte usava tal parole.

Attenti, cavalliero, a quella chioma. . . .[1]

---

[1] Bojardo, *Orlando Innamorato*, l. ii. c. 9. *Ed. di Vinegia*, 1544.

So spake Repentance. With the speed of fire
Orlando followed where the enchantress fled,
Rending and scattering tree and bush and briar,
And leaving wide the vestige of his tread.
Nearer he drew, with feet that could not tire,
And strong in hope to seize her as she sped,
How vain the hope ! Her form he seemed to clasp,
But soon as seized, she vanished from his grasp.

How many times he laid his eager hand
On her bright form, or on her vesture fair ;

" She must have anticipated my coming," said the young gentleman to himself. " She had opened the book at this passage, and has

> But her white robes, and their vermilion band,
> Deceived his touch, and passed away like air.
> But once, as with a half-turned glance she scanned
> Her foe—Heaven's will and happy chance were there—
> No breath for pausing might the time allow—
> He seized the golden forelock of her brow.
>
> Then passed the gloom and tempest from the sky ;
> The air at once grew calm and all serene ;
> And where rude thorns had clothed the mountain high,
> Was spread a plain, all flowers and vernal green.
> Repentance ceased her scourge.　Still standing nigh,
> With placid looks, in her but rarely seen,
> She said : " Beware how yet the prize you lose ;
> The key of fortune few can wisely use."

In the last stanza of the preceding translation, the seventh line is the
essence of the stanza immediately following ; the eighth is from a passage
several stanzas forward, after Orlando has obtained the key, which was the
object of his search :

> Che mal se trova alcun sotto la Luna,
> Ch' adopri ben la chiave de Fortuna.

The first two books of Bojardo's poem were published in 1486.　The first
complete edition was published in 1495.

The Venetian edition of 1544, from which I have cited this passage, and
the preceding one in chapter xx., is the fifteenth and last complete Italian
edition.　The original work was superseded by the *Rifacciamenti* of Berni
and Domenichi.　Mr. Panizzi has rendered a great service to literature in
reprinting the original.　He collated all accessible editions.　*Verum opere
in longo fas est obrepere somnum.*　["There is no blame in one who is overtaken by sleep in the midst of a long work."　Horace : *A.P.* 360.　G.]
He took for his standard, as I think, unfortunately, the Milanese edition
of 1539.　With all the care he bestowed on his task, he overlooked one
fearful perversion in the concluding stanza, which in all editions but the
Milanese reads thus :

> Mentre ch' io canto, ahimè Dio redentore,
> Veggio l' Italia tutta a fiamma e a foco,
> Per questi Galli, che con gran furore
> Vengon per disertar non so che loco.
> Però vi lascio in questo vano amore
> Di Fiordespina ardente a poco a poco :
> Un' altra fiata, se mi fia concesso,
> Racconterovi il tutto per espresso.

left it to say to me for her—choose between love and repentance.
Four times seven days ! This is to ensure calm for the Christmas
holidays. The term will pass over twelfth night. The lovers of
old romance were subjected to a probation of seven years :—

> Seven long years I served thee, fair one,
> Seven long years my fee was scorn.[1]

" But here, perhaps, the case is reversed. She may have feared
a probation of seven years for herself ; and not without reason. And
what have I to expect if I let the four times seven days pass by ?
Why, then, I can read in her looks—and they are interpreted in the
verses before me—I am assigned to repentance, without the hope of
a third opportunity. She is not without a leaning towards Lord
Curryfin. She thinks he is passing from her, and on the twenty-
ninth day, or perhaps in the meantime, she will try to regain him.
Of course she will succeed. What rivalry could stand against her ?
If her power over him is lessened, it is that she has not chosen to
exert it. She has but to will it, and he is again her slave. Twenty-
eight days ! twenty-eight days of doubt and distraction." And
starting up, he walked out into the park, not choosing the swept
path, but wading knee-deep in snow where it lay thickest in the

---

> Even while I sing, ah me, redeeming Heaven !
> I see all Italy in fire and flame,
> Raised by these Gauls, who, by great fury driven,
> Come with destruction for their end and aim.
> The maiden's heart, by vainest passion riven,
> Not now the rudely-broken song may claim ;
> Some future day, if Fate auspicious prove,
> Shall end the tale of Fiodespina's love.

The Milanese edition of 1539 was a reprint of that of 1513, in which year
the French, under Louis XII., had reconquered Milan. The Milanese
editions read *valore* for *furore*.

It was no doubt in deference to the conquerors that the printer of 1513
made this substitution ; but it utterly perverts the whole force of the
passage. The French, under Charles VIII., invaded Italy in September,
1494, and the horror with which their devastations inspired Bojardo not
only stopped the progress of his poem, but brought his life prematurely to
a close. He died in December, 1494. The alteration of this single word
changes almost into a compliment an expression of cordial detestation.

[P.]

[1] Quotation untraced. G.

glades. He was recalled to himself by sinking up to his shoulders in a hollow. He emerged with some difficulty, and retraced his steps to the house, thinking that, even in the midst of love's most dire perplexities, dry clothes and a good fire are better than a hole in the snow.

CHAPTER XXV

Μνηστῆρες δ' ὁμάδησαν ἀνὰ μέγαρα σκιόεντα.

HOMERUS *in Odysseâ.*[1]

The youthful suitors, playing each his part,
Stirred pleasing tumult in each fair one's heart.

Adapted—not translated.

HARRY HEDGEROW had found means on several occasions of delivering farm and forest produce at the Tower, to introduce his six friends to the sisters, giving all the young men in turn to understand that they must not think of Miss Dorothy ; an injunction which, in the ordinary perverse course of events, might have led them all to think of no one else, and produced a complication very disagreeable for their introducer. It was not so, however. " The beauty of it," as Harry said to the Reverend Doctor, was that each had found a distinct favourite among the seven vestals. They had not, however, gone beyond giving pretty intelligible hints. They had not decidedly ventured to declare or propose. They left it to Harry to prosecute his suit to Miss Dorothy, purposing to step in on the rear of his success. They had severally the satisfaction of being assured by various handsome young gipsies, whose hands they had crossed with lucky shillings, that each of them was in love with a fair young woman, who was quite as much in love with him, and whom he would certainly marry before twelve months were over. And they went on their way rejoicing.

Now Harry was indefatigable in his suit, which he had unbounded liberty to plead ; for Dorothy always listened to him complacently, though without departing from the answer she had originally given, that she and her sisters would not part with each other and their young master.

[1] I. 365. *et alia.* G.

The sisters had not attached much importance to Mr. Falconer's absences ; for on every occasion of his return, the predominant feeling he had seemed to express was that of extreme delight at being once more at home.

One day, while Mr. Falconer was at the Grange, receiving admonition from *Orlando Innamorato*, Harry, having the pleasure to find Dorothy alone, pressed his suit as usual, was listened to as usual, and seemed likely to terminate without being more advanced than usual, except in so far as they both found a progressive pleasure, she in listening, and he in being listened to. There was to both a growing charm in thus "dallying with the innocence of love,"[1] and though she always said No with her lips, he began to read Yes in her eyes.

HARRY. Well, but Miss Dorothy, though you and your sisters will not leave your young master, suppose somebody should take him away from you, what would you say then ?

DOROTHY. What do you mean, Master Harry ?

HARRY. Why, suppose he should get married, Miss Dorothy ?

DOROTHY. Married !

HARRY. How should you like to see a fine lady in the Tower, looking at you as much as to say, This is mine ?

DOROTHY. I will tell you very candidly, I should not like it at all. But what makes you think of such a thing ?

HARRY. You know where he is now ?

DOROTHY. At Squire Gryll's, rehearsing a play for Christmas.

HARRY. And Squire Gryll's niece is a great beauty, and a great fortune.

DOROTHY. Squire Gryll's niece was here, and my sisters and myself saw a great deal of her. She is a very nice young lady ; but he has seen great beauties and great fortunes before ; he has always been indifferent to the beauties, and he does not care about fortune. I am sure he would not like to change his mode of life.

[1] *Twelfth Night*, Act II, Sc. 4. G.

HARRY. Ah, Miss Dorothy! you don't know what it is to fall in love. It tears a man up by the roots, like a gale of wind.

DOROTHY. Is that your case, Master Harry?

HARRY. Indeed it is, Miss Dorothy. If you didn't speak kindly to me, I do not know what would become of me. But you always speak kindly to me, though you won't have me.

DOROTHY. I never said won't, Master Harry.

HARRY. No; but you always say can't, and that's the same as won't, so long as you don't.

DOROTHY. You are a very good young man, Master Harry. Everybody speaks well of you. And I am really pleased to think you are so partial to me. And if my young master and my sisters were married, and I were disposed to follow their example, I will tell you very truly, you are the only person I should think of, Master Harry.

Master Harry attempted to speak, but he felt choked in the attempt at utterance; and in default of words, he threw himself on his knees before his beloved, and clasped his hands together with a look of passionate imploring, which was rewarded by a benevolent smile. And they did not change their attitude till the entrance of one of the sisters startled them from their sympathetic reverie.

Harry having thus made a successful impression on one of the Theban gates, encouraged his six allies to carry on the siege of the others; for which they had ample opportunity, as the absences of the young gentleman became longer, and the rumours of an attachment between him and Miss Gryll obtained more ready belief.

CHAPTER XXVI

Οὐ χρὴ κακοῖσι θυμὸν ἐπιτρέπειν·
Προκόψομεν γὰρ οὐδὲν, ἀσάμενοι,
Ὦ Βακχί· φάρμακον δ' ἄριστον
Οἶνον ἐνεικαμένοις μεθύσθαι.

ALCAEUS.[1]

Bacchis ! 'tis vain to brood on care,
  Since grief no remedy supplies ;
Be ours the sparkling bowl to share,
  And drown our sorrows as they rise.

MR. FALCONER saw no more of Miss Gryll till the party assembled in the drawing-rooms. She necessarily took the arm of Lord Curryfin for dinner, and it fell to the lot of Mr. Falconer to offer his to Miss Niphet, so that they sate at remote ends of the table, each wishing himself in the other's place ; but Lord Curryfin paid all possible attention to his fair neighbour. Mr. Falconer could see that Miss Gryll's conversation with Lord Curryfin was very animated and joyous : too merry, perhaps, for love : but cordial to a degree that alarmed him. It was, however, clear by the general mirth at the head of the table, that nothing very confidential or sentimental was passing. Still, a young lady who had placed the destiny of her life on a point of brief suspense ought not to be so merry as Miss Gryll evidently was. He said little to Miss Niphet ; and she, with her habit of originating nothing, sate in her normal state of statue-like placidity, listening to the conversation near her. She was on the left hand of Mr. Gryll. Miss Ilex was on his right, and on her right was the Reverend Doctor Opimian. These three kept up an animated dialogue. Mr. MacBorrowdale was in the middle of the table, and amused his two immediate fair neighbours with remarks appertaining to the matter immediately before them, the preparation and arrangement of a good dinner : remarks that would have done honour to Francatelli.[2]

After a while, Mr. Falconer bethought him that he would try to draw out Miss Niphet's opinion on the subject nearest his heart. He said to her : " They are very merry at the head of the table."

---

[1] *Fragm.* Bergk. 35.   G.

[2] Charles Elmé Francatelli, pupil of Carême, maître d'hôtel and chief cook to Queen Victoria and author of *The Modern Cook* (1846).   G.

MISS NIPHET. I suppose Lord Curryfin is in the vein for amusing his company, and he generally succeeds in his social purposes.

MR. FALCONER. You lay stress on social, as if you thought him not successful in all his purposes.

MISS NIPHET. Not in all his inventions, for example. But in the promotion of social enjoyment he has few equals. Of course, it must be in congenial society. There is a power of being pleased, as well as a power of pleasing. With Miss Gryll and Lord Curryfin, both meet in both. No wonder that they amuse those around them.

MR. FALCONER. In whom there must also be a power of being pleased.

MISS NIPHET. Most of the guests here have it. If they had not they would scarcely be here. I have seen some dismal persons, any one of whom would be a kill-joy to a whole company. There are none such in this party. I have also seen a whole company all willing to be pleased, but all mute from not knowing what to say to each other : not knowing how to begin. Lord Curryfin would be a blessing to such a party. He would be the steel to their flint.

MR. FALCONER. Have you known him long ?

MISS NIPHET. Only since I met him here.

MR. FALCONER. Have you heard that he is a suitor to Miss Gryll ?

MISS NIPHET. I have heard so.

MR. FALCONER. Should you include the probability of his being accepted in your estimate of his social successes ?

MISS NIPHET. Love affairs are under influences too capricious for the calculation of probabilities.

MR. FALCONER. Yet I should be very glad to hear your opinion. You know them both so well.

MISS NIPHET. I am disposed to indulge you, because I think it is not mere curiosity that makes you ask the question. Otherwise I should not be inclined to answer it. I do not think he will ever be the affianced lover of Morgana. Perhaps he might have been if he had persevered as he began. But he has been used to smiling audiences. He did not find the exact reciprocity he looked for. He fancied that it was, or would be, for another. I believe he was right.

MR. FALCONER. Yet you think he might have succeeded if he had persevered.

MISS NIPHET. I can scarcely think otherwise, seeing how much he has to recommend him.

MR. FALCONER. But he has not withdrawn.

MISS NIPHET. No, and will not. But she is too high-minded to hold him to a proposal not followed up as it commenced ; even if she had not turned her thoughts elsewhere.

MR. FALCONER. Do you not think she could recall him to his first ardour if she exerted all her fascinations for the purpose ?

MISS NIPHET. It may be so. I do not think she will try. (*She added, to herself :*) I do not think she would succeed.

Mr. Falconer did not feel sure she would not try : he thought he saw symptoms of her already doing so. In his opinion Morgana was, and must be, irresistible. But as he had thought his fair neighbour somewhat interested in the subject, he wondered at the apparent impassiveness with which she replied to his questions.

In the meantime he found, as he had often done before, that the more his mind was troubled, the more Madeira he could drink without disordering his head.

CHAPTER XXVII

Il faut avoir aimé une fois en sa vie, non pour le moment où l'on aime, car on n'éprouve alors que des tourmens, des regrets, de la jalousie : mais peu à peu ces tourmens-là deviennent des souvenirs, qui charment notre arrière saison : . . . et quand vous verrez le vieillesse douce, facile et tolérante, vous pourrez dire comme Fontenelle : L'amour a passé par-là. SCRIBE : *La Vieille.*

MISS GRYLL carefully avoided being alone with Mr. Falconer, in order not to give him an opportunity of speaking on the forbidden subject. She was confident that she had taken the only course which promised to relieve her from a life of intolerable suspense ; but she wished to subject her conduct to dispassionate opinion, and she thought she could not submit it to a more calmly-judging person than her old spinster friend, Miss Ilex, who had, moreover, the great advantage of being a woman of the world. She therefore took an early opportunity of telling her what had passed between herself and Mr. Falconer, and asking her judgment on the point.

MISS ILEX. Why, my dear, if I thought there had been the slightest chance of his ever knowing his own mind sufficiently to come to the desired conclusion himself, I should have advised your giving him a little longer time ; but as it is clear to me that he never would have done so, and as you are decidedly partial to him, I think you have taken the best course which was open to you. He had all but declared to you more than once before ; but this " all but " would have continued, and you would have sacrificed your life to him for nothing.

MISS GRYLL. But do you think you would in my case have done as I did ?

MISS ILEX. No, my dear, I certainly should not : for, in a case very similar, I did not. It does not follow that I was right. On the contrary, I think you are right ; and I was wrong.[1] You have shown true moral courage where it was most needed.

MISS GRYLL. I hope I have not revived any displeasing recollections.

MISS ILEX. No, my dear, no ; the recollections are not displeasing. The day-dreams of youth, however fallacious, are a composite of pain and pleasure : for the sake of the latter the former is endured, nay, even cherished in memory.

MISS GRYLL. Hearing what I hear you were, seeing what I see you are, observing your invariable cheerfulness, I should not have thought it possible that you could have been crossed in love, as your words seem to imply.

[1] Peacock's views on the education of women carried out with his own daughters, and his views on the relations of the sexes, were those of the twentieth rather than the nineteenth century. G.

MISS ILEX. I was, my dear, and have been foolish enough to be constant all my life to a single idea ; and yet I would not part with this shadow for any attainable reality.

MISS GRYLL. If it were not opening the fountain of an ancient sorrow, I could wish to know the story, not from idle curiosity, but from my interest in you.

MISS ILEX. Indeed, my dear Morgana, it is very little of a story : but such as it is, I am willing to tell it you. I had the credit of being handsome and accomplished. I had several lovers ; but my inner thoughts distinguished only one ; and he, I think, had a decided preference for me, but it was a preference of present impression. If some Genius had commanded him to choose a wife from any company of which I was one, he would, I feel sure, have chosen me ; but he was very much of an universal lover, and was always overcome by the smiles of present beauty. He was of a romantic turn of mind : he disliked and avoided the ordinary pursuits of young men : he delighted in the society of accomplished young women, and in that alone. It was the single link between him and the world. He would disappear for weeks at a time, wandering in forests, climbing mountains, and descending into the dingles of mountain-streams, with no other companion than a Newfoundland dog ; a large black dog, with a white breast, four white paws, and a white tip to his tail : a beautiful affectionate dog : I often patted him on the head, and fed him with my hand. He knew me as well as Bajardo [1] knew Angelica.

[1] Rinaldo's horse : he had escaped from his master, and had repelled Sacripante with his heels :—

> Indi va mansueto alla donzella,
> Con umile sembiante e gesto umano :
> Come intorno al padrone il can saltella,
> Che sia due giorni o tre stato lontano.
> Bajardo ancora avea memoria d' ella,
> Che in Albracca il servia già di sua mano.
>   *Orlando Furioso*, c. i. s. 75. [P.]

[" Then he goes gently to the maiden, with humble countenance and human gesture : just as a dog jumps around his master who has been away for two or three days. Bajardo still remembered her, since in Albracca he had already eaten from her hand." G.]

Tears started into her eyes at the recollection of the dog. She paused for a moment.

MISS GRYLL.   I see the remembrance is painful.   Do not proceed.

MISS ILEX.   No, my dear.   I would not, if I could, forget that dog. Well, my young gentleman, as I have said, was a sort of universal lover, and made a sort of half-declaration to half the young women he knew : sincerely for the moment to all : but with more permanent earnestness, more constant return, to me than to any other.   If I had met him with equal earnestness, if I could have said or implied to him in any way, " Take me while you may, or think of me no more," I am persuaded I should not now write myself spinster. But I wrapped myself up in reserve.   I thought it fitting that all advances should come from him : that I should at most show nothing more than willingness to hear, not even the semblance of anxiety to receive them.   So nothing came of our love but remembrance and regret.   Another girl, whom I am sure he loved less, but who understood him better, acted towards him as I ought to have done, and became his wife.   Therefore, my dear, I applaud your moral courage, and regret that I had it not when the occasion required it.

MISS GRYLL.   My lover, if I may so call him, differs from yours in this : that he is not wandering in his habits, nor versatile in his affections.

MISS ILEX.   The peculiar system of domestic affection, in which he was brought up and which his maturer years have confirmed, presents a greater obstacle to you than any which my lover's versatility presented to me, if I had known how to deal with it.

MISS GRYLL.   But how was it, that, having so many admirers as you must have had, you still remained single ?

MISS ILEX.   Because I had fixed my heart on one who was not like any one else.[1]   If he had been one of a class, such as most persons in this world are, I might have replaced the first idea by another ; but " his soul was like a star, and dwelt apart." [2]

[1] Compare Miss Evergreen, *Melincourt*, p. 252.   G.
[2] Wordsworth : *London 1802.*   G.

MISS GRYLL. A very erratic star, apparently. A comet, rather.

MISS ILEX. No. For the qualities which he loved and admired in the object of his temporary affection, existed more in his imagination than in her. She was only the frame-work of the picture of his fancy. He was true to his idea, though not to the exterior semblance on which he appended it, and to or from which he so readily transferred it. Unhappily for myself, he was more of a reality to me than I was to him.

MISS GRYLL. His marriage could scarcely have been a happy one. Did you ever meet him again ?

MISS ILEX. Not of late years, but for a time occasionally in general society, which he very sparingly entered. Our intercourse was friendly ; but he never knew, never imagined, how well I loved him, nor even, perhaps, that I had loved him at all. I had kept my secret only too well. He retained his wandering habits, disappearing from time to time, but always returning home. I believe he had no cause to complain of his wife. Yet I cannot help thinking that I could have fixed him and kept him at home. Your case is in many respects similar to mine ; but the rivalry to me was in a wandering fancy : to you it is in fixed domestic affections. Still, you were in as much danger as I was of being the victim of an idea and a punctilio : and you have taken the only course to save you from it. I regret that I gave in to the punctilio : but I would not part with the idea. I find a charm in the recollection far preferable to

The waveless calm, the slumber of the dead,[1]

which weighs on the minds of those who have never loved, or never earnestly.

[1] Quotation untraced. G.

CHAPTER XXVIII

Non duco contentionis funem, dum constet inter nos, quod fere totus mundus exerceat histrioniam.—Petronius Arbiter.

I do not draw the rope of contention,[1] while it is agreed amongst us, that almost the whole world practises acting.

All the world's a stage.—Shakespeare.[2]

En el teatro del mundo
Todos son representantes.[3]—Calderon.

Tous les comédiens ne sont pas au théâtre.—*French Proverb.*

Rain came, and thaw, followed by drying wind. The roads were in good order for the visitors to the Aristophanic Comedy. The fifth day of Christmas was fixed for the performance. The theatre was brilliantly lighted, with spermaceti candles in glass chandeliers for the audience, and argand lamps[4] for the stage. In addition to Mr. Gryll's own houseful of company, the beauty and fashion of the surrounding country, which comprised an extensive circle, adorned the semicircular seats; which, however, were not mere stone benches, but were backed, armed, and padded, into comfortable stalls. Lord Curryfin was in his glory, in the capacity of stage-manager.

The curtain rising, as there was no necessity for its being made to fall,[5] discovered the scene, which was on the London bank of the Thames, on the terrace of a mansion occupied by the Spirit-rapping Society, with an archway in the centre of the building, showing a

---

[1] A metaphor apparently taken from persons pulling in opposite directions at each end of a rope. I cannot see, as some have done, that it has anything in common with Horace's *Tortum digna sequi potius quam ducere funem* : " More worthy to follow than to lead the tightened cord : " [*Ep.* I. x. 48. G.] which is a metaphor taken from a towing line, or any line acting in a similar manner, where one draws and another is drawn. Horace applies it to money, which, he says, should be the slave, and not the master of its possessor. [P.]

[2] *As You Like It*, Act II, Sc. 7. G.

[3] " In the theatre of the world all are actors." G.

[4] Lamps with cylindrical wicks named from their inventor. G.

[5] The Athenian theatre was open to the sky, and if the curtain had been made to fall it would have been folded up in mid air, destroying the effect of the scene. Being raised from below, it was invisible when not in use.

[P.]

street in the background. Gryllus was lying asleep. Circe, standing
over him, began the dialogue.

CIRCE.

Wake, Gryllus, and arise in human form.

GRYLLUS.

I have slept soundly, and had pleasant dreams.

CIRCE.

I, too, have soundly slept. Divine how long.

GRYLLUS.

Why, judging by the sun, some fourteen hours.

CIRCE.

Three thousand years.

GRYLLUS.

That is a nap, indeed.
But this is not your garden, nor your palace.
Where are we now ?

CIRCE.

Three thousand years ago,
This land was forest, and a bright pure river
Ran through it to and from the Ocean stream.
Now, through a wilderness of human forms,
And human dwellings, a polluted flood
Rolls up and down, charged with all earthly poisons,
Poisoning the air in turn.

GRYLLUS.

I see vast masses
Of strange unnatural things.

CIRCE.

Houses, and ships,
And boats, and chimneys vomiting black smoke,
Horses, and carriages of every form,
And restless bipeds, rushing here and there
For profit or for pleasure, as they phrase it.

GRYLLUS.

Oh, Jupiter and Bacchus ! what a crowd,
Flitting, like shadows without mind or purpose,
Such as Ulysses saw in Erebus.
But wherefore are we here ?

CIRCE.

There have arisen
Some mighty masters of the invisible world,
And these have summoned us.

GRYLLUS.

With what design ?

CIRCE.

That they themselves must tell.   Behold they come,
Carrying a mystic table, around which
They work their magic spells.   Stand by, and mark.

Three spirit-rappers appeared, carrying a table, which they placed
on one side of the stage :

    1. Carefully the table place,
       Let our gifted brother trace
       A ring around the enchanted space.
    2. Let him tow'rd the table point,
       With his first fore-finger joint,
       And, with mesmerized beginning
       Set the sentient oak-slab spinning.
    3. Now it spins around, around,
       Sending forth a murmuring sound,
       By the initiate understood
       As of spirits in the wood.
ALL. Once more Circe we invoke.

CIRCE.

Here : not bound in ribs of oak,
Nor, from wooden disk revolving,
In strange sounds strange riddles solving,
But in native form appearing,
Plain to sight, as clear to hearing.

THE THREE.

Thee with wonder we behold.
By thy hair of burning gold,
By thy face with radiance bright,
By thine eyes of beaming light,
We confess thee, mighty one,
For the daughter of the Sun.
On thy form we gaze appalled.

CIRCE.

Gryllus, too, your summons called.

THE THREE.

Him of yore thy powerful spell
Doomed in swinish shape to dwell :
Yet such life he reckoned then
Happier than the life of men.
Now, when carefully he ponders
All our scientific wonders,
Steam-driven myriads, all in motion,
On the land and on the ocean,
Going, for the sake of going,
Wheresoever waves are flowing,
Wheresoever winds are blowing ;
Converse through the sea transmitted,
Swift as ever thought has flitted ;
All the glories of our time,
Past the praise of loftiest rhyme ;
Will he, seeing these, indeed,
Still retain his ancient creed,
Ranking, in his mental plan,
Life of beast o'er life of man ?

CIRCE.

Speak, Gryllus.

GRYLLUS.

It is early yet to judge :
But all the novelties I yet have seen
Seem changes for the worse.

THE THREE.

If we could show him
Our triumphs in succession, one by one,
'Twould surely change his judgment : and herein
How might'st thou aid us, Circe !

CIRCE.

I will do so :
And calling down, like Socrates of yore,
The Clouds to aid us, they shall shadow forth,
In bright succession, all that they behold,
From air, on earth and sea.   I wave my wand :
And lo ! they come, even as they came in Athens,
Shining like virgins of ethereal life.

The Chorus of Clouds descended, and a dazzling array of female beauty was revealed by degrees through folds of misty gauze. They sang their first choral song :

CHORUS OF CLOUDS [1]

I.

Clouds ever-flowing, conspicuously soaring,
  From loud-rolling Ocean, whose stream [2] gave us birth,
To heights, whence we look over torrents down-pouring
  To the deep quiet vales of the fruit-giving earth,—
As the broad eye of Æther, unwearied in brightness,
  Dissolves our mist-veil in its glittering rays,
Our forms we reveal from its vapoury lightness,
  In semblance immortal, with far-seeing gaze.

II.

Shower-bearing Virgins, we seek not the regions
  Whence Pallas, the Muses, and Bacchus have fled,
But the city, where Commerce embodies her legions,
  And Mammon exalts his omnipotent head.
All joys of thought, feeling, and taste are before us,
  Wherever the beams of his favour are warm :
Though transient full oft as the veil of our chorus,
  Now golden with glory, now passing in storm.

Reformers, scientific, moral, educational, political, passed in succession, each answering a question of Gryllus. Gryllus observed, that so far from everything being better than it had been, it seemed that everything was wrong and wanted mending. The chorus sang its second song.

Seven competitive examiners entered with another table, and sate down on the opposite side of the stage to the spirit-rappers. They brought forward Hermogenes [3] as a crammed fowl to argue with Gryllus. Gryllus had the best of the argument ; but the examiners adjudged the victory to Hermogenes. The chorus sang its third song.

Circe, at the request of the spirit-rappers, whose power was limited to the production of sound, called up several visible spirits, all

---

[1] The first stanza is pretty closely adapted from the strophe of Aristophanes : 'Aέναοι Νεφέλαι. The second is only a distant imitation of the antistrophe : Παρθένοι ὀμβροφόροι. [P.]

[2] In Homer, and all the older poets, the ocean is a river surrounding the earth, and the seas are inlets from it. [P.]

[3] See Chapter XV, pp. 855–6. [P.]

illustrious in their day, but all appearing as in the days of their early youth, " before their renown was around them." They were all subjected to competitive examination, and were severally pronounced disqualified for the pursuit in which they had shone. At last came one whom Circe recommended to the examiners as a particularly promising youth. He was a candidate for military life. Every question relative to his profession he answered to the purpose. To every question not so relevant he replied, that he did not know and did not care. This drew on him a reprimand. He was pronounced disqualified, and ordered to join the rejected, who were ranged in a line along the back of the scene. A touch of Circe's wand changed them into their semblance of maturer years. Among them were Hannibal and Oliver Cromwell ; and in the foreground was the last candidate, Richard Cœur-de-Lion. Richard flourished his battle-axe over the heads of the examiners, who jumped up in great trepidation, overturned their table, tumbled over one another, and escaped as best they might in haste and terror. The heroes vanished. The chorus sang its fourth song.

CHORUS

I.

As before the pike will fly
Dace and roach and such small fry ;
As the leaf before the gale,
As the chaff beneath the flail ;
As before the wolf the flocks,
As before the hounds the fox ;
As before the cat the mouse,
As the rat from falling house ;
As the fiend before the spell
Of holy water, book, and bell ;
As the ghost from dawning day,—
So has fled, in gaunt dismay,
This septemvirate of quacks,
From the shadowy attacks
Of Cœur-de-Lion's battle-axe.

II.

Could he in corporeal might,
Plain to feeling as to sight,[1]
Rise again to solar light,

---

[1] Misquoted from *Macbeth*, Act II, Sc. 1.   G.

How his arm would put to flight
All the forms of Stygian night,
That round us rise in grim array,
Darkening the meridian day :
Bigotry, whose chief employ
Is embittering earthly joy ;
Chaos, throned in pedant state,
Teaching echo how to prate ;
And " Ignorance, with looks profound," [1]
Not " with eye that loves the ground."
But stalking wide, with lofty crest,
In science's pretentious vest.

III.

And now, great masters of the realms of shade,
    To end the task which called us down from air,
We shall present, in pictured show arrayed,
    Of this your modern world the triumphs rare,
That Gryllus's benighted spirit
May wake to your transcendent merit,
And, with profoundest admiration thrilled,
 He may with willing mind assume his place
In your steam-nursed, steam-borne, steam-killed,
And gas-enlightened race.

CIRCE.

Speak, Gryllus, what you see.

GRYLLUS.

                              I see the ocean,
And o'er its face ships passing wide and far ;
Some with expanded sails before the breeze,
And some with neither sails nor oars, impelled
By some invisible power against the wind,
Scattering the spray before them.   But of many
One is on fire, and one has struck on rocks
And melted in the waves like fallen snow.
Two crash together in the middle sea,
And go to pieces on the instant, leaving
No soul to tell the tale ; and one is hurled
In fragments to the sky, strewing the deep
With death and wreck.   I had rather live with Circe
Even as I was, than flit about the world
In those enchanted ships, which some Alastor
Must have devised as traps for mortal ruin.

CIRCE.

Look yet again.

---

[1] Gray : *Installation Ode.* G.

GRYLLUS.

Now the whole scene is changed.
I see long trains of strange machines on wheels,
With one in front of each, puffing white smoke
From a black hollow column.   Fast and far
They speed, like yellow leaves before the gale,
When autumn winds are strongest.   Through their windows
I judge them thronged with people ; but distinctly
Their speed forbids my seeing.

SPIRIT-RAPPER.

This is one
Of the great glories of our modern time.
" Men are become as birds," and skim like swallows
The surface of the world.

GRYLLUS.

For what good end ?

SPIRIT-RAPPER.

The end is in itself—the end of skimming
The surface of the world.

GRYLLUS.

If that be all,
I had rather sit in peace in my old home :
But while I look, two of them meet and clash,
And pile their way with ruin.   One is rolled
Down a steep bank ; one through a broken bridge
Is dashed into a flood.   Dead, dying, wounded,
Are there as in a battle-field.   Are these
Your modern triumphs ?   Jove preserve me from them.

SPIRIT-RAPPER.

These ills are rare.   Millions are borne in safety
Where one incurs mischance.   Look yet again.

GRYLLUS.

I see a mass of light brighter than that
Which burned in Circe's palace, and beneath it
A motley crew dancing to joyous music.
But from that light explosion comes, and flame ;
And forth the dancers rush in haste and fear
From their wide-blazing hall.

SPIRIT-RAPPER.

Oh, Circe ! Circe !
Thou show'st him all the evil of our arts
In more than just proportion to the good.
Good without evil is not given to man.
Jove, from his urns dispensing good and ill,

Gives ill unmixed to some, and good and ill
Mingled to many—good unmixed to none.[1]
Our arts are good. The inevitable ill
That mixes with them, as with all things human,
Is as a drop of water in a goblet
Full of old wine.

GRYLLUS.

More than one drop, I fear,
And those of bitter water.

CIRCE.

There is yet
An ample field of scientific triumph :
What shall we show him next ?

SPIRIT-RAPPER.

Pause we awhile.
He is not in the mood to feel conviction
Of our superior greatness. He is all
For rural comfort and domestic ease,
But our impulsive days are all for moving :
Sometimes with some ulterior end, but still
For moving, moving, always. There is nothing
Common between us in our points of judgment.

---

[1] This is the true sense of the Homeric passage :—

Δοιοὶ γάρ τε πίθοι κατακείαται ἐν Διὸς οὔδει
Δώρων, οἷα δίδωσι, κακῶν, ἕτερος δὲ ἐάων·
Ὧι μὲν καμμίξας δώῃ Ζεὺς τερπικέραυνος,
Ἄλλοτε μὲν τε κακῷ ὅγε κύρεται, ἄλλοτε δ᾽ ἐσθλῷ·
Ὧι δέ κε τῶν λυγρῶν δώῃ, λωβητὸν ἔθηκε,
Καὶ ἐ κακὴ βούβρωστις ἐπὶ χθόνα δῖαν ἐλαύνει·
Φοιτᾷ δ᾽ οὔτε θεοῖσι τετιμένος, οὔτε βροτοῖσιν.

Homer : *Il.* xxiv. [527–33. G.]

There are only two distributions : good and ill mixed, and unmixed ill.
None, as Heyne has observed, receive unmixed good : *Ex dolio bonorum
nemo meracius accipit : hoc memorare omisit.* [No one received unmixed
wine from the urn that contained blessings : he omitted to record this. G.]
This sense is implied, not expressed. Pope missed it in his otherwise
beautiful translation.

Two urns by Jove's high throne have ever stood,
The source of evil one, and one of good ;
From thence the cup of mortal man he fills,
Blessings to these, to those distributes ills,
To most he mingles both : the wretch decreed
To taste the bad, unmixed, is curst indeed :
Pursued by wrongs, by meagre famine driven,
He wanders, outcast both of earth and heaven. Pope. [P.]

He takes his stand upon tranquillity,
We ours upon excitement.   There we place
The being, end, and aim of mortal life.
The many are with us : some few, perhaps,
With him.   We put the question to the vote
By universal suffrage.   Aid us, Circe !
On talismanic wings your spells can waft
The question and reply.   Are we not wiser,
Happier, and better, than the men of old,
Of Homer's days, of Athens, and of Rome ?

VOICES WITHOUT.

Aye. No. Aye, aye.   No. Aye, aye, aye, aye, aye.
We are the wisest race the earth has known,
The most advanced in all the arts of life,
In science, and in morals.

SPIRIT-RAPPER.

The Ayes have it.
What is that wondrous sound, that seems like thunder,
Mixed with gigantic laughter ?

CIRCE.

It is Jupiter,
Who laughs at your presumption ; half in anger,
And half in mockery.   Now, my worthy masters,
You must in turn experience in yourselves
The mighty magic thus far tried on others.

The table turned slowly, and by degrees went on spinning with accelerated speed.   The legs assumed motion, and it danced off the stage.   The arms of the chairs put forth hands, and pinched the spirit-rappers, who sprang up and ran off, pursued by their chairs. This piece of mechanical pantomime was a triumph of Lord Curryfin's art, and afforded him ample satisfaction for the failure of his resonant vases.

CIRCE.

Now, Gryllus, we may seek our ancient home
In my enchanted isle.

GRYLLUS.

Not yet, not yet.
Good signs are toward of a joyous supper.
Therein the modern world may have its glory,
And I, like an impartial judge, am ready
To do it ample justice.   But, perhaps,
As all we hitherto have seen are shadows,
So too may be the supper.

CIRCE.

Fear not, Gryllus.
That you will find a sound reality,
To which the land and air, seas, lakes, and rivers,
Have sent their several tributes. Now, kind friends,
Who with your smiles have graciously rewarded
Our humble but most earnest aims to please,
And with your presence at our festal board
Will charm the winter midnight, Music gives
The signal : Welcome and old wine await you.

THE CHORUS.

Shadows to-night have offered portraits true
Of many follies which the world enthrall.
" Shadows we are, and shadows we pursue : " [1]
But in the banquet's well-illumined hall,
Realities, delectable to all,
Invite you now our festal joy to share.
Could we our Attic prototype recall,
One compound word should give our bill of fare : [2]
But where our language fails, our hearts true welcome bear.

Miss Gryll was resplendent as Circe ; and Miss Niphet, as leader of
the Chorus, looked like Melpomene herself, slightly unbending her
tragic severity into that solemn smile which characterized the chorus
of the old comedy. The charm of the first acted irresistibly on Mr.
Falconer. The second would have completed, if anything had been
wanted to complete it, the conquest of Lord Curryfin.

The supper passed off joyously, and it was a late hour of the
morning before the company dispersed.

CHAPTER XXIX

Within the temple of my purer mind
One imaged form shall ever live enshrined,
And hear the vows, to first affection due,
Still breathed : for love, that ceases, ne'er was true.
LEYDEN'S *Scenes of Infancy.* [3]

AN interval of a week was interposed between the comedy and the
intended ball. Mr. Falconer having no fancy for balls, and disturbed

[1] Burke : Speech at Bristol on Declining the Poll, 1780. G.
[2] As at the end of the *Ecclesiazusæ*. [P.]
[3] John Leyden, 1775–1811. Assisted Scott with *Border Minstrelsy.* G.

beyond endurance by the interdict which Miss Gryll had laid on him
against speaking for four times seven days on the subject nearest
his heart, having discharged with becoming self-command his share
in the Aristophanic comedy, determined to pass his remaining days
of probation in the Tower, where he found in the attentions of the
seven sisters, not a perfect Nepenthe, but the only possible antidote
to intense vexation of spirit. It is true, his two Hebes, pouring out
his Madeira, approximated as nearly as anything could do to Helen's
administration of the true Nepenthe. He might have sung of
Madeira, as Redi's Bacchus sang of one of his favourite wines :—

> Egli è il vero oro potabile,
> Che mandar suole in esilio
> Ogni male inrimediabile :
> Egli è d' Elena il Nepente,
> Che fa stare il mondo allegro,
> Dai pensieri
> Foschi e neri
> Sempre sciolto, e sempre esente.[1]

Matters went on quietly at the Grange. One evening Mr. Gryll
said to the Reverend Doctor Opimian—

I have heard you, Doctor, more than once, very eulogistic of hair
as indispensable to beauty. What say you to the Bald Venus of the
Romans—*Venus Calva ?*

THE REVEREND DOCTOR OPIMIAN. Why, sir, if it were a question
whether the Romans had any such deity, I would unhesitatingly
maintain the *negatur*. Where do you find her ?

MR. GRYLL. In the first place, I find her in several dictionaries.

THE REVEREND DOCTOR OPIMIAN. A dictionary is nothing without
an authority. You have no authority but that of one or two very
late writers, and two or three old grammarians, who had found the

---

[1] Redi : *Bacco in Toscana.* [P.]
> [" 'Tis the true old Aurum Potabile
> Gilding life when it wears shabbily :
> Helen's old Nepenthe 'tis,
> That in the drinking
> Swallowed thinking,
> And was the receipt for bliss."
> Leigh Hunt's translation. G.]

word and guessed at its meaning. You do not find her in any genuine classic. A bald Venus! It is as manifest a contradiction in terms as hot ice or black snow.

LORD CURRYFIN. Yet I have certainly read, though I cannot at this moment say where, that there was in Rome a temple to *Venus Calva*, and that it was so dedicated in consequence of one of two circumstances : the first being, that through some divine anger the hair of the Roman women fell off, and that Ancus Martius set up a bald statue of his wife, which served as an expiation, for all the women recovered their hair, and the worship of the Bald Venus was instituted ; the other being, that when Rome was taken by the Gauls, and when they had occupied the city and were besieging the Capitol, the besieged having no materials to make bowstrings, the women cut off their hair for the purpose, and after the war a statue of the Bald Venus was raised in honour of the women.

THE REVEREND DOCTOR OPIMIAN. I have seen the last story trans-ferred to the time of the younger Maximin.[1] But when two or three explanations of which only one can possibly be true, are given of any real or supposed fact, we may safely conclude that all are false. These are ridiculous myths, founded on the misunderstanding of an obsolete word. Some hold that *Calva*, as applied to Venus, signifies Pure ; but I hold with others that it signifies alluring, with a sense of deceit. You will find the cognate verbs, *calvo* and *calvor*, active,[2] passive,[3] and deponent,[4] in Servius, Plautus, and Sallust. Nobody

---

[1] Julius Capitolinus : *Max. Jun. c.* 7. [P.]

[2] Est et Venus Calva, ob hanc causam, quod cum Galli Capitolium obsiderent, et deessent funes Romanis ad tomenta facienda, Prima Domitia crinem suum, post cæteræ matronæ, imitatæ eam, exsecuerunt, unde facta tormenta ; et post bellum statua Veneri hoc nomine collocata est : licet alii Calvam Venerem quasi puram tradant : *alii Calvam, quod corda calviat, id est, fallat atque eludat.* Quidam dicunt, porrigine olim capillos cecidisse fœminis, et Ancum regem suæ uxori statuam Calvam posuisse, quod constitit piaculo ; nam mox omnibus fœminis capilli renati sunt : unde institutum ut Calva Venus coleretur.—Servius ad *Aen.* i. 720.

The substance of this passage is given in the text. [P.]

[3] Contra ille *calvi* ratus.—Sallust : *Hist.* iii.

Thinking himself to be deceitfully allured. [P.]

[4] Nam ubi domi sola sum, sopor manus *calvitur*.

Plautus *in Casinâ.*

For when I am at home alone, sleep alluringly deceives my hands. [P.]

pretends that the Greeks had a bald Venus. The *Venus Calva* of the
Romans was the *Aphrodité Dolié* of the Greeks.[1] Beauty cannot
co-exist with baldness ; but it may and does co-exist with deceit.
Homer makes deceitful allurement an essential element in the girdle
of Venus.[2] Sappho addresses her as craft-weaving Venus.[3] Why
should I multiply examples, when poetry so abounds with complaints
of deceitful love, that I will be bound every one of this company
could, without a moment's hesitation, find a quotation in point ?—
Miss Gryll, to begin with.

MISS GRYLL. Oh, Doctor, with every one who has a memory for
poetry, it must be *l'embarras de richesses*. We could occupy the time
till midnight in going round and round on the subject. We should
soon come to an end with instances of truth and constancy.

THE REVEREND DOCTOR OPIMIAN. Not so soon, perhaps. If we
were to go on accumulating examples, I think I could find you a
Penelope for a Helen, a Fiordiligi for an Angelica, an Imogene for a
Calista, a Sacripant for a Rinaldo, a Romeo for an Angelo, to nearly
the end of the chapter.[4] I will not say quite, for I am afraid at
the end of the catalogue the numbers of the unfaithful would
predominate.

MISS ILEX. Do you think, Doctor, you would find many examples
of love that is one, and once for all ; love never transferred from its
first object to a second ?

THE REVEREND DOCTOR OPIMIAN. Plato holds that such is the
essence of love, and poetry and romance present it in many instances.

MISS ILEX. And the contrary in many more.

THE REVEREND DOCTOR OPIMIAN. If we look, indeed, into the
realities of life, as they offer themselves to us in our own experience,

---

[1] *'Αφροδίτη Δολίη*. [P.] [" guileful Aphrodite." G.]

[2] *Πάρφασις, ἥτ' ἔκλεψε νόον πύκα περ φρονεόντων.—Il.* xiv. 217. [P.]
[" Persuasion that steals the mind even of wise philosophers." G.]

[3] *Παῖ Διὸς δολοπλόκε.* [P.] [" Craft-weaving child of Zeus." G.]

[4] Penelope and Helen in Homer's *Odyssey* and *Iliad* ; Fiordiligi, Angelica,
Sacripant and Rinaldo in Ariosto's *Orlando Furioso* ; Imogen in *Cymbeline* ;
Romeo in *Romeo and Juliet* ; Angelo in *Measure for Measure* ; Calista in
Beaumont and Fletcher's *The Lovers Progress*. G.

in history, in biography, we shall find few instances of constancy to first love ; but it would be possible to compile a volume of illustrious examples of love which, though it may have previously ranged, is at last fixed in single, unchanging constancy.   Even Iñez de Castro was only the second love of Don Pedro of Portugal ; yet what an instance is there of love enduring in the innermost heart as if it had been engraved on marble.

MISS GRYLL.   What is that story, Doctor ?   I know it but imperfectly.

THE REVEREND DOCTOR OPIMIAN.   Iñez de Castro was the daughter, singularly beautiful and accomplished, of a Castilian nobleman, attached to the Court of Alphonso the Fourth of Portugal.   When very young, she became the favourite and devoted friend of Constance, the wife of the young Prince Don Pedro.   The Princess died early, and the grief of Iñez touched the heart of Pedro, who found no consolation but in her society.   Thence grew love, which resulted in secret marriage.   Pedro and Iñez lived in seclusion at Coimbra, perfectly happy in each other, and in two children who were born to them, till three of Alphonso's courtiers, moved by I know not what demon of mischief—for I never could discover an adequate motive— induced the king to attempt the dissolution of the marriage, and failing in this, to authorize them to murder Iñez during a brief absence of her husband.   Pedro raised a rebellion, and desolated the estates of the assassins, who escaped, one into France, and two into Castille. Pedro laid down his arms on the entreaty of his mother, but would never again see his father, and lived with his two children in the strictest retirement in the scene of his ruined happiness.   When Alphonso died, Pedro determined not to assume the crown till he had punished the assassins of his wife.   The one who had taken refuge in France was dead ; the others were given up by the King of Castille. They were put to death, their bodies were burned, and their ashes were scattered to the winds.   He then proceeded to the ceremony of his coronation.   The mortal form of Iñez, veiled and in royal robes, was enthroned by his side : he placed the queenly crown on her head, and commanded all present to do her homage.   He raised in a monastery side by side, two tombs of white marble, one for her, one for himself. He visited the spot daily, and remained inconsolable till he rejoined her in death. This is the true history, which has been sadly perverted by fiction.

MISS ILEX. There is, indeed, something grand in that long-enduring constancy : something terribly impressive in that veiled spectral image of robed and crowned majesty. You have given this, Doctor, as an instance that the first love is not necessarily the strongest, and this, no doubt, is frequently true. Even Romeo had loved Rosalind before he saw Juliet. But love which can be so superseded, is scarcely love. It is acquiescence in a semblance : acquiescence, which may pass for love through the entire space of life, if the latent sympathy should never meet its perfect counterpart.

THE REVEREND DOCTOR OPIMIAN. Which it very seldom does ; but acquiescence in the semblance is rarely enduring, and hence there are few examples of lifelong constancy. But I hold with Plato that true love is single, indivisible, unalterable.

MISS ILEX. In this sense, then, true love is first love : for the love which endures to the end of life, though it may be the second in semblance, is the first in reality.

The next morning Lord Curryfin said to Miss Niphet : " You took no part in the conversation of last evening. You gave no opinion on the singleness and permanence of love."

MISS NIPHET. I mistrust the experience of others and I have none of my own.

LORD CURRYFIN. Your experience, when it comes, cannot but confirm the theory. The love which once dwells on you can never turn to another.

MISS NIPHET. I do not know that I ought to wish to inspire such an attachment.

LORD CURRYFIN. Because you could not respond to it ?

MISS NIPHET. On the contrary ; because I think it possible I might respond to it too well.

She paused a moment, and then, afraid of trusting herself to carry on the dialogue, she said : " Come into the hall and play at battle-dore and shuttlecock."

He obeyed the order : but in the exercise her every movement developed some new grace, that maintained at its highest degree the intensity of his passionate admiration.

CHAPTER XXX

——— dum fata sinunt, jungamus amores :
Mox veniet tenebris Mors adoperta caput.
Jam subrepet iners ætas, nec amare licebit,
Dicere nec cano blanditias capite. TIBULLUS.[1]

Let us, while Fate allows, in love combine,
Ere our last night its shade around us throw,
Or Age, slow-creeping, quench the fire divine,
And tender words befit not locks of snow.

THE shuttlecock had been some time on the wing, struck to and fro with unerring aim, and to all appearances would never have touched the ground, if Lord Curryfin had not seen, or fancied he saw, symptoms of fatigue on the part of his fair antagonist.   He therefore, instead of returning the shuttlecock, struck it upward, caught it in his hand, and presented it to her, saying, "I give in.   The victory is yours." She answered, " The victory is yours, as it always is, in courtesy."

She said this with a melancholy smile, more fascinating to him than the most radiant expression from another.   She withdrew to the drawing-room, motioning to him not to follow.

In the drawing-room she found Miss Gryll, who appeared to be reading ; at any rate, a book was open before her.

MISS GRYLL.   You did not see me just now, as I passed through the hall.   You saw only two things : the shuttlecock, and your partner in the game.

MISS NIPHET.   It is not possible to play, and see anything but the shuttlecock.

MISS GRYLL.   And the hand that strikes it.

[1] *El.* I. ii. 83–6.   G.

MISS NIPHET. That comes unavoidably into sight.

MISS GRYLL. My dear Alice, you are in love, and do not choose to confess it.

MISS NIPHET. I have no right to be in love with your suitor.

MISS GRYLL. He was my suitor, and has not renounced his pursuit : but he is your lover. I ought to have seen long ago, that from the moment his eyes rested on you, all else was nothing to him. With all that habit of the world, which enables men to conceal their feelings in society, with all his exertion to diffuse his attentions as much as possible among all the young ladies in his company, it must have been manifest to a careful observer, that when it came, as it seemed in ordinary course, to be your turn to be attended to, the expression of his features was changed from complacency and courtesy to delight and admiration. I could not have failed to see it, if I had not been occupied with other thoughts. Tell me candidly, do you not think it is so ?

MISS NIPHET. Indeed, my dear Morgana, I did not designedly enter into rivalry with you ; but I do think you conjecture rightly.

MISS GRYLL. And if he were free to offer himself to you, and if he did so offer himself, you would accept him ?

MISS NIPHET. Assuredly I would.

MISS GRYLL. Then, when you next see him, he shall be free. I have set my happiness on another cast, and I will stand the hazard of the die.

MISS NIPHET. You are very generous, Morgana : for I do not think you give up what you do not value.

MISS GRYLL. No, indeed. I value him highly. So much so, that I have hesitated, and might have finally inclined to him, if I had not perceived his invincible preference of you. I am sorry, for your sake, and his, that I did not clearly perceive it sooner ; but you see what it is to be spoiled by admirers. I did not think it possible that any one could be preferred to me. I ought to have thought it possible, but I had no experience in that direction. So now you see a striking specimen of mortified vanity.

MISS NIPHET. You have admirers in abundance, Morgana : more than have often fallen to the lot of the most attractive young women. And love is such a capricious thing, that to be the subject of it is no proof of superior merit. There are inexplicable affinities of sympathy, that make up an irresistible attraction, heaven knows how.

MISS GRYLL. And these inexplicable affinities Lord Curryfin has found in you, and you in him.

MISS NIPHET. He has never told me so.

MISS GRYLL. Not in words : but looks and actions have spoken for him. You have both struggled to conceal your feelings from others, perhaps even from yourselves. But you are both too ingenuous to dissemble successfully. You suit each other thoroughly : and I have no doubt you will find in each other the happiness I most cordially wish you.

Miss Gryll soon found an opportunity of conversing with Lord Curryfin, and began with him somewhat sportively : " I have been thinking," she said, " of an old song which contains a morsel of good advice—

> Be sure to be off with the old love,
> Before you are on with the new.[1]

You begin by making passionate love to me, and all at once you turn round to one of my young friends, and say, ' Zephyrs whisper how I love you.' "

LORD CURRYFIN. Oh, no! no, indeed. I have not said that, nor anything to the same effect.

[1] These well-known lines first appear in the form

> " It's gude to be off wi' the old love
> Before ye be an wi' the new."

in what is probably an old song sent by Burns to Johnson's *Scots' Musical Museum.* Allan Cunningham states that there was an old song, " It's best to be off wi' the auld ring." (*The Songs of Scotland,* Vol. II, p. 352.) G.

MISS GRYLL. Well, if you have not exactly said it, you have
implied it. You have looked it. You have felt it. You cannot
conceal it. You cannot deny it. I give you notice, that, if I die for
love of you, I shall haunt you.

LORD CURRYFIN. Ah ! Miss Gryll, if you do not die till you die for
love of me, you will be as immortal as Circe, whom you so divinely
represented.

MISS GRYLL. You offered yourself to me, to have and to hold, for
ever and aye. Suppose I claim you. Do not look so frightened.
You deserve some punishment, but that would be too severe. But,
to a certain extent, you belong to me, and I claim the right to transfer
you. I shall make a present of you to Miss Niphet. So, according
to the old rules of chivalry, I order you, as my captive by right, to
present yourself before her, and tell her that you have come to receive
her commands, and obey them to the letter. I expect she will keep
you in chains for life. You do not look much alarmed at the
prospect. Yet you must be aware, that you are a great criminal ;
and you have not a word to say in your own justification.

LORD CURRYFIN. Who could be insensible to charms like yours,
if hope could have mingled with the contemplation ? But there
were several causes by which hope seemed forbidden, and therefore——

MISS GRYLL. And therefore when beauty, and hope, and sympathy
shone under a more propitious star, you followed its guidance.
You could not help yourself :

> What heart were his that could resist
> That melancholy smile ? [1]

I shall flatter myself that I might have kept you, if I had tried hard
for it at first ; but

> Il pentirsi da sesto nulla giova. [2]

---

[1] Southey : *Thalaba*, XI. 33. " Resist " should be " gainsay." G.
[2] Quotation untraced. The line as printed by Peacock makes no sense,
but if " sezzo " be substituted for " sesto," it may be translated " It is no
use repenting at the end." G.

No doubt you might have said with the old song,

> I ne'er could any lustre see
> In eyes that would not look on me.[1]

But you scarcely gave me time to look on you before you were gone. You see, however, like our own Mirror of Knighthood,[2] I make the best of my evil fate, and

> Cheer myself up with ends of verse,
> And sayings of philosophers.[3]

LORD CURRYFIN. I am glad to see you so merry ; for even if your heart were more deeply touched by another than it ever could have been by me, I think I may say of you, in your own manner,

> So light a heel
> Will never wear the everlasting flint.[4]

I hope and I believe you will always trip joyously over the surface of the world. You are the personification of L'Allegro.

MISS GRYLL. I do not know how that may be. But go now to the personification of La Penserosa. If you do not turn her into a brighter Allegro than I am, you may say I have no knowledge of woman's heart.

It was not long after this dialogue that Lord Curryfin found an opportunity of speaking to Miss Niphet alone. He said, " I am charged with a duty, such as was sometimes imposed on knights in the old days of chivalry. A lady, who claims me as her captive by right, has ordered me to kneel at your feet, to obey your commands, and to wear your chains, if you please to impose them."

MISS NIPHET. To your kneeling I say, Rise ; for your obedience, I have no commands ; for chains, I have none to impose.

LORD CURRYFIN. You have imposed them. I wear them already, inextricably, indissolubly.

---

[1] Sheridan : *The Duenna*, Act I, Sc. 2. G.
[2] Butler : *Hudibras*, Pt. I, Canto i, l. 16. G.
[3] *Ibid.*, Pt. I, Canto iii, lines 1011–12. G.
[4] *Romeo and Juliet*, Act II, Sc. 6. G.

MISS NIPHET. If I may say, with the witch in *Thalaba*,

> Only she,
> Who knit his bonds, can set him free,[1]

I am prepared to unbind the bonds. Rise, my lord, rise.

LORD CURRYFIN. I will rise, if you give me your hand to lift me up.

MISS NIPHET. There it is. Now that it has helped you up, let it go.

LORD CURRYFIN. And do not call me, my lord.

MISS NIPHET. What shall I call you?

LORD CURRYFIN. Call me Richard, and let me call you Alice.

MISS NIPHET. That is a familiarity only sanctioned by longer intimacy than ours has been.

LORD CURRYFIN. Or closer?

MISS NIPHET. We have been very familiar friends during the brief term of our acquaintance. But let go my hand.

LORD CURRYFIN. I have set my heart on being allowed to call you Alice, and on your calling me Richard.

MISS NIPHET. It must not be so—at least, not yet.

LORD CURRYFIN. There is nothing I would not do to acquire the right.

MISS NIPHET. Nothing?

LORD CURRYFIN. Nothing.

MISS NIPHET. How thrives your suit with Miss Gryll?

LORD CURRYFIN. That is at an end. I have her permission—her command she calls it—to throw myself at your feet, and on your mercy.

MISS NIPHET. How did she take leave of you, crying or laughing?

[1] Bk. IX, St. 8. G.

LORD CURRYFIN. Why, if anything, laughing.

MISS NIPHET. Do you not feel mortified ?

LORD CURRYFIN. I have another and deeper feeling, which predominates over any possible mortification.

MISS NIPHET. And that is——

LORD CURRYFIN. Can you doubt what it is !

MISS NIPHET. I will not pretend to doubt. I have for some time been well aware of your partiality for me.

LORD CURRYFIN. Partiality ! Say love, adoration, absorption of all feelings into one.

MISS NIPHET. Then you may call me Alice. But once more, let go my hand.

LORD CURRYFIN. My hand, is it not ?

MISS NIPHET. Yours, when you claim it.

LORD CURRYFIN. Then thus I seal my claim.

He kissed her hand as respectfully as was consistent with " master-less passion ; " and she said to him, " I will not dissemble. If I have had one wish stronger than another—strong enough to exclude all others—it has been for the day when you might be free to say to me what you have now said. Am I too frank with you ? "

LORD CURRYFIN. Oh, heaven, no ! I drink in your words as a stream from paradise.

He sealed his claim again, but this time it was on her lips. The rose again mantled on her cheeks, but the blush was heightened to damask. She withdrew herself from his arms, saying, " Once for all, till you have an indisputable right."

CHAPTER XXXI

Sic erimus cuncti, postquam nos auferet Orcus :
Ergo vivamus, dum licet esse bene.

So must we be, when ends our mortal day :
Then let us live, while yet live well we may.
TRIMALCHIO, *with the silver skeleton : in*
PETRONIUS, c. 34.

TWELFTH NIGHT was the night of the ball. The folding-doors of the drawing-rooms, which occupied their entire breadth, were thrown wide open. The larger room was appropriated to grown dancers ; the smaller to children, who came in some force, and were placed within the magnetic attraction of an enormous twelfthcake, which stood in a decorated recess. The carpets had been taken up, and the floors were painted with forms in chalk [1] by skilful artists, under the superintendence of Mr. Pallet. The library, separated from all the apartments by ante-chambers with double doors, was assigned, with an arrangement of whist-tables, to such of the elder portion of the party as might prefer that mode of amusement to being mere spectators of the dancing. Mr. Gryll, with Miss Ilex, Mr. Mac-Borrowdale, and the Reverend Doctor Opimian, established his own quadrille party in a corner of the smaller drawing-room, where they could at once play and talk, and enjoy the enjoyment of the young. Lord Curryfin was Master of the Ceremonies.

After two or three preliminary dances, to give time for the arrival of the whole of the company, the twelfthcake was divided. The characters were drawn exclusively among the children, and the little king and queen were duly crowned, placed on a theatrical throne, and paraded in state round both drawing-rooms, to their own great delight and that of their little associates. Then the ball was supposed to commence, and was by general desire opened with a minuet by Miss Niphet and Lord Curryfin. Then came alternations of quadrilles and country dances, interspersed with occasional waltzes and polkas. So the ball went merrily, with, as usual, abundant love-making in mute signs and in *sotto voce* parlance.

---

[1] These all wear out of me, like forms, with chalk
Painted on rich men's floors, for one feast-night :
says Wordsworth, of " chance acquaintance " in his neighbourhood.—
Miscellaneous Sonnets, No. 39. [P.]

Lord Curryfin, having brought his own love-making to a satisfactory close, was in exuberant spirits, sometimes joining in the
dance, sometimes—in his official capacity—taking the round of the
rooms to see that everything was going on to everybody's satisfaction.
He could not fail to observe that his proffered partnership in the
dance, though always graciously, was not so ambitiously accepted as
before he had disposed of himself for life.   A day had sufficed to ask
and obtain the consent of Miss Niphet's father, who now sate on the
side of the larger drawing-room, looking with pride and delight on his
daughter, and with cordial gratification on her choice ; and when it
was once, as it was at once, known that Miss Niphet was to be Lady
Curryfin, his lordship passed into the class of married men, and was
no longer the object of that solicitous attention which he had received
as an undrawn prize in the lottery of marriage, while it was probable
that somebody would have him, and nobody knew who.

The absence of Mr. Falconer was remarked by several young
ladies, to whom it appeared that Miss Gryll had lost her two most
favoured lovers at once.   However, as she had still many others, it
was not yet a decided case for sympathy.   Of course she had no lack
of partners, and whatever might have been her internal anxiety, she
was not the least gay among the joyous assembly.

Lord Curryfin, in his circuit of the apartments, paused at the
quadrille-table, and said, " You have been absent two or three days,
Mr. MacBorrowdale—what news have you brought from London ? "

MR. MACBORROWDALE. Not much, my lord. Tables turn as
usual, and the ghost-trade appears to be thriving : for instead of being
merely audible, the ghosts are becoming tangible, and shake hands
under the tables with living wiseacres, who solemnly attest the fact.
Civilized men ill-use their wives ; the wives revenge themselves in
their own way, and the Divorce Court has business enough on its
hands to employ it twenty years at its present rate of progression.
Commercial bubbles burst, and high-pressure boilers blow up, and
mountebanks of all descriptions flourish on public credulity.   Everywhere there are wars and rumours of wars.   The Peace Society has
wound up its affairs in the Insolvent Court of Prophecy.   A great
tribulation is coming on the earth, and Apollyon in person is to be

perpetual dictator of all the nations. There is, to be sure, one piece of news in your line, but it will be no news to you. There is a meeting of the Pantopragmatic Society, under the presidency of Lord Facing-both-ways, who has opened it with a long speech, philanthropically designed as an elaborate exercise in fallacies, for the benefit of young rhetoricians. The society has divided its work into departments, which are to meddle with everything, from the highest to the lowest—from a voice in legislation to a finger in Jack Horner's pie. I looked for a department of Fish, with your lordship's name at the head of it ; but I did not find it. It would be a fine department. It would divide itself naturally into three classes—living fish, fossil fish, and fish in the frying-pan.

LORD CURRYFIN. I assure you, Mr. MacBorrowdale, all this seems as ridiculous now to me as it does to you. The third class of fish is all that I shall trouble myself with in future, and that only at the tables of myself and my friends.

MR. GRYLL. I wonder the Pantopragmatics have not a department of cookery ; a female department, to teach young wives how to keep their husbands at home, by giving them as good dinners as they can get abroad, especially at clubs. Those antidomestic institutions receive their chief encouragement from the total ignorance of cookery on the part of young wives : for in this, as in all other arts of life, it is not sufficient to order what shall be done : it is necessary to know how it ought to be done. This is a matter of more importance to social well-being, than nine-tenths of the subjects the Pantopragmatics meddle with.

THE REVEREND DOCTOR OPIMIAN. And therefore I rejoice that they do not meddle with it. A dinner, prepared from a New Art of Cookery, concocted under their auspices, would be more comical and more uneatable than the Roman dinner in Peregrine Pickle.[1] Let young ladies learn cookery by all means : but let them learn under any other tuition than that of the Pantopragmatic Society.

MR. GRYLL. As for the tribulation coming on the earth, I am afraid there is some ground to expect it, without looking for its

[1] Smollett : *Peregrine Pickle*, Ch. 44. G.

foreshadowing exclusively to the Apocalypse. Niebuhr,[1] who did not draw his opinions from prophecy, rejoiced that his career was coming to a close, for he thought we were on the eve of a darker middle age.

THE REVEREND DOCTOR OPIMIAN. He had not before his eyes the astounding march of intellect, drumming and trumpeting science from city to city. But I am afraid that sort of obstreperous science only gives people the novel " use of their eyes to see the way of blindness." [2]

> Truths which, from action's paths retired,
> My silent search in vain required,[3]

I am not likely to find in the successive gabblings of a dozen lecturers of Babel.

MR. GRYLL. If you could so find them, they would be of little avail against the new irruption of Goths and Vandals, which must have been in the apprehension of Niebuhr. There are Vandals on northern thrones,[4] anxious for nothing so much as to extinguish truth and liberty wherever they show themselves—Vandals in the bosom of society everywhere, even amongst ourselves, in multitudes, with precisely the same aim, only more disguised by knaves, and less understood by dupes.

THE REVEREND DOCTOR OPIMIAN. And, you may add, Vandals dominating over society throughout half America, who deal with free

---

[1] Barthold Georg Niebuhr, 1776–1831, German Statesman, historian and archæologist. The first historian to deal with the ancient history of Rome in a scientific spirit. G.

[2] *Gaoler.* For look you, sir : you know not which way you shall go.
Posthumus. Yes, indeed, do I, fellow.
Gaoler. Your death has eyes in's head, then : I have not seen him so pictured.
Posthumus. I tell thee, fellow, there are none want eyes to direct them the way I am going, but such as wink, and will not use them.
Gaoler. What an infinite mock is this, that a man should have the best use of eyes to see the way of blindness !
Cymbeline, Act v. Scene 4. [P.]

[3] Collins : *Ode on the Manners.* [P.]

[4] Written just after the Crimean War : Tsar Nicholas I in Russia and King Frederick William IV of Prussia who had held aloof from the Allies during the war. G.

speech and even the suspicion of free thought, just as the Inquisition dealt with them, only substituting Lynch law and the gallows for a different mockery of justice, ending in fire and faggot.

MR. GRYLL. I confine my view to Europe. I dread northern monarchy, and southern anarchy; and rabble brutality amongst ourselves, smothered and repressed for the present, but always ready to break out into inextinguishable flame, like hidden fire under treacherous ashes.[1]

MR. MACBORROWDALE. In the meantime, we are all pretty comfortable : and sufficient for the day is the evil thereof; which in our case, so far as I can see, happens to be precisely none.

MISS ILEX. Lord Curryfin seems to be of that opinion, for he has flitted away from the discussion, and is going down a country-dance with Miss Niphet.

THE REVEREND DOCTOR OPIMIAN. He has chosen his time well. He takes care to be her last partner before supper, that he may hand her to the table. But do you observe, how her tragic severity has passed away ? She was always pleasant to look on, but it was often like contemplating ideal beauty in an animated statue. Now she is the image of perfect happiness, and irradiates all around her.

MISS ILEX. How can it be otherwise ? The present and the future are all brightness to her. She cannot but reflect their radiance.

Now came the supper, which, as all present had dined early, was unaffectedly welcomed and enjoyed. Lord Curryfin looked carefully to the comfort of his idol, but was unremitting in his attentions to her fair neighbours. After supper, dancing was resumed, with an apparent resolution in the greater portion of the company not to go home till morning. Mr. Gryll, Mr. MacBorrowdale, the Reverend Doctor Opimian, and two or three elders of the party, not having had their usual allowance of wine after their early dinner, remained at the

---

[1] ———incedis per ignes
Suppositos cineri doloso.
      Hor : *Carm.* II, i. [P.]
[" You make your way through life through fires covered over with treacherous ashes." G.]

supper table over a bowl of punch, which had been provided in ample quantity, and, in the intervals of dancing, circulated, amongst other refreshments, round the sides of the ball-room, where it was gratefully accepted by the gentlemen, and not absolutely disregarded even by the young ladies. This may be conceded on occasion, without admitting Goldoni's facetious position, that a woman, masked and silent, may be known to be English by her acceptance of punch.[1]

CHAPTER XXXII

Ὑμεῖς δε, πρέσβεις, χαίρετ', ἐν κακοῖς ὅμως
Ψυχῇ διδόντες ἡδονὴν καθ' ἡμέραν,
Ὡς τοῖς θανοῦσι πλοῦτος οὐδὲν ὠφελεῖ.

The Ghost of Darius to the Chorus, in the Persæ of Æschylus.[2]

Farewell, old friends : and even if ills surround you,
Seize every joy the passing day can bring,
For wealth affords no pleasure to the dead.

Dorothy had begun to hope that Harry's news might be true, but even Harry's sanguineness began to give way : the pertinacity with

---

[1] Lord Runebif, in Venice, meets Rosaura, who is masked, before a *bottega di caffè*. She makes him a curtsey in the English fashion.

Milord. Madama, molto compita, volete caffè ?
Rosaura. (*Fa cenno di no.*)
Milord. Cioccolata ?
Rosaura. (*Fa cenno di no.*)
Milord. Volete ponce ?
Rosaura. (*Fa cenno di sì.*)
Milord. Oh ! è Inglese.

La Vedova Scaltra, A. iii. S. 10.

He does not offer her tea, which, as a more English drink than either coffee or choclate, might have entered into rivalry with punch : especially if, as Goldoni represented in another comedy, the English were in the habit of drinking it, not with milk, but with arrack. Lord Arthur calls on his friend Lord Bonfil in the middle of the day, and Lord Bonfil offers him tea, which is placed on the table with sugar and arrack. While they are drinking it, Lord Coubrech enters.

Bonfil. Favorite, bevete con noi.
Coubrech. Il tè non si rifiuta.
Artur. È bevanda salutifera.
Bonfil. Volete rak ?
Coubrech. Sì, rak.
Bonfil. Ecco, vi servo.

Pamela Fanciulla, A. i. S. 15. [P.]

[2] 840-2. G.

which the young master remained at home, threw a damp on their expectations. But having once fairly started, in the way of making love on the one side and responding to it on the other, they could not but continue as they had begun, and she permitted him to go on building castles in the air, in which the Christmas of the ensuing year was arrayed in the brightest apparel of fire and festival.

Harry, walking home one afternoon, met the Reverend Doctor Opimian, who was on his way to the Tower, where he purposed to dine and pass the night. Mr. Falconer's absence from the ball had surprised him, especially as Lord Curryfin's rivalry had ceased, and he could imagine no good cause for his not returning to the Grange. The Doctor held out his hand to Harry, who returned the grasp most cordially. The Doctor asked him, "How he and his six young friends were prospering in their siege of the hearts of the seven sisters."

HARRY HEDGEROW. Why, sir, so far as the young ladies are concerned, we have no cause to complain. But we can't make out the young gentleman. He used to sit and read all the morning, at the top of the Tower. Now he goes up the stairs, and after a little while he comes down again, and walks into the forest. Then he goes up stairs again, and down again, and out again. Something must be come to him, and the only thing we can think of is, that he is crossed in love. And he never gives me a letter or a message to the Grange. So putting all that together, we haven't a merry Christmas, you see, sir.

THE REVEREND DOCTOR OPIMIAN. I see, still harping on a merry Christmas. Let us hope that the next may make amends.

HARRY HEDGEROW. Have they a merry Christmas at the Grange, sir?

THE REVEREND DOCTOR OPIMIAN. Very merry.

HARRY HEDGEROW. Then there's nobody crossed in love there, sir.

THE REVEREND DOCTOR OPIMIAN. That is more than I can say. I cannot answer for others. I am not, and never was, if that is any comfort to you.

HARRY HEDGEROW. It is a comfort to me to see you, and hear the sound of your voice, sir. It always does me good.

THE REVEREND DOCTOR OPIMIAN. Why then, my young friend, you are most heartily welcome to see and hear me whenever you please, if you will come over to the Vicarage. And you will always find a piece of cold roast beef and a tankard of good ale ; and just now a shield of brawn. There is some comfort in them.

HARRY HEDGEROW. Ah ! thank ye, sir. They are comfortable things in their way. But it isn't for them I should come.

THE REVEREND DOCTOR OPIMIAN. I believe you, my young friend. But a man fights best when he has a good basis of old English fare to stand on, against all opposing forces, whether of body or mind. Come and see me. And whatever happens in this world, never let it spoil your dinner.

HARRY HEDGEROW. That's father's advice, sir. But it won't always do. When he lost mother, that spoiled his dinner for many a day. He has never been the same man since, though he bears up as well as he can. But if I could take Miss Dorothy home to him, I'm sure that would all but make him young again. And if he had a little Harry to dandle next Christmas, wouldn't he give him the first spoonful out of the marrow-bone !

THE REVEREND DOCTOR OPIMIAN. I doubt if that would be good food for little Harry, notwithstanding it was Hector's way of feeding Astyanax.[1] But we may postpone the discussion of his diet till he makes his appearance. In the meantime, live in hope ; but live on beef and ale.

The Doctor again shook him heartily by the hand, and Harry took his leave.

The Doctor walked on, soliloquising as usual. "This young man's father has lost a good wife, and has never been the same man since. If he had had a bad wife, he would have felt it as a happy release. This life has strange compensations. It helps to show the truth of

[1] *Il.* xxii. vv. 500, 501. [P.]

Juvenal's remark, that the gods alone know what is good for us.[1] Now, here again is my friend at the Tower. If he had not, as I am sure he has, the love of Morgana, he would console himself with his Vestals. If he had not their sisterly affection, he would rejoice in the love of Morgana, but having both the love and the affection, he is between two counter-attractions, either of which would make him happy, and both together make him miserable. Who can say which is best for him ? or for them ? or for Morgana herself ? I almost wish the light of her favour had shone on Lord Curryfin. That chance has passed from her; and she will not easily find such another. Perhaps she might have held him in her bonds, if she had been so disposed. But Miss Niphet is a glorious girl, and there is a great charm in such perfect reciprocity. Jupiter himself, as I have before had occasion to remark, must have pre-arranged their consentaneity. The young lord went on some time, adhering, as he supposed, to his first pursuit, and falling unconsciously and inextricably into the second : and the young lady went on, devoting her whole heart and soul to him, not clearly perhaps knowing it herself, but certainly not suspecting that any one else could dive into the heart of her mystery. And now they both seem surprised that nobody seems surprised at their sudden appearance in the character of affianced lovers. His is another example of strange compensation ; for if Morgana had accepted him on his first offer, Miss Niphet would not have thought of him ; but she found him a waif and stray, a flotsam on the waters of love, and landed him at her feet without art or stratagem. Artlessness and simplicity triumphed, where the deepest design would have failed. I do not know if she had any compensation to look for ; but if she had, she has found it ; for never was a man with more qualities for domestic happiness, and not Pedro of Portugal himself was more overwhelmingly in love. When I first knew him, I saw only the comic side of his character : he has a serious one too, and not the least agreeable part of it : but the comic still shows itself. I cannot well define whether his exuberant good-humour is contagious, and makes me laugh by anticipation as soon as I fall into his company, or whether it is impossible to think of him, gravely lecturing on Fish, as a member of the Pantopragmatic Society, without perceiving a ludicrous

[1] Juvenal: *Sat.* x. v. 346, sqq.

contrast between his pleasant social face and the unpleasant social impertinence of those would-be meddlers with everything. It is true, he has renounced that folly ; but it is not so easy to dissociate him from the recollection. No matter : if I laugh, he laughs with me : if he laughs, I laugh with him. ' Laugh when you can ' is a good maxim : between well-disposed sympathies a very little cause strikes out the fire of merriment—

> As long liveth the merry man, they say,
> As doth the sorry man, and longer by a day.

And a day so acquired is a day worth having. But then—

> Another sayd sawe doth men advise,
> That they be together both merry and wise.[1]

Very good doctrine, and fit to be kept in mind : but there is much good laughter without much wisdom, and yet with no harm in it."

The Doctor was approaching the Tower when he met Mr. Falconer, who had made one of his feverish exits from it, and was walking at double his usual speed. He turned back with the Doctor, who having declined taking anything before dinner but a glass of wine and a biscuit, they went up together to the library.

They conversed only on literary subjects. The Doctor, though Miss Gryll was uppermost in his mind, determined not to originate a word respecting her, and Mr. Falconer, though she was also his predominant idea, felt that it was only over a bottle of Madeira he could unbosom himself freely to the Doctor.

The Doctor asked, "What he had been reading of late ? " He said, " I have tried many things, but I have always returned to *Orlando Innamorato*. There it is on the table, an old edition of the original poem." The Doctor said, " I have seen an old edition, something like this, on the drawing-room table at the Grange." He was about to say something touching sympathy in taste, but he checked himself in time. The two younger sisters brought in lights. " I observe," said the Doctor, "that your handmaids always move in pairs. My hot water for dressing is always brought by two inseparables, whom it seems profanation to call housemaids."

---

[1] These two quotations are from the oldest comedy in the English language : *Ralph Roister Doister*, 1566. Republished by the Shakspeare Society, 1847. [P.]

MR. FALCONER. It is always so on my side of the house, that not a breath of scandal may touch their reputation. If you were to live here from January to December, with a houseful of company, neither you, nor I, nor any of my friends, would see one of them alone for a single minute.

THE REVEREND DOCTOR OPIMIAN. I approve the rule. I would stake my life on the conviction that these sisters are

> Pure as the new-fall'n snow,
> When never yet the sullying sun
> Has seen its purity,
> Nor the warm zephyr touched and tainted it.[1]

But as the world is constituted, the most perfect virtue needs to be guarded from suspicion. I cannot, however, associate your habits with a houseful of company.

MR. FALCONER. There must be sympathies enough in the world to make up society for all tastes : more difficult to find in some cases than in others ; but still always within the possibility of being found. I contemplated, when I arranged this house, the frequent presence of a select party. The Aristophanic comedy and its adjuncts brought me into pleasant company elsewhere. I have postponed the purpose, not abandoned it.

Several thoughts passed through the Doctor's mind. He was almost tempted to speak them. " How beautiful was Miss Gryll in Circe ; how charmingly she acted. What was a select party without women ? And how could a bachelor invite them ? " But this would be touching a string which he had determined not to be the first to strike. So, *apropos* of the Aristophanic comedy, he took down Aristophanes, and said, " What a high idea of Athenian comedy is given by this single line, in which the poet opines ' The bringing out of comedy to be the most difficult of all arts.' [2] It would not seem to be a difficult art now-a-days, seeing how much new comedy is nightly produced in London, and still more in Paris, which, whatever

[1] Southey : *Thalaba.* [P.] [Bk. II, St. 33. G.]
[2] Κωμῳδοδιδασκαλίαν εἶναι χαλεπώτατον ἔργον ἁπάντων. *Equites.* [P.] [516. G.]

may be its literary value, amuses its audiences as much as Aristophanes amused the Athenians."

MR. FALCONER. There is this difference, that though both
audiences may be equally amused, the Athenians felt they had
something to be proud of in the poet, which our audiences can
scarcely feel, as far as novelties are concerned. And as to the
atrocious outrages on taste and feeling perpetrated under the name
of burlesques, I should be astonished if even those who laugh at them
could look back on their amusement with any other feeling than that
of being most heartily ashamed of the author, the theatre, and
themselves.

When the dinner was over, and a bottle of claret had been placed
by the side of the Doctor, and a bottle of Madeira by the side of his
host, who had not been sparing during dinner of his favourite
beverage, which had been to him for some days, like ale to the
Captain and his friends in Beaumont and Fletcher,[1] almost " his
eating and his drinking solely," the Doctor said, "I am glad to
perceive that you keep up your practice of having a good dinner ;
though I am at the same time sorry to see that you have not done
your old justice to it."

MR. FALCONER. A great philosopher had seven friends, one of
whom dined with him in succession on each day of the week. He
directed, amongst his last dispositions, that during six months after
his death the establishment of his house should be kept on the same
footing, and that a dinner should be daily provided for himself and
his single guest of the day, who was to be entreated to dine there in
memory of him, with one of his executors (both philosophers) to
represent him in doing the honours of the table alternately.

THE REVEREND DOCTOR OPIMIAN. I am happy to see that the
honours of your table are done by yourself, and not by an executor,
administrator, or assign. The honours are done admirably, but the
old justice on your side is wanting. I do not, however, clearly see

---

[1] Ale is their eating and their drinking solely.
                               Scornful Lady, Act iv. Scene 2. [P.]

what the *feralis cœna* of guest and executor has to do with the dinner of two living men.

MR. FALCONER. Ah, Doctor, you should say one living man and a ghost. I am only the ghost of myself. I do the honours of my departed conviviality.

THE REVEREND DOCTOR OPIMIAN. I thought something was wrong; but whatever it may be, take Horace's advice—" Alleviate every ill with wine and song, the sweet consolations of deforming anxiety." [1]

MR. FALCONER. I do, Doctor. Madeira, and the music of the Seven Sisters, are my consolations, and great ones ; but they do not go down to the hidden care that gnaws at the deepest fibres of the heart, like Ratatosk at the roots of the Ash of Ygdrasil.

THE REVEREND DOCTOR OPIMIAN. In the Scandinavian mythology: one of the most poetical of all mythologies. I have a great respect for Odin and Thor. Their adventures have always delighted me ; and the system was admirably adapted to foster the high spirit of a military people. Lucan has a fine passage on the subject.[2]

The Doctor repeated the passage of Lucan with great emphasis. This was not what Mr. Falconer wanted. He had wished that the Doctor should inquire into the cause of his trouble ; but independently of the Doctor's determination to ask no questions, and to let his young friend originate his own disclosures, the unlucky metaphor had carried the Doctor into one of his old fields, and if it had not been that he awaited the confidence, which he felt sure his host would spontaneously repose in him, the Scandinavian mythology would have formed his subject for the evening. He paused, therefore, and went on quietly sipping his claret.

Mr. Falconer could restrain himself no longer, and without preface or note of preparation, he communicated to the Doctor all that had passed between Miss Gryll and himself, not omitting a single word of

---

[1] Illic omne malum vino cantuque levato,
     Deformis ægrimoniæ dulcibus alloquiis.
                                   Epod. xiii. [P.]

[2] *Pharsalia*, i. vv. 458–462. [P.]

the passages of Bojardo, which were indelibly impressed on his memory.

THE REVEREND DOCTOR OPIMIAN.   I cannot see what there is to afflict you in all this.   You are in love with Miss Gryll.   She is disposed to receive you favourably.   What more would you wish in that quarter ?

MR. FALCONER.   No more in that quarter, but the seven sisters are as sisters to me.   If I had seven real sisters, the relationship would subsist, and marriage would not interfere with it ; but, be a woman as amiable, as liberal, as indulgent, as confiding as she may, she could not treat the unreal, as she would the real tie.

THE REVEREND DOCTOR OPIMIAN.   I admit, it is not to be expected. Still there is one way out of the difficulty.   And that is by seeing all the seven happily married.

MR. FALCONER.   All the seven married !   Surely that is impossible.

THE REVEREND DOCTOR OPIMIAN.   Not so impossible as you apprehend.

The Doctor thought it a favourable opportunity to tell the story of the seven suitors, and was especially panegyrical on Harry Hedgerow, observing, that if the maxim *Noscitur à sociis* might be reversed, and a man's companions judged by himself, it would be a sufficient recommendation of the other six ; whom, moreover, the result of his inquiries had given him ample reason to think well of.   Mr. Falconer received with pleasure at Christmas, a communication which at the Midsummer preceding, would have given him infinite pain.   It struck him all at once, that, as he had dined so ill, he would have some partridges for supper, his larder being always well stocked with game.   They were presented accordingly, after the usual music in the drawing-room, and the Doctor, though he had dined well, considered himself bound in courtesy to assist in their disposal ; when recollecting how he had wound up the night of the ball, he volunteered to brew a bowl of punch, over which they sate till a late hour, discoursing of many things, but chiefly of Morgana.

CHAPTER XXXIII

'Η σοφὸς ἦ σοφὸς ἦν,
'Ος πρῶτος ἐν γνώμᾳ τόδ' ἐβάστασε,
Καὶ γλώσσᾳ διεμυθολόγησεν,
'Ως τὸ κηδεῦσαι καθ' ἑαυτὸν ἀριστεύει μακρῷ·
Καὶ μήτε τῶν πλούτῳ διαθρυπτομένων,
Μήτε τῶν γέννᾳ μεγαλυνομένων,
'Οντα χερνήταν ἐραστεῦσαι γάμων.

ÆSCHYLUS : *Prometheus.*[1]

Oh ! wise was he, the first who taught
This lesson of observant thought,
That equal fates alone may dress
The bowers of nuptial happiness ;
That never, where ancestral pride
Inflames, or affluence rolls its tide,
Should love's ill-omened bonds entwine
The offspring of an humbler line.

MR. FALCONER, the next morning, after the Doctor had set out on his return walk, departed from his usual practice of not seeing one of the sisters alone, and requested that Dorothy would come to him in the drawing-room. She appeared before him, blushing and trembling.

" Sit down," he said, " dear Dorothy ; I have something to say to you and your sisters ; but I have reasons for saying it first to you. It is probable, at any rate possible, that I shall very soon marry, and perhaps, in that case, you may be disposed to do the same. And I am told, that one of the best young men I have ever known is dying for love of you."

" He is a good young man, that is certain," said Dorothy ; then becoming suddenly conscious of how much she had undesignedly admitted, she blushed deeper than before. And by way of mending the matter, she said, " but I am not dying for love of him."

" I daresay you are not," said Mr. Falconer ; " you have no cause to be so, as you are sure of him, and only your consent is wanting."

" And yours," said Dorothy, " and that of my sisters ; especially my elder sisters ; indeed, they ought to set the example."

" I am not sure of that," said Mr. Falconer. " So far, if I understand rightly, they have followed yours. It was your lover's indefatigable devotion that brought together suitors to them all. As to my

[1] Lines 887–93. G.

consent, that you shall certainly have. So the next time you see Master Harry, send him to me."

" He is here now," said Dorothy.

" Then ask him to come in," said Mr. Falconer.

And Dorothy retired in some confusion. But her lips could not contradict her heart. Harry appeared.

MR. FALCONER. So, Harry, you have been making love in my house, without asking my leave.

HARRY HEDGEROW. I couldn't help making love, sir ; and I didn't ask your leave, because I thought I shouldn't get it.

MR. FALCONER. Candid, as usual, Harry. But do you think Dorothy would make a good farmer's wife ?

HARRY HEDGEROW. I think, sir, she is so good, and so clever, and so ready and willing to turn her hand to anything, that she would be a fit wife for anybody, from a lord downwards. But it may be most for her own happiness to keep in the class in which she was born.

MR. FALCONER. She is not very pretty, you know.

HARRY HEDGEROW. Not pretty, sir ! If she isn't a beauty, I don't know who is.

MR. FALCONER. Well, no doubt she is a handsome girl.

HARRY HEDGEROW. Handsome is not the thing, sir. She's beautiful.

MR. FALCONER. Well, Harry, she is beautiful, if that will please you.

HARRY HEDGEROW. It does please me, sir. I ought to have known you were joking when you said she was not pretty.

MR. FALCONER. But, you know, she has no fortune.

HARRY HEDGEROW. I don't want fortune. I want her, and nothing else, and nobody else.

MR. FALCONER. But I cannot consent to her marrying without a fortune of her own.

HARRY HEDGEROW. Why, then, I'll give her one beforehand.
Father has saved some money, and she shall have that. We'll settle
it on her, as the lawyers say.

MR. FALCONER. You are a thoroughly good fellow, Harry, and
I really wish Dorothy joy of her choice ; but that is not what I
meant. She must bring you a fortune, not take one from you ;
and you must not refuse it.

Harry repeated that he did not want fortune ; and Mr. Falconer
repeated that, so far as depended on him, he should not have Dorothy
without one. It was not an arduous matter to bring to an amicable
settlement.

The affair of Harry and Dorothy being thus satisfactorily arranged,
the other six were adjusted with little difficulty ; and Mr. Falconer
returned with a light heart to the Grange, where he presented himself
at dinner on the twenty-seventh day of his probation.

He found much the same party as before ; for though some of
them absented themselves for a while, they could not resist Mr.
Gryll's earnest entreaties to return. He was cordially welcomed by
all, and with a gracious smile from Morgana.

CHAPTER XXXIV

> *Jane.* . . . We'll draw round
> The fire, and grandmamma perhaps will tell us
> One of her stories.
> *Harry.*   Aye, dear grandmamma !
> A pretty story ! something dismal now !
> A bloody murder.
> *Jane.*   Or about a ghost.
>   SOUTHEY : *The Grandmother's Tale.*

IN the evening Miss Gryll said to the Doctor,

" We have passed Christmas without a ghost story. This is not
as it should be. One evening at least of Christmas ought to be
devoted to *merveilleuses histoires racontées autour du foyer* ; which
Chateaubriand enumerates among the peculiar enjoyments of those

qui n'ont pas quitté leur pays natal.   You must have plenty of ghosts in Greek and Latin, Doctor."

THE REVEREND DOCTOR OPIMIAN. No doubt. All literature abounds with ghosts.   But there are not many classical ghosts that would make a Christmas tale, according to the received notion of a ghost story.   The ghosts of Patroclus in Homer, of Darius in Æschylus, of Polydorus in Euripides, are fine poetical ghosts : but none of them would make a ghost story.   I can only call to mind one such story in Greek : but even that, as it has been turned into ballads by Goethe in the *Bride of Corinth*, and by Lewis in the *Gay Gold Ring*,[1] would not be new to any one here.   There are some classical tales of wonder, not ghost stories, but suitable Christmas tales.   There are two in Petronius, which I once amused myself by translating as

---

[1] Lewis says, in a note on the *Gay Gold Ring* :—" I once read in some Grecian author, whose name I have forgotten, the story which suggested to me the outline of the foregoing ballad. It was as follows : a young man arriving at the house of a friend, to whose daughter he was betrothed, was informed that some weeks had passed since death had deprived him of his intended bride. Never having seen her, he soon reconciled himself to her loss, especially as, during his stay at his friend's house, a young lady was kind enough to visit him every night in his chamber, whence she retired at daybreak, always carrying with her some valuable present from her lover. This intercourse continued till accident showed the young man the picture of his deceased bride, and he recognised, with horror, the features of his nocturnal visitor. The young lady's tomb being opened, he found in it the various presents which his liberality had bestowed on his unknown *innamorata*."—M. G. Lewis : *Tales of Wonder,* v. i. p. 99.

The Greek author here alluded to was Phlegon, whom some assign to the age of Augustus, and others, more correctly, to that of Hadrian. He wrote a treatise, Περὶ Θαυμασίων : *On Wonderful Things.* The first, in what remains of the treatise, is the story in question, and the beginning of the story is lost. There is no picture in the case. The lover and his nocturnal visitor had interchanged presents, and the parents recognised those which had belonged to their daughter : a gold ring, and a neckerchief. They surprised their daughter on her third nightly visit, and she said to them :—" Oh, mother and father ! how unjustly have you envied me the passing three days with your guest under my paternal roof. Now deeply will you lament your curiosity. I return to my destined place : for not without divine will came I hither." Having spoken thus, she fell immediately dead. The tomb was opened, and they found an iron ring and a gilt cup, which she had received from her lover : who, in grief and horror, put an end to his life. It appears to be implied, that, if the third night had passed like the two preceding, she would have regained her life, and been restored to her parents and bridegroom. [P.]

closely as possible to the originals, and, if you please, I will relate
them as I remember them. For I hold with Chaucer :

> Whoso shall telle a tale after a man,
> He moste reherse, as nigh as ever he can,
> Everich word, if it be in his charge,
> All speke he never so rudely and so large :
> Or elles he moste tellen his tale untrewe,
> Or feinen things, or finden wordes newe.[1]

This proposal being received with an unanimous " By all means,
Doctor," the Doctor went on :

These stories are told at the feast of Trimalchio : the first by
Niceros, a freedman, one of the guests :

" While I was yet serving, we lived in a narrow street where now
is the house of Gavilla.   There, as it pleased the gods, I fell in love
with the wife of Terentius, the tavern-keeper—Melissa Tarentiana—
many of you knew her, a most beautiful kiss-thrower."

MISS GRYLL.   That is an odd term, Doctor.

THE REVEREND DOCTOR OPIMIAN.   It relates, I imagine, to some
graceful gesture of pantomimic dancing : for beautiful hostesses were
often accomplished dancers.   Virgil's Copa, which, by the way, is
only half panegyrical, gives us, nevertheless, a pleasant picture in
this kind.   It seems to have been one of the great attractions of a
Roman tavern : and the host, in looking out for a wife, was probably
much influenced by her possession of this accomplishment.   The
dancing, probably, was of that kind which the moderns call
demicaractère, and was performed in picturesque costume. . . .

The Doctor would have gone off in a dissertation on dancing
hostesses; but Miss Gryll recalled him to the story, which he continued, in the words of Niceros :

" But, by Hercules, mine was pure love ; her manners charmed
me, and her friendliness.   If I wanted money, if she had earned an *as*,
she gave me a *semis*.   If I had money, I gave it into her keeping.
Never was woman more trustworthy.   Her husband died at a farm,

---

[1] *Canterbury Tales*, vv. 733–738. [P.]

which they possessed in the country. I left no means untried to
visit her in her distress ; for friends are shown in adversity. It so
happened, that my master had gone to Capua, to dispose of some
cast-off finery. Seizing the opportunity, I persuaded a guest of ours
to accompany me to the fifth milestone. He was a soldier, strong as
Pluto. We set off before cock-crow ; the moon shone like day ; we
passed through a line of tombs. My man began some ceremonies
before the pillars. I sate down, singing, and counting the stars.
Then, as I looked round to my comrade, he stripped himself, and laid
his clothes by the wayside. My heart was in my nose : I could no
more move than a dead man. But he walked three times round his
clothes, and was suddenly changed into a wolf. Do not think I am
jesting. No man's patrimony would tempt me to lie. But, as I had
begun to say, as soon as he was changed into a wolf, he set up a long
howl, and fled into the woods. I remained a while, bewildered ; then
I approached to take up his clothes, but they were turned into stone.
Who was dying of fear but I ? But I drew my sword, and went on
cutting shadows till I arrived at the farm. I entered the narrow
way. The life was half boiled out of me ; perspiration ran down me
like a torrent : my eyes were dead. I could scarcely come to myself.
My Melissa began to wonder why I walked so late ; ' and if you had
come sooner,' she said, ' you might at least have helped us ; for a wolf
entered the farm and fell on the sheep, tearing them, and leaving
them all bleeding. He escaped ; but with cause to remember us ;
for our man drove a spear through his neck.' When I heard these
things, I could not think of sleep ; but hurried homeward with the
dawn ; and when I came to the place where the clothes had been
turned into stone, I found nothing but blood. When I reached
home, my soldier was in bed, lying like an ox, and a surgeon was
dressing his neck. I felt that he was a turnskin, and I could never
after taste bread with him, not if you would have killed me. Let
those who doubt of such things look into them. If I lie, may the
wrath of all your Genii fall on me."

This story being told, Trimalchio, the lord of the feast, after giving
his implicit adhesion to it, and affirming the indisputable veracity of
Niceros, relates another, as a fact of his own experience.

"While yet I wore long hair, for from a boy I led a Chian

life,[1] our little Iphis, the delight of the family, died ; by Hercules, a pearl ; quick, beautiful, one of ten thousand.   While, therefore, his unhappy mother was weeping for him, and we all were plunged in sorrow, suddenly witches came in pursuit of him, as dogs, you may suppose, of a hare.   We had then in the house a Cappadocian, tall, brave to audacity, capable of lifting up an angry bull.   He boldly, with a drawn sword, rushed out through the gate, having his left hand carefully wrapped up, and drove his sword through a woman's bosom ; here as it were ; safe be what I touch ! We heard a groan ; but, assuredly I will not lie, we did not see the women.   But our stout fellow returning, threw himself into bed, and all his body was livid, as if he had been beaten with whips ; for the evil hand had touched him.   We closed the gate, and resumed our watch over the dead ; but when the mother went to embrace the body of her son, she touched it, and found it was only a figure, of which all the interior was straw, no heart, nothing.   The witches had stolen away the boy, and left in his place a straw-stuffed image.   I ask you—it is impossible not—to believe, that there are women with more than mortal knowledge, nocturnal women, who can make that which is uppermost downmost.   But our tall hero after this was never again of his own colour ; indeed, after a few days, he died raving."

" We wondered and believed," says a guest who heard the story, " and kissing the table, we implored the nocturnals to keep themselves to themselves, while we were returning from supper."

MISS GRYLL.   Those are pleasant stories, Doctor ; and the peculiar style of the narrators testifies to their faith in their own marvels. Still, as you say, they are not ghost stories.

LORD CURRYFIN.   Shakspeare's are glorious ghosts, and would make good stories, if they were not so familiarly known.   There is a ghost much to my mind in Beaumont and Fletcher's *Lover's Progress*. Cleander has a beautiful wife, Calista, and a friend, Lisander. Calista and Lisander love each other, *en tout bien, tout honneur*. Lisander, in self-defence and in fair fight, kills a court favourite, and

---

[1] Free boys wore long hair.   A Chian life is a delicate and luxurious life. Trimalchio implies that, though he began life as a slave, he was a pet in the household, and was treated as if he had been free.   [P.]

is obliged to conceal himself in the country. Cleander and Dorilaus, Calista's father, travel in search of him. They pass the night at a country inn. The jovial host had been long known to Cleander, who had extolled him to Dorilaus ; but on inquiring for him they find he has been dead three weeks. They call for more wine, dismiss their attendants, and sit up alone, chatting of various things, and, among others, of mine host, whose skill on the lute and in singing is remembered and commended by Cleander. While they are talking, a lute is struck within ; followed by a song, beginning

> 'Tis late and cold, stir up the fire,—
> Sit close, and draw the table nigher :
> Be merry, and drink wine that's old.

And ending :—

> Welcome, welcome, shall go round,
> And I shall smile, though underground.

And when the song ceases, the host's ghost enters. They ask him why he appears ? He answers, to wait once more on Cleander, and to entreat a courtesy :—

> —— to see my body buried
> In holy ground : for now I lie unhallowed,
> By the clerk's fault : let my new grave be made
> Amongst good fellows, that have died before me,
> And merry hosts of my kind.

Cleander promises that it shall be done ; and Dorilaus, who is a merry old gentleman throughout the play, adds :—

> And forty stoops of wine drank at thy funeral.

Cleander asks him :—

> Is't in your power, some hours before my death,
> To give me warning ?

The host replies :—

> I cannot tell you truly :
> But if I can, so much on earth I loved you,
> I will appear again.

In a subsequent scene, the ghost forewarns him, and he is soon after assassinated : not premeditatedly, but as an accident in the working out, by subordinate characters, of a plot to bring into question the purity of Calista's love for Lisander.

MISS ILEX.   In my young days ghosts were so popular, that the first question asked about any new play was, Is there a ghost in it ? The *Castle Spectre*[1] had set this fashion.   It was one of the first plays I saw, when I was a very little girl.   The opening of the folding-doors disclosing the illuminated oratory ; the extreme beauty of the actress who personated the ghost ; the solemn music to which she moved slowly forward to give a silent blessing to her kneeling daughter ; and the chorus of female voices chanting *Jubilate* ; made an impression on me which no other scene of the kind has ever made. That is my ghost, but I have no ghost-story worth telling.

MR. FALCONER.   There are many stories in which the supernatural is only apparent, and is finally explained.   But some of these, especially the novels of Brockden Brown, carry the principle of terror to its utmost limits.[2]   What can be more appalling than his *Wieland* ? It is one of the few tales in which the final explanation of the apparently supernatural does not destroy or diminish the original effect.

MISS GRYLL.   Generally, I do not like that explaining away.   I can accord a ready faith to the supernatural in all its forms, as I do to the adventures of Ulysses and Orlando.   I should be sorry to see the enchantments of Circe expounded into sleights of hand.

THE REVEREND DOCTOR OPIMIAN.   I agree with you, Miss Gryll. I do not like to find a ghost, which has frightened me through two volumes, turned into a Cock lane ghost in the third.[3]

MISS GRYLL.   We are talking about ghosts, but we have not a ghost story.   I want a ghost story.

---

[1] By M. G. Lewis (1798).   G.

[2] Charles Brockden Brown, 1771–1810, American novelist.   His novels are full of the weird, wild and wonderful, but not the supernatural.   The plot of *Wieland* turns on ventriloquism.   He was greatly influenced by Godwin.   G.

[3] In 1762 London was agog with tales of ghostly rappings in Cock Lane, Stockwell, which were finally traced to a maidservant.   G.

MISS NIPHET. I will try to tell you one, which I remember imperfectly. It relates, as many such stories do, to a buried treasure. An old miser had an only daughter ; he denied himself everything, but he educated her well, and treated her becomingly. He had accumulated a treasure, which he designed for her, but could not bear the thought of parting with it, and died without disclosing the place of its concealment. The daughter had a lover, not absolutely poor, nor much removed from it. He farmed a little land of his own. When her father died, and she was left destitute and friendless, he married her, and they endeavoured by economy and industry to make up for the deficiencies of fortune. The young husband had an aunt, with whom they sometimes passed a day of festival, and Christmas Day especially. They were returning home late at night on one of these occasions ; snow was on the ground ; the moon was in the first quarter, and nearly setting. Crossing a field, they paused a moment to look on the beauty of the starry sky ; and when they again turned their eyes to the ground, they saw a shadow on the snow ; it was too long to have any distinct outline ; but no sub-stantial form was there to throw it. The young wife clung trembling to the arm of her husband. The moon set, and the shadow dis-appeared. New Year's Day came, and they passed it at the aunt's. On their return the moon was full, and high in heaven. They crossed the same field, not without hesitation and fear. In the same spot as before, they again saw the shadow ; it was that of a man in a large loose wrapper, and a high-peaked hat. They recognised the outline of the old miser. The husband sustained his nearly fainting wife ; as their eyes were irresistibly fixed on it, it began to move, but a cloud came over the moon, and they lost sight of it. The next night was bright, and the wife had summoned all her courage to follow out the mystery ; they returned to the spot at the same hour ; the shadow again fell on the snow, and again it began to move, and glided away slowly over the surface of the snow. They followed it fearfully. At length it stopped on a small mound in another field of their own farm. They walked round and round it, but it moved no more. The husband entreated his wife to remain, while he sought a stick to mark the place. When she was alone, the shadow spread out its arms as in the act of benediction, and vanished. The husband found her extended on the snow ; he raised her in his arms ; she recovered, and they walked home. He returned in the morning with pick-axe and spade, cleared away the snow, broke into the ground, and found a pot of gold, which was unquestionably their own. And then, with the usual end of a nurse's tale, " they lived happily all the rest of their lives."

MISS ILEX. Your story, though differing in all other respects, reminds me of a ballad in which there is a shadow on the snow,

> Around it, and round, he had ventured to go,
> But no form that had life threw that stamp on the snow.[1]

MR. GRYLL. In these instances, the shadow has an outline, without a visible form to throw it. I remember a striking instance of shadows without distinguishable forms. A young chevalier was riding through a forest of pines, in which he had before met with fearful adventures, when a strange voice called on him to stop. He did not stop, and the stranger jumped up behind him. He tried to look back, but could not turn his head. They emerged into a glade, where he hoped to see in the moonlight the outline of the unwelcome form. But " unaccountable shadows fell around, unstamped with delineations of themselves." [2]

MISS GRYLL. Well, Mr. MacBorrowdale, have you no ghost story for us ?

MR. MACBORROWDALE. In faith, Miss Gryll, ghosts are not much in my line : the main business of my life has been among the driest matters of fact : but I will tell you a tale of a bogle, which I remember from my boyish days.

There was a party of witches and warlocks assembled in the refectory of a ruined abbey, intending to have a merry supper, if they could get the materials. They had no money, and they had for servant a poor bogle, who had been lent to them by his Satanic

---

[1] Miss Bannerman's *Tales of Superstition and Chivalry*. [P.]

[2] *The Three Brothers*, vol. iv. p. 193. [P.] [A novel by Joshua Pickersgill, junior, 1803. In the Advertisement to *The Deformed Transformed*, Byron says : " This production is founded partly on the story of a novel called *The Three Brothers* . . . from which M. G. Lewis's *Wood Demon* was also taken." G.]

majesty, on condition that he should provide their supper if he could ; but without buying or stealing. They had a roaring fire, with nothing to roast, and a large stone table, with nothing on it but broken dishes and empty mugs. So the fire-light shone on an uncouth set of long hungry faces. Whether there was among them " ae winsome wench and wawlie " [1] is more than I can say ; but most probably there was, or the bogle would scarcely have been so zealous in the cause. Still he was late on his quest. The friars of a still flourishing abbey were making preparations for a festal day, and had despatched a man with a cart to the nearest town, to bring them a supply of good things. He was driving back his cart well loaded with beef, and poultry, and ham ; and a supply of choice rolls, for which a goodwife in the town was famous ; and a new arrival of rare old wine, a special present to the Abbot from some great lord. The bogle having smelt out the prize, presented himself before the carter in the form of a sailor with a wooden leg, imploring charity. The carter said he had nothing for him, and the sailor seemed to go on his way. He re-appeared in various forms, always soliciting charity, more and more importunately every time, and always receiving the same denial. At last he appeared as an old woman, leaning on a stick, who was more pertinacious in her entreaties than the preceding semblances ; and the carter, after asseverating with an oath, that a whole ship-load of beggars must have been wrecked that night on the coast, reiterated that he had nothing for her. " Only the smallest coin, master," said the old woman. " I have no coin," said the carter. " Just a wee bite and sup of something," said the old woman ; " you are scarcely going about without something to eat and drink ; something comfortable for yourself. Just look in the cart : I am sure you will find something good." " Something, something, something," said the carter ; " if there is anything fit to eat or drink in the cart, I wish a bogle may fly away with it." " Thank you," said the bogle, and changed himself into a shape which laid the carter on his back, with his heels in the air. The

---

[1] But Tam kend what was what fu' brawlie :
  There was ae winsome wench and wawlie,
  That night enlisted in the core,
  Lang after kend on Carrick shore.
                    Tam o' Shanter. [P.] [Burns. G.]

bogle made lawful prize of the contents of the cart.   The refectory
was soon fragrant with the odour of roast, and the old wine flowed
briskly, to the great joy of the assembly, who passed the night in
feasting, singing, and dancing, and toasting Old Nick.

MISS GRYLL.   And now, Mr. Falconer, you who live in an old
tower, among old books, and are deep in the legends of saints, surely
you must have a ghost-story to tell us.

MR. FALCONER.   Not exactly a ghost-story, Miss Gryll, but there
is a legend which took my fancy, and which I turned into a ballad.
If you permit me, I will repeat it.

The permission being willingly granted, Mr. Falconer closed the
series of fireside marvels by reciting

THE LEGEND OF SAINT LAURA.

Saint Laura, in her sleep of death,
     Preserves beneath the tomb
—'Tis willed where what is willed must be— [1]
In incorruptibility
     Her beauty and her bloom.

So pure her maiden life had been,
     So free from earthly stain,
'Twas fixed in fate by Heaven's own Queen,
That till the earth's last closing scene
     She should unchanged remain.

Within a deep sarcophagus
     Of alabaster sheen,
With sculptured lid of roses white,
She slumbered in unbroken night,
     By mortal eyes unseen.

Above her marble couch was reared
     A monumental shrine,
Where cloistered sisters, gathering round,
Made night and morn the aisle resound
     With choristry divine.

---

[1] Vuolsi cosí colà dove si puote
Ciò che si vuole, e più non domandare.
          Dante. [P.]   [*Inferno*, III, 95–96.   G.]

The abbess died : and in her pride
　　Her parting mandate said,
They should her final rest provide,
The alabaster couch beside,
　　Where slept the sainted dead.

The abbess came of princely race :
　　The nuns might not gainsay :
And sadly passed the timid band,
To execute the high command
　　They dared not disobey.

The monument was opened then :
　　It gave to general sight
The alabaster couch alone :
But all its lucid substance shone
　　With præternatural light.

They laid the corpse within the shrine :
　　They closed its doors again :
But nameless terror seemed to fall,
Throughout the live-long night, on all
　　Who formed the funeral train.

Lo ! on the morrow morn, still closed
　　The monument was found :
But in its robes funereal drest,
The corpse they had consigned to rest
　　Lay on the stony ground.

Fear and amazement seized on all:
　　They called on Mary's aid :
And in the tomb, unclosed again,
With choral hymn and funeral train,
　　The corpse again was laid.

But with the incorruptible
　　Corruption might not rest :
The lonely chapel's stone-paved floor
Received the ejected corpse once more,
　　In robes funereal drest.

So was it found when morning beamed :
　　In solemn suppliant strain
The nuns implored all saints in heaven,
That rest might to the corpse be given,
　　Which they entombed again.

On the third night a watch was kept
    By many a friar and nun :
Trembling, all knelt in fervent prayer,
Till on the dreary midnight air
    Rolled the deep bell-toll, " One ! "

The saint within the opening tomb
    Like marble statue stood :
All fell to earth in deep dismay :
And through their ranks she passed away,
    In calm unchanging mood.

No answering sound her footsteps raised
    Along the stony floor :
Silent as death, severe as fate,
She glided through the chapel gate,
    And none beheld her more.

The alabaster couch was gone :
    The tomb was void and bare :
For the last time, with hasty rite,
Even 'mid the terror of the night,
    They laid the abbess there.

'Tis said, the abbess rests not well
    In that sepulchral pile :
But yearly, when the night comes round,
As dies of " One " the bell's deep sound
    She flits along the aisle.

But whither passed the virgin saint,
    To slumber far away,
Destined by Mary to endure,
Unaltered in her semblance pure,
    Until the judgment day ?

None knew, and none may ever know:
    Angels the secret keep :
Impenetrable ramparts bound,
Eternal silence dwells around,
    The chamber of her sleep.

CHAPTER XXXV

Σοὶ δὲ θεοὶ τόσα δοῖεν, ὅσα φρεσὶ σῆσι μενοινᾶς,
Ἄνδρα τε καὶ οἶκον, καὶ ὁμοφροσύνην ὀπάσειαν
Ἐσθλήν· οὐ μὲν γὰρ τοῦ γε κρεῖσσον καὶ ἄρειον,
Ἢ ὅθ᾽ ὁμοφρονέοντε νοήμασιν οἶκον ἔχητον
Ἀνὴρ ἠδὲ γυνή.

May the gods grant what your best hopes pursue,
A husband, and a home, with concord true :
No greater boon from Jove's ethereal dome
Descends, than concord in the nuptial home.
ULYSSES *to* NAUSICAA, *in the sixth book of the Odyssey*.[1]

WHAT passed between Algernon and Morgana, when the twenty-eighth morning brought his probation to a close, it is unnecessary to relate. The gentleman being predetermined to propose, and the lady to accept, there was little to be said, but that little was conclusive.

Mr. Gryll was delighted. His niece could not have made a choice more thoroughly to his mind.

" My dear Morgana," he said, " all's well that ends well. Your fastidiousness in choice has arrived at a happy termination. And now you will perhaps tell me why you rejected so many suitors, to whom you had in turn accorded a hearing. In the first place, what was your objection to the Honourable Escor A'Cass ?[2] He was a fine, handsome, dashing fellow. He was the first in the field, and you seemed to like him."

MISS GRYLL.   He was too dashing, uncle : he gambled. I did like him, till I discovered his evil propensity.

MR. GRYLL.   To Sir Alley Capel ?

MISS GRYLL.   He speculated ; which is only another name for gambling. He never knew from day to day whether he was a rich man or a beggar. He lived in a perpetual fever, and I wish to live in tranquillity.

MR. GRYLL.   To Mr. Ballot ?

---

[1] Lines 180–4. G.

[2] *Ἐς κόρακας* : *To-the-Crows* : the Athenian equivalent for our *to-the-Devil* : a gambler's journey ; not often a long one. [P.]

MISS GRYLL. He thought of nothing but politics : he had no feeling of poetry. There was never a more complete negation of sympathy, than between him and me.

MR. GRYLL. To Sir John Pachyderm ?

MISS GRYLL. He was a mere man of the world, with no feeling of any kind : tolerable in company, but tiresome beyond description in a tête-à-tête. I did not choose that he should bestow all his tediousness on me.

MR. GRYLL. To Mr. Enavant ?

MISS GRYLL. He was what is called a fast man, and was always talking of slow coaches. I had no fancy for living in an express train. I like to go quietly through life, and to see all that lies in my way.

MR. GRYLL. To Mr. Geront ?

MISS GRYLL. He had only one fault, but that one was unpardonable. He was too old. To do him justice, he did not begin as a lover. Seeing that I took pleasure in his society, he was led by degrees into fancying that I might accept him as a husband. I liked his temper, his acquirements, his conversation, his love of music and poetry, his devotion to domestic life. But age and youth cannot harmonize in marriage.

MR. GRYLL. To Mr. Long Owen ?

MISS GRYLL. He was in debt, and kept it secret from me. I thought he only wanted my fortune : but be that as it might, the concealment destroyed my esteem.

MR. GRYLL. To Mr. Larvel ?

MISS GRYLL. He was too ugly. Expression may make plain features agreeable, and I tried if daily intercourse would reconcile me to his. But no. His ugliness was unredeemed.

MR. GRYLL. None of these objections applied to Lord Curryfin.

MISS GRYLL. No, uncle ; but he came too late. And besides, he soon found what suited him better.

MR. GRYLL. There were others. Did any of the same objections apply to them all ?

MISS GRYLL. Indeed, uncle, the most of them were nothing ; or at best, mere suits of good clothes ; men made, as it were, to pattern by the dozen ; selfish, frivolous, without any earnest pursuit, or desire to have one ; ornamental drawing-room furniture, no more distinguishable in memory than a set of chairs.

MR. GRYLL. Well, my dear Morgana, for mere negations there is no remedy ; but for positive errors, even for gambling, it strikes me they are curable.

MISS GRYLL. No, uncle. Even my limited observation has shown me, that men are easily cured of unfashionable virtues, but never of fashionable vices.

Miss Gryll and Miss Niphet arranged that their respective marriages and those of the seven sisters, should be celebrated at the same time and place. In the course of their castle-building before marriage, Miss Niphet said to her intended :

" When I am your wife, I shall release you from your promise of not trying experiments with horses, carriages, boats, and so forth ; but with this proviso, that if ever you do try a dangerous experiment, it shall be in my company."

" No, dear Alice," he answered ; " you will make my life too dear to me, to risk it in any experiment. You shall be my guiding star, and the only question I shall ask respecting my conduct in life, will be, Whether it pleases you ? "

Some natural tears they shed, but wiped them soon ; [1]

might have been applied to the sisters, when they stepped, on their bridal morning, into the carriages which were to convey them to the Grange.

It was the dissipation of a dream too much above mortal frailty, too much above the contingencies of chance and change, to be

[1] Milton : *Paradise Lost*, Bk. XII, l. 645. G.

permanently realized. But the damsels had consented, and the suitors rejoiced ; and if ever there was a man on earth with " his saul abune the moon," it was Harry Hedgerow, on the bright February morning that gave him the hand of his Dorothy.

There was a grand *déjeûner* at Gryll Grange. There were the nine brides, and the nine bridegrooms ; a beautiful array of bridesmaids ; a few friends of Mr. Gryll, Mr. Niphet, Lord Curryfin, and Mr. Falconer ; and a large party at the lower end of the hall, composed of fathers, mothers, and sisters of the bridegrooms of the seven Vestals. None of the bridegrooms had brothers, and Harry had neither mother nor sister ; but his father was there in rustic portliness, looking, as Harry had anticipated, as if he were all but made young again.

Among the most conspicuous of the party were the Reverend Doctor Opimian and his lady, who had on this occasion stepped out of her domestic seclusion. In due course, the Reverend Doctor stood up and made a speech, which may be received as the epilogue of our comedy.

THE REVEREND DOCTOR OPIMIAN. We are here to do honour to the nuptials ; first, of the niece of our excellent host, a young lady whom to name is to show her title to the love and respect of all present ; with a young gentleman, of whom to say that he is in every way worthy of her, is to say all that can be said of him in the highest order of praise : secondly, of a young lord and lady, to whom those who had the pleasure of being here last Christmas are indebted for the large share of enjoyment which their rare and diversified accomplishments, and their readiness to contribute in every way to social entertainment, bestowed on the assembled party ; and who, both in contrast and congeniality,—for both these elements enter into perfect fitness of companionship—may be considered to have been expressly formed for each other : thirdly, of seven other young couples, on many accounts most interesting to us all, who enter on the duties of married life, with as fair expectation of happiness as can reasonably be entertained in this diurnal sphere. An old Greek poet says :—
" Four things are good for man in this world ; first, health ; second, personal beauty ; third, riches not dishonourably acquired ; fourth.

to pass life among friends." [1] But thereon says the comic poet Anaxandrides : " Health is rightly placed first ; but riches should have been second ; for what is beauty ragged and starving ? " [2] Be this as it may, we here see them all four ; health in its brightest bloom ; riches in two instances ; more than competence in the other seven ; beauty in the brides, good looks, as far as young men need them, in the bridegrooms, and as bright a prospect of passing life among friends as ever shone on any. Most earnestly do I hope that the promise of their marriage morning may be fulfilled in its noon and in its sunset ; and when I add, may they all be as happy in their partners as I have been, I say what all who know the excellent person beside me will feel to be the best good wish in my power to bestow. And now, to the health of the brides and bridegrooms, in bumpers of champagne. Let all the attendants stand by, each with a fresh bottle, with only one uncut string. Let all the corks, when I give the signal, be discharged simultaneously ; and we will receive it as a peal of Bacchic ordnance, in honour of the Power of Joyful Event, [3] whom we may assume to be presiding on this auspicious occasion.

THE END

---

[1] Ὑγιαίνειν μὲν ἄριστον ἀνδρὶ θνατῷ·
Δεύτερον δέ, φυὰν καλὸν γενέσθαι·
Τρίτον δέ, πλουτεῖν ἀδόλως·
Καὶ τὸ τέταρτον, ἡβᾷν μετὰ τῶν φίλων.
Simonides. [P.] [cp. Athen. 694E. G.]

[2] Athenæus : l. xv. p. 694. [P.]

[3] This was a Roman deity. *Invocato hilaro atque prospero Eventu.*— Apuleius : *Metamorph.* 1. iv. [P.] [" Having called upon the God of happy and successful issues." G.]